Geoffrey Chaucer's
The Canterbury Ta[les]
In Plain and Simple En[glish]

BookCaps Study Guides
www.bookcaps.com

Cover Image © Fotolia.com

© 2012. All Rights Reserved.

Table of Contents:

About This Series **4**
Comparative Version **5**
   The Prologue **6**
   The Knight's Tale **25**
   The Miller's Tale **73**
      Prologue 74
      The Tale 76
   The Reeve's Tale **91**
      Prologue 92
      The Tale 94
   The Cook's Tale **104**
      The Prologue 105
      The Tale 107
   The Lawyer's Tale **109**
      Introduction 110
      Prologue 113
      The Tale 114
   The Wife of Bath's Tale **141**
      Prologue 142
      The Tale 162
   The Friar's Tale **174**
      The Prologue 175
      The Tale 176
   The Summoner's Tale **186**
      The Prologue 187
      The Tale 189
   The Clerks Tale **203**
      The Prologue 204
      The Tale 206
   The Merchant's Tale **235**
      The Prologue 236
      The Tale 237
   The Squier's Tale **263**
      Introduction 264

- The Tale 265
- The Franklin's Tale **281**
  - The Prologue 282
  - The Tale 283
- The Physician's Tale **303**
- The Pardoner's Tale **310**
  - The Tale 316
- The Shipman's Tale **328**
- The Prioress' Tale **338**
  - Prologue 339
- The Tale of Sir Thopas **346**
- The Tale of Melibee **351**
- The Monk's Tale **391**
- The Nun's Priest's Tale **413**
  - Prologue 413
  - The Tale 414
- The Second Nun's Tale **432**
- The Canon's Yeoman's Tale **443**
  - Prologue 443
  - The Tale 447
- The Manciple's Tale **465**
  - Prologue 465
  - The Tale 467
- The Parsons's Tale **474**
  - Prologue 474
  - The Tale 475
- Chaucer's retraction **545**

About This Series

The "Classic Retold" series started as a way of telling classics for the modern reader—being careful to preserve the themes and integrity of the original. Whether you want to understand Shakespeare a little more or are trying to get a better grasp of the Greek classics, there is a book waiting for you!

Comparative Version

The Prologue

WHEN that Aprilis, with his showers swoot,	When the sweet showers of April
The drought of March hath pierced to the root,	Have soaked down through the drought of March,
And bathed every vein in such licour,	Washing every shoot with such sweet liquid
Of which virtue engender'd is the flower;	That all the flowers start to bloom;
When Zephyrus eke with his swoote breath	When the sweet breezes blow
Inspired hath in every holt and heath	Through every field and forest, encouraging
The tender croppes and the younge sun	The tender crops, and the young sun
Hath in the Ram his halfe course y-run,	Has run his course halfway through the Ram,
And smalle fowles make melody,	And the small birds sing
That sleepen all the night with open eye,	Which sleep all night with eyes open
(So pricketh them nature in their corages);	(This is the nature in their hearts)
Then longe folk to go on pilgrimages,	The people long to go on pilgrimages,
And palmers for to seeke strange strands,	Seeking out foreign lands,
To ferne hallows couth in sundry lands;	Distant shrines in diverse countries,
And specially, from every shire's end	And especially from every corner
Of Engleland, to Canterbury they wend,	Of England they go to Canterbury,
The holy blissful Martyr for to seek,	Looking for the sweet holy martyr
That them hath holpen, when that they were sick.	Who had helped them when they were sick.
Befell that, in that season on a day,	Now it happened that one day in that season,
In Southwark at the Tabard as I lay,	As I stayed at the Tabard in Southwark,
Ready to wenden on my pilgrimage	Ready to go on my pilgrimage
To Canterbury with devout corage,	To Canterbury in great high spirits,
At night was come into that hostelry	At night there came into that inn
Well nine and twenty in a company	A group of twenty-nine
Of sundry folk, by aventure y-fall who had by chance fallen	Diverse people, who had by chance
In fellowship, and pilgrims were they all, into company.	Fallen in with each other, and they were all pilgrims,
That toward Canterbury woulde ride.	That wanted to ride to Canterbury.
The chamber, and the stables were wide,	The rooms and stables there were spacious,
And well we weren eased at the best.	And we were well served with fine food and drink,
And shortly, when the sunne was to rest,	And by the time the sun had set
So had I spoken with them every one,	I had spoken to each of them and had
That I was of their fellowship anon,	Become one of their fellowship,
And made forword early for to rise,	And we all agreed that we would get up early
To take our way there as I you devise.	To go on our way, as I shall describe.
But natheless, while I have time and space,	But before that, while I have time and space,
Ere that I farther in this tale pace,	Before I carry on with my story,
Me thinketh it accordant to reason,	I think it would make sense
To tell you alle the condition	To tell you how each of them
Of each of them, so as it seemed me,	Appeared to me,
And which they weren, and of what degree;	And who they were, and of what rank,
And eke in what array that they were in:	And also their appearance:
And at a Knight then will I first begin.	And I shall start with a knight.
A KNIGHT there was, and that a worthy man,	There was a knight, he was a good man,
That from the time that he first began	Who from the time that he first

To riden out, he loved chivalry,	Rode out was in love with chivalry,
Truth and honour, freedom and courtesy.	Truth and honour, freedom and courtesy.
Full worthy was he in his Lorde's war,	He was a great fighter on the Crusades,
And thereto had he ridden, no man farre,	And to fight for his Lord he had ridden farther
As well in Christendom as in Heatheness,	Than any man, in Christendom or heathen lands,
And ever honour'd for his worthiness	And was always respected for his goodness.
At Alisandre he was when it was won.	He was at Alexandria when it was captured.
Full often time he had the board begun	Many times he had been placed at the head of the table
Above alle nations in Prusse.	Above knights of any other country, in Prussia.
In Lettowe had he reysed, and in Russe,	He had travelled in Lithuania and Russia,
No Christian man so oft of his degree.	No Christian man had done that more.
In Grenade at the siege eke had he be	He was also at the siege of Algesir,
Of Algesir, and ridden in Belmarie.	In Granada, and he had ridden in Belmarie.
At Leyes was he, and at Satalie,	He was at Leyes and at Satelie,
When they were won; and in the Greate Sea	When they were captured; and he had joined
At many a noble army had he be.	Many noble armies all around the Mediterranean.
At mortal battles had he been fifteen,	He had been in fifteen great battles,
And foughten for our faith at Tramissene.	and fought for the Christians at Tramissene.
In listes thries, and aye slain his foe.	He had fought in three jousts, and each time killed his enemy.
This ilke worthy knight had been also	This same good knight had also
Some time with the lord of Palatie,	Fought alongside the Lord of Palestine
Against another heathen in Turkie:	Against some other heathens in Turkey:
And evermore he had a sovereign price	And he was always held in high esteem.
And though that he was worthy he was wise,	Although he was great he was wise,
And of his port as meek as is a maid.	And carried himself with the modesty of a girl.
He never yet no villainy ne said	He never undertook a bad thing
In all his life, unto no manner wight.	in his whole life, in any way at all.
He was a very perfect gentle knight.	He was the model of a perfect gentle knight.
But for to telle you of his array,	To tell you how he was dressed,
His horse was good, but yet he was not gay.	He had a good horse, but he was not showy.
Of fustian he weared a gipon,	He wore a short jacket of coarse cloth,
Alle besmotter'd with his habergeon,	Stained by his armour,
For he was late y-come from his voyage,	And he had recently returned from abroad,
And wente for to do his pilgrimage.	To go on his pilgrimage.
With him there was his son, a younge SQUIRE,	With him was his son, a young squire,
A lover, and a lusty bacheler,	A lusty young single fellow,
With lockes crulle as they were laid in press.	With his hair carefully curled,
Of twenty year of age he was I guess.	I imagine about twenty years old.
Of his stature he was of even length,	He was very tall,
And wonderly deliver, and great of strength.	Wonderfully nimble and very strong;
And he had been some time in chevachie,	He had at one time fought with the cavalry
In Flanders, in Artois, and Picardie,	In Flanders, Artois and Picardy,
And borne him well, as of so little space,	And acquitted himself well in a very short time,
In hope to standen in his lady's grace.	Hoping to win his lady's favour.
Embroider'd was he, as it were a mead	He wore embroidered clothes, he looked like a field
All full of freshe flowers, white and red.	Full of fresh flowers, red and white.
Singing he was, or fluting all the day;	He was always singing or playing his flute;
He was as fresh as is the month of May.	He was as fresh as the month of May.

Short was his gown, with sleeves long and wide.	He wore a short gown
Well could he sit on horse, and faire ride.	With long wide sleeves.
He coulde songes make, and well indite,	He had a good seat on his horse, he rode well.
Joust, and eke dance, and well pourtray and write.	He could write songs and recite poetry,
So hot he loved, that by nightertale	Joust and dance, paint and write.
He slept no more than doth the nightingale.	He was such an ardent lover that at night
Courteous he was, lowly, and serviceable,	He got no more sleep than the nightingale.
And carv'd before his father at the table.	He was polite, humble and hard working,
	Carving his father's meat at table.
A YEOMAN had he, and servants no mo'	He had a yeoman, and no other servants,
At that time, for him list ride so it pleased him so to ride	For that was his style at that time,
And he was clad in coat and hood of green.	Who wore a green cloak and hood.
A sheaf of peacock arrows bright and keen	He carried a quiver of arrows tipped with peacock feathers
Under his belt he bare full thriftily.	Carefully tucked into his belt.
Well could he dress his tackle yeomanly:	He was dressed in the true Yeoman style:
His arrows drooped not with feathers low;	His arrows were not shabby with common feathers,
And in his hand he bare a mighty bow.	And he carried a great bow in his hands.
A nut-head had he, with a brown visiage:	He had a head like a nut, with a brown face,
Of wood-craft coud he well all the usage:	And he knew all about woodcraft:
Upon his arm he bare a gay bracer,	On his arm he carried a bright shield,
And by his side a sword and a buckler,	And at his side a sword and belt,
And on that other side a gay daggere,	And on the other side a handsome dagger,
Harnessed well, and sharp as point of spear:	In a fine sheath, as sharp as a spear:
A Christopher on his breast of silver sheen.	He wore a silver St.Christopher on his chest.
An horn he bare, the baldric was of green:	He carried a horn hung from a green strap:
A forester was he soothly as I guess.	I could certainly see he was a forester.
There was also a Nun, a PRIORESS,	There was also a nun, a prioress,
That of her smiling was full simple and coy;	Who smiled openly and sweetly;
Her greatest oathe was but by Saint Loy;	Her worst oath was to swear by St Loy;
And she was cleped Madame Eglentine.	And she was called Madam Eglentine.
Full well she sang the service divine,	She sang divine service perfectly,
Entuned in her nose full seemly;	Singing through her nose tunefully;
And French she spake full fair and fetisly	She spoke French beautifully and accurately
After the school of Stratford atte Bow,	After the style of the school of Stratford at Bow,
For French of Paris was to her unknow.	For she did not know Parisian French.
At meate was she well y-taught withal;	She had beautiful table manners;
She let no morsel from her lippes fall,	She didn't let any crumbs fall from her lips,
Nor wet her fingers in her sauce deep.	Nor would she get her fingers covered in sauce.
Well could she carry a morsel, and well keep,	She could hold her food so daintily and well
That no droppe ne fell upon her breast.	That not a drop would fall on her breast.
In courtesy was set full much her lest.	She took great pleasure in good manners.
Her over-lippe wiped she so clean,	She wiped her top lip so clean
That in her cup there was no farthing seen	That not a speck of grease could be seen
Of grease, when she drunken had her draught;	On her cup when she had drunk;
Full seemely after her meat she raught:	She always reached for her food politely,
And sickerly she was of great disport,	And she was certainly amiable,
And full pleasant, and amiable of port,	Very pleasant and she carried herself cheerfully,

And pained her to counterfeite cheer	And she took pains to behave
Of court, and be estately of mannere,	In a courtly manner, and be dignified,
And to be holden digne of reverence.	And to be worthy of respect.
But for to speaken of her conscience,	But to speak of her conscience
She was so charitable and so pitous,	She was so charitable and full of pity
She woulde weep if that she saw a mouse	That she would weep if she saw a mouse
Caught in a trap, if it were dead or bled.	Caught in a trap, if it was dead or bleeding.
Of smalle houndes had she, that she fed	She had small dogs, that she fed
With roasted flesh, and milk, and wastel bread.	On roast meat, milk and the finest white bread,
But sore she wept if one of them were dead,	And she wept terribly if one of them died,
Or if men smote it with a yarde smart:	Or if a man struck it with a stick:
And all was conscience and tender heart.	She was all conscience and tender heart.
Full seemly her wimple y-pinched was;	Her wimple was beautifully styled;
Her nose tretis; her eyen gray as glass;	her nose was well shaped, her eyes grey as glass;
Her mouth full small, and thereto soft and red;	Her mouth was small and soft and red;
But sickerly she had a fair forehead.	But she certainly had a lovely forehead.
It was almost a spanne broad I trow;	I think it was almost a hand's width across;
For hardily she was not undergrow.	She certainly wasn't small.
Full fetis was her cloak, as I was ware.	Her cloak, I could see, was very neat,
Of small coral about her arm she bare	And around her arm she wore a bracelet
A pair of beades, gauded all with green;	Of a pair of green coral beads;
And thereon hung a brooch of gold full sheen,	And from it hung a shiny gold brooch,
On which was first y-written a crown'd A,	On which was written a A with a crown over it,
And after, Amor vincit omnia.	Followed by, "Love conquers all."
Another Nun also with her had she,	She had another nun with her also,
That was her chapelleine, and PRIESTES three.	Who was her chaplain, and also three priests.
A MONK there was, a fair for the mast'ry,	There was a monk there, more handsome than the rest,
An out-rider, that loved venery;	A horseman, who loved hunting;
A manly man, to be an abbot able.	A man's man, and a competent abbot.
Full many a dainty horse had he in stable:	He had many fine horses in his stable:
And when he rode, men might his bridle hear	And when he rode, men could hear his bridle
Jingeling in a whistling wind as clear,	Jingling in the whistling breeze as clear
And eke as loud, as doth the chapel bell,	And loud as the chapel bell,
There as this lord was keeper of the cell.	In the monastery this lord ruled over.
The rule of Saint Maur and of Saint Benet,	The rules of St Maurus and St Benedictine,
Because that it was old and somedeal strait	Which were old and somewhat strict,
This ilke monk let olde thinges pace,	This same monk didn't care for,
And held after the newe world the trace.	He liked the modern world.
He gave not of the text a pulled hen,	He didn't give a damn for the text
That saith, that hunters be not holy men:	Which said that monks can't be hunters,
Ne that a monk, when he is cloisterless;	Or the saying that a monk out of his cloister
Is like to a fish that is waterless;	Is like a fish out of water;
This is to say, a monk out of his cloister.	That's what they say about a monk in the world,
This ilke text held he not worth an oyster;	But he didn't think those words were worth an oyster,
And I say his opinion was good.	And I say that his opinion was right.
Why should he study, and make himselfe wood	Why should he study, and drive himself mad,
Upon a book in cloister always pore,	Always poring over books in the cloisters,
Or swinken with his handes, and labour,	Or ruining his hands with labour,
As Austin bid? how shall the world be served?	As St Augustine ordered? What good will that

Let Austin have his swink to him reserved.	do?
Therefore he was a prickasour aright:	Let St Augustine keep that grief for himself.
Greyhounds he had as swift as fowl of flight;	So instead that monk was a fine horseman;
	He had greyhounds who were as fast as birds in flight;
Of pricking and of hunting for the hare	Riding and hunting hares
Was all his lust, for no cost would he spare.	Was all he cared for, and he spared no expense.
I saw his sleeves purfil'd at the hand	I saw that his sleeves were trimmed with
With gris, and that the finest of the land.	The finest fur that could be had,
And for to fasten his hood under his chin,	And to fasten his hood under his chin
He had of gold y-wrought a curious pin;	He had a strange pin made of gold;
A love-knot in the greater end there was.	It had a love knot in its larger end.
His head was bald, and shone as any glass,	He was bald and his head shone like a mirror,
And eke his face, as it had been anoint;	And so did his face, as if it had been polished;
He was a lord full fat and in good point;	He was a portly Lord, full figured;
His eyen steep, and rolling in his head,	His eyes were deep-set in his head,
That steamed as a furnace of a lead.	And they flashed like lead smelting furnaces.
His bootes supple, his horse in great estate,	His boots were supple, his horse well kitted out,
Now certainly he was a fair prelate;	He certainly was a handsome churchman;
He was not pale as a forpined ghost;	He wasn't pale like a starving ghost;
A fat swan lov'd he best of any roast.	His favourite meat was a fat roast swan.
His palfrey was as brown as is a berry.	His horse was brown as a berry.
A FRIAR there was, a wanton and a merry,	There was a friar, jolly and lusty,
A limitour, a full solemne man.	A licensed beggar, a very dignified man.
In all the orders four is none that can	There was no religious person
So much of dalliance and fair language.	Who was so good at backchat and fair speech.
He had y-made full many a marriage	He had married off many
Of younge women, at his owen cost.	young women, to his regret.
Unto his order he was a noble post;	He was an ornament to his order;
Full well belov'd, and familiar was he	He was much liked and well known
With franklins over all in his country,	To all the men of his region,
And eke with worthy women of the town:	And also the good women of the town:
For he had power of confession,	For he gave the best confessions,
As said himselfe, more than a curate,	He said himself, better than a curate,
For of his order he was licentiate.	For his position allowed him.
Full sweetely heard he confession,	He listened sweetly to confessions
And pleasant was his absolution.	And gave easy punishments.
He was an easy man to give penance,	He knew the best way to go about it,
There as he wist to have a good pittance:	How to get himself well paid
For unto a poor order for to give get good payment	For leading men to forgiveness.
Is signe that a man is well y-shrive.	For he often liked to say
For if he gave, he durste make avant,	That he knew when a
He wiste that the man was repentant.	man was repentant,
For many a man so hard is of his heart,	For many men are so hard
He may not weep although him sore smart.	That they won't weep even if they're suffering,
Therefore instead of weeping and prayeres,	So instead of weeping or praying,
Men must give silver to the poore freres.	They have to give the poor friars silver.
His tippet was aye farsed full of knives	His cloak was full of fine
And pinnes, for to give to faire wives;	Jewellery, to give to pretty women;
And certainly he had a merry note:	He certainly had a fine voice:
Well could he sing and playen on a rote;	And he was
Of yeddings he bare utterly the prize.	the finest singer.

His neck was white as is the fleur-de-lis.	*His neck was as white as a lily,*
Thereto he strong was as a champion,	*Though he was strong as a prizefighter,*
And knew well the taverns in every town.	*And well known in all the taverns.*
And every hosteler and gay tapstere,	*He knew every landlord and barman*
Better than a lazar or a beggere,	*Better than he knew lepers or beggars,*
For unto such a worthy man as he	*For a man of his high station*
Accordeth not, as by his faculty,	*Would not want, in his position,*
To have with such lazars acquaintance.	*To hang out with lepers.*
It is not honest, it may not advance,	*It certainly wouldn't be profitable*
As for to deale with no such pouraille,	*To hang around with such dregs,*
But all with rich, and sellers of vitaille.	*He preferred the rich and merchants,*
And ov'r all there as profit should arise,	*And anyone from whom he could get a profit.*
Courteous he was, and lowly of service;	*He was polite and obsequious,*
There n'as no man nowhere so virtuous.	*And nobody knew a better man.*
He was the beste beggar in all his house:	*He was the best beggar of his order,*
And gave a certain farme for the grant,	*And he paid a good fee for his license to beg;*
None of his brethern came in his haunt.	*Non of his fellows could match him.*
For though a widow hadde but one shoe,	*A widow might have next to nothing,*
So pleasant was his In Principio,	*But his reading of scripture was so lovely*
Yet would he have a farthing ere he went;	*She would give him a farthing before he left;*
His purchase was well better than his rent.	*He always got more than he gave,*
And rage he could and play as any whelp,	*So he could romp around like a puppy,*
In lovedays; there could he muchel help.	*And on festival days he was much involved,*
For there was he not like a cloisterer,	*And he was not like some monk then,*
With threadbare cope as is a poor scholer;	*With a threadbare cloak like some poor scholar,*
But he was like a master or a pope.	*But he was like a lord or a pope.*
Of double worsted was his semicope,	*His short cloak was fine and thick,*
That rounded was as a bell out of press.	*Swelling like a new-cast bell.*
Somewhat he lisped for his wantonness,	*He affected a lisp in his indulgence,*
To make his English sweet upon his tongue;	*To make his language sound sweeter;*
And in his harping, when that he had sung,	*When he sang along to the harp*
His eyen twinkled in his head aright,	*His eyes twinkled in his head*
As do the starres in a frosty night.	*Like stars on a frosty night.*
This worthy limitour was call'd Huberd.	*This good begging friar was called Hubert.*
A MERCHANT was there with a forked beard,	*There was a merchant with a forked beard,*
In motley, and high on his horse he sat,	*Wearing jester's clothes, sat on a high horse,*
Upon his head a Flandrish beaver hat.	*Wearing a Dutch fur hat on his head.*
His bootes clasped fair and fetisly.	*His boots were snug and well fitting.*
His reasons aye spake he full solemnly,	*He always spoke in a serious tone,*
Sounding alway th' increase of his winning.	*Letting everyone know how successful he was.*
He would the sea were kept for any thing	*He was obsessed with the protection of the sea-routes*
Betwixte Middleburg and Orewell	*Between England and Holland,*
Well could he in exchange shieldes sell	*For dealing in foreign exchange*
This worthy man full well his wit beset;	*Was the good man's main business;*
There wiste no wight that he was in debt,	*Nobody guessed that he was in debt,*
So estately was he of governance	*Because he managed his affairs so smoothly,*
With his bargains, and with his chevisance.	*With his dealing and his contracts,*
For sooth he was a worthy man withal,	*And after all he was a good man,*
But sooth to say, I n'ot how men him call.	*But I must admit I never discovered his name.*
A CLERK there was of Oxenford also,	*There was also a clerk from Oxford,*
That unto logic hadde long y-go.	*Who had devoted his life to logic.*

As leane was his horse as is a rake,	His horse was thin as a rake,
And he was not right fat, I undertake;	And I can tell you he wasn't much fatter;
But looked hollow, and thereto soberly.	He looked thin and ill,
Full threadbare was his overest courtepy,	And his topcoat was very threadbare,
For he had gotten him yet no benefice,	For he had no real position;
Ne was not worldly, to have an office.	He was too dreamy to get a post.
For him was lever have at his bed's head	He would rather have at his bedside
Twenty bookes, clothed in black or red,	Twenty books bound in red or black leather,
Of Aristotle, and his philosophy,	About Aristotle and his philosophy,
Than robes rich, or fiddle, or psalt'ry.	Than rich clothes, or a fiddle or ornaments.
But all be that he was a philosopher,	For all that he was a philosopher
Yet hadde he but little gold in coffer,	He had no money in the bank,
But all that he might of his friendes hent,	But everything he got from his friends
On bookes and on learning he it spent,	He spent on books and education,
And busily gan for the soules pray	And he prayed fervently for the souls
Of them that gave him wherewith to scholay	Of those who gave him money for study,
Of study took he moste care and heed.	For that was what he cared about most.
Not one word spake he more than was need;	He never said an unnecessary word,
And that was said in form and reverence,	Always speaking to the point,
And short and quick, and full of high sentence.	Briefly and full of high meaning.
Sounding in moral virtue was his speech,	What he said was full of moral virtue,
And gladly would he learn, and gladly teach.	And he loved to learn and loved to teach.
A SERGEANT OF THE LAW, wary and wise,	There was a Sergeant of the Law, clever and suspicious,
That often had y-been at the Parvis,	Who often plied his trade at St.Paul's,
There was also, full rich of excellence.	He was full of good virtues.
Discreet he was, and of great reverence:	He was discreet, and very pious:
He seemed such, his wordes were so wise,	He seemed so good and spoke so well
Justice he was full often in assize,	That he had often served as a trial judge,
By patent, and by plein commission;	Commissioned with full authority;
For his science, and for his high renown,	Because of his knowledge and fame
Of fees and robes had he many one.	He was given many fees and had many robes.
So great a purchaser was nowhere none.	Nobody made money like he did.
All was fee simple to him, in effect	He had plenty of lands,
His purchasing might not be in suspect	He bought so much that no-one thought
Nowhere so busy a man as he there was	There could be anyone busier than him,
And yet he seemed busier than he was.	Though he pretended to be busier than he was.
In termes had he case' and doomes all	He knew all the laws which had been passed
That from the time of King Will. were fall.	Since the Norman conquest,
Thereto he could indite, and make a thing	And he could quote them and construct a case
There coulde no wight pinch at his writing.	That nobody would be able to bring down,
And every statute coud he plain by rote	Knowing every law by heart.
He rode but homely in a medley coat,	He had no great style in his patchwork cloak,
Girt with a seint of silk, with barres small;	With a silken sash and small clasps;
Of his array tell I no longer tale.	That's all I'll say about his clothes.
A FRANKELIN was in this company;	There was also a Franklin in the group;
White was his beard, as is the daisy.	His beard was as white as daisies.
Of his complexion he was sanguine.	He had a ruddy complexion.
Well lov'd he in the morn a sop in wine.	He loved to dip his bread in wine for breakfast.
To liven in delight was ever his won,	He really did live for pleasure,
For he was Epicurus' owen son,	He was a true epicurean,
That held opinion, that plein delight	Who thought that great pleasure

Was verily felicity perfite.	Was the most perfect thing on earth.
An householder, and that a great, was he;	He was a great landowner;
Saint Julianhe was in his country.	In his region he was thought of like St Julian.
His bread, his ale, was alway after one;	He always insisted one tried his bread and beer;
A better envined man was nowhere none;	Nobody had a better wine cellar;
Withoute bake-meat never was his house,	His house was never lacking in cooked meat,
Of fish and flesh, and that so plenteous,	He had so much meat and fish that
It snowed in his house of meat and drink,	It was as if it was snowing meat and drink in his house,
Of alle dainties that men coulde think.	Every dainty a man could think of.
After the sundry seasons of the year,	At the different times of year
So changed he his meat and his soupere.	He would have different meats and meals.
Full many a fat partridge had he in mew,	He had many fat partridges in cages,
And many a bream, and many a luce in stew	And many bream and pike in his fishpond;
Woe was his cook, his sauce were	His cook was in trouble unless his sauce was
Poignant and sharp, and ready all his gear.	Tasty and sharp, and he had to be always ready.
His table dormant in his hall alway	His table was fixed in his hallway,
Stood ready cover'd all the longe day.	Always ready for a meal throughout the day.
At sessions there was he lord and sire.	He was the greatest man in his district.
Full often time he was knight of the shire	And many times he had been a member of Parliament.
An anlace, and a gipciere all of silk,	A dagger and a silk purse,
Hung at his girdle, white as morning milk.	White as new milk hung from his belt.
A sheriff had he been, and a countour	He had been a sheriff and the county treasurer;
Was nowhere such a worthy vavasour.	There wasn't a landowner to match him.
An HABERDASHER, and a CARPENTER,	There were also a haberdasher, a carpenter,
A WEBBE, a DYER, and a TAPISER,	a weaver, a dyer and a tapestry maker,
Were with us eke, cloth'd in one livery,	All dressed in the same uniform,
Of a solemn and great fraternity.	Of their great and respected guild.
Full fresh and new their gear y-picked was;	Their gear was all fresh and spruce;
Their knives were y-chaped not with brass,	Their knives did not have brass hilts,
But all with silver wrought full clean and well,	But were well made of shining silver,
Their girdles and their pouches every deal.	And every part of their belts and purses
Well seemed each of them a fair burgess,	Made them look like a good townsman,
To sitten in a guild-hall, on the dais.	Who would sit in a Guildhall at the high table.
Evereach, for the wisdom that he can,	Each one knew that he was
Was shapely for to be an alderman.	Suitable to be an alderman.
For chattels hadde they enough and rent,	They had enough property and money coming in from rent,
And eke their wives would it well assent:	And also their wives would be very pleased about it:
And elles certain they had been to blame.	And they certainly would have been unhappy otherwise.
It is full fair to be y-clep'd madame,	It is nice to be addressed as madame,
And for to go to vigils all before,	And to be at the forefront of processions,
And have a mantle royally y-bore.	Wearing the noblest of clothes.
A COOK they hadde with them for the nones,	They had a cook with them for the occasion,
To boil the chickens and the marrow bones,	To boil the chicken and the marrow bones,
And powder merchant tart and galingale.	And to season their tarts with ginger.
Well could he know a draught of London ale.	He was a good judge of London ale.

He could roast, and stew, and broil, and fry,	*He could roast and stew, boil and fry,*
Make mortrewes, and well bake a pie.	*Brew up a good broth and bake excellent pies.*
But great harm was it, as it thoughte me,	*I thought it was a great shame that*
That, on his shin a mormal hadde he.	*He has a nasty ulcer on his leg,*
For blanc manger, that made he with the best.	*For his blancmange could match any man's.*
A SHIPMAN was there, wonned far by West:	*There was a shipman, who lived far in the West,*
For ought I wot, he was of Dartemouth.	*For I knew that he had come from Dartmouth.*
He rode upon a rouncy, as he couth,	*He rode upon an old hack, what he could afford,*
All in a gown of falding to the knee.	*Wearing a long gown of coarse cloth.*
A dagger hanging by a lace had he	*He had a dagger hanging on a piece of string,*
About his neck under his arm adown;	*Around his neck and under his arm;*
The hot summer had made his hue all brown;	*The hot summer had given him a good tan;*
And certainly he was a good fellow.	*And he certainly was a good chap.*
Full many a draught of wine he had y-draw	*He had helped himself to many a drink from*
From Bourdeaux-ward, while that the chapmen sleep;	*The barrels of Bordeaux, whilst tradesmen slept;*
Of nice conscience took he no keep.	*He didn't let his conscience bother him much.*
If that he fought, and had the higher hand,	*If he had to fight, and triumphed,*
By water he sent them home to every land.	*He would drown his prisoners,*
But of his craft to reckon well his tides,	*But he knew all the tides,*
His streames and his strandes him besides,	*The rivers and spits,*
His herberow, his moon, and lodemanage,	*The harbours and channels, and he could read the moon,*
There was none such, from Hull unto Carthage;	*Nobody could match him, from Carthage to Hull;*
Hardy he was, and wise, I undertake:	*He was very strong, and I think also wise:*
With many a tempest had his beard been shake.	*He had ridden out many a storm.*
He knew well all the havens, as they were,	*He knew all the best shelters*
From Scotland to the Cape of Finisterre,	*From Scotland to Cape Finisterre,*
And every creek in Bretagne and in Spain:	*And every creek in Brittany and Spain:*
His barge y-cleped was the Magdelain.	*His ship was called The Magdalene.*
With us there was a DOCTOR OF PHYSIC;	*There was also a doctor of medicine,*
In all this worlde was there none him like	*And there was nobody in the world like him*
To speak of physic, and of surgery:	*In knowledge of medicine and of surgery:*
For he was grounded in astronomy.	*He also knew astronomy.*
He kept his patient a full great deal	*He treated his pateients at different times*
In houres by his magic natural.	*Depending when the medicine would be strongest.*
Well could he fortune the ascendent	*He could tell by the movement of the stars*
Of his images for his patient,.	*What treatment would suit the patient best.*
He knew the cause of every malady,	*He knew the cause of every illness,*
Were it of cold, or hot, or moist, or dry,	*Whether it was cold, hot, moist or dry,*
And where engender'd, and of what humour.	*And where it came from and what it affected.*
He was a very perfect practisour	*He was an excellent practitioner,*
The cause y-know, and of his harm the root,	*And once he knew the cause he could at once*
Anon he gave to the sick man his boot	*Provide the sick man with a remedy;*
Full ready had he his apothecaries,	*He had his chemists ready to provide*
To send his drugges and his lectuaries,	*Any drugs or medicine he needed,*
For each of them made other for to win	*For their mutual benefit,*
Their friendship was not newe to begin.	*For they had a longstanding relationship.*
Well knew he the old Esculapius,	*He knew all the work of old Escalpius,*

And Dioscorides, and eke Rufus;	And Dioscorides, and also Rufus;
Old Hippocras, Hali, and Gallien;	Old Hippocras, Hali, and Gallien;
Serapion, Rasis, and Avicen;	Serapion, Rasis, and Avicen;
Averrois, Damascene, and Constantin;	Averrois, Damascene, and Constantin;
Bernard, and Gatisden, and Gilbertin.	Bernard, and Gatisden, and Gilbertin.
Of his diet measurable was he,	He ate a balanced diet,
For it was of no superfluity,	In which nothing was taken excessively,
But of great nourishing, and digestible.	But it was all very nourishing and easy to digest.
His study was but little on the Bible.	He didn't bother with much Bible study.
In sanguine and in perse he clad was all	He was dressed all in red and blue,
Lined with taffeta, and with sendall,	Lined with taffeta and fine silk,
And yet he was but easy of dispense:	But he spent very little money,
He kept that he won in the pestilence.	Keeping the money he earned during the plague,
For gold in physic is a cordial;	For gold is a very fine medicine,
Therefore he loved gold in special.	And so he loved it best of all.
A good WIFE was there OF beside BATH,	There was a housewife from near Bath,
But she was somedeal deaf, and that was scath.	Who sadly was deaf in both ears.
Of cloth-making she hadde such an haunt,	She was so good at making cloth,
She passed them of Ypres, and of Gaunt.	She outdid those from Ypres and even Ghent.
In all the parish wife was there none,	There was no good wife in the whole parish
That to the off'ring before her should gon,	Who would give to charity ahead of her,
And if there did, certain so wroth was she,	And indeed if they did she would be so angry
That she was out of alle charity	She would quite forget her charitable temper.
Her coverchiefs were full fine of ground	Her headcloths were of the finest workmanship;
I durste swear, they weighede ten pound	I daresay the ones she wore wrapped round her head
That on the Sunday were upon her head.	On Sunday weighed about ten pounds.
Her hosen weren of fine scarlet red,	Her stockings were the best deep scarlet,
Full strait y-tied, and shoes full moist and new	Tied round tight, and her shoes were soft and new.
Bold was her face, and fair and red of hue.	She had a pretty, determined face, which was very red.
She was a worthy woman all her live,	She'd been a good woman all her life,
Husbands at the church door had she had five,	Having been married to five different husbands,
Withouten other company in youth;	Not to mention the company she kept when young;
But thereof needeth not to speak as nouth.	But we needn't go mentioning that, I'm sure.
And thrice had she been at Jerusalem;	She'd made the pilgrimage to Jerusalem three times,
She hadde passed many a strange stream	And crossed over many foreign rivers;
At Rome she had been, and at Bologne,	She'd been to Rome, and Bolougne,
In Galice at Saint James, and at Cologne;	And Santiago in Spain and at Cologne.
She coude much of wand'rng by the Way.	She could tell many tales of her wanderings:
Gat-toothed was she, soothly for to say.	And I can tell you she was bucktoothed.
Upon an ambler easily she sat,	She sat comfortably on a walking horse,
Y-wimpled well, and on her head an hat	With a large wimple covered by a hat
As broad as is a buckler or a targe.	As wide as a shield or a target;
A foot-mantle about her hippes large,	She had a rug tucked round her plump buttocks,
And on her feet a pair of spurres sharp.	And a pair of sharp spurs on her feet.

In fellowship well could she laugh and carp	In company she enjoyed a laugh a joke.
Of remedies of love she knew perchance	She knew all about the game of love,
For of that art she coud the olde dance.	Having learned its rules long ago.

A good man was ther of religioun,	There was a good religious man there,
And was a povre PERSOUN OF A TOUN,	He was the poor parson of a town,
But riche he was of hooly thoght and werk.	But he was rich in holy thoughts and works.
He was also a lerned man, a clerk,	He was also an educated man, a scholar.
That Cristes gospel trewely wolde preche;	He tried to preach Christ's gospel truly;
His parisshens devoutly wolde he teche.	He devoutly taught his parishioners.
Benynge he was, and wonder diligent,	He was kind and very hard-working,
And in adversitee ful pacient,	And very patient in the face of adversity,
And swich he was ypreved ofte sithes.	And he had proven this many times.
Ful looth were hym to cursen for his tithes,	He would not curse people to try and get his tax,
But rather wolde he yeven, out of doute,	But would actually give, there is no doubt,
Unto his povre parisshens aboute	To his poor parishioners
Of his offryng and eek of his substaunce.	Some of his income, even some of his property.
He koude in litel thyng have suffisaunce.	He could manage himself with very little.
Wyd was his parisshe, and houses fer asonder,	He had a large parish, with the houses scattered wide
But he ne lefte nat, for reyn ne thonder,	But he never failed, whatever the weather,
In siknesse nor in meschief to visite	To visit the sick or sinful, or any others,
The ferreste in his parisshe, muche and lite,	The farthest away, however poor they were,
Upon his feet, and in his hand a staf.	Going on foot, carrying a stick in his hand.
This noble ensample to his sheep he yaf,	In this way he gave his flock a fine example,
That first he wroghte, and afterward he taughte.	That he did first and then taught afterwards;
Out of the gospel he tho wordes caughte,	He taught them the text from the gospel,
And this figure he added eek therto,	And to it he added this metaphor:
That if gold ruste, what shal iren do?	If gold will rust, what will happen to iron?
For if a preest be foul, on whom we truste,	If the priest whom we trust is wicked,
No wonder is a lewed man to ruste;	Is it any wonder his parishioners misbehave?
And shame it is, if a prest take keep,	It is shameful if the priest is greedy,
A shiten shepherde and a clene sheep.	A shitty shepherd looking after clean sheep.
Wel oghte a preest ensample for to yive,	The priest ought to set a good example
By his clennesse, how that his sheep sholde lyve.	Through his chastity, showing his flock how to live.
He sette nat his benefice to hyre	He never rented out his church lands,
And leet his sheep encombred in the myre	To leave his sheep wallowing in the mud,
And ran to Londoun unto Seinte Poules	Running up to London, to St Paul's,
To seken hym a chaunterie for soules,	To get himself a better position,
Or with a bretherhed to been witholde;	Nor did he join some secret brotherhood,
But dwelt at hoom, and kepte wel his folde,	He stayed at home and looked after his flock so well
So that the wolf ne made it nat myscarie;	That no wolf could never lead them astray;
He was a shepherde and noght a mercenarie.	He was a shepherd, not a mercenary.
And though he hooly were and vertuous,	Although he was wholly and virtuous,
He was to synful men nat despitous,	He did not despise sinful men,
Ne of his speche daungerous ne digne,	He didn't look down on them or preach too much,
But in his techyng discreet and benygne;	He just taught them politely and kindly.
To drawen folk to hevene by fairnesse,	He wanted to show people the gentle path to heaven,
By good ensample, this was his bisynesse.	Through his good example, that was his business.

But it were any persone obstinat,	But if anybody carried on sinning,
What so he were, of heigh or lough estat,	Whoever he was, rich or poor,
Hym wolde he snybben sharply for the nonys.	He would certainly give him a sharp rebuke.
A bettre preest I trowe, that nowher noon ys.	I believe there never was a better priest.
He waited after no pompe and reverence,	He didn't want ceremony and worship,
Ne maked him a spiced conscience,	Nor did he ever try to behave badly,
But Cristes loore, and Hise apostles twelve	He just taught the law of Christ and his twelve Apostles,
He taughte, but first he folwed it hymselve.	But firstly he followed it himself.
With hym ther was a PLOWMAN, was his brother,	With him there was his brother, a ploughman,
That hadde ylad of dong ful many a fother;	Who had loaded many carts with dung,
A trewe swynkere and a good was he,	He was a hard and loyal worker,
Lyvynge in pees and parfit charitee.	Who lived in peace and was very kind.
God loved he best with al his hoole herte	He loved God most of all with the whole of his heart,
At alle tymes, thogh him gamed or smerte,	At all times, although it might damage or wound him,
And thanne his neighebor right as hym-selve.	And then he loved his neighbour as much as himself.
He wolde thresshe, and therto dyke and delve,	He would thresh and dig and shift,
For Cristes sake, for every povre wight	For every poor person, for the sake of Christ,
Withouten hire, if it lay in his myght.	Without asking for payment, if he could manage it.
Hise tithes payed he ful faire and wel,	He paid his tax in full and on time,
Bothe of his propre swynk and his catel.	For his labour and and on his property.
In a tabard he rood, upon a mere.	He wore a sleeveless coat and rode a mare.
Ther was also a REVE and a MILLERE,	A reeve and a miller were also there;
A SOMNOUR and a PARDONER also,	A summoner, manciple and pardoner,
A MAUNCIPLE, and myself - ther were namo.	And those were the whole company, apart from myself.
The MILLERE was a stout carl for the nones;	The miller was a strong present, it should be known,
Ful byg he was of brawn and eek of bones-	He was very muscular and heavily built;
That proved wel, for over al ther he cam	This was always proved in wrestling tournaments
At wrastlynge he wolde have alwey the ram.	When he would win the prize of a ram.
He was short-sholdred, brood, a thikke knarre,	He was thickset, broad and heavy,
Ther was no dore that he nolde heve of harre,	There was no door he couldn't lift off its hinges,
Or breke it at a rennyng with his heed.	Or break through it by running at head down.
His berd as any sowe or fox was reed,	His beard was as red as a sow or fox,
And therto brood, as though it were a spade.	And broad as a spade.
Upon the cop right of his nose he hade	Right on top of his nose he had
A werte, and thereon stood a toft of herys,	A wart, from which a tuft of hair grew,
Reed as the brustles of a sowes erys;	As red as the bristles in a pig's ear;
Hise nosethirles blake were and wyde.	His nostrils were black and broad.
A swerd and bokeler bar he by his syde.	He carried a sword and belt at his side.
His mouth as greet was as a greet forneys.	His mouth was the size of a great oven.
He was a janglere and a goliardeys,	He was a joker and could recite poetry,
And that was moost of synne and harlotrics.	Though it was mostly about sin and obscene things.
Wel koude he stelen corn, and tollen thries;	He would steal corn, and charge three times the fair price;

And yet he hadde a thombe of gold, pardee.	*He certainly had the Midas touch.*
A whit cote and a blew hood wered he.	*He wore a white coat with a blue hood;*
A baggepipe wel koude he blowe and sowne,	*He could play the bagpipes very well,*
And therwithal he broghte us out of towne.	*And he paged us out of town with them.*
A gentil MAUNCIPLE was ther of a temple,	*There was a Manciple from one of the temples,*
Of which achatours myghte take exemple	*Whom buyers might regard as an example,*
For to be wise in byynge of vitaille;	*In the matter of buying foodstuffs;*
For wheither that he payde or took by taille,	*For whether he paid or took it on credit,*
Algate he wayted so in his achaat	*He always knew the time to buy,*
That he was ay biforn, and in good staat.	*So he always made a profit, he did well.*
Now is nat that of God a ful fair grace,	*Now isn't it proof of the goodness of God*
That swich a lewed mannes wit shal pace	*That such a vulgar man could outwit*
The wisdom of an heep of lerned men?	*A whole crowd of educated men?*
Of maistres hadde he mo than thries ten,	*No more than thirty people could compete with him,*
That weren of lawe expert and curious,	*And they were all experts in the law,*
Of whiche ther weren a duszeyne in that hous	*And there were a dozen in his place*
Worthy to been stywardes of rente and lond	*Who were fit to run the business affairs*
Of any lord that is in Engelond,	*Of any lord of England,*
To maken hym lyve by his propre good,	*And help him live off his own wealth,*
In honour dettelees (but if he were wood),	*Honourably, debt-free (unless he was mad),*
Or lyve as scarsly as hym list desire,	*Or to live as frugally as he wished,*
And able for to helpen al a shire	*For these men could have run a whole county,*
In any caas that myghte falle or happe-	*Under any circumstances at all;*
And yet this Manciple sette hir aller cappe.	*But this manciple could easily outwit them.*
The REVE was a sclendre colerik man.	*The Reeve was a skinny irritable man,*
His berd was shave as ny as ever he kan;	*With his beard shaved as close as he could get it;*
His heer was by his erys ful round yshorn;	*His hair was cut close to his ears,*
His top was dokked lyk a preest biforn.	*And the top was cut like that of a priest.*
Ful longe were his legges, and ful lene,	*He had very long skinny legs*
Ylyk a staf, ther was no calf ysene.	*Like sticks, they went straight down.*
Wel koude he kepe a gerner and a bynne;	*He knew how to manage a granary and a store,*
Ther was noon auditour koude on him wynne.	*No auditor could ever trip him up.*
Wel wiste he by the droghte and by the reyn,	*He knew, by observing the sun and the rain,*
The yeldynge of his seed and of his greyn.	*How much seed and grain he could harvest.*
His lordes sheep, his neet, his dayerye,	*His lord's sheep, cattle and dairy cows,*
His swyn, his hors, his stoor, and his pultrye,	*His pigs, horses, stores and poultry,*
Was hoolly in this Reves governynge,	*Were all at this reeve's command,*
And by his covenant yaf the rekenynge,	*And by arrangement he had kept the books*
Syn that his lord was twenty yeer of age,	*Since this lord was twenty years old,*
Ther koude no man brynge hym in arrerage.	*And no-one had ever found irregularities.*
Ther nas baillif, ne hierde, nor oother hyne,	*No bailiff, shepherd or servant could cheat him,*
That he ne knew his sleighte and his covyne;	*He always knew what they were up to;*
They were adrad of hym as of the deeth.	*They were afraid of him as death itself.*
His wonyng was ful faire upon an heeth;	*He had a fine cottage on a heath,*
With grene trees shadwed was his place.	*Shaded by green trees.*
He koude bettre than his lord purchace.	*He actually was wealthier than his lord,*
Ful riche he was astored pryvely:	*He had amassed a great secret fortune;*
His lord wel koude he plesen subtilly,	*He knew how to keep his lord happy,*
To yeve and lene hym of his owene good,	*By giving or lending him his own goods,*

And have a thank, and yet a cote and hood.
In youthe he hadde lerned a good myster;
He was a wel good wrighte, a carpenter.

This Reve sat upon a ful good stot,
That was al pomely grey, and highte Scot.
A long surcote of pers upon he hade,
And by his syde he baar a rusty blade.
Of Northfolk was this Reve, of which I telle,
Bisyde a toun men clepen Baldeswelle.
Tukked he was as is a frere aboute,
And evere he rood the hyndreste of oure route.

A SOMONOUR was ther with us in that place,
That hadde a fyr-reed cherubynnes face,
For saucefleem he was, with eyen narwe.
As hoot he was and lecherous as a sparwe,

With scalled browes blake, and piled berd,

Of his visage children were aferd.
Ther nas quyk-silver, lytarge, ne brymstoon,
Boras, ceruce, ne oille of tartre noon,
Ne oynement, that wolde clense and byte,
That hym myghte helpen of his whelkes white,
Nor of the knobbes sittynge on his chekes.
Wel loved he garleek, oynons, and eek lekes,
And for to drynken strong wyn, reed as blood;
Thanne wolde he speke and crie as he were wood.
And whan that he wel dronken hadde the wyn,
Than wolde he speke no word but Latyn.
A fewe termes hadde he, two or thre,
That he had lerned out of som decree-
No wonder is, he herde it al the day,
And eek ye knowen wel how that a jay
Kan clepen "Watte" as wel as kan the pope.
But whoso koude in oother thyng hym grope,
Thanne hadde he spent al his philosophie;
Ay "Questio quid iuris" wolde he crie.
He was a gentil harlot and a kynde;
A bettre felawe sholde men noght fynde;
He wolde suffre, for a quart of wyn,
A good felawe to have his concubyn
A twelf-monthe, and excuse hym atte fulle;
Ful prively a fynch eek koude he pulle.

And if he foond owher a good felawe,
He wolde techen him to have noon awe,
In swich caas, of the ercedekenes curs,
But if a mannes soule were in his purs;
For in his purs he sholde ypunysshed be.

"Purs is the erchedekenes helle," seyde he.

And so he got thanks, but also wealth.
When young he had trained in a good trade,
And he had been a skilful workman as a carpenter.

The reeve sat on a good trotting horse,
All dapple grey, called Scot.
He had a long topcoat of blue,
And he carried a rusty sword at his side.
This reeve I'm talking of was from Norfolk,
Next to a town named Baldeswelle.
His coat was tightly belted like a friar's habit,
And he always rode at the back of our procession.

There was a summoner with us there,
With a bright red cherubic face,
Covered in pimples with narrow eyes.
He was as hot tempered and lecherous as a sparrow,
With black scabby eyebrows and a threadbare beard;

His face could frighten children.
No mercury, sulphur, lyes,
Borax, ceruse, or oil of tartar,
No ointment that could clean or scrub,
Would get rid of his white pimples
Or the great boils on his cheeks.
He loved garlic, onions and leeks,
And to drink strong wine, blood-red;
Then he would speak and shout as if mad.
And after he'd had a good drink,
He would speak nothing but Latin.
He had a few phrases, two or three,
That he had learned from some document;
No wonder, as he heard them all day,
And everyone knows that a jay bird
Can give a good imitation of the pope.
But if you tried to investigate him further,
You'd find that was his limit;
He'd cry out, "Questio quid juris".
He was a courteous scoundrel and a kind one;
Nobody could imagine a better companion;
In exchange for a quart of wine
He'd let another chap have his tart
For a year, stepping right out of the way
(Though secretly he'd make sure he still got plenty).
And if he met up with some good fellow,
He would teach him never to be afraid
Of the curse of any archdeacon,
Unless he kept his soul inside his purse,
For it was his purse which would take the punishment.

"Archdeacons hit your purse like devils," he said,

19

But wel I woot he lyed right in dede;	But I know full well he was lying;
Of cursyng oghte ech gilty man him drede,	Every guilty man should dread being cursed
For curs wol slee, right as assoillyng savith,	(Curses can kill just as absolution saves),
And also war him of a Significavit.	And also he should look out for excommunication orders.
In daunger hadde he at his owene gise	He had power over all of
The yonge girles of the diocise,	The young girls in his diocese,
And knew hir conseil, and was al hir reed.	And knew what they thought, he was their confidant.
A gerland hadde he set upon his heed	He put a garland on his head
As greet as it were for an ale-stake;	That was the size of a tavern sign;
A bokeleer hadde he maad him of a cake.	He had made himself a sword belt out of bread.
With hym ther rood a gentil PARDONER	With him there rode a noble pardoner
Of Rouncivale, his freend and his compeer,	Of Roncesvalles, his friend and equal;
That streight was comen fro the court of Rome.	He had come straight from Rome.
Ful loude he soong "Com hider, love, to me!"	He sang loudly, "Come here to me, love,"
This Somonour bar to hym a stif burdoun;	And the summoner came in with a strong bass;
Was nevere trompe of half so greet a soun.	No trumpet was ever half as loud.
This Pardoner hadde heer as yelow as wex,	This pardoner's hair was yellow as wax,
But smothe it heeng as dooth a strike of flex;	But it hung straight down as threads;
By ounces henge his lokkes that he hadde,	It hung down behind in clumps,
And therwith he hise shuldres overspradde;	Spreading over his shoulders,
But thynne it lay by colpons oon and oon.	But it was thin and stringy.
But hood, for jolitee, wered he noon,	But he was a merry chap and wore no hood,
For it was trussed up in his walet.	Keeping it packed in his luggage.
Hym thoughte he rood al of the newe jet;	He thought he was following the latest fashion,
Dischevelee, save his cappe, he rood al bare.	With his hair loose and head bear apart from his cap.
Swiche glarynge eyen hadde he as an hare.	He had shining eyes, bright like a hare's,
A vernycle hadde he sowed upon his cappe.	And a "Veronica cloth" sewn into his cap.
His walet lay biforn hym in his lappe	He carried his bag in front of him on his lap,
Bretful of pardoun come from Rome al hoot.	Stuffed full of pardons, brought fresh from Rome.
A voys he hadde as smal as hath a goot,	His voice was like a bleating goat,
No berd hadde he, ne nevere sholde have;	And he had no beard, nor ever would have,
As smothe it was as it were late shave,	His face was as smooth as if he'd just shaved;
I trowe he were a geldyng or a mare.	I think he was either a gelding or a mare.
But of his craft, from Berwyk into Ware,	But in his job, from Berwick all the way to Ware,
Ne was ther swich another pardoner;	There was no pardoner so successful;
For in his male he hadde a pilwe-beer,	In his bag he had a pillow case,
Which that he seyde was Oure Lady veyl:	Which he said was the veil of Our Lady;
He seyde he hadde a gobet of the seyl	He said he had a fragment of the sail
That Seint Peter hadde, whan that he wente	Which St.Peter had, when he sailed on the sea,
Upon the see, til Jesu Crist hym hente.	Until Jesus called him.
He hadde a croys of latoun ful of stones,	He had a brass cross set with stones,
And in a glas he hadde pigges bones.	And some pig bones in a bottle.
But with thise relikes, whan that he fond	With these relics, when he found
A povre persoun dwellyng upon lond,	Some simple parson in the countryside,
Upon a day he gat hym moore moneye	He made more money from him in one day
Than that the person gat in monthes tweye;	Than the parson could make in two months;
And thus, with feyned flaterye and japes,	So, with false flatery and jokes,
He made the persoun and the peple his apes.	He made a monkey out of the parson and his

But trewely to tellen atte laste,	But, to sum up the whole business truthfully,
He was in chirche a noble ecclesiaste.	He was a fine pious man in church.
Wel koude he rede a lessoun or a storie,	He was expert at reading a lesson or a parable,
But alderbest he song an offertorie;	But he was best when he sang for the offertory,
For wel he wiste, whan that song was songe,	For he was well aware, when that song was sung,
He moste preche, and wel affile his tonge	That he should preach, and with his smooth tongue
To wynne silver, as he ful wel koude;	Get as much silver from the congregation as he could;
Therfore he song the murierly and loude.	So he sang out merrily and loud.
Now have I toold you shortly in a clause,	Now I have told you briefly, in a few words,
Th'estaat, th'array, the nombre, and eek the cause	The rank, order and number, and the reason
Why that assembled was this compaignye	That all these people assembled
In Southwerk, at this gentil hostelrye	In Southwark, at this fine hostelry
That highte the Tabard, faste by the Belle.	Known as the Tabard Inn, close by the Bell.
But now is tyme to yow for to telle	But now the time has come for me to tell
How that we baren us that ilke nyght,	Of what we did with ourselves on that first night
Whan we were in that hostelrie alyght;	When we all met up at the inn.
And after wol I telle of our viage	Afterwards I'll begin telling you
And all the remenaunt of oure pilgrimage.	The story of our pilgrimage.
But first I pray yow, of youre curteisye,	But first, I beg you, politely indulge me,
That ye n'arette it nat my vileynye,	Don't think that I am being vulgar
Thogh that I pleynly speke in this mateere,	When I address the matter plainly,
To telle yow hir wordes and hir cheere,	Telling you what they said and how they enjoyed themselves;
Ne thogh I speke hir wordes proprely.	Even though I will be using their exact words.
For this ye knowen also wel as I,	For you know this as well as I do:
Whoso shal telle a tale after a man,	That when somebody repeats a story told by a man,
He moot reherce as ny as evere he kan	He must try to remember as closely as possible
Everich a word, if it be in his charge,	Every single word, if he can,
Al speke he never so rudeliche or large,	However rude or vulgar they might be,
Or ellis he moot telle his tale untrewe,	Or otherwise he will be telling an untrue story,
Or feyne thyng, or fynde wordes newe.	Making things up, putting words in their mouths.
He may nat spare, al thogh he were his brother;	He shouldn't spare them, even if he were talking of his brother;
He moot as wel seye o word as another.	He must report him word for word.
Crist spak hymself ful brode in hooly writ,	Christ himself spoke very plainly in the holy book,
And, wel ye woot, no vileynye is it.	And you know very well there's nothing bad there.
Eek Plato seith, whoso kan hym rede,	Also Plato says, to those who can read,
The wordes moote be cosyn to the dede.	"The words must be matching to the deeds."
Also I prey yow to foryeve it me,	I also beg you to forgive me
Al have I nat set folk in hir degree	If I have not put people in their proper place
Heere in this tale, as that they sholde stonde.	Here in this story, as they ought to be.
My wit is short, ye may wel understonde.	I'm not that clever, as you will see.
Greet chiere made oure Hoost us everichon,	Our host provided a warm welcome for flock.

And to the soper sette he us anon.	And settled us down to supper at once.
He served us with vitaille at the beste;	He served us with the finest foods,
Strong was the wyn, and wel to drynke us leste.	The wine was strong and everyone liked it.
A semely man OURE HOOSTE was withalle	Our host was a very elegant man,
For to been a marchal in an halle.	For he had worked in elegant places.
A large man he was, with eyen stepe -	He was a large man, with piercing eyes,
A fairer burgeys was ther noon in Chepe -	There wasn't a better citizen in Cheapside;
Boold of his speche, and wys, and well ytaught,	He spoke openly, and was wise, and well educated,
And of manhod hym lakkede right naught.	And he wasn't lacking anything that goes to make up a man.
Eek therto he was right a myrie man,	He was also a very jolly man,
And after soper pleyen he bigan,	And after supper he began some fun,
And spak of myrthe amonges othere thynges,	And spoke of mirth amongst other things,
Whan that we hadde maad our rekenynges,	When we had all paid our bills,
And seyde thus: "Now lordynges, trewely,	And said, "Now my Lords, truly
Ye been to me right welcome hertely;	I give you all a hearty welcome;
For by my trouthe, if that I shal nat lye,	I give you my word, and that's no lie,
I saugh nat this yeer so myrie a compaignye	That I haven't had a group in this inn this year,
Atones in this herberwe, as is now.	Ready for fun, who were as merry as you.
Fayn wolde I doon yow myrthe, wiste I how.	I can see you want some sport, and I know how to provide it.
And of a myrthe I am right now bythoght,	Just now I have thought of great entertainment,
To doon yow ese, and it shal coste noght.	To pass your time, and it will cost nothing.
Ye goon to Caunterbury - God yow speede,	You are going to Canterbury; may God speed you,
The blisful martir quite yow youre meede!	And may the holy martyr listen to your prayers!
And wel I woot, as ye goon by the weye,	I am sure, as you go on your journey,
Ye shapen yow to talen and to pleye,	You will have fun and tell tales,
For trewely, confort ne myrthe is noon	For truly there is no comfort or fun
To ride by the weye doumb as stoon;	Riding along dumb as stones;
And therfore wol I maken yow disport,	And so I will set up a game,
As I seyde erst, and doon yow som confort.	As I just said, that will entertain you.
And if yow liketh alle by oon assent	And if you will all agree unanimously
For to stonden at my juggement,	To allow yourselves to be judged by me,
And for to werken as I shal yow seye,	And to do what I tell you,
To-morwe, whan ye riden by the weye,	Tomorrow, when you go follow the way,
Now, by my fader soule that is deed,	I swear on the soul of my dead father
But ye be myrie, I wol yeve yow myn heed!	That if you're not jolly, you can cut off my head!
Hoold up youre hond, withouten moore speche."	No more speech, put up your hand if you agree."
Oure conseil was nat longe for to seche.	It didn't take us long to decide,
Us thoughte it was noght worth to make it wys,	We thought there was no reason to disagree,
And graunted hym, withouten moore avys,	And without further debate we told him
And bad him seye his voirdit, as hym leste.	To tell us his idea, as he wished.
"Lordynges," quod he, "now herkneth for the beste;	"Lords," he said, "now listen carefully;
But taak it nought, I prey yow, in desdeyn.	And don't sneer at my idea, I pray.
This is the poynt, to speken short and pleyn,	I will speak briefly and to the point;
That ech of yow, to shorte with oure weye,	To make our journey seem shorter, each of you

In this viage shal telle tales tweye To Caunterbury-ward I mene it so, And homward he shal tellen othere two, Of aventures that whilom han bifalle. And which of yow that bereth hym best of alle, That is to seyn, that telleth in this caas Tales of best sentence and moost solaas, Shal have a soper at oure aller cost	*In this company shall tell two stories as we* *Make our way to Canterbury; and each of you* *Will tell two more as we come home,* *About things that have happened in the past.* *And whoever acquits himself the best,* *That is to say, who tells us the best* *Stories, and the most amusing,* *Will have a supper at the expense of the others,*
Heere in this place, sittynge by this post, Whan that we come agayn fro Caunterbury. And for to make yow the moore mury, I wol myselven goodly with yow ryde Right at myn owene cost, and be youre gyde; And who so wole my juggement withseye Shal paye al that we spenden by the weye.	*Sitting right here in this room,* *When we come back from Canterbury.* *And to make sure you enjoy yourselves* *I will gladly ride with you myself* *At my own expense, and I will be your guide.* *But anyone who disagrees with my judgement* *Will pay for everything we spend along the way.*
And if ye vouche sauf that it be so, Tel me anon, withouten wordes mo, And I wol erly shape me therfore."	*If you agree to this* *Tell me at once, with no more discussion,* *And I will make sure I'm ready early tomorrow.*
This thyng was graunted, and oure othes swore With ful glad herte, and preyden hym also That he wolde vouche sauf for to do so, And that he wolde been oure governour, And of our tales juge and reportour, And sette a soper at a certeyn pris, And we wol reuled been at his devys In heigh and lough; and thus by oon assent We been acorded to his juggement. And therupon the wyn was fet anon; We dronken, and to reste wente echon, Withouten any lenger taryynge.	*His wish was granted and we swore oaths* *Very gladly, and also asked him* *That he would do as he suggested* *And be our leader,* *And be the judge of our tales,* *And arrange that supper at a set price,* *And that we would follow his plan* *In every respect; and so unanimously* *We accepted his rule over us.* *At that the wine was fetched at once* *And we drank to it and went off to bed* *Without any further ado.*
Amorwe, whan that day bigan to sprynge, Up roos oure Hoost, and was oure aller cok, And gadrede us to gidre alle in a flok, And forth we riden, a litel moore than paas Unto the wateryng of Seint Thomas; And there oure Hoost bigan his hors areste And seyde, "Lordynges, herkneth if yow leste. Ye woot youre foreward, and I it yow recorde. If even-song and morwe-song accorde, Lat se now who shal telle the firste tale. As evere mote I drynke wyn or ale,	*Next morning at daybreak* *Our host got up and woke us all* *And gathered us together in a group,* *And out we rode at a jog trot,* *Until we reached St Thomas' well;* *And there our host pulled up his horse* *And said, "Lords, listen if you please.* *You know the agreement, and I'll remind you.* *If what you said last night stands good,* *Let's now decide who will tell the first tale.* *I swear by my hope that I will always drink wine and beer*
Whoso be rebel to my juggement Shal paye for al that by the wey is spent. Now draweth cut, er that we ferrer twynne, He which that hath the shorteste shal bigynne. Sire Knyght," quod he, "my mayster and my lord, Now draweth cut, for that is myn accord. Cometh neer," quod he, "my lady Prioresse, And ye, Sir Clerk, lat be youre shamefastnesse,	*That whoever disagrees with my judgement* *Will pay for everything we spend on the way.* *Now let's draw straws before we go farther,* *And whoever draws the longest one will begin.* *Sir Knight," he said, "my master and my lord,* *You draw first, that's my decision.* *Come here," he said, "my lady prioress,* *And you, Sir Clerk, drop your shyness,*

Ne studieth noght; ley hond to, every man!"
Anon to drawen every wight bigan,
And shortly for to tellen as it was,
Were it by aventure, or sort, or cas,
The sothe is this, the cut fil to the Knyght,
Of which ful blithe and glad was every wyght.
And telle he moste his tale, as was resoun,
By foreward and by composicioun,-
As ye han herd, what nedeth wordes mo?
And whan this goode man saugh that it was so,

As he that wys was and obedient
To kepe his foreward by his free assent,

He seyde, "Syn I shal bigynne the game,
What, welcome be the cut, a Goddes name!
Now lat us ryde, and herkneth what I seye."
And with that word we ryden forth oure weye,
And he bigan with right a myrie cheere
His tale anon, and seyde as ye may heere.

No more discussion, everyone draw lots!"
At once everyone drew a straw,
And to cut a long story short it happened,
Whether by chance or luck or design,
The truth is, the Knight drew the short straw,
Which everyone else was very pleased with.
So he had to tell his story first as we'd agreed,
According to what we had sworn to before,
As I've told you, what more need I say?
And when this good man saw what had happened,
As he was wise and obedient,
He said, to keep his promise he had freely given,
"Since it's me to start the game,
Why, I thank God for letting me win the cut!
Now let's ride on, and listen to what I say."
When he said that we carried on our way,
And he began at once to tell very merrily
His story, as you will hear.

The Knight's Tale

Whilom, as olde stories tellen us,	*Once upon a time, as the old stories say,*
Ther was a duc that highte Theseus;	*There was a duke who was called Theseus:*
Of Atthenes he was lord and governour,	*He was lord and governor of Athens,*
And in his tyme swich a conquerour,	*And in his time he was such a conqueror*
That gretter was ther noon under the sonne.	*That there was no match for him on Earth.*
Ful many a riche contree hadde he wonne,	*He had won over many rich countries,*
What with his wysdom and his chivalrie;	*With his wisdom and chivalry;*
He conquered al the regne of Femenye,	*He won over that kingdom of women,*
That whilom was ycleped Scithia,	*That in ancient times was called Scythia,*
And weddede the queene Ypolita,	*And he married Queen Hippolyta,*
And broghte hir hoom with hym in his contree,	*And brought her back to his own country,*
With muchel glorie and greet solempnytee,	*With great glory and ceremony,*
And eek hir yonge suster Emelye.	*And also he brought her younger sister, Emily.*
And thus with victorie and with melodye	*So, victorious and with music playing,*
Lete I this noble duc to Atthenes ryde,	*I bring this noble duke riding to Athens,*
And al his hoost, in armes hym bisyde.	*With all his forces marching armed beside him.*
And certes, if it nere to long to heere,	*And honestly, if it wasn't too long a tale,*
I wolde have toold yow fully the manere	*I would have described in full how*
How wonnen was the regne of Femenye	*He won over that kingdom of women,*
By Theseus, and by his chivalrye,	*This Theseus, with his chivalry,*
And of the grete bataille for the nones	*And also of the great battle fought*
Bitwixen Atthenes and Amazones,	*Between Athens and the Amazons,*
And how asseged was Ypolita	*And how he laid siege to Hippolyta,*
The faire hardy queene of Scithia,	*The beautiful strong Queen of Scythia,*
And of the feste that was at hir weddynge,	*And of the great feast they had for their wedding,*
And of the tempest at hir hoom-comynge;	*And the storm they encountered coming home;*
But al the thyng I moot as now forbere,	*But I must leave all that aside for now,*
I have, God woot, a large feeld to ere,	*I have, God knows, plenty to tell you,*
And wayke been the oxen in my plough,	*And it's going to be a hard enough job;*
The remenant of the tale is long ynough.	*The rest of my tale will take long enough.*
I wol nat letten eek noon of this route,	*I don't want to get in anyone's way,*
Lat every felawe telle his tale aboute,	*Let everyone tell his story in turn*
And lat se now who shal the soper wynne;-	*And let's see who will win the supper;*
And ther I lefte, I wol ayeyn bigynne.	*So, where I left off, I will start again.*
This duc of whom I make mencioun,	*This Duke whom I have mentioned,*
Whan he was come almoost unto the toun,	*When he had almost got into town,*
In al his wele and in his mooste pride,	*Feeling fine and very proud,*
He was war, as he caste his eye aside,	*He noticed, as he looked aside,*
Where that ther kneled in the hye weye	*Where there were kneeling in the road*
A compaignye of ladyes, tweye and tweye,	*A group of ladies, all in pairs,*
Ech after oother, clad in clothes blake;	*All the same, dressed in black;*
But swich a cry and swich a wo they make,	*They were making such a cry of sorrow*
That in this world nys creature lyvynge	*That no person living*
That herde swich another waymentynge;	*Had ever heard such lamentation;*
And of this cry they nolde nevere stenten,	*And they did not hold back on their cries*
Til they the reynes of his brydel henten.	*Until they had hold of his bridle.*
"What folk been ye, that at myn hom-comynge	*"Who are you, who disturbs my homecoming,*
Perturben so my feste with criynge?"	*Spoiling my triumph with such sorrow?"*
Quod Theseus. "Have ye so greet envye	*Asked Theseus. "Are you so jealous*

Of myn honour, that thus compleyne and crye?	Of my honour, that you complain and wail?
Or who hath yow mysboden or offended?	Otherwise who has wronged you, who offended?
And telleth me if it may been amended,	Tell me if it can be put right,
And why that ye been clothed thus in blak?"	And why you are all dressed in black?"
The eldeste lady of hem alle spak-	The oldest lady of them all spoke,
Whan she hadde swowned with a deedly cheere,	After she had swooned, pale cheeked,
That it was routhe for to seen and heere-	it was pitiful to see them and hear them—
And seyde, "Lord, to whom Fortune hath yiven	And she said, "Lord, Fortune has given you
Victorie, and as a conqueror to lyven,	Victory, allowing you to live as a conqueror,
Nat greveth us youre glorie and youre honour,	And we do not regret your glory and your honour,
But we biseken mercy and socour.	But we are seeking mercy and assistance.
Have mercy on oure wo and oure distresse,	Have mercy on our sorrow and distress,
Som drope of pitee thurgh thy gentillesse	Through your kindness give us some drop of pity,
Upon us wrecched wommen lat thou falle;	Let it fall on us wretched women;
For certes, lord, ther is noon of us alle,	For truthfully, Lord, there is not one of us
That she ne hath been a duchesse or a queene.	Who has not been a duchess or queen.
Now be we caytyves, as it is wel seene,	Now we're prisoners, as you can clearly see,
Thanked be Fortune, and hir false wheel,	Thanks to Fortune and her treacherous ways,
That noon estaat assureth to be weel.	Which mean nobody can rest assured of happiness.
And certes, lord, to abyden youre presence,	Truly Lord, we have been waiting for you,
Heere in the temple of the goddesse Clemence	Here in the temple of the goddess of pity,
We han ben waitynge al this fourtenyght;	For the whole of the last fortnight;
Now help us, lord, sith it is in thy myght!	Now help us, Lord, you have the power!
I wrecche, which that wepe and waille thus,	This wretch whom you see weeping and wailing like this
Was whilom wyf to kyng Cappaneus,	Was once the wife of King Cappaneus,
That starf at Thebes -cursed be that day!-	Who died at Thebes—may that day be cursed!-
And alle we that been in this array	And everyone you see in this group
And maken al this lamentacioun,	Makes the same lamentation,
We losten alle oure housbondes at that toun,	We all lost our husbands in that town,
Whil that the seege theraboute lay.	While it was under siege.
And yet now the olde Creon, weylaway!	And even now old Creon, alas!
That lord is now of Thebes the Citee,	That lord is now governor of Thebes,
Fulfild of ire and of iniquitee,	Filled with anger and injustice,
He, for despit and for his tirannye,	Out of spite and from tyranny
To do the dede bodyes vileynye,	He wants to shame the dead bodies
Of alle oure lordes, whiche that been slawe,	Of all our lords who have been killed.
Hath alle the bodyes on an heep ydrawe,	He has piled all the bodies in a heap
And wol nat suffren hem, by noon assent,	And will not allow them in any way
Neither to been yburyed nor ybrent,	To be either buried or burnt;
But maketh houndes ete hem in despit."	He lets his dogs eat them out of spite."
And with that word, withouten moore respit,	Having said that without a pause
They fillen gruf, and criden pitously,	They all fell the ground and cried out piteously,
"Have on us wrecched wommen som mercy	"Have some mercy on we wretched women,
And lat oure sorwe synken in thyn herte."	Let our sorrows sink into your heart!"
This gentil duc doun from his courser sterte	This noble Duke got down from his horse
With herte pitous, whan he herde hem speke;	With his heart full of pity, when he had heard them speak;

Hym thoughte that his herte wolde breke,	He thought that his heart would break
Whan he saugh hem so pitous and so maat,	When he saw them in such a pitiful state
That whilom weren of so greet estaat.	Who previously had been so exalted.
And in his armes he hem alle up hente,	He lifted them all with his arms,
And hem conforteth in ful good entente,	And comforted them as well as he could,
And swoor his ooth, as he was trewe knyght,	And swore on his oath as a true knight
He wolde doon so ferforthly his myght	That he would use his power so mightily
Upon the tiraunt Creon hem to wreke,	That he would take vengeance against the tyrant Creon
That all the peple of Grece sholde speke	So great that all of Greece would speak
How Creon was of Theseus yserved,	Of how he was treated by Theseus,
As he that hadde his deeth ful wel deserved.	As one who had fully deserved to die.
And right anoon, withouten moore abood,	And straight away, without further ado,
His baner he desplayeth, and forth rood	He raised his banners and rode out
To Thebes-ward, and al his hoost biside,	Towards Thebes, with all his forces beside him;
No neer Atthenes wolde he go ne ride,	He would not go any farther towards Athens,
Ne take his ese fully half a day,	Nor would he rest for even half a day,
But onward on his wey that nyght he lay,	But he started his journey that very night,
And sente anon Ypolita the queene,	And he sent his queen Hippolyta
And Emelye, hir yonge suster sheene,	And her beautiful younger sister Emily
Unto the toun of Atthenes to dwelle,	To live in the town of Athens
And forth he rit; ther is namoore to telle.	As he rode out; that's all there is to say about that.
The rede statue of Mars, with spere and targe,	The red image of Mars, with his spear and shield,
So shyneth, in his white baner large,	Shone so brightly on his snow white banner
That alle the feeldes gliteren up and doun,	That all the fields glittered in its reflection,
And by his baner gorn is his penoun	And next to the banner was his pennant,
Of gold ful riche, in which ther was ybete	On which there was the image in beaten gold
The Mynotaur which that he slough in Crete.	Of the Minotaur, which he had killed in Crete.
Thus rit this duc, thus rit this conquerour,	So on rode this duke, this conqueror,
And in his hoost of chivalrie the flour,	With his army, the flower of chivalry,
Til that he cam to Thebes, and alighte	Until he came to Thebes, and dismounted
Faire in a feeld, ther as he thoughte to fighte.	Right in the field where he wished to fight.
But shortly for to speken of this thyng,	But to speak as briefly as possible,
With Creon, which that was of Thebes kyng,	He fought with Creon, King of Thebes,
He faught, and slough hym manly as a knight	And killed him manfully, as a knight should,
In pleyn bataille, and putte the folk to flyght;	In open battle, and he put his army to flight;
And by assaut he wan the citee after,	Then he attacked the city and captured it,
And rente adoun bothe wall, and sparre, and rafter.	And tore down its walls and its roofs.
And to the ladyes he sestored agayn	He gave back to the ladies
The bones of hir freendes that weren slayn,	The bodies of their friends who had been killed,
To doon obsequies as was tho the gyse.	So they could perform the proper burial ceremonies.
But it were al to longe for to devyse	It would take far too long to describe
The grete clamour and the waymentynge	The great clamour of grief
That the ladyes made at the brennynge	That the ladies made as they burned
Of the bodies, and the grete honour	The bodies, and the great honour
That Theseus, the noble conquerour,	That Theseus, the noble conqueror,
Dooth to the ladyes, whan they from hym wente;	Paid to the ladies when they left him;
But shortly for to telle is myn entente.	I want to keep my story short.
Whan that his worthy duc, this Theseus,	When this good Duke, this Theseus,

Hath Creon slayn, and wonne Thebes thus,	Had killed Creon and captured his city of Thebes,
Stille in that feeld he took al nyght his reste,	He rested at night on the battlefield,
And dide with al the contree as hym leste.	And disposed of the country as he thought best.
To ransake in the taas of bodyes dede,	Ransacking the bodies of the dead,
Hem for to strepe of harneys and of wede,	To take away their gear and their clothes,
The pilours diden bisynesse and cure,	The pillagers did excellent business,
After the bataille and disconfiture;	After the battle and the overthrow;
And so bifel, that in the taas they founde	And so it happened that in the heap they discovered,
Thurgh-girt with many a grevous blody wounde,	Pierced with many terrible bloody wounds,
Two yonge knyghtes liggynge by and by,	Two young knights lying side by side,
Bothe in oon armes, wroght ful richely,	Both with the same crest, richly made,
Of whiche two Arcita highte that oon,	One of them was called Arcite
And that oother knyght highte Palamon.	And the other was called Palamon.
Nat fully quyke, ne fully dede they were,	They seem to be neither alive nor dead,
But by here cote-armures and by hir gere,	But from their coats of arms and their armour
The heraudes knewe hem best in special	The heralds could easily see that
As they that weren of the blood roial	They were members of the royal family
Of Thebes, and of sustren two yborn.	Of Thebes, and that they were cousins.
Out of the taas the pilours han hem torn,	The pillagers pulled them out of the heap
And had hem caried softe unto the tente	And carried them gently to the tent
Of Theseus, and he ful soone hem sente	Of Theseus, and soon he had them sent
To Atthenes to dwellen in prisoun	To Athens to live in prison
Perpetuelly, he nolde no raunsoun.	Forever, he wouldn't hear of ransom.
And whan this worthy duc hath thus ydon,	And when this good Duke had done this
He took his hoost, and hoom he rit anon,	He gathered up his forces and soon rode home,
With laurer crowned, as a conquerour;	Crowned with laurels as a conqueror;
And ther he lyveth in joye and in honour	And he lived there happily and with honour
Terme of his lyve; what nedeth wordes mo?	For his whole life; what more needs to be said?
And in a tour, in angwissh and in wo,	And this Palamon and also Arcite
Dwellen this Palamon and eek Arcite	Lived in a tower, in anguish and sorrow,
For evermoore, ther may no gold hem quite.	Forever, where no gold could free them.
This passeth yeer by yeer, and day by day,	So the days and years passed
Till it fil ones, in a morwe of May,	Until it happened on a May morning
That Emelye, that fairer was to sene	That Emily, who was more beautiful to see
Than is the lylie upon his stalke grene,	Than a lily on its green stalk,
And fressher than the May with floures newe—	And fresher than the May flowers blooming—
For with the rose colour stroof hir hewe,	For her colour competed with that of the rose,
I noot which was the fairer of hem two—	I couldn't say which one was more lovely—
Er it were day, as was hir wone to do,	Before dawn, as she often did,
She was arisen, and al redy dight—	She had risen, and was already dressed,
For May wole have no slogardie a-nyght;	For May doesn't encourage people to lie in;
The sesoun priketh every gentil herte,	That season stimulates every kind heart,
And maketh hym out of his slepe to sterte,	Making people rise out of their sleep,
And seith, "Arys and do thyn observaunce."	Saying, "Get up and pay your respects."
This maked Emelye have remembraunce	This made Emily remember
To doon honour to May, and for to ryse.	To show honour to May, and to get up.
Yclothed was she fressh, for to devyse,	She dressed in fresh clothes, and to describe

Hir yelow heer was broyded in a tresse,	Her yellow hair was braided in a plait
Bihynde hir bak, a yerde long, I gesse,	Behind her back, I would guess a yard long,
And in the gardyn, at the sonne upriste,	And in the garden, at sunrise,
She walketh up and doun, and as hir liste	She walked up and down, and as she went
She gadereth floures, party white and rede,	She gathered flowers, some white and some red,
To make a subtil gerland for hir hede,	To make a delicate garland for her head,
And as an aungel hevenysshly she soong.	And she sang like an angel from heaven.
The grete tour, that was so thikke and stroong,	The great tower, that was so thick and strong,
Which of the castel was the chief dongeoun,	Which was the main dungeon of the castle,
(Ther as the knyghtes weren in prisoun,	(Which was where the knights were imprisoned,
Of whiche I tolde yow, and tellen shal)	As I mentioned, and I shall tell you more)
Was evene joynant to the gardyn wal	Was directly adjacent to the garden wall,
Ther as this Emelye hadde hir pleyynge.	Just where Emily went for a stroll;
Bright was the sonne, and cleer that morwenynge,	The sun was bright, and the morning was clear,
And Palamoun, this woful prisoner,	And Palamon, this sorrowful prisoner,
As was his wone, by leve of his gayler,	As he usually did, with his jailer's permission,
Was risen, and romed in a chambre on heigh,	Had risen, and was walking in a high room,
In which he al the noble citee seigh,	From which he could see all of the great city,
And eek the gardyn, ful of braunches grene,	And also the garden, full of green branches,
Ther as this fresshe Emelye the shene	Where bright serene Emily
Was in hire walk, and romed up and doun.	Was taking her walk, roaming up and down.
This sorweful prisoner, this Palamoun,	This sorrowful prisoner, this Palamon,
Goth in the chambre romynge to and fro,	Went walking to and fro in the room,
And to hym-self compleynynge of his wo.	And complained to himself of his sorrows.
That he was born, ful ofte he seyde, "allas!"	He often cried "Alas!" for the fact he was born,
And so bifel, by aventure or cas,	And so it happened, by chance or design,
That thurgh a wyndow, thikke of many a barre	That through a thickly barred iron window,
Of iren greet, and square as any sparre,	Which was as strong as a ship's mast,
He cast his eye upon Emelya,	He happened to spy Emily, and cried "Ah!"
And therwithal he bleynte, and cryede "A!"	As though he had been stabbed to the heart.
As though he stongen were unto the herte.	At that cry Arcite sprang up
And with that cry Arcite anon up sterte	And said, "My cousin, what's wrong,
And seyde, "Cosyn myn, what eyleth thee,	Why do you look so deathly pale?
That art so pale and deedly on to see?	Why did you cry out? What's harmed you?
Why cridestow? who hath thee doon offence?	For the love of God, endure our prison
For Goddess love, taak al in pacience	Patiently, it cannot be helped;
Oure prisoun, for it may noon oother be;	Fortune has given us this trial,
Fortune hath yeven us this adversitee.	Some evil conjunction of Saturn
Som wikke aspect or disposicioun	With some other constellation
Of Saturne, by sum constellacioun	Has brought us here, against our will;
Hath yeven us this, al though we hadde it sworn;	Has given us this, although we had sworn it would not be;
So stood the hevene, whan that we were born.	That's how the stars were when we were born,
We moste endure it, this the short and playn."	We must put up with it, and that's the end of it."
This Palamon answerde and seyde agayn:	This is how Palamon answered him:
"Cosyn, for sothe, of this opinioun	"Cousin, I swear, you have got the
Thow hast a veyn ymaginacioun.	Wrong end of the stick.
This prison caused me nat for to crye,	It wasn't this prison which made me cry out,

But I was hurt right now thurgh-out myn ye	But I just received a wound through my eye
Into myn herte, that wol my bane be.	Right down to my heart, that will be the death of me.
The fairnesse of that lady, that I see	The beauty of that lady that I see,
Yond in the gardyn romen to and fro,	Out there in the garden wandering to and fro,
Is cause of al my criyng and my wo.	Is what makes me cry and brings me sorrow.
I noot wher she be womman or goddesse,	I don't know whether she is a woman or goddess,
But Venus is it, soothly as I gesse."	But I swear my guess would be that she is Venus."
And therwithal, on knees doun he fil,	And on the spot he fell down on his knees,
And seyde, "Venus, if it be thy wil,	And said, "Venus, if it is your wish
Yow in this gardyn thus to transfigure	To appear disguised in this garden
Bifore me, sorweful wrecched creature,	Showing yourself to me, this sad creature,
Out of this prisoun helpe that we may scapen!	Help us to escape from this prison!
And if so be my destynee be shapen	And if it is my destiny, shaped by
By eterne word to dyen in prisoun,	The gods, to die in prison,
Of oure lynage have som compassioun,	Have pity on we so nobly born
That is so lowe ybroght by tirannye."	Who have been brought down by tyranny."
And with that word Arcite gan espye	As he said this Arcite went to see
Wher-as this lady romed to and fro,	This lady roaming to and fro,
And with that sighte hir beautee hurte hym so,	And the sight of her beauty hurt him so
That, if that Palamon was wounded sore,	That if Palamon was badly wounded
Arcite is hurt as moche as he, or moore.	Arcite was hurt as much, if not more.
And with a sigh he seyde pitously:	With a sigh he said piteously:
"The fresshe beautee sleeth me sodeynly	"Such fresh beauty has killed me suddenly,
Of hire, that rometh in the yonder place,	That of the one who is wandering there,
And but I have hir mercy and hir grace	And if I don't have her pity and her grace,
That I may seen hir atte leeste weye,	Allowing me to at least look on her every day,
I nam but deed, ther is namoore to seye."	I'm as good as dead, that's the end of it."
This Palamon, whan he tho wordes herde,	When Palamon heard these words,
Dispitously he looked and answerde,	He looked dispassionately at him and answered,
"Wheither seistow this in ernest or in pley?"	"Are you in earnest or are you joking?"
"Nay," quod Arcite, "in ernest by my fey,	"No," said Arcite, "I'm telling you I'm earnest,
God helpe me so, me list ful yvele pleye."	So help me God, I'm not messing about."
This Palamon gan knytte his browes tweye;	Then Palamon began to frown sternly;
"It nere," quod he, "to thee no greet honour	"It would be dishonourable of you," he said,
For to be fals, ne for to be traitour	"To be false and a traitor
To me, that am thy cosyn and thy brother,	To me, who is your cousin and your brother,
Ysworn ful depe, and ech of us til oother,	Sworn to be loyal to each other as we are,
That nevere for to dyen in the peyne,	Sworn that we would, on pain of death, never,
Til that the deeth departe shal us tweyne,	Even until death parts us,
Neither of us in love to hyndre other,	Block the other in love,
Ne in noon oother cas, my leeve brother,	Nor in any other way, my dear brother,
But that thou sholdest trewely forthren me	Indeed you should be loyally helping me
In every cas, as I shal forthren thee, -	In every way, as I shall help you;
This was thyn ooth, and myn also certeyn,	This was what you swore, and so did I,
I woot right wel thou darst it nat withseyn.	I know well that you will not deny it.
Thus artow of my conseil, out of doute;	So you are on my side, beyond doubt;
And now thou woldest falsly been aboute	And now you treacherously want to go and
To love my lady, whom I love and serve	Love my lady, whom I love and serve
And evere shal, til that myn herte sterve.	And always will, until my heart gives out.

Nay, certes, false Arcite, thow shalt nat so! I loved hire first, and tolde thee my wo As to my conseil, and to my brother sworn, To forthre me as I have toold biforn, For which thou art ybounden as a knyght To helpen me, if it lay in thy myght, Or elles artow fals, I dar wel seyn."	No, false Arcite, I certainly won't allow it! I loved her first, and told you of my sorrow, As my advisor and my brother who is sworn To help me, as I told you before, And you are bound by the laws of chivalry To help me, if there's anything you can do, Or otherwise I say you are false."
This Arcite ful proudly spak ageyn, "Thow shalt," quod he, "be rather fals than I.	Arcite proudly spoke again, "It would be you," he said, "who is false, not me,
But thou art fals, I telle thee outrely, For paramour I loved hir first er thow.	And you are utterly false, I tell you, For you know that I loved her as a lover before you,
What, wiltow seyn thou wistest nat yet now Wheither she be a womman or goddesse? Thyn is affeccioun of hoolynesse, And myn is love, as to a creature; For which I tolde thee myn aventure As to my cosyn and my brother sworn. I pose, that thow lovedest hir biforn; Wostow nat wel the olde clerkes sawe That `who shal yeve a lovere any lawe?' Love is a gretter lawe, by my pan, Than may be yeve of any erthely man. And therfore positif lawe and swich decree Is broken al day for love in ech degree. A man moot nedes love, maugree his heed, He may nat fleen it, thogh he sholde be deed, Al be she mayde, or wydwe, or elles wyf. And eek it is nat likly, al thy lyf, To stonden in hir grace, namoore shal I,	What, didn't you just say that you didn't know Whether she was a woman or a goddess? You are worshipping her in a holy way, And I am loving her as a mortal creature; I told you how I felt As my cousin and my sworn brother. Imagine that you loved her before me; Don't you know what the old writers said, "All's fair in love and war?" Love is more powerful, in my opinion, Than any law created by mortal men. So the statute laws and things like that Are broken every day for every sort of love. A man needs love, whatever he is thinking, He cannot flee it even if it would kill him, And whether she is a maid, a widow or a wife, It is unlikely that in this life You will get any favour from her, and nor shall I;
For wel thou woost thyselven, verraily, That thou and I be dampned to prisoun Perpetuelly, us gayneth no raunsoun. We stryven as dide the houndes for the boon, They foughte al day, and yet hir part was noon. Ther cam a kyte, whil they weren so wrothe,	For you know perfectly well That you and I are condemned to prison For ever, we cannot be ransomed. We are fighting like dogs fighting over a bone, They fought all day but got nothing, Then a kite came, when they were still fighting,
And baar awey the boon bitwixe hem bothe.	And carried the bone away from under their noses.
And therfore at the kynges court, my brother, Ech man for hymself, ther is noon oother.	And so at the king's court, my brother, It's every man for himself, not helping any other.
Love if thee list, for I love, and ay shal;	You can love if you want, for I do, and always shall;
And soothly, leeve brother, this is al.	And truly, dear brother, that's all I have to say.
Heere in this prisoun moote we endure, And everich of us take his aventure."	We have to stay in this prison cell, And each of us put up with his fate."
Greet was the strif and long bitwix hem tweye,	The arguments between the two were long and passionate,
If that I hadde leyser for to seye.	If I just had time to describe them.

But to th'effect; it happed on a day,	*But to summarise; it happened that one day,*
To telle it yow as shortly as I may,	*To cut the story as short as I may,*
A worthy duc, that highte Perotheus,	*A noble duke, called Perotheus,*
That felawe was unto duc Theseus	*Who had been a friend of Duke Theseus*
Syn thilke day that they were children lite,	*Since they were little children*
Was come to Atthenes his felawe to visite,	*Came to Athens to see his friend,*
And for to pleye as he was wont to do—	*To enjoy themselves as they used to do,*
For in this world he loved no man so,	*For he loved no man in the world as well as Theseus,*
And he loved hym als tendrely agayn.	*And Theseus felt the same about him.*
So wel they lovede, as olde bookes sayn,	*They were so close, old stories say,*
That whan that oon was deed, soothly to telle,	*That when one died, and this is truth,*
His felawe wente and soughte hym doun in helle.	*His friend went to look for him in hell.*
But of that storie list me nat to write;	*But I don't have time to tell that story;*
Duc Perotheus loved wel Arcite,	*Duke Perotheus was very fond of Arcite,*
And hadde hym knowe at Thebes yeer by yere,	*And had known him at Thebes for many years,*
And finally, at requeste and preyere	*And finally at the fervent request*
Of Perotheus, withouten any raunsoun,	*Of Perotheus, without any ransom,*
Duc Theseus hym leet out of prisoun	*Duke Theseus let him out of prison*
Frely to goon, wher that hym liste overal,	*To go freely wherever he wanted,*
In swich a gyse as I you tellen shal.	*And I shall tell you what he did next.*
This was the forward, pleynly for t'endite,	*This was the agreement, to explain simply,*
Bitwixen Theseus and hym Arcite,	*Between Theseus and Arcite:*
That if so were that Arcite were yfounde	*That if Arcite was ever found*
Evere in his lif, by day or nyght or stounde,	*In his life, day or night,*
In any contree of this Theseus,	*On any land of Theseus,*
And he were caught, it was acorded thus,	*And was caught, it was agreed*
That with a swerd he sholde lese his heed;	*That he would be beheaded with a sword,*
Ther nas noon oother remedie ne reed,	*And so there was nothing else that he could do*
But taketh his leve and homward he him spedde;	*But to take his leave and go home;*
Lat hym be war! His nekke lith to wedde!	*Let him be warned! His neck was at risk!*
How greet a sorwe suffreth now Arcite!	*What great sorrow Arcite now suffered!*
The deeth he feeleth thurgh his herte smyte,	*He felt death strike its heavy blow through his heart,*
He wepeth, wayleth, crieth pitously,	*He wept, wailed, cried out piteously,*
To sleen hymself he waiteth prively.	*And thought of doing away with himself.*
He seyde, "Allas, that day that he was born!	*He said, "Alas for the day I was born!*
Now is my prisoun worse than biforn;	*I'm in a worse prison than I was before;*
Now is me shape eternally to dwelle	*Now I am condemned to live eternally*
Nat in purgatorie, but in helle.	*Not in purgatory but in hell.*
Allas, that evere knew I Perotheus!	*I wish I had never known Perotheus!*
For elles hadde I dwelled with Theseus,	*For otherwise I would have stayed with Theseus,*
Yfetered in his prisoun evermo;	*Locked up in his prison forever;*
Thanne hadde I been in blisse, and nat in wo.	*Then I would have been happy, not sad.*
Oonly the sighte of hire whom that I serve,	*Just the sight of her whom I worship,*
Though that I nevere hir grace may deserve,	*Even though I would never have her,*
Wolde han suffised right ynough for me.	*Would have been enough for me.*
O deere cosyn Palamon," quod he,	*Oh dear cousin Palamon," he said,*
"Thyn is the victorie of this aventure.	*"You have won the day here.*
Ful blisfully in prison maistow dure.—	*You can live happily in your prison.*
In prisoun? certes, nay, but in paradys!	*In prison? It's not prison, it's paradise!*
Wel hath Fortune yturned thee the dys,	*Fortune's dice have favoured you,*

That hast the sighte of hir, and I th'absence;	Because you can see her and I cannot;
For possible is, syn thou hast hir presence,	It's possible, since you are near her,
And art a knyght, a worthy and an able,	And are a knight, good and able,
That by som cas, syn Fortune is chaungeable,	That in some way, since Fortune is so changeable,
Thow maist to thy desir som tyme atteyne.	You might at some point get what you desire.
But I, that am exiled and bareyne	But I, exiled and stripped
Of alle grace, and in so greet dispeir	Of all grace, and in such despair
That ther nys erthe, water, fir, ne eir,	That neither earth or water, fire or air,
Ne creature, that of hem maked is,	Nor any creature made of them
That may me helpe or doon confort in this,	Can help me or bring me comfort in this,
Wel oughte I sterve in wanhope and distresse,	As I suffer in my despair and distress;
Farwel, my lif, my lust, and my gladnesse!	Farewell, my life, strength and happiness!
Allas, why pleynen folk so in commune	Alas! Why do folk complain so much
On purveiaunce of God or of Fortune,	Of what God or Fortune preordain,
That yeveth hem ful ofte in many a gyse	When what they actually give them
Wel bettre than they kan hemself devyse?	Is better than anything they could have thought of?
Som man desireth for to han richesse,	Some men want to be rich,
That cause is of his mordre of greet siknesse.	And that might kill them or make them ill.
And som man wolde out of his prisoun fayn,	Some man wants to get out of prison,
That in his hous is of his meynee slayn.	And then he's killed inside his own house.
Infinite harmes been in this mateere,	There are great evils all over the earth,
We witen nat what thing we preyen heere.	And we don't know what we are praying for.
We faren as he that dronke is as a mous;	We carry on like someone drunk as a mouse;
A dronke man woot wel he hath an hous,	A drunken man knows full well he has a house,
But he noot which the righte wey is thider,	But he doesn't know the way there,
And to a dronke man the wey is slider.	And to a drunkard the path is slippery.
And certes, in this world so faren we;	And that's how we are in this world;
We seken faste after felicitee,	We're always chasing after happiness,
But we goon wrong ful often trewely.	But we often go completely the wrong way.
Thus may we seyen alle, and namely I,	This applies to all, especially me,
That wende and hadde a greet opinioun	Who thought sincerely that if I
That if I myghte escapen from prisoun,	Could escape from my prison,
Thanne hadde I been in joye and perfit heele,	Then I would be happy and well,
Ther now I am exiled fro my wele.	And now I'm exiled from my happiness.
Syn that I may nat seen you, Emelye,	Since I cannot see you, Emily,
I nam but deed, ther nys no remedye."	I'm good as dead, there is no cure.
Upon that oother syde, Palamon,	On the other side, Palamon,
Whan that he wiste Arcite was agon,	When he found Arcite gone,
Swich sorwe he maketh that the grete tour	Was so sorrowful that the great tower
Resouneth of his youlyng and clamour.	Echoed with the sound of his wailing and cries.
The pure fettres on his shynes grete	The iron chains around his legs
Weren of his bittre salte teeres wete.	Were wet with bitter salt tears.
"Allas," quod he, "Arcite, cosyn myn!	"Alas," he said, "Arcite, my cousin!
Of al oure strif, God woot, the fruyt is thyn.	God knows, after all our arguments, you're the winner.
Thow walkest now in Thebes at thy large,	You are now walking free in Thebes,
And of my wo thow yevest litel charge.	Taking little notice of my sorrow.
Thou mayst, syn thou hast wysdom and manhede,	You can, since you are wise and manly,
Assemblen alle the folk of oure kynrede,	Gather all the people of our family
And make a werre so sharp on this citee,	And wage such vicious war on this city

That by som aventure, or som tretee,
Thow mayst have hir to lady and to wyf,
For whom that I moste nedes lese my lyf.
For as by wey of possibilitee,
Sith thou art at thy large, of prisoun free,
And art a lord, greet is thyn avauntage
Moore than is myn, that sterve here in a cage.
For I moot wepe and wayle, whil I lyve,
With al the wo that prison may me yeve,
And eek with peyne that love me yeveth also,
That doubleth al my torment and my wo."

Therwith the fyr of jalousie up-sterte
Withinne his brest, and hente him by the herte
So woodly, that he lyk was to biholde
The boxtree, or the asshen dede and colde.

Thanne seyde he, "O cruel Goddes, that governe
This world with byndyng of youre word eterne,
And writen in the table of atthamaunt
Youre parlement and youre eterne graunt,
What is mankynde moore unto you holde
Than is the sheep that rouketh in the folde?
For slayn is man right as another beest,
And dwelleth eek in prison and arreest,
And hath siknesse, and greet adversitee,
And ofte tymes giltelees, pardee.
What governance is in this prescience
That giltelees tormenteth innocence?
And yet encresseth this al my penaunce,
That man is bounden to his observaunce,
For Goddes sake, to letten of his wille,
Ther as a beest may al his lust fulfille.
And whan a beest is deed, he hath no peyne,
But man after his deeth moot wepe and pleyne,
Though in this world he have care and wo.

Withouten doute it may stonden so.
The answere of this lete I to dyvynys,
But well I woot, that in this world greet pyne ys.
Allas, I se a serpent or a theef,
That many a trewe man hath doon mescheef,
Goon at his large, and where hym list may turne!

But I moot been in prisoun thurgh Saturne,
And eek thurgh Juno, jalous and eek wood,
That hath destroyed wel ny al the blood
Of Thebes with hise waste walles wyde.
And Venus sleeth me on that oother syde
For jalousie and fere of hym Arcite."
Now wol I stynte of Palamon a lite,

And lete hym in his prisoun stille dwelle,
And of Arcita forth I wol yow telle.

*That with some luck, or some agreement,
You can have the lady for your wife,
The one for whom I must lay down my life.
For it is surely possible,
Since you are wandering, free from prison,
And are a lord, you have a great advantage
Over me, dying here in a cage.
For I must weep and wail my whole life long,
With all the sorrow that prison provides,
And also the pain that love gives me as well,
That makes all my torment and sorrow double."

Then the fire of jealousy flamed up
In his breast and burned his heart
So madly that he looked like
A burnt tree, or dead cold ashes.

Then he said, "O cruel gods, that govern
This world with your eternally binding words,
Who have written on diamond tablets
Your laws and the fates of men,
Do you care any more about mankind
Than you do about sheep huddled in a pen?
For men must die just like any other beast,
And also suffer arrest and prison,
Illness, and great adversity,
And often they are innocent, by God!
What sort of management is this
That tortures the guiltless innocent?
And what makes all my torment worse
Is that man is duty bound to obey,
To follow the will of God,
When a beast can let his lusts run free.
And when a beast is dead, he feels no pain,
But after his death a man must go on suffering,
Even though in this world he had nothing but sorrow.
There is no doubt that this is how it is.
I'll leave it to the priests to explain why it is,
But what I know is that this world is hell.
Alas, I have seen serpents and thieves
Bringing down many good men,
Then wandering around free, doing as they please!
But because of Saturn I must stay in prison,
And also Juno, jealous and mad,
Who has spilled virtually all the blood
Of Thebes with her destroyed walls,
And Venus tortures me on the other side
With jealousy and fear of what Arcite will do."
Now I will leave off talking of Palamon for awhile,
Leaving him to stay in his prison,
And now I will tell you about Arcite.*

The somer passeth, and the nyghtes longe	*The summer passed and the long nights*
Encressen double wise the peynes stronge	*Doubled the great pains*
Bothe of the lovere and the prisoner;	*Of both the lover and the prisoner;*
I noot which hath the wofuller mester.	*I don't know who had the sadder time.*
For shortly for to seyn, this Palamoun	*To put it briefly, this Palamon*
Perpetuelly is dampned to prisoun	*Is condemned to prison forever,*
In cheynes and in fettres to been deed,	*Chained and fettered until his death,*
And Arcite is exiled upon his heed	*And on threat of beheading Arcite is exiled*
For evere mo as out of that contree,	*Eternally from that country,*
Ne nevere mo he shal his lady see.	*And can never see his lady again.*
Yow loveres axe I now this questioun,	*Now I ask you lovers this question,*
Who hath the worse, Arcite or Palamoun?	*Who's worse off, Arcite or Palamon?*
That oon may seen his lady day by day,	*One can see his lady every day,*
But in prison he moot dwelle alway;	*But he must spend his whole life in prison;*
That oother wher hym list may ride or go,	*The other can go wherever he wishes,*
But seen his lady shal he nevere mo.	*But never see his lady again.*
Now demeth as yow liste ye that kan,	*Say what you think, whoever wants to,*
For I wol telle forth, as I bigan.	*While I will carry on with my tale.*
Whan that Arcite to Thebes comen was,	*Now that Arcite had come to Thebes*
Ful ofte a day he swelte and seyde `Allas,'	*He languished and often said, "Alas!"*
For seen his lady shal he nevere mo;	*For he was never going to see his lady again;*
And shortly to concluden al his wo,	*And to describe his sorrow in brief,*
So muche sorwe hadde nevere creature,	*No creature was ever so sad,*
That is, or shal whil that the world may dure.	*Now or until the end of the world.*
His slep, his mete, his drynke is hym biraft,	*He did not sleep or eat or drink,*
That lene he wex and drye as is a shaft.	*And he became thin and dry as a pole.*
Hise eyen holwe and grisly to biholde,	*His eyes were hollow and horrible to see,*
His hewe falow and pale as asshen colde;	*His face was grey and cold,*
And solitarie he was and evere alone	*And he kept himself apart and alone,*
And waillynge al the nyght, makynge his mone.	*Moaning all night, mourning his lost.*
And if he herde song or instrument,	*And if he heard music or song*
Thanne wolde he wepe, he myghte nat be stent.	*Then he would weep uncontrollably.*
So feble eek were hise spiritz, and so lowe,	*His spirits were so feeble and low*
And chaunged so, that no man koude knowe	*And so changed that neither he or any other*
His speche nor his voys, though men it herde.	*Could recognize his words or voice,*
And in his geere for al the world he ferde	*And in this change he did not only seem*
Nat oonly lik the loveris maladye	*To have the pangs of love*
Of Hereos, but rather lyk manye	*Of Heroes, but rather like many*
Hath Theseus doon wroght in noble wyse Engendred of humour malencolik	
But to have that deep depression	
Biforen in his celle fantastik,	*Where fantasy takes over the mind,*
And shortly turned was al up so doun	*And soon he was completely changed*
Bothe habit and eek disposicioun	*In both his habits and temper,*
Of hym, this woful lovere daun Arcite.	*This sad lover, Arcite.*
What sholde I al day of his wo endite?	*What can I say of his daily woes?*
Whan he endured hadde a yeer or two	*When he had suffered a year or two*
This crueel torment, and this peyne and wo,	*Of this cruel torment, this pain and sorrow,*
At Thebes in his contree, as I seyde,	*In his country of Thebes, as I said,*
Upon a nyght in sleep as he hym leyde,	*One night as he slept in his bed*
Hym thoughte how that the wynged god Mercurie	*He dreamed that the winged god Mercury stood*
Biforn hym stood, and bad hym to be murie.	*Before him and told him to be happy.*
His slepy yerde in hond he bar uprighte,	*He was carrying his sleep giving staff in his*

An hat he werede upon hise heris brighte.	And wore a hat upon his bright hair.
Arrayed was this god, as he took keep,	This god was dressed as he was
As he was whan that Argus took his sleep;	When he put Argus to sleep,
And seyde hym thus, "To Atthenes shaltou wende,	And he said to him, "You must go to Athens,
Ther is thee shapen of thy wo an ende."	For that is where your sorrow is destined to end."
And with that word Arcite wook and sterte.	At those words Arcite awoke with a start.
"Now trewely, how soore that me smerte,"	"Now I swear, however sorely I'm hurt,"
Quod he, "to Atthenes right now wol I fare,	He said, "I shall go to Athens at once,
Ne for the drede of deeth shal I nat spare	And the fear of death will not stop me
To se my lady that I love and serve,	Seeing the lady I love and worship,
In hire presence I recche nat to sterve."	To see her I don't care about death."
And with that word he caughte a greet mirour,	As he said that he looked in a great mirror,
And saugh that chaunged was al his colour,	And saw how his colour had all changed,
And saugh his visage al in another kynde.	And how his face was completely different.
And right anon it ran hym in his mynde,	At once it came into his mind
That sith his face was so disfigured	That now his face was so disfigured
Of maladye, the which he hadde endured,	From the suffering he had undergone
He myghte wel, if that he bar hym lowe,	He could easily, if he lived humbly,
Lyve in Atthenes, everemoore unknowe,	Live in Athens, never recognized,
And seen his lady wel ny day by day.	And see his lady virtually every day.
And right anon he chaunged his array,	Straight away he changed his clothes,
And cladde hym as a povre laborer,	Dressing himself as a poor labourer,
And al allone, save oonly a squire	And alone apart from one squire
That knew his privetee and al his cas,	Who knew his secret and his situation,
Which was disgised povrely, as he was,	And who was dressed as poorly as he was,
To Atthenes is he goon, the nexte way.	He went to Athens by the quickest route.
And to the court he wente, upon a day,	Then one day he went to the court,
And at the gate he profreth his servyse,	And offered his service at the gate,
To drugge and drawe, what so men wol devyse.	To do lowly work, whatever was needed.
And shortly of this matere for to seyn,	And to cut a long story short
He fil in office with a chamberleyn,	He got a job with a chamberlain,
The which that dwellynge was with Emelye,	Who was serving in Emily's house;
For he was wys and koude soone espye	For he was wise and soon spied out
Of every servant which that serveth here.	All the servants who were working there.
Wel koude he hewen wode, and water bere,	He was good at chopping wood and carrying water,
For he was yong and myghty for the nones,	For he was young and strong,
And therto he was strong and big of bones	Muscular and well built,
To doon that any wight kan hym devyse.	Ready to do whatever he was asked.
A yeer or two he was in this servyse	He worked in this job a year or two,
Page of the chambre of Emelye the brighte;	As a page in the rooms of lovely Emily;
And Philostrate he seyde that he highte.	And he said that he was called Philostrate.
But half so wel biloved a man as he	No man of his position was ever
Ne was ther nevere in court, of his degree;	As well loved in that court as he was;
He was so gentil of condicioun	His nature was so kind and gentle
That thurghout al the court was his renoun.	That he was known for it throughout the court.
They seyden, that it were a charitee,	They said it would be a kindly gesture
That Theseus wolde enhauncen his degree,	For Theseus to promote him
And putten hym in worshipful servyse	And give him a position
Ther as he myghte his vertu exercise.	Where he could employ his talents.
And thus withinne a while his name is spronge	And so in a little while his name was famous

Middle English	Modern English
Bothe of hise dedes and his goode tonge, / That Theseus hath taken hym so neer,	Both for his good deeds and the things he said, / So that Theseus brought him in his inner circle,
That of his chambre he made hym a squier, / And gaf hym gold to mayntene his degree. / And eek men broghte hym out of his contree / From yeer to yeer, ful pryvely, his rente.	And made him a squire of his bedroom, / And gave him gold to support his position. / Also men brought him the rents from / His own property in his country secretly each year.
But honestly and slyly he it spente, / That no man wondred how that he it hadde. / And thre yeer in this wise his lif he ladde, / And bar hym so in pees, and eek in werre, / Ther was no man that Theseus hath derre. / And in this blisse lete I now Arcite, / And speke I wole of Palamon a lite.	But he spent this honestly and secretly, / So that nobody wondered how he got it. / He lived his life this way for three years, / And carried himself so well in peace and war / That there was no man more dear to Theseus. / I shall leave Arcite in this happy state, / And speak for a little about Palamon.
In derknesse and horrible and strong prisoun / Thise seven yeer hath seten Palamoun, / Forpyned, what for wo and for distresse. / Who feeleth double soor and hevynesse / But Palamon, that love destreyneth so, / That wood out of his wit he goth for wo? / And eek therto he is a prisoner, / Perpetuelly, noght oonly for a yer. / Who koude ryme in Englyssh properly / His martirdom? For sothe it am nat I, / Therfore I passe as lightly as I may. / It fel that in the seventhe yer, in May, / The thridde nyght, (as olde bookes seyn, / That al this storie tellen moore pleyn) / Were it by aventure or destynee - / As, whan a thyng is shapen, it shal be -	In darkness, in a horrible strong prison, / Palamon had been kept for these seven years, / Wasting away with sorrow and distress. / Who had a greater double injury / Palamon, whom love was destroying so badly / That he was half out of his mind with sorrow? / And added to that he was a prisoner, / Permanently, not only for a year. / Who could properly write the story / Of his martyrdom? I'm sure that it's not me, / So I'll pass over it as lightly as I can. / It happened that in the seventh year, in May, / On the third night (as the old books say, / Which all tell this story in more detail) / Whether it was by chance or destiny— / Since, when a thing is destined, it must happen—
That soone after the mydnyght Palamoun / By helpyng of a freend, brak his prisoun	Soon after midnight Palamon / Managed to escape prison with the help of a friend,
And fleeth the citee faste as he may go; / For he hade yeve his gayler drynke so / Of a clarree maad of a certeyn wyn, / With nercotikes and opie of Thebes fyn, / That al that nyght, thogh that men wolde him shake, / The gayler sleep, he myghte nat awake. / And thus he fleeth as faste as evere he may; / The nyght was short and faste by the day, / That nedes-cost he moot hymselven hyde; / And til a grove, faste ther bisyde, / With dredeful foot thanne stalketh Palamoun. / For shortly, this was his opinioun, / That in that grove he wolde hym hyde al day, / And in the nyght thanne wolde he take his way / To Thebes-ward, his freendes for to preye / On Theseus to helpe hym to werreye;	And fled from the city as fast as he could go; / For he had given his guard a drink / Of punch made with a certain wine / Spiked with narcotics and Theban opiates, / So that all night, though men shook him, / The jailer would sleep, he would not wake up. / And so he fled as fast as he could; / The night was short and day was coming, / And so he had to find a place to hide; / So he went to the grove that grew close by; / Palamon walked there with trepidation. / Briefly, he had decided that / He would hide in that grove all day, / And in the night he would make his way / Towards Thebes, to find his friends / To come back to help him fight against Theseus;
And shortly, outher he wolde lese his lif,	And in a little while he would either lose his life

Or wynnen Emelye unto his wyf;	Or win over Emily as his wife;
This is th'effect and his entente pleyn.	This was the substance of his whole plan.
Now wol I turne to Arcite ageyn,	Now I will turn back to Arcite,
That litel wiste how ny that was his care,	Who didn't know how close misery was,
Til that Fortune had broght him in the snare.	Until Fortune had caught him in her trap.
The bisy larke, messager of day,	The busy lark, herald of the day,
Salueth in hir song the morwe gray,	Was saluting the grey morning with her song,
And firy Phebus riseth up so brighte	And the fiery sun had risen up so bright
That al the orient laugheth of the light,	That the whole east was laughing with light,
And with hise stremes dryeth in the greves	And with its beams it dried
The silver dropes hangynge on the leves.	The silver dew drops hanging on the leaves.
And Arcita, that is in the court roial	Arcite was in the royal court
With Theseus, his squier principal,	With Theseus as his chief Squire,
Is risen, and looketh on the myrie day.	And had risen and looked at the happy day.
And for to doon his observaunce of May,	And to pay his respects to May,
Remembrynge on the poynt of his desir	Remembering the object of his desire,
He on a courser startlynge as the fir	He jumped on a horse which leapt like fire,
Is riden into the feeldes, hym to pleye,	And on into the fields to think and exercise
Out of the court, were it a myle or tweye.	A mile or two away from the court;
And to the grove of which that I yow tolde	And by accident he began to make his way
By aventure his wey he gan to holde,	Towards the grove which I recently mentioned,
To maken hym a gerland of the greves,	To make himself a garland from the leaves,
Were it of wodebynde or hawethorn leves.	Either of the woodbine or the hawthorn.
And loude he song ayeyn the sonne shene,	And he sang aloud in the sunshine,
"May, with alle thy floures and thy grene,	"May, with all your flowers and greenery,
Welcome be thou, faire fresshe May,	You are very welcome, fair fresh May,
In hope that I som grene gete may."	And I hope that I can get some greenery."
And from his courser, with a lusty herte,	And he leapt from his horse with a jolly heart,
Into a grove ful hastily he sterte,	And he dashed into the grove,
And in a path he rometh up and doun	And he wandered up and down a path
Ther as by aventure this Palamoun	Where by chance Palamon was hiding
Was in a bussh, that no man myghte hym se;	In a bush so no one could see him;
For soore afered of his deeth was he.	For he was very afraid of being killed.
No thyng ne knew he that it was Arcite,	He had no idea that it was Arcite,
God woot, he wolde have trowed it ful lite.	God knows he would have had trouble believing it.
But sooth is seyd, go sithen many yeres,	But it has been a truthful saying for many years,
That "feeld hath eyen and the wode hath eres."	That "fields have eyes and woods have ears."
It is ful fair a man to bere hym evene,	A man must try and stay well balanced,
For al day meeteth men at unset stevene.	For every day we face the unexpected.
Ful litel woot Arcite of his felawe,	Arcite little suspected his friend was nearby,
That was so ny to herknen al his sawe,	Listening to everything that happened,
For in the bussh he sitteth now ful stille.	Sitting in the bush, keeping still.
Whan that Arcite hadde romed al his fille	When Arcite had walked around enough,
And songen al the roundel lustily,	And sung his lusty song,
Into a studie he fil al sodeynly,	He suddenly started to meditate,
As doon thise loveres in hir queynte geres,	As these lovers do with their strange desires,
Now in the croppe, now doun in the breres,	Now amongst the trees, now down in the brambles,
Now up, now doun as boket in a welle.	Up and down like a bucket in a well.
Right as the Friday, soothly for to telle,	To tell the truth it was just like a Friday,
Now it shyneth, now it reyneth faste,	When one minute the sun shines, the next it

Right so kan geery Venus overcaste	That's the way fickle Venus can cast shadows
The hertes of hir folk; right as hir day	Over the hearts of her people; as emotions
Is gereful, right so chaungeth she array.	Change, so she changes her appearance.
Selde is the Friday al the wowke ylike.	Friday is very rarely like the rest of the week.
Whan that Arcite had songe, he gan to sike,	When Arcite had finished singing, he began to speak,
And sette hym doun withouten any moore;	And he sat down without further ado;
"Allas," quod he, "that day that I was bore!	"Alas," he said, "that I was ever born!
How longe, Juno, thurgh thy crueltee	How long, Juno, because of your cruelty,
Woltow werreyen Thebes the Citee?	Will you wage war against the city of Thebes?
Allas, ybroght is to confusioun	Alas, the royal blood of Cadmus and Amphion
The blood roial of Cadme and Amphioun, –	Has all been thrown into confusion;
Of Cadmus, which that was the firste man	Cadmus was the first man to build at Thebes,
That Thebes bulte, or first the toun bigan,	He was the founder of the town,
And of the citee first was crouned kyng,	And he was the first king of the city;
Of his lynage am I, and his ofspryng,	I am descended from him
By verray ligne, as of the stok roial,	In direct line, of the royal blood,
And now I am so caytyf and so thral	And now I am trapped in the lowly service
That he that is my mortal enemy	Of him who is my mortal enemy,
I serve hym as his squier povrely.	Humbly serving him as his squire.
And yet dooth Juno me wel moore shame,	And yet Juno wants me to suffer more shame
For I dar noght biknowe myn owene name,	For I dare not acknowledge who I am;
But theras I was wont to highte Arcite,	My rightful name is highborn Arcite,
Now highte I Philostrate, noght worth a myte.	But now I'm called Philostrate, not worth a damn.
Allas, thou felle Mars! allas, Juno!	Alas, you cruel Mars! Alas, Juno!
Thus hath youre ire oure lynage al fordo,	Your anger has destroyed our family,
Save oonly me, and wrecched Palamoun	Apart from me and the wretched Palamon,
That Theseus martireth in prisoun.	Whom Theseus tortures in that prison.
And over al this, to sleen me outrely,	And to truly finish me off
Love hath his firy dart so brennyngly	Love has thrust his fiery dart
Ystiked thurgh my trewe careful herte,	Into my faithful and suffering heart,
That shapen was my deeth erst than my sherte.	My death was planned before my birth.
Ye sleen me with youre eyen, Emelye!	You kill me with your eyes, Emily!
Ye been the cause wherfore that I dye.	You are the reason that I must die.
Of al the remenant of myn oother care	I wouldn't care sixpence for all the other
Ne sette I nat the montance of a tare,	Cares that I suffer from,
So that I koude doon aught to youre plesaunce."	If I could do anything to make you happy."
And with that word he fil doun in a traunce	And saying that he fell down in a trance
A longe tyme, and after he upsterte.	For a long time, and then he jumped up.
This Palamoun, that thoughte that thurgh his herte	This Palamon, who felt that a cold sword
He felte a coold swerd sodeynliche glyde,	Had suddenly been thrust through his heart,
For ire he quook, no lenger wolde he byde.	Shook with anger, he could no longer wait.
And whan that he had herd Arcites tale,	And when he had heard what Arcite said,
As he were wood, with face deed and pale,	It was as if he were mad, with his face deathly pale,
He stirte hym up out of the buskes thikke,	And he jumped out of the thick bushes,
And seide, "Arcite, false traytour wikke!	And said, "Arcite, you wicked false traitor!
Now artow hent that lovest my lady so,	Now you who love my lady so are caught,
For whom that I have al this peyne and wo,	You for whom I suffer all this pain and sorrow,
And art my blood, and to my conseil sworn,	You are my relative, and my sworn counsellor,
As I ful ofte ofte have seyd thee heerbiforn,	As I have often said to you before,
And hast byjaped heere duc Theseus,	And you have deceived Duke Theseus,

And falsly chaunged hast thy name thus. I wol be deed, or elles thou shalt dye; Thou shalt nat love my lady Emelye, But I wol love hire oonly, and namo, For I am Palamon, thy mortal foo! And though that I no wepene have in this place, But out of prison am astert by grace, I drede noght that outher thow shalt dye, Or thow ne shalt nat loven Emelye. Chees which thou wolt, for thou shalt nat asterte!"	*And falsely changed your name.* *Either you or I must die;* *You will not love my Lady Emily,* *Only I will love her, nobody else.* *For I am Palamon, your mortal enemy!* *And although I have no weapon with me,* *I have escaped from prison by grace of God,* *And I do not doubt that either you will die,* *Or give up your love for Emily.* *Choose which one you want, for you will not leave until you do!"*
This Arcite, with ful despitous herte, Whan he hym knew, and hadde his tale herd,	*Then Arcite, with scorn and anger in his heart,* *When he recognised him, and heard what he said,*
As fiers as leoun pulled out his swerd, And seyde thus: "By God that sit above, Nere it that thou art sik and wood for love,	*Pulled out his sword, fierce as a lion,* *And said, "By God who sits above,* *If it wasn't for the fact that you are sick and mad with love,*
And eek that thow no wepne hast in this place, Thou sholdest nevere out of this grove pace, That thou ne sholdest dyen of myn hond. For I defye the seurete and the bond Which that thou seist that I have maad to thee. What, verray fool, thynk wel that love is free, And I wol love hir, maugree al thy myght! But for as muche thou art a worthy knyght, And wilnest to darreyne hire by bataille, Have heer my trouthe; tomorwe I wol nat faille Withoute wityng of any oother wight That heere I wol be founden as a knyght, And bryngen harneys right ynough for thee, And ches the beste, and leef the worste for me.	*And also that you have no weapon here,* *You would never get out of this grove,* *You would die at my hands.* *I reject the bond which you* *Say that I have made with you.* *Why, you absolute fool, love does as it wishes,* *And I will love her, despite all your strength!* *But seeing as you are a good knight,* *And willing to fight for her in battle,* *Listen to what I say; tomorrow I will not fail,* *Without anyone else knowing it,* *To come here in the armour of a knight,* *And I will bring good armour for you as well,* *You shall choose the best and leave the worst for me.*
And mete and drynke this nyght wol I brynge Ynough for thee, and clothes for thy beddynge; And if so be that thou my lady wynne, And sle me in this wode ther I am inne, Thow mayst wel have thy lady as for me." This Palamon answerde, "I graunte it thee." And thus they been departed til amorwe, Whan ech of hem had leyd his feith to borwe.	*I will bring you meat and drink tonight,* *And bedding for you as well;* *And if it happens that you win my lady,* *And kill me in this wood which I am in,* *Then you can have the lady over me."* *Palamon answered, "I agree with you."* *And so they parted until the next day,* *When each of them had faithfully promised to return.*
O Cupide, out of alle charitee! O regne, that wolt no felawe have with thee! Ful sooth is seyd that love ne lordship Wol noght, hir thankes, have no felaweshipe. Wel fynden that Arcite and Palamoun. Arcite is riden anon unto the toun, And on the morwe, er it were dayes light, Ful prively two harneys hath he dight, Bothe suffisaunt and mete to darreyne The bataille in the feeld bitwix hem tweyne. And on his hors, allone as he was born,	*Oh Cupid, you have no kindness!* *You tyrant, who allows no man to be with you!* *It is truly said that love is like a lord,* *And does not thank any who try to join him.* *They certainly knew that, Arcite and Palamon.* *Soon Arcite had ridden into town,* *And the next day, before daybreak,* *He secretly got two sets of armour,* *Both good and suitable for* *The battle in the field between the two of them.* *So on his horse, as alone as the day he was*

He carieth al this harneys hym biforn,	He carried all this along with him,
And in the grove, at tyme and place yset,	And in the grove, at the agreed time and place,
This Arcite and this Palamon ben met.	Arcite and Palamon met to fight.
To chaungen gan the colour in hir face	The colour in both their faces changed,
Right as the hunters in the regne of Trace,	They were just like Thracian hunters,
That stondeth at the gappe with a spere,	Standing in a clearing with a spear,
Whan hunted is the leoun and the bere,	When they are hunting lion or bear,
And hereth hym come russhyng in the greves,	And hear him come rushing through the forest,
And breketh bothe bowes and the leves,	Breaking branches and leaves,
And thynketh, "Heere cometh my mortal enemy,	And thinks, "Here comes my deadly enemy,
Withoute faille he moot be deed or I,	Without fail either he or I must die,
For outher I moot sleen hym at the gappe,	For either I must kill him in this clearing,
Or he moot sleen me, if that me myshappe"-	Or he must kill me, if that is my fate."
So ferden they in chaungyng of hir hewe,	That was what they were like with their changing colours,
As fer as everich of hem oother knewe.	For each one knew the strength of the other.
Ther nas no good day ne no saluyng,	They did not greet each other nor salute,
But streight, withouten word or rehersyng,	But at once, without speech or rehearsal,
Everich of hem heelp for to armen oother,	Each of them helped to arm the other,
As freendly as he were his owene brother.	As friendly as if they were blood brothers.
And after that with sharpe speres stronge	And after that with strong sharp spears,
They foynen ech at oother wonder longe.	They battled with each other for an incredible time.
Thou myghtest wene that this Palamoun	You might have thought that this Palamon
In his fightyng were a wood leon,	As he fought was a mad lion,
And as a crueel tigre was Arcite.	And Arcite was like cruel tiger.
As wilde bores gonne they to smyte,	They began to fight like two wild boar,
That frothen white as foom for ire wood.	frothing at the mouth in their madness.
Up to the ancle foghte they in hir blood.	They fought up to the ankles in their own blood.
And in this wise I lete hem fightyng dwelle,	I will leave them to their battle,
And forth I wole of Theseus yow telle.	And now I will tell you about Theseus.
The destinee, ministre general,	Destiny, minister general,
That executeth in the world overall	That rules over everything in this world,
The purveiaunce that God hath seyn biforn,	Imposing the predestined will of God,
So strong it is, that though the world had sworn	Is so strong that although the whole world swore
The contrarie of a thyng, by ye or nay,	Something different, by hook or by crook
Yet somtyme it shal fallen on a day	Something will happen on a particular day
That falleth nat eft withinne a thousand yeere.	Even if it would never happen again in a thousand years.
For certeinly, oure appetites heere,	It's certain that what we wish for here,
Be it of werre, or pees, or hate, or love,	Whether in war or peace, hate or love,
Al is this reuled by the sighte above.	Everything is ruled by the ones above.
This mene I now by myghty Theseus,	I'll show you this now through mighty Theseus,
That for to hunten is so desirus	Who is so anxious to go hunting,
And namely at the grete hert in May,	Particularly the great deer in May,
That in his bed ther daweth hym no day	That there is no dawn that finds him in bed,
That he nys clad, and redy for to ryde	He is always dressed and ready to ride
With hunte and horn, and houndes hym bisyde	With his hunters and horn, and hounds alongside,
For in his huntyng hath he swich delit	For he takes such pleasure in hunting
That it is al his joye and appetite	That it is all his happiness desires,

| To been hymself the grete hertes bane- | To be the death of the great deer, |
| For after Mars he serveth now Dyane. | For besides Mars he is a servant of Diana. |

Cleer was the day, as I have toold er this,	It was a clear day, as I have mentioned before,
And Theseus, with alle joye and blis,	And Theseus, full of joy and happiness,
With his Ypolita, the faire quene,	With his Hippolyta, his lovely Queen,
And Emelye, clothed al in grene,	And Emily, dressed all in green,
On huntyng be they riden roially,	Rode out on their royal hunt,
And to the grove, that stood ful faste by,	And they went straight to the nearby grove,
In which ther was an hert, as men hym tolde,	In which there was a deer, men had said,
Duc Theseus the streighte wey hath holde,	Which made to Theseus go straight there,
And to the launde he rideth hym ful right,	He rode directly to the clearing,
For thider was the hert wont have his flight,	For that was the way the deer usually ran
And over a brook, and so forth in his weye.	He crossed a stream, and went on his way.
This duc wol han a cours at hym, or tweye,	This Duke would have a chase or two with him,
With houndes swiche as that hym list comaunde.	With his hounds which he loved to command.

And whan this duc was come unto the launde,	And when the Duke came into the glade,
Under the sonne he looketh, and anon	He looked in out of the sunlight,
He was war of Arcite and Palamon,	And once he saw Arcite and Palamon,
That foughten breme, as it were bores two;	Who were fighting so strongly, like two bears;
The brighte swerdes wenten to and fro	The bright swords flashed to and fro
So hidously, that with the leeste strook	So fearfully, that it seemed their smallest stroke

It semed as it wolde felle an ook;	Would be enough to bring down an oak tree;
But what they were, nothyng he ne woot.	But he knew nothing of who they were.
This duc his courser with his spores smoot,	The Duke urged on his horse with his spurs,
And at a stert he was bitwix hem two,	And at once he was between the two of them,
And pulled out a swerd, and cride, "Hoo!	Pulling out his sword, and crying, "Hey!
Namoore, up peyne of lesynge of youre heed!	No more of this or you will lose your heads!
By myghty Mars, he shal anon be deed	I swear by great Mars, the man will soon die
That smyteth any strook, that I may seen.	Whom I see strike another blow.
But telleth me what myster men ye been,	But tell me what sort of men you are,
That been so hardy for to fighten here	Who are so reckless to fight out here
Withouten juge or oother officere,	Without a judge or other official,
As it were in a lystes roially?"	As if you were fighting in a royal tournament?"

This Palamon answerde hastily,	Palamon answered him hastily,
And seyde, "Sire, what nedeth wordes mo?	And said, "Sir, what more words are needed?
We have the deeth disserved, bothe two.	Both of us deserve to die.
Two woful wrecches been we, two caytyves,	We are two pitiful wretches, two prisoners,
That been encombred of oure owene lyves,	Weighed down by our own lives,
And as thou art a rightful lord and juge,	And as you are a righteous lord and judge,
Ne yeve us neither mercy ne refuge,	Do not show us mercy or give us refuge,
But sle me first for seinte charitee!	But out of blessed charity kill me first!
But sle my felawe eek as wel as me-	But also kill my companion along with me,
Or sle hym first, for, though thow knowest it lite,	Or kill him first, for although you find out late,
This is thy mortal foo, this is Arcite,	This is your mortal enemy, this is Arcite,
That fro thy lond is banysshed on his heed,	Who has been banished from your land on pain of death,

For which he hath deserved to be deed.	And so he also deserves to die.
For this is he, that cam unto thy gate,	For this is the one who came to your gate,
And seyde that he highte Philostrate.	And said that he was called Philostrate.

Thus hath he japed thee ful many a yer,	So he has fooled you for many years,
And thou hast maked hym thy chief Squier,	And you have made him your chief squire,
And this is he that loveth Emelye.	And he is in love with Emily.
For sith the day is come that I shal dye,	Since the day of my death has come,
I make pleynly my confessioun	I will openly confess
That I am thilke woful Palamoun,	That I am the same sorrowful Palamon
That hath thy prisoun broken wikkedly.	Who viciously broke out of your prison.
I am thy mortal foo, and it am I	I am your mortal enemy, and I also
That loveth so hoote Emelye the brighte,	Love the beautiful Emily so passionately
That I wol dye present in hir sighte;	That I will be happy to die under her gaze;
Wherfore I axe deeth and my juwise-	And so I ask for death as my penalty,
But sle my felawe in the same wise	But kill my companion in the same way,
For bothe han we deserved to be slayn."	For both of us are deserving of death."
This worthy duc answered anon agayn,	This good Duke then answered him,
And seyde, "This is a short conclusioun,	Saying, "This doesn't take much thought,
Youre owene mouth, by your confessioun,	You are condemned by your own confession,
Hath dampned yow, and I wol it recorde.	This has damned you, I will remember it.
It nedeth noght to pyne yow with the corde,	There is no need for you to be tortured,
Ye shal be deed, by myghty Mars the rede!"	You shall die, I swear by great red Mars!"
The queene anon, for verray wommanhede,	At once the Queen, like a true woman,
Gan for to wepe, and so dide Emelye,	Began to weep, and so did Emily,
And alle the ladyes in the compaignye.	And all the ladies in the company.
Greet pitee was it, as it thoughte hem alle,	They all thought it was very piteous
That evere swich a chaunce sholde falle.	That such a thing should ever happen.
For gentil men they were of greet estaat,	For they were gentlemen of great nobility,
And no thyng but for love was this debaat,	And all they were fighting for was love,
And saugh hir blody woundes wyde and soore,	They saw their great bloody wounds,
And alle crieden, both lasse and moore,	and they all cried out, higher and lower,
"Have mercy, lord, upon us wommen alle!"	"Have mercy Lord, on all we women!"
And on hir bare knees adoun they falle,	They fell down upon their bare knees,
And wolde have kist his feet ther as he stood;	And would have kissed his feet as he stood there;
Til at the laste aslaked was his mood,	Until at last his anger began to cool,
For pitee renneth soone in gentil herte.	For pity comes quickly to the noble heart.
And though he first for ire quook and sterte,	Although at first he was shaking with anger,
He hath considered shortly in a clause	To put it briefly he soon thought of
The trespas of hem bothe, and eek the cause,	What they had done, and why they did it,
And although that his ire hir gilt accused,	And although he was still angry with their trespass
Yet in his resoun he hem bothe excused.	His reason saw that they could both be excused.
As thus: he thoghte wel, that every man	His reasoning was that every man
Wol helpe hymself in love, if that he kan,	Will do what he can for love, if he is able,
And eek delivere hym-self out of prisoun;	Even break out of prison;
And eek his herte hadde compassioun	And also in his heart he had pity
Of wommen, for they wepen evere in oon.	For the women, for they were all weeping together.
And in his gentil herte he thoughte anon,	In his kind heart he then thought,
And softe unto hymself he seyde, "Fy	And said softly to himself,
Upon a lord that wol have no mercy,	"Any lord who cannot show mercy,
But been a leon, bothe in word and dede,	But acts like a lion in both word and deed,
To hem that been in repentaunce and drede,	To those who are repentant and afraid,
As wel as to a proud despitous man,	As well as to the unrepentant man
That wol maynteyne that he first bigan.	Who wants to carry on his crimes.

43

That lord hath litel of discrecioun	Any lord would be lacking in judgement
That in swich cas kan no divisioun,	Who cannot discern any difference in cases
But weyeth pride and humblesse after oon."	But treats pride and humility just the same."
And shortly, whan his ire is thus agoon,	And shortly, as his anger faded,
He gan to looken up with eyen lighte,	He looked up to the sky with burning eyes,
And spak thise same wordes al on highte:	And spoke these words to the heavens:
"The God of love, a benedicite!	"Blessings to the God of love!
How myghty and how greet a lord is he!	What a great and mighty Lord he is
Ayeyns his myght ther gayneth none obstacles,	No obstacles can block his might,
He may be cleped a god for his myracles,	His miracles show he is truly a god,
For he kan maken at his owene gyse	For he can impose his image
Of everich herte as that hym list divyse.	On every heart that he chooses.
Lo heere, this Arcite and this Palamoun	See here, this Arcite and this Palamon,
That quitly weren out of my prisoun,	Who managed to escape my prison,
And myghte han lyved in Thebes roially,	And could have lived a royal life in Thebes,
And witen I am hir mortal enemy,	Knowing that I am their mortal enemy,
And that hir deth lith in my myght also;	And that I held their lives in my hand;
And yet hath love, maugree hir eyen two,	Yet love, despite what they could see,
Ybroght hem hyder bothe for to dye.	Has brought them here for them both to die.
Now looketh, is nat that an heigh folye?	Now think, is that not the height of madness?
Who may been a fole, but if he love?	Who can be called a fool, if not a lover?
Bihoold, for Goddes sake that sit above,	And in the name of God who sits above,
Se how they blede! Be they noght wel arrayed?	Look how they bleed! Aren't they well armoured?
Thus hath hir lord, the God of Love, ypayed	This is how their lord, the God of love, repaid
Hir wages and hir fees for hir servyse!	Them for all their service to him!
And yet they wenen for to been ful wyse,	And yet those who serve love are supposed to be wise
That serven love, for aught that may bifalle!	whatever may happen to them!
But this is yet the beste game of alle,	But this is the best joke of all,
That she, for whom they han this jolitee,	That the one for whom they are fighting
Kan hem therfore as muche thank, as me!	Knows as little about it as I do!
She woot namoore of al this hoote fare,	She knew no more of this whole business,
By God, than woot a cokkow or an hare!	By God, than a cuckoo or a hare!
But all moot ben assayed, hoot and coold;	But everything must play out, hot and cold;
A man moot ben a fool, or yong or oold;	A man can be a fool, whether young or old;
I woot it by myself ful yore agon,	I remember it myself in times gone by,
For in my tyme a servant was I oon.	For I also have been a servant of love.
And therfore, syn I knowe of loves peyne,	And so, since I know of the pain of love,
And woot how soore it kan a man distreyne,	And am well aware how much it can provoke a man,
As he that hath ben caught ofte in his laas,	As one who has often been caught in his net,
I yow foryeve al hoolly this trespaas,	I now completely forgive you your trespasses,
At requeste of the queene that kneleth heere,	At the request of the queen who kneels here,
And eek of Emelye, my suster deere.	And also of Emily, my dear sister.
And ye shul bothe anon unto me swere,	And shortly you will both swear to me
That nevere mo ye shal my contree dere,	That you will never come to my country again,
Ne make werre upon me, nyght ne day,	Nor attack me, night or day,
But been my freendes in al that ye may,	But will be friends to me in every way you can;
I yow foryeve this trespas, every deel."	So I will forgive your trespass, in every respect."
And they hym sworen his axyng, faire and weel,	Then they swore to what he asked,
And hym of lordship and of mercy preyde,	And prayed for his lordly mercy,
And he hem graunteth grace, and thus he seyde:	And he granted them forgiveness, and said:

"To speke of roial lynage and richesse,
Though that she were a queene or a princesse,
Ech of you bothe is worthy doutelees
To wedden whan tyme is, but nathelees
I speke as for my suster Emelye,
For whom ye have this strif and jalousye:
Ye woot yourself, she may nat wedden two
Atones, though ye fighten everemo.
That oon of you, al be hym looth or lief,
He moot go pipen in an yvy leef-
This is to seyn, she may nat now han bothe,
Al be ye never so jalouse, ne so wrothe.
And forthy, I yow putte in this degree;
That ech of yow shal have his destynee
As hym is shape, and herkneth in what wyse;
Lo, heere your ende of that I shal devyse.
My wyl is this, for plat conclusioun,
Withouten any repplicacioun, -
If that you liketh, take it for the beste,
That everich of you shal goon where hym leste,
Frely, withouten raunson, or daunger,
And this day fifty wykes fer ne ner,
Everich of you shal brynge an hundred knyghtes
Armed for lystes up at alle rightes,
Al redy to darreyne hire by bataille.
And this bihote I yow withouten faille,
Upon my trouthe, and as I am a knyght,
That wheither of yow bothe that hath myght,
This is to seyn, that wheither he, or thow
May with his hundred, as I spak of now,

Sleen his contrarie, or out of lystes dryve,

Thanne shal I yeve Emelya to wyve
To whom that Fortune yeveth so fair a grace.
Tho lystes shal I maken in this place,
And God so wisly on my soule rewe,
As I shal evene juge been, and trewe.
Ye shul noon oother ende with me maken,
That oon of yow ne shal be deed or taken.
And if yow thynketh this is weel ysayd,
Seyeth youre avys and holdeth you apayd;
This is youre ende and youre conclusioun."

Who looketh lightly now but Palamoun?
Who spryngeth up for joye but Arcite?
Who kouthe tellen, or who kouthe endite
The joye that is maked in the place,
Whan Theseus hath doon so fair a grace?
But doun on knees wente every maner wight,
And thonken hym with al hir herte and myght,
And namely the Thebans, often sithe.
And thus with good hope and with herte blithe
They taken hir leve, and homward gonne they ride

"To ask to marry into royalty and riches,
Even with a queen or princess,
Each of you is doubtless deserving,
When it comes time to marry, but nonetheless
I am speaking of my sister Emily,
The cause of all this strife and jealousy:
You know yourself that she cannot marry two
At the same time, even if you fought eternally.
So one of you, willingly or not,
Will have to accept that he cannot win—
That is to say, she cannot have both,
However jealous or angry you are.
So, I impose this upon you;
Each of you will learn your destiny
As it is decreed for you, and the shape it takes;
Listen to the fate I have decided for you.
I order that the business be concluded,
Settled once and for all:
Whatever you feel, accept it's for the best;
Each of you will go wherever he pleases,
Freely, without ransom or threats,
And on this day fifty weeks from now
Each of you will bring here a hundred knights
All armoured, ready for the fight,
To settle your disagreement in battle.
I promise this to you without fail,
I swear on my honour as a knight,
That whichever one of you should triumph,
That is to say, that whichever one,
Along with his hundred men, which I spoke of just now,
Kills his opponent, or drives him over the boundaries,
I shall give Emily as his wife,
The one whom Fortune has made so beautiful.
I shall mark out the battlefield in this place,
And may God show mercy to my soul
And let me be a fair and honest judge.
I will not hear of any other solution;
One of you must either die or be captured.
And if you think this is a good idea,
Say what you think and agree to it;
This is how these matters will be settled."

Now who was happier than Palamon?
Who was more joyful than Arcite?
Who could tell or who could write
Of the happy scenes that took place there
When Theseus showed such a fair judgement?
But everyone went down on their knees,
And thanked him with all their heart and soul,
And especially grateful were the Thebans.
And so with high hopes and merry hearts
They took their leave, and rode homeward

To Thebes with hise olde walles wyde.

I trowe men wolde deme it necligence,
If I foryete to tellen the dispence
Of Theseus, that gooth so bisily
To maken up the lystes roially;
That swich a noble theatre as it was,
I dar wel seyen, in this world ther nas.

The circuit a myle was aboute,
Walled of stoon, and dyched al withoute.
Round was the shap, in manere of compas,
Ful of degrees the heighte of sixty pas,
That whan a man was set on o degree,
He lette nat his felawe for to see.
Estward ther stood a gate of marbul whit,
Westward, right swich another in the opposit;
And shortly to concluden, swich a place
Was noon in erthe, as in so litel space.
For in the lond ther was no crafty man
That geometrie or ars-metrike kan,
Ne portreytour, ne kervere of ymages,
That Theseus ne yaf him mete and wages,

The theatre for to maken and devyse.

And for to doon his ryte and sacrifise,
He estward hath upon the gate above,
In worshipe of Venus, goddesse of love,
Doon make an auter and an oratorie.
And on the gate westward, in memorie
Of Mars, he maked hath right swich another,
That coste largely of gold a fother.
And northward, in a touret on the wal
Of alabastre whit, and reed coral,
An oratorie, riche for to see,
In worshipe of Dyane, of chastitee,
Hath Theseus doon wroght in noble wyse.

But yet hadde I foryeten to devyse
The noble kervyng and the portreitures,
The shap, the contenaunce, and the figures,
That weren in thise oratories thre.
First in the temple of Venus maystow se
Wroght on the wal, ful pitous to biholde,
The broken slepes and the sikes colde,
The sacred teeris and the waymentynge,
The firy strokes, and the desirynge
That loves servantz in this lyf enduren;
The othes that her covenantz assuren;

Plesaunce and Hope, Desir, Foolhardynesse,
Beautee and Youthe, Bauderie, Richesse,
Charmes and Force, Lesynges, Flaterye,

To Thebes, sitting inside her ancient walls.

I think that men would call me negligent,
If I forgot to mention the efforts
Of Theseus, who worked so hard
To make a truly royal battleground;
He built such a noble theatre
That I daresay that there was nothing to match it in the world.

It was a mile in circumference,
Stone walled, with trenches all round.
It was circular, as a compass traces,
And the tiers reached a height of sixty paces,
So that when a man was sat on one level,
He did not obscure the view of those behind.
To the east there was a gate of white marble,
To the west, its twin, right opposite;
In brief, there was no other such place
Anywhere on earth built in such quick time.
For there was no craftsman in the land
With skill at geometry or arithmetic,
No portrait painter and sculptor
Whom Theseus did not ply with food and wages,
In order for them to design and build that theatre.

In order to observe all the proper rites
He built above the gates in the east,
In worship of Venus, goddess of love,
An altar and a temple.
On the west gate, in memory
Of Mars, he made one just the same,
At great expense and much effort.
To the north, on top of a turret set in the wall,
Theseus had a rich temple built
Of white alabaster and red coral,
For the worship of Diana, the virgin.
Has Thesesus done wrong in the eyes of the noble

And still I have not yet mentioned
The noble carvings and the portraits,
The shapes, faces and figures,
That filled all these temples.
First, in the temple of Venus could be seen,
Painted on the wall, pitiful to behold,
The broken sleep and cold sighs,
The sacred tears and lamentations,
The burning of fierce desire
That the servants of love endure in life;
The oaths that they swear to keep their promises;

Pleasure and hope, desire, foolishness,
Beauty and youth, bawdiness, riches,
Charms and force, lying, flattery,

Despense, Bisynesse, and Jalousye,	Expense, effort and jealousy,
That wered of yelewe gooldes a gerland,	Who wore a garland of yellow marigolds,
And a cokkow sittynge on hir hand;	And had a cuckoo sitting on her hand;
Festes, instrumentz, caroles, daunces,	Feasts, instruments, carols, dances,
Lust and array, and alle the circumstaunces	Lust and ornamentation, and all the parts
Of love, whiche that I rekned, and rekne shal,	Of love, which I know of now or ever will,
By ordre weren peynted on the wal,	Were painted on that wall by order,
And mo than I kan make of mencioun;	More than I have time to mention;
For soothly, al the mount of Citheroun,	For truly, the whole Mount of Citheroun,
Ther Venus hath hir principal dwellynge,	Where Venus has her chief residence,
Was shewed on the wal in portreyynge,	Was shown in the painting on that wall,
With al the gardyn and the lustynesse.	With all the gardens and their loveliness.
Nat was foryeten the Porter Ydelnesse,	Nor was the gatekeeper Idleness forgotten,
Ne Narcisus the faire, of yore agon,	Nor Narcissus the lovely, from times gone by,
Ne yet the folye of kyng Salamon,	Nor the folly of King Solomon,
And eek the grete strengthe of Ercules -	And also the great strength of Hercules,
Th'enchauntementz of Medea and Circes -	The enchantments of Medea and Circe,
Ne of Turnus, with the hardy fiers corage,	Nor Turnus with his strong fierce courage,
The riche Cresus, kaytyf in servage.	Rich Croesus, a slave to his riches.
Thus may ye seen, that wysdom ne richesse,	So it could be seen that neither wisdom nor riches,
Beautee ne sleighte, strengthe ne hardynesse,	Beauty nor skill, strength nor hardiness,
Ne may with Venus holde champartie,	Could compete with Venus,
For as hir list, the world than may she gye.	For when she wishes she can lead the world.
Lo, alle thise folk so caught were in hir las,	See, all these folk were caught in her trap,
Til they for wo ful ofte seyde "allas!"	Until they often cried aloud in sorrow, "Alas!"
Suffiseth heere ensamples oon or two-	It's enough to mention one or two examples here,
And, though, I koude rekene a thousand mo.	Although I think I could give you a thousand more.
The statue of Venus, glorious for to se,	The statue of Venus, which was glorious to see,
Was naked, fletynge in the large see,	Was naked, floating on the open sea,
And fro the navele doun al covered was	And from the navel down it was all covered
With wawes grene, and brighte as any glas.	With green waves, shining bright as glass.
A citole in hir right hand hadde she,	She held a fiddle in her right hand,
And on hir heed, ful semely for to se,	And on her head, beautiful to see,
A rose gerland, fressh and wel smellynge;	Was a garland of roses, fresh and sweet smelling;
Above hir heed hir dowves flikerynge.	Above her head flew fluttering doves.
Biforn hir stood hir sone Cupido,	In front of her stood her son Cupid,
Upon his shuldres wynges hadde he two,	With two wings on his shoulders,
And blynd he was, as it was often seene.	He was blind, as has often been shown;
A bowe he bar, and arwes brighte and kene.	He carried a bow, and bright sharp arrows.
Why sholde I noght as wel eek telle yow al	Why should I not also tell you of
The portreiture, that was upon the wal	All the paintings that were on the walls
Withinne the temple of myghty Mars the rede?	Inside the temple of great red Mars?
Al peynted was the wal in lengthe and brede	The whole wall was painted, length and breadth,
Lyk to the estres of the grisly place	Like the inside of that ghastly place,
That highte the grete temple of Mars in Trace,	The great Temple of Mars in Thrace,
In thilke colde frosty regioun	In that same cold and frosty region
Ther as Mars hath his sovereyn mansioun.	Where Mars keeps his royal palace.

First on the wal was peynted a forest	Firstly on the wall there was painted a forest,
In which ther dwelleth neither man ne best,	In which neither man nor beast dwelt,
With knotty, knarry, bareyne trees olde,	With knotty, gnarled, old barren trees,
Of stubbes sharpe and hidouse to biholde,	With sharp stumps, horrible to see,
In which ther ran a rumbel and a swough	Through which there ran a rumbling shudder
As though a storm sholde bresten every bough.	As if the storm was shaking every branch.
And dounward from an hille, under a bente,	And farther down the hill, under a crag,
Ther stood the temple of Mars Armypotente,	There stood the temple of Mars in Armour,
Wroght al of burned steel, of which the entrée	Made of burnished steel, and the gate
Was long and streit, and gastly for to see,	Was huge and ghastly to look at,
And therout came a rage and suche a veze,	And from it such a gale exploded
That it made al the gate for to rese.	That it made the whole gate shake.
The northren lyght in at the dores shoon,	The northern light shone in at the doors,
For wyndowe on the wal ne was ther noon,	For there were no windows in the walls,
Thurgh which men myghten any light discerne.	Through which men could see any light.
The dore was al of adamant eterne,	The door was made of eternal diamond,
Yclenched overthwart and endelong	Encased both sides and along its edges
With iren tough, and for to make it strong	With tough iron, to make it strong.
Every pyler, the temple to sustene,	Every pillar which held up this temple
Was tonne-greet of iren bright and shene.	Was thick as a barrel, of shining iron.
Ther saugh I first the dirke ymaginyng	There I first saw the dark thoughts
Of Felonye, and al the compassyng,	Of Felony, and all that entailed,
The crueel Ire, reed as any gleede,	Cruel Anger, red as burning coal,
The pykepurs, and eek the pale Drede,	Pickpockets, and also pale Dread,
The smylere with the knyf under the cloke,	The smiling villain with his knife under his cloak,
The shepne brennynge with the blake smoke,	Barns burning with black smoke,
The tresoun of the mordrynge in the bedde,	The treachery to men murdered in their beds,
The open werre, with woundes al bibledde;	The open battle with bleeding wounds;
Contek, with blody knyf and sharp manace,	Strife, with its bloody knife and sharp menace,
Al ful of chirkyng was that sory place.	That whole dismal place groaned with sorrow.
The sleere of hymself yet saugh I ther,	I also saw the suicide there,
His herte-blood hath bathed al his heer;	His heart's blood matted in his hair;
The nayl ydryven in the shode anyght,	The nail that's driven into the skull at night,
The colde deeth, with mouth gapyng upright.	And cold death, with its open mouth gaping.
Amyddes of the temple sat Meschaunce,	In the middle of the temple sat mischance,
With Disconfort and Sory Contenaunce.	With its gloomy woeful expression.
Yet saugh I Woodnesse laughynge in his rage,	I also saw madness laughing in his rage,
Armed Compleint, Outhees, and fiers Outrage;	Armed rebellion, riots and fearsome outrages;
The careyne in the busk with throte ycorve,	Dead meat in the bush with its throat slit,
A thousand slayn, and nat of qualm ystorve,	A thousand killed, not of plague or starvation,
The tiraunt with the pray by force yraft,	The tyrant with his plunder taken by force,
The toun destroyed, ther was nothyng laft.	The town destroyed, with nothing left.
Yet saugh I brent the shippes hoppesteres,	I also saw the great ships burnt,
The hunte strangled with the wilde beres,	The hunter strangled by wild bears,
The sowe freten the child right in the cradel,	The sow devouring the child in its cradle,
The cook yscalded, for al his longe ladel.	The cook scalded, despite his long ladle.
Noght was foryeten by the infortune of Marte,	Nothing escapes the misfortunes of Mars,
The cartere overryden with his carte,	The carter run over by his own cart,
Under the wheel ful lowe he lay adoun.	Crushed underneath its wheels.
Ther were also, of Martes divisioun,	There were also, in that house of Mars,
The barbour, and the bocher, and the smyth	The surgeon, and the butcher, and the

That forgeth sharpe swerdes on his styth.	blacksmith
And al above, depeynted in a tour,	Who makes sharp swords on his anvil.
Saugh I Conquest sittynge in greet honour,	Above them all, painted on a tower,
With the sharpe swerd over his heed	I saw Conquest sitting in great honour,
Hangynge by a soutil twyned threed.	With a sharp sword hung over his head
Depeynted was the slaughtre of Julius,	Held up by a single twisted thread.
Of grete Nero, and of Antonius;	Also shown was the slaughter of Julius,
Al be that thilke tyme they were unborn,	Of great Nero, and of Antony;
Yet was hir deth depeynted ther-biforn	And although that they had yet to be born,
By manasynge of Mars, right by figure;	Yet their deaths were shown, predicted
So was it shewed in that portreiture,	In the mansion of Mars, accurate and true;
As is depeynted in the sterres above	Things were shown in that picture,
Who shal be slayn or elles deed for love.	That are predicted in the stars above;
Suffiseth oon ensample in stories olde,	Who will be killed or otherwise die for love.
I may nat rekene hem alle though I wolde.	That's just one example of the old stories,
	I couldn't tell them all even if I wanted to.
The statue of Mars upon a carte stood	The statue of Mars stood upon a chariot,
Armed, and looked grym as he were wood,	Armed, looking as grim as if he were mad,
And over his heed ther shynen two figures	And over his head there were two shining pictures
Of sterres, that been cleped in scriptures	Of stars, that have been named in writings,
That oon Puella, that oother Rubeus.	One being Puella, and the other Rubeus.
This god of armes was arrayed thus:	The God of War was shown like this:
A wolf ther stood biforn hym at his feet,	There was a wolf standing at his feet,
With eyen rede, and of a man he eet.	With red eyes, eating a man.
With soutil pencel was depeynt this storie,	A cunning artist had painted this story,
In redoutynge of Mars and of his glorie.	To worship Mars and all his glory.
Now to the temple of Dyane the chaste	Now I will go to the temple of Diana the virgin,
As shortly as I kan I wol me haste,	As quickly as ever I can,
To telle yow al the descripsioun.	To give you a full description of it.
Depeynted been the walles up and doun	The walls were painted up and down
Of huntyng and of shamefast chastitee.	With images of hunting and modest chastity.
Ther saugh I, how woful Calistopee	There I saw how poor Callisto,
Whan that Diane agreved was with here,	When Diana was angry with her,
Was turned from a womman til a bere,	Was changed from a woman into a bear,
And after was she maad the loode-sterre.	And afterwards made into the lonely polestar.
Thus was it peynted, I kan sey yow no ferre -	There it was, that's all I can say—
Hir sone is eek a sterre, as men may see.	Her son is also a star, which men can see.
Ther saugh I Dane, yturned til a tree,	There I saw Daphne, turned into a tree,
I mene nat the goddesse Diane,	I don't mean the goddess Diana,
But Penneus doughter, which that highte Dane.	But the daughter of Peneus, who was called Daphne.
Ther saugh I Attheon an hert ymaked,	There I saw Actaeon turned into a deer,
For vengeaunce that he saugh Diane al naked.	As punishment for seeing Diana naked.
I saugh how that hise houndes have hym caught	I saw how his hounds caught him
And freeten hym, for that they knewe hym naught.	And ate him, not knowing it was him.
Yet peynted was a litel forther moor	Painted a little farther on
How Atthalante hunted the wilde boor,	Was how Atalanta hunted the wild boar,
And Meleagree, and many another mo,	Also Meleager, and many others with him,
For which Dyane wroghte hym care and wo.	For which Diana gave him sorrow and suffering.
Ther saugh I many another wonder storie,	There I also saw many other wonderful

The which me list nat drawen to memorie.	stories, Which I will not call to mind just now.
This goddesse on an hert ful hye seet, With smale houndes al aboute hir feet; And undernethe hir feet she hadde a moone, Wexynge it was, and sholde wanye soone. In gaude grene hir statue clothed was, With bowe in honde, and arwes in a cas. Hir eyen caste she ful lowe adoun, Ther Pluto hath his derke regioun. A womman travaillynge was hir biforn; But for hir child so longe was unborn Ful pitously Lucyna gan she calle, And seyde, "Help, for thou mayst best of alle!"	The goddess was sitting on a great deer, With little hounds around her feet, And underneath her feet there was a moon, It was waxing, but it should be full soon. Her statue was clothed in gold green robes, With her bow in hand and arrows in a quiver. Her eyes were cast down upon the ground To where Pluto has his dark kingdom. In front of her there was a woman suffering, Having been so long in childbirth That she pitifully cried out for Lucina, And said, "You are the only one who can help me!"
Wel koude he peynten lyfly, that it wroghte, With many a floryn he the hewes boghte. Now been thise listes maad, and Theseus, That at his grete cost arrayed thus The temples, and the theatre every deel, Whan it was doon, hym lyked wonder weel.-	It was a fine painter who had depicted this, And he had spent plenty on his paints. Now the arena was finished, and Theseus, Who had built these things at such great cost, The temples and the arena, as I've told, When it was finished, he was very pleased with it.
But stynte I wole of Theseus a lite, And speke of Palamon and of Arcite.	But I will stop talking of Theseus for a while And speak of Palamon and Arcite.
The day approcheth of hir retournynge, That everich sholde an hundred knyghtes brynge	The day of their return approached, When each of them would bring a hundred knights,
The bataille to darreyne, as I yow tolde. And til Atthenes, hir covenantz for to holde, Hath everich of hem broght an hundred knyghtes, Wel armed for the werre at alle rightes. And sikerly, ther trowed many a man, That nevere sithen, that the world bigan, As for to speke of knyghthod of hir hond, As fer as God hath maked see or lond, Nas of so fewe so noble a compaignye. For every wight that lovede chivalrye, And wolde, his thankes, han a passant name, Hath preyed that he myghte been of that game; And wel was hym that therto chosen was. For if ther fille tomorwe swich a cas Ye knowen wel, that every lusty knyght That loveth paramours, and hath his myght,	To join in the battle, as I told you. And so to Athens, to keep their promise, Each of them brought a hundred knights, Carrying all the equipment of war, And certainly many men believed That never since the world began, Thinking of good knights, good fighters, Wherever God had created sea or land, Was there ever a great and noble company Of every man who loved chivalry, And was eager to win his spurs, And wanted to be part of that great game; And every man who was chosen was delighted. For if there was such an opportunity tomorrow You know full well that every lusty knight Who loves the ladies and keeps up his strength,
Were it in Engelond or elles where, They wolde, hir thankes, wilnen to be there, To fighte for a lady, benedicitee! It were a lusty sighte for to see.	Weather in England or elsewhere, They would be desperate to be invited there, To fight for a lady, with God's blessing! That would be a fine sight to see.
And right so ferden they with Palamon,	This was how it was with those who were with Palamon,
With hym ther wenten knyghtes many on.	With the great company of knights riding with him.

Som wol ben armed in an haubergeoun,	*Some were well armed in chain mail,*
In a bristplate, and in a light gypoun,	*With breastplates, and light tunics over,*
And som wol have a paire plates large,	*And some wore large plates back and front,*
And som wol have a Pruce sheeld, or a targe,	*And some carried a Prussian shield,*
Som wol ben armed on hir legges weel,	*Some were well armoured round their legs,*
And have an ax, and somme a mace of steel.	*Carrying axes, and some had steel maces.*
Ther is no newe gyse, that it nas old;	*There is nothing new under the sun;*
Armed were they, as I have yow told,	*They were armed as I have described to you,*
Everych after his opinioun.	*Every one according to his liking.*
Ther maistow seen comyng with Palamoun,	*There could be seen, coming with Palamon,*
Lygurge hym-self, the grete kyng of Trace.	*Lycurgus himself, the mighty king of Thrace;*
Blak was his berd, and manly was his face,	*He had a black beard and a manly face,*
The cercles of hise eyen in his heed,	*The eyes which sat there in his head*
They gloweden bitwyxen yelow and reed,	*Alternated glowing between yellow and red,*
And lik a grifphon looked he aboute,	*And he glared around him like a griffin,*
With kempe heeris on hise browes stoute,	*From underneath his bushy eyebrows,*
Hise lymes grete, hise brawnes harde and stronge,	*His limbs were huge, his muscles hard and strong,*
Hise shuldres brode, hise armes rounde and longe;	*His shoulders broad, his arms both large and long;*
And as the gyse was in his contree,	*And as was the fashion in his country*
Ful hye upon a chaar of gold stood he,	*He stood in a high golden chariot,*
With foure white boles in the trays.	*Pulled by four white bulls.*
In stede of cote-armure, over his harnays	*Instead of a coat of arms over his armour*
With nayles yelewe and brighte as any gold	*He wore a very old black bearskin*
He hadde a beres skyn, col-blak, for old;	*Which had claws as yellow and bright as gold;*
His longe heer was kembd bihynde his bak,	*His long hair was combed down behind his back,*
As any ravenes fethere it shoon for-blak.	*As shiny and black as any raven's feather.*
A wrethe of gold arm-greet, of huge wighte,	*He wore a gold wreath, of great weight,*
Upon his heed, set ful of stones brighte,	*On his head, shining with precious stones,*
Of fyne rubyes and of dyamauntz.	*Fine rubies and also diamonds.*
Aboute his chaar ther wenten white alauntz,	*Around his chariot there were white wolfhounds,*
Twenty and mo, as grete as any steer,	*Twenty or more, as large as any steer,*
To hunten at the leoun or the deer,	*To hunt for lion or for deer,*
And folwed hym, with mosel faste ybounde,	*They followed him, with their muzzles bound up tight,*
Colored of gold, and tourettes fyled rounde.	*Wearing gold collars, of smooth round links.*
An hundred lordes hadde he in his route,	*A hundred lords followed on behind him,*
Armed ful wel, with hertes stierne and stoute.	*All well armed, with strong steadfast hearts.*
With Arcita, in stories as men fynde,	*With Arcite, so the stories tell,*
The grete Emetreus, the kyng of Inde,	*Was great Emetreus, king of India,*
Upon a steede bay, trapped in steel,	*On a bay horse, armoured in steel,*
Covered in clooth of gold dyapred weel,	*Covered in well cut cloth of gold,*
Cam ridynge lyk the god of armes, Mars.	*He rode like Mars, the god of war.*
His cote-armure was of clooth of Tars,	*His coat of arms was made of Tartar cloth,*
Couched with perles white and rounde and grete.	*Sewn with great white round pearls.*
His sadel was of brend gold newe ybete;	*His saddle was beaten out of fresh mined gold;*
A mantelet upon his shuldre hangynge	*A cloak hung from his shoulders*
Bret-ful of rubyes rede, as fyr sparklynge.	*Covered in red rubies, sparkling like fire.*
His crispe heer lyk rynges was yronne,	*His crisp hair curled down in ringlets,*
And that was yelow, and glytered as the sonne.	*His nose was high,*

His nose was heigh, hise eyen bright citryn,	his eyes bright yellow,
Hise lippes rounde, his colour was sangwyn;	Full lipped, with a good red colour;
A fewe frakenes in his face yspreynd,	There were a few freckles dotted around his face,
Bitwixen yelow and somdel blak ymeynd,	Coloured somewhere between yellow and black,
And as a leoun he his looking caste.	And he looked around him like a lion.
Of fyve and twenty yeer his age I caste;	I would say he was twenty-five years old;
His berd was wel bigonne for to sprynge,	His beard was beginning to flourish on his face,
His voys was as a trompe thonderynge.	His voice was like a thundering trumpet.
Upon his heed he wered of laurer grene	On his head he wore a garland of
A gerland, fressh and lusty for to sene.	Green laurels, fresh and cheering to see.
Upon his hand he bar for his deduyt	On his wrist he carried for his delight
An egle tame, as any lilye whyt.	A tame eagle, white as any lily.
An hundred lordes hadde he with hym there,	He had a hundred lords along with him,
Al armed, save hir heddes, in al hir gere,	Wearing all their armour apart from their helmets,
Ful richely in alle maner thynges.	Very finely kitted out in everything.
For trusteth wel, that dukes, erles, kynges,	For believe you me, dukes, earls and kings
Were gadered in this noble compaignye,	Were gathered in this noble company,
For love, and for encrees of chivalrye.	For love and to fight for chivalry.
Aboute this kyng ther ran on every part	Around this king there ran on every side
Ful many a tame leoun and leopard,	Many tame lions and leopards,
And in this wise thise lordes, alle and some	And in this way these lords, every one,
Been on the sonday to the citee come,	Came to the city on Sunday,
Aboute pryme, and in the toun alight.	Round about noon, and they settled in the town.
This Theseus, this duc, this worthy knyght,	This Theseus, this duke, this worthy knight,
Whan he had broght hem into his citee,	When he had brought them into his city,
And inned hem, everich in his degree,	And quartered them, each according to his station,
He festeth hem, and dooth so greet labour	He gave a feast for them, and took great trouble
To esen hem and doon hem al honour,	To make them comfortable and do them honour,
That yet men wenen that no maner wit	So that men say there is no way that anyone,
Of noon estaat ne koude amenden it.	High or low, could have done better.
The mynstralcye, the service at the feeste,	The minstrels, the service at the feast,
The grete yiftes to the mooste and leeste,	The great gifts to the highest and the lowest,
The riche array of Theseus paleys,	The rich decoration of Theseus' palace,
Ne who sat first ne last upon the deys,	Of who sat in what place on the dais,
What ladyes fairest been, or best daunsynge,	What ladies were loveliest, or the best turned out,
Or which of hem kan dauncen best and synge,	Or which of them was the best answer or singer,
Ne who moost felyngly speketh of love,	Or who could speak the words of love the best,
What haukes sitten on the perche above,	Or the hawks which sat on the perches above,
What houndes liggen in the floor adoun-	Or the hounds which laid on the floor below—
Of al this make I now no mencioun;	I will not mention anything about this now;
But, al th'effect, that thynketh me the beste,	But I will tell my tale, I think that's best,
Now cometh the point, and herkneth if yow leste.	It's coming to the point, listen if you will.
The Sonday nyght, er day bigan to sprynge,	On Sunday night, before daybreak,

Whan Palamon the larke herde synge,	When Palamon heard the lark singing,
(Al though it nere nat day by houres two,	(Although it was two hours before sunrise,
Yet song the larke) and Palamon right tho.	The lark still sang) and Palamon sang with him.
With hooly herte and with an heigh corage	With a pious heart and his courage high
He roos, to wenden on his pilgrymage,	He rose to go on his pilgrimage,
Unto the blisful Citherea benigne,	To the blessed shrine of Citherea,
I mene Venus, honurable and digne.	By which I mean Venus, honourable and kind.
And in hir houre he walketh forth a pas	At her time he then walked out quickly
Unto the lystes, ther hire temple was,	To the arena, where her temple was,
And doun he kneleth, with ful humble cheere,	And he knelt down, in all humility,
And herte soor, and seyde in this manere.	And with an aching heart he said these words.
"Faireste of faire, O lady myn, Venus,	"Fairest of all fair, my Lady Venus,
Doughter to Jove, and spouse of Vulcanus,	Daughter of Jove, wife of Vulcan,
Thow glader of the Mount of Citheron,	You who beautify the Mount of Citheron,
For thilke love thow haddest to Adoon,	Because of your great love for Adonis,
Have pitee of my bittre teeris smerte,	Have pity on my bitter stinging tears,
And taak myn humble preyere at thyn herte.	And take my humble prayer into your heart.
Allas, I ne have no langage to telle	Alas, I do not have the words to describe
Th'effectes, ne the tormentz of myn helle!	The effect of all the tortures in my hell!
Myn herte may myne harmes nat biwreye,	My heart cannot describe all its suffering,
I am so confus that I kan noght seye.	I am so confused that I have nothing to say.
But 'Mercy, lady bright! that knowest weele	But mercy, Lady bright, you know full well
My thought, and seest what harmes that I feele.'	What I think, and you see all my suffering.
Considere al this, and rewe upon my soore,	Think of all this and take pity on my anguish,
As wisly, as I shal for everemoore,	As truly, I will for ever afterwards
Emforth my myght, thy trewe servant be,	Be your true servant, to the best of my ability,
And holden werre alwey with chastitee.	And from now on fight a war against chastity.
That make I myn avow, so ye me helpe.	This is what I promise if you help me now.
I kepe noght of armes for to yelpe,	I don't care about boasting of knightly strength,
Ne I ne axe nat tomorwe to have victorie,	Nor am I asking you for victory tomorrow,
Ne renoun in this cas, ne veyne glorie	I don't want fame or any empty glory
Of pris of armes blowen up and doun,	Or prizes for acts of chivalry,
But I wolde have fully possessioun	All I want is to have possession
Of Emelye, and dye in thy servyse.	Of Emily, and to die serving you;
Fynd thow the manere how, and in what wyse-	You tell me how this should be done and in what way;
I recche nat, but it may bettre be	I do not care, unless it helps my aims,
To have victorie of hem, or they of me-	If I beat them, or if they beat me,
So that I have my lady in myne armes.	As long as I have my lady in my arms.
For though so be, that Mars is god of armes,	For although it's Mars who is the god of war,
Youre vertu is so greet in hevene above	You have such great powers in heaven above
That if yow list, I shal wel have my love.	That if you order it I shall get my love.
Thy temple wol I worshipe everemo,	I will worship you for evermore,
And on thyn auter, where I ride or go,	And on your altar, wherever I travel,
I wol doon sacrifice and fires beete.	I will make sacrifices and feed your fires.
And if ye wol nat so, my lady sweete,	If you won't do this, my sweet lady,
Thanne preye I thee, tomorwe with a spere	Then I pray to you that tomorrow
That Arcita me thurgh the herte bere.	Arcite runs my heart through with a spear.
Thanne rekke I noght, whan I have lost my lyf,	I will not care, when my life has gone,
Though that Arcita wynne hir to his wyf.	If Arcite wins her as his wife.
This is th'effect and ende of my preyere,	This is all I ask, and ends my prayer,
Yif me my love, thow blisful lady deere!"	Give me my love, sweet lady fair!"

Whan the orison was doon of Palamon,	When Palamon was finished with his prayers
His sacrifice he dide, and that anon,	He straight away made his sacrifice,
Ful pitously with alle circumstaunces,	Very piously in the proper fashion,
Al telle I noght as now his observaunces.	Although I won't describe all that now.
But atte laste, the statue of Venus shook,	But at the end, the statue of Venus shook,
And made a signe wherby that he took	And made a sign which he took to mean
That his preyere accepted was that day.	That his prayers had been accepted that day.
For thogh the signe shewed a delay,	Although the sign showed there could be a delay,
Yet wiste he wel that graunted was his boone,	He knew very well that his prayers were answered,
And with glad herte he wente hym hoom ful soone.	And happily he took himself straight back home.
The thridde houre inequal, that Palamon	Three hours or thereabouts after Palamon
Bigan to Venus temple for to gon,	Had left to go to the temple of Venus,
Up roos the sonne, and up roos Emelye,	The sun rose up, and so did Emily,
And to the temple of Dyane gan hye.	And she took herself to the temple of Diana.
Hir maydens that she thider with hir ladde,	She took her handmaids along with her,
Ful redily with hem the fyr they ladde,	And they gladly took along fire,
Th'encens, the clothes, and the remenant al	Incense, robes, and everything else
That to the sacrifice longen shal.	Suitable for a sacrifice.
The hornes fulle of meeth, as was the gyse,	They had horns full of mead, as was their way,
Ther lakked noght to doon hir sacrifise,	There was not one thing missing from their sacrifice.
Smokynge the temple, ful of clothes faire.	In the smoky temple, hung with beautiful cloths,
This Emelye, with herte debonaire,	Emily, with her gracious heart,
Hir body wessh with water of a welle-	Washed her body in the water of a well—
But how she dide hir ryte I dar nat telle,	But how she did that rite I dare not tell,
But it be any thing in general;	Except to mention it generally;
And yet it were a game to heeren al,	But it was a thing well worth hearing of,
To hym that meneth wel it were no charge,	For someone who is well-meaning,
But it is good a man been at his large.-	But it is best for me to be discreet.
Hir brighte heer was kembd, untressed al,	Her bright hair was unbound and combed,
A coroune of a grene ook cerial	And she wore a crown of green oak
Upon hir heed was set, ful fair and meete.	Upon her head, beautiful and fitting.
Two fyres on the auter gan she beete,	She began to fan two fires on the altar,
And dide hir thynges as men may biholde	And performed her ceremonies as described
In Stace of Thebes, and thise bookes olde.	In the ancient books of Stace of Thebes.
Whan kyndled was the fyr, with pitous cheere	When the fire was kindled, with a pious expression
Unto Dyane she spak as ye may heere.	She spoke to Diana, as you shall hear.
"O chaste goddesse of the wodes grene,	"Oh chaste goddess of the green woods,
To whom bothe hevene and erthe and see is sene,	Who can see over heaven and earth and sea,
Queene of the regne of Pluto derk and lowe,	Queen of the kingdom of Pluto, dark underground,
Goddesse of maydens, that myn herte hast knowe	Goddess of virgins, who has known my heart
Ful many a yeer, and woost what I desire,	For many years, and sees what I desire,
As keep me fro thy vengeaunce and thyn ire,	Save me from your vengeance and your anger,
That Attheon aboughte cruelly.	That you impose so cruelly onto Actaeon.
Chaste goddesse, wel wostow that I	Pure goddess, you know well that I
Desire to ben a mayden al my lyf,	Wish to remain a virgin all my life,
Ne nevere wol I be no love ne wyf.	And I don't want to be any man's love or wife.

I am, thow woost, yet of thy compaignye,	*I am, you know, one of your devotees,*
A mayde, and love huntynge and venerye,	*A virgin, who loves hunting and the countryside,*
And for to walken in the wodes wilde,	*And to walk in the wild woods,*
And noght to ben a wyf, and be with childe.	*Not to be a wife and have a child.*
Noght wol I knowe the compaignye of man;	*I do not want the company of a man;*
Now helpe me, lady, sith ye may and kan,	*Now help me, lady, since you are able to,*
For tho thre formes that thou hast in thee.	*Through the three beings that are one in you.*
And Palamon, that hath swich love to me,	*For Palamon, who has such love for me,*
And eek Arcite, that loveth me so soore,	*For Arcite also, who loves me so madly,*
This grace I preye thee, withoute moore,	*I pray you for this favour, and nothing else,*
As sende love and pees bitwixe hem two,	*To create love and peace between those two,*
And fro me turne awey hir hertes so,	*And let their hearts turn away from me,*
That al hir hoote love and hir desir,	*So that all their hot love and their desire,*
And al hir bisy torment and hir fir,	*And all their endless torment and their fire,*
Be queynt, or turned in another place.	*Shall be quenched, or turned towards someone else.*
And if so be thou wolt do me no grace,	*And if you choose not to do me this favour,*
And if my destynee be shapen so	*And if it's my destiny that I*
That I shal nedes have oon of hem two,	*Have to have one of the two,*
As sende me hym that moost desireth me.	*Give me the one who loves me the most.*
Bihoold, goddesse, of clene chastitee,	*See, goddess of pure chastity,*
The bittre teeris that on my chekes falle.	*The bitter tears that run down my cheeks.*
Syn thou art mayde and kepere of us alle,	*Since you are a virgin and preserver of us all,*
My maydenhede thou kepe and wel conserve,	*Let me keep my virginity, protect me,*
And whil I lyve a mayde, I wol thee serve."	*And while I remain a virgin, I will serve you."*
The fires brenne upon the auter cleere,	*The fires blazed upon the pure altar,*
Whil Emelye was thus in hir preyere;	*While Emily was making these prayers;*
But sodeynly she saugh a sighte queynte,	*But suddenly she saw a very strange sight,*
For right anon oon of the fyres queynte,	*For instantly one fire shrank,*
And quyked agayn, and after that anon	*Then blazed again, and straight after that*
That oother fyr was queynt and al agon;	*The other fire withered and was gone;*
And as it queynte, it made a whistelynge	*And as it disappeared, it made a whistling sound*
As doon thise wete brondes in hir brennynge;	*Like wet branches do when they are burned;*
And at the brondes ende out ran anon	*And from the end of the branches there ran*
As it were blody dropes many oon;	*What looked like many drops of blood;*
For which so soore agast was Emelye	*And Emily was so terrified by this*
That she was wel ny mad, and gan to crye;	*That she almost went mad, and began to cry;*
For she ne wiste what it signyfied.	*For she did not know what it signified.*
But oonly for the feere thus hath she cried,	*But all she could do was cry with terror,*
And weep that it was pitee for to heere.	*And weep in a way that was pitiful to hear.*
And therwithal Dyane gan appeere,	*Suddenly Diana began to appear,*
With bowe in honde, right as an hunteresse,	*With her bow in hand, as befits a huntress, and said,*
And seyde,	
"Doghter, stynt thyn hevynesse.	*"Daughter, throw off this heaviness.*
Among the goddes hye it is affermed,	*It has been agreed amongst the gods,*
And by eterne word writen and confermed,	*And written in the eternal Word,*
Thou shalt ben wedded unto oon of tho	*That you shall be the wife of one of those*
That han for thee so muchel care and wo.	*Who go through so much suffering and sorrow for you;*
But unto which of hem I may nat telle,	*But which of them it will be I cannot tell.*
Farwel, for I ne may no lenger dwelle.	*I cannot say here, so farewell.*

The fires whiche that on myn auter brenne	The fires that burn incense on my altar
Shule thee declaren, er that thou go henne,	Should tell you everything, before you go from here,
Thyn aventure of love, as in this cas."	About what will happen to love in your case."
And with that word, the arwes in the caas	As she said this the hunting arrows
Of the goddesse clateren faste and rynge,	The goddess carried clattered and rang,
And forth she wente, and made a vanysshynge,	And she stepped out and vanished,
For which this Emelye astoned was,	Which astonished Emily,
And seyde, "What amounteth this, allas!	Who said, "What does this mean, alas!
I putte me in thy proteccioun,	I put yourself under your protection,
Dyane, and in thy disposicioun!"	Diana, I'm yours to do with as you will!"
And hoom she goth anon the nexte weye.	And then she took the fastest way home.
This is th'effect, ther is namoore to seye.	This is all that happened, there is no more to say.
The nexte houre of Mars folwynge this	In the next hour of Mars following this
Arcite unto the temple walked is	Arcite walked to the temple dedicated
Of fierse Mars, to doon his sacrifise	To fierce Mars, to make his sacrifice,
With alle the rytes of his payen wyse.	With all the full rites of a pagan.
With pitous herte and heigh devocioun	With a pious heart and great devotion
Right thus to Mars he seyde his orisoun.	He began to make his prayers to Mars.
"O stronge god, that in the regnes colde	"O mighty God, who is honoured
Of Trace honoured art and lord yholde,	In the cold regions of Thrace, where you are lord,
And hast in every regne and every lond	And who has in every kingdom and every country
Of armes al the brydel in thyn hond,	The control of every single battle,
And hem fortunest as thee lyst devyse,	And hands out fortune as you wish,
Accepte of me my pitous sacrifise.	Accept my pious sacrifice to you.
If so be that my youthe may deserve,	If one so young deserves the honour,
And that my myght be worthy for to serve	If my strength is thought great enough to serve
Thy godhede, that I may been oon of thyne,	Your divinity, so I can be one of yours,
Thanne preye I thee to rewe upon my pyne.	Then I pray you to take pity on my pain.
For thilke peyne, and thilke hoote fir,	For the same pain and the same hot fire
In which thou whilom brendest for desir	With which you once burned with desire
Whan that thow usedest the greet beautee	When you used the great beauty
Of faire yonge fresshe Venus free,	Of the fair young virgin Venus,
And haddest hir in armes at thy wille-	Holding her in your arms, in your power,
Although thee ones on a tyme mysfille	Although with you you had bad luck,
Whan Vulcanus hadde caught thee in his las,	With Vulcan catching you in his net when
And foond thee liggynge by his wyf, allas!-	He found you lying with his wife, alas!
For thilke sorwe that was in thyn herte	Remember the sorrow that was in your heart,
Have routhe as wel, upon my peynes smerte!	And take pity on my pains now!
I am yong and unkonnynge as thow woost,	I am young and ignorant as you know,
And, as I trowe, with love offended moost	And I believe I am more hurt by love now
That evere was any lyves creature,	Than any living creature ever was,
For she that dooth me al this wo endure	For she who puts me through all this sorrow
Ne reccheth nevere wher I synke or fleete.	Does not care whether I sink or swim.
And wel I woot, er she me mercy heete,	And I am well aware that before she shows me mercy
I moot with strengthe wynne hir in the place.	I must show my strength and win her in this place.
And,. wel I woot, withouten help or grace	And I also know that without your help and favour
Of thee, ne may my strengthe noght availle.	My strength will be completely worthless.

Thanne help me, lord, tomorwe in my bataille	So help me, lord, tomorrow in my battle
For thilke fyr that whilom brente thee,	Remembering the fire that once burned in you,
As wel as thilke fyr now brenneth me!	Which is the fire that now burns in me!
And do that I tomorwe have victorie,	If tomorrow I have the victory
Myn be the travaille and thyn be the glorie!	It will be my work but all your glory!
Thy sovereyn temple wol I moost honouren	I will honour your royal temple in every way,
Of any place, and alwey moost labouren	More than any other, and always work
In thy plesaunce, and in thy craftes stronge,	For your pleasure, to learn your will,
And in thy temple I wol my baner honge,	And I will hang my banner in your temple,
And alle the armes of my compaignye;	And all weapons of my companions;
And evere-mo, unto that day I dye,	And ever afterwards, to the day I die,
Eterne fir I wol biforn thee fynde.	I will make sure the eternal fire burns for you.
And eek to this avow I wol me bynde;	I also make this binding vow;
My beerd, myn heer, that hongeth long adoun,	My beard and my hair, that hangs down so long,
That nevere yet ne felte offensioun	That has never before been touched
Of rasour, nor of shere, I wol thee yeve,	By a razor or by shears, I will give to you,
And ben thy trewe servant whil I lyve.	and be your loyal servant while I live.
Now lord, have routhe upon my sorwes soore;	Now lord, have pity on my anguish;
Yif me victorie, I aske thee namoore!"	If you give me victory, that's all I ask!"
The preyere stynt of Arcita the stronge;	This was the prayer of strong Arcite;
The rynges on the temple dore that honge,	The rings that hung on the door of the temple
And eek the dores clatereden ful faste,	And also the doors rattled so loudly
Of which Arcita somwhat hym agaste.	That Arcite was rather terrified.
The fyres brenden upon the auter brighte,	The fires on the altar blazed brightly,
That it gan al the temple for to lighte,	Until the whole temple was filled with light,
And sweete smel the ground anon up yaf,	And a sweet smell rose up from the ground.
And Arcita anon his hand up haf,	Arcite whirled his arm around
And moore encens into the fyr he caste,	And threw more incense on the fire,
With othere rytes mo, and atte laste	And did other rites, and at last
The statue of Mars bigan his hauberk rynge,	The armour on the statue of Mars began to ring,
And with that soun he herde a murmurynge,	And along with that sound there came a murmuring,
Ful lowe and dym, and seyde thus, "Victorie!"	Low and unclear, but saying, "Victory!"
For which he yaf to Mars honour and glorie;	For which he gave to Mars honour and glory;
And thus with joye and hope wel to fare,	And so with joy and hope of success
Arcite anon unto his in is fare,	Arcite returned to his lodging,
As fayn as fowel is of the brighte sonne.	As happy as a bird in the bright sunlight.
And right anon swich strif ther is bigonne	Right away there began a great quarrel
For thilke grauntyng, in the hevene above	In heaven over this granting of wishes
Bitwixe Venus, the Goddesse of Love,	Between Venus, the goddess of love,
And Mars the stierne God armypotente,	And mars the stern god of war,
That Jupiter was bisy it to stente;	So that Jupiter had to work hard to settle it;
Til that the pale Saturnus the colde,	Until pale cold Saturn,
That knew so manye of aventures olde,	Who knew so much of what had happened in the past,
Foond in his olde experience an art	Found from his store of experience a solution
That he ful soone hath plesed every part.	That soon managed to please every person.
As sooth is seyd, elde hath greet avantage;	What they say is true, age has great advantages;
In elde is bothe wysdom and usage;	Age gives both wisdom and experience;
Men may the olde atrenne, and noght atrede.	Men can outrun the old, but they can't outwit

57

Saturne anon, to stynten strif and drede,	So Saturn, to remove this strife and fear,
Al be it that it is agayn his kynde,	Even though this was against his nature,
Of al this strif he gan remedie fynde.	Proposed his plan to solve everything.
"My deere doghter Venus," quod Saturne,	"My dear daughter Venus," said Saturn,
"My cours, that hath so wyde for to turne,	"My path, which goes in such a wide orbit,
Hath moore power than woot any man.	Has more power than any man knows.
Myn is the drenchyng in the see so wan,	I am the one who drowns men in the sea,
Myn is the prison in the derke cote,	I own the dungeon in the dark basement,
Myn is the stranglyng and hangyng by the throte,	Mine is the strangling and the hanging by the throat,
The murmure, and the cherles rebellyng,	The rebellion when the peasants grumble,
The groynynge, and the pryvee empoysonyng.	The groaning and the secret poisonings,
I do vengeance and pleyn correccioun,	Vengeance and punishment are mine,
Whil I dwelle in the signe of the leoun.	When I am living in the sign of the lion.
Myn is the ruyne of the hye halles,	I am the one who ruins great palaces,
The fallynge of the toures and of the walles	Who makes the towers and the walls fall down
Upon the mynour, or the carpenter.	On the miner or the carpenter.
I slow Sampsoun, shakynge the piler,	I killed Sampson, the one who shook the pillars,
And myne be the maladyes colde,	And all the dark diseases belong to me,
The derke tresons, and the castes olde;	The terrible treasons, the evil plans;
My lookyng is the fader of pestilence.	The plague comes from the power of my glance.
Now weep namoore, I shal doon diligence	Now stop your weeping, I shall promise you
That Palamon, that is thyn owene knyght,	That Palamon, who is your own true knight,
Shal have his lady, as thou hast him hight.	Will have his lady, as you told him he would.
Though Mars shal helpe his knyght, yet nathelees	Mars will help his knight, but nonetheless
Bitwixe yow ther moot be somtyme pees,	You two must at some point make your peace,
Al be ye noght of o compleccioun-	Even if you are not in agreement,
That causeth al day swich divisioun.	And have been rowing about this for so long.
I am thyn aiel, redy at thy wille,	I am your grandfather and will do as you wish;
Weep now namoore, I wol thy lust fulfille."	So weep no more, I'll give you your desire."
Now wol I stynten of the goddes above,	Now I will stop speaking about the gods in heaven,
Of Mars and of Venus, goddesse of Love,	About Mars and Venus, goddess of love,
And telle yow, as pleynly as I kan,	And I'll tell you as plainly as I can
The grete effect for which that I bygan.	The great conclusion, which is why I started.
Greet was the feeste in Atthenes that day,	There was great feasting in Athens that day,
And eek the lusty seson of that May	And also the merry season of May
Made every wight to been in such plesaunce	Gave everyone such joy and pleasure
That al that Monday justen they and daunce,	That all that Monday all they did was joust and dance,
And spenten it in Venus heigh servyse.	Or devote themselves to the service of Venus.
But by the cause that they sholde ryse	But because they all had to get up early
Eerly, for to seen the grete fight,	To see the great fight,
Unto hir rest wenten they at nyght.	They all turned in early that night.
And on the morwe, whan that day gan sprynge,	In the morning, as day began to break,
Of hors and harneys noyse and claterynge	There was a great noise and clattering of horses and harness
Ther was in hostelryes al aboute.	In all the inns of the town.
And to the paleys rood ther many a route	Up to the palace rode a great crowd
Of lordes upon steedes and palfreys.	Of lords on walking horses and chargers.

Ther maystow seen devisynge of harneys	There you could see their fine harness
So unkouth and so riche, and wroght so weel	Of such unusual rich design, made so well,
Of goldsmythrye, of browdynge, and of steel;	Fine work in gold, embroidery and steel;
The sheeldes brighte, testeres, and trappures,	The bright shields, helmets, and trappings,
Gold-hewen helmes, hauberkes, cote-armures;	Golden helmets and coats of chain mail;
Lordes in parementz on hir coursers,	Lords in rich clothes on their chargers,
Knyghtes of retenue and eek squieres,	Knights with their retinues and also squires,
Nailynge the speres, and helmes bokelynge,	Putting heads on spears, buckling helmets,
Giggynge of sheeldes, with layneres lacynge.	Strapping on shields and lacing straps.
There as nede is, they weren nothyng ydel.	Everything needful was being done.
The fomy steedes on the golden brydel	The foaming chargers chewed at the golden bits,
Gnawynge, and faste the armurers also	And the armourers also worked fast,
With fyle and hamer prikynge to and fro;	Rushing to and fro with files and hammers.
Yemen on foote and communes many oon,	Yeomen on foot and many common soldiers turned out,
With shorte staves thikke as they may goon,	With short staves, great crowds of them,
Pypes, trompes, nakers, clariounes,	Pipes, trumpets, drums and bugles,
That in the bataille blowen blody sounes;	That blow such bloody tunes in battle;
The paleys ful of peples up and doun,	The palace was packed to the rafters,
Heere thre, ther ten, holdynge hir questioun,	People in different groups discussing
Dyvynynge of thise Thebane knyghtes two.	The virtues of those two Theban knights.
Somme seyden thus, somme seyde "it shal be so";	Some said this would happen, some said that;
Somme helden with hym with the blake berd,	Some supported the one with the great beard,
Somme with the balled, somme with the thikke-herd,	Some went for the bald headed, some for the thick haired,
Somme seyde he looked grymme, and he wolde fighte,	Some said "He looks stern, he will be a good fighter,
"He hath a sparth of twenty pound of wighte."	His battleaxe must weigh twenty pounds."
Thus was the halle ful of divynynge,	So the whole hall was full of gossip,
Longe after that the sonne gan to sprynge.	Long after the sun had risen.
The grete Theseus, that of his sleep awaked	Great Theseus, who was woken from his sleep
With mynstralcie and noyse that was maked,	By the singing and ceaseless noise,
Heeld yet the chambre of his paleys riche,	Stayed in his rooms in his rich palace
Til that the Thebane knyghtes, bothe yliche	Until the Theban knights, with equal
Honured, were into the paleys fet.	Ceremony, were led into the palace.
Duc Theseus was at a wyndow set,	Duke Theseus sat at a window,
Arrayed, right as he were a god in trone.	Dressed as if he were a god on a throne.
The peple preesseth thiderward ful soone,	People pressed forward to see him,
Hym for to seen and doon heigh reverence.	And to show him their great respect,
And eek to herkne his heste and his sentence.	And also to listen to his wise judgements.
An heraud on a scaffold made an "Oo!"	A herald on a scaffold cried out, "Ho!"
Til al the noyse of peple was ydo,	Until all the people's noise stopped,
And whan he saugh the peple of noyse al stille,	And when he saw that everyone was silent
Tho shewed he the myghty dukes wille.	He read out the proclamation of the great duke.
"The lord hath of his heigh discrecioun	"The lord has in his great wisdom,
Considered that it were destruccioun	Decided that it would be a great waste
To gentil blood, to fighten in the gyse	Of noble blood, to settle this matter
Of mortal bataille, now in this emprise;	In a deadly battle;
Wherfore, to shapen that they shal nat dye,	So, to stop unnecessary death,
He wolde his firste purpos modifye.	He has changed his earlier plan.
No man therfore, up peyne of los of lyf,	So no man, on pain of death,
No maner shot, ne polax, ne short knyf	Should take any arrows, poleaxes or daggers

Into the lystes sende, ne thider brynge.
Ne short swerd for to stoke, with poynt bitynge,
No man ne drawe, ne bere by his syde;
Ne no man shal unto his felawe ryde
But o cours, with a sharpe ygrounde spere.

Foyne, if hym list on foote, hymself to were.

And he that is at meschief shal be take,
And noght slayn, but be broght unto the stake

That shal ben ordeyned on either syde,
But thider he shal by force, and there abyde.

And if so be the chevetayn be take
On outher syde, or elles sleen his make,
No lenger shal the turneiynge laste.
God spede you! Gooth forth, and ley on faste!
With long swerd and with maces fight youre fille.
Gooth now youre wey, this is the lordes wille."

The voys of peple touchede the hevene,
So loude cride they with murie stevene,
"God save swich a lord, that is so good
He wilneth no destruccion of blood."
Up goon the trompes and the melodye,
And to the lystes rit the compaignye,
By ordinance, thurghout the citee large
Hanged with clooth of gold, and nat with sarge.

Ful lik a lord this noble duc gan ryde,
Thise two Thebanes upon either syde,
And after rood the queene and Emelye,
And after that another compaignye,
Of oon and oother, after hir degree.
And thus they passen thurghout the cite
And to the lystes come they by tyme.
It nas nat of the day yet fully pryme
Whan set was Theseus ful riche and hye,

Ypolita the queene, and Emelye,
And othere ladys in degrees aboute.

Unto the seettes preesseth al the route,
And westward thurgh the gates under Marte,
Arcite, and eek the hondred of his parte,
With baner reed is entred right anon.
And in that selve moment Palamon
Is under Venus estward in the place,
With baner whyt, and hardy chiere and face.
In al the world, to seken up and doun
So evene, withouten variacioun
Ther nere swiche compaignyes tweye;
For ther was noon so wys, that koude seye

On to the battlefield, bring nothing,
No short stabbing swords with biting points,
Will be drawn or carried by any man,
And nobody shall ride against his opponent,
Except in one single charge with a sharp ground spear,
And when overthrown and on foot he may fight as he wishes;
If someone's overcome like this,
And not killed, he should be brought to the fence,
Set up upon either side,
But he must go forward by force, and remain there.
And if it happens that the captain
Of either side goes there, or is killed,
That will be the end of the tournament.
God speed! Off you go, and fight well!
Fight all you wish with long sword and mace.
Go on your way, this is what your lord decrees."

The voices of the people reached up to heaven,
So loud were their merry cries,
"God save a lord like this, who is so good
That he will not tolerate any waste of blood."
The trumpets started their melody,
And the knights rode out to the arena,
By order the whole of the great city
Was hung with golden cloth, not with common stuff.

Like a great lord this duke rode,
With the two Thebans on either side,
And following them rode the queen and Emily,
After that came the two companies
Of the two men, in their ranks.
They passed like this through the city,
And came to the arena in good time.
The day had not yet reached noon
When Theseus took his place on his rich high throne,
And Queen Hippolyta and Emily
And the other ladies took their places according to rank.
Then the common people filled the other seats,
And from the west through the gates of Mars
Arcite came and also his hundred knights,
With his great red banner.
At the same moment Palamon
Came through the gate of Venus in the east,
With his white banner, and a stern face.
They were so equal, identical,
That nowhere in the world
Could two such forces be found;
No man was wise enough to be able

That any hadde of oother avauntage,	To point to any difference between them,
Of worthynesse ne of estaat ne age,	In reputation, rank or age,
So evene were they chosen, for to gesse.	They were so evenly matched, I think,
And in two renges faire they hem dresse,	And they lined up in two great ranks,
Whan that hir names rad were everichon,	And when their rollcall had been read,
That in hir nombre gyle were ther noon.	So that neither side could have more than the right number,
Tho were the gates shet and cried was loude,	The gates were closed and the cry went up,
"Do now youre devoir, yonge knyghtes proude!"	"Now do your best, young proud knights!"
The heraudes lefte hir prikyng up and doun;	The heralds left off prancing up and down;
Now ryngen trompes loude and clarioun.	And now the trumpets sound the call.
Ther is namoore to seyn, but west and est	There's no more to say, from the East and West
In goon the speres ful sadly in arrest,	All the spears are levelled and ready,
In gooth the sharpe spore into the syde.	And the sharp spurs are jabbed into the horses' sides.
Ther seen men who kan juste, and who kan ryde,	Now the men who could joust and ride were seen,
Ther shyveren shaftes upon sheeldes thikke;	Now the spears clatter on the thick shields;
He feeleth thurgh the herte-spoon the prikke.	One feels the point stabbed through his chest.
Up spryngen speres twenty foot on highte;	Spears are hurled twenty feet in the air;
Out goon the swerdes as the silver brighte.	The swords flash out like polished silver.
The helmes they tohewen and toshrede,	Helmets are split, torn to shreds,
Out brest the blood, with stierne stremes rede,	And the blood bursts out in gushing red streams.
With myghty maces the bones they tobreste.	Bones are crushed by mighty maces.
He thurgh the thikkeste of the throng gan threste;	One begins to charge where the crowd is thickest;
Ther stomblen steedes stronge, and doun gooth al;	There the strong horses tumble down, bringing everyone with them;
He rolleth under foot as dooth a bal,	One rolls under their feet like a ball,
He foyneth on his feet with his tronchoun,	One lays about him with his club,
And he hym hurtleth with his hors adoun.	While another rides him down with his horse.
He thurgh the body is hurt and sithen ytake,	One is pierced through the body and then taken,
Maugree his heed, and broght unto the stake,	Regardless of his struggles, off to the fence,
As forward was, right there he moste abyde;	As had been agreed, and he has to stay there;
Another lad is on that oother syde.	There is another there from the other side.
And som tyme dooth hem Theseus to reste,	Sometimes Theseus ordered them to rest,
Hem to refresshe, and drynken if hem leste.	To catch their breath, and drink if they wished.
Ful ofte a day han thise Thebanes two	Many times throughout the day those two Thebans
Togydre ymet, and wroght his felawe wo.	Came together, and did each other damage.
Unhorsed hath ech oother of hem tweye,	Each one managed to unhorse the other;
Ther nas no tygre in the vale of Galgopheye	There was no tigress in the Vale of Galgopheye
Whan that hir whelp is stole, whan it is lite,	Who had lost her cub when it was young
So crueel on the hunte, as is Arcite	Who was so vicious as Arcite
For jelous herte upon this Palamon;	Was to Palamon due to his jealousy;
Ne in Belmarye ther nys so fel leon	And there is no starving lion hunting
That hunted is, or for his hunger wood,	In Belmarie who is so keen for blood
Ne of his praye desireth so the blood,	As Palamon was to kill his enemy Arcite.
As Palamon to sleen his foo Arcite.	Their jealous blows crashed down on their helmets,
The jelous strokes on hir helmes byte,	

Out renneth blood on bothe hir sydes rede.	And the blood ran out, staining them both red.
Som tyme an ende ther is of every dede.	Eventually everything comes to an end;
For er the sonne unto the reste wente,	Before the sun had set
The stronge kyng Emetreus gan hente	Mighty King Emetreus had caught
This Palamon, as he faught with Arcite,	This Palamon, as he fought with Arcite,
And made his swerd depe in his flessh to byte.	And driven his sword deep into his flesh.
And by the force of twenty is he take	And twenty men dragged him away,
Unyolden, and ydrawen unto the stake.	Struggling, over to the fence.
And in the rescus of this Palamoun	Trying hard to rescue Palamon
The stronge kyng Lygurge is born adoun,	The mighty King Lygurgus came charging,
And kyng Emetreus, for al his strengthe,	And King Emetreus, despite his strength
Is born out of his sadel a swerdes lengthe,	Was thrown from his saddle by a blow from a sword,
So hitte him Palamoun er he were take;	Struck by Palamon before he was captured;
But al for noght, he was broght to the stake.	But it was all for nothing, he was brought to the fence.
His hardy herte myghte hym helpe naught,	His brave heart could not help him now;
He moste abyde, whan that he was caught,	He had to stay there, when he had been caught,
By force, and eek by composicioun.	Fairly according to the agreed rules.
Who sorweth now but woful Palamoun,	Who now was more sorrowful than woeful Palamon,
That moot namoore goon agayn to fighte?	Who could no longer continue with the fight?
And whan that Theseus hadde seyn this sighte	When Theseus saw what had happened
Unto the folk that foghten thus echon	With the fighting warriors, he called out
He cryde, "Hoo! namoore, for it is doon.	"Stop! No more, it's over!
I wol be trewe juge, and no partie;	I will be a true impartial judge;
Arcite of Thebes shal have Emelie,	Arcite of Thebes shall have Emily,
That by his fortune hath hir faire ywonne!"	He has been lucky enough to win her fair and square!"
Anon ther is a noyse of peple bigonne	At once the people began to cheer,
For joye of this so loude and heighe withalle	Because of their happiness at this, so loud and shrill
It semed that the lystes sholde falle.	It seemed the whole arena would collapse.
What kan now faire Venus doon above?	Now what can the fair Venus do up above?
What seith she now? What dooth this queene of Love,	What can she say? What can this queen of love do
But wepeth so, for wantynge of hir wille,	But shed tears for her thwarted plans,
Til that hir teeres in the lystes fille.	Until her tears began to fall on the arena.
She seyde, "I am ashamed, doutelees."	She said, "I have been shamed, it's obvious."
Saturnus seyde, "Doghter, hoold thy pees,	Saturn said, "Daughter, hold your tongue,
Mars hath his wille, his knyght hath al his boone,	Mars has won, his knight has what he wanted,
And, by myn heed, thow shalt been esed soone."	But I swear, your pain will be eased soon."
The trompes with the loude mynstralcie,	The trumpets and the loud singers,
The heraudes that ful loude yolle and crie,	The heralds that loudly yelled and cried,
Been in hir wele for joye of daun Arcite.	Celebrated the victory of Arcite.
But herkneth me, and stynteth noyse a lite,	But listen to me, keep quiet a little longer,
Which a myracle ther bifel anon.	While I tell you the miracle that then happened.
This fierse Arcite hath of his helm ydon,	Now fierce Arcite had removed his helmet,
And on a courser for to shewe his face	And jumped on a horse to show his face;

He priketh endelong the large place,	He galloped from end to end of the great arena,
Lokynge upward upon this Emelye,	Looking up towards his Emily,
And she agayn hym caste a freendlich eye,	And she looked down on him with a friendly eye,
(For wommen, as to speken in comune,	(For women, to speak generally,
Thei folwen alle the favour of Fortune)	Follow whoever has the best fortune)
And she was al his chiere, as in his herte.	And she brought great happiness to his heart.
Out of the ground a furie infernal sterte,	Out of the ground came a great tremor,
From Pluto sent, at requeste of Saturne,	Sent from Pluto, at the request of Saturn,
For which his hors for fere gan to turne,	And this made his horse begin to turn in fear,
And leep aside and foundred as he leep.	And he leapt aside and stumbled as he did so.
And er that Arcite may taken keep,	Before Arcite could do anything,
He pighte hym on the pomel of his heed,	He was thrown down and landed on his head,
That in the place he lay as he were deed,	And he lay in that place as if he were dead,
His brest tobrosten with his sadel-bowe.	His chest crushed by the pommel of his saddle.
As blak he lay as any cole or crowe,	He lay there looking black as coal or any crow,
So was the blood yronnen in his face.	So much blood came rushing into his face.
Anon he was yborn out of the place,	Soon they carried him out of that place
With herte soor, to Theseus paleys.	With heavy hearts, to the palace of Theseus.
Tho was he korven out of his harneys,	Then he was cut out of his armour,
And in a bed ybrought ful faire and blyve,	And placed in a great soft bed,
For he was yet in memorie and alyve,	For he still had his faculties and was alive,
And alwey criynge after Emelye.	And was always calling out for Emily.
Duc Theseus, with al his compaignye,	Duke Theseus, and all his company,
Is comen hoom to Atthenes his citee,	Came back into Athens, his city,
With alle blisse and greet solempnitee;	With much celebration and ceremony;
Al be it that this aventure was falle,	Although this terrible thing had happened
He nolde noght disconforten hem alle.	He could not dampen all their high spirits.
Men seyde eek that Arcite shal nat dye,	Men were saying that Arcite was not going to die,
He shal been heeled of his maladye.	But that he would be healed of his wounds soon.
And of another thyng they weren as fayn,	There was another thing of which they were certain,
That of hem alle was ther noon yslayn,	Which was that not one man had been killed,
Al were they soore yhurt, and namely oon,	Albeit they were all wounded, especially one,
That with a spere was thirled his brest boon.	Who had had a spear thrust straight through his chest.
To othere woundes, and to broken armes,	For other wounds, and broken arms,
Somme hadden salves, and somme hadden charmes,	Some had ointment, some had charms,
Fermacies of herbes and eek save	And medicines made of many different herbs,
They dronken, for they wolde hir lymes have.	Which they drank, to comfort their damaged limbs.
For which this noble duc as he wel kan,	In all of this the noble duke, as well as he could,
Conforteth and honoureth every man,	Comforted and praised every single man,
And made revel al the longe nyght	And the celebrations went long into the night
Unto the straunge lordes, as was right.	For these foreign lords, as was only right.
Ne ther was holden no disconfitynge	Nor was anybody feeling in any way bad,
But as a justes or a tourneiynge,	Apart from their wounds from the combat,
For soothly ther was no disconfiture.	For truly there was no shame for anyone,
For fallyng nys nat but an aventure-	For falling is just the luck of the draw;

Ne to be lad by force unto the stake	Nor is it shameful to be forced out of the combat
Unyolden, and with twenty knyghtes take,	Without surrendering, being pulled by twenty knights,
O persone allone, withouten mo,	One man alone, with no support,
And haryed forth by arme, foot, and too,	Driven by armour and dragged out by the feet,
And eke his steede dryven forth with staves,	With a horse beaten away with sticks
With footmen, bothe yemen and eek knaves,	By footmen, yeomen and also servants,
It nas aretted hym no vileynye,	This did not bring any dishonour,
Ther may no man clepen it cowardye.	And nobody could call it cowardice.
For which anon duc Theseus leet crye,	Because of this Duke Theseus straight away called out
To stynten alle rancour and envye,	So that there would be no rancour or jealousy,
The gree, as wel of o syde as of oother,	That each side was just as good as the other,
And eyther syde ylik as oothers brother,	Both of them recall, as if they were brothers,
And yaf hem yiftes after hir degree,	And he gave them all gifts according to their rank,
And fully heeld a feeste dayes three,	And held a full festival for fully three days,
And conveyed the kynges worthily	And then escorted these kings with great ceremony
Out of his toun a journee largely;	Out of the town, accompanying them for a whole day;
And hoom wente every man, the righte way.	And every man took the quickest way home.
Ther was namoore but "Fare-wel, have good day."	There was nothing more to say but, "Farewell, and good day."
Of this bataille I wol namoore endite,	I'll say no more about this combat,
But speke of Palamoun and of Arcite.	Now I shall speak of Palamon and Arcite.
Swelleth the brest of Arcite, and the soore	The chest of Arcite was swelling, and the pain
Encreesseth at his herte moore and moore.	In his heart increased more and more.
The clothered blood for any lechecraft	In spite of all the doctors' efforts the clotted blood
Corrupteth, and is in his bouk ylaft,	Rotted inside his body,
That neither veyne-blood, ne ventusynge,	And neither bloodletting nor cupping,
Ne drynke of herbes may ben his helpynge.	Nor any medicine could help him.
The vertu expulsif, or animal,	He could not use his natural
Fro thilke vertu cleped natural	Powers of expulsion
Ne may the venym voyden, ne expelle.	To get rid of the poison.
The pipes of his longes gonne to swelle,	His windpipe began to swell,
And every lacerte in his brest adoun	And every laceration in his breast
Is shent with venym and corrupcioun.	Was full of poison and corruption.
Hym gayneth neither for to gete his lif	It did no good in the struggle for life
Vomyt upward, ne dounward laxatif;	For him to vomit or take a laxative;
Al is tobrosten thilke regioun,	Everything inside him was so broken
Nature hath now no dominacioun.	That Nature could not fight against it.
And certeinly, ther Nature wol nat wirche,	And certainly it's true that when Nature will not work,
Fare wel phisik! Go ber the man to chirche!	Enough of medicine! Take the man to church!
This al and som, that Arcita moot dye;	To sum it all up, Arcite was bound to die;
For which he sendeth after Emelye	And so he sent word to Emily
And Palamon, that was his cosyn deere.	And Palamon, his own dear cousin.
Thanne seyde he thus, as ye shal after heere:	Then he said this, as you shall hear:
"Naught may the woful spirit in myn herte	"The sorrowing spirit in my heart
Declare o point of alle my sorwes smerte	cannot say anything of all my grief
To yow, my lady, that I love moost.	To you, my lady, whom I love the most.

But I biquethe the servyce of my goost	But I declare my ghost shall serve
To yow aboven every creature.	You beyond all others.
Syn that my lyf may no lenger dure,	Now my life here is ended.
Allas, the wo! Allas, the peynes stronge,	Alas, the sorrow! Alas, the pain is so strong,
That I for yow have suffred, and so longe!	That I have suffered for you, for so long!
Allas, the deeth! Allas, myn Emelye!	Alas, death! Alas, my Emily!
Allas, departynge of our compaignye!	Alas, that we must part company!
Allas, myn hertes queene! allas, my wyf!	Alas, Queen of my heart! Alas, my wife!
Myn hertes lady, endere of my lyf!	Lady of my heart, who has ended my life!
What is this world? What asketh men to have?	What is this world? What do men want?
Now with his love, now in his colde grave,	Now I take my love to my cold grave,
Allone, withouten any compaignye.	Alone, without any company.
Fare-wel, my swete foo, myn Emelye!	Farewell, my sweet enemy! My Emily!
And softe taak me in youre armes tweye,	Take me in your two soft arms,
For love of God, and herkneth what I seye.	For the love of God, and listen to what I have to say.
"I have heer with my cosyn Palamon	I have in this place with my cousin Palamon
Had strif and rancour many a day agon,	Had arguments and fights for many long days,
For love of yow, and for my jalousye.	Out of love for you, and because of my jealousy.
And Juppiter so wys my soule gye,	And Jupiter will surely guide my soul
To speken of a servaunt proprely,	To allow me to speak of love properly,
With alle circumstances trewely,	And truthfully about all the circumstances,
That is to seyen, trouthe, honour, and knyghthede,	That is to say, about truth, honour and knighthood,
Wysdom, humblesse, estaat, and heigh kynrede,	Wisdom, humbleness, rank and great kinship,
Fredom, and al that longeth to that art -	Generosity, and everything associated with it—
So Juppiter have of my soule part	Now Jupiter can take away my soul,
As in this world right now ne knowe I non	And I know of nobody living in this world
So worthy to ben loved, as Palamon	Who so deserves love as Palamon
That serveth yow, and wol doon al his lyf;	Who is your servant and will be all his life;
And if that evere ye shul ben a wyf,	And if you ever wish to be a wife,
Foryet nat Palamon, the gentil man."	Do not forget Palamon, that noble man."
And with that word his speche faille gan,	And with these words his speech began to fail,
And from his herte up to his brest was come	And from his heart up to his breast there came
The coold of deeth, that hadde hym overcome.	The chill of death, that had overcome him.
And yet moreover in hise armes two	From both his arms also
The vital strengthe is lost and al ago.	All vitality was lost and gone.
Oonly the intellect, withouten moore,	Only his intellect was all that remained,
That dwelled in his herte syk and soore	Living within his heart, sick and sore,
Gan faillen, when the herte felte deeth.	And it began to fail now when his heart sensed death.
Dusked hise eyen two, and failled breeth,	Both his eyes then darkened, and his breath failed,
But on his lady yet caste he his eye.	But he still looked towards his lady.
His laste word was "Mercy, Emelye!"	His last words were, "Mercy, Emily!"
His spirit chaunged hous, and wente ther	His spirit changed its residence, and went away,
As I cam nevere, I kan nat tellen wher,	And as I was not there, I cannot say where,
Therfore I stynte; I nam no divinistre;	So I shall forbear; I am not a divine;
Of soules fynde I nat in this registre,	I can't tell what happens to souls,
Ne me ne list thilke opinions to telle	Nor would I presume to think I can talk
Of hem, though that they writen wher they dwelle.	About them, though others have written of their dwellings.
Arcite is coold, ther Mars his soule gye!	Arcite is cold, Mars has taken his soul to

Now wol I speken forthe of Emelye.	Now I will tell you about Emily.
Shrighte Emelye, and howleth Palamon,	Emily shrieked and Palamon howled,
And Theseus his suster took anon	And Theseus quickly took his sister away,
Swownynge, and baar hir fro the corps away.	Swooning, from the corpse.
What helpeth it to tarien forth the day	What use would it be to pass the day
To tellen how she weep bothe eve and morwe?	Telling of her endless weeping?
For in swich cas wommen have swich sorwe	Always in these circumstances women have this grief
Whan that hir housbond is from hem ago,	When they lose their husbands,
That for the moore part they sorwen so,	Most of them will mourn like this,
Or ellis fallen in swich maladye,	Or otherwise collapse into such a decline
That at the laste certeinly they dye.	That eventually they will certainly die.
Infinite been the sorwes and the teeres	There were infinite sorrows and tears
Of olde folk, and eek of tendre yeeres	From both young and old
In al the toun, for deeth of this Theban.	Throughout the town, for the death of this Theban.
For hym ther wepeth bothe child and man;	Both children and men wept for him;
So greet a wepyng was ther noon, certayn,	I swear there was not such grieving
Whan Ector was ybroght al fressh yslayn	When Hector was brought back newly slain
To Troye. Allas, the pitee that was ther,	To Troy. Alas, what sorrow there was,
Cracchynge of chekes, rentynge eek of heer;	Cracking of cheeks and tearing of hair;
"Why woldestow be deed," thise wommen crye,	"Oh why did you have to die," the women cried,
"And haddest gold ynough, and Emelye?"	"You who had so much wealth, and also Emily?"
No man myghte gladen Theseus,	Then there was no man who could comfort Theseus,
Savynge his olde fader, Egeus,	Apart from his old father, Aegeus,
That knew this worldes transmutacioun,	Who knew the way the world could change,
As he hadde seyn it chaunge bothe up and doun,	Having seen it go both up and down,
Joye after wo, and wo after gladnesse,	Joy after sorrow, sorrow after gladness,
And shewed hem ensamples and liknesse.	And gave them examples of this.
"Right as ther dyed nevere man," quod he,	"Just as no man ever died," he said,
"That he ne lyvede in erthe in som degree,	"Who had never lived in some way on earth,
Right so ther lyvede never man," he seyde,	No man ever lived," he said,
"In al this world that somtyme he ne deyde.	"In the whole world who did not have to die at some point.
This world nys but a thurghfare ful of wo,	This world is just a passing journey of sorrow,
And we been pilgrymes passynge to and fro.	And we are pilgrims going to through.
Deeth is an ende of every worldes soore."	Death is the end of all the pain in the world."
And over al this yet seyde he muchel moore,	And after this he told them more
To this effect ful wisely to enhorte	In the same vein, to sensibly persuade
The peple, that they sholde hem reconforte.	The people to take some comfort.
Duc Theseus, with al his bisy cure,	Duke Theseus, with all his pressing business,
Caste now, wher that the sepulture	Now took time to think where the grave
Of goode Arcite may best ymaked be,	Of good Arcite should be best situated,
And eek moost honurable in his degree.	What would be most suited to his honour.
And at the laste he took conclusioun	And in the end he decided
That ther as first Arcite and Palamoun	That where initially Arcite and Palamon
Hadden for love the bataille hem bitwene,	Had fought between themselves for love,
That in that selve grove swoote and grene	Right there in that same grove, sweet and

Ther as he hadde hise amorouse desires,	*green,*
His compleynte, and for love hise hoote fires,	*Where he had thought about his burning love,*
He wolde make a fyr, in which the office	*Complaining of the hot passion he suffered,*
Funeral he myghte al accomplice.	*He would make a pyre and use it*
And leet comande anon to hakke and hewe	*To undertake the funeral.*
	So straight away he gave a command to cut down
The okes olde, and leye hem on a rewe	*The ancient oaks, and lay them out in rows,*
In colpons, wel arrayed for to brenne.	*Split into kindling, ready to burn.*
His officers with swifte feet they renne	*His officers swiftly ran*
And ryden anon at his comandement;	*And rode to do his bidding;*
And after this, Theseus hath ysent	*And after this, Theseus ordered*
After a beere, and it al over-spradde	*A bier, and spread over it*
With clooth of gold, the richeste that he hadde.	*Cloth of gold, the richest that he had.*
And of the same suyte he cladde Arcite,	*He dressed Arcite in a suit of the same material,*
Upon his hondes hadde he gloves white,	*And put white gloves upon his hands,*
Eek on his heed a coroune of laurer grene,	*And on his head a green laurel wreath,*
And in his hond a swerd ful bright and kene.	*In his hand a bright sharp sword.*
He leyde hym bare the visage on the beere,	*He laid him on the bier with his face uncovered,*
Therwith he weep that pitee was to heere.	*And wept so much that it was pitiful to hear him.*
And for the peple sholde seen hym alle,	*And so that all the people could see him*
Whan it was day, he broghte hym to the halle,	*He brought him into the hall at daybreak,*
That roreth of the criyng and the soun.	*And the place soon echoed to the sound of their crying.*
Tho cam this woful Theban, Palamoun,	*Then this sorrowing Theban, Palamon,*
With flotery berd and ruggy asshy heeres,	*With his beard unkempt and matted, ash covered hair,*
In clothes blake, ydropped al with teeres,	*In black clothes, wet with his tears, came,*
And, passynge othere of wepynge, Emelye,	*Along with, weeping more than any other, Emily,*
The rewefulleste of al the compaignye.	*The most sorrowful of all the company.*
In as muche as the servyce sholde be	*So that the service would be*
The moore noble and riche in his degree,	*More noble and rich in its honour,*
Duc Theseus leet forth thre steedes brynge	*Duke Theseus commanded three horses brought,*
That trapped were in steel al gliterynge,	*Covered in glittering chainmail,*
And covered with the armes of daun Arcite.	*Carrying the weapons of great Arcite.*
Upon thise steedes that weren grete and white	*On these great white stallions*
Ther sitten folk, of whiche oon baar his sheeld,	*There were men riding, one carrying his shield,*
Another his spere up in his hondes heeld,	*Another holding his spear,*
The thridde baar with hym his bowe Turkeys,	*And the third carrying his Turkish bow,*
(Of brend gold was the caas, and eek the harneys;)	*(The quiver was of polished gold, and so was the strap)*
And riden forth a paas, with sorweful cheere,	*And they rode slowly, mournfully,*
Toward the grove, as ye shul after heere.	*Towards the grove, as you will hear now.*
The nobleste of the Grekes that ther were	*The noblest of all the Greeks that were there*
Upon hir shuldres caryeden the beere,	*Carried the bier upon their shoulders,*
With slakke paas, and eyen rede and wete,	*With measured tread, and eyes all red and wet,*
Thurghout the citee by the maister strete,	*Right through the city by the main street,*

That sprad was al with blak, and wonder hye	Which was all hung with black, and right up high
Right of the same is the strete ywrye.	The houses were covered with the same cloth.
Upon the right hond wente olde Egeus,	On the right hand went old Aegeus,
And on that oother syde duc Theseus,	And on the other side was Duke Theseus,
With vessel in hir hand of gold ful fyn,	Carrying fine golden vessels in their hands,
Al ful of hony, milk, and blood, and wyn.	All full of honey, milk, blood and wine.
Eek Palamon, with ful greet compaignye,	There was also Palamon with a great retinue,
And after that cam woful Emelye,	And after that came sorrowing Emily,
With fyr in honde, as was that tyme the gyse,	Carrying a burning torch, in order to
To do the office of funeral servyse.	Help perform the funeral rites.
Heigh labour, and ful greet apparaillynge,	Great labour and great craftsmanship
Was at the service and the fyr-makynge,	Went into the service and the making of the pyre,
That with his grene top the heven raughte,	Which reached up to heaven with its green top,
And twenty fadme of brede the armes straughte;	And spread out to a width of twenty fathoms;
This is to seyn, the bowes weren so brode.	That's how far the branches stretched.
Of stree first ther was leyd ful many a lode,	There was a great load of straw to help the fire,
But how the fyr was maked upon highte,	But how it was made, to climb so high,
Ne eek the names that the trees highte,	Nor the names of the trees that were there,
As, ook, firre, birch, aspe, alder, holm, popeler,	Such as oak, fir, birch, asp, alder, poplar, holm,
Wylugh, elm, plane, assh, box, chasteyn, lynde, laurer,	Willow, plane, ash, box, chestnut, linden, elm,
Mapul, thorn, bech, hasel, ew, whippeltree -	Laurel, thorn, maple, beech, yew, dogwood tree,
How they weren fild shal nat be toold for me,	I shall not tell of how they were felled,
Ne how the goddes ronnen up and doun	Nor how the gods of the woods ran up and down,
Disherited of hir habitacioun,	Driven out of their homes,
In whiche they woneden in reste and pees,	In which they had dwelt at ease, in peace,
Nymphes, Fawnes, and Amadrides;	Nymphs, fawns and dryads;
Ne how the beestes and the briddes alle	Nor how all the beasts and the birds
Fledden for fere, whan the wode was falle;	Had fled in terror when the wood was cut down;
Ne how the ground agast was of the light,	Nor how petrified the ground was in the light,
That was nat wont to seen the sonne bright;	That was not used to seeing the bright sunshine;
Ne how the fyr was couched first with stree,	Nor how the fire was first begun with straw,
And thanne with drye stokkes cloven a thre,	And then with dry kindling,
And thanne with grene wode and spicerye,	Then with green wood and spices,
And thanne with clooth of gold and with perrye,	Then with cloth of gold and precious stones,
And gerlandes hangynge with ful many a flour,	And garlands hung with blooming flowers,
The mirre, th'encens, with al so greet odour;	And myrrh, incense, with such sweet perfume;
Ne how Arcite lay among al this,	Nor how Arcite lay amongst all this stuff,
Ne what richesse aboute his body is,	Nor what great riches were spread round his body,
Ne how that Emelye, as was the gyse,	Nor how Emily, as was the custom,
Putte in the fyr of funeral servyse;	Lit the sacred pyre to start the service;

Ne how she swowned whan men made the fyr,	Nor how she swooned when the men stoked the fire,
Ne what she spak, ne what was hir desir;	Nor what she said, nor what she wanted;
Ne what jeweles men in the fyre caste,	Nor what jewels men through in the fire,
Whan that the fyr was greet and brente faste;	When it was up and burning strong.
Ne how somme caste hir sheeld, and somme hir spere,	Nor how some threw their shields, and some their spears,
And of hire vestimentz whiche that they were,	And the clothes which they were wearing,
And coppes fulle of wyn, and milk, and blood,	And cups of wine and milk and blood,
Into the fyr, that brente as it were wood,	Onto the fire, burning like mad.
Ne how the Grekes, with an huge route,	Nor how the Greeks, in one great procession,
Thries riden al the fyr aboute,	Rode three times around the fire,
Upon the left hand with a loud shoutynge,	Anticlockwise, shouting loud,
And thries with hir speres claterynge,	And clattering their spears,
And thries how the ladyes gonne crye,	And three times the ladies burst out wailing,
And how that lad was homward Emelye;	Nor how Emily was led back to her home;
Ne how Arcite is brent to asshen colde,	Nor how Arcite was burned to cold ashes,
Ne how that lyche-wake was yholde	Nor of how they held a wake
Al thilke nyght, ne how the Grekes pleye	All through that night, nor how the Greeks played
The wake-pleyes ne kepe I nat to seye,	The funeral games, I don't wish to say,
Who wrastleth best naked, with oille enoynt,	Who was the best wrestler, naked, covered in oil,
Ne who that baar hym best in no disjoynt;	Nor who did best in all the customary deeds;
I wol nat tellen eek, how that they goon	I also won't describe how they went
Hoom til Atthenes, whan the pley is doon;	Home to Athens, when the games were finished;
But shortly to the point thanne wol I wende,	I will now speak briefly, to the point,
And maken of my longe tale an ende.	And make an end of my lengthy tale.
By processe, and by lengthe of certeyn yeres,	As time went by, as the years passed,
Al stynted is the moornynge and the teres	All the mourning and the tears of the Greeks
Of Grekes, by oon general assent.	Were put aside, by general agreement.
Thanne semed me ther was a parlement	Then I hear there was a Parliament held
At Atthenes, upon certein pointz and caas,	At Athens, to address certain matters,
Among the whiche pointz yspoken was	And among the things discussed there
To have with certein contrees alliaunce,	Was the making of alliances with certain countries,
And have fully of Thebans obeisaunce,	To have full tribute from the Thebans,
For which this noble Theseus anon	For which reason noble Theseus soon
Leet senden after gentil Palamon,	Invited noble Palamon to come,
Unwist of hym what was the cause and why.	Not telling him the reason he wanted him.
But in hise blake clothes sorwefully	But he came sorrowing in his mourning clothes,
He cam at his comandement in hye;	Doing the bidding of the Duke;
Tho sente Theseus for Emelye.	And Theseus also sent for Emily.
Whan they were set, and hust was al the place,	When they were all sitting, and the place was quiet,
And Theseus abiden hadde a space	Theseus thought for a little while,
Er any word cam fram his wise brest,	Before any words came from his wise heart;
Hise eyen sette he ther as was his lest,	He fixed his eyes on those two whom he loved best,
And with a sad visage he siked stille,	Then with a sad face he gave a great sigh,
And after that right thus he seyde his wille:	And then began to say what he wanted:

"The Firste Moevere of the cause above
Whan he first made the faire cheyne of love,
Greet was th'effect, and heigh was his entente;

Wel wiste he why, and what therof he mente,
For with that faire cheyne of love he bond
The fyr, the eyr, the water, and the lond,
In certeyn boundes that they may nat flee.

That same prince and that same moevere," quod he,
"Hath stablissed in this wrecched world adoun
Certeyne dayes and duracioun
To al that is engendred in this place,
Over the whiche day they may nat pace;
Al mowe they yet tho dayes wel abregge,
Ther nedeth noght noon auctoritee t'allegge,
For it is preeved by experience,
But that me list declaren my sentence.

Thanne may men by this ordre wel discerne
That thilke Moevere stable is and eterne.
Wel may men knowe, but it be a fool,
That every part deryveth from his hool;
For nature hath nat taken his bigynnyng
Of no partie nor cantel of a thyng,
But of a thyng that parfit is and stable,
Descendynge so til it be corrumpable;

And therfore, of his wise purveiaunce,
He hath so wel biset his ordinaunce,
That speces of thynges and progressiouns
Shullen enduren by successiouns,
And nat eterne, withouten any lye.
This maystow understonde and seen at ye.

"Loo the ook, that hath so long a norisshynge
From tyme that it first bigynneth sprynge,
And hath so long a lif, as we may see,
Yet at the laste wasted is the tree.
"Considereth eek, how that the harde stoon
Under oure feet, on which we trede and goon,
Yet wasteth it, as it lyth by the weye.
The brode ryver somtyme wexeth dreye,
The grete toures se we wane and wende,
Thanne may ye se that al this thyng hath ende.

"Of man and womman seen we wel also,
That nedeth, in oon of thise termes two -
This is to seyn, in youthe or elles age -
He moot be deed, the kyng as shal a page.

Som in his bed, som in the depe see,
Som in the large feeld, as men may se;
Ther helpeth noght, al goth that ilke weye,
Thanne may I seyn that al this thyng moot deye.

"The great Creator who sits above,
When he first created the chains of love,
Had a great effect, which matched his high purpose;
He knew well why he did it, and his intentions,
For with the sweet chain of love he bound
Fire, air, water and land
In certain boundaries so they could not escape.

That same prince and creator," he said,
"Has settled in this wretched world
A certain length of days allotted
To everyone who is born in this place,
And they cannot exceed their allotted number;
Although anyone can make the time shorter,
None can give orders to make them longer;
I have learned this through long experience,
But now I'm pleased to tell you what I have decided,

Then men can see clearly through my orders
That God above is unchanging and eternal.
Every man must know, unless he is a fool,
That everything is part of one great whole;
For nature did not create itself
From any part or section of a thing,
But comes from a perfect stable substance,
That then comes here and becomes corrupted.

And so, with His wise provision,
He has organised everything so well
That all species of things must progress,
If they are to endure, by succession,
They cannot be eternal, that's the truth.
You can see the proof of this by looking around.

Look at the oak, which lasts so long,
From the time that it first begins to sprout,
And lives for so long, as we can see,
But in the end the tree must fall.
Think also how even the hard stone
Under our feet, which we tread on as we pass,
Eventually will erode as it lies beside the path.
One day the great river will dry up,
The great towns will decline and fall,
And you will see everything come to an end.

We can see this also in men and women,
Who have to be in one state or another—
That is to say, either young or old—
All men must die, the king the same as his servant.

Some die in bed, some in the deep sea,
Some on the battlefield, as you can see;
Nothing can prevent it, all go the same way,
And so I say that everything must die.

"What maketh this, but Juppiter the kyng,	Who has decided this, apart from Jupiter the King,
That is prince and cause of alle thing	Who is the Prince and mover of everything,
Convertynge al unto his propre welle	Converting everything back to the primal stream
From which it is deryved, sooth to telle,	From which it came, that's the truth,
And heer-agayns no creature on lyve	And there is no point for any creature alive
Of no degree availleth for to stryve.	To try and fight against this process.
"Thanne is it wysdom, as it thynketh me,	So it is wise, it seems to me,
To maken vertu of necessitee,	To make a virtue from necessity,
And take it weel, that we may nat eschue;	And welcome things that we cannot change;
And namely, that to us alle is due.	Especially that which will come to us all.
And who so gruccheth ought, he dooth folye,	So anyone who fights it, he's a fool,
And rebel is to hym that al may gye.	A rebel against the one who gives us everything.
And certeinly, a man hath moost honour	Certainly it's most honourable front man
To dyen in his excellence and flour,	To die in the prime of life,
Whan he is siker of his goode name,	When he is certain of his fine reputation,
Thanne hath he doon his freend ne hym no shame.	Then he does not shame himself or his friends.
And gladder oghte his freend been of his deeth,	His friends should be glad that he has died,
Whan with honour up yolden in his breeth,	When he has given up his breath while still honourable,
Than whan his name apalled is for age;	Rather than when his reputation has been ruined through age;
For al forgeten is his vassellage.	All his courage will then be forgotten.
Thanne is it best as for a worthy fame,	So then it's best for a noble man
To dyen whan that he is best of name.	To die when his reputation is highest.
"The contrarie of al this is wilfulnesse:	To do opposite of this is idiocy:
Why grucchen we, why have we hevynesse,	Why do we grumble, why are we sad,
That goode Arcite, of chivalrie flour,	That good Arcite, most chivalrous of men,
Departed is with duetee and honour	Has gone honourably, doing his duty,
Out of this foule prisoun of this lyf?	From the filthy prison of this life?
Why grucchen heere his cosyn and his wyf	Why do his cousin and his wife grumble here
Of his welfare, that loved hem so weel?	About what has happened to the one who loved them so much?
Kan he hem thank? Nay, God woot never a deel,	Can he thank them for it? No, God knows he can't,
That bothe his soule and eek hemself offende,	And they are insulting his soul and themselves,
And yet they mowe hir lustes nat amende.	And yet they still persist in their sorrow.
"What may I concluden of this longe serye,	What can I say with this long speech,
But after wo I rede us to be merye,	Except that I want us all to be happy,
And thanken Juppiter of al his grace?	And thank Jupiter for all his grace?
And er that we departen from this place	And before we take our leave of this place
I rede that we make, of sorwes two,	I want us to make, from two sorrows,
O parfit joye lastyng everemo.	One perfect joy, lasting forever.
And looketh now, wher moost sorwe is her inne,	You shall see, the one who has the worst grief,
Ther wol we first amenden and bigynne.	Is the one with whom we shall begin.
"Suster," quod he, "this is my fulle assent,	"Sister," he said, "I have fully agreed,
With all th'avys heere of my parlement,	On the advice of my parliament here,
That gentil Palamon thyn owene knyght,	That noble Palamon shall be your own true knight,
That serveth yow with wille, herte, and myght,	Serving you with all his heart and strength,

And evere hath doon, syn that ye first hym knewe, \
That ye shul of your grace upon hym rewe, \
And taken hym for housbonde and for lord. \
Lene me youre hond, for this is oure accord.

Lat se now of youre wommanly pitee; \
He is a kynges brother sone, pardee, \
And though he were a povre bacheler, \
Syn he hath served yow so many a yeer, \
And had for yow so greet adversitee, \
It moste been considered, leeveth me, \
For gentil mercy oghte to passen right."

Thanne seyde he thus to Palamon the knyght: \
"I trowe ther nedeth litel sermonyng \
To make yow assente to this thyng. \
Com neer, and taak youre lady by the hond." \
Bitwixen hem was maad anon the bond \
That highte matrimoigne or mariage, \
By al the conseil and the baronage.

And thus with alle blisse and melodye \
Hath Palamon ywedded Emelye; \
And God, that al this wyde world hath wroght, \
Sende hym his love that hath it deere aboght, \
For now is Palamon in alle wele, \
Lyvynge in blisse, in richesse, and in heele, \
And Emelye hym loveth so tendrely, \
And he hir serveth al so gentilly, \
That nevere was ther no word hem bitwene,

Of jalousie, or any oother teene. \
Thus endeth Palamon and Emelye, \
And God save al this faire compaignye! Amen.

Heere is ended the Knyghtes Tale.

As he always has since you first knew him, \
And you shall show graceful kindness to him, \
By taking him as your husband and your lord. \
Give me your hand, this is what we have all agreed.

Let us see your feminine forgiveness; \
He is the nephew of a king, by God, \
And even if he were an impoverished knight, \
As he has served you for so many years, \
And undergone such great trials for you, \
It seems to me you must consider \
Allowing sweet kindness to overcome all."

Then he spoke to Palamon the knight: \
"I don't think you will need much persuading \
To get you to agree to this proposal. \
Come here, and take your lady by the hand." \
And so the bond was made between them \
That we call matrimony or marriage, \
With the agreement of all the council and the peers.

And so with all happiness and song \
Palamon married Emily; \
And God, who has made the whole world, \
Sent love to him who had paid so dearly for it, \
For now Palamon has everything, \
Living with happiness, riches and health, \
And Emily loved him so tenderly, \
And he served her so faithfully, \
That no argument ever spoiled their happiness,

No jealousy, or any other thing. \
This is how Palamon and Emily finished up, \
And may God preserve all this fair company! Amen.

This is the end of the Knight's Tale.

The Miller's Tale

Prologue

Heere folwen the wordes bitwene the Hoost and the Millere

There follow the words between the Host and the Miller

Whan that the Knyght had thus his tale ytoold,
In al the route ne was ther yong ne oold

That he ne seyde it was a noble storie,
And worthy for to drawen to memorie;
And namely the gentils everichon.
Oure Hooste lough, and swoor, "So moot I gon,

This gooth aright; unbokeled is the male,
Lat se now who shal telle another tale,
For trewely the game is wel bigonne.
Now telleth on, sir Monk, if that ye konne
Somwhat to quite with the Knyghtes tale."

The Millere that for dronken was al pale,
So that unnethe upon his hors he sat,
He nolde avalen neither hood ne hat,
Ne abyde no man for his curteisie,
But in Pilates voys he gan to crie,
And swoor, "By armes and by blood and bones,

I kan a noble tale for the nones,
With which I wol now quite the Knyghtes tale."
Oure Hooste saugh that he was dronke of ale,
And seyde, "Abyd, Robyn, my leeve brother,
Som bettre man shal telle us first another,
Abyd, and lat us werken thriftily."

"By Goddes soule," quod he, "that wol nat I,

For I wol speke, or elles go my wey."
Oure Hoost answerde, "Tel on, a devel wey!

Thou art a fool, thy wit is overcome!
"Now herkneth," quod the Miller, "alle and some,
But first I make a protestacioun
That I am dronke, I knowe it by my soun;
And therfore, if that I mysspeke or seye,

Wyte it the ale of Southwerk I you preye.
For I wol telle a legende and a lyf
Bothe of a carpenter and of his wyf,
How that a clerk hath set the wrightes cappe."

The Reve answerde and seyde, "Stynt thy clappe,

Lat be thy lewed dronken harlotrye,

It is a synne and eek a greet folye

*When the Knight had finished his tale,
There was no one in our company, young or old,
Who did not say that it was a fine story,
And well worth remembering;
This was especially true of all the gentlefolk.
Our host laughed, and swore, "I think I can say
That went down well; now the armour is off;
Let's see who can tell us another tale:
For now the game is truly on.
Now come on then, sir Monk, if you can,
Give us a challenge to the Knight's tale."

The Miller then was pale from drinking,
Sitting unsteadily on his horse,
He would not take off his hood or his hat,
Nor politely let anyone other man go first,
But he began to cry, with a voice like Pilate,
And swear, "By my arms and blood and bones,

I have a noble tale for this occasion,
To reply to the Knight\s tale."
Our host saw that he was drunk on pale,
And said, "Wait, Robin, my dear brother,
First let a better man tell us another,
You wait, and let us go sensibly."

"By the soul of God," he said, "I won't do that,
I shall speak, or else I'm leaving."
Our host answered, "Go on then, on your way to hell!

You are a fool, your senses are overwhelmed!"
"Now listen," said the Miller, "one and all,
But first I must excuse myself by saying
That I am drunk, I can hear it in my voice;
And so, should I happen to say anything wrong,
Blame it on the ale of Southwark, please.
I will tell you a story and biography
Of both a carpenter and his wife,
And how a scholar made a fool of him."

The Reeve answered and said, "Shut your mouth,
We don't want your ill mannered drunk ribaldry,
It is a sin, and also stupid,*

To apeyren any man or hym defame, And eek to bryngen wyves in swich fame; Thou mayst ynogh of othere thynges seyn." This dronke Millere spak ful soone ageyn, And seyde, "Leve brother Osewold, Who hath no wyf, he is no cokewold.	*To slander any man or insult him,* *And also to do the same to their wives:* *There are plenty of other stories to tell."* *The drunken Miller replied at once,* *Saying, "My dear brother Oswald,* *If you don't have a wife, you haven't been cheated on.*
But I sey nat therfore that thou art oon, Ther been ful goode wyves many oon, And evere a thousand goode ayeyns oon badde; That knowestow wel thyself, but if thou madde. Why artow angry with my tale now? I have a wyf, pardee, as wel as thow, Yet nolde I for the oxen in my plogh Take upon me moore than ynogh, As demen of myself that I were oon; I wol bileve wel, that I am noon. An housbonde shal nat been inquisityf Of Goddes pryvetee, nor of his wyf. So he may fynde Goddes foysoun there, Of the remenant nedeth nat enquere."	*But I'm not saying that you have been:* *There are plenty of faithful wives,* *A thousand good ones to every bad,* *As you must know, unless you're mad.* *So why are you getting angry with my story?* *I have a wife, by God, the same as you,* *But I wouldn't take the oxen from my plough,* *To trouble myself in thinking that she* *Had made a cuckold out of me;* *I'm very sure that she has not.* *A husband mustn't be too questioning* *Of either God nor his wife.* *As long as he gets the good things of God,* *He needn't care too much about the rest."*
What sholde I moore seyn, but this Millere He nolde his wordes for no man forbere, But tolde his cherles tale in his manere; Me thynketh that I shal reherce it heere. And therfore every gentil wight I preye, For Goddes love, demeth nat that I seye Of yvel entente, but that I moot reherce Hir tales alle, be they bettre or werse, Or elles falsen som of my mateere.	*What more can I say except that this miller* *Would not hold his tongue for any man,* *But told his vulgar tale in his own way;* *I think that I will repeat it here.* *And so I pray to every gentle soul,* *For love of God, don't think that what I say* *Is meant evilly, but that I must tell* *All of their tales, the good and the bad,* *Otherwise I won't be doing what I said I would.*
And therfore who-so list it nat yheere, Turne over the leef, and chese another tale; For he shal fynde ynowe, grete and smale, Of storial thyng that toucheth gentillesse, And eek moralitee, and hoolynesse. Blameth nat me if that ye chese amys; The Millere is a cherl, ye knowe wel this,	*And so whoever does not like this one,* *Turn over the page, choose another tale;* *You shall find many stories, long and short,* *Which deal with matters of nobility,* *Holiness and morality;* *Do not blame me if you choose wrongly;* *The Miller is a vulgar man, you know this well,*
So was the Reve, and othere manye mo, And harlotrie they tolden bothe two. Avyseth yow, and put me out of blame, And eek men shal nat maken ernest of game.	*So was the Reeve, and many of the others,* *And they both let rip with vulgar stories.* *So be advised, and don't blame me,* *It's only a game, you don't need to be serious.*

The Tale

Heere bigynneth the Millere his Tale | *Here the Miller began his Tale*

Whilom ther was dwellynge at Oxenford
A riche gnof, that gestes heeld to bord,
And of his craft he was a carpenter.
With hym ther was dwellynge a poure scoler,

Hadde lerned art, but al his fantasye

Was turned for to lerne astrologye,
And koude a certeyn of conclusiouns,
To demen by interrogaciouns,

If that men asked hym in certain houres

Whan that men sholde have droghte or elles shoures,
Or if men asked hym what sholde bifalle
Of every thyng; I may nat rekene hem alle.

This clerk was cleped hende Nicholas.
Of deerne love he koude and of solas;

And therto he was sleigh and ful privee,

And lyk a mayden meke for to see.
A chambre hadde he in that hostelrye
Allone, withouten any compaignye,
Ful fetisly ydight with herbes swoote;

And he hymself as sweete as is the roote
Of lycorys, or any cetewale.
His Almageste, and bookes grete and smale,

His astrelabie, longynge for his art,
His augrym stones layen faire apart,

On shelves couched at his beddes heed;
His presse ycovered with a faldyng reed
And al above ther lay a gay sautrie,
On which he made a-nyghtes melodie
So swetely that all the chambre rong;
And Angelus ad virginem he song;
And after that he song the Kynges Noote.
Ful often blessed was his myrie throte.
And thus this sweete clerk his tyme spente
After his freendes fyndyng and his rente.

This carpenter hadde newe a wyf,
Which that he lovede moore than his lyf;
Of eighteteene yeer she was of age.
Jalous he was, and heeld hire narwe in cage,

Once there was living at Oxford
A rich man, who took in paying guests,
And by trade he was a carpenter.
There was a poor scholar living with him there,
Who was learned in all the arts, but his imagination
Was fired by study of astrology;
And he had various cunning methods
Through which he could discover by investigation
The answer if men asked him if at certain times
There was going to be drought or rain,

And he could answer many other questions,
Too many to mention here.

This scholar was called clever Nicholas;
He knew all about forbidden love and its ways,
And he kept the information to himself, he was sly
And looked almost like a girl.
He had a room in that boarding house,
Alone, without any company,
And it was decked out very nicely with sweet smelling herbs;
And he himself smelt as sweet as the root
Of liquorice, or ginger.
His almanac, and his books both great and small,
His astrolabe, which he used for his work,
And his counting stones were all placed separately
On shelves which ran at the head of his bed;
His table was covered with a red cloth,
And over everything there hung a bright heart,
On which at night he played melodies
So sweetly that the whole room sang with it;
And he sung "Of angels and the virgin",
And after that he sang "The King's Note".
He was blessed with a very fine voice.
This is how this gentle scholar spent his time
Supported by his friends, and a little income.

Now this carpenter was newly married,
And he loved his wife more than life itself;
She was just eighteen years old.
He was jealous, and kept her within tight

For she was wylde and yong, and he was old,	boundaries,
And demed hymself, been lik a cokewold.	For she was wild and young, and he was old,
	And he thought that she might well be unfaithful.
He knew nat Catoun, for his wit was rude,	He didn't know Cato, for he was uneducated,
That bad man sholde wedde his simylitude.	Who advised that men should marry their equals.
Men sholde wedden after hire estaat,	Men should marry according to their position,
For youth and elde is often at debaat.	For young and old are often at loggerheads.
But sith that he was fallen in the snare,	But since he had fallen into this trap,
Her moste endure, as oother folk, his care.	He would have to take what was coming to him, as we all do.
Fair was this yonge wyf, and therwithal	This young wife was beautiful, and also
As any wezele hir body gent and smal.	Her body was as slim and lithe as a weasel's.
A ceynt she werede, barred al of silk,	She wore a striped silk girdle,
A barmclooth as whit as morne milk	And an apron as white as new milk
Upon her lendes, ful of many a goore.	Around her loins, with many folds and tucks.
Whit was hir smok, and broyden al bifoore	Her smock was white, embroidered all around,
And eek bihynde, on hir coler aboute,	Even behind, and around her collar,
Of col-blak silk, withinne and eek withoute.	Which was made of coal black silk, inside and out.
The tapes of hir white voluper	The tapes of her white hat
Were of the same suyte of his coler;	Were of the same material as her collar;
Hir filet brood of silk, and set ful hye.	Her headband was broad silk, worn high on her head.
And sikerly she hadde a likerous ye;	She certainly had a flirtatious eye;
Ful smale ypulled were hire browes two,	She'd carefully plucked her eyebrows,
And tho were bent and blake as any sloo.	And they were as arched and black as sloe berries.
She was ful moore blisful on to see	She was far more beautiful to see
Than is the newe pere-jonette tree,	Than a newly blossoming pear tree,
And softer than the wolle is of a wether.	And softer than the wool still on the sheep.
And by hir girdel heeng a purs of lether,	From her belt there hung a purse of leather,
Tasseled with silk, and perled with latoun.	With silken tassles, ornamented with beads.
In al this world, to seken up and doun,	In all the world, wherever you looked,
There nys no man so wys that koude thence	There was no man who could find
So gay a popelote or swich a wenche.	Such a bright butterfly, such a girl.
Ful brighter was the shynyng of hir hewe	She shone far more brightly
Than in the Tour the noble yforged newe.	Than the golden coins in the Tower, newly minted.
But of hir song, it was as loude and yerne	Her singing was as sweet and pretty
As any swalwe sittynge on a berne.	As as a swallow chirping from a barn.
Therto she koude skippe and make game,	And she could also dance and play games,
As any kyde or calf folwynge his dame.	Gambolling like a kid or calf with its mother.
Hir mouth was sweete as bragot or the meeth,	Her mouth was as sweet as honey or ale,
Or hoord of apples leyd in hey or heeth.	Or a store of apples packed in hay.
Wynsynge she was, as is a joly colt,	She was as fidgety as a spirited colt,
Long as a mast, and upright as a bolt.	Tall as a mast, straight as an arrow.
A brooch she baar upon hir lowe coler,	She wore a brooch upon her low collar,
As brood as is the boos of a bokeler.	As broad as the boss of a shield.
Hir shoes were laced on hir legges hye.	Her shoes were laced high up her legs.
She was a prymerole, a piggesnye,	She was a primrose, a little chick,
For any lord to leggen in his bedde,	That any lord would want in bed,

77

Or yet for any good yeman to wedde.

Now, sire, and eft, sire, so bifel the cas,
That on a day this hende Nicholas
Fil with this yonge wyf to rage and pleye,
Whil that her housbonde was at Oseneye,
As clerkes ben ful subtile and ful queynte;
And prively he caughte hire by the queynte,

And seyde, "Ywis, but if ich have my wille,
For deerne love of thee, lemman, I spille."

And heeld hire harde by the haunchebones,
And seyde, "Lemman, love me al atones,
Or I wol dyen, also God me save!"
And she sproong as a colt dooth in the trave,
And with hir heed she wryed faste awey,
And seyde, "I wol nat kisse thee, by my fey!
Why, lat be," quod she, "lat be, Nicholas,

Or I wol crie 'out harrow' and 'allas!'
Do wey youre handes, for youre curteisye!"

This Nicholas gan mercy for to crye,
And spak so faire, and profred him so faste,
That she hir love hym graunted atte laste,
Ans swoor hir ooth, by seint Thomas of Kent,
That she wol been at his comandement,
Whan that she may hir leyser wel espie.
"Myn housbonde is so ful of jalousie
That but ye wayte wel and been privee,
I woot right wel I nam but deed," quod she.
"Ye moste been ful deerne, as in this cas."
"Nay, therof care thee noght," quod Nicholas.
"A clerk hadde litherly biset his whyle,
But if he koude a carpenter bigyle."
And thus they been accorded and ysworn
To wayte a tyme, as I have told biforn.
Whan Nicholas had doon thus everideel,
And thakked hire aboute the lendes weel,
He kiste hire sweete and taketh his sawtrie,
And pleyeth faste, and maketh melodie.

Thanne fil it thus, that to the paryssh chirche,
Cristes owene werkes for to wirche,
This goode wyf went on a haliday.
Hir forheed shoon as bright as any day,

So was it wasshen whan she leet hir werk.

Now was ther of that chirche a parissh clerk,
The which that was ycleped Absolon.
Crul was his heer, and as the gold it shoon,
And strouted as a fanne large and brode;
Ful streight and evene lay his joly shode;

And any yeoman would want to marry her.

Now, sir, and also you, sir, it so happened
That one day this clever Nicholas
Began to mess around with this young wife,
While her husband was visiting Oseneye,
Scholars being subtle and crafty chaps;
And he sneaked up and caught her round the snatch,
And said, "I tell you, if I can't have my way,
My love for you, woman, will make me explode."
And he grabbed her hard around the ass,
And said, "Darling, love me now, at once,
Or I will die, God help me!"
She jumped like a colt does when it is penned,
And she twisted her head away quickly,
Saying, "I will not kiss you, I swear!
Y, leave me alone," she said, "leave me alone, Nicholas,
Or I shall be crying out for help!
Remember your manners, get your hands off!"

This Nicholas began to beg for mercy,
Spoke so sweetly, wooed her so well,
At last she agreed that she would love him,
And swore on the grave of St Thomas of Kent
That she would be at his disposal,
When she managed to get a chance.
"My husband is so terribly jealous
That unless you be patient and keep secret
I know that I am as good as dead," she said.
"You must be totally discreet in this matter."
"No, don't worry about that," said Nicholas.
"A scholar has truly been a lazy chap
If he can't outwit a carpenter."
So they agreed, and they swore
To wait for their chance, as I've already said.
When Nicholas had sorted all this out,
And stroked her around her loins awhile,
He gave her sweet kisses, then took his heart,
And played it fast, creating tunes.

So it happened that this good wife went
Upon a holy day to the parish church,
To work for the Lord Jesus Christ;
Her forehead was as clear as a bright sunny day,
So well had she washed it when she finished work.

Now in that church there was a parish clerk,
And his name was Absolon.
He had curly hair, shining like gold,
Sprouting out like a great fan;
It was beautifully parted and combed on top;

His rode was reed, his eyen greye as goos.	He had red cheeks, goose grey eyes,
With Poules wyndow corven on his shoos,	With fashionable ornaments on his shoes,
In hoses rede he wente fetisly.	And he wore elegant red stockings.
Yclad he was ful smal and properly	He was dressed very fashionably
Al in a kirtel of a lyght waget;	In a coat of blue which had
Ful faire and thikke been the poyntes set.	Plenty of holes for fancy lacing.
And therupon he hadde a gay surplys	Over that he wore a fine surplice
As whit as is the blosme upon the rys.	As white as the blossom on the hawthorn.
A myrie child he was, so God me save.	He was a merry lad as well, I swear;
Wel koude he laten blood and clippe and shave,	He was good at bloodletting, haircutting and shaving,
And maken a chartre of lond or acquitaunce.	He could draw up contracts, for land or business.
In twenty manere koude he trippe and daunce	He knew twenty different sorts of dance,
After the scole of Oxenforde tho,	In the manner of the Oxford school,
And with his legges casten to and fro,	And with his legs swinging to and fro
And pleyen songes on a smal rubible;	He could play songs on a little fiddle;
Therto he song som tyme a loud quynyble;	And he sang along in a loud treble;
And as wel koude he pleye on a giterne.	And he also was a fine guitarist.
In al the toun nas brewhous ne tavern	There was no inn or pub in the town
That he ne visited with his solas,	That he had not visited for his pleasure,
Ther any gaylard tappestere was.	As long as there were pretty barmaids there.
But sooth to seyn, he was somdeel squaymous	But to tell the truth, he was a little squeamish
Of fartyng, and of speche daungerous.	About farting, and he didn't like braggarts.
This Absolon, that jolif was and gay,	This Absolon, who was jolly and gay,
Gooth with a sencer on the haliday,	Went with a censer on the holy day,
Sensynge the wyves of the parisshe faste;	Enthusiastically perfuming the wives of the parish;
And many a lovely look on hem caste,	And he cast many loving looks at them,
And namely on this carpenteris wyf.	And especially on the wife of this carpenter.
To looke on hire hym thoughte a myrie lyf,	It made him very happy to look at her,
She was so propre and sweete and likerous.	She was so pretty and sweet and flirty.
I dar wel seyn, if she hadde been a mous,	I daresay that if she had been a mouse
And I the cat, he wolde hire hente anon.	And he a cat, he would have done her some harm!
This parissh clerk, this joly Absolon,	This parish clerk, this jolly Absolon,
Hath in his herte swich a love-longynge	Had such a yearning for love in his heart
That of no wyf took he noon offrynge;	That he would take no donations from any wife;
For curteisie, he seyde, he wolde noon.	He said it would be rude to do so.
The moone, whan it was nyght, ful brighte shoon,	On a night when the moon was shining brightly
And Absolon his gyterne hath ytake,	Then Absolon took his guitar,
For paramours he thoghte for to wake.	Hoping to awake his lady's passion.
And forth he gooth, jolif and amorous,	Out he went, jolly and amorous,
Til he cam to the carpenters hous	Until he came to the carpenter's house,
A litel after cokkes hadde ycrowe,	A little after the cocks had crowed,
And dressed hym up by a shot-wyndowe	And stationed himself by a little window
That was upon the carpenteris wall.	In the wall of the carpenter's house.
He syngeth in his voys gentil and smal,	He sung in his pleasant whispering voice,
'Now, deere lady, if thy wille be,	"Now, dear lady, if you would,
I praye yow that ye wole rewe on me,'	I pray that you take pity on me."
Ful wel acordaunt to his gyternynge.	He played his guitar in harmony with his

This carpenter awook, and herde him synge,	The carpenter awoke, and heard him singing,
And spak unto his wyf, and seyde anon,	And spoke to his wife, saying at once,
"What! Alison! Herestow nat Absolon,	"What! Alison! Can you not hear Absolon,
That chaunteth thus under oure boures wal?"	Playing and singing under our bedroom wall?"
Ans she answerde hir housbonde therwithal,	And she answered her husband straight away,
"Yis, God woot, John, I heere it every deel."	"Yes, God knows, John, I hear it clearly."
This passeth forth; what wol ye bet than weel?	So this went on; what more should I say?
Fro day to day this joly Absolon	Every day this jolly Absolon
So woweth hire that hym is wo bigon.	Wooed the one who was making him so sad.
He waketh al the nyght and al the day;	He lay awake all through the night and day;
He kembeth his lokkes brode, and made hym gay;	He combed his long hair, and dressed up handsomely;
He woweth hire by meenes and brocage,	He wooed her through agents and go-betweens,
And swoor he wolde been hir owene page;	And swore he would be her loyal servant;
He syngeth, brokkynge as a nyghtyngale;	He sang, quavering like a nightingale;
He sente hire pyment, meeth, and spiced ale,	He sent her mead, sweet wine and spiced ale,
And wafres, pipyng hoot out of the gleede;	And waffles, piping hot from the oven;
And, for she was of towne, he profred meede.	And, as she was a townswoman, he offered her money.
For som folk wol ben wonnen for richesse,	Some people can be won over by offers of wealth,
And somme for strokes, and somme for gentillesse.	Some by tricks, and some by courtesy.
Somtyme, to shewe his lightnesse and maistrye,	Once, to show his cleverness and skill,
He pleyeth Herodes upon a scaffold hye.	He played Herod up upon a high stage.
But what availleth hym as in the cas?	But what good did that do him?
She loveth so this hende Nicholas	She was so in love with this charming Nicholas
That Absolon may blowe the bukkes horn;	That he might as well have blown a horn;
He ne hadde for his labour but a scorn.	All he got for his work was scorn.
And thus she maketh Absolon hire ape,	So she made a monkey out of Absolon,
And al his ernest turneth til a jape.	And made a joke out of all his earnestness.
Ful sooth is this proverbe, it is no lye,	The proverb is very true, it does not lie,
Men seyn right thus, 'Alwey the nye slye	What men say, "The one who's always around
Maketh the ferre leeve to be looth.'	Can slyly make the absent lover be hated."
For though that Absolon be wood or wrooth,	For however much Absolon was mad and passionate,
By cause that he fer was from hire sight,	Because he was out of her sight,
This nye Nicholas stood in his light.	The young Nicholas could always block his efforts.
Now ber thee wel, thou hende Nicholas,	Now hold your nerve, crafty Nicholas,
For Absolon may waille and synge 'allas.'	And Absolon will wail and cry, "alas!"
And so bifel it on a Saturday,	So it happened on one Saturday
This carpenter was goon til Osenay;	That the carpenter had to go to Osney;
And hende Nicholas and Alison	And crafty Nicholas and Alison
Acorded been to this conclusioun,	Had come to this agreement,
That Nicholas shal shapen hym a wyle	That Nicholas would play a trick
This sely jalous housbonde to bigyle;	To fool this silly jealous husband;
And if so be the game wente aright,	And if things happened to go the right way,
She sholde slepen in his arm al nyght,	She would be sleeping in his arms all night,

For this was his desir and hire also.	For this is what he wanted and she did too.
And right anon, withouten wordes mo,	So straight away, with no more talking,
This Nicholas no lenger wolde tarie,	Nicholas wasted no more time,
But dooth ful softe unto his chambre carie	But secretly carried up to his room
Bothe mete and drynke for a day or tweye,	Enough food and drink for a day or two,
And to hire housbonde bad hire for to seye,	And told her to say to her husband,
If that he axed after Nicholas,	If she asked where he was,
She sholde seye she nyste where he was,	That she had no idea,
Of al that day she saugh hym nat with ye;	That she had not seen him all day;
She trowed that he was in maladye,	To say that she thought he must be ill,
For for no cry hir mayde koude hym calle,	For he did not answer the chambermaid's knock,
He nolde answere for thyng that myghte falle.	He would not answer, whatever happened.
This passeth forth al thilke Saterday,	And so for the whole of that Saturday,
That Nicholas stille in his chambre lay,	Nicholas lay quietly in his chamber,
And eet and sleep, or dide what hym leste,	And ate and slept, or did what he liked best,
Til Sonday, that the sonne gooth to reste.	Until Sunday, after sunset.
This sely carpenter hath greet merveyle	The simple carpenter was much astonished
Of Nicholas, or what thyng myghte hym eyle,	At Nicholas, or at what might ail him,
And seyde, "I am adrad, by Seint Thomas,	And said, "I am afraid, by St Thomas,
It stondeth nat aright with Nicholas.	That there is something wrong with Nicholas.
God shilde that he deyde sodeynly!	Please God that he has not suddenly died!
This world is now ful tikel, sikerly.	The world is certainly most unpredictable.
I saugh today a cors yborn to chirche	Today I saw a body being carried to church
That now, on Monday last, I saugh hym wirche.	Of a man whom I saw at work last Monday.
"Go up," quod he unto his knave anoon,	"Go up," he said to his serving boy,
"Clepe at his dore, or knokke with a stoon.	"Call through his door, or knock on it with a stone.
Looke how it is, and tel me boldely."	Find out what's going on, and come and tell me."
This knave gooth hym up ful sturdily,	The servant went up boldly,
And at the chambre dore whil that he stood,	And standing in front of the door of the room
He cride and knokked as that he were wood,	He called and knocked as if he were mad,
"What! how! what do ye, maister Nicholay?	"What! Hello! What are you doing, Master Nicholas?
How may ye slepen al the longe day?"	How can you sleep through the whole day?"
But al for noghte, he herde nat a word.	But for all his knocking, he did not get a reply.
An hole he foond, ful lowe upon a bord,	He found a hole low down in the door
Ther as the cat was wont in for to crepe,	Through which the cat used to pass to and fro,
And at that hole he looked in ful depe,	And he bent down and peered in through it.
And at the laste he hadde of hym a sight.	And finally he got sight of him.
This Nicholas sat evere capyng upright,	Nicholas sat there gaping, upright,
As he had kiked on the newe moone.	As if he had stared too long at the new moon.
Adoun he gooth, and tolde his maister soone	He went downstairs, and told his master at once
In what array he saugh this ilke man.	What he had seen of this man.
This carpenter to blessen hym bigan,	This carpenter began to cross himself,
And seyde, "Help us, seinte Frydeswyde!	And said, "Help us, St Frideswide!
A man woot litel what hym shal bityde.	A man can't predict what's going to happen.
This man is falle, with his astromye,	This man has fallen, through his studies,
In som woodnesse or in som agonye,	Into some madness or some illness,
I thoghte ay wel how that it sholde be!	I always thought that this would happen!

Men sholde nat knowe of Goddes pryvetee. Ye, blessed be alwey a lewed man That noght but oonly his bileve kan! So ferde another clerk with astromye;	Men should not meddle with God's plan. Yes, the ignorant man is truly blessed, Who only believes in the holy word! This happened to another scholar of astronomy;
He walked in the feeldes, for to prye Upon the sterres, what ther sholde bifalle, Til he was in a marle-pit yfalle; He saugh nat that. But yet, by seint Thomas, Me reweth soore of hende Nicholas. He shal be rated of his studiyng, If that I may, Jhesus, hevene kyng!	He walked in the fields, to look at The stars, to predict the future, And he fell into a clay pit, He didn't predict that. Still, by St Thomas, I pity this clever Nicholas. I shall put a stop to his studying, If I can, with the help of Jesus, King of Heaven!
Get me a staf, that I may underspore, Whil that thou, Robyn, hevest up the dore. He shal out of his studiyng, as I gesse" And to the chambre dore he gan hym dresse. His knave was a strong carl for the nones, And by the haspe he haaf it of atones; Into the floor the dore fil anon. This Nicholas sat ay as stille as stoon, And evere caped upward into the eir.	Get me a stick, so that I can pry the door, While you, Robin, push against it. I think we can stop him studying." He began to attack the bedroom door. His boy was a strong if simple lad, And he pushed the door off the hinges; It fell forward onto the floor. Nicholas was sitting there, still as stone, Gaping upwards into the air.
This carpenter wende he were in despeir, And hente hym by the sholdres myghtily And shook him harde, and cride spitously, "What! Nicholay! what, how! what, looke adoun!	The carpenter thought he was in despair, And gripped him hard around the shoulders, And shook him vigourously, crying loudly, "What! Nicholas! What's this! Look downwards!
Awak, and thenk on Christes passioun! I crouche thee from elves and fro wightes. Therwith the nyght-spel seyde he anon-rightes	Wake up, and think of the Passion of Christ! I call you back from elves and ghosts!" Then he spoke of the night spell quite correctly,
On foure halves of the hous aboute, And on the tresshfold of the dore withoute: "Jhesu Crist and seinte Benedight, Blesse this hous from every wikked wight, For nyghtes verye, the white pater-noster! Where wentestow, seinte Petres soster?" And atte laste this hende Nicholas Gan for to sike soore, and seyde, "Allas! Shal al the world be lost eftsoones now?" This carpenter answerde, "What seystow? What! Thynk on God, as we doon, men that swynke." This Nicholas answerde, "Fecche me drynke, And after wol I speke in pryvetee Of certeyn thyng that toucheth me and thee. I wol telle it noon oother man, certeyn."	All round the four corners of the house, And on the threshold of the outside door: "Jesus Christ and St Benedict, Protect this house from every wicked ghost, From the night hag, the white Paternoster, Where are you, Saint Peter's sister?" And at last this clever Nicholas Began to give great sighs, saying, "Alas! The Carpenter answered, "What are you saying? What! Think about God, as we working men do." Nicholas answered, "Fetch me drink, And afterwards I will tell you privately Of certain things affecting you and me. I swear I won't tell any other man."
This carpenter gooth doun, and comth ageyn, And broghte of myghty ale a large quart; And whan that ech of hem had dronke his part, This Nicholas his dore faste shette, And doun the carpenter by hym he sette.	The carpenter went downstairs, and came back up, Bringing a large quart of strong ale; And when each of them had drunk their share, Then Nicholas closed his door tight, And sat down next to the carpenter.

He seyde "John, myn hooste, lief and deere,	He said, "John, my host, whom I love dearly,
Thou shalt upon thy trouthe swere me here	You must swear on your true faith
That to no wight thou shalt this conseil wreye;	That you will not breathe a word of this to any other man;
For it is Cristes conseil that I seye,	For I am going to tell you the word of Christ,
And if thou telle it man, thou art forlore;	And if you tell anyone else, you are damned,
For this vengeaunce thou shalt han therfore,	This punishment will come your way,
That if thou wreye me, thou shalt be wood."	That if you betray me, you will go insane."
"Nay, Crist forbede it, for his hooly blood!"	"No, Christ forbid it, by his holy blood!"
Quod tho this sely man, "I nam no labbe;	Then this simple man said, "I'm no blabbermouth;
Ne, though I seye, I nam nat lief to gabbe.	Though I say it myself, I don't like gossip.
Sey what thou wolt, I shal it nevere telle	Say what you want, I will never tell,
To child ne wyf, by hym that harwed helle!"	To my child nor my wife, by him who harrowed hell!"
"Now John," quod Nicholas, "I wol nat lye;	"Now John," said Nicholas, "I will not lie;
I have yfounde in myn astrologye,	I have found through my astrology,
As I have looked in the moone bright,	As I looked upon the shining moon,
That now a Monday next, at quarter nyght,	That come next Monday, at nine o'clock,
Shal falle a reyn, and that so wilde and wood,	There will be such rain, so wild and mad,
That half so greet was nevere Noes flood.	That it will be twice as bad as Noah's flood.
This world," he seyde, "in lasse than an hour	This world," he said, "in less than an hour
Shal al be dreynt, so hidous is the shour.	Will all be drowned, so terrible the storm will be.
Thus shal mankynde drenche, and lese hir lyf."	So all men will be drowned, and lose their lives."
This carpenter answerde, "Allas, my wyf!	The carpenter answered, "Alas, my wife!
And shal she drenche? Allas, myn Alisoun!"	Will she be drowned? Alas, my Alison!"
For sorwe of this fil almoost adoun,	He almost fainted in his grief,
And seyde, "Is ther no remedie in this cas?"	And said, "Is there nothing that can be done?"
"Why, yis, for Gode," quod hende Nicholas,	"Why yes, by God," said clever Nicholas,
"If thou wolt werken after loore and reed.	"If you follow the advice of the wise.
Thou mayst nat werken after thyn owene heed;	You must not do what you think of yourself;
For thus seith Salomon, that was ful trewe,	That's what Solomon said, and it was very true,
'Werk al by conseil, and thou shalt not rewe.'	'Follow advice, and you won't regret it.'
And if thou werken wolt by good conseil,	If you will follow good advice,
I undertake, withouten mast and seyl,	I promise, without a mast or sail,
Yet shal I saven hire and thee and me.	I will save you and her and me.
Hastow nat herd hou saved was Noe,	Haven't you heard how Noah was saved,
Whan that oure Lord hadde warned hym biforn	When our Lord warned him in advance
That al the world with water sholde be lorn?"	That the world would be covered in water?"
"Yis," quod this Carpenter, "ful yoore ago."	"Yes," said the carpenter, "many years ago."
"Hastou nat herd," quod Nicholas, "also	"Haven't you heard," said Nicholas, "also
The sorwe of Noe with his felawshipe,	Of the terrible time Noah had with his companions
Er that he myghte gete his wyf to shipe?	To persuade his wife to come on board the ship?
Hym hadde be levere, I dar wel undertake,	He would have preferred, I daresay,
At thilke tyme, than alle wetheres blake	At that time, and despite all the stormy weather,
That she hadde had a ship hirself allone.	For her to have one ship just to herself.
And therfore, woostou what is best to doone?	And so, do you know what the best plan is?

This asketh haste, and of an hastif thing	We must be quick, and when speed is needed
Men may nat preche or maken tariyng.	Men must not waste their time in preaching."
"Anon go gete us faste into this in	"As soon as you can, go and bring here,
A knedyng-trogh, or ellis a kymelyn,	A kneading trough, or a brewing barrel,
For ech of us, but looke that they be large,	For each of us, but make sure they are large,
In which we mowe swymme as in a barge,	So we can float in them like boats,
And han therinne vitaille suffisant	And put inside enough provisions
But for a day - fy on the remenant!	To keep us going for a day–that should be enough!
The water shal aslake and goon away	The water will dry up and go away
Aboute pryme upon the nexte day.	Around about the middle of the next day.
But Robyn may nat wite of this, thy knave,	But don't let your boy Robin know anything about this,
Ne eek thy mayde Gille I may nat save;	And also I can't save your maid Jill;
Axe nat why, for though thou aske me,	Do not ask why, for even if you do
I wol nat tellen Goddes pryvetee.	I will not tell you about the plans of God.
Suffiseth thee, but if thy wittes madde,	It should be enough for you, unless you are mad,
To han as greet a grace as Noe hadde.	To be given the same grace which Noah had.
Thy wyf shal I wel saven, out of doute.	I will save your wife, I promise you that.
Go now thy wey, and speed thee heer-aboute.	Now get going, and be quick about it.
"But whan thou hast, for hire and thee and me,	"But when you have, for her and you and me,
Ygeten us thise knedyng-tubbes three,	Got us those three vessels,
Thanne shaltow hange hem in the roof ful hye,	You must hang them high up in the roof,
That no man of oure purveiaunce espye.	So that no man can see our conveyances.
And whan thou thus hast doon, as I have seyd,	And when you have done this, as I have said,
And hast oure vitaille faire in hem yleyd	And also put in the provisions we need,
And eek an ax, to smyte the corde atwo,	And also an axe, to cut the cord in half,
Whan that the water comth, that we may go,	When the water comes, so we can float away,
And breke an hole an heigh, upon the gable,	And cut a hole high up in the roof,
Unto the gardyn-ward, over the stable,	On the garden side, above the stable,
That we may frely passen forth oure way,	So that we can freely go up on our way,
Whan that the grete shour is goon away,	When the great storm has disappeared,
Thanne shaltou swymme as myrie, I undertake,	I promise you will float away as happily
As dooth the white doke after hire drake.	As a white duck following her drake.
Thanne wol I clepe, 'How, Alison! how, John	Then I will call out, "Hello, Alison! Hello, John,
Be myrie, for the flood wol passe anon.'	Be happy, for the flood will soon go."
And thou wolt seyn, 'Hayl, maister Nicholay!	And you will say, "Hello there, Master Nicholas!
Good morwe, I see thee wel, for it is day.'	Good day to you, I can see you well, it is now light."
And thanne shul we be lordes al oure lyf	And so we shall spend our lives as lords
Of al the world, as Noe and his wyf.	Of the whole world, like Noah and his wife.
"But of o thyng I warne thee ful right:	"But there's one thing I really must warn you about:
Be wel avysed on that ilke nyght	Be careful that on that very night
That we ben entred into shippes bord,	When we have climbed on board our boats,
That noon of us ne speke nat a word,	That none of us must speak a word,
Ne clepe, ne crie, but be in his preyere;	Not speak or cry, just silently pray;
For it is Goddes owene heeste deere.	This is what the good Lord orders.
"Thy wyf and thou moote hange fer atwynne;	Your wife and you must hang apart;
For that bitwixe yow shal be no synne,	For you must have no sin between you,

Namoore in lookyng than ther shal in deede,	Either in looks or in deed,
This ordinance is seyd. Go, God thee speede!	This is how it is ordered. Go, God speed!
Tomorwe at nyght, whan men ben alle aslepe,	Tomorrow night, when all men are sleep,
Into oure knedyng-tubbes wol we crepe,	We will creep into our kneading tubs,
And sitten there, abidyng Goddes grace.	And sit there, waiting for the grace of God.
Go now thy wey, I have no lenger space	Now go on your way, I don't have longer
To make of this no lenger sermonyng.	To tell you any more than this.
Men seyn thus, 'sende the wise, and sey no thyng:'	There is a saying, 'Work with the wise, you won't need to speak.'
Thou art so wys, it needeth thee nat teche.	You are so wise that you don't need teaching.
Go, save oure lyf, and that I the biseche."	Go, save our lives, I beg of you."
This sely carpenter goth forth his wey.	The foolish carpenter went on his way.
Ful ofte he seide 'Allas' and 'weylawey,'	He often cried out, "Alas!" and "Woe is me!"
And to his wyf he tolde his pryvetee,	He told his wife his secret,
And she was war, and knew it bet than he,	Though actually she knew it better than him,
What als his queynte cast was for to seye.	And what was going to happen.
But natheless she ferde as she wolde deye,	However, she acted as if she would die,
And seyde, "Allas! go forth thy wey anon,	And said, "Alas! Go about your business,
Help us to scape, or we been dede echon!	Help us to escape, or we're all dead!
I am thy trewe, verray wedded wyf;	I am you true, lawful wife;
Go, deere spouse, and help to save oure lyf."	Go, dear husband, and help save our lives."
Lo, with a greet thyng is affeccioun!	What a great thing is imagination!
Men may dyen of ymaginacioun,	I swear men can die from it,
So depe may impressioun be take.	So powerful ideas can be.
This sely carpenter bigynneth quake;	This foolish carpenter began to shake;
Hym thynketh verraily that he may see	He truly thought that he could see
Noees flood come walwynge as the see	Noah's flood come sweeping in like the sea
To drenchen Alisoun, his hony deere.	To drown Alison, his sweet wife.
He wepeth, weyleth, maketh sory cheere;	He wept and wailed and was thoroughly miserable;
He siketh with ful many a sory swogh;	He sighed with many sobbing moans;
He gooth and geteth hym a knedyng-trogh,	He went and found a kneading-trough,
And after that a tubbe and a kymelyn,	And after that he found a couple of tubs,
And pryvely he sente hem to his in,	And he had them secretly brought to his inn,
And heng hem in the roof in pryvetee.	And hung them up from the rafters.
His owene hand he made laddres thre,	With his own hand he then made three ladders,
To clymben by the ronges and the stalkes	To climb up on the rungs and get into
Unto the tubbes hangynge in the balkes,	The tubs he had hanging from the beams.
And hem vitailled, bothe trogh and tubbe,	He loaded up both the tubs and the trough
With breed and chese, and good ale in a jubbe,	With bread and cheese, and good ale in a jug,
Suffisynge right ynogh as for a day.	Enough to last them for a day.
But er that he hadde maad al this array,	But before he made all these arrangements
He sente his knave, and eek his wenche also,	He sent his boy and also his maid
Upon his nede to London for to go.	To go on an errand to London.
And on the Monday, whan it drow to nyght,	On Monday, when the night had come,
He shette his dore withoute candel-lyght,	He closed his door without lighting the candles,
And dressed alle thyng as it sholde be.	And had everything organised as it should be.
And shortly, up they clomben alle thre;	Shortly they all three climbed up;
They seten stille wel a furlong way.	They sat there for the time it takes to plough a furlong.
"Now, Pater-noster, clom!" seyde Nicholay,	"Now, by our father, hush!" said Nicholas,
And "Clom," quod John, and "clom," seyde Alisoun.	And John and Alison repeated, "Hush!"

This carpenter seyde his devocioun,	The carpenter had done his devotions,
And stille he sit, and biddeth his preyere,	And he sat still, praying inside,
Awaitynge on the reyn, if he it heere.	Waiting to hear the rain.
The dede sleep, for wery bisynesse,	The deathly sleep of exhaustion
Fil on this carpenter right, as I gesse,	Came to this carpenter, as I guess,
Aboute corfew-tyme, or litel moore;	Round about curfew time, or a little later;
For travaille of his goost he groneth soore	He moaned with a tortured spirit,
And eft he routeth, for his heed myslay.	And soon he was snoring, lying awkwardly.
Doun of the laddre stalketh Nicholay,	Nicholas crept down his ladder,
And Alisoun ful softe adoun she spedde;	And Alison slipped quietly down hers;
Withouten wordes mo they goon to bedde,	Without another word they went off to bed,
Ther as the carpenter is wont to lye.	Right where the carpenter usually slept.
Ther was the revel and the melodye;	That was when the party started!
And thus lith Alison and Nicholas,	And so Alison and Nicholas lay together,
In bisynesse of myrthe and of solas,	Busy having their fun with each other,
Til that the belle of laudes gan to rynge,	Until the bells for the early morning service began to ring,
And freres in the chauncel gonne synge.	And the friars went into their chapel to sing.
This parissh clerk, this amorous Absolon,	This parish clerk, amorous Absolon,
That is for love alwey so wo bigon,	Who was always so woebegone for love,
Upon the Monday was at Oseneye	On Monday was down at Oseny
With compaignye, hym to disporte and pleye,	With friends, looking for some fun,
And axed upon cas a cloisterer	And he happened to ask a monk
Ful prively after John the carpenter;	Secretly about John the carpenter;
And he drough hym apart out of the chirche,	He took him aside from the church,
And seyde, "I noot, I saugh hym heere nat wirche	And said, "I haven't seen him working here
Syn Saterday; I trowe that he be went	Since Saturday; I think our abbot
For tymber, ther oure abott hath hym sent;	Sent him off to get some timber,
For he is wont for tymber for to go,	So maybe he'll be stopping at our farm a couple of days,
And dwellen at the grange a day or two;	
Or elles he is at his hous, certeyn.	Or else he has gone home to his house,
Where that he be, I kan nat soothly seyn."	But I can't tell you for certain which it might be."
This Absolon ful joly was and light,	Then Absolon was happy and lighthearted,
And thoghte, "Now is tyme to wake al nyght;	And thought, "Now's the time to be up all night,
For sikirly I saugh hym nat stirynge	For certainly I haven't seen him stirring
Aboute his dore, syn day bigan to sprynge.	From his threshold since day began.
So moot I thryve, I shal, at cokkes crowe,	"So I can get my way I shall, at cock crow,
Ful pryvely knokken at his wyndowe	Secretly knock upon that window,
That stant ful lowe upon his boures wal.	That's so low down on his bedroom wall.
To Alison now wol I tellen al	Then I will tell Alison all about
My love-longynge, for yet I shal nat mysse	How my love yearns for her, and that way
That at the leeste wey I shal hire kisse.	At least I will have her lips to kiss.
Som maner confort shal I have, parfay.	I tell you I will get something this time.
My mouth hath icched al this longe day;	My mouth's been itching this whole day;
That is a signe of kissyng atte leeste.	That means I will at least be kissed.
Al nyght me mette eek I was at a feeste.	Also all last night I dreamed that I was at a feast.
Therfore I wol go slepe an houre or tweye,	So I will go and sleep for an hour or two,
And al the nyght thanne wol I wake and pleye."	And then I'll be awake and having fun all night."

Whan that the firste cok hathe crowe, anon	So when the cock crow had come, at once
Up rist this joly lovere Absolon,	This jolly lover Absalon got up,
And hym arraieth gay, at poynt-devys.	And dressed himself smartly, all laced up,
But first he cheweth greyn and lycorys,	But firstly he chewed some liquorice and ginger,
To smellen sweete, er he hadde kembd his heer.	To be sweet smelling, and then he combed his hair.
Under his tonge a trewe-love he beer,	He slipped some herbs under his tongue,
For therby wende he to ben gracious.	Thinking that would make him more classy.
He rometh to the carpenteres hous,	He went to the house of the carpenter,
And stille he stant under the shot-wyndowe -	And stood silent beneath the little window-
Unto his brest it raughte, it was so lowe -	It was next to his chest, it was so low-
And softe he cougheth with a semy soun:	And he called in a little whisper:
"What do ye, hony-comb, sweete Alisoun,	"What are you doing, honeycomb, sweet Alison,
My faire bryd, my sweete cynamome?	My fair bird, sweet cinnamon?
Awaketh, lemman myn, and speketh to me!	Wake up, my darling, and speak to me!
Wel lithel thynken ye upon me wo,	You don't care much for me and my sorrow,
That for youre love I swete ther I go.	The one who sweats for your love wherever I go.
No wonder is thogh that I swelte and swete;	It's no wonder that I'm fainting and sweating;
I moorne as dooth a lamb after the tete.	I long for you like a lamb for the teat.
Ywis, lemman, I have swich love-longynge,	Truly, sweetheart, I am so desperate for love
That lik a turtel trewe is my moornynge.	That I yearn for you like a turtledove,
I may nat ete na moore than a mayde."	And I can eat no more than a girl."
"Go fro the wyndow, Jakke fool," she sayde;	"Get away from my window, jackass," she said,
"As help me God, it wol not be 'com pa me.'	"So help me God, you won't be kissing me.
I love another - and elles I were to blame -	I love someone else, and that's not my fault,
Wel bet than thee, by Jhesu, Absolon.	He's far better than you, Absalon, by Jesus!
Go forth thy wey, or I wol caste a ston,	Go on your way, or I will stone you,
And lat me slepe, a twenty devel wey!"	And let me sleep, may the devils take you away!"
"Allas," quod Absolon, "and weylawey,	"Alas," said Absalon, "woe now is me,
That trewe love was evere so yvel biset!	That true love was ever so badly treated!
Thanne kysse me, syn it may be no bet,	Then kiss me, since you can do no more,
For Jhesus love, and for the love of me."	For the love of Jesus, and the love of me."
"Wiltow thanne go thy wey therwith?" quod she.	"Will you go away if I do?" she asked.
"Ye, certes, lemman," quod Absolon.	"Yes, I promise, sweetheart," said Absalon.
"Thanne make thee redy," quod she, "I come anon."	"Then get ready," she said, "here I come."
And unto Nicholas she seyde stille,	And she whispered then to Nicholas,
"Now hust, and thou shalt laughen al thy fille."	"Now keep quiet and you'll get a good laugh."
This Absolon doun sette hym on his knees	Then Absolon got down upon his knees
And seyde, "I am a lord at alle degrees;	And said, "I am as lucky as a lord,
For after this I hope ther cometh moore.	For after this I hope she'll give me more.
Lemman, thy grace, and sweete bryd, thyn oore!"	Darling, sweet bird, I'm waiting for you!"
The wyndow she undoth, and that in haste.	She unlocked the window, and said swiftly,
"Have do," quod she, "com of, and speed the faste,	"Come on, do it quickly,
Lest that oure neighebores thee espie."	Before any of the neighbours see us."
This Absolon gan wype his mouth ful drie.	Absolon wiped his mouth clean and dry.
Derk was the nyght as pich, or as a cole,	The night was pitch black, dark as coal,
And at the wyndow out she putte hir hole,	And she then stuck her hole out of the window,

And Absolon, hym fil no bet ne wers, But with his mouth he kiste hir naked ers Ful savorly, er he were war of this.	And Absalon, none the wiser, Kissed her naked arse with his mouth, Very greedily, before he knew what was happening.
Abak he stirte, and thoughte it was amys, For wel he wiste a womman hath no berd.	He jumped back, thinking something was odd, For he knew very well that women don't have beards.
He felte a thyng al rough and long yherd, And seyde, "Fy! allas! what have I do?" "Tehee!" quod she, and clapte the wyndow to,	He'd felt something rough and covered in hair, And said, "Alas! What have I done?" "Tee-hee!" she said, and slammed the window shut,
And Absolon gooth forth a sory pas. "A berd! a berd!" quod hende Nicholas, "By Goddes corpus, this goth faire and weel."	And Absolom sadly trudged away. "A beard! A beard!" said crafty Nicholas, "By the body of Christ, that was a good trick!"
This sely Absolon herde every deel, And on his lippe he gan for anger byte, And to hymself he seyde, "I shall thee quyte." Who rubbeth now, who frotheth now his lippes With dust, with sond, with straw, with clooth, with chippes, But Absolon, that seith ful ofte, "Allas!" My soule bitake I unto Sathanas, But me were levere than al this toun," quod he, "Of this despit awroken for to be. Allas," quod he, "allas, I ne hadde ybleynt!" His hoote love was coold and al yqueynt; For fro that tyme that he hadde kist her ers, Of paramours he sette nat a kers; For he was heeled of his maladie. Ful ofte paramours he gan deffie, And weep as dooth a child that is ybete. A softe paas he wente over the street Until a smyth men cleped daun Gerveys, That in his forge smythed plough harneys; He sharpeth shaar and kultour bisily.	Foolish Absolon heard every word, And began to bite his lip angrily, And said to himself, "I'll get even." He rubbed roughly away at his lips With dust, sand, straw, cloth and woodchips, But Absolon often wailed, "Alas! I give my soul now to Satan, If I were offered this whole town," he said, "I would turn it down in favour of revenge. Alas," he said, "I went full on for that kiss!" His hot love was all cold and quenched; From the moment he had kissed her arse He had decided to give up on lovers; He was cured of his lovesickness. In fact he cursed all lovely women, And wept like a child who's been beaten. He stealthily crept across the street To a smith whose name was Jarvis, Who made parts for ploughs in his forge; He was busy sharpening shears and ploughshares.
This Absolon knokketh al esily, And seyde, "Undo, Gerveys, and that anon." "What, who artow?" "It am I, Absolon."	Absolon knocked softly on the door, And said, "Jarvis, open up, quickly." "What, who's there?" "It's me, Absolon."
"What, Absolon! For Cristes sweete tree,	"What, Absolon! In the name of the Holy Cross,
Why rise ye so rathe? Ey, benedicitee! What eyleth yow? Som gay gerl, God it woot,	Why are you up so early? Bless me! What's the matter with you? Some jolly girl, God knows,
Hath broght yow thus upon the viritoot. By seinte Note, ye woot wel what I mene."	Has brought you here to my forge. By St.Neot, you know perfectly well what I mean."
This Absolon ne roghte nat a bene Of all his pley; no word agayn he yaf; He hadde moore tow on his distaff	Absolon didn't give a damn For all these jokes; he didn't answer back, He had other things to think about
Than Gerveys knew, and seyde, "Freend so deere,	Than Jarvis knew, and he said, "My dear friend,

That hoote kultour in the chymenee heere,	This red hot poker here in the fireplace,
As lene it me, I have therwith to doone,	Lend it to me, I need it for a while,
And I wol brynge it thee agayn ful soone."	And I'll bring it back to you very soon."
Gerveys answerde, "Certes, were it gold,	Jarvis answered, "Of course, if it were gold,
Or in a poke nobles alle untold,	Or a purse full of countless gold coins,
Thou sholdest have, as I am trewe smyth.	You would have it, as I am a true smith.
Ey, Cristes foo! What wol ye do therwith?"	But what the devil do you want it for?"
"Therof," quod Absolon, "be as be may.	"Don't you worry yourself about that," said Absolon.
I shal wel telle it thee to-morwe day" -	I'll tell you all about it tomorrow."
And caughte the kultour by the colde stele,	And he grabbed the poker by its cold end,
Ful softe out at the dore he gan to stele,	And quietly began to steal out of the door,
And wente unto the carpenteris wal.	And went back to the wall of the carpenter's house.
He cogheth first, and knokketh therwithal	He coughed at first, and then he knocked
Upon the wyndowe, right as he dide er.	On the window, just as he had before.
This Alison answerde, "Who is ther	Alison answered him, "Who's out there
That knokketh so? I warante it a theef."	Knocking like that? I think it's a thief."
"Why, nay," quod he, "God woot, my sweete leef,	"Why no," he said, "God knows, sweet roseleaf,
I am thyn Absolon, my deerelyng.	I am your Absolon, my darling.
Of gold," quod he, "I have thee broght a ryng.	I have brought you a gold ring," he said,
My mooder yaf it me, so God me save;	"Which I swear my mother gave to me;
Ful fyn it is, and therto wel ygrave.	It's very fine gold, and well engraved,
This wol I yeve thee, if thou me kisse."	And you can have it for another kiss."
This Nicholas was risen for to pisse,	Nicholas had got up to have a piss,
And thoughte he wolde amenden al the jape;	And thought he would carry on the joke,
He sholde kisse his ers er that he scape.	And get this jackass to kiss his arse.
And up the wyndowe dide he hastily,	He threw open the window quickly
And out his ers he putteth pryvely	And stuck out his arse quietly,
Over the buttok, to the haunche-bon;	Right up to the hipbone;
And therwith spak this clerk, this Absolon,	And then this clerk Absolon spoke out:
"Spek, sweete bryd, I noot nat where thou art."	"Speak, sweet bird, I don't know where you are."
This Nicholas anon leet fle a fart,	Then Nicholas let fly with a fart,
As greet as it had been a thonder-dent,	As loud as a great thunderclap,
That with the strook he was almoost yblent;	So that Absolon was nearly blinded;
And he was redy with his iren hoot,	But he was ready with his hot iron,
And Nicholas amydde the ers he smoot,	And got Nicholas right in the arse,
Of gooth the skyn an hande brede aboute,	And stripped off the skin for a hand's breadth around,
The hoote kultour brende so his toute,	The poker burned his arse so badly
And for the smert he wende for to dye.	That he thought he would die of the pain.
As he were wood, for wo he gan to crye,	He started to cry out as though he had gone mad,
"Help! Water! Water! Help for Goddes herte!"	"Help! Water, water! For God's sake!"
This carpenter out of his slomber sterte,	The carpenter woke up out of his slumber,
And herde oon crien 'water' as he were,	And when he heard, "Water!" he went mad,
And thoughte, "Allas, now comth Nowelis flood!"	And thought, "Alas, here come's Noah's flood!"
He sit hym up withouten wordes mo,	He sat up without saying any more,
And with his ax he smoot the corde atwo,	And with his axe he chopped the rope in two,

And doun gooth al; he foond neither to selle, Ne breed ne ale, til he cam to the celle Upon the floor, and ther aswowne he lay.	And everything collapsed; he didn't have time To catch his breath until he reached the cellar And lay down there swooning on the floor.
Up stirte hire Alison and Nicholay, And criden "Out" and "Harrow" in the strete. The neighebores, bothe smale and grete, In ronnen for to gauren on this man, That yet aswowne lay, bothe pale and wan, For with the fal he brosten hadde his arm. But stonde he moste unto his owene harm; For whan he spak, he was anon bore doun	Up jumped Alison and Nicholas, Calling, "Help!" and "Hello!" down the street. The neighbours, the great and the lowly, Came running to stare at this man, Who lay fainting, pale and wan, For as he fell he had broken his arm. He had to also suffer another injury, For when he spoke he was at once shouted down
With hende Nicholas and Alisoun. They tolden every man that he was wood, He was agast so of Nowelis flood Thurgh fantasie, that of his vanytee He hadde yboght hym knedyng-tubbes thre,	By cunning Nicholas and Alison, Who told everyone there that he was mad, So afraid of "Noel's" flood Through his mad imagination That he had bought himself three kneading-tubs,
And hadde hem hanged in the roof above; And that he preyed hem, for Goddes love, To sitten in the roof, par compaignye.	And hung them up in his loft; And he had begged them, for the love of God, To sit up there with him and keep him company.
The folk gan laughen at his fantasye; Into the roof they kiken and they cape; And turned al his harm unto a jape. For what so that this carpenter answerde, It was for noght, no man his reson herde. With othes grete he was so sworn adoun That he was holde wood in al the toun;	The people began to laugh at this fantasy; They looked up at the roof open mouthed; So they made his injury into a great joke. Whatever the carpenter tried to say It was useless, nobody listened to him; The others swore so convincingly That everyone in the town thought he was mad,
For every clerk anonright heeld with oother. They seyde, "The man is wood, my leeve brother"; And every wight gan laughen at this stryf. Thus swyved was this carpenteris wyf, For al his kepyng and his jalousye; And Absolon hath kist hir nether ye; And Nicholas is scalded in the towte. This tale is doon, and God save al the rowte!	For all the clerks agreed with each other, And said, "This man is mad, my dear brother!" And everyone mocked him in his trouble. So the carpenter's wife got screwed, For all his watchful jealousy; And Absolon kissed her arsehole, And Nicholas got a burned arse. That's the end of the story, God save you all!
Heere endeth the Millere his Tale.	*This is the end of the Miller's tale.*

The Reeve's Tale

Prologue

The Prologe of the Reves Tale

Whan folk hadde laughen at this nyce cas

Of Absolon and hende Nicholas,
Diverse folk diversely they seyde,
But for the moore part they loughe and pleyde.
Ne at this tale I saugh no man hym greve,
But it were oonly Osewold the Reve.
Bycause he was of carpenteres craft,
A litel ire is in his herte ylaft;
He gan to grucche, and blamed it a lite.
"So theek," quod he, "ful wel koude I thee quite
With bleryng of a proud milleres eye,
If that me liste speke of ribaudye.
But ik am oold, me list no pley for age,
Gras-tyme is doon, my fodder is now forage,

This white top writeth myne olde yeris,
Myn herte is also mowled as myne heris,
But if I fare as dooth an open-ers, -
That ilke fruyt is ever lenger the wers,
Til it be roten in mullok or in stree.
We olde men, I drede, so fare we,
Til we be roten kan we nat be rype.
We hoppen ay whil that the world wol pype,
For in oure wyl ther stiketh evere a nayl,

To have an hoor heed and a grene tayl,
As hath a leek, for thogh oure myght be goon,
Oure wyl desireth folie evere in oon.
For whan we may nat doon, than wol we speke,
Yet in oure asshen olde is fyr yreke.

"Foure gleedes han we whiche I shal devyse, -

Avauntyng, liyng, anger, coveitise;
Thise foure sparkles longen unto eelde.

Oure olde lemes mowe wel been unweelde,
But wyl ne shal nat faillen, that is sooth.
And yet ik have alwey a coltes tooth,
As many a yeer as it is passed henne
Syn that my tappe of lif bigan to renne.
For sikerly, whan I was bore, anon
Deeth drough the tappe of lyf, and leet it gon,
And ever sithe hath so the tappe yronne,
Til that almoost al empty is the tonne.
The streem of lyf now droppeth on the chymbe;
The sely tonge may wel rynge and chymbe

The Reeve's Prologue

When everyone had laughed at this funny business
Of Absolon and crafty Nicholas,
Different people said different things about it,
But most of them laughed and were happy.
I didn't see anyone upset by this story,
Except for Oswald the Reeve,
Because he was a carpenter by trade,
And so he was somewhat annoyed,
And he began to grumble, and criticise.
"I think," he said, "I could very well respond
By making a proud miller look stupid,
If I wanted to be vulgar.
But I am old, too old for this nonsense,
My time at pasture has gone, all I need now is straw,
My white hair shows how old I am,
And my heart is as worn out as my hair,
Unless I have the virtues of a medlar,
That fruit which is better as it gets worse,
Until it's at its best when it's quite rotten.
I'm afraid we old men are the same as that;
We can't be ripe until we're rotten.
We still have hope while the world goes on,
But something always happens to drag us back,
We have a white head, but green tail,
Just like a leek, although our strength is gone
We still wish for foolishness always.
Things which we can't do, we will speak of,
For there is still fire burning in our old ashes.

"There are four burning embers, I shall describe them:
Boasting, lying, anger and covetousness;
These are the four sparks belonging to old age.
Our old limbs might well be unwieldy,
But the desire never leaves us, that is true.
I have always had a young man's tastes,
And many years have passed away
Since the course of my life began.
For certainly, when I was born, so long ago,
Death turned on the tap of life, letting it flow,
And ever since the tap has been running,
Until now the barrel is almost empty.
The stream of life is now running out in drips;
This silly tongue can certainly tell you a story

Of wrecchednesse that passed is ful yoore.
With olde folk, save dotage, is namoore!"

Whan that oure Hoost hadde herd this sermonyng,
He gan to speke as lordly as a kyng,
He seide, "What amounteth al this wit?
What shul we speke alday of hooly writ?
The devel made a reve for to preche,
And of a soutere a shipman, or a leche.

Sey forth thy tale, and tarie nat the tyme.
Lo Depeford, and it is half-wey pryme.

Lo Grenewych, ther many a shrewe is inne!
It were al tyme thy tale to bigynne."
"Now sires," quod this Osewold the Reve,
"I pray yow alle, that ye nat yow greve,
Thogh I answere, and somdeel sette his howve,

For leveful is with force force of-showve.
This dronke Millere hath ytoold us heer
How that bigyled was a carpenteer,
Peraventure in scorn, for I am oon.
And, by youre leve, I shal hym quite anoon;
Right in his cherles termes wol I speke.
I pray to God his nekke mote to-breke;
He kan wel in myn eye seen a stalke,
But in his owene he kan nat seen a balke."

Of foolish things done a long time before.
With old folk, apart from senility, that's all there is left!"
When our host had heard all this sermonising,
He began to speak as grandly as a king,
Saying, "What's the point of all this wit?
Are we going to speak of holy things all day?
A Reeve as a preacher is devilish,
And the same goes for a cobbler, a sailor or doctor.
Let's have your tale, stop wasting time.
Look, there's Deptford, and it's halfway to midday.
There's Greenwich, where many rascals live!
It's time for you to get on with your story."
"Now gentlemen," said this Oswald the Reeve,
"I hope that none of you will be annoyed
At the way I answer him, and make a fool of him,
It's quite lawful to meet force with force.
This drunken Miller here has told us
Of how a carpenter was tricked,
Perhaps to mock me, for I am one.
With your permission, I will pay him back;
I'll speak to him in his own vulgar language.
I pray that God will break his neck;
He can easily find the straw in my eye,
But he can't see the timber in his own."

The Tale

Heere bigynneth the Reves Tale

At TRUMPYNGTOUN, nat fer fro Cantebrigge,
Ther gooth a brook, and over that a brigge,
Upon the whiche brook ther stant a melle;
And this is verray sooth that I yow telle.
A millere was ther dwellynge many a day;

As any pecok he was proud and gay.
Pipen he koude and fisshe, and nettes beete,

And turne coppes, and wel wrastle and sheete;
Ay by his belt he baar a long panade,
And of a swerd ful trenchant was the blade.

A joly poppere baar he in his pouche;
Ther was no man, for peril, dorste hym touche.
A Sheffeld thwitel baar he in his hose.

Round was his face, and camus was his nose;
As piled as an ape was his skulle.
He was a market-betere atte fulle.
Ther dorste no wight hand upon hym legge,
That he ne swoor he sholde anon abegge.

A theef he was for sothe of corn and mele,
And that a sly, and usaunt for to stele.
His name was hoote deynous Symkyn.
A wyf he hadde, ycomen of noble kyn;
The person of the toun hir fader was.
With hire he yaf ful many a panne of bras,
For that Symkyn sholde in his blood allye.
She was yfostred in a nonnerye;
For Symkyn wolde no wyf, as he sayde,
But she were wel ynorissed and a mayde,
To saven his estaat of yomanrye.
And she was proud, and peert as is a pye.
A ful fair sighte was it upon hem two;
On halydayes biforn hire wolde he go
With his typet wound aboute his heed,
And she cam after in a gyte of reed;
And Symkyn hadde hosen of the same.
Ther dorste no wight clepen hire but 'dame';
Was noon so hardy that went by the weye

That with hire dorste rage or ones pleye,
But if he wolde be slayn of Symkyn
With panade, or with knyf, or boidekyn.
For jalous folk ben perilous everemo;

The Reeve's Tale

At Trumpington, not far from Cambridge,
There is a stream, crossed by a bridge,
And on that stream there is a mill;
And this is the absolute truth I am telling you.
There was a miller who had lived there a good long time;
He was proud and gay as any peacock.
He could play the flute and fish, and mend nets,
Make cups, wrestle and shoot;
In his belt he carried a long machete,
And the blade was as strong as a full-sized sword.
In his pocket he carried a pretty little dagger;
Every man was afraid to lay a finger on him.
He carried a long Sheffield knife in his stockings.
His face was round, with an upturned nose;
His skull was as bald as an ape's.
He was a great swaggering bully.
Nobody dared to lay a hand upon him,
Because he swore that he would make anyone pay.

He was a thief of corn and meal,
And a sly one, experienced in theft.
He was called arrogant Simpkin.
He had a wife, who came from a good family;
Her father was the parson of the town.
He gave many brass pans as a dowry,
To persuade Simpkin to join the family.
She was brought up in a nunnery;
For Simpkin would have no wife, he said,
Unless she was a virgin and well bred,
So as not to disgrace his yeoman's stock.
And she was proud, and bold as a magpie.
A pretty picture the two of them made;
On holy days he would walk in front of her
With his scarf wrapped around his head,
And she followed after him in a red skirt;
And Simpkin had stockings the same colour.
Nobody dared call her anything but "lady";
And there was no one so bold of all those they passed
Who dared to flirt with her or try anything on,
Because he knew that Simpkin would kill him
With his machete, knife or dagger.
Jealous people are always dangerous;

Algate they wolde hire wyves wenden so.	At least that's what they want their wives to think.
And eek, for she was somdel smoterlich,	And also, because she was somewhat tarnished in reputation,
She was as digne as water in a dich,	She was as snobbish as you can imagine,
And ful of hoker and of bisemare.	Full of sneering disdain.
Hir thoughte that a lady sholde hire spare,	She thought that she should be treated like a lady,
What for hire kynrede and hir nortelrie	On account of her family and the upbringing
That she hadde lerned in the nonnerie.	That she had had in the nunnery.
A doghter hadde they bitwixe hem two	They had a daughter between the two of them,
Of twenty yeer, withouten any mo,	Who was twenty years old, an only child,
Savynge a child that was of half yeer age;	Apart from a baby who was only six months old;
In cradel it lay and was a propre page.	It lay in its cradle and was a solid lad.
This wenche thikke and wel ygrowen was,	This girl was thickset and well-developed,
With kamus nose, and eyen greye as glas,	With an upturned nose and eyes as grey as glass,
With buttokes brode, and brestes rounde and hye;	With a wide backside, and round high breasts,
But right fair was hire heer, I wol nat lye.	But I must be honest, she had nice hair.
This person of the toun, for she was feir,	The parson of the town, because she was pretty,
In purpos was to maken hire his heir,	Intended to make her into his heir,
Bothe of his catel and his mesuage,	Both of his possessions and his lands,
And straunge he made it of hir mariage.	Provided that she got married.
His purpos was for to bistowe hire hye	He intended to marry her into a family
Into som worthy blood of auncetrye;	Which would be suitable for one of her ancestry;
For hooly chirches good moot been despended	For the money of the Holy Church must be spent
On hooly chirches blood, that is descended.	On the descendants, by blood, of the Holy Church.
Therfore he wolde his hooly blood honoure	So he would honour his holy blood,
Though that he hooly chirche sholde devoure.	Whatever it ended up costing the Holy Church.
Greet sokene hath his millere, out of doute,	There's no doubting that this miller took great profits
With whete and malt of al the land aboute;	Out of the wheat and malt of all the surrounding country;
And nameliche ther was a greet college	And particularly there was a great college
Men clepen the Soler Halle at Cantebregge;	Which men call the King's Hall at Cambridge;
Ther was hir whete and eek hir malt ygrounde.	And he ground all their wheat and also their malt.
And on a day it happed, in a stounde,	One day it happened to come to pass
Sik lay the maunciple on a maladye;	That their business agent had become very ill;
Men wenden wisly that he sholde dye.	All the wise men thought that he would die.
For which this millere stal bothe mele and corn	So this miller stole both meal and corn
And hundred tyme moore than biforn;	A hundred times more than he had before;
For therbiforn he stal but curteisly,	Previously he had just stolen cautiously,
But now he was a theef outrageously,	But now he was an outrageous thief,
For which the wardeyn chidde and made fare.	The warden scolded him and made a fuss,
But therof sette the millere nat a tare;	But the miller didn't care at all;
He cracketh boost, and swoor it was nat so.	He blustered and boasted and denied it all.

Thanne were ther yonge povre scolers two,	There were two young impoverished scholars
That dwelten in this halle, of which I seye.	Living in this college which I mentioned.
Testif they were, and lusty for to pleye,	They were very spirited, always up for fun,
And oonly for hire myrthe and revelrye,	And just for their own amusement
Upon the wardeyn bisily they crye	They nagged away at the college warden
To yeve hem leve, but a litel stounde,	To give them permission, just for a little while,
To goon to mille and seen hir corn ygrounde;	To go to the mill and see their corn being ground;
And hardily they dorste leye hir nekke	And they boldly said they would bet their necks
The millere sholde not stele hem half a pekke	That the miller wouldn't steal the tiniest bit
Of corn by sleighte, ne by force hem reve;	Of grain with his tricks, neither would he get it by force;
And at the laste the wardeyn yaf hem leve.	And in the end the warden gave them permission.
John highte that oon, and Aleyn highte that oother;	One of them was called John, and the other was called Alan;
Of o toun were they born, that highte Strother,	They were born in a town called Strother,
Fer in the north, I kan nat telle where.	Which is far in the North, I don't know where.
This Aleyn maketh redy al his gere,	Then Alan got all his gear prepared,
And on an hors the sak he caste anon.	And loaded his sack on a horse.
Forth goth Aleyn the clerk, and also John,	And out went Alan the clerk, and also John,
With good swerd and with bokeler by hir syde.	With good swords and bucklers by their sides.
John knew the wey, - hem nedede no gyde, -	John knew the way—he didn't need a guide—
And at the mille the sak adoun he layth.	And he put down the sack of grain at the mill.
Aleyn spak first, "Al hayl, Symond, y-fayth!	Alan spoke first, "Hello there, Simpkin, by God!
Hou fares thy faire doghter and thy wyf?"	How are your lovely daughter and your wife?"
"Aleyn, welcome," quod Symkyn, "by my lyf!	"Alan, welcome," said Simpkin, "on my life!
And John also, how now, what do ye heer?"	And John as well, hello there, what are you doing here?"
"Symond," quod John, "by God, nede has na peer.	"Simpkin," said John, "by God, needs must.
Hym boes serve hymself that has na swayn,	Someone who doesn't have a servant must serve himself,
Or elles he is a fool, as clerkes sayn.	Or else he is a fool, so the scholars say.
Oure manciple, I hope he wil be deed,	Our agent, I expect he's going to die,
Swa werkes ay the wanges in his heed;	The teeth in his head are all aching so;
And forthy is I come, and eek Alayn,	And I have come here, along with Alan,
To grynde oure corn and carie it ham agayn;	To grind our corn and carry it back home;
I pray yow spede us heythen that ye may."	Please give us as much help as you can."
"It shal be doon," quod Symkyn, "by my fay!	"This shall be done," said Simpkin, I swear to you!
What wol ye doon whil that is in hande?"	What will you do while that's being done?"
"By God, right by the hopur wil I stande,"	"By God, I will stand right by the hopper,"
Quod John, "and se howgates the corn gas in.	Said John, "and see how the corn is poured in.
Yet saugh I nevere, by my fader kyn,	I have never seen, I swear to you,
How that the hopur wagges til and fra."	The way the hopper actually works."
Aleyn answerde, "John, and wiltow swa?	Allen said, "So, John, that's what you'll do?
Thanne wil I be bynethe, by my croun,	Then I'll go underneath, I swear,
And se how that the mele falles doun	And see how the meal comes running
Into the trough; that sal be my disport.	Into the trough; that will be my entertainment.
For John, y-faith, I may been of youre sort;	For John, I swear, I must be like you;

I is as ille a millere as ar ye."	I'm as ignorant of milling as you are."
This millere smyled of hir nycetee,	The miller smiled at their naivete,
And thoghte, "Al this nys doon but for a wyle.	And thought, "All of this is just a trick.
They wene that no man may hem bigyle,	They think that nobody can deceive them,
But by my thrift, yet shal I blere hir ye,	But with my skill I'll hoodwink them,
For al the sleighte in hir philosophye.	For all their educated ways.
The moore queynte crekes that they make,	The more cunning strategies they use,
The moore wol I stele whan I take.	The more I'll steal from them when I start.
In stide of flour yet wol I yeve hem bren.	I will give them flour instead of bran.
'The gretteste clerkes been noght wisest men,'	"The greatest scholars are not the wisest men,"
As whilom to the wolf thus spak the mare.	As the wolf once said to the mare.
Of al hir art ne counte I noght a tare."	I don't give a damn for all their learning."
Out at the dore he gooth ful pryvely,	Then he sneaked secretly out of the door,
Whan that he saugh his tyme, softely.	Quietly, when he saw a chance.
He looketh up and doun til he hath founde	He searched about until he found
The clerkes hors, ther as it stood ybounde	The students' horse, where it was tied up
Bihynde the mille, under a levesel;	Behind the mill, under a tree;
And to the hors he goth hym faire and wel;	And he got up to it without being seen;
He strepeth of the brydel right anon.	He took off the bridle straight away,
And whan the hors was laus, he gynneth gon	And when the horse was loose, he shot off
Toward the fen, ther wilde mares renne,	Towards the fen, where the wild mares live,
And forth with 'wehee,' thurgh thikke and thurgh thenne.	And neighing, he charged off through thick and thin.
This millere gooth agayn, no word he seyde,	The miller went back in again, without saying a word,
But dooth his note, and with the clerkes pleyde,	Just doing his business, chatting with the students,
Til that hir corn was faire and weel ygrounde.	Until the corn was well and truly ground.
And whan the mele is sakked and ybounde,	But when the flour was bagged and fastened,
This John goth out and fynt his hors away,	John went out and found his horse was gone,
And gan to crie "Harrow!" and "Weylaway!	And began to cry "Hello!" And "Alas!
Oure hors is lorn, Alayn, for Goddes banes,	Our horse has gone, Alan, for God's sake,
Step on thy feet! Com of man, man, al atanes!	Look lively! Come out man, at once!
Allas, our wardeyn has his palfrey lorn."	Alas, our warden's horse has gone!"
This Aleyn al forgat, bothe mele and corn;	Alan forgot everything, the corn and the flour;
Al was out of his mynde his housbonderie.	All caution had gone clean out of his mind.
"What, whilk way is he geen?" he gan to crie.	"What? Which way did he go?" he cried.
The wyf cam lepynge inward with a ren.	The wife came running from the house,
She seyde, "Allas! youre hors goth to the fen	Saying, "Alas! Your horse has gone to the fen
With wilde mares, as faste as he may go.	To see the wild mares, as fast as he could go.
Unthank come on his hand that boond hym so,	You should curse the person who tied him like that,
And he that bettre sholde han knyt the reyne!"	He should have taken more care with the reins!"
"Allas," quod John, "Aleyn, for Cristes peyne,	"Alas," said John, "Alan, for Christ's sake,
Lay doun thy swerd, and I wil myn alswa.	Take off your sword, I will do the same.
I is ful wight, God waat, as is a raa;	God knows, I'm as quick as a deer;
By Goddes herte, he sal nat scape us bathe!	I swear he won't get away from us both!
Why ne had thow pit the capul in the lathe?	Why didn't you put the horse in a barn?
Ilhayl! by God, Alayn, thou is a fonne!"	By God, Alan, you are a fool!"

Thise sely clerkes han ful faste yronne	These foolish students set off as fast as they could
Toward the fen, bothe Aleyn and eek John.	Towards the fen, Alan and also John.
And whan the millere saugh that they were gon,	And when the Miller saw that they had gone,
He half a busshel of hir flour hath take,	He took half a bushel of their flour,
And bad his wyf go knede it in a cake.	And told his wife to go and make it into a loaf.
He seyde, "I trowe the clerkes were aferd	He said, "I know those students were on the lookout
Yet kan a millere make a clerkes berd,	But a miller can make a fool of a student,
For al his art; now lat hem goon hir weye!	For all their learning; let them go about their business!
Lo, wher he gooth! ye, lat the children pleye.	Look where he goes! Let the children play.
They gete hym nat so lightly, by my croun."	They won't catch him easily, I swear."
Thise sely clerkes rennen up and doun	These foolish clerks ran up and down
With 'Keep! keep! stand! stand! jossa, warderere,	Shouting, "Stay there! Wait! Wait! Go round the back,
Ga whistle thou, and I shal kepe hym heere!'	You whistle, and I will keep him here!"
But shortly, til that it was verray nyght,	To cut a a long story short, it wasn't until the evening
They koude nat, though they dide al hir myght,	That they could, although they did their best,
Hir capul cacche, he ran alwey so faste,	Catch their horse, he ran away so fast,
Til in a dych they caughte hym atte laste.	Until at last they caught him in a ditch.
Wery and weet, as beest is in the reyn,	Tired and wet, like animals in the rain,
Comth sely John, and with him comth Aleyn.	came foolish John, and with him came Alan.
"Allas," quod John, "the day that I was born!	"Alas," said John, "for the day I was born!
Now are we dryve til hethyng and til scorn.	Now we shall suffer misery and scorn.
Oure corn is stoln, men wil us fooles calle,	Our corn has been stolen, men will call us fools,
Bathe the wardeyn and oure felawes alle,	Both the warden and our fellow students,
And namely the millere, weylaway!"	And especially the Miller, alas!"
Thus pleyneth John as he gooth by the way	So John complained as he went on his way
Toward the mille, and Bayard in his hond.	Towards the mill, leading the horse.
The millere sittynge by the fyr he fond,	He found the Miller sitting by the fire,
For it was nyght, and forther myghte they noght;	For it was night, and they could not go any further;
But for the love of God they hym bisoght	They begged him for the love of God
Of herberwe and of ese, as for hir peny.	To give them food and shelter, for payment.
The millere seyde agayn, "If ther be eny,	The miller replied, "If there's any to be had,
Swich as it is, yet shal ye have youre part.	Whatever it is, you will have your share.
Myn hous is streit, but ye han lerned art;	My house is small, but you are clever men;
Ye konne by arguments make a place	You can with your philosophy make a place
A myle brood of twenty foot of space.	Twenty feet wide into a palace.
Lat se now if this place may suffise,	Let's see if this place is good enough,
Or make it rowm with speche, as is your gise."	Or you can make it bigger with your speech, as is your custom."
"Now, Symond," seyde John, "by seint Cutberd,	"Now Simon," said John, "by St Cuthbert,
Ay is thou myrie, and this is faire answerd.	You are a funny chap, and that's a good answer.
I have herd seyd, 'Man sal taa of twa thynges	I've heard it said a man can have two things,
Slyk as he fyndes, or taa slyk as he brynges.'	The things he finds, or what he brings.
But specially I pray thee, hooste deere,	But I beg you especially, my dear host,
Get us som mete and drynke, and make us cheere,	To get some meat and drink, to cheer us up,

And we wil payen trewely atte fulle.	And we will truly pay you the full price.
With empty hand men may na haukes tulle;	No man should expect anything from nothing;
Loo, heere oure silver, redy for to spende."	Look, here is our silver, ready to be spent."
This millere into toun his doghter sende	The miller sent his daughter into town
For ale and breed, and rosted hem a goos,	To get ale and bread, and he roasted a goose for them,
And booned hire hors, it sholde namoore go loos;	And tied up their horse, so that it would no longer escape;
And in his owene chambre hem made a bed,	And in his own bedroom he made them a bed,
With sheetes and with chalons faire yspred,	Spread with fine sheets and blankets,
Noght from his owene bed ten foot or twelve.	Only a few feet away from his own bed.
His doghter hadde a bed, al by hirselve,	His daughter had a bed all to herself,
Right in the same chambre by and by.	Right there in the same bedroom.
It myghte be no bet, and cause why?	It had to be like that, and why?
Ther was no roumer herberwe in the place.	There wasn't any other room in the place.
They soupen and they speke, hem to solace,	They ate and chatted, and felt a little better,
And drynken evere strong ale atte beste.	And drank a lot of the best strong ale.
Aboute mydnyght wente they to reste.	About midnight they went to bed.
Wel hath this millere vernysshed his heed;	This miller had properly filled up his head;
Ful pale he was for dronken, and nat reed.	He was completely pale with drink, and not red.
He yexeth, and he speketh thurgh the nose	He hicupped and spoke through his nose,
As he were on the quakke, or on the pose.	As if he had chill, or a blocked throat.
To bedde he goth, and with hym goth his wyf.	He went to bed, and with him went his wife.
As any jay she light was and jolyf,	She was as jolly and as light as a jay;
So was hir joly whistle wel ywet.	She had had plenty to drink.
The cradel at hir beddes feet is set,	The cradle was set at the foot of her bed,
To rokken, and to yeve the child to sowke.	So it could be rocked, and so she could feed the child.
And whan that dronken al was in the crowke,	And when they are drunk up everything in the jug
To bedde wente the doghter right anon;	The daughter went straight up to bed;
To bedde goth Aleyn and also John;	So did Alan and also John;
Ther nas na moore, - hem nebede no dwale.	That was all of them; none of them needed a sleeping potion.
This millere hath so wisely bibbed ale	The miller had swilled down so much ale
That as an hors he fnorteth in his sleep,	That he snorted like a horse in his sleep,
Ne of his tayl bihynde he took no keep.	And he didn't take any account of what was behind them.
His wyf bar hym a burdon, a ful strong;	His wife joined in with a chorus, very strong;
Men myghte hir rowtyng heere two furlong;	Men could have heard her snoring two furlongs away;
The wenche rowteth eek, par compaignye.	The girl joined in as well, to keep them company.
Aleyn the clerk, that herde this melodye,	Alan the student, who heard this melody,
He poked John, and seyde, "Slepestow?	Poked John, and said, "Are you asleep?
Herdestow evere slyk a sang er now?	Did you ever hear a noise like this before now?
Lo, swilk a complyn is ymel hem alle,	Look, what a service they are all singing!
A wilde fyr upon thair bodyes falle!	May a wildfire fall down on their bodies!
Wha herkned evere slyk a ferly thyng?	Whoever heard of such a terrible racket?
Ye, they sal have the flour of il endyng.	But they shall be the ones to come out worst.

This lange nyght ther tydes me na reste;	All through this long night I will not get any rest;
But yet, nafors, al sal be for the beste.	But never mind, it will all be for the best.
For, John," seyde he, "als evere moot I thryve,	For, John," he said, "I would be eternally happy
If that I may, yon wenche wil I swyve.	If by some chance I could screw that girl.
Som esement has lawe yshapen us;	The law allows us some compensation;
For, John, ther is a lawe that says thus,	For, John, the law says that
That gif a man in a point be agreved,	If a man has been cheated in one way,
That in another he sal be reveled.	He can be recompensed in another.
Oure corn is stoln, sothly, it is na nay,	Our corn has been stolen, that can't be denied,
And we han had an il fit al this day;	And we have had a bad day of it;
And syn I sal have neen amendement	But since I won't get compensation
Agayn my los, I will have esement.	For my loss, I'll get my recompense,
By Goddes sale, it sal neen other bee!"	By God, I'll make sure I do!"
This John answerde, "Alayn, avyse thee!	John answered him, "Alan, you be careful!
The millere is a perilous man, "he seyde,	The miller is a dangerous man," he said,
"And gif that he out of his sleep abreyde,	"And if he is woken from his sleep
He myghte doon us bathe a vileynye."	He could do us both great harm."
Aleyn answerde, "I counte hym nat a flye."	Alan answered, "He's less than a flea to me."
And up he rist, and by the wenche he crepte.	And he got up, and crept over to the girl.
This wenche lay uprighte, and faste slepte,	She was lying on her back, and fast asleep,
Til he so ny was, er she myghte espie,	So he got so close, before she could see him,
That it had been to late for to crie,	That it was too late for her to cry out,
And shortly for to seyn, they were aton.	And to put things briefly, they were soon joined together.
Now pley, Aleyn, for I wol speke of John.	Now enjoy yourself, Alan, I shall speak about John.
This John lith stille a furlong wey or two,	John lay still for a few minutes or so,
And to hymself he maketh routhe and wo.	And he began to feel very sorry for himself.
"Allas!" quod he, "this is a wikked jape;	"Alas!" he said, "this is a nice state of affairs;
Now may I seyn that I is but an ape.	Now I'm the only one who's been made a monkey.
Yet has my felawe somwhat for his harm;	My friend has got some compensation;
He has the milleres doghter in his arm.	He's got the miller's daughter in his arms.
He auntred hym, and has his nedes sped,	He took his chance, and he's got what he needs,
And I lye as a draf-sak in my bed;	While I lie here in my bed like an old sack;
And when this jape is tald another day,	And when this story is told on other days,
I sal been halde a daf, a cokenay!	I'll be called an idiot, a weakling!
I wil arise and auntre it, by my fayth!	I will get up and do the same, I swear!
'Unhardy is unseely,' thus men sayth."	'The weak man is unhappy,' is what men say."
And up he roos, and softely he wente	So up he got, and quietly crept
Unto the cradel, and in his hand it hente,	Over to the cradle, and took it in his hands,
And baar it softe unto his beddes feet.	And carried it quietly to the foot of his bed.
Soon after this the wyf hir rowtyng leet,	Soon after this the wife let up her snoring,
And gan awake, and wente hire out to pisse,	And she woke up, and went out to have a piss,
And cam agayn, and gan hir cradel mysse	And came back in again, and couldn't find her cradle,
And groped heer and ther, but she found noon.	She looked here and there, but she could not find it.
"Allas!" quod she, "I hadde almoost mysgoon;	"Alas!" she said, "I almost missed my way;

I hadde almoost goon to the clerkes bed.	*I almost got into the students' bed.*
Ey, benedicite! thanne hadde I foule ysped."	*Praise be to God! That would have been a bad mistake."*
And forth she gooth til she the cradel fond. She gropeth alwey forther with hir hond, And foond the bed, and thoghte noght but good, By cause that the cradel by it stood, And nyste wher she was, for it was derk;	*And she went on until she found the cradle. Groping farther on with her hand She found the bed, and thought all was well, Because it was standing next to the cradle, And she didn't know where she was, for it was dark;*
But faire and wel she creep in to the clerk, And lith ful stille, and wolde han caught a sleep.	*She happily climbed in beside the student, And lay there silent, and would have gone to sleep.*
Withinne a while this John the clerk up leep, And on this goode wyf he leith on soore.	*After a moment John the student leapt up, And flung himself right on top of this good wife.*
So myrie a fit ne hadde she nat ful yoore;	*She hadn't had such a good bout in many years;*
He priketh harde and depe as he were mad.	*He pricked her hard and deep as if he'd gone mad.*
This joly lyf han thise two clerkes lad Til that the thridde cok bigan to synge.	*The two students certainly had a jolly time Until the third cock began to grow.*
Aleyn wax wery in the dawenynge, For he had swonken al the longe nyght,	*Alan became very tired as dawn approached, For he had been screwing the whole night through,*
And seyde, "Fare weel, Malyne, sweete wight! The day is come, I may no lenger byde; But everemo, wher so I go or ryde, I is thyn awen clerk, swa have I seel!" "Now, deere lemman," quod she, "go, far weel! But er thow go, o thyng I wol thee telle: Whan that thou wendest homward by the melle, Right at the entre of the dore bihynde Thou shalt a cake of half a busshel fynde That was ymaked of thyn owene mele, Which that I heelp my sire for to stele. And, goode lemman, God thee save and kepe!"	*And he said, "Farewell, Melanie, lovely girl! Day has come, I cannot stay here; But from now on, wherever I go, I will always be your man, I swear to it!" "Now, sweetheart," she said, "Go, farewell! But before you go, I will tell you one thing. When you walk home past the mill, Right at the entrance, just behind the door, You will find a loaf made of half a bushel, Which was made with your own flour, Which I helped my father to steal. And, darling, may God save you and keep you!"*
And with that word almoost she gan to wepe.	*And with the words she almost began to weep.*
Aleyn up rist, and thoughte, "Er that it dawe I wol crepen in by my felawe," And fond the cradel with his hand anon. "By God," thoughte he, al wrang I have mysgon. Myn heed is toty of my swynk to-nyght, That makes me that I ga nat aright. I woot wel by the cradel I have mysgo; Heere lith the millere and his wyf also."	*Alan got up, and thought, "Before dawn comes I'll slip into bed next to my friend," And he quickly found the cradle by feel. "By God," he thought, "I have gone all wrong. I must be dizzy through all that screwing, And that has put me on the wrong path. I can tell from this cradle I've made a mistake; This is where the miller and his wife are lying."*
And forth he goth, a twenty devel way, Unto the bed ther as the millere lay. He wende have cropen by his felawe John,	*On he went, the devil's way, Up to the bed where the miller lay. He thought he was creeping in next to his friend John,*
And by the millere in the creep anon,	*And so he got in next to the miller,*

And caughte hym by the nekke, and softe he spak.	And caught him by the neck, and quietly he spoke.
He seyde, "Thou John, thou swynes-heed, awak, / For Cristes saule, and heer a noble game.	Saying: "John, you old pig's head, wake up, / For Christ's sake, and hear about a fabulous trick.
For by that lord called is seint Jame, / As I have thries in this shorte nyght / Swyved the milleres doghter bolt upright, / Whil thow hast, as a coward, been agast."	For I shall swear by good St James, / That three times in this short night / I screwed that miller's daughter on her back, / While you were lying here scared like a coward."
"Ye, false harlot," quod the millere, "hast? / A, false traitor! false clerk!" quod he, / Tow shalt be deed, by Goddes dignitee! / Who dorste be so boold to disparage / My doghter, that is come of swich lynage?' / And by the throte-bolle he caughte Alayn, / And he hente hym despitously agayn, / And on the nose he smoot hym with his fest. / Doun ran the blody streem upon his brest; / And in the floor, with nose and mouth tobroke,	"You scoundrel," said the miller, "have you? / You false traitor! You false student!" he said, / "You're going to die, I swear to God! / Who dares be so bold as to slander / My daughter, who is so highborn?" / And he caught Alan by the throat / And threw him around without pity, / And smashed him in the nose with his fist. / The bloody stream ran down his chest; / And he fell to the floor, with a broken nose and teeth,
They walwe as doon two pigges in a poke; / And up they goon, and doun agayn anon,	They rolled around like two pigs in a bag; / And up they got, and then again they were down,
Til that the millere sporned at a stoon, / And doun he fil bakward upon his wyf, / That wiste no thyng of this nyce stryf; / For she was falle aslepe a lite wight / With John the clerk, that waked hadde al nyght,	Until the miller tripped over a stone, / And fell down backwards on his wife, / Who knew nothing about this foolish fight; / For she had fallen asleep a little while before / With John the student, who had kept her awake all night,
And with the fal out of hir sleep she breyde. / "Help! hooly croys of Bromeholm," she seyde, / 'In manus tuas! Lord, to thee I calle!	But with the fall she jumped out of her sleep. / "Help! Holy cross of Bromholm!" she shouted, / "I put myself in your hands! Lord I call on you!
Awak, Symond! The feend is on me falle. / Myn herte is broken; help! I nam but deed / Ther lyth oon upon my wombe and on myn heed.	Wake up, Simon! The devil has fallen on me. / My heart is broken, help, I'm almost dead! / There's one lying on my stomach, and one across my head.
Help. Symkyn, for the false clerkes fighte!"	Help, Simpkin, these treacherous students are fighting!"
This John stirte up as faste as ever he myghte, / And graspeth by the walles to and fro,	John got up as quickly as he possibly could, / And started feeling along the sides of the walls,
To fynde a staf; and she stirte up also, / And knew the estres bet than dide this John,	To find a stick; she got up also, / And as she knew the room better than this John did
And by the wal a staf she foond anon, / And saugh a litel shymeryng of a light, / For at an hole in shoon the moone bright;	She soon found a stick against the wall, / And she saw a little glimpse of light, / For the moon was shining in brightly through a hole;
And by that light she saugh hem bothe two, / But sikerly she nyste who was who, / But as she saugh a whit thyng in hir ye.	And in that light she saw the two of them, / But she certainly didn't know who was who, / But then she saw a white thing with her eye,

And whan she gan this white espye,	*And when she had seen this white,*
She wende the clerk hadde wered a volupeer,	*She remembered the clerk had worn a nightcap,*
And with the staf she drow ay neer and neer,	*And so she came nearer and nearer with her stick,*
And wende han hit this Aleyn at the fulle, And smoot the millere on the pyled skulle, That doun he gooth, and cride, "Harrow! I dye!"	*And meaning to smash Alan over the head, She hit the Miller on his bald white skull, So that he collapsed, crying, "Help me! I'm dying!"*
Thise clerkes beete hym weel and lete hym lye;	*These students gave them a good beating, and left him lying there;*
And greythen hem, and tooke hir hors anon, And eek hire mele, and on hir wey they gon. And at the mille yet they tooke hir cake	*Then they got dressed, and got their horse, And also their flour, and went on their way. And they looked in at the mill to take their loaf,*
Of half a busshel flour, ful wel ybake.	*Which had been well baked from their own half bushel of flour.*
Thus is the proude millere wel ybete, And hath ylost the gryndynge of the whete, And payed for the soper everideel Of Aleyn and of John, that bette hym weel.	*And so the arrogant miller was well beaten, And lost his contract for grinding the wheat, And also paid for the whole two suppers Of Alan and John, who gave him a good beating.*
His wyf is swyved, and his doghter als.	*His wife has been screwed, and his daughter also,*
Lo, swich it is a millere to be fals! And therfore this proverbe is seyd ful sooth, 'Hym thar nat wene wel that yvele dooth'; A gylour shal hymself bigyled be. And God, that sitteth heighte in magestee, Save al this compaignye, grete and smale! Thus have I quyt the Millere in my tale.	*That's what happens to a miller who cheats! And so this proverb is proved well true: "Evil comes to those who do evil"; A fraudster will be cheated himself. And God, who sits in judgement on high, Save all this company, great and small! So I have paid the miller back with my tale.*
Heere is ended the Reves Tale	*This is the end of the Reeve's tale.*

The Cook's Tale

The Prologue

The Prologe of the Cokes Tale

The COOK of Londoun, whil the Reve spak,

For joye him thoughte, he clawed him on the bak.

"Ha! ha!" quod he, "for Criste passioun,
This miller hadde a sharp conclusioun
Upon his argument of herbergage.
Wel seyde Salomon in his langage,
`Ne bryng nat every man into thyn hous,'
For herberwynge by nyghte is perilous.

Wel oghte a man avysed for to be,
Whom that be broghte into his pryvetee.
I pray to God so yeve me sorwe and care,
If evere sitthe I highte Hogge of Ware,

Herde I a millere bettre yset awerk.

He hadde a jape of malice in the derk.
But God forbede that we stynte heere,
And therfore, if ye vouche-sauf to here
A tale of me that am a povre man,
I wol yow telle, as wel as evere I kan,
A litel jape that fil in oure citee."

Oure Hoost answerde and seide, "I graunte it thee,

Now telle on, Roger, looke that it be good,
For many a pastee hastow laten blood,
And many a Jakke of Dovere hastow sold
That hath been twies hoot and twies coold.
Of many a pilgrim hastow Cristes curs,
For of thy percely yet they fare the wors,

That they han eten with thy stubbel goos,
For in thy shoppe is many a flye loos.
Now telle on, gentil Roger, by thy name,
But yet I pray thee, be nat wroth for game;
A man may seye ful sooth in game and pley."
"Thou seist ful sooth," quod Roger, "by my fey;

But `sooth pley quaad pley,' as the Flemyng seith.

And therfore, Herry Bailly, by thy feith,
Be thou nat wrooth, er we departen heer,
Though that my tale be of an hostileer.
But nathelees I wol nat telle it yit,

The Cook's Prologue

*The cook from London, while the Reeve was speaking,
Was filled with pleasure, and slapped him on the back.
"Ha ha!" he said, "in the name of Christ,
That miller got a pretty sharp punishment
For letting strangers stay.
What Solomon said was very true,
"Be careful who you let into your house,"
For harbouring strangers by night can be dangerous.
A man should certainly be careful
Who he brings into his private home.
May God punish me with sorrow and care
If I have ever, since I have been called Hogge of Ware,
Heard of a miller getting a better comeuppance.
A wicked joke was played on him in the dark.
But God forbid that we should stop here,
And therefore, if you will listen to me,
And hear a tale from one who is a poor man,
I will tell you, as best as I possibly can
Of a little trick that was played in our city."*

*Our host answered and said, "I grant that to you,
Now speak on, Roger, make sure it's good,
For you have kept meat out of many a pasty,
And many Jack Dover cakes you have sold
That have been reheated more than once.
Many pilgrims have given you Christ's curse,
For the suffering they've got from the parsley you used,
When they have eaten your produce,
For there are many flies in your shop.
Now speak on, sweet Roger, on you go,
But please, don't be angry with my jokes;
There's many a true word is said in jest."
"You're telling the truth," said Roger, "I don't think;
But as the Flemish say, if it's true it's not a good joke.
And so, Harry Bailey, by your faith,
Don't you be cross, before we're finished here,
If my tale is about an innkeeper.
But still, I won't tell that one yet,*

But er we parte, ywis, thou shalt be quit."

And ther-with-al he lough and made cheere,
And seyde his tale, as ye shul after heere.

But before we part I'll pay you back for your jokes."

And then he laughed, and with great jollity
He told his tale, as you shall hear.

The Tale

Heere bigynneth the Cookes Tale

A prentys whilom dwelled in oure citee,
And of a craft of vitailliers was hee.
Gaillard he was as goldfynch in the shawe,
Broun as a berye, a propre short felawe,
With lokkes blake, ykembd ful fetisly.
Dauncen he koude so wel and jolily
That he was cleped Perkyn Revelour.
He was as ful of love and paramour
As is the hyve ful of hony sweete:
Wel was the wenche with hym myghte meete.
At every bridale wolde he synge and hoppe;

He loved bet the taverne than the shoppe.
For whan ther any ridyng was in Chepe,
Out of the shoppe thider wolde he lepe -
Til that he hadde al the sighte yseyn,

And daunced wel, he wolde nat come ayeyn -
And gadered hym a meynee of his sort

To hoppe and synge and maken swich disport;
And ther they setten stevene for to meete
To pleyen at the dys in swich a streete.
For in the toune nas ther no prentys
That fairer koude caste a paire of dys
Than Perkyn koude, and therto he was free
Of his dispense, in place of pryvetee.

That fond his maister wel in his chaffare;
For often tyme he foond his box ful bare.
For sikerly a prentys revelour
That haunteth dys, riot, or paramour,
His maister shal it in his shoppe abye,
Al have he no part of the mynstralcye.
For thefte and riot, they been convertible
Al konne he pleye on gyterne or ribible.

Revel and trouthe, as in a lowe degree,
They been ful wrothe al day, as men may see.
This joly prentys with his maister bood,
Til he were ny out of his prentishood,
Al were he snybbed bothe erly and late,
And somtyme lad with revel to Newegate.

But atte laste his maister hym bithoghte,
Upon a day, whan he his papir soughte,
Of a proverbe that seith this same word,

The beginning of the Cook's tale

There was an apprentice who lived in our city,
And his profession was that of a grocer.
He was as happy as a goldfinch in the wood,
Brown has a berry, well built and short,
With black hair, very well combed.
He could dance so well and prettily
That he was called Perkyn the reveller.
He was as packed full of love and passion
As the hive is of sweet honey:
It was a lucky girl who came across him.
At every wedding feast he would sing and dance,
And he loved the tavern better than his shop.
If there was any party there in Cheapside,
He would rush straight out of the shop,
Until he had seen everything that was going on,
And danced his fill, he would not return,
And he gathered to him many fellows of his type
To dance and sing and make that sort of fun;
And they would make appointments to meet
To play at dice in such and such a street.
In the whole town there was no apprentice
Who was better at throwing the dice
Than Perkyn was, and so he could be generous
With his cash, when he was in trusted company.

His master discovered this to his expense;
For often he found his cash box empty.
For certainly a revelling apprentice
Who loves dice, dancing and the women,
Will make his master pay the price,
Even though he hasn't been having any fun.
Riotous behaviour and theft go hand-in-hand,
And he played both on the guitar and the fiddle.
Revelling and truth, for a lowborn man,
Are always at odds, as everyone can see.
This jolly apprentice lived with his master,
Until his apprenticeship was nearly finished,
Though he was punished day in day out,
And sometimes imprisoned in Newgate for drinking.
But at last his master suddenly thought,
One day, when he was looking for his ledger,
Of the proverb which says this:

107

'Wel bet is roten appul out of hoord	"It's better to take a rotten apple out of the barrel
Than that it rotie al the remenaunt.'	Than to let it infect all the others."
So fareth it by a riotous servaunt;	That's what should be done with a drunken servant;
It is ful lasse harm to lete hym pace,	It does less harm to let him go,
Than he shende alle the servantz in the place	Than to let him ruin all the other servants.
Therfore his maister yaf hym acquitance,	Therefore his master turned him out,
And bad hym go, with sorwe and with meschance!	And told him to go, and wished him bad luck!
And thus this joly prentys hadde his leve.	And so the jolly apprentice took his leave.
Now lat hym riote al the nyghte or leve.	Now he could dance all night, or not, as he pleased,
And for ther is no theef withoute a lowke,	And since there is no thief without an accomplice
That helpeth hym to wasten and to sowke	To help him waste away all the things
Of that he brybe kan or borwe may,	That he can steal or borrow on the way,
Anon he sente his bed and his array	He straight away sent his bedding and his clothes
Unto a compeer of his owene sort,	To a friend, a man after his own heart,
That lovede dys, and revel, and disport,	Who loved dice, and dancing, and fun,
And hadde a wyf that heeld for contenance	And had a wife who kept a shop for appearance sake,
A shoppe, and swyved for hir sustenance.	But sold herself to make a living.

(Chaucer did not finish this tale.)

The Lawyer's Tale

Introduction

Introduction to the Man of Law's Tale

The wordes of the Hoost to the compaignye.

Oure Hooste saugh wel that the brighte sonne
The ark of his artificial day hath ronne
The ferthe part, and half an houre and moore;

And though he were nat depe expert in loore,

He wiste it was the eightetethe day
Of Aprill, that is messager to May;
And saugh wel, that the shadwe of every tree

Was as in lengthe the same quantitee
That was the body erect that caused it,
And therfore by the shadwe he took his wit
That Phebus, which that shoon so clere and brighte,
Degrees was fyve and fourty clombe on highte;

And for that day, as in that latitude,
It was ten at the clokke, he gan conclude,
And sodeynly he plighte his hors aboute.-

"Lordynges," quod he, "I warne yow, al this route,
The fourthe party of this day is gon.
Now for the love of God and of Seint John,
Leseth no tyme, as ferforth as ye may.

Lordynges, the tyme wasteth nyght and day,
And steleth from us, what pryvely slepynge,

And what thurgh necligence in oure wakynge,
As dooth the streem, that turneth nevere agayn,
Descendynge fro the montaigne into playn.
Wel kan Senec and many a philosopher

Biwaillen tyme, moore than gold in cofre.

For 'Los of catel may recovered be,
But los of tyme shendeth us,' quod he.
It wol nat come agayn, withouten drede,
Namoore than wole Malkynes maydenhede,
Whan she hath lost it in hir wantownesse.
Lat us nat mowlen thus in ydelnesse;

Sir Man of Lawe," quod he, "so have ye blis,
Telle us a tale anon, as forward is.
Ye been submytted thurgh youre free assent

Introduction to the Lawyer's Tale

What the host said to the company

*Our host could clearly see that the bright sun
Had run through the course of his day
A quarter of the way, plus half an hour or more;*

And though he wasn't an expert in such matters,

*He knew that it was the eighteenth day
Of April, the precursor to May;
And he could clearly see that shadow of every tree*

*Was the same in length as the height
Of the tree which caused it,
And so he could calculate from shadow
That the sun, shining so clear and bright,
Had climbed up to an angle of forty-five degrees to the Earth;*

*So that for that day, in that place,
He could tell it was ten o'clock,
And suddenly he wheeled his horse around.*

*"My lords," he said, "I must warn you all
That a quarter of the day has passed.
Now for the love of God and St John
Let's waste no more time, let's do the best we can.*

*My Lords, time runs away night and day,
Always slipping away from us, what with sleeping,*

*And what we waste when we are awake,
Like a stream that never turns back
Falling down from the mountain to the plains.
Well might Seneca, and many other philosophers,*

Think that lost time was more valuable than gold.

*He said, "Loss of property can be recovered,
But loss of time ruins us."
It will never come back, once it's gone,
Any more than Malkin's virginity,
Once she's lost it through her sluttiness.
Let's not sit here and rot through laziness;*

*Sir Lawyer," he said, "for your salvation,
Tell us a tale now, as the agreement is.
You freely agreed*

110

To stonden in this cas at my juggement.	To submit yourself to my judgement in this matter.
Acquiteth yow as now of youre biheeste,	Now you must discharge your promise,
Thanne have ye do youre devoir atte leeste."	So at the least you'll have done your duty."
"Hooste," quod he, "Depardieux ich assente,	"My host," he said, "with the grace of God, I agree,
To breke forward is nat myn entente.	I don't intend to break our agreement.
Biheste is dette, and I wole holde fayn	A promise is a debt, and I will swear
Al my biheste, I kan no bettre sayn.	I keep all mine, that's all I can say.
For swich lawe as a man yeveth another wight,	If a man imposes laws on other people,
He sholde hymselven usen it by right;	He himself must stick to it as well;
Thus wole oure text, but nathelees certeyn	That's what we say, however I must say
I kan right now no thrifty tale seyn;	I haven't really got a suitable tale for you;
That Chaucer, thogh he kan but lewedly	That man Chaucer, although he only speaks the vulgar tongue,
On metres and on rymyng craftily,	Can use meter and crafty rhymes,
Hath seyd hem in swich Englissh as he kan,	Telling his stories in what English he has,
Of olde tyme, as knoweth many a man.	Of the olden days, as many people know.
And if he have noght seyd hem, leve brother,	If he hasn't told them, dear brother,
In o book, he hath seyd hem in another.	In one book, he told them in another.
For he hath toold of loveris up and doun	He told of lovers and their doings,
Mo than Ovide made of mencioun,	More of them than Ovid ever mentioned,
In hise Episteles that been ful olde;	In his very ancient Epistles;
What sholde I tellen hem, syn they ben tolde?	Why should I retell them, when they have been told?
In youthe he made of Ceys and Alcione,	When young he told stories of Ceyx and Alcyon,
And sitthen hath he spoken of everichone	And since then he has told of everyone,
Thise noble wyves and thise loveris eke.	Speaking of noble wives and also lovers.
Whoso that wole his large volume seke	Anyone who looks out that great book
Cleped the Seintes Legende of Cupide,	Called the Legend of Good Women,
Ther may he seen the large woundes wyde	Can see the great wounds done
Of Lucresse, and of Babilan Tesbee,	To Lucrece, and Babylonian Thisbe,
The swerd of Dido for the false Enee,	The sword Dido used when wronged by false Aeneas,
The tree of Phillis for hir Demophon,	The tree which Phyllis planted for her Demophon,
The pleinte of Dianire and Hermyon,	The sorrows of Dianire and Hermyon,
Of Adriane and of Isiphilee,	Of Ariadne and Isiphilee,
The bareyne yle stondynge in the see,	Of the barren island standing in the sea;
The dreynte Leandre for his Erro,	Drowned Leander and his fair hero,
The teeris of Eleyne, and eek the wo	The tears of Helen, and also the woe
Of Brixseyde, and of the, Ladomea,	Of Briseis and of Laodomea,
The crueltee of the, queene Medea,	The cruelty of Queen Medea,
Thy litel children hangyng by the hals	Her little children hanging by the neck
For thy Jason, that was in love so fals.	Because of Jason, who was so false in love.
O Ypermystra, Penolopee, Alceste,	Oh Hypermnestra, Penelope, Alcestis,
Youre wyfhede he comendeth with the beste!	He recommends your wifely ways as the best!
But certeinly no word ne writeth he	But it's certain he hasn't written anything
Of thilke wikke ensample of Canacee,	About that wicked woman, Canace,
That loved hir owene brother synfully; -	Who sinfully loved her own brother;
Of swiche cursed stories I sey fy!-	I say let horrible stories like that stay untold!
Or ellis of Tyro Appollonius,	He hasn't told about Tyrian Apollonius;

How that the cursed kyng Antiochus	*Or how cursed King Antiochus*
Birafte his doghter of hir maydenhede,	*Took his daughter's virginity,*
That is so horrible a tale for to rede,	*Which is such a horrible story to read,*
Whan he hir threw upon the pavement.	*When he threw her down onto the cobbles.*
And therfore he, of ful avysement,	*And so he, very wisely,*
Nolde nevere write, in none of his sermouns,	*Would never write, in one of his stories,*
Of swiche unkynde abhomynaciouns;	*Of such unnatural abominations.*
Ne I wol noon reherce, if that I may.	*And if it's alright, neither will I.*
But of my tale how shall I doon this day?	*But what shall I tell for my tale today?*
Me were looth be likned, doutelees,	*I wouldn't like to be compared to*
To Muses that men clepe Pierides -	*The muses that men call Pierides—*
Methamorphosios woot what I mene -	*The Metamorphoses know what I mean—*
But nathelees, I recche noght a bene	*Nevertheless, I don't care a damn,*
Though I come after hym with hawebake,	*Even though I follow him with my poor fare.*
I speke in prose, and lat him rymes make."	*I'll speak in prose, let him do the rhyming."*
And with that word he, with a sobre cheere,	*Having said that, with a sober face,*
Bigan his tale, as ye shal after heere.	*He began his story, as you shall now hear.*

Prologue

The prologe of the Mannes Tale of Lawe.

O hateful harm, condicion of poverte!
With thurst, with coold, with hunger so confoundid!
To asken help thee shameth in thyn herte,
If thou noon aske, so soore artow so wounded

That verray nede unwrappeth al thy wounde hid;
Maugree thyn heed thou most for indigence

Or stele, or begge, or borwe thy despence!

Thow blamest Crist, and seist ful bitterly
He mysdeparteth richesse temporal.

Thy neighebore thou wytest synfully,
And seist thou hast to lite and he hath al.

"Parfay!" seistow, "somtyme he rekene shal,

Whan that his tayl shal brennen in the gleede,
For he noght helpeth needfulle in hir neede."

Herkne what is the sentence of the wise,
"Bet is to dyen than have indigence."
Thy selve neighebor wol thee despise,
If thou be povre, farwel thy reverence!
Yet of the wise man take this sentence,
"Alle dayes of povre men been wikke;"
Be war therfore, er thou come to that prikke.

If thou be povre, thy brother hateth thee,
And alle thy freendes fleen from thee; allas,
O riche marchauntz, ful of wele been yee!
O noble, o prudent folk, as in this cas!
Youre bagges been nat fild with ambes as,
But with sys cynk, that renneth for youre chaunce,

At Cristemasse myrie may ye daunce!

Ye seken lond and see for your wynnynges,

As wise folk ye knowen all th'estaat
Of regnes; ye been fadres of tydynges
And tales, bothe of pees and of debaat.
I were right now of tales desolaat
Nere that a marchant, goon is many a yeere,

Me taughte a tale, which that ye shal heere.

The prologue of the lawyer's tale

What a horrible thing it is to live in poverty!
Thirsty, cold, so terribly hungry!
To ask for help makes you deeply ashamed,
If you don't ask for any, you will be so wounded

That your needs will be exposed in any case;
In spite of your scruples you must from necessity

Either steal, or beg, or borrow.

You blame Christ, and you say bitterly,
That he does not share out the riches of this world properly.

You criticise your neighbour, sinfully,
Saying you don't have enough and he has everything.

"By God!" you say, "sometime he will get his comeuppance,

His backside will be burned in the fire
For not helping those who are in need.

Now listen to the judgement of the wise,
"It's better to die than to live in poverty."
Even your neighbours will despise you,
If you are poor, forget any respect!
But listen to the words of wise men,
"Poor men sin everyday;"
So make sure you do not end up in that state.

If you are poor, your brother will hate you,
And all your friends will run from you; alas,
O rich merchants, you are truly rich!
O noble, prudent folk, you're in a fine state!
Your dice cups are not filled with bad luck,
You throw sixes and fives in your games of chance,

So at Christmas you can have a fine time!

You travel overland and sea for your winnings,

And as wise folk you know the conditions
In every country; you make things happen
In both peace and war.
Right now I would not have any stories
If it wasn't for a merchant, who has been dead for many years,

Who taught me a story, which I will tell you now.

The Tale

Heere begynneth the Man of Lawe his Tale.	*Here the lawyer began his tale*
In Surrye whilom dwelte a compaignye	In Syria once there lived a company
Of chapmen riche, and therto sadde and trewe,	Of rich traders, all sober men and true,
That wyde-where senten hir spicerye,	They sent their spices throughout the world,
Clothes of gold, and satyns riche of hewe.	And cloth of gold, and richly coloured satin.
Hir chaffare was so thrifty and so newe	Their goods were so excellent and unique
That every wight hath deyntee to chaffare	That everyone wanted to trade
With hem, and eek to sellen hem hir ware.	With them, and to sell them their goods.
Now fil it, that the maistres of that sort	Now it happened that the leaders of this company
Han shapen hem to Rome for to wende;	Decided that they would go to Rome;
Were it for chapmanhode, or for disport,	Either for business or just for fun;
Noon oother message wolde they thider sende,	They wouldn't send any messages there,
But comen hemself to Rome, this is the ende,	They would go to Rome themselves, that is certain,
And in swich place as thoughte hem avantage	And they chose a place that they thought was best
For hir entente, they take hir herbergage.	For their accommodation, and settled down there.
Sojourned han thise marchantz in that toun	These merchants had stayed in that town
A certein tyme, as fil to hire plesance.	For a certain amount of time, according to their pleasure.
And so bifel, that th'excellent renoun	And it so happened that the great reputation
Of the Emperoures doghter, dame Custance,	Of the Emperor's daughter, Dame Constance,
Reported was, with every circumstance	Was told, with everything about her,
Unto thise Surryen marchantz in swich wyse	To these Syrian merchants in a way
Fro day to day, as I shal yow devyse.	Which I shall now tell you about.
This was the commune voys of every man:	This was what every man in Rome said:
"Oure Emperour of Rome, God hym see,	"Our Roman emperor, God bless him,
A doghter hath that, syn the world bigan,	Has a daughter that has not been matched,
To rekene as wel hir goodnesse as beautee,	For either her goodness or her beauty,
Nas nevere swich another as is shee.	Ever since the world began.
I prey to God in honour hir susteene	I pray to God that he looks after her
And wolde she were of all Europe the queene!	And I wish that she were queen of all of Europe!
In hir is heigh beautee, withoute pride,	She is a great beauty, with no pride,
Yowthe, withoute grenehede or folye,	She is young, without being crude or vulgar;
To alle hir werkes vertu is hir gyde,	In everything she does, virtue guides her;
Humblesse hath slayn in hir al tirannye,	Her meekness removes any chance of tyranny,
She is mirour of alle curteisye,	She is the model of courtesy,
Hir herte is verray chambre of hoolynesse,	Her heart is truly a holy shrine,
Hir hand ministre of fredam for almesse."	And her hand seems to be made for generosity."
And al this voys was sooth, as God is trewe!	And all this was true, I swear to God!

But now to purpos, lat us turne agayn;	But let's get back to our story;
Thise marchantz han doon fraught hir shippes newe,	These merchants had built their new ships,
And whan they han this blisful mayden sayn,	And when they had seen this lovely girl
Hoom to Surrye been they went ful fayn,	They wanted to get back home to Syria,
And doon hir nedes as they han doon yoore,	And carry on with their business as they had done before,
And lyven in wele, I kan sey yow namoore.	Living in luxury, I can't tell you more.
Now fil it, that thise marchantz stode in grace	Now so happened that these merchants were viewed favourably
Of hym, that was the Sowdan of Surrye.	By the one who was Sultan of Syria.
For whan they cam from any strange place,	When they came from any foreign place
He wolde, of his benigne curteisye,	He would, from his kind courtesy,
Make hem good chiere, and bisily espye	Give them a good welcome, and eagerly ask them
Tidynges of sondry regnes, for to leere	For details of other countries, to learn
The wondres that they myghte seen or heere.	About the wonders that might be seen or heard there.
Amonges othere thynges, specially	Amongst other things, these merchants
Thise marchantz han hym toold of dame Custance	Especially told him of Dame Constance,
So greet noblesse in ernest, ceriously,	Who was so noble, they told of her so earnestly
That this Sowdan hath caught so greet plesance	That the Sultan got a very good impression of her,
To han hir figure in his remembrance,	And began to think of her all the time,
That all his lust and al his bisy cure	So that all of his desires, and his plans,
Was for to love hir, while his lyf may dure.	Were to love her for the rest of his life.
Paraventure in thilke large book,	Now it happened that in that great book
Which that men clepe the hevene, ywriten was	Which men call heaven, it was written
With sterres, whan that he his birthe took,	In the stars, when he was born,
That he for love sholde han his deeth, allas!	That he would die for love, alas!
For in the sterres clerer than is glas	For it is written in the stars, more clearly than glass,
Is writen, God woot, whoso koude it rede,	God knows, if someone knows how to read it,
The deeth of every man, withouten drede.	Of the death of every man, it's true.
In sterres many a wynter therbiforn	In the stars, many years ago,
Was writen the deeth of Ector, Achilles,	Were written the deaths of Hector, Achilles,
Of Pompei, Julius, er they were born,	Pompey, Julius, long before they were born;
The strif of Thebes, and of Ercules,	The trouble at Thebes, and of great Hercules,
Of Sampson, Turnus, and of Socrates	Of Sampson, Turnus, and of Socrates,
The deeth, but mennes wittes ben so dulle	Each of their deaths, but men are so stupid
That no wight kan wel rede it atte fulle.	That nobody can read the whole thing.
This Sowdan for his privee conseil sente,	This sultan sent for his privy council,
And, shortly of this matiere for to pace,	And, to cut a long story short,
He hath to hem declared his entente	He told them all about his purpose,
And seyde hem, certein, but he myghte have grace	And said to them that if he was not lucky enough
To han Custance withinne a litel space,	To get Constance for himself in a short time
He nas but deed; and charged hem in hye	He would surely die; and he ordered them to hurry
To shapen for his lyf som remedye.	To find some way to save his life.

Diverse men diverse thynges seyden;	Different men said different things;
They argumenten, casten up and doun,	They argued, going to and fro,
Many a subtil resoun forth they leyden,	Putting out many subtle theories,
They speken of magyk and abusioun;	Talking of magic and deception;
But finally, as in conclusioun,	But finally, in conclusion,
They kan nat seen in that noon avantage,	They could not see any alternative
Ne in noon oother wey, save mariage.	But for him to marry her, there was no other way.
Thanne sawe they therin swich difficultee	They saw so many difficulties appear
By wey of reson, for to speke al playn	When they were thinking of it, to say plainly,
By cause that ther was swich diversitee	Because there was such a great difference
Bitwene hir bothe lawes, that they sayn	Between the laws of the two places, that they said
They trowe that "no Cristene prince wolde fayn	They thought that "no Christian prince would allow
Wedden his child under oure lawes swete	His child to be married under our sweet laws,
That us were taught by Mahoun oure prophete."	Which were taught to us by Mohamed our profit."
And he answerde: "Rather than I lese	He answered: "Rather than lose
Custance, I wol be cristned, doutelees.	Constance, I am willing to be christened.
I moot been hires, I may noon oother chese;	I must be hers, I can belong to no other;
I prey yow, hoold youre argumentz in pees.	I pray you, do not try to argue with me.
Saveth my lyf, and beth noght recchelees	Save my life, and don't be negligent
To geten hir that hath my lyf in cure,	In your efforts to get the one who can save my life,
For in this wo I may nat longe endure."	For otherwise I won't be here for long."
What nedeth gretter dilatacioun?	Is there a greater explanation needed?
I seye, by tretys and embassadrye	I tell you, that through treaties and ambassadors,
And by the popes mediacioun,	And the intervention of the Pope,
And al the chirche and al the chivalrie,	And the whole of the church, and all the aristocracy,
That in destruccioun of Mawmettrie	That, because it would destroy Mohammedism
And in encrees of Cristes lawe deere,	And boost the Christian faith,
They been acorded, so as ye shal heere:	They all agreed, as you shall hear:
How that the Sowdan and his baronage	The Sultan and all his noblemen
And alle hise liges sholde ycristned be-	And all his servants, must all be christened–
And he shal han Custance in mariage,	And that will get him Constance as his wife,
And certein gold, I noot what quantitee,	Along with gold, I can't say how much,
And heerto founden suffisant suretee.	Which was demanded as security.
This same accord was sworn on eyther syde.	The agreement was sworn to by both sides,
Now, faire Custance, almyghty God thee gyde!	Now, fair Constance, may Almighty God be your guide!
Now wolde som men waiten, as I gesse,	Now I imagine some men are expecting
That I sholde tellen al the purveiance	That I will tell them all about the provision
That th'Emperour, of his grete noblesse,	That that Emperor, through his great nobility,
Hath shapen for his doghter dame Custance;	Had made for his daughter Dame Constance;
Wel may men knowen that so greet ordinance	But everyone should know that such a great preparation

May no man tellen in a litel clause As was arrayed for so heigh a cause.	*Cannot be told in a short space,* *Not what was arranged there.*
Bisshopes been shapen with hir for to wende, Lordes, ladies, knyghtes of renoun, And oother folk ynogh, this is th'ende, And notified is, thurghout the toun,	*Bishops were chosen to go with her,* *Lords, ladies, famous knights,* *Along with other folk, that's all I'll say,* *Except that it was ordered through the whole town*
That every wight with greet devocioun Sholde preyen Crist, that he this mariage Receyve in gree, and spede this viage.	*That every person should show great devotion* *And pray to Christ that he would bless* *Their marriage, and speed their voyage.*
The day is comen of hir departynge, I seye, the woful day fatal is come, That ther may be no lenger tariynge, But forthward they hem dressen, alle and some. Custance, that was with sorwe al overcome, Ful pale arist, and dresseth hir to wende,	*The day came when they were to leave,* *I tell you, the sorrowful fatal day had come,* *When they could no longer wait,* *But all and sundry got ready to go.* *Constance, who was overcome with sorrow,* *Got up, very pale, and dressed herself for her journey,*
For wel she seeth ther is noon oother ende.	*For she could clearly see there was no alternative.*
Allas, what wonder is it thogh she wepte, That shal be sent to strange nacioun Fro freendes that so tendrely hir kepte,	*Alas, is it any wonder that she wept,* *Being sent away to a strange country,* *Away from the friends who had looked after her so kindly,*
And to be bounden under subjeccioun Of oon, she knoweth nat his condicioun? Housbondes been alle goode, and han ben yoore,	*And to be placed under the command* *Of someone whom she knew nothing about?* *Husbands are all good, and have been for years,*
That knowen wyves! I dar sey yow namoore.	*Their wives know that! I can't say any more.*
"Fader," she seyde, "Thy wrecched child Custance,	*"Father," she said, "your wretched child Constance,*
Thy yonge doghter, fostred up so softe,	*Your young daughter, whom you brought up in such luxury,*
And ye my mooder, my soverayn plesance, Over alle thyng, out-taken Crist on-lofte,	*And you, my mother, my chief delight* *Over everything else, except for Christ who rules on high,*
Custance, youre child, hir recomandeth ofte	*Constance, your child, would like to be remembered*
Unto your grace, for I shal to Surrye Ne shal I nevere seen yow moore with eye.	*Often in your prayers, for I am going to Syria,* *And I shall never set eyes on you again.*
Allas! unto the Barbre nacioun I moste goon, syn that it is youre wille, But Crist, that starf for our savacioun, So yeve me grace hise heestes to fulfille,- I, wrecche womman, no fors though I spille! Wommen are born to thraldom and penance, And to been under mannes governance."	*Alas! I'm going to a barbarian country,* *Since that is what you have decreed,* *But Christ, who died for our salvation,* *Give me grace, I will do what he says—* *I, wretched woman, it doesn't matter if I die!* *Women are born to servitude and penance,* *And to be ruled over by men."*
I trowe at Troye, whan Pirrus brak the wal,	*I think Troy, when Pyrrhus broke through the wall;*
Or Ilion brende, ne at Thebes the Citee,	*Or Illium burned, nor when Thebes fell,*

N'at Rome for the harm thurgh Hanybal	Nor when Rome was so injured by Hannibal
That Romayns hath venqysshed tymes thre,	That the Romans were completely defeated,
Nas herd swich tendre wepyng for pitee	None of them caused such piteous weeping
As in the chambre was, for his departynge;	As there was in her room, as she left;
But forth she moot, wher-so she wepe or synge.	But she had to go, whether she wept or sang.
O firste moevyng! Crueel firmament,	Oh primaeval, cruel stars,
With thy diurnal sweigh, that crowdest ay	With your influence throwing all of them
And hurlest al from Est til Occident	From East to West,
That naturelly wolde holde another way,	Who naturally would have gone some other way,
Thy crowdyng set the hevene in swich array	Your pressure set the heavens in such a state
At the bigynnyng of this fiers viage,	At the beginning of this dangerous voyage
That cruel Mars hath slayn this mariage.	That cruel Mars killed this marriage.
Infortunat ascendent tortuous,	Alas for the unfortunate conjunction
Of which the lord is helplees falle, allas!	Which fell upon the helpless Lord!
Out of his angle into the derkeste hous!	It came into his constellation from the darkest house!
O Mars! O Atazir! As in this cas,	Oh Mars, oh Atazir, in this present case,
O fieble Moone, unhappy been thy paas!	You feeble moon, you have been too slow!
Thou knyttest thee, ther thou art nat receyved;	You are in a place where you should not be,
Ther thou were weel, fro thennes artow weyved.-	You have not reached where you ought to be.
Imprudent Emperour of Rome, allas!	Foolish emperor of Rome, alas!
Was ther no philosophre in al thy toun?	Was there no philosopher in your whole town?
Is no tyme bet than oother in swich cas?	Is there no time better than any other in this case?
Of viage is ther noon eleccioun,	Can't you choose a time to travel,
Namely to folk of heigh condicioun,	Especially for people of such nobility,
Noght whan a roote is of a burthe yknowe?	When everybody knows the days they were born?
Allas, we been to lewed or to slowe!	Alas, we are too ignorant or too slow!
To ship is brought this woful faire mayde	This poor sorrowful girl was brought to her ship,
Solempnely, with every circumstance,	With great ceremony and solemnity,
"Now Jesu Crist be with yow alle," she seyde.	"Now may Jesus Christ be with all of you," she said.
Ther nys namoore but, "Farewel faire Custance!"	There was nothing more to be said but, "Farewell, fair Constance!"
She peyneth hir to make good contenance,	She did her best to put on a brave face,
And forth I lete hir saille in this manere,	And so I will let her sail away like this,
And turne I wole agayn to my matere.	And turn back to my subject.
The mooder of the Sowdan, welle of vices,	The mother of the Sultan, who was full of vice,
Espied hath hir sones pleyne entente,	Had got news of all of her son's plans,
How he wol lete hise olde sacrifices,	How he wanted to leave the old religion,
And right anon she for hir conseil sente,	And at once she sent for her own counsel,
And they been come, to knowe what she mente,	And they came to find out what she wanted,
And whan assembled was this folk in-feere,	And when all these people were assembled,
She sette hir doun, and seyde as ye shal heere.	She sat down, and spoke as you will hear.
"Lordes," quod she, "ye knowen everichon,	"Lords," she said, "every one of you knows very well

How that my sone in point is for to lete	*That my son is intending to relinquish*
The hooly lawes of oure Alkaron,	*The holy laws of our Koran,*
Yeven by Goddes message, Makomete.	*Given to us by God's messenger, Muhammad.*
But oon avow to grete God I heete,	*But I shall make a promise to great God,*
The lyf shal rather out of my body sterte,	*I would rather lose my life*
Than Makometes lawe out of myn herte!	*Than lose the law of Mohammed from my heart!*
What sholde us tyden of this newe lawe	*What should we get from this new creed*
But thraldom to our bodies, and penance,	*But slavery for our bodies, and punishment,*
And afterward in helle to be drawe	*And afterwards we will be thrown into hell*
For we reneyed Mahoun oure creance?	*For reneging on our belief in Muhammad?*
But lordes, wol ye maken assurance	*But lords, if you will promise to do*
As I shal seyn, assentynge to my loore,	*As I say, follow my instructions,*
And I shal make us sauf for everemoore."	*I will save us all for eternity."*
They sworen and assenten every man	*Every one of them agreed and swore*
To lyve with hir, and dye, and by hir stonde,	*That they would live and die for her,*
And everich in the beste wise he kan	*And each of them, as best he could,*
To strengthen hir shal alle hise frendes fonde,	*Would recruit all his friends to her cause,*
And she hath this emprise ytake on honde,	*And she would take the business into her hands,*
Which ye shal heren, that I shal devyse.	*As you shall hear, I shall tell you about it.*
And to hem alle she spak right in this wyse:	*And she spoke to all of them in this fashion:*
"We shul first feyne us cristendom to take, -	*"At first we will pretend to become Christians,*
Coold water shal nat greve us but a lite-	*And their holy water will only annoy us—*
And I shal swich a feeste and revel make,	*And I will organise such feasting and revelry*
That, as I trowe, I shal the Sowdan quite;	*That I am sure the Sultan will believe in me;*
For thogh his wyf be cristned never so white,	*For although his wife may have been christened ever so white*
She shal have nede to wasshe awey the rede,	*Before she's finished she will have to wash off the red,*
Thogh she a font-ful water with hir lede!"	*Even if she brought a whole font full of water with her!"*
O Sowdanesse, roote of iniquitee!	*Oh Sultana, you inspirer of evil!*
Virage, thou Semyrame the secounde!	*You virago, you second Semiramis!*
O serpent under femynyntee,	*You snake dressed as a woman,*
Lik to the serpent depe in helle ybounde!	*You are like the serpent deep down in hell!*
O feyned womman, al that may confounde	*You pseudo woman, who wants to destroy*
Vertu and innocence thurgh thy malice	*Virtue and innocence through your malice,*
Is bred in thee, as nest of every vice!	*That is bred in you, you are the mother of every vice!*
O Sathan, envious syn thilke day	*O Satan, you have been envious since the day*
That thou were chaced from oure heritage,	*That you were thrown out of our inheritance,*
Wel knowestow to wommen the olde way!	*You know how to convert women to your ways!*
Thou madest Eva brynge us in servage;	*You made Eve bring us all into servitude;*
Thou wolt fordoon this Cristen mariage.	*You want to destroy this Christian marriage.*
Thyn instrument, so weylawey the while!	*You make women, alas,*
Makestow of wommen, whan thou wolt bigile.	*Your instruments, when you want to play tricks.*

This Sowdanesse, whom I thus blame and warye,	This Sultana, whom I blame and curse,
Leet prively hir conseil goon hir way.	Let her council go on their way secretly.
What sholde I in this tale lenger tarie?	What more do I have to say about this?
She rydeth to the Sowdan on a day,	She rode to see the sultan one day,
And seyde hym, that she wolde reneye hir lay,	And said to him that she would renounce her faith,
And cristendom of preestes handes fonge,	And be christened by the priests,
Repentynge hir she hethen was so longe;	Repenting for having been a heathen for so long;
Bisechynge hym to doon hir that honour	She begged him to do her the honour
That she moste han the Cristen folk to feeste.	Of letting her entertain all the Christian folk.
"To plesen hem I wol do my labour."	"I want to do my best to please them."
The Sowdan seith, "I wol doon at youre heeste,"	The Sultan said, "I will do as you wish,"
And knelynge thanketh hir of that requeste.	And he knelt down, thanking her for asking.
So gald he was, he nyste what to seye;	He was so glad that he did not know what to say;
She kiste hir sone, and hoom she gooth hir weye.	She kissed her son, and made her way home.
Arryved been this Cristen folk to londe,	Now these Christian folk reached land
In Surrye, with a greet solempne route,	In Syria, with great solemn ceremony,
And hastifliche this Sowdan sente his sonde	And at once the Sultan sent his command
First to his mooder and all the regne aboute,	First to his mother, and then to the whole kingdom,
And seyde his wyf was comen, oute of doute,	Saying his wife had definitely arrived,
And preyde hir for to ryde agayn the queene,	And asking her to ride out and meet the queen,
The honour of his regne to susteene.	To uphold the honour of his Majesty.
Greet was the prees, and riche was th'array	There was a great crush, and a rich display
Of Surryens and Romayns met yfeere;	From the Syrians and the Romans meeting there;
The mooder of the Sowdan, riche and gay,	The mother of the Sultan, richly and brightly dressed,
Receyveth hir with also glad a cheere	Gave her such a warm welcome,
As any mooder myghte hir doghter deere,	It was like that of any mother to a dear daughter,
And to the nexte citee ther bisyde	And they journeyed towards the nearest city,
A softe pass solempnely they ryde.	Riding at a solemn, stately pace.
Noght trowe I the triumphe of Julius,	I don't think that the triumph of Julius Caesar,
Of which that Lucan maketh swich a boost,	Which Lucan made such a fuss about,
Was roialler, ne moore curius	Was more royal, or more singular
Than was th'assemblee of this blisful hoost.	Than the march of this happy crowd.
But this scorpioun, this wikked goost,	But this scorpion, this wicked ghost
The Sowdanesse, for all hir falterynge	The Sultana, for all her flattery,
Caste under this ful mortally to stynge.	Was preparing to give her fatal sting.
The Sowdan comth hymself soone after this	The Sultan comes soon after this
So roially, that wonder is to telle,	So high and mighty that it is a wonder to everyone
And welcometh hir with alle joye and blis,	And welcomes her with all joy
And thus in murthe and joye I lete hem dwelle-	And thus in joy I let him stay
The fruyt of this matiere is that I telle.-	The important part of this story is what I tell
Whan tyme cam, men thoughte it for the beste,	When the time came, the men thought it was for the best

The revel stynte, and men goon to hir reste.	*That revel should stint, and the people go to their rest*
The tyme cam, this olde Sowdanesse Ordeyned hath this feeste of which I tolde, And to the feeste Cristen folk hem dresse In general, ye, bothe yonge and olde. Heere may men feeste and roialtee biholde,	*The time came when this old Sultana Had ordered up the feast which I mentioned, And the Christian folk prepared for it, Both young and old. There men could feast and see the royal family,*
And deyntees mo than I kan yow devyse;	*With more rare foods that I can describe to you;*
But al to deere they boghte it er they ryse!	*But they will have paid a high price for it before they leave the table!*
O sodeyn wo, that evere art successour To worldly blisse, spreynd with bitternesse! The ende of the joye of oure worldly labour!	*Oh sudden sorrow, that always follows Worldly happiness, full of bitterness! The end result of happiness in our worldly toils!*
Wo occupieth the fyn of oure gladnesse! Herke this conseil for thy sikernesse, Upon thy galde day have in thy minde The unwar wo or harm that comth bihynde.	*Sorrow always eventually replaces joy! Listen to this maxim to confirm this for you; On your happiest day always remember That unknown sorrow and harm is following.*
For shortly for to tellen at o word, The Sowdan and the Cristen everichone Been al tohewe and stiked at the bord,	*For, to tell you briefly, in a word, The Sultan and the Christians, all of them, Were all cut down and run through at the table,*
But it were oonly dame Custance allone. This olde Sowdanesse, cursed krone, Hath with hir freendes doon this cursed dede, For she hirself wolde all the contree lede.	*Except for the Dame Constance. This old Sultana, this cursed crone, Did this wicked thing with her supporters, For she wanted to rule the country herself.*
Ne was ther Surryen noon, that was converted, That of the conseil of the Sowdan woot, That he nas al tohewe er he asterted. And Custance han they take anon foot-hoot And in a ship all steerelees, God woot, They han hir set, and biddeth hir lerne saille Out of Surrye agaynward to Ytaille.	*No Syrian who had been converted, On the orders of the Sultan, Was spared from the slaughter. And now they rushed Constance Onto a ship without a rudder; They put her in it, and told her to learn to sail From Syria back to Italy.*
A certein tresor that she thider ladde,	*They put in some of the treasures she had brought,*
And, sooth to seyn, vitaille greet plentee They han hir yeven, and clothes eek she hadde, And forth she sailleth in the salte see. O my Custance, ful of benignytee, O Emperoures yonge doghter deere, He that is lord of Fortune be thy steere!	*And, to tell the truth, plenty of food, And they also gave her clothing, And she set out upon the salty sea. Oh my Constance, full of goodness, Oh dear young daughter of the Emperor, May the Lord of Fortune guide you!*
She blesseth hir, and with ful pitous voys Unto the croys of Crist thus seyde she, "O cleere, o welful auter, hooly croys, Reed of the lambes blood, ful of pitee, That wesshe the world fro the olde iniquitee, Me fro the feend and fro his clawes kepe,	*She crossed herself, and in a sorrowing voice She spoke to the cross of Jesus, "Oh bright, wonderful altar, holy cross, Red with the blood of the Lamb, full of sorrow, Who saved the world from its ancient sins, Keep the devil and his claws away from me,*

That day that I shal drenchen in the depe.

Victorious tree, proteccioun of trewe,
That oonly worthy were for to bere
The Kyng of Hevene with his woundes newe,

The white lamb that hurt was with the spere,

Flemere of feendes out of hym and here
On which thy lymes feithfully extenden,
Me keep, and yif me myght my lyf tamenden."

Yeres and dayes fleteth this creature
Thurghout the See of Grece unto the Strayte
Of Marrok, as it was hir aventure.
On many a sory meel now may she bayte;
After hir deeth ful often may she wayte,
Er that the wilde wawes wol hire dryve
Unto the place ther she shal arryve.

Men myghten asken why she was nat slayn?
Eek at the feeste who myghte hir body save?
And I answere to that demande agayn,

Who saved Danyel in the horrible cave,
Ther every wight save he, maister and knave,
Was with the leoun frete, er he asterte?

No wight but god, that he bar in his herte.

God liste to shewe his wonderful miracle
In hir, for we sholde seen his myghty werkis.

Crist, which that is to every harm triacle,
By certeine meenes ofte, as knowen clerkis,
Dooth thyng for certein ende, that ful derk is
To mannes wit, that for oure ignorance
Ne konne noght knowe his prudent purveiance.

Now, sith she was nat at the feeste yslawe,
Who kepte hir fro the drenchyng in the see?
Who kepte Jonas in the fisshes mawe
Til he was spouted up at Nynyvee?
Wel may men knowe it was no wight but he
That kepte peple Ebrayk from hir drenchynge,
With drye feet thurghout the see passynge.

Who bad the foure spirites of tempest,
That power han t'anoyen lond and see,

"Bothe north and south, and also west and est,
Anoyeth neither see, ne land, ne tree?"
Soothly, the comandour of that was he,
That fro the tempest ay this womman kepte,

On the day when I drown in the deep.

Victorious tree, Protector of the faithful,
The only thing that was good enough to carry
The King of Heaven with his new wounds,

The white lamb that was run through with the spear,
The exorciser of daemons from all people
Who give themselves into your arms,
Protect me, and give me strength to repent my sins."

For many days and years this maiden drifted
Across the seas of Greece, to the Strait
Of Gibraltar, this was how it chanced.
By now she was eating pitiful meals;
She was expecting her death at any time,
Before the wild waves would drive her
To the place where she would land.

Men might ask, "Why was she not killed?
Who was there at the feast who saved her?"
And I will answer your question with a question;

Who saved Daniel in that horrible cave,
Where every other man, master and servant,
Was killed by the lions before he could escape?

No one but God, whom he kept in his heart.

God chose to work this wonderful miracle
For her, so that we could see his mighty works.

Christ, who is the medicine for all ills,
In certain ways, as all learned men know,
Does things with a purpose in mind which
Men cannot see, in our ignorance
We cannot know his protecting foresight.

Now, since she was not killed at the feast,
Who kept her from drowning in the sea?
Who kept Jonah in the fish's mouth
Until he was spat out at Nineveh?
All men know it was no one but the one
Who saved the Hebrew people from drowning,
Letting them cross the sea with dry feet.

Who commanded the four spirits of storms,
That have the power to destroy on land and sea,

"Both north and south, and also west and east,
Do not attack the sea, the land nor the trees?"
Truly, it was the commander of all these things
Who kept the storm away from this woman,

As wel eek when she wook as whan she slepte.	*As much when she was sleeping as when she was awake.*
Where myghte this womman mete and drynke have? Thre yeer and moore how lasteth hir vitaille?	*How did this woman get her meat and drink? How did her provisions last her three years or more?*
Who fedde the Egypcien Marie in the cave, Or in desert? No wight but Crist, sanz faille.	*Who gave the Egyptian Mary food in her cave, In the desert? No one but Christ, without doubt.*
Fyve thousand folk it was as greet mervaille	*In a great miracle five thousand people were fed*
With loves fyve and fisshes two to feede; God sente his foyson at hir grete neede.	*With five loaves and two fish; God sent her his plenty in her hour of need.*
She dryveth forth into oure occian Thurghout oure wilde see, til atte laste Under an hoold that nempnen I ne kan, Fer in Northhumberlond, the wawe hir caste,	*She sailed out into our ocean, Right across our wild seas, until at last By a castle which I cannot name, Far off in Northumberland, her ship came ashore,*
And in the sond hir ship stiked so faste That thennes wolde it noght of al a tyde, The wyl of Crist was that she sholde abyde.	*And stuck so fast in the stands That it could not be moved by any tide, It was the will of Christ that she should stay there.*
The constable of the castel doun is fare To seen his wrak, and al the ship he soghte, And foond this wery womman ful of care,	*The constable of the castle came down To see the wreck, and he searched the ship, And found this exhausted woman, full of sorrow;*
He foond also the tresor that she broghte, In hir langage mercy she bisoghte,	*He also found the treasure that she brought, And she asked him for mercy in his own language,*
The lyf out of hire body for to twynne, Hir to delivere of wo that she was inne.	*Asking him to cut the life out of her body, To free her from all of her sorrow.*
A maner Latyn corrupt was hir speche, But algates therby was she understonde. The constable, whan hym lyst no lenger seche,	*She spoke a kind of pidgin Latin, By which however she was understood. The constable, when he had finished searching,*
This woful womman broghte he to the londe. She kneleth doun and thanketh Goddes sonde; But what she was, she wolde no man seye, For foul ne fair, thogh that she sholde deye.	*Brought this sorrowing woman onto the land. She knelt down and gave thanks to God; But she would tell no man who she was, For threats or bribes, even if it cost her her life.*
She seyde, she was so mazed in the see	*She said that she had become so bewildered at sea*
That she forgat hir mynde, by hir trouthe. The constable hath of hir so greet pitee, And eke his wyf, that they wepen for routhe. She was so diligent, withouten slouthe To serve and plesen everich in that place, That alle hir loven that looken on hir face.	*That she had lost her mind, she swore to it. The constable felt very sorry for her, And so did his wife, so that they wept with pity. She worked so hard, never slacking, To serve and please everyone in that place, That everyone who saw her loved her.*
This constable and dame Hermengyld his wyf	*This constable and his wife, Dame*

Were payens, and that contree everywhere;	Hermengild, Were pagans, and so were all the people of that country;
But Hermengyld loved hir right as hir lyf,	But Hermengild loved her as much as life itself,
And Custance hath so longe sojourned there In orisons, with many a bitter teere,	And Constance stayed there for so long, Saying so many prayers, with many bitter tears,
Til Jesu hath converted thurgh his grace Dame Hermengyld, constablesse of that place.	Until eventually through the grace of Christ Dame Hermengild, the lady of that place, was converted.
In al that lond no Cristen dorste route,	No Christians dared to travel through that land,
Alle Cristen folk been fled fro that contree Thurgh payens that conquereden al aboute The plages of the North by land and see. To Walys fledde the Cristyanytee Of olde Britons, dwellynge in this ile; Ther was hir refut for the meene-while.	All Christian folk had fled the country, For it had been conquered by pagans, All the lands of the North, from land and sea. The ancient British Christians living On this island fled away to Wales; That was their refuge for the time being.
But yet nere cristene Britons so exiled	But Christianity had not been so driven out of Britain
That ther nere somme that in hir privetee Honoured Crist, and hethen folk bigiled,	That there were none who did not privately Honour Christ, and deceive the heathen people,
And ny the castel swiche ther dwelten three;	And near the castle there were three such men;
That oon of hem was blynd, and myghte nat see, But it were with thilke eyen of his mynde, With whiche men seen, after that they ben blynde.	One of them was blind, and could not see, Except by using the eyes of his mind, With which men can see, after they go blind.
Bright was the sonne as in that someres day, For which the constable and his wyf also And Custance han ytake the righte way Toward the see, a furlong wey or two, To pleyen, and to romen, to and fro, And in hir walk this blynde man they mette, Croked and oold, with eyen faste yshette.	It was a bright and sunny summer's day When the constable and also his wife And Constance took the path Down to the sea, a furlong or so away, To exercise and to stroll to and fro, And on their walk they met this blind man, Crooked and old, with his eyes shut tight.
"In name of Crist," cride this olde Britoun, "Dame Hermengyld, yif me my sighte agayn." This lady weex affrayed of the soun, Lest that hir housbonde, shortly for to sayn, Wolde hir for Jesu Cristes love han slayn, Til Custance made hir boold, and bad hir wirche	"In the name of Christ," this old Briton cried, "Dame Hermengild, give me back my sight." The lady was terrified when she heard this, In case her husband, to put it bluntly, Would kill her for her love of Jesus, Until Constance strengthened her, and told her to do
The wyl of Crist, as doghter of his chirche.	The will of Christ, as a daughter of his church.
The constable weex abasshed of that sight, And seyde, "What amounteth all this fare!" Custance answerde, "Sire, it is Cristes myght,	The constable was astonished by that sight, And asked, "What is going on here!" Constance answered, "Sir, it is the strength of Christ,
That helpeth folk out of the feendes snare."	Who keeps people out of the traps of the devil."

And so ferforth she gan oure lay declare,	And she so fervently described our faith
That she the constable, er that it were eve	That before the evening she had converted the constable
Converteth, and on Crist maketh hym bileve.	To believing in the church of Christ.
This constable was no-thyng lord of this place	This constable was not the lord of this place
Of which I speke, ther he Custance fond;	Of which I have spoken, where he found Constance;
But kepte it strongly many wyntres space	But he had ruled over it for many years
Under Alla, kyng of al Northhumbrelond,	Under the rule of Alla, King of Northumberland,
That was ful wys and worthy of his hond	Who was very wise and great in battle
Agayn the Scottes, as men may wel heere;-	Against the Scots, as many men know;
But turne I wole agayn to my mateere.	But I will go back to my subject.
Sathan, that ever us waiteth to bigile,	Satan, who is always waiting to trick us,
Saugh of Custance al hir perfeccioun	Saw Constance in all her perfection
And caste anon how he myghte quite hir while;	And wondered how he could take revenge on her;
And made a yong knyght, that dwelte in that toun,	And he made a young knight who lived in that town
Love hir so hoote of foul affeccioun	Love her so madly with such foul passion
That verraily hym thoughte he sholde spille,	That he truly thought his life would end
But he of hir myghte ones have his wille.	Unless he could have his way with her.
He woweth hir, but it availleth noght,	He tried to woo her, but it did no good,
She wolde do no synne, by no were;	She would not sin in any way;
And for despit he compassed in his thought	And out of spite he formed a plan
To maken hir on shameful deeth to deye.	To make her die a shameful death.
He wayteth whan the constable was aweye	He waited until the constable was away
And pryvely upon a nyght he crepte	And he secretly crept in at night
In Hermengyldes chambre whil she slepte.	Into Hermengild's bedroom while she slept.
Wery, for-waked in hir orisouns,	Tired from keeping her prayer vigil,
Slepeth Custance, and Hermengyld also.	Constance was asleep, and so was Hermengild.
This knyght, thurgh Sathanas temptaciouns,	This knight, through Satan's temptations,
All softely is to the bed ygo,	Crept softly up to the bedside
And kitte the throte of Hermengyld atwo,	And slit open the throat of Hermengild,
And leyde the blody knyf by dame Custance,	Leaving the bloody knife next to Dame Constance,
And wente his wey, ther God yeve hym meschance!	And went on his way, may God punish him!
Soone after cometh this constable hoom agayn,	Soon after this constable came home again,
And eek Alla, that kyng was of that lond,	Bringing with him Alla, who was king of that country,
And saugh his wyf despitously yslayn,	And saw his wife, mercilessly slain,
For which ful ofte he weep and wroong his hond,	And he wept and wrung his hands,
And in the bed the blody knyf he fond	And he found a bloody knife in bed
By Dame Custance; allas, what myghte she seye?	Next to Dame Constance; alas, what could she say?
For verray wo hir wit was al aweye!	Her wit was destroyed by sorrow!
To kyng Alla was toold al this meschance,	King Alla was told of this sad happening,
And eek the tyme, and where, and in what wise	And also the time, where and how

That in a ship was founden dame Custance,	Dame Constance was found in a ship,
As heer-biforn that ye han herd devyse.	As you have already heard me tell.
The kynges herte of pitee gan agryse,	Pity rose up in the heart of the king
Whan he saugh so benigne a creature	When he saw such a kind creature
Falle in disese and in mysaventure.	Distressed in such unhappy circumstances.
For as the lomb toward his deeth is broght,	Like a lamb brought to the slaughter,
So stant this innocent bifore the kyng.	This innocent stood before the king.
This false knyght, that hath this tresoun wroght,	The false knight who had done the foul deed
Berth hir on hond that she hath doon thys thyng,	Swore it was her who had done this thing,
But nathelees, ther was greet moornyng	But despite this there was much sorrow
Among the peple, and seyn, they kan nat gesse	Amongst the people, who said that they wouldn't believe
That she had doon so greet a wikkednesse;	That she had done something so wicked;
For they han seyn hir evere so vertuous,	For they had seen that she was always virtuous,
And lovyng Hermengyld right as hir lyf:	And loved Hermengild as much as her own life:
Of this baar witnesse everich in that hous	Of this bear witness in that house
Save he that Hermengyld slow with his knyf.	Apart from the one who had killed Hermengild with his knife.
This gentil kyng hath caught a greet motyf	This kind king suspected perverted motives
Of this witnesse, and thoghte he wolde enquere	Of this man, and thought he would enquire
Depper in this, a trouthe for to lere.	Deeper into the matter, to find the truth.
Allas, Custance, thou hast no champioun!	Alas, Constance, you have no champion!
Ne fighte kanstow noght, so weylaway!	You can't fight for yourself, so woe is you!
But he, that starf for our redempcioun,	But he who died to redeem us all
And boond Sathan-and yet lith ther he lay-	And to imprison Satan–who still lives where he put him–
So be thy stronge champion this day!	He will be your champion this day!
For but if Crist open myracle kithe,	For unless Christ makes a miracle happen
Withouten gilt thou shalt be slayn as swithe.	You will be killed at once, though you are guiltless.
She sette hir doun on knees, and thus she sayde,	She went down on her knees, and said,
"Immortal God, that savedest Susanne	"Immortal God, who saved Susanna
Fro false blame, and thou, merciful Mayde,	From false accusations, and you, merciful virgin,
Marie I meene, doghter to Seynte Anne,	I mean Mary, daughter of St Anne,
Bifore whos child angeles synge Osanne,	To whose child the angels sang hosanna,
If I be giltlees of this felonye,	If I am guiltless of this crime
My socour be, for ellis shal I dye."	Then save me, otherwise I will die."
Have ye nat seyn som tyme a pale face	Haven't you sometimes seen a pale face
Among a prees, of hym that hath be lad	In the crowd, of someone being led
Toward his deeth, wher as hym gat no grace,	Towards his death, someone who has not been forgiven,
And swich a colour in his face hath had,	And who had such a colour in his face
Men myghte knowe his face, that was bistad,	That men would be able to tell who was facing death
Amonges alle the faces in that route?	Amongst all the faces in the crowd?
So stant Custance, and looketh hir aboute.	That is what Constance looked like, as she looked around.

O queenes, lyvynge in prosperitee,	Oh queens, who live in prosperity,
Duchesses, and ladyes everichone,	Duchesses, and all you ladies, everyone,
Haveth som routhe on hir adversitee;	Have pity on her now in her troubles;
An Emperoures doghter stant allone,	The daughter of an emperor standing alone,
She hath no wight to whom to make hir mone.	She had nobody to whom she could plead.
O blood roial, that stondest in this drede,	O woman of royal blood, standing in such danger,
Fer been thy freendes at thy grete nede!	In your time of great need your friends are far away.
This Alla kyng hath swich compassioun,	This king Alla was so compassionate,
As gentil herte is fulfild of pitee,	Because kind hearts are filled with pity,
That from hise eyen ran the water doun.	That the tears ran down from his eyes.
"Now hastily do fecche a book," quod he,	"Now quickly go and bring a sacred book," he said,
"And if this knyght wol sweren how that she	"And if this knight will swear that it was her
This womman slow, yet wol we us avyse,	Who killed this woman, then we shall follow
Whom that we wole, that shal been oure justise."	The laws of our country."
A Britoun book, written with Evaungiles,	A book of Gospels written in English
Was fet, and on this book he swoor anoon	Was fetched, and he swore on this book
She gilty was, and in the meene-whiles	That she was guilty, and as he did
An hand hym smoot upon the nekke-boon,	A hand smashed him on his collarbone
That doun he fil atones, as a stoon;	So that he fell stunned to the floor;
And bothe hise eyen broste out of his face,	And both of his eyes burst out of his face
In sighte of every body in that place.	In sight of every person in that place.
A voys was herd in general audience,	A voice was heard by all the people,
And seyde, "Thou hast desclaundred, giltelees	Saying, "You have slandered this guiltless
The doghter of hooly chirche in heigh presence,	Daughter of the holy Church in front of all these noble people,
Thus hastou doon, and yet holde I my pees."	You did this, that's all I shall say."
Of this mervaille agast was al the prees,	The whole crowd was astonished by this miracle,
As mazed folk they stoden everichone	And every one of them stood there like men stunned,
For drede of wreche, save Custance allone.	Dreading vengeance, all apart from Constance.
Greet was the drede and eek the repentance	There was great fear and also repentance
Of hem that hadden wronge suspecioun	Amongst those who had wrongly suspected
Upon this sely innocent, Custance;	This simple innocent, Constance;
And for this miracle, in conclusioun,	And because of this miracle I can tell you
And by Custances mediacioun,	(And also because of the prayers of Constance)
The kyng, and many another in that place,	The king, and many others in that place,
Converted was, thanked be Cristes grace.	Were converted, thanks be to Christ.
This false knyght was slayn for his untrouthe,	The false knight was executed for his slander,
By juggement of Alla hastifly-	Swiftly, through the sentence of Alla,
And yet Custance hadde of his deeth greet routhe-	Although Constance felt great pity for him.
And after this Jesus, of His mercy,	After this Jesus, in his mercy,
Made Alla wedden ful solempnely	Caused Alla to solemnly marry
This hooly mayden, that is so bright and sheene,	This holy maiden, shining bright,

And thus hath Crist ymaad Custance a queene.	And so Christ made a queen of Constance.
But who was woful, if I shal nat lye,	The false knight was executed for his slander,
Of this weddyng but Donegild, and namo,	Swiftly, through the sentence of Alla,
The kynges mooder, ful of tirannye?	Although Constance felt great pity for him.
Hir thoughte hir cursed herte brast atwo,	After this Jesus, in his mercy,
She wolde noght hir sone had do so,	Caused Alla to solemnly marry
Hir thoughte a despit, that he sholde take	This holy maiden, shining bright,
So strange a creature unto his make.	And so Christ made a queen of Constance.
Me list nat of the chaf nor of the stree	I'm not going to bother with the chaff or the straw
Maken so long a tale, as of the corn;	Of this long story, I shall concentrate on the corn;
What sholde I tellen of the roialtee	Why should I tell you all about the royalty
At mariages, or which cours goth biforn,	At the wedding, or who went first in the procession,
Who bloweth in the trumpe, or in an horn?	Who was blowing trumpets, or the horns?
The fruyt of every tale is for to seye;	The thing can be put in a nutshell by saying
They ete, and drynke, and daunce, and synge, and pleye.	That they ate, drank, danced, sang, and played.
They goon to bedde, as it was skile and right,	They went to bed, as was fitting and right,
For thogh that wyves be ful hooly thynges,	For even if wives are very holy people
They moste take in pacience at nyght	They must endure in patience in the night
Swiche manere necessaries as been plesynges	The things which are necessary to give pleasure
To folk that han ywedded hem with rynges,	To the men whom they have been bound with rings,
And leye a lite hir hoolynesse aside	And forget their holiness for a little while,
As for the tyme, it may no bet bitide.	That does not do them any harm.
On hire he gat a knave childe anon,	Soon they made a baby boy together,
And to a bisshop and his constable eke	And he asked his bishop and his constable
He took his wyf to kepe, whan he is gon	To look after his wife, when he went
To Scotlond-ward, his foomen for to seke.	To Scotland, to look for his enemies.
Now faire Custance, that is so humble and meke,	Now fair Constance, who is so humble and meek,
So longe is goon with childe, til that stille	Was so far gone in her pregnancy that she stayed
She halt hire chambre, abidyng Cristes wille.	Quietly in her room, waiting for the will of Christ.
The tyme is come; a knave child she beer,	The time came; she gave birth to a boy,
Mauricius at the fontstoon they hym calle.	And they had him christened Maurice.
This constable dooth forth come a messageer,	The constable sent out a messenger,
And wroot unto his kyng, that cleped was Alle,	Writing to his King, who was called Alla,
How that this blisful tidyng is bifalle,	Of this happy event,
And othere tidynges spedeful for to seye;	Along with other urgent news;
He taketh the lettre, and forth he gooth his weye.	The messenger took the letter, and went on his way.
This messager, to doon his avantage,	The messenger, to further his own ends,
Unto the kynges mooder rideth swithe,	Rode quickly to the king's mother,
And salueth hir ful faire in his langage,	And saluted her, bowing down,
"Madame," quod he, "ye may be glad and blithe,	"Madam," he said, "you can be joyful,

And thanketh God an hundred thousand sithe.	And thank God a hundred thousand times.
My lady queene hath child, withouten doute,	My lady the queen has had a child
To joye and blisse to al this regne aboute.	To the great joy of this whole country.
Lo, heere the lettres seled of this thyng,	Look, here are sealed letters telling of this thing,
That I moot bere with al the haste I may.	That I must take as fast as I can.
If ye wol aught unto youre sone, the kyng,	If you want to add a message to your son, the king,
I am youre servant both nyght and day."	I am at your service, night and day."
Donegild answerde, "as now at this tyme, nay,	Donegild answered, "At the moment, no,
But heere al nyght I wol thou take thy reste,	But tonight I'd like you to stay here,
Tomorwe wol I seye thee what me leste."	Tomorrow I will think of something to say."
This messager drank sadly ale and wyn,	This messenger drank lots of ale and wine,
And stolen wer hise lettres pryvely	And his letters were secretly stolen
Out of his box, whil he sleep as a swyn	From his bag, while he slept like a pig;
And countrefeted was ful subtilly	And another letter was forged,
Another lettre wroght ful synfully,	Very skilfully and sinfully,
Unto the kyng direct of this mateere	To the king as if it came directly
Fro his constable, as ye shal after heere.	From his constable, as you shall hear.
The lettre spak, the queene delivered was	The letter said that the Queen had given birth
Of so horrible a feendly creature	To such a horrible devilish creature
That in the castel noon so hardy was	That there was no one in the castle so brave
That any while dorste ther endure;	That they could stay with it for any length of time;
The mooder was an elf, by aventure,	It was thought the mother was an elf,
Ycomen by charmes or by sorcerie,	Brought there by chance or sorcery,
And every wight hateth hir compaignye.	And everybody hated her company.
Wo was this kyng whan he this lettre had sayn,	The king was greatly distressed by this letter,
But to no wight he tolde his sorwes soore,	But he did not tell anyone of his sorrow,
But of his owene hand he wroot agayn:	But he wrote back in his own hand:
"Welcome the sonde of Crist for everemoore	"I welcome everything that's sent from Christ
To me, that am now lerned in his loore!	To me, who have now learned his ways!
Lord, welcome be thy lust and thy plesaunce,	My lord, your desires and your pleasure are welcome to me,
My lust I putte al in thyn ordinaunce.	All I want to do is to do your bidding.
Kepeth this child, al be it foul or feire,	Guard this child, whether it is foul or fair,
And eek my wyf, unto myn hoom-comynge;	And also my wife, until I return;
Crist, whan hym list, may sende me an heir	When Christ decides he may send me an heir
Moore agreable than this to my likynge."	Whom I will prefer to this one."
This lettre he seleth, pryvely wepynge,	He sealed this letter, privately weeping,
Which to the messager was take soone	And it was quickly given to the messenger
And forth he gooth, ther is namoore to doone.	And off he went; that's an end of the matter.
O messager, fulfild of dronkenesse,	O messenger, filled with drink,
Strong is thy breeth, thy lymes faltren ay,	Your breath reeks, and you stumble,
And thou biwreyest alle secreenesse.	You have given away all your secrets.
Thy mynde is lorn, thou janglest as a jay,	You've lost your mind, you jabber like a jay;
Thy face is turned in a newe array;	Your face has turned a different colour;
Ther dronkenesse regneth in any route,	Where drunkenness rules amongst men
Ther is no conseil hyd, withouten doute.	It's quite clear there is no wisdom.

O Donegild, I ne have noon Englissh digne	Oh Donegild, I don't have words in my language
Unto thy malice and thy tirannye;	To describe your malice and your evil;
And therfore to the feend I thee resigne,	So I will leave you to the devil,
Lat hym enditen of thy traitorie!	Let him describe your treachery!
Fy, mannysh, fy? - O nay, by God, I lye -	Damn you like a man! No, I'm lying,
Fy, feendlych spirit! for I dar wel telle,	Damn you like a devil! For I am certain
Thogh thou heere walke, thy spirit is in helle.	That though you walk on earth, your spirit is in hell.
This messager comth fro the kyng agayn,	The messenger from the King came again,
And at the kynges moodres court he lighte	And arrived at the court of the king's mother,
And she was of this messager ful fayn,	And she was delighted to see him
And plesed hym in al that ever she myghte.	And gave him the warmest welcome she could.
He drank, and wel his girdel underpighte.	He drank until his belt was bulging,
He slepeth, and he fnorteth in his gyse	He slept and snored drunkenly
Al nyght until the sonne gan aryse.	All night, until sunrise.
Eft were hise lettres stolen everychon	Again all of his letters were stolen
And countrefeted lettres in this wyse,	And fake ones put in their place, saying,
"The king comandeth his constable anon	"The king orders his constable at once,
Up peyne of hangyng and on heigh juyse	On pain of death,
That he ne sholde suffren in no wyse	That he should not allow, for any reason,
Custance inwith his reawme for t'abyde,	Constance to remain within his kingdom
Thre dayes and o quarter of a tyde.	More than three days and three hours.
But in the same ship as he hir fond,	She and her baby and all her gear
Hire, and hir yonge sone, and al hir geere,	Should be put into the same ship he found her in
He sholde putte, and croude hir fro the lond,	And pushed away from the land,
And chargen hir she never eft coome theere."	And she should be told that she may never return."
O my Custance, wel may thy goost have fere,	Oh my Constance, your spirit is right to fear,
And slepynge in thy dreem been in penance,	Seeing suffering in your dreams
Whan Donegild cast al this ordinance.	When Donegild planned all these things.
This messager, on morwe whan he wook,	When the messenger awoke the next morning
Unto the Castel halt the nexte way,	He took the shortest path to the castle,
And to the constable he the lettre took.	Taking the letters of a constable.
And whan that he this pitous lettre say,	And when he knew the contents of the letter
Ful ofte he seyde, "Allas and weylaway!"	He started to cry out, "alas, oh sorry day!
"Lord Crist," quod he, "how may this world endure,	Lord Christ," he said, "how can the world carry on,
So ful of synne is many a creature?	When so many people are so sinful?
O myghty God, if that it be thy wille,	O mighty God, if this is your will,
Sith thou art rightful juge, how may it be	Since you are the true judge, how can it be
That thou wolt suffren innocentz to spille,	That you will allow the innocent to suffer,
And wikked folk regnen in prosperitee?	And wicked folk to rule prosperously?
O goode Custance, allas, so wo is me,	Oh good Constance, alas, I am so sorry
That I moot be thy tormentour, or deye	That I must either be your tormentor, or die
On shames deeth! Ther is noon oother weye!"	A shameful death! There is no alternative!"
Wepen bothe yonge and olde in al that place,	Both the young and the old people of the

Whan that the kyng this cursed lettre sente,	country wept
And Custance, with a deedly pale face,	Because of this cursed letter of the King,
The ferthe day toward the ship she wente;	And Constance, with a deadly pale face,
But nathelees she taketh in good entente	Went to her ship on the fourth day;
	Nevertheless, she submitted herself
The wyl of Crist, and knelynge on the stronde,	To the will of Christ, and kneeling on the shore,
She seyde, "Lord, ay welcome be thy sonde!	She said, "Lord, all your commands are welcome!
He that me kepte fro the false blame,	He protected me from false accusations
While I was on the lond amonges yow,	When I lived amongst you on the land,
He kan me kepe from harm and eek fro shame	He will now keep me from harm and shame
In salte see, al thogh I se noght how.	On the salt sea, although I do not see how.
As strong as evere he was, he is yet now;	He is as strong as he ever was,
In hym triste I, and in his mooder deere,	And I trust in him, and in his dear mother,
That is to me my seyl and eek my steere."	They are my sails, and my helmsmen."
Hir litel child lay wepyng in hir arm,	Her little child lay weeping in her arms,
And knelynge, pitously to hym she seyde,	And kneeling down, she said sorrowfully to him,
"Pees, litel sone, I wol do thee noon harm."	"Peace, little son, I will do you no harm."
With that hir coverchief on hir heed she breyde,	And with that she took her kerchief off her head
And over hise litel eyen she it leyde,	And laid it over his little eyes,
And in hir arm she lulleth it ful faste,	And she rocked him in her arms
And into hevene hir eyen up she caste.	While she gazed up into the heavens.
"Mooder," quod she, "and mayde bright, Marie,	"Mother," she said, "bright virgin, Mary,
Sooth is that thurgh wommanes eggement	It's true that it was a woman who caused
Mankynde was lorn and damned ay to dye,	Mankind to be banished, and damned to die,
For which thy child was on a croys yrent;	And your child was torn on a cross for this;
Thy blisful eyen sawe al his torment;	Your blessed eyes saw all of his torture;
Thanne is ther no comparison bitwene	So there can be no comparison between
Thy wo, and any wo man may sustene.	Your sorrow, and that which any man can suffer.
Thow sawe thy child yslayn bifore thyne eyen,	You saw them kill your child in front of your eyes,
And yet now lyveth my litel child, parfay.	And yet my little child is still living, perfect.
Now, lady bright, to whom alle woful cryen,	Now, bright lady, to whom every sorrowing person cries,
Thow glorie of wommanhede, thow faire may,	You glory of womanhood, you fair lady,
Thow haven of refut, brighte sterre of day,	You harbour of refuge, you bright star of day,
Rewe on my child, that of thy gentillesse	Have pity on my child, you whose kindness
Ruest on every reweful in distresse.	Has pity on every soul in distress.
O litel child, allas, what is thy gilt,	O little child, alas, what have you done wrong,
That nevere wroghtest synne as yet, pardee!	You who has yet to commit a single sin, by God!
Why wil thyn harde fader han thee spilt?	Why does your merciless father want you killed?
O mercy, deere Constable," quod she,	Have mercy, dear Constable," she said,
"As lat my litel child dwelle heer with thee;	"And let my little child live here with you;

And if thou darst nat saven hym for blame,	And if you are too scared of being punished
Yet kys hym ones in his fadres name."	Then kiss him once, in his father's name."
Therwith she looketh bakward to the londe,	With that she looked back towards the land,
And seyde, "Farwel, housbonde routheless!"	And said, "Farewell, my pitiless husband!"
And up she rist, and walketh doun the stronde,	And she got up and walked down the shore
Toward the ship. - hir folweth al the prees -	Towards the ship–the whole crowd followed her–
And evere she preyeth hir child to holde his pees,	And all the time she was asking her child not to cry,
And taketh hir leve, and with an hooly entente	And she made her farewell, piously
She blisseth hir, and into ship she wente.	Crossing herself, and she went into the ship.
Vitailled was the ship, it is no drede,	The ship was well provisioned, it is true,
Habundantly for hir ful longe space;	There was enough to keep her for a long time;
And othere necessaries that sholde nede	And there were plenty of the other things
She hadde ynogh, heried be Goddes grace;	She would need, thanks be to God;
For wynd and weder almyghty God purchace,	May God find a way through the wind and weather
And brynge hir hoom, I kan no bettre seye!	To bring her home! That's the best I can ask for;
But in the see she dryveth forth hir weye.	But she set out upon the sea.
Alla the kyng comth hoom, soone after this	King Alla came home soon after this
Unto his castel of the which I tolde,	To the castle which I mentioned,
And asketh where his wyf and his child is.	And asked where his wife and child were.
The constable gan aboute his herte colde,	The constable's blood ran cold,
And pleynly al the manere he hym tolde,	And he told him all that had happened,
As ye han herd - I kan telle it no bettre -	As you have heard – I've told you as well as I can –
And sheweth the kyng his seel and eek his lettre,	And he showed the king his seal and the letter.
And seyde, "Lord, as ye comanded me,	He said, "Lord, as you ordered me,
Up peyne of deeth, so have I doon, certein."	On pain of death, I have followed your orders."
This messager tormented was til he	The messenger was tortured until he
Moste biknowe, and tellen plat and pleyn	Revealed everything, plain and clear,
Fro nyght to nyght in what place he had leyn,	Where he had stopped each evening,
And thus, by wit and sotil enquerynge,	And so, through clever cunning questioning,
Ymagined was, by whom this harm gan sprynge.	It was reasoned out who was to blame.
The hand was knowe that the lettre wroot,	Now it was clear who wrote the letter,
And al the venym of this cursed dede,	And all the hatred in this horrid deed,
But in what wise certeinly I noot.	But how this came about, I do not know.
Th'effect is this, that Alla, out of drede,	But the result was that Alla, for punishment,
His mooder slow - that may men pleynly rede -	Killed his mother – you can read that in the books –
For that she traitoure was to hir ligeance,	For being a disloyal traitor,
Thus endeth olde Donegild, with meschance!	And so old Donegild died, evilly!
The sorwe that this Alla, nyght and day,	The sorrow which Alla felt for his wife, night and day,
Maketh for his wyf, and for his child also,	For his wife and also for his child,
Ther is no tonge that it telle may-	No tongue could possibly describe;

But now wol I unto Custance go,	But now I will go back to Constance,
That fleteth in the see in peyne and wo,	Who drifted on the sea, with pain and sorrow,
Fyve yeer and moore, as liked Cristes sonde,	For five years and more, as Christ willed,
Er that hir ship approched unto londe.	Before her ship reached the shore.
Under an hethen castel, atte laste,	At last she came to a heathen castle,
Of which the name in my text toght I fynde,	The name of which I cannot discover,
Custance and eek hir child the see upcaste.	And Constance and her child came ashore.
Almyghty god that saved al mankynde,	Almighty God who saved all of mankind,
Have on Custance and on hir child som mynde,	Keep Constance and her child in mind,
That fallen is in hethen hand eft soone,	Who will soon fall into heathen hands
In point to spille, as I shal telle yow soone.	And nearly die, as I shall tell.
Doun fro the castel comth ther many a wight	Many people came down from the castle
To gauren on this ship and on Custance,	To stare at this ship and at Constance,
But shortly from the castel on a nyght	And briefly, from the castle, one night,
The lordes styward - God yeve hym meschance!-	The lord's steward – may God curse him –
A theef that hadde reneyed oure creance,	A thief who had renounced God,
Cam into the ship allone, and seyde he sholde	Came on to the ship and said he would
Hir lemman be, wherso she wolde or nolde.	Be her lover, whether she liked it or not.
Wo was this wrecched womman tho bigon!	A terrible time then began for this woman!
Hir child cride, and she cride pitously,	Her child cried, and she wept pitifully,
But blisful Marie heelp hir right anon,	But blessed Mary came quickly to her aid,
For with hir struglyng wel and myghtily,	For with her struggling well and mighty
The theef fil over bord al sodeynly,	And the thief suddenly fell overboard,
And in the see he dreynte for vengeance,	And he was drowned in the sea as punishment,
And thus hath Crist unwemmed kept Custance.	And so Christ kept Constance pure.
O foule lust of luxurie, lo, thyn ende!	Oh foul lustful desires, this is how you will end!
Nat oonly that thou feyntest mannes mynde,	Not only do you damage a man's mind,
But verraily thou wolt his body shende.	But you also destroy his body.
Th'ende of thy werk or of thy lustes blynde	The end result of all your efforts and blind lust
Is compleynyng. Hou many oon may men fynde,	Is suffering. How many men have we seen
That noght for werk somtyme, but for th'entente	Who have been shamed or killed,
To doon this synne, been outher slayn or shente!	Not even for doing this sin, just for intending to.
How may this wayke womman han this strengthe	How could this weak woman have the strength
Hire to defende agayn this renegat?	To defend herself against that thug?
O Golias, unmesurable of lengthe,	Oh Goliath, immeasurably tall,
Hou myghte David make thee so maat,	How could David have brought you down,
So yong, and of armure so desolaat?	When he was so young, with no armour?
Hou dorste he looke upon thy dredful face?	How did he dare to look on your dreadful face?
Wel may men seen, it nas but Goddes grace!	It's obvious, it must have been through God's grace.
Who yaf Judith corage or hardynesse	Who gave Judith the strength and courage
To sleen hym, Olofernus, in his tente,	To kill Holofernes in his tent
And to deliveren out of wrecchednesse	
The peple of God? I seyde, for this entente	And so save the people of God? I tell you, for this reason,

That right as God spirit of vigour sente To hem, and saved hem out of meschance,	That God sent strength to both of them, And saved them from their evil luck.
So sente he myght and vigour to Custance.	Just as he sent strength and courage to Constance.
Forth gooth hir ship thurghout the narwe mouth Of Jubaltar and Septe, dryvynge alway, Somtyme west, and somtyme north and south,	Out went her ship through the narrow mouth Of Gibraltar and Ceuta, driving with the wind, Sometimes west, and sometimes north and south,
And somtyme est, ful many a wery day; Til Cristes mooder - blessed be she ay! -	And sometimes east, for many long days; Until Christ's mother – may she be forever blessed! –
Hath shapen, thurgh hir endelees goodnesse, To make an ende of al hir hevynesse.	Decided, through her eternal goodness, To make an end of all her sorrows.
Now lat us stynte of Custance but a throwe, And speke we of the Romayn Emperour, That out of Surrye hath by lettres knowe The slaughtre of Cristen folk, and dishonour	Now let us leave Constance for a while, And talk about the Roman emperor, Who knew through messages from Syria About the slaughtre of Christian folk, and the harm
Doon to his doghter by a fals traytour, I mene the cursed wikked Sowdanesse, That at the feeste leet sleen both moore and lesse;	Done to his daughter by a false traitor, I mean the cursed Sultana, Who at the feast had killed the great and lowly.
For which this emperour hath sent anon His senatour with roial ordinance, And othere lordes, God woot many oon, On Surryens to taken heigh vengeance. They brennen, sleen, and brynge hem to meschance	Because of this the emperor quickly sent A senator, with royal commands, And with other lords, God knows how many, To take great vengance against the Syrians. They burned and killed, gave thme all suffering,
Ful many a day, but shortly, this is th'ende, Homward to Rome they shapen hem to wende.	For many days, but to cut a long story short They went back home victorious.
This senatour repaireth with victorie To Rome-ward saillynge ful roially, And mette the ship dryvynge, as seith the storie, In which Custance sit ful pitously.	The senator went back, victorious, Sailing in full state, to Rome, And the stories tell that he met the drifting ship In which Constance was sitting, in a pitiful state.
Nothyng ne knew he what she was, ne why She was in swich array, ne she nyl seye Of hire estaat, thogh that she sholde deye.	He didn't know who she was, nor why She was in such a state, and she would not say Who she was, even if her life was at stake.
He bryngeth hire to Rome, and to his wyf He yaf hire, and hir yonge sone also, And with the senatour she ladde hir lyf. Thus kan oure Lady bryngen out of wo Woful Custance, and many another mo. And longe tyme dwelled she in that place, In hooly werkes evere, as was hir grace.	He brought her to Rome, and gave her To his wife, along with his young son, And she lived with the senator for a while. So Our Lady rescued from her misery Sad Constance, and many more besides. She lived for a long time in that place, Doing holy works, as always, through her piety.
The senatoures wyf hir aunte was,	The senator's wife was her aunt,

But for all that she knew hir never the moore. I wol no lenger tarien in this cas,	But she has no idea of that. I won't carry on talking of her,
But to kyng Alla, which I spake of yoore,	But return to King Alla, of whom I spoke before,
That wepeth for his wyf and siketh soore, I wol retourne, and lete I wol Custance Under the senatoures governance. Kyng Alla, which that hadde his mooder slayn, Upon a day fil in swich repentance That, if I shortly tellen shal and playn, To Rome he comth, to receyven his penance; And putte hym in the popes ordinance In heigh and logh, and Jesu Crist bisoghte Foryeve hise wikked werkes that he wroghte.	Weeping for his wife and sighing sorrowfully, And I will leave Constance In the care of the senator. King Alla, who had killed his mother, Was one day filled with such grief That, to tell it briefly, He came to Rome, to receive his punishment; He put himself in the hands of the pope In all things, and asked Jesus Christ To forgive all evil things he had done.
The fame anon thurgh Rome toun is born How Alla kyng shal comen on pilgrymage,	Throughout the city of Rome the news Spread of how King Alla had come on pilgrimage,
By herbergeours that wenten hym biforn, For which the Senatour, as was usage, Rood hym agayns, and many of his lynage, As wel to shewen his heighe magnificence As to doon any kyng a reverence.	Through messengers who went ahead of him, And the senator, as was the custom, Rode out to meet him, with many of his peers, To show off his own magnificence As well as to pay his respects to the king.
Greet cheere dooth this noble senatour To kyng Alla, and he to hym also, Everich of hem dooth oother greet honour; And so bifel, that inwith a day or two This senatour is to kyng Alla go To feste; and shortly, if I shal nat lye,	This noble senator gave a great welcome To King Alla, which he reciprocated, Each of them honouring the other; And so it happened that within a day or two The senator went to King Alla For a banquet, and I'll say briefly and truthfully
Custances sone wente in his compaignye.	That Constance's son went with him.
Som men wolde seyn, at requeste of Custance This senatour hath lad this child to feeste;	Some men claim that Constance Asked the senator to take her son to the banquet;
I may nat tellen every circumstance, Be as be may, ther was he at the leeste,	I can't tell you for certain, But whatever the truth is, he was there, at least,
But sooth is this, that at his moodres heeste	But it's certainly true that at his mother's request
Biforn Alla durynge the metes space, The child stood, lookynge in the kynges face.	He stood in front of Alla during the feasting And looked in the face of the king.
This Alla kyng hath of this child greet wonder, And to the senatour he seyde anon, "Whos is that faire child, that stondeth yonder?" "I noot," quod he, "by God and by Seint John!	King Alla was astonished by the child, And at once he said the senator, "Who is that fair child, standing over there?" "I don't know," he said, "I swear by God and Saint John!
A mooder he hath, but fader hath he noon,	He has a mother, but he does not have a father,
That I of woot." But shortly, in a stounde, He tolde Alla how that this child was founde.	That I know of." He briefly and quickly Told Alla how the child was found.

"But God woot," quod this senatour also,	"But God knows," the senator said also,
"So vertuous a lyvere in my lyf	"I never saw anybody in my life who lived
Ne saugh I nevere as she, ne herde of mo	Such a virtuous life as she, I've never heard
Of worldly wommen, mayde, ne of wyf;	Of any earthly woman, girl or wife like her.
I dar wel seyn, hir hadde levere a knyf	I daresay she would rather have a knife stabbed
Thurghout hir brest, than ben a womman wikke,	Through her heart than be an evil woman,
There is no man koude brynge hir to that prikke."	Nobody could make her be like that."
Now was this child as lyke unto Custance,	Now this child was as identical to Constance
As possible is a creature to be.	As it is possible for a creature to be.
This Alla hath the face in remembrance	Alla remembered the face
Of dame Custance, and theron mused he,	Of Dame Constance, and so he wondered
If that the childes mooder were aught she	If maybe the mother of the child was
That is his wyf; and prively he sighte	His wife; and he sighed inwardly
And spedde hym fro the table that he myghte.	And left the table as quickly as he could.
"Parfay," thoghte he, "fantome is in myn heed!	"My God," he thought, "I have a phantom in my head!
I oghte deme, of skilful juggement,	I ought to accept, by any logic,
That in the salte see my wyf is deed."	That my wife has been drowned in the sea."
And afterward he made his argument:	Afterwards he argued to himself:
"What woot I, if that Crist have hyder ysent	"How do I know that Christ hasn't sent
My wyf by see, as wel as he hir sente	My wife here by sea, in the same way that
To my contree fro thennes that she wente?"	He sent her to my country?"
And, after noon, hoom with the senator	And, after noon, Alla went with the senator
Goth Alla, for to seen this wonder chaunce.	To his home, to explore this amazing circumstance.
This senatour dooth Alla greet honour,	The senator gave Alla a great welcome,
And hastifly he sente after Custance.	And quickly he sent for Constance.
But trusteth weel, hir liste nat to daunce	But believe me, she wasn't exactly dancing
Whan that she wiste wherfore was that sonde;	When she heard why she had been sent for;
Unnethe upon hir feet she myghte stonde.	She could hardly stand upright on her feet.
Whan Alla saugh his wyf, faire he hir grette,	When Alla saw his wife, he greeted her warmly,
And weep, that it was routhe for to see.	And he wept, it was pitiful to see.
For at the firste look he on hir sette,	As soon as he saw her
He knew wel verraily that it was she.	He knew that it was definitely her.
And she for sorwe, as doumb stant as a tree,	And in her grief she stood as silent as a tree,
So was hir herte shet in hir distresse,	Her heart was so cold through her distress
Whan she remembred his unkyndenesse.	When she remembered how unkind he'd been.
Twyes she swowned in his owene sighte.	Twice she fainted away in front of him.
He weep, and hym excuseth pitously.	He wept, and excused himself piteously.
"Now God," quod he, "and alle hise halwes brighte	"Now God," he said, "and all his bright angels,
So wisly on my soule as have mercy,	Please have mercy on my soul, knowing
That of youre harm as giltelees am I	That I am as innocent of your troubles as you yourself,
As is Maurice my sone, so lyk youre face;	And so is my son Maurice, who looked so like you,
Elles the feend me fecche out of this place!"	If I'm lying may the devil drag me out of here!"

Long was the sobbyng and the bitter peyne	*There were many tears and much pain*
Er that hir woful hertes myghte cesse,	*Before their sorrowful hearts could find comfort,*
Greet was the pitee for to heere hem pleyne,	*It was absolutely piteous to hear them,*
Thurgh whiche pleintes gan hir wo encresse.	*And their moaning surely made them sadder.*
I pray yow alle my labour to relesse;	*I must ask you all to excuse me;*
I may nat telle hir wo until tomorwe,	*I can't tell you of their grief until tomorrow,*
I am so wery for to speke of sorwe.	*I am so exhausted speaking of their sorrow.*
Twyes she swowned in his owene sighte.	*Twice she fainted away in front of him.*
He weep, and hym excuseth pitously.	*He wept, and excused himself piteously.*
"Now God," quod he, "and alle hise halwes brighte	*"Now God," he said, "and all his bright angels,*
So wisly on my soule as have mercy,	*Please have mercy on my soul, knowing*
That of youre harm as giltelees am I	*That I am as innocent of your troubles as you yourself,*
As is Maurice my sone, so lyk youre face;	*And so is my son Maurice, who looked so like you;*
Elles the feend me fecche out of this place!"	*If I'm lying may the devil drag me out of here!"*
Long was the sobbyng and the bitter peyne	*There were many tears and much pain*
Er that hir woful hertes myghte cesse,	*Before their sorrowful hearts could find comfort,*
Greet was the pitee for to heere hem pleyne,	*It was absolutely piteous to hear them,*
Thurgh whiche pleintes gan hir wo encresse.	*And their moaning surely made them sadder.*
I pray yow alle my labour to relesse;	*I must ask you all to excuse me;*
I may nat telle hir wo until tomorwe,	*I can't tell you of their grief until tomorrow,*
I am so wery for to speke of sorwe.	*I am so exhausted speaking of their sorrow.*
But finally, whan that the sothe is wist,	*But finally, when the truth was known,*
That Alla giltelees was of hir wo,	*And it was shown that Alla had not caused her pain,*
I trowe an hundred tymes been they kist,	*I think they must have kissed each other a hundred times,*
And swich a blisse is ther bitwix hem two,	*And there was such happiness between the two of them*
That, save the joye that lasteth everemo	*That, apart from the joy of heaven,*
Ther is noon lyk that any creature	*Nobody has ever seen anything like it*
Hath seyn, or shal, whil that the world may dure.	*And will not, in the history of the world.*
Tho preyde she hir housbonde mekely,	*Then she asked her husband meekly*
In relief of hir longe pitous pyne,	*To help relieve her long suffering*
That he wolde preye hir fader specially	*By asking her father specially*
That, of his magestee, he wolde enclyne	*That he would in his Majesty agree*
To vouche sauf som day with hym to dyne.	*To come and dine with him one day;*
She preyde hym eek, he wolde by no weye	*She also asked him not*
Unto hir fader no word of hir seye.	*To tell her father a word about her.*
Som men wolde seyn, how that the child Maurice	*Some men claim that the child Maurice*
Dooth this message unto this emperour,	*Took this message to the Emperor,*
But, as I gesse, Alla was nat so nyce	*But I imagine Alla was not so disrespectful*
To hym that was of so sovereyn honour,	*To the person who was so royal,*
As he that is of Cristen folk the flour,	*The greatest man in Christendom,*
Sente any child, but it is bet to deeme	*As to send a child, I believe*

He wente hymself, and so it may wel seeme.	He went himself, as would be proper.

This emperour hath graunted gentilly	The emporer graciously agreed to come to dinner
To come to dyner, as he hym bisoughte,	As he had been asked,
And wel rede I he looked bisily	And I can imagine that he looked intently
Upon this child, and on his doghter thoghte.	At this child, and thought about his daughter.
Alla goth to his in, and as him oghte	Alla went to his lodging, and as he should,
Arrayed for this feste in every wise	Prepared everyhting for this feast
As ferforth as his konnyng may suffise.	In the best way he could imagine.
The morwe cam, and Alla gan hym dresse	The next day came, and Alla dressed himself,
And eek his wyf, this emperour to meete,	As did his wife, to meet the Emperor,
And forth they ryde in joye and in galdnesse,	And they rode out with much joy and happiness,
And whan she saugh hir fader in the strete,	And when she saw her father in the street,
She lighte doun and falleth hym to feete.	She dismounted and fell at his feet.
"Fader," quod she, "youre yonge child Custance	"Father," he said, "your young daughter Constance
Is now ful clene out of youre remembrance.	Has been completely forgotten by you.
I am youre doghter Custance," quod she,	I am your daughter Constance," she said,
"That whilom ye han sent unto Surrye.	"The one whom you sent to Syria.
It am I, fader, that in the salte see	It is me, father, who was set adrift
Was put allone, and dampned for to dye.	On the salt sea, alone, doomed to die.
Now goode fader, mercy I yow crye,	Now good father, I ask you for mercy,
Sende me namoore unto noon hethenesse,	Do not send me any more into heathen regions,
But thonketh my lord heere of his kyndenesse."	But give thanks to my husband for his kindness."
Who kan the pitous joye tellen al	Who can describe all the tearful joy
Bitwixe hem thre, syn they been thus ymette?	Which they all experienced at this meeting?
But of my tale make an ende I shal,	But I will finish up my tale;
The day goth faste, I wol no lenger lette.	The day is going quickly, I won't keep you any longer.
This glade folk to dyner they hem sette,	These happy people all sat down to dinner,
In joye and blisse at mete I lete hem dwelle,	And I will leave them there with their joy and bliss,
A thousand foold wel moore than I kan telle.	A thousand times more happy than I can describe.
This child Maurice was sithen emperor	Since then the child Maurice was made Emperor
Maad by the pope, and lyved cristenly.	By the Pope, and lived a good Christian life.
To Cristes chirche he dide greet honour;	He did great service to the Church of Christ;
But I lete all his storie passen by—	But I will not tell you this story,
Of Custance is my tale specially—	My tale is specifically about Constance—
In the olde Romayn geestes may men fynde	In the ancient Roman histories men can read
Maurices lyf; I bere it noght in mynde.	Of the life of Maurice, that's not my business now.
This kyng Alla, whan he his tyme say,	This king Alla, when the time was right,
With his Custance, his hooly wyf so sweete,	Came straight back to England with
To Engelond been they come the righte way,	His Constance, his sweet holy wife,

Wher as they lyve in joye and in quiete.	And they lived peacefully and happily.
But litel while it lasteth, I yow heete,	But I can tell you that happiness in this world
Joye of this world, for tyme wol nat abyde;	Never lasts for very long;
Fro day to nyght it changeth as the tyde.	It can change around in a day like the tide.
Who lyved evere in swich delit o day	Who is there who ever lived in such happiness for one day
That hym ne moeved outher conscience	Without being disturbed by his conscience,
Or ire, or talent, or som-kyn affray,	Or anger, or desire, or some other kind of commotion,
Envye, or pride, or passion, or offence?	Envy, pride, passion or taking offence?
I ne seye but for this ende this sentence,	I will just say one thing about this:
That litel while in joye or in pleasance	That the happiness of Alla and Constance
Lasteth the blisse of Alla with Custance.	Only lasted a little while.
For deeth, that taketh of heigh and logh his rente,	For death, who demands payment from both high and low,
Whan passed was a yeer, evene as I gesse,	Snatched King Alla out of this world
Out of this world this kyng Alla he hente,	When only a year had passed,
For whom Custance hath ful greet hevynesse.	And this brought great sorrow to Constance.
Now lat us praye God his soule blesse,	Now let us pray that God will bless his soul,
And dame Custance, finally to seye,	And I will tell you finally that Dame Constance
Toward the toun of Rome goth hir weye.	Made her way towards the city of Rome.
To Rome is come this hooly creature,	This holy person came to Rome,
And fyndeth ther hir freendes hoole and sounde.	And found her friends there were safe and healthy.
Now is she scaped al hire aventure,	And when she came to her father
Doun on hir knees falleth she to grounde,	She fell down upon her knees,
Wepynge for tendrenesse, in herte blithe,	Weeping with happiness, with a joyful heart,
She heryeth God an hundred thousande sithe.	And thanked God a hundred thousand times.
In vertu and in hooly almus-dede	They all lived virtuously and charitably,
They lyven alle, and never asonder wende	And were never separated
Til deeth departed hem; this lyf they lede;-	Until death parted them, they lived like this;
And fareth now weel, my tale is at an ende.	And now farewell, that's the end of my tale.
Now Jesu Crist, that of his myght may sende	Now may Jesus Christ, who through his power can give
Joye after wo, governe us in his grace,	Joy after sorrow, rule over us with his grace,
And kepe us alle that been in this place. Amen.	And watch over all of us who are here. Amen.
Heere endeth the tale of the Man of Lawe.	This is the end of the lawyer's tale
Owre Hoost upon his stiropes stood anon,	At once our host stood up in his stirrups,
And seyde, "Goode men, herkeneth everych on!	And said, "Good men, listen, all of you!
This was a thrifty tale for the nones!	This was a good story for this occasion!
Sir Parisshe Prest," quod he, "for Goddes bones,	Sir Parish Priest," he said, "in the name of God,
Telle us a tale, as was thi forward yore.	Tell us a tale, as you agreed to before.
I se wel that ye lerned men in lore	I can see that you learned men
Can moche good, by Goddes dignitee!"	Can do a good job, by God!"
The Parson him answerde, "Benedicite!	The Parson answered him: "Bless you!
What eyleth the man, so synfully to swere?"	What's wrong with this man, who is swearing so sinfully?"

Oure Host answerde, "O Jankin, be ye there?	Our host answered, "Hello Jenkin, is that you?
I smelle a Lollere in the wynd," quod he.	I think I smell an anti-churchman," he said.
"Now! goode men," quod oure Hoste, 'herkeneth me;	"Now! Good men," our host said, "listen to me;
Abydeth, for Goddes digne passioun,	Just wait a while, in God's name,
For we schal han a predicacioun;	For I can predict what's going to happen;
This Lollere heer wil prechen us somwhat."	This Lollard here will give us a sermon."
"Nay, by my fader soule, that schal he nat!"	"No, by the soul of my father, he will not do that!"
Seyde the Shipman, "Heer schal he nat preche;	Said the sailor, "I won't have him preaching here;
He schal no gospel glosen here ne teche.	He's not going to précis the scriptures or try and teach us.
We leven alle in the grete God," quod he;	We all believe in the great God," he said;
"He wolde sowen som difficulte,	"But this one would cause dissension amongst us,
Or springen cokkel in oure clene corn.	Causing our clean crops to rot.
And therfore, Hoost, I warne thee biforn,	And so, host, I warn you in advance,
My joly body schal a tale telle,	Jolly old me will tell you such a tale
And I schal clynken you so merry a belle,	And I will get the bells ringing for you so merrily
That I schal waken al this compaignie.	That all of this company will be woken up.
But it schal not ben of philosophie,	But I won't be talking about philosophy,
Ne phislyas, ne termes queinte of lawe.	Nor physics, nor using complex legal terms,
Ther is but litel Latyn in my mawe!"	I'm not one who knows a lot of Latin!"

The Wife of Bath's Tale

Prologue

"Experience, though noon auctoritee	"If there were no other written authority
Were in this world, were right ynogh to me	In the world, experience would give me the right
To speke of wo that is in mariage;	To speak of the sorrow one finds in marriage;
For, lordynges, sith I twelf yeer was of age,	For, my lords, since I was twelve years old,
Thonked be God, that is eterne on lyve,	Thanks be to God, who lives eternally,
Housbondes at chirche dore I have had fyve -	I have had five husbands at the church door–
For I so ofte have ywedded bee -	That's how many times I've been married–
And alle were worthy men in hir degree.	And they were all good men in their way.
But me was toold, certeyn, nat longe agoon is,	But someone told me not long ago
That sith that Crist ne wente nevere but onis	That since Christ never went to a wedding
To weddyng in the Cane of Galilee,	Except the one at Cana in Galilee,
That by the same ensample, taughte he me,	He was showing me an example, teaching me
That I ne sholde wedded be but ones.	That I should have only been married once.
Herkne eek, lo, which a sharpe word for the nones,	Also listen to the sharp words
Biside a welle Jhesus, God and Man,	Which Lord Jesus, both God and man,
Spak in repreeve of the Samaritan.	Spoke when he told off the Samaritan.
"Thou hast yhad fyve housbondes," quod he,	"For you have had five husbands," he said,
"And thilke man the which that hath now thee	"And the man who has you now
Is noght thyn housbonde;" thus seyde he certeyn.	Is not your husband;" that's definitely what he said.
What that he mente ther by, I kan nat seyn;	What he meant by that, I can't say;
But that I axe, why that the fifthe man	But I'm asking you, why was the fifth man
Was noon housbonde to the Samaritan?	Not a husband to the Samaritan?
How manye myghte she have in mariage?	How many was she allowed to marry?
Yet herde I nevere tellen in myn age	I have never heard at any time in my life
Upon this nombre diffinicioun.	A definition of the number allowed.
Men may devyne, and glosen up and doun,	Men can take a guess, and argue the matter,
But wel I woot, expres, withoute lye,	But I certainly know, and I'll tell you truthfully,
God bad us for to wexe and multiplye;	That God ordered us to go forth and multiply;
That gentil text kan I wel understonde.	I can certainly understand that great text.
Eek wel I woot, he seyde, myn housbonde	And I also know very well that he said my husband
Sholde lete fader and mooder, and take to me;	Should leave his father and mother and come to me;
But of no nombre mencioun made he,	But he didn't mention a specific number,
Of bigamye, or of octogamye;	Whether somebody married twice or eight times;
Why sholde men speke of it vileynye?	Why do men talk of it as if it was a crime?
Lo, heere the wise kyng, daun Salomon;	Let's think about the wise King, old Solomon;
I trowe he hadde wyves mo than oon-	I believe that he had more than one wife–
As, wolde God, it leveful were to me	I wish to God that I was allowed
To be refresshed half so ofte as he!	Half as many new ones as him!
Which yifte of God hadde he, for alle hise wyvys!	What a gift from God he had, all those wives!
No man hath swich that in this world alyve is.	There is no man like him alive today.
God woot, this noble kyng, as to my wit,	God knows, this noble king, to my mind,
The firste nyght had many a myrie fit	Must have had a wonderful wedding night
With ech of hem, so wel was hym on lyve!	With each of them, what a great life!
Yblessed be God, that I have wedded fyve;	Praise be to God that I married five;

(Of whiche I have pyked out the beste,	(I picked out the best available,
Bothe of here nether purs and of here cheste.	For their endowments, financial and physical.
Diverse scoles maken parfyt clerkes,	Different teachers make scholars perfect,
And diverse practyk in many sondry werkes	And different methods learned in different milieus
Maketh the werkman parfyt sekirly;	Certainly make a workman perfect;
Of fyve husbondes scoleiyng am I.)	I've been taught by five different husbands.)
Welcome the sixte, whan that evere he shal.	I shall welcome the sixth, whenever he comes;
For sothe I wol nat kepe me chaast in al.	I certainly won't remain celibate forever.
Whan myn housbonde is fro the world ygon,	When my husband leaves the world,
Som Cristen man shal wedde me anon.	Some Christian man will soon marry me.
For thanne th'apostle seith that I am free,	For the apostle says that I am free
To wedde, a Goddes half, where it liketh me.	To marry, in God's name, whom I like.
He seith, that to be wedded is no synne,	He says that it is no sin to be married,
Bet is to be wedded than to brynne.	It's better to be married than to burn in hell.
What rekketh me, thogh folk seye vileynye	What do I care if people speak badly
Of shrewed Lameth and of bigamye?	Of cursed Lamech and his bigamy?
I woot wel Abraham was an hooly man,	I'm convinced that Abraham was a holy man,
And Jacob eek, as ferforth as I kan,	And also Jacob, as far as I know,
And ech of hem hadde wyves mo than two,	And each of them had more than two wives,
And many another holy man also.	As did many other holy men.
Whanne saugh ye evere in any manere age,	Can anybody honestly say
That hye God defended marriage	That God has ever forbidden marriage
By expres word? I pray you, telleth me,	Explicitly? Please, tell me,
Or where comanded he virginitee?	Where did he say one had to be a virgin?
I woot as wel as ye it is no drede,	I know as well as ye it's nothing to be afraid of;
Th'apostel, whan he speketh of maydenhede;	When the apostle spoke about virginity
He seyde that precept therof hadde he noon.	He said that there was no law enforcing it.
Men may conseille a womman to been oon,	Men can advise a woman to remain virgin,
But conseillyng is no comandement;	But advice is not a law;
He putte it in oure owene juggement.	He left it to our own judgement.
For hadde God comanded maydenhede,	For if God had ordered virginity
Thanne hadde he dampned weddyng with the dede;	Then he would have damned marriage along with it;
And certein, if ther were no seed ysowe,	And certainly, if nobody ever mated,
Virginitee, wherof thanne sholde it growe?	Then where would all these virgins come from?
Poul dorste nat comanden, atte leeste,	Paul at least didn't dare to forbid us
A thyng of which his maister yaf noon heeste.	Something his master had given no orders about.
The dart is set up of virginitee;	The target of virginity is set up;
Cacche who so may, who renneth best lat see.	Let's see who can hit the bull's-eye.
But this word is nat taken of every wight,	But what I'm saying isn't right for everybody,
But ther as God lust gyve it of his myght.	Only for the ones God thinks suitable.
I woot wel, th'apostel was a mayde;	I know full well that the apostle was a virgin;
But nathelees, thogh that he wroot and sayde	Nevertheless, although he wrote and said
He wolde that every wight were swich as he,	That he wanted everyone to be like him,
Al nys but conseil to virginitee;	That is not advising virginity;
And for to been a wyf, he yaf me leve	And he has given me permission
Of indulgence, so it is no repreve	To be a wife, so it's no sin
To wedde me, if that my make dye,	For me to marry, if my husband dies,
Withouten excepcioun of bigamye.	Without being accused of bigamy.

were it good no womman for to touche,
He mente, as in his bed or in his couche;
For peril is bothe fyr and tow t'assemble;

Ye knowe what this ensample may resemble.
This is al and som, he heeld virginitee
Moore parfit than weddyng in freletee.

Freletee clepe I, but if that he and she
Wolde leden al hir lyf in chastitee.

I graunte it wel, I have noon envie,
Thogh maydenhede preferre bigamye;

Hem liketh to be clene, body and goost.

Of myn estaat I nyl nat make no boost,
For wel ye knowe, a lord in his houshold,
He nath nat every vessel al of gold;
Somme been of tree, and doon hir lord servyse.

God clepeth folk to hym in sondry wyse,
And everich hath of God a propre yifte -
Som this, som that, as hym liketh shifte.

Virginitee is greet perfeccioun,
And continence eek with devocioun.
But Crist, that of perfeccioun is welle,
Bad nat every wight he sholde go selle
Al that he hadde, and gyve it to the poore,
And in swich wise folwe hym and his foore.
He spak to hem that wolde lyve parfitly,
And lordynges, by youre leve, that am nat I.

I wol bistowe the flour of myn age
In the actes and in fruyt of mariage.

Telle me also, to what conclusion
Were membres maad of generacion,
And of so parfit wys a wright ywroght?
Trusteth right wel, they were maad for noght.

Glose whoso wole, and seye bothe up and doun,
That they were maked for purgacioun
Of uryne, and oure bothe thynges smale
Were eek to knowe a femele from a male,
And for noon other cause, -say ye no?
The experience woot wel it is noght so.
So that the clerkes be nat with me wrothe,
I sey this: that they maked ben for bothe,
That is to seye, for office and for ese
Of engendrure, ther we nat God displese.

Although he said it was good not to touch women,
He meant in his own bed, or on his couch;
For it's dangerous to put fire next to the kindling;

I'm sure you understand my metaphor.
To sum it all up, he thought that virginity
Was a better thing for weak persons than marriage.

I think it's weak for men and women
To spend their whole lives as virgins.

I'll tell you truthfully, I don't have regrets,
Although virginity may be preferred to bigamy;

Let those who want to be clean in body and spirit.

I'll make no such boast about my position,
For you all know well that a lord in his castle
Doesn't have every utensil made out of gold;
Some are made of wood, and they do good service.

God calls people to him in different ways,
And everyone has a specific gift from God—
Some have this, some that, depending on his will.

Virginity is a very perfect state,
And moderation also shows devotion.
But Christ, from whom all perfection comes,
Didn't say that each individual man should sell
Everything he had, and give it to the poor,
And do exactly as he did.
He was telling people how to live perfectly,
And my lords, if you'll excuse me, I don't want to.

I will give the best years of my life
To all the business of marriage.

Now tell me also for what reason
Were the sexual organs made,
And why were humans made so perfect?
You can be certain, they weren't made for nothing.

People can argue as much as they like,
That they were made for passing
Urine, and that they were just made different
So that we could separate women from men,
And for no other reason—do you say no?
Experience tells us this is not the case.
To stop the churchmen being angry with me,
I will say this: they were made for both,
That is to say, for work and for pleasure
Of procreation, and that does not displease

Why sholde men elles in hir bookes sette	Why else would men say in their books
That man shal yelde to his wyf hire dette?	That a man owes a debt to his wife?
Now wherwith sholde he make his paiement,	Now tell me how he is going to pay her
If he ne used his sely instrument?	Without using his blessed instrument?
Thanne were they maad upon a creature	These things were put upon the body
To purge uryne, and eek for engendrure.	To pass urine, and also for breeding.
But I seye noght that every wight is holde,	But I tell you that not every person is obliged,
That hath swich harneys as I to yow tolde,	Who has the equipment I've just described,
To goon and usen hem in engendrure.	To go and use it for procreation.
Thanne sholde men take of chastitee no cure.	Then men wouldn't care at all about chastity.
Crist was a mayde, and shapen as a man,	Christ was a virgin, though he had a man's body,
And many a seint, sith that the world bigan;	As many saints were, since the beginning of the world;
Yet lyved that evere in parfit chastitee.	But they always lived perfectly chaste.
I nyl envye no virginitee.	I don't have any envy towards virginity.
Lat hem be breed of pured whete-seed,	Let virgins be the pure white bread,
And lat us wyves hoten barly-breed;	And let we wives just be called barley bread;
And yet with barly-breed, Mark telle kan,	But if you look in the Gospel of Mark you'll see
Oure Lord Jhesu refresshed many a man.	That Jesus refreshed many men with barley bread.
In swich estaat as God hath cleped us	I will keep on going in the position
I wol persevere; I nam nat precius.	God chose for me; I'm not fussy.
In wyfhod I wol use myn instrument	As a wife I will use my organ
As frely as my Makere hath it sent.	As generously as my maker who gave it to me.
If I be daungerous, God yeve me sorwe!	If I am mean with it, may God punish me!
Myn housbonde shal it have bothe eve and morwe,	My husband will have it morning and night,
Whan that hym list come forth and paye his dette.	When he wants to come and pay his debts.
An housbonde I wol have, I wol nat lette,	I will have a husband, I won't let up,
Which shal be bothe my dettour and my thral,	And he will be debtor and my slave,
And have his tribulacioun withal	And he will experience the suffering
Upon his flessh whil that I am his wyf.	Of the flesh while I am his wife.
I have the power durynge al my lyf	I have the power throughout my life
Upon his propre body, and noght he.	Over his body, not him.
Right thus the Apostel tolde it unto me,	This is what the apostle said to me,
And bad oure housbondes for to love us weel.	And he told our husbands to love us well.
Al this sentence me liketh every deel" -	And that is perfectly fine by me."
Up stirte the Pardoner, and that anon;	Up jumped the Pardoner, straight away;
"Now, dame," quod he, "by God and by Seint John!	"Now, Lady," he said, "in the name of God and Saint John!
Ye been a noble prechour in this cas.	You are talking sense in this matter.
I was aboute to wedde a wyf; allas!	I was about to get married, alas!
What sholde I bye it on my flessh so deere?	Why should I put myself through such suffering?
Yet hadde I levere wedde no wyf to-yeere!"	No, I'd rather not marry this year!"
"Abyde," quod she, "my tale in nat bigonne.	"Wait," she said, "I have not begun my story.
Nay, thou shalt drynken of another tonne,	No, you will drink from a different barrel
Er that I go, shal savoure wors than ale.	Before I'm finished, and it won't taste as good as beer.

145

And whan that I have toold thee forth my tale	And when I have told you my story
Of tribulacioun in mariage,	Of the suffering in marriage,
Of which I am expert in al myn age,	Which my life has made me an expert at,
This to seyn, myself have been the whippe, -	That is to say, that I have been the whip;
Than maystow chese wheither thou wolt sippe	Then you can choose whether you will drink
Of thilke tonne that I shal abroche,	Out of the barrel which I open for you,
Be war of it, er thou to ny approche;	Be careful of it, before you get too near;
For I shal telle ensamples mo than ten.	For I will give you more than ten examples.
Whoso that nyl be war by othere men,	People who won't take the warnings of other men
By hym shul othere men corrected be.	End up being punished by other men instead.
The same wordes writeth Ptholomee;	This is what Ptolemy wrote;
Rede it in his Almageste, and take it there."	Look in his almanac, you'll find it there."
"Dame, I wolde praye yow, if youre wyl it were,"	"Lady, I pray you, if it is your will,"
Seyde this Pardoner, "as ye bigan,	Said the Pardoner, "carry on with your tale
Telle forth youre tale, spareth for no man,	The way you began, don't spare any man,
And teche us yonge men of your praktike."	Teach us young men from your experience."
"Gladly," quod she, "sith it may yow like.	"Certainly," she said, since it may please you.
But yet I praye to al this compaignye,	But I must beg this whole company,
If that I speke after my fantasye,	If I speak according to my imagination,
As taketh not agrief of that I seye,	Don't take what I say the wrong way,
For myn entente nis but for to pleye."	All I'm doing is having a bit of fun.
Now, sire, now wol I telle forth my tale,	Now, sir, I will tell you my tale,
As evere moote I drynken wyn or ale,	As willingly as I would drink wine or ale,
I shal seye sooth, tho housbondes that I hadde,	I will tell you all about the husbands that I've had,
As thre of hem were goode, and two were badde.	There were three of them were good, and two were bad.
The thre men were goode, and riche, and olde;	The three were good, rich and old;
Unnethe myghte they the statut holde	They didn't find it very easy
In which that they were bounden unto me-	To give me what I had a right to expect—
Ye woot wel what I meene of this, pardee!	By God, you know what I'm talking about!
As help me God, I laughe whan I thynke	So help me God, I laugh when I think
How pitously a-nyght I made hem swynke.	How mercilessly I made them work at night.
And, by my fey, I tolde of it no stoor,	And by my faith, it didn't make any difference
They had me yeven hir gold and hir tresoor;	That they had given me their gold and other possessions;
Me neded nat do lenger diligence	I didn't need any other efforts
To wynne hir love, or doon hem reverence,	To win their love, or show them respect.
They loved me so wel, by God above,	They all loved me so much, I swear to God,
That I ne tolde no deyntee of hir love.	That I did not put any value on their love.
A wys womman wol sette hire evere in oon	A wise woman will always do her best
To gete hire love, ther as she hath noon.	To make sure she's loved, if she is not.
But sith I hadde hem hoolly in myn hond,	But since I had them in the palm of my hand,
And sith they hadde me yeven all hir lond,	And they had given me all of their land,
What sholde I taken heede hem for to plese,	Why did I have to try and use them
But it were for my profit and myn ese?	Unless it was for my own enjoyment?
I sette hem so a-werke, by my fey,	I made them work so hard, I swear,
That many a nyght they songen "weilawey!"	That many nights they cried out, "Woe is me!"
The bacon was nat fet for hem, I trowe,	I don't think that they got the same pleasure
That som men han in Essex at Dunmowe.	As the men of Essex have in their Dunmowe bacon.

I governed hem so wel after my lawe,	I governed them so well, by my own rules,
That ech of hem ful blisful was, and fawe	That each of them was very happy, and wanted
To brynge me gaye thynges fro the fayre.	To bring me pretty things from the fair.
They were ful glad whan I spak to hem faire,	They were delighted when I spoke to them kindly
For, God it woot, I chidde hem spitously.	For God knows I nagged them mercilessly.
Now herkneth hou I baar me proprely,	Now listen to how well I carried on,
Ye wise wyves, that kan understonde.	You wise wives, who can understand.
Thus shul ye speke and bere hem wrong on honde;	This is how you should speak, and make wrongful accusations;
For half so boldely kan ther no man	For there is no man who can swear and lie
Swere and lyen, as a womman kan.	Half as brazenly as a woman can.
I sey nat this by wyves that been wyse,	I'm not saying this to wives who are canny,
But if it be whan they hem mysavyse.	But those ones who behave mistakenly.
A wys wyf, it that she kan hir good,	A wise wife, if she knows what's good for her,
Shal beren hym on hond the cow is wood,	Will swear that all the gossips are mad,
And take witnesse of hir owene mayde,	And back it up with evidence from her own maid,
Of hir assent; but herkneth how I sayde.	Who will be in it with her; but now listen to what I said.
"Sir olde kaynard, is this thyn array?	"Why you old fool, is this the best you can do?
Why is my neighebores wyf so gay?	Why is the wife of my neighbour so well kitted out?
She is honoured overal ther she gooth;	She is respected where she goes;
I sitte at hoom, I have no thrifty clooth.	I stay at home, I have no decent clothes.
What dostow at my neighebores hous?	What are you doing in my neighbour's house?
Is she so fair? Artow so amorous?	Is she so lovely? Are you so randy?
What rowne ye with oure mayde? Benedicite,	Why are you whispering with our maid? For God's sake,
Sir olde lecchour, lat thy japes be!	You old lech, give up your games!
And if I have a gossib or a freend	And if I have a confidant or friend,
Withouten gilt, thou chidest as a feend	Completely innocently, you curse me like a devil
If that I walke or pleye unto his hous.	If I just go over to his house.
Thou comest hoom as dronken as a mous	You come home absolutely drunk
And prechest on thy bench, with yvel preef!	And sit there on your bench evilly cursing me!
Thou seist to me, it is a greet mischief	You say to me that it's a terrible thing
To wedde a povre womman, for costage,	To marry a poor woman, because of the expense,
And if she be riche and of heigh parage,	And that if she is rich and nobly born
Thanne seistow it is a tormentrie	Then it is torture
To soffre hire pride and hir malencolie.	To put up with her pride and sorrow.
And if she be fair, thou verray knave,	And if she is beautiful, you scoundrel,
Thou seyst that every holour wol hir have;	You say that every randy man will have her;
She may no while in chastitee abyde	There is no way that she will remain chaste
That is assailled upon ech a syde.	When she's attacked from every angle.
Thou seyst, som folk desiren us for richesse,	You say that some folk want us for our wealth,
Somme for oure shape, and somme for oure fairnesse,	Some for our bodies, some for our beauty,
And som for she kan outher synge or daunce,	And some for our skills in singing and dancing,
And som for gentillesse and daliaunce,	And some for our gentility and flirting.

Som for hir handes and hir armes smale;	Some for their little hands and arms;
Thus goth al to the devel by thy tale.	So according to you we all go to the devil.
Thou seyst, men may nat kepe a castel wal,	You say that men cannot defend a castle
It may so longe assailled been overal.	That is attacked on all sides for so long.
And if that she be foul, thou seist that she	And if she is ugly, you say that she
Coveiteth every man that she may se;	Must lust after every man that she sees;
For as a spaynel she wol on hym lepe	She will leap on them like a spaniel,
Til that she fynde som man hir to chepe;	Until she manages to trap some man;
Ne noon so grey goos gooth ther in the lake	There is no goose in the lake that is so grey
As, seistow, wol been withoute make;	As, so you say, to stop it getting a mate;
And seyst, it is an hard thyng for to welde	You say it would be hard to make
A thyng that no man wole, his thankes, helde.	A woman whom no man wanted.
Thus seistow, lorel, whan thow goost to bedde,	You say this, you worthless thing, when you go to bed,
And that no wys man nedeth for to wedde,	And say that no wise man should marry,
Ne no man that entendeth unto hevene -	And nor should any man who wants to get to heaven.
With wilde thonder-dynt and firy levene	May your wrinkled old neck be broken
Moote thy welked nekke be tobroke!	With wild thunderclaps and fiery lightning!
Thow seyst that droppyng houses, and eek smoke,	You say that collapsing houses, and also smoke,
And chidyng wyves maken men to flee	And nagging wives will make men flee
Out of hir owene hous, a! benedicitee!	From their own homes; alas, God bless us!
What eyleth swich an old man for to chide?	Why does an old man have to be so critical?
Thow seyst, we wyves wol oure vices hide	You say that we women hide all our vices,
Til we be fast, and thanne we wol hem shewe, -	Until we've trapped you, then we show them to you;
Wel may that be a proverbe of a shrewe!	That's the saying of a scoundrel, I tell you!
Thou seist, that oxen, asses, hors, and houndes,	You say that oxen, asses, horses and hounds
They been assayd at diverse stoundes;	Are always tested in various ways;
Bacyns, lavours, er that men hem bye,	So are basins and bowls, before you buy them,
Spoones and stooles, and al swich housbondrye,	And spoons and stools, and other household goods,
And so been pottes, clothes, and array;	The same with pots, clothes and finery;
But folk of wyves maken noon assay	But people can't try out their wives
Til they be wedded, olde dotard shrewe!	Until they are married, you nagging old fool!
And thanne, seistow, we wol oure vices shewe.	And then, you say, we show our evil side.
Thou seist also, that it displeseth me	You also says that I'm unhappy
But if that thou wolt preyse my beautee,	If you don't always praise my beauty,
And but thou poure alwey upon my face,	And spend your whole time looking at my face,
And clepe me "faire dame" in every place,	And call me, "beautiful lady" everywhere,
And but thou make a feeste on thilke day	And if you don't organise a great feast,
That I was born, and make me fressh and gay,	On my birthday, and dress me in finery,
And but thou do to my norice honour,	And behave respectfully to my nurse,
And to my chamberere withinne my bour,	As well as to my chambermaid,
And to my fadres folk and hise allyes-	And my father's people and all his friends—
Thus seistow, olde barel-ful of lyes!	That's what you say, you old barrel of lies!
And yet of oure apprentice Janekyn,	And then you suspect our apprentice Young Jenkin, with his crisp hair,
For his crispe heer, shynynge as gold so fyn,	Shining as beautifully as spun gold,

And for he squiereth me bothe up and doun,	Because he escorts me when I go out,
Yet hastow caught a fals suspecioun.	You wrongly think there's something going on.
I wol hym noght, thogh thou were deed tomorwe!	He would get nothing from me, even if you died tomorrow!
But tel me this, why hydestow, with sorwe,	But tell me this, why do you keep the keys
The keyes of my cheste awey fro me?	To your strongbox hidden from me?
It is my good as wel as thyn, pardee;	Those are my goods as well as yours, by God;
What, wenestow make an ydiot of oure dame?	Do you want to make a fool out of your lady?
Now by that lord that called is Seint Jame,	Now by St James I swear
Thou shalt nat bothe, thogh that thou were wood,	That you shall not, even if you were mad,
Be maister of my body and of my good;	Be the master of my body and my property;
That oon thou shalt forgo, maugree thyne eyen.	You will give one of them up, despite what you think.
What nedeth thee of me to enquere or spyen?	Why do you question me and spy on me?
I trowe thou woldest loke me in thy chiste.	I think you'd like to lock me up in your strongbox.
Thou sholdest seye, "Wyf, go wher thee liste,	You should say, "Wife, go where if you like,
Taak youre disport, I wol not leve no talys,	Enjoy yourself, I won't listen to gossip,
I knowe yow for a trewe wyf, dame Alys."	I know you are loyal wife, lady Alice."
We love no man that taketh kepe or charge	We don't love men who imprison us
Wher that we goon, we wol ben at our large.	Or order where we can go, we want to be free.
Of alle men yblessed moot he be,	Of all men the one who is most blessed,
The wise astrologien, Daun Ptholome,	The wise astrologer, old Ptolemy,
That seith this proverbe in his Almageste:	Said this in his almanac:
`Of alle men his wysdom is the hyeste,	"Of all men the wisest is he
That rekketh nevere who hath the world in honde.'	Who cares nothing for what others have."
By this proverbe thou shalt understonde,	You should understand from this proverb,
Have thou ynogh, what thar thee recche or care	That if you have enough, why should you observe or care
How myrily that othere folkes fare?	How other people are doing?
For certeyn, olde dotard, by youre leve,	It's certain, you old fool, if you'll excuse me,
Ye shul have queynte right ynogh at eve.	That you will get plenty of snatch in the evening.
He is to greet a nygard, that wolde werne	It's a mean man who won't allow
A man to lighte his candle at his lanterne;	Somebody to light his candle from his lantern;
He shal have never the lasse light, pardee,	He wouldn't lose any light thereby, by God;
Have thou ynogh, thee thar nat pleyne thee.	Since you've got enough, you shouldn't complain.
Thou seyst also, that if we make us gay	You also say, if we dress ourselves up
With clothyng and with precious array,	With nice clothes and finery,
That it is peril of oure chastitee:	That this puts our chastity in danger;
And yet, with sorwe, thou most enforce thee,	And still, pitifully, you back yourself up
And seye thise wordes in the Apostles name,	By repeating the words of the apostle,
"In habit, maad with chastitee and shame,	"Your women should be dressed in clothes
Ye wommen shul apparaille yow," quod he,	Appropriate for chastity, not for lust," he says,
"And noght in tressed heer and gay perree,	"And she shouldn't have her hair braided or wear jewellery,
As perles, ne with gold, ne clothes riche."	Such as pearls, gold, nor rich clothes."
After thy text, ne after thy rubriche	I couldn't give a gnat for
I wol nat wirche, as muchel as a gnat!	All your sermonising and your texts!
Thou seydest this, that I was lyk a cat;	Then you told me that I was like a cat;
For whoso wolde senge a cattes skyn,	For anyone who burns a cat's fur

149

Thanne wolde the cat wel dwellen in his in.	Can be sure the cat will stay in the house.
And if the cattes skyn be slyk and gay,	And if the cat is sleek and pretty
She wol nat dwelle in house half a day,	She won't stay in the house for half a day,
But forth she wole, er any day be dawed,	She will be off before dawn
To shewe hir skyn, and goon a-caterwawed.	To show off her skin and mewl and play.
This is to seye, if I be gay, sire shrewe,	What you mean is that if I dress nicely, you old miser,
I wol renne out, my borel for to shewe.	I'll spend the whole day out showing off my clothes.
Sire olde fool, what eyleth thee to spyen,	You old fool, why do you bother spying,
Thogh thou preye Argus, with his hundred eyen,	If you asked Argus, with his hundred eyes
To be my warde-cors, as he kan best,	To be my bodyguard and do his best,
In feith, he shal nat kepe me but me lest;	I swear he couldn't keep track of me;
Yet koude I make his berd, so moot I thee.	I could make a fool of him, as I can of you.
Thou seydest eek, that ther been thynges thre,	You also said that there are three things,
The whiche thynges troublen al this erthe,	Things which cause such trouble on this earth
And that no wight ne may endure the ferthe.	That nobody would be able to put up with a fourth.
O leeve sire shrewe, Jesu shorte thy lyf!	My dear old scoundrel, may Jesus cut your life short!
Yet prechestow, and seyst an hateful wyf	You go on preaching and say that a bad wife
Yrekened is for oon of thise meschances.	Is one of those three bad things.
Been ther none othere maner resemblances	Is there nothing else that you can
That ye may likne youre parables to,	Use as a metaphor for your sermons,
But if a sely wyf be oon of tho?	Do you have to use your unfortunate wife?
Thou likenest wommenes love to helle,	You compare a woman's love to hell,
To bareyne lond, ther water may nat dwelle.	To desert lands where there is no water.
Thou liknest it also to wilde fyr;	You also compare it to wildfire;
The moore it brenneth, the moore it hath desir	The more it burns, the more it wants
To consume every thyng that brent wole be.	To consume everything that's flammable.
Thou seyest, right as wormes shende a tree,	You say that just as worms destroy a tree
Right so a wyf destroyeth hir housbond.	That's how a wife destroys her husband.
This knowe they, that been to wyves bonde."	Men who have been tied to wives know this."
Lordynges, right thus, as ye have understonde,	My lords, you must understand from this
Baar I stifly myne olde housbondes on honde,	That this is what I accused my old husbands
That thus they seyden in hir dronkenesse;	Of saying when they were drunk;
And al was fals, but that I took witnesse	And it was all untrue, but it was witnessed
On Janekyn and on my nece also.	By Jenkins, and also my niece.
O lord! The pyne I dide hem, and the wo	Oh Lord! What pain I gave them, and
Ful giltelees, by Goddes sweete pyne!	What sorrow, when, by God, they were completely innocent!
For as an hors I koude byte and whyne,	Like a horse I could whinny and bite,
I koude pleyne, thogh I were in the gilt,	I would criticise, though I was the guilty one,
Or elles often tyme hadde I been spilt.	Otherwise I would have come a cropper.
Who so that first to mille comth first grynt;	Whoever is first at the mill is the first to get their corn;
I pleyned first, so was oure werre ystynt.	I got my complaints in early, and so confounded them.
They were ful glad to excuse hem ful blyve	They were quick to make full apologies
Of thyng of which they nevere agilte hir lyve.	For the things which they had never done in their lives.

Of wenches wolde I beren hym on honde,	*I accused him of messing with women*
Whan that for syk unnethes myghte he stonde,	*When to tell the truth he hardly had the strength to stand up.*
Yet tikled it his herte, for that he!	*But all this tickled his heart, for he*
Wende that I hadde of hym so greet chiertee.	*Imagined it was love that was making me jealous.*
I swoor that al my walkynge out by nyghte	*I swore that all my nighttime strolls*
Was for t'espye wenches that he dighte.	*Were to look out for the girls he was after.*
Under that colour hadde I many a myrthe;	*I had a lot of fun under cover of that;*
For al swich wit is yeven us in oure byrthe,	*For we are given that sort of cunning when we are born,*
Deceite, wepyng, spynnyng, God hath yive	*Deceit, weeping, spinning yarns, is what God gives*
To wommen kyndely whil they may lyve.	*To women to use throughout their lives.*
And thus of o thyng I avaunte me,	*And so I am truly able to boast,*
Atte ende I hadde the bettre in ech degree,	*That in the end I got the better of each one*
By sleighte, or force, or by som maner thyng,	*By cunning, or force, or in some other way,*
As by continueel murmur or grucchyng.	*As well as by continual nagging and grouching.*
Namely a bedde hadden they meschaunce;	*They had a bad time in bed especially;*
Ther wolde I chide and do hem no plesaunce,	*There I would nag them and give them no pleasure,*
I wolde no lenger in the bed abyde,	*I would not stay in bed*
If that I felte his arm over my syde	*If I felt his arm on my side*
Til he had maad his raunsoun unto me;	*Until he had paid an appropriate penalty;*
Thanne wolde I suffre hym do his nycetee.	*Then I would let him get what he wanted.*
And therfore every man this tale I telle,	*And so I'm telling this tale to every man,*
Wynne who so may, for al is for to selle;	*And may those who wish to benefit from it, it's there for everyone;*
With empty hand men may none haukes lure.	*You won't trap hawks with empty hands.*
For wynnyng wolde I al his lust endure	*I would put up with all his lust for money,*
And make me a feyned appetit;	*And pretend that I was as keen as him;*
And yet in bacon hadde I nevere delit;	*But old meat never gave me pleasure;*
That made me that evere I wolde hem chide.	*That's why I used to nag so much.*
For thogh the pope hadde seten hem biside,	*Even if the Pope had been sitting with them,*
I wolde nat spare hem at hir owene bord,	*I would not spare them at their own table,*
For by my trouthe I quitte hem word for word.	*I swear to you I matched them word for word.*
As help me verray God omnipotent,	*So help me omnipotent God,*
Though I right now sholde make my testament,	*If I was brought to judgement right now,*
I ne owe hem nat a word, that it nys quit.	*They did not say anything to me that I didn't answer back.*
I broghte it so aboute by my wit,	*I worked the whole business so cleverly*
That they moste yeve it up as for the beste,	*That they had to give in in the end,*
Or elles hadde we nevere been in reste.	*Or otherwise there would never have been any peace.*
For thogh he looked as a wood leon,	*He could scowl at me like a mad lion,*
Yet sholde he faille of his conclusioun.	*But he never got what he wanted.*
Thanne wolde I seye, "Goode lief, taak keep,	*Then I would say, "My dear, remember*
How mekely looketh Wilkyn oure sheep!	*How meek our sheep Wilkin is!*
Com neer, my spouse, lat me ba thy cheke!	*Come here, husband, let me kiss your cheek!*
Ye sholde been al pacient and meke,	*You should always be patient and meek,*
And han a sweete spiced conscience,	*And be kind and conscientiously sweet,*

Sith ye so preche of Jobes pacience.	Since you are always talking of the patience of Job.
Suffreth alwey, syn ye so wel kan preche,	You can preach so well of him, you must suffer everything,
And but ye do, certein we shal yow teche	And if you don't, you can be certain we will teach you
That it is fair to have a wyf in pees.	That a peaceful wife is the best thing to have.
Oon of us two moste bowen, doutelees;	One of the two of us must back down, it's certain;
And sith a man is moore resonable,	And since men are more reasonable
Than womman is, ye moste been suffrable."	Than women, you are the one who must suffer."
What eyleth yow to grucche thus and grone?	What's so wrong that you grumble and groan?
Is it for ye wolde have my queynte allone?	Is it because you want my snatch all to yourself;
Wy, taak it al! lo, have it every deel!	Why, have it all! Go on, take the lot;
Peter! I shrewe yow, but ye love it weel;	Peter! Damn you, you're very keen on it;
For if I wolde selle my bele chose,	For if I wanted to sell it around
I koude walke as fressh as is a rose	I could certainly make a fine profit,
But I wol kepe it for youre owene tooth.	But I will save it just for you.
Ye be to blame, by God! I sey yow sooth."	It's your fault, by God! I'm telling you the truth."
Swiche manere wordes hadde we on honde.	This is the way we spoke to each other.
Now wol I speken of my fourthe housbonde.	Now I will talk about my fourth husband.
My fourthe housbonde was a revelour -	He was a reveller—
This is to seyn, he hadde a paramour -	That is to say, he had a mistress—
And I was yong and ful of ragerye,	And I was young and full of passion,
Stibourn and strong, and joly as a pye.	Stubborn and strong, and jolly as a magpie.
Wel koude I daunce to an harpe smale,	I could dance beautifully to the little harp,
And synge, ywis, as any nyghtyngale,	And sing as well as any nightingale,
Whan I had dronke a draughte of sweete wyn.	When I had had a good drink of sweet wine.
Metellius, the foule cherl, the swyn,	Metellius, that foul peasant, the swine,
That with a staf birafte his wyf hire lyf,	Beat his wife to death with a stick
For she drank wyn, thogh I hadde been his wyf,	For drinking wine, though if I had been his wife
He sholde nat han daunted me fro drynke.	He wouldn't have been able to stop me drinking.
And after wyn on Venus moste I thynke,	After wine, it's love that I most think about,
For al so siker as cold engendreth hayl,	For just as when it's cold it hails,
A likerous mouth moste han a likerous tayl.	Liquor in the mouth creates a lascivious ass.
In wommen vinolent is no defence,	The drunken woman doesn't put up a fight,
This knowen lecchours by experience.	That's what all lecherous men have learnt.
But, Lord Crist! whan that it remembreth me	But, by Christ! When I remember
Upon my yowthe and on my jolitee,	All my youth and my happiness,
It tikleth me aboute myn herte roote.	It really warms my heart deep down.
Unto this day it dooth myn herte boote	To this day it does my heart good
That I have had my world, as in my tyme.	To think of what I had in my day.
But age, allas, that al wole envenyme,	But age, alas, that poisons everything,
Hath me biraft my beautee and my pith!	Has taken away my beauty and my spirit!
Lat go, farewel, the devel go therwith!	Leave go, farewell, go to the devil!
The flour is goon, ther is namoore to telle,	The bloom has gone, there is no more to tell,
The bren as I best kan, now moste I selle;	Now I have to try and sell the stalks;

But yet to be right myrie wol I fonde.	*But still I'll try to keep cheerful,*
Now wol I tellen of my fourthe housbonde.	*And tell you about my fourth husband.*
I seye, I hadde in herte greet despit	*I tell you that I hated it deep down*
That he of any oother had delit;	*When he was off with any other woman.*
But he was quit, by God and by Seint Joce!	*But he was paid back, by God and St John!*
I made hym of the same wode a croce;	*I made a stick to beat him with of the same would,*
Nat of my body in no foul manere,	*I didn't use my body in any foul way,*
But certeinly, I made folk swich cheere	*But certainly, I acted in such a jolly way*
That in his owene grece I made hym frye	*That I made him fry in his own fat*
For angre and for verray jalousye.	*With anger and with jealousy.*
By God, in erthe I was his purgatorie,	*By God, I made the world purgatory for him,*
For which I hope his soule be in glorie,	*And I hope that his soul now lives in heaven,*
For, God it woot, he sat ful ofte and song	*For God knows, many times he sat and sang*
Whan that his shoo ful bitterly hym wrong!	*Of the pain which he was suffering!*
Ther was no wight save God and he, that wiste	*There was nobody, apart from him and God, who knew*
In many wise how soore I hym twiste.	*How much pain I caused him.*
He deyde whan I cam fro Jerusalem,	*He died when I came back from Jerusalem,*
And lith ygrave under the roode-beem,	*And he is buried under the cross,*
Al is his tombe noght so curyus	*Although his tomb is not as exotic*
As was the sepulcre of hym Daryus,	*As the grave of Darius,*
Which that Appelles wroghte subtilly.	*Which Appelles built so cleverly;*
It nys but wast to burye hym preciously,	*It would have been a waste of money to bury him expensively,*
Lat hym fare-wel, God yeve his soule reste,	*May he go well, may God rest his soul,*
He is now in his grave, and in his cheste.	*Now he's in his coffin in his grave.*
Now of my fifthe housbonde wol I telle.	*Now I will tell you about my fifth husband,*
God lete his soule nevere come in helle!	*May God keep his soul out of hell!*
And yet was he to me the mooste shrewe;	*But he was the one who was most brutal to me;*
That feele I on my ribbes al by rewe,	*I can still feel the pain in my ribs,*
And evere shal, unto myn endyng day.	*And always shall until my dying day.*
But in oure bed he was ful fressh and gay,	*But in our bed he was so fresh and jolly*
And therwithal so wel koude he me glose	*And he could flatter me so well*
Whan that he solde han my bele chose,	*When he wanted to get hold of me,*
That thogh he hadde me bet on every bon	*That though he had beaten me black and blue*
He koude wynne agayn my love anon.	*He could quickly win my love again.*
I trowe I loved hym beste, for that he	*I think I loved him most of all, because he*
Was of his love daungerous to me.	*Was begrudging in his love for me.*
We wommen han, if that I shal nat lye,	*We women have, to tell the truth,*
In this matere a queynte fantasye;	*Strange tastes in this matter;*
Wayte what thyng we may nat lightly have,	*Show us something we can't get easily,*
Therafter wol we crie al day and crave.	*And we will cry and desire it all day.*
Forbede us thyng, and that desiren we;	*Forbid us something, and we will want it;*
Preesse on us faste, and thanne wol we fle;	*Try and force it on us, and we'll run away from it.*
With daunger oute we al oure chaffare.	*We only offer our wares sparingly;*
Greet prees at market maketh deere ware,	*The more people who are in the market the better price you get,*
And to greet cheep is holde at litel prys;	*And what's cheap doesn't attract much interest;*
This knoweth every womman that is wys.	*Every wise woman knows this.*

My fifthe housbonde, God his soule blesse,	My fifth husband, God bless his soul,
Which that I took for love and no richesse,	Whom I married for love, not wealth,
He somtyme was a clerk of Oxenford,	Had at one time been a student at Oxford,
And hadde left scole, and wente at hom to bord	But he had left college, and come home to lodge
With my gossib, dwellynge in oure toun,	With my close friend, living in our town,
God have hir soule! hir name was Alisoun.	God rest her soul! Her name was Alison.
She knew myn herte and eek my privetee	She knew what was in my heart and all my secrets
Bet than oure parisshe preest, as moot I thee.	Better than our parish priest, I swear.
To hir biwreyed I my conseil al,	I confided everything in her,
For hadde myn housbonde pissed on a wal,	For if my husband so much as pissed on the wall,
Or doon a thyng that sholde han cost his lyf,	Or if he did something that risked his life,
To hir, and to another worthy wyf,	I would tell her and another good woman,
And to my nece, which that I loved weel,	And my niece, whom I loved very much,
I wolde han toold his conseil every deel.	Everything about it.
And so I dide ful often, God it woot,	I did this so many times, God knows,
That made his face ful often reed and hoot	He was often made to blush fearlessly
For verray shame, and blamed hym-self, for he	In shame, blaming himself for
Had toold to me so greet a pryvetee.	Telling me such great secrets.
And so bifel that ones, in a Lente -	And so it happened once, in Lent—
So often tymes I to my gossyb wente,	I frequently went to see my friend,
For evere yet I loved to be gay,	For I always loved to be jolly,
And for to walke in March, Averill, and May,	And to go out walking in March, April and May,
Fro hous to hous to heere sondry talys -	Going from house to house to hear the gossip—
That Jankyn Clerk and my gossyb, dame Alys,	This clerk Jenkins and my friend, lady Alison,
And I myself into the feeldes wente.	And myself went out into the fields.
Myn housbonde was at London al that Lente;	My husband was in London all through that Lent;
I hadde the bettre leyser for to pleye,	So I had more time to enjoy myself,
And for to se, and eek for to be seye	And to look for, and also be seen by,
Of lusty folk; what wiste I, wher my grace	Lusty people; how did I know what my fate
Was shapen for to be, or in what place?	Was going to be, or where it would happen?
Therfore I made my visitaciouns	And so I went around visiting
To vigilies and to processiouns,	Vigils and religious processions,
To prechyng eek, and to thise pilgrimages,	Going to see preachers, and sites of pilgrimage,
To pleyes of myracles, and to mariages;	To miracle plays, and to weddings;
And wered upon my gaye scarlet gytes.	And I wore my cheerful red skirts.
Thise wormes ne thise motthes, ne thise mytes,	The worms and moths and mites
Upon my peril, frete hem never a deel;	I swear, never ate a morsel of them;
And wostow why? for they were used weel!	Do you know why? Because I wore them all the time!
Now wol I tellen forth what happed me.	Now I'll tell you what happened to me.
I seye, that in the feeldes walked we,	I said, that we went out into the fields,
Til trewely we hadde swich daliance,	Until we really became so flirtatious,
This clerk and I, that of my purveyance	This clerk and I, that thinking of the future
I spak to hym, and seyde hym, how that he,	I told him that if I were a widow
If I were wydwe, sholde wedde me.	Then I would marry him.
For certeinly, I sey for no bobance,	For I can certainly say without boasting

Yet was I nevere withouten purveyance	That I was never lacking in offers
Of mariage, n'of othere thynges eek.	Of marriage, nor of other things.
I holde a mouses herte nat worth a leek	I don't think a mouse is safe
That hath but oon hole for to sterte to,	If it only has one hole to run to,
And if that faille, thanne is al ydo.	Because if that one fails, he's lost.
I bar hym on honde, he hadde enchanted me, -	I led him on, letting him think I was enchanted by him—
My dame taughte me that soutiltee.	My mother taught me all the tricks.
And eek I seyde, I mette of hym al nyght,	And I also said that I had dreams of him all night,
He wolde han slayn me as I lay upright,	That he killed me as I lay on my back,
And al my bed was ful of verray blood;	And all my bed was swamped with blood;
But yet I hope that he shal do me good,	But still I hoped that he would be good to me,
For blood bitokeneth gold, as me was taught-	For I have been taught that blood represents gold—
And al was fals, I dremed of it right naught,	And this was all lies, I didn't dream it at all,
But as I folwed ay my dames lore	But I followed my mother's rules
As wel of this, as of othere thynges moore.	In this as well as in other things.
But now sir, lat me se, what I shal seyn?	But now Sir, let me see, what was I going to say?
A ha, by God, I have my tale ageyn.	By God, I remember, this is how it went.
Whan that my fourthe housbonde was on beere,	When my fourth husband was lying dead,
I weep algate, and made sory cheere,	I wept all day, and put on a miserable face,
As wyves mooten, for it is usage-	As wives have to, for it is the custom,
And with my coverchief covered my visage;	And I covered my face with a handkerchief;
But for that I was purveyed of a make,	But since I had another mate,
I wepte but smal, and that I undertake.	I only really wept a little, I swear.
To chirche was myn housbonde born amorwe	My husband was carried to church the next day,
With neighebores that for hym maden sorwe;	By neighbours who showed their mourning for him;
And Janekyn oure clerk was oon of tho.	And our clerk Jenkins was one of them.
As help me God! whan that I saugh hym go	So help me God! When I saw him following
After the beere, me thoughte he hadde a paire	The coffin, I thought he had a pair
Of legges and of feet so clene and faire,	Of legs and feet which was so clean and lovely
That al myn herte I yaf unto his hoold.	That I surrendered my heart to him completely.
He was, I trowe, a twenty wynter oold,	He was, I thought, a twenty year old
And I was fourty, if I shal seye sooth,	And I was forty, to tell the truth,
But yet I hadde alwey a coltes tooth.	But I always loved the young ones.
Gat-tothed I was, and that bicam me weel,	I was gap toothed, and that suited me well,
I hadde the prente of Seinte Venus seel.	That was the imprint of holy Venus.
As help me God, I was a lusty oon,	So help me God, I was a lusty one,
And faire, and riche, and yong, and wel bigon,	Pretty, rich, young and well set up
And trewely, as myne housbondes tolde me,	And truly, as my husbands told me,
I hadde the beste quonyam myghte be.	I had the loveliest snatch imaginable.
For certes, I am al Venerien	Truly, Venus rules over all
In feelynge, and myn herte is Marcien.	My emotions, whereas my brain is ruled by Mars.
Venus me yaf my lust, my likerousnesse,	Venus gives me my lustiness, my licentiousness,
And Mars yaf me my sturdy hardynesse.	And Mars gives me my sturdy hardiness.

Myn ascendent was Taur, and Mars therinne,	Taurus was in the ascendance, along with Mars, when I was born,
Allas, allas, that evere love was synne!	Alas that love was ever counted as a sin!
I folwed ay myn inclinacioun	I always followed my inclinations,
By vertu of my constellacioun;	Due to the star sign I was born under;
That made me I koude noght withdrawe	It made me so that I would never refuse
My chambre of Venus from a good felawe.	To let a good man enter me.
Yet have I Martes mark upon my face,	But I have the sign of Mars upon my face,
And also in another privee place.	And also somewhere else, private.
For God so wys be my savacioun,	For as God will be my salvation,
I ne loved nevere by no discrecioun,	I have never been cautious about my love,
But evere folwede myn appetit,	But always followed my appetites,
Al were he short, or long, or blak, or whit.	Whether the chap was short or tall, fair or dark.
I took no kep, so that he liked me,	I didn't care, as long as he liked me,
How poore he was, ne eek of what degree.	How poor he was, or what rank he held.
What sholde I seye, but at the monthes ende	What more can I say, but at the end of the month
This joly clerk Jankyn, that was so hende	This jolly clerk Jenkins, who was so pleasant,
Hath wedded me with greet solempnytee,	Married me with great ceremony,
And to hym yaf I al the lond and fee	And I handed over to him all the land
That evere was me yeven therbifoore;	That had ever been given to me previously;
But afterward repented me ful soore;	But afterwards I had to regret this;
He nolde suffre nothyng of my list.	He never let me do anything I wanted.
By God, he smoot me ones on the lyst	By God, once he hit me over the ear
For that I rente out of his book a leef,	For taking a page out of his book,
That of the strook myn ere wax al deef.	So hard that now that ear is completely deaf.
Stibourne I was as is a leonesse,	I was a stubborn as a lioness,
And of my tonge a verray jangleresse,	And chatted away like a jay,
And walke I wolde, as I had doon biforn,	And I would stroll, as I had before,
From hous to hous, although he had it sworn,	From house to house, although he had sworn
For which he often-tymes wolde preche,	I would not, and he would often preach
And me of olde Romayn geestes teche,	About the old Roman stories,
How he Symplicius Gallus lefte his wyf,	How the one called Sulpicius Gallus left his wife,
And hir forsook for terme of al his lyf,	Abandoning her for the rest of his life,
Noght but for open-heveded he hir say,	Just because he saw her looking out the door
Lookynge out at his dore, upon a day.	One time with no head covering on.
Another Romayn tolde he me by name,	He told me about another Roman chap
That for his wyf was at a someres game	Who because his wife went to a summer game
Withoute his wityng, he forsook hir eke.	Without his permission, left her at once.
And thanne wolde he upon his Bible seke	And then he would look inside his Bible
That like proverbe of Ecclesiaste,	For the proverb of Ecclesiastes,
Where he comandeth, and forbedeth faste,	Where he orders against, and strictly forbids,
Man shal nat suffre his wyf go roule aboute,	A man to allow his wife to go around enjoying herself,
Thanne wolde he seye right thus, withouten doute:	And he would repeat it, believing it:
"Who so that buyldeth his hous al of salwes,	"Someone who builds his whole house of straw,
And priketh his blynde hors over the falwes,	And spurs his blind horse over the fields,
And suffreth his wyf to go seken halwes,	And lets his wife go on solo pilgrimages
Is worthy to been hanged on the galwes!"	Deserves to be hung upon the gallows."

But al for noght, I sette noght an hawe
Of his proverbes, n'of his olde sawe,
Ne I wolde nat of hym corrected be.
I hate hym that my vices telleth me;

And so doo mo, God woot, of us than I.
This made hym with me wood al outrely,
I nolde noght forbere hym in no cas.
 Now wol I seye yow sooth, by seint Thomas,
Why that I rente out of his book a leef,
For which he smoot me so that I was deef.

He hadde a book that gladly, nyght and day,
For his desport he wolde rede alway.
He cleped it Valerie and Theofraste,
At whiche book he lough alwey ful faste.

And eek ther was som tyme a clerk at Rome,
A cardinal that highte Seint Jerome,
That made a book agayn Jovinian,
In whiche book eek ther was Tertulan,
Crisippus, Trotula, and Helowys,
That was abbesse nat fer fro Parys,
And eek the Parables of Salomon,
Ovides Art, and bookes many on,
And alle thise were bounden in o volume,
And every nyght and day was his custume
Whan he hadde leyser and vacacioun
From oother worldly occupacioun
To reden on this book of wikked wyves.
He knew of hem mo legendes and lyves
Than been of goode wyves in the Bible.
For trusteth wel, it is an impossible
That any clerk wol speke good of wyves,
But if it be of hooly seintes lyves,

Ne of noon oother womman never the mo.
Who peyntede the leon, tel me, who?
By God! if wommen hadde writen stories,
As clerkes han withinne hire oratories,
They wolde han writen of men moore wikkednesse

Than all the mark of Adam may redresse.

The children of Mercurie and Venus
Been in hir wirkyng ful contrarius,
Mercurie loveth wysdam and science,
And Venus loveth ryot and dispence.
And for hire diverse disposicioun
Ech falleth in otheres exaltacioun,
And thus, God woot, Mercurie is desolate
In Pisces, wher Venus is exaltat;
And Venus falleth ther Mercurie is reysed.

Therfore no womman of no clerk is preysed.

But it was all for nothing, I didn't care
Of his proverbs, none of his age saw
Nor would I let him order me about.
I hate someone telling me what I'm doing wrong;
As do most of us, God knows.
This made him very cross with me,
Because I wouldn't do what he wanted.
Now I'll tell you truthfully, by St Thomas,
Why I tore a page out of his book,
Which is why he hit me and made me deaf.

He had a book that he happily, night and day,
Would read all the time for his amusement.
He called it Valerie and Theofraste,
And this book would make him laugh enormously.

Also there was one time a clerk at Rome,
A cardinal, called St Jerome,
Who wrote a book against Jovinian,
And in that book there was also Terullian,
Crispus, Trotula and Heloise,
Who was an abbess not far from Paris,
And also the parables of Solomon,
Ovid's "Art", and many other books,
All bound up in one volume,
And every night and day it was his habit,
When he had any spare time
From all his other worldly occupations
To read in this book about wicked wives.
He knew more stories and biographies of them
Then there are good wives in the Bible.
For believe me, it is impossible
For any cleric to speak well of wives,
Unless they are talking about the lives of the holy saints,
They care nothing for any other women.
Tell me, who first painted the lion?
By God! If women had written the stories,
That these clerics have in their libraries,
They would have written more about the wickedness of men
Than any of Adam's descendants could atone for.

The children of Mercury and Venus
Are always working against each other,
Mercury loves wisdom and science,
And Venus loves pleasure and excess.
Because they are so very different
Each one declines when the other rises,
And so, God knows, Mercury is abandoned
In Pisces, when Venus is ascendant;
And Venus falls down there when Mercury rises.

So no woman is praised by any cleric.

...an he is oold and may noght do	The cleric, when he is old and can't do anything
...verkes worth his olde sho,	Worthwhile in the games of love,
... he doun, and writ in his dotage	Then he sits down, and in his old age he writes
That wommen kan nat kepe hir mariage.	That women are not worthy of marriage.
But now to purpos, why I tolde thee	But now to the point, to tell you why
That I was beten for a book, pardee.	I was beaten because of the book, by God.
Upon a nyght Jankyn, that was oure sire,	One night Jenkins, who was my husband,
Redde on his book as he sat by the fire	Was reading his book as he sat by the fire,
Of Eva first, that for hir wikkednesse	Of the first Eve, whose wickedness
Was al mankynde broght to wrecchednesse,	Brought wretchedness to all mankind,
For which that Jhesu Crist hymself was slayn,	Which is why Jesus Christ himself was killed,
That boghte us with his herte blood agayn.	Who saved us again with his heart's blood.
Lo, heere expres of womman may ye fynde,	Here you can find it expressly said
That womman was the los of al mankynde.	That woman was the downfall of all mankind.
Tho redde he me how Sampson loste hise heres,	Then he read to me of how Samson lost his hair,
Slepynge, his lemman kitte it with hir sheres,	Sleeping, with his lover cutting it with her shears,
Thurgh whiche tresoun loste he bothe hise yen.	And because of this treason he lost both his eyes.
Tho redde he me, if that I shal nat lyen,	Then he read to me, I'm telling you the truth,
Of Hercules and of his Dianyre,	About Hercules and Deinanira,
That caused hym to sette hymself afyre.	And how he ended up on fire.
No thyng forgat he the penaunce and wo	Nor did he forget the pain and sorrow
That Socrates hadde with hise wyves two,	That Socrates had with his two wives,
How Xantippa caste pisse upon his heed.	How Xantippe threw piss over his head;
This sely man sat stille as he were deed;	The unfortunate man sat still as if he were dead;
He wiped his heed, namoore dorste he seyn	He wiped off his head, he didn't dare say anything more
But, "Er that thonder stynte, comth a reyn."	Than, "Once the thunder finishes, then comes the rain."
Of Phasipha, that was the queene of Crete,	He liked the story of Pasiphae, Queen of Crete,
For shrewednesse hym thoughte the tale swete-	Her wickedness appealed to him in that tale-
Fy! Speke namoore - it is a grisly thyng -	I'll speak no more of it, it's a horrible thing,
Of hir horrible lust and hir likyng.	Her revolting lust and her insatiable desires.
Of Clitermystra for hire lecherye,	He read with great enjoyment
That falsly made hir housbonde for to dye,	About Clytemnestra and her lechery,
He redde it with ful good devocioun.	Who brought her husband down through treachery.
He tolde me eek for what occasioun	He also told me the reason why
Amphiorax at Thebes loste his lyf.	Amphiorax lost his life at Thebes.
Myn housbonde hadde a legende of his wyf	My husband had a legend about his wife
Eriphilem, that for an ouche of gold	Eriphyle, who for a golden brooch
Hath prively unto the Grekes told	Secretly told the Greeks
Wher that hir housbonde hidde hym in a place,	Where her husband was hiding out,
For which he hadde at Thebes sory grace.	And he did not receive any mercy at Thebes.
Of Lyvia tolde he me, and of Lucye,	He told me about Livia and Lucia,
They bothe made hir housbondes for to dye,	Who both caused the death of their husbands,

That oon for love, that oother was for hate.	One out of love, the other from hate.
Lyvia hir housbonde, on an even late,	Late one evening Livia made her husband
Empoysoned hath, for that she was his fo.	Drink some poison, for she was his enemy.
Lucia, likerous, loved hir housbonde so,	Lucia, lecherous, loved her husband so much
That for he sholde alwey upon hire thynke,	That she gave him such a strong love potion,
She yaf hym swich a manere love-drynke	So he would never look at anyone else,
That he was deed, er it were by the morwe.	That he was dead by the morning.
And thus algates housbondes han sorw.	And so all husbands end up suffering.
Thanne tolde he me, how that Latumyus	Then he told me how Latumius
Compleyned unto his felawe Arrius,	Complained to his friend Arrius
That in his gardyn growed swich a tree,	That in his garden there was growing an evil tree
On which he seyde how that hise wyves thre	On which he had seen his three wives
Hanged hemself, for herte despitus.	Hang themselves, from heartache.
"O leeve brother," quod this Arrius,	"Oh dear brother," said this Arrius,
"Yif me a plante of thilke blissed tree,	"Give me a graft of that blessed tree,
And in my gardyn planted it shal bee."	And I shall have it planted in my garden."
Of latter date of wyves hath he red,	He also read of wives from later times,
That somme han slayn hir housbondes in hir bed,	Some of whom had killed their husbands in their beds,
And lete hir lecchour dighte hir al the nyght,	And let their lovers screw them all night long,
Whan that the corps lay in the floor upright.	With the corpses lying there on the floor.
And somme han dryve nayles in hir brayn	And some had nails driven into their heads
Whil that they slepte, and thus they han hem slayn.	While they slept, and so they were killed.
Somme han hem yeve poysoun in hir drynke.	Some of them put poison in their drinks.
He spak moore harm than herte may bithynke,	He told me of more evil than the mind can imagine,
And therwithal he knew of mo proverbs	And also he knew more proverbs
Than in this world ther growen gras or herbes.	Than there is grass or herbs in the world.
"Bet is," quod he, "thyn habitacioun	"It is better," he said, "to live
Be with a leon, or a foul dragoun,	With a lion, or a foul dragon,
Than with a womman usynge for to chyde."	Than it is to be with a nagging woman.
"Bet is," quod he, "hye in the roof abyde	It's better," he said, "to live up on the roof
Than with an angry wyf doun in the hous,	Than be with an angry wife down in your house,
They been so wikked and contrarious.	They are so wicked and argumentative,
They haten that hir housbondes loveth ay."	They hate anything that their husbands love."
He seyde, "a womman cast hir shame away	He said, "A woman throws away her shame
Whan she cast of hir smok," and forther mo,	When she takes off her dress," and also,
"A fair womman, but she be chaast also,	"A pretty woman, unless she is chaste,
Is lyk a goldryng in a sowes nose."	Is like a gold ring through the nose of a pig."
Who wolde leeve, or who wolde suppose	Can anybody possibly imagine
The wo that in myn herte was, and pyne?	What grief and pain this gave my heart?
And whan I saugh he wolde nevere fyne	When I saw he would never stop
To reden on this cursed book al nyght,	Reading this bloody book all night,
Al sodeynly thre leves have I plyght	I suddenly ripped three pages
Out of his book, right as he radde, and eke	Out of it, just as he was reading, and also
I with my fest so took hym on the cheke,	I punched him in the face so hard
That in oure fyr he ril bakward adoun.	That the staggered backwards into the fire.
And he up-stirte as dooth a wood leoun,	And he jumped up like a wild lion,
And with his fest he smoot me on the heed	And with his fist he smashed me in the head
That in the floor I lay, as I were deed.	So that I lay on the floor, as if I were dead.

And whan he saugh how stille that I lay,
He was agast, and wolde han fled his way,
Til atte laste out of my swogh I breyde.
'O, hastow slayn me, false theef,' I seyde,
'And for my land thus hastow mordred me?
Er I be deed, yet wol I kisse thee.'

And neer he cam and kneled faire adoun,
And seyde, 'Deere suster Alisoun,
As help me God, I shal thee nevere smyte.
That I have doon, it is thyself to wyte,
Foryeve it me, and that I thee biseke.'
And yet eftsoones I hitte hym on the cheke,
And seyde, 'Theef, thus muchel am I wreke;
Now wol I dye, I may no lenger speke.'
But atte laste, with muchel care and wo,
We fille acorded by us selven two.
He yaf me al the bridel in myn hond,
To han the governance of hous and lond,
And of his tonge, and of his hond also,
And made hym brenne his book anon right tho.
And whan that I hadde geten unto me
By maistrie, al the soveraynetee,
And that he seyde, 'Myn owene trewe wyf,
Do as thee lust the terme of al thy lyf,
Keepe thyn honour, and keep eek myn estaat,' -

After that day we hadden never debaat.

God help me so, I was to hym as kynde
As any wyf from Denmark unto Ynde,
And also trewe, and so was he to me.

I prey to God, that sit in magestee,
So blesse his soule for his mercy deere.
Now wol I seye my tale, if ye wol heere.

Biholde the wordes bitwene the Somonour and the Frere.

The Frere lough whan he hadde herd al this.-
"Now dame," quod he, "so have I joye or blis,
This is a long preamble of a tale."
And whan the Somonour herde the Frere gale,
"Lo," quod the Somonour, "Goddes armes two,
A frere wol entremette hym everemo.
Lo goode men, a flye and eek a frère

Wol falle in every dyssh and eek mateere.
What spekestow of preambulacioun?
What, amble, or trotte, or pees, or go sit doun,
Thou lettest oure disport in this manere."
"Ye, woltow so, sire Somonour?" quod the Frere,

And when he saw how still I was lying,
He was terrified, and would have run away,
Until at last I came round and said,
"Oh, you have killed me, you false thief,
Have you murdered me like this for my land?
Kiss me just once before I die."

And he came close to me and then knelt down,
And said, "Dear sister Alison,
So help me God, I'll never hit you again.
You're to blame for the fact that I did,
But still I ask you to forgive me for it."
And straight away I punched him in the face,
And said, "You bad man, I take my revenge;
Now I shall die, I can say no more."
But at last, with much effort and sorrow,
We patched it up between the two of us.
He gave me all the power
Over the running of the house and land,
And also over his tongue, and of his hands;
And I made him burn his book at once.
And when I had got for myself
Through my efforts, all the power,
And he had said, "My own true wife,
Do as you wish for the rest of your life,
Protect your honour, and look after my estate,"
From that day onwards we never argued again.
God help me, I was as good to him
As any wife between Denmark and India,
And also I was faithful, and he was the same to me.
I pray to God, who sits above in judgement,
To bless his soul through his sweet mercy.
Now I will tell you my tale, if you want to listen."

Now see what the Summoner and the Friar said

The Friar laughed when he heard all this.
"Now my lady," he said, "I swear to you,
That this was a long introduction!"
And when the Summoner heard this he said,
"Look at this, I swear by the hand of God,
A friar will always try to interfere.
All you good men, you must see that a fly and also a friar
Will stick their noses into anything they can.
What are you talking about, introduction?
Amble or trot, keep your peace, or sit down,
You're getting in the way of our fun."
"Is that what you say, Mr Summoner?" asked the Friar,

"Now by my feith, I shal er that I go Telle of a somonour swich a tale or two That alle the folk shal laughen in this place." "Now elles, frere, I bishrewe thy face,"	*"Now I swear, before I leave, I will tell a tale or two about summoners Which will set all these folk laughing." "If it were otherwise, friar, I would damn your face,"*
Quod this Somonour, "and I bishrewe me, But if I telle tales two or thre Of freres, er I come to Sidyngborne, That I shal make thyn herte for to morne, For wel I woot thy pacience in gon." Oure Hooste cride, "Pees, and that anon!"	*Said the summoner, "and I will damn myself Unless I tell two or three tales About friars, before we reach Sittingbourne, That will certainly give you plenty of grief, You will be completely fed up." Our host cried out, "Shut up, and straight away!*
And seyde, "lat the womman telle hire tale, Ye fare as folk that dronken were of ale. Do, dame, telle forth youre tale, and that is best."	*Let this woman tell her story, You're behaving like a pair of drunkards. Lady, you go ahead and tell your story, that's what we want."*
"Al redy, sire," quod she, "right as yow lest, If I have licence of this worthy Frere." "Yis, dame," quod he, "tel forth, and I wol heere."	*"I am ready to, sir," she said, "as you request, As long as this good Friar agrees." "Yes, lady," he said, "you speak and I will listen."*
Heere endeth the Wyf of Bathe hir Prologe.	*This is the end of the Wife of Bath's Prologue*

The Tale

In tholde dayes of the Kyng Arthour,	*In the old days of King Arthur,*
Of which that Britons speken greet honour,	*Of whom Britons speak with such reverence,*
All was this land fulfild of Fayerye.	*This whole land was filled with magic.*
The elf-queene, with hir joly compaignye,	*The Queen of the elves, with her jolly companions,*
Daunced ful ofte in many a grene mede;	*Often danced in the green fields;*
This was the olde opinion, as I rede.	*That's what men used to believe, I have read.*

Here begins the Wife of Bath's tale

I speke of manye hundred yeres ago;	*I'm talking about many hundreds of years ago;*
But now kan no man se none elves mo,	*Now no man ever sees elves any more,*
For now the grete charitee and prayers	*For now the great charity and prayers*
Of lymytours, and othere hooly freres,	*Of the mendicants, and other holy friars,*
That serchen every lond and every streem	*Who have swamped every land and river*
As thikke as motes in the sonne-beem,	*As thick as dust in the sunbeams,*
Blessynge halles, chambres, kichenes, boures,	*Blessing halls, bedrooms, kitchens, chambers,*
Citees, burghes, castels, hye toures,	*Cities, towns, castles, great towers,*
Thropes, bernes, shipnes, dayeryes,	*Hamlets, barns, stables, dairies,*
This maketh that ther been no Fayeryes.	*That makes sure there are no more fairies.*
For ther as wont to walken was an elf,	*For where once the elf used to walk,*
Ther walketh now the lymytour hymself	*Now the mendicant walks himself,*
In undermeles and in morwenynges,	*In the mornings, late and early,*
And seyth his matyns and his hooly thynges	*Saying matins and other holy offices,*
As he gooth in his lymytacioun.	*As he goes around begging.*
Wommen may go saufly up and doun;	*Women can safely travel about;*
In every bussh or under every tree	*In every bush and every tree*
Ther is noon oother incubus but he,	*There is no other spirit except him,*
And he ne wol doon hem but dishonour.	*And he won't do them any harm.*
And so bifel it that this kyng Arthour	*It so happened that this King Arthur*
Hadde in his hous a lusty bachelor,	*Had a lusty bachelor in his establishment*
That on a day cam ridynge fro ryver;	*Who one day came riding home from hawking,*
And happed that, allone as she was born,	*And he happened to see a maiden walking*
He saugh a mayde walkynge hym biforn,	*In front of him, as alone as the day she was born,*
Of whiche mayde anon, maugree hir heed,	*And at once, despite her resistance,*
By verray force he rafte hir maydenhed;	*He raped her of her virginity;*
For which oppressioun was swich clamour	*This crime caused such outrage*
And swich pursute unto the kyng Arthour,	*And such were the demands made to King Arthur*
That dampned was this knyght for to be deed	*That this knight was sentenced to death*
By cours of lawe, and sholde han lost his heed,	*By the course of law, and he should have lost his head,*
Paraventure, swich was the statut tho,	*Because that was the way the laws were then,*

But that the queene and othere ladyes mo	But the queen and also other ladies
So longe preyeden the kyng of grace,	Begged the king to show mercy,
Til he his lyf hym graunted in the place,	Until he agreed to spare his life,
And yaf hym to the queene al at hir wille,	And he handed over to the queen to do what she would,
To chese, wheither she wolde hym save or spille.	To choose whether she would save him or kill him.
The queene thanketh the kyng with al hir myght,	The queen thanked the king most sincerely,
And after this thus spak she to the knyght,	And afterwards she spoke to the knight,
Whan that she saugh hir tyme, upon a day,	When she decided the time was right.
Thou standest yet, quod she, in swich array	"You are in a position," she said,
That of thy lyf yet hastow no suretee.	"Where you have no guarantee of staying alive.
I grante thee lyf, if thou kanst tellen me	I shall spare your life, if you can tell me
What thyng is it that wommen moost desiren.	What it is that women desire the most.
Be war and keep thy nekke-boon from iren,	"Be careful, and keep your neck from the axe,
And if thou kanst nat tellen it anon,	And if you can't give me the answer straight away,
Yet shal I yeve thee leve for to gon	I give you permission to go away
A twelf-month and a day to seche and leere	For a year and a day to see if you can find
An answere suffisant in this mateere;	A proper answer for my question;
And suretee wol I han, er that thou pace,	And before you go I will have a guarantee
Thy body for to yelden in this place.	That you will turn yourself in back here."
Wo was this knyght, and sorwefully he siketh,	This knight was very sad and sighed sorrowfully,
But what! he may nat do al as hym liketh;	But there was no way he could do as he pleased;
And at the laste he chees hym for to wende,	And at last he chose to depart,
And come agayn right at the yeres ende,	And come back at the end of the year,
With swich answere as God wolde hym purveye;	With whatever answer God gave to him;
And taketh his leve, and wendeth forth his weye.	And he said his farewells, and went on his way.
He seketh every hous and every place,	He looked in every house and every place,
Where as he hopeth for to fynde grace	Hoping that it would be vouchsafed to him
To lerne what thyng wommen loven moost;	The thing that women love the most;
But he ne koude arryven in no coost	But there was no place to which he went
Wher as he myghte fynde in this mateere	Where he could discover, in this business,
Two creatures accordynge in feere.	Two people who agreed with each other.
Somme seyde, wommen loven best richesse,	Some said women loved wealth the best,
Somme seyde honour, somme seyde jolynesse,	Some said honour, some said fun,
Somme riche array, somme seyden lust abedde,	Some fine clothes, some said sex,
And oftetyme to be wydwe and wedde.	And many said to be married and widowed.
Somme seyde, that oure hertes been moost esed	Some said that our hearts are best pleased
Whan that we been yflatered and yplesed—	When we have been flattered and spoilt—
he gooth ful ny the sothe, I wol nat lye,	He was getting near the truth, I will not lie,

a man shal Wynne us best with flaterye;	Flattery is the best way for a man to get us;
and with attendance and with bisynesse	Paying attention, doing things for us,
been we ylymed, bothe moore and lesse.	Can easily catch us, the great and small.
And somme seyn, how that we loven best	And some said, that what we loved best
For to be free, and do right as us lest,	Was to be free, and do as we wished,
And that no man repreve us of oure vice,	With no man telling us what to do,
But seye that we be wise, and nothyng nyce.	Admitting that we are wise, not stupid.
For trewely, ther is noon of us alle,	For truthfully, there isn't a single one of us,
If any wight wol clawe us on the galle,	If anyone touches us on the sore spot,
That we nel kike; for he seith us sooth;	That we won't kick out at him; he's telling us the truth;
Assay, and he shal fynde it that so dooth.	Try it, and you'll find that's what will happen.
For be we never so vicious withinne,	However vicious we are inside,
We sol been holden wise, and clene of synne.	We want to be thought wise, and innocent.
And somme seyn, that greet delit han we	And some say that we take great delight
For to been holden stable and eke secree,	In being thought reliable and discreet,
And in o purpos stedefastly to dwelle,	Being able to follow through a plan,
And nat biwerye thyng that men us telle.	Not betraying secrets that men tell us.
But that tale is nat worth a rake-stele,	But that idea is entirely worthless,
Pardee, we wommen konne no thyng hele.	By God, we women can't keep a secret.
Witnesse on Myda-wol ye heere the tale?	Look at Midas—do you want to hear the story?
Ovyde, amonges othere thynges smale,	Ovid, amongst other little stories,
Seyde, Myda hadde under his longe heres	Said that under his long hair Midas had
Growynge upon his heed two asses eres,	Growing on his head two asses' ears,
The whiche vice he hydde, as he best myghte,	And he hid this deformity he well as he could,
Ful subtilly from every mannes sighte;	Very cunningly keeping them out of sight,
That, save his wyf, ther wiste of it namo,	So that nobody apart from his wife knew anything about them,
He loved hir moost and trusted hir also.	He loved her best of all, and trusted her as well.
He preyede hir, that to no creature	He begged her to tell nobody
She sholde tellen of his disfigure.	About his disfigurement.
She swoor him nay, for al this world to wynne,	She swore to him that she would not, for the world,
She nolde do that vileynye or synne,	Commit that evil sin,
To make hir housbonde han so foul a name,	To give her husband such an evil reputation,
She nolde nat telle it for hir owene shame!	That would reflect on her as well!
But nathelees, hir thoughte that she dyde,	Nonetheless, she thought she would die,
That she so longe sholde a conseil hyde,	Having to keep a secret for so long,
Hir thoughte it swal so soore aboute hir herte	The thought of it pressed so heavy on her heart
That nedely som word hir moste asterte.	That it was impossible for her to keep it in.

And sith she dorste telle it to no man,	And since she did not dare to say it to any man,
Doun to a mareys faste by she ran,	She went down to a nearby marsh,
Til she came there, hir herte was afyre,	And when she got there, her heart was on fire,
And as a bitore bombleth in the myre,	And like a wading bird with its beak in the water,
She leyde hir mouth unto the water doun;-	She lowered her mouth down close to the surface;
Biwreye me nat, thou water, with thy soun,	"Don't betray me, you water, with your babbling,"
Quod she, to thee I telle it and namo,	She said, "I'll tell it to you and no one else,
Myn housbonde hath longe asses erys two!	My husband has two long asses' ears!
Now is myn herte al hool, now is it oute,	Now my heart is eased, now I've let it out,
I myghte no lenger kepe it, out of doute.	It's certain I couldn't have kept it in any longer."
Heere may ye se, thogh we a tyme abyde,	Through this you can see, though we keep secrets for a while,
Yet out it moot, we kan no conseil hyde.-	They must come out in the end, we cannot hide them.
The remenant of the tale, if ye wol heere,	If you want to hear the rest of the story,
Redeth Ovyde, and ther ye may it leere.-	Read Ovid, you can learn it there.
This knyght, of which my tale is specially,	This knight, the subject of my story,
Whan that he saugh he myghte nat come therby,	When he saw that he wasn't going to find it,
This is to seye, what wommen love moost,	That is to say, what women love best,
Withinne his brest ful sorweful was the goost.	His spirit mourned within his breast.
But hoom he gooth, he myghte nat sojourne;	But he headed homewards, he could not delay;
The day was come that homward moste he tourne,	The day came when he had to turn for home,
And in his wey it happed hym to ryde	And on his journey he happened to ride,
In al this care under a forest syde,	Full of care, under the eaves of a forest,
Wher as he saugh upon a daunce go	And there he saw dancing
Of ladyes foure and twenty, and yet mo;	Twenty-four ladies, or maybe more;
Toward the whiche daunce he drow ful yerne,	He headed towards the dancers eagerly,
In hope that som wysdom sholde he lerne.	Hoping that he would learn something.
But certeinly, er he came fully there,	But the truth is, before he got there,
Vanysshed was this daunce, he nyste where;	All the dancers vanished, he did not know where;
No creature saugh he that bar lyf,	He couldn't see a single living creature,
Save on the grene he saugh sittynge a wyf,	Except in the glade he saw an old woman sitting,
A fouler wight ther may no man devyse.	A more disgusting person than anyone could imagine.
Agayn the knyght this olde wyf gan ryse,	This old woman got to her feet before the knight,
And seyde, Sire knyght, heer-forth ne lith no wey;	And said, "Sir knight, listen to me for a

Tel me what that ye seken, by your fey.	Tell me what you're looking for, in faith.
Paraventure it may the bettre be,	Perhaps that would be good for you,
Thise olde folk kan muchel thyng, quod she.	We old folk know many things," she said.
My leeve mooder, quod this knyght, certeyn,	"My dear mother," said the knight, "it's certain
I nam but deed, but if that I kan seyn	That I am dead, unless I can find out
What thyng it is, that wommen moost desire.	What it is that women want the most.
Koude ye me wisse, I wolde wel quite youre hire.	If you can tell me, I'll be completely in your debt."
Plight me thy trouthe, heere in myn hand, quod she,	"Give me your promise, handed to me," she said,
The nexte thyng that I requere thee,	"That the next thing I ask you to do,
Thou shalt it do, if it lye in thy myght,	You will do it, if it is within your power,
And I wol telle it yow, er it be nyght.	And I'll tell you the answer, before nightfall."
Have heer my trouthe, quod the knyght, I grante.	"Take my promise," said the knight, "I give it to you."
Thanne, quod she, I dar me wel avante,	"Then," she said, "I venture to say
Thy lyf is sauf, for I wol stonde therby	That your life is saved, for I will bet
Upon my lyf, the queene wol seye as I.	My life that the Queen will say the same thing as me.
Lat se which is the proudeste of hem alle,	Let us see if any of the greatest
That wereth on a coverchief or a calle,	Of all these noble women
That dar seye nay of that I shal thee teche.	Dare deny what I will tell you.
Lat us go forth withouten lenger speche.	Let's head there without any more talk."
Tho rowned she a pistel in his ere,	Then she whispered in his ear,
And bad hym to be glad and have no fere.	And told him to be happy, and not to worry.
Whan they be comen to the court, this knyght	When they arrived at the court, this knight
Seyde he had holde his day, as he hadde hight,	Announced he had come as he had promised,
And redy was his answere, as he sayde.	And was ready with his answer, as he had said.
Ful many a noble wyf, and many a mayde,	Many noble wives, and many girls,
And many a wydwe, for that they been wise,	And many widows, because they were wise,
The wueene hirself sittynge as a justise,	And the Queen herself sitting as judge,
Assembled been, his answere for to heere;	Were assembled, to listen to his answer;
And afterward this knyght was bode appeere.	And so the knight was ordered to appear.
To every wight comanded was silence,	Every person was ordered to be silent,
And that the knyght sholde telle in audience	So that the knight could tell the gathering
What thyng that worldly wommen loven best.	The thing that women love best in the world.
This knyght ne stood nat stille, as doth a best,	The knight wasn't silent, like a dumb animal,
But ot his questioun anon answered	But straight away gave his answer
With manly voys, that al the court it herde:	In a manly voice, that could be heard throughout the court:
My lige lady, generally, quod he,	"My royal lady, in general," he said,
Wommen desiren to have sovereynetee	"Women want to rule over their husbands

As wel over hir housbond as hir love,	and lovers,
And for to been in maistrie hym above.	To have sovereignty over them.
This is youre mooste desir, thogh ye me kille,	"This is what you want most, even if you kill me,
Dooth as yow list, I am heer at youre wille.	Do what you want, I am at your mercy."
In al the court ne was ther wyf ne mayde	Throughout the court there was neither a wife nor
Ne wydwe that contraried that he sayde,	A widow who disagreed with what he said,
But seyden he was worthy han his lyf.	They all said that he had earned his life.
And with that word up stirte the olde wyf,	At their words up jumped the old wife,
Which that the knyght saugh sittynge in the grene.	Whom the knight had seen sitting in the glade.
Mercy, quod she, my sovereyn lady queene,	"Please," she said, "my royal queen,
Er that youre court departe, do me right.	Before your court breaks up, do justice to me.
I taughte this answere unto the knyght,	I told the knight this answer,
For which he plighte me his trouthe there,	In return for which he gave me his promise
The firste thyng I wolde of hym requere,	That he would do the first thing
He wolde it do, if it lay in his myght.	I asked of him, if he was capable of it.
Bifor the court thanne preye I thee, sir knyght,	"So in front of this court then I ask you, sir knight,"
Quod she, that thou me take unto thy wyf,	She said, "to take me as your wife,
For wel thou woost that I have kept thy lyf.	For you are well aware that I have saved your life.
If I seye fals, sey nay, upon thy fey!	If I'm not telling the truth, then refuse me, on your faith!"
This knyght answerde, Allas and weylawey!	The knight answered, "Alas, unhappy day!
I woot right wel that swich was my biheste!	I know perfectly well that was my promise!
For Goddes love, as chees a newe requeste,	For the love of God, please choose something else,
Taak al my good, and lat my body go!	Take all my possessions, and leave me my body!"
Nay, thanne, quod she, I shrewe us bothe two,	"No then," she said, "I would curse us both,
For thogh that I be foul, and oold, and poore,	For although I am horrid, and old, and poor,
I nolde for al the metal, ne for oore,	I would not, for all the metal, all the ore,
That under erthe is grave, or lith above,	That is buried under the earth, or is out in the open,
But if thy wyf I were, and eek thy love.	Give up being your wife and also your love."
My love? quod he, nay, my dampnacioun!	"My love?" He said, "no, my damnation!
Allas, that any of my nacioun	How terrible, that any of my countrymen
Sholde evere so foule disparaged be!	Would ever fall into such a terrible trap!"
But al for noght, the ende is this, that he	But it was all in vain, the result was that he
Constreyned was, he nedes moste hir wedde,	Was forced to marry her,
And taketh his olde wyf, and gooth to bedde.	And he took his old wife, and went to bed.

Middle English	Modern English
Now wolden som men seye, paraventure,	Now I expect that some men will say
That for my necligence I do no cure	That I am being negligent
To tellen yow the joye and al tharray,	In not telling you of all the ceremony and revelling
That at the feeste was that ilke day;	That took place for that wedding feast;
To whiche thyng shortly answere I shal.	I shall explain that at once.
I seye, ther nas no joye ne feeste at al,	I tell you, there was no happiness and no feasting,
Ther nas but hevynesse and muche sorwe,	When he secretly married her the next morning,
For prively he wedde hir on a morwe,	And all day he hid himself away like an owl,
And al day after hidde hym as an owle,	
So wo was hym, his wyf looked so foule.	He was so sorrowful, his wife was so hideous.
Greet was the wo the knyght hadde in his thoght,	This knight was extremely depressed,
Whan he was with his wyf abedde ybroght,	When he had to take his wife to bed,
He walweth and he turneth to and fro.	He tossed and turned incessantly.
His olde wyf lay smylynge everemo,	His old wife lay continually smiling,
And seyde, O deere housbonde, benedicitee,	And said, "Oh dear husband, please God,
Fareth every knyght thus with his wyf, as ye?	Is this how every knight treats his wife?
Is this the lawe of Kyng Arthures hous?	Is this what goes on in the house of King Arthur?
Is every knyght of his so dangerous?	Is every one of his knights so cold?
I am youre owene love, and eek your wyf;	I am your own love, and also your wife;
I am she which that saved hath youre lyf.	I am the woman who saved your life.
And certes, yet dide I yow nevere unright;	And certainly, I have never done you wrong;
Why fare ye thus with me this firste nyght?	So why are you treating me like this on our wedding night?
Ye faren lyk a man had lost his wit.	You are behaving like a man who's gone mad.
What is my gilt? for Goddes love, tel it,	What have I done wrong? For God's sake, tell me,
And it shal been amended, if I may.	And I'll make up for it, if I can."
Amended, quod this knyght, allas! nay! nay!	"Make up for it," said the knight, "alas! No! No!
It wol nat been amended nevere mo;	You can never make up for this;
Thou art so loothly and so oold also	You're so hideous and also so old,
And therto comen of so lough a kynde,	And also so lowly born,
That litel wonder is thogh I walwe and wynde.	It's no surprise that I toss and turn.
So wolde God, myn herte wolde breste!	I swear to God, my heart will break!"
Is this, quod she, the cause of youre unreste?	"Is this," she asked, "why you are so restless?"
Ye certeinly, quod he, no wonder is!	"Yes certainly," he said, "it's not surprising!"
Now, sire, quod she, I koude amende al this,	"Now, sir," she said, "I can change all this,
If that me liste, er it were dayes thre,	If I want to, before three days are passed,
So wel ye myghte bere yow unto me.	If you decide to treat me properly.
But for ye speken of swich gentillesse	But you're talking of such nobility,

As is descended out of old richesse,	Descended out of old money,
That therfore sholden ye be gentil men,	Thinking you are a gentleman,
Swich arrogance nis nat worth an hen.	Such arrogance is not worth a damn.
Looke who that is moost vertuous alway,	Look at who is always most virtuous,
Pryvee and apert, and moost entendeth ay	In public and in private, and who always wants
To do the gentil dedes that he kan,	To do as many good deeds as he can,
Taak hym for the grettest gentil-man.	That person is the greatest gentleman.
Crist wole, we clayme of hym oure gentillesse,	Our gentility is inherited from Christ,
Nat of oure eldres for hire old richesse.	Not from our ancestors and their money.
For thogh they yeve us al hir heritage,	Although they give us our lineage,
For which we clayme to been of heigh parage,	From which we claim that we are high born,
Yet may they nat biquethe for no thyng	They can't pass down to us anything
To noon of us hir vertuous lyvyng,	Of their virtuous way of life,
That made hem gentil men ycalled be,	That made them be called gentlemen,
And bad us folwen hem in swich degree.	And makes us want to imitate them so much.
Wel kan the wise poete of Florence,	The wise poet of Florence knew this well,
That highte Dant, speken in this sentence.	The one called Dante, when he said this.
Lo in swich maner rym is Dantes tale:	This is what it says in Dante's poem:
`Ful selde upriseth by his branches smale	'It's very rarely that a little man
Prowesse of man, for God of his goodnesse	Grows on his own, for God in his goodness
Wole, that of hym we clayme oure gentillesse.'	Has decreed that we should get our nobility from him.'
For of oure eldres may we no thyng clayme	We can claim nothing from our ancestors
But temporel thyng, that man may hurte and mayme.	But worldly things, that men can hurt and damage.
Eek every wight woot this as wel as I,	Every person knows this as well as I do,
If gentillesse were planted natureelly	That if nobility was a natural virtue,
Unto a certeyn lynage doun the lyne,	Handed down through the family tree,
Pryvee nor apert, thanne wolde they nevere fyne	Then in private or in public they would never fail
To doon of gentillesse the faire office,	To behave in a noble fashion,
They myghte do no vileynye or vice.	And would never do anything wrong.
Taak fyr, and ber it in the derkeste hous	If you take fire and put it in the darkest house
Bitwix this and the mount of Kaukasous,	Between this place and the Caucasus,
And lat men shette the dores and go thenne,	And let people close the doors and go away,
Yet wole the fyr as faire lye and brenne	The fire will still burn as brightly
As twenty thousand men myghte it biholde;	As if twenty thousand men were looking at it;
His office natureel ay wol it holde,	It will perform its natural task,
Up peril of my lyf, til that it dye.	I swear on my life, until it dies out.
Heere may ye se wel, how that genterye	So you can see that nobility
Is nat annexed to possessioun,	Is not related to possessions,

Sith folk ne doon hir operacioun Alwey, as dooth the fyr, lo, in his kynde. For God it woot, men may wel often fynde A lordes sone do shame and vileynye,	Since folks do not always behave Like the fire, never changing. For God knows, men often discover That a lord's son can behave shamefully and wickedly,
And he that wole han pris of his gentrye,	And someone who wants to be praised for nobility,
For he was boren of a gentil hous, And hadde hise eldres noble and vertuous, And nel hym-selven do no gentil dedis, Ne folwen his gentil auncestre that deed is,	Because he was born into a noble family, And had noble and virtuous ancestors, But who does not do noble things himself, Who doesn't follow the example of his noble ancestors,
He nys nat gentil, be he duc or erl;	He is not noble, whether he is a duke or an earl;
For vileyns synful dedes make a cherl.	For evil sinful deeds make him into a peasant.
For gentillesse nys but renomee Of thyne auncestres for hire heigh bountee, Which is a strange thyng to thy persone. Thy gentillesse cometh fro God allone, Thanne comth oure verray gentillesse of grace, It was no thyng biquethe us with oure place.	Nobility is nothing but the fame Of your ancestors for their good deeds, Which has nothing to do with you. Your nobility can only come from God That is where true grace comes from, It is not something handed down to us with our titles.
Thenketh hou noble, as seith Valerius, Was thilke Tullius Hostillius, That out of poverte roos to heigh noblesse. Reedeth Senek, and redeth eek Boece, Ther shul ye seen expres that it no drede is,	Think how noble, as Valerius tells us, Tullius Hostillius was, Who rose out of poverty to great nobility. Read Seneca, and also read Boethius, And there you will see it said without doubt
That he is gentil that dooth gentil dedis.	That the noble man is the one who does noble deeds.
And therfore, leeve housbonde, I thus conclude, Al were it that myne auncestres weren rude,	And so, dear husband, I will conclude That even though my ancestors were common,
Yet may the hye God-and so hope I,- Grante me grace to lyven vertuously.	The great God–and this is what I hope– Will give me grace to live a good life.
Thanne am I gentil whan that I bigynne To lyven vertuously, and weyve synne. And ther as ye of poverte me repreeve,	So I will be noble when I begin To live a good life, and renounce sin. And just as you reproach me for my poverty,
The hye God, on whom that we bileeve In wilful poverte chees to lyve his lyf.	Great God, the one in whom we believe, Deliberately chose to live his life in poverty.
And certes every man, mayden or wyf,	And it's certain that every man, girl or woman,
May understonde that Jesus, hevene kyng, Ne wolde nat chesen vicious lyvyng.	Knows that Jesus, the King of Heaven, Would not have chosen an evil way to live.
Glad poverte is an honeste thyng, certeyn,	Happy poverty is certainly an honest thing,
This wole Senec and othere clerkes seyn.	This is what Seneca and other scholars say.

Who so that halt hym payd of his poverte,	If someone is satisfied with his poverty,
I holde hym riche, al hadde he nat a sherte;	I count him as a rich man, even if he has no shirt;
He that coveiteth is a povre wight,	The person who is covetous is a poor man,
For he wolde han that is nat in his myght,	For he wants things he cannot get,
But he that noght hath, ne coveiteth have,	But the person who has nothing, covets nothing,
Is riche, although ye holde hym but a knave.	He is rich, although you hold him in contempt.
Verray poverte, it syngeth proprely.	True poverty, it can really sing out.
Juvenal seith of poverte myrily,	Juvenal merrily said about poverty,
'The povre man, whan he goth by the weye,	'The poor man, as he goes along the road,
Bifore the theves he may synge and pleye.'	Can sing and dance in front of the thieves.'
Poverte is hateful good, and, as I gesse,	Poverty is both horrid and good, and I imagine
A ful greet bryngere out of bisynesse;	It takes away many cares;
A greet amender eek of sapience	It will bring much wisdom
To hym that taketh it in pacience.	To the person who suffers it patiently.
Poverte is this, although it seme elenge;	This is what poverty is, though it seems miserable;
Possessioun, that no wight wol chalenge.	A possession no one will want to steal from you.
Poverte ful ofte, whan a man is lowe,	Poverty often, when a man is laid low,
Maketh his God and eek hymself to knowe;	Allows him to know his God and also himself;
Poverte a spectacle is, as thynketh me,	Poverty is a lens, I believe,
Thurgh which he may hise verray freendes see.	Which allows a man to see who his real friends are.
And therfore, sire, syn that I noght yow greve,	And therefore, sir, as I do you no harm,
Of my poverte namoore ye me repreve.	You cannot criticise me for my poverty.
Now sire, of elde ye repreve me,	Now sir, you criticise me for being old,
And certes, sire, thogh noon auctoritee	And it is certain, sir, although it is not written
Were in no book, ye gentils of honour	In any book, that you noblemen
Seyn, that men sholde an oold wight doon favour,	Say that men should show respect for old people,
And clepe hym fader for youre gentillesse,	And be polite and call him "Father",
And auctours shal I fynden, as I gesse.	And I could find authors who agreed, I imagine.
Now, ther ye seye that I am foul and old,	Now, you say that I am foul and old,
Than drede you noght to been a cokewold;	That means you need not fear being a cuckold;
For filthe and eelde, al so moot I thee,	For hideousness and age, I propose,
Been grete wardeyns upon chastitee;	Are great guardians of chastity;
But nathelees, syn I knowe youre delit,	But nonetheless, since I know what you like,
I shal fulfille youre worldly appetit.	I shall assuage your worldly appetite.
Chese now, quod she, oon of thise thynges tweye:	Now choose," she said, "one of these two things:

To han me foul and old til that I deye, And be to yow a trewe humble wyf, And nevere yow displese in al my lyf;	*To have me hideous and old until I die,* *Acting as a true humble wife to you,* *And never causing you any displeasure my whole life long;*
Or elles ye wol han me yong and fair,	*Or otherwise you can have me young and fair,*
And take youre aventure of the repair	*And take your chances with the crowd of men*
That shal be to youre hous, by cause of me,	*Who will flock to your house, because of me,*
Or in som oother place may wel be. Now chese yourselven wheither that yow liketh.	*Or maybe in some other place.* *Go ahead, make your choice."*
This knyght avyseth hym and sore siketh,	*The knight thought about this long and hard,*
But atte laste, he seyde in this manere: My lady and my love, and wyf so deere, I put me in youre wise governance. Cheseth yourself, which may be moost plesance And moost honour to yow and me also.	*But at last, he said these words:* *"My lady and my love, and my dear wife,* *I put myself in your wise hands.* *You choose what would be best* *And most honourable for you and also for me.*
I do no fors the wheither of the two, For, as yow liketh, it suffiseth me.	*I will not object to either choice,* *For whatever pleases you is good enough for me."*
Thanne have I gete of yow maistrie, quod she, Syn I may chese and governe as me lest?	*"Then I am the master of you," she said,* *"Since I can choose and decide what I think is best?"*
Ye, certes, wyf, quod he, I holde it best.	*"Yes, certainly, wife," he said, "I think that's best."*
Kys me, quod she, we be no lenger wrothe,	*"Kiss me," she said, "we will no longer argue,*
For, by my trouthe, I wol be to yow bothe! This is to seyn, ye, bothe fair and good.	*For, I swear to you, I will be both to you!* *That is to say, I will be both beautiful and good.*
I prey to God that I moote sterven woo	*I pray to God that I will starve and go mad*
But I to yow be al so good and trewe As evere was wyf, syn that the world was newe.	*If I am not as good and true to you* *As any wife ever was, since the beginning of the world.*
And but I be tomorn as fair to seene As any lady, emperice or queene, That is bitwixe the est and eke the west, Dooth with my lyf and deth right as yow lest.	*And tomorrow I will be as fair to look at* *As any lady, empress or queen,* *In any land on earth,* *Now you may do what you please with my life.*
Cast up the curtyn, looke how that it is.	*Lift up the curtain, and see how things are."*
And whan the knyght saugh verraily al this, That she so fair was, and so yong therto,	*And when the knight saw all this was true,* *That she was so beautiful and also so young,*
For joye he hente hire in hise armes two. His herte bathed in a bath of blisse, A thousand tyme arewe he gan hir kisse,	*He took her happily into his arms.* *His heart was swimming in happiness,* *And he kissed her thousands of times,*

And she obeyed hym in every thing That myghte doon hym plesance or likyng.	*And she obeyed him in every way* *That could bring him happiness and pleasure.*
And thus they lyve unto hir lyves ende In parfit joye;-and Jesu Crist us sende	*And so they lived to the end of their lives* *In perfect happiness, and may Jesus Christ send us*
Housbondes meeke, yonge, fressh abedde, And grace toverbyde hem that we wedde.	*Obedient young husbands, strong in bed,* *And the grace to outlive the ones we marry.*
And eek I praye Jesu shorte hir lyves, That nat wol be governed by hir wyves;	*And also I pray that Jesus gives short lives* *To those who will not be ruled by their wives;*
And olde and angry nygardes of dispence, God sende hem soone verray pestilence!	*And any old tight fisted misers,* *May God send them the plague at once!*
Heere endeth the Wyves Tale of Bathe	*This is the end of the Wife of Bath's tale*

The Friar's Tale

The Prologue

The Prologue of the Freres Tale

This worthy lymytour, this noble frere,
He made alwey a maner louryng chiere
Upon the Somonour, but for honestee
No vileyns word as yet to hym spak he.
But atte laste he seyde unto the wyf,

Dame, quod he, God yeve yow right good lyf!

Ye han heer touched, also moot I thee,
In scole-matere greet difficultee.
Ye han seyd muche thyng right wel, I seye.
But dame, heere as we ryde by the weye
Us nedeth nat to speken but of game,
And lete auctoritees, on Goddes name,

To prechyng and to scole eek of clergye.

But if it lyke to this compaignye,
I wol yow of a somonour telle a game.
Pardee, ye may wel knowe bby the name
That of a somonour may no good be sayd;

I praye that noon of you be yvele apayd.
A somonour is a renner up and doun
With mandementz for fornicacioun,
And is ybet at every townes ende.

Oure Hoost tho spak, A sire, ye sholde be hende

And curteys, as a man of youre estaat.
In compaignye we wol have no debaat.
Telleth youre tale, and lat the Somonour be.

Nay, quod the Somonour, lat hym seye to me
What so hym list. Whan it comth to my lot,

By God I shal hym quiten every grot.
I shal hym tellen which a greet honour
It is to be a flaterynge lymytour,
And his office I shal hym teele, ywis.
Oure Hoost answerde, Pees, namoore of this!
And after this he seyde unto the Frere,
Tel forth youre tale, leeve maister deere.

The prologue to the Friar's tale

This good mendicant, this noble friar,
Was always scowling away
At the Summoner, but to tell the truth
He had never said a bad word to him as yet.
But at last he said to the wife,

"Lady," he said, "May God grant you a wonderful life!
You have touched upon, I swear,
Matters which scholars find very difficult.
You've spoken very well, I'm telling you.
But lady, as we ride along the road,
We only need to speak as we wish,
We can leave the search for proof, in God's name,
To preachers and clergymen scholars.

But if it pleases this company
I'll tell you a story about a summoner.
By God, you know from the name
That nothing good can be said about a summoner;
I hope that it won't annoy any of you.
A summoner goes running up and down
Carrying warrants against fornication,
And he's beaten from pillar to post."

Our host then spoke, "Oh Sir, you should be courteous
And polite, as befits a man of your position.
We won't have any arguments in our company.
Tell your story, and leave the summoner alone."

"No," said the summoner, "let him say
What he likes to me. When it comes round to my turn,
By God I'll pay him back, every penny.
I'll show him what a great honour it is
To be a lying mendicant,
I'll tell him all about what his job is like."
Our host answered, "Peace, stop this!"
Afterwards he said to the friar,
"Now tell us your story, beloved master."

The Tale

Heere bigynneth the Freres Tale

The Friar's tale

Whilom ther was dwellynge in my contree

Once there was living in my part of the country

And erchedeken, a man of heigh degree,
That boldely dide execucioun
In punysshynge of fornicacioun,
Of wicchecraft, and eek of bawderye,
Of difamacioun, and avowtrye,
Of chirche reves, and of testamentz,

And Archdeacon, a man of high rank,
Who boldly enforced the laws
In punishment of fornication
Witchcraft, and lewd behaviour,
Defamation, also adultery
By churchwardens, and failure to carry out wills,

Of contractes and of lakke of sacramentz,

Breaking of contracts and failure to take the sacraments,

Of usure, and of symonye also.

Usury, and bribery as well.

But certes, lecchours dide he grettest wo;

But the people he made suffer most were lechers;

They sholde syngen if that they were hent;
And smale tytheres weren foule yshent,

They would regret it when they were caught;
People who tried to short change on their taxes

If any persoun wolde upon hem pleyne.

Got heavily punished if anyone informed against them.

Ther myghte asterte hym no pecunyal peyne.

Nobody could escape his financial punishments.

For smale tithes and for smal offrynge

If anyone tried to shirk their taxes or their offerings

He made the peple pitously to synge.

He would come down hard upon them.

For er the bisshop caughte hem with his hook,
They weren in the erchedeknes book.

For before the bishop handed out punishment,
They were written down in the Archdeacon's book.

Thanne hadde he, thurgh his jurisdiccioun,
Power to doon on hem correccioun.
He hadde a somonour redy to his hond;
A slyer boye nas noon in engelond;
For subtilly he hadde his espiaille,
That taughte hym wel wher that hym myghte availle.

And then he had, due to his position,
The power to hand out punishments to them.
He had a summoner always with him;
There wasn't a more cunning chap in England;
He would secretly spy out the land,
Which showed him where he could get rich pickings.

He koude spare of lecchours oon or two,
To techen hym to foure and twenty mo.

He would spare one or two lechers,
If they would give evidence against twenty four others.

For thogh this somonour wood were as an hare,
To telle his harlotrye I wol nat spare;
For we been out of his correccioun.
They han of us no jurisdiccioun,
Ne nevere shullen, terme of alle hir lyves. --
Peter! so been the wommen of the styves,

Even if he was as mad as a hare,
I wouldn't cover up his bad behaviour;
He can't hand out punishments to us,
They have no jurisdiction over us,
And they never shall, throughout their lives."
"By St Peter, the same applies to the women of the slums!"

Quod the somonour, yput out of oure cure!

Said the summoner, "I can't get them either!"

Pees! with myschance and with mysaventure!	"Quiet! Or else be damned!"
Thys seyde oure hoost, and lat hym telle his tale.	That's what our host said, "and let him tell his story.
Now telleth forth, thogh that the somonour gale;	Now you carry on, however much the summoner complains;
Ne spareth nat, myn owene maister deere. --	Don't spare anybody, my dear master."
This false theef, this somonour, quod the frere,	"This false thief, this summoner," said the fryer,
Hadde alwey bawdes redy to his hond,	"Always had a few whores around him,
As any hauk to lure in engelond,	Like any person trying to lure a hawk;
That tolde hym al the secree that they knewe;	They told him all the secrets that they knew,
For hire acqueyntace was nat come of newe.	For they had been in the game long enough.
They weren his approwours prively.	They were his secret agents,
He took hymself a greet profit therby;	And he made great profits from them;
His maister knew nat alwey what he wan.	His master didn't always know how much he got.
Withouten mandement a lewed man	Without official backing he would summon
He koude somne, on peyne of cristes curs,	Ignorant people, on pain of being cursed by Christ,
And they were glade for to fille his purs,	And they were glad to give him money,
And make hym grete feestes atte nale.	And also entertain him in the taverns.
And right as judas hadde purses smale,	Just as Judas had his little purses,
And was a theef, right swich a theef was he;	Got through thieving, that was the sort of thief he was;
His maister hadde but half his duetee.	His master only got half his taxes.
He was, if I shal yeven hym his laude,	He was, if I'm to give him his full June,
A theef, and eek a somnour, and baude.	A thief, and also a summoner, and a pimp.
He hadde eek wenches at his retenue,	He had a load of tarts in his company,
That, wheither that sir robert or sir huwe,	So that whether it was Sir Robert or Sir Hugh,
Or jakke, or rauf, or whoso that it were	Or Jack or Ralph, whoever it was
That lay by hem, they tolde it in his ere.	Who slept with them, they told him about it.
Thus was the wenche and he of oon assent;	So the tarts and he worked hand-in-hand;
And he wolde fecche a feyned mandement,	And he would bring out a forged warrant,
And somne hem to chapitre bothe two,	And summon both of them to the chapter house,
And pile the man, and lete the wenche go.	And he would fine the man, and let the tart go.
Thanne wolde he seye, freend, I shal for thy sake	Then he would say, "My friend, for your sake
Do striken hire out of oure lettres blake;	I will erase your name from the record;
Thee thar namoore as in this cas travaille.	You'll have no more trouble over this business.
I am thy freend, ther I thee may availle.	I am your friend, so I will help you."
Certeyn he knew of briberyes mo	It's certain he got up to so much bribery
Than possible is to telle in yeres two.	It would take more than a couple of years to tell it.
For in this world nys dogge for the bowe	For there is no hunting dog in the world
That kan an hurt deer from an hool yknowe	Who could tell a wounded deer from a sound one
Bet than this somnour knew a sly lecchour,	Better than this summoner could spy out a crafty lecher,

Or an avowtier, or a paramour.	Or an adulterer, or a kept woman.
And for that was the fruyt of al his rente,	That was how he made his living,
Therfore on it he sette al his entente.	So he gave his full attention to it.
And so bifel that ones on a day	And so it came to pass that one day
This somnour, evere waityng on his pray,	This summoner, always looking for his prey,
Rood for to somne an old wydwe, a ribibe,	Rode out to summon an old widow, an old crone,
Feynynge a cause, for he wolde brybe.	With a made up accusation, for he wanted a bribe.
And happed that he saugh bifore hym ryde	It so happened that he saw riding ahead of him
A gay yeman, under a forest syde,	A jolly yeoman, under the eaves of the forest,
A bowe he bar, and arwes brighte and kene;	He was carrying a bow, with bright sharp arrows;
He hadde upon a courtepy of grene,	He was wearing a green jacket,
An hat upon his heed with frenges blake.	And he had a black fringed hat on his head.
Sire, quod this somnour, hayl, and wel atake!	"Sir," said this summoner, "greetings to you!
Welcome, quod he, and every good felawe!	"Welcome," he said, "and the same to every good man!
Wher rydestow, under this grene-wode shawe?	Where are you riding to, in the shade of these green woods?"
Seyde this yeman, wiltow fer to day?	The yeoman asked, "Are you going far today?"
This somnour hym answerde and seyde, nay;	The summoner answered him, "No;
Heere faste by, quod he, is myn entente	Just near here," he said, "is my destination,
To ryden, for to reysen up a rente	I'm riding there to collect a rent
That longeth to my lordes duetee.	Which is long overdue, for my lord."
Artow thanne a bailly? ye, quod he.	"So you are a bailiff?" "Yes," he said.
He dorste nat, for verray filthe and shame	He didn't want, because he was ashamed,
Seye that he was a somonour, for the name.	To admit that he was a summoner.
Depardieux, quod this yeman, deere broother,	"By God," said this yeoman, "dear brother,
Thou art a bailly, and I am another.	You are a bailiff, and so am I.
I am unknowen as in this contree;	I'm not familiar with this area;
Of thyn aqueyntance I wolde praye thee,	I should like to make your acquaintance,
And eek of bretherhede, if that yow leste.	And be your brother, if you permit it.
I have gold and silver in my cheste;	I have gold and silver in my chest;
If that thee happe to comen in oure shire,	If you happen to come to my region
Al shal be thyn, right as thou wolt desire.	I will treat you to everything you want."
Grantmercy, quod this somonour, by my feith!	"God have mercy," said this summoner, "I'll swear to that!"
Everych on ootheres hand his trouthe leith,	Both of them joined hands and
For to be sworne bretheren til they deye.	Swore to be brothers until they died.
In daliance they ryden forth and pleye.	They rode out happily together.
This somonour, which that was as ful of jangles,	This summoner was always full of gossip,
As ful of venym been thise waryangles,	And as poisonous as these butcher birds,
And evere enqueryng upon every thyng,	Was always trying to find out about everything.
Brother, quod he, where is now youre dwellyng	"Brother," he said, "where do you live,
Another day if that I sholde yow seche?	If I try to find you some other day?"
This yeman hym answerde in softe speche,	The yeoman answered him politely,
Brother, quod he, fer in the north contree,	"Brother," he said, "I live far away in the north country,

Where-as I hope som tyme I shal thee see.	*Where I hope I shall see you sometime.*
Er we departe, I shal thee so wel wisse	*Before we part I will give you such clear directions*
That of myn hous ne shaltow nevere mysse.	*That there is no chance you would miss my house."*
Now, brother, quod this somonour, I yow preye,	*"Now brother," said this summoner, "I pray you,*
Teche me, whil that we ryden by the weye,	*Teach me, as we ride along,*
Syn that ye been a baillif as am I,	*Since you are a bailiff just like me,*
Som subtiltee, and tel me feithfully	*Some of your tricks, and tell me truthfully*
In myn office how that I may moost wynne;	*How I can make the most profit from my job;*
And spareth nat for conscience ne synne,	*Don't be at all fastidious about it,*
But as my brother tel me, how do ye.	*But tell me as my brother what you get up to."*
Now, by my trouthe, brother deere, seyde he,	*"Now I swear, dear brother," he said,*
As I shal tellen thee a feithful tale,	*"I shall tell you the whole truth,*
My wages been ful streite and ful smale.	*My wages are very small.*
My lord is hard to me and daungerous,	*My lord is very harsh and tightfisted,*
And myn office is ful laborous,	*And my job is extremely hard work,*
And therfore by extorcions I lyve.	*And so I live through extortion.*
For sothe, I take al that men wol me yive.	*In truth, I take everything I can from men.*
Algate, by gleyghte or by violence,	*Either by cunning or violence*
Fro yeer to yeer I wynne al my dispence.	*I make my wages from year to year.*
I kan no bettre telle, feithfully.	*I'm telling you the whole truth."*
Now certes, quod this somonour, so fare I.	*"Now I swear," said the summoner, "that's what I do.*
I spare nat to taken, God it woot,	*I don't leave anything, God knows,*
But if it be to hevy or to hoot.	*Unless it is too heavy all too hot to handle.*
What I may gete in conseil prively,	*Whatever I can lay my hands on secretly,*
No maner conscience of that have I.	*I don't have any conscience at all about it.*
Nere myn extorcioun, I myghte nat lyven,	*Without my extortions, I couldn't live,*
Ne of swiche japes wol I nat be shryven.	*And I will never confess do what I get up to.*
Stomak ne conscience ne knowe I noon;	*I have no compassion and no conscience;*
I shrewe thise shrifte-fadres everychoon.	*I curse every one of these confessors.*
Wel be we met, by God and by seint jame!	*By God and St James, it's good that we've met!*
But, leeve brother, tel me thanne thy name,	*But, dear brother, tell me your name,"*
Quod this somonour. In this meene while	*The summoner asked. In the meantime*
This yeman gan a litel for to smyle.	*The yeoman began to smile a little.*
Brother, quod he, wiltow that I thee telle?	*"Brother," he said, "do you want me to tell you?*
I am a feend; my dwellyng is in helle,	*I am a devil; my home is in hell,*
And heere I ryde aboute my purchasyng,	*And I ride around here acquiring*
To wite wher men wol yeve me any thyng.	*Anything which men will give me.*
My purchas is th' effect of al my rente.	*What I get is my entire income.*
Looke how thou rydest for the same entente,	*See how you ride for the same purpose,*
To wynne good, thou rekkest nevere how;	*You're not bothered how you make a profit;*
Right so fare I, for ryde wolde I now	*You're just the same as me, for I would*
Unto the worldes ende for a preye.	*Ride to the end of the world for a victim."*

Al! quod this somonour, benedicite! sey ye?	"Good heavens!" said this summoner, "is that the truth?
I wende ye were a yeman trewely.	I thought that you were really a yeoman.
Ye han a mannes shap as wel as I;	You have a human shape just like mine;
Han ye a figure thanne determinat	Do you have a different figure
In helle, ther ye been in youre estat?	When you're at home in hell?"
Nay, certeinly, quod he, ther have we noon;	"No, truly," he said, "there we have none,
But whan us liketh, we kan take us oon,	But we can assume any shape we wish,
Or elles make yow seme we been shape	Or at least make you think that is our shape,
Somtyme lyk a man, or lyk an ape,	Looking like a man, or like an ape,
Or lyk an angel kan I ryde or go.	Or even like an angel I can ride or walk.
It is no wonder thyng thogh it be so;	It's no surprise that this can be done;
A lowsy jogelour kan deceyve thee,	A lousy conjurer can fool you,
And pardee, yet kan I moore craft than he.	And by God, I'm more cunning than him."
Why, quod this somonour, ryde ye thanne or goon	"But why," asked this summoner, "do you ride or walk
In sondry shap, and nat alwey in oon?	In different shapes, and not always in the same one?"
For we, quod he, wol us swiche formes make	"Because," he said, "we take on whatever shape
As moost able is oure preyes for to take.	Is most suitable for capturing our prey."
What maketh yow to han al this labour?	"And why do you take all this trouble?"
Ful many a cause, leeve sire somonour,	"For many reasons, my dear summoner,"
Seyde this feend, but alle thyng hath tyme.	Said this devil, "but all in good time.
The day is short, and it is passed pryme,	The day is short, and it's gone noon,
And yet ne wan I nothyng in this day.	And yet I have got nothing yet today.
I wol entende to wynnyng, if I may,	I shall focus on my profits, if I may,
And nat entende oure wittes to declare.	And not waste time explaining what's in our minds.
For, brother myn, thy wit is al to bare	For, my brother, you wouldn't be able to understand
To understonde, althogh I tolde hem thee.	Even if I explained it all for you.
But, for thou axest why labouren we --	But since you ask why we take so much trouble—
For somtyme we been goddes instrumentz,	Once upon a time we were the tools of God,
And meenes to doon his comandementz,	His way of carrying his orders,
Whan that hym list, upon his creatures,	When he wanted us to, to his creation,
In divers art and in diverse figures.	In various ways and in different disguises.
Withouten hym we have no myght, certayn,	It's certain that without him we have no power,
If that hym list stonden ther-agayn.	If he ever wanted to fight against us again.
And somtyme, at oure prayere, han we leve	And sometimes, at our request, we get permission
Oonly the body and nat the soule greve;	To aggravate the body and not the soul;
Witnesse on job, whom that we diden wo.	Look at the trouble we gave to Job.
And somtyme han we myght of bothe two,	And sometimes we have power over both,
This is to seyn, of soule and body eke.	That is to say, over the soul and the body as well.
And somtyme be we suffred for to seke	And sometimes we are allowed to hunt
Upon a man, and doon his soule unreste,	A man, and cause pain to his soul,

And nat his body, and al is for the beste.	And not his body, and everything is for the best.
Whan he withstandeth oure temptacioun,	When he resists our temptations,
It is a cause of his savacioun,	That brings about his salvation,
Al be it that it was nat oure entente	Even though it was not our purpose
He sholde be sauf, but that we wolde hym hente.	For him to be saved, we want to capture him.
And somtyme be we servant unto man,	And sometimes we serve men,
As to the erchebisshop seint dunstan,	Like we did the Archbishop St Dunstan,
And to the apostles servent eek was I.	And I was also a servant to the apostles."
Yet tel me, quod the somonour, feithfully,	"But tell me," said the summoner, "truthfully,
Make ye yow newe bodies thus alway	Do you always make new bodies
Of elementz? the feend answerde, nay.	From the elements?" The fiend answered, "No.
Somtyme we feyne, and somtyme we aryse	Sometimes we imitate them, and sometimes reuse
With dede bodyes, in ful sondry wyse,	Dead bodies, in various different ways,
And speke as renably and faire and wel	And speak as comprehensibly and elegantly
As to the phitonissa dide samuel.	As Samuel did to the Phitnissa.
(and yet wol som men seye it was nat he;	(Although some men say it wasn't him;
I do no fors of youre dyvynytee.)	Your theology has nothing to do with me)
But o thyng warne I thee, I wol nat jape, --	But one thing I'll warn you about, I won't joke;
Thou wolt algates wite how we been shape;	You will always be able to recognise us,
Thou shalt herafterward, my brother deere,	From now on, my dear brother,
Come there thee nedeth nat of me to leere.	You won't need to ask who I am.
For thou shalt, by thyn owene experience,	You will, through your own experience,
Konne in a chayer rede of this sentence	Sitting in a red chair understand
Bet than virgile, while he was on lyve,	Better than Virgil, when he was alive,
Or dant also. Now lat us ryde blyve,	And also Dante. Now let us ride on quickly,
For I wole holde compaignye with thee	For I will keep you company
Til it be so that thou forsake me.	Until you decide to leave me.
Nay, quod this somonour, that shal nat bityde!	"No," said this summoner, "that will never happen!
I am a yeman, knowen is ful wyde;	I am a yeoman, everybody knows that;
My trouthe wol I holde, as in this cas.	I will stay faithful in this instance.
For though thou were the devel sathanas,	Even if you were Satan himself,
My trouthe wol I holde to my brother,	I would keep my promise to my brother,
As I am sworn, and ech of us til oother,	As I have sworn, as we both swore,
For to be trewe brother in this cas;	To be true brothers to each other;
And bothe we goon abouten oure purchas.	And we must both go about our business.
Taak thou thy part, what that men wol thee yive,	You do your part, taking what men will give you,
And I shal myn; thus may we bothe lyve.	And I shall do mine; so we will both thrive.
And if that any of us have moore than oother,	And if either of us gets more than the other,
Lat hym be trewe, and parte it with his brother.	Let him be faithful, and share it with his brother.
I graunte, quod the devel, by my fey.	"I swear that I agree," said the devil.
And with that word they ryden forth hir wey.	With those words they rode on their way.
And right at the entryng of the townes ende,	As they came into the end of the town,
To which this somonour shoop hym for to wende,	Which this summoner had been making for,
They saugh a cart that charged was with hey,	They saw a cart which was full of hay,

Which that a cartere droof forth in his wey.	Which a carter was driving on its way.
Deep was the wey, for which the carte stood.	The road on which the cart was going was very muddy,
The cartere smoot, and cryde as he were wood,	And the carter beat his horses, crying as if he were mad,
Hayt, brok! hayt, scot! what spare ye for the stones?	"Get on, Badger! Come on, Scot! What do you care for stones?
The feend, quod he, yow fecche, body and bones,	"May the devil," he said, "take you, body and bones,
As ferforthly as evere were ye foled,	Just as certainly as you ever born,
So muche wo as I have with yow tholed!	You have given me so much grief!
The devel have al, bothe hors and cart and hey!	The devil take everything, the horses and cart and the hay!"
This somonour seyde, heere shal we have a pley.	The summoner said, "Here we shall have some fun."
And neer the feend he drough, as noght ne were,	And he crept over to the fiend, as if he were doing nothing,
Ful prively, and rowned in his ere	And secretly whispered in his ear,
Herkne, my brother, herkne, by thy feith!	"Listen, my brother, listen, in faith!
Herestow nat how that the cartere seith?	Did you hear what the carter said?
Hent it anon, for he hath yeve it thee,	Grab it at once, for he has given it to you,
Bothe hey and cart, and eek his caples thre.	Both the hay and the cart, and also his three horses."
Nay, quod the devel, God woot, never a deel!	"No," said the devil, "God knows, he hasn't!
It is nat his entente, trust me weel.	That's not what he meant, trust me.
Axe hym thyself, it thou nat trowest me;	Ask him yourself, if you don't believe me;
Or elles stynt a while, and thou shalt see.	Or just wait a while, and you will see."
This cartere thakketh his hors upon the croupe,	The carter thwacked his horses on the backside,
And they bigonne to drawen and to stoupe.	And they began to pull and strain.
Heyt! now, quod he, ther jhesu crist yow blesse,	"Giddyup! Now," he said, "may Jesus Christ bless you,
And al his handwerk, bothe moore and lesse!	And everything that he makes, the great and small!
That was wel twight, myn owene lyard boy.	That was well done, my dappled lad.
I pray God save thee, and seinte loy!	I pray that God will save you, and St Loy!
Now is my cart out of the slow, pardee!	Now my cart is out of the swamp, by God!"
Lo, brother, quod the feend, what tolde I thee?	"Look, brother," said the fiend, "what did I tell you?
Heere may ye se, myn owene deere brother,	Here you can see, my friend and brother,
The carl spak oo thing, but he thoghte another.	That hasn't said one thing, but he was thinking another.
Lat us go forth abouten oure viage;	Let's carry on on our journey;
Heere wynne I nothyng upon cariage.	I'm not getting any cart tax today."
Whan that they coomen somwhat out of towne,	When they had gone some way out of town,
This somonour to his brother gan to rowne	This summoner began to whisper to his brother:
Brother, quod he, heere woneth an old rebekke,	"Brother," he said, "there's an old crone living here,
That hadde almoost as lief to lese hire nekke	Who would almost rather lose her neck
As for to yeve a peny of hir good.	Than lose a penny of her wealth.

I wole han twelf pens, though that she be wood,	I will have twelvepence from her, even if it drives her mad,
Or I wol sompne hire unto oure office;	Or I will summon her to our office;
And yet, God woot, of hire knowe I no vice.	And yet, God knows, I don't know of any vice in her.
But for thou kanst nat, as in this contree,	But seeing as it seems that you cannot, in this region,
Wynne thy cost, taak heer ensample of me.	Make any profits, take your example from me."
This somonour clappeth at the wydwes gate.	This summoner not on the widow's gate.
Com out, quod he, thou olde virytrate!	"Come out," he said, "you old hag!
I trowe thou hast som frere or preest with thee.	I think you've got some friar or priest in there with you."
Who clappeth? seyde this wyf, benedicitee!	"Who's that knocking?" asked this wife, "God bless me!
God save you, sire, what is youre sweete wille?	God save you, sir, what is your sweet desire?"
I have, quod he, of somonce here a bille;	"I have," he said, "a bill of summons here;
Up peyne of cursyng, looke that thou be	If you don't wish to be cursed, make sure that you
To-morn bifore the erchedeknes knee,	Appear before the Archdeacon tomorrow,
T' answere to the court of certeyn thynges.	To face certain accusations in court."
Now, lord, quod she, crist jhesu, kyng of kynges,	"Now, Lord," she said, "Jesus Christ, King of Kings,
So wisly helpe me, as I ne may.	Please send me help, I can't help myself.
I have been syk, and that ful many a day.	I have been ill, for a very long time.
I may nat go so fer, quod she, ne ryde,	I can't go that far," she said, "nor ride,
But I be deed, so priketh it in my syde.	It would kill me, it gives me such pain.
May I nat axe a libel, sire somonour,	Can't I ask for a written accusation, sir summoner,
And answere there by my procuratour	And answer through a proxy
To swich thyng as men wole opposen me?	Whatever it is I'm accused of?"
Yis, quod this somonour, pay anon, lat se,	"Yes," said the summoner, "pay at once, let's see,
Twelf pens to me, and I wol thee acquite.	Twelvepence to me, and I will let you off.
I shal no profit han therby but lite;	I shan't be making any profit from it,
My maister hath the profit, and nat I.	All of that goes to my master, not me.
Com of, and lat me ryden hastily;	Hurry up, and let me be on my way;
Yif me twelf pens, I may no lenger tarye.	Give me twelvepence, I can't wait any longer."
Twelf pens! quod she, now, lady seinte marie	"Twelvepence!" she said, "now, Lady St Mary
So wisly help me out of care and synne,	Keep me from trouble and soon,
This wyde world thogh that I sholde wynne,	Even if I could have the whole world for it,
Ne have I nat twelf pens withinne myn hoold.	I don't have twelvepence to spare.
Ye knowen wel that I am povre and oold;	You well know that I am poor and old;
Kithe youre almesse on me povre wrecche.	Show some pity for a poor wretch."
Nay thanne, quod he, the foule feend me fecche	"No then," he said, "may the devil take me away
If I th' excuse, though thou shul be spilt!	If I let you off, even if it would kill you!
allas! quod she, God woot, I have no gilt.	"Alas!" she said, "God knows, I'm innocent."
Pay me, quod he, or by the swete seinte anne,	"Pay me," he said, "or by sweet St Anne
As I wol bere awey thy newe panne	I will take away your new pan,
For dette which thou owest me of old.	Which you owe me for an old debt;

183

Whan that thou madest thyn housbonde cokewold,	When you cheated on your husband,
I payde at hoom for thy correccioun.	I paid the fine for your punishment."
Thou lixt! quod she, by my savacioun,	"You're lying!" she said, "by my salvation,
Ne was I nevere er now, wydwe ne wyf,	Never have I before now, either as widow or wife,
Somoned unto youre court in al my lyf;	Been summoned to your court in my whole life;
Ne nevere I nas but of my body trewe!	And furthermore I have never been unfaithful!
Unto the devel blak and rough of hewe	I give the rough black devil
Yeve I thy body and my panne also!	Your body, and my pan!"
And whan the devel herde hire cursen so	And when the devil heard her cursing like this,
Upon hir knees, he seyde in this manere,	Upon her knees, he spoke in this fashion;
Now, mabely, myn owene mooder deere,	Now, Mabel, my own dear mother,
Is this youre wyl in ernest that ye seye?	Are you earnest in what you're saying?"
The devel, quod she, so fecche hym er he deye,	"The devil," she said, "may come and get him efore he dies,
And panne and al, but he wol hym repente!	And take the pan and everything, if only he will repent!"
Nay, olde stot, that is nat myn entente,	"No, you old baggage, I'm not doing that,"
Quod this somonour, for to repente me	Said this summoner, "I shan't repent
For any thyng that I have had of thee.	Of anything that I've had from you.
I wolde I hadde thy smok and every clooth!	I wish I had your dress and all your clothes!"
Now, brother, quod the devel, be nat wrooth;	"Now, brother," said the devil, "don't be angry;
Thy body and this panne been myne by right.	Your body and this pan are mine by rights.
Thow shalt with me to helle yet to-nyght,	You shall come to hell with me tonight,
Where thou shalt knowen of oure privetee	Where you will learn more about our business
Moore than a maister of dyvynytee.	Than any master of theology knows."
And with that word this foule feend hym hente;	And saying that the foul fiend grabbed him;
Body and soule he with the devel wente	His body and soul both went with the devil
Where as that somonours han hir heritage.	To where summoners get what they deserve.
And god, that maked after his ymage	And may God, who made mankind in his image,
Mankynde, save and gyde us, alle and some,	Save and guide us, every one,
And leve thise somonours goode men bicome!	And help these summoners to become good men!
Lordynges, I koude han toold yow, quod this frere,	"My Lords, I could have told you," said this friar,
Hadde I had leyser for this somonour heere,	"If I hadn't been interrupted by this summoner here,
After the text of crist, poul, and john,	From the text of Christ, Paul and John,
And of oure othere doctours many oon,	And many of our other learned men,
Swiche peynes that youre hertes myghte agryse,	Of such tortures that your hearts would shake,
Al be it so no tonge may it devyse,	No tongue could ever describe them,
Thogh that I myghte a thousand wynter telle	Even if I spent a thousand years telling you
The peynes of thilke cursed hous of helle.	The pains suffered by the damned in hell.
But for to kepe us fro that cursed place,	But to keep us from that cursed place,

Waketh, and preyeth jhesu for his grace
So kepe us from the temptour sathanas.
Herketh this word! beth war, as in this cas

The leoun sit in his awayt alway
To sle the innocent, if that he may.
Disposeth ay youre hertes to withstonde
The feend, that yow wolde make thral and bonde.
He may nat tempte yow over youre myght,

For crist wol be youre champion and knyght.

And prayeth that thise somonours hem repente
Of hir mysdedes, er that the feend hem hente!

Heere endeth the Freres Tale

*Wake up, and pray to Jesus for his grace
To protect us from the tempter Satan.
Listen to what I say! Be warned, like in this story,*

*The lion is always sitting in wait
To kill the innocent, if he can.
Dispose always your hearts to withstand
The devil, who wants to make you his slave.
He cannot tempt you if you use all your strength,
For Christ will be your champion and your knight.
And pray that these summoners repent
Their sins, before the Devil grabs them!"*

The end of the Friar's tale

The Summoner's Tale

The Prologue

The Prologue of the Somonours Tale.

This somonour in his styropes hye stood;
Upon this frere his herte was so wood
That lyk an aspen leef he quook for ire.
Lordynges, quod he, but o thyng I desire;

I yow biseke that, of youre curteisye,
Syn ye han herd this false frere lye,

As suffreth me I may my tale telle.
This frere bosteth that he knoweth helle,
And God it woot, that it is litel wonder;
Freres and feendes been but lyte asonder.

For, pardee, ye han ofte tyme herd telle
How that a frere ravyshed was to helle
In spirit ones by a visioun;
And as an angel ladde hym up and doun,
To shewen hym the peynes that the were,
In al the place saugh he nat a frere;
Of oother folk he saugh ynowe in wo.

Unto this angel spak the frere tho
Now, sire, quod he, han freres swich a grace

That noon of hem shal come to this place?
Yis, quod this aungel, many a millioun!

And unto sathanas he ladde hym doun.

-- And now hath sathanas, -- seith he, -- a tayl

Brodder than of a carryk is the sayl.
Hold up thy tayl, thou sathanas! -- quod he;
-- shewe forth thyn ers, and lat the frere se
Where is the nest of freres in this place! --
And er that half a furlong wey of space,

Right so as bees out swarmen from an hyve,
Out of the develes ers ther gonne dryve
Twenty thousand freres on a route,
And thurghout helle swarmed al aboute,
And comen agayn as faste as they may gon,

And in his ers they crepten everychon.

He clapte his tayl agayn and lay ful stille.
This frere, whan he looked hadde his fille
Upon the tormentz of this sory place,

The Summoner's prologue

This summoner stood up in his stirrups;
He was so furious with this friar
That he shook with anger like an aspen leaf.
"My lords," he said, "I only ask you for one thing;
That you are polite enough,
Since you have listened to the lies of this false friar,
That you will now listen to my story.
This friar boasts that he knows about hell,
And God knows, that's no surprise;
Friars and Demons are much the same thing.

For, by God, you will have often heard
About a friar being carried off to hell
His spirit being taken in a vision;
And as he was led up and down by an angel,
Showing him the suffering that was there,
He didn't see a single friar in the whole place;
He saw plenty of other types of people suffering.
Then the friar spoke to the angel:
"Now, sir," he said, "have friars been granted such grace
That none of them ever come to this place?"
"Yes," said the angel, "many millions of them have come!"
And he took him down to see Satan.

"And now you will see that Satan," he said, "has a tail
Which is wider than the sail of a great ship.
Hold up your tail, Satan!" he said;
"Reveal your arse, and let the friar see
Where they keep the friars in this place!"
And in less time than it takes to plough half a furlong,
Like bees swarming out of a hive,
Out of the Devil's backside there began to rush
Twenty thousand friars in a great crowd,
Swarming around throughout hell,
Then going back again as fast as they came out,
Creeping back into his ass, every one.

He dropped his tail again and lay very still.
This friar, when he had seen enough
Of the torments of that unhappy place,

His spirit God restored, of his grace,
Unto his body agayn, and he awook.
But natheles, for fere yet he quook,
So was the develes ers ay in his mynde,
That is his heritage of verray kynde.
God save yow alle, save this cursed frere!

My prologe wol I ende in this manere.

Had his spirit replaced by God's grace
Back into his body, and he woke up.
Nevertheless, he was shaking with fear,
With the devil's ass always on his mind,
That's his natural inheritance.
May God save you all, except for this cursed friar!
This is where I shall end my prologue.

The Tale

Heere bigynneth the Somonour his Tale

The Summoner's tale

Lordynges, ther is in yorkshire, as I gesse,
A mersshy contree called holdernesse,
In which ther wente a lymytour aboute,
To preche, and eek to begge, it so no doute.

*My lords, there is in Yorkshire, I believe,
A marshy country called Holderness,
In which there was a licensed beggar,
Who went round preaching, and also begging, doubtless.*

And so bifel that on a day this frere
Hadde preched at a chirche in his manere,
And specially, aboven every thyng,
Excited he the peple in his prechyng
To trentals, and to yeve, for goddes sake,

*And it happened one day that this friar
Had preached at a church in his usual way,
And especially, more than anything,
He encouraged the people with his preaching
To hold masses for the dead, and to give, for the sake of God,*

Wherwith men myghte hooly houses make,
Ther as divine servyce is honoured,
Nat ther as it is wasted and devoured,
Ne ther it nedeth nat for to be yive,
As to possessioners, that mowen lyve,
Thanked be god, in wele and habundaunce.

*Money which men could use to build churches,
Where the divine service would be celebrated,
Not in places where it would be wasted,
Nor where it is not needed,
To licensed clergymen, who can live,
God be thanked, in prosperity and plenty.*

Trentals, seyde he, deliveren fro penaunce

Hir freendes soules, as wel olde as yonge, --

Ye, whan that they been hastily ysonge,
Nat for to holde a preest holy and gay --
He syngeth nat but o masse in a day.
Delivereth out, quod he, anon the soules!
Ful hard it is with flesshhook or with oules
To been yclawed, or to brenne or bake.
Now spede yow hastily, for cristes sake!

*"Masses for the dead," he said, "take away punishments
From the souls of your friends, the old as well as the young,
Yes, when they have been quickly performed,
Not just done in order to keep a priest happy–
He would only sing one mass a day.
Save all the souls at once!" he said,
"They are suffering greatly, being tortured,
Torn, burning and baking.
Now get on with it, for Christ's sake!"*

And whan this frere had seyd al his entente,
With qui cum patre forth his wey he wente.

*And when this friar had spoken his piece,
He gave the prayer "with the father" and went on his way.*

Whan folk in chirche had yeve him what hem leste,

He wente his wey, no lenger wolde he reste,
With scrippe and tipped staf, ytukked hye,

*When the people in the church had given him all they wished
Then off he went; he would stay no longer.
He went with his bag and his metal tipped staff, with his robe tucked up high,*

In every hous he gan to poure and prye,
And beggeth mele and chese, or elles corn.

*And he stuck his nose into every single house,
Begging for porridge and cheese, or otherwise corn.*

His felawe hadde a staf tipped with horn,
A peyre of tables al of yvory,
And a poyntel polysshed fetisly,
And wrooth the names alwey, as he stood,
Of alle folk that yaf hym any good,
Ascaunces that he wolde for hem preye.

*His companion had a staff tipped with horn,
And a pair of ivory tablets,
And a carefully sharpened pen,
And he always wrote down the names at once
Of all people who gave him anything good,
Promising they would be remembered in his prayers.*

189

Yif us a busshel whete, malt, or reye,	"Give us a bushel of wheat, malt or rye,
A goddes kechyl, or a trype of chese,	A piece of cake, or a bit of cheese,
Or elles what yow lyst, we may nat cheese;	Or whatever else you have, we do not choose;
A goddes halfpeny, or a masse peny,	A God's halfpenny, or a mass penny,
Or yif us of youre brawn, if ye have eny;	Or give us some meat, if you have any;
A dagon of youre blanket, leeve dame,	A piece of cloth, dear lady,
Oure suster deere, -- lo! heere I write youre name, --	Our beloved sister–look! I'm writing down your name–
Bacon or beef, or swich thyng as ye fynde.	Bacon or beef, or anything else you have."
A sturdy harlot wente ay hem bihynde,	A well built rascal always followed them,
That was hir hostes man, and bar a sak,	He was the servant of their host, and carried the sack,
And what men yaf hem, leyde it on his bak.	And whatever men gave them, he carried on his back.
And whan that he was out at dore, anon	And as soon as he was out the door, he immediately
He planed awey the names everichon	Scraped off the names of everyone
That he biforn had writen in his tables;	That he previously had written on his tablets;
He served hem with nyfles and with fables.	He deceived them with his tricks and his lies.
Nay, ther thou lixt, thou somonour! quod the frere.	"No, you are lying, you summoner!" said the friar.
Pees, quod oure hoost, for cristes mooder deere!	"Quiet," our host said, "for the sake of holy Mary!
Tel forth thy tale, and spare it nat at al.	Tell us your story, don't leave anything out."
So thryve I, quod this somonour, so I shal!	"As I hope to flourish," said the summoner, "that's what I'll do!"
So longe he wente, hous by hous, til he	So along he went, from house to house, until he
Cam til an hous ther he was wont to be	Came to a house where he was used to being
Refresshed moore than in an hundred placis.	More welcomed than in a hundred other places.
Syk lay the goode man whos that the place is;	The good man who owned the place was sick,
Bedrede upon a couche lowe he lay.	And he lay bedridden upon a couch.
Deus hic! quod he, o thomas, freend, good day!	"May God be here!" he said, "O Thomas, my friend, good day!"
Seyde this frere, curteisly and softe.	This is what the friar said, courteous and soft.
Thomas, quod he, God yelde yow! ful ofte	"Thomas," he said, "May God reward you! Very often
Have I upon this bench faren ful weel;	I have done well at your table;
Heere have I eten many a myrie meel.	I've had many good meals here."
And fro the bench he droof awey the cat,	And he pushed the cat off the bench,
And leyde adoun his potente and his hat,	And put down his staff and his hat,
And eek his scrippe, and sette hym softe adoun.	And also his satchel, and quietly sat down.
His felawe was go walked into toun	His companion had gone walking into town
Forth with his knave, into that hostelrye	With his servant, to the hostel
Where as he shoop hym thilke nyght to lye.	Where he meant to stay that night.
O deere maister, quod this sike man,	"Oh dear master," said the sick man,
How han ye fare sith that march bigan?	"How have you been doing since the beginning of March?
I saugh yow noght this fourtenyght or moore.	I haven't seen you for a fortnight or more."

God woot, quod he, laboured have I ful soore,	"God knows," he said, "I have been working hard,
And specially, for thy savacion	Especially for your salvation,
Have I seyd many a precious orison,	I've said many valuable prayers for you,
And for oure othere freendes, God hem blesse!	And for our other friends, may God bless them!
I have to day been at youre chirche at messe,	Today I was like your church at mass,
And seyd a sermon after my symple wit,	And read a sermon in my simple style;
Nat al after the text of hooly writ;	Not entirely following the text of the Bible,
For it is hard to yow, as I suppose,	For I think that's hard for you to understand,
And therfore wol I teche yow al the glose.	And so I give you all my interpretation.
Glosynge is a glorious thyng, certeyn,	Interpretation is certainly a wonderful thing,
For lettre sleeth, so as we clerkes seyn.	for words can kill, we scholars say;
There have I taught hem to be charitable,	I have taught them to be charitable,
And spende hir good ther it is resonable;	And share out their wealth when the time is right;
And there I saugh oure dame, -- a! where is she?	And I saw our lady there–where is she?"
Yond in the yerd I trowe that she be,	"I think that she is out in the yard,"
Seyde this man, and she wol come anon.	The man said, "and she will coming soon."
Ey, maister, welcome be ye, by seint john!	"Ah, master, you are welcome, by St John!"
Seyde this wyf, how fare ye, hertely?	Said this wife, "how are you, I kindly ask?"
The frere ariseth up ful curteisly,	The friar he got up politely,
And hire embraceth in his armes narwe,	And hugged her tightly,
And kiste hire sweete, and chirketh as a sparwe	And kissed her sweetly, and chirped like a sparrow
With his lyppes: dame, quod he, right weel,	Through his lips: "Lady," he said, "I'm very well,
As he that is youre servent every deel,	And as someone who is your devoted servant,
Thanked be god, that yow yaf soule and lyf!	I give thanks to God, that he gave you your soul and life!
Yet saugh I nat this day so fair a wyf	I swear to God I didn't see a more lovely
In al the chirche, God so save me!	Wife in church today!"
Ye, God amende defautes, sire, quod she.	"Yes, may God help me to change my ways," she said,
Algates, welcome be ye, by my fey!	"In any case, I swear you are very welcome!"
Graunt mercy, dame, this have I founde alwey.	"I have always been treated well by you, lady.
But of youre grete goodnesse, by youre leve,	But in your great kindness, with your permission,
I wolde prey yow that ye nat yow greve,	I ask you now not to be annoyed,
I wole with thomas speke a litel throwe.	I want to speak with Thomas for a little while.
Thise curatz been ful necligent and slowe	These curates are very lazy and slow
To grope tendrely a conscience	About carefully examining a conscience
In shrift; in prechyng is my diligence,	In confession; preaching is my business,
And studie in petres wordes and in poules.	And the study of the words of Peter and Paul.
I walke, and fisshe cristen mennes soules,	I walk and fish for the souls of Christian men,
To yelden jhesu crist his propre rente;	Asking them to pay their dues to Jesus Christ;
To sprede his word is set al myn entente.	It is my business to spread his word."
Now, by youre leve, o deere sire, she,	"Now, with your permission, oh dear sir," she said,
Chideth him weel, for seinte trinitee!	"Tell him off, in the name of the holy Trinity!
He is as angry as a pissemyre,	He is as angry as an ant,
Though that he have al that he kan desire,	Although he has everything he could want;

Though I hym wrye a-nyght and make hym warm,	*Even though I lie with him at night and keep him warm,*
And over hym leye my leg outher myn arm,	*Laying my legs and arms over him,*
He groneth lyk oure boor, lith in oure sty.	*He groans like the boar pig we have in our sty.*
Oother desport right noon of hym have I;	*I don't get any pleasure out of him;*
I may nat plese hym in no maner cas.	*Nothing I do seems to please him."*
O thomas, je vous dy, thomas! thomas!	*"Oh Thomas, I'm telling you, Thomas, Thomas!*
This maketh the feend; this moste ben amended.	*This is the devil's work, this must be changed.*
Ire is a thyng that hye God defended,	*Anger is something that God forbids,*
And therof wol I speke a word or two.	*And I will tell you a thing or two about it."*
Now, maister, quod the wyf, er that I go,	*"Now, master," said the wife, "before I go,*
What wol ye dyne? I wol go theraboute.	*What will you have to eat? I will see to it."*
Now dame, quod he, now je vous dy sanz doute,	*"Now, lady," he said, "I will tell you definitely*
Have I nat of a capon but the lyvere,	*That I will just have some chicken liver,*
And of youre softe breed nat but a shyvere,	*And just a tiny slice of your best bread,*
And after that a rosted pigges heed --	*And after that a roasted pig's head—*
But that I nolde no beest for me were deed --	*I don't want any animal killed for me—*
Thanne hadde I with yow hoomly suffisaunce.	*I'm quite happy to make do with plain food.*
I am a man of litel sustenaunce;	*I don't need much to keep me going;*
My spirit hath his fostryng in the bible.	*My spirit gets its nourishment from the Bible.*
The body is ay so redy and penyble	*My body is so used to*
To wake, that my stomak is destroyed.	*Staying awake praying that I have little appetite.*
I prey yow, dame, ye be nat anoyed,	*Please, lady, don't be annoyed,*
Though I so freendly yow my conseil shewe.	*By my sharing these confidences with you.*
By god! I wolde nat telle it but a fewe.	*My God! There aren't many I would tell."*
Now, sire, quod she, but o word er I go.	*"Now, sir," she said, "just one word before I go.*
My child is deed withinne thise wykes two,	*My child died within this fortnight,*
Soone after that ye wente out of this toun.	*Soon after you left the town."*
His deeth saugh I by revelacioun,	*"I saw his death in a vision,"*
Seide this frere, at hoom in oure dortour.	*Said the friar, "at home in my dormitory.*
I dar wel seyn that, er that half an hour	*I can promise you that just half an hour*
After his deeth, I saugh hym born to blisse	*After his death I saw him carried up to heaven*
In myn avision, so God me wisse!	*In my vision, as I swear to God!*
So didde oure sexteyn and oure fermerer,	*So did our sexton, and our physician,*
That han been trewe freres fifty yeer;	*Who have been true friars for fifty years;*
They may now -- God be thanked of his loone! --	*They may now—thank God for his grace!—*
Maken hir jubilee and walke allone.	*Celebrate their anniversary in peace.*
And up I roos, and al oure covent eke,	*I rose up, along with all my fellows,*
With many a teere trillyng on my cheke,	*With many tears running down my cheeks,*
Withouten noyse or claterynge of belles;	*Without any noise or ringing of bells;*
Te deum was oure song, and nothyng elles,	*We sung praises to God, nothing else,*
Save that to crist I seyde an orison,	*Except I said a prayer to Christ,*
Thankynge hym of his revelacion.	*Thanking him for his revelation.*
For, sire and dame, trusteth me right weel,	*For, sir and lady, you must believe me,*
Oure orisons been moore effectueel,	*Our prayers are more effective,*
And moore we seen of cristes secree thynges,	*And we see more of the plans of Christ,*
Than burel folk, although they weren kynges.	*Than ordinary people, even if they are kings.*
We lyve in poverte and in abstinence,	*We live in poverty and abstinence,*

And burell folk in richesse and despence	And other people have wealth and spend money
Of mete and drynke, and in hir foul delit.	On food and drink, indulging their lusts.
We han this worldes lust al in despit.	We reject all the excesses of the world.
Lazar and dives lyveden diversly,	Lazarus and Dives lived differently,
And divers gerdon hadden they therby.	And so they got different rewards.
Whoso wol preye, he moot faste and be clene,	Whoever prays, he must fast and be pure,
And fatte his soule, and make his body lene.	He must feed up his soul, and let his body starve.
We fare as seith th' apostle; clooth and foode	We do what the apostle says; clothes and food
Suffisen us, though they be nat ful goode.	Are enough for us, even though they may be poor.
The clennesse and the fastynge of us freres	The purity and fasting of we friars
Maketh that crist accepteth oure preyeres.	Is what makes Christ accept our prayers.
Lo, moyses fourty dayes and fourty nyght	Moses fasted for forty days and forty nights
Fasted, er that the heighe God of myght	Before Almighty God
Spak with hym in the mountayne of synay.	Spoke to him on the mountain of Sinai.
With empty wombe, fastynge many a day,	With his stomach empty, from many days of fasting,
Receyved he the lawe that was writen	He was given the laws that were written
With goddes fynger; and elye, wel ye witen,	By God's hand; and you are well aware that Elijah
In mount oreb, er he hadde any speche	On Mount Horeb, before he spoke
With hye god, that is oure lyves leche,	To Almighty God, who is the healer of our lives,
He fasted longe, and was in contemplaunce.	He fasted for a long time and meditated.
Aaron, that hadde the temple in governaunce,	Aaron, who ruled over the temple,
And eek the othere preestes everichon,	And also all the other priests,
Into the temple whan they sholde gon	When they had to go into the Temple
To preye for the peple, and do servyse,	To pray for the people and worship God,
They nolden drynken in no maner wyse	They would not drink any sort of
No drynke which that myghte hem dronke make,	Drink which could make them drunk,
But there in abstinence preye and wake,	They remained abstinent whilst they prayed and kept a vigil,
Lest that they deyden. Taak heede what I seye!	In fear of of death. Listen to what I say!
But they be sobre that for the peple preye,	Unless people who pray for others are sober,
War that I seye -- namoore, for it suffiseth.	Watch out–I'll say no more, that's enough.
Oure lord jhesu, as hooly writ devyseth,	Our Lord Jesus, as the Bible tells us,
Yaf us ensample of fastynge and preyeres.	Set us an example of fasting and prayer.
Therfore we mendynantz, we sely freres,	So we mendicants, we innocent friars,
Been wedded to poverte and continence,	Are married to poverty and chastity,
To charite, humblesse, and abstinence,	Charity, humility, and abstinence,
To persecucioun for rightwisnesse,	To persecution for following the right path,
To wepynge, misericorde, and clennesse.	To weep, show kindness, and be pure.
And therfore may ye se that oure preyeres --	And so you can see that our prayers–
I speke of us, we mendynantz, we freres --	I'm talking of we mendicant friars–
Been to the hye God moore acceptable	Are more acceptable to Almighty God
Than youres, with youre feestes at the table.	Than yours, with all your stuffing at the table.
Fro paradys first, if I shal nat lye,	To tell you the truth, man was banished
Was man out chaced for his glotonye;	From Paradise initially for his greed;
And chaast was man in paradys, certeyn.	When he was in paradise man was certainly pure.

But herkne now, thomas, what I shal seyn.	But listen now, Thomas, to what I say.
I ne have no text of it, as I suppose,	I don't think I'll use any Scripture for it,
But I shal fynde it in a maner glose,	But I will employ my own interpretation,
That specially oure sweete lord jhesus	And say that our sweet Lord Jesus
Spak this by freres, whan he seyde thus	Was particularly thinking of friars when he said this:
-- Blessed be they that povere in spirit been. --	"Blessed are those who are poor in spirit."
And so forth al the gospel may ye seen,	And so you can see in the gospel
Wher it be likker oure professioun,	Whether He preferred our profession
Or hirs that swymmen in possessioun.	Or those who are loaded with goods.
Fy on hire pompe and on hire glotonye!	A curse on their showiness and their greed!
And for hir lewednesse I hem diffye.	I reject their ignorance.
My thynketh they been lyk jovinyan,	I think they are like Jovinian,
Fat as a whale, and walkynge as a swan,	As fat as a whale, walking like a swan,
Al vinolent as botel in the spence.	As full of wine as an unopened bottle.
Hir preyere is of ful greet reverence, it;	Their prayers are full of reverence
Lo, -- buf! -- they seye, -- cor meum eructavit! --	When they say the psalm of David for their souls: They think they have said something good when they belch.
Who folweth cristes gospel and his foore,	Who is there who follows the words of Christ and his path,
But we that humble been, and chaast, and poore,	Except for we who are humble, and chaste and poor,
Werkeris of goddes word, nat auditours?	The ones who do the Word of God, don't just listen to it?
Therfore, right as an hauk up at a sours	So, just like a hawk flying upwards
Up springeth into th' eir, right so prayeres	Leaping into the air, so the prayers
Of charitable and chaste bisy freres	Of charitable and pure hard-working friars
Maken hir sours to goddes eres two.	Fly straight up to the ears of God.
Thomas! thomas! so moote I ryde or go,	Thomas, Thomas! Whether I ride or walk,
And by that lord that clepid is seint yve,	I swear by the lord called St Yve,
Nere thou oure brother, sholdestou nat thryve.	If we didn't help you, you would be in trouble.
In our chapitre prayer we day and nyght	In our history we pray day and night
To crist, that he thee sende heele and might	To Christ, to give you health and strength,
Thy body for to weelden hastily.	And to work his cure on your body."
God woot, quod he, nothyng therof feele i!	"God knows," he said, "I don't feel anything of it!
As help me crist, as I in fewe yeres,	So help me Christ, in a few years
Have spent upon diverse manere freres	I have spent many pounds on
Ful many a pound; yet fare I never the bet.	Different sorts of friars, but I never feel better.
Certeyn, my good have I almoost biset.	I swear, I have spent almost all my money.
Farwel, my gold, for it is al ago!	Farewell, my gold, it is all gone!"
The frere answerde, o thomas, dostow so?	The friar answered, "O Thomas, do you say so?
What nedeth yow diverse freres seche?	Why have you tried different friars?
What nedeth hym that hath a parfit leche	Why does the person who has a perfect doctor need
To sechen othere leches in the toun?	To go and try any others?
Youre inconstance is youre confusioun.	It's your inconstancy that has ruined you.
Holde ye thanne me, or elles oure covent,	Do you think that I, or my monastery,
To praye for yow been insufficient?	Are not good enough to pray for you?
Thomas, that jape nys nat worth a myte.	Thomas, your behaviour has been worthless.

Youre maladye is for we han to lyte.	*You are ill because we have not been given enough.*
A! yif that covent half a quarter otes!	*Give our monastery four bushels of oats!*
A! yif that covent foure and twenty grotes!	*Give us fourpence!*
A! yif that frere a peny, and lat hym go!	*Give the friar a penny, and let him go!*
Nay, nay, thomas, it may no thyng be so!	*No, no, Thomas, it can't be like this!*
What is a ferthyng worth parted in twelve?	*What is a farthing worth when it's divided between twelve?*
Lo, ech thyng that is oned in himselve	*Everything that stays together*
Is moore strong than whan it is toscatered.	*Is stronger than things which are scattered.*
Thomas, of me thou shalt nat been yflatered;	*Thomas, I will not flatter you;*
Thou woldest han oure labour al for noght.	*You want all our work for nothing.*
The hye god, that al this world hath wroght,	*Almighty God, who made the whole world,*
Seith that the werkman worthy is his hyre.	*Said that the labourer is worthy of his hire.*
Thomas, noght of youre tresor I desire	*Thomas, I don't want any of your treasure*
As for myself, but that al oure covent	*For myself, but because our whole monastery*
To preye for yow is ay so diligent,	*Has worked so hard to pray for you,*
And for to buylden cristes owene chirche.	*And we need it to build the church of Christ.*
Thomas, if ye wol lernen for to wirche,	*Thomas, if you want to find out about*
Of buyldynge up of chirches may ye fynde,	*The construction of churches you can see*
If it be good, in thomas lyf of inde.	*In the life of Thomas of India whether it's a good thing.*
Ye lye heere ful of anger and of ire,	*You lie here full of anger and temper,*
With which the devel set youre herte afyre,	*Which the devil has placed in your heart,*
And chiden heere the sely innocent,	*And you criticise the poor innocent,*
Youre wyf, that is so meke and pacient.	*Your wife, who is so meek and patient.*
And therfore, thomas, trowe me if thee leste,	*And so, Thomas, believe me if you will,*
Ne stryve nat with thy wyf, as for thy beste;	*Do not fight with your wife, for your own good;*
And ber this word awey now, by thy feith,	*And pay attention to these words;*
Touchynge swich thyng, lo, what the wise seith	*In this business, think of what the wise man said:*
-- Withinne thyn hous ne be thou no leon;	*"Inside your house do not be a lion;*
To thy subgitz do noon oppression,	*Do not oppress those under you,*
Ne make thyne aqueyntances nat to flee. --	*And do not make your friends forsake you."*
And, thomas, yet eft-soones I charge thee,	*And, Thomas, again I order you*
Be war from hire that in thy bosom slepeth;	*To be wary of that anger which sleeps in your heart;*
War fro the serpent that so slily crepeth	*Beware of the serpent that slyly creeps*
Under the gras, and styngeth subtilly.	*Through the grass and ambushes you with its sting.*
Be war, my sone, and herkne paciently,	*Beware, my son, and listen patiently;*
That twenty thousand men han lost hir lyves	*Twenty thousand men have lost their lives*
For stryvyng with hir lemmans and hir wyves.	*Fighting with their sweethearts and their wives.*
Now sith ye han so hooly and meke a wyf,	*Since you have such a holy humble wife,*
What nedeth yow, thomas, to maken stryf?	*Thomas, why do you need to argue?*
Ther nys, ywys, no serpent so cruel,	*There is no serpent who is so cruel, it's certain,*
Whan man tret on his tayl, ne half so fel,	*When a man treads on his tail, nor half as fierce,*
As womman is, whan she hath caught an ire;	*As a woman who has been made angry;*

Vengeance is thanne al that they desire.	Revenge is then all that they want.
Ire is a synne, oon of the grete of sevene,	Anger is a sin, one of the worst of the seven,
Abhomynable unto the God of hevene;	Which God in heaven despises;
And to hymself it is destruccion.	It destroys the person who feels it.
This every lewed viker or person	Every ignorant vicar or parson
Kan seye, how ire engendreth homycide.	Can see how anger causes murder.
Ire is, in sooth, executour of pryde.	Anger is truly the instrument of pride.
I koude of ire seye so muche sorwe,	I could say so many bad things about anger
My tale sholde laste til to-morwe.	That I would still be speaking tomorrow.
And therfore preye I god, bothe day and nyght,	And so I pray to God both day and night
An irous man, God sende hym litel myght!	That God does not give strength to an angry man!
It is greet harm and certes greet pitee	It is very harmful and certainly a shame
To sette an irous man in heigh degree.	To put an angry man in a high position.
Whilom ther was an irous potestat,	There was once an angry prince,
As seith senek, that, durynge his estaat,	So Seneca says, and during his reign
Upon a day out ryden knyghtes two,	Two knights rode out together,
And as fortune wolde that it were so,	And it so turned out that
That oon of hem cam hoom, that oother noght.	One of them came home, and the other didn't.
Anon the knyght bifore the juge is broght,	Straight away the knight was brought before a judge,
That seyde thus, -- thou hast thy felawe slayn,	Who said, "You have killed your companion,
For which I deme thee to the deeth, certayn. --	For which I condemn you to death."
And to another knyght comanded he,	And he ordered a another knight,
-- Go lede hym to the deeth, I charge thee, --	"Take him to be executed, I order you."
And happed, as they wente by the weye	And it so happened, as they went on their way
Toward the place ther he sholde deye,	Towards the place of execution,
The knyght cam which men wenden had be deed.	The other knight came, the one whom they thought was dead.
Thanne thoughte they it were the beste reed	They thought the best thing to do would be
To lede hem bothe to the juge agayn.	To take them both back to the judge.
They seiden,-lord, the knyght ne hath nat slayn	They said, "Lord, this knight did not kill
His felawe; heere he standeth hool alyve. --	His companion; here he is, alive in one piece."
-- Ye shul be deed, -- quod he, -- so moot I thryve!	"You shall die," he said, "I swear by my life!
That is to seyn, bothe oon, and two, and thre! --	That is to say, all three of you will die!"
And to the firste knyght right thus spak he,	And he spoke directly to the first knight,
-- I dampned thee; thou most algate be deed.	"I condemned you, and so you must die.
And thou also most nedes lese thyn heed,	And you also must lose your head,
For thou art cause why thy felawe deyth. --	For you are the reason your companion is going to die."
And to the thridde knyght right thus he seith,	And to the third knight he said,
-- Thou hast nat doon that I comanded thee. --	"You have not done what I ordered you to do."
And thus he dide doon sleen hem alle thre.	And so he condemned all three to death.
Irous cambises was eek dronkelewe,	Angry Cambises was also a drunkard,
And ay delited hym to been a shrewe.	And he revelled in foul behaviour.
And so bifel, a lord of his meynee,	It so happened that a Lord from his household
That loved vertuous moralitee,	Who loved virtue and morality
Seyde on a day bitwix hem two right thus	Said these words to him one day:
-- A lord is lost, if he be vicius;	"If a lord is vicious, he is lost;
And dronkenesse is eek a foul record	And to be a drunkard is also a horrible thing
Of any man, and namely in a lord.	In any man, and especially in a lord.
Ther is ful many an eye and many an ere	There are many eyes and many years

Awaityng on a lord, and he noot where.	Watching lords, they don't know all of them.
For goddes love, drynk moore attemprely!	For God's sake, show some temperance!
Wyn maketh man to lesen wrecchedly	Wine makes a man wretchedly lose control
His mynde and eek his lymes everichon. --	Of his limbs and also his mind."
-- The revers shaltou se, -- quod he, -- anon,	"You will see differently," he said, "at once,
And preve it by thyn owene experience,	And you will experience it yourself,
That wyn ne dooth to folk no swich offence.	That wine doesn't do anyone any harm.
Ther is no wyn bireveth me my myght	There is no wine that takes away my
Of hand ne foot, ne of myne eyen sight. --	Physical power, nor that makes me blind."
And for despit he drank ful muchel moore,	And to spite him he drank a lot more,
An hondred part, than he hadde don bifoore;	A hundred times more than he had done before;
And right anon this irous, cursed wrecche	And at once this angry cursed wretch
Leet this knyghtes sone bifore hym fecche,	Had his knight's son brought before him,
Comandynge hym he sholde bifore hym stonde.	Telling him to stand in front of him.
And sodeynly he took his bowe in honde,	He suddenly picked up his bow
And up the streng he pulled to his ere,	And drew the string back to his ear,
And with an arwe he slow the child right there.	And he killed the child right there with an arrow.
-- Now wheither have I a siker hand or noon? --	"Now tell me, do I have a steady hand or not?"
Quod he; -- is al my myght and mynde agon?	He said, "has all my power and my mind deserted me?
Hath wyn bireved me myn eyen sight? --	Has wine taken away my sight?"
What sholde I telle th' answere of the knyght?	Why should I mention what the knight said?
His sone was slayn, ther is namoore to seye.	His son was killed, there's nothing more to be said.
Beth war, therfore, with lordes how ye pleye.	So be careful how you behave around lords.
Syngeth placebo, and -- I shal, if I kan, --	Always sing songs of obedience,
But if it be unto a povre man.	Unless you're dealing with a poor man.
To a povre man men sholde his vices telle,	You should always tell a poor man when he is wrong,
But nat to a lord, thogh he sholde go to helle.	But not a lord, even though he will go to hell.
Lo irous cirus, thilke percien,	Think of angry Cyrus, that Persian,
How he destroyed the ryver of gysen,	Who destroyed the river of Gysen
For that an hors of his was dreynt therinne,	Because one of his horses drowned in it,
Whan that he wente babiloigne to wynne.	When he went to conquer Babylon.
He made that the ryver was so smal	He reduced the river so much
That wommen myghte wade it over al.	That a woman could wade over it everywhere.
Lo, what seyde he that so wel teche kan?	What did the great teachers say?
-- Ne be no felawe to an irous man,	"Do not be friends with an angry man,
Ne with no wood man walke by the weye,	And do not journey alongside him,
Lest thee repente; -- I wol no ferther seye.	In case you regret it;" that's all I will say.
Now, thomas, leeve brother, lef thyn ire;	"Now, Thomas, dear brother, leave aside your anger,
Thou shalt me fynde as just as is a squyre.	You will find that I am as true as a set square.
Hoold nat the develes knyf ay at thyn herte --	Don't keep the devil's knife inside your heart–
Thyn angre dooth thee al to soore smerte --	Your anger is what's causing your suffering–
But shewe to me al thy confessioun.	Confess everything to me."
nay, quod the sike man, by seint symoun!	"No," said the sick man, "by St Simon!
I have be shryven this day at my curat.	I have been to confession today with my curate.
I have hym toold hoolly al myn estat;	I told him everything about myself;

Nedeth namoore to speken of it, seith he,	There is no need to say any more," he said,
But if me list, of myn humylitee.	"Unless I want to, through my humility."
Yif me thanne of thy gold, to make oure cloystre,	"Then give me money for our church buildings,"
Quod he, for many a muscle and many an oystre,	He said, "for we have lived on oysters and mussels
Whan othere men han ben ful wel at eyse,	When other men have been stuffed with food
Hath been oure foode, our cloystre for to reyse.	To get the money to build our cloister.
And yet, God woot, unnethe the fundement	And yet, God knows, even the foundation
Parfourned is, ne of our pavement	Is hardly finished, and there is not
Nys nat a tyle yet withinne oure wones.	A single stone of the floor laid down.
By god! we owen fourty pound for stones.	By God, we owe forty pounds for stones.
Now help, thomas, for hym that harwed helle!	Now help us, Thomas, for the sake of he who harrowed hell!
For elles moste we oure bookes selle.	For otherwise we will have to sell our books.
And if yow lakke oure predicacioun,	If you don't have our preaching,
Thanne goth the world al to destruccioun.	The whole world will fall apart.
For whoso wolde us fro this world bireve,	Anyone who wants to remove us from this world,
So God me save, thomas, by youre leve,	So help me God, Thomas, I'm telling you,
He wolde bireve out of this world the sonne.	Would be taking the sun from the world.
For who kan teche and werchen as we konne?	Who can teach and work as we can?
And that is nat of litel tyme, quod he,	And it has been so not just recently," he said,
But syn elye was, or elise,	"But since the time of Elijah or Elisha,
Han freres been, that funde I of record,	There have been friars—I find that in the records—
In charitee, ythanked be oure lord!	Of charity, thanks be to God!
Now thomas, help, for seinte charitee!	Now, Thomas, help, for holy charity!"
And doun anon he sette hym on his knee.	And down he went on his knees.
This sike man wax wel ny wood for ire;	The sick man almost went mad with anger;
He wolde that the frere had been on-fire,	He would have liked to burn the friar
With his false dissymulacioun.	For his dishonest efforts.
Swich thyng as is in my possessioun,	"I have something in my possession,"
Quod he, that may I yeve yow, and noon oother.	He said, "that only I can give.
Ye sey me thus, how that I am youre brother?	Are you saying to me that I am your brother?"
Ye, certes, quod the frere, trusteth weel.	"Yes, certainly," said the fryer, "you can trust me.
I took oure dame oure lettre with oure seel.	I gave our lady a letter with our seal on it."
Now wel, quod he, and somwhat shal I yive	"Well now," he said, "I shall give something
Unto youre hooly covent whil I lyve;	To your holy monastery while I'm alive;
And in thyn hand thou shalt it have anon,	And I shall put it in your hand right now,
On this condicion, and oother noon,	On this condition, and no other,
That thou departe it so, my deere brother,	That you divide it up, my dear brother,
That every frere have also muche as oother.	So that every friar gets as much as the others.
This shaltou swere on thy professioun,	You must swear this on your profession,
Withouten fraude or cavillacioun.	Honestly and without argument."
I swere it, quod this frere, by my feith!	"I swear it," said the fryer, "on my faith!"
And therwithal his hand in his he leith,	And he took his hand in his, saying,
Lo, heer my feith; in me shal be no lak.	"Here I pledge my faith; I shall not fail you."
Now thanne, put in thyn hand doun by my bak,	"Now then, put your hand down my back,"
Seyde this man, and grope wel bihynde.	Said this man, "and have a good feel around.
Bynethe my buttok there shaltow fynde	Beneath my buttocks there you will find
A thyng that I have hyd in pryvetee.	Something I have secretly hidden."

A! thoghte this frere, that shal go with me!	"Aha!" the friar thought, "this will now be mine!"
And doun his hand he launcheth to the clifte,	And he shoved his hand down the crack
In hope for to fynde there a yifte.	Hoping to find a gift there.
And whan this sike man felte this frere	And when this sick man felt that the friar
Aboute his tuwel grope there and heere,	Was groping all around his arse
Amydde his hand he leet the frere a fart,	He farted straight into the friar's hand;
Ther nys no capul, drawynge in a cart,	There was no horse, drawing a cart,
That myghte have lete a fart of swich a soun.	Who could have let off such an impressive fart.
The frere up stirte as dooth a wood leoun, --	The friar jumped up like a mad lion–
A! false cherl, quod he, for goddes bones!	"Oh, you lying peasant," he said, "by God!
This hastow for despit doon for the nones.	You do this on purpose, spitefully.
Thou shalt abye this fart, if that I may!	I shall make you pay for your fart, if I can!"
His meynee, whiche that herden this affray,	His servants, who heard all the fuss,
Cam lepynge in and chaced out the frere;	Came running in and chased the friar away;
And forth he gooth, with a ful angry cheere,	And he went out, looking very angry,
And fette his felawe, ther as lay his stoor.	And fetched his companion, who was with his goods.
He looked as it were a wilde boor;	He looked like he were a wild boar;
He grynte with his teeth, so was he wrooth.	He ground his teeth, he was so angry.
A sturdy paas doun to the court he gooth,	He walked quickly down to the court,
Wher as ther woned a man of greet honour,	Where there was a very honourable man
To whom that he was alwey confessour.	Whose confessions he always heard.
This worthy man was lord of that village.	This good man was the lord of the village.
This frere cam as he were in a rage,	The friar came to him in a rage,
Where as this lord sat etyng at his bord;	As the lord sat eating at his table;
Unnethes myghte the frere speke a word,	The friar could hardly get a word out,
Til atte laste he seyde, God yow see!	Until at last he said, "God can see you!"
This lord gan looke, and seide, benedicitee!	The lord looked at him, and said, "Bless me!
What, frere john, what maner world is this?	What on earth is the matter, Friar John?
I se wel that som thyng ther is amys;	I can see that there is something wrong;
Ye looken as the wode were ful of thevys.	You look as if the woods were full of thieves.
Sit doun anon, and tel me what youre grief is,	Sit down at once, tell me what is wrong,
And it shal been amended, if I may.	And I will make it better, if I can."
I have, quod he, had a despit this day,	"I have," he said, "been so insulted this day,
God yelde yow, adoun in youre village,	By God, down in your village,
That in this world is noon so povre a page	That there is no servant so lowly in the world
That he nolde have abhomynacioun	That he would not have been revolted
Of that I have receyved in youre toun.	By what I have been given in your town.
And yet ne greveth me nothyng so soore,	And yet nothing gives me so much pain
As that this olde cherl with lokkes hoore	As to know that this old peasant with his white hair
Blasphemed hath oure hooly covent eke.	Has also insulted our holy monastery."
Now, maister, quod this lord, I yow biseke, --	"Now, Master," said this Lord, "I beg you–"
No maister, sire, quod he, but servitour,	"I am not your master, Sir," he said, "but your servant,
Thogh I have had in scole that honour.	Although I have been called that in school.
God liketh nat that -- raby -- men us calle,	God does not like men to call us 'rabbi',
Neither in market ne in youre large halle.	Not in the market, nor in your great halls."
No fors, quod he, but tel me al youre grief.	"Whatever," he said, "just tell me what is wrong."
Sire, quod this frere, and odious meschief	"Sir," said the friar, "a revolting trick

This day bityd is to myn ordre and me,	Has been played on both my order and me today,
And so, per consequens, to ech degree	And so, by implication, to every part
Of hooly chirche, God amende it soone!	Of the holy Church–may God punish it soon!"
Sire, quod the lord, ye woot what is to doone.	"Sir," said the lord, "you know what must be done.
Distempre yow noght, ye be my confessour;	Do not be angry; you are my confessor;
Ye been the salt of the erthe and the savour.	You are the salt of the earth and its pleasures.
For goddes love, youre pacience ye holde!	In the name of God, be patient!
Tel me youre grief; and anon hym tolde,	Tell me what's wrong." And at once he told him,
As ye han herd biforn, ye woot wel what.	What I have already told you, you know all about it.
The lady of the hous ay stille sat	The lady of the house sat perfectly still
Til she had herd what the frere sayde.	Until she heard what he had to say.
Ey, goddes mooder, quod she, blisful mayde!	"Why, by the mother of God," she said, "blessed maiden!
Is ther oght elles? telle me feithfully.	Is there anything else? Tell me truthfully."
Madame, quod he, how thynke ye herby?	"Madam," he said, "what do you think of this?"
How that me thynketh? quod she, so God me speede,	"What do I think?" She said. "So help me God,
I seye, a cherl hath doon a cherles dede.	I say a peasant has behaved like a peasant.
What shold I seye? God lat hym nevere thee!	What should I say? May God never help him!
His sike heed is ful of vanytee;	His sick head is full of stupidity;
I holde hym in a manere frenesye.	I think that he is rather mad."
Madame, quod he, by god, I shal nat lye	"Madam," he said, "by God, I will not lie,
But in on oother wyse may be wreke,	Unless I get revenge in some other way,
I shal disclaundre hym over al ther I speke,	I will slander him wherever I speak,
This false blasphemour, that charged me	This false blasphemer who ordered me
To parte that wol nat departed be,	To split up something which cannot be divided
To every man yliche, with meschaunce!	Equally to every man, bad luck to him!"
The lord sat stille as he were in a traunce,	The Lord sat as still as if he were in a trance,
And in his herte he rolled up and doun,	And he contemplated what had happened,
How hadde this cherl ymaginacioun	"How did this peasant have the imagination
To shewe swich a probleme to the frere?	To create this problem for the friar?
Nevere erst er now herde I of swich mateere.	Never before have I heard of such a business.
I trowe the devel putte it in his mynde.	I think the devil put in his mind.
In ars-metrike shal ther no man fynde,	In all of arithmetic nobody could find
Biforn this day, of swich a question.	Such a problem, before today.
Who sholde make a demonstracion	Who could show us how
That every man sholde have yliche his part	Every man would equally have his part
As of the soun or savour of a fart?	Of the sound or smell of a fart?
O nyce, proude cherl, I shrewe his face!	Clever, arrogant peasant, I curse him!
Lo, sires, quod the lord, with harde grace!	Now, sirs," said the lord, "bad luck to him!
Who evere herde of swich a thyng er now?	Who has ever heard of such a thing?
To every man ylike, tel me how?	Share it equally? Tell me how.
It is an inpossible, it may nat be.	It is impossible; it cannot be.
Ey, nyce cherl, God lete him nevere thee!	You clever peasant, may God abandon you!
The rumblynge of a fart, and every soun,	The rumbling of a fart, like all other sounds,
Nis but of eir reverberacioun,	Is nothing but the air vibrating,
And evere it wasteth litel and litel awey.	And then it fades away little by little.
Ther is no man kan deemen, by my fey,	Nobody can judge, I swear,

If that it were departed equally.
What, lo, my cherl, lo, yet how shrewdly
Unto my confessour to-day he spak!
I holde hym certeyn a demonyak!
Now ete youre mete, and lat the cherl go pleye;

Lat hym go honge hymself a devel weye!

Now stood the lordes squier at the bord,

That karf his mete, and herde word by word
Of alle thynges whiche I have yow sayd.
My lord, quod he, be ye nat yvele apayd,

I koude telle, for a gowne-clooth,

To yow, sire frere, so ye be nat wrooth,
How that this fart sholde evene deled be
Among youre covent, if it lyked me.
Tel, quod the lord, and thou shalt have anon
A gowne-clooth, by God and by seint john!

My lord, quod he, whan that the weder is fair,
Withouten wynd or perturbynge of air,
Lat brynge a cartwheel heere into this halle;
But looke that it have his spokes alle, --
Twelve spokes hath a cartwheel comunly.
And bryng me thanne twelve freres, woot ye why?

For thritteene is a covent, as I gesse.
Youre confessour heere, for his worthynesse,
Shal parfoune up the nombre of his covent,
Thanne shal they knele doun, by oon assent,
And to every spokes ende, in this manere,
Ful sadly leye his nose shal a frere.
Youre noble confessour -- there God hym save! --
Shal holde his nose upright under the nave.
Thanne shal this cherl, with bely stif and toght

As any tabour, hyder been ybroght;
And sette hym on the wheel right of this cart.
Upon the nave, and make hym lete a fart.
And ye shul seen, up peril of my lyf,
By preeve which that is demonstratif,
That equally the soun of it wol wende,
And eke the stynk, unto the spokes ende.
Save that this worthy man, youre confessour,
By cause he is a man of greet honour,
Shal have the firste fruyt, as resoun is.
The noble usage of freres yet is this,
The worthy men of hem shul first be served;
And certeinly he hath it well disserved.
He hath to-day taught us so muche good
With prechyng in the pulpit the he stood,

How to divide it equally.
Well then, my peasant, how cunningly
He has dealt with my confessor!
I think he must be possessed by a daemon!
Now eat your meat and forget about the peasant;
Let him go to hell!"

Now the lord's squire was standing by the table,
Carving the meat, and he heard every word
Of all the things I have told you.
"My Lord," he said, "if it would not annoy you,
I could tell you, in return for some material for a gown,
And you, sir friar, if you will not be angry,
How this fart could easily be divided
Amongst your monastery, if I wanted."
"Tell us," said the Lord, "and you shall have
The material at once, I swear by God and St John!"

"My Lord," he said, "when the weather is fair,
And there is no wind or breeze,
Bring a cartwheel into the hall;
Make sure it has all of its spokes—
A cartwheel usually has twelve.
And then bring me twelve friars. Do you know why?
For thirteen make up a monastery, I believe.
Your confessor here, for his goodness,
Will make up the complete complement.
Then they can all kneel down together,
And at the end of each spoke, like this,
Each friar will place his nose.
Your noble confessor—God save him!–
Shall plays his nose right under the middle.
Then this peasant, with his belly as stiff and taut
As a drum, shall be brought here;
And we'll put him on this cartwheel,
Right in the middle, and tell him to fart.
And you will see, I swear on my life,
It will be clearly proved
That the sound and also the smell
Will travel up the spokes equally,
Except that this good man, your confessor,
Because he is a man of great honour,
Will get the first taste, as is proper.
The noble custom of friars is this,
That the best man gets served first;
And he has certainly deserved it.
Today he taught us so many good things
When he was preaching in the pulpit

That I may vouche sauf, I sey for me,	That I can say on my part
He hadde the firste smel of fartes thre;	That he got the first whiff of three farts;
And so wolde al his covent hardily,	And I'm sure all his monastery would agree to this,
He bereth hym so faire and hoolily.	Because he keeps himself so holy and pure."
The lord, the lady, and ech man, save the frere,	The lord, the lady, and everyone except the friar,
Seyde that jankyn spak, in this matere,	Said that Jankyn was speaking, in this matter,
As wel as euclide dide or ptholomee.	As much sense as Euclid or Ptolemy.
Touchynge the cherl, they seyde, subtiltee	They said that the peasant had spoken as he did
And heigh wit made hym speken as he spak;	Through good sense and great intelligence;
He nys no fool, ne no demonyak.	He wasn't a fool, nor possessed by a daemon.
And jankyn hath ywonne a newe gowne. --	And Jankyn has a new gown:
My tale is doon; we been almost at towne.	My story is finished; we've almost reached town.

The Clerks Tale

The Prologue

Heere folweth the Prologe of the Clerkes Tale of Oxenford.

The prologue of the clerk's tale

Sire clerk of Oxenford, oure Hooste sayde,
Ye ryde as coy and stille as dooth a mayde,
Were newe spoused, sittynge at the bord.

"Sir Clerk of Oxford," said our host,
"You ride as quiet and still as a girl
Who has just been married, sitting at the dinner table;

This day ne herde I of youre tonge a word.
I trowe ye studie about som sophyme;

I haven't heard a word from you all day.
I suppose you're thinking about some philosophy;

But Salomon seith, `every thyng hath tyme.'
For Goddes sake, as beth of bettre cheere;
It is no tyme for to studien heere,
Telle us som myrie tale, by youre fey.
For what man that is entred in a pley,
He nedes moot unto the pley assente;
But precheth nat as freres doon in Lente,
To make us for oure olde synnes wepe,
Ne that thy tale make us nat to slepe.
Telle us som murie thyng of aventures;
Youre termes, youre colours, and youre figures,

But as Solomon says, "everything in its place."
For God's sake, cheer up!
This is no time for studying.
Tell us some jolly tale, by God!
When a man joins in with a game,
He must play by the rules.
But don't preach to us, like friars in Lent,
To make us weep for our ancient sins,
And don't let your story put us to sleep.
Tell us some jolly business of adventures,
Keep your technical terms, fancy language, rhetoric,

Keep hem in stoor, til so be that ye endite
Heigh style, as whan that men to kynges write.

In store until you are writing
In a high style, which men use to write to kings.

Speketh so pleyn at this tyme, we yow preye,
That we may understonde what ye seye.

We pray you, speak plainly at this time,
So we can understand what you're saying."

This worthy clerk benignely answerde,
Hooste, quod he, I am under youre yerde.
Ye han of us as now the governance;
And therfore wol I do yow obeisance
As fer as resoun axeth, hardily.
I wol yow telle a tale, which that I
Lerned at Padwe of a worthy clerk,
As preved by his wordes and his werk.

This good clerk graciously answered:
"Host," he said, "I bow to your authority;
You rule over all of us now,
And so I will obey you,
Gladly, as far as possible.
I will tell you a tale which I
Had from a fine student at Padua,
His reputation was established by his words and his work.

He is now deed, and nayled in his cheste;
I prey to God so yeve his soule reste.
Fraunceys Petrark, the lauriat poete,
Highte this clerk, whos rethorike sweete

He is now dead and in his coffin;
I pray God will have mercy on his soul.
Francis Petrarch, the poet Laureate,
Was the name of this student, whose sweet rhetoric

Enlumyned al Ytaille of poetrie,
As Lynyan dide of philosophie,
Or lawe, or oother art particuler.
But deeth, that wol nat suffre us dwellen heer
But as it were a twynklyng of an eye,
Hem bothe hath slayn, and alle shul we dye.

Lit up Italy with his poetry,
As Lynyan did with his philosophy,
Or law, or other specialised area;
But death, who will not let us stay here,
In just the twinkling of an eye
Has killed them both, and we shall die.

But forth to tellen of this worthy man,

But to tell you about this good man

That taughte me this tale as I bigan,	*Who told me this story, as I intended,*
I seye, that first with heigh stile he enditeth	*I will tell you that firstly he composes in a high style,*
Er he the body of his tale writeth,	*Before he writes his main story,*
A prohemye in the which discryveth he	*A prologue, in which he describes*
Pemond, and of Saluces the contree,	*Piedmont and the country of Saluces,*
And speketh of Apennyn, the hilles hye,	*And the Apennines, the great hills*
That been the boundes of Westlumbardye;	*That are the frontiers of West Lombardy,*
And of Mount Vesulus in special,	*And he particularly talks of Mount Vesulus,*
Where as the Poo out of a welle small	*Where the Po comes from a small well,*
Taketh his firste spryngyng and his sours,	*Its spring and its source,*
That estward ay encresseth in his cours	*Always growing as it goes eastwards*
To Emeleward, to Ferrare, and Venyse;	*Towards Emelia, Ferrara and Venice,*
The which a long thyng were to devyse.	*Which would take a long time to tell you.*
And trewely, as to my juggement,	*And to be honest, in my judgement,*
Me thynketh it a thyng impertinent,	*I think that is is irrelevant,*
Save that he wole convoyen his mateere;	*Except as an introduction for his story;*
But this his tale, which that ye may heere.	*But here is the story, which you shall hear."*

The Tale

Heere bigynneth the Tale of the Clerk of Oxenford.

Ther is, at the west syde of Ytaille,	*There is, on the west side of Italy,*
Doun at the roote of Vesulus the colde,	*Down at the foot of cold Vesulus,*
A lusty playne, habundant of vitaille,	*A fertile plain, bursting with crops,*
Where many a tour and toun thou mayst biholde	*Where you can see many towns and towers,*
That founded were in tyme of fadres olde,	*That were established in ancient times,*
And many another delitable sighte,	*And many other delightful sights,*
And Saluces this noble contree highte.	*And this noble country is called Saluces.*
A markys whilom lord was of that lond,	*Once a marquis was lord of that land,*
As were hise worthy eldres hym bifore,	*As his good ancestors were before him;*
And obeisant and redy to his hond	*And his subjects were obedient, always ready*
Were alle hise liges, bothe lasse and moore.	*To obey his commands, both the high and low.*
Thus in delit he lyveth, and hath doon yoore,	*So he lived in happiness, and had done for a long time,*
Biloved and drad thurgh favour of Fortune,	*Loved and feared, favoured by Fortune,*
Bothe of hise lordes and of his commune.	*Both by his noblemen, and his citizens.*
Therwith he was, to speke as of lynage,	*Furthermore he was, in terms of ancestry,*
The gentilleste yborn of Lumbardye;	*The noblest man in Lombardy,*
A fair persone, and strong, and yong of age,	*A handsome person, young and strong,*
And ful of honour and of curteisye,	*Full of honour and courtesy;*
Discreet ynogh his contree for to gye,	*He was very sensible in governing his country,*
Save that in somme thynges that he was to blame,	*Except for certain mistakes he made;*
And Walter was this yonge lordes name.	*And this young lord's name was Walter.*
I blame hym thus, that he considereth noght	*What he was to blame for is that he did not think*
In tyme comynge what hym myghte bityde,	*What might happen to him in times to come,*
But in his lust present was al his thoght,	*He only thought of his present pleasure,*
As for to hauke and hunte on every syde.	*Such as hawking and hunting everywhere.*
Wel ny alle othere cures leet he slyde;	*He let all other worries slip away,*
And eek he nolde,–and that was worst of alle–	*And also he would not–and this was the worst thing–*
Wedde no wyf, for noght that may bifalle.	*Take a wife, whatever happened.*
Oonly that point his peple bar so soore,	*This matter worried his people so much*
That flokmeele on a day they to hym wente,	*That they gathered together and went to him one day,*
And oon of hem, that wisest was of loore,	*And one of them, who was the wisest of them,*
Or elles that the lord best wolde assente,	*Or perhaps the one the lord would be most willing to listen to*
That he sholde telle hym what his peple mente,	*If he told him how his people were feeling,*
Or elles koude he shewe wel swich mateere,	*Or otherwise he was the one who knew how to put the case best;*
He to the markys seyde as ye shul heere:	*He spoke to the marquis like this:*
O noble Markys, youre humanitee	*"O noble marquis, your kindness*
Asseureth us, and yeveth us hardinesse,	*Gives us confidence and strength,*
As ofte as tyme is of necessitee	*To do what must be done,*
That we to yow mowe telle oure hevynesse.	*Which is to tell you of our sorrow.*

Accepteth, lord, now for youre gentillesse	*Accept, lord, through your nobility,*
That we with pitous herte unto yow pleyne,	*That we have a right to complain to you of our sorrows,*
And lat youre eres nat my voys desdeyne,	*And do not close your ears to my voice.*
Al have I noght to doone in this mateere	*Although I don't have any more to do with this*
Moore than another man hath in this place;	*Than any other man in this place,*
Yet for as muche as ye, my lord so deere,	*But inasmuch as you, my dear lord,*
Han alwey shewed me favour and grace,	*Have always shown me kindness and grace*
I dar the bettre aske of yow a space	*That gives me the confidence to ask you for an appointment*
Of audience to shewen oure requeste,	*When we can present our case to you,*
And ye, my lord, to doon right as yow leste.	*And you, my lord, can do what pleases you.*
For certes, lord, so wel us liketh yow	*For certainly lord, we like you so much,*
And al youre werk, and evere han doon that we	*And everything you do, and always have, that we*
Ne koude nat us-self devysen how	*Can't imagine how*
We myghte lyven in moore felicitee,	*We could be happier,*
Save o thyng, lord, if it youre wille be,	*Except for one thing, Lord, if you agree,*
That for to been a wedded man yow leste,	*And that is for you to be married,*
Thanne were youre peple in sovereyn hertes reste.	*Then your people would be completely happy.*
Boweth youre nekke under that blisful yok	*Bow your neck to that sweet burden*
Of soveraynetee, noght of servyse,	*As a master, not as a slave,*
Which that men clepeth spousaille or wedlock;	*Which men call marriage or wedlock;*
And thenketh, lord, among youre thoghtes wyse	*And think, Lord, amongst your wise thoughts,*
How that oure dayes passe in sondry wyse,	*How we pass our days in different ways,*
For thogh we slepe, or wake, or rome, or ryde,	*Whether we sleep, wake, roam about or ride,*
Ay fleeth the tyme, it nyl no man abyde.	*Time is always slipping away; it waits for no man.*
And thogh youre grene youthe floure as yit,	*And although you are still in the first flush of youth*
In crepeth age alwey, as stille as stoon,	*Age is always creeping up on you, silently,*
And deeth manaceth every age, and smyt	*And death threatens everyone, and falls*
In ech estaat, for ther escapeth noon;	*On every rank, nobody escapes;*
And al so certein as we knowe echoon	*And although every one of us is certain*
That we shul deye, as uncerteyn we alle	*That we will die one day, we do not know*
Been of that day, whan deeth shal on us falle.	*The day when death will come to us.*
Accepteth thanne of us the trewe entente	*So accept our loyal intentions,*
That nevere yet refuseden thyn heeste;	*We who have never yet disobeyed you,*
And we wol, lord, if that ye wole assente,	*And we will, lord, if you will agree,*
Chese yow a wyf in short tyme atte leeste,	*Choose a wife for you, as quickly as possible,*
Born of the gentilleste and of the meeste	*A noblewoman of the highest rank*
Of al this land, so that it oghte seme	*In this whole land, so that it will be*
Honour to God, and yow, as we kan deeme.	*An honour to God and to you, as far as we can make it.*
Delivere us out of al this bisy drede,	*Save us from this constant fear,*
And taak a wyf for hye Goddes sake,	*And take a wife, for the sake of Almighty God!*
For if it so bifelle, as God forbede,	*For if it came about, God forbid,*
That thurgh your deeth your lyne sholde slake,	*That through your death your family would die out,*

And that a straunge successour sholde take Youre heritage, o wo were us alyve!	And a foreigner would take Command, what sorrow it would be to we who were left!
Wherfore we pray you hastily to wyve.	So we ask you to quickly choose a wife."
Hir meeke preyere and hir pitous cheere Made the markys herte han pitee. Ye wol, quod he, myn owene peple deere, To that I nevere erst thoughte, streyne me.	Their humble prayer and fair pitiful demeanour Filled the heart of the marquis with pity. "You want," he said, "my own dear people, Something which I never thought I would have to force myself to.
I me rejoysed of my liberte, That seelde tyme is founde in mariage. Ther I was free, I moot been in servage.	I have enjoyed my freedom, And that is seldom found in marriage; Where once I was free, now I must be a slave.
But nathelees I se youre trewe entente, And truste upon youre wit, and have doon at;	But still I can see your honest motivation, And I trust your intelligence, as I always have done;
Wherfore of my free wyl I wole assente To wedde me, as soone as evere I may. But ther as ye han profred me this day To chese me a wyf, I yow relesse That choys, and prey yow of that profre cesse.	So I freely agree To be married, as soon as possible. But as for the offer that you have made me today Of choosing me a wife, I don't want you To make that choice, and I ask you not to offer again.
For God it woot, that children ofte been Unlyk hir worthy eldres hem bifore. Bountee comth al of God, nat of the streen,	For God knows, children are often Different to their worthy ancestors; All good things come from God, not from one's descent
Of which they been engendred and ybore. I truste in Goddes bontee; and therfore My mariage, and myn estaat and reste,	Through which they were conceived and born. I trust that God is good, and therefore I will leave the business of my marriage, my property
I hym bitake, he may doon as hym leste.	And my peace of mind to him; he can do as he pleases.
Lat me allone in chesynge of my wyf, That charge upon my bak I wole endure; But I yow preye, and charge upon youre lyf That what wyf that I take, ye me assure To worshipe hir, whil that hir lyf may dure, In word and werk, bothe heere and everywheere, As she an emperoures doghter weere.	Let me choose my wife myself— I will take that responsibility on my own back. But I ask you, and order you on your life, Whatever wife I choose, you promise me To respect her, whilst she is alive, In word and deed, here and elsewhere, As if she were an emperor's daughter.
And forthermoore, this shal ye swere, that ye Agayn my choys shul neither grucche ne stryve,	And furthermore you must swear this: that you Will not argue with the fight against my choice;
For sith I shal forgoon my libertee At youre requeste, as evere moot I thryve, Ther as myn herte is set, ther wol I wyve! And but ye wole assente in this manere, I prey yow, speketh namoore of this matere.	For since I must give up my freedom At your request, then I swear That I will take the wife my heart chooses; And unless you will agree to this Then I ask you to never speak of this matter again."

With hertely wyl they sworen and assenten	They heartily agreed and swore
To al this thyng, ther seyde no wight nay,	To all these things—no person disagreed—
Bisekynge hym of grace er that they wenten,	Begging him, before they went, to kindly
That he wolde graunten hem a certein day	Fix a particular day
Of his spousaille, as soone as evere he may,	For his wedding, as soon as he possibly could;
For yet alwey the peple somwhat dredde	For still the people were rather apprehensive
Lest that this markys no wyf wolde wedde.	That the marquis would not take a wife.
He graunted hem a day, swich as hym leste,	He appointed a day of his own choosing,
On which he wolde be wedded sikerly,	On which he would definitely be married,
And seyde he dide al this at hir requeste;	And he said he was doing all this at their request.
And they with humble entente, buxomly,	And they, with humble respect, obediently,
Knelynge upon hir knees ful reverently	Knelt down on their knees dutifully
Hym thonken alle, and thus they han an ende	And they all thanked him; and so things transpired
Of hir entente, and hoom agayn they wende.	According to their wishes, and they went back home.
And heerupon he to hise officers	And so he called his officers
Comaundeth for the feste to purveye,	To give them commands for the feast,
And to hise privee knyghtes and squieres	And to his household knights and squires
Swich charge yaf, as hym liste on hem leye.	He gave them whatever orders he wanted;
And they to his comandement obeye,	And they did as they were told,
And ech of hem dooth al his diligence	And each of them did his best
To doon unto the feeste reverence:	To show respect for the feast.
Explicit prima pars.	The end of the first part
Incipit secunda pars.	The beginning of the second part
Noght fer fro thilke paleys honorable	Not far from that noble palace
Ther as this markys shoop his mariage,	Where the marquis was planning his marriage,
Ther stood a throop, of site delitable,	There was a small village, in a beautiful place,
In which that povre folk of that village	Where the poor folk of that village
Hadden hir beestes and hir herbergage,	Had their animals and their houses,
And of hir lobour tooke hir sustenance,	And got what they had through labour,
After that the erthe yaf hem habundance.	Depending on what the earth provided.
Amonges thise povre folk ther dwelte a man	Amongst these poor folk there was a man living
Which that was holden povrest of hem alle;	Who was thought to be the poorest of all of them;
(But hye God somtyme senden kan	But Almighty God can sometimes send
His grace into a litel oxes stalle)	His grace into the stable of an ox;
Janicula men of that throop hym calle.	Men of the village called him Janicula.
A doghter hadde he, fair ynogh to sighte,	He had a daughter, who was good looking,
And Grisildis this yonge mayden highte.	And her name was Griselda.
But for to speke of vertuous beautee,	If we're talking about virtuous beauty,
Thanne was she oon the faireste under sonne,	Then she was the loveliest woman on earth;
For povreliche yfostred up was she,	Because she had grown up with poverty
No likerous lust was thurgh hir herte yronne.	No foul lusts ran through her heart.
Wel ofter of the welle than of the tonne	She drank water far more often than wine,
She drank, and for she wolde vertu plese	And because she wished to live a good life

She knew wel labour but noon ydel ese.	She was very familiar with work, but not with laziness.
But thogh this mayde tendre were of age, Yet in the brest of hire virginitee Ther was enclosed rype and sad corage; And in greet reverence and charitee Hir olde povre fader fostred shee. A fewe sheepe, spynnynge on feeld she kepte,	But although she was only a young girl, Inside the case of her maidenhood Was kept a mature and strong courage; And with great respect and kindness She cared for her poor old father. She watched a few sheep in the fields, while she was spinning,
-She wolde noght been ydel, til she slepte.	And she never rested except when she slept.
And whan she homward cam, she wolde brynge Wortes, or othere herbes tymes ofte, The whiche she shredde and seeth for hir lyvynge,	When she came home she would bring Cabbages or other green vegetables often, Which she shredded and boiled for their goodness,
And made hir bed ful harde and no thyng softe; And ay she kepte hir fadres lyf on lofte With everich obeisaunce and diligence That child may doon to fadres reverence.	And she slept on a hard bed, with nothing soft, And she kept her father alive With all the obedience and care That a child can offer to respect its father.
Upon Grisilde, this povre creature, Ful ofte sithe this markys caste his eye, As he on huntyng rood paraventure. And whan it fil that he myghte hire espye, He noght with wantowne lookyng of folye Hise eyen caste on hir, but in sad wyse, Upon hir chiere he wolde hym ofte avyse, Commendynge in his herte hir wommanhede And eek hir vertu, passynge any wight Of so yong age, as wel in chiere as dede.	On this poor creature Griselda This marquis very often looked If he happened to ride past as he was hunting; And if he happened to see her He didn't look at her with lustful Stupidity, but in a serious fashion, He would often think about her carriage, Praising her womanly qualities in his heart, And also her virtue, greater than any other Of such a young age, both in her manner and her deeds.
For thogh the peple hadde no greet insight In vertu, he considered ful right Hir bountee, and disposed that he wolde	Although the people had no great vision Of virtue, he thought very carefully About her goodness, and decided that he would
Wedde hir oonly, if evere he wedde sholde.	Only marry her, if he had to marry.
The day of weddyng cam, but no wight kan	The day of the wedding came, but nobody could
Telle what womman that it sholde be, For which merveille wondred many a man, And seyden, whan that they were in privetee, Wol nat oure lord yet leve his vanytee? Wol he nat wedde? allas, allas, the while!	Tell whom the bride was going to be; Many men tried to guess, And said, when they were alone, "Why won't our lord stop being so vain? Why won't he marry? Alas! Alas what times these are!
Why wole he thus hymself and us bigile?	Why will he deceive both us and himself like this?"
But nathelees this markys hath doon make Of gemmes set in gold and in asure Brooches and rynges, for Grisildis sake, And of hir clothyng took he the mesure,	However this marquis had ordered made, With jewels, set in gold and azure, Brooches and rings, all for Griselda; And he had her clothes measured up

By a mayde lyk to hir stature,	On a girl of the same size,
And eek of othere ornementes alle	And he also ordered all the other embellishments
That unto swich a weddyng sholde falle.	Appropriate for such a wedding.
The time of undren of the same day	Mid-morning on the day of this wedding
Approcheth, that this weddyng sholde be;	Was approaching,
And al the paleys put was in array,	And the palace was all prepared,
Bothe halle and chambres, ech in his degree;	Both the hall and the rooms, as they should be;
Houses of office stuffed with plentee	The storerooms were bursting with provisions,
Ther maystow seen, of deyntevous vitaille,	There you would have seen the most delicious foods
That may be founde as fer as last Ytaille.	That could be found from anywhere in Italy.
This roial markys, richely arrayed,	This royal marquis, richly dressed,
Lordes and ladyes in his compaignye,	With the lords and ladies in his company,
The whiche that to the feeste weren yprayed,	Who were invited to the feast,
And of his retenue the bachelrye,	And his company of knights,
With many a soun of sondry melodye	With much music
Unto the village, of the which I tolde,	Headed straight for
In this array the righte wey han holde.	The village I have mentioned, in a splendid procession.
Grisilde (of this, God woot, ful innocent,	God knows, Griselda knew nothing of this,
That for hir shapen was al this array)	She didn't know all this display was for her,
To fecchen water at a welle is went,	She had gone to fetch water from a well,
And cometh hoom as soone as ever she may;	And came home as quickly as she could;
For wel she hadde herd seyd, that thilke day	For she had heard tell that on that day
The markys sholde wedde, and if she myghte,	The marquis would be married, and if she could
She wolde fayn han seyn som of that sighte.	She wanted to go and watch the celebrations.
She thoghte, I wole with othere maydens stonde,	She thought, "I shall stand with the other girls,
That been my felawes, in oure dore, and se	Who are my companions, at our door, and see
The markysesse, and therfore wol I fonde	The Marchioness, and so I will try
To doon at hoom as soone as it may be	To do my housework
The labour, which that longeth unto me,	As quickly as I possibly can,
And thanne I may at leyser hir biholde,	And then I will have the time to go and look at her,
If she this wey unto the castel holde.	If she comes past here on her way to the castle."
And as she wolde over hir thresshfold gon	And as she was going to leave
The markys cam and gan hire for to calle,	The marquis came and called for her;
And she set doun hir water pot anon	And she put down her water pot quickly,
Biside the thresshfold in an oxes stalle,	On the doorstep, next to an ox's stall,
And doun up-on hir knes she gan to falle,	And she began to go down on her knees,
And with sad contenance kneleth stille,	And she knelt there solemnly without speaking
Til she had herd what was the lordes will.	Until she heard what her lord wanted.
This thoghtful markys spak unto this mayde	The thoughtful marquis spoke to this girl
Ful sobrely, and seyde in this manere,	Very solemnly, and said to her:
Where is youre fader, O Grisildis? he sayde,	"Where is your father, oh Griselda?"

And she with reverence in humble cheere Answerde, Lord, he is al redy heere. And in she gooth, withouten lenger lette, And to the markys she hir fader fette.	And she respectfully, in a humble fashion, Answered, "Lord, he is just here." And she went inside with no further delay, And brought her father back to the marquis.
He by the hand thanne took this olde man, And seyde thus, whan he hym hadde asyde, Janicula, I neither may ne kan Lenger the plesance of myn herte hyde; If that thou vouchsauf, what so bityde, Thy doghter wol I take, er that I wende, As for my wyf unto hir lyves ende.	Then he took the old man by the hand, And said to him, when he had him on one side: "Janicula, I can no longer Hide my heart's desire. If you agree, whatever happens, Before I go away I will take your daughter As my bride, for the rest of her life.
Thou lovest me, I woot it wel certeyn, And art my feithful lige man ybore, And all that liketh me, I dar wel seyn, It liketh thee; and specially therfore Tel me that poynt that I have seyd bifore, If that thou wolt unto that purpos drawe, To take me as for thy sone-in-lawe.	I know very well that you love me, And were born my faithful servant, And I dare say that everything that pleases me Will please you, and so I ask you particularly To answer the question I have put to you, Tell me if you will agree to my proposal And have me as your son-in-law."
This sodeyn cas this man astonyed so, That reed he wax abayst and al quakyng He stood, unnethes seyde he wordes mo, But oonly thus, Lord, quod he, my willynge Is as ye wole, ne ayeyns youre likynge I wol no thyng, ye be my lord so deere; Right as yow lust governeth this mateere.	This sudden event astonished this man so That he blushed red; he stood embarrassed And shaking; he could hardly say anything, Only: "Lord," he said, "I agree To what you wish, I will do nothing Against your desire, you are my beloved lord; Whatever you want, that's what you should do."
Yet wol I, quod this markys softely, That in thy chambre I and thou and she Have a collacioun, and wostow why? For I wol axe, if it hir wille be To be my wyf, and reule hir after me; And al this shal be doon in thy presence, I wol noght speke out of thyn audience.	"But I want," the marquis said softly, "For you and her and me to have a discussion In your room, and do you know why? For I must ask if she wants To be my wife and follow me. And all this will be done in your presence; I won't say anything when you're not there."
And in the chambre whil they were aboute Hir tretys which as ye shal after heere,	And while they were in the room, discussing Their agreement, which you will hear about later,
The peple cam unto the hous withoute, And wondred hem in how honeste manere And tentifly she kepte hir fader deere.	The people gathered outside the house, And were amazed by how virtuously And attentively she looked after her dear father.
But outrely Grisildis wondre myghte For nevere erst ne saugh she swich a sighte.	Griselda would certainly have been amazed, For she had never seen anything like it.
No wonder is thogh that she were astoned To seen so greet a grest come in that place; She nevere was to swiche gestes woned, For which she looked with ful pale face- But shortly forth this tale for to chace, Thise arn the wordes that the markys sayde To this benigne verray feithful mayde.	It's no surprise that she was astonished To see such a great guest come into that place; She was not accustomed to such company, And she looked very pale in the face. But to cut a long story short, These are the words that the marquis said To this sweet, true and loyal girl:

Grisilde, he seyde, ye shal wel understonde It liketh to youre fader and to me That I yow wedde, and eek it may so stonde, As, I suppose, ye wol that it so be. But thise demandes axe I first, quod he,	"Griselda," he said, "you must understand That your father and I would both be pleased If you would marry me, and this will happen If it is what you want. But I must ask you these questions first," he said,
That sith it shal be doon in hastif wyse, Wol ye assente, or elles yow avyse?	"Since everything is being done in a rush, Will you agree, or do you want to think it over?
I seye this, be ye redy with good herte To al my lust, and that I frely may, As me best thynketh, do yow laughe or smerte,	I say this: are you ready to gladly agree To all my desires, and allow me freely, As seems best to me, to make you laugh or give you pain,
And nevere ye to grucche it nyght ne day,	And for you never to complain about it, night or day?
And eek whan I sey ye, ne sey nat nay, Neither by word, ne frownyng contenance? Swere this, and heere I swere yow alliance.	And also never to disagree with me, Neither with words nor by frowning? Swear to this, and we will be joined together."
Wondrynge upon this word, quakynge for drede, She seyde, Lord, undigne and unworthy	Amazed by these words, trembling with fear, She said, "My lord, I am too lowly and unworthy
Am I to thilke honour, that ye me beede, But as ye wole yourself, right so wol I.	Of the honour which you offer me, But whatever you wish for yourself, that is what I wish.
And heere I swere, that nevere willyngly In werk ne thoght I nyl yow disobeye, For to be deed, though me were looth to deye.	And I swear that I will never deliberately, In my deeds nor my thoughts, disobey you, Even if it would kill me, though I don't want to die."
This is ynogh, Grisilde myn, quod he, And forth he gooth with a ful sobre cheere Out at the dore, and after that cam she; And to the peple he seyde in this manere, This is my wyf, quod he, that standeth heere; Honoureth hir, and loveth hir, I preye, Whoso me loveth; ther is namoore to seye.	"That's good enough, my Griselda," he said. He went very solemnly Out of the door, and she followed him, And he said these words to his people: "This is my wife," he said, "standing here. Respect and love her, I ask you, If you love me; that's all I have to say."
And for that nothyng of hir olde geere	And so that she would bring none of her old possessions
She sholde brynge into his hous, he bad That wommen sholde dispoillen hir right theere;-	Into his house, he ordered That his women should undress her on the spot;
Of which thise ladyes were nat right glad To handle hir clothes, wherinne she was clad-	These ladies were quite unhappy About handling the clothes which she was wearing.
But nathelees, this mayde bright of hewe Fro foot to heed they clothed han al newe.	But nevertheless, this shining maid Was dressed head to foot in new clothes.
Hir heris han they kembd, that lay untressed Ful rudely, and with hir fyngres smale A corone on hir heed they han ydressed, And sette hir ful of nowches grete and smale.	They combed her hair, that was not dressed, Very thoroughly, and with their little fingers They placed a crown upon her head, And covered her with jewellery of every sort.

Of hir array what sholde I make a tale?	Why should I make a long story out of her appearance?
Unnethe the peple hire knew for hir fairnesse	The people could hardly recognise her, she was so beautiful,
Whan she translated was in swich richesse.	When she had been transformed with such riches.
This markys hath hir spoused with a ryng	The Marquis had engaged her with a ring
Broght for the same cause, and thanne hir sette	Which he had brought for that purpose, and then he sat her
Upon an hors, snow-whit and wel amblyng,	On a horse, snow white with an excellent gait,
And to his paleys, er he lenger lette,	And he took her to his palace, without delay,
With joyful peple that hir ladde and mette	With the people, joyful, leading and greeting her,
Convoyed hir; and thus the day they spende	And so they spent the day
In revel, til the sonne gan descende.	Celebrating, until sunset.
And shortly forth this tale for to chace,	To cut a long story short
I seye, that to this newe markysesse	I tell you that this new marchioness
God hath swich favour sent hir of his grace,	Was so favoured by God
That it ne semed nat by liklynesse	That looking at her it didn't seem possible
That she was born and fed in rudenesse	That she had been born and raised in poverty,
As in a cote or in an oxe-stalle,	In a hut or stable,
But norissed in an emperoures halle.	She looked as though she had been brought up in a palace.
To every wight she woxen is so deere	She became so dear to every person
And worshipful, that folk ther she was bore	And so respected that her townspeople,
And from hir birthe knewe hir yeer by yeere,	Who had known her as she grew up
Unnethe trowed they, but dorste han swore	Could hardly believe, though they could swear,
That she to Janicle, of which I spak bifore,	That she was the daughter of Janiclus,
She doghter nere, for as by conjecture,	Of whom I spoke before, because one could imagine
Hem thoughte she was another creature.	That she was a completely different person.
For though that evere vertuous was she,	Although she remained completely virtuous,
She was encressed in swich excellence,	She had been wonderfully embellished
Of thewes goode, yset in heigh bountee,	With fine characteristics, great goodness,
And so discreet and fair of eloquence,	And was so kind and elegant in speaking,
So benigne, and so digne of reverence,	So generous and worthy of respect,
And koude so the peples herte embrace,	And the people took her so much to their hearts
That ech hir lovede, that looked on hir face.	That everyone who looked at her loved her.
Noght oonly of Saluces in the toun	Not only was the town of Saluces
Publiced was the bountee of hir name,	Ringing with the praise of her name,
But eek biside in many a regioun,	But in many other regions,
If oon seide wel, another seyde the same;	If someone thought well of her, then so did another;
So spradde of hir heighe bountee the fame	So the reputation of her great goodness spread
That men and wommen, as wel yonge as olde,	And men and women, young and old,
Goon to Saluce upon hir to biholde.	All went to Saluce to look at her.

Thus Walter lowely, nay! but royally	*So Walter married lowly, but royally,*
Wedded with fortunat honestetee,	*To a fine woman,*
In Goddes pees lyveth ful esily	*Lived happily in the peace of God,*
At hoom, and outward grace ynogh had he,	*At home, and he seemed to be very happy;*
And for he saugh that under low degree	*And because he could see that lowly people*
Was ofte vertu hid, the peple hym heeled	*Were often the most virtuous, the people considered him*
A prudent man, and that is seyn ful seelde.	*A wise man, and one doesn't see many of those.*
Nat oonly this Grisildis thurgh hir wit	*Not only did this Griselda, through her intelligence,*
Koude al the feet of wyfly humblenesse,	*Know all the skills of a fine housewife,*
But eek, whan that the cas required it,	*She could also, when it was needed,*
The commune profit koude she redresse.	*Act on behalf of all the people.*
Ther nas discord, rancour, ne hevynesse	*There was no disagreement, argument nor sadness*
In al that land, that she ne koude apese,	*In that whole land which she could not solve,*
And wisely brynge hem alle in reste and ese.	*And bring peace and happiness to everyone.*
Though that hir housbonde absent were anon	*Even if her husband was absent at the time,*
If gentil men, or othere of hir contree	*If noblemen other people in her country*
Were wrothe, she wolde bryngen hem aton.	*Were angry, she would bring them to agreement;*
So wise and rype wordes hadde she,	*She spoke so wisely and so well,*
And juggementz of so greet equitee,	*Handing down such fair judgements,*
That she from hevene sent was, as men wende,	*That men thought she was sent from heaven*
Peple to save and every wrong tamende.	*To save the people and to put every wrong right.*
Nat longe tyme after that this Grisild	*It wasn't long after this Griselda*
Was wedded, she a doghter hath ybore-	*Was married that she had a daughter,*
Al had hir levere have born a man child;	*Although she would rather have had a boy;*
Glad was this markys and the folk therfore,	*The marquis and the people were happy,*
For though a mayde child coome al bifore,	*For although a girl may come first,*
She may unto a knave child atteyne	*She could easily have a boy later,*
By liklihede, syn she nys nat bareyne.	*She had proved she was not barren.*
Explicit secundus pars.	*The end of the second part.*
Incipit tercia pars.	*The beginning of the third part*
Ther fil, as it bifalleth tymes mo,	*Then it came to pass, as it often does,*
Whan that this child had souked but a throwe,	*That shortly after this child was born,*
This markys in his herte longeth so	*The marquis in his heart longed to*
To tempte his wyf, hir sadnesse for to knowe,	*Test the faithfulness of his wife,*
That he ne myghte out of his herte throwe	*And he couldn't get rid of this strange*
This merveillous desir his wyf tassaye.	*Desire in his heart to tempt her;*
Nedelees, God woot, he thoghte hir for taffraye.	*He meant to do it, though God knows there was no need.*
He hadde assayed hir ynogh bifore,	*He had tested her often enough before,*
And foond hir evere good; what neded it	*And always found her to be good; why did he need*
Hir for to tempte and alwey moore and moore?	*To test her, always more and more,*

Though som men preise it for a subtil wit,	Even if some men think it's clever?
But as for me, I seye that yvele it sit	As for me, I say that nobody
To assaye a wyf, whan that it is no nede,	Should test his wife when there is no need,
And putten hir in angwyssh and in drede.	And cause her pain and anguish.
For which this markys wroghte in this manere;	This marquis carried out his plan in this way;
He cam allone a nyght, ther as she lay,	He came alone at night time to where she lay,
With stierne face and with ful trouble cheere,	With a stern face, and looking very troubled,
And seyde thus, Grisilde, quod he, that day	And said, "Griselda, the day
That I yow took out of your povere array,	That I took you from your poverty,
And putte yow in estaat of heigh noblesse,	And raised you to this position of nobility—
Ye have nat that forgeten, as I gesse.	You have not forgotten about that, I should imagine?
I seye, Grisilde, this present dignitee	I say, Griselda, your current high position,
In which that I have put yow, as I trowe	In which I put you, I think
Maketh yow nat foryetful for to be	Requires that you do not forget
That I yow took in povre estaat ful lowe	That I took you from your terrible poverty,
For any wele ye moot youreselven knowe.	You must recognise this yourself.
Taak heede of every word that y yow seye,	Pay attention to everything I say to you;
Ther is no wight that hereth it but we tweye.	There is nobody who can hear it but us.
Ye woot yourself wel how that ye cam heere	You are well aware how you came
Into this hous, it is nat longe ago.	Into this house, it wasn't long ago;
And though to me that ye be lief and deere,	And though you are beloved and dear to me,
Unto my gentils ye be no thyng so.	My noblemen do not feel the same.
They seyn, to hem it is greet shame and wo	They say it is a great shame and sorrow
For to be subgetz, and to been in servage,	For them to be subjects and servants of
To thee that born art of a smal village.	You, who was born in a small village.
And namely, sith thy doghter was ybore,	And especially since your daughter was born
Thise wordes han they spoken, doutelees;	They have said these things, it's true.
But I desire, as I have doon bifore,	But I want to live my life with them
To lyve my lyf with hem in reste and pees.	Peacefully, as I did before.
I may nat in this caas be recchelees,	I can't take any risks in this matter;
I moot doon with thy doghter for the beste,	I must do what is best with your daughter,
Nat as I wolde, but as my peple leste.	Not as I would like to, but as my people wish.
And yet God woot, this is ful looth to me!	And yet, God knows, this is horrible for me;
But nathelees, withoute youre wityng	But nonetheless, without your knowing of it,
I wol nat doon, but this wol I, quod he,	I will not do anything; but this is what I want," he said,
That ye to me assente as in this thyng.	"That you agree to what I decide.
Shewe now youre pacience in youre werkyng,	Show your faithfulness by your actions,
That ye me highte and swore in youre village,	That which you promised me and swore in your village
That day that maked was oure mariage.	The day we agreed to marry."
Whan she had herd al this, she noght ameved	When she had heard all this, she did not change
Neither in word, or chiere, or countenaunce;	In words, actions or expression,
For as it semed she was nat agreved.	For it seems that she was not offended.
She seyde, Lord, al lyth in youre plesaunce,	She said, "Lord, everything awaits your pleasure.
My child, and I, with hertely obeisaunce	My child and I, with heartfelt obedience,

Been youres al, and ye mowe save and spille	*Belong to you, and you can save or kill*
Your owene thyng, werketh after youre wille.	*Your own things; do as you wish.*
Ther may no thyng, God so my soule save,	*There can be nothing, may God save me,*
Liken to yow, that may displese me,	*That pleases you which will displease me;*
Ne I ne desire no thyng for to have,	*There is nothing which I desire*
Ne drede for to leese save oonly yee;	*Or dread to lose, except you.*
This wyl is in myn herte, and ay shal be;	*This is my fixed position, and always will be;*
No lengthe of tyme or deeth may this deface,	*No passing of time or death can change this,*
Ne chaunge my corage to another place.	*Or make my heart feel differently."*
Glad was this markys of hir answeryng,	*The marquis was pleased with her answer,*
But yet he feyned as he were nat so.	*But he pretended that he was not;*
Al drery was his cheere and his lookyng,	*He looked as if he was upset,*
Whan that he sholde out of the chambre go.	*When he left the room.*
Soone after this, a furlong wey or two,	*Soon after this, a few minutes later,*
He pryvely hath toold al his entente	*He secretly told his plan*
Unto a man, and to his wyf hym sente.	*To a man, and he sent him to his wife.*
A maner sergeant was this privee man,	*This confidant was a sort of sergeant,*
The which that feithful ofte he founden hadde	*Whom he had often found loyal*
In thynges grete, and eek swich folk wel kan	*In important matters, one of those people*
Doon execucioun on thynges badde.	*Who would follow orders, no matter how bad.*
The lord knew wel that he hym loved and dradde;–	*The lord knew that he loved and feared him;*
And whan this sergeant wiste the lordes wille,	*And when this sergeant knew what his lord wanted,*
Into the chambre he stalked hym ful stille.	*He crept quietly into the chamber.*
Madame, he seyde, ye moote foryeve it me	*"Madam," he said, "you must forgive me*
Though I do thyng to which I am constreyned,	*For doing what I am bound to do.*
Ye been so wys, that ful wel knowe ye	*You are so wise that you know full well*
That lordes heestes mowe nat been yfeyned,	*That I cannot fake obedience to my lord;*
They mowe wel been biwailled and compleyned,	*I might disagree or hate his orders,*
But men moote nede unto hir lust obeye;	*But men must do as he says,*
And so wol I, ther is namoore to seye.	*And I will; that's all I can say.*
This child I am comanded for to take.	*I have been ordered to take this child,"*
And spak namoore, but out the child he hente	*And he said no more, but grabbed the baby*
Despitously, and gan a cheere makeq	*Without pity, and he looked as though*
As though he wolde han slayn it er he wente.	*He was going to kill it before he left.*
Grisildis moot al suffren and consente,	*Griselda had to suffer and agree to everything,*
And as a lamb she sitteth meke and stille,	*And she sat as quiet and still as a lamb*
And leet this crueel sergeant doon his wille.	*While the cruel sergeant did as he wished.*
Suspecious was the diffame of this man,	*This man had a bad reputation,*
Suspect his face, suspect his word also,	*His face was suspect, and so was his word;*
Suspect the tyme in which he this bigan.	*So was the time he began all this.*
Allas, hir doghter that she loved so!	*Alas! She loved her daughter so,*
She wende he wolde han slawen it right tho;	*And she thought he was going to kill it on the spot.*
But nathelees she neither weep ne syked,	*But nevertheless, she neither wept nor sighed,*
Consentynge hir to that the markys lyked.	*Following the orders of the marquis.*
But atte laste speken she bigan,	*But at last she began to speak,*
And mekely she to the sergeant preyde,	*And she meekly asked the sergeant*

So as he was a worthy gentil man,	If as a good and kind man
That she moste kisse hire child, er that it deyde,	He would let her kiss her child before it died.
And in hir barm this litel child she leyde,	She put the little child in her lap
With ful sad face, and gan the child to kisse,	With a sorrowful face, and blessed it,
And lulled it, and after gan it blisse.	And rocked it, and then kissed it.
And thus she seyde in hir benigne voys,	And then she said in her kind voice,
Fareweel, my child, I shal thee nevere see,	"Farewell, my child! I will never see you again.
But sith I thee have marked with the croys	But since I have marked you with the cross
Of thilke fader blessed moote thou be,	Of that Father—may be blessed!—
That for us deyde upon a croys of tree.	Who died for us on a wooden cross,
Thy soule, litel child, I hym bitake,	I trust your soul, little child, to him,
For this nyght shaltow dyen for my sake.	For tonight you will die for my sake.
I trowe, that to a norice in this cas	I believe that in this case a nurse
It had been hard this reuthe for to se;	Would have found it hard to face this terrible sorrow;
Wel myghte a mooder thanne han cryd `allas!'	So a mother might well have cried, "alas!"
But nathelees so sad and stidefast was she,	However she was so steadfast
That she endured al adversitee,	That she tolerated all adversity,
And to the sergeant mekely she sayde,	And she said meekly to the sergeant,
Have heer agayn your litel yonge mayde.	"Here, take back this tiny girl.
Gooth now, quod she, and dooth my lordes heeste;	"Now go," she said, "and do what my lord has ordered,
But o thyng wol I prey yow of youre grace,	But I will ask you one thing out of kindness,
That, but my lord forbad yow atte leeste,	That, unless my lord forbids it, at least
Burieth this litel body in son place	Bury the little body in some place
That beestes ne no briddes it torace.	Where no beasts and birds can violate it."
But he no word wol to that purpos seye,	But he would not give his word to do that,
But took the child, and wente upon his weye.	He just took the child and went on his way.
This sergeant cam unto his lord ageyn,	This sergeant then came back to his Lord,
And of Grisildis wordes and hir cheere	And he told him every detail, simply,
He tolde hym point for point, in short and pleyn,	About Griselda's words and demeanour,
And hym presenteth with his doghter deere.	And gave him his dear daughter.
Somwhat this lord hath routhe in his manere,	It seems the lord did feel some pity,
But nathelees his purpos heeld he stille,	However he stuck to his plan,
As lordes doon whan they wol han hir wille;	As lords will, when they have decided on something;
And bad his sergeant, that he pryvely	And he ordered his sergeant to secretly
Sholde this child ful softe wynde and wrappe,	And gently wrap this child up,
With alle circumstances tendrely,	Taking every possible care,
And carie it in a cofre or in a lappe,	And carry it in a box or a sling;
But upon peyne his heed of for to swappe	But, on pain of being beheaded,
That no man sholde knowe of his entente,	He must let no man know what he was doing,
Ne whenne he cam, ne whider that he wente.	Or where he came from, nor where he was going;
But at Boloigne to his suster deere,	But he should go to his dear sister
That thilke tyme of Panik was Countesse,	At Bologna, who was the Countess of Panik,
He sholde it take, and shewe hir this mateere,	And show her the baby and explain the business,

Bisekynge hir to doon hir bisynesse	Asking her to do her best
This child to fostre in alle gentillesse,	To bring the child up as a noblewoman;
And whos child that it was, he bad hire hyde	And he told her to keep the child's parentage secret
From every wight, for oght that may bityde.	From every person, no matter what might happen.
The sergeant gooth, and hath fulfild this thyng,	The sergeant went, and obeyed these orders;
But to this markys now retourne we,	But now we must go back to the marquis.
For now gooth he ful faste ymaginyng,	For now he spent a lot of time wondering
If by his wyves cheere he myghte se	If he could see in his wife's appearance,
Or by hir word aperceyve that she	Or by anything she said, if she
Were chaunged, but he nevere hir koude fynde,	Had changed; but he could see nothing,
But evere in oon ylike sad and kynde.	She was just the same, loyal and kind.
As glad, as humble, as bisy in servyse,	She was as happy, as humble, as hardowrking,
And eek in love, as she was wont to be,	And also as loving, as she had always been,
Was she to hym in every maner wyse,	In every possible way towards him,
Ne of hir doghter noght a word spak she.	And she never said a word about her daughter.
Noon accident for noon adversitee	No sign of any misfortune
Was seyn in hir, ne nevere hir doghter name	Could be seen in her, and she never mentioned
Ne nempned she, in ernest nor in game.	Her daughter's name, in any circumstance.
Explicit tercia pars.	The end of the third part.
Sequitur pars quarta.	Here follows the fourth part
In this estaat ther passed been foure yeer	Four years passed by in this fashion
Er she with childe was; but as God wolde,	Before she was pregnant again, but as God willed it
A knave child she bar by this Walter,	She gave this Walter a male child,
Ful gracious and fair for to biholde.	Very noble and beautiful to see.
And whan that folk it to his fader tolde,	And when his father was told about this,
Nat oonly he, but al his contree, merye	Not only he but all his people were happy
Was for this child, and God they thanke and herye.	To welcome the child, and they gave God their thanks and praise.
Whan it was two yeer old, and fro the brest	When it was two years old, and had been
Departed of his norice, on a day	Weaned from his nurse, one day
This markys caughte yet another lest	The marquis suddenly wanted again
To tempte his wyf yet ofter if he may.	To test his wife, if he could.
O, nedelees was she tempted in assay!	How pointless it was to put her to the test!
But wedded men ne knowe no mesure,	But married men can't stop themselves
Whan that they fynde a pacient creature.	When they find a loyal creature.
Wyf, quod this markys, ye han herd er this	"Wife," said this marquis, "you've heard before now
My peple sikly berth oure mariage;	That my people are unhappy at our marriage;
And namely sith my sone yboren is,	And especially since my son was born,
Now is it worse than evere in al oure age.	Now it is worse than it's ever been.
The murmure sleeth myn herte and my corage,	The discontent crushes my heart and my courage,
For to myne eres comth the voys so smeerte,	The attacks beat so harshly on my ears
That it wel ny destroyed hath myn herte.	That they have almost destroyed me.

Now sey they thus, `whan Walter is agon,	Now they are saying this: 'When Walter is dead,
Thanne shal the blood of Janicle succede,	Then the descendants of Janiclus will take q over
And been oure lord, for oother have we noon.'	And be our rulers, for we have no other.'
Swiche wordes seith my peple, out of drede,	This is what my people are saying, it's certain.
Wel oughte I of swich murmur taken heede,	I really have to take notice of this grumbling,
For certeinly I drede swich sentence,	For I truly dread their opinions.
Though they nat pleyn speke in myn audience.	Even if they don't voice them plainly to me.
I wolde lyve in pees, if that I myghte;	I would like to live in peace, if I can;
Wherfore I am disposed outrely	And so I have firmly decided
As I his suster servede by nyghte,	That I shall deal with him secretly
Right so thenke I to serve hym pryvely.	In the same way as I did with his sister in the night.
This warne I yow, that ye nat sodeynly	I warn you this so that you don't suddenly
Out of yourself for no wo sholde outreye.	Go mad with any sort of sorrow;
Beth pacient, and therof I yow preye.	I must ask you to remain calm."
I have, quod she, seyd thus, and evere shal,	"I have," she said, "promised that, and I will stick to it:
I wol no thyng, ne nyl no thyng, certayn,	I don't want anything, and I never will,
But as yow list, naught greveth me at al	Except what you desire. It doesn't grieve me at all,
Though that my doughter and my sone be slayn-	Even though my daughter and my son are killed—
At youre comandement, this is to sayn-	For it is at your orders.
I have noght had no part of children tweyne	I have had nothing from my two children
But first siknesse, and after wo and peyne.	But sickness, followed by sorrow and pain.
Ye been oure lord, dooth with your owene thyng	You are our Lord; do with your possessions
Right as yow list, axeth no reed at me;	Exactly as you wish; don't ask me for advice.
For as I lefte at hoom al my clothyng,	For just as I left all my clothes at home
Whan I first cam to yow, right so, quod she,	When I first came to you," she said,
Lefte I my wyl and al my libertee,	"I also left my will and my freedom,
And took youre clothyng, wherfore I yow preye,	And I took your clothes; so I beg you,
Dooth youre plesaunce; I wol youre lust obeye.	Do as you wish; I'll do what you want.
And certes, if I hadde prescience	And certainly, if I had had foresight
Youre wyl to knowe, er ye youre lust me tolde,	Of what you wanted, before you told me,
I wolde it doon withouten necligence.	I would make sure that it was done;
But now I woot your lust and what ye wolde,	But now I know what you want, your desire,
Al your plesance ferme and stable I holde,	I remain steadfast to whatever you wish;
For wiste I that my deeth wolde do yow ese,	If I thought my death would make you happy,
Right gladly wolde I dyen yow to plese.	I would happily die, to please you.
Deth may noght make no comparisoun	Death is nothing compared
Unto youre love! and whan this markys say	To your love." And when this marquis saw
The constance of his wyf, he caste adoun	How loyal his wife was, he looked down
Hise eyen two, and wondreth that she may	At the ground, and was amazed that she could
In pacience suffre al this array;	Suffer all this treatment without complaint;
And forth he goth with drery contenance,	And he went out with a sad face,
But ot his herte it was ful greet plesance.	But his heart was full of pleasure.

This ugly sergeant, in the same wyse That he hir doghter caughte, right so he Or worse, if men worse kan devyse, Hath hent hir sone, that ful was of beautee, And evere in oon so pacient was she, That she no chiere maade of hevynesse, But kiste hir sone, and after gan it blesse.	*This horrible sergeant, in the same way* *That he took her daughter, did the same—* *Or even worse, if one can imagine it—* *In seizing her son, who was so beautiful.* *And she was always so patient* *That she did not show the slightest sorrow,* *But she kissed her son, and after she blessed it;*
Save this, she preyde hym, that if he myghte, Hir litel sone he wolde in erthe grave His tendre lymes, delicaat to sighte, Fro foweles and fro beestes for to save. But she noon answere of hym myghte have, He wente his wey, as hym nothyng ne roghte, But to Boloigne he tendrely it broghte.	*All she asked him was that if he could* *He would bury her little son in the earth,* *To save his tender limbs, so beautiful,* *From the birds and beasts.* *But she could get no answer from him.* *He went on his way, as if he didn't care,* *But he took the baby tenderly to Bologna.*
This markys wondred evere lenger the moore Upon hir pacience, and if that he Ne hadde soothly knowen therbifoore That parfitly hir children loved she, He wolde have wend that of som subtiltee, And of malice, or for crueel corage, That she hadde suffred this with sad visage.	*This marquis was even more astonished* *By her patience, and if he* *Hadn't been absolutely certain beforehand* *That she was devoted to her children,* *He would have suspected some deception,* *And thought that she was evil or unfeeling* *In suffering what had happened so calmly.*
But wel he knew that next hymself, certayn, She loved hir children best in every wyse; But now of wommen wolde I axen fayn, If thise assayes myghte nat suffise, What koude a sturdy housbonde moore devyse To preeve hire wyfhod or hir stedefastnesse, And he continuynge evere in sturdinesse?	*But he certainly knew that next to himself* *She loved her children most of all.* *But now I would like to ask women* *If these tests were not enough?* *What more cruelty could a husband invent* *To test her wifely virtues and her loyalty,* *Carrying on with his cruelty forever?*
But ther been folk of swich condicioun, That whan they have a certein purpos take They kan nat stynte of hir entencioun, But right as they were bounden to that stake They wol nat of that firste purpos slake. Right so this markys fulliche hath purposed To tempte his wyf, as he was first disposed.	*But there are people who are so stubborn* *That when they have decided on a certain plan* *They cannot bring themselves to change it,* *They are like somebody tied to a stake,* *They will not give up their original plan.* *This was the case with this marquis, who decided* *To carry on testing his wife as he had planned.*
He waiteth, if by word or contenance That she to hym was changed of corage; But nevere koude he fynde variance, She was ay oon in herte and in visage.	*He waited to see if in speech or expression* *She had changed her feelings towards him,* *But he could never find anything different.* *She was always the same in her heart and her face,*
And ay the forther that she was in age, The moore trewe-if that it were possible- She was to hym in love, and moore penyble.	*And the older that she got* *The more loyal, if it were possible,* *She became to him in love, and was more caring.*
For which it semed thus, that of hem two Ther nas but o wyl; for, as Walter leste, The same lust was hir plesance also,	*And so it seemed that between the two of them* *There was only one will, that of Walter,* *For his desires matched hers exactly.*

And, God be thanked, al fil for the beste.	And, thanks be to God, everything turned out for the best.
She shewed wel, for no worldly unreste	She showed herself good, and caused no
A wyf as of hirself no thing ne sholde	Discord, as a wife should, only wanting
Wille in effect, but as hir housbonde wolde.	Exactly what her husband did.
The sclaundre of Walter ofte and wyde spradde,	The infamy of Walter spread far and wide,
That of a crueel herte he wikkedly,	Telling how with his cruel heart he had wickedly,
For he a povre womman wedded hadde,	Because he had married a poor woman,
Hath mordred bothe his children prively.-	Had both his children secretly murdered.
Swich murmure was among hem comunly;	This was the rumour amongst all the people.
No wonder is, for to the peples ere	It's no surprise, for all the people heard
Ther cam no word, but that they mordred were.	Was that the children had been murdered.
For which, wher as his peple therbifore	Because of this, just as his people before
Hadde loved hym wel, the sclaundre of his diffame	Had loved him very much, the disgrace
Made hem, that they hym hatede therfore.	Made them hate him.
To been a mordrere is an hateful name;	To be called a murderer is a terrible thing;
But nathelees, for ernest ne for game	But still, there was nothing at all
He of his crueel purpos nolde stente:	Which could make him swerve from his cruel plan;
To tempte his wyf was set al his entente.	All he wanted to do was test his wife.
Whan that his doghter twelf yeer was of age,	When his daughter was twelve years old
He to the court of Rome in subtil wyse	He sent to the court of Rome, which had been secretly
Enformed of his wyl sente his message,	Informed of his true plans, his messenger,
Comaundynge hem swiche bulles to devyse	Asking them to put out such proclamations
As to his crueel purpos may suffyse,	As would fit in with his cruel plans–
How that the pope as for his peples reste	Saying that the Pope, in order to have peace,
Bad hym to wedde another, if hym leste.	Had told him to marry someone else, if he wanted.
I seye, he bad they sholde countrefete	As I say, he ordered that they should forge
The popes bulles, makynge mencioun	Papal orders, saying that
That he hath leve his firste wyf to lete	He had permission to leave his first wife,
As by the popes dispensacioun,	As if the Pope agreed to it,
To stynte rancour and dissencioun	To end any disagreement
Bitwixe his peple and hym, thus seyde the bulle,	Between him and his people; this is what the proclamation said,
The which they han publiced atte fulle.	And it was published far and wide.
The rude peple, as it no wonder is,	The ignorant people, it's no surprise to say,
Wenden ful wel that it hadde be right so;	Imagined that all this was true;
But whan thise tidynges cam to Grisildis,	But when the news came to Griselda,
I deeme that hir herte was ful wo.	I think that her heart was full of sorrow.
But she, ylike sad for everemo,	But she, eternally steadfast,
Disposed was, this humble creature,	Was prepared, this humble creature,
The adversitee of Fortune al tendure,	To endure everything fortune could throw at her,
Abidynge evere his lust and his pleasance	Suffering whatever he desired,
To whom that she was yeven, herte and al,	Having given him her heart and soul,

As to hir verray worldly suffisance.	*Making him the centre of the world.*
But shortly, if this storie I tellen shal,	*But to move the story onwards I'll tell you*
This markys writen hath in special	*That the marquis had written out*
A lettre, in which he sheweth his entente,	*A letter, revealing his plans,*
And secreely he to Boloigne it sente;	*And he secretly sent it to Bologna.*
To the Erl of Panyk, which that hadde tho	*He specifically asked the Earl of Panyk,*
Wedded his suster, preyde he specially	*Who was married to his sister,*
To bryngen hoom agayn hise children two,	*To bring his two children back home again,*
In honurable estaat al openly;	*In a great public procession.*
But o thyng he hym preyede outrely,	*But he asked him one thing in particular,*
That he to no wight, though men wolde enquere,	*That no matter who asked him*
Sholde nat telle whos children that they were,	*He would never reveal whose children they were.*
But seye, the mayden sholde ywedded be	*He should say that the girl should be married*
Unto the Markys of Saluce anon.	*At once to the Marquis of Saluce,*
And as this Erl was preyed, so dide he;	*And the Earl did exactly as he was asked;*
For at day set he on his wey is goon	*On the appointed day he made his way*
Toward Saluce, and lordes many oon,	*Towards Saluce, with many other lords*
In riche array this mayden for to gyde,	*In a rich procession, leading this girl,*
Hir yonge brother ridynge hir bisyde.	*With her young brother riding beside her.*
Arrayed was toward hir marriage	*She was dressed ready for her marriage,*
This fresshe mayde, ful of gemmes cleere;	*This beautiful girl, her clothes covered in bright jewels;*
Hir brother, which that seven yeer was of age,	*Her brother, who was seven years old,*
Arrayed eek ful fressh in his manere.	*Was also beautifully dressed in his own way.*
And thus in greet noblesse, and with glad cheere,	*And so this very noble and happy procession*
Toward Saluces shapynge hir journey,	*Made its way towards Saluces,*
Fro day to day they ryden in hir wey.	*Getting closer day by day.*
Explicit quarta pars.	*The end of the fourth part*
Sequitur pars quinta.	*The second part follows.*
Among al this, after his wikke usage,	*Meanwhile, continuing his wicked plans,*
This markys yet his wyf to tempte moore	*This marquis, to test his wife even more,*
To the outtreste preeve of hir corage,	*To find the outer limits of her heart,*
Fully to han experience and loore,	*To discover to the fullest extent*
If that she were as stidefast as bifoore,	*If she were as loyal to him as before,*
He on a day in open audience	*One day, with everybody listening,*
Ful boistously hath seyd hir this sentence.	*He rudely spoke to her in this fashion:*
Certes, Grisilde, I hadde ynogh plesance,	*"I certainly, Griselda, had enough pleasure*
To han yow to my wyf for your goodnesse,	*Having you as my wife due to your goodness,*
As for youre trouthe, and for your obeisance-	*For your truth and your obedience,*
Noght for youre lynage, ne for youre richesse;	*Not for your ancestry, or your wealth;*
But now knowe I, in verray soothfastnesse,	*But now I know for certain*
That in greet lordshipe, if I wel avyse,	*That being a great lord, if I am correct,*
Ther is greet servitute in sondry wyse.	*Imposes many great obligations on me.*
I may nat doon as every plowman may;	*I can't behave just like any ordinary ploughman;*
My peple me constreyneth for to take	*My people are asking me to choose*

Another wyf, and crien day by day,	Another wife, and they complain about it daily;
And eek the pope, rancour for to slake,	And also the Pope, to quell their anger,
Consenteth it, that dar I undertake-	Has agreed to it–I can say that with confidence-
And treweliche thus muche I wol yow seye,	And so I have to say this to you:
My newe wyf is comynge by the weye.	My new wife is coming this way.
Be strong of herte, and voyde anon hir place,	Keep strong in courage, and give up your place at once;
And thilke dower that ye broghten me	And the dowry that you brought to me,
Taak it agayn, I graunte it of my grace.	You can take it back; I kindly give it to you.
Retourneth to youre fadres hous, quod he;	Go back to your father's house," he said;
No man may alwey han prosperitee.	"Nobody can always have prosperity.
With evene herte I rede yow tendure	I advise you to suffer with a calm heart
This strook of Fortune or of aventure.	The brickbats of Fortune and chance."
And she answerde agayn in pacience,	Again she answered him patiently:
My lord, quod she, I woot and wiste alway	"My lord," she said, "I know, and always knew,
How that bitwixen youre magnificence	How nobody can make a comparison
And my poverte, no wight kan ne may	Between your magnificence
Maken comparisoun, it is no nay.	And my poverty; this cannot be denied.
I ne heeld me nevere digne in no manere	Of being your wife, not even your chambermaid.
And in this hous ther ye me lady maade,	And in this house, where you made me the lady,
The heighe God take I for my witnesse,	I ask Almighty God to witness,
And also wysly he my soule glaade,	And I swear on my hopes for my soul,
I nevere heeld me lady ne maistresse,	That I never considered myself lady or mistress,
But humble servant to youre worthynesse,	Just a humble servant to your greatness,
And evere shal whil that my lyf may dure	And though I shall be, as long as I live,
Aboven every worldly creature.	Serving you better than anyone in the world.
That ye so longe of youre benignitee	That you so long and so kindly
Han holden me in honour and nobleye,	Have kept me in this honourable and noble position,
Wher as I was noght worthy for to bee,	Where I had no right to be,
That thonke I God and yow, to whom I preye	I thank you and God, whom I pray
Foryelde it yow; ther is namoore to seye.	Will reward you for it; that's all I have to say.
Unto my fader gladly wol I wende,	I will gladly go back to my father,
And with hym dwelle unto my lyves ende.	And live with him until the end of my life.
Ther I was fostred of a child ful smal,	I was brought up there when I was a child,
Til I be deed, my lyf ther wol I lede,	And I will live there until I die.
A wydwe clene in body, herte, and al,	I shall be a widow clean in body, heart and soul.
For sith I yaf to yow my maydenhede	Since I gave you my virginity,
And am youre trewe wyf, it is no drede,	And I am your true wife, no doubt about that,
God shilde swich a lordes wyf to take	God forbid the wife of such a lord
Another man, to housbonde or to make.	Should take another man as a husband or a mate!

And of youre newe wyf, God of his grace	And with your new wife may God in his grace
So graunte yow wele and prosperitee,	Grant to happiness and prosperity!
For I wol gladly yelden hir my place	I will gladly give up my place for her,
In which that I was blisful wont to bee.	Where I used to be happy.
For sith it liketh yow my lord, quod shee,	Since it pleases you, my lord," she said,
That whilom weren al myn hertes reste,	"Who was once my entire world,
That I shal goon, I wol goon whan yow leste.	For me to go, then I will go when you wish.
But ther as ye me profre swich dowaire	But when you tell me to take the dowry
As I first broghte, it is wel in my mynde	That I brought with me first, all I can think of
It were my wrecched clothes, no thyng faire,	Is my wretched clothes, which were very poor,
The whiche to me were hard now for to fynde.	And which it would be hard for me to find now.
O goode God! how gentil and how kynde	Oh good God! How gentle and kind
Ye semed by youre speche and youre visage	You seemed in your speech and your appearance
The day that maked was oure mariage!	On the day that we got married!
But sooth is seyd, algate I fynde it trewe,	But it is truthfully said–I have always found it true,
(For in effect it preeved is on me)	For I am the living proof of it–
Love is noght oold, as whan that it is newe,	That old love is not the same as new.
But certes, lord, for noon adversitee,	But certainly, lord, no adversity,
To dyen in the cas it shal nat bee	Even if I died, could make me
That evere in word or werk I shal repente	Repent in word or deed the fact
That I yow yaf myn herte in hool entente.	That I gave you the whole of my heart.
My lord, ye woot that in my fadres place	My lord, you know that in my father's house
Ye dide me streepe out of my povre weede,	You stripped me of my clothes,
And richely me cladden of youre grace.	And dressed me richly, in your kindness.
To yow broghte I noght elles, out of drede,	I brought you nothing else, it's certain,
But feith, and nakednesse, and maydenhede.	Except my faith, my nakedness, and my virginity;
And heere agayn my clothyng I restoore,	And here I give you back your clothes,
And eek my weddyng ryng for everemo.	And also your wedding ring, for eternity.
The remenant of youre jueles redy be	I can safely say that the rest of your jewels
In-with youre chambre, dar I saufly sayn.	Are waiting for you in your chamber.
Naked out of my fadres hous, quod she,	I left my father's house naked," she said,
I cam, and naked moot I turne agayn.	"To come here, and I must go back naked.
Al your plesance wol I folwen fayn,	I will gladly do exactly as you ask;
But yet I hope it be nat your entente	But I hope that you are not planning
That I smoklees out of your paleys wente.	For me to leave your palace completely unclothed.
Ye koude nat doon so dishoneste a thyng,	You could not do such a shameful thing,
That thilke wombe in which your children leye,	That the womb in which your children lay
Sholde biforn the peple in my walking	Should be seen bare in front of
Be seyn al bare; wherfore I yow preye,	Everybody as I walk out, so I beg you,
Lat me nat lyk a worm go by the weye!	Do not let me leave here like a worm.
Remembre yow, myn owene lord so deere,	Remember, my own dear Lord,
I was your wyf, though I unworthy weere.	I was your wife, even if I was unworthy of you.
Wherfore, in gerdoun of my maydenhede	So, to pay me for my virginity,

Which that I broghte, and noght agayn I bere,	Which I brought here, and have nothing to take back,
As voucheth sauf to yeve me to my meede	Allow me to have, in recompense,
But swich a smok as I was wont to were,	Just a peasant smock like I used to wear,
That I therwith may wrye the wombe of here	Which I can use to cover the womb of she
That was your wyf, and heer take I my leeve	Who was your wife. And now I leave
Of yow, myn owene lord, lest I yow greve.	You, my own lord, in case I upset you."
The smok, quod he, that thou hast on thy bak,	"The smock," he said, "that you have on your back,
Lat it be stille, and bere it forth with thee.	You can keep that, take away with you."
But wel unnethes thilke word he spak,	But hardly had he spoken the words
But wente his wey for routhe and for pitee.	When he disappeared, full of grief and pity.
Biforn the folk hirselven strepeth she,	She stripped her clothes off in front of everyone,
And in hir smok, with heed and foot al bare,	And in her smock, with her head and feet all bare,
Toward hir fader hous forth is she fare.	She made her way to her father's house.
The folk hir folwe, wepynge in hir weye,	The people followed her, weeping on their way,
And Fortune ay they cursen, as they goon.	And they cursed fate as they went;
But she fro wepyng kepte hir eyen dreye,	But she did not weep, her eyes were dry,
Ne in this tyme word ne spak she noon.	And she did not say anything.
Hir fader, that this tidynge herde anoon,	Her father, who had already heard the news,
Curseth the day and tyme that nature	Cursed the day and time
Shoop hym to been a lyves creature.	That he was born upon the earth.
For out of doute this olde povre man	For there is no doubt that this poor old man
Was evere in suspect of hir mariage,	Was always suspicious about her marriage;
For evere he demed, sith that it bigan,	He had always believed, since it began,
That whan the lord fulfild hadde his corage,	That when the Lord had got his desire
Hym wolde thynke it were a disparage	He would think that it was degrading
To his estaat, so lowe for talighte,	To his position to bend so low,
And voyden hir as soone as ever he myghte.	And he would get rid of her as soon as he possibly could.
Agayns his doghter hastiliche goth he,	He went quickly to meet his daughter,
For he by noyse of folk knew hir comynge,	For he could tell from the noise of the crowd she was coming,
And with hir olde coote, as it myghte be,	And he covered her as well as possible
He covered hir, ful sorwefully wepynge,	With her old coat, weeping sorrowfully.
But on hir body myghte he it nat brynge.	But he couldn't bring himself to put it
For rude was the clooth, and moore of age	On her body, for it was rough, and older
By dayes fele, than at hir mariage.	Than her marriage by many days.
Thus with hir fader for a certeyn space	So this flower of womanly patience
Dwelleth this flour of wyfly pacience,	Stayed with her father for a certain time,
That neither by hir wordes ne hir face,	And neither in her words nor her expression,
Biforn the folk ne eek in hir absence,	In public nor in private,
Ne shewed she that hir was doon offence,	Did she show that anyone had done her wrong;
Ne of hir heighe estaat no remembraunce	She looked as though she could not remember
Ne hadde she, as by hir contenaunce.	Anything about her previous position.

No wonder is, for in hir grete estaat	This was no surprise, for when she had a great position
Hir goost was evere in pleyn humylitee.	Her spirit was always full of humility;
No tendre mouth, noon herte delicaat,	No affectations, no self-indulgence,
No pompe, no semblant of roialtee,	No ceremony, no outward shows of royalty,
But ful of pacient benyngnytee,	But she had been full of patient goodness,
Discreet and prideless, ay honurable,	Quiet and modest, always honourable,
And to hir housbonde evere meke and stable.	And always obedient and loyal to her husband.
Men speke of Job, and moost for his humblesse,	Men talk about Job, and speak of his humility,
As clerkes whan hem list konne wel endite,	And scholars, when they want to, use him as an example,
Namely of men; but as in soothfastnesse,	For mankind, but to tell the truth,
Though clerkes preise wommen but a lite,	Although scholars don't give women much praise,
Ther kan no man in humblesse hym acquite,	No man can show the same humility
As womman kan, ne kan been half so trewe	As a woman, nor be half as loyal
As wommen been, but it be falle of newe.	As women are, unless something's happened I haven't heard of.
(Pars sexta.)	The sixth part
Fro Boloigne is this Erl of Panyk come,	The Earl of Panyk came from Bologna,
Of which the fame up sprang to moore and lesse,	And everybody heard what was going on,
And in the peples eres, alle and some,	And everybody heard what was going on,
Was kouth eek that a newe markysesse	They knew that a new marchioness
He with hym broghte, in swich pompe and richesse,	Was coming with him, with such ceremony and wealth
That nevere was ther seyn with mannes eye	That nobody had ever seen anything like it,
So noble array in al Westlumbardye.	Never such a great display in all of West Lombardy.
The markys, which that shoop and knew al this,	The marquis, who had arranged the whole thing,
Er that thise Erl was come, sente his message	Sent his messenger, before the Earl came,
For thilke sely povre Grisildis;	To fetch poor innocent Griselda;
And she with humble herte and glad visage,	And with a humble heart and happy face,
Nat with no swollen thoght in hire corage	With no proud thoughts swelling in her heart,
Cam at his heste, and on hir knees hire sette,	Came at his command, and put herself down on her knees,
And reverently and wysely she hym grette.	And she respectfully and humbly greeted him.
Grisilde, quod he, my wyl is outrely	"Griselda," he said, "my wish is that
This mayden, that shal wedded been to me,	This girl, who will be married to me,
Received be to morwe as roially	Shall be welcomed tomorrow as royally
As it possible is in myn hous to be;	As it is possible for her to be in my house,
And eek that every wight in his degree	And also that every person, according to rank,
Have his estaat in sittyng and servyse	Will take his proper place, at the ceremony and the feast,
And heigh plesaunce, as I kan best devyse.	And enjoy themselves to the best of my ability.
I have no wommen, suffisaunt, certayn,	I don't have any women capable
The chambres for tarraye in ordinaunce	Of arranging the rooms
After my lust, and therfore wolde I fayn	As I wished, and so I want

That thyn were al swich manere governaunce;	You to take care of the business.
Thou knowest eek of olde al my plesaunce,	You know the sort of thing I like;
Thogh thyn array be badde and yvel biseye,	Although you are dressed poorly and roughly
Do thou thy devoir at the leeste weye.	Make sure that you do your duty."
Nat oonly lord, that I am glad, quod she,	"Not only, lord, am I glad," she said,
To doon your lust, but I desire also	To do your wishes, but I would also like
Yow for to serve and plese in my degree	To serve you and please you according to my position
Withouten feyntyng, and shal everemo.	Without any excuses, and I always shall;
Ne nevere, for no wele ne no wo,	And never, whether in happiness or sorrow,
Ne shal the goost withinne myn herte stente	Will the spirit within my heart stop
To love yow best with al my trewe entente.	Loving you heart and soul."
And with that word she gan the hous to dighte,	Having said that she began to prepare the house,
And tables for to sette, and beddes make,	And to set tables, make beds;
And peyned hir to doon al that she myghte,	She made sure she did all that she could,
Preyynge the chambereres for Goddes sake	Asking the chambermaids for God's sake
To hasten hem, and faste swepe and shake,	To hurry up, and quickly sweep and dust;
And she, the mooste servysable of alle,	And she, the hardest working of all,
Hath every chambre arrayed, and his halle.	Got every room and also the halls ready.
Abouten undren gan this Erl alighte,	Around mid-morning the Earl arrived,
That with hym broghte thise noble children tweye,	Bringing with him those two noble children,
For which the peple ran to seen the sighte	And people ran to see the sight
Of hir array, so richely biseye;	Of their wonderful rich clothes;
And thanne at erst amonges hem they seye,	And then they said to each other
That Walter was no fool, thogh that hym leste	That Walter was no fool, and though he wanted
To chaunge his wyf, for it was for the beste.	To change his wife, it was for the best.
For she is fairer, as they deemen alle,	For they all decided she was more beautiful
Than is Grisilde, and moore tendre of age,	Than Griselda, and also younger,
And fairer fruyt bitwene hem sholde falle,	And they would make wonderful children,
And moore plesant for hir heigh lynage.	Even better due to her high birth.
Hir brother eek so faire was of visage,	Her brother was also good-looking,
That hem to seen the peple hath caught plesaunce,	And people took pleasure from seeing them,
Commendynge now the markys governaunce.	Applauding the choice of the marquis.
O stormy peple, unsad and evere untrewe!	"You stormy people! Unfaithful and always untrue!
Ay undiscreet and chaungynge as a vane,	You swing around like a weather vane!
Delitynge evere in rumbul that is newe;	You take pleasure in every new rumour,
For lyk the moone ay wexe ye and wane,	You wax and wane like the moon!
Ay ful of clappyng, deere ynogh a jane,	You're always full of your worthless gossip!
Youre doom is fals, youre constance yvele preeveth,	Your judgement is wrong and you are horribly faithless;
A ful greet fool is he that on yow leeveth!	Anyone who puts trust in you is an idiot."
Thus seyden sadde folk in that citee,	This is what the serious people of the city said,
Whan that the peple gazed up and doun,	When they saw how the people were behaving,
For they were glad right for the noveltee	For they were very glad to have something new,
To han a newe lady of hir toun.	To have a new lady in their town.

Namoore of this make I now mencioun,	I won't say any more about this,
But to Grisilde agayn wol I me dresse,	But I will go back to Griselda,
And telle hir constance and hir bisynesse.	And tell you about her loyalty and hard work.
Ful bisy was Grisilde in every thyng	Griselda was busy with everything
That to the feeste was apertinent.	To do with the feast.
Right noght was she abayst of hir clothyng,	She wasn't embarrassed by her clothes,
Thogh it were rude and somdeel eek torent,	Even though they were rough and rather tattered;
But with glad cheere to the yate is went	But she cheerfully went down to the gate
With oother folk to greete the markysesse,	With the other people to greet the marchioness,
And after that dooth forth hir bisynesse.	And after that she carried on with her work.
With so glad chiere hise gestes she receyveth,	With a cheerful demeanour she welcomed his guests,
And konnyngly everich in his degree,	With such dignity, behaving correctly towards each rank,
That no defaute no man aperceyveth,	That nobody could find any fault with her,
But ay they wondren what she myghte bee	But they were all set to wondering whom she might be,
That in so povre array was for to see,	Dressed in such a poor outfits,
And koude swich honour and reverence;	Who knew courtly behaviour so well,
And worhtily they preisen hire prudence.	And they justly sang her praises.
In al this meenewhile she ne stente	During all this she did not stop
This mayde and eek hir brother to commende	Praising the girl and also her brother
With al hir herte, in ful benyngne entente,	With all her heart, meaning only kindliness,
So wel that no man koude hir pris amende	Doing so well that she couldn't be praised enough.
But atte laste, whan that thise lordes wende	But in the end, when these lords went
To sitten doun to mete, he gan to calle	In to dinner, he called
Grisilde, as she was bisy in his halle.	Griselda, as she worked in his hall.
Grisilde, quod he, as it were in his pley,	"Griselda," he said, as if he were making a joke,
How liketh thee my wyf and hir beautee?	"What do you think of my wife and her beauty?"
Right wel, quod she, my lord, for in good fey	"I like her very much," she said, "my lord; for, I swear,
A fairer saugh I nevere noon than she.	I never saw someone as beautiful as her.
I prey to God yeve hir prosperitee,	I pray that God will make her prosperous,
And so hope I that he wol to yow sende	And I also hope that he will keep you
Plesance ynogh unto youre lyves ende.	Happy all through your lives.
O thyng biseke I yow, and warne also	Just one thing I ask of you, and I also warn you,
That ye ne prikke with no tormentynge	Don't oppress this tender girl with
This tendre mayden, as ye han doon mo;	Any tortures, as you have done before;
For she is fostred in hir norissynge	She has been brought up
Moore tendrely, and to my supposynge	More tenderly than I, and I think
She koude nat adversitee endure,	That she would not be able to endure the pain
As koude a povre fostred creature.	Like someone raised in rougher circumstances."

And whan this Walter saugh hir pacience,	And when Walter saw how patient she was,
Hir glade chiere, and no malice at al,	What a glad expression she had, with no malice at all,
And he so ofte had doon to hir offence	When he had done so much wrong to her,
And she ay sad and constant as a wal,	And she had remained a steadfast loyal bulwark,
Continuynge evere hir innocence overal,	Remaining forever innocent,
This sturdy markys gan his herte dresse	This harsh marquis felt in his heart
To rewen upon hir wyfly stedfastnesse.	That he should have pity on her feminine loyalty.
This is ynogh Grisilde myn, quod he,	"This is enough, my Griselda," he said;
Be now namoore agast, ne yvele apayed.	Don't be afraid of evil any more.
I have thy feith and thy benyngnytee	I have tested your loyalty and your goodness
As wel as evere womman was, assayed	As harshly as any woman was ever tested,
In greet estaat, and povreliche arrayed;	Both in a high position and in poverty.
Now knowe I, goode wyf, thy stedfastnesse!	Now I know, dear wife, how true you are."
And hir in armes took, and gan hir kesse.	And he took her in his arms and kissed her.
And she for wonder took of it no keep.	In her astonishment she took no notice of it;
She herde nat, what thyng he to hir seyde.	She didn't hear what he was saying to her;
She ferde as she had stert out of a sleep,	She looked like someone who had just awoken,
Til she out of hire mazednesse abreyde.	Until she suddenly broke out of her bewilderment.
Grisilde, quod he, by God that for us deyde,	"Griselda," he said, "by God, who died for us,
Thou art my wyf, ne noon oother I have,	You're my wife, I shall not have any other,
Ne nevere hadde, as God my soule save.	And I never have had, may God save my soul!
This is thy doghter which thou hast supposed	This is your daughter, whom you thought
To be my wyf; that oother faithfully	Was going to be my wife; that other child is truly
Shal be myn heir, as I have ay purposed;	My heir, as I have always intended;
Thou bare hym in thy body trewely.	I swear he came from your womb.
At Boloigne have I kept hem prively.	I have been keeping them secretly at Bologna;
Taak hem agayn, for now maystow nat seye	Take them back, no longer can you say
That thou hast lorn noon of thy children tweye.	That you have lost two of your children.
And folk that ootherweys han seyd of me,	People who have accused me of other things,
I warne hem wel that I have doon this deede	I tell them openly that I have done this deed
For no malice, ne for no crueltee,	Not out of malice, or through cruelty,
But for tassaye in thee thy wommanheede,	But to test your womanhood,
And not to sleen my clildren, God forbeede!	And I have not killed my children—God forbid!—
But for to kepe hem pryvely and stille,	But kept them secretly and quietly,
Til I thy purpos knewe and al thy wille.	Until I discovered your true worth."
Whan she this herde, aswowne doun she falleth	When she heard this, she fell down in a swoon
For pitous joye, and after hir swownynge	In pitiful joy, and when she had recovered
She bothe hir yonge children unto hir calleth,	She called both her young children to her,
And in hir armes pitously wepynge	And in her arms, pitifully weeping,
Embraceth hem, and tendrely kissynge	She embraced them, tenderly kissed them
Ful lyk a mooder, with hir salte teeres	Just like a mother, with her salty tears
She bathed bothe hir visage and hir heeres.	Streaming over their hair and their faces.
O, which a pitous thyng it was to se	O what a pitiful thing it was to see

Hir swownyng, and hir humble voys to heere!	How she fainted, and to hear her humble voice!
Grauntmercy, lord, that thanke I yow, quod she,	"I give you great thanks, my lord, may God repay you," she said,
That ye han saved me my children deere.	"That you have saved my dear children for me!
Now rekke I nevere to been deed right heere. Sith I stonde in your love and in your grace, No fors of deeth, ne whan my spirit pace!	Now I wouldn't care if I died right here; Since I have your love and kindness Death has no power, it doesn't matter when I go!
O tendre, O deere, O yonge children myne! Your woful mooder wende stedfastly That crueel houndes, or som foul vermyne Hadde eten yow; but God of his mercy And youre benyngne fader tendrely Hath doon yow kept, and in that same stounde Al sodeynly she swapte adoun to grounde.	Oh sweet, dear, oh my young children! Your sorrowing mother truly believed That cruel hounds or foul vermin Had eaten you; but God in his mercy And your kind father have tenderly Protected you-" and at the same moment She suddenly fell down on the ground.
And in hir swough so sadly holdeth she Hir children two, whan she gan hem tembrace, That with greet sleighte and greet difficultee The children from hir arm they gonne arace.	In her faint she held so tightly to the Two children, embracing them, That it was only with great effort and difficulty The children managed to get away from her arms.
O many a teere on many a pitous face Doun ran, of hem that stooden hir bisyde;	There were many tears on many pitying faces, Falling from the eyes of those who stood around;
Unnethe abouten hir myghte they abyde.	They could hardly bear to be with her.
Walter hir gladeth, and hir sorwe slaketh,	But they comforted her and her sorrow abated;
She riseth up abaysed from hir traunce, And every wight hir joye and feeste maketh, Til she hath caught agayn hir contenaunce. Walter hir dooth so feithfully plesaunce, That it was deyntee for to seen the cheere. Bitwixe hem two, now they been met yfeere.	She got up, embarrassed, from her trance, And everyone celebrated for her Until she regained her composure. Walter made such great efforts to please her That it was wonderful to see the happiness Between the two of them, now they had reconciled.
Thise ladyes, whan that they hir tyme say, Han taken hir and into chambre gon, And strepen hir out of hir rude array And in a clooth of gold that brighte shoon,	The ladies, when they saw the time was right, Took her into her bedroom, And stripped off all her rough clothes, And dressed her in cloth of gold, shining brightly,
With a coroune of many a riche stoon Upon hir heed, they into halle hir broghte,	With a richly jewelled crown On her head, and they brought her into the hall,
And ther she was honured as hir oghte.	And there she was revered as was her right.
Thus hath this pitous day a blisful ende, For every man and womman dooth his myght This day in murthe and revel to dispende, Til on the welkne shoon the sterres lyght. For moore solempne in every mannes syght	So this sad day had a happy ending, For every man and woman did their best To spend the day in happy celebrations, Until the sky was full of stars. The feast was more splendid, every man

This feste was, and gretter of costage,
Than was the revel of hire mariage.

Ful many a yeer in heigh prosperitee
Lyven thise two in concord and in reste.
And richely his doghter maryed he

Unto a lord, oon of the worthieste
Of al Ytaille, and thanne in pees and reste
His wyves fader in his court he kepeth,
Til that the soule out of his body crepeth.

His sone succedeth in his heritage
In reste and pees, after his fader day,

And fortunat was eek in mariage—
Al putte he nat his wyf in greet assay;
This world is nat so strong, it is no nay,
As it hath been of olde tymes yoore.
And herkneth what this auctour seith therfore.

This storie is seyd, nat for that wyves sholde
Folwen Grisilde as in humylitee,
For it were inportable though they wolde,

But for that every wight in his degree
Sholde be constant in adversitee
As was Grisilde. Therfore Petrark writeth
This storie, which with heigh stile he enditeth.

For sith a womman was so pacient
Unto a mortal man, wel moore us oghte

Receyven al in gree that God us sent.
For greet skile is, he preeve that he wroghte.

But he ne tempteth no man that he boghte,

As seith Seint Jame, if ye his pistel rede;

He preeveth folk al day, it is no drede,

And suffreth us, as for oure excercise,
With sharpe scourges of adversitee
Ful ofte to be bete in sondry wise,
Nat for to knowe oure wyl, for certes he
Er we were born knew al oure freletee,
And for oure beste is al his governaunce.
Lat us thanne lyve in vertuous suffraunce.

But o word, lordynges, herkneth er I go,

---

thought,
And also of far greater expense,
Than the one they had had to celebrate their marriage.

For many years in great prosperity
These two lived together peacefully,
And he made a great marriage for his daughter
To a lord, one of the best
In Italy, and then he brought his wife's father
To court to live in peace and luxury,
Staying there until the day he died.

His son inherited his titles
In peace and prosperity, once his father was gone,
And he also made a good marriage,
Although he did not put his wife to the test.
The world is not as strong, it has to be said,
As it was in the old days,
And listen to what the author says about this story.

This story has not been told for wives to
Copy Griselda's humility,
That would be impossible, even if they wanted to,

But so that every person, whatever his rank,
Should try to be as patient in adversity
As Griselda was; that's why Petrarch wrote
This story, which he set out in such high style.

For since a woman was so patient
With a mortal man, then how much more so should we

Be with all the things which God sends us;
For he has a right to test the things he has made.

But he does not test any man whom he has saved,

That's what St James says, if you read his Epistle;

There is no doubt that He tests people every day.

He makes us suffer, for our own good,
The sharp whips of adversity,
We get beaten often in different ways;
Not to test our will, for he certainly
Knew how frail we were before we were born;
Everything he does to us is for the best,
So let us suffer with virtuous patience.

But one word, my lords, before I go:

It were ful hard to fynde nowadayes	*It would be very difficult to find in these days*
In al a toun Grisildis thre or two,	*More than two or three Griseldas in a town;*
For it that they were put to swiche assayes,	*For if they were tested in the same way,*
The gold of hem hath now so badde alayes	*Their gold is now so badly adulterated*
With bras, that thogh the coyne be fair at eye,	*With brass, that although the coin might be nice to look at,*
It wolde rather breste atwo than plye.	*It will snap in two rather than bend.*
For which, heere for the Wyves love of Bathe,	*And so, out of love of the wife of Bath—*
Whos lyf and al hir seete God mayntene	*May God look after her and all her kind,*
In heigh maistrie, and elles were it scathe,	*Keep them powerful, it would be a shame otherwise—*
I wol with lusty herte fressh and grene	*I will with a strong heart, fresh and young,*
Seyn yow a song, to glade yow, I wene,	*Sing a song which I think will make you happy;*
And lat us stynte of ernestful matere.	*Let's stop talking about serious things.*
Herkneth my song, that seith in this manere.	*Hear my song, that says this:*
Grisilde is deed, and eek hir pacience,	*Griselda is dead, and so is her patience,*
And bothe atones buryed in Ytaille,	*And both are buried in Italy;*
For which I crie in open audience	*And so I cry out to all of you here*
No wedded man so hardy be tassaille	*That no married man should be so foolish as to test*
His wyves pacience, in hope to fynde	*The patience of his wife, thinking he will find*
Grisildis, for in certein he shal faille.	*Griselda, for he will certainly fail.*
O noble wyves, ful of heigh prudence,	*Oh noble wives, with your great wisdom,*
Lat noon humylitee youre tonge naille,	*Don't let humility curb your tongue,*
Ne lat no clerk have cause or diligence	*Nor let any scholar have a reason*
To write of yow a storie of swich mervaille	*To write a story about you of such wonderful things*
As of Grisildis, pacient and kynde,	*As we heard of patient and kind Griselda,*
Lest Chichivache yow swelwe in hire entraille.	*In case the monster which swallows good women gobbles you up!*
Folweth Ekko, that holdeth no silence,	*Be like Echo, who is never silent,*
But evere answereth at the countretaille;	*But always has to answer everything.*
Beth nat bidaffed for youre innocence,	*Don't be fooled through your innocence,*
But sharply taak on yow the governaille.	*Grab the upper hand for yourself.*
Emprenteth wel this lessoun in youre mynde	*Make sure you keep this lesson in mind,*
For commune profit, sith it may availle.	*Because it may do good for everyone.*
Ye archiwyves, stondeth at defense,	*You great fat wives, get ready for battle,*
Syn ye be strong as is a greet camaille.	*Since you are strong as a mighty camel;*
Ne suffreth nat that men yow doon offense,	*Don't allow men to offend you.*
And sklendre wyves, fieble as in bataille,	*And slim wives, who are weak in battle,*
Beth egre as is a tygre yond in Ynde,	*Be as fierce as a tiger from faraway India;*
Ay clappeth as a mille, I yow consaille.	*Always let your tongues spin on like a windmill.*
Ne dreed hem nat, doth hem no reverence,	*Don't be afraid of them, don't show them any respect,*
For though thyn housbonde armed be in maille,	*For although your husband might be fully armoured,*
The arwes of thy crabbed eloquence	*The arrows of your spiteful speech*

Shal perce his brest and eek his aventaille.	Will get through and stab him in the heart.
In jalousie I rede eek thou hym bynde,	I advise that you tie him up with jealousy,
And thou shalt make hym couche as doth a quaille.	And you will make him just as timid as a quail.
If thou be fair, ther folk been in presence	If you're beautiful, when there are people around,
Shewe thou thy visage and thyn apparaille;	Show off your face and your clothes;
If thou be foul, be fre of thy dispence,	If you are ugly, spend plenty of money;
To gete thee freendes ay do thy travaille,	Always try and have plenty of friends;
Be ay of chiere as light as leef on lynde,	Always be as light as a leaf on the linden tree,
And lat hym care, and wepe, and wryng, and waille.	Let him do the grieving, weeping, wringing of hands and wailing!

Bihoold the murye Wordes of the Hoost. — *Listen to the jolly words of the host*

This worthy clerk, whan ended was his tale,	When this good scholar had finished his tale,
Oure hoost seyde, and swoor: "By goddes bones,	Our host said, and swore, "By the bones of God,
Me were levere than a barel ale	I would give a barrel of ale
Me wyf at hoom had herd this legende ones;	For my wife at home to have heard this story!
This is a gentil tale for the nones,	That would be a great story for her to listen to,
As to my purpos, wiste ye my wille,-	To let her know what I thought of her;
But thyng that wol nat be, lat it be stille."	But since that cannot be, I'll leave it."

Heere endeth the Tale of the Clerk of Oxenford. — *This is the end of the Clerk's tale*

The Merchant's Tale

The Prologue

The Prologe of the Marchantes Tale

Wepyng and waylyng, care and oother sorwe,

I knowe ynogh, on even and a morwe,
Quod the Marchant, and so doon othere mo

That wedded been, I trowe that it be so.
For wel I woot, it fareth so with me.
I have a wyf, the worste that may be,
For thogh the feend to hire ycoupled were,
She wolde hym overmacche, I dar wel swere.

What sholde I yow reherce in special
Hir hye malice? She is a shrewe at al!
Ther is a long and large difference
Bitwix Grisildis grete pacience
And of my wyf the passyng crueltee.
Were I unbounden, al so moot I thee,
I wolde nevere eft comen in the snare.
We wedded men lyve in sorwe and care;
Assaye who so wole, and he shal fynde
I seye sooth, by Seint Thomas of Ynde-

As for the moore part, I seye nat alle;
God shilde, that it sholde so bifalle!

Ay, goode Sir Hoost, I have ywedded bee
Thise monthes two, and moore nat, pardee;
And yet I trowe, he that al his lyve
Wyflees hath been, though that men wolde him ryve
Unto the herte, ne koude in no manere
Tellen so muchel sorwe as I now here
Koude tellen of my wyves cursednesse!
Now quod our hoost, Marchant, so God yow blesse,

Syn ye so muchel knowen of that art,
Ful hertely I pray yow telle us part.

Gladly, quod he, but of myn owene soore,
For soory herte I telle may namoore.

The Merchant's Prologue

"Weeping and wailing, grief and other sorrows
Are familiar to me, morning and evening,"
Said the merchant, "as they are too many others
Who are married. I think this is true,
And that's certainly how things go with me.
I have a wife, the worst you can imagine;
Even if the devil were married to her,
I think I can swear she would beat him.

Why should I tell you the details
Of her evil? She is a shrew in everything.
There is a very great difference
Between Griselda's great patience
And the great cruelty of my wife.
If I were set free, I can tell you,
I would never fall back into that trap.
We married men live with sorrow and grief.
Whoever tries it, he will find
That I'm telling the truth, by St Thomas of India,
For most of them—I don't say everyone.
May God prevent this happening!

Ah, my good host, I have been married
For the past two months, no more, by God;
And yet, I believe that someone who has
Never been married could be stabbed
Through the heart and he still wouldn't know
The pain which I can tell you about
Caused by my wife's wicked ways!"
"Now," said our host, "merchant, may God bless you,
Since you know so much about it
I heartily request you to tell us something of it."
"Gladly," he said, "but it depresses me so
That I can't tell you any more about my own sorrow."

The Tale

Heere bigynneth the Marchantes Tale

Whilom ther was dwellynge in lumbardye	*Once there was living in Lombardy*
A worthy knyght, that born was of pavye,	*A good knight, who was born in Pavia,*
In which he lyved in greet prosperitee;	*Where he lived a very rich life;*
And sixty yeer a wyflees man was hee,	*And for sixty years he was a bachelor,*
And folwed ay his bodily delyt	*And always chased after whichever*
On wommen, ther as was his appetyt,	*Woman he fancied, just as he liked,*
As doon thise fooles that been seculeer.	*As all these irreligious fools do.*
And whan that he was passed sixty yeer,	*And when he had passed sixty years,*
Were it for hoolynesse or for dotage,	*Whether it was through holiness or because of age*
I kan nat seye, but swich a greet corage	*I cannot say, but he had such a great wish*
Hadde this knyght to been a wedded man	*To be married*
That day and nyght he dooth al that he kan	*That day and night he did all he could*
T' espien where he myghte wedded be,	*To find himself a bride,*
Preyinge oure lord to graunten him that he	*Praying to God to allow him*
Mighte ones knowe of thilke blisful lyf	*To experience the happy life*
That is bitwixe an housbonde and his wyf,	*That exists between a husband and his wife,*
And for to lyve under that hooly boond	*And to live in the holy state*
With which that first God man and womman bond.	*Which God first ordered for men and women.*
Noon oother lyf, seyde he, is worth a bene;	*"There is no other life," he said, "worth a bean,*
For wedlok is so esy and so clene,	*Marriage is so happy and pure,*
That in this world it is paradys.	*That it is paradise in this world."*
Thus seyde this olde knyght, that was so wys.	*This is what this wise old knight said.*
And certeinly, as sooth as God is kyng,	*And certainly, as sure as God is king,*
To take a wyf it is a glorious thyng,	*It's a wonderful thing to be married,*
And namely whan a man is oold and hoor;	*Especially when a man is old and grey–*
Thanne is a wyf the fruyt of his tresor.	*Then a wife is the best thing he has.*
Thanne sholde he take a yong wyf and a feir,	*He should take a young beautiful wife,*
On which he myghte engendren hym and heir,	*Through which he can breed an heir for himself,*
And lede his lyf in joye and in solas,	*Spending his life in joy and pleasure,*
Where as thise bacheleris synge allas,	*Whilst bachelors all bemoan their lot*
Whan that they funden any adversitee	*When they find any setbacks*
In love, which nys but childyssh vanytee.	*In love, which is just their childish foolishness.*
And trewely it sit wel to be so,	*And truly it is proper for it to be this way,*
That bacheleris have often peyne and wo;	*For bachelors to have all the pain and sorrow;*
On brotel ground they buylde, and brotelnesse	*They build their castles on sand, and*
They fynde, whan they wene sikernesse.	*They never know any security.*
They lyve but as a bryd or as a beest,	*They live like birds or beasts,*
In libertee, and under noon arreest,	*Free and with no restraints,*
Ther as a wedded man in his estaat	*Whereas a married man*
Lyveth a lyf blisful and ordinaat,	*Lives a happy and ordered life,*
Under this yok of mariage ybounde.	*Tied up in the bonds of marriage.*
Wel may his herte in joy and blisse habounde,	*He may well have a heart full of joy,*
For who kan be so buxom as a wyf?	*For who can be so obedient as a wife?*
Who is so trewe, and eek so ententyf	*Who is so loyal, and also so willing*
To kepe hym, syk and hool, as is his make?	*To look after him, sick and well, as his mate?*

For wele or wo she wole hym nat forsake;	In happiness or in sorrow she will not leave him;
She nys nat wery hym to love and serve,	She never tires of loving and serving him,
Thogh that he lye bedrede, til he sterve.	Even though he might be bedridden until death.
And yet somme clerkes seyn it nys nat so,	And yet some scholars say this is not the case,
Of whiche he theofraste is oon of tho.	Theofrastus is one of those.
What force though theofraste liste lye?	But who cares if he wants to live?
Ne take no wyf, quod he, for housbondrye,	"Do not take a wife," he says, "to keep house for you,
As for to spare in houshold thy dispence.	Thinking you will save money on your establishment.
A trewe servant dooth moore diligence	A true servant does better work
Thy good to kepe, than thyn owene wyf,	Looking after your property than your own wife,
For she wol clayme half part al hir lyf.	For she will always demand half of what you've got.
And if that thou be syk, so God me save,	And if you are sick, I swear,
Thy verray freendes, or a trewe knave,	Your true friends, or a good servant,
Wol kepe thee bet than she that waiteth ay	Will take better care of you that someone who is always
After thy good and hath doon many a day.	And has always been thinking about inheriting your property.
And if thou take a wyf unto thyn hoold,	If you take a wife into your household
Ful lightly maystow been a cokewold.	You can very much expect to be cheated on."
This sentence, and an hundred thynges worse,	This opinion, and a hundred worse ones,
Writeth this man, ther God his bones corse!	Has been written by this man, may God curse his bones!
But take no kep of al swich vanytee;	But don't pay attention to such nonsense;
Deffie theofraste, and herke me.	Reject Theofrastus, and listen to me.
A wyf is goddes yifte verraily;	A wife is truly a gift from God;
Alle othere manere yiftes hardily,	All other types of gifts are certainly–
As londes, rentes, pasture, or commune,	Gifts like lands, rents, pastures or common land,
Or moebles, alle been yiftes of fortune,	Or household possessions - all given by Fortune,
That passen as a shadwe upon a wal.	And they slip by like shadows.
But drede nat, if pleynly speke I shal,	But do not doubt, I tell you plainly:
A wyf wol laste, and thyn hous endure,	A wife will stay and embellish your household,
Wel lenger than thee list, paraventure.	Maybe even longer than you want her to.
Mariage is a ful greet sacrement.	Marriage is a very great sacrament.
He which that hath no wyf, I holde hym shent;	If a man has no wife, I think he is destroyed;
He lyveth helplees and al desolat, --	He lives helpless and desolate–
I speke of folk in seculer estaat.	I'm talking of people in secular life.
And herke why, I sey nat this for noght,	And here my reasoning –I'm not saying this for nothing–
That womman is for mannes helpe ywroght.	A woman is created to help her man.
The hye god, whan he hadde adam maked,	Almighty God when he had made Adam,
And saugh him al allone, bely-naked,	And saw him all alone, completely naked,
God of his grete goodnesse syde than,	God in his great goodness then said,
Lat us now make an helpe unto this man	"Now let me make a helper for this man

Lyk to hymself; and thanne he made him eve.	Similar to himself"; and then he made Eve.
Heere may ye se, and heerby may ye preve,	Here you can see that it is proven
That wyf is mannes helpe and his confort,	That a wife is here to help and comfort a man,
His paradys terrestre, and his disport.	She is his earthly paradise, and his pleasure.
So buxom and so vertuous is she,	She is so obedient and good
They moste nedes lyve in unitee.	That they simply have to be united.
O flessh they been, and o fleesh, as I gesse,	They are of the same flesh, and one body, I imagine,
Hath but oon herte, in wele and in distresse.	Only has one heart, in joy or sorrow.
A wyf! a, seinte marie, benedicite!	A wife! Bless me, by St Mary!
How myghte man han any adversitee	How could any man have any troubles
That hath a wyf? certes, I kan nat seye.	If he is married? I certainly can't say.
the blisse which that is bitwixe hem tweye	The happiness that exists between the two of them
Ther may no tonge telle, or herte thynke.	No time can tell, no heart can imagine.
If he be povre, she helpeth hym to swynke;	If he is poor, she helps him with his work;
She kepeth his good, and wasteth never a deel;	She looks after his property, and never wastes anything;
Al that hire housbonde lust, hire liketh weel;	Anything her husband wants, delights her;
She seith nat ones nay, whan he seith ye.	She never says no when he says yes.
Do this, seith he; al redy, sire, seith she.	"Do this," he says; "Everything is ready, Sir," she says.
O blisful ordre of wedlok precious,	Oh happy state of precious marriage,
Thou art so murye, and eek so vertuous,	You are so jolly, and also so good,
And so commended and appreved eek	And so recommended and approved also
That every man that halt hym worth a leek,	That every man who thinks he's worth anything
Upon his bare knees oughte al his lyf	Should go down on his bare knees throughout his life
Thanken his God that hym hath sent a wyf,	To thank God for sending him a wife,
Or elles preye to God hym for to sende	Or otherwise pray to God to send him
A wyf, to laste unto his lyves ende.	A wife to be with him for the rest of his life.
For thanne his lyf is set in sikernesse;	For then his life has security;
He may nat be deceyved, as I gesse,	He cannot be cheated, I think,
So that he werke after his wyves reed.	Providing that he follows his wife's advice.
Thanne may he boldely beren up his heed,	Then he can proudly hold his head high,
They been so trewe, and therwithal so wyse;	For they are so true and also so wise;
For which, if thou wolt werken as the wyse,	So I say, if you want to be like a wise man,
Do alwey so as wommen wol thee rede.	Always do what women tell you.
Lo, how that jacob, as thise clerkes rede,	See how Jacob, as scholars tell us,
By good conseil of his mooder rebekke,	Through the good advice of his mother Rebecca,
Boond the kydes skyn aboute his nekke,	Wrapped the skin of a kid around his neck,
For which his fadres benyson he wan.	And won his father's blessing.
Lo, how that jacob, as thise clerkes rede,	Look how Judith, as the story also tells,
By wys conseil she goddes peple kepte,	Looked after God's people with good advice,
And slow hym olofernus, whil he slepte.	And killed Holofernes while he slept.
Lo abigayl, by good conseil, how she	See how Abigail cleverly
Saved hir housbonde nabal, whan that he	Saved her husband Nabal when he
Sholde han be slayn; and looke, ester also	Should've been killed; see how Esther
By good conseil delyvered out of wo	Cleverly saved the people of God
The peple of god, and made hym mardochee	From their sorrows, and made Mordechai
Of assuere enhaunced for to be.	Praised by Ahasuerus.

Ther nys no thyng in gree superlatyf,	There is nothing to equal,
As seith senek, above and humble wyf.	As Seneca says, a humble wife.
Suffre thy wyves tonge, as catoun bit;	Tolerate your wife's criticism, as Plato orders;
She shal comande, and thou shalt suffren it,	She shall command you, and you will obey,
And yet she wole obeye of curteisye.	But she will still pretend to obey out of politeness.
A wyf is kepere of thyn housbondrye;	A wife is the one who runs your household;
Wel may the sike man biwaille and wepe,	Sick men might well moan and weep,
Ther as ther nys no wyf the hous to kepe.	When they have no wife to keep their house.
I warne thee, if wisely thou wolt wirche,	I warn you, if you want to be wise,
Love wel thy wyf, as crist loved his chirche.	Love your wife well, as Christ loved his church.
If thou lovest thyself, thou lovest thy wyf;	If you love yourself, you love your wife;
No man hateth his flessh, but in his lyf	No man hates his own body, but in his life
He fostreth it, and therfore bidde I thee,	He looks after it, and so I tell you,
Cherisse thy wyf, or thou shalt nevere thee.	Cherish your wife, or you will never prosper.
Housbonde and wyf, what so men jape or pleye,	Husbands and wives, however much men joke about it,
Of worldly folk holden the siker weye;	Are the safest people in the world;
They been so knyt ther may noon harm bityde,	They are so tightly joined no harm can come to them,
And namely upon the wyves syde.	Especially to the wife.
For which this januarie, of whom I tolde,	This is what this January, whom I spoke of,
Considered hath, inwith his dayes olde,	Was thinking of, in his old age,
The lusty lyf, the vertuous quyete,	The happy life, the virtuous peace,
That is in mariage hony-sweete;	That exists in sweet marriage,
And for his freendes on a day he sente,	And one day he sent his friends,
To tellen hem th' effect of his entente.	To tell them what he intended to do.
With face sad his tale he hath hem toold.	He soberly told them his story:
He seyde, freendes, I am hoor and oold,	He said, "Friends, I am grey and old,
And almost, God woot, on my pittes brynke;	And God knows I am almost on the edge of the grave;
Upon my soule somwhat moste I thynke.	I must give consideration to my soul.
I have my body folily despended;	I have foolishly wasted my body;
Blessed be God that it shal been amended!	May God be blessed that he will repair it!
For I wol be, certeyn, a wedded man,	For I am determined to be married,
And that anoon in al the haste I kan.	As quickly as I can,
Unto som mayde fair and tendre of age,	To some fair young maid.
I prey yow, shapeth for my mariage	But seeing as you are in better shape than me,
Al sodeynly, for I wol nat abyde;	You are the ones who can find out more easily
And I wol fonde t' espien, on my syde,	And I will attempt to discover, on my side,
To whom I may be wedded hastily.	Whom it would be best for me to marry.
But forasmuche as ye been mo than I,	But I warn you of one thing, my dear friends,
Ye shullen rather swich a thyng espyen	You shall rather such a thing discover
Than I, and where me best were to allyen.	Than I, and where it would be best to myself
But o thyng warne I yow, my freendes deere,	"But one thing warn I you, my friends,
I wol noon oold wyf han in no manere.	I will in no circumstances take an old wife.
She shal nat passe twenty yeer, certayn;	She must not be more than twenty years old;
Oold fissh and yong flessh wolde I have ful fayn.	I want old fish and young flesh.
Bet is, quod he, a pyk than a pykerel,	A pike is better than a pickerel,
And bet than old boef is the tendre veel.	But tender veal is better than old beef.
I wol no womman thritty yeer of age;	I don't want some thirty-year-old woman;
It is but bene-straw and greet forage.	That is just dry straw and rough forage.

And eek thise olde wydwes, God it woot,	*And also these old widows, God knows,*
They konne so muchel craft on wades boot,	*They have learnt so much trickery,*
So muchel broken harm, whan that hem leste,	*They do so much harm, when they choose,*
That with hem sholde I nevere lyve in reste.	*That I could never live peacefully with them.*
For sondry scoles maken sotile clerkis;	*Clever scholars go to several schools,*
Womman of manye scoles half a clerk is.	*And a woman who has had much schooling is almost a scholar.*
But certeynly, a yong thyng may men gye,	*But certainly one can guide a young girl,*
Right as men may warm wex with handes plye.	*In the same way a man can mould warm wax in his hands.*
Wherfore I sey yow pleynly, in a clause,	*So I'm telling you straight, in brief,*
I wol noon oold wyf han right for this cause.	*For this reason I will not go near an old wife.*
For if so were I hadde swich myschaunce,	*For if it so happened that I had the bad luck*
That I in hire ne koude han no plesaunce,	*Not to be able to take any pleasure from her,*
Thanne sholde I lede my lyf in avoutrye,	*Then I would have to be an adulterer,*
And go streight to the devel, whan I dye.	*And go straight to hell when I died.*
Ne children sholde I none upon hire geten;	*Nor would I get any children through her;*
Yet were me levere houndes hand me eten,	*But I would rather be eaten by the hounds*
Than that myn heritage sholde falle	*Than for my inheritance to fall*
In straunge hand, and this I telle yow alle.	*Into the hands of a stranger, I'm telling you all this.*
I dote nat, I woot the cause why	*I'm not senile; I know why*
Men sholde wedde, and forthermoore woot I,	*One should be married, and furthermore I know*
Ther speketh many a man of mariage	*That many men speak of marriage*
That woot namoore of it than woot my page,	*Who know no more about it than my pageboy,*
For whiche causes man sholde take a wyf.	*They don't know why a man should get married.*
If he ne may nat lyven chaast his lyf,	*If he can't live a chaste life,*
Take hym a wyf with greet devocioun,	*Let him devote himself to his wife,*
By cause of leverful procreacioun	*For the sake of lawful procreation*
Of children, to th' onour of God above,	*Of children in order to honour God,*
And nat oonly for paramour or love;	*Not just for sex or for love;*
And for they sholde leccherye eschue,	*And to keep themselves out of lechery,*
And yelde hir dette whan that it is due;	*And pay the marriage debts when they are due;*
Or for that ech of hem sholde helpen oother	*Also that each of them could help the other*
In meschief, as a suster shal the brother;	*When they are in distress, like a sister will a brother,*
And lyve in chastitee ful holily.	*And live in holy chastity.*
But sires, by youre leve, that am nat I.	*But gentlemen, if you'll excuse me, that wouldn't suit me.*
For, God be thanked! I dar make avaunt,	*For—God be thanked—I dare to boast*
I feele my lymes stark and suffisaunt	*That I can feel my body is strong enough*
To do al that a man bilongeth to;	*To do all the things a man should do;*
I woot myselven best what I may do.	*I know best what I'm capable of.*
Though I be hoor, I fare as dooth a tree	*Even though I'm grey-haired, I'm like a tree*
That blosmeth er that fruyt ywoxen bee;	*That blossoms before the fruit has grown;*
And blosmy tree nys neither drye ne deed.	*And a tree covered in blossom is not dry or dead.*
I feele me nowhere hoor but on myn heed;	*I don't feel grey anywhere except on my head;*
Myn herte and alle my lymes been as grene	*My heart and all my limbs are as green*
As laurer thurgh the yeer is for to sene.	*As the laurel which you see all year round.*
And syn that ye han herd al myn entente,	*And since you've heard what I intend to do,*

I prey yow to my wyl ye wole assente.	I ask you all to agree to it."
Diverse men diversely hym tolde	Different men told him different things,
Of mariage manye ensamples olde.	Telling him many old examples of marriage.
Somme blamed it, somme preysed it, certeyn;	Some criticised it, some certainly praised it,
But atte laste, shortly for to seyn,	But in the end, to say it briefly,
As al day falleth altercacioun	Just as every day disagreements occur
Bitwixen freendes in disputisoun,	Between friends,
Ther fil a stryf bitwixe his bretheren two,	An argument started between his two brothers,
Of whiche that oon was cleped placebo,	One of whom was called Placebo;
Justinus soothly called was that oother.	And the other was named Justinus.
Placebo seyde, o januarie, brother,	Placebo said, "Oh January, my brother,
Ful litel nede hadde ye, my lord so deere,	There was no need for you, my dear lord,
Conseil to axe of any that is heere,	To ask the advice of anyone here,
But that ye been so ful of sapience	Except that you have so much wisdom
That yow ne liketh, for youre heighe prudence,	That with your great sense you did not wish
To weyven fro the word of salomon.	To go against the word of Solomon.
This word seyde he unto us everychon	He said these words to all of us:
Wirk alle thyng by conseil, -- thus seyde he,	'Do everything with agreement,' he said,
-- And thanne shaltow nat repente thee. --	'And then you will not repent it.'
But though that salomon spak swich a word,	But although Solomon said these things,
Myn owene deere brother and my lord,	My own dear brother and my lord,
So wysly God my soule brynge at reste,	I swear on my immortal soul
I holde youre owene conseil is the beste.	That I think your own advice is the best.
For, brother myn, of me taak this motyf,	For, my brother, take this advice from me:
I have now been a court-man al my lyf,	I have been a courtier throughout my life,
And God it woot, though I unworthy be,	And God knows, although I am unworthy,
I have stonden in ful greet degree	I have been raised to a very high position
Abouten lordes of ful heigh estaat;	Amongst all these noble lords;
Yet hadde I nevere with noon of hem debaat.	But I've never disagreed with any of them.
I nevere hem contraried, trewely;	I say truthfully, I have never contradicted them;
I woot wel that my lord kan moore than I.	I'm well aware that my lord knows more than I do.
With that he seith, I holde it ferme and stable;	Whatever he says, I'm sure that that's the truth;
I seye the same, or elles thyng semblable.	I agree, or otherwise say something similar.
A ful greet fool is any conseillour	Any councillor would be a great fool,
That serveth any lord of heigh honour,	If he serves any honourable lord,
That dar presume, or elles thanken it,	To dare to presume, or even think,
That his conseil sholde passe his lordes wit.	That his advice would be better than his lord's.
Nay, lordes been no fooles, by my fay!	Lords are not fools, I swear!
Ye han youreselven shewed heer to-day	You have showed yourselves here today
So heigh sentence, so holily and weel,	To have such great judgement, so holy and good,
That I consente and conferme everydeel	That I agree to every single thing
Youre wordes alle and youre opinioun.	You have said and are thinking.
By god, ther nys no man in al this toun,	By God there is no man in this whole town,
Ne in ytaille, that koude bet han sayd!	Nor in Italy, who could have put it better!
Crist halt hym of this conseil ful wel apayd.	Christ will be very pleased with this counsel.
And trewely, it is an heigh corage	And to speak truthfully, it is a bold act
Of any man that stapen is in age	For any man getting on in years
To take a yong wyf; by my fader kyn,	To take a young wife; by my father's family,
Youre herte hangeth on a joly pyn!	You have a merry heart!
Dooth now in this matiere right as yow leste,	Do exactly as you want to in this matter,

For finally I holde it for the beste.	For I think it will be for the best."
Justinus, that ay stille sat and herde,	Justinus, who had been sitting and listening,
Right in this wise he to placebo answered	Right away answered Placebo in this manner:
Now, brother myn, be pacient, I preye,	"Now, my brother, I pray you, be patient,
Syn ye han seyd, and herkneth what I seye.	You have said your piece, hear what I have to say.
Senek, amonges othere wordes wyse,	Seneca, amongst his other wise words,
Seith that a man oghte hym right wel avyse	Says that a man ought to think very carefully
To whom he yeveth his lond or his catel.	About to whom he is leaving his land and his possessions.
And syn I oghte avyse me right wel	And since one ought to think very carefully
To whom I yeve my good awey from me,	About to whom one hands one's goods,
Wel muchel moore I oghte avysed be	One ought to think even more carefully
To whom I yeve my body for alwey.	About whom one gives one's body for ever.
I warne yow wel, it is no childes pley	I'm warning you, it isn't a children's game
To take a wyf withouten avysement.	To take a wife without thinking about it.
Men moste enquere, this is myn assent,	Men must find out—this is what I think—
Wher she be wys, or sobre, or dronkelewe,	Whether she is wise, sober, or a drunkard,
Or proud, or elles ootherweys a shrewe,	Arrogant, or otherwise a shrew,
A chidestere, or wastour of thy good,	A nagger, or a profligate,
Or riche, or poore, or elles mannyssh wood.	Rich, poor, or crazy for men.
Al be it so that no man fynden shal	Although it is the case that nobody will find
Noon in this world that trotteth hool in al,	Anything in this world that is completely perfect,
Ne man, ne beest, swich as men koude devyse;	There is neither man nor beast that could be that,
But nathelees it oghte ynough suffise	Nevertheless one should try to find
With any wyf, if so were that she hadde	A wife who has
Mo goode thewes than hire vices badde;	More good qualities than bad ones;
And al this axeth leyser for t' enquere.	And this takes time to discover.
For, God it woot, I have wept many a teere	For, God knows, I have wept many tears
Ful pryvely, syn I have had a wyf.	In private, since I've been married.
Preyse whoso wole a wedded mannes lyf,	However much anyone praises married life,
Certein I fynde in it but cost and care	I find nothing in it but cost and care
And observances, of alle blisses bare.	And duties, with no happiness.
And yet, God woot, my neighebores aboute,	And yet, God knows, all my neighbours,
And namely of wommen many a route,	And especially all of the women,
Seyn that I have the mooste stedefast wyf,	Say that I have a wonderful wife,
And eek the mekeste oon that bereth lyf;	And the meekest one alive;
Ye mowe, for me, right as yow liketh do;	But I think I know best where my shoe pinches me. As far as I'm concerned you can do as you please;
Avyseth yow -- ye been a man of age --	But think - you are an old man -
How that ye entren into mariage,	About how you enter into marriage,
And namely with a yong wyf and a fair.	And especially with a young and beautiful wife.
By hym that made water, erthe, and air,	By the one who created water, earth and air,
The yongeste man that is in al this route	The youngest man among us
Is bisy ynough to bryngen it aboute	Has enough trouble trying
To han his wyf allone. Trusteth me,	To cope with his wife. Trust me,
Ye shul nat plesen hire fully yeres thre, --	You won't please her for three years—
This is to seyn, to doon hire ful plesaunce.	Meaning, you won't give her pleasure.
A wyf axeth ful many an observaunce.	A wife needs all your attention.
I prey yow that ye be nat yvele apayd.	Please don't be annoyed with me."

Wel, quod this januarie, and hastow sayd?	"Well," said this January, "have you finished?
Straw for thy senek, and for thy proverbes!	I don't give a damn for Seneca, or your proverbs!
I counte nat a panyer ful of herbes	I wouldn't give a basket full of herbs
Of scole-termes. Wyser men than thow,	For your academic chatter. Wiser men than you,
As thou hast herd, assenteden right now	As you have heard, agreed at once
To my purpos. Placebo, what sey ye?	To my idea. Placebo, what do you say?"
I seye it is a cursed man, quod he,	"I say that a man should be cursed," he said,
That letteth matrimoigne, sikerly.	"if he gets in the way of marriage, certainly."
And with that word they rysen sodeynly,	And with those words they all got up,
And been assented fully that he sholde	And were fully agreed that he should
Be wedded whanne hym liste, and where he wolde.	Be married as and when he pleased.
Heigh fantasye and curious bisynesse	Great fantasies and agitation
Fro day to day gan in the soule impresse	Became daily more embedded in the soul
Of januarie aboute his mariage.	Of January about his marriage.
Many fair shap and many a fair visage	Many fair bodies and many sweet faces
Ther passeth thurgh his herte nyght by nyght,	Passed through his mind night after night,
As whoso tooke a mirour, polisshed bryght,	Like one who took a mirror, polished bright,
And sette it in a commune market-place,	And put it up in the marketplace,
Thanne sholde he se ful many a figure pace	Who would then see many bodies passing
By his mirour; and in the same wyse	Through his mirror; and in the same way
Gan januarie inwith his thoght devyse	January created in his imagination
Of maydens whiche that dwelten hym bisyde.	Fantasies about the girls living around him.
He wiste nat wher that he myghte abyde.	He didn't know which one he might choose;
For if that oon have beaute in hir face,	For if one had a beautiful face,
Another stant so in the peples grace	Another was so praised by the people
For hire sadnesse and hire benyngnytee	For her seriousness and her goodness,
That of the peple grettest voys hath she;	That she had the greatest praise from them;
And somme were riche, and hadden badde name.	And one was rich but had a bad reputation.
But nathelees, bitwixe ernest and game,	But nonetheless, having gone through the lot,
He atte laste apoynted hym on oon,	He at last decided on one,
And leet alle othere from his herte goon,	And let all the others go from his heart,
And chees hire of his owene auctoritee;	And he made her his definite choice;
For love is blynd alday, and may nat see.	For love is always blind, and cannot see.
And whan that he was in his bed ybroght,	And as he lay there in his bed,
He purtreyed in his herte and in his thoght	He pictured in his heart and his thoughts
Hir fresshe beautee and hir age tendre,	Her fresh beauty and her young age,
Hir myddel smal, hire armes longe and sklendre,	Her tiny waist, her long slender arms,
Hir wise governaunce, hir gentillesse,	Her sober behaviour, her nobility,
Hir wommanly berynge, and hire sadnesse.	Her womanly carriage, and her seriousness.
And whan that he on hire was condescended,	And when he had definitely chosen her,
Hym thoughte his choys myghte nat ben amended.	He thought that his choice could not be bettered.
For whan that he hymself concluded hadde,	Once he had decided for himself,
Hym thoughte ech oother mannes wit so badde	He thought everyone else was so foolish
That inpossible it were to repplye	That it would be impossible for them to argue
Agayn his choys, this was his fantasye.	With his choice; this is what he imagined.
His freendes sente he to, at his instaunce,	He sent for his friends, insisting
And preyed hem to doon hym that plesaunce,	That they would give him the pleasure
That hastily they wolden to hym come;	Of coming to him at once;
He wolde abregge hir labour, alle and some.	He would recompense their labour, all of them.
Nedeth namoore for hym to go ne ryde;	He didn't need to travel around any more;

He was apoynted ther he wolde abyde.	He had decided on his choice.
Placebo cam, and eek his freendes soone,	Placebo came, and also his other friends,
And alderfirst he bad hem alle a boone,	And firstly he asked them all for a favour,
That noon of hem none argumentes make	That none of them would start any arguments
Agayn the purpos which that he hath take,	Against the choice which he had made,
Which purpos was plesant to god, seyde he,	Which he said was very pleasing to God,
And verray ground of his prosperitee.	And would be the basis of his good fortune.
He seyde ther was a mayden in the toun,	He said that there was a maiden in the town,
Which that of beautee hadde greet renoun,	Who was very famous for her beauty,
Al were it so she were of smal degree;	Even though she was of humble birth;
Suffiseth hym hir yowthe and hir beautee.	Her youth and her beauty were enough for him.
Which mayde, he seyde, he wolde han to his wyf,	He said he would have this maiden for his wife,
To lede in ese and hoolynesse his lyf;	And they would live a peaceful and holy life together;
And thanked God that he myghte han hire al,	And he thanked God that he could have her all to himself,
That no wight his blisse parten shal.	So that nobody would share in his happiness.
And preyed hem to laboure in this nede,	He asked them all to work for him,
And shapen that he faille nat to spede;	And make sure that he had success;
For thanne, he seyde, his spirit was at ese.	For then, he said, his spirit would be at ease.
Thanne is, quod he, no thyng may me displese,	"Then," he said, "nothing would displease me,
Save o thyng priketh in my conscience,	Except for one thing which sticks in my conscience,
The which I wol reherce in youre presence.	Which I will tell you about now you're all here.
I have, quod he, herd seyd, ful yoore ago,	I have," he said, "heard it said, long ago,
Ther may no man han parfite blisses two, --	That no man can be perfectly happy twice–
This is to seye, in erthe and eek in hevene.	That is to say, on Earth and also in heaven.
For though he kepe hym fro the synnes sevene,	Even if he keeps himself from the seven sins,
And eek from every branche of thilke tree,	Right away from every part of that tree,
Yet is ther so parfit felicitee	There is such perfect happiness
And so greet ese and lust in mariage,	And such satisfaction and pleasure in marriage
That evere I am agast now in myn age	That I am worried that in my old age
That I shal lede now so myrie a lyf,	I will now have such a happy life,
So delicat, withouten wo and stryf,	So wonderful, without sorrow or strife,
That I shal have myn hevene in erthe heere.	That I will be given my heaven here on earth.
For sith that verray hevene is boght so deere	Since the true heaven is paid for so dearly
With tribulation and greet penaunce,	With suffering and great penance,
How sholde I thanne, that lyve in swich plesaunce	How would I, living with such pleasure,
As alle wedded men doon with hire wyvys,	As all married men do with their wives,
Come to the blisse ther crist eterne on lyve ys?	Find happiness with Christ in eternity?
This is my drede, and ye, my bretheren tweye,	This is what I dread, and you, my two brothers,
Assoilleth me this question, I preye.	Help me with this problem, I beg you."
Justinus, which that hated his folye,	Justinus, who hated his foolishness,
Answerde anon right in his japerye;	Answered straight away by mocking him;
And for he wolde his longe tale abregge,	And because he wanted to keep his words short,
He wolde noon auctoritee allegge,	He wouldn't quote any authorities,
But seyde, sire, so ther be noon obstacle	But he said, "Sir, if this is the only obstacle

Oother than this, God of his hygh myracle	You have, God through his great miracles
And of his mercy may so for yow wirche	And through his mercy could work for you
That, er ye have youre right of hooly chirche,	So that before you receive the last sacrament
Ye may repente of wedded mannes lyf,	You will repent having been married,
In which ye seyn ther is no wo ne stryf.	Even though you think there will be nothing to repent.
And elles, God forbede but he sente	Otherwise, God forbid that he would not send
A wedded man hym grace to repente	A married man the ability to repent
Wel ofte rather than a sengle man!	More than he would a single man!
And therfore, sire -- the beste reed I kan --	And so, sir, this is the best advice I can give,
Dispeire yow noght, but have in youre memorie,	Do not despair, but always remember,
Paraunter she may be youre purgatorie!	Perhaps she will prove to be your Purgatory!
She may be goddes meene and goddes whippe;	She might be the instrument of God, his whip,
Thanne shal youre soule up to hevene skippe	So then your soul would fly up to heaven
Swifter than dooth and arwe out of bowe.	Quicker than an arrow from a bow.
I hope to god, herafter shul ye knowe	I hope to God, that afterwards you will know
That ther nys no so greet felicitee	That there is not such great happiness
In mariage, ne nevere mo shal bee,	In marriage, and there never will be,
That yow shal lette of youre savacion,	Not enough to keep you from your salvation,
So that ye sue, as skile is an reson,	Providing that you use, sensibly and wisely,
The lustes of youre wyf attemprely,	The pleasures of your wife temperately,
And that ye plese hire nat to amorously,	Not giving her too much sensual pleasure,
And that ye kepe yow eek from oother synne.	And also keeping yourself from other sins.
My tale is doon, for my wit is thynne.	That's all I have to say, I don't have great wit.
Beth nat agast herof, my brother deere,	Don't worry about this, my dear brother,
But lat us waden out of this mateere.	Let's forget about this matter.
The wyf of bethe, if ye han understonde,	The wife of Bath, if you have understood correctly,
Of mariage, which we have on honde,	Has said all that needs to be said
Declared hath ful wel in litel space.	About marriage, as we speak of it.
Fareth now wel, God have yow in his grace.	Now farewell. May God protect you."
And with this word this justyn and his brother	And having said this Justinus and his brother
Han take hir leve, and ech of hem of oother.	Left him, and parted from each other.
For whan they saughe that it moste nedes be,	For when they saw it was bound to happen,
They wroghten so, by sly and wys tretee,	They arranged matters, with secret and clever negotiations,
That she, this mayden, which that mayus highte,	So that this maiden, who was called May,
As hastily as evere that she myghte,	Might be as quickly as possible
Shal wedded be unto this januarie.	Married to this January.
I trowe it were to longe yow to tarie,	I think it would bore you
If I yow tolde of every scrit and bond	If I told you of every document and bond
By which that she was feffed in his lond,	Which endowed her with his land,
Or for to herknen of hir riche array.	Or told you all about her rich clothing.
But finally ycomen is the day	But finally the day came
That to the chirche bothe be they went	That they both went to church
For to receyve the hooly sacrament.	To be married.
Forth comth the preest, with stole aboute his nakke,	The priest came out, with his stole around his neck,
And bad hire be lyk sarra and rebekke	And ordered her to be like Sarah and Rebecca,
In wysdom and in trouthe of mariage;	In wisdom and in faithfulness;
And seyde his orisons, as is usage,	And he said his prayers, as is customary,
And croucheth hem, and bad God sholde hem blesse,	And made the sign of the cross, and asked God to bless them,
And made al siker ynogh with hoolynesse.	And made everything secure and holy.

Thus been they wedded with solempnitee,	So they were solemnly married,
And at the feeste sitteth he and she	And they sat at the feast,
With othere worthy folk upon the deys.	With other noble folk on the dais.
Al ful of joye and blisse is the paleys,	The palace was full of joy and happiness,
And ful of instrumentz and of vitaille,	And music and food,
The mooste deyntevous of al ytaille.	The loveliest in all of Italy.
Biforn hem stoode instrumentz of swich soun	In front of them there were instruments playing sounds
That orpheus, ne of thebes amphioun,	That Orpheus, nor Amphioun of Thebes,
Ne maden nevere swich a melodye.	Had never produced themselves.
At every cours thanne cam loud mynstralcye,	With every course there came loud singing
That nevere trompede joab for to heer,	Better than Joab ever heard,
Nor he theodomas, yet half so cleere,	Nor did Theodomas, half as clearly,
At thebes, whan the citee was in doute.	At Thebes when the city was in danger.
Bacus the wyn hem shynketh al aboute,	Bacchus poured out the wine for them,
And venus laugheth upon every wight,	And Venus smiled on every person,
For januarie was bicome hir knyght,	For January had become her knight,
And wolde bothe assayen his corage	And she would put him to the test
In libertee, and eek in mariage;	In freedom, and also marriage;
And with hire fyrbrond in hire hand aboute	And carrying her torch in her hand
Dauncheth biforn the bryde and al the route.	She danced in front of the bride and everyone there.
And certeinly, I dar right wel seyn this,	And certainly, I can say this,
Ymeneus, that God of weddyng is,	Hymen, who is the God of marriage,
Saugh nevere his lyf so myrie a wedded man.	Never saw such a happy married man in his life.
Hoold thou thy pees, thou poete marcian,	Hold your peace, you poet Marcian,
That writest us that ilke weddyng murie	Who wrote about the same merry wedding
Of hire philologie and hym mercurie,	Of Philology and Mercury,
And of the songes that the muses songe!	And of the song that the Muses sang!
To smal is bothe thy penen, and eek thy tonge,	Your pen and also your tongue are too weak
For to descryven of this mariage.	To describe this marriage.
Whan tendre youthe hath wedded stoupyng age,	When tender youth has been wedded to stooping age,
Ther is swich myrthe that it may nat be writen.	There's such happiness that it cannot be written.
Assayeth it youreself, thanne may ye witen	Try it yourself; then you will know
If that I lye or noon in this matiere.	If I'm telling the truth in this matter.
Mayus, that sit with so benyngne a chiere,	May sat there looking so kindly
Hire to biholde it semed fayerye.	That it seemed she was a fairy.
Queene ester looked nevere with swich an ye	Queen Esther never looked the same way
On assuer, so meke a look hath she.	On Ahasuerus, she looks so meek.
I may yow nat devyse al hir beautee.	I can't describe her beauty to you.
But thus muche of hire beautee telle I may,	But I can tell you this much about it,
That she was lyk the brighte morwe of may,	That she was like a bright May morning,
Fulfild of alle beautee and plesaunce.	Filled with beauty and delight.
This januarie is ravysshed in a traunce	January was absolutely entranced,
At every tyme he looked on hir face;	Every time he looked on her face;
But in his herte he gan hire to manace	But in his heart he began to plan
That he that nyght in armes wolde hire streyne	That at night he would squeeze her in his arms
Harder than evere parys dide eleyne.	Harder than Paris ever did Helen of Troy.
But nathelees yet hadde he greet pitee	But nevertheless he was very sad

That thilke nyght offenden hire moste he,	That in the night he would have to offend her,
And thoughte, allas! o tendre creature,	And he thought, "Alas! You tender creature,
Now wolde God ye myghte wel endure	I hope to God that you can withstand
Al my corage, it is so sharp and keene!	All my passion, it's so sharp and keen!
I am agast ye shul it nat sustene.	I'm afraid that you won't be able to cope with it.
But God forbede that I dide al my myght!	But God forbid that I should hold back!
Now wolde God that it were woxen nyght,	Now I wish to God that it were night,
And that the nyght wolde lasten everemo.	And that the night would last forever.
I wolde that al this peple were ago.	I wish all these people would go away."
And finally he dooth al his labour,	And finally he did all he could,
As he best myghte, savynge his honour,	As well as he could, as far as honour permitted,
To haste hem fro the mete in subtil wyse.	To subtly hurry them away from the dinner.
The tyme cam that resoun was to ryse;	The time came when it was reasonable to leave the table;
And after that men daunce and drynken faste,	And after that men danced and drank plenty,
And spices al aboute the hous they caste,	And passed spicy cakes around the house,
And ful of joye and blisse is every man, --	And every man was full of joy and happiness—
Al but a squyer, highte damyan,	Except for a squire, called Damien,
Which carf biforn the knyght ful many a day.	Who had often carved for the knight.
He was so ravysshed on his lady may	He was so taken with his lady May
That for the verray peyne he was ny wood.	That he was nearly mad with pain.
Almoost he swelte and swowned ther he stood,	He almost fainted and fell down on the spot,
So soore hath venus hurt hym with hire brond,	Venus had touched him so painfully with her torch,
As that she bar it daunsynge in hire hond;	As she carried it in her hand as she danced;
And to his bed he wente hym hastily.	He went swiftly to his bed.
Namoore of hym as at this tyme speke I,	I won't say any more about him now,
But there I lete hym wepe ynogh and pleyne,	But I'll leave him there weeping and moaning
Til fresshe may wol rewen on his peyne.	Until fresh May takes pity on his pain.
O perilous fyr, that in the bedstraw bredeth!	What a dangerous fire burns in bed straw!
O famulier foo, that his servyce bedeth!	What enemies one can have amongst one's servants!
O servant traytour, false hoomly hewe,	You traitorous servant, you false domestic,
Lyk to the naddre in bosom sly untrewe,	You are like a sly and faithless adder in the heart,
God shilde us alle from youre aqueyntaunce!	May God protect us all from knowing you!
O januarie, dronken in plesaunce	Oh January, drunk with pleasure,
In mariage, se how thy damyan,	About your marriage, see how your Damian,
Thyn owene squier and thy borne man,	Your own squire and your servant from birth,
Entendeth for to do thee vileynye.	Intends to do you wrong.
God graunte thee thyn hoomly fo t' espye!	May God give you the strength to see the enemy in your house!
For in this world nys worse pestilence	There is nothing worse in the world
Than hoomly foo al day in thy presence.	Than an enemy in the household, for they are always with you.
Parfourned hath the sonne his ark diurne;	The sun had finished its daily journey;
No lenger may the body of hym sojurne	No longer did his body rest
On th' orisonte, as in that latitude.	On the horizon, at that place.
Night with his mantel, that is derk and rude,	The cloak of night, that is dark and rough,
Gan oversprede the hemysperie aboute;	Began to spread over the hemisphere;
For which departed is this lusty route	And so the cheerful crowd went away
Fro januarie, with thank on every syde.	From January, with everyone thanking him.

Hoom to hir houses lustily they ryde,	They cheerfully rode home to their houses,
Where as they doon hir thynges as hem leste,	Where they did whatever they pleased,
And whan they sye hir tyme, goon to reste.	And went to bed when the time is right.
Soone after than, this hastif januarie	Soon after that, impatient January
Wolde go to bedde, he wolde no lenger tarye.	Wanted to go to bed; he could no longer wait.
He drynketh ypocras, clarree, and vernage	He had drunk mulled wine, claret and white wine,
Of spices hoote, t' encreessen his corage;	With hot spices to help his passion;
And many a letuarie hath he ful fyn,	And he had many fine aphrodisiacs,
Swiche as the cursed monk, daun constantyn,	Like the ones the cursed monk, Dan Constantine,
Hath writen in his book de coitu;	Had written about in his book, "On Sex";
To eten hem alle he nas no thyng eschu.	He tried every one of them.
And to his privee freendes thus seyde he	To his closest confidants he said:
For goddes love, as soone as it may be,	"For the love of God as soon as possible,
Lat voyden al this hous in curteys wyse.	Politely get everyone out of this house."
And they han doon right as he wol devyse.	And they did exactly as he asked.
Men drynken, and the travers drawe anon.	Men drank and drew the curtain across the room at once.
The bryde was broght abedde as stille as stoon;	The bride was brought to bed as still as stone,
And whan the bed was with the preest yblessed,	And when the bed had been blessed by the priest,
Out of the chambre hath every wight hym dressed;	Everyone left the room,
And januarie hath faste in armes take	And January clasped his arms around
His fresshe may, his paradys, his make.	His fresh May, his paradise, his mate.
He lulleth hire, he kisseth hire ful ofte;	He rocked her; he kissed her often;
With thikke brustles of his berd unsofte,	With the bristles of his beard pricking her,
Lyk to the skyn of houndfyssh, sharp as brere --	Like dogfish skin, as sharp as brambles,
For he was shave al newe in his manere --	For he was freshly shaved in his own way—
He rubbeth hire aboute hir tendre face,	He robbed them all over her tender face,
And seyde thus, allas! I moot trespace	And said, "Alas! I must harm
To yow, my spouse, and yow greetly offende,	You, my wife, and greatly offend you
Er tyme come that I wil doun descende.	Before I give up my passion.
But nathelees, considereth this, quod he,	But nonetheless, think of this," he said,
Ther nys no werkman, whatsoevere he be,	"There is no workman, whoever he is,
That may bothe werke wel and hastily;	Who can do good work if he hurries;
This wol be doon at leyser parfitly.	We shall take our time and do it perfectly.
It is no fors how longe that we pleye;	It doesn't matter how long we go on;
In trewe wedlok coupled be we tweye;	We are joined in true wedlock,
And blessed be the yok that we been inne,	And so we are in a blessed state,
For in oure actes we mowe do no synne.	And whatever we do is not a sin.
A man may do no synne with his wyf,	A man cannot commit a sin with his wife,
Ne hurte hymselven with his owene knyf;	Nor hurt himself with his own knife,
For we han leve to pleye us by the lawe.	For the law says that we can have fun."
Thus laboureth he til that the day gan dawe;	So he worked away until the morning came;
And thanne he taketh a sop in fyn clarree,	Then he had some bread soaked in fine claret,
And upright in his bed thanne sitteth he,	And then he sat upright in his bed,
And after that he sang ful loude and cleere,	And sang loudly and clearly,
And kiste his wyf, and made wantown cheere	And kissed his wife, and was very saucy.
He was al coltissh, ful of ragerye,	He was like a colt, full of lust,
And ful of jargon as a flekked pye.	And chattering away like a speckled magpie.
The slakke skyn aboute his nekke shaketh,	The loose skin around his neck shook
Whil that he sang, so chaunteth he and craketh.	While he sang, he was chanting and croaking so much.

But God woot what that may thoughte in hir herte,	But God knows what May was thinking in her heart,
Whan she hym saugh up sittynge in his sherte,	When she saw him sitting up in his shirt,
In his nyght-cappe, and with his nekke lene;	And his nightcap, with his skinny neck;
She preyseth nat his pleyyng worth a bene.	She didn't think all his lovemaking was worth a bean.
Thanne seide he thus, my reste wol I take;	Then he said, "Now I will have a rest;
Now day is come, I may no lenger wake.	Now morning is here, I can't stay awake."
And doun he leyde his heed, and sleep til pryme.	And he put his head down and slept until midday.
And afterward, whan that he saugh his tyme,	And afterwards, when he saw the time was right,
Up ryseth januarie; but fresshe may	January got up; but fresh May
Heeld hire chambre unto the fourthe day,	Stayed in her room until four days later,
As usage is of wyves for the beste.	As the best wives do, by tradition.
For every labour somtyme moot han reste,	For every labourer must have rest sometimes,
Or elles longe may he nat endure;	Otherwise he will not live long;
This is to seyn, no lyves creature,	I mean, no living creature can,
Be it of fyssh, or bryd, or beest, or man.	Whether it is a fish, bird, beast or man.
Now wol I speke of woful damyan,	Now I will speak of sorrowful Damian,
That langwissheth for love, as ye shul heere;	Who is suffering for love, as you shall hear;
Therfore I speke to hym in this manere	So I will say this about him:
I seye, o sely damyan, allas!	I say, "Oh innocent Damien, alas!
Andswere to my demaunde, as in this cas.	Answer my question, in this matter.
How shaltow to thy lady, fresshe may,	How will you tell your lady, fresh May,
Telle thy wo? she wole alwey seye nay.	All your sorrow? She will always refuse you.
Eek if thou speke, she wol thy wo biwreye.	Also if you speak to her, she will betray you.
God be thyn helpe! I kan no bettre seye.	May God help you! That's all I can say."
This sike damyan in venus fyr	This sick Damien was burning so badly
So brenneth that he dyeth for desyr,	In the fire of Venus that he was dying with desire,
For which he putte his lyf in aventure.	And he was willing to risk his life.
No lenger myghte he in this wise endure,	He could no longer stand the pain,
But prively a penner gan he borwe,	But he secretly borrowed a pen,
And in a lettre wroot he al his sorwe,	And wrote down all his sorrows in a letter,
In manere of a compleynt or a lay,	As a poem, a lament or a song,
Unto his faire, fresshe lady may;	To his fair fresh lady May;
And in a purs of sylk, heng on his sherte	And in a silk purse which hung on his shirt
He hath it put, and leyde it at his herte.	He put it, next to his heart.
The moone, that at noon was thilke day	The moon, which was full the day
That januarie hath wedded fresshe may	That January married fresh May
In two of tawr, was into cancre glyden;	Had moved through Taurus and into Cancer,
So longe hath mayus in hir chambre abyden,	May had stayed in her room for so long,
As custume is unto thise nobles alle.	As is customary for these noble women.
A bryde shal nat eten in the halle	A bride cannot eat in the hall
Til dayes foure, or thre dayes atte leeste,	Until four days have passed, or at least three,
Ypassed been; thanne lat hire go to feeste.	Then she can join the company.
The fourthe day compleet fro noon to noon,	The fourth day was passed, noon to noon,
Whan that the heighe masse was ydoon,	When high mass was finished,
In halle sit this januarie and may,	And January and May sat in the hall,
As fressh as is the brighte someres day.	Fresh as a bright summer's day.
And so bifel how that this goode man	And so happened that this good man
Remembred hym upon this damyan,	Thought about Damien,

And seyde, seynte marie! how may this be,	And said, "By St Mary! Why is it
That damyan entendeth nat to me?	That Damien is not serving me?
Is he ay syk, or how may this bityde?	Is he sick, or what has happened?"
His squieres, whiche that stooden ther bisyde,	His squires, who were standing near him,
Excused hym by cause of his siknesse,	Excused him, saying he was sick,
Which letted hym to doon his bisynesse;	And they said they stopped him doing his duty;
Noon oother cause myghte make hym tarye.	There was no other reason he would not be there.
That me forthynketh, quod this januarie,	"I'm sorry to hear that," said this January,
He is a gentil squier, by my trouthe!	"He is a good squire, I swear!
If that he deyde, it were harm and routhe.	If he died, it would be a great shame.
He is as wys, discreet, and as secree	He is as wise, discreet and as trustworthy
As any man I woot of his degree,	As any man I know of his rank,
And therto manly, and eek servysable.	And he is also manly, and hard-working,
And for to been a thrifty man right able.	And really a proper good man.
But after mete, as soone as evere I may,	After dinner, as soon as I can,
I wol myself visite hym, and eek may,	I'll go myself, and also May,
To doon hym al the confort that I kan.	To bring him any comfort I can."
And for that word hym blessed every man,	So saying that every man blessed him,
That of his bountee and his gentillesse	For the fact that through his kind goodness
He wolde so conforten in siknesse	He would think about comforting
His squier, for it was a gentil dede.	His ill squire, for it was a good deed.
Dame, quod this januarie, taak good hede,	"My lady," said this January, "pay attention,
At after-mete ye with youre wommen alle,	When you and all of your women go out
Whan ye han been in chambre out of this halle,	Of this hall to your room after dinner,
That alle ye go se this damyan.	All of you must go and see this Damian.
Dooth hym disport -- he is a gentil man;	Cheer him up—he's a good man;
And telleth hym that I wol hym visite,	And tell him that I will visit him,
Have I no thyng but rested me a lite;	When I have had a little rest;
And spede yow faste, for I wole abyde	And be quick about it, for I shall be waiting
Til that ye slepe faste by my syde.	Until you are lying by my side."
And with that word he gan to hym to calle	And having said that, he called up
A squier, that was marchal of his halle,	A squire, who was the marshall of his hall,
And tolde hym certeyn thynges, what he wolde.	And told him about certain things he wanted.
This fresshe may hath streight hir wey yholde,	Fresh May went straight
With alle hir wommen, unto damyan.	To Damien with the other women.
Doun by his beddes syde sit she than,	She sat down by his bedside,
Confortynge hym as goodly as she may.	Comforting him as kindly as she could.
This damyan, whan that his tyme he say,	This Damian, when he saw his chance,
In secree wise his purs and eek his bille,	Secretly took his purse and his letter,
In which that he ywriten hadde his wille,	In which he had written down his desires,
Hath put into hire hand, withouten moore,	And put it into her hand, that was all,
And softely to hire right thus seyde he	Apart from giving a tremendously deep sigh, And softly saying to her:
Mercy! and that ye nat discovere me,	"Show me mercy! And please don't betray me,
For I am deed if that this thyng be kyd.	For I am dead if this is discovered."
This purs hath she inwith hir bosom hyd,	She hid the purse in her bosom,
And wente hire wey; ye gete namoore of me.	And went on her way; that's all I shall say of that.
But unto januarie ycomen is she,	But she came in to January,
That on his beddes syde sit ful softe.	Who was sitting waiting on the side of his bed.
He taketh hire, and kisseth hire ful ofte,	He took her, and kissed her often,
And leyde hym doun to slepe, and that anon.	And laid down to sleep, straight away.

She feyned hire as that she moste gon Ther as ye woot that every wight moot neede;	She pretended she had to go To the place where everyone sometimes has to go,
And whan she of this bille hath taken heede, She rente it al to cloutes atte laste, And in the pryvee softely it caste.	And when she had absorbed this letter She tore it all into pieces, And quietly threw it down the toilet.
Who studieth now but faire fresshe may? Adoun by olde januarie she lay, That sleep til that the coughe hath hym awaked. Anon he preyde hire strepen hire al naked; He wolde of hire, he seyde, han som plesaunce, And seyde hir clothes dide hym encombraunce, And she obeyeth, be hire lief or looth. But lest that precious folk be with me wrooth, How that he wroghte, I dar nat to yow telle; Or wheither hire thoughte it paradys or helle.	Who is now confused if not fair fresh May? She lay down by old January, Who slept until his cough woke him up. At once he asked her to strip naked; He wanted some pleasure from her, he said; He said her clothes were an encumbrance, And she obeyed, whether she wanted to or not. But in case prudish people are angry with me, I do not tell you what he got up to, Or whether she thought it was paradise or hell.
But heere I lete hem werken in hir wyse Til evensong rong, and that they moste aryse.	I'll let them go on in their own way Until the bell for Evensong rang, and they had to get up.
Were it by destynee or aventure, Were it by influence or by nature,	Whether it was fate or chance, The influence of the stars, or the natural order of things,
Or constellacion, that in swich estaat The hevene stood, that tyme fortunaat Was for to putte a bille of venus werkes -- For alle thyng hath tyme, as seyn thise clerkes --	Or the way the stars stood, in such a way That heaven was favourable at that time To a petition concerning the work of love— For there is a time for everything, the scholars say—
To any womman, for to gete hire love, I kan nat seye; but grete God above, That knoweth that noon act is causeless, He deme of al, for I wole hole my pees. But sooth is this, how that this fresshe may Hath take swich impression that day Of pitee of this sike damyan, That from hire herte she ne dryve kan The remembrance for to doon hym ese. Certeyn, thoghte she, whom that this thyng displese,	For a woman to get her love, I cannot say; but Almighty God, Who knows everything that happens, Can be the judge of it, I will say nothing. But the truth is, this fresh May Had been so filled on that day With pity for this sick Damien That she could not drive out The desire to comfort him from her heart. "Certainly," she thought, "whomever this might upset,
I rekke noght, for heere I hym assure To love hym best of any creature, Though he namoore hadde than his sherte. Lo, pitee renneth soone in gentil herte! Heere may ye se how excellent franchise In wommen is, whan they hem narwe avyse. Som tyrant is, as ther be many oon,	I don't care, for I now promise I will love him more than any other creature, However poor he might be." This is how pity affects a kind heart! Here you can see the great generosity That women have, when they think about it. There are some tyrants, there are many of them,
That hath an herte as hard as any stoon, Which wolde han lat hym sterven in the place Wel rather than han graunted hym hire grace; And hem rejoysen in hire crueel pryde,	Who have hearts as hard as stone, Who would rather have let him die there Than show him any kindness, And they would have rejoiced in her cruelty if he had,
And rekke nat to been an homycide.	And wouldn't care that it was murder.

This gentil may, fulfilled of pitee,	*This kind May, full of pity,*
Right of hire hand a lettre made she,	*Wrote a letter in her own hand,*
In which she graunteth hym hire verray grace.	*In which she gave him her true kindness.*
Ther lakketh noght, oonly but day and place,	*All that was lacking was a day and a place*
Wher that she myghte unto his lust suffise;	*When she could satisfy his desire,*
For it shal be right as he wole devyse.	*For she would do just as he wished.*
And whan she saugh hir tyme, upon a day,	*And when she saw a chance, one day,*
To visite this damyan gooth may,	*May went to visit this Damian,*
And sotilly this lettre doun she threste	*And craftily pushed the letter down*
Under his pilwe, rede it if hym leste.	*Under his pillow; let him read it if he wants.*
She taketh hym by the hand, and harde hym twiste	*She took his hand and squeezed it hard,*
So secrely that no wight of it wiste,	*Secretly so that nobody saw it,*
And bad hym been al hool, and forth she wente	*And told him to get well, and went out*
To januarie, whan that he for hire sente.	*To January, when he sent for her.*
Up riseth damyan the nexte morwe;	*Damian got up the next morning,*
Al passed was his siknesse and his sorwe.	*With all his sickness and his sorrow gone.*
He kembeth hym, he preyneth hym and pyketh,	*He combed his hair, he preened and pricked himself,*
He dooth al that his lady lust and lyketh;	*He did everything that his lady would like,*
And eek to januarie he gooth as lowe	*And also he went to January as humbly*
As evere dide a dogge for the bowe.	*As any hunting dog ever did.*
He is so plesant unto every man	*He was so pleasant to every man*
(for craft is al, whoso that do it kan)	*(For cunningness is everything, if you can do it)*
That every wight is fayn to speke hym good;	*So that everyone was eager to speak well of him,*
And fully in his lady grace he stood.	*And he was completely in his lady's favour.*
Thus lete I damyan aboute his nede,	*So I shall leave Damian to do his business,*
And in my tale forth I wol procede.	*And carry on with my story.*
Somme clerkes holden that felicitee	*Some scholars think that happiness*
Stant in delit, and therfore certeyn he,	*Is made of only pleasure, and certainly he,*
This noble januarie, with al his myght,	*This noble January, with all his might,*
In honest wyse, as longeth to a knyght,	*In a respectable fashion, as appropriate for a knight,*
Shoop hym to lyve ful deliciously.	*Arranged for himself to have a luxurious life.*
His housynge, his array, as honestly	*His house, his clothes were as fine*
To his degree was maked as a kynges.	*As those suited to a king.*
Amonges othere of his honeste thynges,	*Among other good things he had,*
He made a gardyn, walled al with stoon;	*He made a garden, walled around with stone;*
So fair a gardyn woot I nowher noon.	*I've never heard of such a lovely garden anywhere else.*
For, out of doute, I verraily suppose	*I am certain, I really think*
That he that wroot the romance of the rose	*That the person who wrote the Romance of the Rose*
Ne koude of it the beautee wel devyse;	*Would not be able to describe the beauty of it;*
Ne priapus ne myghte nat suffise,	*Nor would Priapus be adequate,*
Though he be God of gardyns, for to telle	*Even though he is the god of gardens, to describe*
The beautee of the gardyn and the welle,	*The beauty of the garden and the well*
That stood under a laurer alwey grene.	*That stood under a flourishing green laurel.*
Ful ofte tyme he pluto and his queene,	*Often Pluto and his queen*
Proserpina, and al hire fayerye,	*Proserpine, and all their fairies,*
Disporten hem and maken melodye	*Amused themselves and sang*
Aboute that welle, and daunced, as men tolde.	*Around that well, and danced, so men said.*

This noble knyght, this januarie the olde,	This noble knight, this ancient January,
Swich deyntee hath in it to walke and pleye,	Took such pleasure from walking there
That he wol no wight suffren bere the keye	That he would not allow anyone to hold the key
Save he hymself; for of the smale wyket	Except for himself; he always carried a silver latchkey
He baar alwey of silver a clyket,	To the small gate,
With which, whan that hym leste, he it unshette.	Which he used to unlock it when he wished.
And whan he wolde paye his wyf hir dette	And when he wanted to give his wife her conjugal rights
In somer seson, thider wolde he go,	In the days of summer, he would go there,
And may his wyf, and no wight but they two;	With May his wife, just the two of them;
And thynges whiche that were nat doon abedde,	And anything he hadn't done in bed
He in the gardyn parfourned hem and spedde.	He did with her in the garden.
And in this wyse, many a murye day,	So in this way, for many merry days,
Lyved this januarie and fresshe may.	Lived this January and fresh May.
But worldly joye may nat alwey dure	But worldly pleasure will not last forever
To januarie, ne to creature.	For January, or for any other creature.
O sodeyn hap! o thou fortune unstable!	Oh cruel chance! Unstable fortune!
Lyk to the scorpion so deceyvable,	You're like the deceitful scorpion,
That flaterest with thyn heed whan thou wolt stynge;	Who shows his head when he's going to sting;
Thy tayl is deeth, thurgh thyn envenymynge.	Your tail is death, through your poison.
O brotil joye! o sweete venym queynte!	What brittle joy! What sweet subtle poison!
O monstre, that so subtilly kanst peynte	You monster, who can so cunningly disguise
Thy yiftes under hewe of stidefastnesse,	Your gifts by looking loyal,
That thou deceyvest bothe moore and lesse!	You who deceives everyone!
Why hastow januarie thus deceyved,	Why have you deceived January like this,
That haddest hym for thy fulle freend receyved?	When you had treated him like your closest friend?
And now thou hast biraft hym bothe his ye,	And now you have taken away his eyes,
For sorwe of which desireth he to dyen.	And made him so sad that he would like to die.
Allas! this noble januarie free,	Alas, this noble generous January,
Amydde his lust and his prosperitee,	Amidst all his pleasure and prosperity,
Is woxen blynd, and that al sodeynly,	Became blind, it happened suddenly.
He wepeth and he wayleth pitously;	He wept and wailed pitifully;
And therwithal the fyr of jalousie,	And also burned with jealousy,
Lest that his wyf sholde falle in som folye,	In case his wife should get up to no good,
So brente his herte that he wolde fayn	His heart burned so badly he truly wished
That som man bothe hire and hym had slayn.	That somebody had killed both him and her.
For neither after his deeth, nor in his lyf,	For neither after his death nor in his life
Ne wolde he that she were love ne wyf,	Did he want her to be lover nor wife to anyone else,
But evere lyve as wydwe in clothes blake,	He wanted her to live as a black cloaked widow always,
Soul as the turtle that lost hath hire make,	As alone as a turtle dove who has lost her mate.
But atte laste, after a month or tweye	But at last, after a month or two,
His sorwe gan aswage, sooth to seye;	I can truthfully say his sorrow began to abate;
For whan he wiste it may noon oother be,	When he knew that there was nothing to be done
He paciently took his adversitee,	He patiently accepted his trials,
Save, out of doute, he may nat forgoon	Except that, certainly, he couldn't give up
That he nas jalous everemoore in oon;	Getting more and more jealous constantly;
Which jalousye it was so outrageous,	His jealousy was so great

That neither in halle, n' yn noon oother hous,	That he would not let her ride or walk,
Ne in noon oother place, neverthemo,	In the hall, nor in any other house,
He nolde suffre hire for to ryde or go,	Nor in any other place,
But if that he had hond on hire alway;	Unless he always had a hand resting on her;
For which ful ofte wepeth fresshe may,	And because of this fresh May wept very often,
That loveth damyan so benyngnely	For she had such sweet love for Damian
That she moot oother dyen sodeynly,	That she felt that she must consummate it
Or elles she moot han hym as hir leste.	Or else she was going to die.
She wayteth whan hir herte wolde breste.	She thought that her heart was going to burst.
Upon that oother syde damyan	On the other side Damien
Bicomen is the sorwefulleste man	Had become the saddest man
That evere was; for neither nyght ne day	That there ever was, for never, night or day
Ne myghte he speke a word to fresshe may,	Could he have one word with fresh May,
As to his purpos, of no swich mateere,	Regarding the things he wanted,
But if that januarie moste it heere,	Without January hearing it,
That hadde an hand upon hire everemo.	Who always had his hand upon her.
But nathelees, by writyng to and fro,	Nevertheless, by writing to and fro
And privee signes, wiste he what she mente,	And making secret signs he knew what she meant,
And she knew eek the fyn of his entente.	And she knew what he was planning.
O januarie, what myghte it thee availle,	Oh January, what use would it be to you,
Thogh thou myghte se as fer as shippes saille?	If you could see over the farthest oceans?
For as good is blynd deceyved be	It's just as bad being tricked when blind
As to be deceyved whan a man may se.	As it is being tricked when you can see.
Lo, argus, which that hadde an hondred yen,	Look at Argus, who had a hundred eyes,
For al that evere he koude poure or pryen,	Letting him see into everything,
Yet was he blent, and, God woot, so been mo,	But he was cheated, and God knows, so have others been,
That wenen wisly that it be nat so.	Who were absolutely sure it wasn't happening to them.
Passe over is an ese, I sey namoore.	Ignorance is bliss, that's all I'll say.
This fresshe may, that I spak of so yoore,	This fresh maid, of whom I have already spoken,
In warm wex hath emprented the clyket	Took an impression of the latchkey in warm wax,
That januarie bar of the smale wyket,	The key which January used for the small gate,
By which into his gardyn ofte he wente;	Which he used to go into his garden;
And damyan, that knew al hire entente,	And Damian, who knew everything she was planning,
The cliket countrefeted pryvely.	Made a secret copy of it.
Ther nys namoore to seye, but hastily	That's all there is to be said, but soon
Som wonder by this clyket shal bityde,	Something amazing will happen due to this latchkey,
Which ye shul heeren, if ye wole abyde.	Which you will hear about, if you go on listening.
O noble ovyde, ful sooth seystou, God woot,	O noble Ovid, God knows you were telling the whole truth;
What sleighte is it, thogh it be long and hoot,	What trick is there, though it may take a long time,
That love nyl fynde it out in som manere?	That love will not discover in some way?
By piramus and tesbee may men leere;	Men can learn from Pyramus and Thisbe;
Thogh they were kept ful longe streite overal,	Although they were strictly separated,
They been accorded, rownynge thurgh a wal,	They joined together by whispering through a wall,

Ther no wight koude han founde out swich a sleighte.	Where no other could have found out that trick.
But now to purpos er that dayes eighte	But to the point: before eight days
Were passed, er the month of juyn, bifil	Of June had passed, it happened
That januarie hath caught so greet a wil,	That January had a great desire,
Thurgh eggyng of his wyf, hym for to pleye	Encouraged by his wife, to enjoy himself
In his gardyn, and no wight but they tweye,	In his garden, with no one there but them,
That in a morwe unto his may seith he	So one morning he said to his May:
Rys up, my wyf, my love, my lady free!	"Get up, my wife, my love, my noble lady!
The turtles voys is herd, my dowve sweete;	I can hear the voice of the turtledove, my sweet dove;
The wynter is goon with alle his reynes weete.	The winter has gone with all his wet rains.
Com forth now, with thyne eyen columbyn!	Come out now, with your eyes like a dove!
How fairer been thy brestes than is wyn!	How much sweeter your breasts are than wine!
The gardyn is enclosed al aboute;	The garden is walled all round;
Com forth, my white spouse! out of doute	Come out, my white wife! It is beyond doubt
Thou hast me wounded in myn herte, o wyf!	You have wounded me in my heart, O my wife!
No spot of thee ne knew I al my lyf.	I didn't know of any stain on you, ever.
Com forth, and lat us taken oure disport;	Come out, and let's have fun;
I chees thee for my wyf and my confort.	I chose you as my wife and my pleasure."
Swiche olde lewed wordes used he.	These were the ignorant words he used.
On damyan a signe made she,	She made a sign to Damian,
That he sholde go biforn with his cliket.	That he should go ahead with his latchkey.
This damyan thanne hath opened the wyket,	Then Damien opened up the gate,
And in he stirte, and that in swich manere	And hurried in, in such a way
That no wight myghte it se neither yheere,	That nobody could see or hear him,
And stille he sit under a bussh anon.	And at once he hid himself under a bush.
This januarie, as blynd as is a stoon,	This January, as blind as a stone,
With mayus in his hand, and no wight mo,	With May in his hand, and no one else,
Into his fresshe gardyn is ago,	Went into his fresh garden,
And clapte to the wyket sodeynly.	And quickly shut the gate.
Now wyf, quod he, heere nys but thou and I,	"Now, wife," he said, "there's no one here but you and I,
That art the creature that I best love.	You are the creature that I love best.
For by that lord that sit in hevene above,	For by the Lord who sits in heaven above,
Levere ich hadde to dyen on a knyf,	I would rather be stabbed to death
Than thee offende, trewe deere wyf!	Than offend you, my true dear wife!
For goddes sake, thenk how I thee chees,	For God's sake, think how I chose you,
Noght for no coveitise, doutelees,	Not through greed, honestly,
But oonly for the love I had to thee.	But only because of the love I had for you.
And though that I be oold, and may nat see,	And although I am old and cannot see,
Beth to me trewe, and I wol telle yow why.	Be faithful to me, and I will tell you why.
Thre thynges, certes, shal ye wynne therby	There are three things, certainly, which you will get through that:
First, love of crist, and to youreself honour,	Firstly, the love of Christ, and honour to yourself,
And al myn heritage, toun and tour;	And all my inheritance, the town and the castle;
I yeve it yow, maketh chartres as yow leste;	I give it to you, draw up the deeds as you wish;
This shal be doon to-morwe er sonne reste,	We shall do this tomorrow before sunset,
So wisly God my soule brynge in blisse.	I swear by my hopes of heaven.
I prey yow first, in covenant ye me kisse;	I pray you, to seal the contract, kiss me;

And though that I be jalous, wyte me noght.	And don't blame me if I am jealous.
Ye been so depe enprented in my thoght	You are so deeply buried in my thoughts
That, whan that I considere youre beautee,	That, when I think of your beauty
And therwithal the unlikly elde of me,	And also my unpleasant old-age,
I may nat, certes, though I sholde dye,	I cannot, certainly, even if I would die,
Forbere to been out of youre compaignye	Bear to be without you,
For verray love; this is withouten doute.	Because of my true love; this much is certain.
Now kys me, wyf, and lat us rome aboute.	Now kiss me, wife, and let us walk around."
This fresshe may, whan she thise wordes herde,	This fresh May, when she heard these words,
Benyngnely to januarie answerde,	Sweetly answered January,
But first and forward she bigan to wepe.	But before beginning she began to weep.
I have, quod she, a soule for to kepe	"I have," she said, "a soul to save
As wel as ye, and also myn honour,	As much as you do, and also my honour,
And of my wyfhod thilke tendre flour,	And the tender flower of wifehood,
Which that I have assured in youre hond,	Which I have placed in your hands,
Whan that the preest to yow my body bond;	When the priest bound my body to you;
Wherfore I wole answere in this manere,	And so I will answer you in this fashion,
By the leve of yow, my lord so deere	With your permission, my dear lord:
I prey to God that nevere dawe the day	I pray to God that the day never comes
That I ne sterve, as foule as womman may,	When I do not die, as horribly as a woman can,
If evere I do unto my kyn that shame,	If I ever bring any shame on my family,
Or elles I empeyre so my name,	Or do any other damage to my name,
That I be fals; and if I do that lak,	By being untrue; and if I do anything like that,
Do strepe me and put me in a sak,	Strip me off and put me in a sack,
And in the nexte ryver do me drenche.	And drown me in the nearest river.
I am a gentil womman and no wenche.	I am a gentlewoman, not a serving girl.
Why speke ye thus? but men been evere untrewe,	Why are you talking like this? But men are always faithless,
And wommen have repreve of yow ay newe.	And women are always being blamed by you.
Ye han noon oother contenance, I leeve,	You don't know any other way of behaving, I believe,
But speke to us of untrust and repreeve.	Except for treating us with distrust and criticism."
And with that word she saugh wher damyan	As she said this she saw where Damian
Sat in the bussh, and coughen she bigan,	Was sitting in the bush, and she began to cough,
And with hir fynger signes made she	And with her fingers she made signs
That damyan sholde clymbe upon a tree,	That Damien should climb up a tree
That charged was with fruyt, and up he wente.	That was loaded with fruit, and up he went.
For verraily he knew al hire entente,	He certainly knew what she was up to,
And every signe that she koude make,	And every sign that she could make,
Wel bet than januarie, hir owene make;	Much better than January, her own husband,
For in a lettre she hadde toold hym al	For in a letter she had told him everything
Of this matere, how he werchen shal.	About this business, and what he should do.
And thus I lete hym sitte upon the pyrie,	So I will leave him sitting in a pear tree,
And januarie and may romynge ful myrie.	With January and May roaming around happily.
Bright was the day, and blew the firmament;	It was a bright day, with a blue sky;
Phebus hath of gold his stremes doun ysent,	The sun was sending down golden beams
To gladen every flour with his warmnesse.	To please every flower with its warmth.
He was that tyme in geminis, as I gesse,	At that time, I would guess, he was in Gemini,
But litel fro his declynacion	Just a little way from
Of cancer, jovis exaltacion.	Cancer, the pleasure of Jove.

And so bifel, that brighte morwe-tyde,
That in that gardyn, in the ferther syde,
Pluto, that is kyng of fayerye,
And many a lady in his compaignye,
Folwynge his wyf, the queene proserpyna,
Which that he ravysshed out of ethna
Whil that she gadered floures in the mede --
In claudyan ye may the stories rede,
How in his grisely carte he hire fette --

This kyng of fairye thanne adoun hym sette
Upon a bench of turves, fressh and grene,
And right anon thus seyde he to his queene
My wyf, quod he, ther may no wight seye nay;
Th' experience so preveth every day
The tresons whiche that wommen doon to man.
Ten hondred thousand (tales) tellen I kan
Notable of youre untrouthe and brotilnesse.
O salomon, wys, and richest of richesse,
Fulfild of sapience and of worldly glorie,
Ful worthy been thy wordes to memorie
To every wight that wit and reson kan.
Thus preiseth he yet the bountee of man
-- Amonges a thousand men yet foond I oon,
But of wommen alle foond I noon. --
Thus seith the kyng that knoweth youre wikkednesse.
And jhesus, filius syrak, as I gesse,
Ne speketh of yow but seelde reverence.
A wylde fyr and corrupt pestilence
So falle upon youre bodyes yet to-nyght!
Ne se ye nat this honurable knyght,
By cause, allas! that he is blynd and old,
His owene man shal make hym cokewold.
Lo, where he sit, the lechour, in the tree!
Now wol I graunten, of my magestee,
Unto this olde, blynde, worthy knyght
That he shal have ayen his eyen syght,
Whan that his wyf wold doon hym vileynye.
Thanne shal he knowen al hire harlotrye,
Bothe in repreve of hire and othere mo.

Ye shal? quod proserpyne, wol ye so?
Now by my moodres sires soule I swere

That I shal yeven hire suffisant answere,
And alle wommen after, for hir sake;

That, though they be in any gilt ytake,
With face boold they shulle hemself excuse,

And bere hem doun that wolden hem accuse.
For lak of answere noon of hem shal dyen.
Al hadde man seyn a thyng with bothe his yen,

Yit shul we wommen visage it hardily, And wepe, and swere, and chyde subtilly,	*We women will face it boldly,* *And weep, and swear, and dishonestly criticise,*
So that ye man shul been as lewed as gees.	*So that you men will remain as ignorant as geese.*
What rekketh me of youre auctoritees? I woot wel that this jew, this salomon, Foond of us wommen fooles many oon. But though that he ne foond no good womman, Yet hath ther founde many another man Wommen ful trewe, ful goode, and vertuous. Witnesse on hem that dwelle in cristes hous; With martirdom they preved hire constance. The romayn geestes eek make remembrance Of many a verray, trewe wyf also. But, sire, ne be nat wrooth, al be it so, Though that he seyde he foond no good womman,	*What do I care about your precedents?* *I know perfectly well that this Jew, Solomon,* *Thought that many of we women were false.* *But though he found no good women,* *Many other men have found* *Women to be true, good and virtuous.* *Look at the ones who live in heaven;* *They prove their loyalty through martyrdom.* *The Roman historians also tell us* *Of many genuine true wives.* *But, sir, do not be angry, even if it is the case* *That he said he could not find any good women,*
I prey yow take the sentence of the man; He mente thus, that in sovereyn bontee Nis noon but god, but neither he ne she. Ey! for verray god, that nys but oon, What make ye so muche of salomon? What though he made a temple, goddes hous? What though he were riche and glorious? So made he eek a temple of false goddis. How myghte he do a thyng that moore forbode is? Pardee, as faire as ye his name emplastre, He was a lecchour and an ydolastre, And in his elde he verray God forsook; And if this God ne hadde, as seith the book, Yspared hem for his fadres sake, he sholde Have lost his regne rather than he wolde. I sette right noght, of al the vileynye That ye of wommen write, a boterflye! I am a womman, nedes moot I speke, Of elles swelle til myn herte breke. For sithen he seyde that we been jangleresses, As evere hool I moote brouke my tresses, I shal nat spare, for no curteisye, To speke hym harm that wolde us vileynye.	*I must ask you to think of his true meaning;* *What he meant was that's nobody is perfect* *Except for God, neither man nor woman.* *Ah! I ask by the only true God,* *Why do you make such a fuss about Solomon?* *So what if he made a temple, house of God?* *So what if he was rich and glorious?* *He also made a temple for false gods.* *How could he do anything more shameful?* *By God, however good you say he was,* *He was a lecher and an idolater,* *And in his old age he abandoned the true God;* *And if God had not, as the Bible says,* *Spared him for the sake of his father, he would* *Have lost his kingdom before he wanted to.* *I don't think that all the wickedness you write* *About women is worth a butterfly!* *I am a woman, I have to speak,* *Or else my heart will burst.* *Since he said that we were chatterers,* *While I remain alive* *I will not stop, no matter what,* *To criticise the one who criticises us."*
Dame, quod this pluto, be no lenger wrooth; I yeve it up! but sith I swoor myn ooth That I wolde graunten hym his sighte ageyn, My word shal stonde, I warne yow certeyn. I am a kyng, it sit me noght to lye. And I, quod she, a queene of fayerye! Hir answere shal she have, I undertake. Lat us namoore wordes heerof make; For sothe, I wol no lenger yow contrarie.	*"Lady," said this Pluto, "don't be angry;* *I give up! But since I swore an oath* *That I would give him back his sight,* *I must keep my word, I warn you.* *I am the King; it is wrong for me to lie."* *"And I," she said, "and a queen of the fairies!* *I swear that she shall have her answer.* *Let us no longer talk about this;* *For I swear, I will not argue with you any more."*
Now lat us turne agayn to januarie, That in the gardyn with his faire may Syngeth ful murier than the papejay,	*Now let us go back to January,* *Who in his garden with his fair May* *Was singing merrier than a popinjay,*

Yow love I best, and shal, and oother noon.	"It is you I love the best, and I shall love no other."
So longe aboute the aleyes is he goon,	He wandered along the garden paths,
Til he was come agaynes thilke pyrie	Until he came up to the same pear tree
Where as this damyan sitteth ful myrie	Where Damien was sitting, full of mirth,
An heigh among the fresshe leves grene.	High up amongst the fresh green leaves.
This fresshe may, that is so bright and sheene,	This fresh May, so bright and shining,
Gan for to syke, and seyde, allas, my syde!	Began to sigh, and said, "Alas, I'm hungry!
Now sire, quod she, for aught that may bityde,	Now Sir," she said, "whatever happens,
I moste han of the peres that I see,	I must have some of those pears I can see,
Or I moot dye, so soore longeth me	Or I shall die, I am so desperate
To eten of the smale peres grene.	To eat some of the small green pears.
Help, for hir love that is of hevene queene!	Help me, for the love of the Queen of Heaven!
I telle yow wel, a womman in my plit	I'm telling you, a woman in my condition
May han to fruyt so greet an appetit	Can get such a great appetite for fruit
That she may dyen, but she of it have.	That she can die if she doesn't get it."
Allas! quod he, that I ne had heer a knave	"Alas," he said, "I don't have a servant here
That koude clymbe! allas, allas, quod he,	Who can climb up! Alas, alas," he said,
For I am blynd! ye, sire, no fors, quod she;	"For I am blind!" "Yes, sir, it doesn't matter," she said;
-- But wolde ye vouche sauf, for goddes sake,	"But please would you, for God's sake,
The pyrie inwith youre armes for to take,	Wrap your arms around the pear tree,
For wel I woot that ye mystruste me,	For I know that you could support me,
Thanne sholde I clymbe wel ynogh, quod she,	I would be able to climb up,
So I my foot myghte sette ypon youre bak.	If I could put my foot on your back."
Certes, quod he, theron shal be no lak,	"Certainly," he said, "I shall do that,
Mighte I yow helpen with myn herte blood.	I would give my blood to help you."
He stoupeth doun, and on his bak she stood,	He bent down, and she stood on his back,
And caughte hire by a twiste, and up she gooth --	And caught a branch, and up she went—
Ladyes, I prey yow that ye be nat wrooth;	Ladies, please don't be angry with me;
I kan nat glose, I am a rude man --	I can't use euphemisms, I'm uneducated—
And sodeynly anon this damyan	All at once this Damian
Gan pullen up the smok, and in he throng.	Pulled up her dress, and piled in.
And whan that pluto saugh this grete wrong,	And when Pluto saw this great wrong,
To januarie he gaf agayn his sighte,	He gave January back his sight,
And made hym se as wel as evere he myghte.	So that he could see as well as he ever could.
And whan that he hadde caught his sighte agayn,	And when he had got back his sight,
Ne was ther nevere man of thyng so fayn,	No man was ever so happy about anything,
But on his wyf his thoght was everemo.	But he immediately thought about his wife.
Up to the tree he caste his eyen two,	He turned his eyes up to the trees
And saugh that damyan his wyf had dressed	And saw Damien treating his wife
In swich manere it may nat been expressed,	In a way which cannot be described
But if I wolde speke uncurteisly;	Unless I spoke very rudely;
And up he yaf a roryng and a cry,	And he set up such a shouting and wailing
As dooth the mooder whan the child shal dye	Like a mother when her child is about to die:
Out! he gan to crye,	"Get out! Help! Alas! Help!" He began to shout,
O stronge lady stoore, what dostow?	"Oh you hussey, what are you doing?"
And she answerde, sire, what eyleth yow?	And she answered, "Sir, what is the matter?
Have pacience and resoun in youre mynde!	Calm down and be sensible.
I have yow holpe on bothe youre eyen blynde.	I have helped you with your blind eyes.
Up peril of my soule, I shal nat lyen,	I swear on my soul, I will not lie,
As me was taught, to heele with youre eyen,	I was taught how to heal your eyes,

Was no thyng bet, to make yow to see,

Than strugle with a man upon a tree.
God woot, I dide it in ful good entente.
Strugle! quod he, ye algate in it wente!
God yeve yow bothe on shames deth to dyen!
He swyved thee, I saugh it with myne yen,
And elles be I hanged by the hals!
thanne is, quod she, my medicyne fals;

For certeinly, if that ye myghte se.
Ye wolde nat seyn thise wordes unto me.
Ye han som glymsyng, and no parfit sighte.

I se, quod he, as wel as evere I myghte,

Thonked be god! with bothe myne eyen two,
And by my trouthe, me thoughte he dide thee so.

ye maze, maze, goode sire, quod she;

This thank have I for I have maad yow see.
Allas, quod she, that evere I was so kynde!

Now, dame, quod he, lat al passe out of mynde.
Com doun, my lief, and if I have myssayd,

God helpe me so, as I am yvele apayd.
But, by my fader soule, I wende han seyn
How that this damyan hadde by thee leyn,
And that thy smok hadde leyn upon his brest.

Ye sire, quod she, ye may wene as yow lest.

But, sire, a man that waketh out of his sleep,
He may nat sodeynly wel taken keep
Upon a thyng, ne seen it parfitly,
Til that he be adawed verraily.
Right so a man that longe hath blynd ybe,

Ne may nat sodeynly so wel yse,
First whan his sighte is newe come ageyn,
As he that hath a day or two yseyn.

Til that youre sighte ysatled be a while,
Ther may ful many a sighte yow bigile.
Beth war, I prey yow; for, by hevene kyng,
Ful many a man weneth to seen a thyng,
And it is al another than it semeth.
He that mysconceyveth, he mysdemeth.
And with that word she leep doun fro the tree,

This januarie, who is glad but he?
He kisseth hire, and clippeth hire ful ofte,

I was told that nothing was more likely to make you see
Then for me to fight with a man in a tree.
God knows, I did it with good intentions."
"Fight?" He said, "yes, in it went!
May God give you both shameful deaths!
He screwed you; I saw it with my own eyes,
Hang me by the neck if I didn't!"
"Then," she said, "my medicine can't have worked,
For certainly, if you could see,
You would not say those words to me.
You've just got a glimpse, you don't have perfect sight."
"I can see," he said, "just as well as I always could,
Thanks be to God! with both of my eyes,
And I swear, it looked to me as if he was doing you."
"You are confused, confused, good sir," she said;
"This is the thanks I get for making you see.
Alas," she said, "I wish I'd never been so kind!"
"Now, lady," he said, "let's forget all of that.
Come down, my dear, and if I said something wrong,
God help me, I am very sorry.
But, on my father's soul, I thought I saw
This Damien lying next to you,
With your dress pulled up on his chest."
"Yes, sir," she said, "you can think what you like.
But, sir, a man who wakes from his sleep,
He does not suddenly understand
Everything, nor see everything perfectly,
Until he is properly awake.
In just the same way a man who has been blind for a long time
Can't suddenly see just as well
When his sight returns to him,
As he can when he has been seeing for a day or two.
Until your sight settles down
Many things you see might deceive you.
Be careful, please, by the King of Heaven,
Many men think they seen a thing,
When it is something entirely different.
Someone who misunderstands misjudges."
Having said that she jumped down from the tree.
This January, who was happier than him?
He kissed her, and hugged her many times,

261

And on hire wombe he stroketh hire ful softe,
And to his palays hoom he hath hire lad.
Now, goode men, I pray yow to be glad.
Thus endeth heere my tale of januarie;
God blesse us, and his mooder seinte marie!

Here is ended The Marchantes Tale of Januarie

Ey, Goddes mercy! seyde oure Hooste tho,
Now swich a wyf I pray God kepe me fro!
Lo, whiche sleightes and subtilitees
In wommen been, for ay as bisy as bees
Been they us sely men for to deceyve;
And from a sooth evere wol they weyve,
By this Marchantes tale it preveth weel.
But doutelees, as trewe as any steel,
I have a wyf, though that she povre be,
But of hir tonge a labbyng shrewe is she.
And yet she hath an heep of vices mo-

Ther-of no fors, lat alle swiche thynges go.
But wyte ye what, in conseil be it seyd,

Me reweth soore I am unto hire teyd;
For and I sholde rekenen every vice,
Which that she hath, ywis, I were to nyce.
And cause why? it sholde reported be,
And toold to hir of somme of this meynee;
Of whom, it nedeth nat for to declare,
Syn wommen konnen outen swich chaffare.
And eek my with suffiseth nat therto,
To tellen al, wherfore my tale is do.

And he stroked her womb softly,
And took her home to his palace.
Now, good men, I hope you're happy.
This is the end of my tale of January;
God bless us, and also his mother St Mary!

The end of the Merchant's tale

"Why! God have mercy!" said our host then,
"May God keep me away from a wife like that!
Look at what tricks and cunning
Women have! They are always as busy as bees
To deceive we innocent men,
And they are always straying from the truth;
This tale from the merchant proves it well.
But I swear, I have a wife
Who is as true as steel, although she is poor,
But she is also a chattering nag,
And there are many other things wrong with her as well;
But who cares! Let these things pass.
But do you know what? May it be said secretly,
That I very much regret being tied to her.
For if I added up all the vices
Which she has, I would certainly look foolish.
And why? Because it would be reported
To her by some of this company–
I need not say who it would be,
Since women know how to get what they want;
And also I'm not clever enough to
Tell you everything; so I'm finished."

The Squier's Tale

Introduction

The Squier's Tale (introduction)

Squier, come neer, if it your wille be,
And sey somwhat of love, for certes, ye

Konnen theron as muche as any man.
Nay sir, quod he, but I wol seye as I kan,
With hertly wyl, for I wol nat rebelle
Agayn your lust. A tale wol I telle,
Have me excused if I speke amys;
My wyl is good, and lo, my tale is this.

The introduction to the Squire's tale

"Squire, come closer, if you will,
And tell us something about love, for certainly you
Know as much about it as anybody."
"No, sir," he said, "but I'll say what I can
Gladly, I won't go against
Your desires; I will tell you a story.
Please excuse me if I displease you;
I'm doing my best, and this is my story."

The Tale

Heere bigynneth the Squieres Tale.

At Sarray, in the land of Tartarye,
Ther dwelte a kyng, that werreyed Russye,

Thurgh which ther dyde many a doughty man.
This noble kyng was cleped Cambynskan,
Which in his tyme was of so greet renoun,
That ther was nowher in no regioun
So excellent a lord in alle thyng.
Hym lakked noght that longeth to a kyng;

And of the secte, of which that he was born,

He kepte his lay, to which that he was sworn;
And therto he was hardy, wys, and riche,
Pitous, and just, and everemoore yliche,
Sooth of his word, benigne, and honurable,
Of his corage as any centre stable,
Yong, fressh, strong, and in armes desirous

As any bacheler of al his hous.

A fair persone he was, and fortunat,
And kepte alwey so wel roial estat

That ther was nowher swich another man.
This noble kyng, this Tarte Cambynskan,
Hadde two sones on Elpheta his wyf,
Of whiche the eldeste highte Algarsyf,
That oother sone was cleped Cambalo.
A doghter hadde this worthy kyng also,
That yongest was, and highte Canacee.

But for to telle yow al hir beautee,
It lyth nat in my tonge nyn my konnyng.
I dar nat undertake so heigh a thyng;
Myn Englissh eek is insufficient.
I moste been a rethor excellent,
That koude hise colours longynge for that art,
If he sholde hir discryven every part.
I am noon swich; I moot speke as I kan.

And so bifel, that whan this Cambynskan

Hath twenty wynter born his diademe,
As he was wont fro yeer to yeer, I deme,
He leet the feeste of his nativitee
Doon cryen thurghout Sarray his citee,
The last Idus of March after the yeer.

The beginning of the Squire's tale

*At Sarray, in the country of the Tartars,
There lived a king who fought a war against Russia,
Which caused the death of many good men.
This noble king was called Cambyuskan,
And in his time he was so famous
That no other place in the world
Had such a good lord in everything:
He was missing none of the attributes of a king.
With regard to the religion into which he was born
He kept its law, which he had sworn to;
Furthermore he was strong, wise and rich,
Compassionate and just, always fair;
True to his word, kind and honourable;
His heart was as firm as any fixed point;
Young, lively and strong, wanting to be as good a fighting man
As any young knight in his household.*

*He was a handsome man and blessed,
And he always maintained such a royal demeanour
That there was nobody like him in the world.
This noble king, this Tartar Cambyuskan,
Had two sons with his wife Elpheta,
Of whom the elder one was called Algarsyf,
And the other was called Cambalo.
This good King also had a daughter,
The youngest of them, who was called Canacee.
To tell you of her beauty
Is not within my capabilities;
I wouldn't dare to try such a great thing.
My English couldn't match up to it.
It would need an excellent speaker,
Knowing all the tricks of rhetoric,
To describe her in every detail.
I'm not such a person, I must say what I can.*

*And so it happened that when this Cambyuskan
Had been king for twenty years,
Just as he did every single year
He held a feast on his birthday,
Announced all through his city of Sarray,
On March the fifteenth, every year.*

Phebus the sonne ful joly was and cleer,	The sun shone bright and clear,
For he was neigh his exaltacioun	For it had almost reached its highest point
In Martes face, and in his mansioun	In front of Mars, in the house of
In Aries, the colerik hoote signe.	Aries, that burning hot sign.
Ful lusty was the weder, and benigne,	The weather was very pleasant and mild,
For which the foweles agayn the sonne sheene,	And the birds, because of the sunshine,
What for the sesoun and the yonge grene,	What with the season and the young greenery,
Ful loude songen hir affecciouns;	Sang loudly about their desires.
Hem semed han geten hem protecciouns	They seemed to have been protected
Agayn the swerd of wynter, keene and coold.	Against the keen cold sword of winter.
This Cambynskan, of which I have yow toold,	This Cambyuskan, of whom I have told you,
In roial vestiment sit on his deys,	Sat on his dais in his royal robes,
With diademe, ful heighe in his paleys,	And his crown, noble in his palace,
And halt his feeste so solempne and so ryche,	And he held a feast so ceremonious and rich
That in this world ne was ther noon it lyche.	That there wasn't anything to match it in the world;
Of which, if I shal tellen al tharray,	If I were to describe the whole scene
Thanne wolde it occupie a someres day,	It would take the whole of a summer's day,
And eek it nedeth nat for to devyse,	But anyway it's not necessary to describe
At every cours, the ordre of hire servyse.	Every little detail of the celebrations.
I wol nat tellen of hir strange sewes,	I won't tell you about their strange stews,
Ne of hir swannes, nor of hire heronsewes;	Nor about the swans, nor the young herons.
Eek in that lond, as tellen knyghtes olde,	Also in that land, knights of old have told us,
Ther is som mete that is ful deynte holde,	There are foods that are thought of as delicacies
That in this lond men recche of it but smal-	That in this country are thought worthless;
Ther nys no man that may reporten al.	No man can describe everything.
I wol nat taryen yow, for it is pryme,	I won't keep you, because it is nine o'clock,
And for it is no fruyt but los of tyme.	And all it would do would be to waste your time;
Unto my firste I wole have my recours.	I'll go back to my point.
And so bifel, that after the thridde cours	So it happened that after the third course
Whil that htis kyng sit thus in his nobleye,	While the king was sitting on his throne,
Herknynge hise mynstrals hir thynges pleye	Listening to his minstrels play
Biforn hym at the bord deliciously,	Delightfully in front of them at the table,
In at the halle dore al sodeynly	Suddenly in at the hall door
Ther cam a knyght, upon a steede of bras,	There came a knight on a brass horse,
And in his hand a brood mirour of glas,	And in his hand he held a wide glass mirror.
Upon his thombe he hadde of gold a ryng,	On his thumb he had a gold ring,
And by his syde a naked swerd hangyng.	And an unsheathed sword was hanging at his side;
And up he rideth to the heighe bord.	And so he rode up to the high table.
In al the hall ne was ther spoken a word	Throughout the hall nobody said a word,
For merveille of this knyght; hym to biholde	Amazed by this apparition; they all
Ful bisily ther wayten yonge and olde.	Stared at him intently, young and old.
This strange knyght, that cam thus sodeynly	This strange knight, who appeared so suddenly,
Al armed, save his heed, ful richely,	Fully armed apart from his head, with rich armour,
Saleweth kyng, and queene, and lordes alle,	Saluted the king and queen and all the lords,
By ordre, as they seten in the halle,	In the order in which they were sat,
With so heigh reverence and obeisaunce,	With such great reverence and respect
As wel in speche as in contenaunce,	In his speech as well as in his appearance,
That Gawayn, with his olde curteisye,	That Gawain, with his old beautiful manners,

Though he were comen ayeyn out of Fairye,	If he came back from fairyland,
Ne koude hym nat amende with a word.	Wouldn't have said a single word differently.
And after this, biforn the heighe bord	And after this, in front of the high table,
He with a manly voys seith his message,	He delivered a message in a manly voice,
After the forme used in his langage,	In the style used in his language,
Withouten vice of silable or of lettre.	Without a single mistake in anything;
And for his tale sholde seme the bettre,	And so that his tale would seem better
Accordant to hise wordes was his cheere,	He matched his facial expression to his words,
As techeth art of speche hem that it leere.	As those who study rhetoric are taught.
Al be it that I kan nat sowne his stile,	Although I cannot copy his style,
Ne kan nat clymben over so heigh a style,	I can't aspire to such heights,
Yet seye I this, as to commune entente,	I will say this, as to what he meant:
Thus muche amounteth al that evere he mente,	This describes what he meant to say,
If it so be that I have it in mynde.	If I have it straight in my mind.
He seyde, The kyng of Arabe and of Inde,	He said, "The king of Arabia and of India,
My lige lord, on this solempne day	My dear lord, on this special day,
Saleweth yow, as he best kan and may;	Salutes you, in the best way he knows how,
And sendeth yow, in honour of your feeste,	And has sent you, to honour your feast,
By me, that am al redy at your heeste,	Through me, who am at your command,
This steede of bras, that esily and weel	This brass horse, that can easily,
Kan in the space of o dday natureel,	In the space of a single day,
This is to seyn, in foure and twenty houres,	That is to say, in twenty-four hours,
Wherso yow lyst, in droghte or elles shoures,	Wherever you desire, whatever the weather,
Beren youre body into every place	Take you to any place
To which youre herte wilneth for to pace,	That your heart wishes to go,
Withouten wem of yow, thurgh foul or fair.	Without any harm to you, foul or fair climates,
Or if yow lyst to fleen as hye in the air	Or, if you want to fly as high in the air
As dooth an egle, whan that hym list to soore,	As an eagle does when he is soaring,
This same steede shal bere yow evere moore	This same horse will carry you there,
Withouten harm, til ye be ther yow leste,	With no danger, until you reach your goal,
Though that ye slepen on his bak or reste;	Even if you fall asleep on his back,
And turne ayeyn, with writhyng of a pyn.	And he will come back by twisting a peg.
He that it wroghte, koude ful many a gyn;	The one who built it knew many clever tricks.
He wayted many a constellacioun	He looked at many different constellations
Er he had doon this operacioun;	Before he had finished his work,
And knew ful many a seel, and many a bond.	And he knew many magical seals and joining spells.
This mirrour eek, that I have in myn hond,	This mirror also, that I have in my hand,
Hath swich a myght, that men may in it see	Has a power to allow men to see
Whan ther shal fallen any adversitee	When any bad thing is coming
Unto your regne, or to yourself also,	To attack your kingdom or yourself,
And openly who is your freend, or foo.	And it will show clearly who is your friend and who your enemy.
And over al this, if any lady bright	As well as all this, if any beautiful lady
Hath set hir herte in any maner wight,	Has set her heart on any man,
If he be fals, she shal his tresoun see,	If he is false, she will see his treason,
His newe love, and al his subtiltee	His new love, and all his tricks,
So openly, that ther shal no thyng hyde.	So clearly, that there will be nothing to hide.
Wherfore, ageyn this lusty someres tyde,	For this reason, for protection in this lusty springtime,
This mirrour and this ryng that ye may see,	He has sent this mirror and this ring
He hath sent unto my lady Canacee,	That you can see to my lady Canacee,
Your excellente doghter that is heere.	Your excellent daughter here.

The vertu of the ryng, if ye wol heere,	*The power of the ring, I can tell you,*
Is this, that if hir lust it for to were	*Is this: if she wants to wear it*
Upon hir thombe, or in hir purs it bere,	*On her thumb, or put it in her purse,*
Ther is no fowel that fleeth under the hevene	*There is no bird flying under the skies*
That she ne shal wel understonde his stevene,	*That she will not be able to understand,*
And knowe his menyng openly and pleyn,	*She will know his meaning openly and clear,*
And answere hym in his langage ageyn.	*And answer him in his own language;*
And every gras that groweth upon roote,	*And every herb that grows on a stalk*
She shal eek knowe, and whom it wol do boote,	*She will also know, and whom it will be good for,*
Al be hise woundes never so depe and wyde.	*However deep and wide his wounds.*
This naked swerd, that hangeth by my syde	*This unsheathed sword, that hangs by my side,*
Swich vertu hath, that what man so ye smyte	*Has the power to cut through the armour*
Thurghout his armure it wole hym kerve and byte,	*Of any man you strike with it,*
Were it as thikke as is a branched ook.	*If it is as thick as an ancient oak;*
And what man that is wounded with a strook	*And any man who is wounded by it*
Shal never be hool, til that yow list of grace	*Will never recover unless you wish to kindly*
To stroke hym with the plate in thilke place	*Touching with the flat side in the same place*
Ther he is hurt; this is as muche to seyn,	*You have wounded him; that is to say,*
Ye moote with the plate swerd ageyn	*You must touch again*
Strike hym in the wounde, and it wol close.	*On his wound with the blunt side, and it will close.*
This is a verray sooth withouten glose.	*This is absolutely true, no exaggeration;*
It faileth nat, whils it is in youre hoold.	*It will not fail you while you keep it."*
And whan this knyght hath thus his tale toold,	*And when this knight had told his tale,*
He rideth out of halle, and doun he lighte.	*He rode out of the hall and jumped down.*
His steede, which that shoon as sonne brighte,	*His horse, which was shining as bright as the sun,*
Stant in the court, as stille as any stoon.	*Stood in the court, as still as stone.*
This knyght is to his chambre lad anoon,	*The knight was shown at once to his room,*
And is unarmed and unto mete yset.	*His armour was taken off, and he sat down to dinner.*
The presentes been ful roially yfet,	*The presents were ceremoniously fetched–*
This is to seyn, the swerd and the mirrour,	*That is to say, the sword and the mirror–*
And born anon into the heighe tour	*And carried at once to the high tower*
With certeine officers ordeyned therfore.	*By officers appointed for the task;*
And unto Canacee this ryng was bore,	*And the ring was taken to Canacee*
Solempnely, ther she sit at the table.	*Solemnly, where she was sitting at the table.*
But sikerly, withouten any fable,	*But certainly, with no lie,*
The hors of bras, that may nat be remewed,	*The brass horse, that could not be moved,*
It stant as it were to the ground yglewed.	*Stood as if it were glued to the ground.*
Ther may no man out of the place it dryve,	*No man could move it from the place*
For noon engyn of wyndas ne polyve;	*Whatever they tried with rope or pulley;*
And cause why, for they kan nat the craft,	*And why? Because they didn't understand the skill.*
And therfore in the place they han it laft,	*And so they left it in the place*
Til that the knyght hath taught hem the manere	*Until the knight taught them the way*
To voyden hym, as ye shal after heere.	*To move him, as you will hear afterwards.*
Greety was the prees that swarmeth to and fro	*A great crowd swarmed to and fro*
To gauren on this hors, that stondeth so.	*To stare at the horse standing there,*
For it so heigh was, and so brood, and long,	*For it was so tall, and so broad and long,*
So wel proporcioned for to been strong,	*So very muscular,*
Right as it were a steede of Lumbardye;	*It was like a steed of Lombardy;*
Therwith so horsly and so quyk of eye,	*Such a splendid horse, with such a quick eye,*

As it a gentil Poilleys courser were.	*It was like a noble Apulian hunting horse.*
For certes, fro his tayl unto his ere,	*Certainly, from his tail to his ear,*
Nature ne art ne koude hym nat amende	*Neither nature nor art could make him any better*
In no degree, as al the peple wende.	*In any way, as all the people agreed.*
But everemoore hir mooste wonder was	*But all the time their greatest astonishment was*
How that it koude go, and was of bras.	*That it could move, although made of brass;*
It was a fairye, as al the peple semed.	*It was magical, it seemed to them.*
Diverse folk diversely they demed;	*Different people thought different things;*
As many heddes, as manye wittes ther been.	*There were as many opinions as there were heads.*
They murmureden as dooth a swarm of been,	*They murmured like a swarm of bees,*
And maden skiles after hir fantasies,	*And constructed theories with their imaginations,*
Rehersynge of thise olde poetries,	*Retelling ancient poems,*
And seyde that it was lyk the Pegasee,	*Saying it was like Pegasus,*
The hors that hadde wynges for to flee;	*The horse that had wings to fly with;*
Or elles, it was the Grekes hors Synoun,	*Or else it was the Greek horse of Synon,*
That broghte Troie to destruccioun,	*That brought destruction to Troy,*
As men in thise olde geestes rede.	*As men have read in the old romances.*
Myn herte, quod oon, is everemoore in drede.	*"My heart," said one, "is very disturbed;*
I trowe som men of armes been therinne,	*I believe there are some soldiers inside,*
That shapen hem this citee for to wynne.	*Preparing to conquer this city.*
It were right good that al swich thyng were knowe.	*It would be a good thing to investigate this."*
Another rowned to his felawe lowe,	*Another whispered quietly to his friend,*
And seyde, He lyeth; it is rather lyk	*And said, "He's lying, it's more like*
An apparence ymaad by som magyk,	*An illusion created with magic,*
As jogelours pleyen at thise feestes grete.	*Like the conjurors show us at the great feasts."*
Of sondry doutes thus they jangle and trete,	*They tested and debated their various theories,*
As lewed peple demeth comunly	*As ignorant people often speak*
Of thynges that been maad moore subtilly	*Of things that are made more cleverly*
Than they kan in hir lewednesse comprehende;	*Than they can understand in their ignorance;*
They demen gladly to the badder ende.	*They always imagine the worst.*
And somme of hem wondred on the mirror	*And some of them wondered about the mirror,*
That born was up into the maister tour-	*That was carried up into the great tower,*
How men myghte in it swiche thynges se.	*Asking how men could see such things in it.*
Another answerde, and seyde, It myghte wel be	*Someone else answered and said it might well be*
Naturelly by composiciouns	*Natural, through arrangements*
Of anglis and of slye reflexiouns;	*Of angles and clever reflections,*
And seyden, that in Rome was swich oon.	*And said that there was one like it in Rome.*
They speken of Alocen and Vitulon,	*They spoke of Alocen, and Vitulon,*
And Aristotle, that writen in hir lyves	*And Aristotle, who wrote in their lifetimes*
Of queynte mirrours and of perspectives,	*Of cunning mirrors and optical lenses,*
As knowen they that han hir bookes herd.	*Known to those who had heard the books read.*
And oother folk han wondred on the swerd,	*Other folk speculated about the sword,*
That wolde percen thurgh out every thyng;	*That could pierce through anything,*
And fille in speche of Thelophus the kyng	*And spoke about King Thelophus,*
And of Achilles with his queynte spere,	*And Achilles with his magical spear,*
For he koude with it bothe heele and dere,	*With which he could both harm and heal,*

Right in swich wise as men may with the swerd,	In the same way as men could do with the sword
Of which right now ye han yourselven herd.	Which I have just told you about.
They speken of sondry hardyng of metal,	They spoke of various ways of hardening metal,
And speke of medicynes therwithal,	And also of different chemicals,
And how and whanne it sholde yharded be,	And how and when it could be hardened,
Which is unknowe, algates unto me.	Skills which are unknown, at least to me.
Tho speeke they of Canacees ryng,	They also spoke about Canacee's ring,
And seyden alle, that swich a wonder thing	And everyone said it was such a wonderful thing
Of craft of rynges herde they nevere noon;	That they had never heard such a skill in aking rings,
Save that he Moyses, and kyng Salomon	Apart from Moses and King Solomon
Hadde a name of konnyng in swich art.	Who had a reputation for their skill in such arts.
Thus seyn the peple, and drawen hem apart.	That's what the people said, standing aside.
But nathelees, somme seiden that it was	Nevertheless some said that it was
Wonder to maken of fern asshen glas,	Amazing to make glass from the ashes of ferns,
And yet nys glas nat lyk asshen of fern;	When glass is nothing like the ashes of ferns;
But for they han knowen it so fern,	But, because they have seen it done so long
Therfore cesseth hir janglyng and hir wonder.	They don't find this amazing any more.
As soore wondren somme on cause of thonder,	Some think deeply about the cause of thunder,
On ebbe, on flood, on gossomer, and on myst,	The tides, floods, spiders' webs and mist,
And alle thyng, til that the cause is wyst.	And all other things, until what causes them is known.
Thus jangle they, and demen, and devyse,	So they chattered, and speculated, and imagined
Til that the knyg gan fro the bord aryse.	Until the King got up from his table.
Phebus hath laft the angle meridional,	The sun was descending from high noon,
And yet ascendynge was the beest roial,	But the royal beast was in the ascendant,
The gentil Leoun, with his Aldrian,	The noble lion, with his star Aldrian,
Whan that this Tartre kyng, this Cambynskan	When this Tartar king, Cambyuskan,
Roos fro his bord, ther that he sat ful hye.	Rose from his table, where he sitting great state.
Toforn hym gooth the loude mynstralcye	In front of him went the loud musicians
Til he cam to his chambre of parementz,	Until he came to his presence chamber,
Ther as they sownen diverse intrumentz	Where they played different instruments
That it is lyk an hevene for to heere.	In a way which sounded like heaven.
Now dauncen lusty Venus children deere,	Now the lusty children of Venus danced,
For in the Fyssh hir lady sat ful hye,	For that lady sat high in Pisces,
And looketh on hem with a freendly eye.	And looked on them with a friendly eye.
This noble kyng is set up in his trone;	The noble king sat upon his throne,
This strange knyght is fet to hym ful soone,	And the foreign knight was brought to him at once,
And on the daunce he gooth with Canacee.	And he began dancing with Canacee.
Heere is the revel and the jolitee	There was such joy and celebration
That is nat able a dul man to devyse;	That a dull-witted man can't describe it.
He moste han knowen love and his servyse,	Someone would have had to known love and its ways
And been a feestlych man as fressh as May,	And been as jolly a man as the fresh new May
That sholde yow devysen swich array.	To describe such splendid things for you.
Who koude telle yow the forme of daunces,	Who could tell you how they danced
So unkouthe and so fresshe contenaunces,	In such strange ways, with such happy faces,

Swich subtil lookyng and dissymulynges,	Such subtle glances and pretences
For drede of jalouse mennes aperceyvynges?	Out of dread for what jealous men might think?
No man but Launcelet, and he is deed.	Nobody but Lancelot, and he is dead.
Therfore I passe of al this lustiheed;	So I will pass over all these pleasures;
I sey namoore, but in this jolynesse	I will say no more, but in this jolly state
I lete hem, til men to the soper dresse.	I will leave them until they go into supper.
The styward bit the spices for to hye,	The steward ordered the spiced cakes to be brought,
And eek the wyn, in al this melodye;	And also the wine, amongst all this music.
The usshers and the squiers been ygoon,	The ushers and squires were gone,
The spices and the wyn is come anoon,	And the spice cakes and wine were brought quickly.
They ete and drynke, and whan this hadde an ende,	They ate and drank, and when they had finished,
Unto the temple, as reson was, they wende.	They went to the temple, as they should.
The service doon, they soupen al by day;	When the service was done, they drank all day long.
What nedeth me rehercen hir array?	What need is there to tell you how splendid it was;
Ech man woot wel, that at a kynges feeste	Every man knows full well that the feast of a king
Hath plentee, to the mooste and to the leeste,	Has plenty for both the highest and the lowest,
And deyntees mo than been in my knowyng.	And more delicacies than I can tell.
At after soper gooth this noble kyng,	After supper this noble king went
To seen this hors of bras, with al the route	To see this brass horse, with a great crowd
Of lordes, and of ladyes hym aboute.	Of lords and ladies around him.
Swich wondryng was ther on this hors of bras,	There was such amazement at this brass horse,
That syn the grete sege of Troie was,	That since the siege of Troy,
Ther as men wondreden on an hors also,	When men also were amazed by a horse,
Ne was ther swich a wondryng as was tho.	There had never been such wondering.
But fynally, the kyng axeth this knight	But finally the king asked the knight
The vertu of this courser, and the myght;	About the power of the horse and its strength,
And preyde hym to telle his governaunce.	And asked him to tell him how to control it.
This hors anoon bigan to trippe and daunce,	The horse at once began to trip and dance,
Whan that this knyght leyde hand upon his reyne,	When the knight laid his hand on his reins,
And seyde, Sire, ther is namoore to seyne,	And he said, "Sir, all there is to say
But whan yow list to ryden any where,	You must turn a peg, here by his ear,
Ye mooten trille a pyn, stant in his ere,	Which I shall explain to you secretly.
Which I shal telle yow bitwix us two.	You must tell him where you want to go,
Ye moote nempne hym to what place also,	What place to which you want to ride.
Or to what contree, that yow list to ryde,	And when you get where you want to go,
And whan ye com ther as yow list abyde,	Tell him to go down, and turn another peg,
Bidde hym descende, and trille another pyn,	That is all there is to making it work,
(For therin lith theffect of al the gyn)	He will then fly down and do as you wish,
And he wol doun descende, and doon youre wille.	And he will stand still in that place.
And in that place he wol stonde stille,	Though all the world try to make it different,
Though al the world the contrarie hadde yswore;	He will not be drawn away from that place.
He shal nat thennes been ydrawe ne ybore.	Or, if you want him to leave,
Or, if yow liste, bidde hym thennes goon,	Turn this peg, and he will vanish at once
Trille this pyn, and he wol vanysshe anoon	Out of sight of every creature,
Out of the sighte of every maner wight,	And he will come again, day or night,
And com agayn, be it day or nyght,	When you want to call him back,
Whan that yow list to clepen hym ageyn,	Using a method I will describe

271

In swich a gyse as I shal to yow seyn,
Bitwixe yow and me, and that ful soone.

Ride whan yow list; ther is namoore to doone.

Enformed whan the kyng was of that knyght,
And hath conceyved in his wit aright
The manere and the forme of al this thyng,
Thus glad and blithe this noble doughty kyng
Repeireth to his revel as biforn,
The brydel is unto the tour yborn,
And kept among hise jueles, leeve and deere.
The hors vanysshed, I noot in what manere,
Out of hir sighte; ye gete namoore of me.

But thus I lete in lust and jolitee
This Cambynskan, hise lordes festeiynge,
Til wel ny the day bigan to sprynge.

Explicit prima pars. Sequitur pars secunda.

Sequitur pars secunda.

The norice of digestioun, the sleepe,
Gan on hem wynke, and bad hem taken keepe,
That muchel drynke and labour wolde han reste;

And with a galpyng mouth hem alle he keste,
And seyde, It was tyme to lye adoun,
For blood was in his domynacioun.
Cherisseth blood, natures freend, quod he.

They thanken hym, galpynge, by two, by thre,

And every wight gan drawe hym to his reste,
As sleep hem bad; they tooke it for the beste.

Hir dremes shul nat been ytoold for me;
Ful were hir heddes of fumositee,
That causeth dreem, of which ther nys no charge.

They slepen til that it was pryme large,
The mooste part, but it were Canacee;
She was ful mesurable, as wommen be.
For of hir fader hadde she take leve
To goon to reste, soone after it was eve.
Hir liste nat appalled for to be,
Ne on the morwe unfeestlich for to se:
And slepte hir firste sleepe, and thanne awook;

For swich a joye she in hir herte took,
Bothe of hir queynte ryng and hire mirrour,
That twenty tyme she changed hir colour,

Shortly, just between you and me.
Ride when you want to; that's all you need to know."

When the King had been told this by that knight,
And had got straight in his mind
The details of all these matters,
Very happy, this noble strong king
Went back to his revels as before.
The bridle was carried up to the tower
And kept amongst his precious loved jewels.
The horse vanished, I do not know how,
Out of their sight; that's all I can tell you.
So I will leave Cambyuskan entertaining his lords
With pleasure and jollity,
Until the sunrise of the next day came.

The end of the first part.

Here follows the second part

The nurse of digestion, sleep,
Started to signal them to be aware
That lots of drink and exercise mean man needs rest;
And yawning he kissed them all,
Saying that it was time to lie down,
For blood was ruling the body.
"Take care of your blood, the friend of nature," he said.
They thanked him, yawning, in twos and threes,
And everybody went off to rest,
As sleep ordered them; they thought it was for the best.
I shan't now tell you about their dreams;
Their heads were full of the fumes of wine,
Which gives a man dreams which mean nothing.
They slept until nine in the morning,
Most of them, but not Canacee.
She was abstemious, as women are;
She had left her father
To go to rest soon after sunset.
She did not wish to become pale,
Or look unhappy in the morning,
And she had her first sleep, and then woke up.

She had such happiness in her heart
At both her strange ring and her mirror,
That she changed colour twenty times;

And in hir sleep right for impressioun	And in her sleep, because of the impression the mirror
Of hir mirrour she hadde a visioun.	Had made on her mind, she had a vision.
Wherfore, er that the sonne gan up glyde,	And so, before the sun had risen,
She cleped on hir maistresse, hir bisyde,	She called on her governess beside her,
And seyde, that hir liste for to ryse.	And said that she wanted to get up.
Thise olde wommen that been gladly wyse,	These old women are often wise,
As hir maistresse answerde hir anon,	And her governess was, who answered her once,
And seyde, Madame, whider wil ye goon	Saying, "Madam, where do you want to go
Thus erly, for the folk been alle on reste?	This early, when everyone is sleeping?"
I wol, quod she, arise, for me leste	"I want," she said, "to get up, for I no longer wish
No lenger for to slepe; and walke aboute.	To sleep, I want to walk around."
Hir maistresse clepeth wommen a greet route,	Her governess called up a great crowd of women,
And up they rysen wel an ten or twelve.	And up they got, ten or twelve of them;
Up riseth fresshe Canacee hirselve,	And up fresh Canacee rose herself,
As rody and bright as dooth the yonge sonne,	As bright and red as the young sun,
That in the Ram is foure degrees upronne,	When it has gone four degrees across the Ram,
Noon hyer was he, whan she redy was;	He was no higher than that when she was ready,
And forth she walketh esily a pas,	And out she strolled,
Arrayed after the lusty sesoun soote,	Dressed, as the blooming season directed,
Lightly for to pleye and walke on foote,	In light clothes, to amuse herself and stroll about,
Nat but with fyve or sixe of hir meynee;	With no more than five or six of her companions;
And in a trench forth in the park gooth she.	And she followed a path into the park.
The vapour, which that fro the erthe glood,	The mists that were rising from the earth
Made the sonne to seme rody and brood;	Made the sun seem wide and red;
But natheless, it was so fair a sighte	But nevertheless it was such a lovely sight
That it made alle hir hertes for to lighte,	That it lightened all their hearts,
What for the sesoun and the morwenynge,	What with the season and the sunrise,
And for the foweles that she herde synge;	And the birds that she heard singing.
For right anon she wiste what they mente	At once she knew what they meant
Right by hir song, and knew al hir entente.	Precisely through their song, understanding everything.
The knotte, why that every tale is toold,	The main reason for telling every story,
If it be taried til that lust be coold	If you keep it until the interest has gone cold
Of hem that han it after herkned yoore,	Of those who have been listening to it,
The savour passeth ever lenger the moore,	The desire for it gets less and less,
For fulsomnesse of his prolixitee;	Because of the teller's verbosity;
And by the same resoun thynketh me,	And for the same reason, I think,
I sholde to the knotte condescende,	I should get to the point,
And maken of hir walkyng soone an ende.	And quickly finish off her stroll.
Amydde a tree fordryed, as whit as chalk,	In a tree, which was as white as chalk with dryness,
As Canacee was pleyyng in hir walk,	As Canacee was amusing herself in her walk,
Ther sat a faucon over hir heed ful hye,	There was sitting a falcon right over her head,
That with a pitous voys so gan to crye	That with a pitiful voice began to cry
That all the wode resouned of hir cry.	In a way which made all the woods echo with it.
Ybeten hath she hirself so pitously	She had beaten herself so mercilessly

273

With bothe hir wynges, til the rede blood	With both her wings that the red blood
Ran endelong the tree ther as she stood,	Ran down the trunk of the tree in which she stood.
And evere in oon she cryde alwey and shrighte,	She perpetually cried and shrieked,
And with hir beek hirselven so she prighte,	And she stabbed herself so with her beak
That ther nys tygre, ne noon so cruel beest	That there is no tiger, nor any other cruel beast,
That dwelleth outher in wode or in forest	Dwelling in either the wood or the forest,
That nolde han wept, if that he wepe koude	That would not have wept, if he could weep,
For sorwe of hir, she shrighte alwey so loude.	From sorrow to see her, she was always shrieking so loud.
For ther nas nevere yet no man on lyve	There has never been any man living,
(If that I koude a faucon wel discryve),	If I could describe this falcon,
That herde of swich another of fairnesse,	Who had seen her equal in beauty,
As wel of plumage as of gentillesse	Such noble plumage,
Of shape and al that myghte yrekened be.	Such a wonderful shape, so perfect.
A faucon peregryn thanne semed she	She seemed to be a peregrine falcon
Of fremde land, and everemoore as she stood	From a foreign land; and over and over again, as she stood there,
She swowneth now and now for lakke of blood,	She fainted every now and then from lack of blood,
Til wel neigh is she fallen fro the tree.	Until she had almost fallen from the tree.
This faire kynges doghter Canacee,	This fair Princess, Canacee,
That on hir fynger baar the queynte ryng,	Who was wearing the strange ring on her finger,
Thurgh which she understood wel every thing	Through which she understood everything
That any fowel may in his leden seyn,	That any bird could say in his language,
And koude answeren hym in his ledene ageyn,	And could answer him back in the same way,
Hath understonde what this faucoun seyde,	Understood what this falcon meant,
And wel neigh for the routhe almoost she deyde.	And she almost died with pity.
And to the tree she gooth ful hastily,	She went quickly to the tree,
And on this faucoun looketh pitously,	And looked on this falcon with pity,
And heeld hir lappe abroad, for wel she wiste	And she spread her skirt wide, for she well knew
The faucoun moste fallen fro the twiste,	That the falcon must fall from the branch,
Whan that it swowned next, for lakke of blood.	Next time it fainted, from lack of blood.
A longe while to wayten hir she stood,	She waited a long time for her,
Til atte laste she spak in this manere	Until at last she finally said this
Unto the hauk, as ye shal after heere.	To the hawk, as you shall hear:
what is the cause, if it be for to telle,	"For what reason, if you can say,
That ye be in this furial pyne of helle?'	Are you suffering these terrible pains of hell?"
Quod Canacee unto the hauk above,	Said Canacee to the hawk above,
Is this for sorwe of deeth, or los of love?	"Is this through the sorrow of death, or loss of love?
For, as I trowe, thise been causes two	For, as I believe, those are the two things
That causeth moost a gentil herte wo.	That give my sorrow to a kind heart;
Of oother harm it nedeth nat to speke,	There's no need to mention any other harm.
For ye yourself upon yourself yow wreke,	For now you are taking things out on yourself,
Which proveth wel, that oother love or drede	Which proves that either anger or fear
Moot been enchesoun of your cruel dede,	Must be the reason for your cruel behaviour,
Syn that I see noon oother wight yow chace.	Since I can see no other creature chasing you.
For love of God as dooth yourselven grace.	For love of God, be kind to yourself,

Or what may been your helpe? for west nor est	*Or how can you be helped? For west nor east*
Ne saugh I nevere er now no bryd ne beest	*I never before have seen a bird nor beast*
That ferde with hymself so pitously.	*Treating itself so horribly.*
Ye sle me with your sorwe, verraily,	*Your sorrow truly is killing me,*
I have of yow so greet compassioun.	*I have such great pity for you.*
For Goddes love com fro the tree adoun,	*For the love of God, come down from the tree;*
And as I am a kynges doghter trewe,	*And as I am a true princess,*
If that I verraily the cause knewe	*If I truly knew the cause*
Of your disese, if it lay in my might	*Of your pain, if it lay my power,*
I wolde amenden it er that it were nyght,	*I would make amends for it before nightfall,*
As wisly helpe me, grete god of kynde!	*So help me Almighty God!*
And herbes shal I right ynowe yfynde,	*I shall find herbs right now*
To heele with youre hurtes hastily.	*Which will heal your hurts quickly."*
Tho shrighte this faucoun moore yet pitously	*Then the falcon shrieked even more pitifully*
Than ever she dide, and fil to grounde anon	*Than she had before, and fell down at once to the ground,*
And lith aswowne, deed, and lyk a stoon,	*Lying in a swoon, dead as a stone,*
Til Canacee hath in hir lappe hir take	*Until Canacee took her in her lap,*
Unto the tyme she gan of swough awake.	*Waiting for her to recover from her faint.*
And after that she of hir swough gan breyde,	*And after she had recovered*
Right ibn hir hsukes ledene thus she seyde:	*At once she said in her hawk's language:*
That pitee renneth soone in gentil herte,	*"That pity which quickly comes to kind hearts,*
Fellynge his similitude in peynes smerte,	*Feeling its opposite in stabbing pain,*
Is preved al day, as men may it see,	*Is shown every day, as men may see,*
As wel by werk as by auctoritee.	*By deeds as well as in knowledge;*
For gentil herte kitheth gentillesse.	*A kind heart shows its great kindness.*
I se wel, that ye han of my distresse	*I can see that you have pity*
Compassioun, my faire Canacee,	*For my distress, my fair Canacee,*
Of verray wommanly benignytee	*From the true womanly goodness*
That nature in youre principles hath set.	*That nature has given you.*
But for noon hope for to fare the bet,	*But I have no hope of getting better,*
But for to obeye unto youre herte free,	*Just follow your noble heart*
And for to maken othere be war by me,	*And let others be warned by me,*
As by the whelp chasted is the leoun,	*Like a whelp chastised by the lion,*
Right for that cause and that condlusioun	*For that reason and for that purpose,*
Whil that I have a leyser and a space,	*While I still have the strength and opportunity,*
Myn harm I wol confessen, er I pace.	*I will tell you what is wrong before I depart."*
And evere whil that oon hir sorwe tolde,	*And always, whilst the one was telling her sorrow,*
That oother weep, as she to water wolde,	*The other wept as if she was turned to water,*
Til that the faucoun bad hire to be stille;	*Until the falcon told her to be calm*
And with a syk right thus she seyde hir wille.	*And, sighing, told her what was on her mind:*
Ther I was bred, allas, that harde day!	*"I was born–curse the day!–*
And fostred in a roche of marbul gray	*And brought up on a marble grey cliff,*
So tendrely, that no thyng eyled me;	*So tenderly that nothing harmed me,*
I nyste nat what was adversitee,	*I didn't know anything about hardship*
Til I koude flee ful hye under the sky.	*Until I could fly high in the sky.*
Tho dwelte a tercelet me faste by	*A male falcon lived very near to me,*
That semed welle of alle gentillesse,	*Who seemed to exemplify nobility;*
Al were he ful of tresoun and falsnesse;	*Although he was full of treason and lies,*
It was so wrapped under humble cheere,	*It was so covered by a humble manner,*
And under hewe of trouthe in swich manere,	*And the false appearance of truth,*
Under plesance, and under bisy peyne,	*Pleasantness, and great attentiveness,*

That I ne koude han wend he koude feyne,	That nobody could have imagined he was false,
So depe in greyn he dyed his colours.	So deeply had he dyed his true colours.
Right as a serpent hit hym under floures	Just like a serpent which hides under the flowers
Til he may seen his tyme for to byte,	Until he sees the opportunity to bite,
Right so this god of love, this ypocryte,	So this hypocrite to the god of love
Dooth so hise cerymonyes and obeisaunces,	Performed his ceremonies and observances,
And kepeth in semblant alle hise observaunces	And gave such an impression of piety
That sowneth into gentillesse of love.	That he seemed to be full of love.
As in a toumbe is al the faire above,	As a tomb which is beautiful above,
And under is the corps swich as ye woot,	But underneath has a corpse, as you know,
Swich was this ypocrite, bothe coold and hoot;	That was what this hypocrite was like in every way.
And in this wise he served his entente,	And in this way he served his own purpose
That-save the feend-noon wiste what he mente;	So that, except for the devil, nobody knew what he was up to,
Til he so longe hadde wopen and compleyned,	Until he had wept and wailed for so long,
And many a yeer his service to me feyned,	And pretended to be a servant to me for so many years,
Til that myn herte, to pitous and to nyce,	That my heart, too kind and naive,
Al innocent of his corouned malice,	Knowing nothing of his great malice,
For-fered of his deeth, as thoughte me,	Terrified that he would die, it seemed to me,
Upon hise othes and his seuretee,	When I was given his oaths and his promises,
Graunted hym love up this condicioun	I gave him my love, upon the condition
That everemoore myn honour and renoun	That my honour and reputation
Were saved, bothe privee and apert.	Would be safe, in every way;
This is to seyn, that after his desert	I am saying, that as I thought he deserved,
I yaf hym al myn herte and al my thoght-	I gave him all my heart and my thoughts-
God woot and he, that ootherwise noght!-	God and he both know, I would never otherwise have agreed-
And took his herte in chaunge for myn for ay.	And I took his heart in exchange for mine for eternity.
But sooth is seyd, goon sithen many a day,	But it is truly said, and has been for many ages,
`A trewe wight and a theef thenken nat oon.'	"A true creature and a thief do not think the same way."
And whan he saugh the thyng so fer ygoon,	And when he saw the matter so advanced
That I hadde graunted hym fully my love,	That I gave him all my love
In swich a gyse as I have seyd above,	In the way in which I have described above,
And yeven hym my trewe herte, as free	And given him my true heart as freely
As he swoor he his herte yaf to me,	As he swore he gave his to me,
Anon this tigre ful of doublenesse	At once this tiger, full of doubledealing,
Fil on hise knees, with so devout humblesse,	Fell on his knees with such devout humility,
With so heigh reverence, and as by his cheere	With such great respect, and, as it seemed,
So lyk a gentil lovere of manere,	So like a gentle lover in his manners,
So ravysshed, as it semed, for the joye,	So ecstatic, it seemed, with happiness
That nevere Jason, ne Parys of Troye,	That neither Jason nor Paris of Troy-
Jason? certes, ne noon oother man	Jason? Certainly, nor any other man
Syn Lameth was, that alderfirst bigan	Since the time of Lameth, who first began
To loven two, as writen folk biforn,	To love another, as folks wrote long ago-
Ne nevere syn the firste man was born,	Never, since the first man was born,
Ne koude man, by twenty thousand part,	Could any man, by a factor of many thousands,

Countrefete the sophymes fo his art;	Be so cunning in counterfeiting his art,
Ne were worhty unbokelen his galoche,	There were none worthy to unbuckle his shoe,
Ther doublenesse or feynyng sholde approche,	Where deceitfulness or forgery were concerned,
Ne so koude thonke a wight as he dide me.	Nor has any other creature been treated as he did me!
His manere was an hevene for to see	His manner was heavenly to see
Til any womman, were she never so wys;	For any woman, however wise she was,
So peynted he and kembde at point-devys	He made himself look so wonderful in all things,
As wel hise wordes as his contenaunce	Both in his words and his expression,
And I so loved hym for his oveisaunce	And I loved him so much for his worship,
And for the trouthe I demed in his herte,	And for the truth I thought was in his heart,
That if so were that any thyng hym smerte,	That if there was anything which caused him pain,
Al were it nevere so lite, and I it wiste,	Even if it was a tiny thing, and I found out about it,
Me thoughte I felte deeth myn herte twiste.	I felt as though death was twisting my heart.
And shortly so ferforth this thyng is went,	And soon, the matter had gone so far
That my wyl was his willes instrument;	That my will was completely under his control;
This is to seyn, my wyl obeyed his wyl	That is to say, I did what he wanted
In alle thyng as fer as resoun fil,	In everything, as far as was reasonable,
Kepynge the boundes of my worship evere.	Keeping within the limits of my honour.
Ne nevere hadde I thyng so lief, ne levere,	Nobody ever loved more, or even as much,
As hym, God woot! ne nevere shal namo.	As him, God knows, and never shall again.
This lasteth lenger than a yeer or two,	This lasted longer than a couple of years,
That I supposed of hym noght but good.	And I thought nothing but good of him,
But finally, thus atte laste it stood,	But finally, it came out in the end
That Fortune wolde that he moste twynne	That fate wanted him to leave
Out of that place, which that I was inne.	The place where I was.
Wher me was wo that is no questioun;	There is no question as to whether I was sorrowful;
I kan nat make of it discripcioun.	I cannot describe it.
For o thyng dare I tellen boldely,	One thing I boldly dare say:
I knowe what is the peyne of deeth therby.	This has shown me what the pain of death is like;
Swich harme I felte, for he ne myghte bileve;	I felt such pain because he would not stay.
So on a day of me he took his leve	So one day he left me,
So sosrwefully eek, that I wende verraily,	With such sorrow that I truly believed
That he had felt as muche harm as I,	That he felt as much harm as I did,
Whan that I herde hym speke, and saugh his hewe.	When I heard him speak and saw how he looked.
But nathelees, I thoughte he was so trewe,	But nonetheless, I thought he was so loyal,
And eek that he repaire sholde ageyn	And also that he would come back again
Withinne a litel while, sooth to seyn,	In a little while, to tell the truth;
And resoun wolde eek that he moste go	And it also seemed reasonable that he had to go
For his honour, as ofte it happeth so,	For his honour, as so often happens,
That I made vertu of necessitee,	That I made a virtue from necessity,
And took it wel, syn that it moste be.	And took it well, since it had to be.
As I best myghte, I hidde fro hym my sorwe,	As best I could, I hid my sorrow from him,
And took hym by the hond, seint John to borwe,	And took him by the hand, swearing by St John,

And seyde hym thus, `Lo I am youres al.
Beth swich as I to yow have been, and shal.'

What he answerde, it nedeth noght reherce,

Who kan sey bet than he? who kan do werse?

Whan he hath al wel seyd, thanne hath he doon;

`Therfore bihoveth hire a ful long spoon
That shal ete with a feend,' thus herde I seye.
So atte laste he moste forth his weye,
And forth he fleeth, til he cam ther hym leste.

Whan it cam hym to purpos for to reste,
I trowe he hadde thilke text in mynde
That `alle thyng repeirynge to his kynde

Gladeth hymself;' thus seyn men, as I gesse.

Men loven of propre kynde newefangelnesse,
As briddes doon, that men in cages fede,
For though thou nyght and day take of hem hede,
And strawe hir cage faire and softe as silk,
And yeve hem sugre, hony, breed, and milk,
Yet right anon as that his dore is uppe,
He with his feet wol spurne adoun his cuppe,
And to the wode he wole and wormes ete;
So newefangel been they of hir mete,
And loven novelrie of propre kynde.
No gentillesse of blood ne may hem bynde.
So ferde this tercelet, allas, the day!
Though he were gentil born, and fressh, and gay,
And goodlich for to seen, humble and free,

He saugh upon a tyme a kyte flee,
And sodeynly he loved this kyte so
That al his love is clene fro me ago,
And hath his trouthe falsed in this wyse.
Thus hath the kyte my love in hire servyse,
And I am lorn withouten remedie.
And with that word this faucoun gan to crie,
And swowned eft in Canacees barm.

Greet was the sorwe for the haukes harm
That Canacee and alle hir wommen made.
They nyste hou they myghte the faucoun glade;

But Canacee hom bereth hir in hir lappe,

And softely in plastres gan hir wrappe,
Ther as she with hir beek hadde hurt hirselve.
Now kan nat Canacee but herbes delve

Out of the ground, and make saves newe

And said this to him: "See, I am all yours;
Treat me in the same way as I have treated you and always shall."
I need not repeat what he answered;

Who can speak better than him, and who can act worse?

When he had spoken everything well, then he was finished.

"She who sups with the devil
Needs a very long spoon," I have heard said.
So finally he had to go on his way,
And he sped off until he came to where he wanted.

When he wanted to rest,
I think he had that proverb in mind,
That 'everything, by going back to its natural state,

Makes himself happy;' that's what men say, I believe.

Men, because of their nature, love new things,
Like the birds that men feed in cages.
For though you look after them day and night,
And cover their cages with fine soft straw,
And give them sugar, honey, bread and milk,
Yet just as soon as the door is left open
He will kick away his cup,
And go to the wood and eat worms;
They are so fond of new tastes for their food,
And love novelties due to their nature,
No nobility can control them.
This is what this falcon did, alas!
Although he was noble, and fresh and gay,
And sweet to look on and humble and generous,

One time he saw a kite fly by,
And he was suddenly so in love with this kite
That all his love vanished from me,
And he became false to his promises.
So this kite has my lover serving her,
And I am lost, with nothing to be done!"
And with those words the falcon cried out
And fainted again in Canacee's lap.

A great sorrow for the harm done to this hawk
Filled Canacee and all of her women;
They did not know how they could make it happy.

But Canacee carried her home wrapped in her dress,

And softly began to wrap her in bandages,
Where she had harmed herself with her beak.
Now Canacee could do nothing but dig for herbs

From the ground, and make new ointments

Of herbes preciouse and fyne of hewe,	*Of the precious fine coloured herbs,*
To heelen with this hauk; fro day to nyght	*To heal this hawk. All day and night*
She dooth hir bisynesse and al hir myght.	*She worked as hard as she could,*
And by hir beddes heed she made a mewe,	*And by the head of her bed she made a pen*
And covered it with veluettes blewe,	*And covered it with blue velvet cloth,*
In signe of trouthe that is in wommen sene.	*As a sign of the truth that can be seen in women.*
And al withoute, the mewe is peynted grene,	*And on the outside, the pen was painted green,*
In which were ypeynted alle thise false fowles,	*The colour of all these false birds,*
As beth thise tidyves, tercelettes, and owles,	*Like these little birds, falcons and owls;*
Right for despit were peynted hem bisyde,	*Scornfully alongside them were painted*
And pyes on hem for to crie and chyde.	*Magpies, to cry out and criticise them.*
Thus lete I Canacee hir hauk kepyng;	*So I will leave Canacee looking after her hawk;*
I wol namoore as now speke of hir ryng,	*I won't say anything more about her ring*
Til it come eft to purpos for to seyn	*Until there is a point to explaining*
How that this faucoun gat hire love ageyn	*How this falcon got her love back,*
Repentant, as the storie telleth us,	*Repentant, so the story goes,*
By mediacioun of Cambalus,	*Through the intervention of Cambalus,*
The kynges sone, of which that I yow tolde.	*The son of the king, of whom I told you.*
But hennesforth I wol my proces holde	*But for now I will keep my story*
To speken of aventures and of batailles,	*To adventures and battles,*
That nevere yet was herd so grete mervailles.	*So wonderful their like has never been heard before.*
First wol I telle yow of Cambynskan,	*First I will tell you about Cambyuskan,*
That in his tyme many a citee wan;	*Who in his time conquered many cities;*
And after wol I speke of Algarsif,	*And after that I will speak of Algarsif,*
How that he wan Theodora to his wif,	*And how he won over Theodora as his wife,*
For whom ful ofte in greet peril he was,	*For whom he braved great dangers,*
Ne hadde he be holpen by the steede of bras;	*If he hadn't been helped by his brass horse;*
And after wol I speke of Cambalo	*And after that I will speak of Cambalo,*
That faught in lystes with the bretheren two	*That fought in tournaments with the two brothers*
For Canacee, er that he myghte hir wynne.	*For Canacee, before he could win her,*
And ther I lefte, I wol ayeyn bigynne.	*And then I will go back to where I left off.*
Explicit secunda pars.	***The end of the second part***
Incipit pars tercia.	***The start of the third part***
Appollo whirleth up his chaar so hye	*Apollo whirled his chariot up so high*
Til that the god Mercurius hous, the slye-	*To the house of the god Mercury, the sly–*

(This is all that remains of the Squire's Tale)

Heere folwen the wordes of the Frankelyn to the Squier, and the wordes of the hoost to the Frankelyn.

What the Franklin said to the Squire, and what the Host said to the Franklin

"In feith, Squier, thow hast thee wel yquit,	*"By God, Squire, you have done so well.*
And gentilly I preise wel thy wit,"	*I nobly praise your intelligence,"*
Quod the Frankeleyn, "considerynge thy yowthe,	*Said the Franklin, "considering your youth,*
So feelyngly thou spekest, sire, I allow the;	*You speak with such feeling, sir, I salute you!*
As to my doom, ther is noon that is here	*In my opinion, there is no one here*

Of eloquence that shal be thy peere,
If that thou lyve; God yeve thee good chaunce,
And in vertu sende thee continuance!
For of thy speche I have greet deyntee;
I have a sone, and, by the Trinitee,
I hadde levere than twenty pound worth lond,
Though it right now were fallen in myn hond,
He were a man of swich discrecioun
As that ye been! Fy on possessioun
But if a man be vertuous withal!
I have my sone snybbed, and yet shal,
For he to vertu listneth nat entende,
But for to pleye at dees, and to despende
And lese al that he hath, is his usage.
And he hath levere talken with a page
Than to comune with any gentil wight
Where he myghte lerne gentillesse aright."

    "Straw for youre gentillesse," quod our Hoost,
"What, Frankeleyn, pardee! sire, wel thou woost
That ech of yow moot tellen atte leste
A tale or two, or breken his biheste."

    "That knowe I wel, sire," quod the Frankeleyn,
"I prey yow, haveth me nat in desdeyn
Though to this man I speke a word or two."

    "Telle on thy tale, withouten wordes mo."

    "Gladly, sire Hoost," quod he, "I wole obeye
Unto your wyl; now herkneth what I seye.
I wol yow nat contrarien in no wyse
As fer as that my wittes wol suffyse;
I prey to God that it may plesen yow,
Thanne woot I wel that it is good ynow."

*Who will be able to speak so well,
If you live; May God give you good luck,
And through his kindness let you go on,
For your speech has delighted me.
I have a son, and by the holy Trinity,
I would give twenty pounds' worth of land,
Even if I had it right here and now,
For him to be a man of such talents
As you are! Damnation to possessions,
Unless a man is good as well!
I have told off my son, and will again,
Because he doesn't care about virtue;
He just likes playing dice, and spending
And losing everything that he has.
He would rather talk with a servant
Than chat with any noble person;
From him he might learn proper nobility."*

*"A curse on your nobility!" said our host.
"What, Franklin! By God, sir, you well know
That each of you must at least tell
A tale or two, or break your promise."*

*"I know that very well, sir," said Franklin.
"Please, don't be contemptuous to me,
Just because I say a word or two to this man."*

"Get on with your story without further ado."

*"Gladly, Sir host," he said, "I will obey
Your instructions; now listen to what I say.
I will not offend you in any way,
As far as my wits allow it.
I pray to God that you will be pleased with it;
That will show me that it is good enough.*

The Franklin's Tale

The Prologue

The prologe of the Frankeleyns tale.

Thise olde gentil Britouns in hir dayes
Of diverse aventures maden layes,
Rymeyed in hir firste Briton tonge;
Whiche layes with hir instrumentz they songe,
Or elles redden hem, for hir plesaunce.
And oon of hem have I in remembraunce,
Which I shal seyn, with good-wyl, as I kan.
But sires, by cause I am a burel man,
At my bigynnyng first I yow biseche,
Have me excused of my rude speche.
I lerned nevere rethorik, certeyn;
Thyng that I speke, it moot be bare and pleyn.
I sleep nevere on the Mount of Parnaso,
Ne lerned Marcus Tullius Scithero.
Colours ne knowe I none, withouten drede,

But swiche colours as growen in the mede,
Or elles swiche, as men dye or peynte.
Colours of rethoryk been me to queynte,
My spirit feeleth noght of swich mateere;
But if yow list, my tale shul ye heere.

The Franklin's Prologue

*These ancient noble Britons in there times
Made songs about various adventures,
Rhyming in their early British tongue,
And they sang their songs with instruments
Or read them out for their pleasure;
And I have one in my memory,
Which I shall tell as well as I can.
But, sirs, because I am an uneducated man,
As I begin I beg of you
To excuse me for my crude way of speaking.
I certainly never learned rhetoric;
Whatever I say, it must be plain and simple.
I never slept on Mount Parnassus,
Nor learned Marcus Tullius Cicero.
I know no rhetorical touches, that's for certain,
Only what comes naturally,
Or the ones that are common amongst men.
Figures of speech are strangers to me;
I don't have any feeling for them in my soul.
But if you want, you can hear my tale.*

The Tale

Heere bigynneth the Frankeleyns tale.

In Armorik, that called is Britayne,
Ther was a knyght that loved and dide his payne

To serve a lady in his beste wise;
And many a labour, many a greet emprise,
He for his lady wroghte, er she were wonne.
For she was oon the faireste under sonne,
And eek therto comen of so heigh kynrede

That wel unnethes dorste this knyght for drede
Telle hir his wo, his peyne, and his distresse.
But atte laste, she for his worthynesse,
And namely for his meke obeysaunce,
Hath swiche a pitee caught of his penaunce,
That pryvely she fil of his accord
To take hym for hir housbonde and hir lord-
Of swich lordshipe as men han over hir wyves-

And for to lede the moore in blisse hir lyves,
Of his free wyl he swoor hir as a knyght,
That nevere in al his lyf he, day ne nyght,
Ne sholde upon hym take no maistrie
Agayn hir wyl, ne kithe hir jalousie,
But hir obeye and folwe hir wyl in al

As any lovere to his lady shal;
Save that the name of soveraynetee,

That wolde he have, for shame of his degree.

She thanked hym, and with ful greet humblesse
She seyde, Sire, sith of youre gentillesse
Ye profre me to have so large a reyne,
Ne wolde nevere God bitwixe us tweyne,

As in my gilt, were outher werre or stryf.
Sir, I wol be youre humble trewe wyf,
Have heer my trouthe til that myn herte breste.

Thus been they bothe in quiete and in reste.
For o thyng, sires, saufly dar I seye,

That freendes everych oother moot obeye,
If they wol longe holden compaignye.
Love wol nat been constreyned by maistrye;
Whan maistrie comth, the God of Love anon

Beteth hise wynges, and farewel, he is gon!

Here the Franklin's Tale begins

In Armorica, which is called Brittany,
There was a knight who loved and worked hard
To serve a lady as best he could;
And many labours, many great endeavours,
He did for his lady before she was won over.
For she was one of the fairest women on earth,
And also came from such a distinguished background
That this knight hardly dared, out of fear,
To tell of his sorrow, his pain and his distress.
But at last she, because of his goodness,
And also for his meek obedience,
Took such pity on his suffering
That privately she agreed with him
To have him as her husband and her lord,
With such power as men have over their wives.

And so their lives would be happier,
He freely swore to her as a knight
That never in his life would he, day or night,
Assume any power for himself
Against her will, and he would not be jealous,
He would obey her, and follow her wishes in everything,
As any love should with his lady,
As long as they keep up the appearance of the man ruling,
Which he needed to avoid shaming his knighthood.
She thanked him, and very humbly
She said, "Sir, since in your nobility
You have given me such freedom,
And I pray to God that there will never be between us
Any war or strife caused by me.
Sir, I will be your true and humble wife–
I promise you this–until the day I die."

So they were both calm and content.
There is one thing, gentlemen, I dare say with confidence,
That friends must obey each other,
If they want to stay together long.
Love cannot be bullied.
When someone becomes master, the God of love immediately
Flaps its wings, and farewell, he is gone!

Love is a thyng as any spirit free.	Love is as free as any spirit.
Wommen of kynde desiren libertee,	Women, by nature, want freedom,
And nat to been constreyned as a thral-	And will not be constrained like slaves;
And so doon men, if I sooth seyen shal.	And men are the same, to tell the truth.
Looke who that is moost pacient in love,	See the person who keeps his patience when in love,
He is at his avantage al above.	He has a better position than anyone.
Pacience is an heigh vertu, certeyn,	Patience certainly is a noble virtue,
For it venquysseth, as thise clerkes seyn,	For it triumphs over, so the scholars say,
Thynges that rigour sholde nevere atteyne.	Things that force can never defeat.
For every word men may nat chide or pleyne,	Men cannot criticise all complain over every word.
Lerneth to suffre, or elles, so moot I goon,	Learn to suffer, or otherwise, I swear,
Ye shul it lerne, wherso ye wole or noon.	You will learn to, whether you like it or not;
For in this world, certein, ther no wight is	For in this world, certainly, there is nobody
That he ne dooth or seith som tyme amys.	Who doesn't sometimes do or say something wrong.
Ire, siknesse, or constellacioun	Anger, illness, or the position of the stars,
Wyn, wo, or chaungynge of complexioun	Drunkenness, sorrow, or an imbalance of humours
Causeth ful ofte to doon amys or speken.	Often causes people to do or say something wrong.
On every wrong a man may nat be wreken;	A man cannot take revenge for every wrong.
After the tyme moste be temperaunce	He must be remain temperate, suit himself to the times,
To every wight that kan on governaunce.	Everyone who knows about ruling does this.
And therfore hath this wise worthy knyght,	And so this wise and good knight,
To lyve in ese, suffrance hir bihight,	To have a peaceful life, promised to be patient with her,
And she to hym ful wisly gan to swere	And she swore to him very truly
That nevere sholde ther be defaute in here.	That he would never find fault in her.
Heere may men seen an humble wys accord!	Here men can see a humble and wise agreement;
Thus hath she take hir servant and hir lord,	This is how she took her servant and her lord–
Servant in love, and lord in mariage;	Servant in love, and husband in marriage.
Thanne was he bothe in lordship and servage-	So he was both a lord and a servant.
Servage? nay but in lordshipe above,	Servant? No, but still a lord,
Sith he hath bothe his lady and his love-	Since he had both his lady and his love;
His lady, certes, and his wyf also,	His lady, certainly, and also his wife,
The which that lawe of love acordeth to.	According to the laws of love.
And whan he was in this prosperitee,	And when he was in this happy situation,
Hoom with his wyf he gooth to his contree,	He took wife home to his country,
Nat fer fro Pedmark, ther his dwellyng was,	Not far from Pedmark, where his home was,
Where as he lyveth in blisse and in solas.	Where he lived in joy and happiness.
Who koude telle, but he hadde wedded be,	Who can know, unless he has been married,
The joye, the ese, and the prosperitee	The joy, the care, and the happiness
That is bitwixe an housbonde and his wyf?	That exists between a husband and wife?
A yeer and moore lasted this blisful lyf,	This happy life lasted for a year or more,
Til that the knyght of which I speke of thus,	Until the knight of whom I speak,
That of Kayrrud was cleped Arveragus,	Who was called Arveragus of Kayrrud,
Shoop hym to goon, and dwelle a yeer or tweyne,	Prepared to go and live for a year or two
In Engelond, that cleped was eek Briteyne,	In England, which was also called Britain,

To seke in armes worship and honour-	To try and get a reputation and honour from his prowess in arms–
For al his lust he sette in swich labour-	He had set his heart on this–
And dwelled there two yeer, the book seith thus.	And he lived there for two years; that's what the book says.
Now wol I stynten of this Arveragus	Now I will leave off talking of Arveragus,
And speken I wole of Dorigene his wyf,	And speak about his wife Dorigen,
That loveth hir housbonde as hir hertes lyf.	Who loved her husband as she did her life.
For his absence wepeth she and siketh,	She wept and sighed over his absence,
As doon thise noble wyves whan hem liketh.	As these noble wives do when they wish.
She moorneth, waketh, wayleth, fasteth, pleyneth,	She mourned, stayed awake, wailed, fasted and moaned;
Desir of his presence hir so destreyneth,	The desire for his presence was so distressing
That al this wyde world she sette at noght,	That she thought the whole wide world was worthless.
Hir freendes whiche that knewe hir hevy thoght,	Her friends, who knew how unhappy she was,
Conforten hir in al that ever they may.	Comforted her in every way they could.
They prechen hir, they telle hir nyght and day	They preached to her, they told her night and day
That causelees she sleeth hirself, allas!	That she was harming herself for no reason, alas!
And every confort possible in this cas	They gave every possible comfort in the situation,
They doon to hir, with all hir bisynesse,	Working as hard as they could to help her,
Al for to make hir leve hir hevynesse.	To persuade her not to be so sad.
By proces, as ye knowen everichoon,	Over time, as you all know,
Men may so longe graven in a stoon,	Men can scrape a stone for so long
Til som figure therinne emprented be.	That some shape will be imprinted on it.
So longe han they conforted hir, til she	They comforted her for so long until she
Receyved hath by hope and by resound	Accepted, through hope and reason,
The empryntyng of hir consolacioun,	The imprint of their consolation,
Thurgh which hir grete sorwe gan aswage;	And so her great sorrow began to be lessened;
She may nat alwey duren in swich rage.	She couldn't carry on in such passionate grief for ever.
And eek Arveragus, in al this care,	And also Arveragus, during her troubles,
Hath sent hir lettres hoom of his welfare,	Had written letters home telling how he was,
And that he wol com hastily agayn,	Saying he would come back soon;
Or elles hadde this sorwe hir herte slayn.	Otherwise the sorrow would have killed her.
Hir freendes sawe hir sorwe gan to slake,	Her friends saw that her sorrow was listening
And preyden hir on knees, for Goddes sake,	And prayed her, on their knees, for the sake of God,
To com and romen hir in compaignye,	To come out, and walk around with them,
Awey to dryve hir derke fantasye.	To drive away her black thoughts.
And finally she graunted that requeste,	And finally she agreed to that request,
For wel she saugh that it was for the beste.	For she could see that it really was for the best.
Now stood hir castel faste by the see;	Now her castle stood close by the sea,
And often with hir freendes walketh she	And she often walked with her friends
Hir to disporte, upon the bank an heigh,	To amuse herself on the high cliffs,
Where as she many a ship and barge seigh	Seeing many ships and sailing vessels
Seillynge hir cours, where as hem liste go.	Going on their journeys, wherever they chose.
But thanne was that a parcel of hir wo,	But then that also caused her sorrow,
For to hirself ful ofte allas, seith she,	For she often said to herself, "alas!"

Is ther no ship of so many as I se	"Is there no ship, of all these ones I see,
Wol bryngen hoom my lord? thanne were myn herte	To bring home my lord? Then my heart would be
Al warisshed of hisse bittre peynes smerte.	Cured of these sharp bitter pains."
Another tyme ther wolde she sitte and thynke	At other times she would sit and think there,
And caste hir eyen dounward fro the brynke;	Looking down from the brink.
But whan she saugh the reisly rokkes blake,	But when she saw the horrid black rocks,
For verray feere, so wolde hir herte quake	Her heart would shake with terrible fear,
That on hir feet she myghte hir noght sustene.	And she could not remain on her feet.
Thanne wolde she sitte adoun upon the grene,	Then she would sit down on the grass,
And pitously into the see biholde,	And piteously look at the sea,
And seyn right thus, with sorweful sikes colde:	And say this, with sorrowful, cold sighs:
Eterne God, that thurgh thy purveiaunce	"The eternal God, who with your foreknowledge
Ledest the world by certein governaunce,	Leads the world with perfect government,
In ydel, as men seyn, ye no thyng make.	Men say that you make no thing for no reason.
But, lord, thise grisly feendly rokkes blake,	But, Lord, these horrid devilish black rocks,
That semen rather a foul confusioun	Who seem to be an evil mess
Of werk, than any fair creacioun	Of work rather than any fair creation
Of swich a parfit wys God and a stable,	Of such a perfect wise and consistent God,
Why han ye wroght this werk unresonable?	Why have you built these horrible things?
For by this werk, south, north, ne west ne eest	For through this work, south, north, west, nor east,
Ther nys yfostred man, ne bryd, ne beest.	There is no benefit for any man, bird nor beast;
It dooth no good, to my wit, but anoyeth,	As far as I know it does no good, only harm.
Se ye nat, lord, how mankynde it destroyeth?	Can you not see, Lord, how it destroys mankind?
An hundred thousand bodyes of mankynde	A hundred thousand mortal men
Han rokkes slayn, al be they nat in mynde;	Have been killed by rocks, although their names are forgotten,
Which mankynde is so fair part of thy werk	And mankind is such a wonderful part of your creation
That thou it madest lyk to thyn owene merk.	That you made him in your own image.
Thanne semed it ye hadde a greet chiertee	Then it seemed that you had great love
Toward mankynde; but how thanne may it bee	Towards mankind; so how can it be
That ye swiche meenes make it to destroyen,	That you make things like this to destroy it,
Whiche meenes do no good, but evere anoyen?	Which do no good, but always cause trouble?
I woot wel clerkes wol seyn, as hem leste,	I know that scholars will say as they wish,
By argumentz, that al is for the beste,	And argue logically that everything is for the best,
Though I ne kan the causes nat yknowe,	Although I cannot see the reasoning.
But thilke God, that made wynd to blowe,	But the same God who made this blowing wind,
As kepe my lord; this my conclusioun.	Please protect my lord! That's what I say.
To clerkes lete I al this disputisoun-	I'll leave the arguments to the scholars.
But wolde God, that alle thise rokkes blake,	But I would to God that all these black rocks
Were sonken into helle for his sake!	Were sunk into hell for his sake!
Thise rokkes sleen myn herte for the feere!	These rocks are stabbing my heart with fear."
Thus wolde she seyn, with many a pitous teere.	So she would speak, with many sorrowful tears.
Hir freendes sawe that ti was no disport	Her friends saw that it gave her no pleasure
To romen by the see, but disconfort,	To walk by the sea, just discomfort,

And shopen for to pleyen somwher elles;	And decided they would amuse themselves elsewhere.
They leden hir by ryveres and by welles,	They took her along rivers and by springs,
And eek in othere places delitables,	And other delightful places;
They dauncen, and they pleyen at ches and tables.	They danced and they played chess and backgammon.
So on a day, right in the morwe tyde,	So one day, early in the morning,
Unto a gardyn that was ther bisyde,	They went to a garden that was nearby,
In which that they hadde maad hir ordinaunce	Where they had arranged
Of vitaille and of oother purveiaunce,	Food and other provisions,
They goon and pleye hem al the longe day.	And they amused themselves the whole long day.
And this was in the sixte morwe of May,	This was on the sixth morning of May,
Which May hadde peynted with his softe shoures	A May which had painted, with his soft showers,
This gardyn ful of leves and of floures,	This garden full of leaves and flowers;
And craft of mannes hand so curiously	And cunning craftsmanship had skilfully
Arrayed hadde this gardyn trewely,	Embellished this garden, truly,
That nevere was ther gardyn of swich prys	There was never such a wonderful garden
But if it were the verray Paradys.	Unless it was the original paradise.
The odour of floures and the fresshe sighte	The smell of flowers and the fresh sights
Wolde han maked any herte lighte	Would have pleased any heart
That evere was born, but if to greet siknesse	That was ever born, unless its illness
Or to greet sorwe helde it in distresse;	Or sorrow was too great and kept it in distress,
So ful it was of beautee with plesaunce.	There was so much beauty and pleasure there.
At after dyner gonne they to daunce	After dinner they went to dance,
And synge also, save Dorigen allone,	And also sing, apart from Dorigen,
Which made alwey hir compleint and hir moone	Who maintained her complaining and moaning,
For she ne saugh hym on the daunce go	For in the dance she could not see the one
That was hir housbonde, and hir love also.	Who was her husband and also her lover.
But nathelees she moste a tyme abyde,	Nevertheless she had to bide her time
And with good hope lete hir sorwe slyde.	And let hope triumph over her sorrow.
Upon this daunce, amonges othere men,	At this dance, amongst other men,
Daunced a squier biforn Dorigen	There was a squire dancing in front of Dorigen,
That fressher was, and jolyer of array,	Who was fresher and more merrily dressed,
As to my doom, than is the monthe of May.	In my opinion, than the month of May.
He syngeth, daunceth, passynge any man	He sang and danced, better than any man
That is or was, sith that the world bigan.	Ever has or ever will, since the world began.
Therwith he was, if men sholde hym discryve,	So he was, if one wanted to describe him,
Oon of the beste farynge man of lyve;	One of the best looking men alive;
Yong, strong, right vertuous, and riche, and wys,	Young, strong, very brave, rich and wise,
And wel biloved, and holden in greet prys.	Much loved, and very respected.
And shortly, if the sothe I tellen shal,	And soon, if I tell the truth,
Unwityng of this Dorigen at al,	Completely unknown to Dorigen,
This lusty squier, servant to Venus,	This lusty squire, a servant of Venus,
Which that ycleped was Aurelius,	Who was called Aurelius,
Hadde loved hir best of any creature	Had loved her more than any creature
Two yeer and moore, as was his aventure;	For more than two years, such was his fate,
But nevere dorste he tellen hir his grevaunce,	But he never dared to tell her how he felt.
Withouten coppe he drank al his penaunce.	He wallowed in his suffering.

He was despeyred, no thyng dorste he seye

Save in his songes somwhat wolde he wreye
His wo, as in a general compleynyng.
He seyde he lovede, and was biloved no thyng,

Of swich matere made he manye layes,
Songes, compleintes, roundels, virelayes,
How that he dorste nat his sorwe telle,
But langwissheth, as a furye dooth in helle,
And dye he moste, he seyde, as dide Ekko

For Narcisus, that dorste nat telle hir wo,

In oother manere than ye heere me seye,
Ne dorste he nat to hir his wo biwreye,
Save that paraventure som tyme at daunces,

Ther yonge folk kepen hir observaunces,
It may wel be he looked on hir face,
In swich a wise as man that asketh grace;
But no thyng wiste she of his entente.
Nathelees it happed, er they thennes wente,
By cause that he was hir neighebour,
And was a man of worship and honour,

And hadde yknowen hym of tyme yoore,
They fille in speche, and forthe moore and moore

Unto this purpos drough Aurelius.
And whan he saugh his tyme, he seyde thus:

Madame, quod he, by God that this world made,

So that I wiste it myghte your herte glade,

I wolde that day that youre Arveragus
Wente over the see, that I, Aurelius,
Hadde went ther nevere I sholde have come agayn.

For wel I woot my servyce is in vayn,

My gerdoun is but brestyng of myn herte.
Madame, reweth upon my peynes smerte,
For with a word ye may me sleen or save.
Heere at your feet, God wolde that I were grave,

I ne have as now no leyser moore to seye,
Have mercy, sweete, or ye wol do me deye.

She gan to looke upon Aurelius:
Is this youre wyl! quod she, and sey ye thus?

Nevere erst, quod she, ne wiste I what ye mente.

He was in despair; he didn't dare say anything,	
Except sometimes in his songs he would reveal	
His sorrow, in a general sort of way;	
He said that he was in love and was not loved back;	
He made many verses on this subject,	
Songs, laments, chants and melodies,	
Saying how he dared not tell his sorrow,	
But he was suffering like a fury in hell;	
And he said that he would have to die, as Echo did	
For Narcissus, whom she dared not tell her sorrow.	
There were other ways which I may not tell	
In which he dared not tell her his sorrow,	
Except that occasionally, by chance, at dances,	
Where young folk courted each other,	
Maybe that he looked at her face	
In the same way as a man asking for kindness;	
But she knew nothing of his intentions.	
However it happened, before they left,	
Because he was her neighbour,	
And was a man of good reputation and honour,	
And she had known him for a long time,	
They started talking; and in their talk, Aurelius	
Came closer and closer to his meaning,	
And when he saw his opportunity, he said these words:	
"Madam," he said, "by the God that made this world,	
Providing that I knew it might make you happy,	
I wish that on the day your Arveragus	
Went over the sea that I, Aurelius,	
Had gone somewhere from whence I could never return.	
For I am well aware that all my service is useless;	
All my reward is the breaking of my heart.	
Madam, have pity on my horrible pain;	
For with a word you can kill me or save me.	
I wish to God that I was buried here at your feet!	
I don't have the chance to say any more;	
Have mercy on me, sweet, or you will kill me!"	
She then looked at Aurelius:	
"Is this your desire," she said, "and this is what you say?	
Never before," she said, "did I know what you meant.	

But now, Aurelie, I knowe youre entente.	But now, Aurelius, I know what you mean,
By thilke God, that yaf me soule and lyf,	And by the same God that gave me my soul and life,
Ne shal I nevere been untrewe wyf,	I will never be a disloyal wife,
In word ne werk, as fer as I have wit.	In word nor deed, as long as I keep my sense;
I wol been his to whom that I am knyt.	I will belong to the one with whom I am joined.
Taak this for fynal answere as of me.	Take this as my final answer."
But after that, in pley thus seyde she,	But after that, as a joke, she then said:
Aurelie, quod she, by heighe God above,	"Aurelius," she said, "by great God above,
Yet wolde I graunte yow to been youre love,	I would still agree to be your lover,
Syn I yow se so pitously complayne.	Since I see that you are so terribly sad.
Looke, what day that endelong Britayne	On whatever day that from one end to the other of Brittany
Ye remoeve alle the rokkes, stoon by stoon,	You can remove all the rocks, stone by stone,
That they ne lette shipe ne boot to goon,	So that they do not block the passage of any ship or boat—
I seye, whan ye han maad the coost so clene	I say when you have made the coast so clean
Of rokkes that ther nys no stoon ysene,	Of rocks that is not a stone can be seen,
Thanne wol I love yow best of any man!	Then I will love you better than any man;
Have heer my trouthe in al that evere I kan.	I promise you this, as truly as I can."
Is ther noon oother grace in yow? quod he.	"Can you not give me any other kindness?" he said.
No, by that lord, quod she, that maked me;	"No, by the Lord," she said, "that made me!
For wel I woot that it shal nevere bityde;	For I am certain that it will never happen.
Lat swiche folies out of your herte slyde.	Let such foolishness leave your heart.
What deyntee sholde a man han in his lyf	How should a man enjoy his life
For to go love another mannes wyf,	If he tries to love another man's wife,
That hath hir body whan so that hym liketh?	Who can have her body whenever he pleases?"
Aurelius ful ofte soore siketh,	Aurelius gave many very bitter sighs;
Wo was Aurelie, whan that he this herde,	Aurelius was sorrowful when he heard this,
And with a sorweful herte he thus answered.	And with a sorrowing heart he answered her:
Madame, quod he, this were an inpossible;	"Madam," he said, "this is impossible!
Thanne moot I dye of sodeyn deth horrible.	So I must die a sudden horrible death."
And with that word he turned hym anon.	Saying that he turned away at once.
Tho coome hir othere freendes many oon,	Then many other friends came up to her,
And in the aleyes romeden up and doun,	Roaming up and down the garden paths,
And no thyng wiste of this conclusioun,	Knowing nothing about the business,
But sodeynly bigonne revel newe,	But they suddenly began their revels anew
Til that the brighte sonne loste his hewe,	Until the bright sun had lost its shine;
For thorisonte hath reft the sonne his lyght-	For the horizon cut off the light of the sun,
This is as muche to seye as, ti was nyght-	In other words it was night,
And hoom they goon in joye and in solas,	And they went home, joyful and happy,
Save oonly wrecche Aurelius, allas!	Apart from wretched Aurelius, alas!
He to his hous is goon with sorweful herte;	He went to his house with a sorrowing heart.
He seeth he may nat fro his deeth asterte;	He saw that he could not escape his death;
Hym semed that he felte his herte colde;	He thought that he felt his heart grow cold.
Up to the hevene hise handes he gan holde,	He held his hands up to the heavens,
And on hise knowes bare he sette hym doun,	And put himself down on his bare knees,
And in his ravyng seyde his orisoun.	And raving, said his prayer.
For verray wo out of his wit he breyde;	In sorrow he had suddenly gone out of his mind.
He nyste what he spak, but thus he seyde:	He didn't know what he was saying, but this is what he said:

With pitous herte his pleynt hath he bigonne	With a sorrowing heart he began to complain
Unto the goddes, and first unto the sonne	To the gods, firstly to the sun:
He seyde, Appollo, God and governour	He said, "Apollo, god and governor
Of every plaunte, herbe, tree, and flour	Of every plant, herb, tree and flower,
That yevest after thy declinacioun	Who gives, according to your position in the sky,
To ech of hem his tyme and his sesoun,	Each of them their time and season,
As thyn herberwe chaungeth lowe or heighe,	As your position changes, low or high,
Lord Phebus, cast thy mericiable eighe	Lord Phoebus, cast your merciful eye
On wrecche Aurelie, which that am but lorn.	On wretched Aurelius, who is almost lost.
Lo, lord, my lady hath my deeth ysworn	Look, Lord! My lady has sworn to my death,
Withoute gilt, but thy benignytee	Guiltless, unless your kindness
Upon my dedly herte have som pitee.	Take some pity on my dying heart.
For wel I woot, lord Phebus, if yow lest,	For I well know, Lord Phoebus, if you wish,
Ye may me helpen, save my lady, best.	You can help me best of anybody, apart from my lady.
Now voucheth sauf that I may yow devyse	Now grant that I can tell you
How that I may been holpen and in what wyse.	How I can be helped and in what way.
Your blisful suster, Lucina the sheene,	Your beautiful sister, bright Luchina,
That of the see is chief goddesse and queene,	Who is the chief goddess and queen of the sea
(Though Neptunus have deitee in the see,	(Though Neptune is the god of the sea,
Yet emperisse aboven hym is she)	She is Empress over him),
Ye knowen wel, lord, that right as hir desir	You know very well, lord, that just as she wishes
Is to be quyked and lightned of youre fir,	To be kindled and lit by your fire,
For which she folweth yow ful bisily,	And so she follows you very closely,
Right so the see desireth naturelly	In the same way sea naturally desires
To folwen hir, as she that is goddesse	To follow her, as she is the goddess
Bothe in the see and ryveres moore and lesse.	Of both the sea and rivers great and small.
Wherfore, lord Phebus, this is my requeste;	So, Lord Phoebus, this is what I ask—
Do this miracle, or do myn herte breste,	Do this miracle, or break my heart—
That now next at this opposicioun	That at the next change in the heavens,
Which in the signe shal be of the Leoun,	Which will be in the sign of the Lion,
As preieth hir, so greet a flood to brynge	Ask her to bring such a great tide
That fyve fadme at the leeste it oversprynge	That it rises at least five fathoms above
The hyeste rokke in Armorik Briteyne,	The highest rock in Armorican Brittany;
And lat this flood endure yeres tweyne.	And let this tide last for two years.
Thanne, certes, to my lady may I seye	Then I can certainly say to my lady,
`Holdeth youre heste, the rokkes been aweye.'	'Keep your promise, the rocks have gone.'
Lord Phebus, dooth this miracle for me,	Lord Phoebus, do this miracle for me.
Preye hir she go no faster cours than ye.	Ask her to go no faster than you;
I seye, preyeth your suster that she go	I say, ask your sister to go
No faster cours than ye thise yeres two.	No faster than you for these two years.
Thanne shal she been evene atte fulle alway;	Then she will always match you,
And spryng flood laste bothe nyght and day;	And the spring tide will last through night and day.
And but she vouche sauf in swich manere	Unless she agrees in this way
To graunte me my sovereyn lady deere,	To let me have my dear lady,
Prey hir to synken every rok adoun	Ask her to sink every rock down
Into hir owene dirke regioun	Into her own dark region
Under the ground ther Pluto dwelleth inne,	Underground, where Pluto lives,
Or nevere mo shal I my lady wynne.	Or else I will never win my lady.
Thy temple in Delphos wol I barefoot seke,	I will walk barefoot to your temple in Delphi.
Lord Phebus; se the teeris on my cheke,	Lord Phoebus, see the tears on my cheeks,
And of my peyne have som compassioun!	And have some pity on my suffering."

And with that word in swowne he fil adoun,	And with that word he fell down in a faint,
And longe tyme he lay forth in a traunce.	And for a long time he lay there in a trance.
His brother, which that knew of his penaunce,	His brother, who knew what he was suffering,
Up caughte hym, and to bedde he hath hym broght.	Lifted him up and brought him to his bed.
Dispeyred in this torment and this thought	He despaired of his pain and thought
Lete I this woful creature lye;	I will leave this sorrowing creature here;
Chese he for me wheither he wol lyve or dye.	Let him choose, for all I care, life or death.
Arveragus with heele and greet honour,	Arveragus, with his health and great honour,
As he that was of chivalrie the flour,	As he was the very flower of chivalry,
Is comen hoom, and othere worthy men.	Had come home, with other good men.
O blisful artow now, thou Dorigen!	Now you are happy, Dorigen,
That hast thy lusty housbonde in thyne armes,	You have your lusty husband in your arms,
The fresshe knyght, the worthy man or armes,	The fresh knight, the worthy man of arms,
That loveth thee, as his owene hertes lyf.	Who loves you as much as life itself.
No thyng list hym to been ymaginatyf	There was nothing to make him suspicious,
If any wight hadde spoke, whil he was oute,	Wondering if any person had spoken, while he was away,
To hire of love; he hadde of it no doute,	Of love to her; he had no fear of that.
He noght entendeth to no swich mateere,	He paid no attention to such matters,
But daunceth, justeth, maketh hir good cheere,	But he danced, jousted, and made her happy;
And thus in joye and blisse I lete hem dwelle,	And so I will leave them in joy and happiness,
And of the sike Aurelius I wol telle.	And tell you of the sick Aurelius.
In langour and in torment furyes	In suffering and terrible torment
Two yeer and moore lay wrecche Aurelyus,	Wretched Aurelius lay for two years or more,
Eer any foot he myghte on erthe gon;	Before he could walk again;
Ne confort in this tyme hadde he noon,	Nobody comforted him in this time,
Save of his brother, which that was a clerk.	Except for his brother, who was a clerk.
He knew of al this wo and al this werk;	He knew all about his sorrow and suffering,
For to noon oother creature, certeyn,	But he dared tell no other creature
Of this matere he dorste no word seyn.	Anything about the matter.
Under his brest he baar it moore secree	He kept it hidden in his heart more secretly
Than evere dide Pamphilus for Galathee.	Than Pamphilus ever did for Galathee.
His brest was hool withoute for to sene,	Outwardly, his chest looked undamaged,
But in his herte ay was the arwe kene.	But the sharp arrow was always in his heart.
And wel ye knowe that of a sursanure	And you know well that they wound only healed on the surface
In surgerye is perilous the cure,	In surgery is not certain to be cured,
But men myghte touche the arwe, or come therby.	Unless one can touch the arrow or pull it out.
His brother weep and wayled pryvely,	His brother wept and wailed secretly,
Til atte laste hym fil in remembraunce	Until at last he remembered
That whiles he was at Orliens in Fraunce,	That while he was at Orleans in France–
As yonge clerkes, that been lykerous	As young students are eager
To reden artes that been curious,	To read of strange arts,
Seken in every halke and every herne	And look in every nook and cranny
Particular sciences for to lerne,	To learn arcane sciences–
He hym remembred, that upon a day	He remembered that, one day,
At Orliens in studie a book he say	At Orleans in a library he saw a book
Of magyk natureel, which his felawe,	Of natural magic, which his friend,
That was that tyme a bacheler of lawe-	Who was at that time a student of law,
Al were he ther to lerne another craft-	Although he was there to learn another trade,
Hadde prively upon his desk ylaft;	Had secretly left on his desk;
Which book spak muchel of the operaciouns,	This book said much about the matters
Touchynge the eighte and twenty mansiouns	Concerning the twenty-eight houses

That longen to the moone, and swich folye	*Of the moon, and other such nonsense*
As in oure dayes is nat worth a flye.	*That in our day is not worth a flea—*
For hooly chirches feith in oure bileve	*For the holy Church trusts us to believe*
Ne suffreth noon illusioun us to greve.	*And does not allow any illusion to disturb us.*
And whan this book was in his remembraunce,	*And when he remembered this book,*
Anon for joye his herte gan to daunce,	*At once his heart began to dance,*
And to hymself he seyde pryvely,	*And he secretly said to himself,*
My brother shal be warisshed hastily;	*"My brother will be cured at once;*
For I am siker that ther be sciences	*For I am certain that there are sciences*
By whiche men make diverse apparences	*Through which men can make different illusions,*
Swiche as thise subtile tregetoures pleye;	*Like the ones the cunning conjurors create.*
For ofte at feestes have I wel herd seye	*Often at feasts I have heard it well said*
That tregetours withinne an halle large	*That illusionists in a great hall*
Have maad come in a water and a barge,	*Have made it seem that water and a barge have come in*
And in the halle rowen up and doun.	*And that they have rowed up and down the hall.*
Somtyme hath semed come a grym leoun;	*Sometimes it does seem like a grim lion has come in;*
And somtyme floures sprynge as in a mede,	*Sometimes as if flowers sprang up in a field;*
Somtyme a vyne, and grapes white and rede,	*Sometimes there are vines, with white and red grapes;*
Somtyme a castel al of lym and stoon;	*Sometimes a castle, made of mortar and stone;*
And whan hem lyked, voyded it anoon,	*And when they wanted, it suddenly vanished.*
Thus semed it to every mannes sighte.	*Everyone thought that they'd seen it.*
Now thanne conclude I thus, that if I myghte	*So I reach this conclusion: that if I could*
At Orliens som oold felawe yfynde	*Find some old fellow at Orleans*
That hadde this moones mansions in mynde,	*Who remembered these stations of the moon,*
Or oother magyk natureel above,	*Or other natural magic better than that,*
He sholde wel make my brother han his love;	*He could easily get my brother his love.*
For with an apparence a clerk may make	*For with an apparition a clerk could make it seem*
To mannes sighte, that alle the rokkes blake	*To the eyes of man, that all the black rocks*
Of Britaigne weren yvoyded everichon,	*Of Brittany have all been removed,*
And shippes by the brynke comen and gon,	*And ships could sail up and down close to shore,*
And in swich forme enduren a wowke or two.	*And this illusion could last a week or two.*
Thanne were my brother warisshed of his wo;	*Then my brother would be cured of his sorrows;*
Thanne moste she nedes holden hire biheste,	*She would have to keep her promise,*
Or elles he shal shame hire atte leeste.	*Or else at the very least he could make her ashamed."*
what sholde I make a lenger tale of this?	*Why should I make this tale any longer?*
Unto his brotheres bed he comen is,	*He came to his brother's bed,*
And swich confort he yaf hym for to gon	*And he made him so enthusiastic to go*
To orliens that he up stirte anon,	*To Orleans that he jumped up at once,*
And on his wey forthward thanne is he fare	*And he started to make his way there*
In hope for to been lissed of his care.	*In the hope of being relieved of his sorrows.*
whan they were come almoost to that citee,	*When they had almost come to that city,*
But if it were a two furlong or thre,	*Not more than a couple of furlongs away,*
A yong clerk romynge by hymself they mette,	*They met a young clerk wandering alone,*
Which that in latyn thriftily hem grette,	*Who politely greeted them in Latin,*
And after that he seyde a wonder thyng --	*And after that he said an amazing thing:*

I knowe, quod he, the cause of youre comyng.	"I know," he said, "why you are here."
And er they ferther any foote wente,	And before they went a foot farther
He tolde hem al that was in hire entente.	He told them what it was they were after.
this briton clerk hym asked of felawes	This Breton clerk asked him about fellows
The whiche that he had knowe in olde dawes,	Whom he had known in the old days,
And he answerde hym that they dede were,	And he told him that they were dead,
For which he weep ful ofte many a teere.	And he shared many a tear for them.
doun of his hors aurelius lighte anon,	Aurelius jumped straight down from his horse,
And with this magicien forth is he gon	And went off with this magician,
Hoom to his hous, and maden hem wel at ese.	Home to his house, and he made them very comfortable.
Hem lakked no vitaille that myghte hem plese.	They certainly weren't lacking for good food.
So wel arrayed hous as ther was oon	The house was so well appointed that
Aurelius in his lyf saugh nevere noon.	Aurelius had never in his life seen one better.
he shewed hym, er he wente to sopeer,	He showed him, before he went to supper,
Forestes, parkes ful of wilde deer;	Forests, with parks full of wild deer;
Ther saugh he hertes with hir hornes hye,	There he saw harts with their tall horns,
The gretteste that evere were seyn with ye.	The largest that any man had ever seen.
He saugh of hem an hondred slayn with houndes,	He saw a hundred of them killed with dogs,
And somme with arwes blede of bittre woundes.	And others bled with bitter arrow wounds.
He saugh, whan voyded were thise wilde deer,	He saw, when the wild deer had gone,
Thise fauconers upon a fair ryver,	Hunters with falcons on a lovely riverbank,
That with hir haukes han the heron slayn.	Who had killed a heron with their hawks.
tho saugh he knyghtes justyng in a playn;	Then he saw knights jousting on a plain;
And after this he dide hym swich plesaunce	And after this he gave him pleasure
That he hym shewed his lady on a daunce,	By showing him his lady dancing,
On which hymself he daunced, as hym thoughte.	Dancing with himself, so he thought.
And whan this maister that this magyk wroughte	And when this master who made this magic
Saugh it was tyme, he clapte his handes two,	Saw the time was up, he clapped his hands together,
And farewel! al oure revel was ago,	And farewell! All the pleasures were gone.
And yet remoeved they nevere out of the hous,	And yet they had never left the house,
Whil they saugh al this sighte merveillous,	In seeing any of these marvellous sights,
But in his studie, ther as his bookes be,	But were still in his study, with his books,
They seten stille, and no wight but they thre.	Sitting still, and there was nobody there but the three of them.
to hym this maister called his squier,	This master called his squire to him,
And seyde hym thus -- is redy oure soper?	And asked him, "Is our supper ready?
Almoost an houre it is, I undertake,	I think it's almost an hour
Sith I yow bad oure soper for to make,	Since I ordered you to make it,
Whan that thise wrothy men wenten with me	When these good men went with me
Into my studie, ther as my bookes be.	Into my study, where my books."
sire, quod this squier, whan it liketh yow,	"Sir," said this squire, "when you wish
It is al redy, though ye wol right now.	It is all ready, even if you want it right now."
Go we thanne soupe, quod he, as for the beste.	"Then let's go to supper," he said, "that's the best thing.
Thise amorous folk somtyme moote han hir reste.	These passionate folk need rest sometimes."
at after-soper fille they in tretee	After supper they began to speak of
What somme sholde this maistres gerdon be,	How much this master should be rewarded,
To remoeven alle the rokkes of britayne,	For removing all the rocks of Brittany,
And eek from gerounde to the mouth of sayne.	From the Gironde to the mouth of the Seine.
he made it straunge, and swoor, so God hym save,	He made it difficult, and swore, that as God was his witness,

Middle English	Modern English
Lasse than a thousand pound he wolde nat have,	He would not take less than a thousand pounds,
Ne gladly for than somme he wolde nat goon. aurelius, with blisful herte anoon,	And even that amount wouldn't make him happy. Aurelius, with a happy heart, at once
Answerde thus -- fy on a thousand pound!	Answered thus: "A thousand pounds be damned!
This wyde world, which that men seye is round,	This wide world, which men say is round,
I wolde it yeve, if I were lord of it.	I would give, if I were lord of it.
This bargayn is ful dryve, for we been knyt.	The bargain has been made, we are agreed.
Ye shal be payed trewely, by my trouthe!	You will honestly be paid, I swear to you!
But looketh now for no necligence or slouthe	But make sure that there is no negligence or laziness,
Ye tarie us heere, no lenger than to-morwe.	You mustn't keep us here past tomorrow."
Nay, quod this clerk, have heer my feith to borwe.	"No," said this clerk, "I pledge my faith to you."
To bedde is goon Aurelius whan hym leste,	Aurelius went to bed when he felt like it,
And wel ny al that nyght he hadde his reste;	And he slept almost the whole night through.
What for his labour and his hope of blisse,	What with his labours and his hopes of happiness
His woful hrete of penaunce hadde a lisse.	His sorrowing heart felt relief.
Upon the morwe, whan that it was day,	On the next morning, when day came,
To Britaigne tooke they the righte way,	They went straight to Brittany,
Aurelie and this magicien bisyde,	Aurelius and this magician at his side,
And been descended ther they wolde abyde.	And they came to where they would stay.
And this was, as thise bookes me remembre,	At this time it was, as the books remind me,
The colde frosty sesoun of Decembre.	The cold, frosty season of December.
Phebus wax old, and hewed lyk latoun,	The sun grew old, and was coloured like tin,
That in this hoote declynacioun	When he had been at his height
Shoon as the burned gold, and stremes brighte;	He had shone like polished gold with bright rays;
But now in Capricorn adoun he lighte,	But now he declined in Capricorn,
Where as he shoon ful pale, I dar wel seyn.	Where I can tell you his light was very pale.
The bittre frostes, with the sleet and reyn,	The bitter frosts, with the sleet and rain,
Destroyed hath the grene in every yerd;	Had destroyed all the greenery in every garden.
Janus sit by the fyr, with double berd,	Janus sat by the fire, with his two faces,
And drynketh of his bugle horn the wyn.	And drank wine from his buffalo horn;
Biforn hym stant brawen of the tusked swyn,	In front of him was the meat of the wild boar,
And `Nowel' crieth every lusty man.	And "Noel!" cried every happy man.
Aurelius, in al that evere he kan,	Aurelius, in every way he could
Dooth to his master chiere and reverence,	Provided entertainments and respect for this master,
And preyeth hym to doon his diligence	And prayed that he would work hard
To bryngen hym out of his peynes smerte,	To save him from his bitter pains,
Or with a swerd that he wolde slitte his herte.	Or else he would cut his heart out with a sword.
This subtil clerk swich routhe had of this man,	This cunning clerk had such pity on this man
That nyght and day he spedde hym that he kan	That he worked night and day, as well as he could,
To wayten a tyme of his conclusioun,	To find a right time for his experiment;
This is to seye, to maken illusioun	By which I mean, to make an illusion,
By swich an apparence or jogelrye-	With some sleight of hand or conjuring-
I ne kan no termes of astrologye-	I don't know the nitty-gritty of astrology-

Middle English	Modern English
That she and every wight sholde wene and seye	So that she and every other person would believe and say
That of Britaigne the rokkes were aweye,	That all the rocks of Brittany had been taken away,
Or ellis they were sonken under grounde.	Or else they were sunk underground.
So atte laste he hath his tyme yfounde	So at last he found the time
To maken hise japes and his wrecchednesse	To do his tricks and his wretched deeds
Of swich a supersticious cursednesse.	Of such cursed superstition.
Hise tables Tolletanes forth he brought,	He brought out his astronomical tables from Toledo,
Ful wel corrected, ne ther lakked nought,	Perfectly adjusted, and there was nothing missing,
Neither his collect ne hise expans yeeris,	Neither his yearly tables nor the extended ones,
Ne hise rootes, ne hise othere geeris,	Nor his calculations, nor his other apparatus,
As been his centris and hise argumentz,	Like his geometrical instruments
And hise proporcioneles convenientz	And his reckoner for the motions of the planets,
For hise equacions in every thyng.	He knew every angle of the astrological sphere.
And by his eighte speere in his wirkyng	From the eighth sphere in his working
He knew ful wel how fer Alnath was shove	He knew exactly how far Alnath was above
Fro the heed of thilke fixe Aries above	The head of the fixed point of Aries,
That in the ninthe speere considered is.	Who is in the ninth sphere;
Ful subtilly he kalkuled al this.	He calculated all this very cleverly.
Whan he hadde founde his firste mansioun,	When he had found the first position of the moon
He knew the remenaunt by proporcioun,	He knew the rest by calculation,
And knew the arisyng of his moone weel,	And he knew when the moon would rise,
And in whos face and terme, and everydeel;	By which planet, and in which Zodiac, and everything;
And knew ful weel the moones mansioun	And he was well aware of the position of the Moon
Acordaunt to his operacioun,	In relation to his experiment,
And knew also hise othere observaunces	And he also knew other observations
For swiche illusiouns and swiche meschaunces	For such tricks and evil practices
As hethen folk useden in thilke dayes;—	As heathen folks employed in those days.
For which no lenger maked he delayes,	He no longer wasted any time,
But thurgh his magik, for a wyke or tweye,	But through his magic, for a week or two,
It semed that alle the rokkes were aweye.	It seemed that all the rocks were gone.
Aurelius, which that yet despeired is,	Aurelius, who was still in despair,
Wher he shal han his love, or fare amys,	Not knowing whether he would have his love or go wrong,
Awaiteth nyght and day on this myracle.	Was waiting for this miracle night and day;
And whan he knew that ther was noon obstacle,	And when he knew nothing had stopped it,
That voyded were thise rokkes everychon,	That all of these rocks had disappeared,
Doun to hise maistres feet he fil anon,	He fell down at once at his mistress' feet,
And seyde, I woful wrecche, Aurelius,	And said, "I, woeful, wretched Aurelius,
Thanke yow, lord, and lady myn, Venus,	Thank you, lord, and my Lady Venus,
That me han holpen fro my cares colde.	Who have helped me from my terrible sorrows."
And to the temple his wey forth hath he holde	And he went on his way to the temple,
Where as he knew he sholde his lady see,	Where he knew he would see his lady,
And whan he saugh his tyme, anon right hee	And when he saw his time he immediately,
With dredful herte and with ful humble cheere	With a fearful heart and a humble manner,

Salewed hath his sovereyn lady deere.

My righte lady, quod this woful man,
Whom I moost drede and love as I best kan,

And lothest were of al this world displese,

Nere it that I for yow have swich disese

That I moste dyen heere at youre foot anon,
Noght wolde I telle how me is wo bigon;

But, certes, outher moste I dye or pleyne,
Ye sle me giltelees for verray peyne.
But of my deeth thogh that ye have no routhe,

Avyseth yow er that ye breke youre trouthe.

Repenteth yow for thilke God above,
Er ye me sleen by cause that I yow love.
For madame, wel ye woot what ye han hight;

Nat that I chalange any thyng of right
Of yow, my sovereyn lady, but youre grace;

But in a gardyn yond at swich a place

Ye woot right wel what ye bihighten me,
And in myn hand youre trouthe plighten ye
To love me best, God woot ye seyde so,

Al be that I unworthy be therto.
Madame, I speke it for the honour of yow,
Moore than to save myn hertes lyf right now.
I have do so as ye comanded me,
And if ye vouchesauf, ye may go see.
Dooth as yow list, have youre biheste in mynde,
For, quyk or deed, right there ye shal me fynde.
In yow lith al, to do me lyve of deye,
But wel I woot the rokkes been aweye!

He taketh his leve, and she astonied stood,
In al hir face nas a drope of blood.
She wende nevere han come in swich a trappe.

Allas, quod she, that evere this sholde happe.

For wende I nevere, by possibilitee,
That swich a monstre or merveille myghte be.
It is agayns the proces of nature.
And hoom she goth a sorweful creature,
For verray feere unnethe may she go.
She wepeth, wailleth, al a day or two,
And swowneth that it routhe was to see;
But why it was, to no wight tolde shee,

Saluted his dear sovereign lady:

"My true lady," said this sorry man,
"Whom I most dread and love the best I can,

And would hate to displease more than anyone in the world,

If it wasn't for the fact that you have caused me such sorrow

That I must die right now here at your feet,
I would not tell you of how much sorrow I suffer.

But I must either say it or die;
You are killing me, guiltless, with sheer pain.
But although you have no pity concerning my death,

Think carefully before you break your promise.

Repent, for God above,
Before you kill me for loving you,
For, madam, you know very well what you promised—

I'm not claiming anything as a right
From you, my sovereign lady, except your kindness—

But in the garden over there, in a particular place,

You know very well what you promised;
You took my hand as you gave your word
That you would love me best—God knows, you said so,

Although I do not deserve it.
Madam, I am saying this for your honour
More than I am for my own life right now—
I have done as you ordered me;
With your permission, we can go and see.
Do what you wish; keep your promise in mind,
For, alive or dead, you will find me right here.
You have the power of life or death over me—
But I certainly know that the rocks have gone."

He left her, and she stood astounded;
There wasn't a drop of blood in her face.
She never expected that she would be in such a fix.

"Alas," she said, "that this should ever happen!

I never imagined the possibility
Of such an astonishing thing happening!
It is against the laws of nature."
And she went home a sorrowful creature;
She could hardly walk from fear.
She wept, wailed, for a couple of days,
And fainted, so that it was pitiful to see.
But she didn't tell anyone the reason,

For out of towne was goon Arveragus.	For Averagus had left town.
But to hirself she spak, and seyde thus,	But she spoke to herself, and said this,
With face pale and with ful sorweful cheere,	With a pale face and sorrowful manner
In hire compleynt, as ye shal after heere.	As she complained, as you shall hear:
Allas! quod she, on thee, Fortune, I pleyne,	"Alas," she said, "I complain to you, Fate,
That unwar wrapped hast me in thy cheyne;	Who has caught me unwary in your chain,
For which tescape woot I no socour	From which I don't know how to escape,
Save oonly deeth or elles dishonour;	Except through death or otherwise dishonour;
Oon of thise two bihoveth me to chese.	I have to choose one of these two.
But nathelees, yet have I levere to lese	Nevertheless, I would rather lose
My lyf, thanne of my body have a shame,	My life than for my body to be so shamed,
Or knowe myselven fals or lese my name,	Or to be disloyal, or lose my good name;
And with my deth I may be quyt, ywis;	And with my death I will pay my debt, I think.
Hath ther nat many a noble wyf er this	Haven't there been many noble wives before now,
And many a mayde yslayn hirself, allas,	And many maids, who have killed themselves, alas,
Rather than with hir body doon trespas?	Rather than sin with their bodies?
Yis, certes, lo, thise stories beren witnesse,	It has certainly happened, these stories show it:
Whan thritty tirauntz, ful of cursednesse,	When thirty tyrants, very evil,
Hadde slayn Phidoun in Atthenes, at feste,	Killed Phidon at the feast at Athens,
They comanded hise doghtres for tareste,	They ordered that his daughters be seized
And bryngen hem biforn hem in despit,	And brought before them to be insulted,
Al naked, to fulfille hir foul delit,	All naked, so they could have their foul pleasures,
And in hir fadres blood they made hem daunce	And they made them dance in their father's blood
Upon the pavement, God yeve hem myschaunce;	On the pavement, may God damn them!
For which thise woful maydens ful of drede,	And so these sad maidens, full of dread,
Rather than they wolde lese hir maydenhede,	Rather than lose their virginity,
They prively been stirt into a welle	They secretly jumped into a well
And dreynte hemselven, as the bookes telle.	And drowned themselves, so the story says.
They of Mecene leete enquere and seke	Those from Messene had people find
Of Lacedomye fifty maydens eke,	Fifty Spartan maidens also,
On whiche they wolden doon hir lecherye;	Whom they wanted to abuse.
But was ther noon of al that compaignye	But there was none of that group
That she nas slayn, and with a good entente	Who was not killed, with the noble desire
Chees rather for to dye than assente	To die rather than agree
To been oppressed of hir maydenhede.	To be deprived of their virginity.
Why sholde I thanne to dye been in drede?	So why should I be afraid to die?
Lo, eek the tiraunt Aristoclides,	Remember also the tyrant Aristoclides,
That loved a mayden heet Stymphalides,	Who loved the maiden, called Stymphalides,
Whan that hir fader slayn was on a nyght,	And when her father was killed one night,
Unto Dianes temple goth she right,	She went straight to the temple of Diana,
And hente the ymage in hir handes two;	And grabbed the statue in both her hands,
Fro which ymage wolde she nevere go,	And refused to let go of the image.
No wight ne myghte hir handes of it arace,	Nobody could pull her hands away
Til she was slayn right in the selve place.	Until she was dead, right in that place.
Now sith that maydens hadden swich despit,	Now since these maidens were so unwilling
To been defouled with mannes foul delit,	To be defiled by the foul pleasures of man,
Wel oghte a wyf rather hirselven slee,	A wife certainly ought to kill herself
Than be defouled, as it thynketh me.	Rather than be defiled, so I think.
What shal I seyn of Hasdrubales wyf	What shall I say about the wife of Hasdrubal,
That at Cartage birafte hirself hir lyf?	Who committed suicide at Carthage?

For whan she saugh that Romayns wan the toun,

She took hir children alle and skipte adoun
Into the fyr, and chees rather to dye
Than any Romayn dide hir vileynye.
Hath nat Lucresse yslayn hirself, allas,
At Rome whan that she oppressed was
Of Tarquyn, for hir thoughte it was a shame
To lyven whan she hadde lost hir name?
The sevene maydens of Melesie also
Han slayn hemself, for verray drede and wo
Rather than folk of Gawle hem sholde oppresse.

Mo than a thousand stories, as I gesse,

Koude I now telle as touchynge this mateere.
Whan Habradate was slayn, his wyf so deere
Hirselven slow, and leet hir blood to glyde
In Habradates woundes depe and wyde;
And seyde, My body at the leeste way
Ther shal no wight defoulen, if I may.

What sholde I mo ensamples heer of sayn?
Sith that so manye han hemselven slayn,
Wel rather than they wolde defouled be,
I wol conclude that it is bet for me
To sleen myself, than been defouled thus.
I wol be trewe unto Arveragus,
Or rather sleen myself in som manere,
As dide Demociones doghter deere,
By cause that she wolde nat defouled be.
O Cedasus, it is ful greet pitee
To reden how thy doghtren deyde, allas,
That slowe hemself, for swich manere cas!
As greet a pitee was it, or wel moore,
The Theban mayden, that for Nichanore
Hirselven slow right for swich manere wo.
Another Theban mayden dide right so;
For oon of Macidonye hadde hire oppressed,

She with hire deeth hir maydenhede redressed.

What shal I seye of Nicerates wyf,
That for swich cas birafte hirself hir lyf?
How trewe eek was to Alcebiades
His love that rather for to dyen chees
Than for to suffre his body unburyed be.
Lo, which a wyf was Alceste, quod she,
What seith Omer of goode Penalopee?
Al Grece knoweth of hire chastitee.
Pardee of Lacedomya is writen thus,
That whan at Troie was slayn Protheselaus,
No lenger wolde she lyve after his day.
The same of noble Porcia telle I may,
Withoute Brutus koude she nat lyve,

For when she saw that the Romans had conquered the town,
She took all her children, and jumped down
Into the fire, and chose to die
Rather than have any Roman dishonour her.
Didn't Lucrecia kill herself, alas,
At Rome, when she was raped
By Tarquin, believing that it was shameful
To live when she had lost her good name?
The seven maidens of Miletus also
Killed themselves, from fear and sorrow,
Rather than allowing the people of Galatia to rape them.
There are more than a thousand stories, I should guess,
Which I could tell concerning this matter.
When Habradate was killed, his dear wife
Killed herself, and let her blood pour
Into his deep wide wounds,
And said, 'My body, at least,
Will be defiled by nobody else, if I have my way.'
Why should I speak of any more examples,
Since so many have killed themselves
Rather than be defiled?
I must conclude it is better for me
To kill myself than to be defiled like this.
I will be loyal to Arveragus,
And would rather kill myself in some way,
Like Demotion's dear daughter did
Rather than be defiled.
Oh Cedasus, it is a very great pity
To read of how your daughters died, alas,
Who killed themselves in a similar situation.
Just such a great pity it was, or even more,
When the Theban maiden killed herself
For Nichanore, for just such a sorrow.
Another Theban maiden did exactly the same;
Because one of the Macedonians had raped her,
And she restored her maidenhead with her eath.
What should I say about Nicerate's wife,
Who killed herself in a similar situation?
How true also was Alcibades' love
To him, who chose to die
Rather than allow his body to go unburied.
What a wife Alcestis was," she said.
"What does Homer say about good Penelope?
All of Greece knew of her chastity.
By God, it is written of Laodomia
That when Protheselaus was killed,
She refused to stay alive after his death.
I can say the same of noble Portia;
She could not live without Brutus,

To whom she hadde al hool hir herte yeve.	To whom she had given the whole of her heart.
The parfit wyfhod of Arthemesie	The perfect wifehood of Arthemesie
Honured is thurgh al the Barbarie.	Is venerated throughout Barbary.
O Teuta queene, thy wyfly chastitee	Oh Teuta, queen, your wifely chastity
To alle wyves may a mirrour bee!	Is an example to all wives, always.
The same thyng I seye of Bilyea,	I say the same thing about Bilia,
Of Rodogone, and eek Valeria.	Of Rodogone, and also Valeria."
Thus pleyned Dorigene a day or tweye,	So Dorigen complained for a day or two,
Purposynge evere that she wolde deye.	Always meaning to die.
But nathelees, upon the thridde nyght	However, on the third night,
Hoom cam Arveragus, this worthy knyght,	The good knight Arveragus came home,
And asked hir why that she weep so soore.	And asked her why she was weeping so bitterly;
And she gan wepen ever lenger the moore.	And she began to weep even harder than before.
Allas! quod she, that evere I was born.	"Alas," she said, "that I was ever born!
Thus have I seyd, quod she, thus have I sworn;	This is what I have said," she said, "this is what I have sworn,"
And toold hym al as ye han herd bifore,	And told him everything you have already heard;
It nedeth nat reherce it yow namoore.	There's no need to repeat it to you.
This housbonde with glad chiere in freendly wyse	This husband, with a cheerful face, in a friendly way,
Answerde and seyde, as I shal yow devyse,	Answered and said these words:
Is ther oght elles, Dorigen, but this?	"Is that all, Dorigen?"
Nay, nay, quod she, God helpe me so, as wys,	"No, no," she said, "so help me God!
This is to muche, and it were Goddes wille.	This is too much, even if it were ordered by God."
Ye, wyf, quod he, lat slepen that is stille.	"Yes, wife," he said, "let sleeping dogs lie.
It may be wel paraventure yet to-day.	Everything may still turn out all right.
Ye shul youre trouthe holden, by my fay.	You shall keep your promise, I swear!
For God so wisly have mercy upon me,	For as surely as God will have mercy on me,
I hadde wel levere ystiked for to be	I would definitely rather be stabbed
For verray love which that I to yow have,	Due to the pure love which I have for you,
But if ye sholde your trouthe kepe and save.	Than for you to do anything to break your promise.
Trouthe is the hyeste thyng that man may kepe.	A pledge is the greatest thing a man must stick to."
But with that word he brast anon to wepe	But as he said that he immediately burst into tears,
And seyde, I yow forbede, up peyne of deeth,	And said, "I forbid you, on pain of death,
That nevere whil thee lasteth lyf ne breeth,	That never, while the life or breath lasts,
To no wight telle thou of this aventure;	From telling anybody about this matter;
As I may best, I wol my wo endure.	I will suffer my sorrow as best I can,
Ne make no contenance of hevynesse,	And I will not show any sign of sadness,
That folk of yow may demen harm or gesse.	Which would allow people to guess that you have done anything wrong."
And forth he cleped a squier and a mayde;	And he called for a squire and a maid:
Gooth forth anon with Dorigen, he sayde,	"Go out right now with Dorigen," he said,
And bryngeth hir to swich a place anon,	"And take her to such and such a place quickly."
They take hir leve, and on hir wey they gon,	They left him, and went on their way,
But they ne weste why she thider wente,	But they did not know why she was going there.

He nolde no wight tellen his entente.
Paraventure, an heep of yow, ywis,
Wol holden hym a lewed man in this,
That he wol putte his wyf in jupartie.

Herkneth the tale er ye upon hire crie;

She may have bettre fortune than yow semeth,
And whan that ye han herd the tale, demeth.

This squier, which that highte Aurelius,
On Dorigen that was so amorus,
Of aventure happed hir to meete
Amydde the toun, right in the quykkest strete,
As she was bown to goon the wey forth-right
Toward the gardyn, ther as she had hight.
And he was to the gardynward also,
For wel he spyed whan she wolde go
Out of hir hous to any maner place.

But thus they mette, of aventure or grace
And he saleweth hir with glad entente,
And asked of hir whiderward she wente.
And she answerde, half as she were mad,
Unto the gardyn as myn housbonde bad,
My trouthe for to holde, allas! allas!
Aurelius gan wondren on this cas,
And in his herte hadde greet compassioun
Of hir and of hir lamentacioun,
And of Arveragus, the worthy knyght,
That bad hire holden al that she had hight,
So looth hym was his wyf sholde breke hir trouthe;
And in his herte he caughte of this greet routhe,
Considerynge the beste on every syde

That fro his lust yet were hym levere abyde
Than doon so heigh a cherlyssh wrecchednesse

Agayns franchise and alle gentillesse.-
For which in fewe wordes seyde he thus:
Madame, seyeth to your lord Arveragus,
That sith I se his grete gentillesse
To yow, and eek I se wel youre distresse,
That him were levere han shame-and that were routhe-
Than ye to me sholde breke thus youre trouthe,
I have wel levere evere to suffre wo
Than I departe the love bitwix yow two.
I yow relesse, madame, into youre hond
Quyt every surement and every bond,
That ye han maad to me as heer biforn,
Sith thilke tyme which that ye were born.
My trouthe I plighte, I shal yow never repreve
Of no biheste, and heere I take my leve,
As of the treweste and the beste wyf

He wouldn't tell anyone what he was doing.
Perhaps many of you, certainly,
Will think that he is foolish,
Putting his wife in such jeopardy

Listen to the story before you shout out about her.
It may turn out better than you think;
Judge when you have heard the whole story.

This squire, called Aurelius,
Who was so passionate about Dorigen,
Happened by chance to meet her
There in the town, in the busiest street,
As she was about to go straight
To the garden as she had promised.
He was also going towards the garden;
For he had kept watch so he would know
When she was leaving her house to go anywhere.

But so they met, through chance or fate,
And he greeted her cheerfully,
And asked her where she was going;
And she answered, as if she were half mad,
"To the garden, as my husband has ordered,
To keep my promise–alas, alas!"
Aurelius began to wonder about the matter,
And in his heart he felt great pity
For her and her sorrow,
And for Arveragus, that good knight,
Who ordered her to keep her promises,
He was so reluctant for her to break her word;
And in his heart this caused him great pity,
And made him think what would be best for everybody,
Would be for him to give up his desire
Rather than doing such a horrible wretched act
Which would be so uncharitable and ignoble;
And so in a few words he said this:
"Madam, say to your Lord Arveragus
That now I see his great kindness
To you, and I also see your distress,
That he would rather the shamed
(and that would be a shame)
Than for you to break your promise to me,
I would rather always suffer sorrow
Than harm this love between the pair of you.
I release you, madam, I give back to you
Every promise and pledge
Which you have made to me before,
Since the day you were born.
I pledge my word, I will never prosecute you
For any promise, and now I shall leave you,
Who is the truest and best wife

That evere yet I knew in al my lyf.	*That I have ever known in my life.*
But every wyf be war of hir biheeste,	*But let every wife be careful about her promises!*
On Dorigene remembreth atte leeste!	*Remember Dorigen, at least.*
Thus kan a squier doon a gentil dede	*So a squire can do a kind deed*
As wel as kan a knyght, with outen drede.	*The same as a knight, it's certain."*
She thonketh hym upon hir knees al bare,	*She went down on her bare knees to thank him,*
And hoom unto hir housbonde is she fare,	*And she went home to her husband,*
And tolde hym al, as ye han herd me sayd;	*And told him everything which you have heard me describe;*
And be ye siker, he was so weel apayd	*And you can be sure, he was so pleased*
That it were inpossible me to wryte.	*That it would be impossible for me to describe it.*
What sholde I lenger of this cas endyte?	*What else can I say about this matter?*
Arveragus and Dorigene his wyf	*Arveragus and his wife Dorigen*
In sovereyn blisse leden forth hir lyf,	*Lived their lives in perfect bliss.*
Nevere eft ne was ther angre hem bitwene.	*There was never again any anger between them.*
He cherisseth hir as though she were a queene,	*He cherished her as though she were a queen,*
And she was to hym trewe for everemoore.-	*And she was loyal to him for ever.*
Of thise two folk ye gete of me namoore.	*That's all I shall tell you about these people.*
Aurelius, that his cost hath al forlorn	*Aurelius, who had spent all his fortune,*
Curseth the tyme that evere he was born.	*Cursed the day that he was born:*
Allas, quod he, allas, that I bihighte	*"Alas!" he said, "alas, that I promised*
Of pured gold a thousand pound of wighte	*A thousand pounds of pure gold*
Unto this philosophre! how shal I do?	*To this scientist! What shall I do?*
I se namoore but that I am fordo;	*I can only think that I will be ruined.*
Myn heritage moot I nedes selle	*I must sell all of my inheritance,*
And been a beggere; heere may I nat dwelle,	*And be a beggar; I cannot stay here*
And shamen al my kynrede in this place,	*And bring shame to my family in this place,*
But I of hym may gete bettre grace.	*Unless he will agree to more favourable terms.*
But nathelees I wole of hym assaye	*Still, I will try him, I will offer*
At certeyn dayes yeer by yeer to paye,	*To pay on certain dates, year after year,*
And thanke hym of his grete curteisye;	*And thank him for his great kindness.*
My trouthe wol I kepe, I wol nat lye.	*I will keep my word, I will not lie."*
With herte soor he gooth unto his cofre,	*With a sore heart he went to his strongbox,*
And broghte gold unto this philosopher	*And brought gold to this scientist,*
The value of fyve hundred pound, I gesse,	*Worth five hundred pounds, I would guess,*
And hym bisecheth of his gentillesse	*And begged him, through his kindness,*
To graunte hym dayes of the remenaunte,	*To allow him to pay the rest in instalments;*
And seyde, Maister, I dar wel make avaunt,	*And said, "Master, I dare to boast*
I failled nevere of my trouthe as yit.	*That I have never yet broken my word.*
For sikerly my dette shal be quyt	*My debt will certainly be repaid*
Towareds yow, how evere that I fare,	*To you, even if I have*
To goon a begged in my kirtle bare!	*To go begging in rags.*
But wolde ye vouche sauf upon seuretee	*But if you would agree, on my word,*
Two yeer or thre, for to respiten me,	*To allow me two or three years' grace,*
Thanne were I wel, for elles moot I selle	*Everything would be good; otherwise I must sell*
Myn heritage, ther is namoore to telle.	*My inheritance; that's all I can tell you."*
This philosophre sobrely answerde,	*This scientist answered soberly,*
And seyde thus, whan he thise wordes herde,	*And said this, when he heard these words:*

Have I nat holden covenant unto thee?	"Did I not keep my agreement with you?"
Yes, certes, wel and trewely, quod he.	"Yes, certainly, well and truly," he said.
Hastow nat had thy lady, as thee liketh?	"Haven't you had the lady as you wished?"
No, no, quod he, and sorwefully he siketh.	"No, no," he said, and sighed sorrowfully.
What was the cause, tel me if thou kan?	"Why not? Tell me if you can."
Aurelius his tale anon bigan,	Aurelius immediately began his story,
And tolde hym al, as ye han herd bifoore,	And told him everything, as you have already heard;
It nedeth nat to yow reherce it moore.	There is no need to repeat it to you.
He seide, Arveragus of gentillesse	He said, "Arveragus, in his nobility,
Hadde levere dye in sorwe and in distresse	Would rather have died with sorrow and distress
Than that his wyf were of hir trouthe fals;	Than for her wife to break a promise."
The sorwe of Dorigen he tolde hym als,	He also told him of the sorrow of Dorigen,
How looth hir was to been a wikked wyf,	And how she hated the idea of being a wicked wife,
And that she levere had lost that day hir lyf,	And that she would rather have lost her life,
And that hir trouthe she swoor, thurgh innocence,	And that she made her promise through ignorance,
She nevere erst hadde herd speke of apparence.	Never before having heard of such illusions.
That made me han of hir so greet pitee;	"That made me feel such great pity for her,
And right as frely as he sente hir me,	And as freely as he sent her to me,
As frely sente I hir to hym ageyn.	I sent her back to him again.
This al and som, ther is namoore to seyn.	That is the whole business; that's all I can say."
This philosophre answerde, Leeve brother,	The scientist answered, "Dear brother,
Everich of yow dide gentilly til oother.	All of you treated the others well.
Thou art a squier, and he is a knyght;	You are a squire, and he is a knight;
But God forbede, for his blisful myght,	But God forbid, in his sweet kindness,
But if a clerk koude doon a gentil dede	That a clerk shouldn't do a kind deed
As wel as any of yow, it is no drede.	As well as any of you, there's no doubt he can!
Sire, I releesse thee thy thousand pound,	Sir, I release you from your debt of a thousand pounds,
As thou right now were cropen out of the ground,	As if you had just been born
Ne nevere er now ne haddest knowen me;	And I had never known you.
For, sire, I wol nat taken a peny of thee	For, sir, I will not take a penny from you
For al my craft, ne noght for my travaille.	For all my skills, nor anything for my labour.
Thou hast ypayed wel for my vitaille,	You have repaid my expenses well.
It is ynogh, and farewel, have good day.	That is enough, Farewell, have a good day!"
And took his hors, and forth he goth his way.	And he took his horse, and went on his way.
Lordynges, this questioun wolde I aske now,	Gentlemen, now I will ask you this question,
Which was the mooste fre, as thynketh yow?	Who was the most generous, do you think?
Now telleth me, er that ye ferther wende,	Now tell me, before we go any further.
I kan namoore, my tale is at an ende.	That's all I know; that's the end of my story.
Heere is ended the Frankeleyns Tale	*This is the end of the Franklin's tale*

The Physician's Tale

Heere folweth the Phisiciens Tale.

Ther was, as telleth Titus Livius,
A knyght that called was Virginius,
Fulfild of honour and of worthynesse,
And strong of freendes, and of greet richesse.
This knyght a doghter hadde by his wyf,
No children hadde he mo in al his lyf.
Fair was this mayde in excellent beautee
Aboven every wight that man may see.
For Nature hath with sovereyn diligence
Yformed hir in so greet excellence,
As though she wolde seyn, Lo, I, Nature,
Thus kan I forme and peynte a creature
Whan that me list; who kan me countrefete?
Pigmalion noght, though he ay forge and bete,

Or grave, or peynte, for I dar wel seyn
Apelles, Zanzis sholde werche in veyn

Outher to grave or peynte, or forge, or bete,
If they presumed me to countrefete.
For He that is the former principal
Hath maked me his vicaire general
To forme and peynten erthely creaturis
Right as me list, and ech thyng in my cure is
Under the Moone, that may wane and waxe,
And for my werk right nothyng wol I axe.
My lord and I been ful of oon accord;
I made hir to the worship of my lord,
So do I alle myne othere creatures,
What colour that they han, or what figures.

Thus semeth me that Nature wolde seye.
This mayde of age twelf yeer was and tweye,
Is which that Nature hadde swich delit.
For right as she kan peynte a lilie whit,
And reed a rose, right with swich peynture
She peynted hath this noble creature,
Er she were born, upon hir lymes fre,
Where as by right swiche colours sholde be.
And Phebus dyed hath hir treses grete,
Lyk to the stremes of his burned heete;
And if that excellent was hir beautee,
A thousand foold moore vertuous was she.
In hire ne lakked no condicioun
That is to preyse, as by discrecioun;
As wel in goost as body chast was she,
For which she floured in virginitee

The Physician's Tale

*There was, so Titus Livius tells us,
A knight who was called Virginius,
Very honourable and good,
With great friends, and much wealth.
This knight had a daughter with his wife;
He didn't have any other children.
This girl was very lovely and beautiful,
More than any other person one might see;
For nature with her royal work
Shaped her so wonderfully,
As if she was saying, "Look! I, nature,
Can make and colour a creature like this
Whenever I wish; who can copy me?
Not Pygmalion, although he was always casting and hammering,
Or carving, or painting; for I can certainly say
That Apelles or Zeuxis would be working in vain
Either to carve, paint, cast or beat out,
If they thought they could forge my work.
For He who created everything
Has made me his representative,
To shape and paint the creatures of Earth
Just as I wish, and everything under the moon
Is in my control, great or small,
And I ask for no reward for my work;
My lord and I are of one accord.
I made her as a gesture of worship to my lord;
As I do with all my other creatures,
Whatever colour they have or whatever shape."*

*That seems to me what nature would say.
This girl was fourteen years of age,
The one whom nature was so delighted with.
For just as she can paint a lily white,
And a rose red, those were the colours
She had used to paint this wonderful creature,
Before she was born, on her sweet limbs,
Where colours like that should properly be;
And the sun had coloured her streaming hair
To resemble the rays of his burning sunbeams.
And if her beauty was wonderful,
She was a thousand times more virtuous.
She lacked none of the things
That are praised by those with fine morals.
In spirit and in body she was chaste,
And she flourished in her virginity*

With alle humylitee and abstinence,	With all humility and abstinence,
With alle attemperaunce and pacience,	With all temperance and patience,
With mesure eek of beryng and array.	Properly humble in bearing and dress.
Discreet she was in answeryng alway,	She was always polite in conversation;
Though she were wise Pallas, dar I seyn,	Although I dare say she was as wise as Pallas
Hir facound eek ful wommanly and pleyn,	She spoke in a very feminine and simple manner,
No countrefeted termes hadde she	Not using any highflown expressions
To seme wys, but after hir degree	To make herself look clever, but she spoke as appropriate
She spak, and alle hir wordes, moore and lesse,	To her position, and all her words, long and short,
Sownynge in vertu and in gentillesse.	Were full of virtue and nobility.
Shamefast she was in maydens shamefastnesse,	She always retained her maidenly modesty,
Constant in herte, and evere in bisynesse	Was very loyal, and always working
To dryve hir out of ydel slogardye.	To keep herself away from idleness.
Bacus hadde of hire mouth right no maistrie;	Bacchus had no power over her mouth;
For wyn and youthe dooth Venus encresse,	For wine combined with youth increases the power of Venus,
As man in fyr wol casten oille or greesse.	As when men throw oil or grease into a fire.
And of hir owene vertu unconstreyned,	From her own virtue, her own free will,
She hath ful ofte tyme syk hir feyned,	She very often pretended to be ill,
For that she wolde fleen the compaignye	Because she wanted to leave the company
Wher likly was to treten of folye,	If there was likely to be foolish talk,
As is at feestes, revels, and at daunces	As there is at feasts, revels and dances,
That been occasions of daliaunces.	That give opportunities for flirtatiousness.
Swich thynges maken children for to be	These things make children
To soone rype and boold, as men may se,	Grow up too quickly, as everyone knows,
Which is ful perilous, and hath been yoore;	Which is very dangerous and has been always,
For al to soone may they lerne lore	For she will learn the ways
Of booldnesse, whan she woxen is a wyf.	Of sexuality quickly enough, when she becomes a wife.
And ye maistresses, in youre olde lyf,	And you ladies, who in your old age
That lordes doghtres han in governaunce,	Are governesses to the daughters of lords,
Ne taketh of my wordes no displesaunce;	Don't be annoyed by my words.
Thenketh that ye been set in governynges	Remember that you have been given charge
Of lordes doghtres, oonly for two thynges;	Of the daughters of lords for just two reasons:
Outher for ye han kept youre honestee,	Either because you remained chaste,
Or elles ye han falle in freletee,	Or else you have become frail,
And knowen wel ynough the olde daunce,	And although you know the old dance well enough,
And han forsaken fully swich meschaunce	You have completely given up such behaviour
For everemo; therfore for Cristes sake,	For eternity; and so, for Christ's sake,
To teche hem vertu looke that ye ne slake.	Make sure you never leave off teaching them to be good.
A theef of venysoun, that hath forlaft	A poacher, who has abandoned
His likerousnesse, and al his olde craft,	His greed and all his old trade,
Kan kepe a forest best of any man.	Is a better gamekeeper than any other man.
Now kepeth wel, for if ye wole, ye kan.	Now keep guard well, if you want to, you can.
Looke wel that ye unto no vice assente,	Take care that you do not agree to any vice,
Lest ye be dampned for your wikke entente.	In case you should be damned for your wicked plans;
For who so dooth, a traitour is, certeyn;	For anyone who does is definitely a traitor.

And taketh kepe of that that I shal seyn,	And pay attention to what I say:
Of alle tresons, sovereyn pestilence	Of all betrayals the very worst
Is whan a wight bitrayseth innocence.	Is when a person betrays an innocent.
Ye fadres and ye moodres, eek also,	You fathers and you mothers also,
Though ye han children, be it oon or two,	If you have children, whether one or more,
Youre is the charge of al hir surveiaunce	It's up to you to look after them,
Whil that they been under youre governaunce.	While you are their governors.
Beth war, if by ensample of youre lyvynge,	Beware, in case your way of life,
Or by youre necligence in chastisynge,	Or your failure to punish them,
That they perisse, for I dar wel seye,	Brings them to death; for I can certainly say
If that they doon ye shul it deere abeye;	That if they do, you will dearly pay for it.
Under a shepherde softe and necligent	When the shepherd is soft and neglectful
The wolf hath many a sheep and lamb to-rent.	The wolf tears many sheep and lambs limb from limb.
Suffyseth oon ensample now as here,	Let that just be one example for now,
For I moot turne agayn to my mateere.	For I must return to my subject.
This mayde, of which I wol this tale expresse,	This maiden, of whom I'm telling this tale,
So kepte hirself, hir neded no maistresse.	Looked after herself so well she needed no governess,
For in hir lyvyng maydens myghten rede,	For other maidens might read in her way of life,
As in a book, every good word or dede	As if reading a book, about every good word or deed
That longeth to a mayden vertuous,	That a virtuous maiden should do,
She was so prudent and so bountevous.	She was so well-behaved and good.
For which the fame out-sprong on every syde	Her reputation spread far and wide,
Bothe of hir beautee and hir bountee wyde,	Both of her beauty and her goodness,
That thurgh that land they preised hire echone	So that throughout the land everybody praised her
That loved vertu; save encye allone,	If they loved virtue, and only envy did not,
That sory is of oother mennes wele,	Who resents the good of other men,
And glad is of his sorwe and his unheele-	And is glad when he is sad and miserable.
The doctour maketh this descripcioun.	(St Augustine describes this).
This mayde upon a day wente in the toun	One day this maiden went into town
Toward a temple, with hir mooder deere,	Going to temple, with her dear mother,
As is of yonge maydens the namere.	As young maidens do.
Now was ther thanne a justice in that toun,	Now there was a judge in that town,
That governour was of that regioun,	Who was the governor of the region.
And so bifel this juge hise eyen caste	And it so happened that this judge saw
Upon this mayde, avysynge hym ful faste	This maiden, and he stared very hard at her,
As she cam forby, ther as this juge stood.	As she passed by where he was standing.
Anon his herte chaunged and his mood,	Immediately his heart and his mood both changed,
So was he caught with beautee of this mayde,	He was so entranced with the beauty of this maid,
And to hymself ful pryvely he sayde,	And he secretly said to himself,
This mayde shal be myn, for any man.	"No man shall stop that girl being mine!"
Anon the feend into his herte ran,	At once the devil came into his heart,
And taughte hym sodeynly, that he by slyghte	And showed him at once that by trickery
The mayden to his purpos wynne myghte.	He could win the maiden for himself.
For certes, by no force, ne by no meede,	For certainly, he thought that he could not succeed through
Hym thoughte he was nat able for to speede;	Any sort of force or bribery;

For she was strong of freends, and eek she Confermed was in swich soverayn bountee, That wel he wiste he myghte hir nevere wynne, As for to maken hir with hir body synne.	*For she had powerful friends, and also she* *Was well known to be of such goodness* *That he knew he could never win over her* *And make her commit bodily sins.*
For which, by greet deliberacioun, He sente after a cherl, was in the toun, Which that he knew for subtil and for boold. This Juge unto this cherl his tale hath toold In secree wise, and made hym to ensure He sholde telle it to no creature, And if he dide, he sholde lese his heed. Whan that assented was this cursed reed, Glad was this juge, and maked hym greet cheere,	*So, after much thought,* *He sent for a peasant, who was in the town,* *Whom he knew was tricky and bold.* *The judge told this peasant his story* *Secretly, and made him swear* *That he would tell nobody else,* *On pain of losing his head.* *When this horrible plot was agreed to* *The judge was very glad, and spoiled the peasant,*
And yaf hym yiftes preciouse and deere. Whan shapen was al hir conspiracie	*Giving him precious expensive gifts.* *When their whole conspiracy had been planned*
Fro point to point, how that his lecherie Parfourned sholde been ful subtilly, (As ye shul heere it after openly) Hoom gooth the cherl, that highte Claudius.	*In every detail, how his filthy designs* *Should be accomplished very cunningly,* *As you will hear clearly shortly,* *The peasant, who was called Claudius, went home.*
This false juge, that highte Apius, So was his name-for this is no fable, But knowen for historial thyng notable; The sentence of it sooth is out of doute- This false juge gooth now faste aboute To hasten his delit al that he may.	*This false judge, who was called Apius,* *(That truly was his name, for this is no story* *But true historical fact;* *The substance of it is certainly true),* *This false judge now hurried* *To get his pleasure as quickly as he could.*
And so bifel soone after on a day,	*And so it happened soon after, on a particular day,*
This false juge, as telleth us the storie, As he was wont, sat in his consistorie, And yaf his doomes upon sondry cas. This false cherl cam forth a ful greet pas And seyde, Lord, if that it be youre wille, As dooth me right upon this pitous bille In which I pleyne upon Virginius; And if that he wol seyn it is nat thus, I wol it preeve, and fynde good witnesse That sooth is, that my bille wol expresse. The juge answerde, Of this in his absence, I may nat yeve diffynytyve sentence. Lat do hym calle, and I wol gladly heere.	*That this false judge, so the story tells us,* *As he usually did, sat in his court,* *Giving his judgement on various cases.* *This false peasant came rushing to him,* *And said, "Lord, if you will,* *Give me justice in this horrible case* *Which I have against Virginius;* *And if he says it is not true,* *I will prove it, and show good witnesses,* *That my complaint against him is true."* *The judge answered, "As he is not here* *I cannot give you a definitive judgement.* *Let him be called, and I will gladly hear the case;*
Thou shalt have al right and no wrong heere.	*There shall be justice for all, everything shall be right."*
Virginius cam to wite the juges wille, And right anon was rad this cursed bille. The sentence of it was, as ye shul heere: To yow, my lord, Sire Apius so deere, Sheweth youre povre servant Claudius, How that a knyght called Virginius Agayns the lawe, agayn al equitee,	*Virginius came to hear the judge's decision,* *And at once this cursed petition was read;* *The gist of it was what you shall hear now:* *"To you, my lord, Sir Apius so dear,* *Your poor servant Claudius tells* *How a knight, called Virginius,* *Against the law, against all fairness,*

Holdeth expres agayn the wyl of me	Is holding, against my express desire,
My servant, which that is my thral by right,	My servant, who is bound to me by right,
Which fro myn hous was stole upon a nyght,	Who was stolen from my house one night,
Whil that she was ful yong; this wol I preeve	When she was very young; I will prove this
By witnesse, lord, so that it nat yow greeve.	With evidence, lord, as long as you allow it.
She nys his doghter, nat what so he seye.	She is not his daughter, whatever he says.
Wherfore to yow, my lord the Juge, I preye	So to you, my lord judge, I pray,
Yeld me my thral, if that it be youre wille.	Give me back my servant, if you would."
Lo, this was al the sentence of his bille.	You see, this was his case in a nutshell.
Virginius gan upon the cherl biholde,	Virginius started to stare at the peasant,
But hastily, er he his tale tolde,	And he would have liked, before the story was over,
And wolde have preeved it as sholde a knyght,	To have settled the matter with arms,
And eek by witnessyng of many a wight,	And also with the evidence of many people,
That it was fals, that seyde his adversarie,	Which would have proved his enemy was lying,
This cursed juge wolde no thyng tarie,	But the cursed judge did not give him time,
Ne heere a word moore of Virginius,	He would not hear a single word from Virginius,
But yaf his juggement and seyde thus:	But he gave his judgement, saying this:
I deeme anon this cherl his servant have,	"I rule that this peasant should have his servant at once;
Thou shalt no lenger in thyn hous hir save.	You will no longer keep her in your house.
Go, bryng hir forth, and put hir in our warde.	Bring her here, and hand over to us.
The cherl shal have his thral, this I awarde.	I rule that the peasant will have his slave back."
And whan this worthy knyght Virginius,	And when this good knight Virginius,
Thurgh sentence of this justice Apius,	Because of the sentence of this judge Apius,
Moste by force his deere doghter yeven	Had been forced to hand over his dear daughter
Unto the juge in lecherie to lyven,	To the judge, to live in lechery,
He gooth hym hoom, and sette him in his halle,	He went home, and sat in his hall,
And leet anon his deere doghter calle,	And called his dear daughter to him at once,
And with a face deed as asshen colde,	And with a face as grey as cold ashes
Upon hir humble face he gan biholde	He looked at her humble face,
With fadres pitee stikynge thurgh his herte,	With a father's pity stabbing through his heart,
Al wolde he from his purpos nat converte.	But he would not give up his purpose.
Doghter, quod he, Virginia, by thy name,	"Daughter," he said, "Virginia, I swear by your name,
Ther been two weyes, outher deeth or shame	There are two options, either death or shame,
That thou most suffre, allas, that I was bore!	That you must suffer; curse the day I was born!
For nevere thou deservedest wherefore	You never did anything to deserve
To dyen with a swerd, or with a knyf.	Death by sword or by knife.
O deere doghter, ender of my lyf,	Oh dear daughter, the death of my life,
Which I have fostred up with swich plesaunce,	Whom I have raised with such pleasure,
That thou were nevere out of my remembraunce.	So that you were never out of my thoughts!
O doghter, which that art my laste wo,	O daughter, who is my greatest sorrow,
And in my lyf my laste joye also,	And also the greatest joy of my life,
O gemme of chastitee, in pacience	You gem of chastity, suffer your death
Take thou thy deeth, for this is my sentence,	Patiently, for this is what I have decided.
For love and nat for hate, thou most be deed;	You must die, for love, not for hate;
My pitous hand moot smyten of thyn heed.	My sorrowing hand must chop off your head.

Middle English	Modern English
Allas, that evere Apius the say!	Alas for the fact that Apius ever saw you!
Thus hath he falsly jugged the to day.	Because of that he has given a false judgement today"—
And tolde hir al the cas, as ye bifore	And he told her everything, as you have already
Han herd, nat nedeth for to telle it moore.	Heard; there is no need to repeat it.
O mercy, deere fader, quod this mayde,	"Oh mercy, dear father!" said this maiden,
And with that word she bothe hir armes layde	And as she said it she threw both her arms
About his nekke, as she was wont to do.	Around his neck, as she often did.
The teeris bruste out of hir eyen two,	The tears streamed from her eyes,
And seyde, Goode fader, shal I dye?	And she said, "Good father, must I die?
Is ther no grace? is ther no remedye?	Is there no grace, is there nothing else to be done?"
No certes, deere doghter myn, quod he.	"No, certainly, my dear daughter," he said.
Thanne yif me leyser, fader myn, quod she,	"Then give me a little space, my father," she said,
My deeth for to compleyne a litel space,	"To grieve a little while for my death;
For, pardee, Jepte yaf his doghter grace	For, by God, Jephthah gave his daughter a space
For to compleyne, er he hir slow, allas!	To lament, before he killed her, alas!
And God it woot, no thyng was hir trespass	And, God knows, she had done nothing wrong,
But for she ran hir fader for to see	Except that she was the first one to run to see her father,
To welcome hym with greet solempnitee.	To give him a proper welcome."
And with that word she fil aswowne anon;	And as she said that she fell down in a faint,
And after whan hir swownyng is agon	And afterwards, when she had recovered
She riseth up and to hir fader sayde,	She got up, and said her father,
Blissed be God that I shal dye a mayde;	"Thanks be to God that I will die a virgin!
Yif me my deeth, er that I have a shame.	Give me death, before dishonour;
Dooth with youre child youre wyl, a Goddes name.	Do what you want with your child, in the name of God!"
And with that word she preyed hym ful ofte	Having said that she asked him repeatedly
That with his swerd he wolde smyte softe,	To use his sword on her;
And with that word aswowne doun she fil.	And as she said it she fell down faint again.
Hir fader with ful sorweful herte and wil	Her father, greatly sorrowing in heart and spirit,
Hir heed of smoot, and by the top it hente,	Struck off her head, and picked it up by the hair,
And to the juge he gan it to presente	And he gave it to the judge,
As he sat yet in doom, in consistorie.	As he sat giving judgement in court.
And whan the juge it saugh, as seith the storie,	And when the judge saw it, so the story goes,
He bad to take hym and anhange hym faste.	He ordered his men to take the knight and hang him at once;
But right anon a thousand peple in thraste	But straight away a thousand people burst in
To save the knyght for routhe and for pitee;	To save the knight, from compassion and pity,
For knowen was the false iniquitee.	For the false wickedness had become known.
The peple anon hath suspect of this thyng,	The people at once had their suspicions in the matter,
By manere of the cherles chalangyng,	Because of the way the peasant presented his claim,
That it was by the assent of Apius-	They thought they could see the hand of Apius;
They wisten wel that he was lecherus;	They knew perfectly well that he was a lecher.
For which unto this Apius they gon	And so they sought out this Apius

And caste hym in a prisoun right anon,
Ther as he slow hymself, and Claudius
That servant was unto this Apius,
Was demed for to hange upon a tree,
But that Virginius, of his pitee,
So preyde for hym, that he was exiled;
And elles, certes, he had been bigyled.
The remenant were anhanged, moore and lesse,
That were consentant of this cursednesse.

Heere men may seen, how synne hath his merite.
Beth war, for no man woot whom God wol smyte
In no degree, ne in which manere wyse
The worm of conscience may agryse
Of wikked lyf, though it so pryvee be
That no man woot therof but God and he.
For be he lewed man, or ellis lered,
He noot how soone that he shal been afered.

Therfore I rede yow this conseil take,
Forsaketh synne, er synne yow forsake.

Heere is ended the Phisiciens Tale

And threw him into prison at once,
Where he killed himself; and Claudius,
The servant of this Apius,
Was condemned to hang from a tree,
Except Virginius, through his pity,
Interceded for him so he was exiled;
Because he had certainly been tricked.
The rest were hanged, the great and the lowly,
Who were accessories to this wickedness.

So men can see how sin is rewarded.
Beware, nobody knows whom God will smite,
It could be any rank, and we do not know how;
The worm of conscience may tremble
Because of its wicked life, even if it is so secret
That no man knows of it but him and God.
Whether he is an ignorant man, or educated,
He does not know when judgement will come to him.
And so I give you this advice:
Give up sin, before it brings you down.

The end of the Physician's Tale

The Pardoner's Tale

The Wordes of the Hoost to the Phisicien and the Pardoner

Oure Hooste gan to swere as he were wood;
Harrow! quod he, by nayles and by blood!

This was a fals cherl and a fals justice!
As shameful deeth as herte may devyse
Come to thise juges and hire advocatz!
Algate this sely mayde is slayn, allas!

Allas! to deere boughte she beautee!
Wherfore I seye al day, as men may see
That yiftes of Fortune and of Nature
Been cause of deeth to many a creature.
(Hir beautee was hir deeth, I dar wel sayn;
Allas, so pitously as she was slayn!)
Of bothe yiftes that I speke of now
Men han ful ofte moore harm than prow.

But trewely, myn owene maister deere,
This is a pitous tale for to heere.
But nathelees, passe over is no fors;

I pray to God so save thy gentil cors,
And eek thyne urynals and thy jurdanes,
Thyn ypocras and eek thy Galianes
And every boyste ful of thy letuarie,
God blesse hem, and oure lady Seinte Marie!
So moot I theen, thou art a propre man,
And lyk a prelat, by Seint Ronyan.
Seyde I nat wel? I kan nat speke in terme;

But wel I woot thou doost myn herte to erme,

That I almoost have caught a cardyacle.
By corpus bones, but I have triacle,

Or elles a draughte of moyste and corny ale,
Or but I heere anon a myrie tale,
Myn herte is lost, for pitee of this mayde!

Thou beelamy, thou Pardoner, he sayde,
Telle us som myrthe or japes right anon.
It shal be doon, quod he, by Seint Ronyon;
But first, quod he, heere at this ale-stake,
I wol bothe drynke and eten of a cake.
And right anon the gentils gonne to crye,
Nay, lat hym telle us of no ribaudye!
Telle us som moral thyng that we may leere

What the Host said to the Physician and the Pardoner

*Our host began to swear as if he were mad;
"alas!" He said, "by the nails and blood of Christ!
This was a false peasant and a false judge.
May a death as shameful as one can imagine
Come to these judges and their lawyers!
Anyway, this innocent maiden has been killed, alas!*

*Alas, she paid to dearly for her beauty!
I've always said that men can always see
That the gifts of Fate and of Nature
Have brought death to many creatures.
Her beauty was the death of her, I daresay.
Alas, she was killed so mercilessly!
Both of those gifts that I have mentioned
Very often do more harm than good for their owners.*

*But truly, my dear master,
This was a sad tale to listen to.
But nevertheless, let's move on; there's nothing to be done.*

*I pray to God to save your gentle body,
And all your physician's equipment,
Your filters and your medicines,
And every bottle of potions;
God bless them, and our Lady St Mary!
As I live, you are a good man,
Like a bishop, by St Ronyan!
Haven't I spoken rightly? I can't speak classically;*

But I know that you have made my heart so sorrowful

*That you have almost broken it.
By the bones of Christ! Unless I have some medicine,*

*Or otherwise a draft of fresh strong ale,
Or else soon hear a merry tale,
My heart will be lost through my pity for this maiden.*

*You dear old rascal, you Pardoner," he said,
"Tell us some jolly comic story at once."
"It shall be done," he said, "by St Ronyon!
But first," he said, "at this tavern here
I will drink and have some cake."
But once all the gentlefolk began to cry out,
"No, don't let him tell us anything smutty!
Tell us some moral tale, so that we can learn*

Som wit, and thanne wol we gladly heere!

I graunte, ywis, quod he, but I moot thynke

Upon som honeste thyng, while that I drynke.

Some useful knowledge, which we will gladly listen to."

"I agree, certainly," he said, "but I'll have to think
About something respectable whilst I have a drink."

Prologue

Heere folweth the Prologe of the Pardoners Tale.
Radix malorum est Cupiditas: Ad Thimotheum, 6°.

Lordynges-quod he-in chirches whan I preche,

I peyne me to han an hauteyn speche,
And rynge it out as round as gooth a belle,
For I kan al by rote that I telle.
My theme is alwey oon and evere was,

Radix malorum est Cupiditas.
First I pronounce whennes that I come,
And thanne my bulles shewe I, alle and some;
Oure lige lordes seel on my patente,
That shewe I first, my body to warente,
That no man be so boold, ne preest ne clerk,

Me to destourbe of Cristes hooly werk.
And after that thanne telle I forth my tales,
Bulles of popes and of cardynales,

Of patriarkes and bishopes I shewe,
And in Latyn I speke a wordes fewe,
To saffron with my predicacioun,
And for to stire hem to devocioun.
Thanne shewe I forth my longe cristal stones,
Yerammed ful of cloutes and of bones;
Relikes been they, as wenen they echoon.
Thanne have I in latoun a sholder-boon
Which that was of an hooly Jewes sheepe.

Goode men, I seye, taak of my wordes keepe:
If that this boon be wasshe in any welle,
If cow, or calf, or sheep, or oxe swelle,
That any worm hath ete, or worm ystonge,

Taak water of that welle, and wassh his tonge,

And it is hool anon; and forthermoor,
Of pokkes and of scabbe and every soor

Shal every sheepe be hool that of this welle
Drynketh a draughte; taak kepe eek what I telle,
If that the goode man that the beestes oweth,
Wol every wyke, er that the cok hym croweth,
Fastynge, drinken of this welle a draughte,
As thilke hooly Jew oure eldres taughte,
Hise beestes and his stoor shal multiplie.
And, sire, also it heeleth jalousie;

Here follows the prologue to the Pardoner's tale
"Greed is the root of all evil": Paul's Epistle to Timothy, chapter 6.

"My lords," he said, "when I preach in church,
I make sure I speak out loudly,
Bringing out my words like a peal of bells,
For I know everything I say by heart.
My theme is always the same, and always has been;
'Greed is the root of all evil.'
First I tell them where I come from,
And then I show them all of my papal bulls.
The seal of our ruling Lord on my credentials,
I show that first, to protect my body,
So that nobody would dare, neither priest nor clerk,
To stop me doing the holy work of Christ.
After that I tell my stories;
I tell of the indulgences of popes and cardinals,
Patriarchs and bishops,
And I say a few words in Latin,
To add spice to my sermons,
And to inspire holy feelings.
Then I show my long crystal stones,
Packed full of rags and bones–
Men love relics, so they will believe.
I have mounted in brass a shoulder bone
Which came from the sheep of a holy Jew.
Good men,' I say, 'pay attention to my words;
If this bone is rinsed in any well,
Then if a cow, a calf, a sheep or an ox swell up
From having eaten worms, or being stung by snakes,
Take the water from that well and wash its tongue,
And it will be well at once; and furthermore,
Every sheep that drinks from this well will be cured
Of pox and of scab, and every sore.
Also pay attention to this:
If the owner of these beasts
Will, before dawn every week,
Having fasted, drink from this well,
As that same holy Jew taught our ancestors,
His stock and his stores will increase.
And, sirs, it also heals jealousy;

312

For though a man be falle in jalous rage,	For even though a man has fallen into a jealous rage,
Lat maken with this water his potage,	Let him use this water in his soup,
And nevere shal he moore his wyf mystriste,	And he will no longer mistrust his wife,
Though he the soothe of hir defaute wiste,	However much he sees what she has done wrong,
Al had she taken preestes two or thre.	Even if she has had a few priests.
Heere is a miteyn, eek, that ye may se:	I also have a mitten, as you can see.
He that his hand wol putte in this mitayn,	If anyone puts his hand into this mitten,
He shal have multipliyng of his grain	His grain shall increase,
What he hath sowen, be it whete or otes,	When he sows it, whether it is wheat or oats,
So that he offre pens, or elles grotes.	Providing he offers me some pennies, or groats.
Goode men and wommen, o thyng warne I yow,	Good men and women, I warn you of one thing:
If any wight be in this chirche now,	If there is anybody in this church now
That hath doon synne horrible, that he	Who has committed such horrible sins that he
Dar nat for shame of it yshryven be,	Dares not, for shame, they admit to it,
Or any womman, be she yong or old,	Or any woman, young or old,
That hath ymaad hir housbonde cokewold,	Who has cheated on her husband,
Swich folk shal have no power ne no grace	These people will have no power or grace
To offren to my relikes in this place.	To benefit from these relics of mine.
And who so fyndeth hym out of swich fame,	Anyone who is blameless of such offences,
He wol come up and offre, on Goddes name,	He can come up and make an offering in the name of God,
And I assoille him, by the auctoritee	And I will absolve him with the authority
Which that by tulle ygraunted was to me.	Which has been granted to me by the Pope.'
By this gaude have I wonne, yeer by yeer,	Through this trick I have won, year-on-year,
An hundred mark, sith I was pardoner.	A hundred marks since I became a pardoner.
I stonde lyk a clerk in my pulpet,	I stand like a clerk in my pulpit,
And whan the lewed peple is doun yset,	And when the ignorant people have sat down,
I preche so, as ye han heerd bifoore,	I preach as I have told you,
And telle an hundred false japes moore.	And tell a hundred more false tales.
Thanne peyne I me to strecche forth the nekke,	Then I make a special effort to stretch out my neck,
And est and west upon the peple I bekke,	Nodding to the people east and west,
As dooth a dowve sittynge on a berne.	Like a dove sitting on top of a barn.
Myne handes adn my tonge goon so yerne	My hands and tongue work so quickly
That it is joye to se my bisynesse.	That it is a joy to see how much I get done.
Of avarice and of swich cursednesse	All my preaching is about avarice
Is al my prechyng, for to make hem free	And other such scenes, to make them generous
To yeven hir pens; and namely, unto me!	With their pennies, particularly to me.
For myn entente is nat but for to wynne,	All I care about is making a profit,
And no thyng for correccioun of synne.	And I don't care at all about correcting sin.
I rekke nevere, whan that they been beryed,	I don't care, once they're dead,
Though that hir soules goon a blakeberyed,	If their souls go picking blackberries!
For certes, many a predicacioun	For certainly, many sermons
Comth ofte tyme of yvel entencioun.	Are inspired by evil intentions;
Som for plesance of folk, and flaterye,	Some want to give the people pleasure and flatter them,
To been avaunced by ypocrisye,	So that they can get on through hypocrisy,
And som for veyne glorie, and som for hate.	And some are inspired by vaingloriousness, and some by hate.

Middle English	Modern English
For whan I dar noon oother weyes debate,	For when I have no other way of getting at a man,
Thanne wol I stynge hym with my tonge smerte	I can sting him with my sharp tongue
In prechyng, so that he shal nat astert	In my preaching, so that he will not escape
To been defamed falsly, if that he	Being falsely accused, if he
Hath trespased to my bretheren, or to me.	Has gone against me or my brethren.
For though I telle noght his propre name,	Although I don't specifically mention his name,
Men shal wel knowe that it is the same	Men will know of whom I'm talking,
By signes, and by othere circumstances.	Through certain clues and other details.
Thus quyte I folk that doon us displesances,	This is how I repay folk who make trouble for we pardoners;
Thus spitte I out my venym, under hewe	So I spill out my bile disguised
Of hoolynesse, to semen hooly and trewe.	As holiness, to appear holy and true.
But shortly, myn entente I wol devyse;	I can quickly tell you all my plans:
I preche of no thyng but for coveityse.	All I preach for is for greed.
Therfore my theme is yet, and evere was,	And so my theme is still, and always has been,
Radix malorum est Cupiditas.	'Greed is the root of all evil.'
Thus kan I preche agayn that same vice	So I preach against the same vice
Which that I use, and that is avarice.	Of which I am guilty, and that is avarice.
But though myself be gilty in that synne,	But although I am myself guilty of that soon,
Yet kan I maken oother folk to twynne	I can still make other folk turn away
From avarice, and soore to repente;	From avarice and to sorrowfully repent.
But that is nat my principal entente.	But that's not the main reason I do it;
I preche no thyng but for coveitise;	I am only preaching for greed.
Of this mateere it oghte ynogh suffise.	That ought to tell you enough.
Thanne telle I hem ensamples many oon	Then I give them many examples
Of olde stories longe tyme agoon,	From old stories from long ago.
For lewed peple loven tales olde;	Ignorant people love old stories;
Swiche thynges kan they wel reporte and holde.	They can easily repeat such things and keep them in their minds.
What? trowe ye, the whiles I may preche,	What, do you imagine that while I can preach,
And wynne gold and silver for I teche,	And win gold and silver through my teaching,
That I wol lyve in poverte wilfully?	That I would choose to live in poverty?
Nay, nay, I thoghte it nevere, trewely.	No, no, that's never crossed my mind, I swear!
For I wol preche and begge in sondry landes,	I will preach and beg in various regions;
I wol nat do no labour with myne handes,	I won't do any work with my hands,
Ne make baskettes, and lyve therby,	I shan't make baskets for a living,
By cause I wol nat beggen ydelly.	Because I'll put my energy into begging.
I wol noon of the apostles countrefete,	I won't copy any of the Apostles;
I wol have moneie, wolle, chese, and whete,	I want money, wool, cheese and wheat,
Al were it yeven of the povereste page,	Even if it is given by the poorest servant,
Or of the povereste wydwe in a village,	Or the most impoverished widow in a village,
Al sholde hir children sterve for famyne.	Even if that means her children dying of hunger.
Nay, I wol drynke licour of the vyne,	No, I will drink good wine,
And have a joly wenche in every toun.	And have a fine wench in every town.
But herkneth, lordynges, in conclusioun:	But listen, my lords, in conclusion:
Your likyng is, that I shal telle a tale.	What you want is for me to tell a tale.
Now have I dronke a draughte of corny ale,	Now I have had a draft of strong ale,
By God, I hope I shal yow telle a thing	By God, I hope I can tell you something
That shal by resoun been at youre likyng.	That will with good reason be to your liking.
For though myself be a ful vicious man,	Although I myself am a very vicious man,
A moral tale yet I you telle kan,	I can still tell you a moral tale,
Which I am wont to preche, for to wynne.	Which I use in my preaching for profit.

Now hoold youre pees, my tale I wol bigynne.   *Now keep quiet! I shall begin my story."*

The Tale

Heere bigynneth the Pardoners Tale	*The Pardoner's Tale*
In Flaundres whilom was a compaignye / Of yonge folk, that haunteden folye, / As riot, hasard, stywes, and tavernes,	*Once in Flanders there was a company / Of young folk who behaved stupidly, / Debauched, gambling, haunting brothels and taverns,*
Wher as with harpes, lutes, and gyternes / They daunce and pleyen at dees, bothe day and nyght, / And eten also and drynken over hir myght, / Thurgh which they doon the devel sacrifise	*Where with harps, lutes and guitars / And they danced and played dice all day and night, / And also ate and drank more than they should, / Which meant they were making sacrifices to the devil*
Withinne that develes temple in cursed wise, / By superfluytee abhomynable. / Hir othes been so grete and so dampnable / That it is grisly for to heere hem swere. / Oure blissed lordes body they to-tere,	*In a cursed fashion in the Devil's Temple / Through their disgusting excesses. / They swore so horribly and hellishly / That it was terrible to hear them. / They tore the body of our Blessed Lord in pieces—*
Hem thoughte that Jewes rente hym noght ynough,	*They thought that the Jews had not punished him enough—*
And ech of hem at otheres synne lough.	*And each of them laughed at the sins of the others.*
And right anon thanne comen tombesteres, / Fetys and smale, and yonge frutesteres, / Syngeres with harpes, baudes, wafereres,	*And at once there came dancing girls, / Slim and shapely, and girls selling fruit, / Singers with harps, bawds, girls selling wafers,*
Whiche been the verray develes officers / To kyndle and blowe the fyr of lecherye, / That is annexed unto glotonye. / The hooly writ take I to my witnesse, / That luxurie is in wyn and dronkenesse.	*Who were the officers of the devil, / Kindling and blowing on the fire of lechery, / Which goes hand-in-hand with gluttony. / I take the Bible as my witness / That lechery comes from wine and drunkenness.*
Lo, how that dronken Looth unkyndely / Lay by hise doghtres two unwityngly; / So dronke he was, he nyste what he wroghte.	*Look how drunken Lot unnaturally / Lay with his two daughters, unknowingly; / He was so drunk he didn't know what he was doing.*
Herodes, whoso wel the stories soghte, / Whan he of wyn was repleet at his feeste, / Right at his owene table he yaf his heeste / To sleen the Baptist John, ful giltelees. / Senec seith a good word, doutelees; / He seith, he kan no difference fynde / Bitwix a man that is out of his mynde, / And a man which that is dronkelewe, / But that woodnesse fallen in a shrewe	*Herod, as anyone can find in the stories, / When he was full of wine at his feast, / Right there at his own table he ordered / The death of the guiltless John the Baptist. / There is no doubt that Seneca was right; / He said that he can find no difference / Between a madman / And one who is drunk, / Except that madness, when it comes to an evil person,*
Persevereth lenger than dooth dronkenesse.	*Lasts longer than drunkenness does.*

O glotonye, ful of cursednesse!	Oh gluttony, so cursed!
O cause first of oure confusioun!	The cause of our first sin!
O original of oure dampnacioun	The origin of our damnation,
Til Crist hadde boght us with his blood agayn!	Until Christ saved us with his blood!
Lo, how deere, shortly for to sayn,	See how dearly, to speak briefly,
Aboght was thilke cursed vileynye!	The price was paid for that villainy!
Corrupt was al this world for glotonye!	The whole world was corrupted by gluttony.
Adam oure fader, and his wyf also,	Our father Adam, and his wife also,
Fro Paradys to labour and to wo	Went from Paradise to labour and sorrow
Were dryven for that vice, it is no drede;	Because of that vice, that is certain.
For whil that Adam fasted, as I rede,	For while Adam fasted, so I read,
He was in Paradys, and whan that he	He was in Paradise; and when he
Eet of the fruyt deffended on the tree,	Ate the forbidden fruit from the tree,
Anon he was out-cast to wo and peyne.	He was immediately thrown out to suffer sorrow and pain.
O glotonye, on thee wel oghte us pleyne!	Oh gluttony, we certainly should blame you!
O, wiste a man how manye maladyes	Oh, if a man knew how many maladies
Folwen of excesse and of goltonyes,	Came from excess and gluttony,
He wolde been the moore measurable	He would be more careful
Of his diete, sittynge at his table.	About his diet, when he sits down to table.
Allas, the shorte throte, the tendre mouth,	Alas, the greedy throat, the tender mouth,
Maketh that est and west and north and south	Means that all around the world,
In erthe, in eir, in water, man to swynke	On the earth, in the air, in water, men work
To gete a glotoun deyntee mete and drynke.	To provide gluttons with dainty meat and drink!
Of this matiere, O Paul! wel kanstow trete,	On this matter, oh Paul, you spoke very well:
Mete unto wombe and wombe eek unto mete	"Food into the belly, and belly into food,
Shal God destroyen bothe, as Paulus seith.	God shall destroy both," as Paul says.
Allas, a foul thyng is it, by my feith!	Alas, it is a horrible thing, I swear,
To seye this word, and fouler is the dede	To say these things, and the act is even worse,
Whan man so drynketh of the white and rede,	When a man drinks red and white wine
That of his throte he maketh his pryvee	He makes a lavatory of his throat
Thurgh thilke cursed superfluitee.	Through his cursed excesses.
The Apostel wepyng seith ful pitously,	Weeping the apostle says sorrowfully,
Ther walken manye of whiche yow toold have I,	"I have told you of many living—
I seye it now wepyng with pitous voys,	I am weeping as I say it, with a sorrowful voice—
That they been enemys of Cristes croys,	Who are enemies of the cross of Christ,
Of whiche the ende is deeth, wombe is hir god.	And death shall be their end; their God is their belly!"
O wombe! O bely! O stynkyng cod!	Oh guts! Oh belly! Those stinking bags,
Fulfilled of donge and of corrupcioun,	Filled with dung and corruption!
At either ende of thee foul is the soun;	The sound coming from either end of you is revolting.
How greet labour and cost is thee to fynde,	What great work and expense is used to feed you!
Thise cookes, how they stampe, and streyne, and grynde,	These crooks, how they pound and strain and grind,
And turnen substaunce into accident,	Turning plain things into extravagant ones
To fulfillen al thy likerous talent!	To fulfil all your gluttonous desires!
Out of the harde bones knokke they	They knock the marrow out of the
The mary, for they caste noght awey,	Hard bones, for they throw nothing away

That may go thurgh the golet softe and swoote;	That can pass through the gullet softly and sweetly.
Of spicerie, of leef, and bark, and roote,	They use seasonings of leaf, bark and roots
Shal been his sauce ymaked by delit,	To make a sauce to please him,
To make hym yet a newer appetit.	To pique his appetite still further.
But certes, he that haunteth swiche delices	But certainly, the one who always needs such delicacies
Is deed, whil that he lyveth in tho vices.	Is dead, if he keeps to those vices.
A lecherous thyng is wyn, and dronkenesse	Wine and drunkenness is a lecherous thing,
Is ful of stryvyng and of wrecchednesse.	Causing much strife and wretchedness.
O dronke man, disfigured is thy face!	A drunken man, your face is disfigured,
Sour is thy breeth, foul artow to embrace,	Your breath is sour, you are revolting to embrace,
And thurgh thy dronke nose semeth the soun,	And through your drunken nose it sounds as if
As though thow seydest ay, Sampsoun! Sampsoun!	You are always saying, "Sampson, Samson!"
And yet, God woot, Sampsoun drank nevere no wyn!	And yet, God knows, Sampson never drank any wine.
Thou fallest, as it were a styked swyn;	You fall down like a stuck pig;
Thy tonge is lost, and al thyn honeste cure	Your tongue is lost, and all sense of decency,
For dronkenesse is verray sepulture	For truly drunkenness is the grave
Of mannes wit and his discrecioun.	Of the wit and discretion of mankind.
In whom that drynke hath dominacioun.	The one who is ruled by drink
He kan no conseil kepe, it is no drede;	Can keep no secrets; there's no doubt about that.
Now kepe yow fro the white and fro the rede,	Keep yourself away from white and red wine,
And namely, fro the white wyn of Lepe,	And especially from the white wine of Lepe
That is to selle in fysshstrete, or in Chepe.	That can be bought in Fish Street or Cheapside.
This wyn of Spaigne crepeth subtilly	This Spanish wine creeps cunningly
In othere wynes, growynge faste by,	Into other wines which grow nearby,
Of which ther ryseth swich fumositee,	And such fumes rise from it
That whan a man hath dronken draughtes thre	That when a man has had three draughts of it,
And weneth that he be at hoom in Chepe,	And imagines that he is at home in Cheapside,
He is in Spaigne, right at the toune of Lepe,	He's actually in Spain, in the town of Lepe–
Nat at the Rochele, ne at Bur deux toun;	Not in La Rochelle, nor in Bordeaux–
And thanne wol he seye Sampsoun, Sampsoun!	And then he will cry out, "Samson, Sampson!"
But herkneth, lordes, o word I yow preye,	But listen, my lords, just a word, I pray you,
That alle the sovereyn actes, dar I seye,	All the great deeds, I daresay,
Of victories in the Olde Testament,	And victories in the old Testament,
Thurgh verray God that is omnipotent,	Through the true God, who is omnipotent,
Were doon in abstinence and in preyere.	Were done by men who were abstinent and prayed.
Looketh the Bible, and ther ye may it leere.	Look in the Bible, and you will see it.
Looke, Attilla, the grete conquerour,	Think how Attila, the great conqueror,
Deyde in his sleepe, with shame and dishonour,	Died in his sleep, shamed and dishonoured,
Bledynge ay at his nose in dronkenesse.	Bleeding from the nose in his drunkenness.
A capitayn sholde lyve in sobrenesse;	A captain should be sober.
And over al this avyseth yow right wel,	And more than all this, think carefully
What was comaunded unto Lamwel,	What Lamuel was ordered–
Nat Samuel, but Lamwel, seye I;	Not Samuel, but Lamuel, I say;

Redeth the Bible and fynde it expresly,	*Read the Bible, you will find it explicitly mentioned*
Of wyn yevyng to hem that han justise.	*About giving wine to the justices.*
Namoore of this, for it may wel suffise.	*That's enough of this, it will do.*
And now that I have spoken of glotonye,	*And now I have spoken of gluttony,*
Now wol I yow deffenden hasardrye.	*I will now warn you against gambling.*
Hasard is verray mooder of lesynges,	*Dice is the mother of lying,*
And of dedeite and cursed forswerynges,	*And of deceit, and cursed perjury,*
Blasphemyng of Crist, manslaughtre and wast also,	*Blaspheming of Christ, manslaughter and also a waste*
Of catel and of tyme, and forthermo	*Of both possessions and time; and furthermore,*
It is repreeve and contrarie of honour	*It is disgraceful and against honour*
For to ben holde a commune hasardour.	*To be thought of as a common gambler.*
And ever the hyer he is of estaat,	*And the higher in rank the gambler is,*
The moore is he holden desolaat;	*The more disgraceful it is for him to fall.*
If that a prynce useth hasardrye,	*If a Prince plays dice*
In all governaunce and policye	*With his government and policies*
He is as by commune opinioun	*Then he is, by common opinion,*
Yholde the lasse in reputacioun.	*Thought the less of.*
Stilboun, that was a wys embassadour,	*Stilboun, who was a wise ambassador,*
Was sent to Corynthe in ful greet honour,	*Was sent to Corinth with great ceremony*
Fro Lacidomye to maken hire alliaunce.	*To conclude a treaty with Sparta.*
And whan he cam hym happede par chaunce,	*And when he came, he happened, by chance,*
That alle the gretteste that were of that lond	*To find all the greatest men in the land*
Pleyynge atte hasard he hem fond.	*Playing at dice.*
For which, as soone as it myghte be,	*Because of this, as soon as he could,*
He stal hym hoom agayn to his contree,	*He sneaked back home to his own country,*
And seyde, Ther wol I nat lese my name,	*And said, "I won't lose my reputation there,*
Ne I wol nat take on me so greet defame.	*Or do such harm to my honour*
Yow for to allie unto none hasardours.	*To make an alliance with any dice players.*
Sendeth othere wise embassadours,	*Send other wise ambassadors there;*
For by my trouthe me were levere dye	*For, I swear, I would rather die*
Than I yow sholde to hasardours allye.	*Than put you into an alliance with gamblers.*
For ye that been so glorious in honours	*For you, who have such glorious honour,*
Shul nat allyen yow with hasardours,	*Should not be in alliance with gamblers,*
As by my wyl, ne as by my tretee,	*And I won't be any part of it."*
This wise philosophre, thus seyde hee.	*This is what this wise philosopher said.*
Looke eek, that to the kyng Demetrius	*Think also about King Demetrius;*
The kyng of Parthes, as the book seith us,	*The King of Parthia, so the books tell us,*
Sente him a paire of dees of gold, in scorn,	*Sent him a pair of gold dice to mock him,*
For he hadde used hasard therbiforn,	*Because he had been a gambler before that;*
For which he heeld his glorie or his renoun	*And because of this he thought nothing*
At no value or reputacioun.	*Of any of his glory or renown.*
Lordes may fynden oother maner pley	*Lords can find other sorts of entertainments*
Honeste ynough, to dryve the day awey.	*Which are respectable, to pass the time.*
Now wol I speke of othes false and grete	*Now I will talk of oaths false and great*
A word or two, as olde bookes trete.	*For a few words, in the way old books speak of them*
Gret sweryng is a thyng abhominable,	*Excessive swearing is a horrible thing,*
And fals sweryng is yet moore reprevable.	*And false swearing is still more revolting.*

The heighe God forbad sweryng at al,	Almighty God forbade all swearing,
Witnesse on Mathew; but in special	You can see that in Matthew; but particularly
Of sweryng seith the hooly Jeremye,	Holy Jeremiah said of swearing,
Thou shalt seye sooth thyne othes, and nat lye,	"You must swear your oaths truthfully, and do not lie,
And swere in doom, and eek in rightwisnesse,	Think carefully about swearing and be righteous";
But ydel sweryng is a cursednesse.	But careless swearing is a cursed thing.
Bihoold and se, that in the firste table	Look and see that in the first three
Of heighe Goddes heestes honourable	Of Almighty God's honourable commandments,
How that the seconde heeste of hym is this:	How the second one says this:
Take nat my name in ydel or amys.	"Do not take my name in vain."
Lo, rather he forbedeth swich sweryng	So, he forbids swearing before
Than homycide, or any cursed thyng!	Murder or many other cursed things;
I seye, that as by ordre thus it stondeth,	I say that his orders are still in place;
This knowen that hise heestes understondeth	Anyone who understands the commandments knows this,
How that the seconde heeste of God is that.	How that was the second commandment of God.
And forther-over I wol thee telle al plat,	And furthermore, I will tell you straight
That vengeance shal nat parten from his hous	That the house of he who swears excessively
That of hise othes is to outrageous-	Shall not escape punishment.
By Goddes precious herte and by his nayles,	"By the precious art of God," and "By his nails,"
And by the blood of Crist that is in Hayles,	And, "By the blood of Christ that is in Hales Abbey,
Sevene is my chaunce and thyn is cynk and treye.	I have rolled a seven, and you a five and three!"
By Goddes armes, if thou falsly pleye,	"By the arms of God, if you play false,
This dagger shal thurghout thyn herte go!	This dagger shall stand through your heart!"
This fruyt cometh of the bicched bones two,	This is what comes from the cursed dice,
Forsweryng, ire, falsnesse, homycide!	Perjury, anger, lying and murder.
Now for the love of Crist, that for us dyde,	Now, for the love of Christ, who died for us,
Lete youre othes bothe grete and smale.	Leave aside your oaths, both great and small.
But, sires, now wol I telle forth my tale.	But, sirs, now I'll tell you my story.
Thise riotoures thre, of whiche I telle,	These three roisterers of whom I speak,
Longe erst er prime rong of any belle,	Long before any bell had rung nine o'clock,
Were set hem in a taverne for to drynke.	Had gathered in a tavern to drink,
And as they sat, they herde a belle clynke	And as they sat there, they heard a bell ringing
Biforn a cors, was caried to his grave.	Leading a corpse, being taken to its grave.
That oon of hem gan callen to his knave,	Then one of them called out to his servant:
Go bet, quod he, and axe redily	"Go quickly," he said, "and ask immediately
What cors is this, that passeth heer forby,	Whose corpse this is passing by here;
And looke, that thou reporte his name weel.	Make sure you get his name right."
Sir, quod this boy, it nedeth neveradeel;	"Sir," said the boy, "there is no need for that;
It was me toold, er ye cam heer two houres.	I was told this two hours before you came here.
He was, pardee, an old felawe of youres,	He was, by God, an old companion of yours,
And sodeynly he was yslayn to-nyght,	And he was killed suddenly last night,
Fordronke, as he sat on his bench upright.	Completely drunk, as he sat up on his bench.
Ther cam a privee theef men clepeth Deeth,	The sneak thief that men called death,
That in this contree al the peple sleeth,	Who kills everyone in this country,

And with his spere he smoot his herte atwo,	*Came and split his heart with his spear,*
And wente his wey withouten wordes mo.	*And went on his way without saying any more.*
He hath a thousand slayn this pestilence,	*He has killed a thousand during this plague.*
And maister, er ye come in his presence,	*And, master, before you meet him,*
Me thynketh that it were necessarie	*I think you would be well advised*
For to be war of swich an adversarie.	*To be wary of such an enemy.*
Beth redy for to meete hym everemoore,	*Always be ready to meet him;*
Thus taughte me my dame, I sey namoore.	*This is what my mother taught me; that's all I will say."*
By Seinte Marie,: seyde this taverner,	*"By St Mary!" said the innkeeper,*
The child seith sooth, for he hath slayn this yeer	*"The child is telling the truth, for this year he has killed,*
Henne over a mile, withinne a greet village	*Just a mile from here, in a great village,*
Bothe man and womman, child, and hyne, and page.	*Both men and women, children, labourers and servants;*
I trowe his habitacioun be there.	*I believe that's where he lives.*
To been avysed, greet wysdom it were,	*It would be very wise to be prepared,*
Er that he dide a man a dishonour.	*Before he did harm to any man."*
Ye, Goddes armes, quod this riotour,	*"Well, by the arms of God!" said this roisterer,*
Is it swich peril with hym for to meete?	*"Is it so dangerous to meet with him?*
I shal hym seke, by wey and eek by strete,	*I shall look for him everywhere,*
I make avow to Goddes digne bones.	*I swear to the sacred bones of God!*
Herkneth, felawes, we thre been al ones;	*Listen, friends, we three are all agreed;*
Lat ech of us holde up his hand til oother,	*Let each of us hold up his hand to the other,*
And ech of us bicomen otheres brother,	*And swear to be the others' brother,*
And we wol sleen this false traytour Deeth.	*And we will kill this false traitor Death.*
He shal be slayn, which that so manye sleeth,	*The one who has killed so many will be killed himself,*
By Goddes dignitee, er it be nyght.	*By Almighty God, before nightfall!*
Togidres han thise thre hir trouthes plight,	*So these three all swore together*
To lyve and dyen, ech of hem for oother,	*That they would live and die for each other,*
As though he were his owene ybore brother;	*As if each was the natural brother of the other.*
And up they stirte al dronken in this rage,	*And up they jumped, all in a drunken rage,*
And forth they goon towardes that village,	*And they set off for the village*
Of which the taverner hadde spoke biforn.	*Which the innkeeper had mentioned before.*
And many a grisly ooth thanne han they sworn,	*They swore many horrid oaths,*
And Cristes blessed body they to-rente,	*Tearing the blessed body of Christ to pieces—*
`Deeth shal be deed, if that they may hym hente.'	*Death would die, if they could catch him!*
Whan they han goon nat fully half a mile,	*When they had not gone farther than half a mile,*
Right as they wolde han troden over a stile,	*Just as they were climbing over a stile,*
An oold man and a povre with hem mette.	*An old poor man met them.*
This olde man ful mekely hem grette,	*This old man humbly greeted them,*
And seyde thus, Now, lordes, God yow see.	*and said, "Now, Lords, may God protect you!"*
The proudeste of thise riotoures three	*The most arrogant of these three roisterers*
Answerde agayn, What, carl, with sory grace,	*Answered back, "What, peasant, bad cess to you!*
Why artow al forwrapped save thy face?	*Why are you all wrapped up apart from your face?*
Why lyvestow so longe in so greet age?	*Why have you lived so long, to get so old?"*

This olde man gan looke in his visage,	*This old man looked in his face,*
And seyde thus, For I ne kan nat fynde	*Saying, "Because I cannot find*
A man, though that I walked in to Ynde,	*A single man, even though I walked to India,*
Neither in citee nor in no village,	*In any city or any village,*
That wolde chaunge his youthe for myn age.	*Who would exchange his youthful my age;*
And therfore mooth I han myn age stille	*And so I have to remain old,*
As longe tyme as it is Goddes wille.	*For as long as God orders.*
Ne deeth, allas, ne wol nat han my lyf!	*Death, alas, will not take my life.*
Thus walke I lyk a restelees kaityf,	*So I will live like a restless wretch,*
And on the ground, which is my moodres gate,	*And on the ground, where my mother lives,*
I knokke with my staf bothe erly and late,	*I knock with my staff, all the time,*
And seye, 'leeve mooder, leet me in!	*Saying, "Dear mother, let me in!*
Lo, how I vanysshe, flessh and blood and skyn!	*Look how I am wasting away, flesh, blood and skin!*
Allas, whan shul my bones been at reste?	*Alas, when shall my bones have rest?*
Mooder, with yow wolde I chaunge my cheste,	*Mother, I would give all my valuables,*
That in my chambre longe tyme hath be,	*That have been in my room for a long time,*
Ye, for an heyre-clowt to wrappe me.'	*In exchange for a shroud!"*
But yet to me she wol nat do that grace;	*But still she won't do me the favour,*
For which ful pale and welked is my face.	*And so my face is very pale and wizened.*
But, sires, to yow it is no curteisye	*But, sirs, it is impolite of you*
To speken to an old man vileynye,	*To speak so rudely to an old man,*
But he trespasse in word, or elles in dede.	*Unless he has done or said anything wrong.*
In hooly writ ye may yourself wel rede,	*You can read for yourselves in holy writ:*
`Agayns an oold man, hoor upon his heed,	*"When you are with an old man, with grey hair,*
Ye sholde arise;' wherfore I yeve yow reed,	*You should stand up;" so I advise you,*
Ne dooth unto an oold man noon harm now,	*Don't do any harm to an old man,*
Namoore than that ye wolde men did to yow	*Treat him as you would want to be treated yourself*
In age, if that ye so longe abyde,	*In your old age, if you live for so long.*
And God be with yow where ye go or ryde.	*May God go with you, wherever you walk or ride!*
I moote go thider, as I have to go.	*I must carry on my journey."*
Nay, olde cherl, by God, thou shalt nat so,	*"No, old peasant, by God, you shall not,"*
Seyde this oother hasardour anon.	*Said this other gambler quickly;*
Thou partest nat so lightly, by Seint John.	*"You can't leave so quickly, by St John!*
Thou spak right now of thilke traytour Deeth,	*You spoke just now of that traitor Death,*
That in this contree alle oure freendes sleeth.	*Who is killing all our friends in this country.*
Have heer my trouthe, as thou art his espye,	*I swear to you, as you are his spy,*
Telle where he is, or thou shalt it abye,	*That you will tell us where he is or you will pay for it,*
By God and by the hooly sacrament,	*By God and the holy sacrament!*
For soothly thou art oon of his assent	*For truly you are one of his accomplices,*
To sleen us yonge folk, thou false theef?	*Who kills we young folk, you false thief!"*
Now, sires, quod he, if that ye be so leef	*"Now, sirs," he said, "if you're so keen*
To fynde Deeth, turne up this croked wey,	*To find Death, turn up this crooked path,*
For in that grove I lafte hym, by my fey,	*For I left him in that grove, I swear,*
Under a tree, and there he wole abyde.	*Under a tree, and he is waiting there;*
Noght for your boost he wole him nothyng hyde,	*Your boasting won't make him hide away.*
Se ye that ook? right ther ye shal hym fynde,	*You see that oak? You will find him right there.*

God save yow that boghte agayn mankynde,	May God protect you, who saved mankind,
And yow amende. Thus seyde this olde man;	And make you change your ways!" So the old man said;
And everich of thise riotoures ran	And each of these roisterers ran
Til he cam to that tree, and ther they founde	Until they got that tree, where they found
Of floryns fyne of gold ycoyned rounde	Nearly eight bushels of fine
Wel ny an eighte busshels, as hem thoughte.	Gold florins, as they thought.
No lenger thanne after Deeth they soughte,	They no longer looked for death,
But ech of hem so glad was of that sighte,	But each of them was so pleased by the sight,
For that the floryns been so faire and brighte,	Because the florins were so pretty and bright,
That doun they sette hem by this precious hoord.	That they sat themselves down by this precious treasure.
The worste of hem, he spak the firste word,	The worst of them spoke first:
Bretheren, quod he, taak kepe what I seys;	"Brothers," he said, "pay attention to what I say;
My wit is greet, though that I bourde and pleye.	I am very clever, although I mess around.
This tresor hath Fortune unto us yeven,	Fortune has given us this treasure
In myrthe and jolitee oure lyf to lyven.	So we can live our lives in happiness and merriment,
And lightly as it comth, so wol we spende.	And we shall spend it as easily as it has come to us.
Ey, Goddes precious dignitee, who wende	Ah, by the precious dignity of God! Who would have imagined
Today that we sholde han so fair a grace?	That we would get such good fortune today?
But myghte this gold be caried fro this place	But if this gold could be carried away from this place
Hoom to myn hous or elles unto youres,	Home to my house, or otherwise to yours—
(For wel ye woot that al this gold is oures)	For you know full well that all this gold is ours—
Thanne were we in heigh felicitee.	Then we should be extremely happy.
But trewely, by daye it may nat bee;	But truly, we can't do it by day.
Men wolde seyn that we were theves stronge,	Men would say that we were clearly thieves,
And for oure owene tresor doon us honge.	And have us hanged for our own treasure.
This tresor moste ycaried be by nyghte,	This treasure must be carried by night
As wisely and as slyly as it myghte.	As cunningly and secretly as can be.
Wherfore I rede that cut among us alle	So I suggest that we all
Be drawe, and lat se wher the cut wol falle,	Draw straws, and see who gets the short one;
And he that hath the cut, with herte blithe	The one who does shall with a happy heart
Shal renne to the towne, and that ful seithe,	Run to the town, and do that very quickly,
And brynge us breed and wyn, ful prively;	And secretly bring us bread and wine.
And two of us shul kepen subtilly	The other two will carefully guard
This tresor wel, and if he wol nat tarie,	This treasure; and if he doesn't waste time,
Whan it is nyght, we wol this tresor carie,	When night comes, we will carry this treasure,
By oon assent, where as us thynketh best.	By mutual agreement, to where we think best."
That oon of hem the cut broghte in his fest,	One of them put the straws in his fist,
And bad hym drawe, and looke where it wol falle;	And told them to draw and see what happened;
And it fil on the yongeste of hem alle,	And the choice fell on the youngest of them,
And forth toward the toun he wente anon.	And he headed for town at once.
And al so soone, as that he was agon,	And as soon as he had gone,
That oon of hem spak thus unto that oother,	One of them spoke to the other:
Thou knowest wel thou art my sworen brother,	"You know full well you are my sworn brother,
Thy profit wol I telle thee anon.	I will tell you at once what's good for you.

Thou woost wel, that oure felawe is agon,	You know that our friend has now gone.
And heere is gold, and that ful greet plentee,	And here we have gold, a very great quantity,
That shal departed been among us thre.	That will be divided between the three of us.
But nathelees, if I kan shape it so	However, if I can arrange matters
That it departed were among us two,	So that it is only shared between the two of us,
Hadde I nat doon a freendes torn to thee?	Won't I have done you a good turn?"
That oother answerde, I noot hou that may be;	The other answered, "I don't know how that could be.
He woot how that the gold is with us tweye;	He knows that we have the gold;
What shal we doon? what shal we to hym seye?	What shall we do? What shall we say to him?"
Shal it be conseil? seyde the firste shrewe,	"Shall we keep it secret?" said the first scoundrel
And I shal tellen, in a wordes fewe,	"And I will tell you in just a few words
What we shal doon, and bryngen it wel aboute.	What we shall do, and I will make it happen."
I graunte, quod that oother, out of doute,	"I agree," said the other, "without doubt,
That by my trouthe I shal thee nat biwreye.	I promise I will not betray you."
Now, quod the firste, thou woost wel we be tweye,	"Now," said the first, "you know full well that there are two of us,
And two of us shul strenger be than oon;	And two are stronger than one.
Looke whan that he is set, that right anoon	When he sits down, make sure that at once
Arys, as though thou woldest with hym pleye,	You get up as though you were playing with him,
And I shal ryve hym thurgh the sydes tweye,	And I will stab him through his sides
Whil that thou strogelest with hym as in game.	While you wrestle with him as if you were playing,
And with thy daggere looke thou do the same,	And make sure you do the same with your dagger;
And thanne shal al this gold departed be,	And then we shall divide this gold,
My deere freend, bitwixen me and thee.	My dear friend, between you and I.
Thanne may we bothe oure lustes all fulfille,	Then we can both do everything we want,
And pleye at dees right at oure owene wille.	And gamble away just as we wish."
And thus acorded been thise shrewes tweye	And so these two scoundrels agreed
To sleen the thridde, as ye han herd me seye.	To kill the third, as I have said.
This yongeste, which that wente unto the toun,	This youngest one, who went to town,
Ful ofte in herte he rolleth up and doun	Continually rolled these beautiful
The beautee of thise floryns newe and brighte.	Florins up and down in his imagination.
O lorde, quod he, if so were that I myghte	"O Lord!" he said, "if it were the case that
Have al this tresor to my-self allone,	I could have this treasure all to myself,
Ther is no man that lyveth under the trone	There is no man living
Of god, that sholde lyve so murye as I.	On earth who would be as happy as me!"
And atte laste the feend, oure enemy,	And eventually our enemy the devil
Putte in his thought that he sholde poyson beye,	Put the thought his mind that he should buy poison,
With which he myghte sleen hise felawes tweye.	With which he could kill his two friends;
For why, the feend foond hym in swich lyvynge,	Because the devil found he lived in such a way
That he hadde leve hem to sorwe brynge;	That he had permission to bring sorrow to him.
For this was outrely his fulle entente,	For this was his plan, completely,
To sleen hem bothe, and nevere to repente.	That he would kill them both and never repent it.
And forth he gooth, no lenger wolde he tarie,	And so out he went, he would no longer wait,
Into the toun unto a pothecarie	Into the town, to a chemist,

And preyde hym that he hym wolde selle	And asked him to sell him
Som poysoun, that he myghte hise rattes quelle,	Some poison, so he could kill his rats;
And eek ther was a polcat in his hawe,	And he also pretended there was a polecat in his yard,
That, as he seyde, hise capouns hadde yslawe;	That, he said, had killed his chickens,
And fayn he wolde wreke hym, if he myghte,	And he wanted to take revenge, if he could,
On vermyn that destroyed hym by nyghte.	On the vermin that ruined him in the night.
The pothecarie answerde, and thou shalt have	The chemist answered, "And you shall have
A thyng, that al so God my soule save,	Something that, I swear to God,
In al this world ther is no creature	There is not a creature in the world
That eten or dronken hath of this confiture	Who has eaten or drunk this preparation,
Noght but the montance of a corn of whete,	A piece just the size of a grain of wheat,
That he ne shal his lif anon forlete;	That has not lost its life at once;
Ye, sterve he shal, and that in lasse while	Yes, it will die, and in less time
Than thou wolt goon a paas nat but a mile,	Than it would take you to walk a mile,
This poysoun is so strong and violent.	This poison is so strong and deadly."
This cursed man hath in his hond yhent	This accursed man took in his hand
This poysoun in a box, and sith he ran	The poison in a box, and then he ran
Into the nexte strete unto a man	Into the next street to a man,
And borwed hym of large botels thre;	And borrowed three large bottles from him,
And in the two his poyson poured he,	And poured poison into two of them;
The thridde he kepte clene for his owene drynke,	He kept the third clean for his drink.
For al the nyght he shoop hym for to swynke	He intended to work all night
In cariynge of the gold out of that place.	Carrying the gold out of that place.
And whan this riotour, with sory grace,	And when this roisterer, bad cess to him,
Hadde filed with wyn his grete botels thre,	Had filled his three big bottles with wine,
To hise felawes agayn repaireth he.	He went back again to his friends.
What nedeth it to sermone of it moore?	Why should I speak of it any longer?
For right as they hadde cast his deeth bifoore	For just as they had already planned his death,
Right so they han him slayn, and that anon;	That was how they killed him, at once.
And whan that this was doon, thus spak that oon,	And when this was done, one of them said:
Now lat us sitte and drynke, and make us merie,	"Now let us sit down and drink, and have a jolly time,
And afterward we wol his body berie.	And afterwards we will bury the body."
And with that word it happed hym, par cas,	As he spoke it happened that, by chance,
To take the botel ther the poysoun was,	He picked up the bottle which had poison in it,
And drank, and yaf his felawe drynke also,	And drank, and passed it to his friend to drink also,
For which anon they storven bothe two.	And so both of them died at once.
But certes, I suppose that Avycen	But certainly, I don't imagine that Avicenna
Wroot nevere in no canoun, ne in no fen,	Ever wrote in any book, or in any chapter,
Mo wonder signes of empoisoning	More astonishing signs of poisoning
Than hadde thise wrecches two, er hir endyng.	Than these two wretches had, before they died.
Thus ended been thise homycides two,	So these two murderers were finished
And eek the false empoysoner also.	And also the false poisoner as well.
O cursed synne ful of cursednesse!	O cursed sin, worst of all of them!
O traytours homycide! O wikkednesse!	O treacherous murder, o wickedness!
O glotonye, luxurie, and hasardrye!	O gluttony, lechery and gambling!
Thou blasphemour of Crist, with vileynye,	You blasphemer of Christ with evil
And othes grete, of usage and of pride,	And great oathes, through habits and pride!

Allas, mankynde! how may it betide	Alas, mankind, how can it happen
That to thy Creatour which that the wroghte,	That to your Creator, who made you,
And with His precious herte-blood thee boghte,	And saved you with his precious heart's blood,
Thou art so fals and so unkynde, allas!	You can be so false and unkind, alas?
Now, goode men, God foryeve yow youre trespas,	Now, good men, may God forgive your sins,
And ware yow fro the synne of avarice;	And protect you from the sin of avarice!
Myn hooly pardoun may yow alle warice,	My holy pardon can cure each one of you,
So that ye offre nobles or sterlynges,	Providing you offer me gold coins or silver pennies,
Or elles silver broches, spoones, rynges;	Or otherwise silver brooches, spoons, rings.
Boweth youre heed under this hooly bulle,	Bow down before this holy document!
Com up, ye wyves, offreth of youre wolle;	Come forward, you wives, give me some wool!
Youre names I entre heer in my rolle anon,	I shall put your names down on my scroll at once;
Into the blisse of hevene shul ye gon.	You shall go straight into heaven.
I yow assoille by myn heigh power,	I absolve you, through my high power,
Yow that wol offre, as clene and eek as cleer	Those of you who will pay will be as clear of sin
As ye were born-and lo, sires, thus I preche;	As the day you were born.—And so, sirs, that's how I preach.
And Jesu Crist, that is oure soules leche,	And Jesus Christ, who is the doctor to our souls,
So graunte yow his pardoun to receyve,	May he give you his pardon,
For that is best, I wol yow nat deceyve.	For that is the best; I will not deceive you.
But sires, o word forgat I in my tale,	But, sirs, there's one thing I forgot to say:
I have relikes and pardoun in my male	I have relics and pardons in my bag,
As faire as any man in Engelond,	As good as any man in England,
Whiche were me yeven by the popes hond.	Which were given to me directly by the Pope.
If any of yow wole of devocioun	If any of you want, out of devotion,
Offren and han myn absolucioun,	To pay me and have my absolution
Com forth anon, and kneleth heere adoun,	Come forward at once, and kneel down here,
And mekely receyveth my pardoun,	And humbly receive my pardon;
Or elles taketh pardoun as ye wende,	Or otherwise I can pardon you as you travel,
Al newe and fressh at every miles ende,	So you will be clean at the end of every mile,
So that ye offren alwey newe and newe	Providing you offer me, again and again,
Nobles or pens, whiche that be goode and trewe.	Gold coins or silver pennies, genuine ones.
It is an honour to everich that is heer,	It is a fine thing for everyone here
That ye mowe have a suffisant pardoner	That you have a pardoner with sufficient power
Tassoille yow in contree as ye ryde,	To give you absolution as you ride through the country,
For aventures whiche that may bityde.	No matter what accidents may happen.
Paraventure ther may fallen oon or two	Maybe one or two of you
Doun of his hors, and breke his nekke atwo.	Down off his horse Aurelius alighted quickly,
Look, which a seuretee is it to yow alle	Look what security it offers you all
That I am in youre felaweship yfalle,	To have me in your company,
That may assoille yow, bothe moore and lasse,	Someone who can absolve you, no matter what your rank,
Whan that the soule shal fro the body passe.	When your soul passes from your body.
I rede that oure Hoost heere shal bigynne,	I recommend that we start with our host,
For he is moost envoluped in synne.	For he is the one most steeped in sin.
Com forth, sire Hoost, and offre first anon,	Come to me, sir host, make the first offering,
And thou shalt kisse my relikes everychon,	And you can kiss all the relics,

Ye, for a grote, unbokele anon thy purs.-	*Yes, just for a groat! Open up your purse at once."*
Nay, nay, quod he, thanne have I Cristes curs!	*"No, no!" he said, "then I will be cursed by Christ!*
Lat be, quod he, it shal nat be, so theech, Thou woldest make me kisse thyn olde breech, And swere it were a relyk of a seint, Though it were with thy fundement depeint. But by the croys which that seint Eleyne fond, I wolde I hadde thy coillons in myn hond In stide of relikes or of seintuarie. Lat kutte hem of, I wol thee helpe hem carie, They shul be shryned in an hogges toord. This Pardoner answerde nat a word; So wrooth he was, no word ne wolde he seye.	*Leave it," he said, "it won't happen, as I live! You would make me kiss your old pants, And swear they were relics of a saint, Even though your arse had stained them! But, by the cross which St Helen found, I wish I had your balls in my hand Rather than relics or reliquaries. Let's cut them off, I'll help you to carry them; They should be enshrined in a hog's turd!" The pardoner didn't say a word; He was so angry, he could say nothing.*
Now, quod oure Hoost, I wol no lenger pleye With thee, ne with noon oother angry man. But right anon the worthy knyght bigan, Whan that he saugh that al the peple lough, Namoore of this, for it is right ynough. Sir Pardoner, be glad and myrie of cheere; And ye, sir Hoost, that been to me so deere, I prey yow, that ye kisse the pardoner; And Pardoner, I prey thee, drawe thee neer, And, as we diden lat us laughe and pley. Anon they kiste, and ryden forth hir weye.	*"Now," said our host, "I will no longer joke With you, nor with any other angry man." But straight away the good knight began, When he saw all the people laughing, "Enough of this, it's true enough! Sir Pardoner, be happy and merry; And you, sir host, whom I like so much, I ask you please to kiss the Pardoner. And Pardoner, I beg you, come closer, And let us laugh and play as we did before." At once they kissed, and carried on their way.*
Heere is ended the Pardoners tale.	***The end of the Pardoner's tale***

The Shipman's Tale

Heere bigynneth the Shipmannes Tale

The beginning of the Shipman's tale

A merchant whilom dwelled at seint-denys,
That riche was, for which men helde hym wys.

A wyf he hadde of excellent beautee;
And compaignable and revelous was she,
Which is a thyng that causeth more dispence
Than worth is al the chiere and reverence
That men hem doon at festes and at daunces.
Swiche salutaciouns and contenances
Passen as dooth a shadwe upon the wal;
But wo is hym that payen moot for al!
The sely housbonde, algate he moot paye,
He moot us clothe, and he moot us arraye,
Al for his owene worshipe richely,
In which array we daunce jolily.
And if that he noght may, par aventure,
Or ellis list no swich dispence endure,
But thynketh it is wasted and ylost,
Thanne moot another payen for oure cost,
Or lene us gold, and that is perilous.

This noble marchaunt heeld a worthy hous,
For which ne hadde alday so greet repair
For his largesse, and for his wyf was fair,
That wonder is; but herkneth to my tale.
Amonges alle his gestes, grete and smale,
Ther was a monk, a fair man and a boold --
I trowe a thritty wynter he was oold --
That evere in oon was drawynge to that place.
This yonge monk, that was so fair of face,
Aqueynted was so with the goode man,
Sith that hir firste knoweliche bigan,
That in his hous as famulier was he
As it is possible any freend to be.

And for as muchel as this goode man,
And eek this monk, of which that I began,
Were bothe two yborn in o village,
The monk hym claymeth as for cosynage;
And he agayn, he seith nat ones nay,
But was as glad therof as fowel of day;
For to his herte it was a greet plesaunce.
Thus been they knyt with eterne alliaunce,
And ech of hem gan oother for t'assure
Of bretherhede, whil that hir lyf may dure.
Free was daun john, and namely of dispence,
As in that hous, and ful of diligence
To doon plesaunce, and also greet costage.
He noght forgat to yeve the leeste page

*There was once a merchant living at St. Denis,
Who was rich, and so men thought he was wise.
He had a very beautiful wife;
And she was sociable and fond of partying,
Which is something causing greater expense
Than all the good cheer and observances
Men have at festivals and dances.
The greetings and courtesies
Vanish like a shadow on a wall,
But woe betide the man who's paying for it!
The hopeless husband, he always pays,
He must clothe us all, with rich
Ornamentation, for his own reputation,
And we have a jolly dance in this finery.
And if it turns out he cannot pay,
Or that he doesn't want to spend such sums,
Thinking that it's all a waste,
Then someone else must pay the bills,
Or lend us money, which is dangerous.*

*This noble merchant kept a good house,
And he always had many visitors,
Because of his generosity and his lovely wife,
It was extraordinary; but hear my tale.
Amongst all his guests, high and low,
There was a monk, handsome and bold-
I think he was about thirty-
Who was always coming to that place.
This young monk, who was so handsome,
Was so friendly with the householder,
And had been since they first met,
That he was as welcome in that house
As any friend could possibly be.*

*And because this good man,
And also the monk of whom I've told you,
Were both born in the same village,
The monk claimed they were related,
And he agreed; he never said, 'no',
But was as glad of it as a bird of the sun,
And it gave him very great pleasure.
So they were sworn brothers,
And each of them promised the other
That they were brothers for life.
This John was generous and free spending
In that household, and very keen
To give pleasure, and also to spend money.
He always remembered to give to the lowliest*

In al that hous; but after hir degree,	servant
He yaf the lord, and sitthe al his meynee,	In the house; but according to rank
	He gave to the lord, and then to all the household,
Whan that he cam, som manere honest thyng;	When he visited, some appropriate gift,
For which they were as glad of his comyng	And so they were as glad when he came
As fowel is fayn whan that the sonne up riseth.	As a fowl is when the sun rises.
Na moore of this as now, for it suffiseth.	That's enough about this for now.
But so bifel, this marchant on a day	But it so happened that one day
Shoop hym to make redy his array	This merchant decided to get ready
Toward the toun of brugges for to fare,	To make a trip to Bruges,
To byen there a porcioun of ware;	To purchase some merchandise;
For which he hath to parys sent anon	So he sent a messenger at once
A messager, and preyed hat daun john	To Paris, asking Don John
That he sholde come to seint-denys to pleye	To come to St.Denis and visit
With hym and with his wyf a day or tweye,	Him and his wife for a couple of days
Er he to brugges wente, in alle wise.	Before he made his trip to Bruges.
This noble monk, of which I yow devyse,	This noble monk, whom I am describing,
Hath of his abbot, as hym list, licence,	Had standing permission from his abbot,
By cause he was a man of heigh prudence,	Because he was a very well behaved man,
And eek an officer, out for to ryde,	And also an officer, to ride out
To seen hir graunges and hire bernes wyde,	To visit their farms and great barns,
And unto seint-denys he comth anon.	And he quickly came to St.Denis.
Who was so welcome as my lord daun john,	Was there anyone as welcome as my lord Don John,
Oure deere cosyn, ful of curteisye?	Our dear kind cousin?
With hym broghte he a jubbe of malvesye,	He brought a jug of malmsey wine with him,
And eek another, ful of fyn vernage,	And also another of good white,
And volatyl, as ay was his usage.	And game birds, as he always did.
And thus I lete hem ete and drynke and pleye,	So I'll leave them to eat and drink and have fun,
This marchant and this monk, a day or tweye.	This merchant and monk, for a day or two.
The thridde day, this marchant up ariseth,	On the third day, the merchant got up,
And on his nedes sadly hym avyseth,	And thought seriously about his business,
And up into his countour-hous gooth he	And he went into his counting house,
To rekene with hymself, as wel may be,	To reckon up, as clearly as he could,
Of thilke yeer how that it with hym stood,	Where his finances stood that year,
And how that he despended hadde his good,	How he had spent his money,
And if that he encressed were or noon.	And whether or not he had made a profit.
His bookes and his bagges many oon	He took his accounts and all his moneybags,
He leith biforn hym on his countyng-bord.	And laid them out on a counting board.
Ful riche was his tresor and his hord,	He had a very great store of treasure,
For which ful faste his countour-dore he shette;	And so he closed his counting house door tight;
And eek he nolde that no man sholde hym lette	He didn't want anyone to interrupt him
Of his acountes, for the meene tyme;	Whilst he made his accounts, for the moment;
And thus he sit til it was passed pryme.	And so he sat until past nine in the morning.
Daun john was rysen in the morwe also,	Don John had also risen,
And in the gardyn walketh to and fro,	And he walked to and fro in the garden,
And hath his thynges seyd ful curteisly.	And said his prayers very diligently.
This goode wyf cam walkynge pryvely	The good wife came walking alone

Into the gardyn, there he walketh softe,	Into the garden, where he walked quietly,
And hym saleweth, as she hath doon ofte.	And greeted him, as she often had before.
A mayde child cam in hire compaignye,	A maidservant came with her,
Which as hir list she may governe and gye,	Whom she could order about as she pleased,
For yet under the yerde was the mayde.	For the girl had to obey adults.
O deere cosyn myn, daun john, she sayde,	"Oh my dear cousin, Don John," she said,
What eyleth yow so rathe for to ryse?	"What has made you get up so early?"
Nece, quod he, it oghte ynough suffise	"My niece," he said, "it ought to be enough
Fyve houres for to slepe upon a nyght,	To get five hours sleep in a night,
But it were for an old appalled wight,	Unless one were an old and feeble creature,
As been thise wedded men, that lye and dare	Like these married men, who lie and snooze
As in a fourme sit a wery hare,	Like a tired hare in his burrow,
Were al forstraught with houndes grete and smale.	When it has been harassed by a gang of hounds.
But deere nece, why be ye so pale?	But, dear niece, why are you so pale?
I trowe, certes, that oure goode man	I believe my host must have
Hath yow laboured sith the nyght bigan,	Been working you so hard all night
That yow were nede to resten hastily.	That you now really need a rest."
And with that word he lough ful murily,	Saying that he began to laugh so merrily
And of his owene thought he was reed.	That he blushed crimson at his own thoughts.
This faire wyf gan for to shake hir heed	The fair wife began to shake her head,
And seyde thus, ye, God woot al, quod she.	And said to him: "Well, God knows everything.
Nay, cosyn myn, it stant nat so with me;	No, my cousin, that's not the case;
For, by that God that yaf me soule and lyf,	For, I swear by almighty God,
In al the reawme of france is ther no wyf	That nowhere in France is there a wife
That lasse lust hath to that sory pley.	Who has less appetite for that business.
For I may synge -- allas and weylawey	I might sing, 'Alas and unhappy day
That I was born, -- but to no wight, quod she,	that I was born,' but I don't dare tell
Dar I nat telle how that it stant with me.	Any man how things are with me.
Wherfore I thynke out of this land to wende,	So I mean to leave this country,
Or elles of myself to make an ende,	Or otherwise I shall kill myself,
So ful am I of drede and eek of care.	I am so full of sorrow and care."
This monk bigan upon this wyf to stare,	This monk began to stare at this wife,
And seyde, allas, my nece, God forbede	And said, "Alas, my niece, God forbid
That ye, for any sorwe or any drede,	That you, for any sorrow or fear,
Fordo youreself; but telleth me youre grief.	Should kill yourself; but tell me why you are sad.
Paraventure I may, in youre meschief,	Maybe I can, in your sad position,
Conseille or helpe; and therfore telleth me	Give you advice or help; and so tell me
Al youre anoy, for it shal been secree.	All your troubles, I shall keep it secret.
For on my porthors here I make an ooth	I swear on my prayerbook
That nevere in my lyf, for lief ne looth,	That never in my life, willingly or not,
Ne shal I of no conseil yow biwreye.	Would I betray any secret of yours."
The same agayn to yow, quod she, I seye.	"I say the same to you," she said,
By God and by this porthors I yow swere,	"By God and this prayerbook I swear
Though men me wolde al into pieces tere,	That although men threatened to tear me to pieces,
Ne shal I nevere, for to goon to helle,	I would never, even if I went to hell,
Biwreye a word of thyng that ye me telle,	Betray a word of anything you say,
Nat for no cosynage ne alliance,	Not because of kinship or obligation,
But verraily, for love and affiance.	But because of love and trust."

Thus been they sworn, and heerupon they kiste,	So they swore to each other, and they kissed,
And ech of hem tolde oother what hem liste.	And each told the other what they wished.
Cosyn, quod she, if that I hadde a space,	"Cousin," she said, "if I had time,
As I have noon, and namely in this place,	Which I have not, especially here,
Thanne wolde I telle a legende of my lyf,	Then I would tell you the story of my life,
What I have suffred with I was a wyf	And what I have suffered since I married
With myn housbonde, al be he youre cosyn.	Through my husband, though he is your cousin."
Nay, quod this monk, by God and seint martyn,	"No," said this monk, "by God and St. Martin,
He is na moore cosyn unto me	He is no more my cousin
Than is this leef that hangeth on the tree!	Than the leaf hanging from this tree!
I clepe hym so, by seint denys of fraunce,	I called him that, by St. Denis of France,
To have the moore cause of aqueyntaunce	So I could get closer
Of yow, which I have loved specially	To you, whom I have always loved more
Aboven alle wommen, sikerly.	Than any other woman, that's certain.
This swere I yow on my professioun.	I swear this to you on my vows.
Telleth youre grief, lest that he come adoun;	Tell me your sorrows quickly
And hasteth yow, and gooth youre wey anon.	And then get going, in case he comes down."
My deere love, quod she, o my daun john,	"My dear love," she said, "my dear Don John,
Ful lief were me this conseil for to hyde,	I wish I could keep this secret,
But out it moot, I may namoore abyde.	But I must tell it, I can't wait any longer.
Myn housbonde is to me the worste man	My husband treats me as badly as any man
That evere was sith that the world bigan.	Has done since the world began.
But sith I am a wyf, it sit nat me	But as I am a wife, it doesn't suit me
To tellen no wight of oure privetee,	To tell anyone our private business,
Neither abedde, ne in noon oother place;	What goes on in bed or anywhere else;
God shilde I sholde it tellen, for his grace!	May God forbid me telling, in his grace!
A wyf ne shal nat seyn of hir housbonde	A wife should say nothing of her husband,
But al honour, as I kan understonde;	Except what's good, so I understand;
Save unto yow thus muche I tellen shal	Only I will tell you this much:
As helpe me god, he is noght worth at al	So help me God, he isn't worth
In no degree the value of a flye.	So much as a flea.
But yet me greveth moost his nygardye.	His miserliness is what grieves me most.
And wel ye woot that wommen naturelly	You know well that women naturally
Desiren thynges sixe as wel as I	Want six things, the same as me:
They wolde that hir housbondes sholde be	They want their husbands to be
Hardy, and wise, and riche, and therto free,	Strong and wise, and rich, also generous,
And buxom unto his wyf, and fressh abedde.	Obedient to his wife and keen in bed.
But by that ilke lord that for us bledde,	But by the lord who bled for us,
For his honour, myself for to arraye,	To clothe myself in a way which would honour my husband,
A sonday next I moste nedes paye	Next Sunday I am obliged to pay
An hundred frankes, or ellis I am lorn.	A hundred francs, or else I am lost.
Yet were me levere that I were unborn	I would rather have never been born
Than me were doon a sclaundre or vileynye;	Than to be disgraced or dishonoured;
And if myn housbonde eek it myghte espye,	And if my husband finds out
I nere but lost; and therfore I yow preye,	I would be all but lost; and so I prey you,
Lene me this somme, or ellis moot I deye.	Lend me this money, or I must die.
Daun john, I seye, lene me thise hundred frankes.	Don John, I ask, lend me these hundred francs.
Pardee, I wol nat faille yow my thankes,	By God, you will not find me thankless,
If that yow list to doon that I yow praye.	If you will do as I ask of you.
For at a certeyn day I wol yow paye,	On a certain day I will pay you,
And doon to yow what plesance and service	And do you whatever pleasure and service

That I may doon, right as yow list devise.	*That I can do, just as you wish.*
And but I do, God take on me vengeance	*Unless I do, may God punish me*
As foul as evere hadde genylon of france.	*As horribly as he ever did Genlon of France."*

This gentil monk answerde in this manere	*This kind monk answered in this way:*
Now trewely, myn owene lady deere,	*"No truly, my own dear lady,*
I have, quod he, on yow so greet a routhe	*I have," he said, "such great pity for you*
That I yow swere, and plighte yow my trouthe,	*That I swear to you, and give you my word,*
That whan youre housbonde is to flaundres fare,	*That once your husband has gone to Flanders,*
I wol delyvere yow out of this care;	*I will relieve you of this burden;*
For I wol brynge yow an hundred frankes.	*For I will bring you a hundred francs."*
And with that word he caughte hire by the flankes,	*And having said that he grabbed her by the flanks*

And hire embraceth harde, and kiste hire ofte.	*And hugged her tight, and kissed her many times.*
Gooth now youre wey, quod he, al stille and softe,	*"Now go on your way," he said, "calmly and quietly,*
And lat us dyne as soone as that ye may;	*And let us dine together as soon as we can;*
For by my chilyndre it is pryme of day.	*For my sundial tells me it is almost noon.*
Gooth now, and beeth as trewe as I shal be.	*Go now, and be as true as I will be."*
Now elles God forbede, sire, quod she;	*"God forbid I should be anything else, Sir,"* she said;

And forth she gooth as jolif as a pye,	*And off she went as jolly as a magpie,*
And bad the cookes that they sholde hem hye,	*And told the cooks to hurry up,*
So that men myghte dyne, and that anon.	*So that people could have their meal, and quickly.*
Up to hir housbonde is this wyf ygon,	*This wife went off to find her husband,*
And knokketh at his countour boldely.	*And boldly knocked at the door of his counting house.*

Quy la? quod he. Peter! it am I,	*"Who is there?" he said. "By St Peter! It's me,"*
Quod she; what, sire, how longe wol ye faste?	*She said; "What, sir, how long are you going to be?*
How longe tyme wol ye rekene and caste	*How long will you be totting up*
Youre sommes, and youre bookes, and youre thynges?	*Your sums, and your books, and all your business?*
The devel have part on alle swiche rekenynges!	*The devil take all such matters!*
Ye have ynough, pardee, of goddes sonde;	*You have enough, by God, of the gifts of God;*
Com doun to-day, and lat youre bagges stonde.	*Come down now, and leave your moneybags alone.*

Ne be ye nat ashamed that daun john	*Aren't you ashamed that Don John*
Shal fasting al this day alenge goon?	*Has to go on fasting all through the day?*
What! lat us heere a messe, and go we dyne.	*Come on, let's go to mass and then eat."*

Wyf, quod this man, litel kanstow devyne	*"Wife," said this man, "you have no idea*
The curious bisynesse that we have.	*How complicated business matters are*
For of us chapmen, also God me save,	*For we merchants, God save me,*
And by that lord that clepid is seint yve,	*And by the lord called St Yve,*
Scarsly amonges twelve tweye shul thryve	*Hardly two out of a dozen of us will succeed*
Continuelly, lastynge unto oure age.	*Consistently, right into our old age.*
We may wel make chiere and good visage,	*We might seem cheerful and put on a brave face,*

And dryve forth the world as it may be,	*And put up with the world as it is,*
And kepen oure estaat in pryvetee,	*And keep the true state of affairs secret,*

Til we be deed, or elles that we pleye	Until we are dead, or we go on
A pilgrymage, or goon out of the weye.	A pilgrimage, or go into hiding.
And therfore have I greet necessitee	It is very necessary
Upon this queynte world t' avyse me;	To plan carefully in this difficult world,
For everemoore we moote stonde in drede	For we must always stand in fear
Of hap and fortune in oure chapmanhede.	Of chance and fate in our dealings.
To flaundres wol I go to-morwe at day,	"I will go to Flanders tomorrow at daybreak,
And come agayn, as soone as evere I may.	And come back again, as soon as I can.
For which, my deere wyf, I thee diseke,	And so, my dear wife, I beg you,
As be to every wight buxom and meke,	To be humble and meek to every person,
And for to kepe oure good be curious,	And make sure you look after our possessions,
And honestly governe wel oure hous.	And look after the household well.
Thou hast ynough, in every maner wise,	You have enough, in every conceivable way,
That to a thrifty houshold may suffise.	To make sure the household is all right.
Thee lakketh noon array ne no vitaille;	You don't lack any supplies nor provisions;
Of silver in thy purs shaltow nat faille.	And you shall have plenty of silver in your purse."
And with that word his countour-dore he shette,	Having said that he closed the door of his counting house,
And doun he gooth, no lenger wolde he lette.	And down he went, he wouldn't wait any longer.
But hastily a messe was ther seyd,	A mass was hastily said,
And spedily the tables were yleyd,	And the tables were quickly laid,
And to the dyner faste they hem spedde,	And they hurried in to dinner,
And richely this monk the chapman fedde.	And this merchant gave the monk a fine meal.
At after-dyner daun john sobrely	After dinner Don John quietly
This chapman took apart, and prively	Took the merchant aside, and secretly
He seyde hym thus	Said to him, "Cousin, this is how it stands,
That wel I se to brugges wol ye go.	I see that you are set on going to Bruges.
Go and seint austyn spede yow and gyde!	May God and St Augustine speed and guide you!
I prey yow, cosyn, wisely that ye ryde.	I beg you, cousin, to ride carefully.
Governeth yow also of youre diete	Also be careful about your diet,
Atemprely, and namely in this hete.	Be moderate, especially in this heat.
Bitwix us two nedeth no strange fare;	We needn't have any formalities between us;
Farewel, cosyn; God shilde yow fro care!	Farewell, cousin; may God keep you from all care!
And if that any thyng by day or nyght,	And if there is anything, day or night,
If it lye in my power and my myght,	If I have the strength and power to do it,
That ye me wol comande in any wyse,	That you want from me in any way,
It shal be doon, right as ye wol devyse.	It shall be done exactly as you ask.
O thyng, er that ye goon, if it may be,	"One thing, before you go, if I may,
I wolde prey yow; for to lene me	I want to ask you: lend me
An hundred frankes, for a wyke or tweye,	A hundred francs, for a week or two,
For certein beestes that I moste beye,	For I need to buy certain animals,
To stoore with a place that is oures.	To stock a place of ours.
God helpe me so, I wolde it were youres!	So help me God, I wish it was yours!
I shal nat faille surely of my day,	I promise I will repay you on the due date,
Nat for a thousand frankes, a mile way.	I wouldn't be a minute late, not for a thousand farncs.
But lat this thyng be secree, I yow preye,	But keep this thing a secret, I beg you,
For yet to-nyght thise beestes moot I beye.	For I have to buy these beasts tonight.

And fare now wel, myn owene cosyn deere;	And now farewell, my own dear cousin;
Graunt mercy of youre cost and of youre cheere.	Thank you for your trouble and your hospitality."
This noble marchant gentilly anon	This noble merchant courteously at once
Answerde and seyde, o cosyn myn, daun john,	Answered and said, "Oh my cousin, Don John,
Now sikerly this is a smal requeste.	Now surely this is just a small request.
My gold is youres, whan that it yow leste,	My gold is yours, whenever you wish,
And nat oonly my gold, but my chaffare.	And not only my gold, but my merchandise.
Take what yow list, God shilde that ye spare.	Take what you want; God forbid you don't.
But o thyng is, ye knowe it wel ynogh,	But there is one thing, you know well,
Of chapmen, that hir moneie is hir plogh.	About merchants, that money is like a plough for us.
We may creaunce whil we have a name;	We can borrow while we have a good reputation,
But goldlees for to be, it is no game.	But when you have no money, that's no joke.
Paye it agayn whan it lith in youre ese;	Pay it back when you can;
After my myght ful fayn wolde I yow plese.	I'm happy to help you as much as I can."
Thise hundred frankes he fette forth anon,	He brought out these hundred francs at once,
And prively he took hem to daun john.	And secretly gave them to Don John.
No wight in al this world wiste of this loone,	There wasn't a man in the world who knew of this loan
Savynge this marchant and daun john allone.	Except for this merchant and Don John.
They drynke, and speke, and rome a while and pleye,	They drank, and chatted, and strolled around amusing themselves,
Til that daun john rideth to his abbeye.	Until Don John rode back to his abbey.
The morwe cam, and forth this marchant rideth	The morning came, and the merchant rode out
To flaundres-ward; his prentys wel hym gydeth,	Towards Flanders; his apprentice guided him well
Til he came into brugges murily.	Until he came happily to Bruges.
Now gooth this marchant faste and bisily	Now this merchant went quickly and busily
Aboute his nede, and byeth and creaunceth.	About his business, and bought and borrowed.
He neither pleyeth at the dees ne daunceth,	He didn't gamble, nor did he dance,
But as a marchaunt, shortly for to telle,	But to say it simply, he lived his life
He let him lyf, and there I lete hym dwelle.	As a merchant should, and I will leave him to it.
The sonday next the marchant was agon,	The next Sunday after the merchant left,
To seint-denys ycomen is daun john,	Don John came to St Denis,
With crowne and berd al fressh and newe yshave.	With his head and his beard newly trimmed.
In al the hous ther nas so litel a knave,	In that household there wasn't the humblest serving boy,
Ne no wight elles, that he nas ful fayn	Nor anybody else, who was not very happy
For that my lord daun john was come agayn.	That their Lord Don John had come again.
And shortly to the point right for to gon,	To cut directly to the point,
This faire wyf acorded with daun john	This pretty wife agreed with Don John
That for thise hundred frankes he sholde al nyght	That in exchange for these hundred francs he would
Have hire in his armes bolt upright;	Have her in his arms, on her back, for the whole night;
And this acord parfourned was in dede.	And this agreement was put into practice.
In myrthe al nyght a bisy lyf they lede	They spent the whole night busy with their fun,
Til it was day, that daun john wente his way,	Until daybreak, and Don John went on his way,

And bad the meynee farewel, have good day!	Saying to the household, "Farewell, have a good day!"
For noon of hem, ne no wight in the toun,	For none of them, nor anyone in the town,
Hath of daun john right no suspecioun.	Had any suspicion about Don John at all.
And forth he rydeth hoom to his abbeye,	Off he went home to his abbey,
Or where hym list; namoore of hym I seye.	Or wherever he wanted; that's all I'll say about him.
This marchant, whan that ended was the faire,	This merchant, when the fair was ended,
To seint-denys he gan for to repaire,	Went back to St Denis,
And with his wyf he maketh feeste and cheere,	And feasted and was happy with his wife,
And telleth hire that chaffare is so deere	And told her that the goods were so expensive
That nedes moste he make a chevyssaunce;	That he was forced to take out credit,
For he was bounden in a reconyssaunce	He was bound by a legal agreement
To paye twenty thousand sheeld anon.	To pay twenty thousand shields very soon.
For which this marchant is to parys gon	For that reason the merchant went to Paris
To borwe of certeine freendes that he hadde	To borrow from certain friends he had
A certeyn frankes; and somme with him he ladde.	A certain number of francs; and he brought some back with him.
And whan that he was come into the toun,	When he got to the town,
For greet chiertee and greet affeccioun,	Because of his great affection and goodwill,
Unto daun john he gooth first, hym to pleye;	He went to visit Don John first of all;
Nat for to axe or borwe of hym moneye,	Not to ask him for a loan,
But for to wite and seen of his welfare,	But just to find out how he was,
And for to tellen hym of his chaffare,	And to tell him about his business,
As freendes doon whan they been met yfeere.	As friends do when they meet.
Daun john hym maketh feeste and murye cheere,	Don John feasted him and gave him a warm welcome,
And he hym tolde agayn, ful specially,	And he told him in his turn, in full detail,
How he hadde wel yboght and graciously,	What good things he had bought, how successfully,
Thanked be god, al hool his marchandise;	And he thanked God for all of his goods.
Save that he moste, in alle maner wise,	Except that he had to, no matter what,
Maken a chevyssaunce, as for his beste,	Arrange the credit, as the best thing to do,
And thanne he sholde been in joye and reste.	Otherwise everything would be perfect.
Daun john answerde, certes, I am fayn	Don John answered, "Certainly, I am glad
That ye in heele ar comen hom agayn.	That you have come home again and all well.
And if that I were riche, as have I blisse,	If I were rich, I swear by my chance of heaven,
Of twenty thousand sheeld sholde ye nat mysse,	You wouldn't be lacking those twenty thousand shields,
For ye so kyndely this oother day	For just the other day you so kindly
Lente me gold; and as I kan and may,	Lent me gold; and just as well as I know how to
I thanke yow, by God and by seint jame!	I thank you, by God and St James!
But nathelees, I took unto oure dame,	However, I gave our Lady,
Youre wyf, at hom, the same gold ageyn	Your wife, at home, that same gold back
Upon youre bench; she woot it wel, certeyn,	On your counting board; she knows all about it,
By certeyn tokenes that I kan hire telle.	I can give proof of that.
Now, by youre leve, I may no lenger dwelle;	Now, if you'll excuse me, I can't hang around;
Oure abbot wole out of this toun anon,	Our abbot wants to leave the town soon,
And in his compaignye moot I goon.	And I must go with him.
Grete wel oure dame, myn owene nece sweete,	Give my regards to our lady, my own sweet

	niece,
And fare wel, deere cosyn, til we meete!	*And farewell, dear cousin, until we meet!"*
This marchant, which that was ful war and wys,	*This merchant, who was very sensible and wise,*
Creanced hath, and payd eek in parys	*Had got credit, and also paid in Paris*
To certeyn lumbardes, redy in hir hond,	*To certain bankers of Lombardy, in ready cash,*
The somme of gold, and gat of hem his bond;	*The sum in gold, and he had redeemed his bond;*
And hoom he gooth, murie as a papejay,	*And he went home, as merry as a parrot,*
For wel he knew he stood in swich array	*For he knew well that he was in a position*
That nedes moste he wynne in that viage	*That would enable him to earn from his journey*
A thousand frankes aboven al his costage.	*A clear thousand francs in profit.*
His wyf ful redy mette hym atte gate,	*His wife very gladly met him at the gate,*
As she was wont of oold usage algate,	*As by custom she always did,*
And al that nyght in myrthe they bisette;	*And they spent that night having fun,*
For he was riche and cleerly out of dette.	*For he was rich and had completely cleared his debts.*
Whan it was day, this marchant gan embrace	*When the day came, this merchant embraced*
His wyf al newe, and kiste hire on hir face,	*His wife over again, and kissed her on the face,*
And up he gooth and maketh it ful tough.	*And in he went again, good and hard.*
Namoore, quod she, by god, ye have ynough!	*"No more," she said, "by God, haven't you had enough!"*
And wantownly agayn with hym she pleyde,	*And she played with him again saucily,*
Til atte laste thus this marchant seyde	*Until at the last this merchant said:*
By go, quod he, I am a litel wrooth	*"By God," he said, "I am a little angry*
With yow, my wyf, although it be me looth.	*With you, my wife, although I don't want to be.*
And woot ye why? by god, as that I gesse	*Do you know why? By God, because I think*
That ye han maad a manere straungenesse	*That you have driven a wedge*
Bitwixen me and my cosyn daun john.	*Between me and my cousin Don John.*
Ye sholde han warned me, er I had gon,	*You should have warned me, before I left,*
That he yow hadde an hundred frankes payed	*That he had paid you a hundred francs*
By redy token; and heeld hym yvele apayed,	*In cash; and he thought I was insulting him,*
For that I to hym spak of chevyssaunce;	*Because I spoke to him about borrowing;*
Me semed so, as by his contenaunce.	*It seemed that way to me, from his face.*
But nathelees, by god, oure hevene kyng,	*But nonetheless, by God, our almighty King,*
I thoughte nat to axen hym no thyng.	*I wasn't thinking of asking anything from him.*
I prey thee, wyf, ne do namoore so;	*I pray you, wife, don't do that again;*
Telle me alwey, er that I fro thee go,	*Always tell me, before I leave,*
If any dettour hath in myn absence	*If any debtor has, in my absence,*
Ypayed thee, lest thurgh thy necligence	*Paid you, so that I won't carelessly*
I myghte hym axe a thing that he hath payed.	*Ask him for what he has already paid."*
This wyf was nat afered nor affrayed,	*This wife showed absolutely no fear,*
But boldely she seyde, and that anon;	*She boldly said, at once,*
Marie, I deffie the false monk, daun john!	*"By Mary, I defy that false monk, Don John!*
I kepe nat of his tokenes never a deel;	*I don't care what proof he offers;*
He took me certeyn gold, that woot I weel, --	*I know he gave me a certain amount of gold—*
What! yvel thedam on his monkes snowte!	*What! Bad luck to his monk's snout!*
For, God it woot, I wende, withouten doute,	*For, God knows, I thought, certainly,*

That he hadde yeve it me bycause of yow,	That he had given it to me out of respect for you
To doon therwith myn honour and my prow, For cosynage, and eek for beele cheere	To do things with it for my honour and benefit, Because of your kinship, and also because of the good times
That he hath had ful ofte tymes heere. But sith I se I stonde in this disjoynt, I wol answere yow shortly to the poynt. Ye han mo slakkere dettours than am i!	He has always been offered here. But since I see I'm in this difficult position, I shall answer you straight to the point. You will have debtors who pay you slower than me!
For I wol paye yow wel and redily Fro day to day, and if so be I faille, I am youre wyf; score it upon my taille, And I shal paye as soone as ever I may. For by my trouthe, I have on myn array, And nat on wast, bistowed every deel; And for I have bistowed it so weel For youre honour, for goddes sake, I seye, As be nat wrooth, but lat us laughe and pleye. Ye shal my joly body have to wedde; By god, I wol nat paye yow but abedde! Forgyve it me, myn owene spouse deere; Turne hiderward, and maketh bettre cheere.	For I will pay you well and regularly From day to day, and if I happen to miss, I am your wife; put it on my tab, And I will pay you as soon as I can. For I swear, I have spent every penny On clothes, I haven't wasted it; And because I have spent it so well To make you look good, for God's sake, I say, Don't be angry, let us laugh and play. You shall have my sweet body as my pledge; By God, the only way I'll pay you is in bed! Forgive me this, my own dear husband; Come over here, and cheer yourself up."
This marchant saugh ther was no remedie,	This merchant saw there was nothing to be done,
And for to chide it nere but folie, Sith that the thyng may nat amended be. Now wyf, he seyde, and I foryeve it thee; But, by thy lyf, ne be namoore so large.	And that to criticise would be a waste of time, Since the business could not be changed. "Now wife," he said, "I forgive you for it; But, swear on your life you will no longer be so generous.
Keep bet my good, this yeve I thee in charge.	Take better care of your property, I order this of you."
Thus endeth now my tale, and God us sende Taillynge ynough unto oure lyves ende. Amen	So my tale ends, and may God send us Enough of this sort of thing to keep us going to the end of our lives. Amen

Heere endeth the Shipmannes Tale. **The end of the Shipman's tale**

The Prioress' Tale

Behoold the murie wordes of the Hoost to the Shipman and to the lady Prioresse.

Wel seyd, by corpus dominus, quod our Hoost,
Now longe moote thou saille by the cost,
Sir gentil maister, gentil maryneer.
God yeve this monk a thousand last quade yeer!
A ha! felawes, beth ware of swich a jape.
The monk putte in the mannes hood an ape,
And in his wyves eek, by Seint Austyn;
Draweth no monkes moore unto your in.
But now passe over, and lat us seke aboute
Who shal now telle first of al this route
Another tale? and with that word he sayde,
As curteisly as it had ben a mayde,

My lady Prioresse, by youre leve,
So that I wiste I sholde yow nat greve,
I wolde demen that ye tellen sholde
A tale next, if so were that ye wolde.
Now wol ye vouchesauf, my lady deere?
Gladly, quod she, and seyde as ye shal heere.

The jolly words of the host to the Shipman and the lady Prioress

"Well said, by the body of our Lord," said our host,
"Now may you have many journeys round the coast,
Sir gentle master, sweet mariner!
May God give the monk a thousand bad years!
Aha! Fellows, look out for such a trick!
This monk made a monkey of that man,
And also of his wife, by St Augustine!
Don't have any more monks staying with you.
But enough of that, let's look around and see
Who will now, from all this company, tell
Another tale." And having said that,
He spoke as courteously as if he were a maiden,
"My lady prioress, with your permission,
As long as you have no objections,
I think that you should tell
The next tale, if you would like to.
Will you do this for us, my dear lady?"
"Gladly," she said, and she spoke as you shall hear.

Prologue

The prologe of the Prioresses Tale   *The Prioress' Prologue*

Domine dominus noster   *Our Lord, our Lord*

O lord oure lord, thy name how merveillous   *"Oh Lord, our Lord, how much your wonderful name*

Is in this large world ysprad-quod she-   *Is praised across the wide world," she said,*
For noght oonly thy laude precious   *"For not only is your precious praise*
Parfourned is by men of dignitee,   *Given by high-ranking men,*
But by the mouth of children thy bountee   *But through the mouths of children your goodness*

Parfourned is, for on the brest soukynge   *Is made known, for when they suck at the breast*

Somtyme shewen they thyn heriynge.   *Sometimes they show praise for you.*

Wherfore in laude, as I best kan or may,   *So in your praise, as best I can,*
Of thee, and of the whyte lylye flour   *For you and the white lily flower*
Which that the bar, and is a mayde alway,   *Who bore you, and remains a virgin,*
To telle a storie I wol do my labour;   *I will try to tell a story;*
Nat that I may encreessen hir honour,   *I won't be able to increase her honour,*
For she hirself is honour, and the roote   *For she is honour personified and the fount*
Of bountee, next hir sone, and soules boote.   *Of goodness, next to her son, and the cure for all souls.*

O mooder mayde! O mayde mooder fre!   *O mother maiden, O generous mother and maiden!*

O bussh unbrent, brennynge in Moyses sighte,   *Oh unburnt bush, burning before Moses,*
That ravysedest doun fro the deitee   *That swept down from the godhead,*
Thurgh thyn humblesse, the goost that in thalighte,   *Through your humility, the ghost that entered you,*

Of whos vertu, whan he thyn herte lighte,   *Through whose power, when he lit up your heart,*

Conceyved was the Fadres sapience,   *The wisdom of the father was born,*
Help me to telle it in thy reverence.   *Help me describe it as I worship you!*

Lady, thy bountee, thy magnificence,   *Lady, your goodness, your magnificence,*
Thy vertu, and thy grete humylitee,   *Your virtue and your great humility*
Ther may no tonge expresse in no science,   *Cannot be told in the language of any science;*
For somtyme, lady, er men praye to thee,   *For sometimes, Lady, before men pray to you,*
Thou goost biforn of thy benyngnytee   *You already favour them through your kindness,*

And getest us the lyght, thurgh thy preyere,   *And you show us the light, through your prayers,*

To gyden us unto thy sone so deere.   *To guide us to your dear son.*

My konnyng is so wayk, O blisful queene,   *My skills are so weak, oh wonderful Queen,*
For to declare thy grete worthynesse,   *For declaring your great virtues,*
That I ne may the weighte nat susteene,   *I cannot cope with this great task;*
But as a child of twelf monthe oold, or lesse,   *But as a child a year old or less,*
That kan unnethes any word expresse,   *Who can hardly speak a word,*

Right so fare I; and therfore I yow preye,	That's how I am, and so I pray to you,
Gydeth my song that I shal of yow seye.	Guide my song as I speak of you.

Heere bigynneth the Prioresses Tale.

The Prioress' tale

Ther was in Asye, in a greet citee,	There was in a great city of Asia
Amonges cristene folk a Jewerye,	A Jewish ghetto amongst the Christian folk,
Sustened by a lord of that contree	Maintained by a Lord of that country
For foule usure and lucre of vileynye,	For foul moneylending and the profits of crime,
Hateful to Crist and to his compaignye,	Horrible to Christ and his companions;
And thurgh this strete men myghte ride or wende,	And any man could ride all walk through that street,
For it was free and open at eyther ende.	For it was freely open at both ends.
A litel scole of cristen folk ther stood	There was a little school of Christian people there,
Doun at the ferther ende, in which ther were	Down at the farthest end, in which there were
Children an heep, ycomen of cristen blood,	Many children, who were descended from Christians,
That lerned in that scole yeer by yeer	Who were educated in that school each year,
Swich manere doctrine as men used there,	Taught the doctrines that men use there,
This is to seyn, to syngen and to rede,	That is to say, to sing and to read,
As smale children doon in hir childhede.	As small children do in childhood.
Among thise children was a wydwes sone,	Amongst these children was the son of a widow,
A litel clergeoun, seven yeer of age,	A little schoolboy, seven years old,
That day by day to scole was his wone,	Who used to go to the school every day,
And eek also, wher as he saugh thymage	And also, whenever he saw the image
Of Cristes mooder, he hadde in usage	Of the mother of Christ, it was his custom,
As hym was taught, to knele adoun, and seye	As he had been taught, to kneel down and say
His Ave Marie, as he goth by the weye.	A Hail Mary, as he went on his way.
Thus hath this wydwe hir litel sone ytaught	This was how this widow had taught her little son
Oure blisful lady, Cristes mooder deere,	To worship our blissful lady, the dear
To worshipe ay; and he forgate it naught,	Mother of Christ always, and he never forgot it,
For sely child wol alday soone leere.	For an innocent child is a quick learner.
But ay, whan I remembre on this mateere,	But always, when I think about this business,
Seint Nicholas stant evere in my presence,	St Nicholas is always in my mind,
For he so yong to Crist dide reverence.	Because he worshipped Christ when he was so young.
This litel child, his litel book lernynge,	This little child, learning from his little book,
As he sat in the scole at his prymer,	As he sat in school with his primer,
He Alma redemptoris herde synge	He heard 'Gracious mother of the saviour' being sung,
As children lerned hir anthiphoner;	As the children learned their harmonious hymns;
And as he dorste, he drough hym ner and ner,	And he drew as close as he dared,
And herkned ay the wordes and the noote,	And always listened to the words and notes,
Til he the firste vers koude al by rote.	Until he knew the first verse by heart.

Noght wiste he what this Latyn was to seye,	He didn't know what the Latin words meant,
For he so yong and tendre was of age,	Because he was of such a young age.
But on a day his felawe gan he preye	But one day he begged a friend
Texpounden hym this song in his langage,	To explain the song to him in his own language,
Or telle hym why this song was in usage;	Or to tell him why the song was always sung;
This preyde he hym to construe and declare	He begged him to translate and explain
Ful often tyme upon hise knowes bare.	Very often, down on his bare knees.
His felawe, which that elder was than he,	His friend, who was older than him,
Answerde hym thus, This song, I have herd seye,	Answered him and us: "This song, so I've heard,
Was maked of oure blisful Lady free,	Was composed about our kind and blissful lady,
Hir to salue, and eek hir for to preye	To salute her, and also to pray to her
To been our help, and socour whan we deye.	To be our help and comfort when we die.
I kan namoore expounde in this mateere,	I can't tell you any more about this;
I lerne song, I kan but smal grammere.	I learn songs, but I don't know much grammar."
And is this song maked in reverence	"And is this song composed to worship
Of Cristes mooder? seyde this innocent.	The mother of Christ?" said this innocent.
Now, certes, I wol do my diligence	"Now, certainly, I will do my best
To konne it al, er Cristemasse is went;	To learn it all before Christmas has passed.
Though that I for my prymer shal be shent	Although I will be punished for not learning my primer,
And shal be beten thries in an houre,	And be beaten three times an hour,
I wol it konne, oure lady for to honoure.	I will learn it for the honour of Our Lady!"
His felawe taughte hym homward prively	His friend secretly taught it to him as they headed home,
Fro day to day, til he koude it by rote;	Every day, until he knew it by heart,
And thanne he song it wel and boldely	And then he sang it well and strongly,
Fro word to word acordynge with the note.	Every word, in harmony with the tune.
Twies a day it passed thurgh his throte,	He sang it out twice every day,
To scoleward, and homward whan he wente;	Going to school and coming home;
On Cristes mooder set was his entente.	His mind was full of the mother of Christ.
As I have seyd, thurghout the Jewerie	As I have said, all through the ghetto,
This litel child, as he cam to and fro,	This little child, as he went to and fro,
Ful murily than wolde he synge and crie	Would very merrily sing out
O Alma redemptoris evere-mo.	The song, 'O gracious mother of the saviour'
The swetnesse hath his herte perced so	His heart was so full of the sweetness
Of Cristes mooder, that to hir to preye	Of the mother of Christ that, to pray to her,
He kan nat stynte of syngyng by the weye.	He could not stop himself singing on his journey.
Oure firste foo, the serpent Sathanas,	Our first enemy, the serpent Satan,
That hath in Jewes herte his waspes nest,	Who has built his wasps' nest in the hearts of Jews,
Up swal, and seyde, O Hebrayk peple, allas,	Swelled up, and said, "Oh Jewish people, alas!
Is this to yow a thyng that is honest,	Is this a thing you should allow,
That swich a boy shal walken as hym lest	Letting a boy like that walk as he pleases
In youre despit, and synge of swich sentence,	Scorning you, singing about such things,

Which is agayn oure lawes reverence?

Fro thennes forth the Jewes han conspired
This innocent out of this world to chace.
An homycide therto han they hyred
That in an aleye hadde a privee place;
And as the child gan forby for to pace,
This cursed Jew hym hente and heeld hym faste,

And kitte his throte, and in a pit hym caste.

I seye that in a wardrobe they hym threwe,
Where as this Jewes purgen hire entraille.
O cursed folk of Herodes al newe,
What may youre yvel entente yow availle?
Mordre wol out, certeyn, it wol nat faille,
And namely ther thonour of God shal sprede,
The blood out crieth on youre cursed dede.

O matir, sowded to virginitee,
Now maystow syngen, folwynge evere in oon
The white lamb celestial-quod she-
Of which the grete Evaungelsit Seint John
In Pathmos wroot, which seith that they that goon

Biforn this lamb and synge a song al newe,
That never, fleshly, wommen they ne knewe.

This povre wydwe awaiteth al that nyght
After hir litel child, but he cam noght;
For which, as soone as it was dayes light,
With face pale of drede and bisy thoght,

She hath at scole and elles-where hym soght,
Til finally she gan so fer espie,
That he last seyn was in the Jewerie.

With moodres pitee in hir brest enclosed,
She gooth, as she were half out of hir mynde,

To every place where she hath supposed
By liklihede hir litel child to finde,
And evere on Cristes mooder, meeke and kynde

She cride, and atte laste thus she wroghte,
Among the cursed Jewes she hym soghte.

She frayneth, and she preyeth pitously
To every Jew that dwelte in thilke place,
To telle hir if hir child wente oght forby.
They seyde nay; but Jesu, of his grace,
Yaf in hir thoght, inwith a litel space,
That in that place after hir sone she cryde,
Wher he was casten in a pit bisyde.

Which is against your laws of worship?"

From that moment on the Jews conspired
To chase this innocent out of the world.
For this purpose they hired a murderer,
Who had a secret place in an alleyway;
And as the child began to walk past,
This horrible Jew grabbed him, and held him tight,
And slit his throat, and threw him in a pit.

I'm telling you they threw him in a cesspit,
Where all these Jews emptied their bowels.
Oh you cursed race of new Herods,
What good will all your evil do you?
Murder will be revealed, you can't hide it,
Especially not where God is honoured;
The blood cries out against your cursed deeds.

O martyr, wedded to virginity,
Now you can sing, following eternally
The heavenly white lamb–she said–
Of which the great evangelist, St John,
Wrote when he was on Patmos, who says the ones who go
Before this Lamb and sing a new song
Are those who never knew women sexually.

The poor widow waited all that night
For her little child, but he did not come;
And so, as soon as day had broken,
With a face pale with fear and terrible thoughts,
She looked for him at school and elsewhere,
Until at last she discovered
That he had last been seen in the ghetto.

With the pity of a mother held in her breast
She went there, as if she were almost out of her mind,
To every place where she thought
She might find her little child;
And she always cried out to the mother of Christ,
Meek and kind, and then as her last resort
She looked for him amongst the cursed Jews.

She questioned and pitifully begged
Every Jew who lived in that place
To tell her if her child had passed by there.
They said, "no"; but in his Grace Jesus
Put it into her thoughts very soon
To go and look for her son in that place
Where he had been thrown into the cesspit.

O grete God, that parfournest thy laude	*Oh great God, who takes your praise*
By mouth of innocentz, lo, heer thy myght!	*From the mouths of innocents, see, here is your power!*
This gemme of chastite, this emeraude,	*This jewel of chastity, this emerald,*
And eek of martirdom the ruby bright,	*And also this bright ruby of martyrdom,*
Ther he with throte ykorven lay upright,	*There he lay on his back with his throat slit,*
He Alma redemptoris gan to synge	*And he began to sing 'Gracious mother of the saviour"*
So loude, that al the place gan to rynge.	*So loud that the whole place rang with it.*
The cristene folk that thurgh the strete wente	*The Christian folk who passed through the street*
In coomen, for to wondre upon this thyng,	*Came to wonder at this business,*
And hastily they for the Provost sente.	*And they quickly sent for the justice;*
He cam anon withouten tariyng,	*He came at once, he didn't waste time,*
And herieth Crist that is of hevene kyng,	*And praised Christ who is the King of Heaven,*
And eek his mooder, honour of mankynde;	*And also his mother, the light of humanity,*
And after that, the Jewes leet he bynde.	*And after that he had the Jews arrested.*
This child, with pitous lamentacioun,	*This child was, with pitiful lamentation,*
Uptaken was, syngynge his song alway,	*Picked up, always singing his song,*
And with honour of greet processioun	*And with a great ceremonious procession*
They carien hym unto the nexte abbay;	*They carried him to the nearest abbey.*
His mooder swownynge by his beere lay,	*His mother lay swooning by his bier,*
Unnethe myghte the peple that was theere	*And the people there could hardly*
This newe Rachel brynge fro his beere.	*Prise this new Rachel away from him.*
With torment and with shameful deeth echon	*With torture and shameful deaths for each one,*
This Provost dooth the Jewes for to sterve,	*The magistrate had the Jews put to death*
That of this mordre wiste, and that anon.	*If they knew about this murder, this was done at once.*
He nolde no swich cursednesse observe;	*He would not tolerate any such cursed behaviour.*
Yvele shal have that yvele wol deserve.	*"Evil will get what it deserves";*
Therfore with wilde hors he dide hem drawe,	*And so he had them torn apart with wild horses,*
And after that he heng hem, by the lawe.	*And after that he had them hanged according to the law.*
Upon his beere ay lith this innocent	*This innocent still lay upon his bier*
Biforn the chief auter, whil masse laste,	*In front of the great altar, while the mass lasted;*
And after that, the abbot with his covent	*And after that, the abbot and all his convent*
Han sped hem for to burien hym ful faste,	*Hurried to have him buried at once;*
And whan they hooly water on hym caste,	*And when they sprinkled holy water on him,*
Yet spak this child, whan spreynd was hooly water,	*The child still spoke, when it was done,*
And song O Alma redemptoris mater.	*And sang, 'O gracious mother of the saviour!'*
This abbot, which that was an hooly man,	*This Abbott, who was a holy man,*
As monkes been-or elles oghte be-	*As monks are–or at least as they ought to be–*
This yonge child to conjure he bigan,	*Began to question this young child,*
And seyde, o deere child, I halse thee,	*Saying, "Oh dear child, I beg you,*
In vertu of the hooly trinitee,	*Through the power of the holy Trinity,*
Tel me what is thy cause for to synge,	*Tell me how it is you are singing,*

Sith that thy throte is kut to my semynge?	Since it seems to me that your throat has been cut?"
My throte is kut unto my nekke boon, This yonge child, and, as by wey of kynde,	"My throat has been cut back to my spine," Said this child, "and in the normal way of things
I sholde have dyed, ye, longe tyme agon, But Jesu Crist, as ye in bookes fynde, Wil that his glorie laste and be in mynde,	I should have died a long time ago. But Jesus Christ, as you will find in books, Wants his glory to last and always be thought of,
And for the worship of his mooder deere, Yet may I synge O Alma loude and cleere.	And in worship of his dear mother I still can sing, 'O gracious mother' loud and clear.
This welle of mercy, Cristes mooder swete,	"This well of mercy, the sweet mother of Christ,
I loved alwey as after my konnynge; And whan that I my lyf sholde forlete, To me she cam, and bad me for to synge This antheme, verraily, in my deyynge, As ye han herd, and whan that I hadde songe, Me thoughte she leyde a greyn upon my tonge.	I always loved, as well as I could, And when I had to forfeit my life, She came to me, and asked me to sing This song even as I was dying, As you have heard, and when I sang I thought that she placed a grain upon my tongue.
Wherfore I synge, and synge I moot certeyn In honour of that blisful mayden free, Til fro my tonge oftaken is the greyn. And afterward thus seyde she to me, `My litel child, now wol I fecche thee,	So I sing, and always must sing, In honour of that blissful generous maiden Until the grain is removed from my tongue; And after that she said this to me: "My little child, at that time I will come for you,
Whan that the greyn is fro thy tonge ytake;	When the grain has been taken from your tongue.
Be nat agast, I wol thee nat forsake.'	Do not be afraid; I will not abandon you."
This hooly monk, this Abbot, hym meene I, His tonge out-caughte, and took awey the greyn, And he yaf up the goost ful softely; And whan this Abbot hadde this wonder seyn, Hise salte teeris trikled doun as reyn, And gruf he fil al plat upon the grounde,	This holy monk, this abbot, I mean, Pulled out his tongue, and removed the grain, And he quietly gave up the ghost. And when this abbot had seen this miracle, His salty tears fell like rain, And he threw himself face down upon the ground,
And stille he lay, as he had been ybounde.	Lying as still as if he were in chains.
The covent eek lay on the pavement, Wepynge, and heryen Cristes mooder deere.	All the convent also lay on the pavement Weeping, and praising the dear mother of Christ,
And after that they ryse, and forth been went, And tooken awey this martir from his beere, And in a temple of marbul stones cleere Enclosen they his litel body sweete. Ther he is now, God leve us for to meete!	And after that they got up, and went out, Taking the martyr away from his bier; In a tomb of fine marble They placed his sweet little body. He is still there now, may God allow us to meet him!
O yonge Hugh of Lyncoln, slayn also With cursed Jewes, as it is notable,	Oh young Hugh of Lincoln, also killed By cursed Jews, as everybody knows,

For it nis but a litel while ago,
Preye eek for us, we synful folk unstable,
That of his mercy God so merciable
On us his grete mercy multiplie,
For reverence of his mooder Marie. Amen

Heere is ended the Prioresses Tale.

For it was only a little while ago,
Also pray for us, we changeable sinful folk,
So that in his mercy God who is so merciful
Will increase his great mercy for us,
In worship of his mother Mary. Amen.

The end of the Prioress' tale

The Tale of Sir Thopas

Bihoold the murye wordes of the Hooste to Chaucer

Whan seyd was al this miracle, every man

As sobre was, that wonder was to se,
Til that oure Hooste japen tho bigan,
And thanne at erst he looked upon me,
And seyde thus, What man artow, quod he,
For ever upon the ground I se thee stare.
Approche neer, and looke up murily;
Now war yow, sires, and lat this man have place.
He in the waast is shape as wel as I;
This were a popet in an arm tenbrace
For any womman smal, and fair of face.
He semeth elvyssh by his contenaunce,

For unto no wight dooth he daliaunce.
Sey now somwhat, syn oother folk han sayd,

Telle us a tale of myrthe, and that anon.
Hooste, quod I, ne beth nat yvele apayed,
For oother tale certes kan I noon
But of a ryme I lerned longe agoon.
Ye, that is good, quod he, now shul we here

Som deyntee thyng, me thynketh by his cheere.

Here are the Merry words the host said to Chaucer

When the story of this miracle was finished, every man
Was so solemn, it was incredible to see,
Until our host then began to joke
And he looked at me for the first time,
You look as if you are tracking a hare,
For you are always looking at the ground.
Come closer, and look up and smile.
Make way, gentlemen, give this man a place!
He has a waist shaped just as well as mine;
This would be a nice little doll to embrace
For any woman, small and pretty.
He seems rather like a fairy from his behaviour,
For he is not sociable with any man:
Tell us something now, since the other people have spoken;
Tell us a merry tale, right now."
"Host," I said, "don't be annoyed,
But to tell the truth I only know one tale,
Just a rhyme I learned a long time ago."
"Yes, that is good," he said, "now we will hear
Some dainty thing, I think, judging by his appearance."

Heere bigynneth Chaucers Tale of Thopas

Listeth, lordes, in good entent,
And I wol telle verrayment
Of myrthe and of solas,
Al of a knyght was fair and gent

In bataille and in tourneyment,
His name was Sir Thopas.

Yborn he was in fer contree,
In Flaundres, al biyonde the see,
At Poperyng in the place;
His fader was a man ful free,
And lord he was of that contree,
As it was Goddes grace.

Sir Thopas wax a doghty swayn,
Whit was his face as payndemayn,
Hise lippes rede as rose;
His rode is lyk scarlet in grayn,
And I yow telle, in good certayn,

Listen, my lords, with kindness,
And I will truly tell you
A tale of mirth and pleasure,
About a knight who was handsome and courteous
In battle and in tournaments;
His name was Sir Thopas.

He was born in a faraway country,
In Flanders, over the sea,
At Popering, that was the place.
His father was a very noble man,
And he was the Lord of the whole country,
Since that was the will of God.

Sir Thopas grew up a sturdy chap;
His face was as white as the best white bread,
His lips were red as roses;
His complexion was like a deep red cloth,
And I can tell you for certain

He hadde a semely nose.	*That he had a shapely nose.*
His heer, his berd, was lyk saffroun,	*His hair and his beard were like saffron,*
That to his girdel raughte adoun;	*Reaching right down to his girdel;*
Hise shoon of Cordewane.	*His shoes were made of Cordoba leather.*
Of Brugges were his hosen broun,	*His brown stockings were from Bruges*
His robe was of syklatoun	*And his robe was of silk woven with gold thread,*
That coste many a jane.	*That cost a pretty penny.*
He koude hunte at wilde deer,	*He knew how to hunt for wild deer,*
And ride an haukyng for river,	*And to hunt ducks with hawks,*
With grey goshauk on honde,	*With his grey goshawk on his wrist;*
Therto he was a good archeer,	*Also he was a good archer;*
Of wrastlyng was ther noon his peer,	*Nobody could match him at wrestling,*
Ther any ram shal stonde.	*He always won the prize of a ram.*
Ful many a mayde, bright in bour,	*Many maidens, bright in their bedrooms,*
They moorne for hym, paramour,	*Mourned for him lovingly,*
Whan hem were bet to slepe;	*When they should have been asleep;*
But he was chaast and no lechour,	*But he was chaste and not a lecher,*
And sweete as is the brembulflour	*And as sweet as the dog rose*
That bereth the rede hepe.	*That carries the red buds.*
And so bifel upon a day,	*And so it happened that one day,*
Frosothe as I yow telle may,	*In truth, I can tell you,*
Sir Thopas wolde out ride;	*Sir Thopas wanted to go riding.*
He worth upon his steede gray,	*He climbed upon his grey horse,*
And in his hand a launcegay,	*And in his hand he had a light lance,*
A long swerd by his side.	*With a long sword at his side.*
The priketh thurgh a fair forest,	*He spurred through a lovely forest,*
Therinne is many a wilde best,	*In which there were many wild beasts,*
Ye, both bukke and hare,	*Both deer and hare;*
And as he priketh north and est,	*And as he spurred to the North and East,*
I telle it yow, hym hadde almest	*I'm telling you, he almost*
Bitidde a sory care.	*Had a nasty accident.*
Ther spryngen herbes, grete and smale,	*There were growing large and small plants,*
The lycorys and cetewale,	*Licorice and zedoary,*
And many a clowe-gylofre,	*And also many gillyflowers;*
And notemuge to putte in ale,	*Along with nutmeg to put in ale,*
Wheither it be moyste or stale,	*Either fresh or dried,*
Or for to leye in cofre.	*Or to put in with one's clothes.*
The briddes synge, it is no nay,	*The birds were singing, that must be admitted,*
The sparhauk and the papejay	*The sparrowhawk and the parrot,*
That joye it was to heere,	*It was lovely to hear them;*
The thrustelcok made eek hir lay,	*The male thrush also sang his song,*
The wodedowve upon a spray	*And the wood pigeon on the branch*
She sang ful loude and cleere.	*Sang very loud and clear.*
Sir Thopas fil in love-longynge,	*Sir Thopas began to long for love,*
Al whan he herde the thrustel synge,	*As soon as he heard the thrush sing,*
And pryked as he were wood;	*And he spurred on his horse as if he were mad.*
His faire steede in his prikynge	*His handsome steed, from his spurs,*

So swatte that men myghte him wrynge,	Sweated so much one could wring him out like a sponge;
His sydes were al blood.	His sides were covered in blood.
Sir Thopas eek so wery was	Sir Thopas was also so weary
For prikyng on the softe gras,	From charging across the soft grass,
So fiers was his corage,	His heart was so fierce,
That doun he leyde him in that plas	That he laid down in that place
To make his steede som solas,	To give his horse some rest,
And yaf hym good forage.	And he gave him some good food.
O seinte Marie, benedicite,	"Oh St Mary, bless me!
What eyleth this love at me	What is wrong with this love
To bynde me so soore?	That it gives me such pain?
Me dremed al this nyght, pardee,	I dreamed all last night, by God,
An elf-queene shal my lemman be,	That an elf queen would be my sweetheart,
And slepe under my goore.	And sleep under my coat.
An elf-queene wol I love, ywis,	I will love an elf queen, that is certain,
For in this world no womman is	For in this world there is no woman
Worthy to be my make	Fit to be my mate
In towne;	In the town;
Alle othere wommen I forsake,	I renounce all other women,
And to an elf-queene I me take	And commit myself to an elf queen,
By dale and eek by downe.	By the hills and dales!"
Into his sadel he clamb anon,	And once he jumped back into his saddle,
And priketh over stile and stoon	And charged over stiles and walls
An elf-queene for tespye,	Looking for an elf queen,
Til he so longe hadde riden and goon	Until he had ridden and walked for so long
That he foond, in a pryve woon,	That he found, in a secret place,
The contree of Fairye	Fairyland,
So wilde;	So wild;
For in that contree was ther noon	For in that country there was no one
That to him dorste ryde or goon,	Who dared to ride or walk with him,
Neither wyf ne childe,	Not a woman or child;
Til that ther cam a greet geaunt,	Until up came a huge giant,
His name was Sir Olifaunt,	Who was called Sir Oliphant,
A perilous man of dede;	A dangerous and active man.
He seyde Child, by Termagaunt,	He said, "Child, by Termagant,
But if thou prike out of myn haunt,	Unless you get out of my country,
Anon I sle thy steede	I will kill your horse
With mace.	With my mace.
Heere is the queene of Fayerye,	Here is the queen of fairyland,
With harpe and pipe and symphonye,	With harp and pipe and harmonies,
Dwellyng in this place.	She lives in this place."
The child seyde, Also moote I thee,	The child said, "Well then I swear to you,
Tomorwe wol I meete with thee,	That tomorrow I will meet you
Whan I have myn armoure.	When I have my armour;
And yet I hope, par ma fay,	And yet I hope, I swear,
That thou shalt with this launcegay	That with this light lance
Abyen it ful sowre.	I will make you pay for it.

Thy mawe Shal I percen if I may Er it be fully pryme of day, For heere thow shalt be slawe.	*Your mouth* *I will pierce, if I can,* *Before the day has hardly begun,* *You will be killed here."*
Sir Thopas drow abak ful faste, This geant at hym stones caste Out of a fel staf-slynge; But faire escapeth Child Thopas, And al it was thurgh Goddes gras, And thurgh his fair berynge.	*Sir Thopas retreated very quickly;* *The giant threw stones at him* *From a terrible slingshot.* *But the child Thopas safely escaped,* *All through the grace of God,* *And because of his noble bearing.*
Yet listeth, lordes, to my tale, Murier than the nightyngale, For now I wol yow rowne How Sir Thopas, with sydes smale, Prikyng over hill and dale Is comen agayn to towne.	*Carry on listening, gentlemen, to my story* *Which is merrier than the nightingale,* *For now I will tell you* *How Sir Thopas, with his slender waist,* *Galloping over hill and dale,* *Came back to town.*
His murie men comanded he To make hym bothe game and glee, For nedes moste he fighte With a geaunt with hevedes three, For paramour and jolitee Of oon that shoon ful brighte.	*His merry men he ordered* *To amuse and entertain him,* *For from necessity he had to fight* *With a giant with three heads,* *Out of love and pleasure* *In one who shone so bright.*
Do come,: he seyde, my mynstrales, And geestours, for to tellen tales Anon in myn armynge; Of romances that been roiales, Of Popes and of Cardinales, And eek of love-likynge.	*"Do come," he said, "my musicians,* *And my jesters to tell me stories,* *Come along to my arming,* *Tell me stories of royalty,* *Of popes and cardinals,* *And also of the things of love."*
They fette hym first the sweete wyn, And mede eek in a mazelyn, And roial spicerye, And gyngebreed that was ful fyn, And lycorys, and eek comyn, With sugre that is so trye.	*First they brought him some sweet wine,* *And also mead in a wooden bowl,* *And royal delicacies,* *Gingerbread that was very fine,* *And licorice, and also cumin,* *And excellent sugar.*
He dide next his white leere Of clooth of lake, fyn and cleere, A breech, and eek a sherte, And next his sherte an aketoun, And over that an haubergeoun, For percynge of his herte. And over that a fyn hawberk, Was al ywroght of Jewes werk, Ful strong it was of plate. And over that his cote-armour As whit as is a lilye flour, In which he wol debate.	*Next to his white skin he put on* *A linen cloth, fine and clear,* *Breeches and also a shirt;* *And next to his shirt a padded jacket,* *And over that chainmail,* *To protect his heart;* *And over that a fine armour,* *Which was all made by jewellers,* *It had very strong iron plates;* *And over that he had his topcoat* *As white as any lily,* *Which he would wear for the fight.*
His sheeld was al of gold so reed, And therinne was a bores heed,	*His shield was of such fine gold,* *And on it there was the head of a boar,*

A charbocle bisyde;
And there he swoor on ale and breed,
How that the geaunt shal be deed
Bityde what bityde!

Hise jambeux were of quyrboilly,
His swerdes shethe of yvory,
His helm of laton bright,
His sadel was of rewel-boon,
His brydel as the sonne shoon,
Or as the moone light.

His spere it was of fyn ciprees,
That bodeth werre, and no thyng pees,
The heed ful sharpe ygrounde;
His steede was al dappull-gray,
It gooth an ambil in the way
Ful softely and rounde
In londe.
Loo, lordes myne, heere is a fit;
If ye wol any moore of it,
To telle it wol I fonde.

Now holde youre mouth, par charitee,
Bothe knyght and lady free,
And herkneth to my spelle;
Of batailles and of chivalry
And of ladyes love-drury
Anon I wol yow telle.

Men speken of romances of prys,
Of Hornchild, and of Ypotys,
Of Beves and Sir Gy,
Of Sir Lybeux and Pleyndamour,
But Sir Thopas, he bereth the flour
Of roial chivalry.

His goode steede al he bistrood,
And forth upon his wey he glood
As sparcle out of the bronde.
Upon his creest he bar a tour,
And therinne stiked a lilie-flour;
God shilde his cors fro shonde!

And for he was a knyght auntrous,
He nolde slepen in noon hous,
But liggen in his hoode.
His brighte helm was his wonger,
And by hym baiteth his dextrer
Of herbes fyne and goode.
Hym-self drank water of the well,
As dide the knyght sir Percyvell
So worly under wede,
Til on a day---------

Next to a red jewel;
And then he swore by ale and bread
How the giant was going to die,
Whatever might happen!

His leg guards were made of tough leather,
His sword was in an ivory sheath,
His helmet was made of brass;
His saddle was of fine leather,
His bridle shone like the sun,
Or like the moon.

His spear was made of fine cypress,
Which spoke of war, not peace,
The head was ground very sharp;
His horse was a dappled grey,
And it trotted on the road
Very softly and gently
Across the land.
Look, my lords, we've reached a break!
If you want to hear some more,
I shall try to tell you.

Now keep quiet, if you would be so kind
Both you knights and you noble ladies,
And listen to my tale;
Of battles and chivalry,
And the great love of a lady,
I will tell you right now.

Men speak of fine romances,
Of Horn child and Ypotys,
Of Beves and Sir Guy,
Of Sir Lybeux and Pleyndamour–
But Sir Thopas took the prize
For royal chivalry!

He climbed aboard his fine horse
And glided off on his journey
Like a spark flying from the burning logs;
On top of his helmet there was a tower,
And in it he stuck a lily–
May God protect his body from shame!

Because he was a knight on a mission,
He would not sleep in any house,
He wrapped himself in his cloak;
His bright helmet was his pillow,
And by him his charger grazed
On very fine grass.
He himself drank water from the well,
Like the knight Sir Percival,
So good in his armour,
Until one day–"

The Tale of Melibee

Heere the Hoost stynteth Chaucer of his Tale Thopas.

Here the host cut Chaucer's tale of Thopas of short

Na moore of this, for Goddes dignitee,
Quod oure hooste, for thou makest me
So wery of thy verray lewednesse,
That also wisly God my soule blesse,

Min eres aken of thy drasty speche.
Now swich a rym the devel I biteche!
This may wel be rym dogerel, quod he.

Why so? quod I, why wiltow lette me

Moore of my tale than another man
Syn that it is the beste tale I kan?
By God, quod he, for pleynly at a word

Thy drasty rymyng is nat worth a toord,
Thou doost noght elles but despendest tyme.
Sir, at o word thou shalt no lenger ryme.
Lat se wher thou kanst tellen aught in geeste,

Or telle in prose somwhat, at the leeste,
In which ther be som murthe or som doctryne.

Gladly, quod I, by Goddes sweete pyne,
I wol yow telle a litel thyng in prose,
That oghte liken yow as I suppose,
Or elles, certes, ye been to daungerous.

It is a moral tale vertuous,
Al be it take somtyme in sondry wyse
Of sondry folk as I shal yow devyse.

As thus; ye woot that every Evaungelist
That telleth us the peyne of Jesu Crist
Ne seith nat alle thyng as his felawe dooth,
But, nathelees, hir sentence is al sooth,
And alle acorden as in hir sentence,
Al be her in hir tellyng difference.
For somme of hem seyn moore, and somme seyn lesse,
Whan they his pitous passioun expresse;
I meene of Marke, Mathew, Luc, and John,
But douteless hir sentence is al oon,
Therfore, lordynges alle, I yow biseche
If that yow thynke I varie as in my speche,

"No more of this, in the name of God,"
Our host said, "for you make me
So tired with your great ignorance
That, as surely as I hope God will bless my soul,
My ears ache from your awful speech.
Let's send rhymes like that to the devil!
This is all doggerel," he said.

"Why are you doing this?" I asked, "why will you stop me
Telling my story more than these other men,
Since it's the best rhyme I know?"
"By God," he said, "I can tell you plainly, in one word,
Your crappy rhyming isn't worth a turd!
All you're doing is wasting our time.
Sir, in a word, you will no longer rhyme.
Let's see whether you can tell us something in other verse,
Or at least something in prose,
Which could give us some humour or education."

"Gladly," I said, "by the sweet pain of God!
I will tell you a little thing in prose
That you will like, I think,
Otherwise, you are certainly very hard to please.
It is a virtuous moral tale,
Although it is told in different ways
By different people, as I shall explain.

This is it: you know that every evangelist
Who tells us about the pain of Jesus Christ
Does not exactly speak like his fellow;
Nevertheless they all mean the same thing,
And they all agree with each other,
Although they may speak in different ways.
Some of them say more, and some say less,

When they speak of his horrible suffering—
I mean Mark, Matthew, Luke and John—
But there is no doubt they all mean the same.
Therefore, all you gentlemen, I beg you,
If you think my way of talking is different,

As thus, though that I telle somwhat moore

Of proverbes, than ye han herd bifoore,
Comprehended in this litel tretys heere,
To enforce with theffect of my mateere,
And though I nat the same wordes seye
As ye han herd, yet to yow alle I preye,
Blameth me nat; for, as in my sentence
Ye shul nat fynden moche difference
Fro the sentence of this tretys lyte
After the which this murye tale I write.
And therfore herkneth what that I shal seye,
And lat me tellen al my tale, I preye.

The Tale of Melibee

A yong man called Melibeus, myghty and riche, bigat upon his wyf, that called was Prudence, a doghter which that called was Sophie.

Upon a day bifel that he for his desport is went into the feeldes hem to pleye. His wyf and eek his doghter hath he left inwith his hous, of which the dores weren faste yshette. Thre of his olde foes han it espyed, and setten laddres to the walles of his hous, and by wyndowes been entred, and betten his wyf, and wounded his doghter with fyve mortal woundes in fyve sondry places, this is to seyn, in hir feet, in hire handes, in hir erys, in hir nose, and in hire mouth, and leften hire for deed, and wenten awey.

Whan Melibeus retourned was in to his hous, and saugh al this meschief, he, lyk a mad man, rentynge his clothes, gan to wepe and crie.

Prudence, his wyf, as ferforth as she dorste, bisoghte hym of his wepyng for to stynte; but nat forthy he gan to crie and wepen evere lenger the moore.

This noble wyf Prudence remembred hire upon the sentence of Ovide, in his book that cleped is the remedie of love, where as he seith , "He is a fool that destourbeth the mooder to wepen in the deeth of hire child, til she have wept hir fille as for a certein tyme; and thanne shal man doon his diligence with amyable wordes hire to reconforte, and preyen hire of hir wepyng for to stynte". For which resoun this noble wyf Prudence suffred hir housbonde for to wepe and crie as for a certein space; and whan she saugh hir tyme, she seyde hym in this wise: "Allas, my lord," quod she, "why make ye youreself for to lyk a fool? For sothe it aperteneth nat to a wys man to maken swich a

Like this, although I'm telling you something more
Than proverbs you have heard before
To be heard in my little treatise here,
To make the business stronger;
And those I don't say the same words
You have heard before, but I pray you will
Not blame me; for, in essence,
You won't find any difference
In the meaning of this little treatise,
Which I shall copy for this jolly story.
And listen to what I have say,
And let me tell my tale, I pray you."

A young man called Melibeus, great and wealthy, had with his wife, who was called Prudence, a daughter called Sophie.

It happened one day that for pleasure he went into the fields for his own amusement. His wife and also his daughter he left in his house, with the doors shut tight. Three old enemies of his saw this and put ladders against the walls of his house, and entered in through the windows; they beat his wife, and wounded his daughter with five mortal wounds in five different places–in her feet, her hands, her ears, her nose and her mouth –and left her for dead, and went away.

When Melibeus came back to his house, and saw all these crimes, he, like a madman, tearing at his clothes, began to weep and wail.

His wife Prudence, as much she dared, begged him to stop weeping, however he carried on crying and he could not stop.

His noble wife Prudence remembered what Ovid said, in his book called the Remedy of Love, where he says, "It's a fool who stops a mother from weeping at the death of her child until she has wept as much as she wants for a certain time, and then a man should do his best to comfort her with kind words, and beg her to stop weeping." For this reason this noble wife Prudence allowed her husband to weep and wail for a certain amount of time, and when she saw the time was right, she said these words to him: "Alas, my lord," she said, "why are you making a fool of yourself? Truly it is not proper for a man to be

sorwe. Youre doghter, with the grace of God, shal warisshe and escape. And, al were it so that she right now were deed, ye ne oughte nat, as for hir deeth, youreself to destroye. Senek seith: "The wise man shal nat take to greet disconfort for the deeth of his children; but, certes, he sholde suffren it in pacience as wel as he abideth the deeth of his owene propre persone.'"

This Melibeus answerde anon, and seyde, "what man," quod he, "sholde of his wepyng stente that hath so greet a cause for to wepe? Jhesu Crist, oure lord, hymself wepte for the deeth of Lazarus hys freend."

Prudence answerde: "Certes, wel I woot attempree wepyng is no thyng deffended to hym that sorweful is, amonges folk in sorwe, but it is rather graunted hym to wepe. The apostle Paul unto the Romayns writeth, 'Man shal rejoyse with hem that maken joye, and wepen with swich folk as wepen.' But though attempree wepyng be ygraunted, outrageous wepyng certes is deffended. Mesure of wepyng sholde be considered, after the loore that techeth us Senek: 'Whan that thy frend is deed,' quod he, 'lat nat thyne eyen to moyste been of teeris, ne to muche drye; although the teeris come to thyne eyen, lat hem nat falle; and whan thou hast forgoon thy freend, do diligence to gete another freend; and this is moore wysdom than for to wepe for thy freend which that thou has lorn, for therinne is no boote.'

And therfore, if ye governe yow by sapience, put awey sorwe out of youre herte. Remembre yow that Jhesus Syrak seith, 'a man that is joyous and glad in herte, it hym conserveth florissynge in his age; but soothly sorweful herte maketh his bones drye.' He seith eek thus, that sorwe in herte sleeth ful many a man. Salomon seith that right as motthes in shepes flees anoyeth to the clothes, and the smale wormes to the tree, right so anoyeth sorwe to the herte. Wherfore us oghte, as wel in the deeth of oure children as in the los of oure othere goodes temporels, have pacience.

Remembre yow upon the pacient job. Whan he hadde lost his children and his temporeel substance, and in his body endured and receyved ful many a grevous tribulacion, yet seyde he thus: 'Oure Lord hath yeve it me; oure Lord hath biraft it me; right as oure Lord hath wold, right so it is doon; blessed

so sorrowful. Your daughter, by the grace of God, will recover and escape. And, even if it was the case that she were now dead, you will not, just because she is dead, destroy yourself. Seneca says: "The wise man will not be too disturbed by the death of his children, he should suffer it patiently, just as he should tolerate his own death."

Melibeus answered at once and said, "What man," he said, "should control his weeping, when he has such a good reason for it? Our Lord Jesus Christ himself wept for the death of his friend Lazarus."

Prudence answered: "Certainly, I know that a little weeping is not forbidden for someone who is sorrowing, for sorrowing people certainly have permission to weep. The apostle Paul wrote to the Romans, "One must rejoice with those who are happy, and weep with those who weep." But although moderate weeping is permitted, an excess of it is certainly forbidden. Moderation in weeping should be thought of in terms of the law which Seneca teaches us: 'When your friend is dead,' he said, 'don't let your eyes be too wet with tears, nor too dry; although tears may come to to your eyes, do not let them fall; and when you have lost your friend, go and find yourself another; that is a more sensible thing to do than to weep for your friend whom you have lost, there is no profit in that.'

And so, if you will be ruled by wisdom, push sorrow away from your heart. Remember that Jesus son of Sirach says, 'A man who is joyful and glad in his heart, that will keep him flourishing into old age; but having a sorrowful heart will dry up his bones.' He also says that having sorrow in your heart kills many men. Solomon says that just as moths in the wool of the sheep will harm clothes, and small worms will do harm to a tree, that is what sorrow does to the heart. So we should bear ourselves with patience at the death for children just as we would at the loss of other earthly goods.

Remember the patient Job. When he had lost his children and his property, and taken many tribulations on his body, he still said: 'our Lord gave this to me; our Lord took it away from me; whatever our Lord wished, that is has been done; bless it be the name of our

be the name of oure Lord!'"

To thise forseide thynges answerde Melibeus unto his wyf Prudence: "Alle thy wordes," quod he, "been sothe, and therto profitable; but trewely myn herte is troubled with this sorwe so grievously that I noot what to doone."

"Lat calle," quod Prudence, "thy trewe freendes alle, and thy lynage whiche that been wise. Telleth youre cas, and herkneth what they seye in conseillyng, and yow governe after hire sentence. Salomon seith, 'werk alle thy thynges by conseil, and thou shalt never repente.'"

Thanne, by the conseil of his wyf Prudence, this Melibeus leet callen a greet congregacion of folk; as surgiens, phisiciens, olde folk and yonge, and somme of his olde enemys reconsiled as by hir semblaunt to his love and into his grace; and therwithal ther coomen somme of his neighebores that diden hym reverence moore for drede than for love, as it happeth ofte. Ther coomen also ful many subtille flatereres, and wise advocatz lerned in the lawe.

And whan this folk togidre assembled weren, this Melibeus in sorweful wise shewed hem his cas. And by the manere of his speche it semed that in herte he baar a crueel ire, redy to doon vengeaunce upon his foes, and sodeynly desired that the werre sholde bigynne; but nathelees, yet axed he hire conseil upon this matiere. A surgien, by licence and assent of swiche as weren wise, up roos, and to Melibeus seyde as ye may heere:

"Sire," quod he, "as to us surgiens aperteneth that we do to every wight the beste that we kan, where as we been withholde, and to oure pacientz that we do no damage; wherfore it happeth many tyme and ofte that whan twey men han everich wounded oother, oon same surgien heeleth hem bothe; wherfore unto oure art it is nat pertinent to norice werre ne parties to supporte. But certes, as to the warisshynge of youre doghter, al be it so that she periously be wounded, we shullen do so ententif bisynesse fro day to nyght that with the grace of God she shal be hool and sound as soone as is possible."

Almoost right in the same wise the phisiciens answerden, save that they seyden a fewe woordes

To these things Melibeus answered his wife Prudence: "All your words," he said, "are true and also good, but I swear my heart is so shaken by this sorrow I don't know what to do."

"Call up," said Prudence, "all your true friends and those of your family members who are wise. Tell them what's happened, and listen to what they say, and govern yourself by their advice. Tell them what's happened, and listen to their advice, and do as they say. Solomon says, 'Do all things by agreement, and you will never regret it.'"

So, on the advice of his wife Prudence, this Melibeus called up a great crowd of people, urgeons, physicians, old people and young, and some of his old enemies who were reconciled, so it seemed, to be friendly to him again; and also some of his neighbours came to respected him more out of fear than out of love, as is often the case. They also came many cunning flatterers and wise lawyers.

And when all these people were gathered together, this Melibeus told them his case in a sorrowful fashion. And from the way he spoke it seemed that he had a cruel anger in his heart, ready to take revenge on his enemies, and wanted to begin the war very soon; nevertheless, he still asked them for their advice. A surgeon, with the agreement of all the other wise men, stood up and said this to Melibeus:

"Sir," he said, "for we surgeons it is our duty to do the best we can for everyone, when we are asked, and to do no harm to our patients, so happens many times that two men have wounded each other, and the same surgeon heals them both; so it is not part of our art to encourage conflict nor to support either side. But certainly, with regard to curing your daughter, although she is gravely wounded, we shall work so hard on her, night and day, that with the grace of God she will be back to health as soon as possible."

The physicians answered in almost exactly the same way, except they they used a few more

moore: that right as maladies been cured by hir contraries, right so shul men warisshe werre by vengeaunce. His neighebores ful of envye, his feyned freendes that semeden reconsiled, and his flatereres maden semblant of wepyng, and empeireden and agreggeden muchel of this matiere in preisynge greetly Melibee of myght, of power, of richesse, and of freendes, despisynge the power of his adversaries, and seiden outrely that he anon sholde wreken hym on his foes, and bigynne werre.

Up roos thanne an advocat that was wys, by leve and by conseil of othere that were wise, and seide: "Lordynges, the nede for which we been assembled in this place is a ful hevy thyng and an heigh matiere, by cause of the wrong and of the wikkednesse that hath be doon, and eek by resoun of the grete damages that in tyme comynge been possible to fallen for this same cause, and eek by resoun of the grete richesse and power of the parties bothe; for the whiche resouns it were a ful greet peril to erren in this matiere.

Wherfore, Melibeus, this is oure sentence: we conseille yow aboven alle thyng that right anon thou do thy diligence in kepynge of thy propre persone in swich a wise that thou ne wante noon espie ne wacche, thy persone for to save. And after that, we conseille that in thyn hous thou sette sufficeant garnisoun so that they may as wel thy body as thyn hous defende. But certes, for to moeve werre, ne sodeynly for to doon vengeaunce, we may nat demen in so litel tyme that it were profitable.

Wherfore we axen leyser and espace to have deliberacion in this cas to deme. For the commune proverbe seith thus: 'He that soone deemeth, soone shal repente. and eek men seyn that thilke juge is wys that soone understondeth a matiere and juggeth by leyser; for al be it so that alle tariyng be anoyful, algates it is nat to repreve in yevynge of juggement ne in vengeance takyng, whan it is sufficeant and resonable. And that shewed oure lord Jhesu Crist by ensample; for whan that the womman that was taken in avowtrie was broght in his presence to knowen what sholde be doon with hire persone, al be it so that he wiste wel hymself what that he wolde answere, yet ne wolde he nat answere sodeynly, but he wolde have deliberacion, and in the ground he wroot twies. And thise causes we axen deliberacioun, and we shal thanne, by the grace of God, conseille thee thyng that shal be

more words: that as illnesses are cured by their opposites so men can cure war with vengeance. His neighbours, full of envy, his his pretend friends who seemed to be reconciled with him and his flatterers made a a great show of grief, and made the matter much worse by praising the might of Melibeus, his power, his wealth and his friends, mocking the power of his enemies, and saying straight out that he should immediately take revenge on his enemies and begin a war.

Then an advocate who was wise rose up, with the permission of the other wise men, and said, "Gentlemen, the urgent matter which has brought us here is a very serious one, and important, because of the crime and wickedness that have been done, and also because of the great damage that will be done in the future because of this, and because of the great riches and power of both parties, so it would be very dangerous to get this matter wrong.

So, Melibeus, this is our opinion: we advise above all things that you immediately do the best you can in watching over yourself in such a way that you always have spies and guards to protect your person. As well as that, we advise that you keep enough forces inside your house so that they can defend both your property and your person. But certainly, in the matter of starting a war, or taking some some revenge, we have not had enough time to decide whether that would be advantageous.

So we ask for leisure and the chance to deliberate in considering this case. For the common proverb says, "He who judges to quickly will soon repent." And also men say that a wise judge grasps a matter quickly and judges at leisure; for although all waiting is annoying, it should not be criticised in making judgements nor in taking revenge, when it is proper and reasonable. Our Lord Jesus Christ showed that by example, for when a woman was arrested for adultery and and brought into his presence so that he could say what should be done with her, although he knew perfectly well what he was going to answer, he would not answer quickly, but took time to think, and he wrote twice on the the ground. Because of this we ask for the time to think, and we shall then, by the grace of

profitable.

§16 Up stirten thanne the yonge folk atones, and the mooste partie of that compaignye han scorned this olde wise man, and bigonnen to make noyse, and seyden that right so as, whil that iren is hoot, men sholden smyte, right so men sholde wreken hir wronges whil that they been fresshe and newe; and with loud voys they criden "Werre! Werre!"

§17 Up roos tho oon of thise olde wise, and with his hand made contenaunce that men sholde holden hem stille and yeven hym audience. "Lordynges," quod he, "ther is ful many a man that crieth 'Werre! Werre! that woot ful litel what werre amounteth. Werre at his bigynnyng hath so greet an entryng and so large, that every wight may entre whan hym liketh, and lightly fynde werre; but certes what ende that shal therof bifalle, it is nat light to knowe. For soothly, whan that werre is ones bigonne, ther is ful many a child unborn of his mooder that shal sterve yong by cause of thilke werre, or elles lyve in sorwe and dye in wrecchednesse. And therfore, er that any werre bigynne, men moste have greet conseil and greet deliberacion. And whan this olde man wende to enforcen his tale by resons, wel ny alle atones bigonne they to rise for to breken his tale, and beden hym ful ofte his wordes for to abregge. For soothly, he that precheth to hem that listen nat heeren his wordes, his sermon hem anoieth. For Jhesus Syrak seith that "musik in wepynge is a noyous thyng"; this is to seyn: as muche availleth to speken bifore folk to which his speche anoyeth, as it is to synge biforn hym that wepeth. And whan this wise man saugh that hym wanted audience, al shamefast he sette hym doun agayn. For Salomon seith: "Ther as thou ne mayst have noon audience, enforce thee nat to speke." "I see wel," quod this wise man, "that the commune proverbe is sooth, that good conseil wanteth whan it is moost nede.'"

§18 Yet hadde this Melibeus in his conseil many folk that prively in his eere conseilled hym certeyn thyng, and conseilled hym the contrarie in general audience. Whan Melibeus hadde herd that the gretteste partie of his conseil weren accorded that he sholde maken werre, anoon he consented to hir conseillyng, and fully affermed hire sentence. Thanne dame Prudence, whan that she saugh how that hir housbonde shoop hym for to wreken hym on his foes, and to bigynne werre, she in ful humble wise, whan she saugh hir tyme, seide to

God, give you some good advice."

Then the young folk jumped up at once, and most of the company rejected the advice of this wise old man, and began to make a noise, saying that as men should strike when the iron is hot, so men should take revenge for their wrongs when they are fresh and new; and in loud voices they cried out, "War! War!"

Then one of these wise old men got up and a signal with his hand to say that men should keep still and listen to him. "Gentlemen," he said, "there are many of you calling out, "War, war!" who don't know very much about what war is like. The gates of war are so wide and large that anyone who wants to can enter and find war easily; but it is not so easy to know how things will turn out. For truly, once the war has begun, there are many children as yet unborn who will die young due to that war, or otherwise live in sorrow and die die wretchedly. And therefore, before you begin any war, men must have much debate and consultation." And when this old man meant to back up his argument with quotations, at once they all began to rise up interrupting, and asked him to cut his argument short. For truly, someone who preaches to those who do not want to hear, they are annoyed by the sermon. For Jesus, son of Sirach, says that, "music annoys the person who is crying"; he was saying, it is as much use to speak to people who are annoyed by your speech as it is to sing to someone who is crying. And when this wise man saw that the audience would not listen, shamefaced he sat down again. For Solomon says: "When you do not have an audience, do not speak." "I can see well," said this wise man, "that's the old proverb is true, that where good advice is most needed, that is where it is missing."

Yet amongst his advisers Melibeus heard many people who secretly whispered in his ear about certain matters, and told him to do the opposite with everyone listening. When Melibeus heard that the greatest proportion of his advisers were agreed that he should go to war, he immediately agreed with their advice and confirmed their opinion. Then Dame Prudence, when she saw how her husband was preparing to take revenge on his enemies and go to war, in a very humble

hym thise wordes: "My lord," quod she, "I yow biseche as hertely as I dar and kan, ne haste yow nat to faste, and for alle gerdons, as yeveth me audience. For Piers Alfonce seith, 'Whoso that dooth to thee oother good or harm, haste thee nat to quiten it; for in this wise thy freend wole abyde, and thyn anemy shal the lenger lyve in drede.' The proverbe seith, 'He hasteth wel that wisely kan abyde, and in wikked haste is no profit.'"

§19 This Melibee answerde unto his wyf Prudence: "I purpose nat," quod he, "to werke by thy conseil, for many causes and resouns. For certes, every wight wolde holde me thanne a fool; this is to seyn, if I, for thy conseillyng, wolde chaungen thynges that been ordeyned and affermed by so manye wyse. Secoundely, I seye that alle wommen been wikke, and noon good of hem alle. For 'of a thousand men,' seith Salomon, 'I foond o good man, but certes, of alle wommen, good womman foond I nevere.' And also, certes, if I governed me by thy conseil, it sholde seme that I hadde yeve to thee over me the maistrie; and God forbede that it so weere! For Jhesus Syrak seith 'that if the wyf have maistrie, she is contrarious to hir housbonde.' And Salomon seith: 'Nevere in thy lyf to thy wyf, ne to thy child, ne to thy freend, ne yeve no power over thyself; for bettre it were that thy children aske of thy persone thynges that hem nedeth, than thou see thyself in the handes of thy children.' And also if I wolde werke by thy conseillyng, certes, my conseil moste som tyme be secree, til it were tyme that it moste be knowe, and this ne may noght be.

§20 Whanne dame Prudence, ful debonairly and with greet pacience, hadde herd al that hir housbonde liked for to seye, thanne axed she of hym licence for to speke, and seyde in this wise: "My lord," quod she, "as to youre firste resoun, certes it may lightly been answered. For I seye that it is no folie to chaunge conseil whan the thyng is chaunged, or elles whan the thyng semeth ootherweyes than it was biforn. And mooreover, I seye that though ye han sworn and bihight to perfourne youre emprise, and nathelees ye weyve to perfourne thilke same emprise by juste cause, men sholde nat seyn therfore that ye were a liere ne forswon. For the book seith that 'the wise man maketh no lesyng whan he turneth his corage to the bettre.' And al be it so that youre emprise be establissed and ordeyned by greet multitude of

manner, when she saw her opportunity, said said this to him: "My Lord," she said, "I beg you, as heartily as I dare, do not hurry into this, and, as you hope to prosper, listen to me. For Petrus Alphonsus says, "Whether somebody does good or harm to you, don't rush to pay it back, for in this way your friends will stay and your enemies will live in fear all the longer." The proverb says, "The person who knows how to wait goes faster," and, "there is no benefit in rushing.""

Melibeus answered his wife Prudence: "I do not intend," he said, "to act on your advice, for many different reasons. For certainly, everybody would then think I was a fool; that is to say, if I due to your advice, change things that had been agreed to by so many wise men. Secondly, I say that all women are wicked, and there is not one good one. For Solomon says, "In a thousand men, I found one good one, but certainly amongst all women, I never found a good one." And also, certainly, if I followed your advice, it would seem that I was allowing you to rule over me, and God forbid that! For Jesus son of Sirach says that "if the wife has mastery, she is against her husband." And Solomon says: "never give your wife, or your child, or your friend any power over you, for it would be better that your children ask you for for things that they need rather than you place yourself in the hands of your children." And also I want to follow my advisers, and I must sometimes keep my plans secret, until it is time to reveal them, and this cannot happen.

When Dame Prudence, very calmly and with great patience, had heard everything that her husband wanted to say, she asked for to speak and spoke to him in this fashion: "my Lord," she said, "as for your first reason, I can easily answer that. For I say it is not foolishness to change your plans when the situation has changed, or when things seem different to what they were before. And moreover, I say that although you have sworn that you will go through with your plans, if you then abandon your plans for a good reason, men cannot say that you are a liar or a perjurer. For the book says that 'the wise man is not lying when he decides to do something better.' And although your plans have been established and agreed on by a great number

folk, yet that ye nat accomplice thilke ordinaunce, but yow like. For the trouthe of thynges and the profit been rather founden in fewe folk that been wise and ful of resoun, than by greet multitude of folk ther every man crieth and clatereth what that hym liketh. Soothly swich multitude is nat hones. And as to the seconde resoun, where as ye seyn that alle wommen been wikke; save youre grace, certes ye despisen alle wommen in this wyse, and 'he that al despiseth, al displeseth,' as seith the book. And Senec seith that 'whose wole have sapience shal no man dispreyse, but he shal gladly techen the science that he kan withouten presumpcion or pride, and swiche thynges as he noght ne kan, he shal nat been ashamed to lerne hem, and enquere of lasse folk than hymself.' and, sire That ther hath been many a good womman, may lightly be preved. For certes, sire, oure Lord Jhesu Crist wolde nevere have descended to be born of a womman, if alle wommen hadden been wikke. And after that, for the grete bountee that is in wommen, oure lord Jhesu Crist, whan he was risen fro deeth to lyve, appeered rather to a womman than to his apostles. And though that Salomon seith that he ne foond nevere womman good, it folweth nat therfore that alle wommen ben wikke. For though that he ne foond no good womman, certes, many another man hath founden many a womman ful good and trewe. Or elles, per aventure, the entente of Salomon was this, that, as in sovereyn bounte, he foond no womman; this is to seyn, that ther is no wight that hath sovereyn bountee save God allone, as he hymself recordeth in hys Evaungelie. For ther nys no creature so good that hym ne wanteth somwhat of the perfeccioun of God, that is his makere. Youre thridde reson is this: ye seyn that if ye governe yow by my conseil, it sholde seme that ye hadde yeve me the maistrie and the lordshipe over youre persone. Sire, save youre grace, it is nat so. For if it so were that no man sholde be conseilled but oonly of hem that hadden lordshipe and maistrie of his persone, men wolden nat be conseilled so ofte. For soothly thilke man that asketh conseil of a purpos, yet hath he free choys wheither he wole werke by that conseil or noon. And as to youre fourthe resoun, ther ye seyn that the janglerie of wommen kan hyde thynges that they wot noght, as who seith that a womman kan nat hyde that she woot; sire, thise wordes been understonde of wommen that been jangleresses and wikked; of whiche wommen men seyn that thre thynges dryven a man out of his hous, that is to seyn, smoke, droppyng of reyn, and wikked wyves, and of swiche wommen seith Salomon that 'it were bettre dwelle in desert than with a woman that is

of people, you don't have to carry out the plan unless you want to. For the truth of matters and goodness are found in a few wise folk who are full of reason, rather than the great crowd where every man cries and shouts what he pleases. Truly such a great crowd is not honourable. As for the second reason, when you said that all women are wicked; with all respect, you certainly hate all women in this fashion, and 'someone who hates everybody, pleases nobody,' as the book says. And Seneca says that 'whoever wants wisdom should not criticise any man, but he should gladly teach what he knows without arrogance or pride; and as for the things of which he knows nothing, he should not be ashamed to learn them, and he should ask advice from lower folk than himself.' And, sir, there have certainly been many good women, that can be easily proven. For certainly, sir, our Lord Jesus Christ would never have agreed to be born of a woman, if all women were wicked. And after that, due to the great goodness in women, our Lord Jesus Christ, when he came back to life, appeared to a woman rather than to his apostles. And though Solomon says that he never found a good woman, it does not follow that all women are wicked. For all that he found no good women, many other men have found many women to be good and true. Or otherwise, perhaps, what Solomon meant was this: that, in supreme goodness, he found no woman—that is to say, that there is no creature who has supreme goodness apart from God, as he says himself in his gospels. For there is no creature who is so good that he does not lack some of the perfection of God, who made him. Your third reason is this: you say that if you allow yourself to be governed by my advice, it would as if you had given me power over you. So, with all due respect to you, this is not so. For if it were true that no man should take advice from anyone who did not have lordship and mastery over him, men would not get much advice. For truly, the man who asks for advice about a plan has a free choice as to whether he will follow. As for your fourth reason, where you say that women's gossip hides things that they don't know about, meaning that women cannot hide the things that they know; Sir, these words are true about women who are wicked and gossips; men say about such women that three things drive a

riotous.' And sire, by youre leve, that am nat I; for ye han ful ofte assayed my grete silence and my grete pacience, and eek how wel that I kan hyde and hele thynges that men oghte secreely to hyde. And soothly, as to youre fifthe resoun, where as ye seyn that in wikked conseil wommen venquisshe men, God woot, thilke resoun stant heere in no stede. For understoond now, ye asken conseil to do wikkednesse; and if ye wole werken wikkednesse, and youre wif restreyneth thilke wikked purpos, and overcometh yow by reson and by good conseil, certes youre wyf oghte rather to be preised than yblamed. Thus sholde ye understonde the philosophre that seith, in wikked conseil wommen venquisshen hir housbondes.' Ther as ye blamen alle wommen and hir resouns, I shal shewe yow by manye ensamples that many a womman hath ben ful good, and yet been, and hir conseils ful hoolsome and profitable. Eek som men han seyd that the conseillynge of wommen is outher to deere, or elles to litel of pris. But al be it so that ful many a womman is badde, and hir conseil vile and noght worth, yet han men founde ful many a good womman, and ful discret and wis in conseillynge. Loo, Jacob, by good conseil of his mooder Rebekka, wan the benysoun of Ysaak his fader, and the lordshipe over alle his bretheren. Judith, by hire good conseil, delivered the citee of Bethulie, in which she dwelled, out of the handes of Olofernus, that hadde it biseged and wolde have al destroyed it. Abygail delivered nabal hir housbonde fro David the kyng, that wolde have slayn hym, and apaysed the ire of the kyng by hir wit and by hir good conseillyng. Hester, by hir good conseil, enhaunced greetly the peple of God in the regne of Assuerus the kyng. And the same bountee in good conseillyng of many a good womman may men telle. And mooreover, whan oure lord hadde creat Adam, oure forme fader, he seyde in this wise: it is nat good to been a man alloone; make we to hym an helpe semblable to hymself. May ye se that if that wommen were nat goode, and hir conseils goode and profitable, oure lord God of hevene wolde nevere han wroght hem, ne called hem help of man, but rather confusioun of man. And ther seyde oones a clerk in two vers, 'What is bettre than gold? Jaspre. What is bettre than jaspre? Wisedoom. And what is better than wisedoom? Womman. And what is bettre than a good womman? Nothyng.' And, sire, by manye of othre resons may ye seen that manye wommen been goode, and hir conseils goode and profitable. And therfore, sire, if ye wol triste to my conseil, I shal restoore yow youre

man from his house—that is to say, smoke, raindrops, and wicked wives; and Solomon says about such women that 'it would be better to live in a desert than with a loose woman.' And, sir, by your leave, I am not one of those, for you have often tested my ability to be silent and my great patience, and also how well I can conceal things that ought to be concealed. And truly, as for your fifth reason, where you say that women defeat men with wicked advice, God knows, your reasoning is worthless in this situation. For you must understand, you are asking for advice on how to do a wicked thing; and if you want to do something wicked, and your wife stops your wicked purpose, and overcomes you with reason and good advice, certainly your wife should be praised rather than blamed. So you should understand the philosopher who said, 'Women defeat their husbands with wicked advice.' Whereas you blame all women and their reasoning, I can show you by many examples that many women have been very good, and still are, and their advice is very good and wholesome. Also some men say that the advice of women is either too expensive or too cheap. But although it is the case that many women are bad and their advice is vile and unworthy, but men have found many good women, who are very discreet and wise in giving advice. Through the advice of his mother Rebecca Jacob won the blessing of his father Isaac and became ruler of all his tribe. Through her good advice Judith saved the city of Bethulia, where she lived, from the hands of Holofernes, who had besieged it and wanted to entirely destroyed. Abigail saved her husband Nabal from King David, who would have children, and softened the anger of the King with her wit and good advice. Hester helped the people of God greatly with her good advice during the reign of King Assuerus. And many men can tell of the same goodness in the advice of many good women. Moreover, when our Lord created Adam, our forefather, he said this: 'it is not good for a man to be single; let us make him a helper similar to himself.' You can see that if women were not good, and their advice was not useful, our Lord God in heaven would never have made them, nor called them the helpmeet of man, but he would have called them their destruction. And once a scholar said in two verses, 'What is better than gold?

doghter hool and sound. And eek I wol do to yow so muche that ye shul have honour in this cause."

Jasper. What is better than Jasper? Wisdom. What is better than wisdom? Woman. And what is better than a good woman? Nothing.' And, sir, for many other reasons you can see that women are good, and there advice is worthwhile. And so, Sir, if you will take my advice, I will give you back your daughter whole and healthy. And also I will do so much for you that you will find it is honourable."

§21 Whan Melibee hadde herd the wordes of his wyf Prudence, he seyde thus: "I se wel that the word of Salomon is sooth. He seith that 'wordes that been spoken discreetly by ordinaunce been honycombes, for they yeven swetnesse to the soule and hoolsomnesse to the body.' And, wyf, by cause of thy sweete wordes, and eek for I have assayed and preved thy grete sapience and thy grete trouthe, I wol governe me by thy conseil in alle thyng."

When Melibeus heard what his wife Prudence had to say, he said this: "I can certainly see that what Solomon said is true. He said that, 'words that are spoken sensibly and properly like honeycomb, for they bring sweetness to the soul and health to the body.' And, wife, because of your sweet words, and also because I have examined and proved your great wisdom and truthfulness, I will be governed by your advice in everything."

§22 "Now, sire," quod dame Prudence, "and syn ye vouche sauf to been governed by my conseil, I wol enforme yow how ye shul governe yourself in chesynge of youre conseillours. Ye shul first in alle youre werkes mekely biseken to the heighe God that he wol be youre conseillour; and shapeth yow to swich entente that he yeve yow conseil and confort, as taughte Thobie his sone: 'At alle tymes thou shalt blesse god, and praye hym to dresse thy weyes, and looke that alle thy conseils been in hym for everemoore. Jame eek seith: if any of yow have nede of sapience, axe it of god. and afterward thanne shul ye taken conseil in youreself, and examyne wel youre thoghtes of swich thyng as yow thynketh that is bes for youre profit. And thanne shul ye dryve fro youre herte thre thynges that been contrariouse to good conseil; that is to seyn, ire, coveitise, and hastifnesse.

"Now, sir," said Dame Prudence, "since you have agreed to be ruled by my advice, I will now tell you how you should choose your advisers. Firstly in everything you must meekly beg the Almighty God to be your adviser; and prepare yourself with the aim of his giving you advice and comfort, as Tobias said to his son: 'You shall bless God at all times, and pray to him for guidance, and make sure that you take all your advice from him at all times." St James also says: 'if any of you need wisdom, ask for it from God.' And afterwards then you must take advice from yourself, and examine your thoughts to find the thing which seems of greatest advantage to you. And then you must drive out of your heart the things that are against good advice; that is, anger, greed and haste.

§23 First, he that axeth conseil of hymself, certes he moste been withouten ire, for manye causes. The firste is this: he that hath greet ire and wratthe in hymself, he weneth alwey that he may do thyng that he may nat do. And secoundely, he that is irous and wrooth, he ne may nat wel deme; and he that may nat wel deme, may nat wel conseille. The thridde is this, that he that is irous and wrooth, as seith Senec, ne may nat speke but blameful thynges, and with his viciouse wordes he stireth oother folk to angre and to ire. And eek, sire, ye moste dryve coveitise out of youre herte. For the apostle seith that coveitise is roote of alle harmes. And trust wel

Firstly, someone who looks for advice from himself, he must certainly be without anger, for many reasons. The first is this: someone who has great anger in himself, he always imagines that he can do something he is not capable of. And secondly, someone who is angry does not judge well; and someone who cannot judge well, cannot give good advice. Thirdly, somebody who is angry, as Seneca says, cannot say anything but bad things, and with his vicious words he makes other people angry. And also, Sir, you must rid your heart of greed. For the apostle says that greed is the

that a coveitous man ne kan noght deme ne thynke, but oonly to fulfille the ende of his coveitise; and certes, that ne may nevere been accompliced; For evere the moore habundaunce that he hath of richesse, the moore he desireth. And, sire, ye moste also dryve out of youre herte hastifnesse; for certes, ye ne may nat deeme for the beste by a sodeyn thought that falleth in youre herte, but ye moste avyse yow on it ful ofte. For, as ye herde her biforn, the commune proverbe is this, that he that soone deemeth, soone repenteth. sire, ye ne be nat alwey in lyk disposicioun; for certes, somthyng that somtyme semeth to yow that it is good for to do, another tyme it semeth to yow the contrarie.

§24 Whan ye han taken conseil in youreself, and han deemed by good deliberacion swich thyng as yow semeth bes, thanne rede I yow that ye kepe it secree. Biwrey nat youre conseil to no persone, but if so be that ye wenen sikerly that thurgh youre biwreyyng youre condicioun shal be to yow the moore profitable. for Jhesus Syrak seith, 'neither to thy foo, ne to thy frend, discovere nat thy secree ne thy folie; for they wol yeve yow audience and lookynge and supportacioun in thy presence, and scorne thee in thyn absence.' Another clerk seith that scarsly shaltou fynden any persone that may kepe conseil secrely. The book seith, 'whil that thou kepest thy conseil in thyn herte, thou kepest it in thy prisoun; and whan thou biwreyest thy conseil to any wight, he holdeth thee in his snare.' And therfore yow is bettre to hyde youre conseil in youre herte than praye him to whom ye han biwreyed youre conseil that he wole kepen it cloos and stille. For Seneca seith: 'if so be that thou ne mayst nat thyn owene conseil hyde, how darstou prayen any oother wight thy conseil secrely to kepe?' But nathelees, if thou wene sikerly that the biwreiyng of thy conseil to a persone wol make thy condicion to stonden in the bettre plyt, thanne shaltou tellen hym thy conseil in this wise. First thou shalt make no semblant wheither thee were levere pees or werre, or this or that, ne shewe hym nat thy wille and thyn entente. For trust wel that comunli thise conseillours been flatereres, namely the conseillours of grete Lordes; for they enforcen hem alwey rather to speken plesante wordes, enclynynge to the lordes lust, than wordes that been trewe or profitable. And therfore men seyn that the riche man hath seeld good conseil, but if he have it of hymself.

§25 And after that thou shalt considere thy freendes

root of all evil. You must believe that a greedy man can neither judge nor think of anything, except getting what his greed demands; and certainly, that will never happen, for the greater the riches he has, the more he wants. sir, you must also drive haste from your heart; for certainly, you cannot judge what is for the best with the first thing that comes into your heart, you must reflect upon it very often. For, as you have heard before, the common proverb is that 'swift judgement leads to swift repentance.' Sir, you do not always think the same; for certainly, something that at one time seems good to you, at another does not.

When you have thought the matter over and have judged as best you can what is best to do, then I advise you to keep it secret. Do not reveal your plans to anyone, unless you believe that through revealing them it will be advantageous to you. For Jesus son of Sirach says, 'Neither to your enemy or your friend should you reveal your secrets or your follies, for they will listen to you respectfully and support you when you are there and then mock you when you're not.' Another scholar says that 'you will rarely rarely find any person who can keep your your plans secret.' The book says, 'While you keep your plans in your heart, you keep them them in your prison, and when you reveal your plans to anyone, he has you under his thumb.' And therefore it is better for you to hide your plans in your heart than to ask someone to whom you have told them to keep them secret. For Seneca says: if it is the case that you you can't hide your own plans, how dare you ask anybody else to do so?' But nevertheless, if you really believe that telling your plans to somebody else will be to your advantage, then you should tell them to him in this fashion. Firstly don't give any outward sign as to whether you prefer peace or war, or this or or that, don't show him what it is you mean mean to do. You must be aware that these advisers are flatterers, the advisers of great lords, for they always try to speak pleasant words, the ones the Lord wishes to hear, rather than words that are true or good. And therefore men say that a rich man seldom gets good advice, unless he gives it to himself.

And after that you must think about your

and thyne enemys. And as touchynge thy freendes, thou shalt considere which of hem been moost feithful and moost wise and eldest and most approved in conseillyng; and of hem shalt thou aske thy conseil, as the caas requireth. I seye that first ye shul clepe to youre conseil youre freendes that been trewe. For Salomon seith that 'right as the herte of a man deliteth in savour that is soote, right so the conseil of certes gold ne silver ben nat so muche worth as the goode wyl of a trewe freend.' And eek he seith that 'a trewe freend is a strong deffense; who so that it fyndeth, certes he fyndeth a greet tresour.' Thanne shul ye eek considere if that youre trewe freendes been discrete and wise. For the book seith, 'axe alwey thy conseil of hem that been wise.' And by this same resoun shul ye clepen to youre conseil of youre freendes that been of age, swiche as han seyn and been expert in manye thynges and been approved in conseillynges. For the book seith 'that in olde men is the sapience, and in longe tyme the prudence.' And Tullius seith 'that grete thynges ne been nat ay accomplicéd by strengthe, ne by delivernesse of body, but by good conseil, by auctoritee of persones, and by science; the whiche thre thynges ne been nat fieble by age, but certes they enforcen and encreescen day by day.' And thanne shul ye kepe this for a general reule: first shul ye clepen to youre conseil a fewe of youre freendes that been especiale; for Salomon seith, 'manye freendes have thou, but among a thousand chese thee oon to be thy conseillour.' For al be it so that thou first ne telle thy conseil but to a fewe, thou mayst afterward telle it to mo folk if it be nede. But looke alwey that thy conseillours have thilke thre condiciouns that I have seyd bifore, that is to seyn, that they be trewe, wise, and of oold experience. And werke nat alwey in every nede by oon counseillour allone; for somtyme bihooveth it to been conseilled by manye. For Salomon seith, 'salvacion of thynges is where as ther been manye conseillours.'

§26 Now, sith that I have toold yow of which folk ye sholde been conseilled, now wol I teche yow which conseil ye oghte to eschewe. First, ye shul eschue the conseillyng of fooles; for Salomon seith, 'taak no conseil of a fool, for he ne

enemies. With reference to your friends, you must think which of them are most faithful, wisest, eldest and who have given you the best advice before; and those are the ones you should ask your advice, when you need it. I say that first or you should call to Council your true friends. For Solomon says, 'just as the heart of a man delights in sweet tastes, so the advice of true friends is sweet to the soul.' He also says, 'Nothing compares to a true friend, it's certain that gold and silver are not worth as much as the goodwill of a true friend.' And he also says that 'a true friend is a strong defence; whoever has one, he has great wealth.' Then you must also think about whether your true friends are discreet and wise. For the book says, 'Always ask the advice of wise men.' And for the same same reason, you shall call to your council some of your friends who are of a suitably mature standing, such as those who have seen and are experts in many things, and whose advice has been proven good in the past. For the book says that 'there is wisdom in old men, and prudence in long years.' And Cicero says that 'great things are not always accomplished by power, nor by lissomness, but through good advice, through the power of a person to persuade, and through knowledge; those three things do not get less with age, they gain strength and and increase day by day.' And then you shall obey this as a general rule: firstly you should call to your council a few of your friends, the ones you particularly value; for Solomon says, 'You can have many friends, but out of a thousand only choose one as an adviser.' For it may be that at first you give your advice to only a few, you may afterwards tell more more folk if necessary. But always make sure sure that your advisers fulfil those three conditions I mentioned before—that is to say, that they are true, wise and of great experience. And don't always just use one adviser; for sometimes it is necessary to have the advice of many. For Solomon says, 'Salvation comes when there are many advisers.'

Now, since I have told you which folk you should take advice from, now I will teach what sort of advice you should reject. Firstly, you must reject the advice of fools for Solomon says, 'take no advice from a fool, for he can kan noght conseille but after his owene lust and his affeccioun.' The book seith that 'the propretee of a fool is this: he troweth lightly harm of every wight, and lightly troweth alle bountee in hymself.' Thou shalt eek eschue the conseillyng of alle flatereres, swiche as enforcen hem rather to preise youre persone by flaterye than for to telle yow the soothfastnesse of thynges. Wherfore Tullius seith, 'amonges alle the pestilences that been in freendshipe the gretteste is flaterie.' And therfore is it moore nede that thou eschue and drede flatereres than any oother peple. The book seith, 'thou shalt rather drede and flee fro the sweete wordes of flaterynge preiseres than fro the egre wordes of thy freend that seith thee thy sothes.' Salomon seith that 'the wordes of a flaterere is a snare to cacche with innocentz.' He seith also that 'he that speketh to his freend wordes of swetnesse and of plesaunce, setteth a net biforn his feet to cacche hym.' And therfore Seith Tullius, 'enclyne nat thyne eres to flatereres, ne taak no conseil of the wordes of flaterye.' And Caton seith, 'avyse thee wel, and eschue the wordes of swetnesse and of plesaunce.' And eek thou shalt eschue the conseillyng of thyne olde enemys that been reconsiled. The book seith that 'no wight retourneth saufly into the grace of his olde enemy.' And Isope seith, 'ne trust nat to hem to whiche thou hast had som tyme werre or enemytee, ne telle hem nat thy conseil.' And Seneca telleth the cause why: 'it may nat be,' seith he, 'that where greet fyr hath longe tyme endured, that ther ne dwelleth som vapour of warmnesse.' And therfore seith Salomon, 'in thyn olde foo trust nevere.' For sikerly, though thyn enemy be reconsiled, and maketh thee chiere of hymylitee, and lowteth to thee with his heed, ne trust hym nevere. For certes he maketh thilke feyned humilitee moore for his profit than for any love of thy persone, by cause that he deemeth to have victorie over thy persone by swich feyned contenance, the which victorie he myghte nat have by strif or werre. And Peter Alfonce seith, 'make no felawshipe with thyne olde enemys; for if thou do hem bountee, they wol perverten it into wikkednesse.' And eek thou most eschue the conseillyng of hem that been thy servantz and beren thee greet reverence, for peraventure they seyn it moore for drede than for love. And therfore seith a philosophre in this wise: 'ther is no wight parfitly trewe to hym that he to soore dredeth.' And Tullius seith, 'ther nys no myght so greet of any emperour that longe may endure, but if he have moore love of the peple than drede.' Thou shalt also eschue the conseiling of folk that been

not advise except according to his own ideas.' The book says that, 'the characteristic of a is this: he believes bad things of every person, and thinks that he is perfect.' You must also reject the advice of all flatterers, those who work to praise you with flattery, rather than tell you the truth. Cicero says about this, 'amongst all the diseases that afflict friendship, the greatest is flattery.' And therefore it is more necessary that you reject and dread flatterers than any other people. The book says, 'You should rather dread and flee from the sweet words of flatterers than from the harsh words of a friend who is telling you the truth.' Solomon says that, 'the words of a flatterer are traps with which to catch innocents.' He also says that 'he who speaks to his friend street words and pleasantries put the net in front of his feet to catch them.' And Cicero says of it, 'do not listen to flatterers, and take no advice from flattering words.' And Cato says, 'Think carefully, and reject sweet and pleasant words.' And also you should shun the advice of your old enemies enemies who are now reconciled to you. The book says that 'no person is safe in the protection of an old enemy.' And Aesop says, 'Don't trust those with whom you have at some time had a battle, and do not trust them with your plans.' And Seneca explains why: 'it may not be,' he says, 'that there can have been a great fire for a long time, without some residual warmness remaining.' And Solomon says of the same thing, 'Never trust in your old enemy.' For surely, even if your enemy is reconciled, and appears to be humble to you, and bows down to you, never trust him. For certainly he is feigning humility more for his advantage than for any love of you, because he thinks that he can win you over with such false behaviour, and get a victory which he could not get in war. And Petrus Alphonsus says, 'Do not be friends with your old enemies, for if you do good things for them, they will turn them into wicked ones.' And also you must reject the advice of your servants and those who have great respect for you, for they may be speaking more out of fear than out of of love. And a philosopher said this about that: 'There is no person who is perfectly loyal if he has too much fear.' And Cicero says, 'There is no mighty Emperor who can survive for long, unless he has more love than fear from his people. You must also reject the advice of folk dronkelewe, for they ne kan no conseil hyde. For Salomon seith, 'ther is no privetee ther as regneth dronkenesse.' Ye shul also han in suspect the conseillyng of swich folk as conseille yow o thyng prively, and conseille yow the contrarie openly. For Cassidorie seith that 'it is a manere sleighte to hyndre, whan he sheweth to doon o thyng openly and werketh prively the contrarie.' Thou shalt also have in suspect the conseillyng of wikked folk, for the book seith, 'the conseillyng of wikked folk is alwey ful of fraude.' And David seith, 'blisful is that man that hath nat folwed the conseilyng of shrewes.' Thou shalt also eschue the conseillyng of yong folk, for hir conseil is nat rype.

§27 Now, sire, sith I have shewed yow of which folk ye shul take youre conseil, and of which folk ye shul folwe the conseil, now wol I teche yow how ye shal examyne youre conseil, after the doctrine of Tullius. In the examynynge thanne of youre conseillour ye shul considere manye thynges. Alderfirst thou shalt considere that in thilke thyng that thou purposest, and upon what thyng thou wolt have conseil, that verray trouthe be seyd and conserved; this is to seyn, telle trewely thy tale. For he that seith fals may nat wel be conseilled in that cas of which he lieth. And after this thou shalt considere the thynges that acorden to that thou purposest for to do by thy conseillours, if resoun accorde therto; and eek if thy myght may atteine therto; and if the moore part and the bettre part of thy conseillours acorde therto, or noon. Thanne shaltou considere what thyng shal folwe of that conseillyng, as hate, pees, werre, grace, profit, or damage, and manye othere thynges. And in alle thise thynges thou shalt chese the beste, and weyve alle othere thynges. Thannne shaltow considere of what roote is engendred the matiere of thy conseil, and what fruyt it may conceyve and engendre. Thou shalt eek considere alle thise causes, fro whennes they been sprongen. And whan ye han examyned youre conseil, as I have seyd, and which partie is the bettre and moore profitable, and han approved it by manye wise folk and olde, thanne shaltou considere if thou mayst parfourne it and maken of it a good ende. For certes, resoun wol nat that any man sholde bigynne a thyng, but if he myghte parfourne it as hym oghte; ne no wight sholde take upon hym so hevy a charge that he myghte nat bere it. For the proverbe seith, ;'he that to muche embraceth, distreyneth litel.' And Catoun seith, 'assay to do swich thyng as thou hast power to doon, lest that the charge oppresse thee so soore that

that are drunkards, for they cannot keep secrets. For Solomon says, 'there is no secrecy where drunkenness rules.' You should also be suspicious of the advice of people who advise one thing in private and give you different advice in public. For Cassiodorus says that 'it is difficult to block a plan, when a person seems to do one thing in public and secretly does the opposite.' You should be suspicious of the advice of wicked folk. For the book says, 'The advice of wicked folk is always full of lies.' And David says, 'it is a happy man who has not followed the advice of scoundrels.' You should also reject the advice of young people, for their advice is not mature.

Now, Sir, since I've shown you the people from whom you should take your advice and which people whose advice you should follow, now I I will teach you how you should examine that advice, according to what Cicero said. In questioning your advisor you must consider many things. Firstly you should consider that in the thing you mean to do, and the thing you are asking advice about, that real truth should be spoken and shown; that is to say, tell your story truthfully. For he who speaks deceitfully will not get good advice about the thing which is lying about. And after this you must consider the things that agree with what you intend your advisers to tell you, and also if they can learn of them, and whether the greater number of your advisers agree with you or not. Then you must consider what will happen if you follow their advice, such as hate, peace, war, Grace, profit, damage, and many other things. And in all these things you must choose the best and abandon all others. Then you must consider where your advice springs from and what fruit it may conceive. You must also think of all the reasons they they spring from. And when you have examined the advice, as I have said, and decided what is for the best, and had it approved by many wise old people, then you shall consider if you can do it, and bring it to a good end. For certainly it's common sense for a man not to begin something unless he can carry it out as he should; and no person should take on him such a heavy task that he cannot bear it. For the proverb says, 'He who takes on too much, will keep little of it.' And Cato says, 'Try to do the things you have the power to do, in case the burden presses you so

thee bihoveth to weyve thyng that thou hast bigonne.' And if so be that thou be in doute wheither thou mayst parfourne a thing or noon, chese rather to suffre than bigynne. And Piers Alphonce seith, 'if thou hast myght to doon a thyng of which thou most repente, it is bettre nay than ye. This is to seyn, that thee is bettre holde thy tonge stille than for to speke. Thanne may ye understonde by strenger resons that if thou hast power to parfourne a werk of which thou shalt repente, thanne is it bettre that thou suffre than bigynne. Wel seyn they that defenden every wight to assaye a thyng of which he is in doute wheither he may parfourne it or noon. And after, whan ye han examyned youre conseil, as I have seyd biforn, and knowen wel that ye may parfourne youre emprise, conferme it thanne sadly til it be at and ende.

sorely that you're forced to abandon the project which you have begun.' And if it happens that you're in doubt as to whether you can perform something or not, you should choose to suffer rather than to begin it. And And Petrus Alphonsus says, 'If you have the power to do something which you will repent of, it is better to say no than yes.' He means, that for you it is better to hold your tongue than to speak. Then you can understand better that if you have the power to do something which you will repent of, then it is better for you to suffer than to begin. It is good advice given by those who tell somebody not to try something when he is in doubt as to whether he can do it or not. And afterwards, when you have examined your advice, as I said before, and are certain that you can carry it out, then stick to it diligently until it is finished.

§28 Now is it resoun and tyme that I shewe yow whanne and wherfore that ye may chaunge youre conseillours withouten youre repreve. Soothly, a man may chaungen his purpos and his conseil if the cause cesseth, or whan a newe caas bitydeth. For the lawe seith that 'upon thynges that newely bityden bihoveth newe conseil. And Senec seith, 'if thy conseil is comen to the eeris of thyn enemy, chaunge thy conseil.' Thou mayst also chaunge thy conseil if so be that thou fynde that by errour, or by oother cause, harm or damage may bityde. Also if thy conseil be dishonest, or ellis cometh of dishonest cause, chaunge thy conseil. For the lawes seyn that 'alle bihestes that been dishoneste been of no value'; and eek if so be that it be inpossible, or may nat goodly be parfourned or kept.

Now it is time that I tell you when and in what fashion you can change your plans without being dishonoured. Truly, a man can change as purpose and his plans if the reason for doing them disappears, or when something new happens. For the law says that, 'things that newly happen need new plans.' And Seneca says, 'If your plan comes to the ears of your enemy, change your plan.' You can also change your plan if it happens that you find that through error, or through another cause, some harm may come to you. Also if your plan is not just, or otherwise comes from dishonesty, change your plan. For the laws say that 'no dishonest promises are of any value'; and also if it happens that it is impossible, or cannot be well done, you should change it.'

§29 And take this for a general reule, that every conseil that is affermed so strongly that it may nat be chaunged for no condicioun that may bityde, I seye that thilke conseil is wikked.

And take this as a general rule, that every plan that is so strongly designed that it cannot be changed no matter what happens, I say that plan is wicked.

§30 This Melibeus, whanne he hadde herd the doctrine of his wyf dame Prudence, answerde in this wyse: "Dame," quod he, "as yet into this tyme ye han wel and covenably taught me as in general, how I shal governe me in the chesynge and in the withholdynge of my conseillours. but now wolde I fayn that ye wolde condescende in especial, and telle me how liketh yow, or what semeth yow, by oure conseillours that we han chosen in oure present nede."

This Melibeus, when he had heard the advice of his wife Dame Prudence, answered in this fashion: 'Dame," he said, up until this time you have taught me well in general as to how I should rule myself in the choice and use of my advisers. But now I would very much like you to get down to particular cases and tell me what you think, how it seems to you, about the advisers that we have chosen in our present situation."

§31 "My lord," quod she, "I biseke yow in al humblesse that ye wol nat wilfully replie agayn my resouns, ne distempre youre herte, thogh I speke thyng that yow displese. For God woot that, as in myn entente, I speke it for youre beste, for youre honour, and for youre profite eke. And soothly, I hope that youre benyngnytee wol taken it in pacience. Trusteth me wel," quod she, "that youre conseil as in this caas ne sholde nat, as to speke properly, be called a conseillyng, but a mocioun or a moevyng of folye, in which conseil ye han erred in many a sondry wise.

§32 First and forward, ye han erred in th' assemblynge of youre conseillours. For ye sholde first have cleped a fewe folk to youre conseil, and after ye myghte han shewed it to mo folk, if it hadde been nede. But certes, ye han sodeynly cleped to youre conseil a greet multitude of peple, ful chargeant and ful anoyous for to heere. Also ye han erred, for theras ye sholden oonly have cleped to youre conseil youre trewe frendes olde and wise. Ye han ycleped straunge folk, yonge folk, false flatereres, and enemys reconsiled, and folk that doon yow reverence withouten love. And eek also ye have erred, for ye han broght with yow to youre conseil ire, coveitise, and hastifnesse, the whiche thre thinges been contrariouse to every conseil honest and profitable; the whiche thre thinges ye han nat anientissed or destroyed hem, neither in youreself, ne in youre conseillours, as yow oghte. Ye han erred also, for ye han shewed to youre conseillours youre talent and youre affeccioun to make werre anon, and for to do vengeance. They han espied by youre wordes to what thyng ye been enclyned; and therfore han they rather conseilled yow to youre talent that to youre profit. Ye han erred also, for it semeth that yow suffiseth to han been conseilled by thise conseillours oonly, and with litel avys, whereas in so greet and so heigh a nede it hadde been necessarie mo conseillours and moore deliberacion to parfourne youre emprise. Ye han erred also, for ye ne han nat examyned youre conseil in the forseyde manere, ne in due manere, as the caas requireth. Ye han erred also, for ye han maked no division bitwixe youre conseillours; this is to seyn, bitwixen youre trewe freendes and youre feyned conseillours; ne ye han nat knowe the wil of youre trewe freendes olde and wise; but ye han cast alle hire wordes in an hochepot, and enclyned youre herte to the moore part and to the gretter nombre, and there been ye condescended.

"My Lord," she said, "I beg you with all humility that you will not answer my arguments angrily, nor become upset, even if I say something which displeases you. For God knows that everything I am saying is for the best for you, for your honour and also for your benefit. And truly, I hope that with your kindness you will accept it patiently. You must trust me that in this case, to speak truly, the advice you have been given is all just foolish, and you have made many different mistakes in taking it.

Firstly, you have been mistaken in your choice of advisers. For firstly you should have called a few folk to your council, and you could have told the matter to more folk afterwards, if it was necessary. But certainly, you called a great crowd of people to your counsel at once, a great burden and very annoying to listen to. You have also been mistaken, for you should have only called to your council your true, old and wise friends, and you have summoned foreigners, young people, false flatterers and and old enemies, and people who show you respect without love. And also you have been mistaken in coming to your counsel with anger, greed and haste, three things which are antithetical to every honourable and good counsel; you have not shunned those three things yourself and neither have your advisers, as you ought to have. You have also been mistaken in showing to your advisers your desire and inclination to go to war immediately and take revenge. They saw through what you said the way which you are are inclined; and therefore they advised you according to your wishes, rather than for your benefit. You have also been mistaken, for it seems that to you it has been enough to be advised just by these councillors, with only a little consultation, where is in such a great and urgent situation you should have had more advisers and thought harder about what you were going to do. You have also been mistaken in not questioning your advice in the way which I have already mentioned, nor in a manner suitable to the case. You have also been in error because you have made no distinction between your advisers–that is to say, between your true friends and your false ones–and you have not thought of what your true old and wise friends have said, but have

And sith ye woot wel that men shal alwey fynde a gretter nombre of fooles than of wise men, and therfore the conseils that been at congregaciouns and multitudes of folk, there as men take moore reward to the nombre than to the sapience of persones, ye se wel that in swiche conseillynges fooles han the maistrie."

thrown all their words together in a mixture, and your heart has swung towards the larger larger part, the greater number, and you have have given in to that. And since you know that there will always be more fools than wise men, and so the advice that is available at gatherings of great numbers of folk, where men pay more attention to the number than to wisdom, you can certainly see that in such councils, fools have the upper hand.

§33 Melibeus answerde agayn, and seyde, "I graunte wel that I have erred; but there as thou hast toold me heerbiforn that he nys nat to blame that chaungeth his conseillours in certein caas and for certeine juste causes, I am al redy to chaunge my conseillours right as thow wolt devyse. The proverbe seith that 'for to do synne is mannyssh, but certes for to persevere longe in synne is werk of the devel.'"

Melibeus also again, and said, "I accept I have been mistaken; but since you told me before that someone cannot be blamed if he changes his advisers in certain cases and for certain good reasons, I am ready to change them just as you advise me. The proverb says that, 'to sin is human, but to keep sinning sinning is the work of the devil'"

§34 To this sentence answered anon dame Prudence, and seyde: "examineth," quod she, "youre conseil, and lat us see the whiche of hem han spoken most resonably and taught yow best conseil. And for as muche as that the examynacion is necessarie, lat us bigynne at the surgiens and at the phisiciens, that first speeken in this matiere. I sey yow that the surgiens and phisiciens han seyd yow in youre conseil discreetly, as hem oughte; and in hir speche seyden ful wisely that to the office of hem aperteneth to doon to every wight honour and profit, and no wight for to anoye; and after hir craft to doon greet diligence unto the cure of hem which that they han in hir governaunce. And, sire, right as they han answered wisely and discreetly, right so rede I that they been heighly and sovereynly gerdoned for hir noble speche; and eek for they sholde do the moore ententif bisynesse in the curacion of youre doghter deere. For al be it so that they been youre freendes, therfore shal ye nat suffren that they serve yow for noght, but ye oghte the rather gerdone hem and shewe hem youre largesse. And as touchynge the proposicioun which that the phisiciens encreesceden in this caas, this is to seyn. That in maladies that oon contrarie is warisshed by another contrarie, I wolde fayn knowe hou ye understonde thilke text, and what is youre sentence."

Dame Prudence immediately answered him, saying, "Examine your advisers, and let us see which of them has spoken most reasonably and given you the best advice. And as the examination is necessary, let us begin with the surgeons and physicians, who first spoke of this. I tell you that the surgeons and physicians counselled you very discreetly, as they should, and in their speech they said very wisely that in their position they have to do good for every person, and do no one harm, and the rules of their craft are that they must take great care of those with whom they are entrusted. And, so, just as they have answered wisely and discreetly, so I think that they should be greatly rewarded for their noble speech, and that they should have the greatest greatest part of the care of your dear dear daughter. For although they are your friends, you should not allow them to serve you for nothing, but you should reward them and show them your generosity. As for the theory that the physicians developed in this case–that is to say that in illness one bad thing can be killed by another–I would like to know what you think of that idea, and how how you interpret it."

§35 "Certes," quod Melibeus, "I understonde it in this wise: that right as they han doon me a contrarie, right so sholde I doon hem another. For right as they han venged hem on me and doon me wrong,

"Certainly," said Melibeus, "I understand it to mean this; that just as they have done evil to me, so I should do evil back to them. For just as they took revenge on me and did

367

right so shal I venge me upon hem and doon hem wrong; and thanne have I cured oon contrarie by another."

§36 "Lo, lo," quod dame Prudence, "how lightly is every man enclined to his owene desir and to his owene plesaunce! Certes," quod she, "the wordes of the phisiciens ne sholde nat han been understonden in thys wise. For certes, wikkednesse is nat contrarie to wikkednesse, ne vengeance to vengeaunce, ne wrong to wrong, but they been semblable. And therfore o vengeaunce is nat warisshed by another vengeaunce, ne o wroong by another wroong, but everich of hem encreesceth and aggreggeth oother. But certes, the wordes of the phisiciens sholde been understonden in this wise: for dood and wikkednesse been two contraries, and pees and werre, vengeaunce and suffraunce, discord and accord, and manye othere thynges. But certes, wikkednesse shal be warisshed by goodnesse, discord by accord, werre by pees, and so forth of othere thynges. And hereto accordeth Seint Paul the Apostle in manye places. He seith: 'ne yeldeth nat harm for harm, ne wikked speche for wikked speche; but do wel to hym that dooth thee harm, and blesse hym that seith to thee harm.' And in manye othere places he amonesteth pees and accord. But now wol I speke to yow of the conseil which that was yeven to yow by the men of lawe and the wise folk, that seyden alle by oon accord, as ye han herd bifore, that over alle thynges ye shal doon youre diligence to kepen youre persone and to warnestoore youre hous; and seyden also that in this caas yow oghten for to werken ful avysely and with greet deliberacioun. And, sire, as to the firste point, that toucheth to the kepyng of youre persone, ye shul understonde that he that hath werre shal everemoore mekely and devoutly preyen, biforn alle thynges, that Jhesus Crist of his mercy wol han hym in his proteccion and been his sovereyn helpyng at his nede. For certes, in this world ther is no wight that may be conseilled ne kept sufficeantly withouten the kepyng of oure lord Jhesu Crist. To this sentence accordeth the prophete David, that seith, 'if God ne kepe the citee, in ydel waketh he that it kepeth.' Now, sire, thanne shul ye committe the kepyng of youre persone to youre trewe freendes, that been approved and yknowe, and of hem shul ye axen help youre persone for to kepe. For Catoun seith: 'if thou hast nede of help, axe it of thy freendes; for ther nys noon so good a phisicien as thy trewe freend.' And after this thanne shul ye kepe yow fro alle straunge folk,

me wrong, so I shall revenge myself on them and do them wrong; then I have cured one evil with another."

"Look at this," said Dame Prudence, "how easily every man leans towards his own desires and his own pleasure! Certainly the words of the physicians should not be understood in this fashion. Wickedness is not the opposite of wickedness, revenge of revenge, evil of evil, they are the same thing. And so one revenge is not killed by another, or one evil by another, each of them increases and makes the other worse. The words of the physicians should be understood in this way: and wickedness of opposites, and peace and war, vengeance and forbearance, discord and agreement, and many other things; but certainly, wickedness must be killed with goodness, discord with agreement war with peace, and the same with other things. In many places St Paul the apostle agreed to this. He said, "Don't give back harm for harm, nor evil speech with evil speech, but be good to the one who harms you, and bless the one who speaks harm to you." In many other places he recommends peace and agreement. But now I will speak to you of the advice which was given to you by the lawyers and the wise men, who said in unanimous agreement, as you have heard before, that above all things you should do your best to guard your person and fortify your house; and they also said that in this matter you should take much advice and and deliberate greatly. And, so, as to the first point, looking after the safety of your person, you should understand that someone who is at war should always meekly and devoutly pray, above all else, that Jesus Christ in his mercy will keep him under his protection and be his greatest help when he needs him. For certainly, in this world there is nobody who can be advised nor guarded properly without the protection of our Lord Jesus Christ. The prophet David agrees with this opinion, saying, 'if God does not guard the city, the person who watches it is guarding it in vain.' Now, sir, so you should give the task of guarding your person to your true friends who have proved themselves to you, they are the ones you should ask to help. For Cato says, 'if you need help, ask your friends for it, for there is no physician who is as good as your true friend.' As well as this you should keep

and fro lyeres, and have alwey in suspect hire compaignye. For Piers Alfonce seith, 'ne taak no compaignye by the weye of a straunge man, but if so be that thou have knowe hym of a lenger tyme. And if so be that he falle into thy compaignye paraventure, withouten thyn assent, enquere thanne as subtilly as thou mayst of his conversacion, and of his lyf bifore, and feyne thy wey; seye that thou wolt thider as thou wolt nat go; and if he bereth a spere, hoold thee on the right syde, and if he bere a swerd, hoold thee on the lift syde.' And after this thanne shul ye kepe yow wisely from all swich manere peple as I have seyd bifore, and hem and hir conseil eschewe. And after this thanne shul ye kepe yow in swich manere that, for any presumpcion of youre strengthe, that ye ne dispise nat, ne accompte nat the myght of youre adversarie so litel, that ye lete the kepyng of youre persone for youre presumpcioun; for every wys man dredeth his enemy. And Salomon seith: 'weleful is he that of alle hath drede; for certes, he that thurgh the hardynesse of his herte, and thurghthe hardynesse of hymself, hath to greet presumpcioun, hym shal yvel bityde.' Thanne shul ye everemoore contrewayte embusshementz and alle espiaille. For Senec seith that 'the wise man that dredeth harmes, eschueth harmes, ne he ne falleth into perils that perils eschueth.' And al be it so that it seme that thou art in siker place, yet shaltow alwey do thy diligence in kepynge of thy persone; this is to seyn, ne be nat necligent to kepe thy persone, nat oonly for thy gretteste enemys, but fro thy leeste enemy. Senek seith: 'a man that is well avysed, he dredeth his leste enemy.' Ovyde seith that 'the litel wesele wol slee the grete bole and the wilde hert.' And the book seith, 'a litel thorn may prikke a kyng ful soore, and an hound wol holde the wolde boor.' But nathelees, I sey nat thou shalt be so coward that thou doute ther wher as is no drede. The book seith that somme folk han greet lust to deceyve, but yet they dreden hem to be deceyved. Yet shaltou drede to been empoisoned, and kepe the from the compaignye of Scorneres. For the book seith, 'with scorneres make no compaignye, but flee hire wordes as venym.'

yourself away from all unfamiliar people, and from liars, and always be suspicious of them. For Petrus Alphonsus says, 'do not go in company with strange men, but only with people you have known for longer. And if it so happens that he comes into your company by chance, without your agreement, find out as subtly as you can what is his way of life, and what he did before, and lay a false trail; say that you will go where you are not going; and if he is carrying a spear, keep yourself on his right, and if he is carrying a sword, keep yourself on the left.' So in this way you will sensibly keep yourself away from such people as I have just described and reject them and their advice. And after this you must behave yourself in such a way that, however confident you are in your strength, whether you despise them or not, do not count the strength of your adversary to be so small that you neglect the protection of your person because of overconfidence, for every wise man goes in fear of his enemy. And Solomon says, 'The person who fears is happy, for certainly, the one who through the strength of his heart and of himself is too self-confident, evil will come to him.' Then you must always watch out for ambushes and for spies, for Seneca says that 'the wise man who dreads danger, avoids danger, and the one who avoids peril does not fall into it.' And although you may may feel that you are in a safe place, you must always do your best to God yourself; that is to say, not only God yourself against your greatest enemies but also your smallest enemy. Seneca says, 'A man who is sensible goes in fear of his lowliest enemy.' Ovid says that 'the little weasel can kill the great bull and the wild hart.' And the book says, 'A little can prick a king very badly, and the hound can bring down the wild boar.' But nevertheless, I don't say you should be so cowardly that you fear when there is no reason to. The book says that 'some people are very keen to deceive others, but they have a great fear of being deceived.' But you should go in fear of being poisoned and keep yourself from the company of people who scoff at your fears. For the book says, 'with scoffers do not keep company, but fly from their words as from poison.'

§37 Now, as to the seconde point, where as youre

Now, as for the second point, when your wise

wise conseillours conseilled yow to warnestoore youre hous with gret diligence, I wolde fayn knowe how that ye understonde thilke wordes and what is youre sentence."

§38 Melibeus answerde, and seyde, "certes, I understande it in this wise: that I shal warne store myn hous with toures, swiche as han castelles and othere manere edifices, and armure, and artelries; by whiche thynges I may my persone and myn hous so kepen and deffenden that myne enemys shul been in drede myn hous for to approche."

§39 To this sentence answerde anon Prudence: "Warnestooryng," quod she, "of heighe toures and of grete edifices apperteyneth somtyme to pryde. And eek men make heighe toures, and grete edifices with grete costages and with greet travaille; and whan that they been accomplicéd, yet be they nat worth a stree, but if they be defended by trewe freendes that been olde and wise. And understoond wel that the gretteste and strongeste garnysoun that a riche man may have, as wel to kepen his persone as his goodes, is that he be biloved with hys subgetz and with his neighebores. For thus seith Tullius, that 'ther is a manere garnysoun that no man may vanquysse ne disconfite, and that is a lord to be biloved of his citezeins and of his peple.'

§40 Now, sire, as to the thridde point, where as youre olde and wise conseillours seyden that yow ne oghte nat sodeynly ne hastily proceden in this nede, but that yow oghte purveyen and apparaillen yow in this caas with greet diligence and greet deliberacioun; trewely, I trowe that they seyden right wisely and right sooth. For Tullius seith: 'in every nede, er thou bigynne it, apparaille thee with greet diligence.' Thanne seye I that in vengeance-takyng, in were, in bataille, and in warnestooryng, er thow bigynne, I rede that thou apparaille thee therto, and do it with greet deliberacion. For Tullius seith that 'longe apparaillyng biforn the bataille maketh short victorie.' And Cassidorus seith, 'the garnysoun is stronger, whan it is longe tyme avysed.'

§41 But now lat us speken of the conseil that was accorded by youre neighebores, swiche as doon yow reverence withouten love, youre olde enemys reconsiled, youre flatereres, that conseilled yow certeyne thynges prively, and openly conseilleden yow the contrarie; the yonge folk also, that conseilleden yow to venge yow, and make werre

wise counsellors advise you to fortify your house strongly, I am eager to know how you understand their words and what you will do."

Melibeus answered and said, "Certainly, I understand it to mean this: that I should fortify my house with towers, like those on castles and other buildings, and armour, and artillery, and through things like this I can guard myself and my house so well that my enemies will be frightened to approach."

Prudence immediately answered him: "The fortification of high towers and great buildings buildings sometimes shows pride. And also men make high towers and great buildings with great expense and hard work, and when they are finished, they are not worth anything, unless they are defended by true friends that are old and wise. And you must certainly understand that the greatest and strongest garrison of any rich man, to protect his person as well as his goods, is being loved by his subjects and by his neighbours. For this is what Cicero says, that 'there is a sort of that no man can bring down or destroy, and that is for a lord to be loved by his citizens and his people.'

Now, sir, as for the third point, whereas your old and wise advisers said that you should not rush headlong into this urgent matter, but that you should prepare yourself and get ready with great work and deliberation; truly, I believe that they spoke the truth very wisely. For Cicero says, 'in every urgent matter, before you begin, prepare yourself very carefully.' So I say that in taking revenge, in war, in battle and in fortification, before you begin, I advise you to prepare yourself for it, and do it very carefully. For Cicero says that 'long preparation before the battle makes a quick victory.' And Cassiodorus says, 'Protection is stronger when it has been planned for a long time.'

But now let us speak of the advice that your neighbours agreed on, those who revere you without love, your old enemies reconciled, your flatterers, who advised you of certain things secretly, and advised you in public differently; the young folk also, who advised you to take revenge and make war at once.

anon. And certes, sire, as I have seyd biforn, ye han greetly erred to han cleped swich manere folk to youre conseil, which conseillours been ynogh repreved by the resouns aforeseyd. But nathelees, lat us now descende to the special. Ye shuln first procede after the doctrine of Tullius. Certes, the trouthe of this matiere, or of this conseil, nedeth nat diligently enquere; for it is wel wist whiche they been that han doon to yow this trespas and vileynye, and how manye trespassours, and in what manere they han to yow doon al this wrong and al this vileynye. And after this, thanne shul ye examyne the seconde condicion which that the same Tullius addeth in this matiere. For Tullius put a thyng which that he clepeth 'consentynge'; this is to seyn, who been they, and which been they and how manye, that consenten to thy conseil in thy wilfulnesse to doon hastif vengeance. And lat us considere also who been they, and how manye been they, and whiche been they, that consenteden to youre adversaries. And certes, as to the first poynt, it is wel knowen whiche folk been they that consenteden to youre hastif wilfulnesse; for trewely, alle tho that conseilleden yow to maken sodeyn were ne been nat youre freendes. Lat us now considere whiche been they that ye holde so greetly youre freendes as to youre persone. For al be it so that ye be myghty and riche, certes ye ne been but allone, for certes ye ne han no child but a doghter, ne ye ne han brotheren, ne cosyns germayns, ne noon oother neigh kynrede, wherfore that youre enemys for drede wholde stinte to plede with yow, or to destroye youre persone. Ye knowen also that youre richesses mooten been dispended in diverse parties, and whan that every wight hath his part, they ne wollen taken but litel reward to venge thy deeth. But thyne enemys been thre, and they han manie children, bretheren, cosyns, and oother ny kynrede. And though so were that thou haddest slayn of hem two or three, yet dwellen ther ynowe to wreken hir deeth and to sle thy persone. And though so be that youre kynrede be moore siker and stedefast than the kyn of youre adversarie, yet nathelees youre kynrede nys but a fer kynrede; they been but litel syb to yow, and the kyn of youre enemys been nysyb to hem. And certes, as in that, hir condicioun is bet than youres. Thanne lat us considere also if the conseillung of hem that conseilleden yow to taken sodeyn bengeaunce, wheither it accorde to resoun. And certes, ye knowe wel 'nay'. For, as by right and resoun, ther may no man taken vengeance on no wight. But the juge that hath the jurisdiccioun of it, whan it is graunted hym to take thilke

And certainly, sir, as I've said before, you were very wrong in asking the sort of people to your council, those sorts of advisers have been shunned enough for the reasons I spoke of earlier. But nevertheless, now let us get down to particulars. You should firstly carry on according to the advice of Cicero. Certainly, the truth of this matter, or of his advice, we do not need to carefully enquire, for it is well known who are those who have committed this crime against you, how many of them there are, and the fashion in which they did you all this wrong and villainy. And after this, you should consider the second condition which Cicero adds in this matter. For Cicero spoke of a thing which he called consent; that is to say who are the ones and how many are there who agree with the advice that you should in your anger take hasty revenge. And let us think also who they are, how many of them there are, who agreed with your enemies. And certainly, as to the first point, it is well known who the people are who agreed to your hasty anger, for truly, all those who advise you to go to war once are not your friends. Now let us consider who those are whom you think are your greatest friends. For although it is true that you are powerful and rich, certainly you are alone, you have no child except your daughter, nor do you have brothers, nor first cousins, nor any other close relatives, to make your enemies fear attacking you. You also know that your inheritance will be split into several parts, and when each person has his part, he will not care much about avenging your death. But you have three enemies, and they have many children, brothers, cousins and other close relatives. And although it might be the case that you killed two or three of them, there would be enough living to avenge their deaths and to kill you. And though it would be the case that your family are more trustworthy and more steadfast than the family of your enemies, nevertheless they are distant relations; they are not closely related to you like the family of your enemies are. And certainly, in that respect, they are in a better place than you. So let us consider the advice of those who told you to take a sudden vengeance, whether it is sensible. And certainly, you well know it is not. For, in justice and reason, no man can take vengeance on anybody except for a judge who

vengeance hastily or attemprely, as the lawe requireth. And yet mooreover of thilke word that Tullius clepeth 'consentynge,' thou shalt considere if thy myght and thy power may consenten and suffise to thy wilfulnesse and to thy conseillours. And certes thou mayst wel seyn that 'nay'. For sikerly, as for to speke proprely, we may do no thyng, but oonly swich thyng as we may doon rightfully. And certes rightfully ne mowe ye take no vengeance, as of youre propre auctoritee. Thanne mowe ye seen that youre power ne consenteth nat, ne accordeth nat, with youre wilfulnesse.

§42 Lat us now examyne the thridde point, that Tullius clepeth 'consequent.' Thou shal understonde that the vengeance that thou purposest for to take is the consequent; and therof folweth another vengeaunce, peril, and werre, and othere damages withoute nombre, of whiche we be nat war, as at this tyme.

§43 And as touchynge the fourthe point, that Tullius clepeth 'engendrynge', thou shalt considere that this wrong which that is doon to thee is engendred of the hate of thyne enemys, and of the vengeance-takynge upon that wolde engendre another vengeance, and muchel sorwe and wastynge of richesses, as I seyde.

§44 Now, sire, as to the point that Tullius clepeth 'causes,;' which that is the laste point, thou shalt understonde that the wrong that thou hast receyved hath certeine causes, whiche that clerkes clepen Oriens and Efficiens, and Causa longinqua and Causa propinqua, this is to seyn, the fer cause and the ny cause. The fer cause is almyghty god, that is cause of alle thynges. The neer cause is thy thre enemys. The cause accidental was hate. The cause material been the fyve woundes of thy doghter. The cause formal is the manere of hir werkynge that broghten laddres and cloumben in at thy wyndowes. The cause final was for to sle thy doghter. It letted nat in as muche as in hem was. But for to speken of the fer cause, as to what ende they shul come, or what shal finally bityde of hem in this caas, ne kan I nat deeme but by conjectynge and by supposynge. For we shul suppose that they shul come to a wikked ende, by cause that the Book of Decrees seith, 'seelden, or with greet peyne, been causes ybroght to good ende whanne they been baddely bigonne.'

rules over the matter, when he is given the power to take vengeance quickly or at the right time, as the law requires. With reference to what Cicero calls consent, you should consider if your might and your power are enough to match your headstrong behaviour and that of your advisers. And certainly you can say they are not. For, strictly speaking, we should do nothing except things which are just. And certainly in justice you must take take no revenge on your own authority. You must see that your power does not match or agree with your rashness.

Now let us examine the further point, which Cicero calls consequent. You must understand that the revenge you mean take is consequence; and so it follows that there will be more revenge, danger and war, and other damage which cannot be counted, which we are not aware of, at this time.

With regard to the fourth point, which Cicero calls engendering, you must think that the wrong which is done to you has been engendered by the hatred of your enemies, and taking revenge would cause more revenge, and much sorrow and wasting of resources, as I said.

Now, sir, to the point which Cicero calls causes, which is the last point, you must understand that the wrongs done to you have certain causes, which scholars call Oriens et Efficiens, and Causa Longinqua and Causa Propinqua; that is to say, the far cause and the near cause. The far cause is Almighty God, that causes all things. The near cause is your three enemies. The main motivation was hatred. The material expression of that are the five wounds on your daughter. The formal cause is the way in which they brought ladders and climbed in in at your windows. The final cause was to kill your daughter. They did everything that they could. But to speak of the far cause, and what will happen to them in the end in this case, I cannot judge except through conjecture and guesswork. We can assume that they will come to a wicked end, because the Book of Decrees says, 'Seldom, or only with great great effort, do things end well when they begin badly.'

§45 Now, sire, if men wolde axe me why that God suffred men to do yow this vileynye, certes, I kan nat wel answere, as for no soothfastnesse. For th' apostle seith that 'the sciences and the juggementz of oure Lord God almyghty been ful depe; ther may no man comprehende ne serchen hem suffisantly. 'Nathelees, by certeyne presumpciouns and conjectynges, I holde and bileeve that God, which that is ful of justice and of rightwisnesse, hath suffred this bityde by juste cause resonable.

§46 Thy name is Melibee, this is to seyn, 'a man that drynketh hony.' Thou hast ydronke so muchel hony of sweete temporeel richesses, and delices and honours of this world, that thou art dronken, and hast forgeten Jhesu Crist thy creatour. Thou ne hast nat doon to hym swich honour and reverence as thee oughte, ne thou ne hast nat wel ytaken kep to the wordes of Ovide, that seith, under the hony of the goodes of the body is hyd the venym that sleeth the soule and Salomon seith, 'if thou hast founden hony, ete of it that suffiseth; for if thou ete of it out of mesure, thou shalt spewe,' And be nedy and povre. And peraventure Crist hath thee in despit, and hath turned awey fro thee his face and his eeris of misericorde; and also he hath suffred that thou hast been punysshed in the manere that thow hast ytrespassed. Thou hast doon synne agayn oure lord Crist; for certes, the three enemys of mankynde, - that is to seyn, the flessh, the feend, and the world, - thou hast suffred hem entre in to thyn herte wilfully by the wyndowes of thy body, and hast nat defended thyself suffisantly agayns hire assautes and hire temptaciouns, so that they han wounded thy soule in fyve places; this is to seyn, the deedly synnes that been entred into thyn herte by thy fyve wittes. And in the same manere oure lord Crist hath woold and suffred that thy three enemys been entred into thyn house by the wyndowes, and han ywounded thy doghter in the forseyde manere.
mentioned."

§47 "Certes," quod Melibee, "I se wel that ye enforce yow muchel by wordes to overcome me in swich manere that I shal nat venge me of myne enemys, shewynge me the perils and the yveles that myghten falle of this vengeance. But whoso wolde considere in alle vengeances the perils and yveles that myghte sewe of vengeance-takynge, a man wolde nevere take vengeance, and that were harm; for by the vengeance-takynge been the

Now, sir, if men asked me why God allowed men to commit this crime against you, certainly, I can't give you a definitive answer. For the apostle says that 'the science and judgement of our Lord God Almighty is very deep, no man can understand them and study study them enough.' Nevertheless, through certain assumptions and guesses, I truly believe that God, who is the embodiment of justice and righteousness, has allowed this to happen for a just and reasonable cause.

Your name is Melibeus, which means a man who drinks honey. You have drunk so much of the honey of sweet earthly riches, and had so much pleasure and honour in this world that you have drunk and forgotten your creator Jesus Christ. You have not given him the honour and reverence that you should, nor have you given proper attention to the words of Ovid, who says, 'Hidden under the honey of your body is the poison which kills the soul.' And Solomon says, 'If you have found honey, only eat what you need, for if you eat too much, you will vomit and be sick and poor.' And perhaps Christ despises you, and has turned his face away from you and his merciful ears, and he has allowed you to be punished in the same way in which you sinned. You have sinned against our Lord Jesus Christ, for certainly, the three enemies of mankind, that is to say, the flesh, the Devil and the world—you have allowed them into your heart through the windows of your body, and you have not properly defended yourself against their assaults and temptations, so that they have wounded your soul in five places; that is to say, the deadly sins have come into your heart through your five senses. In the same way our Lord Christ permitted your three enemies to come into your house through the windows and to wound your daughter in the manner already

"Certainly," said Melibeus, "I can see that you are strengthening yourself with words to rule over me in such a way that I will not take vengeance on my enemies, showing me the dangers and the evils that might come about because of this revenge. But if anyone thought, when taking revenge, of all the dangers and evils that might follow on from it, nobody would ever take revenge, and that

wikked men dissevered fro the goode men, and they that han wyl to do wikkednesse restreyne hir wikked purpos, whan they seen the punyssynge and chastisynge of the trespassours.

§48 And yet seye I moore, that right as singuler persone synneth in takynge vengeance of another man, right so synneth the juge if he do no vengeance of hem that it han disserved. For Senec seith thus: 'that maister,' he seith, 'is good that proveth shrewes.' And as Cassidore seith, 'a man dredeth to do outrages whan he woot and knoweth that it despleseth to the juges and the sovereyns.' And another seith, 'the juge that dredeth to do right, maketh men shrewes.' And Seint Paul the apostle seith in his epistle, whan he writeth unto the romayns, that 'the juges beren nat the spere withouten cause, but they beren it to punysse the shrewes and mysdoers, and for to defende the goode men.' If ye wol thanne take vengeance of youre enemys, ye shul retourne or have youre recours to the juge that hath the jurisdiccion upon hem, and he shal punysse hem as the lawe axeth and requireth."

§49 "A!" quod Melibee, "this vengeance liketh me no thyng. I bithenke me now and take heede how fortune hath norissed me fro my childhede, and hath holpen me to passe many a stroong paas. Now wol I assayen hire, trowynge, with goddes help, that she shal helpe me my shame for to venge."

§50 "Certes," quod Prudence, "if ye wol werke by conseil, ye shul nat assaye fortune by no wey, ne ye shul nat lene or bowe unto hire, after the word of Senec; for 'thynges that been folily doon, and that been in hope of fortune, shullen nevere come to good ende.' And, as the same Senec seith, 'the moore cleer and the moore shynyng that Fortune is, the moore brotil and the sonner broken she is.' Trusteth nat in hire, for she nys nat stidefast ne stable; for whan thow trowest to be moost seur or siker of hire help, she wol faille thee and deceyve thee. And where as ye seyn that fortune hath norissed yow fro youre childhede, I seye that in so muchel shul ye the lasse truste in hire and in hir wit. For Senec seith, 'what man that is norissed by Fortune, she maketh hym a greet fool.' Now thanne, syn ye desire and axe vengeance, and the vengeance that is doon after the lawe and bifore the juge ne liketh yow nat, and the vengeance that is doon in hope of fortune is

would be wrong; for taking revenge separates the wicked from the good, and those who want to behave wickedly control themselves, when see the punishment which comes to the trespassers.

And yet I will say more, that just as a private person commits a sin by taking revenge on on another man, in just the same way a judge sins if he does not take revenge on those who deserve it. For Seneca says: 'That master,' he says, 'is good if he punishes scoundrels.' And as Cassiodorus says, 'A man is afraid to do wrong when he knows that it will displease the judges and the rulers.' And someone else else says, 'The judge who is afraid to do justice makes men evil.' And St Paul the apostle says in his Epistle, when he writes of the Romans, that 'the judges do not carry the spear for no reason, they carry it to punish scoundrels and evildoers, and to defend good men' so if you want revenge on your enemies, you must bring your case to the judge who has power over them, and he will punish them as the law demands."

"Ah," said Melibeus, "this form of revenge does not please me at all. I am thinking of how Fortune has favoured me since childhood and has helped me to overcome many difficult situations. Now I will test her, for I believe that, with the help of God, she will help me take revenge for my shame."

"Certainly," said Prudence, "if you follow my advice, you will not test fortune in any way, and you will not rely on or bow down to her, for according to the words of Seneca, 'anything which is foolishly done, hoping for good luck, will never turn out well.' And, as the same Seneca says, 'the more clear and shining fortune is, the more brittle and sooner she breaks.' Do not trust her, for she is not reliable nor stable, for when you believe she is definitely on your side and will help you, she will fail you and desert you. And as for you saying that fortune has watched over you from your childhood, I am telling you that because of that you should have less trust in her and her wisdom. For Seneca says, 'Whenever a man is favoured by fortune, she makes him into a great fool.' Now then, since you wish for and demand revenge, and revenge that is done according to the law, by the judge, does not

perilous and uncertein, thanne have ye noon oother remedie but for to have youre recours unto the sovereyn juge that vengeth alle vileynyes and wronges. And he shal venge yow after that hymself witnesseth, where as he seith, leveth the vengeance to me, and I shal do it'"

please you, and the revenge that is done when when you hope for fortune is dangerous and uncertain, then you have no other alternative but to put your case before the supreme judge who avenges all evil and wrong. And he will take revenge according to what he himself has said, "Leave vengeance to me, and I shall do it."

§51 Melibee answerde, "if I ne venge me nat of the vileynye that men han doon to me, I sompne or warne hem that han doon to me that vileynye, and alle othere, to do me another vileynye. For it is writen, 'if thou take no vengeance of an oold vileynye, thou sompnest thyne adversaries to do thee a newe vileynye.' And also for my suffrance men wolden do me so muchel vileynye that I myghte neither bere it ne susteene, and so sholde I been put and holden overlowe. For men seyn, in muchel suffrynge shul manye thynges falle unto thee whiche thou shalt nat mowe suffre.'"

Melibeus answered, "if I do not take revenge for the evil that men have done to me, I am calling to all of them who have done that wrong, and to all others, to do it all over again. For it is written, 'if you do not take revenge for an ancient evil, you are asking your enemies to do you more evil.' And also if I was so forbearing men would do me so much evil that I would not be able to cope with it, and so I would be thrown down and considered humble. For men say, 'If you have much suffering many things will happen to you which you will not be able to endure.'"

§52 "Certes," quod Prudence, "I graunte yow that over-muchel suffraunce is nat good. But yet ne folweth it nat therof that every persone to whom men doon vileynye take of it vengeance; for that aperteneth and longeth al oonly to the juges, for they shul venge the vileynyes and injuries. And therfore tho two auctoritees that ye han seyd above been oonly understonden in the juges. For whan they suffren over-muchel the wronges and the vileynyes to be doon withouten punysshynge, the sompne nat a man al oonly for to do newe wronges, but they comanden it. Also a wys man seith that 'the juge that correcteth nat the synnere comandeth and biddeth hym do synne.' And the juges and sovereyns myghten in hir land so muchel suffre of the shrewes and mysdoeres that they sholden, by swich suffrance, by proces of tyme wexen of swich power and myght that they sholden putte out the juges and the sovereyns from hir places, and atte laste maken hem lesen hire lordshipes.

"Certainly," said Prudence, "I agree that too much patience is not good. But still it does not follow that every man to whom wrong has been done should take revenge for it, for that is the province of the judges, for they will avenge evil and injuries. And so those two authorities that you have mentioned only applied to the judges, for if they allow too much evil to be done without punishing it, they not only invite a man to do more evil, they demand it. Also a wise man says that 'the judge to does not punish the sinner orders and invites him to sin again.' And the judges and rulers might allow so much evil in their lands through their toleration that in time the evildoers will get so much power that they will throw the judges and rulers from their places, and ultimately make them lose their positions.

§53 But lat us now putte that ye have leve to venge yow. I seye ye been nat of myght and power as now to venge yow; for if ye wole maken comparisoun unto the myght of youre adversaries, ye shul fynde in manye thynges that I have shewed yow er this that hire condicion is bettre than youres. And therfore seye I that it is good as now that ye suffre and be pacient.

But now let us suppose that you have permission to avenge yourself. I say you do not have the might and power at the moment to avenge yourself, for if you compare yourself the might of your adversaries, you will realise that in many of the things that I have showed you before they are better off than you. And so I say that it is good that you should now suffer and the patient.

§54 Forthermoore, ye knowen wel that after the comune sawe, 'it is a woodnesse a man to stryve with a strenger or a moore myghty man than he is hymself; and for to stryve with a man of evene strengthe, that is to seyn, with as strong a man as he is, it is peril; and for to stryve with a weyker man, it is folie.' And therfore sholde a man flee stryvynge as muchel as he myghte. For Salomon seith, 'it is a greet worshipe to a man to kepen hym fro noyse and stryf.' And if it so bifalle or happe that a man of gretter myght and strengthe than thou art do thee grevaunce, studie and bisye thee rather to stille the same grevaunce than for to venge thee. For Senec seith that 'he putteth hym in greet peril that stryveth with a gretter man than he is hymself.' And Catoun seith, 'if a man of hyer estaat or degree, or moore myghty than thou, do thee anoy or grevaunce, suffre hym; for he that oones hath greved thee, may another tyme releeve thee and helpe.' Yet sette I caas, ye have bothe myght and licence for to venge yow, I seye that ther be ful manye thynges that shul restreyne yow of vengeance-takynge, and make yow for to enclyne to suffre, and for to han pacience in the wronges that han been doon to yow. First and foreward, if ye wole considere the defautes that been in youre owene persone, for whiche defautes God hath suffred yow have this tribulacioun, as I have seyd yow heer-biforn. For the poete seith that 'we oghte paciently taken the tribulacions that comen to us, whan we thynken and consideren that we han disserved to have hem.' And Seint Gregorie seith that 'whan a man considereth wel the nombre of his defautes and of his synnes, the peynes and the tribulaciouns that he suffreth semen the lesse unto hym; and in as muche as hym thynketh his synnes moore hevy and grevous, in so muche semeth his peyne the lighter and the esier unto hym.' Also ye owen to enclyne and bowe youre herte to take the pacience of oure lord Jhesu Crist, as seith Seint Peter in his epistles. 'Jhesu Crist,' he seith, 'hath suffred for us and yeven ensample to every man to folwe and sewe hym; for he dide nevere synne, ne nevere cam ther a vileyns word out of his mouth. Whan men cursed hym, he cursed hem noght; And whan men betten hym, he manaced hem noght.' Also the grete pacience which the seintes that been in paradys han had in tribulaciouns that they han ysuffred, withouten hir desert or gilt, oghte muchel stiren yow to pacience. Forthermoore ye sholde enforce yow to have pacience, considerynge that the tribulaciouns of this world but litel while endure,

Furthermore, you are well aware that according to the proverb, 'it is madness for a man to fight with a stronger or greater man than himself, and to strive with a man who is as strong as himself–a man should avoid fighting as much as he can. For Solomon says, 'it is that is dangerous, and to fight with a weaker man, that is stupidity.' And so it is very honourable for a man to keep himself from quarrels and fights.' And if it so happens that a man of great power and strength than you does something wrong to you, put your efforts into stopping that grievance, rather than taking revenge. For Seneca says that, 'someone who fights with a greater man than himself puts himself in great danger.' And Cato says, 'If a man of higher position or power, or stronger than you, upsets you, tolerate it, for the one who has caused you grief may another time help you.' But let us assume for the sake of argument that you have both the power and the right to take revenge, I say that there are many things which should stop you from taking revenge and that should make you accept your suffering, and to tolerate the wrongs which have been done to you. Firstly, if you look at all the faults which you have, the faults for which God has sent you this punishment, as I said to you before. For the poet says that 'we ought to patiently accept the trials which come to us, when we think of the fact that we deserved them.' And St Gregory says that 'when a man thinks properly of how many faults and sins he has committed, the pain and trials that he suffers seem small to him, and the more heavy and grievous he thinks his sins are, the lighter and easier to bear his pains seem to him.' Also you ought to bow down your heart and adopt the patience of our Lord Jesus Christ, as St Peter says in his Epistle. 'Jesus Christ,' he says, 'suffered for us and gave an example to every man to follow and be guided by him, for he never sinned, nor did he ever say an evil thing. When men cursed him, he did not curse them back, and when men beat him, he did not threaten them.' Also the great patience of the saints in Paradise which they showed during the trials they suffered, completely guiltless, ought to inspire you to be patient. Furthermore you you should force yourself to be patient, remembering that the trials of this world only

and soone passed been and goon, and the joye that a man seketh to have by pacience in tribulaciouns is perdurable, after that the apostle seith in his epistle. 'The joye of God,' he seith, 'is perdurable,' that is to seyn, everelastynge. Also troweth and bileveth stedefastly that he nys nat wel ynorissed, ne wel ytaught, that kan nat have pacience, or wol nat receyve pacience. For Salomon seith that 'the doctrine and the wit of a man is knowen by pacience.' And in another place he seith that 'he that is pacient governeth hym by greet prudence.' And the same Salomon seith, 'the angry and wrathful man maketh noyses, and the pacient man atempreth hem and stilleth.' He seith also, 'it is moore worth to be pacient than for to be right strong; and he that may have the lordshipe of his owene herte is moore to preyse than he that by his force or strengthe taketh grete citees. And therfore seith Seint Jame in his epistle that 'pacience is a greet vertu of perfeccioun.'

§55 "Certes," quod Melibee, "I graunte yow, dame Prudence, that pacience is greet vertu of perfeccioun; but every man may nat have the perfeccioun that ye seken; ne I nam nat of the nombre of right parfite men, for myn herte may nevere been in pees unto the tyme it be venged. And al be it so that it was greet peril to myne enemys to do me a vileynye in takynge vengeance upon me, yet tooken they noon heede of the peril, but fulfilleden hir wikked wyl and hir corage. And therfore me thynketh men oghten nat repreve me, though I putte me in a litel peril for to venge me, and though I do a greet excesse, that is to seyn, that I venge oon outrage by another."

§56 "A," quod dame Prudence, "ye seyn youre wyl and as yow liketh, but in no caas of the world a man sholde nat doon outrage ne excesse for to vengen hym. For Cassidore seith that 'as yvele dooth he that vengeth hym by outrage as he that dooth the outrage.' And therfore ye shul venge yow after the ordre of right, that is to seyn, by the lawe, and noght by excesse ne by outrage. And also, if ye wol venge yow of the outrage of youre adversaries in oother manere than right comandeth, ye synne. And therfore seith Senec that 'a man shal nevere vengen shrewednesse by shrewednesse.' And if ye seye that right axeth a man to defenden violence by violence, and fightyng by fightyng, certes ye seye sooth, whan the defense is doon anon withouten intervalle or withouten tariyng or delay, for to deffenden hym

last a little while and are soon gone, and the joy that a man going through injuring his trials patiently is eternal, according to what the apostle says in his Epistle. 'The Joy of God,' he says is 'inperdurable'–which means, everlasting. Also think and keep believing that someone who is not well trained, or well educated, will not show patience, nor will he benefit from it. For Solomon says that 'the belief and wit of man can be shown through his patience.' And in another place he says that 'someone who is patient governs himself himself very wisely.' And the same Solomon says, 'The angry man makes quarrels, and the patient man moderates and calms them.' He also says, 'It is better to be patient than to be very strong; someone who rules over his own his false or strength captures great cities.' And that is why St James in his Epistle says that 'Patience is a great part of perfection.'

"Certainly," said Melibeus, "I grant you, Dame Prudence, that patience is a great part of perfection; but not every man can have the perfection that you seek; nor am I a very perfect man, for my heart will never be at peace until I have my revenge. And although it was very dangerous for my enemies to commit such a crime in taking their revenge on me, they did not take heed of the danger, but carried out their wicked will and their desire. And so it seems to me that men should not criticise me, although I may put myself in a little danger to take my revenge, and although I am very excessive; that is to say, I take revenge for one outrage with another."

"Ah," said Dame Prudence, "you say what you want to do, but there is no case in the world when a man should commit outrages or excess by taking revenge. For Cassiodorus says that 'someone who takes revenge with an outrage is as evil as the one who committed the original outrage.' And so you must avenge yourself by following justice; that is to say, through the law and not through excess nor outrage. And also, if you take revenge for the the outrage of your enemies in any other way than the way which justice commands, you are sinning. And also, if you take revenge for the outrage your enemies have committed in any other fashion than that which justice commands, you are sinning. And so therefore Seneca says that 'a man should never avenge

and nat for to vengen hym. And it bihoveth that a man putte swich attemperance in his deffense that men have no cause ne matiere to repreven hym that deffendeth hym of excesse and outrage, for ellis were it agayn resoun. Pardee, ye knowen wel that ye maken no deffense as now for to deffende yow, but for to venge yow; and so seweth it that ye han no wyl to do youre dede attemprely. And therfore me thynketh that pacience is good; for Salomon seith that 'he that is nat pacient shal have a greet harm.'

§57 "Certes," quod Melibee, "I graunte yow that whan a man is inpacient and wrooth, of that that toucheth hym noght and that aperteneth nat unto hym, though it harme hym, it is no wonder. For the lawe seith that 'he is coupable that entremetteth hym or medleth with swych thyng as aperteneth nat unto hym.' And Salomon seith that 'he that entremetteth hym of the noyse or strif of another man is lyk to hym that taketh an hound by the eris.' For right as he that taketh a straunge hound by the eris is outherwhile biten with the hound, right in the same wise is it resoun that he have harm that by his inpacience medleth hym of the noyse of another man, wheras it aperteneth nat unto hym. But ye knowen wel that this dede, that is to seyn, my grief and my disese, toucheth me right ny. And therfore, though I be wrooth and inpacient, it is no merveille. And, savynge youre grace, I kan nat seen that it myghte greetly harme me though I tooke vengeaunce. For I am richer and moore myghty than myne enemys been; and wel knowen ye that by moneye and by havynge grete possessions been alle the thynges of this world governed. And Salomon seith that 'alle thynges abeyen to moneye.'

§58 Whan Prudence hadde herd hir housbonde avanten hym of his richesse and of his moneye, dispreisynge the power of his adversaries, she spak, and seyde in this wise: "Certes, deere sire, I graunte yow that ye been riche and myghty, and that the richesses been goode to hem that han wel ygeten hem and wel konne usen hem. For right as the body of a man may nat lyven withoute the soule, namoore may it lyve withouten temporeel

wickedness with wickedness.' And if you say that justice demands a man should fight violence with violence and fighting with fighting, you are certainly saying the truth, when the defence is done immediately without any delay, when he is defending himself and not revenging himself. But a man should defend himself with such moderation that men will have no reason nor excuse to criticise him of excess or outrage, for otherwise it would be foolishness. By God, you know full well that you are not now defending yourself, but taking revenge; and so it follows that you are not being moderate in your deeds. And so it seems to me that patience is a good thing. For Solomon says, 'he who is not patient will suffer great harm.'"

Melibeus said, "Certainly, I agree that when when a man is impatient and angry when something which is not directly affecting him, although it harms him, it is no wonder. For the law says that 'the person who intrudes or meddles with things which have nothing to do with him is guilty.' And Solomon says that 'someone who meddles with the quarrels or arguments of another man is like someone who pulls a hound by the ears.' For just as someone who pulls a strange found by the the ears will be at another time bitten by the hound, in the same way it is reasonable that somebody who is impatient enough to meddle with the quarrels of another man, when it does not affect him, deserves harm. But you are well aware that what has happened–I mean, all my grief and suffering–touches me very closely. And therefore, although I am angry and impatient, it is not surprising. And, with all due respect, I can't see what great harm it would do to me to take revenge. For I am richer and more powerful than my enemies; and you know that money and possessions or what rule the world. Solomon says 'everything obeys money.'"

When Prudence heard her husband boast about his wealth and his money, mocking the power of his adversaries, she spoke to him thus: "Certainly, dear Sir, I agree that you are rich and powerful and that riches are good for those who got them in a good fashion and know how to use them properly. For just as the body of a man cannot live without its soul, it can't live without earthly goods either. And

goodes. And by richesses may a man gete hym grete freendes. And therfore seith Pamphilles: 'if a net-herdes doghter,' seith he, 'be riche, she may chesen of a thousand men which she wol take to hir housbonde; for, of a thousand men, oon wol nat forsaken hire ne refusen hire. And this Pamphilles seith also: 'if thow be right happy - that is to seyn, if thou be right riche - thou shalt fynde a greet nombre of felawes and freendes. And if thy fortune change that thou wexe povre, farewel freendshipe and felaweshipe; for thou shalt be alloone withouten any compaignye, but if it be the compaignye of povre folk.' And yet seith this Pamphilles moreover that 'they that been thralle and bonde of lynage shullen been maad worthy and noble by the richesses.' And right so as by richesses ther comen manye goodes, right so by poverte come ther manye harmes and yveles. For greet poverte constreyneth a man to do manye yveles. And therfore clepeth Cassidore poverte the mooder of ruyne, that is to seyn, the mooder of overthrowynge or fallynge doun. And therfore seith Piers Alfonce: 'oon of the gretteste adversitees of this world is whan a free man by kynde or of burthe is constreyned by poverte to eten the almesse of his enemy,' and the same seith innocent in oon of his bookes. He seith that 'sorweful and myshappy is the condicioun of a povre beggere; for if he axe nat his mete, he dyeth for hunger; and if he axe, he dyeth for shame; and algates necessitee constreyneth hym to axe.' And seith Salomon that 'bet it is to dye than for to have swich poverte. And as the same Salomon seith, 'bettre it is to dye of bitter deeth than for to lyven in swich wise.' By thise resons that I have seid unto yow, and by manye othere resons that I koude seye, I graunte yow that richesses been goode to hem that geten hem wel, and to hem that wel usen tho richesses. And therfore wol I shewe yow hou ye shul have yow and how ye shul bere yow in gaderynge of richesses, and in what manere ye shul usen hem.

§59 First, ye shul geten hem withouten greet desir, by good leyser, sokyngly and nat over-hastily. For a man that is to desirynge to gete richesses abaundoneth hym first to thefte, and to alle othere yveles; and therfore seith Salomon, 'he that hasteth hym to bisily to wexe riche shal be noon innocent.' He seith also that 'the richesses that hastily cometh to a man, soone and lightly gooth and passeth fro a man; but that richesse that cometh litel and litel, wexeth alwey and multiplieth.' And, sire richesses by youre wit and by youre travaille unto youre profit; and that withouten wrong or harm doynge

a man can get himself great friends through riches. And so Pamphilles says: 'if the daughter of a cowherd is rich, she can choose any one of a thousand men as her husband, for not a single one of them will abandon her or refuse her.' And he also says, 'If you are very happy–that is to say, if you are very rich– you will find a great number of companions and friends. And if your fortune changes and you become poor, say farewell to companionship and friendship, for you will be alone without any company, except that of the poor.' And he also says that 'those who are born into slavery and bondage will be made worthy and noble through wealth.' And just as through riches many good things come, so poverty brings much harm and evil, for great poverty makes a man do evil things. And so Cassiodorus calls poverty the mother of ruin; that is, the mother of downfall. And so Petrus Alphonsus says, 'One of the greatest adversities in the world is when a man who is free by nature or by birth is forced by poverty to accept the charity of his enemy,' and innocent says the same in one of his books. He says that 'the condition of a poor beggar is sad and unfortunate; for if he does not beg for food, he dies of hunger; and if he does beg, he dies of shame, and yet he is forced to beg.' And Solomon says that 'it is better to die than to be so poor.' And as the same Solomon says, 'It is better to die a bitter death than to live in such a way.' For these reasons I have given you, and many other reasons I can tell you, I agree that riches are good for those who get them honestly and use them well. And so I will tell you how you should behave, and how you should gather riches, and how you should use them."

Firstly, you should get them without great thinking carefully, slowly, not too hastily. For a man who is too keen to acquire riches quickly becomes a thief, and does other evil things; that's why Solomon says, 'He who tries to become rich too quickly will not be innocent.' He also says that 'the riches that a man gains quickly will quickly leave him, those riches which come little by little always grow and multiply.' And, sir, you must get your wealth through your wits and through your work, and without doing wrong or harm to any oother persone. For the lawe seith that 'ther maketh no man himselven riche, if he do harm to another wight.' This is to seyn, that nature deffendeth and fordedeth by right that no man make hymself riche unto the harm of another persone. And Tullius seith that 'no sorwe, ne no drede of deeth, ne no thyng that may falle unto a man, is so muchel agayns nature as a man to encressen his owene profit to the harm of another man. And though the grete man and the myghty men geten richesses moore lightly than thou, yet shaltou nat been ydel ne slow to do thy profit, for thou shalt in alle wise flee ydelnesse. For Salomon seith that 'ydelnesse techeth a man to do manye yveles.' And the same Salomon seith that 'he that travailleth and bisieth hym to tilien his land, shal eten breed; but he that is ydel and casteth hym to no bisynesse ne occupacioun, shal falle into poverte, and dye for hynger.' And he that is ydel and slow kan nevere fynde covenable tyme for to doon his profit. For ther is a versifiour seith that 'the ydel man excuseth hym in wynter by cause of the grete coold, and in somer by enchesoun of the greete heete.' For thise causes seith Caton, 'waketh and enclyneth nat yow over-muchel for to slepe, for overmuchel reste norisseth and causeth manye vices.' And therfore seith Seint Jerome, 'dooth somme goode dedes that the devel, which is oure enemy, ne fynde yow nat unocupied.' For the devel ne taketh nat lightly unto his werkynge swiche as he fyndeth occupied in goode werkes.

§60 Thanne thus, in getynge richesses, ye mosten flee ydelnesse. And afterward, ye shul use the richesses which ye have geten by youre wit and by youre travaille, in swich a manere that men holde yow nat to scars, ne to sparynge, ne to fool-large, that is to seyen, over-large a spendere. For right as men blamen an avaricious man by cause of his scarsetee and chyncherie, in the same wise is he to blame that spendeth over-largely. And therfore seith Caton: 'use,' he seith, 'thy richesses that thou hast geten in swich a manere that men have no matiere ne cause to calle the neither wrecche ne chynche; for it is a greet shame to a man to have a povere herte and a riche purs.' He seith also: 'the goodes that thou hast ygeten, use hem by mesure;' that is to seyn, spende hem mesurably; for they that folily wasten and despenden the goodes that they han, what they han namoore propre of hir owene, they shapen hem to take the goodes of another man. I seye thanne that ye shul fleen avarice; usynge youre richesses in swich manere that men seye nat that youre richesses been yburyed, but that ye have hem in youre myght and in youre weeldynge. For a wys man repreveth the avaricious man, and seith thus in two vers: 'wherto and why burieth a man his goodes by his grete avarice, and knoweth wel that nedes moste he dye? For deeth is the ende of every man as in this present lyf.' And for what cause or enchesoun joyneth he hym or knytteth he hym so faste unto his goodes that alle hise wittes mowen nat disseveren hym or departen hym from his goodes, and knoweth wel, or oghte knowe, that whan he is deed he shal no thyng bere with hym out of this world? And therfore seith Seint Austyn that 'the avaricious man is likned unto helle, that the moore it swelweth. The moore desir it hath to swelwe and devoure.' And as wel as ye wolde eschewe to be called an avaricious man or chynche, as wel sholde ye kepe yow and governe yow in swich a wise that men calle yow nat fool-large. Therfore seith Tullius: 'the goodes,' he seith, 'of thyn hous ne sholde nat been hyd ne kept so cloos, but that they myghte been opened by pitee and debonairetee' -- that is to seyn, to yeven part to hem that han greet nede -- 'ne thy goodes shullen nat been so opene to been every mannes goodes. Afterward, in getynge of youre richesses and in usynge hem, ye shul alwey have thre thynges in youre herte, that is to seyn, oure lord god, conscience, and good name. First, ye shul have God in youre herte, and for no richesse ye shullen do no thyng which may in any manere displese God, that is youre creator and makere. For after the word of Salomon, 'it is bettre to have a litel good with the love of God, than to have muchel good and tresour, and lese the love of his lord God.' And the prophete seith that 'bettre it is to been a good man and have litel good and tresour, than to been holden a shrewe and have grete richesses.' And yet seye I ferthermoore, that ye sholde alwey doon youre bisynesse to gete yow richesses, so that ye gete hem with good conscience. And th' apostle seith that 'ther nys thyng in this world of which we sholden have so greet joye as whan oure conscience bereth us good witnesse.' And the wise man seith, 'the substance of a man is ful good, whan synne is nat in mannes conscience. Afterward, in getynge of youre richesses and in usynge of hem, yow moste have greet bisynesse and greet diligence that youre goode name be alwey kept and conserved. For Salomon seith that 'bettre it is an moore it availleth a man to have a good name, than for to have grete richesses.' And therfore he seith in another place, 'do greet diligence, seith Salomon, 'in kepyng of thy freend and of thy goode name; for it shal lenger

say that your riches are buried, but you have them in your power and under your control. For a wise man reproves the greedy man, and says in two verses: 'why does a man through his great greed bury his goods? When he knows that he is bound to die? For death is the end of the life of every man." So for what reason does he tie himself so fast to his goods that all his wits cannot separate him from them, when he knows full well, or should do, that when he is dead he can carry nothing from the world? And so St Austin says that 'the greedy man is like hell, the more he swallows, the more he wants to swallow.' And as you would not want to be called greedy or a miser, so you should also make sure that men do not call you foolishly spendthrift. Cicero says of this: 'the goods,' he says, 'of your house should not be hidden, nor kept locked up so tight, that they cannot be opened when pity and kindness demands it, but also your goods should not be so available that they become the property of everyone.' Furthermore, in getting your riches and using them you must always have three thoughts in your heart (that is to say, our Lord God, your conscience and good name). Firstly, you must have God in your heart, for you should not do anything for wealth which would displease God in any way, for he is your Creator and maker. For as Solomon says, 'it is better to have few goods and to have the love of God than to have much wealth and treasure and lose the love of the Lord God.' And the prophet says that 'it is better to be a good man and have little wealth and treasure than to be a scoundrel and have much wealth.' And I say furthermore, that you should always be looking for ways to increase your wealth, providing that you do so with a good conscience. The apostle says that 'there is nothing in the world which should give us as much happiness as when our conscience tells us we have been good.' And the wise man says, 'Man is generally very good, when he has no sin in his conscience.' So, in getting your riches and using them, you must make great efforts to ensure that you always keep your good name. Solomon says 'that it is better for a man to have a good name than to have great wealth.' And he also says in another place, 'take great care to keep hold of your friends and your good name; for

abide with thee than any tresour, be it never so precious.' And certes he sholde nat be called a gentil man that after God and good conscience, alle thynges left, ne dooth his diligence and bisynesse to kepen his goode name. And Cassidore seith that 'it is signe of a gentil herte, whan a man loveth and desireth to han a good name.' And therfore seith Seint Austyn that 'ther been two thynges that arn necessarie and nedefulle, and that is good conscience and good loos; that is to seyn, good conscience to thyn owene persone inward, and good loos for thy neighebor outward.' And he that trusteth hym so muchel in his goode conscience that he displeseth, and setteth at noght his goode name or loos, and rekketh noght though he kepe nat his goode neam, nys but a crueel cherl.

§61 Sire, now have I shewed yow how ye shul do in getynge richesses, and how ye shullen usen hem, and I se wel that for the trust that ye han in youre richesses ye wole moeve werre and bataille. I conseille yow that ye bigynne no were in trust of youre richesses, for thay ne suffisen noght werres to mayntene. And therfore seith a philosophre, 'that man that desireth and wole algates han werre, shal nevere have suffisaunce; for the richer that he is, the gretter despenses moste he make, if he wole have worshipe and victorie.' And Salomon seith that 'the gretter richesses that a man hath, the mo despendours he hath.' And, deere sire, al be it so that for youre richesses ye mowe have muchel folk, yet bihoveth it nat, ne it is nat good, to bigynne werre, whereas ye mowe in oother manere have pees unto youre worshipe and profit. For the victorie of batailles that been in this world lyth nat in greet nombre or multitude of the peple, ne in the vertu of man, but it lith in the wyl and in the hand of oure lord God Almyghty. And therfore Judas Machabeus, which was Goddes knyght, whan he sholde fighte agayn his adversarie that hadde a gretter nombre and a gretter multitude of folk and strenger than was this peple of Machabee, yet he reconforted his litel compaignye, and seyde right in this wise: 'als lightly,' quod he, 'may oure lord God Almyghty yeve victorie to a fewe folk as to many folk; for the victorie of a bataille comth nat by the grete nombre of peple, but it cometh from oure Lord God of hevene.' And, deere sire, for as muchel is ther is no man certein if he be worthy that God yeve hym victorie, (ne plus que il est certain se il est digne de l' amour de Dieu), or naught, after that Salomon seith, therfore every man sholde greetly drede werres to bigynne. And by cause that in batailles fallen manye perils, and happeth outher while that as soone is the grete man slayn as the litel man; and as it is written in the seconde Book of Kynges, 'the dedes of Batailles been aventurouse and nothyng certeyne, for as lightly is oon hurt with a spere as another;' and for ther is gret peril in werre; therfore sholde a man flee and eschue werre, in as muchel as a man may goodly. For Salomon seith, 'he that loveth peril shal falle in peril.'"

§62 After that dame Prudence hadde spoken in this manere, Melibee answerde, and seyde: "I see wel, Dame Prudence, that by youre faire wordes, and by youre resouns that ye han shewed me, that the werre liketh yow no thyng; but I have nat yet herd youre conseil, how I shal do in this nede."

§63 "Certes," quod she, "I conseille yow that ye accorde with youre adversaries and that ye have pees with hem. For Seint Jame seith in his Epistles that 'by concord and pees the smale richesses wexen grete, and by debaat and discord the grete richesses fallen doun.' And ye knowen wel that oon of the gretteste and moost sovereyn thyng that is in this world is unytee and pees. And therfore seyde oure lord Jhesu Crist to his apostles in this wise: 'wel happy and blessed been they that loven and purchacen pees, for they been called children of god.'"

§64 "A," quod Melibee, "now se I wel that ye loven nat myn honour ne my worshipe. Ye knowen wel that myne adversaries han bigonnen this debaat and bryge by hire outrage, and ye se wel that they ne requeren ne preyen me nat of pees, ne they asken nat to be reconsiled. Wol ye thanne that I go and meke me and obeye me to hem, and crie hem mercy? For sothe, that were nat my worshipe. For right as men seyn that 'over-greet hoomlynesse engendreth dispreisynge,' so fareth it by to greet hymylitee or mekenesse."

§65 Thanne bigan dame Prudence to maken semblant of wratthe, and seyde: "certes, sire, sauf youre grace, I love youre honour and youre profit as I do myn owene, and evere have doon; ne ye, ne noon oother, seyn nevere the contrarie. And yit if I hadde seyd that ye sholde han purchaced the pees and the reconsilacioun, I ne hadde nat muchel mystaken me, ne seyd amys. For the wise man seith, 'the dissensioun bigynneth

as easily as the lowly one; and as it is written in the second Book of Kings, 'Things that happen in battles are subject to chance and they are uncertain, for one man can be just as easily hurt by a spear as another'; and because there is great danger in war, a man should try to avoid it as much as he can honourably do so. For Solomon says, Someone who loves danger will fall through danger.'"

After Dame Prudence has spoken in this way, Melibeus answered and said, "I see clearly, Dame Prudence, that with your fair words and your reasoning you have shown me that you do not like war; but you have not yet given me your advice as to how I should act in this urgent matter."

"Certainly," she said, "I advise you to make a treaty with your enemies and have peace with them. For St James says in his Epistle that, 'with agreement and peace small riches become great, through argument and discord great riches fall down.' You know well that one of the greatest and most excellent things in the world is unity and peace. That is why our Lord Jesus Christ said to his apostles, 'Happy and blessed are they who love and and bring peace, for they are the children of God.'"

"Ah," said Melibeus, "now I see that you do love my honour nor my goodness. You are well aware that my enemies began this argument with their outrage, and you can certainly see that they will not ask me for peace, and they will not ask to be reconciled. Do you want me to go and abase myself, be subject to them and beg them for mercy? That certainly wouldn't be honourable. For just as men say that 'too much familiarity breeds contempt,' that is also the case when a man is too humble or meek."

Then Dame Prudence began to look angry, and said: "Certainly, sir, with all due respect, I love your honour and care about your health as much as I do my own, and always have; neither you, nor anyone else, can ever say different. And yet if I said that you should start the process of peace and reconciliation, I was not mistaken, I did not say anything wrong. For the wise man says, 'let arguments be

by another man, and the reconsilyng bygynneth by thyself.' And the prophete seith, 'flee shrewednesse and do goodnesse; seke pees and folwe it, as muchel as in thee is.' Yet seye I nat that ye shul rather pursue to youre adversaries for pees than they shuln to yow. For I knowe wel that ye been so hard-herted that ye wol do no thyng for me. And Salomon seith, 'he that hath over-hard an herte, atte laste he shal myshappe and mystyde.'

§66 Whanne Melibee hadde herd dame Prudence maken semblant of wratthe, he seyde in this wise: "dame, I prey yow that ye be nat displesed of thynges that I seye, for ye knowe wel that I am angrey and wrooth, and that is no wonder; and they that been wrothe witen nat wel what they don, ne what they seyn. Therfore the prophete seith that 'troubled eyen han no cleer sighte.' But seyeth and conseileth me as yow liketh, for I am redy to do right as ye wol desire; and if ye repreve me of my folye, I am the moore holden to love yow and to preyse yow. For Salomon seith that 'he that repreveth hym that dooth folye, he shal fynde gretter grace than he that deceyveth hym by sweete wordes.'"

§67 Thanne seide dame Prudence, "I make no semblant of wratthe ne anger, but for youre grete profit. For Salomon seith, 'he is moore worth that repreveth or chideth a fool for his folye, shewynge hym semblant of wratthe, than he that supporteth hym and preyseth hym in his mysdoynge, and laugheth at his folye.' And this same Salomon seith afterward that 'by the sorweful visage of a man, 'that is to seyn by the sory and hevy contenaunce of a man, 'the fool correcteth and amendeth hymself.'"

§68 Thanne seyde Melibee, "I shal nat koone answere to so manye faire resouns as ye putten to me and shewen. Seyeth shortly youre wyl and youre conseil, and I am al redy to fulfille and parfourne it."

§69 Thanne dame Prudence discovered al hir wyl to hym, and seyde, "I conseille yow," quod she, "aboven alle thynges, that ye make pees bitwene God and yow; and beth reconsiled unto hym and to his grace. For, as I have seyd yow heer biforn, God hath suffred yow to have this tribulacioun and disese for youre synnes. And if ye do as I sey yow, God wol sende youre adversaries unto yow, and maken hem fallen at youre feet, redy to do

begun by others,' and the prophet says, 'Reject arguments and do good; look for peace and follow it, as much as you can.' Yet I'm not saying that you should ask your enemies for for peace any more than that they should offer offer it to you. For I know full well that you are so hardhearted that you won't do anything for me. Solomon says, 'Someone whose heart is too hard, ultimately he will have bad luck and misfortune.'"

When Melibeus saw that Dame Prudence looked angry, he said this: "Lady, I beg you you not to be annoyed by the things I say, for you know that I am full of anger, and it is no wonder; and they who are angry do not know clearly what they do or say. That is why the prophet says, 'troubled eyes do not see clearly.' But give me whatever advice you like, for I am ready to do exactly as you wish; and if you criticise me for my stupidity, I am all the more obliged to love and praise you. For Solomon says that 'someone who criticises the person who is being stupid, he will get more grace than the person who deceives him with sweet words.'"

Then Dame Prudence said, "I am not showing my anger except for your great advantage. For Solomon says, 'he is a better person who approves or criticises a fool for his stupidity than someone who supports him and praises him when he does wrong and laughs at his folly.' And this same Solomon said afterwards that the sad face of a man is what makes a fool change his ways."

Then Melibeus said, "I do not know how to answer the great number of good reasons you have shown me. Tell me what you advise, and I am ready to follow you."

Then Dame Prudence revealed all her desires to him and said, "I advise you," she said, "above all things, that you make peace between yourself and God, and that you become reconciled to him and his grace. For, as I have said to you already, God has allowed you to suffer this trial because of your sins. If you do as I tell you, God will send your enemies to you and make them fall at your

youre wyl and youre comande mentz. For Salomon seith, 'whan the condicioun of man is plesaunt and likynge to god, he chaungeth the hertes of the mannes adversaries and constreyneth hem to biseken hym of pees and of grace.' And I prey yow lat me speke with youre adversaries in privee place; for they shul nat knowe that it be of youre wyl or of youre adsent. And thanne, whan I knowe hir wil and hire entente, I may conseille yow the moore seurely.

§70 "Dame," quod Melibee, "dooth youre wil and youre likynge; for I putte me hoolly in youre disposicioun and ordinaunce."

§71 Thanne dame Prudence, whan she saugh the goode wyl of hir housbonde, delibered and took avys in hirself, thinkinge how she myghte brynge this nede unto a good conclusioun and to a good ende. And whan she saugh hir tyme, she sente for this adversaries to come unto hire into a pryvee place, and shewed wisely unto hem the grete goodes that comen of pees, and the grete harmes and perils that been in werre; and seyde to hem in a goodly manere hou that hem oughten have greet repentaunce of the injurie and wrong that they hadden doon to Melibee hir lord, and unto hire, and to hire doghter.

§72 And whan they herden the goodliche wordes of dame Prudence, they weren so supprised and ravysshed, and hadden so greet joye of hire that wonder was to telle. "A, lady," quod they, "ye han shewed unto us the blessynge of swetnesse, after the sawe of David the prophete; for the reconsilynge which we been nat worthy to have in no manere, but we oghte requeren it with greet contricioun and humylitee, ye of youre grete goodnesse have presented unto us. Now se we wel that the science and the konnynge of Salomon is ful trewe. For he seith that 'sweete wordes multiplien and encreescen freendes, and maken shrewes to be debonaire and meeke.'

§73 "Certes," quod they, "we putten oure dede and al oure matere and cause al hooly in youre goode wyl and been redy to obeye to the speche and comandement of my lord Melibee. And therfore, deere and benygne lady, we preien yow and biseke yow as mekely as we konne and mowen, that it lyke unto youre grete goodnesse to fulfillen in dede youre goodliche wordes. For we consideren and knowelichen that we han offended and greved

feet, ready to do exactly as you order. For Solomon says, 'When a man behaves in a way which is pleasant and pleasing to God, he changes the hearts of that man's enemies, and makes them beg him for his peace and kindness.' And I beg you to let me speak to your enemies in private, for they must not know that it is with your agreement. And then, when I know what they intend to do, I can advise you better."

"Lady," said Melibeus, "do what you will; I put myself completely in your hands,"

Then Dame Prudence, when she saw how well disposed her husband was, thought to herself, pondering how she could bring this urgent matter to a satisfactory conclusion. she saw the right time, she sent for these enemies to come to her at a private place, and intelligently showed them the greater good that would come from peace, and the great harm and peril from war, and said to them in a good fashion how they should be very repentant for the injury and wrong they had done to her Lord Melibeus, and to her, and to her daughter.

And when they heard the good words of Dame Prudence, they were so entranced and captivated and were so pleased by her that it was astonishing. "Oh, lady," said they, "you have showed us how blessed is forgiveness, according to the sayings of the the Prophet David, for we are not worthy to to have reconciliation in any way, but we ought to ask for it with great contrition and and humility, what you have offered us through your great goodness. Now we can see that the knowledge and cunning of Solomon is very true, for he said that 'sweet words increase the number of your friends and make villains gentle and meek.'

"Certainly," they said, "we put all of our actions and business in the hands of your goodwill and are ready to obey anything your Lord says. And therefore, dear kind lady, we pray and beg you as meekly as we know how that in your great goodness you can back up your good words, for we now acknowledge that we have offended and grieved my Lord Melibeus infinitely, so much

my lord Melibee out of mesure, so ferforth that we be nat of power to maken his amendes. And therfore we oblige and bynden us and oure freendes for to doon al his wyl and his comandementz. But peraventure he hath swich hevynesse and swich wratthe to us ward, by cause of oure offense, that he wole enjoyne us swich a peyne as we mowe nat bere ne susteene. And therfore, noble lady, we biseke to youre wommanly pitee to taken swich avysement in this nede that we, ne oure freendes, be nat desherited ne destroyed thurgh oure folye."

§74 "Certes," quod Prudence, "it is an hard thyng and right perilous that a man putte hym al outrely in the arbitracioun and juggement, and in the myght and power of his enemys. For Salomon seith, 'leeveth me, and yeveth credence to that I shal seyn: I seye,' quod he, 'ye peple, folk and governours of hooly chirche, to thy sone, to thy wyf, to thy freend, ne to thy broother, ne yeve thou nevere myght ne maistrie of thy body whil thou lyvest.' Now sithen he deffendeth that man sholde nat yeven to his broother ne to his freend the myght of his body, by a strenger resoun he deffendeth and forbedeth a man to yeven hymself to his enemy. And nathelees I conseille you that ye mystruste nat my lord, for I woot wel and knowe verraily that he is debonaire and meeke, large, curteys, and nothyng desirous ne coveitous of good ne richesse. For ther nys nothyng in this world that he desireth, save oonly worshipe and honour. Forthermoore I knowe wel and am right seur that he shal nothyng doon in this nede withouten my conseil; and I shal so werken in this cause that, by the grace of oure lord god, ye shul been reconsiled unto us."

§75 Thanne seyden they with o voys, "worshipful lady, we putten us and oure goodes al fully in youre wil and disposicioun, and been redy to comen, what day that it like unto youre noblesse to lymyte us or assigne us, for to maken oure obligacioun and boond as strong as it liketh unto youre goodnesse, that we mowe fulfille the wille of yow and of my lord Melibee.

§76 Whan dame Prudence hadde herd the answeres of thise men, she bad hem goon agayn prively; and she retourned to hir lord Melibee, and tolde hym how she foond his adversaries ful repentant, knowelechynge ful lowely hir synnes and trespas, and how they were redy to suffren al peyne, requirynge and preiynge hym of mercy and pitee.

so that we do not have the power to make amends. And so we pledge ourselves and all our friends to do whatever he orders. But perhaps he is so angry with us because of what we have done that he will impose a punishment on us that we cannot tolerate. And so, noble lady, we beg you through your womanly pity to take such steps in this urgent matter that neither we nor our friends lose our property or are destroyed through our foolishness."

"Certainly," said Prudence, "it is a hard thing and very dangerous for a man to put himself entirely under the power of the judgement of his enemies. For Solomon says, 'Believe me, listen to what I say: you people, congregation and governors of the holy Church, to your son, to your wife, to your friend nor to your brother should you ever give power or mastery over your body whilst you are alive.' Now since he forbids a man from giving his brother or his friend power over his body, for stronger reasons he forbids a man from handing himself into the power of his enemy. Nevertheless I advise you not to mistrust my Lord, for I know very well and truly that he is gentle, humble, generous, courteous and in no way covetous of goods or riches. There is nothing in this world which he desires, apart from worship and honour. Furthermore I know well, and I'm very sure, that he will do nothing in this urgent matter without my advice, and I shall work in this cause in such a way that by the grace of our Lord God you will be reconciled to us."

Then they said with one voice, "Worshipful lady, we place ourselves and all our goods fully in your power, and we are ready to come on whatever day your nobleness wishes to assign us, to make our pledge and bond in whatever way pleases you, so that we can surrender to the will of you and my lord Melibeus."

When Dame Prudence have the answers from these men, she told them to secretly go away again; and she went back to her Lord Melibeus, and told him how she had found his enemies were very repentant, admitting their sins and trespass very humbly, and saying how they were ready to suffer any punishment, begging him for mercy and pity.

§77 Thanne seyde Melibee: "he is wel worthy to have pardoun and foryifnesse of his synne. That excuseth nat his synne, but knowelecheth it and repenteth hym, axinge indulgence. For Senec seith, 'ther is the remissioun and foryifnesse, where as the confessioun is'; for confessioun is neighebor to innocence. And he seith in another place that 'he that hath shame of his synne and knowlecheth it, is worthy remissioun.' And therfore I assente and conferme me to have pees; but it is good that we do it nat withouten the assent and wyl of oure freendes."

§78 Thanne was Prudence right glad and joyeful, and seyde: "Certes, sire," quod she, "ye han wel and goodly answered; for right as by the conseil, assent, and help of youre freendes ye han been stired to venge yow and maken werre, right so withouten hire conseil shul ye nat accorden yow ne have pees with youre adversaries. For the lawe seith: 'ther nys no thyng so good by wey of kynde as a thyng to be unbounde by hym that it was ybounde.'"

§79 And thanne dame Prudence, withouten delay or tariynge, sente anon hire messages for hire kyn, and for hire olde freendes which that were trewe and wyse, and tolde hem by ordre in the presence of Melibee al this mateere as it is aboven expressed and declared, and preyden hem that they wolde yeven hire avys and conseil what best were to doon in this nede. And whan Melibees freendes hadde taken hire avys and deliberacioun of the forseide mateere, and hadden examyned it by greet bisynesse and greet diligence, they yave ful conseil for to have pees and reste, and that Melibee sholde receyve with good herte his adversaries to foryifnesse and mercy.

§80 And whan dame Prudence hadde herd the assent of hir lord Melibee, and the conseil of his freendes accorde with hire wille and hire entencioun, she was wonderly glad in hire herte, and seyde: "ther is an old proverbe," quod she, "seith that 'the goodnesse that thou mayst do this day, do it, and abide nat ne delaye it nat til tomorwe.' And therfore I conseille that ye sende youre messages, swiche as been discrete and wise, unto youre adversaries, tellynge hem on youre bihalve that if they wole trete of pees and of accord, that they shape hem withouten delay or tariyng to comen unto us." Which thyng parfourned

Then Melibeus said: "Someone is very deserving of being pardoned and forgiven for his sins, if he does not attempt to excuse his sin but acknowledges it and repents, asking for indulgence. For Seneca says, 'when someone confesses, there can be remission and orgiveness,' for confession is the next best thing to innocence. And he says in another place that 'he who knows what his sin is and acknowledges it is worthy of forgiveness.' And so I agree, I am determined that we shall have peace; but it would be best not to do it without the agreement of our friends."

Then Prudence was very glad and joyful and said, "Certainly, sir, you have answered very well, for just as by the advice, agreement and assistance of your friends you were inspired to start a war, so without their advice you will not reconcile or have peace with your enemies. For the law says, 'There is nothing so good in the natural world as for something to be released by the one who tied it up.'

And then Dame Prudence, without further ado, immediately sent messages for her family and her old friends who were wise and true, and told them fully, in the presence of Melibeus, all that had happened as is written above, and prayed them to give their advice as to what it was best to do in this urgent matter. And when the friends of Melibeus had taken her advice on this matter, and had carefully and laboriously looked it over, they all without reservation said that there should be peace, and that Melibeus should welcome his enemies with forgiveness and mercy with a good heart.

And when Dame Prudence heard her Lord Melibeus agree, and also all of her friends, she was wonderfully glad in her heart and said, "There is an old proverb, which says that 'If you can do a good thing on this day, do it, do not wait until tomorrow.' And so I advise you to send your messengers, ones who are wise and discreet, to your enemies, telling them on your behalf that if they want to negotiate peace and harmony they should get ready to come to us without delay. And this was done. And when these trespassers and people repenting their foolishness—that is to

was in dede. And whanne thise trespassours and repentynge folk of hire folies, that is to seyn, the adversaries of Melibee, hadden herd what thise messagers seyden unto hem, they weren right glad and joyeful, and answereden ful mekely and benignely, yeldynge graces and thankynges to hir lord Melibee and to al his compaignye; and shopen hem withouten delay to go with the messagers, and obeye to the comandement of hir Lord Melibee.

§81 And right anon they tooken hire wey to the court of Melibee, and tooken with hem somme of hire trewe freendes to maken feith for hem and for to been hire borwes. And whan they were comen to the presence of Melibee, he seyde hem thise wordes: "it standeth thus," quod Melibee, "and sooth it is, that ye, causelees and withouten skile and resoun, han doon grete injuries and wronges to me and to my wyf Prudence, and to my doghter also. For ye han entred into myn hous by violence, and have doon swich outrage that alle men knowen wel that ye have disserved the deeth. And therfore wol I knowe and wite of yow wheither ye wol putte the punyssement and the chastisynge and the vengeance of this outrage in the wyl of me and of my wyf Prudence, or ye wol nat?"

§82 Thanne the wiseste of hem thre answerde for hem alle, and seyde, "sire," quod he, "we knowen wel that we been unworthy to comen unto the court of so greet a lord and so worthy as ye been. For we han so greetly mystaken us, and han offended and agilt in swich a wise agayn youre heigh lordshipe, that trewely we han disserved the deeth. But yet, for the grete goodnesse and debonairetee that al the world witnesseth of youre persone, we submytten us to the excellence and benignitee of youre gracious lordshipe, and been redy to obeie to alle youre comandementz; bisekynge yow that of youre merciable pitee ye wol considere oure grete repentaunce and lowe submyssioun, and graunten us foryevenesse of oure outrageous trespas and offense. For wel we knowe that youre liberal grace and mercy strecchen hem ferther into goodnesse than doon oure outrageouse giltes and trespas into wikkednesse, al be it that cursedly and dampnablely we han agilt agayn youre heigh lordshipe."

§83 Thanne Melibee took hem up fro the ground ful benignely, and receyved hire obligaciouns and

say, the enemies of Melibeus—heard what these messengers said to them, they were extremely glad and joyful, and answered very meekly and kindly, giving thanks and gratitude to their Lord Melibeus and all his company, and they prepared to go with the messengers without delay and obey the command of their Lord Melibeus.

And at once they made their way to the court of Melibeus, and took with them some of their truest friends to act as hostages for them, and to stand guarantees for them. And when they came into the presence of Melibeus, he said these words to them: "This is how it stands: it is true that you, for no reason and without logical explanation, have done a great injury and harm to me and my wife Prudence and also to my daughter. For you broke into my house with violence, and have committed such outrages that everyone knows that you deserve to die. And so for I want to know whether you will put the punishment and revenge for this outrage in the hands of myself and my wife Prudence or not?"

Then the wisest of the three of them answered for them all and said, "Sir, we are well aware aware that we are unworthy to come into the court of such a great lord who is as good as you are. For we have so greatly transgressed, and have offended and wronged your high Lordship in such a way, that we have truly deserved death. But still, because of the great goodness and gentleness that all the world knows you possess, we hand ourselves over to the excellence and kindness of your gracious lordship, and we are ready to do all your bidding, begging you through your mercy and pity to consider how repentant we are, how we abase ourselves to you, and give us pardon for our outrageous trespass and offence. For we know that your liberal grace and mercy is far greater than our outrageous gilts and wickedness, even though we have so evilly and damnably sinned against your high lordship."

Then Melibeus very kindly picked them up from the ground, and took their pledges and

hir boondes by hire othes upon hire plegges and borwes, and assigned hem a certeyn day to retourne unto his court, for to accepte and receyve the sentence and juggement that Melibee wolde comande to be doon on hem by the causes aforeseyd. Whiche thynges ordeyned, every man retourned to his hous.

§84 And whan that dame Prudence saugh hir tyme, she freyned and axed hir lord Melibee what vengeance he thoughte to taken of his adversaries.

§85 To which Melibee answerde, and seyde: "Certes, quod he, I thynke and purpose me fully to desherite hem of al that evere they han, and for to putte hem in exil for evere.

§86 "Certes," quod dame Prudence, "this were a crueel sentence and muchel agayn resoun. For ye been riche ynough, and han no nede of oother mennes good; and ye myghte lightly in this wise gete yow a coveitous name, which is a vicious thyng, and oghte been eschued of every good man. For after the sawe of the word of the apostle, 'coveitise is roote of alle harmes.' And therfore it were bettre for yow to lese so muchel good of youre owene, than for to taken of hir good in this manere; for bettre it is to lesen good with worshipe, than it is to wynne good with vileynye and shame. And everi man oghte to doon his diligence and his bisynesse to geten hym a good name. And yet shal he nat oonly bisie hym in kepynge of his good name, but he shal also enforcen hym alwey to do somthyng by which he may renovelle his good name. For it is writen that 'the olde good loos or good name of a man is soone goon and passed, whan it is nat newed ne renovelled.' And as touchynge that ye seyn ye wole exile youre adversaries, that thynketh me muchel agayn resoun and out of mesure, considered the power that they han yeve yow upon hemself. And it is writen that 'he is worthy to lesen his privilege, that mysuseth the myght and the power that is yeven hym.' And I sette cas ye myghte enjoyne hem that peyne by right and by lawe, which I trowe ye mowe nat do, I seye ye mighte nat putten it to execucioun peraventure, and thanne were it likly to retourne to the werre as it was biforn. And therfore, if ye wole that men do yow obeisance, ye moste deemen moore curteisly; this is to seyn, ye moste yeven moore esy sentences and juggementz. For it is writen that 'he that moost curteisly comandeth, to hym men moost obeyen.' And therfore I prey yow that in this necessitee and

their bonds with their oaths from their pledges and guarantors, and told them of a certain date when they should return to his court to accept the sentence and judgement that he would impose on them for the reasons already mentioned. With these things arranged, everyone went back to their own home.

And when Dame Prudence saw the time was right, she asked her Lord Melibeus what revenge he meant to take on his enemies.

Melibeus answered her and said, "Certainly, I intend to take away all of their possessions, and to send them into permanent exile."

"Certainly," said Dame Prudence, "this would be a cruel sentence and very wrong. For you are rich enough and do not need the wealth of any other man, and you might easily be thought of as greedy because of this, which is horrible, and should be avoided by every good man. For according to the words of the apostle, 'Greed is the root of all evil.' And so it would be better for you to lose the same amount of your own wealth, rather than take theirs in this fashion, for it is better to lose wealth honourably than it is to gain it with felony and shameful methods. And every man ought to do his best and make it his main concern to have a good name. And yet he should not only make great efforts to keep his good name, he should also always be trying to make it better. For it has been written that, 'the previous good reputation or good name of a man soon passes, if he does not continually restore it.' With reference to you saying you will exile your enemies, I think that is very foolish and disproportionate, when you think of the power they have handed over to you. It is written that 'someone who misuses the power that is given to him deserves to lose it.' And I assume that you wish to impose that punishment on them through justice and law, which I think you cannot do; I think that you could not actually make it happen, and then then we would be back to war as we were before. And so, if you want men to obey you, you must be kind in your judgement; that is to say, you must give easier sentences. For it is written that 'the person who gives the the kindest commands is the one whom most most men will obey.' And so I pray you that in

in this nede ye caste yow to overcome youre herte. For Senec seith that 'he that overcometh his herte, overcometh twies.' And Tullius seith: "ther is no thyng so comendable in a greet lord as whan he is debonaire and meeke, and appeseth him lightly. And I prey yow that ye wole forbere now to do vengeance, in swich a manere that youre goode name may be kept and conserved, and that men mowe have cause and mateere to preyse yow of pitee and of mercy, and that ye have no cause to repente yow of thyng that ye doon. For Senec seith, 'he overcometh in an yvel manere that repenteth hym of his victorie.' Wherfore I pray yow, lat mercy been in youre herte, to th' effect and entente that God almighty have mercy on yow in his laste juggement. For Seint Jame seith in his epistle: 'juggement withouten mercy shal be doon to hym that hath no mercy of another wight.'"

§87 Whanne Melibee hadde herd the grete skiles and resouns of dame Prudence, and hire wise informaciouns and techynges, his herte gan enclyne to the wil of his wif, consideryinge hir trewe entente, and conformed hym anon, and assented fully to werken after hir conseil; and thonked God, of whom procedeth al vertu and alle goodnesse, that hym sente a wyf of so greet discrecioun. And whan the day cam that his adversaries sholde appieren in his presence, he spak unto hem ful goodly, and seyde in this wyse: "al be it so that of youre pride and heigh presumpcioun and folie, and of youre necligence and unkonnynge, ye have mysborn yow and trespassed unto me, yet for as muche as I see and biholde youre grete humylitee, and that ye been sory and repentant of youre giltes, it constreyneth me to doon yow grace and mercy. Wherfore I receyve yow to my grace, and foryeve yow outrely alle the offenses, injuries, and wronges that ye have doon agayn me and myne, to this effect and to this ende that God of his endelees mercy wole at the tyme of oure diyinge foryeven us oure giltes that we han trespassed to hym in this wrecched world. For doutelees, if we be sory and repentant of the synnes and giltes which we han trespassed in the sighte of oure lord God, he is so free and so merciable that he wole foryeven us oure giltes, and bryngen us to the blisse that nevere hath ende." Amen.

Heere is ended Chaucers Tale of Melibee and of Dame Prudence

The Monk's Tale

Whan ended was my tale of Melibee,
And of Prudence, and hir benignytee,
Oure hooste seyde, As I am feithful man,
And by that precious corpus Madrian,
I hadde levere than a barel ale
That goode lief my wyf hadde herd this tale!
She nys nothyng of swich pacience
As was this Melibeus wyf, Prudence.
By Goddes bones, whan I bete my knaves
She bryngeth me forth the grete clobbed staves,
And crieth, Slee the dogges, everichoon,
And brek hem, bothe bak and every boon.

And if that any neighebore of myne
Wol nat in chirche to my wyf enclyne,
Or be so hardy to hir to trespace,
Whan she comth hoom she rampeth in my face,
And crieth, `false coward, wrek thy wyf!
By corpus bones, I wol have thy knyf,
And thou shalt have my distaf and go spynne

Fro day to nyght!' Right thus she wol bigynne.

`Allas,' she seith, `that evere I was shape
To wedden a milksop or a coward ape,
That wol been overlad with every wight;
Thou darst nat stonden by thy wyves right!'

This is my lif, but if that I wol fighte,
And out at dore anon I moot me dighte,
Or elles I am but lost, but if that I
Be lik a wilde leoun fool-hardy.
I woot wel she wol do me slee som day
Som neighebore, and thanne go my way.
For I am perilous with knyf in honde,
Al be it that I dar hir nat withstonde.
For she is byg in armes, by my feith,
That shal he fynde that hir mysdooth or seith—

But lat us passe awey fro this mateere.

My lord the Monk, quod he, be myrie of cheere,
For ye shul telle a tale, trewely.
Loo, Rouchestre stant heer faste by.
Ryde forth, myn owene lord, brek nat oure game.

But, by my trouthe, I knowe nat youre name;
Wher shal I calle yow my lord daun John,
Or daun Thomas, or elles daun Albon?
Of what hous be ye, by youre fader kyn?

When I had finished my tale of Melibeus,
And Prudence and her goodness,
Our host said, "By my faith,
And by the precious body of Madrian,
I would give a barrel of ale
For Goodelief, my wife, to have heard this!
For she has nothing like the sort of patience
Shown by Melibeus' wife Prudence.
By the bones of God, when I beat my servants,
She brings me out great rough clubs
And cries out, ' Kill every one of the dogs,
And break them, their backs and all their bones.'

"And if any neighbour of mine
Won't bow to my wife in church,
Or is so brave as to offend her,
When she comes home she screams in my face,
And cries, 'False coward, defend your wife!
By the bones of God, I will take your knife,
And you will have my spinning staff and do the spinning!'
She will carry on like this from daybreak till nightfall.
'Alas,' she says, 'that I was ever born
To marry a milksop, a cowardly ape,
Who can be lorded over by everybody!
You don't dare to defend your wife's rights!'

This is my life, unless I fight;
And I have to hurry out of our door,
Or else I am pretty much lost, unless I
And as reckless as a wild lion.
I'm sure that one day she will make me kill
Some neighbour, and then I'll be on the run;
For I am dangerous with a knife in my hand,
Even though I don't dare to stand up to her,
For she is a strong fighter, I swear:
Anyone who says or does her wrong will find that out—
But let's talk about something else.

"My Lord, the monk," he said, "be happy,
For you must tell us a good tale.
Look, we're nearly at Rochester!
Come to the front, my own lord, keep the game going.

But, I swear, I don't know your name.
What shall I call you—my Lord Don John,
Or Don Thomas, or Don Albon?
What order of monks do you come from, by

I vowe to God, thou hast a ful fair skyn,	your father's family?
It is a gentil pasture ther thow goost.	I swear to God, you have very fair skin;
Thou art nat lyk a penant or a goost.	You must have eaten in fine pastures.
Upon my feith, thou art som officer,	You don't look like a penitent nor a ghost;
Som worthy sexteyn, or som celerer,	I swear, you are some sort of officer,
For by my fader soule, as to my doom,	Some good sexton, or quartermaster,
Thou art a maister whan thou art at hoom,	For on the sole of my father, as I judge,
No povre cloysterer, ne no novys,	You are the master when you are home;
	You are not some poor cloistered monk, nor are you a novice,
But a governour, wily and wys;	But a governor, cunning and wise,
And therwith-al of brawnes and of bones	And, as well as that, your muscles and bone
A wel-farynge persone, for the nones.	Make you a very handsome person indeed.
I pray to God, yeve hym confusioun	I pray to God, give trouble to the person
That first thee broghte unto religioun.	Who first introduced you to religion!
Thou woldest han been a tredefowel aright;	You would have been a fine old cockerel,
Haddwstow as greet a leeve as thou hast might	If you had as much leeway as you have power
To parfourne al thy lust in engendrure,	To use all your lusts for getting children,
Thou haddest bigeten ful many a creature.	You would have fathered a great many.
Allas, why werestow so wyd a cope?	Alas, why do you wear such a wide cloak?
God yeve me sorwe, but, and I were a pope,	I swear to God, that if I were Pope
Nat oonly thou but every myghty man	Not only you, but every strong man,
Though he were shorn ful hye upon his pan,	Even if he had the monk's haircut,
Sholde have a wyf, for al the world is lorn.	He would have a wife; otherwise the world is lost!
Religioun hath take up al the corn	Religion has taken up all our best
Of tredyng, and we borel men been shrympes.	Breeders, and we laymen are just like shrimps.
Of fieble trees ther comen wrecched ympes.	From such feeble trees you only get weak branches.
This maketh that our heyres ben so sclendre	Our heirs are so scrawny
And feble, that they may nat wel engendre;	And feeble they won't have any good children.
This maketh that oure wyves wole assaye	That's what makes our wives want to try
Religious folk, for ye mowe bettre paye	Religious men, for you are better at playing
Of Venus paiementz than mowe we;	The price of Venus than we are;
God woot no lussheburghes payen ye.	God knows, you don't pay with shabby coins!
But be nat wrooth, my lord, for that I pleye,	But don't be angry, my lord, although I'm joking,
Ful ofte in game a sooth I have herd seye.	I've often heard a true word said in jest!"
This worthy Monk took al in pacience,	This good monk took all this calmly,
And seyde, I wol doon al my diligence,	And said, "I will devote all my efforts,
As fer as sowneth into honestee,	As far as propriety allows,
To telle yow a tale, or two, or three.	To tell you a tale, or two, or three.
And if yow list to herkne hyderward	And if you want to listen to me,
I wol yow seyn the lyf of seint Edward;	I will tell you of the life of St Edward;
Or ellis first tragedies wol I telle	Or otherwise, first, I will tell you some tragedies,
Of whiche I have an hundred in my celle.	Which I have a hundred of in my room.
Tragedie is to seyn, a certeyn storie,	Tragedy means telling a certain story,
As olde bookes maken us memorie,	Once the old books make us remember,
Of hym that stood in greet prosperitee	Or someone who was once in great prosperity,
And is yfallen out of heigh degree	And has fallen from his high degree
Into myserie, and endeth wrecchedly,	Into misery, and comes to a wretched end.
And they ben versified communely	Normally they are in verses
Of six feet, which men clepen exametron.	Of six feet, which men call hexameters.

In prose eek been endited many oon,	There are also many composed in prose,
And eek in meetre, in many a sondry wyse.	And also in metres of many different sorts.
Lo, this declaryng oghte ynogh suffise;	This explanation should be enough.
Now herkneth, if yow liketh for to heere.	Now listen, if you want to hear.
But first, I yow biseeke in this mateere,	But first I must excuse myself,
Though I by ordre telle nat this thynges,	If I don't tell these things in their right order,
Be it of popes, emperours, or kynges,	Whether it be popes, emperors or kings,
After hir ages, as men writen fynde,	According to the times, as men find them,
But tellen hem, som bifore and som bihynde,	But tell of them in the wrong order,
As it now comth unto my remembraunce;	Just as they come to my mind.
Have me excused of myn ignoraunce.	Please excuse my ignorance.

The Monk's Tale

Heere bigynneth the Monkes Tale	*Here begins the Monk's Tale*
De Casibus Virorum Illustrium.	*Concerning the Fates of Famous Men*
I wol biwaille in manere of Tragedie	I will sadly relate in a tragic manner
The harm of hem that stoode in heigh degree,	The harm which came to those who had high position,
And fillen so, that ther nas no remedie	Who fell so low that there was nothing
To brynge hem out of hir adversitee.	Which could save them from adversity.
For certein, whan that Fortune list to flee,	For certainly, when Fortune abandons you,
Ther may no man the cours of hire withholde;	No man can stop her from moving on.
Lat no man truste on blynd prosperitee;	Let no man put his faith in blind prosperity;
Be war of thise ensamples, trewe and olde.	Be warned by these true and ancient examples.
Lucifer	*Lucifer*
At Lucifer, though he an aungel were,	With Lucifer, although he was an angel
And nat a man, at hym wol I biginne,	And not a man, I will begin.
For though Fortune may noon aungel dere,	For although Fortune cannot harm an angel,
From heigh degree yet fel he for his synne	Through his sin he fell from his high position
Doun into helle, where he yet is inne.	Down into hell, where he still is.
O Lucifer, brightest of aungels alle,	O Lucifer, brightest of all Angels,
Now artow Sathanas, that mayst nat twynne	Now you are Satan, who cannot leave
Out of miserie, in which that thou art falle.	His misery, into which you have fallen.
Adam	*Adam*
Loo Adam, in the feeld of Damyssene,	See Adam, in the field of Damascus,
With Goddes owene fynger wroght was he,	Made with God's own hand,
And nat bigeten of mannes sperme unclene,	Not made from the unclean sperm of man,
And welte all Paradys, savynge o tree.	Who ruled over all of paradise except for one tree.
Hadde nevere worldly man so heigh degree	No earthly man ever had such a high position
As Adam, til he, for mysgovernaunce,	As Adam, until he, for misconduct,
Was dryven out of hys hye prosperitee	Was driven out of his great position
To labour, and to helle, and to meschaunce.	To work, and suffer hell and ruin.
Sampson	*Samson*
Loo Sampson, which that was annunciat	Look at Samson, who was announced
By angel, longe er his nativitee,	By the angel long before he was born,
And was to God almyghty consecrat,	And was consecrated to Almighty God,

And stood in noblesse whil he myghte see,	And had a noble position whilst he could still see.
Was nevere swich another as was hee,	There was never another man like him,
To speke of strengthe and therwith hardynesse;	In strength, and also in bravery;
But to hise wyves toolde he his secree,	But he told his secrets to his wives,
Thurgh which he slow hymself for wrecchednesse.	And so he killed himself through wretchedness.
Sampsoun, this noble almyghty champioun,	Samson, this noble great champion,
Withouten wepene, save his handes tweye,	With no weapons but his two hands,
He slow and al torente the leoun	He killed and tore the lion to pieces,
Toward his weddyng walkynge by the weye.	As he was walking on his way to his wedding.
His false wyf koude hym so plese and preye	His false wife could please him and she could pry
Til she his conseil knew, and she untrewe	Until she had found out all his secrets; and she, unfaithful,
Unto hise foos his conseil gan biwreye,	Gave his secrets away to his enemies
And hym forsook, and took another newe.	And abandoned him, taking another lover.
Thre hundred foxes took Sampson for ire,	In his anger Samson took three hundred foxes,
And alle hir tayles he togydre bond,	And tied all their tails together,
And sette the foxes tayles alle on fire;	And set all of them on fire,
For he on every tayl had knyt a brond,	For he had tied a torch to every tail;
And they brende alle the cornes in that lond,	And they burnt all the corn in that land,
And alle hir olyveres and vynes eke.	And all the olive trees, and also the vines.
A thousand men he slow eek with his hond,	He killed a thousand men with his hands,
And hadde no wepene but an asses cheke.	With no weapon except for the jawbone of an ass.
Whan they were slayn, so thursted hym, that he	When they were killed, he was so thirsty that he
Was wel ny lorn, for which he gan to preye	Almost died, and so he prayed
That God wolde on his peyne han som pitee,	For God to take pity on his pain
And sende hym drynke, or elles moste he deye;	And send him some drink, because otherwise he must die;
And of this asses cheke, that was dreye,	And from this dry jawbone of an ass
Out of a wang-tooth sprang anon a welle	A well sprang at once from a molar,
Of which he drank anon, shortly to seye,	And to say briefly, he had plenty to drink;
Thus heelp hym God, as Judicum can telle.	So God helped him, as the book of Judges tells us.
By verray force at Gazan, on a nyght,	Through sheer force, one night at Gaza,
Maugree Philistiens of that citee,	Despite the Philistines in that city,
The gates of the toun he hath upplyght,	He ripped up the town gates,
And on his bak ycaryed hem hath he	And he carried on his back
Hye on an hille, that men myghte hem see.	High up on a hill where men could see them.
O noble almyghty Sampson, lief and deere,	O noble, almighty Samson, beloved and precious,
Had thou nat toold to wommen thy secree,	If you had not told women your secret,
In all this world ne hadde been thy peere.	Nobody in the world could have beaten you!
This Sampson nevere ciser drank, ne wyn,	This Samson never drank any alcohol, no wine,
Ne on his heed cam rasour noon, ne sheere,	And no razor or scissors ever touched his head,

By precept of the messager divyn,	Through the orders of the divine messenger,
For alle hise strengthes in hise heeres weere.	For all his power was in his hair.
And fully twenty wynter, yeer by yeere,	And for fully twenty years in a row
He hadde of Israel the governaunce.	He ruled over Israel.
But soone shal he wepen many a teere,	But soon he would weep many tears,
For wommen shal hym bryngen to meschaunce!	For women would bring him misfortune!
Unto his lemman Dalida he tolde	To his sweetheart Delilah he told the secret
That in hise heeres al his strengthe lay,	That all of his strength was in his hair,
And falsly to hise fooman she hym solde;	And she treacherously sold him to his enemies.
And slepynge in hir barme upon a day	Sleeping with his head on her bosom one day,
She made to clippe or shere hise heres away,	She managed to cut or shear his hair away,
And made hise foomen al this craft espyn.	And let his enemies know of his secret,
And whan that they hym foond in this array,	And when they found him in this state
They bounde hym faste, and putten out hise eyen.	They tied him securely and cut out his eyes.
But er his heer were clipped or yshave,	But before his hair was clipped or shaven,
Ther was no boond with which men myght him bynde,	There were no bonds with which men could tie him;
But now is he in prison in a cave,	But now he was imprisoned in a cave,
Where as they made hym at the queerne grynde.	Where they made him work grinding corn.
O noble Sampson, strongest of mankynde,	O noble Sampson, strongest man of all,
O whilom juge in glorie and in richesse,	Formerly a judge, with glory and riches!
Now maystow wepen with thyne eyen blynde,	Now you can weep with your blind eyes,
Sith thou fro wele art falle in wrecchednesse!	Since you have fallen into wretchedness from prosperity.
The ende of this caytyf was as I shal seye;	The end of this prisoner came as I shall describe.
Hise foomen made a feeste upon a day,	His enemies had a feast one day,
And made hym as hir fool biforn hem pleye.	And they made him caper before them as their fool;
And this was in a temple of greet array;	And this was in a very great temple.
But atte laste he made a foul affray,	But in the end he made a shocking attack,
For he two pilers shook, and made hem falle,	For he shook a pair of pillars and made them fall,
And doun fil temple and al, and ther it lay,	And down fell the whole temple, and there it lay—
And slow hymself, and eek his foomen alle.	It killed him, and also his enemies.
This is to seyn, the prynces everichoon,	That is to say, all of the Princes,
And eek thre thousand bodyes were ther slayn	And also three thousand men, were killed there
With fallynge of the grete temple of stoon.	By the collapse of the great stone temple.
Of Sampson now wol I namoore sayn:	I will now say no more about Sampson.
Beth war by this ensample oold and playn	Be wary of this clear ancient warning
That no men telle hir conseil til hir wyves	That no man should tell his secrets to his wife
Of swich thyng as they solde han secree fayn,	If they really want to keep them secret,
If that it touche hir lymmes or hir lyves.	If it concerns their bodies or their lives.
Hercules	Hercules
Off Hercules the sovereyn conquerour	Of Hercules, the supreme conqueror,
Syngen hise werkes laude and heigh renoun,	His works and frame are greatly praised;
For in his tyme of strengthe he was the flour.	For in his time he was the epitome of strength.
He slow and rafte the skyn of the leoun,	He killed and skinned the lion;

He of Centauros leyde the boost adoun,
He arpies slow, the cruel bryddes felle,
He golden apples refte of the dragoun,
He drow out Cerberus the hound of helle.
He slow the crueel tyrant Busirus,
And made his hors to frete hym, flessh and boon;
He slow the firy serpent venymus,
Of Acheloys two hornes, he brak oon.
And he slow Cacus in a Cave of stoon;
He slow the geaunt Antheus the stronge,
He slow the grisly boor, and that anon,

And bar the hevene on his nekke longe.

Was nevere wight, sith that this world bigan,

That slow so manye monstres as dide he.
Thurghout this wyde world his name ran,

What for his strengthe, and for his heigh bountee,
And every reawme wente he for to see.
He was so stroong that no man myghte hym lette;
At bothe the worldes endes, seith Trophee,
In stide of boundes, he a pileer sette.

A lemman hadde this noble champioun,
That highte Dianira, fressh as May,
And as thise clerkes maken mencioun,
She hath hym sent a sherte fressh and gay.
Allas, this sherte, allas, and weylaway!
Envenymed was so subtilly withalle,
That er that he had wered it half a day
It made his flessh al from hise bones falle.

But nathelees somme clerkes hir excusen
By oon that highte Nessus, that it maked.

Be as be may, I wol hir noght accusen;
But on his bak this sherte he wered al naked,
Til that his flessh was for the venym blaked;
And whan he saugh noon oother remedye,
In hoote coles he hath hym-selven raked,
For with no venym deigned hym to dye.

Thus starf this worthy myghty Hercules.
Lo, who may truste on Fortune any throwe?
For hym that folweth al this world of prees,
Er he be war, is ofte yleyd ful lowe.

Ful wys is he that kan hymselven knowe.
Beth war, for whan that Fortune list to glose,

Thanne wayteth she her man to overthrowe,

He suppressed the arrogance of the centaurs;
He killed the Harpies, those fierce cruel birds;
He stole the golden apples of the dragon;
He dragged the hound Cerberus out of hell;
He killed the cruel tyrant Busirus
And made his horses eat him, flesh and bone;
He killed the fiery poisonous serpent;
He broke one of the two horns of Achelous;
And he killed Cacus in a stone cave;
He killed the strong giant Antheus;
He killed the horrible boar, and that very quickly;
And for a long time carried the skies on his back.

There was never a person, since the beginning of the world,
Who killed as many monsters as he did.
His name was famous throughout the wide world,
What with his strength and his great goodness,
And he travelled through every country.
He was so strong that no man could stop him.
At both ends of the world, so Trophee says,
He placed pillars instead of boundary markers.

This noble champion had a lover,
Who was called Dianira, fresh as May;
And as the scholars mention,
She sent him a shirt, fresh and sweet.
Alas, this shirt–alas, curse the day!–
Was so cunningly poisoned
That before he had worn it for half a day
All his flesh fell from his bones.

Nevertheless some scholars excuse her
Saying that the blame lies with Nessus who made it.

Be that as it may, I will not accuse her;
But he put this shirt on his naked back
Until his flesh turned black from the poison.
And when he could see no other choice,
He had himself buried in hot coals,
For he refused to die from poison.

So the good mighty Hercules died.
See, who can place any trust in fortune?
He who follows the ways of this perilous world
Often is laid low before he knows what's happening.

It's a wise man who knows himself!
Be careful, for when Fortune wants to deceive you,
Then she waits to ambush her man

By swich a wey, as he wolde leest suppose.	*With such means that he would never imagine.*
Nabugodonosor	*Nebuchadnezzar*
The myghty trone, the precious tresor	*The great throne, that precious treasure,*
The golrious ceptre and roial magestee	*The glorious sceptre, and royal majesty*
That hadde the kyng Nabugodonosor,	*That Nebuchadnezzar had*
With tonge unnethe may discryved bee.	*Can hardly be described in speech.*
He twyes wan Jerusalem the citee;	*He twice captured the city of Jerusalem;*
The vessel of the temple he with hym ladde.	*He took the vessels of the temple with him.*
At Babiloigne was his sovereyn see,	*He had his royal throne at Babylon,*
In which his glorie and his delit he hadde.	*Where he enjoyed his glory and his pleasures.*
The faireste children of the blood roial	*The fairest children of the royal blood*
Of Israel he leet do gelde anoon,	*Of Israel he had castrated,*
And make ech of hem to been his thral.	*Making each one of them his slave.*
Amonges othere, Daniel was oon,	*Amongst others there was Daniel,*
That was the wiseste child of everychon;	*Who was the wisest child of all of them,*
For he the dremes of the kyng expouned	*For he explained the dreams of the King,*
Wheras in Chaldeye clerk ne was ther noon	*Whereas in Chaldea there was no scholar*
That wiste to what fyn hise dremes sowned.	*Who could explain what his dreams meant.*
This proude kyng leet maken a statue of gold	*This proud king had a statue made of gold,*
Sixty cubites long, and sevene in brede,	*Sixty cubits long and seven wide,*
To which ymage bothe yonge and oold	*And he ordered both young and old*
Comaunded he to loute and have in drede,	*To bow to this image and worship it,*
Or in a fourneys ful of flambes rede	*Or he would burn the ones who would not obey*
He shal be brent, that wolde noght obeye.	*In a furnace full of red flames.*
But nevere wolde assente to that dede	*But neither Daniel nor his two young companions*
Daniel, ne hise yonge felawes tweye.	*Would ever agree to do that.*
This kyng of kynges proud was and elaat;	*This king of kings was proud and arrogant;*
He wende, that God that sit in magestee	*He thought that God, who sits on high,*
Ne myghte hym nat bireve of his estaat;	*Could not take his position away from him.*
But sodeynly he loste his dignytee,	*But suddenly he lost his great position,*
And lyk a beest hym semed for to bee,	*And he seemed to become like an animal,*
And eet hey as an oxe and lay theroute;	*And he ate hay like an ox, and slept outside*
In reyn with wilde beestes walked hee	*In the rain; he walked with wild beasts*
Til certein tyme was ycome aboute.	*Until a certain period had passed.*
And lik an egles fetheres wex his heres,	*His hair grew like the feathers of an eagle;*
Hise nayles lyk a briddes clawes weere,	*His nails were like the claws of a bird;*
Til God relessed hym a certeyn yeres,	*Then after a certain number of years God released him,*
And yaf hym wit, and thanne, with many a teere,	*And gave him back his wits, and then with many tears*
He thanked God; and evere his lyf in feere	*He thanked God, and for the rest of his life he was afraid*
Was he to doon amys, or moore trespace,	*To do anything wrong or to commit any more sin;*
And til that tyme he leyd was on his beere,	*And until the time he went to his grave*
He knew that God was ful of myght and grace.	*He knew that God was full of strength and grace.*
Balthasar	*Balthazar*

397

His sone which that highte Balthasar, That heeld the regne after his fader day, He by his fader koude noght be war,	His son, who was called Balthazar, Who ruled after his father was gone, Would not take warning from the example of his father,
For proud he was of herte and of array;	For he was arrogant in his soul and his behaviour,
And eek an ydolastre he was ay. His hye estaat assured hym in pryde;	And also he was always an idolater. His great position gave him confidence and arrogance;
But Fortune caste hym doun and ther he lay, And sodeynly his regne gan divide.	But Fortune threw him down, and there he lay, And suddenly his reign began to shatter.
A feeste he made unto hise lordes alle Upon a tyme, and bad hem blithe bee,	He ordered a feast for all his lords At one time and bade them to enjoy themselves;
And thanne hise officeres gan he calle, Gooth, bryngeth forth the vesseles, quod he, Whiche that my fader, in his prosperitee, Out of the temple of Jerusalem birafte, And to oure hye goddes thanke we Of honour, that oure eldres with us lafte.	And then he called his officers: "Go, bring out the vesseles," he said, "Which my father, when he was flourishing, Robbed from the Temple of Jerusalem; And let us give thanks to our high gods For the honour which our predecessors left us."
Hys wyf, hise lordes, and hise concubynes Ay dronken, whil hire appetites laste, Out of thise noble vessels sondry wynes. And on a wal this kyng hise eyen caste, And saugh an hand armlees that wroot ful faste,	His wife, his lords and his mistresses All drank, until they were full, Different wines from these noble cups. And the King looked at the wall And saw a hand without an arm that wrote very fast,
For feere of which he quook and siked soore. This hand, that Balthasar so soore agaste, Wroot `Mame, techel, phares,' and na moore.	And the fear of it made him shake and moan. This hand which terrified Balthazar so much Wrote Mane, techel, phares, that was all.
In al that land magicien was noon That koude expounde what this lettre mente. But Daniel expowned it anon, And seyde, Kyng, God to thy fader lente Glorie and honour, regne, tresour, rente;	In all of that land there was no magician Who could explain what this text meant; But Daniel explained it at once, And said, "King, God lent to your father Glory and honour, power, treasure and income;
And he was proud, and nothyng God ne dradde, And therfore God greet wreche upon hym sente, And hym birafte the regne that he hadde.	And he was proud and did not respect God, And so God took great revenge on him, And took away all of his power.
He was out-cast of mannes compaignye,	He was thrown out of the company of mankind;
With asses was his habitacioun, And eet hey as a beest in weet and drye, Til that he knew by grace and by resound	He had to live with the asses, And he ate hay like an animal in all weathers Until he knew, through grace and through reason,
That God of hevene hath domynacioun Over every regne and every creature, And thanne hadde God of hym compassioun And hym restored his regne and his figure.	That God in heaven rules over Every kingdom, and every creature; And then God took pity on him, And gave him back his power and his body.
Eek thou that art his sone art proud also,	Also you, who are his son, are arrogant,

And knowest alle thise thynges verraily,	*And you know all these things truly,*
And art rebel to God and art his foo.	*And you rebel against God, and you are his enemy.*
Thou drank eek of hise vessels boldely,	*You boldly drank out of his vessels;*
Thy wyf eek, and thy wenches sinfully	*Your wife, and your women, sinfully*
Dronke of the same vessels sondry wynys,	*Drank various wines out of the same vessels;*
And heryest false goddes cursedly;	*And evilly worshiped false gods;*
Therfore to thee yshapen ful greet pyne ys.	*So great pain is coming to you.*
This hand was sent from God, that on the wal	*This hand was sent from God which wrote*
Wroot `Mane techel phares,' truste me!	*Mane, techel, pares on the wall, trust me;*
Thy regne is doon, thou weyest noght at al,	*Your reign is ended, you are now nothing.*
Dyvyded is thy regne, and it shal be	*Your kingdom is broken up, and it will be*
To Medes and to Perses yeve, quod he.	*Given to Medes and the Persians," he said.*
And thilke same nyght this kyng was slawe	*And the same night this King was killed,*
And Darius occupyeth his degree,	*And Darius took over his throne,*
Thogh he therto hadde neither right ne lawe.	*Although he had no right and no legal claim.*
Lordynges, ensample heer-by may ye take	*Gentlemen, you may take the lesson from this*
How that in lordshipe is no sikernesse;	*That there is no security in being a lord,*
For whan Fortune wole a man forsake,	*For when Fortune abandons a man,*
She bereth awey his regne and his richesse,	*She takes away his power and his riches,*
And eek hise freendes, bothe moore and lesse,	*And also his friends, the high and low.*
For what man that hath freendes thurgh Fortune	*For whatever man who has friends due to Fortune,*
Mishap wol maken hem enemys, as I gesse;	*I believe that misfortune will turn them into enemies;*
This proverbe is ful sooth and ful commune.	*This proverb is very true and is often proved.*
Cenobia	*Zenobia*
Cenobia, of Palymerie queene,	*Zenobia, Queen of Palmyra,*
As writen Persiens of hir noblesse,	*According to the Persians who wrote of her nobility,*
So worthy was in armes, and so keene,	*Was so fine in battle and so fierce*
That no wight passed hir in hardynesse,	*That nobody surpassed her bravery,*
Ne in lynage, ne in oother gentillesse.	*Nor her ancestry, nor her other noble attributes.*
Of kynges blood of Perce is she descended.	*She was descended from Kings of Persia.*
I seye nat that she hadde moost fairnesse,	*I won't say that she was the most beautiful,*
But of hire shap she myghte nat been amended.	*But her body could not be improved upon.*
From hir childhede I fynde that she fledde	*From her childhood I have heard that she abandoned*
Office of wommen, and to wode she wente,	*The duties of women, and went into the woods,*
And many a wilde hertes blood she shedde	*And killed many wild deer there with*
With arwes brode, that she to hem sente.	*Broad headed arrows that she fired at them.*
She was so swift that she anon hem hente,	*She was so swift that she quickly captured them;*
And whan that she was elder, she wolde kille	*And when she was older, she would kill*
Leouns, leopardes, and beres al to-rente,	*Lions, leopards, and she would tear bears to pieces,*
And in hir armes weelde hem at hir wille.	*And she could subdue them through the strength of her arms.*

She dorste wilde heestes dennes seke,	*She dared to seek out the dens of wild beasts,*
And rennen in the montaignes al the nyght	*And she ran through the mountains in the night,*
And slepen under the bussh, and she koude eke	*And slept under bushes, and she could also*
Wrastlen by verray force and verray myght	*Wrestle, with great force and strength*
With any yong man, were he never so wight;	*With any young man, however strong he was.*
Ther myghte nothyng in hir armes stonde.	*Nobody could fight against her.*
She kepte hir maydenhod from every wight,	*She kept her virginity from every person;*
To no man deigned hir for to be bonde.	*She refused to be bound to any man.*
But atte laste hir freendes han hir maried	*But in the end her friends married her*
To Odenake, a prynce of that contree,	*To Odenake, a prince of that country,*
Al were it so that she hem longe taried,	*Although she made them wait a very long time.*
And ye shul understonde how that he	*You must understand that he*
Hadde swiche fantasies as hadde she.	*Had the same inclinations as her.*
But nathelees, whan they were knyt infeere,	*But nevertheless, when they were joined together,*
They lyved in joye and in felicitee,	*They lived in joy and happiness,*
For ech of hem hadde oother lief and deere;	*For each of them loved the other very much.*
Save o thyng, that she wolde nevere assente	*Except for one thing: she would never agree*
By no wey that he sholde by hir lye	*In any way for him to sleep with her*
But ones, for it was hir pleyn entente	*Except once, for she very much wanted*
To have a child the world to multiplye;	*To have a child, to increase the population;*
And also soone as that she myghte espye	*And as soon as she could see*
That she was nat with childe with that dede,	*That she was not pregnant from that time,*
Thanne wolde she suffre hym doon his fantasye	*Then she would let him have his way*
Eft-soone and nat but oones, out of drede.	*Again, but certainly only once.*
And if she were with childe at thilke cast,	*And if she then became pregnant,*
Namoore sholde he pleyen thilke game	*He would never be allowed to play that game again*
Til fully fourty dayes weren past;	*Until forty weeks had passed;*
Thanne wolde she ones suffre hym do the same.	*Then she would once again let him do the same thing.*
Al were this Odenake wilde or tame,	*Whether Odenake obeyed or raged,*
He gat no moore of hir, for thus she seyde,	*He could have no more from her, for she said this:*
It was to wyves lecheie and shame	*That it was lascivious and shameful for wives*
In oother caas, it that men with hem pleyde.	*To have sex for any other reason.*
Two sones by this Odenake hadde she,	*She had two sons from this Odenake,*
The whiche she kepte in vertu and lettrure,	*Whom she brought up virtuous and educated.*
But now unto oure tale turne we;	*But now we shall turn to our story.*
I seye, so worshipful a creature,	*I say, that there was never such a respectful creature,*
And wys ther-with, and large with mesure,	*Also wise, generous but not profligate,*
So penyble in the werre, and curteis eke,	*So hardy in war, and also courteous,*
Ne moore labour myghte in werre endure,	*Who would not tolerate any more war,*
Was noon, though al this world men wolde seke.	*Throughout the entire world.*
Hir riche array ne myghte nat be told	*Her rich adornments cannot be described,*
As wel in vessel as in hir clothyng;	*Her household things as well as her clothes.*
She was al clad in perree and in gold,	*She was dressed in precious stones and gold,*

And eek she lafte noght for noon hunting To have of sondry tonges ful knowyng, Whan that she leyser hadde, and for to entende To lerne bookes was al hire likyng, How she in vertu myghte hir lyf dispende.	And she did not neglect any effort To learn various tongues, When she had spare time; and to try To learn from books was all she wanted, To tell her how she could live her life virtuously.
And shortly of this proces for to trete, So doghty was hir housbonde and eek she, That they conquered manye regnes grete In the orient, with many a faire citee, Apertenaunt unto the magestee Of Rome, and with strong hond held hem ful faste,	And to cut a long story short, She and her husband were both so powerful That they conquered many great kingdoms In the orient, with many fair cities Belonging to the majesty Of Rome, and they held them tight with strong hands.
Ne nevere myghte hir foomen doon hem flee, Ay whil that Odenakes dayes laste.	Their enemies could never make them flee, The whole time that Odenake was alive.
Hir batailles, who-so list hem for to rede,	Their battles, if anyone wants to read about them,
Agayn Sapor the kyng and othere mo, And how that al this proces fil in dede, Why she conquered, and what title had therto, And after of hir meschief and hire wo,	Against King Shapur and many others, And how the whole business came about, Why she conquered and what claims she had, And afterwards, of all her troubles and sorrows,
How that she was biseged and ytake, Lat hym unto my maister Petrak go,	How she was besieged and captured— Let anyone who wants to know of this go to my master Petrarch,
That writ ynough of this, I undertake.	Whom I can promise you wrote plenty about this.
Whan Odenake was deed, she myghtily The regnes heeld; and with hir propre hond Agayn hir foos she faught so cruelly That ther nas kyng ne prynce in al that lond	When Odenake died, she strongly held The throne, and with her own hands She fought against her enemies so cruelly That there was not a king or a prince in any land
That he nas glad, if he that grace fond That she ne wolde upon his lond werreye. With hir they makded alliance by bond	Who was not glad, if he had the luck, For her to not fight against his realm. They made friendships with her through treaties
To been in pees, and let hire ride and pleye.	To remain peaceful, and let her do as she wished.
The Emperour of Rome, Claudius, Ne hym bifore, the Romayn Galien, Ne dorste nevere been so corageus, Ne noon Ermyn, ne noon Egipcien, Ne Surrien, ne noon arabyen, With-inne the feeldes that dorste with hir fighte, Lest that she wolde hem with hir handes slen, Or with hir meignee putten hem to flighte.	The emperor of Rome, Claudius, Nor before him, the Roman Galien, Never dared to be so brave, Nor did any Armenian, nor any Egyptian, No Syrian, and no Arabian, Dared to face her in battle, In case she killed them with her hands, Or with her troops made them flee.
In kynges habit wente hir sones two As heires of hir fadres regnes alle,	Her sons went about in the clothes of a king, And they were the heirs to all their father's kingdoms,
And Hermanno, and Thymalao	And they were called Hermanno and Thymalo

Hir names were, as Persiens hem calle.	By the Persians.
But ay Fortune hath in hir hony galle;	But always Fortune has bitterness in her honey;
This myghty queene may no while endure.	This great queen could no longer survive.
Fortune out of hir regne made hir falle	Fortune made her lose her throne
To wrecchednesse and to mysaventure.	In wretchedness and bad luck.
Aurelian, whan that the governaunce	Aurelian, when the rule
Of Rome cam into hise handes tweye,	Of Rome came into his hands,
He shoope upon this queene to doon vengeaunce,	Began to plan vengeance on this queen.
And with hise legions he took his weye	With his legions he made his way
Toward Cenobie, and shortly for to seye,	Towards Zenobia, and to say it briefly,
He made hir flee and atte last hir hente,	He made her flee, and in the end he captured her,
And fettred hir, and eek hir children tweye,	And put her in chains, and also her two children,
And wan the land, and hoom to Rome he wente.	And conquered the land and then he went home to Rome.
Amonges othere thynges that he wan,	Amongst other things which he won,
Hir chaar, that was with gold wroght and perree,	Her chariot, that was covered with gold and precious stones,
This grete Romayn, this Aurelian,	This great Roman, this Aurelian,
Hath with hym lad for that men sholde it see.	Took with him, so that men could see it.
Biforen his triumphe walketh shee,	She walked in front of his triumphal procession,
With gilte cheynes on hir nekke hangynge;	With gold chains hanging round her neck.
Coroned was she, after hir degree,	She was crowned, according to her rank,
And ful of perree charged hir clothynge.	And her clothing was covered with precious stones.
Allas, Fortune! she that whilom was	Alas, Fortune! She that was formerly
Dredful to kynges and to emperoures,	Terrifying to kings and emperors,
Now gaureth al the peple on hir, allas!	Is now stared at by all the people, alas!
And she that helmed was in starke shoures	And she who wore a helmet in terrible battles
And wan by force townes stronge and toures	And won fortified towns by force,
Shal on hir heed now were a vitremyte,	Now has to wear a woman's scarf on her head;
And she that bar the ceptre ful of floures	And she who carried a flourishing sceptre
Shal bere a distaf, hir costes for to quyte.	Must now carry a spinning staff, to earn her living.
De Petro Rege Ispannie	About Pedro, King of Castile
O noble, O worthy Petro, glorie of Spayne!	O noble, O worthy Pedro, Glory of Spain,
Whom Fortune heeld so hye in magestee,	Whom fortune placed in such high position,
Wel oghten men thy pitous deeth complayne;	It's certainly right for men to bemoan your horrible death!
Out of thy land thy brother made thee flee,	Your brother made you run from your land,
And after at a seege by subtiltee	And afterwards, at a siege, through cunning,
Thou were bitraysed, and lad unto his tente	You were betrayed and taken into his tent,
Where as he with his owene hand slow thee,	Where he killed you with his own hand,
Succedynge in thy regne and in thy rente.	Taking your throne and your wealth.
The feeld of snow, with thegle of blak therinne	The field of snow, with a black eagle in it,
Caught with the lymerod, coloured as the gleede,	Caught with bird lime on a stick like burning

He brew this cursednesse and al this synne.

The wikked nest was werker of this nede,
Noght Charles Olyvver, that took ay heede
Of trouthe and honour, but of Armorike
Genyloun Olyver, corrupt for meede,
Broghte this worthy kyng in swich a brike.

De Petro Rege de Cipro
O worthy Petro, kyng of Cipre, also,
That Alisandre wan by heigh maistrie,
Ful many an hethen wroghtestow ful wo,
Of which thyne owene liges hadde envye,
And for nothyng but for thy chivalrie,
They in thy bed han slayn thee by the morwe.
Thus kan Fortune hir wheel governe and gye,

And out of joye brynge men to sorwe.

De Barnabo de Lumbardia
Off Melan grete Barnabo Viscounte,
God of delit and scourge of Lumbardye,

Why sholde I nat thyn infortune acounte,
Sith in estaat thow cloumbe were so hye?

Thy brother sone, that was thy double allye

For he thy nevew was, and sone-in-lawe,

Withinne his prisoun made thee to dye,
But why, ne how, noot I that thou were slawe.

De Hugelino Comite de Pize
Off the Erl Hugelyn of Pyze the languor
Ther may no tonge telle for pitee.
But litel out of Pize stant a tour,
In whiche tour in prisoun put was he,
And with hym been his litel children thre,

The eldeste scarsly fyf yeer was of age.
Allas, Fortune, it was greet crueltee
Swiche briddes for to putte in swiche a cage!

Dampned was he to dyen in that prisoun,
For Roger, which that Bisshop was of Pize,
Hadde on hym maad a fals suggestioun,
Thurgh which the peple gan upon hym rise,
And putten hym to prisoun in swich wise
As ye han herd, and mete and drynke he hadde
So smal that wel unnethe it may suffise,
And therwithal it was ful povre and badde.

coal,
He started all this horrible business, all this sin.
The wicked nest bred all of this horror.
Not Charlemagne's Oliver, who always stuck
To truth and honour, but Amorica,
Ganelon-Oliver, corrupted by bribes,
Brought this worthy king down so low.

Of Pierre de Lusingnan, King of Cyprus
Oh worthy Pierre, King of Cyprus, also,
Who won over Alexandria with his great skill,
You gave great sorrow to many heathens,
So that your own lords envied you,
And for nothing more than your chivalry
They killed you in your bed one morning.
This is how Fortune governs and guides her wheel,
Bringing men sorrow from happiness.

Of Bernabo Visconti of Lombardy
Great Bernabo Visconti of Milan,
A God of pleasure and the scourge of Lombardy,
Why shouldn't I tell of your misfortune,
That came to you after you had climbed so high?
Your brother's son, who was your relative twice over,
For he was both your nephew and your son-in-law,
Caused your death inside his prison—
But I don't know why or how you were killed.

Of Ugolino, Earl of Pisa
Of the torment of Earl Ugolino of Pisa
No tongue can speak out of pity.
But a little way from Pisa there is a tower,
And he was imprisoned in that tower,
And with him there were his three little children;
The oldest was hardly five years of age.
Alas, Fortune, it was terribly cruel
To put birds like that in such a cage!

He was condemned to die in that prison,
For Roger, who was Bishop of Pisa,
Had made a false accusation against him,
Which made the people rise up against him
And put him in prison in the way
You have heard, and he had so little
Meat and drink that it was hardly enough,
And also it was very poor quality and rotten.

And on a day bifil, that in that hour	And one day it happened at the time
Whan that his mete wont was to be broght,	When his meal was usually brought to him,
The gayler shette the dores of the tour;	The jailer closed the doors of the tower.
He herde it wel, but he spak right noght–	He heard it clearly, but he said nothing,
And in his herte anon ther fil a thoght,	And at once he thought in his heart
That they for hunger wolde doon hym dyen.	That they were going to starve him to death.
Allas, quod he, allas, that I was wroght!	"Alas!" he said, "alas for the day I was born!"
Therwith the teeris fillen from hise eyen.	And the tears streamed from his eyes.
His yonge sone, that thre yeer was of age,	His young son, who was three years old,
Unto hym seyde, Fader, why do ye wepe?	Said to him, "Father, why do you weep?
Whanne wol the gayler bryngen our potage?	When will the jailer bring our soup?
Is ther no morsel breed that ye do kepe?	Haven't you got any morsel of bread on you?
I am so hungry that I may nat slepe.	I'm so hungry I cannot sleep.
Now wolde God that I myghte slepen evere!	I wish to God I could sleep forever!
Thanne sholde nat hunger in my wombe crepe,	Then hunger would not creep into my belly;
Ther is nothyng but breed that me were levere.	There is nothing I would rather have than some food."
Thus day by day this child bigan to crye,	And so this child cried like this every day,
Til in his fadres barm adoun it lay,	Until it lay down on his father's chest,
And seyde, Farewel, fader, I moot dye!	And said, "Farewell, father, I must die!"
And kiste his fader, and dyde the same day.	And he kissed his father, and died on that day.
And whan the woful fader deed it say,	And when his sorrowing father saw he was dead
For wo hise armes two he gan to byte,	In sorrow he began to chew on his two arms,
And seyde, Allas, Fortune and weylaway!	Saying, "Alas, Fortune, and what sorrow!
Thy false wheel my wo al may I wyte!	I blame your false wheel for all my sorrow."
Hise children wende that it for hunger was	His children imagined that it was hunger
That he his armes gnow, and nat for wo,	Which made him chew on his arms, and not sorrow,
And seyde, Fader, do nat so, allas!	And said, "Father, do not do this, alas!
But rather ete the flessh upon us two.	Instead eat the flesh of we two.
Oure flessh thou yaf us, take our flessh us fro,	You gave us our flesh, take our flesh from us,
And ete ynogh, right thus they to hym seyde;	And eat your fill"—that's just what they said to him,
And after that withinne a day or two	And after that, within a day or so,
They leyde hem in his lappe adoun, and deyde.	They laid themselves down in his lap and died.
Hymself, despeired, eek for hunger starf,	He, in despair, also died of hunger;
Thus ended is this myghty Erl of Pize.	And so the great Earl of Pisa met his end.
From heigh estaat Fortune awey hym carf,	From his high position fortune pushed him away.
Of this tragedie it oghte ynough suffise.	That is enough about this tragedy;
Whoso wol here it in a lenger wise,	If anybody wants to hear more about it,
Redeth the grete poete of Ytaille	Read the great poet of Italy,
That highte Dant, for he kan al devyse	Who is called Dante, for he told the whole story
Fro point to point, nat o word wol he faille.	In great detail; he didn't omit a word.
Nero	Nero
Al though that Nero were vicius	Although Nero was as vicious
As any feend that lith in helle adoun,	As any daemon in the lowest circles of hell,
Yet he, as telleth us Swetonius,	Yet as Suetonius tells us

This wyde world hadde in subjeccioun,	He had the whole world in his power,
Bothe Est and West, South and Septemtrioun;	The east and the west, south and north.
Of rubies, saphires, and of peerles white	His clothes were covered
Were alle hise clothes brouded up and doun,	With rubies, sapphires and white pearls,
For he in gemmes greetly gan delite.	For he took great pleasure in precious stones.
Moore delicaat, moore pompous of array,	There was never an emperor more fond of luxury, more pompous,
Moore proud was nevere emperour than he.	More arrogant than him;
That ilke clooth that he hadde wered o day,	Once he had worn clothes for one day
After that tyme he nolde it nevere see.	He never wanted to see them again.
Nettes of gold-threed hadde he greet plentee,	He had many nets of gold threads
To fisshe in Tybre, whan hym liste pleye.	To fish in the Tiber, when he wanted amusement.
Hise lustes were al lawe in his decree,	All his lusts were made lawful through his decrees,
For Fortune as his freend hym wolde obeye.	For Fortune obeyed him as his friend.
He Rome brende for his delicasie;	He burned down Rome for his own pleasure;
The senatours he slow upon a day,	One day he killed the senators
To heere how men wolde wepe and crie;	Just to hear them weep and cry;
And slow his brother, and by his suster lay.	And he killed his brother, and slept with his sister.
His mooder made he in pitous array,	He reduced his mother to a piteous state,
For he hir wombe slitte, to biholde	For he slit open her womb to see
Wher he conceyved was, so weilaway	Where he was conceived—what a terrible thing
That he so litel of his mooder tolde!	That he thought so little of his mother!
No teere out of hise eyen for that sighte Ne cam; but seyde, A fair womman was she.	No tears fell from his eyes At that site, but he said, "She was a beautiful woman!"
Greet wonder is how that he koude or myghte	It's amazing that he could
Be domesman of hir dede beautee.	Be a judge of her dead beauty.
The wyn to bryngen hym comanded he,	He ordered that wine should be brought to him,
And drank anon; noon oother wo he made,	And he drank at once—that was all his mourning.
Whan myght is joyned unto crueltee,	When power and cruelty are joined,
Allas, to depe wol the venym wade!	Alas, the poison gets in deep!
In yowthe a maister hadde this emperour	When he was young this Emperor had a master
To techen hym lettrure and curteisye,	To teach him literature and courtesy,
For of moralitee he was the flour,	For he was one of the greatest moralists
As in his tyme, but if bookes lye.	Of his time, if the books tell the truth;
And whil this maister hadde of hym maistrye,	And while this master ruled over him,
He maked hym so konnyng and so sowple,	He made him so skilful and so humble
That longe tyme it was, er tirannye	That it was a long time before tyranny
Or any vice dorste on hym uncowple.	Or any vice dared to raise its head in him.
This Seneca, of which that I devyse,	This Seneca, of whom I'm speaking,
By-cause Nero hadde of hym swich drede,	Nero was in such dread of him,
(For he fro vices wolde hym chastise	For he would always steer him away from vice,
Discreetly as by word, and nat by dede)	Discreetly, with words, not deeds—

Sire, wolde he seyn, an emperour moot need	"Sire," he would say, "an emperor must of necessity
Be vertuous and hate tirannye.-	Be good and hate tyranny—"
For which he in a bath made hym to blede	And for this he made him bleed in a bath
On bothe hise armes, til he moste dye.	From both his arms, until he died.
This Nero hadde eek of acustumaunce	This Nero was also accustomed
In youthe agayns his maister for to ryse,	In his youth to stand in the presence of his master,
Which afterward hym thoughte greet grevaunce;	Which afterwards he thought was a terrible offence;
Therfore he made hym dyen in this wise,	That's why he made him die in this fashion.
But nathelees, this Seneca the wise	But nevertheless this Seneca, the wise,
Chees in a bath to dye in this manere,	Chose to die in this way in a bath
Rather than han anoother tormentise,	Rather than suffer other tortures;
And thus hath Nero slayn his maister deere.	And so Nero killed his dear master.
Now fil it so, that Fortune liste no lenger	Now Fortune no longer wanted
The hye pryde of Nero to cherice;	To care for the great arrogance of Nero,
For though that he was strong, yet was she strenger;	For although he was strong, she was stronger.
She thoughte thus, By God, I am to nyce	She thought this way: "By God! I was too kind
To sette a man that is fulfild of vice	To put a man with so many voices
In heigh degree, and emperour hym calle.	In a high position, and call him emperor.
By God, out of his sete I wol hym trice,	By God, I will drag him from his throne;
Whan he leest weneth, sonnest shal he falle.	When he least expects it, that's when he will fall quickest."
The peple roos upon hym on a nyght	The people rose against him one night
For his defaute, and whan he it espied	Due to his wickedness, and when he saw them,
Out of hise dores anoon he hath hym dight	He ran out of doors at once
Allone, and ther he wende han been allied	Alone, and where he thought he had friends
He knokked faste, and ay the moore he cried,	He knocked hard, and the more he cried out
The faster shette they the dores alle.	The tighter they closed their doors.
For drede of this hym thoughte that he dyed,	Then he knew well that he had deluded himself,
And wente his wey, no lenger dorste he calle.	And he went on his way; he no longer dared to call.
The peple cride, and rombled up and doun,	The people cried out and rioted up and down,
That with his erys herde he how they seyde,	So that he could clearly hear what they said,
Where is this false tiraunt, this Neroun?	"Where is this tyrant, this Nero?"
For fere almoost out of his wit he breyde,	He almost went out of his mind with fear,
And to his goddes pitously he preyed	And he prayed piteously to his gods
For socour, but it myghte nat bityde.	For help, but nothing happened
For drede of this hym thoughte that he deyde,	It seemed to him that he would die of fear
And ran into a gardin hym to hyde.	And he ran into a garden to hide.
And in this gardyn foond he cherles tweye,	And in this garden he found two peasants
That seten by a fyr greet and reed,	Sitting by a fire, huge and red.
And to thise cherles two he gan to preye	He begged these peasants
To sleen hym and to girden of his heed,	To kill him, to strike off his head,
That to his body whan that he were deed,	So that his body, when he was dead,
Were no despit ydoon, for his defame.	Would not be mutilated for his bad reputation.
Hymself he slow, he koude no bettre reed,	He killed himself, he didn't know what else to do,

Of which Fortune lough and hadde a game.	And Fortune laughed, and enjoyed the game.
De Oloferno	**Of Holofernes**
Was nevere capitayn under a kyng	Was there ever a captain serving a king
That regnes mo putte in subjeccioun,	Who conquered more rulers,
Ne strenger was in feeld of alle thyng	And there was never one stronger in warfare,
As ibn his tyme, ne gretter of renoun,	In his time, nor more famous,
Ne moore pompous in heigh presumpcioun,	Nor more arrogant with great presumption
Than Oloferne, which Fortune ay kiste	Than Holofernes, whom fortune always kissed
So likerously, and ladde hym up and doun	So lecherously, leading him up and down
Til that his heed was of er that he wiste.	Until he lost his head, before he knew it.
Nat oonly that this world hadde hym in awe	Not only was the world in awe of him,
For lesynge of richesse or libertee,	Fearing the loss of wealth and liberty,
But he made every man reneyen his lawe.	But he made every man give up his religion.
Nabugodonosor was god, seyde hee,	"Nebuchadnezzar was God," he said;
Noon oother god sholde adoure bee.	"No other gods should be worshipped."
Agayns his heeste no wight dorste trespace,	Nobody dared go against his orders,
Save in Bethulia, a strong citee,	Except in Bethulia, a strong city,
Where Eliachim a preest was of that place.	Where Joachim was a priest.
But taak kepe of the deeth of Oloferne;	But take note of how Holofernes died:
Amydde his hoost he dronke lay a nyght,	He lay drunk in the night in the middle of his army,
Withinne his tente, large as is a berne;	In his tent, as large as a barn,
And yet for al his pompe and al his might	And yet, for all his pomp and his strength,
Judith, a womman, as he lay upright	Judith, a woman, as he lay on his back
Slepynge, his heed of smoot, and from his tente	Sleeping, chopped off his head, and from his tent
Ful prively she stal from every wight,	She secretly sneaked away from everyone,
And with his heed unto hir toun she wente.	And took his head to her town.
De Rege Anthiocho illustri	**Of the famous King Antiochus**
What nedeth it of kyng Anthiochus	Who needs to be told about King Antiochus,
To telle his hye roial magestee,	Of his great royal majesty,
His hye pride, hise werkes venymous?	His great pride, his horrible deeds?
For swich another was ther noon as he,	There has never been anyone like him.
Rede which that he was in Machabee,	You can read who he was in the book of Maccabees,
And rede the proude wordes that he seyde,	And read the terrible words that he said,
And why he fil fro heigh prosperitee,	And why he fell from a great position,
And in an hill how wrecchedly he deyde.	And how he died wretchedly on a hill.
Fortune hym hadde enhaunced so in pride	Fortune had given him such pride
That verraily he wende he myghte attayne	That he truly thought but he could reach
Unto the sterres upon every syde,	Up to the stars on every side,
And in balance weyen ech montayne,	And weigh every mountain on scales,
And alle the floodes of the see restrayne.	And hold back all the tides of the sea,
And Goddes peple hadde he moost in hate;	And he hated the people of God most of all;
Hem wolde he sleen in torment and in payne,	He would kill them with torture, with pain,
Wenynge that God ne myghte his pride abate.	Thinking that God himself could not subdue his pride.
And for that Nichanore and Thymothee	And because Nicanor and Timotheus
Of Jewes weren venquysshed myghtily,	Were completely vanquished by the Jews,
Unto the Jewes swich an hate hadde he	He had such a hatred for the Jews

That he bad greithen his chaar ful hastily,

And swoor, and seyde, ful despitously,
Unto Jerusalem he wolde eft-soone,
To wreken his ire on it ful cruelly;
But of his purpos he was let ful soone.

God for his manace hym so soore smoot

With invisible wounde, ay incurable,

That in hise guttes carf it so and boot
That hise peynes weren importable.
And certeinly, the wreche was resonable,
For many a mannes guttes dide he peyne,
But from his purpos cursed and dampnable
For al his smert he wolde hym nat restreyne;

But bad anon apparaillen his hoost,
And sodeynly, er he was of it war,
God daunted al his pride and al his boost,

For he so soore fil out of his char,
That it hise lemes and his skyn totar,

So that he neyther myghte go ne ryde,
But in a chayer men aboute hym bar
Al forbrused, bothe bak and syde.

The wreche of God hym smoot so cruelly
That thurgh his body wikked wormes crepte;
And therwithal he stank so horribly
That noon of al his meynee that hym kepte
Wheither so he wook or ellis slepte,
Ne myghte noghy for stynk of hym endure.
In this meschief he wayled and eek wepte,
And knew God lord of every creature.

To all his hoost and to hymself also
Ful wlatsom was the stynk of his careyne,
No man ne myghte hym bere to ne fro,
And in this stynk and this horrible peyne
He starf ful wrecchedly in a monteyne.
Thus hath this robbour and this homycide,
That many a man made to wepe and pleyne,
Swich gerdoun as bilongeth unto pryde.

De Alexandro
The storie of Alisaundre is so commune
That every wight that hath discrecioun
Hath herd somwhat or al of his fortune.
This wyde world, as in conclusioun,

That he ordered that his chariot should be prepared at once,
And he swore, and said very angrily
That he would go to Jerusalem at once
And he would cruelly take out his anger on it;
But he was quickly prevented from this aim.

Because of his threats God smote him so harshly
With an invisible wound, which would never heal,
That it cut and bit at his guts
So that his pain was intolerable.
And it certainly was a reasonable punishment,
For he gave many men pains in their guts.
But he would not give up
His cursed and damnable purpose, for all his pain, He would not restrain himself.

He ordered his army to be prepared at once;
And suddenly, before he knew it,
God smashed down his pride and all his boasting.
He had such a terrible fall from his throne
That his limbs and his skin were ripped to pieces,
So that he could neither walk or ride,
But had to be carried around in a chair,
Badly bruised, both on his back and side.

The vengeance of God struck him so cruelly
That wicked worms crept through his body,
And he also stank so horribly
That none of his household who served him,
Whether he was awake or asleep,
Could tolerate the stink of him.
With this affliction he wailed and wept,
And acknowledged that God was Lord of everything.

To all his army, and also to himself,
The stink of his decaying body was revolting;
No man could tolerate him in any way.
And in this stink and horrible pain,
He died very wretchedly on a mountain.
So in this way this robber and murderer,
Who had made many men weep and wail,
Got the reward arrogance deserves.

Of Alexander
The story of Alexander is so commonly known
That anyone who has any intelligence
Has heard something, or maybe all of it.
This wide world, ultimately,

He wan by strengthe, or for his hye renoun	He won through strength, unless due to his great reputation
They weren glad for pees unto hym sende.	People were glad to negotiate peace with him.
The pride of man and beest he leyde adoun	He crushed the pride of men and beasts,
Wher-so he cam, unto the worldes ende.	Wherever he went, to the ends of the world.
Comparison myghte nevere yet been maked	No comparison could ever be made
Bitwixen hym and another conquerour,	Between him and any other conqueror;
For al this world for drede of hym hath quaked.	The whole world shook from fear of him.
He was of knyghthod and of fredom flour,	He was an exemplar of knighthood and nobility;
Fortune hym made the heir of hir honour.	Fortune made him into her heir.
Save wyn and wommen nothyng myghte aswage	Apart from wine and women, nothing could distract him
His hye entente in armes and labour,	From his noble ambitions in battles and struggles,
So was he ful of leonyn corage.	He had such a lion's courage.
What pris were it to hym, though I yow tolde	What honour would it bring him, even if I told you
Of Darius, and an hundred thousand mo,	Of Darius, and a hundred thousand more
Of kynges, princes, erles, dukes bolde,	Kings, princes, dukes, bold earls
Whiche he conquered and broghte hem into wo?	Whom he conquered, and brought to sorrow?
I seye, as fer as man may ryde or go,	I say, as far as a man can ride or walk,
The world was his, what sholde I moore devyse?	The whole world was his—what more can I say?
For though I write or tolde yow everemo,	Even if I wrote or told you forever
Of his knyghthode it myghte nat suffise.	About his achievements, I could not say enough.
Twelf yeer he regned, as seith Machabee,	He ruled for twelve years, so says Maccabees.
Philippes sone of Macidoyne he was,	He was the son of Philip of Macedonia,
That first was kyng in Grece the contree.	Who was the first king of the country of Greece.
O worhty gentil Alisandre, allas,	O worthy, noble Alexander, alas,
That evere sholde fallen swich a cas!	That such a thing should ever happen to you!
Empoysoned of thyn owene folk thou weere;	You were poisoned by your own people;
Thy sys Fortune hath turned into aas	Fortune had turned your six into a one,
And yet for thee ne weep she never a teere.	And she never shed a tear for you.
Who shal me yeven teeris to compleyne	Who will give me tears to mourn
The deeth of gentillesse and of franchise,	The death of nobility and of generosity,
That al the world weelded in his demeyne?	Who ruled over the entire world,
And yet hym thoughte it myghte nat suffise,	And yet it seemed not to be enough for him?
So ful was his corage of heigh emprise.	He had such great courage in his knightly achievements.
Allas, who shal me helpe to endite	Alas who can help me to charge
False Fortune, and poyson to despise,	False Fortune, and to hate poison,
The whiche two of al this wo I wyte?	The two of which I blame for all this sorrow?
De Julio Cesare	Of Julius Caesar
By wisedom, manhede, and by gret labour	Through wisdom, manhood, and with great labour,
From humble bed to roial magestee	From humble beds to royal majesty

Up roos he, Julius the conquerour,	Rose this Julius, the conqueror,
That wan al thoccident by land and see	Who won all of the west through land and sea,
By strengthe of hand, or elles by tretee,	Through force, or otherwise by treaty,
And unto Rome made hem tributarie;	And he made them all subordinate to Rome;
And sitthe of Rome the emperour was he,	And afterwards he became emperor of Rome
Til that Fortune weex his adversarie.	Until Fortune became his enemy.
O myghty Cesar, that in Thessalie	O mighty Caesar, who in Thessaly
Agayn Pompeus, fader thyn in lawe,	Against Pompey, your father-in-law,
That of the Orient hadde al the chivalrye	Who ruled over all of the East
As fer as that the day bigynneth dawe,	As far as the place where the sun rises,
Thou thurgh thy knyghthod hast hem take and slawe,	Who through your prowess took them and killed them,
Save fewe folk that with Pompeus fledde,	Apart from a few folk who fled with Pompey,
Thurgh which thou puttest al thorient in awe,	And because of this the whole of the East was in awe of you.
Thanke Fortune, that so wel thee spedde!	Thank Fortune, who gave you such help!
But now a litel while I wol biwaille	But for a little while I will mourn
This Pompeus, this noble governour	For Pompey, this noble governor
Of Rome, which that fleigh at this bataille,	Of Rome, who fled from the battle.
I seye, oon on hise men, a fals traitour,	I tell you, one of his men, a false traitor,
His heed of-smoot to wynnen hym favour	Cut off his head, to win the favour
Of Julius, and hym the heed he broghte;	Of Julius, and he took the head to him.
Allas, Pompeye, of thorient conquerour,	Alas, Pompey, the conqueror of the East,
That Fortune unto swich a fyn thee broghte!	That fortune should have brought you to such an end!
To Rome agayn repaireth Julius,	Julius went back again to Rome
With his triumphe lauriat ful hye;	In triumph, crowned with a laurel wreath;
But on a tyme Brutus Cassius	But there came a time when Brutus Cassius,
That evere hadde of his hye estaat envye,	Who had always been jealous of his great position,
Ful prively hath maad conspiracye	Secretly made a conspiracy
Agayns this Julius in subtil wise,	Against this Julius in a cunning fashion,
And caste the place in which he sholde dye	And planned the place where he would die
With boydekyns, as I shal yow devyse.	By being stabbed, as I shall tell you.
This Julius to the Capitolie wente	This Julius went to the Capitol
Upon a day, as he was wont to goon;	One day, as he was accustomed to do,
And in the Capitolie anon hym hente	And in the Capitol he was immediately seized
This false Brutus and his othere foor,	By this false Brutus and his other enemies,
And stiked hym with boydekyns anoon	Who all immediately stabbed him
With many a wounde; and thus they lete hym lye.	With many wounds, and they left him lying there;
But nevere gronte he at no strook but oon,	But he never groaned at any of the blows but one,
Or elles at two, but if his sstorie lye.	Or otherwise two, unless the history books lie.
So manly was this Julius of herte	This Julius was so manly in his heart,
And so wel lovede estaatly honestee,	And he so loved dignity and decency,
That though hise deedly woundes soore smerte,	That although his fatal wounds hurt him sorely,
His mantel over hise hypes caste he,	He pulled his cloak over his hips,
For no man sholde seen his privetee.	So that nobody could see him naked;

And as he lay of diyng in a traunce,	*And as he lay dying in a coma,*
And wiste verraily that deed was hee,	*Knowing that he certainly was going to die,*
Of honestee yet hadde he remembraunce.	*He could still think of decency.*
Lucan, to thee this storie I recomende,	*I recommend Lucan's history of this to you,*
And to Sweton, and to Valerie also,	*And also Suetonius, and Valerius,*
That of this storie writen word and ende,	*Who wrote the story of this from beginning to end,*
How that to thise grete conqueroures two	*How these two great conquerors*
Fortune was first freend, and sitthe foo.	*Were first favoured by Fortune, and then opposed.*
No man ne truste upon hire favour longe	*Let no man trust her for too long,*
But have hir in awayt for evere moo!	*But always watch out for her eternally;*
Witnesse on alle thise conqueroures stronge.	*Learn your lesson from these great conquerors.*
Cresus	*Croesus*
This riche Cresus whilom kyng of Lyde,	*This rich Croesus, once king of Lydia,*
Of whiche Cresus Cirus soore hym dradde,	*Of whom Croesus Cyrus was very scared,*
Yet was he caught amyddes al his pryde,	*But he was caught when he was very prosperous,*
And to be brent men to the fyr hym ladde.	*And taken by men to be burned in a fire.*
But swich a reyn doun fro the welkne shadde	*But such a rain poured down from the sky*
That slow the fyr, and made hym to escape;	*That it killed the fire, and allowed him to escape;*
But to be war no grace yet he hadde,	*But he was not allowed to avoid Fortune*
Til Fortune on the galwes made hym gape.	*Until she made him stretch on the gallows.*
Whanne he escaped was, he kan nat stente	*When he had escaped, he could not stop*
For to bigynne a newe werre agayn;	*Himself beginning another war.*
He wende wel, for that Fortune hym sente	*He truly believed, because fortune had sent him*
Swich hap that he escaped thurgh the rayn,	*Such luck in helping him escape because of the rain,*
That of hise foos he myghte nat be slayn;	*That his enemies would not be able to kill him;*
And eek a swevene upon a nyght he mette,	*And also he had a dream one night*
Of which he was so proud and eek so fayn	*Which made him so arrogant and so happy*
That in vengeance he al his herte sette.	*That he set his heart on vengeance.*
Upon a tree he was, as that hym thoughte,	*It seemed to him that he was in a tree,*
Ther Jupiter hym wessh bothe bak and syde,	*And Jupiter washed him, front and back,*
And Phebus eek a fair towaille hym broughte,	*And Phoebus brought him a fine towel*
To dryen hym with; and therfore wax his pryde,	*To dry himself with; and so he grew more proud,*
And to his doghter that stood hym bisyde,	*And to his daughter, who stood beside him,*
Which that he knew in heigh science haboundE,	*Whom he knew was full of good sense,*
He bad hir telle hym what it signyfyde,	*He asked her to tell him what it meant,*
And she his dreem bigan right thus expounde.	*And she began to explain his dream to him like this:*
The tree, quod she, the galwes is to meene,	*"The tree," she said, "symbolises the gallows,*
And Juppiter bitokneth snow and reyn,	*And Jupiter means snow and rain,*
And Phebus with his towaille so clene,	*And Phoebus, with his nice clean towel,*
Tho been the sonne stremes for to seyn.	*Those are the sunbeams.*
Thou shalt anhanged be, fader, certeyn;	*You shall certainly be hanged, father;*

Reyn shal thee wasshe, and sonne shal thee drye.	Rain will wash over you, and the sun will dry you."
Thus warnede hym ful plat and ful pleyn,	That was how he was warned starkly and clearly
His doghter, which that called was Phanye.	By his daughter, who was called Phanye.
Anhanged was Cresus, the proude kyng,	Croesus the proud king was hanged;
His roial trone myghte hym nat availle.	His royal position could not help him.
Tragedie is noon oother maner thyng,	Tragedies have no other theme
Ne kan in syngyng crye ne biwaille,	For all their crying and wailing,
But for that Fortune alwey wole assaille	Fortune will always strike
With unwar strook the regnes that been proude;	Unexpectedly on proud rulers;
For whan me trusteth hir, thanne wol she faille,	When men trust her, she will fail them,
And covere hir brighte face with a clowde.	And cover her bright face with a cloud.
The end of the tragedy	Here the Knight interrupted the Monk's tale

The Nun's Priest's Tale

Prologue

The Prologue of the Nonnes Preestes Tale. — *The Nun's Priest's Prologue*

Hoo! quod the Knyght, good sire, namoore of this,	"Whoa!" said the Knight, "good sire, no more of this!
That ye han seyd is right ynough, ywis,	What you have said is enough, for sure
And muchel moore, for litel hevynesse	And much more; for a little sadness
Is right ynough to muche folk, I gesse.	Is enough for many people, I suppose.
I seye for me, it is a greet disese	I say for myself, it is a great distress,
Where as men han been in greet welthe and ese,	When men have been in great wealth and comfort,
To heeren of hir sodeyn fal, allas!	To Hear of their sudden fall!
And the contrarie is joye and greet solas,	And the contrary is joy and great ease
As whan a man hath been in povre estaat,	As when a man has been in a poor condition
And clymbeth up, and wexeth fortunat,	And climbs up and becomes fortunate
And there abideth in prosperitee.	And there remains in prosperity.
Swich thyng is gladsom, as it thynketh me,	Such a thing is good, as it seems to me,
And of swich thyng were goodly for to telle.	And of such a thing it would be good to tell."
Ye, quod our Hoost, by seinte Poules belle,	"Yes," said our host, "by the bells of St Paul's!
Ye seye right sooth! This Monk, he clappeth lowde,	You are telling the truth; this monk gabbles noisily.
He spak, how Fortune covered with a clowde—	He spoke of how Fortune covered over with a cloud
I noot nevere what-and also of a `Tragedie'—	I don't know what; and also about a tragedy
Right now ye herde; and pardee, no remedie	You heard just now, and by God, there's no cure
It is for to biwaille ne compleyne	In wailing or lamenting
That that is doon; and als it is a peyne,	Things which have happened, and also it causes pain,
As ye han seyd, to heere of hevynesse.	As you have said, to hear of such sadness.
Sire Monk, namoore of this, so God yow blesse!	Sir Monk, no more of this, may God bless you!
Youre tale anoyeth al this compaignye;	Your tale has upset the company.
Swich talkyng is nat worth a boterflye,	Talk like this is not worth a butterfly,
For ther-inne is ther no desport ne game.	For there is no pleasure nor fun in it.
Wherfore sir Monk, or daun Piers by youre name,	So, Sir Monk, Don Piers by name,
I pray yow hertely, telle us somwhat elles,	I earnestly beg you to tell us something else;
For sikerly, nere clynkyng of youre belles	For certainly, if it wasn't for the tinkling of your bells
That on your bridel hange on every syde,	That hang on both sides of your bridle,
By hevene kyng, that for us alle dyde,	By the King of Heaven who died for all of us,
I sholde er this han fallen doun for sleepe,	I would have fallen off in sleep,
Althogh the slough had never been so deepe;	Even if the mud was very deep;
Thanne hadde your tale al be toold in veyn.	Then all your tale would be wasted.
For, certeinly, as that thise clerkes seyn,	For certainly, as these scholars say,
Where as a man may have noon audience,	When nobody is listening to a man

Noght helpeth it to tellen his sentence.	There is no point in him talking.
And wel I woot the substance is in me,	I certainly know that I can be appreciative
If any thyng shal wel reported be.	If something is well told.
Sir, sey somwhat of huntyng, I yow preye.	Sir, tell us something about hunting, I pray you."
Nay, quod this Monk, I have no lust to pleye;	"No," said this monk, "I have no desire for the game.
Not lat another telle as I have toold.	Now let somebody else tell a tale, as I have."
Thanne spak oure Hoost, with rude speche and boold,	Then our host spoke out with rough bold speech,
And seyde unto the Nonnes Preest anon,	And said at once to the nun's priest,
Com neer, thou preest, com hyder, thou, sir John,	"Come closer, you priest, come here, you Sir John!
Telle us swich thyng as may oure hertes glade;	Tell us something to cheer our hearts.
Be blithe, though thou ryde upon a jade.	Be happy, even though you're riding a nag.
What thogh thyn hors be bothe foul and lene?	What's it matter if your horse is a bad skinny one?
If he wol serve thee, rekke nat a bene!	If he can carry you, don't give a damn.
Looke that thyn herte be murie everemo.	Keep your heart happy always."
Yis sir, quod he, yis, Hoost, so moot I go,	"Indeed, sir," he said, "indeed, host, as I hope for heaven,
But I be myrie, ywis, I wol be blamed.	If I'm not merry, I should be criticised."
And right anon his tale he hath attamed,	And that once he began his tale,
And thus he seyde unto us everichon,	And he spoke these words to all of us,
This sweete preest, this goodly man sir John.	This sweet priest, this good man, Sir John.

The Tale

Heere bigynneth the Nonnes Preestes Tale of the Cok and Hen, Chauntecleer and Pertelote	**The Nun's Priest Tale of the cock and the hen, Chaunticleer and Pertelote**
A povre wydwe, somdel stape in age,	A poor widow, getting on in years,
Was whilom dwellyng in a narwe cotage	Was once dwelling in a small cottage,
Biside a greve, stondynge in a dale.	Next to a grove, which stood in dale.
This wydwe, of which I telle yow my tale,	This widow, of whom I am telling you,
Syn thilke day that she was last a wyf,	Since the day on which she was last a wife
In pacience ladde a ful symple lyf,	Had led a very simple life, patiently,
For litel was hir catel and hir rente.	For she had very few possessions and a small income.
By housbondrie, of swich as God hir sente,	Through careful use of what God sent her
She foond hirself and eek hire doghtren two.	She provided for herself and for her two daughters.
Thre large sowes hadde she, and namo,	She had three large sows, that was all,
Three keen, and eek a sheep that highte Malle.	Three cows, and also a sheep called Malle.
Ful sooty was hir bour and eek hire halle,	Her bedroom was covered in soot, as was her hall,
In whidh she eet ful many a sklendre meel—	And she ate many tiny meals there.
Of poynaunt sauce hir neded never a deel.	She didn't need any spicy sauce,
No deyntee morsel passed thurgh hir throte,	No dainty morsels passed through her throat;
Hir diete was accordant to hir cote.	Her diet was what she could get from her farm.
Repleccioun ne made hir nevere sik,	She was never sick from overeating;
Attempree diete was al hir phisik,	A moderate diet was the only medicine she

And exercise, and hertes suffisaunce.	had,
The goute lette hir nothyng for to daunce,	Along with exercise, and a happy heart.
Napoplexie shente nat hir heed.	Gout didn't stop her from dancing,
	And her brain was not harmed through apoplexy.
No wyn ne drank she, neither whit ne reed,	She did not drink wine, neither white nor red,
Hir bord was served moost with whit and blak,	Her table usually had white and black—
Milk and broun breed, in which she foond no lak,	Milk and black bread, which she was satisfied with,
Seynd bacoun, and somtyme an ey or tweye,	Grilled bacon, and sometimes an egg or two,
For she was as it were a maner deye.	For she was, as it were, a sort of dairy farmer.
A yeerd she hadde, enclosed al aboute	She had a yard, fenced all round
With stikkes, and a drye dych withoute,	With sticks, with a dry ditch outside,
In which she hadde a Cok, heet Chauntecleer,	And in it she had a cock, called Chaunticleer.
In al the land of crowyng nas his peer.	In the whole country, there wasn't one who could cry like him.
His voys was murier than the murle orgon	His voice was merrier than the merry organ
On messedayes, that in the chirche gon.	Playing in the church on mass days.
Wel sikerer was his crowyng in his logge,	He kept the time more accurately with his crowing
Than is a clokke, or an abbey orlogge.	Than a clock or a timepiece in an abbey.
By nature he crew eche ascencioun	Nature let him know the time of each ascension
Of the equynoxial in thilke toun;	Of the sun in that town;
For whan degrees fiftene weren ascended,	For when it had risen to fifteen degrees,
Thanne crew he, that it myghte nat been amended.	Then he crowed in such a way that couldn't be improved on.
His coomb was redder than the fyn coral,	His comb was redder than fine coral,
And batailled, as it were a castel wal.	And notched as if it were a castle wall;
His byle was blak, and as the jeet it shoon,	His beak was black, and it shone like jet;
Lyk asure were hise legges and his toon,	His legs and toes were like azure;
Hise nayles whiter than the lylye flour,	His nails were whiter than a lily,
And lyk the burned gold was his colour.	And his colour was like burnished gold.
This gentil cok hadde in his governaunce	This noble cock had under his rule
Sevene hennes, for to doon al his plesaunce,	Seven hens to do as he wished,
Whiche were hise sustres and his paramours,	Who were all his sisters and his mistresses,
And wonder lyk to hym as of colours;	And amazingly like him, in their colours;
Of whiche the faireste hewed on hir throte	The one who had the fairest colour on her throat
Was cleped faire damoysele Pertelote.	Was called the fair damsel Pertelote.
Curteys she was, discreet, and debonaire	She was courteous, dignified and gracious,
And compaignable, and bar hyrself so faire	And friendly, and she carried herself so well
Syn thilke day that she was seven nyght oold,	Since the day on which she was seven nights old
That trewely she hath the herte in hold	That truly she had a hold over the heart of
Of Chauntecleer loken in every lith.	Chaunticleer, she completely ruled him;
He loved hir so, that wel was hym therwith.	He loved her so much that it made him very happy.
But swiche a joye was it to here hem synge	But it was such a joy to hear them sing,
Whan that the brighte sonne gan to sprynge,	When the bright sun began to rise,
In sweete accord, My lief is faren in londe,-	In sweet harmony, "My love has gone to the country!"—
For thilke tyme, as I have understonde,	For at that time, so I understand,
Beestes and briddes koude speke and synge.	Beasts and birds could speak and sing.

And so bifel, that in the dawenynge,	And it so happened that one morning,
As Chauntecleer, among hise wyves alle,	As Chaunticleer sat on his perch
Sat on his perche, that was in the halle,	Amongst all his wives, in the hall,
And next hym sat this faire Pertelote,	And next to him sat this fair Pertelote,
This Chauntecleer gan gronen in his throte	This Chaunticleer began to growl in his throat,
As man that in his dreem is drecched soore.	Like a man having a bad dream.
And whan that Pertelote thus herde hym roore	And when Pertelote heard him making this noise,
She was agast, and seyde, O herte deere,	She was aghast, and said, "dear heart,
What eyleth yow, to grone in this manere?	What ails you, that you groan like this?
Ye been a verray sleper, fy for shame!	You are usually a very sound sleeper; stop this, for shame!"
And he answerde and seyde thus, Madame,	And he answered her saying this: "Madam,
I pray yow that ye take it nat agrief.	Please don't let this cause you grief.
By God, me thoughte I was in swich meschief	By God, I dreamt that I was in such trouble
Right now, that yet myn herte is soore afright.	That my heart is still terribly frightened.
Now God, quod he, my swevene recche aright,	Now God," he said, "show me the meaning of my dream,
And kepe my body out of foul prisoun.	And keep my body out of horrible prison!
Me mette how that I romed up and doun	I dreamt how I wandered up and down
Withinne our yeerd, wheer as I saugh a beest	Inside our yard, where I saw a beast
Was lyk an hound, and wolde han maad areest	Which was like a hound, and it would have seized
Upon my body, and han had me deed.	My body, and would have killed me.
His colour was bitwixe yelow and reed,	Its colour was between yellow and red,
And tipped was his tayl and bothe hise eeris;	And his tail and both his ears were tipped
With blak, unlyk the remenant of hise heeris;	With black, unlike the rest of his fur;
His snowte smal, with glowynge eyen tweye.	His snout was small, with two glowing eyes.
Yet of his look, for feere almoost I deye!	The terror in his look almost killed me;
This caused me my gronyng, doutelees.	That's no doubt why I groaned."
Avoy! quod she, Fly on yow hertelees!	"Shame on you, you coward!" she said,
Allas, quod she, for by that God above	"Alas," she said, "for, by God above,
Now han ye lost myn herte and al my love!	Now you have lost my heart and all my love!
I kan nat love a coward, by my feith,	I swear, I cannot love a coward!
For certes, what so any womman seith,	Full certainly, whatever anyone says,
We alle desiren, if it myght bee,	We all wish, if we can,
To han housbondes hardy, wise, and free,	To have husbands who are strong, wise and generous,
And secree, and no nygard, ne no fool,	And discreet—no miser, and no fool,
Ne hym that is agast of every tool,	Nor somebody who is afraid of weapons,
Ne noon avauntour; by that God above,	Nor any braggart, by God above!
How dorste ye seyn for shame unto youre love	How dare you say, shamefully, to your love,
That any thyng myghte make yow aferd?	That there are things which can make you afraid?
Have ye no mannes herte, and han a berd?	Do you not have the heart of a man, and a beard?
Allas, and konne ye been agast of swevenys?	Alas! Will you be frightened of dreams?
No thyng, God woot, but vanitee in swevene is!	God knows, there is nothing but foolishness in dreams.
Swevenes engendren of replecciouns,	They are made by too much food,
And ofte of fume and of complecciouns,	And fumes from the stomach and bodily humours,
Whan humours been to habundant in a wight.	When you have bred too many.

Certes, this dreem which ye han met tonight	It's certain that this dream, which you had tonight,
Cometh of greet superfluytee	Comes from a superfluity
Of youre rede colera, pardee,	Of red choler, by God,
Which causeth folk to dreden in hir dremes	Which makes folk scared in their dreams
Of arwes, and of fyre with rede lemes,	Of arrows, and of fire with red flames,
Of grete beestes, that they wol hem byte,	Red beasts, fearing they will be bitten,
Of contekes, and of whelpes grete and lyte;	Of strife, and dogs, great and small;
Right as the humour of malencolie	Just as the humour of melancholy
Causeth ful many a man in sleep to crie	Makes many men cry in their sleep
For feere of blake beres, or boles blake,	For fear of black bears, or black bulls,
Or elles blake develes wole hem take.	Or otherwise black devils which will take them.
Of othere humours koude I telle also	I could also tell you about other humours
That werken many a man in sleep ful wo,	That cause many men sorrow in their sleep;
But I wol passe as lightly as I kan.	But I will pass over them as lightly as I can.
Lo Catoun, which that was so wys a man,	Look at Cato, who was such a wise man,
Seyde he nat thus, `ne do no fors of dremes`?	Did he not say, 'Do not give dreams any importance'?
Now sire, quod she, whan ye flee fro the bemes,	Now Sir," she said, "when we fly down from the beams,
For goddes love as taak som laxatyf!	For the love of God, take a laxative.
Up peril of my soule, and of my lyf,	I swear on my soul and my life
I conseille yow the beste, I wol nat lye,	That I am giving you the best advice–I will not lie–
That bothe of colere and of malencolye	You should purge yourself of both choler
Ye purge yow; and for ye shal nat tarie,	And melancholy; and so you won't waste time,
Though in this toun is noon apothecarie,	Although there is no chemist in this town,
I shal myself to herbes techen yow,	I will myself show you which herbs
That shul been for youre hele and for youre prow.	Are the ones for your health and your benefit;
And in oure yeerd tho herbes shal I fynde,	And I will find those herbs in our yard
The whiche han of hir propretee by kynde	Which have the power from nature
To purge yow bynethe and eek above.	To purge you both above and below.
Foryet nat this, for Goddes owene love!	Don't forget this, for the love of God!
Ye been ful coleryk of compleccioun;	You are dominated by your choler;
Ware the sonne in his ascencioun	Beware of the sun when it is high in the sky,
Ne fynde yow nat repleet of humours hoote.	And do not let your humours become overheated.
And if it do, I dar wel leye a grote	And if you do, I will bet fourpence
That ye shul have a fevere terciane,	That you will have a fever every three days,
Or an agu that may be youre bane.	Or an ague that will be the death of you.
A day or two ye shul have digestyves	For a day or two you shall have digestives
Of wormes, er ye take youre laxatyves	Of worms, before you take your laxatives
Of lawriol, centaure, and fumetere,	Of spurge laurel, centuary and fumitory,
Or elles of ellebor that groweth there,	Or otherwise hellebore, that grows there,
Of katapuce, or of gaitrys beryis,	Or caper-spurge or rhamus,
Of herbe yve, growyng in oure yeerd, ther mery is!	And ground ivy, which grows pleasantly in our yard;
Pekke hem up right as they growe, and ete hem yn!	Peck them right up where they are growing and swallow them.
Be myrie, housbonde, for youre fader kyn,	Be happy, husband, for the sake of your father's family!
Dredeth no dreem, I kan sey yow namoore!	Do not worry about dreams; that's all I can tell you."

Madame, quod he, graunt mercy of youre loore,	"Madam," he said, "I thank you for your learning.
But nathelees, as touchyng Daun Catoun,	However, with reference to Cato,
That hath of wysdom swich a greet renoun,	Who was so well known for his wisdom,
Though that he bad no dremes for to drede,	Although he told us not to be afraid of dreams,
By God, men may in olde bookes rede	By God, in ancient books men can read
Of many a man moore of auctorite	Of many men with more authority
Than evere Caton was, so moot I thee,	Than Cato ever had, I swear,
That al the revers seyn of this sentence,	Who say the opposite to him,
And han wel founden by experience	And have discovered through experience
That dremes been significaciouns	That dreams are predictors
As wel of joye as of tribulaciouns	Of happiness and of troubles
That folk enduren in this lif present.	That people suffer in this life on Earth.
Ther nedeth make of this noon argument,	There is no need to argue about this;
The verray preeve sheweth it in dede.	Everyone can see the proof.
Oon of the gretteste auctours that men rede	One of the greatest authors that men read
Seith thus, that whilom two felawes wente	Says this: that once two fellows went
On pilgrimage in a ful good entente;	On a pilgrimage, very well-intentioned,
And happed so, they coomen in a toun	And it so happened, that they came to a town
Wher as ther was swich congregacioun	Where there was such a gathering
Of peple, and eek so streit of herbergage,	Of people, and also so few places to stay,
That they ne founde as muche as o cotage	That they couldn't even find a single cottage
In which they bothe myghte logged bee;	In which they could both be given lodgings.
Wherfore they mosten of necessitee	So they were forced to
As for that nyght departen compaignye,	Part company, for that night;
And ech of hem gooth to his hostelrye,	And each of them went to his lodgings,
And took his loggyng as it wolde falle.	Taking what came to him.
That oon of hem was logged in a stalle,	One of them was lodged in a stall
Fer in a yeerd, with oxen of the plough;	In a far-off farmyard, with ploughing oxen;
That oother man was logged wel ynough,	The other man had good enough lodgings,
As was his aventure or his fortune,	Whether it was through luck or his fortune,
That us governeth alle as in commune.	Which rules over every one of us.
And so bifel, that longe er it were day	And so it happened that, long before daybreak,
This man mette in his bed, ther as he lay,	This man dreamt in his bed, where he lay,
How that his felawe gan upon hym calle	That his friend was calling for him,
And seyde, `Allas, for in an oxes stalle	And said, 'Alas for in an ox stall
This nyght I shal be mordred, ther I lye!	I shall be murdered tonight where I live!
Now help me, deere brother, or I dye;	Now help me, dear brother, or I shall die.
In alle haste com to me! he sayde.	Come to me quickly!' he said.
This man out of his sleep for feere abrayde;	Out of fear this man suddenly awoke from his sleep;
But whan that he was wakened of his sleep,	But when he had woken up,
He turned hym and took of it no keep.	He turned over and paid this no attention.
Hym thoughte, his dreem nas but a vanitee.	He thought his dream was just a fantasy.
Thus twies in his slepyng dremed hee,	So he dreamt the same thing twice;
And atte thridde tyme yet his felawe	And the third time it seemed to him his friend
Cam, as hym thoughte, and seide, `I am now slawe,	Came to him and said, 'Now I have been killed.
Bihoold my bloody woundes depe and wyde;	Look at my bloody wounds, deep and wide!
Arys up erly in the morwe-tyde,	Get up early tomorrow morning,
And at the west gate of the toun,' quod he,	And at the west gate of the town,' he said,
`A carte ful of donge ther shaltow se,	'You shall see a cart full of dung there,

In which my body is hid ful prively. Do thilke carte arresten boldely; My gold caused my mordre, sooth to sayn.'- And tolde hym every point, how he was slayn,	In which my body has been secretly hidden; Have that cart seized at once. I was murdered for my gold, to tell the truth.' And he told him in every detail how he had been killed,
With a ful pitous face, pale of hewe; And truste wel, his dreem he foond ful trewe.	With a very pitiful face pale coloured. And you can believe me, he found his dream to be very true,
For on the morwe, as soone as it was day, To his felawes in he took the way, And whan that he cam to this oxes stalle, After his felawe he bigan to calle.	For all the next day, at daybreak, He went to the lodging of his friend; And when he came to the ox stall He began to call out for his friend.
The hostiler answerde hym anon, And seyde, `Sire, your felawe is agon, As soone as day he wente out of the toun.' This man gan fallen in suspecioun, Remembrynge on hise dremes that he mette, And forth he gooth, no lenger wolde he lette, Unto the westgate of the toun; and fond A dong carte, as it were to donge lond,	The innkeeper answered him at once, Saying, 'Sir, your friend has gone. He left town at daybreak.' This man began to become suspicious, Remembering what he had dreamed, And he went out—he wouldn't wait any longer; To the west gate of the town, and found A manure cart, going as if it were going to fertilise the land,
That was arrayed in that same wise, As ye han herd the dede man devyse. And with an hardy herte he gan to crye,	Which was exactly the same As you have heard the dead man tell. And with a strong heart he began to cry out for
`Vengeance and justice of this felonye; My felawe mordred is this same myght, And in this carte he lith gapyng upright. I crye out on the ministres,' quod he, `That sholden kepe and reulen this citee! Harrow! allas, heere lith my felawe slayn!' What sholde I moore unto this tale sayn? The peple out-sterte, and caste the cart to grounde,	Vengeance and justice for this crime; 'My friend has been murdered tonight, And he is lying dead in this cart. I call upon the officials,' he said, 'Who should be guarding and ruling this city. Help! Alas! Here my friend is lying killed!' What more should I tell you of this tale? The people rushed out and turned over the cart,
And in the myddel of the dong they founde The dede man, that mordred was al newe.	And in the middle of the manure they found The dead man, who had just been murdered.
O blisful God, that art so just and trewe! Lo, howe that thou biwreyest mordre alway! Mordre wol out, that se we, day by day. Mordre is so wlatsom and abhomynable To God that is so just and resonable, That he ne wol nat suffre it heled be, Though it abyde a yeer, or two, or thre.	"Oh sweet God, who is so just and true, Look how you always reveal murder! Murder will out; we see that every day. Murder is so horrid and hated By God, who is so just and reasonable, That he will not allow it to be hidden, Even though one may have to wait a year or more.
Mordre wol out, this my conclusioun. And right anon ministres of that toun Han hent the carter, and so soore hym pyned,	Murder will out, this is my conclusion. And at once the officials of the town Grabbed the carter and tortured him so painfully,
And eek the hostiler so soore engyned That they biknewe hire wikkednesse anon, And were anhanged by the nekke bon.	And they also terribly tortured the innkeeper, So that they both admitted their guilt at once, And they were hanged by the neck.
Heere may men seen, that dremes been to drede!	So you can see here that one should be afraid

And certes, in the same book I rede	of dreams.
Right in the nexte chapitre after this-	And certainly, in the same book which I read,
I gabbe nat, so have I joye or blis-	Right in the next chapter–
Two men that wolde han passed over see	I do not lie, I swear by my hopes of heaven–
For certeyn cause, into a fer contree,	Two men who wanted to go over the sea,
If that the wynd ne hadde been contrarie,	For certain reason, to a faraway country,
That made hem in a citee for to tarie,	If the wind hadn't been against them,
That stood ful myrie upon an haven-syde-	Which made them stop in a city
But on a day, agayn the even-tyde,	That stood prettily right next to a harbour;
The wynd gan chaunge, and blew right as hem leste.	But one day, in the evening,
	The wind began to change, and blew just as they wished.
Jolif and glad they wente unto hir reste,	Jolly and happy they went to their rest,
And casten hem ful erly for to saille,	Planning to sail very early in the morning.
But herkneth, to that o man fil a greet mervaille;	But listen! An amazing thing happened to one man:
That oon of hem, in slepyng as he lay,	One of them, as he lay sleeping,
Hym mette a wonder dreem agayn the day.	Dreamt a wonderful dream before daybreak.
Hym thoughte a man stood by his beddes syde,	He thought a man was standing by the side of his bed,
And hym comanded that he sholde abyde,	Who ordered him to stay,
And seyde hym thus, `If thou tomorwe wende	Saying to him: 'if you travel tomorrow,
Thow shalt be dreynt; my tale is at an ende.'	You will be drowned; that's all I have to say.'
He wook, and tolde his felawe what he mette,	He awoke, and told his friend what he had dreamt,
And preyde hym his viage for to lette,	And begged him to delay his voyage;
As for that day, he preyede hym to byde.	He prayed for him to wait for that day.
His felawe, that lay by his beddes syde,	His friend, who was lying in a bed beside him,
Gan for to laughe and scorned him ful faste.	Began to laugh, and mocked him greatly.
`No dreem,' quod he, `may so myn herte agaste	'No dream,' he said, 'will frighten my heart so much
That I wol lette for to do my thynges.	That I will stop doing what I intend.
I sette nat a straw by thy dremynges,	I don't give a damn for your dreams,
For swevenes been but vanytees and japes.	Dreams are just fantasies and idiocy.
Men dreme al day of owles or of apes,	Men are always dreaming of owls and apes,
And of many a maze therwithal.	And many other amazing things;
Men dreme of thyng that nevere was, ne shal;	Men dream of things that never happened and never will.
But sith I see that thou wolt heere abyde	But since I see that you want to stay here,
And thus forslewthen wilfully thy tyde,	And waste this perfect tide,
God woot it reweth me, and have good day.'	God knows, it makes me sad; good day to you!'
And thus he took his leve and wente his way;	And so he left, and went on his way.
But er that he hadde half his cours yseyled,	But before he had sailed across half his journey,
Noot I nat why, ne what myschaunce it eyled,	I don't know why, or what caused it,
But casuelly the shippes botme rente,	But by chance the bottom of the ship broke open,
And ship and men under the water wente	And both ship and man went under the water
In sighte of othere shippes it bisyde,	In sight of other ships beside it
That with hem seyled at the same tyde.	Which had sailed on the same tide.
And therfore, faire Pertelote so deere,	And so, fair Pertelote so dear,
By swiche ensamples olde yet maistow leere,	From these ancient examples you can learn
That no man sholde been to recchelees	That no man should be too careless
Of dremes, for I seye thee doutelees	About dreams; for I'm telling you, doubtless,

That many a dreem ful soore is for to drede.	*That there are many dreams that one should be frightened of.*
Lo, in the lyf of Seint Kenelm I rede,	*Look, I read in the life of St Kenelm,*
That was Kenulphus sone, the noble kyng,	*Who was the son of Kenulphus, the noble king*
Of Mercenrike how Kenelm mette a thyng.	*Of Mercia, how Kenelm dreamed a thing.*
A lite er he was mordred, on a day	*A little before he was murdered, one day,*
His mordre in his avysioun he say.	*He saw his murder in a vision.*
His norice hym expowned every deel	*His nurse explained everything about his dream*
His swevene, and bad hym for to kepe hym weel	*To him, and told him to watch out*
For traisoun, but he nas but seven yeer oold,	*For treason; but he was only seven years old,*
And therfore litel tale hath he toold	*And so he didn't pay much attention*
Of any dreem, so hooly is his herte.	*To any dream, his heart was so holy.*
By God, I hadde levere than my sherte	*By God! I would give up my shirt*
That ye hadde rad his legende, as have I.	*To have had you read this story, as I have.*
Dame Pertelote, I sey yow trewely,	*Dame Pertelote, I say to you truly,*
Macrobeus, that writ the avisioun	*Macrobius, who wrote down the visions*
In Affrike of the worhty Cipioun,	*Of good Scipio in Africa,*
Affermeth dremes, and seith that they been	*Confirms that dreams can be real, and says they are*
Warnynge of thynges, that men after seen.	*Warnings of things that men will see later.*
And forther-moore I pray yow looketh wel	*And furthermore, I beg you, look carefully*
In the olde testament of Daniel,	*In the old Testament, about Daniel,*
If he heeld dremes any vanitee!	*And see if he thought that dreams were foolishness.*
Reed eek of Joseph, and ther shul ye see	*Read also about Joseph, and there you will see*
Wher dremes be somtyme, I sey nat alle,	*Whether dreams can sometimes—I don't say always—*
Warnynge of thynges that shul after falle.	*Be warnings of things about to happen.*
Looke of Egipte the kyng, daun Pharao,	*Look at the king of Egypt, the Pharaoh,*
His baker and his butiller also,	*His baker and also his butler,*
Wher they ne felte noon effect in dremes!	*See whether or not they were affected by dreams.*
Whoso wol seken actes of sondry remes	*Anyone who looks at the history of different realms*
May rede of dremes many a wonder thyng.	*Can read many wonderful things about dreams.*
Lo Cresus, which that was of Lyde kyng,	*Look at Croesus, who was king of Lydia,*
Mette he nat that he sat upon a tree,	*Did he not dream that he was sitting in a tree,*
Which signified, he sholde anhanged bee?	*Which showed that he was going to be hanged?*
Lo her Adromacha, Ectores wyf,	*Look at Andromache, the wife of Hector,*
That day that Ector sholde lese his lyf	*On the day that Hector lost his life,*
She dremed on the same nyght biforn	*She dreamed on the preceding night*
How that the lyf of Ector sholde be lorn,	*The way he would lose his life*
If thilke day he wente into bataille.	*If he went into battle that day.*
She warned hym, but it myghte nat availle;	*She warned him, but it did no good;*
He wente for to fighte natheles,	*He went out to fight nonetheless,*
But he was slayn anon of Achilles.	*But he was immediately killed by Achilles.*
But thilke is al to longe for to telle,	*But that story would take too long to tell,*
And eek it is ny day, I may nat dwelle.	*And it's nearly daybreak; I cannot wait.*
Shortly I seye, as for conclusioun,	*I tell you, in conclusion*
That I shal han of this avisioun	*That this vision shows I will have*

Adversitee, and I seye forthermoor	Adversity; and I tell you furthermore
That I ne telle of laxatyves no stoor,	That I have no faith in laxatives,
For they been venymes, I woot it weel,	For they are poison, I am certain;
I hem diffye, I love hem never a deel.	I reject them, I do not believe in them!
Now let us speke of myrthe, and stynte al this;	Now let us speak of happiness, and put a stop to this.
Madame Pertelote, so have I blis,	Madam Pertelote, as I might get to heaven,
Of o thyng God hath sent me large grace,	God has sent me one wonderful thing;
For whan I se the beautee of youre face,	For when I see your beautiful face,
Ye been so scarlet reed aboute youre eyen,	You are so scarlet red around your eyes,
It maketh al my drede for to dyen.	It takes away all my fears;
For, al so siker as In principio	For as surely as 'In the beginning
Mulier est hominis confusio,-	Woman brought about the downfall of man—'
Madame, the sentence of this Latyn is,	Madam, this sentence in Latin means,
'Womman is mannes joye and al his blis.'	'Woman is the joy of man and all his happiness.'
For whan I felle a-nyght your softe syde,	For when I feel your soft side in the night—
Al be it that I may nat on yow ryde,	Even if I can't ride on you,
For that oure perche is maad so narwe, allas!	Because our perch is so narrow, alas—
I am so ful of joye and of solas,	I am so full of joy and pleasure,
That I diffye bothe swevene and dreem.	That it makes me reject both my vision and the dream."
And with that word he fly doun fro the beem,	And with those words he flew down from the beam,
For it was day, and eke hise hennes alle;	For it was daybreak, and all his friends followed,
And with a chuk he gan hem for to calle,	And he began to call them to him with clucking,
For he hadde founde a corn lay in the yerd.	Because he had found some corn, lying in the yard.
Real he was, he was namoore aferd;	He was royal, he was no longer afraid.
And fethered Pertelote twenty tyme,	He hugged Pertelote twenty times,
And trad as ofte, er that it was pryme.	And screwed her many times, before nine o'clock.
He looketh as it were a grym leoun,	He looked as if he were a stern lion,
And on hise toos he rometh up and doun,	Roaming up and down on tiptoes;
Hym deigned nat to sette his foot to grounde.	He would not let his foot touch the ground.
He chukketh whan he hath a corn yfounde,	He clucked when he found any corn,
And to hym rennen thanne hise wyves alle.	And then all his wives ran to him.
Thus roial as a prince is in an halle,	So royal, like a prince in his hall,
Leve I this Chauntecleer in his pasture,	I shall leave this Chaunticleer in his yard,
And after wol I telle his aventure.	And afterwards I will tell what happened to him.
Whan that the monthe in which the world bigan	When the month in which the world began,
That highte March, whan God first maked man,	Which is called March, in which God first made man,
Was compleet, and passed were also	Was over, and there had also passed
Syn March bigan, thritty dayes and two,	Since the end of March, thirty-two days,
Bifel that Chauntecleer in al his pryde,	It happened that Chaunticleer in all his pride,
Hise sevene wyves walkynge by his syde,	With his seven wives walking at his side,
Caste up hise eyen to the brighte sonne,	Looked up at the bright sun,
That in the signe of Taurus hadde yronne	That had crossed the sign of Taurus

Twenty degrees and oon, and somwhat moore;
And knew by kynde, and by noon oother loore,

That it was pryme, and crew with blisful stevene.

The sonne, he seyde, is clomben upon hevene
Fourty degrees and oon, and moore, ywis.
Madame Pertelote, my worldes blis,
Herkneth thise blisful briddes how they synge,
And se the fresshe floures how they sprynge.
Ful is myn herte of revel and solas.
But sodeynly hym fil a sorweful cas,
For evere the latter ende of joye is wo.
God woot that worldly joye is soone ago,

And if a rethor koude faire endite,
He in a cronycle saufly myghte it write,
As for a sovereyn notabilitee.
Now every wys man, lat him herkne me:
This storie is al so trewe, I undertake,
As is the book of Launcelot de Lake,
That wommen holde in ful greet reverence.
Now wol I come agayn to my sentence.

A colfox, ful of sly iniquitee,
That in the grove hadde wonned yeres three,
By heigh ymaginacioun forn-cast,
The same nyght thurghout the hegges brast
Into the yerd, ther Chauntecleer the faire
Was wont, and eek hise wyves, to repaire;
And in a bed of wortes stille he lay,
Til it was passed undren of the day,
Waitynge his tyme on Chauntecleer to falle,
As gladly doon thise homycides alle
That in await liggen to mordre men.
O false mordrour, lurkynge in thy den!
O newe Scariot! newe Genyloun!
False dissymulour, O Greek synoun
That broghtest Troye al outrely to sorwe!
O Chauntecleer, acursed be that morwe
That thou into that yerd flaugh fro the bemes!

Thou were ful wel ywarned by thy dremes

That thilke day was perilous to thee;
But what that God forwoot moot nedes bee,
After the opinioun of certein clerkis.
Witnesse on hym, that any parfit clerk is,
That in scole is greet altercacioun

In this mateere, and greet disputisoun,
And hath been of an hundred thousand men;—

But I ne kan nat bulte it to the bren
As kan the hooly doctour Augustyn,

*Through twenty-one degrees, and a little more,
And he knew from nature, through no other learning,
That it was nine o'clock, and he crowed with a happy voice.
"The sun," he said, "has climbed up in heaven
Forty-one degrees, and in fact higher.
Madame Pertelote, the happiness of my world,
Listen to the singing of these happy birds,
And see how the fresh flowers spring up;
My heart is full of joy and pleasure!"
But suddenly a sad thing happened to him,
For sorrow is always waiting at the end of joy.
God knows that joy in this world quickly disappears;
And if a writer could get this straight
He would do well to write it in a Chronicle
As a very important fact.
Now let every wise man listen to me;
This story is as true, I swear,
As the story of Lancelot of the lake,
Which women revere so much.
Now I will turn back to my story.

A fox, full of sly cunning,
Who had lived in the grove for three years,
Predestined by heavenly plans,
That same night broke through the hedges
Into the yard where handsome Chaunticleer
Was accustomed to going with his wives;
And he lay still in a bed of cabbages
Until nine in the morning had passed,
Waiting for his chance to fall on Chaunticleer,
As these murderers do
Who lie in wait to murder men.
Oh false murderer, lurking in your den!
You new Judas, new Genylon,
False deceiver, oh Greek Synon,
Who brought sorrow for all of Troy!
Oh Chaunticleer, may that morning be cursed
When you flew down from the beams into the yard!
You had been given plenty of warning in your dreams
That the day would be dangerous for you;
But what God preordains must happen,
So certain scholars say.
Take the word of any competent scholar,
That in the universities there is great disagreement
About this matter, much debate,
And a hundred thousand men have discussed it.
But I can't sum up the arguments
Like the holy doctor Augustine,*

Or Boece or the Bisshop Bradwardyn,-
Wheither that Goddes worthy forwityng
Streyneth me nedefully to doon a thyng,
(Nedely clepe I symple necessitee)
Or elles, if free choys be graunted me
To do that same thyng, or do it noght,
Though God forwoot it, er that it was wroght;

Or if his wityng streyneth never a deel
But by necessitee condicioneel,-
I wel nat han to do of swich mateere;
My tale is of a Cok, as ye may heere,
That took his conseil of his wyf, with sorwe,
To walken in the yerd, upon that morwe
That he hadde met that dreem, that I of tolde.

Wommennes conseils been ful ofte colde;
Wommannes conseil broghte us first to wo,

And made Adam fro Paradys to go,
Ther as he was ful myrie, and wel at ese.
But for I noot to whom it myght displese,
If I conseil of wommen wolde blame,
Passe over, for I seye it in my game.
Rede auctours, wher they trete of swich mateere,

And what they seyn of wommen ye may heere.
Thise been the cokkes wordes, and nat myne,
I kan noon harm of no womman divyne.

Faire in the soond, to bathe hire myrily,

Lith Pertelote, and alle hir sustres by,
Agayn the sonne; and Chauntecleer so free
Soony murier than the mermayde in the see-

For Phisiologus seith sikerly
How that they syngen wel and myrily.
And so bifel, that as he cast his eye
Among the wortes on a boterflye,
He was war of this fox that lay ful lowe.
Nothyng ne liste hym thanne for to crowe,
But cride anon, cok! cok! and up he sterte,

As man that was affrayed in his herte.
For natureelly a beest desireth flee
Fro his contrarie, if he may it see,
Though he never erst hadde seyn it with his eye.
This Chauntecleer, whan he gan hym espye,
He wolde han fled, but that the fox anon
Seyde, Gentil sire, allas, wher wol ye gon?
Be ye affrayed of me that am youre freend?
Now certes, I were worse than a feend

If I to yow wolde harm or vileynye.

Or Boethius, or Bishop Bradwardyn,
As to whether the good foreknowledge of God
Forces me to do something—
By forces I mean that I have no choice—
Or otherwise, if I have a free choice
To do that same thing, or not do it,
Even though God knew what would happen before I was born;

Or if his knowledge does not control us at all
And we acted according to conditions.
I will not speculate on such matters;
My tale is about a cockerel as you will hear,
He took advice from his wife, sadly,
To walk in the yard that morning
After he had dreamed the dream I told you about.

The advice of women is very often fatal;
It was the advice of a woman which first brought us sorrow

And forced Adam to leave paradise,
Where he was happy and comfortable.
But I don't know who might be upset
If I criticise the advice of women,
Ignore it, I said it as a joke.
Read the authors who write about these matters,

And you can see what they say about women.
These are the words of the cock, not mine;
I don't know of any evil women.

Lying pretty in the sand, to dust herself happily,

Was Pertelote, with all her sisters by her,
In the sunshine, and Chaunticleer so noble
Sang more merrily than the mermaid in the sea
(For Phisiologus said certainly
That they sing well and merrily).
And so it happened that, as he looked at
A butterfly amongst the cabbages,
He noticed this fox that was lying very low.
So then he did not wish to crow,
But cried out at once, "Cock! Cock!" And he leapt up
Like a man who was terrified.
For naturally a beast wants to run
From his predators, if he sees them,
Even if he had never seen one before.
This Chaunticleer, when he saw him,
Would have fled, but the fox at once
Said, "Gentle sir, alas, where are you going?
Are you afraid of me, your friend?
Now, certainly, I would be worse than the devil
If I did you any harm or mischief!

I am nat come your conseil for tespye,	I haven't come to spy on your secrets,
But trewely, the cause of my comynge	But truly, the reason for my coming
Was oonly for to herkne how that ye synge.	Was just to hear how you sing.
For trewely, ye have as myrie a stevene	For truly, you have as jolly a voice
As any aungel hath that is in hevene.	As any angel in heaven.
Therwith ye han in musyk moore feelynge	In it you have more feeling for music
Than hadde Boece, or any that kan synge.	Than Boethius, or anyone who can sing.
My lord youre fader–God his soule blesse!–	My lord your father–God bless his soul!–
And eek youre mooder, of hir gentillesse	And also your mother, so gracious,
Han in myn hous ybeen, to my greet ese;	I have entertained in my house with great pleasure;
And certes, sire, ful fayn wolde I yow plese.	And certainly, sir, I would be delighted to welcome you.
But for men speke of syngyng, I wol seye,	But, in as far as men speak of singing, I will say–
So moote I brouke wel myne eyen tweye,	Because I can use my two eyes–
Save yow I herde nevere man yet synge	Apart from you, I never heard any man sing
As dide youre fader in the morwenynge.	As well as your father did in the morning.
Certes, it was of herte al that he song!	Certainly all that he sang came from the heart.
And for to make his voys the moore strong,	And to make his voice stronger,
He wolde so peyne hym, that with bothe hise eyen	He would make such an effort that both his eyes
He moste wynke, so loude he solde cryen,	Would be screwed up, he was crying so loud,
And stonden on his tiptoon therwithal,	And he would stand on both his tiptoes,
And strecche forth his nekke long and smal.	And stretch out his long thin neck.
And eek he was of swich discrecioun,	And also he had such good judgement
That ther nas no man in no regioun,	That there was no man in any region
That hym in song or wisedom myghte passe.	Who could surpass him in song or wisdom.
I have wel rad in daun Burnel the Asse	I have certainly read in 'Dan Burnel the Ass,'
Among hise vers, how that ther was a cok,	Amongst his verses, how there was a cock,
For that a presstes sone yaf hym a knok,	Who because the son of a priest kicked him
Upon his leg, whil he was yong and nyce,	On his leg when he was young and foolish,
He made hym for to lese his benefice.	He made him lose his living.
But certeyn, ther nys no comparisoun	But certainly, there is no comparison
Bitwixe the wisedom and discrecioun	To the wisdom and discretion
Of youre fader, and of his subtiltee.	Of your father and his skills.
Now syngeth, sire, for seinte charitee,	Now sing, sir, for St Charity;
Lat se konne ye youre fader countrefete!	Can you be as good as your father?"
This Chauntecleer hise wynges gan to bete,	This Chaunticleer began to beat his wings,
As man that koude his traysoun nat espie,	Because he could not see this treason,
So was he ravysshed with his flaterie.	He was so delighted with all this flattery.
Allas, ye lordes! many a fals flatour	Alas, you noble lords, many false flatterers
Is in youre courtes, and many a losengeour,	Are in your courts, and many sycophants,
That plesen yow wel moore, by my feith,	Who please you more, I swear,
Than he that soothfastnesse unto yow seith.	Than somebody who tells you the truth.
Redeth Ecclesiaste of Flaterye;	Read what Ecclesiastes says about flattery;
Beth war, ye lordes, of hir trecherye.	Beware, you lords, their treachery.
This Chauntecleer stood hye upon his toos,	This Chaunticleer stood up high on his toes,
Strecchynge his nekke, and heeld hise eyen cloos,	Stretching out his neck, and closing his eyes,
And gan to crowe loude for the nones,	And he began to crow loudly for a time.
And daun Russell the fox stirte up atones,	And then Russell the fox jumped up at once,
And by the gargat hente Chauntecleer,	And grabbed Chaunticleer by the throat,
And on his bak toward the wode hym beer,	And carried him on his back to the woods,

For yet ne was ther no man that hym sewed.	And no man pursued him.
O destinee, that mayst nat been eschewed!	O destiny, that cannot be escaped!
Allas, that Chauntecleer fleigh fro the bemes!	Alas that Chaunticleer ever flew down from the beam!
Allas, his wyf ne roghte nat of dremes!	Alas, that his wife took no notice of his dream!
And on a Friday fil al this meschaunce.	This unlucky thing happened on Friday.
O Venus, that art goddesse of plesaunce!	O Venus, who is the goddess of pleasure,
Syn that thy servant was this Chauntecleer,	Since this Chaunticleer was your servant,
And in thy servyce dide al his poweer,	And did everything in your service,
Moore for delit, than world to multiplye,	More for enjoyment than to increase the population,
Why woltestow suffre hym on thy day to dye?	Why did you let him die on your day?
O Gaufred, deere Maister soverayn!	Oh Gaufred, dear sovereign master,
That whan thy worthy kyng Richard was slayn	Who when your good King Richard was killed
With shot, compleynedest his deeth so soore,	With an arrow, complained so much about his death,
Why ne hadde I now thy sentence and thy loore,	Why didn't I have your wisdom and learning
The Friday for to chide, as diden ye?–	To criticise the Friday, as you did?
For on a Friday soothly slayn was he.	For truly it was on a Friday that he was killed.
Thanne wolde I shewe yow, how that I koude pleyne	Then I will show you how I would complain
For Chauntecleres drede and for his peyne.	About the fear of Chaunticleer and his pain.
Certes, swich cry ne lamentacioun	Certainly, no such cry or lamentation
Was nevere of ladyes maad, whan Ylioun	Was ever made by ladies when Troy
Was wonne, and Pirrus with his streite swerd,	Was captured, and Pirrus with his drawn sword,
Whan he hadde hent kyng Priam by the berd,	When he took King Priam by the beard,
And slayn hym, as seith us Eneydos,	And killed him as the Aeneid tells us,
As maden alle the hennes in the clos,	As all those hens made in the yard,
Whan they had seyn of Chauntecleer the sighte.	When they saw what happened to Chaunticleer.
But sovereynly dame Pertelote shrighte	But the royal lady Pertelote shrieked
Ful louder than dide Hasdrubales wyf,	Much louder than the wife of Hasdruble,
Whan that hir housbonde hadde lost his lyf,	When her husband lost his life
And that the Romayns hadde brend Cartage;	And the Romans burned Carthage.
She was so ful of torment and of rage	She was so full of suffering and anger
That wilfully into the fyr she sterte,	That she deliberately jumped into the fire
And brende hirselven with a stedefast herte.	And burnt herself with a strong heart.
O woful hennes, right so criden ye,	Oh sorrowing hens, the way you cried was exactly
As whan that Nero brende the Citee	As the wives of the senators of Rome cried
Of Rome, cryden senatoures wyves,	When Nero burnt down the city,
For that hir husbondes losten alle hir lyves,	Because their husbands had all been killed–
Withouten gilt this Nero hath hem slayn.	Nero had killed them although they were innocent.
Now I wole turne to my tale agayn.	Now I will turn back to my tale.
This sely wydwe, and eek hir doghtres two,	The poor widow and also her two daughters
Herden thise hennes crie, and maken wo,	Heard these hens cry out in sorrow,
And out at dores stirten they anon,	And at once they rushed out of doors,
And seyn the fox toward the grove gon,	And saw the fox going towards the grove,
And bar upon his bak the cok away;	Carrying the cock away on his back,

And cryden, Out! harrow! and weylaway!	And they called out, "Help! Help, alas!
Ha! ha! the fox! and after hym they ran,	Ha ha! The fox!" And they ran after him,
And eek with staves many another man,	And also many other men ran with staves.
Ran Colle, oure dogge, and Talbot, and Gerland,	Our dog Colle, and Talbot and Gerland,
And Malkyn with a dystaf in hir hand,	And Malkyn, with a spinning staff in her hand;
Ran cow and calf, and eek the verray hogges,	The cows and calf ran, and also the pigs,
So were they fered for berkying of the dogges,	So frightened by the barking of dogs
And shoutyng of the men and wommen eek,	And also the shouting of the men and women,
They ronne so, hem thoughte hir herte breek;	They ran so hard they thought their hearts would burst.
They yolleden as feends doon in helle,	They shrieked like the devils down in hell
The dokes cryden as men wolde hem quelle,	The ducks cried out as if men had come to kill them;
The gees for feere flowen over the trees,	Out of fear the geese flew over the trees;
Out of the hyve cam the swarm of bees,	A swarm of bees came out of the hive.
So hydous was the noyse, a! benedicitee!	There was such a hideous noise–bless me!–
Certes, he Jakke Straw and his meynee	Certainly, Jack Straw and his company
Ne made nevere shoutes half so shille,	Never made such a terrible racket
Whan that they wolden any Flemyng kille,	When they were going to kill some Flemish person,
As thilke day was maad upon the fox.	As the noise that was shouted out after the fox.
Of bras they broghten bemes and of box,	They brought trumpets of brass, and also of wood,
Of horn, of boon, in whiche they blewe and powped,	Of horn and bone, which they blew and puffed,
And therwithal they skriked and they howped,	Causing a great shrieking and whooping.
It seemed as that hevene sholde falle!	It seemed as if the sky would fall.
Now, goode men, I pray yow, herkneth alle.	Now, good men, I beg you all to listen:
Lo, how Fortune turneth sodeynly	Look how Fortune turned so suddenly
The hope and pryde eek of hir enemy!	On the hope and pride of her enemy!
This cok, that lay upon the foxes bak,	This cock, that was lying on the back of the fox,
In al his drede unto the fox he spak,	In his fear spoke to the fox,
And seyde, Sire, if that I were as ye,	And said, "Sir, if I were you,
Yet wolde I seyn, as wys God helpe me,	I would say, God help me,
`Turneth agayn, ye proude cherles alle,	'Turn back, you proud peasants!
A verray pestilence upon yow falle!	May a plague fall upon you!
Now am I come unto the wodes syde,	Now I have come to the side of the wood;
Maugree youre heed, the cok shal heere abyde,	Despite everything you do, the cock will remain here.
I wol hym ete, in feith, and that anon,'	I will eat him, I swear, and at once!'"
The fox answerde, In feith, it shal be don.	The fox answered, "I swear, I shall do that."
And as he spak that word, al sodeynly	And as he said that, suddenly
This cok brak from his mouth delyverly,	The cock nimbly slipped from his mouth,
And heighe upon a tree he fleigh anon.	And swiftly flew high up into a tree.
And whan the fox saugh that he was gon,	And when the fox saw that the cock had gone,
Allas! quod he, O Chauntecleer, allas!	He said, "Alas! Oh Chaunticleer, alas!
I have to yow, quod he, ydoon trespas,	I have offended you," he said,
In as muche as I maked yow aferd,	"In that I made you afraid
Whan I yow hente and broght into this yerd.	When I grabbed you and took you out of the yard,
But, sire, I dide it of no wikke entente,	But, sir, I had no wicked intention.
Com doun, and I shal telle yow what I mente;	Come down, and I will tell you what I meant;
I shal seye sooth to yow, God help me so.	I'm telling you the truth, so help me God!"

Nay, thanne, quod he, I shrewe us bothe two,	"No no," he said, "I shall curse both of us.
And first I shrewe myself bothe blood and bones,	First I will curse myself, blood and bones,
If thou bigyle me ofter than ones.	If you manage to trick me more than once.
Thou shalt namoore, thurgh thy flaterye,	Your flattery will no longer
Do me to synge and wynke with myn eye;	Make me sing and close my eyes;
For he that wynketh whan he sholde see,	For someone who closes his eyes, when he should be looking,
Al wilfully, God lat him nevere thee.	Deliberately, may God never give him luck!"
Nay, quod the fox, but God yeve hym meschaunce,	"No," said the fox, "May God bring misfortune
That is so undiscreet of governaunce,	To somebody who is so indiscreet
That jangleth, whan he sholde holde his pees.	That he chatters when he should be quiet."
Lo, swich it si for to be recchelees,	This is what happens when you are careless
And necligent, and truste on flaterye!	And negligent, and believe in flattery.
But ye that holden this tale a folye,	But those of you who think this tale is foolish,
As of a fox, or of a cok and hen,	Just about a fox, or a cock and a hen,
Taketh the moralite, goode men;	Take note of the moral, good men.
For seint Paul seith, that al that writen is,	For St Paul says that everything which is written
To oure doctrine it is ywrite, ywis.	Is written for our instruction, certainly;
Taketh the fruyt, and lat the chaf be stille.	Take the fruit and leave the chaff.
Now goode God, if that it be thy wille,	Now, good God, if it is your will,
As seith my lord, so make us alle goode men,	As my Lord says, make us all good men,
And brynge us to his heighe blisse. Amen.	And bring us to his great heaven! Amen.

Here endenth the Nonne's Preest his tale

The Nun's Priest's epilogue

The end of the Nun's Priest's tale

Sire Nonnes Preest, oure Hooste seide anoon,	"Sir Nun's Priest," our host said at once,
I-blessed be thy breche, and every stoon!	"Blessed be your buttocks, and both your testicles!
This was a murie tale of Chauntecleer.	This was a merry tale about Chaunticleer.
But by my trouthe, if thou were seculer,	But I swear, if you were a layman,
Thou woldest ben a trede-foul aright.	You would be an excellent rooster.
For if thou have corage as thou hast myght,	For if you had lusts which matched your strength,
Thee were nede of hennes, as I wene,	You would need, I think,
Ya, moo than seven tymes seventene.	More than a hundred hens.
See, whiche braunes hath this gentil preest	Look at the muscles on this gentle priest,
So gret a nekke, and swich a large breest!	Such a great neck, such a broad chest!
He loketh as a sperhauk with his yen;	His eyes are sharp as a sparrowhawk's;
Him nedeth nat his colour for to dyen	He doesn't need to paint his face
With brasile, ne with greyn of Portyngale.	With red dye or Portuguese grains.
Now, sire, faire falle yow for youre tale!	Now, sir, may you have good fortune for telling us that tale!"
And after that he, with ful merie chere,	And after that he, in a very merry fashion,
Seide unto another, as ye shuln heere.	Spoke to someone else, as you will hear.

The Prologe of the Seconde Nonnes Tale.

The Prologue of the Second Nun's Tale

The ministre and the norice unto vices,	The Minister and encourager of vices,

428

Which that men clepe in Englissh ydelnesse,	Which in English men call Idleness,
That porter of the gate is of delices,	Who is the keeper of the gate of pleasure,
To eschue, and by hir contrarie hir oppresse,	To reject her, and overcome her with her opposite—
(That is to seyn by leveful bisynesse),	That is to say, by doing lawful good work—
Wel oghten we to doon al oure entente,	We ought to try our hardest to do this,
Lest that the feend thurgh ydelnesse us shente.	In case the devil uses idleness to trap us.
For he, that with hise thousand cordes slye	For he with his thousand cunning traps
Continuelly us waiteth to biclappe,	Is continuall lying in wait to grab us,
Whan he may man in ydelnesse espye,	When he sees a man being idle,
He kan so lightly cacche hym in his trappe,	He can catch him so quickly in his trap,
Til that a man be hent right by the lappe,	That until a man is suddenly caught by the hem,
He nys nat war the feend hath hym in honde.	He doesn't know that the devil has hold of him.
Wel oghte us werche, and ydelnesse withstonde.	We certainly ought to work and reject idleness.
And though men dradden nevere for to dye,	And even though a man might not be scared of dying,
Yet seen men wel by resoun, doutelees,	He can certainly see through reason
That ydelnesse is roten slogardye,	That idleness is rotten laziness,
Of which ther nevere comth no good encrees;	Which never engenders any good or profit;
And seen that slouthe hir holdeth in a lees,	And since sloth holds idleness on a leash,
Oonly to slepe, and for to ete and drynke,	Only allowing her to sleep, and to eat and drink,
And to devouren al that othere swynke.	And to gobble up what everyone else pays for with their work,
And for to putte us fro swich ydelnesse,	In order to set us apart from such idleness,
That cause is of so greet confusioun,	Which causes such great ruin,
I have heer doon my feithful bisynesse,	I have here done my faithful work
After the legende, in translacioun	Of translating the legend
Right of thy glorious lyf and passioun,	Correctly of your glorious life and suffering,
Thou with thy gerland wroght with rose and lilie,	You who wore the garland of roses and lilies—
Thee meene I, mayde and martir, seint Cecilie.	I mean you, virgin and martyr, St Cecilia.
Invocacio ad Mariam.	Prayer to Mary
And thow that flour of virgines art alle,	And you who are the exemplar of all virgins,
Of whom that Bernard list so wel to write,	Of whom Bernard was so pleased to write,
To thee at my bigynnyng first I calle,	I call on you as I begin;
Thou confort of us wrecches, do me endite	You are the comfort of we wretches, let me tell
Thy maydens deeth, that wan thurgh hir merite	Of your maidenly death, which won because of your merit
The eterneel lyf, and of the feend victorie,	Eternal life and victory over the devil,
As man may after reden in hir storie.	As any man can read in her story.
Thow mayde and mooder, doghter of thy sone,	You virgin and mother, daughter of your son,
Thow welle of mercy, synful soules cure,	You well of Mercy, the cure for sinful souls,
In whom that God for bountee chees to wone,	Whom God chose as a vessel of goodness,
Thow humble and heigh, over every creature	You humble woman, though higher than every other creature,
Thow nobledest so ferforth oure nature,	Who gave such nobility to our nature,
That no desdeyn the makere hadde of kynde,	That the maker of man did not hesitate

His sone in blood and flessh to clothe and wynde,	To clothe his son in blood and flesh.
Withinne the cloistre blisful of thy sydis	Within the blissful cloister of your sides
Took mannes shape the eterneel love and pees,	Eternal love and peace took the shape of man,
That of the tryne compas lord and gyde is,	Who is the Lord and guide of the triple universe,
Whom erthe and see and hevene out of relees	Whom earth and sea and heaven, without cease,
Ay heryen, and thou, virgine wemmelees,	Always praise; and you, stainless virgin,
Baar of thy body, and dweltest mayden pure,	Carried in your body—and remained a virgin—
The creatour of every creature.	The creator of every creature.
Assembled is in thee magnificence	Magnificence is gathered in you
With mercy, goodnesse, and with swich pitee	With mercy, goodness, and such pity
That thou, that art the sonne of excellence,	That you, who are the sun of excellence
Nat oonly helpest hem that preyen thee,	Not only help those who pray to you,
But oftentyme, of thy benygnytee,	But often in your goodness
Ful frely, er that men thyn help biseche,	Very willingly, before men ask you for help,
Thou goost biforn, and art hir lyves leche.	You go ahead of them and cure their lives.
Now help, thow meeke and blisful faire mayde,	Now help, you meek and blissful fair maiden,
Me, flemed wrecche in this desert of galle;	Me, banished wretch, in this desert of bitterness;
Thynk on the womman Cananee, that sayde	Think of the woman of Cannae, who said
That whelpes eten somme of the crommes alle,	That dogs eat some of the crumbs
That from hir lordes table been yfalle,	That fall from the table of their Lord;
And though that I, unworthy sone of Eve,	And although I, unworthy son of these,
Be synful, yet accepte my bileve.	Am sinful, accept my faith.
And for that feith is deed withouten werkis,	And, because faith is worthless without deeds,
So for to werken yif me wit and space,	Give me the wit and opportunity to work
That I be quit fro thennes that moost derk is.	So that I can be free from the darkest place!
O thou, that art so fair and ful of grace,	Oh you, who are so fair and full of grace,
Be myn advocat in that heighe place	Be my advocate in that high place
Ther as withouten ende is songe Osanne,	Where hosanna is sung unceasingly,
Thow Cristes mooder, doghter deere of Anne!	You mother of Christ, dear daughter of Anne!
And of thy light my soule in prison lighte,	And with your light show the way to my soul in prison,
That troubled is by the contagioun	Which is troubled by the diseases
Of my body, and also by the wighte	Of my body, and also by the burden
Of erthely lust and fals affeccioun,	Of earthly lust and false desire;
O havene of refut, O salvacioune	Oh haven of refuge, oh salvation
Of hem that been in sorwe and in distresse,	Of all those who are in sorrow and distress,
Now help, for to my werk I wol me dresse.	Help me, as I devote myself to my work.
Yet preye I yow that reden that I write,	But I pray to you who reads what I write,
Foryeve me, that I do no diligence	Forgive me for not making any effort
This ilke storie subtilly to endite,	To tell this story in an elaborate way,
For bothe have I the wordes and sentence	For I have both the words and the meaning
Of hym that at the seintes reverence	From the one who, from reverence for the saint,
The storie wroot, and folwe hir legende.	Wrote the story down, and I follow her legend,
I pray yow, that ye wole my werk amende.	And I beg you to correct any faults in my work.

Interpretacio Nominis Caecilie
Quam Ponit Frater Iacobus
Ianuensis in Legenda Aurea.
First wolde I yow the name of seinte Cecile

Expowne, as men may in hir storie see.
It is to seye in Englissh, `hevenes lilie'
For pure chaastnesse of virginitee,
Or for she whitnesse hadde of honestee
And grene of conscience, and of good fame

The soote savour, lilie was hir name.

Or Cecilie is to seye, `the wey to blynde,'
For she ensample was by good techynge;

Or elles, Cecile, as I writen fynde
Is joyned by a manere conjoynynge
Of `hevene' and `lia,' and heere in figurynge

The `hevene' is set for thoght of hoolynesse,
And `lia' for hir lastynge bisynesse.

Cecile may eek be seyd, in this manere,
`Wantynge of blyndnesse,' for hir grete light

Of sapience, and for hire thewes cleere
Or elles, loo, this maydens name bright

Of `hevene' and `leos' comth, for which by right
Men myghte hir wel `the hevene of peple' calle,

Ensample of goode and wise werkes alle.

For `leos' `peple' in Englissh is to seye,
And right as men may in the hevene see
The sonne and moone and sterres every weye,
Right so men goostly, in this mayden free,

Syen of feith the magnanymytee,
And eek the cleernesse hool of sapience,
And sondry werkes, brighte of excellence.

And right so as thise philosophres write
That hevene is swift and round and eek brennynge,

Right so was faire Cecilie the white
Ful swift and bisy evere in good werkynge,

And round and hool in good perseverynge,
And brennynge evere in charite ful brighte.
Now have I yow declared what she highte.

*Explanation of the name of Cecilia
Which Frater Iacobus
Ianuensis in the legend
Firstly I want to explain the name of St Cecilia to you,
The one which men see in her story.
In English it means "the lily of heaven,"
Meaning the pure chastity of virginity;
Or, because she had the whiteness of chastity,
And the green of good conscience and reputation,
The sweet smell of "Lily" was her name.

Cecilia can also mean "the path for the blind,"
Because she set an example through her good teaching;
Or otherwise Cecilia, as I have seen written,
Is joined, a sort of combination
Of "heaven" and "Leah"; and here, symbolically,
Heaven stands for her holy thoughts,
And "Leah" for her unceasing work.

Cecilia can also be explained in this way,
"Lacking in blindness," because of her great light
Of wisdom, and for her pure morals;
Or otherwise, you see, the bright name of this maiden
Comes from "heaven" and "leos", so men
Quite rightly could call her "the heaven of people,"
Because of the example of all her good and wise works.

For in English "leos" means people,
And just as men can see in the heavens
The sun and moon and stars everywhere,
In the same way men can in this generous maiden
See the wonder of the spirit of faith,
And also the complete clarity of wisdom,
And different works, bright in their excellence.

And just as these philosophers write
That heaven is swift and round and also burning,
This was just like fair Cecily the white
Very quick and also always busy with good works,
And round and whole and always persevering,
And always burning with bright charity.
Now I have told you what she was called.*

The Second Nun's Tale

Here bigynneth the Seconde Nonnes Tale of the lyf of Seinte Cecile.	*Here begins the Second Nun's Tale of the life of Saint Cecilia*

This mayden, bright Cecilie, as hir lyf seith,

Was comen of Romayns, and of noble kynde,
And from hir cradel up fostred in the feith

Of Crist, and bar his gospel in hir mynde.
She nevere cessed, as I writen fynde,
Of hir preyere, and God to love and drede,
Bisekynge hym to kepe hir maydenhede.

And whan this mayden sholde unto a man

Ywedded be, that was ful yong of age,
Which that ycleped was Valerian,
And day was comen of hir mariage,
She, ful devout and humble in hir corage,
Under hir robe of gold, that sat ful faire,

Hadde next hir flessh yclad hir in an haire.

And whil the orgnes maden melodie,
To God allone in herte thus sang she:
O Lord, my soule and eek my body gye
Unwemmed, lest that I confounded be.
And for his love that dyde upon a tree,
Every seconde and thridde day she faste,
Ay biddynge in hir orisons ful faste.

The nyght cam, and to bedde moste she gon
With hir housbonde, as ofte is the manere,
And pryvely to hym she seyde anon,
O sweete and wel biloved spouse deere,
Ther is a conseil, and ye wolde it heere,
Which that right fayn I wolde unto yow seye,
So that ye swere ye shul me nat biwreye.

Valerian gan faste unto hire swere
That for no cas, ne thyng that myghte be,
He sholde nevere mo biwreyen here,
And thanne at erst to hym thus seyde she,
I have an Aungel which that loveth me,
That with greet love, wher so I wake or sleepe,

Is redy ay my body for to kepe.

And if that he may feelen out of drede

This bright maiden Cecilia, as her biography says,
Was descended from Romans and nobly born,
And from the cradle was brought up in the faith
Of Christ, and had his gospel in her mind.
She never stopped, as I have found written,
Praying and loving and fearing God,
Begging him to keep her a virgin.

And when this maiden was going to be married
To a man, who was very young
And called Valerian,
And the day of her marriage came,
She, very devout and humble in her heart,
Under her golden robe, that suited her very well,
Had dressed herself in a hair shirt next to her skin.

And as the organs played
She sang in her heart directly to God:
"Oh Lord, save my soul and also my body
Unstained, so that I will not be damned."
And for the love of him who died on the cross,
She fasted every second and third day,
Always praying very fervently.

The night came, and she had to go to bed
With her husband, as is the custom,
And privately she said to him straight away,
"You sweet and well loved dear husband,
There is a secret, if you want to hear it,
Which I am very keen to tell you,
Providing you swear that you will not give it away."

Valerian began to swear to her sincerely
That in no circumstance and for no reason
Would he ever betray her;
And so she said to him for the first time:
"I have an angel who loves me,
Who with great love, whether I am asleep or waking,
Is always ready to guard my body.

And if he feels certain

That ye me touche, or love in vileynye,	That you are touching me, or loving me sexually,
He right anon wol sle yow with the dede,	He will kill you at once,
And in youre yowthe thus ye sholden dye.	And you will die a young man;
And if that ye in clene love me gye,	And if you keep lovingly purely
He wol yow loven as me for youre clennesse,	He will love you the same as me, for your chastity,
And shewen yow his joye and his brightnesse.	And he will show you his joy and his brightness."
Valerian, corrected as God wolde,	Valerian, taking the lesson as God wished,
Answerde agayn, If I shal trusten thee,	Answered her, "If I must trust you,
Lat me that aungel se, and hym biholde,	Let me see that angel and look at him;
And if that it a verray aungel bee,	And if it is a true angel,
Thanne wol I doon as thou hast prayed me;	Then I will do as you have asked me;
And if thou love another man, forsothe	And if you love another man, I swear
Right with this swerd thanne wol I sle yow bothe.	I will certainly kill you both with this sword."
Cecile answerde anon right in this wise,	Cecilia immediately answered in this fashion:
If that yow list, the aungel shul ye see,	"If you wish, you can see the angel,
So that ye trowe in Crist, and yow baptize.	Provided that you believe in Christ and are baptised.
Gooth forth to Via Apia, quod she,	Go out to the Appian Way," she said,
That fro this toun ne stant but miles thre;	"That is not more than three miles from this town,
And to the povre folkes that ther dwelle	And say to the poor folk that live there
Sey hem right thus as that I shal yow telle.	These exact words which I shall tell you.
Telle hem, that I Cecile yow to hem sente,	Tell them that I, Cecilia, sent you to them
To shewen yow the goode Urban the olde,	To show you good Urban the old,
For secree thynges and for good entente;	For secret reasons and for good ones.
And whan that ye Seint Urban han biholde,	And when you have seen St Urban,
Telle hym the wordes whiche that I to yow tolde,	Tell him the words I have said to you;
And whan that he hath purged yow fro synne,	And when he has washed your sin away,
Thanne shul ye se that aungel er ye twynne.	Then you will see the angel, before you leave."
Valerian is to the place ygon,	Valerian went to the place,
And right as hym was taught by his lernynge,	Just as she had taught him,
He foond this hooly olde Urban anon	And he immediately found this holy old Urban
Among the seintes buryeles lotynge.	Hiding amongst the graves of the saints.
And he anon, withouten tariynge,	And at once, without delay,
Dide his message, and whan that he it tolde,	He passed on the message; and when he had said it,
Urban for joye his handes gan up holde.	Urban held up his hands in joy.
The teeris from hise eyen leet he falle.	He let the tears fall from his eyes.
Almyghty lord, O Jesu Crist, quod he,	"Almighty Lord, Jesus Christ," he said,
Sower of chaast conseil, hierde of us alle,	"Sower of pure advice, the shepherd of us all,
The fruyt of thilke seed of chastitee	The fruit of the same seed of chastity
That thou hast sowe in Cecile, taak to thee.	That you have sown in Cecilia, take this man!
Lo, lyk a bisy bee, withouten gile,	See, like a busy bee, with no deceit,
Thee serveth ay thyn owene thral Cecile!	Your servant Cecilia always serves you.
For thilke spouse that she took but now	For the same spouse which she has just married

Ful lyk a fiers leoun, she sendeth heere	Who is so like a fierce lion, she has sent here,
As meke as evere was any lomb, to yow.	As meek as any lamb ever was, to you!"
And with that word anon ther gan appeere	And at those words at once there appeared
An oold man clad in white clothes cleere,	An old man, dressed in clear white clothes,
That hadde a book with lettre of gold in honde,	Who had a book with gold lettering in his hand,
And gan bifore Valerian to stonde.	And he stood in front of Valerian.
Valerian as deed fil doun for drede	Valerian fell then out of fear like a dead man
Whan he hym saugh, and he up hente hym tho,	When he saw him, and the old man then picked him up,
And on his book right thus he gan to rede,	And he began at once to read from his book:
O lord, o feith, o god, withouten mo,	"One Lord, one faith, one God, without others,
O Cristendom, and fader of alle also,	One kingdom, and also the father of all,
Aboven alle, and over alle, everywhere.-	Ruling over everything, everywhere."
Thise wordes al with gold ywriten were.	These words were all written in gold.
Whan this was rad, thanne seyde this olde man,	When this had been read, then the old man said,
Leevestow this thyng or no? sey ye or nay?	"Do you believe in this or not? Say yes or no."
I leeve al this thyng, quod Valerian,	"I believe all of this," said Valerian,
For oother thyng than this, I dar wel say,	"For I dare say that there is nothing truer than this
Under the hevene no wight thynke may.	That anybody could imagine under heaven."
Tho vanysshed this olde man, he nyste where;	Then this old man vanished, he did not know where,
And Pope Urban hym cristned right there.	And Pope Urban christened him on the spot.
Valerian gooth hoom, and fynt Cecile	Valerian went home and found Cecilia
Withinne his chambre with an aungel stonde.	Standing in his room with an angel.
This aungel hadde of roses and of lilie	The angel had two crowns of roses
Corones two, the whiche he bar in honde;	And lilies, which he carried in his hands;
And first to Cecile, as I understonde,	And first to Cecilia, as I understand it,
He yaf that oon, and after gan he take	He gave one, and afterwards he gave
That oother to Valerian hir make.	The other to Valerian, her mate.
With body clene and with unwemmed thoght	"With a clean body and pure thoughts
Kepeth ay wel thise corones, quod he,	Always look after these crowns," he said;
Fro Paradys to yow have I hem broght,	"I have brought them to you from paradise,
Ne nevere mo ne shal they roten bee,	And they will never decay,
Ne lese hir soote savour, trusteth me,	Nor lose their sweet smell, trust me;
Ne nevere wight shal seen hem with his eye	And no person will ever see them,
But he be chaast and hate vileynye.	Unless he is chaste and hates villainy.
And thow Valerian, for thow so soone	And you, Valerian, because you so quickly
Assentedest to good conseil also,	Agreed to good counsel,
Sey what thee list, and thou shalt han thy boone.	Say what you wish, and you shall have it."
I have a brother, quod Valerian tho,	"I have a brother," Valerian then said,
That in this world I love no man so.	"And I don't love any man in the world more.
I pray yow that my brother may han grace,	I beg you to give my brother the Grace
To knowe the trouthe, as I do in this place.	To know the truth, as I have done."
The aungel seyde, God liketh thy requeste,	The angel said, "God approves of your request,
And bothe with the palm of martirdom	And both of you will come to his blissful feast

Ye shullen com unto his blisful feste.	*Carrying the palm of martyrdom."*
And with that word Tiburce his brother coom;	*As he said that his brother Tiburce came.*
And whan that he the savour undernoom,	*And when he smelt the fragrance*
Which that the roses and the lilies caste,	*Of the roses and lilies*
Withinne his herte he gan to wondre faste,	*He began to wonder greatly in his heart,*
And seyde, I wondre, this tyme of the yeer,	*And he said, "I wonder, at this time of year,*
Whennes that soote savour cometh so	*Where that great sweet fragrance comes from,*
Of rose and lilies that I smelle heer.	*The roses and lilies that I can smell here.*
For though I hadde hem in myne handes two,	*For even if I had them in my two hands,*
The savour myghte in me no depper go,	*I would not get any more of the fragrance.*
The sweete smel that in myn herte I fynde	*The sweet smell that I find in my heart*
Hath chaunged me al in another kynde.	*Has completely changed my nature."*
Valerian seyde, Two corones han we,	*Valerian said, "We have two crowns,*
Snow-white and rose-reed that shynen cleere,	*Snow white and rose red, that shine brightly,*
Whiche that thyne eyen han no myght to see,	*Which your eyes do not have the power of seeing;*
And as thou smellest hem thurgh my preyere,	*And just as you can smell them because of my prayers,*
So shaltow seen hem, leeve brother deere,	*You shall also see them, my beloved dear brother,*
If it so be thou wolt, withouten slouthe,	*If you wish it, at once,*
Bileve aright and knowen verray trouthe.	*If you believe correctly and know the truth."*
Tiburce answerde, Seistow this to me?	*Tiburce answered, "Are you saying this to me*
In soothnesse or in dreem I herkne this?	*In reality, or am I hearing this in a dream?"*
In dremes, quod Valerian, han we be	*"Dreams," said Valerian, "are what we have been in*
Unto this tyme, brother myn, ywes;	*Up to this time, my brother, for certain.*
But now at erst in trouthe oure dwellyng is.	*But now for the first time we are living in truth."*
How woostow this, quod Tiburce, in what wyse?	*"How do you know this?" said Tiburce, "How have you learnt it?"*
Quod Valerian, That shal I thee devyse.	*Valerian said, "I shall tell you that.*
The aungel of God hath me the trouthe ytaught	*The angel of God has taught me the truth*
Which thou shalt seen, if that thou wolt reneye	*Which you will see, if you will renounce*
The ydoles and be clene, and elles naught.	*Idols and be pure, otherwise you shall see nothing."*
And of the myracle of thise corones tweye	*And of the miracle of these two crowns*
Seint Ambrose in his preface list to seye.	*St Ambrose is glad to speak in his preface;*
Solempnely this noble doctour deere	*Solemnly this noble dear doctor of the church*
Commendeth it, and seith in this manere;	*Praises it, and he says this:*
The palm of martirdom for to receive	*"In order to receive the palm of martyrdom,*
Seinte Cecile, fulfild of Goddes yifte,	*St Cecilia, filled with the gifts of God,*
The world and eek hire chambre gan she weyve,	*Sacrificed the world and her bedchamber;*
Witnesse Tyburces and Valerians shrifte,	*She was witness to the confessions of Tiburce and Valerian,*
To whiche God of his bountee wolde shifte	*For which God in his goodness would provide*
Corones two, of floures wel smellynge,	*A pair of crowns of sweet smelling flowers,*
And made his aungel hem the corones brynge.	*And he made his angel bring them to them.*

The mayde hath broght thise men to blisse above;	The maiden brought these men to heavenly bliss;
The world hath wist what it is worth, certeyn,	The world has seen how valuable it is, certainly,
Devocioun of chastitee to love. . . .	To be devoted to chastity with love."
Tho shewed hym Cecile, al open and pleyn,	Then Cecilia showed him quite clearly
That alle ydoles nys but a thyng in veyn,	That all idols are just plain things,
For they been dombe and therto they been deve,	For they are dumb and also deaf,
And charged hym hise ydoles for to leve.	And she ordered him to abandon his idols.
Whoso that troweth, nat this, a beest he is,	"Whoever doesn't believe this, he is an animal,"
Quod tho Tiburce, if that I shal nat lye.	Tiburce then said, "if I am truthful."
And she gan kisse his brest, that herde this,	And she who heard this kissed his breast,
And was ful glad he koude trouthe espye.	And was very glad that he could see the truth.
This day I take thee for myn allye,	"Today I take you as my relative,"
Seyde this blisful faire mayde deere,	Said this blissful fair maiden,
And after that she seyde as ye may heere.	And after that she spoke these words which you can hear:
Lo, right so as the love of Crist, quod she,	"See, just as the love of Christ," she said,
Made me thy brotheres wyf, right in that wise	"Made me your brother's wife, in exactly the same way
Anon for myn allyee heer take I thee,	Right now I take you as my kinsman,
Syn that thou wolt thyne ydoles despise.	Since you will reject your idols.
Go with thy brother now, and thee baptise,	Go with your brother now, and get baptised,
And make thee clene, so that thou mowe biholde	And make yourself pure, so that you can see
The aungels face of which thy brother tolde.	The face of the angel which your brother told you of."
Tiburce answerde and seyde, Brother deere,	Tiburce answered and said, "Dear brother,
First tel me whider I shal, and to what man?	Firstly tell me where I should go, to what man?"
To whom? quod he, com forth with right good cheere,	"To whom?" he said, "come out confidently,
I wol thee lede unto the Pope Urban.	I will take you to Pope Urban."
Til Urban? brother myn Valerian,	"To Urban? My brother Valerian,"
Quod tho Tiburce, woltow me thider lede?	Tiburce then said, "will you take me there?
Me thynketh that it were a wonder dede.	I think that would be a wonderful deed.
Ne menestow nat Urban, quod he tho,	You don't mean Urban," he then said,
That is so ofte dampned to be deed,	"Who has so often been condemned to death,
And woneth in halkes alwey to and fro,	And lives in hiding places, going from one to another,
And dar nat ones putte forth his heed;	And does not dare stick his head out?
Men sholde hym brennen in a fyr so reed,	Men should burn him in a fire so red
If he were founde, or that men myghte hym spye;	If he were found, or if any man saw him,
And we also, to bere hym compaignye,	And we would also burn if we were found in his company;
And whil we seken thilke divinitee,	And whilst we seek the same divinity
That is yhid in hevene pryvely,	That is secretly hidden in heaven,
Algate ybrend in this world shul we be!	We would still be burned in this world!"
To whom Cecile answerde boldely,	Cecilia answered him boldly,
Men myghten dreden wel and skilfully	"A man can reasonably and sensibly fear

This lyf to lese, myn owene deere brother,	*Losing this life, my own dear brother,*
If this were lyvynge oonly and noon oother.	*If this were the only life and there was no other.*
But ther is bettre lyf in oother place,	*But there is a better life in another place,*
That nevere shal be lost, ne drede thee noght,	*That can never be lost, do not doubt it,*
Which Goddes sone us tolde thurgh his grace.	*Which the son of God told us of through his grace.*
That fadres sone hath alle thyng ywroght,	*That son of the Father has created everything,*
And al that wroght is with a skilful thoght,	*And everything he made has the power of thought;*
The goost, that fro the fader gan procede,	*The Holy Ghost, which came from the Father,*
Hath sowled hem, withouten any drede.	*Has given us all souls, there is no doubt.*
By word and by myracel Goddes Sone,	*Through words and miracles the son of Almighty God,*
Whan he was in this world, declared here	*When he was in this world, declared here*
That ther was oother lyf ther men may wone.	*That there was another life which men could live."*
To whom answerde Tiburce, O suster deere,	*Tiburce answered her, "Oh dear sister,*
Ne seydestow right now in this manere,	*Did you not just say in the same fashion*
Ther nys but o God, lord in soothfastnesse,	*That there is only one God, the Lord of truthfulness?*
And now of thre how maystow bere witnesse?	*How now you speaking of three?"*
That shal I telle, quod she, er I go.	*"I shall tell you that," she said, "before I go.*
Right as a man hath sapiences thre,	*Just as a man has three types of wisdom—*
Memorie, engyn, and intellect also,	*Memory, imagination, and also judgement—*
So, in o beynge of divinitee	*So in one single God,*
Thre persones may ther right wel bee.	*Three people can be embodied."*
Tho gan she hym ful bisily to preche	*Then she began very eagerly to preach to him*
Of Cristes come, and of hise peynes teche,	*About the coming of Christ, and to teach him of the pain He suffered,*
And many pointes of his passioun;	*And many details of His passion;*
How Goddes sone in this world was withholde	*How the son of God had to stay in this world*
To doon mankynde pleyn remissioun,	*To attain full forgiveness for mankind,*
That was ybounde in synne and cares colde . . .	*Which was bound up with sin and harsh care;*
Al this thyng she unto Tiburce tolde;	*She told Tiburce all these things.*
And after this, Tiburce in good entente	*And after this Tiburce with great content*
With Valerian to Pope Urban he wente;	*Went to see Pope Urban with Valerian,*
That thanked God, and with glad herte and light	*Who thanked God, and with a glad and happy heart*
He cristned hym, and made hym in that place	*He christened him and made him in that place*
Parfit in his lernynge, Goddes knyght.	*Perfect in his learning, a knight of God.*
And after this Tiburce gat swich grace	*And after this Tiburce was granted such grace*
That every day he saugh in tyme and space	*That every day he saw in reality*
The aungel of God, and every maner boone	*The angel of God; and every favour*
That he God axed, it was sped ful soone.	*He asked of God was given to him at once.*
It were ful hard by ordre for to seyn	*It would be very hard to describe in proper order*
How manye wondres Jesu for hem wroghte.	*How many miracles Jesus did for them;*
But atte laste, to tellen short and pleyn,	*But in the end, to tell it simply,*

The sergeantz of the toun of Rome hem soghte,	The officers of the town of Rome sought them out,
And hem biforn Almache the Prefect broghte,	And brought them in front of Almache, the prefect,
Which hem opposed, and knew al hire entente,	Who questioned them, and knew what they thought,
And to the ymage of Juppiter hem sente,	And he sent them to the statue of Jupiter,
And seyde, Whoso wol nat sacrifise,	Saying, "Whoever will not make a sacrifice,
Swap of his heed, this my sentence heer.	Cut off his head; that is my sentence."
Anon thise martirs that I yow devyse,	Immediately these martyrs of whom I'm telling you.
Oon Maximus, that was an officer	One Maximus, who was an officer
Of the prefectes, and his corniculer,	Of the prefect, and his main assistant,
Hem hente, and whan he forth the seintes ladde,	Seized them, and when he led the saints away
Hymself he weepe, for pitee that he hadde.	He himself wept out of pity.
Whan Maximus had herd the seintes loore,	When Maximus had heard the teaching of the saints,
He gat hym of the tormentoures leve,	He got permission from the executioners,
And ladde hem to his hous withoute moore.	And took them to his house without delay,
And with hir prechyng, er that it were eve,	And with their preaching, before evening,
They gonnen fro the tormentours to reve,	They had taken away from the executioners,
And fro Maxime, and fro his folk echone	And from Maximus, and from all his people,
The fals feith, to trowe in God allone.	Their false faith, and taught them to believe in God alone.
Cecile cam whan it was woxen nyght,	Cecilia came, when it was nighttime,
With preestes that hem cristned alle yfeere,	With priests who christened them all at once;
And afterward, whan day was woxen light,	And afterwards, when daylight came,
Cecile hem seyde, with a ful stedefast cheere,	Cecilia said to them steadfastly,
Now Cristes owene knyghtes, leeve and deere,	"Now, beloved dear knights of Christ,
Cast alle awey the werkes of derkness	Reject all the works of darkness,
And armeth yow in armure of brightnesse.	And arm yourselves with light.
Ye han forsothe ydoon a greet bataille,	Truly you have fought a great battle,
Youre cours is doon, youre feith han ye conserved,	Your journey is finished, you have stuck to your faith.
Gooth to the corone of lyf that may nat faille.	Go and seek the crown of the life that cannot end;
The rightful juge which that ye han served	The true Judge, whom you have served,
Shal yeve it yow as ye han it deserved.	Will give it to you, for you have earned it."
And whan this thyng was seyd as I devyse,	And when she said these things I tell you,
Men ledde hem forth to doon the sacrifise.	Men took them out to make the sacrifice.
But whan they weren to the place broght,	When they were brought to the place,
To tellen shortly the conclusioun,	To tell the story briefly,
They nolde encense ne sacrifise right noght,	They would not light incense or make a sacrifice in any way,
But on hir knees they setten hem adoun	But they went down upon their knees
With humble herte and sad devocioun,	With humble hearts and strong devotion,
And losten bothe hir hevedes in the place.	And they both lost their heads in that place.
Her soules wenten to the kyng of grace.	Their souls went to the king of grace.
This Maximus that saugh this thyng bityde,	This Maximus, who saw this happen,

With pitous teeris tolde it anon-right,	With piteous tears spoke at once,
That he hir soules saugh to hevene glyde,	Saying that he saw their souls gliding up to heaven
With aungels ful of cleernesse and of light;	With angels so clear and bright,
And with this word converted many a wight.	And with his words many people were converted;
For which Almachius dide hym so bête	For doing this Almache had him beaten so badly
With whippe of leed, til he the lyf gan lete.	With a lead tipped whip that he died.
Cecile hym took, and buryed hym anon	Cecilia took him and buried him at once
By Tiburce and Valerian softely,	Tenderly next to Tiburce and Valerian
Withinne hir buriyng place under the stoon,	Under their gravestone, in their graves;
And after this Almachius hastily	And after this, Almache hastily
Bad hise ministres fecchen openly	Ordered his ministers to publicly arrest
Cecile, so that she myghte in his presence	Cecilia, so that she would in his presence
Doon sacrifice, and Juppiter encense.	Make sacrifices and burn incense to Jupiter.
But they, converted at hir wise loore,	But they, converted by her wise teaching,
Wepten ful soore, and yaven ful credence	Wept very pitifully, and fully believed
Unto hire word, and cryden moore and moore,	In her words, and cried more and more,
Crist, Goddes sone, withouten difference,	"Christ, son of God, of the same body,
Is verray God, this is al oure sentence,	Is the true God–this is what we all believe–
That hath so good a servant hym to serve	Who has such a good servant working for Him.
This with o voys we trowen, thogh we sterve.	This is what we all believe, even if we die for it!"
Almachius, that herde of this doynge,	Almache, who heard what had happened,
Bad fecchen Cecile, that he myghte hir see,	Ordered Cecilia to be fetched, so that he could see her,
And alderfirst, lo, this was his axynge:	And this was the first question he asked.
What maner womman artow? tho quod he.	"Was sort of woman are you?" he said.
I am a gentil womman born, quod she.	"I am born a gentlewoman," she said.
I axe thee, quod he, though it thee greeve,	"I am asking you," he said, "though you may not like it,
Of thy religioun and of thy bileeve.	About your religion and your beliefs."
Ye han bigonne youre question folily,	"You have started your question foolishly,"
Quod she, that wolden two answeres conclude	She said, "you want two answers
In o demande; ye axed lewedly.	To one question; you asked ignorantly."
Almache answerde unto that similitude,	Almache replied to that rebuttal,
Of whennes comth thyn answeryng so rude?'	"Why do you answer me so rudely?"
Of whennes? quod she, whan that she was freyned,	"Why?" she said, when she was asked,
Of conscience and of good feith unfeyned.	"Because of my conscience and my sincere good faith."
Almachius seyde, Ne takestow noon heede	Almache said, "Do you not care
Of my power? and she answerde hym,	About my power?" And she answered him thus:
Youre myght, quod she, ful litel is to dreede,	"Your power," she said, "is nothing to fear,
For every mortal mannes power nys	For the power of every mortal man is nothing
But lyke a bladdre ful of wynd, ywys;	But a bladder full of wind, it's certain.
For with a nedles poynt, whan it is blowe,	For when it is blown up all its pride
May al the boost of it be leyd ful lowe.	Can be burst with the point of a needle."

Middle English	Modern English
Ful wrongfully bigonne thow, quod he, / And yet in wrong is thy perseveraunce; / Wostow nat how oure myghty princes free / Han thus comanded and maad ordinaunce / That every cristen wight shal han penaunce, / But if that he his cristendom withseye- / And goon al quit, if he wole it reneye?	"You were wrong when you started," he said, / "And you are still wrong as you carry on. / Do you not know how our great noble princes / Have ordered and made a law / That every Christian person will be punished / Unless he renounces his Christianity, / And how he will go free, if he rejects it?"
Youre princes erren, as youre nobleye dooth, / Quod tho Cecile, and with a wood sentence	"Your princes are wrong, as are your nobles," / Cecilia then said, "and with your insane sentence
Ye make us gilty, and it is nat sooth, / For ye, that knowen wel oure innocence,	You find us guilty, and that is not true. / For you, who certainly knows how innocent we are,
For as muche as we doon a reverence / To Crist, and for we bere a cristen name,	Just because we worship Christ, and because we carry the name of Christian,
Ye putte on us a cryme, and eek a blame.	You accuse us of crimes and blame us for it.
But we that knowen thilke name so / For vertuous, we may it nat withseye. / Almache answerde, Chees oon of thise two, / Do sacrifise, or cristendom reneye, / That thou mowe now escapen by that weye. / At which the hooly blisful faire mayde / Gan for to laughe, and to the juge sayde,	But we who know that same name / Is good, we will not deny it." / Almache answered, "Make your choice: / Make a sacrifice, or renounce Christianity, / And in that way you shall escape." / At that the holy blissful fair maiden / Began to laugh, and said to the judge:
O Juge, confus in thy nycetee, / Woltow that I reneye innocence, / To make me a wikked wight, quod shee; / Lo, he dissymuleth heere in audience, / He stareth, and woodeth in his advertence.	"Oh judge, confused in your stupidity, / Do you want me to renounce innocence, / And make myself a wicked person?" she said. / "See, he hides his true feelings in public; / He is staring, and he is going mad in his mind!"
To whom Almachius, Unsely wrecche, / Ne woostow nat how far my myght may strecche?	Almache said to her, "Miserable wretch, / Don't you know how powerful I am?
Han noght oure myghty princes to me yeven / Ye, bothe power and auctoritee / To maken folk to dyen or to lyven? / Why spekestow so proudly thanne to me? / I speke noght but stedfastly, quod she, / Nat proudly, for I speke as for my syde, / We haten deedly thilke vice of pryde.	Haven't our mighty princes given to me / Both the power and authority / Of life and death over people? / So why do you speak to me so arrogantly?" / "I am only speaking with faith," she said, / "Not arrogantly, for I say, on my side, / We hate that deadly sin of pride.
And if thou drede nat a sooth to heere, / Thanne wol I shewe al openly by right / That thou hast maad a ful grete lesyng heere, / Thou seyst, thy princes han thee yeven myght	And if you are not afraid to hear the truth, / Then I will say openly, according to law, / That you have told a very great lie here. / You say that your princes have given you the power
Bothe for to sleen, and for to quyken a wight. / Thou that ne mayst but oonly lyf bireve, / Thou hast noon oother power, ne no leve!	To kill and give life to a person; / You, who can only take life away, / Has no other power or authority.
But thou mayst seyn thy princes han thee maked / Ministre of deeth, for if thou speke of mo,	But you may say your princes have made you / A minister of death; for if you say any more,

Thou lyest, for thy power is ful naked.'	You are lying, for that is all the power you have."
Do wey thy booldnesse, seyde Almachius tho, / And sacrifise to oure goddes er thou go.	"Stop your arrogance," said Almache, "And make a sacrifice to our gods before you go!
I recche na twhat wrong that thou me profre, / For I can suffre it as a philosophre.	I don't care what offence you offer me, I can take it philosophically;
But thilke wronges may I nat endure / That thou spekest of oure goddes heere, quod he. / Cecile answerde, O nyce creature, / Thou seydest no word, syn thou spak to me,	But I will not tolerate you speaking badly Of the gods we have here," he said. Cecilia answered, "Oh you foolish creature! You have said nothing since you've been speaking to me
That I ne knew therwith thy nycetee, / And that thou were in every maner wise / A lewed officer and a veyn justise.	That did not show me your stupidity, Demonstrating to me in every way That you are an ignorant officer and a foolish judge.
Ther lakketh no thyng to thyne outter eyen / That thou nart blynd, for thyng that we seen alle	There is nothing wrong with your outer eyes Except that you are blind; for the thing that we can all see
That it is stoon, that men may wel espyen, / That ilke stoon a god thow wolt it calle. / I rede thee lat thyn hand upon it falle, / And taste it wel, and stoon thou shalt it fynde, / Syn that thou seest nat with thyne eyen blynde.	Is stone—all men can see it— And you call that same stone a God. I advise you, let your hand fall on it And feel it well, and you will find it is stone, Since you cannot see with your blind eyes.
It is a shame that the peple shal / So scorne thee, and laughe at thy folye, / For communly men woot it wel overal / That myghty God is in hise hevenes hye, / And thise ymages, wel thou mayst espye, / To thee ne to hemself mowen noght profite, / For in effect they been nat worth a myte.	It is a shame that the people will Mock you so and laugh at your stupidity, For all men everywhere know well That Almighty God is in his high heaven; And these images, you can certainly see, Can't do any good for you or themselves, For in fact they are completely worthless."
Thise wordes and swiche othere seyde she, / And he weex wrooth, and bad men sholde hir lede	She said these words and others the same, And he became angry, and ordered that men should take her
Hom til hir hous, and in hire hous, quod he,	Home to her house, and, "In her house," he said,
Brenne hire right in a bath of flambes rede. / And as he bad, right so was doon in dede,	"Burn her at once in a bath of red flames." And as he had ordered, that was exactly what they did;
For in a bath they gonne hire faste shetten, / And nyght and day greet fyre they underbetten.	For they shut her up tight in a cauldron, And night and day they maintained a great fire underneath it.
The longe nyght and eek a day also	All through the long night, and also through the day,
For al the fyr and eek the bathes heete / She sat al coold, and feelede no wo; / It made hir nat a drope for to sweete. / But in that bath hir lyf she moste lete, / For he Almachius, with a ful wikke entente, / To sleen hir in the bath his sonde sente.	Despite the fire and the heat of the cauldron She sat completely cool, feeling no pain. She didn't sweat a single drop. But in that cauldron she had to leave her life, For Almache, with completely evil intentions, Sent his servant to kill her there.

Thre strokes in the nekke he smoot hir tho,	He struck her three times on the neck,
The tormentour, but for no maner chaunce	The executioner, but in no way
He myghte noght smyte al hir nekke atwo.	Could he cut her neck in two;
And for ther was that tyme an ordinaunce	And because at that time the law was
That no man sholde doon men swich penaunce	That no man should cause anyone such pain
The ferthe strook to smyten, softe or soore,	As to make a fourth stroke, hard or soft,
This tormentour ne dorste do namoore.	This executioner did not dare to carry on,
But half deed, with hir nekke ycorven there,	But he left her half dead, with her neck
He lefte hir lye, and on his wey is went.	Cut open, and went on his way.
The cristen folk, which that aboute hir were,	The Christian folk, who were around her,
With sheetes han the blood ful faire yhent.	Carefully mopped up the blood with sheets.
Thre dayes lyved she in this torment,	She lived for three days in this agony,
And nevere cessed hem the feith to teche;	And never stopped teaching them the faith
That she hadde fostred, hem she gan to preche.	She had lit in them; she preached to them,
And hem she yaf hir moebles, and hir thyng,	As she gave them all of her possessions,
And to the Pope Urban bitook hem tho,	And she entrusted them to Pope Urban,
And seyde, I axed this at hevene kyng	Saying, "I asked the King of Heaven
To han respit thre dayes, and namo,	To allow me to stay for three days, no more,
To recomende to yow er that I go	To hand over to you, before I go,
Thise soules, lo, and that I myghte do werche	These souls, and so that I could make
Heere of myn hous perpetuelly a chirche.	My house here a church in perpetuity."
Seint Urban with hise deknes prively	St Urban and his deacons secretly
This body fette, and buryed it by nyghte,	Fetched the body and buried it at night,
Among hise othere seintes, honestly.	Decently, amongst the other saints.
Hir hous the chirche of seinte Cecilie highte;	Her house is called the church of St Cecilia;
Seint Urban halwed it, as he wel myghte,	St Urban consecrated it, as best he could;
In which, into this day, in noble wyse	And in that place, to this day, in a noble fashion,
Men doon to Crist and to his seinte servyse.	Men worship Christ and his saint.

Heere is ended the Seconde Nonnes Tale   **The end of the Second Nun's Tale**

The Canon's Yeoman's Tale

Prologue

The Prologe of the Chanounas Yemannes Tale

Whan ended was the lyf of seinte Cecile,
Er we hadde riden fully fyve mile,
At Boghtoun under Blee us gan atake
A man, that clothed was in clothes blake,
And undernethe he wered a whyt surplys.
His hakeney, which that was al pomely grys,
So swatte, that it wonder was to see,

It wemed as he had priked miles thre.

The hors eek that his yeman rood upon
So swatte, that unnethe myghte it gon.

Aboute the peytrel stood the foom ful hye,
He was of fome al flekked as a pye.
A male tweyfoold upon his croper lay,
It semed that he caried lite array.
Al light for somer rood this worthy man,

And in myn herte wondren I bigan
What that he was, til that I understood
How that his cloke was sowed to his hood;
For which, whan I hadde longe avysed me,
I demed hym som Chanoun for to be.

His hat heeng at his bak doun by a laas,
For he hadde riden moore than trot or paas;

He hadde ay priked lik as he were wood.

A clote-leef he hadde under his hood
For swoot, and for to kepe his heed from heete.
But it was joye for to seen hym swete!
His forheed dropped as a stillatorie
Were ful of plantayne and of paritorie.
And whan that he was come, he gan to crye,

God save, quod he, this joly compaignye!
Faste have I priked, quod he, for youre sake,

By cause that I wolde yow atake,
To riden in this myrie compaignye.
His Yeman eek was ful of curteisye,
And seyde, Sires, now in the morwe tyde
Out of youre hostelrie I saugh yow ryde,
And warned heer my lord and my soverayn

The Prologue of the Canon's Yeoman's Tale

When the life of St Cecilia was finished,
Before we had ridden another five miles,
At Boghton under Blee we were overtaken
By a man dressed in black clothes,
Underneath which he had a white surplice.
His horse, which was a dappled grey,
Was sweating so much it was astonishing to see;
It seemed as if it had been galloped for three miles.

The horse that his servant rode on
Was also sweating so much that he could hardly move.

Its bridle was swimming with foam;
He was speckled with foam like a magpie.
A double bag lay across his crupper;
He didn't seem to be carrying much gear.
This good man was wearing light clothes for the summer,

And in my heart I began to wonder
What sort of man he was until I noticed
That his cloak was sewn onto his hood,
Which, when I had thought about it,
Made me think he was some sort of canon.

His hat hung down his back by a strap,
For he had been riding faster than a trot or walk;

He had spurred his horse on as if he were mad.

He had a burdock leaf under his hood,
To soak up the sweat and keep his head cool.
But what a sight it was to see him sweat!
His forehead was dripping like a still,
Full of plantain and pellitory,
And when he came up to us, he began to cry out,

"God save," he said, "this jolly company!
I have galloped on fast," he said, "for your sake,

Because I wanted to overtake you,
To ride with this jolly company."
His servant was also full of courtesy,
And said, "Sirs, just now, in the morning,
I saw you ride out from your inn,
And I alerted my Lord and sovereign here,

Which that to ryden with yow is ful fayn
For his desport; he loveth daliaunce.
Freend, for thy warnyng God yeve thee good chaunce,
Thanne seyde oure Hoost, for certein, it wolde seme
Thy lord were wys, and so I may wel deme.

He is ful jocunde also, dar I leye.
Can he oght telle a myrie tale or tweye
With which he glade may this compaignye?
Who, sire, my lord? ye, ye, with-outen lye!
He kan of murthe and eek of jolitee
Nat but ynough, also, sire, trusteth me.
And ye hym knewen as wel as do I,
Ye wolde wondre how wel and craftily

He koude werke, and that in sondry wise.
He hath take on hym many a greet emprise,
Which were ful hard for any that is here

To brynge aboute, but they of hym it leere.

As hoomly as he rit amonges yow,
If ye hym knewe, it wolde be for youre prow,
Ye wolde nat forgoon his aqueyntaunce
For muchel good, I dar leye in balaunce
Al that I have in my possessioun.
He is a man of heigh discrecioun,
I warne yow wel, he is a passyng man.

Wel, quod oure Hoost, I pray thee, tel em than,
Is he a clerk, or noon? telle what he is?
Nay, he is gretter than a clerk, ywis,
Seyde this Yeman, and in wordes fewe,
Hoost, of his craft somwhat I wol yow shewe.
I seye my lord kan swich subtilitee-
But al his craft ye may nat wite for me,
And somwhat helpe I yet to his wirkyng-
That al this ground on which we been rydyng
Til that we come to Caunterbury toun,
He koude al clene turne it up so doun
And pave ti al of silver and of gold.
And whan this Yeman hadde this tale ytold
Unto oure Hoost, he seyde, Benedicitee,
This thyng is wonder merveillous to me,
Syn that thy lord is of so heigh prudence,
By cause of which men sholde hym reverence,
That of his worship rekketh he so lite.
His overslope nys nat worth a myte
As in effect to hym, so moot I go.
It is al baudy and to-tore also,
Why is thy lord so sluttissh, I the preye,
And is of power bettre clooth to beye,
If that his dede accorde with thy speche?

*Who is very keen to ride with you
For pleasure; he loves company."
"My friend, may God bless you for telling him,"
Said our host, "for certainly it seems
That your Lord is wise, and as far as I can judge
Is also a very cheerful man, I dare bet!
Would he be able to tell a merry tale or two,
To please all of this company?"
"Who, sir? My lord? Yes, yes, definitely,
He knows all about mirth and jollity,
More than enough; also, Sir, believe me,
If you knew him as well as I do,
You would be amazed at how skilfully and cunningly
He can work, in various different ways.
He has undertaken many great enterprises,
Which it would be very difficult for anyone here
To undertake, unless they had learned it from him.
Despite how modestly he is riding with you,
If you knew him, it would be beneficial to you.
You would not give up his friendship
For great wealth, I dare bet
All I have on me on that.
He is a man of great discretion;
I tell you truthfully, he is an amazing man."
"Well," said our host, "I beg you, tell me,
Is he a clerk, or not? Tell us what he is."
"No, he is certainly greater than a clerk,"
This yeoman said, "and in a few words,
Host, I will show you something of his craft.
I say, my lord knows such cunning things-
But I can't tell you all about his craft,
Although I sometimes help with his work—
That all of this ground we are riding over,
From here until we get to Canterbury,
He could turn completely upside down,
And pave it over with silver and gold."
And when this Yeoman had told this tale
To our host, he said, "God bless you!
This is quite amazing to me,
Since your lord is so skilful,
So that men should revere him,
That he seems to care so little for himself.
His cloak is virtually worthless,
Because in fact, to him, I swear,
It is filthy and torn as well.
Why is your lord such a mess, I ask you,
When he has the power to buy better cloth,
If he can do what you say he can?*

Telle me that, and that I thee biseche.	I beg you to answer me that."
Why, quod this Yeman, wherto axe ye me?	"Why?" this Yeoman said, "why do you ask me?
God help me so, for he shal nevere thee!	So help me God, he'll never help you!
But I wol nat avowe that I seye,	But I won't publicly admit what I'm telling you,
And therfore keepe it secree, I yow preye;	And so I beg you to keep it secret.
He is to wys, in feith, as I bileeve!	He is too wise, I swear, I think.
That that is overdoon, it wol nat preeve	Something which is overdone, it will not have
Aright; as clerkes seyn, it is a vice.	Good results, the clerks say; it is a vice.
Wherfore in that I holde hym lewed and nyce;	So I think he is ignorant and foolish.
For whan a man hath over-greet a wit,	When a man is highly intelligent,
Ful oft hym happeth to mysusen it.	He very often misuses his gift.
So dooth my lord, and that me greveth soore.	That's what my lord does, and that gives me much grief;
God it amende, I kan sey yow namoore.	May God change him! I can't tell you any more."
Therof no fors, good Yeman, quod oure Hoost,	"It doesn't matter, good yeoman," said our host;
Syn of the konnyng of thy lord thow woost,	"Since you know the skills of your and lord,
Telle how he dooth, I pray thee hertely,	Tell us how he does things, I beg you,
Syn that he is so crafty and so sly.	Since he is so skilful and cunning.
Wher dwelle ye, if it to telle be?	Where'd you live, if you can tell us?"
In the suburbes of a toun, quod he,	"In the suburbs of a town," he said,
Lurkynge in hernes and in lanes blynde,	"Lurking in hiding places and blind alleys,
Where as thise robbours and thise theves by kynde	Where these robbers and thieves naturally
Holden hir pryvee fereful residence,	Keep their appalling secret hideouts,
As they that dar nat shewen hir presence.	The ones who dare not show themselves;
So faren we if I shal seye the sothe.	That's where we stay, to tell you the truth."
Now, quod oure Hoost, yit lat me talke to the,	"Now," said our host, "let me carry on talking to you.
Why artow so discoloured of thy face?	Why is your face so discoloured?"
Peter, quod he, God yeve it harde grace,	"By St Peter!" he said, "May God curse it,
I am so used in the fyr to blowe,	I am so used to blowing on the fire
That it hath chaunged my colour, I trowe.	That I believe it has changed my colour.
I am nat wont in no mirrour to prie,	I don't usually look in the mirror,
But swynke soore, and lerne multiplie.	I work hard and learn to change metal.
We blondren evere, and pouren in the fir,	We are always blundering and staring in the fire,
And, for al that, we faille of oure desir.	And despite all that, we don't get what we want,
For evere we lakke of oure conclusioun;	For we are always missing the result we want.
To muchel folk we doon illusioun,	We deceive many people,
And borwe gold, be it a pound or two,	And borrow gold, a pound or two,
Or ten, or twelve, or manye sommes mo,	Or ten or twelve, sometimes more,
And make hem wenen at the leeste weye	And make them believe, at the very least,
That of a pound we koude make tweye.	That we could turn one pound into two.
Yet is it fals, but ay we han good hope	But it is false, but we are always hopeful
It for to doon, and after it we grope.	That we can do it, and we grope after the solution.
But that science is so fer us biforn,	But that knowledge is so far from us,
We mowen nat, although we hadden sworn,	We cannot, although we have sworn to it,
It over-take, it slit awey so faste.	Overtake it, it always slides away so quickly.
It wole us maken beggars atte laste.	It will make us into beggars in the end."

Whil this yeman was thus in his talkyng,	While this yeoman was saying this,
This Chanoun drough hym neer, and herde al thyng	The Canon drew near and heard everything
Which this Yeman spak, for suspecioun	Which he spoke, for this Canon
Of mennes speche evere hadde this Chanoun.	Was always suspicious of what men were saying.
For Catoun seith, that he that gilty is	For Cato says that someone who is guilty
Demeth alle thyng be spoke of hym, ywis.	Believes that everyone is always talking of him.
That was the cause he gan so ny hym drawe	That was the reason he drew so near
To his yeman, to herknen al his sawe.	To his servant, to hear everything he said.
And thus he seyde unto his yeman tho,	And so he said then to his yeoman:
Hoold thou thy pees, and spek no wordes mo,	"Hold your tongue and stop speaking,
For if thou do, thou shalt it deere abye.	For if you do, you will pay dearly for it.
Thou sclaundrest me heere in this compaignye,	You are slandering me to this company,
And eek discoverest that thou sholdest hyde.	And also revealing what should remain hidden."
Ye, quod oure Hoost, telle on, what so bityde,	"Yes," said our host, "carry on, whatever happens.
Of al his thretyng rekke nat a myte.	Don't give a damn for his threats!"
In feith, quod he, namoore I do but lyte.	"Truthfully," he said, "that's all I do give for him."
And whan this Chanoun saugh it wolde nat bee,	And when this Canon saw it would not stop,
But his Yeman wolde telle his pryvetee,	But that his servant would tell all his secrets,
He fledde awey for verray sorwe and shame.	He fled away from us in sorrow and shame.
A! quod the Yeman, heere shal arise game.	"Ah ha!" said the Yeoman, "this will cause you some amusement;
Al that I kan, anon now wol I telle,	Right away I will tell you everything I know.
Syn he is goon, the foule feend hym quelle!	Since he has gone, may the devil take him!
For nevere heer after wol I with hym meete,	I will never associate with him again,
For peny ne for pound, I yow biheete.	Not for a penny or pound, I promise you.
He that me broghte first unto that game,	He introduced me to that game,
Er that he dye, sorwe have he and shame.	Before he dies, may he find sorrow and shame!
For it is ernest to me, by my feith,	For it is serious, not a game, to me, I swear;
That feele I wel, what so any man seith.	I can certainly feel, whatever anyone says.
And yet, for al my smert and al my grief,	And yet, for all my pain and grief,
For al my sorwe, labour, and meschief,	For all my sorrow, labour and trouble,
I koude never leve it in no wise.	I could never get away from it.
Now wolde God, my wit myghte suffise	Now I wish to God that my wit were enough
To tellen al that longeth to that art,	To tell you everything about that art!
And nathelees yow wol I tellen part.	But nevertheless you want me to tell you something.
Syn that my lord is goon, I wol nat spare,	Since my lord is gone, I will not spare him;
Swich thyng as that I knowe, I wol declare.	I will tell you everything I know.

Heere endeth the Prologe of the Chanouns Yemannes Tale

The end of the Canon Yeoman's Prologue

The Tale

Heere bigynneth the Chanouns Yeman his Tale.	***Here begins the Canon's Yeoman's Tale***
Prima Pars	***First Part***

With this chanoun I dwelt have seven yeer,	*I have lived with this canon for seven years,*
And of his science am I never the neer.	*And we have not got any further with his experiments.*
Al that I hadde I have lost therby,	*I have lost everything I had because of it,*
And, God woot, so hath many mo than I.	*And, God knows, so have many more than I.*
Ther I was wont to be right fressh and gay	*Where I once used to be fresh and colourful*
Of clothyng and of oother good array,	*In my clothes and with other splendid ornaments,*
Now may I were an hose upon myn heed;	*Now I wear stockings as a hat;*
And wher my colour was bothe fressh and reed	*And where my complexion used to be fresh and red,*
Now is it wan and of a leden hewe --	*Now it is pale and leaden--*
Whoso it useth, soore shal he rewe! --	*Whoever does these things, they will sorely regret it!--*
And of my swynk yet blered is myn ye.	*And from my work my eyes are bleary.*
Lo! which avantage is to multiplie!	*See how profitable it is to try and change metals!*
That slidynge science hath me maad so bare	*That slippery science has stripped me down*
That I have no good, wher that evere I fare;	*So that I have no possessions, wherever I go;*
And yet I am endetted so therby,	*And also I have so many debts*
Of gold that I have borwed, trewely,	*Due to the gold I have borrowed, truly,*
That whil I lyve I shal it quite nevere.	*That I can never repay them as long as I live.*
Lat every man be war by me for evere!	*Let every man always take a warning from me!*
What maner man that casteth hym therto,	*Whatever sort of man chooses this path,*
If he continue, I holde his thrift ydo.	*So help me God, he will not get any profit from it,*
For so helpe me god, therby shal he nat wynne,	*It will empty his purse and drive him mad.*
But empte his purs, and make his wittes thynne.	*And when through his madness and folly*
And whan he, thurgh his madnesse and folye,	*He has lost his own goods in this dangerous business,*
Hath lost his owene good thurgh jupartye,	*Then he will encourage other folk to join in,*
Thanne he exciteth oother folk therto,	*To lose their possessions just like him.*
To lesen hir good, as he hymself hath do.	*For to scoundrels it is happiness and comfort*
For unto shrewes joye it is and ese	*To bring their fellows to pain and hardship.*
To have hir felawes in peyne and disese.	*To have their fellows in pain and disease.*
Thus was I ones lerned of a clerk.	*I was taught this once by a scholar.*
Of that no charge, I wol speke of oure werk.	*But never mind that; I will tell you of our work.*
Whan we been there as we shul exercise	*When we are in the place where we carry out*
Oure elvysshe craft, we semen wonder wise,	*Our magical craft, we seem amazingly wise,*
Oure termes been so clerigal and so queynte.	*We talk in such a scholarly and mysterious fashion.*
I blowe the fir til that myn herte feynte.	*I blow the fire until my heart is faint.*
What sholde I tellen ech proporcion	*Why should I bother telling you every proportion*

Of thynges whiche that we werche upon	Of the things that we work on—
As on fyve or sixe ounces, may wel be,	For example it might be five or six ounces
Of silver, or som oother quantitee --	Of silver, or some other quantity—
And bisye me to telle yow the names	And make an effort to tell you the names
Of orpyment, brent bones, iren squames,	Of arsenic, burnt bones, iron flakes,
That into poudre grounden been ful smal;	That we ground down very fine;
And in an erthen pot how put is al,	And how it is all put in an earthenware pot,
And salt yput in, and also papeer,	With salt and also pepper,
Biforn thise poudres that I speke of heer;	Before those powders which I have mentioned;
And wel ycovered with a lampe of glas;	And well covered with a glass lamp;
And of muche oother thyng which that ther was;	And of many other things which were there;
And of the pot and glasses enlutyng,	And of the sealing of the pot and the glasses
That of the eyr myghte passe out nothyng;	So that no air could escape;
And of the esy fir, and smart also,	And of the slow fire, and also quick
Which that was maad, and of the care and wo	Which was made, and of the care and pain
That we hadde in oure matires sublymyng,	That we had in purifying our materials,
And in amalgamyng and calcenyng	And in blending and making a powder
Of quyksilver, yclept mercurie crude?	Of quicksilver, which is called raw mercury?
For alle oure sleightes we kan nat conclude.	For all our cunning, we could not succeed.
Oure orpyment and sublymed mercurie,	Our arsenic and purified mercury,
Oure grounden litarge eek on the porfurie,	Our lead monoxide, ground up in a mortar,
Of ech of thise of ounces a certeyn --	A certain number of ounces of each—
Noght helpeth us, oure labour is in veyn.	Nothing helped us; our labour was wasted.
Ne eek oure spirites ascencioun,	Neither the vaporised spirits,
Ne oure materes that lyen al fix adoun,	Nor the materials that remained in the pot,
Mowe in oure werkyng no thyng us availle,	Could in any way help us with our work,
For lost is al oure labour and travaille;	All our labour and efforts were wasted;
And al the cost, a twenty devel waye,	And all the money, in the name of twenty devils,
Is lost also, which we upon it laye.	We also lost, everything we spent.
Ther is also ful many another thyng	There are also many other things
That is unto oure craft apertenyng.	That pertain to our craft.
Though I by ordre hem nat reherce kan,	Though I cannot list them in the right order,
By cause that I am a lewed man,	Because I am not a learned man,
Yet wol I telle hem as they come to mynde,	I will tell you of them as I think of them,
Thogh I ne kan nat sette hem in hir kynde	Although I can't put them in the right categories:
As boole armonyak, verdegrees, boras,	Such as red clay, verdigris, borax,
And sondry vessels maad of erthe and glas,	And various vessels made of clay and glass,
Oure urynales and oure descensories,	Urinals and retorts,
Violes, crosletz, and sublymatories,	Vials, crucibles and boiling vessels,
Cucurbites and alambikes eek,	Distilleries and alembics as well,
And othere swiche, deere ynough a leek.	And others, quite pricey—
Nat nedeth it for to reherce hem alle, --	There is no need to list them all—
Watres rubifyng, and boles galle,	Liquids to turn things red, and bull's gall,
Arsenyk, sal armonyak and brymstoon;	Arsenic, sal ammoniac, and brimstone;
And herbes koude I telle eek many oon,	And I can also tell you of many herbs,
As egremoyne, valerian, and lunarie,	Such as agrimony, valerian and moonwort,
And othere swiche, if that me liste tarie;	And other such things, if I wanted to waste time;
Oure lampes brennyng bothe nyght and day,	Our lamps burnt both night and day,
To brynge aboute oure purpos, if we may;	To fulfil our purpose, if we could;
Oure fourneys eek of calcinacioun,	Also our furnace for making powders,
And of watres albificacioun;	And of the whitening of liquids;

Unslekked lym, chalk, and gleyre of an ey,	*Unslaked lime, chalk and egg white,*
Poudres diverse, asshes, donge, pisse, and cley,	*Various powders, ashes, dung, piss and clay,*
Cered pokkets, sal peter, vitriole,	*Waterproof packets, saltpetre, sulphuric acid,*
And diverse fires maad of wode and cole;	*And different fires made of coal and wood;*
Sal tartre, alkaly, and sal preparat,	*Potassium nitrate, alkali, and purified salt,*
And combust materes and coagulat;	*Combustible materials and solid ones;*
Cley maad with hors of mannes heer, and oille	*Clay made with the hairs of horses or men, and oil*
Of tartre, alum glas, berme, wort, and argoille,	*Of tartar, crystallised alum, yeast, malt and argol,*
Resalgar, and oure materes enbibyng,	*Arsenic, and soaking of our materials,*
And eek of oure materes encorporyng,	*And also making compounds of them,*
And of oure silver citrinacioun,	*And turning silver yellow,*
Oure cementyng and fermentacioun,	*Joining things through heat and fermentation,*
Oure yngottes, testes, and many mo.	*Our moulds, testing crucibles, and many more.*
I wol yow telle, as was me taught also,	*I will tell you, as I was taught,*
The foure spirites and the bodies sevene,	*Of the four spirits and the seven metals*
By ordre, as ofte I herde my lord hem nevene.	*In order, as I often heard my lord mention them.*
The firste spirit quyksilver called is,	*The first spirit is called quicksilver,*
The seconde orpyment, the thridde, ywis,	*The second arsenic, the third, certainly,*
Sal armonyak, and the ferthe brymstoon.	*Sal ammoniac, and the fourth, brimstone.*
The bodyes sevene eek, lo! hem heere anoon	*The seven metals also, hear them now:*
Sol gold is, and luna silver we threpe,	*The sun is gold, and we say the moon is silver,*
Mars ire, mercurie quyksilver we clepe,	*Mars is iron, Mercury is quicksilver,*
Saturnus leed, and juppiter is tyn,	*Saturn is lead, and Jupiter is tin,*
And venus coper, by my fader kyn!	*And Venus is copper, by my father's family!*
This cursed craft whoso wole excercise,	*Whoever decides to try this cursed craft,*
He shal no good han that hym may suffise;	*There will be no wealth sufficient for him,*
For al the good he spendeth theraboute	*For all the money he spends on this*
He lese shal; therof have I no doute.	*He shall lose; I have no doubt about that.*
Whoso that listeth outen his folie,	*Whoever wants to make is foolishness public,*
Lat hym come forth and lerne multiplie;	*Let him come out and become an alchemist;*
And every man that oght hath in his cofre,	*And every man who has anything in his strongbox,*
Lat hym appiere, and wexe a philosophre.	*Let him show himself and be an alchemist.*
Ascaunce that craft is so light to leere?	*Is the craft so easy to learn?*
Nay, nay, God woot, al be he monk or frere,	*No, no, God knows, whether he is a monk or a friar,*
Preest or chanoun, or any oother wyght,	*A priest or a canon, or any other sort of person,*
Though he sitte at his book bothe day and nyght	*Although he sits with his books both day and night*
In lernyng of this elvysshe nyce loore,	*Learning this magical stupid lore,*
Al is in veyn, and parde! muchel moore.	*It is all in vain, and by God, there is much more to it.*
To lerne a lewed man this subtiltee --	*To teach and ignorant man this skill—*
Fy! spek nat therof, for it wol nat bee;	*Fie! Don't speak of that, for it will not happen.*
And konne he letterure, or konne he noon,	*And whether he has learned from books or not,*
As in effect, he shal fynde it al oon.	*The end result will all be the same.*
For bothe two, by my savacioun,	*For both of them, I swear,*
Concluden in multiplicacioun	*Will succeed in alchemy*
Ylike wel, whan they han al ydo;	*Both as well, when they have finished;*
This is to seyn, they faillen bothe two.	*This is to say, they will both fail.*

Yet forgat I to maken rehersaille	But I forgot to mention
Of watres corosif, and of lymaille,	Acidic waters, and metal filings,
And of bodies mollificacioun,	And how we softened materials,
And also of hire induracioun;	And also how we harden them;
Oilles, ablucions, and metal fusible, --	Oils, cleansers, and fusing metal–
To tellen al wolde passen any bible	If I told you all it would be longer than any
That owher is; wherfore, as for beste,	Bible anywhere; so, for the best,
Of alle thise names now wol I me reste.	I will keep these names to myself,
For, as I trowe, I have yow toold ynowe	For, I believe, I have told you enough
To reyse a feend, al looke he never so rowe.	To raise a devil, even if it would be a rough one.
A!nay! lat be; the philosophres stoon,	Ah! No! Leave it; the philosophers' stone,
Elixer clept, we sechen faste echoon;	Called Elixir, is what each one of us earnestly seeks;
For hadde we hym, thanne were we siker ynow.	For if we had it, then things would be good.
But unto God of hevene I make avow,	But I swear to the God of heaven,
For al oure craft, whan we han al ydo,	Despite all our craft, when we are finished,
And al oure sleighte, he wol nat come us to.	And all our skill, he will not come to us.
He hath ymaad us spenden muchel good,	He has made this invest so much money,
For sorwe of which almoost we wexen wood,	The sadness of which drives us almost mad,
But that good hope crepeth in oure herte,	But hope still creeps into our heart,
Supposynge evere, though we sore smerte,	Always imagining, through all are suffering,
To be releeved by hym afterward.	That he will relieve us afterwards.
Swich supposyng and hope is sharp and hard;	This sort of imagination and hope is sharp and hard;
I warne yow wel, it is to seken evere.	I'm warning you, it will keep you seeking forever.
That futur temps hath maad men to dissevere,	Hoping for the future has separated men
In trust therof, from al that evere they hadde.	Who believe in it from everything they ever had.
Yet of that art they kan nat wexen sadde,	But they can never have enough of that art,
For unto hem it is a bitter sweete, --	For it is bittersweet to them–
So semeth it, -- for nadde they but a sheete,	So it seems–for if they had nothing but a sheet
Which that they myghte wrappe hem inne a-nyght,	To wrap themselves in at night,
And a brat to walken inne by daylyght,	And a rough cloak to walk about in the daylight,
They wolde hem selle and spenden on this craft.	They would sell them and spend it on this craft.
They kan nat stynte til no thyng be laft.	They cannot stop until there's nothing left.
And everemoore, where that evere they goon	And always, wherever they go,
Men may hem knowe by smel of brymstoon.	Men will know them by the smell of brimstone.
For al the world they stynken as a goot;	To all the world they stink just like a goat;
Hir savour is so rammyssh and so hoot	Their smell is so ramlike and intense
That though a man from hem a mile be,	That although a man can be a mile away from them,
The savour wole infecte hym, trusteth me.	The odour will infect him, trust me.
And thus by smel, and by threedbare array,	So, from their smell and their threadbare clothing,
If that men liste, this folk they knowe may.	If men wish, they can identify these folk.
And if a man wole aske hem pryvely	And if a man secretly asks them
Why they been clothed so unthriftily,	Why they are wearing such poor clothes,
They right anon wol rownen is his ere,	They will immediately whisper in his ear,
And seyn that if that they espied were,	And say that if they were recognised,

Men wolde hem slee by cause of hir science.	Men would kill them because of their knowledge.
Lo, thus this folk bitrayen innocence!	This is how these people cheat innocence!
Passe over this; if go my tale unto.	Enough of this; I will start my tale.
Er that the pot be on the fir ydo,	Before the pot on the fire is finished,
Of metals with a certeyn quantitee,	My lord tempers the certain quantity
My lord hem trempreth, and no man be he --	Of metals in there, nobody but him—
Now he is goon, I dar seyn boldely --	Now he has gone, I dare say it straight—
For, as men seyn, he kan doon craftily.	For, so men say, he can work cunningly.
Algate I woot wel he hath swich a name,	Although I am well aware he has that reputation;
And yet ful ofte he renneth in a blame.	But very often he gets into trouble.
And wite ye how? ful ofte it happeth so,	Do you know how? It very often happens
The pot tobreketh, and farewel, al is go!	That the pot breaks, and farewell, all is lost!
Thise metals been of so greet violence,	These metals are so very powerful
Oure walles mowe nat make hem resistence,	That our equipment cannot handle them,
But if they weren wroght of lym and stoon;	Unless it is made of lime and stone;
They percen so, and thurgh the wal they goon.	They can stab through, and they go through the wall.
And somme of hem synken into the ground --	And some of them sink into the ground—
Thus han we lost by tymes many a pound --	In that way we have swiftly lost many pounds—
And somme are scatered al the floor aboute;	And some are scattered all over the floor;
Somme lepe into the roof. Withouten doute,	Some fly up to the ceiling. Without doubt,
Though that the feend noght in oure sighte hym shewe,	Although the devil does not show himself to us,
I trowe he with us be, that ilke shrewe!	I believe he is with us, the scoundrel!
In helle, where that he lord is and sire,	In hell, where he is lord and father,
Nis ther moore wo, ne moore rancour ne ire.	There is no greater sorrow, no greater anger, than here.
Whan that oure pot is broke, as I have sayd,	When our pot breaks, as I have said,
Every man chit, and halt hym yvele apayd.	Every man criticises us and thinks he has been cheated.
Somme seyde it was long on the fir makyng;	Some said it was due to the way the fire was made;
Somme seyde nay, it was on the blowyng, --	Some said no, it was the way it was blown—
Thanne was I fered, for that was myn office.	Then I was afraid, for that was my job.
Straw! quod the thridde, ye been lewed and nyce.	"Rubbish!" said a third, "you are ignorant and stupid.
It was nat tempred as it oghte be.	It was not tempered as it should have been."
Nay, quod the fourthe, stynt and herkne me.	"No," said a fourth, "be quiet and listen to me.
By cause oure fir ne was nat maad of beech,	It was because our fire was not made of beech,
That is the cause, and oother noon, so theech!	That is the cause and no other, I swear!"
I kan nat telle wheron it was long,	I can't tell what caused it,
But wel I woot greet strif is us among.	But I certainly know there was great disagreement amongst us.
What, quod my lord, ther is namoore to doone;	"Well," said my lord, "there is no more to be done;
Of thise perils I wol be war eftsoone.	I will watch out for these dangers next time.
I am right siker that the pot was crased.	I am certain that the pot was cracked.
Be as be may, be ye no thyng amased;	Be that as it may, don't be shocked;
As usage is, lat swepe the floor as swithe,	As we always do, sweep up the floor quickly,
Plukke up youre hertes, and beeth glad and blithe.	Pluck up your spirits and be calm and happy."

The mullok on an heep ysweped was,	The rubbish was swept into a heap,
And on the floor ycast a canevas,	And a canvas was thrown across the floor,
And al this mullok in a syve ythrowe,	And all this rubbish was thrown into a sieve
And sifted, and ypiked mayn a throwe.	And sifted, and carefully picked over.
Pardee, quod oon, somwhat of oure metal	"By God," said one, "there is something of our metal
Yet is ther heere, though that we han nat al.	Still in here, although we don't have it all.
Although this thyng myshapped have as now,	And although things didn't go well this time,
Another tyme it may be well ynow.	Some other time it might be perfect.
Us moste putte oure good in aventure.	We must risk all our possessions.
A marchant, pardee, may nat ay endure,	A merchant, by God, will not enjoy
Trusteth me wel, in his prosperitee.	Prosperity forever, trust me.
Somtyme his good is drowned in the see,	Sometimes his goods are lost at sea,
And somtyme comth it sauf unto the londe.	And sometimes they come safely to the harbour."
Pees! quod my lord, the nexte tyme I wol fonde	"Quiet!" said my lord, "the next time I will try
To bryngen oure craft al in another plite,	To do our experiment in a quite different way,
And but I do, sires, lat me han the wite.	And unless I manage it, sirs, you can blame me.
Ther was defaute in somwhat, wel I woot,	There was something wrong, I'm certain."
Another seyde the fir was over-hoot, --	Another said the fire was too hot—
But, be it hoot or coold, I dar seye this,	But whether it was hot or cold, I dare say this,
That we concluden everemoore amys.	That we always finished with something going wrong.
We faille of that which that we wolden have,	We failed to get what we wanted,
And in oure madnesse everemoore we rave.	And we always raved in our madness.
And whan we been togidres everichoon,	And when we are all together
Every man semeth a salomon.	Every man seems as wise as Solomon.
But al thyng which that shineth as the gold	But not everything that shines like gold
Nis nat gold, as that I have herd it told;	Is gold, I have heard it said;
Ne every appul that is fair at eye	Not every apple that looks good to the eye
Ne is nat good, what so men clappe or crye.	Is good to eat, whatever chattering men may say.
Right so, lo, fareth it amonges us	That's how it goes with us:
He that semeth the wiseste, by jhesus!	Whoever seems the wisest, by Jesus,
Is moost fool, whan it cometh to the preef;	Is the most stupid, when it comes round to it;
And he that semeth trewest is the theef.	And the one who seems most trustworthy is a thief.
That shul ye knowe, er that I fro yow wende,	You will know that, before I leave you,
By that I of my tale have maad an ende.	By the time I have finished my tale.
Explicit prima pars.	**The end of the first part**
Et sequitur pars secunda.	**Here follows the second part**
Ther is a chanoun of religioun	There is a canon of religion
Amounges us, wolde infecte al a toun,	Amongst us, who would infect a whole town,
Thogh it as greet were as was nynyvee,	Even if it were as big as Nineveh,
Rome, alisaundre, troye, and othere three.	Rome, Alexandria, Troy and any other three.
His sleightes and his infinite falsnesse	His tricks and his infinite deceitfulness
Ther koude no man writen, as I gesse,	Could not be described by any man, I think,
Though that he myghte lyve a thousand yeer.	Even if he lived a thousand years.
In al this world of falshede nis his peer;	In the whole world nobody can match him for falseness,

For in his termes he wol hym so wynde,	For he will wrap himself up in technical terms,
And speke his wordes in so sly a kynde,	And speak so slyly,
Whanne he commune shal with any wight,	When he talks to anyone,
That he wol make hym doten anonright,	That he makes a fool of them at once,
But it a feend be, as hymselven is.	Unless he is talking to a daemon, the same as him.
Ful many a man hath he bigiled er this,	He has tricked many men before now,
And wole, if that he lyve may a while;	And will trick more, if he lives longer;
And yet men ride and goon ful many a mile	And yet men ride and walk many miles
Hym for to seke and have his aqueyntaunce,	To look for him and to have his acquaintance,
Noght knowynge of his false governaunce.	Not knowing how false he is.
And if yow list to yeve me audience,	And if you want to listen to me,
I wol it tellen heere in youre presence.	I will tell you about it right here.
But worshipful chanons religious,	But proper worshipful religious canons,
Ne demeth nat that I sclaundre youre hous,	Do not think that I am slandering you,
Although that my tale of a chanoun bee.	Even though my tale is about a canon.
Of every ordre som shrewe is, pardee,	There are scoundrels in every order, by God,
And God forbede that al a compaignye	And God forbid that a whole group
Sholde rewe o singuleer mannes folye.	Should be criticised because of a single man.
To sclaundre yow is no thyng myn entente,	I have no intention to slander you,
But to correcten that is mys I mente.	But I want to correct what is wrong.
This tale was nat oonly toold for yow	This tale was told not only for you,
But eek for othere mo; ye woot wel how	But also for many others; you know well
That among cristes apostelles twelve	That in the twelve Apostles of Christ
Ther nas no traytour but judas hymselve.	There was no traitor apart from Judas.
Thanne why sholde al the remenant have a blame	So why would all the rest get the blame
That giltlees were? by yow I seye the same,	When they were guiltless? I say the same about you,
Save oonly this, if ye wol herke me	Except for this, if you will listen to me:
If any judas in youre covent be,	If you have any Judas in your convent,
Remoeveth hym bitymes, I yow rede,	Get rid of him quickly, I warn you,
If shame or los may causen any drede.	If the idea of shame or dishonour worries you.
And beeth no thyng displesed, I yow preye,	And don't be annoyed, I beg you,
But in this cas herkneth what I shal seye.	But listen to what I have to say.
In londoun was a preest, an annueleer,	In London there was a priest, a chantry priest,
That therinne dwelled hadde mayn a yeer,	Who had lived there for many years,
Which was so plesaunt and se servysable	Who was so pleasant and attentive
Unto the wyf, where as he was at table,	To the woman in the place where he ate
That she wolde suffre hym no thyng for to paye	That she would not let him pay for anything,
For bord ne clothyng, wente he never so gaye;	Not board or clothing, however flashy his clothes were,
And spendyng silver hadde he right ynow.	And he had plenty of silver to spend.
Therof no fors; I wol procede as now,	That is not relevant; I will carry on
And telle forth my tale of the chanoun	And tell you my tale of the canon
That broghte this preest to confusioun.	Who brought this priest down.
This false chanon cam upon a day	This false canon came one day
Unto this preestes chambre, wher he lay,	To the chamber of this priest, where he was staying,
Bisechynge hym to lene hym a certeyn	Begging him to lend him a certain amount
Of gold, and he wolde quite it hym ageyn.	Of gold, saying he would pay him back again.
Leene me a marc, quod he, but dayes three,	"Just lend me a mark," he said, "for just three days,

And at my day I wol it quiten thee.
And if so be that thow me fynde fals,
Another day do hange me by the hals!

This preest hym took a marc, and that as swithe,
And this chanoun hym thanked ofte sithe,
And took his leve, and wente forth his weye,
And at the thridee day broghte his moneye,
And to the preest he took his gold agayn,
Wherof this preest was wonder glad and fayn.

Certes, quod he, no thyng anoyeth me
To lene a man a noble, or two, or thre,
Or what thyng were in my possessioun,
Whan he so trewe is of condicioun
That in no wise he breke wole his day;

To swich a man I kan never seye nay.

What! quod this chanoun, sholde I be untrewe?
Nay, that were thyng yfallen al of newe.

Trouthe is a thyng that I wol evere kepe
Unto that day in which that I shal crepe
Into my grave, and ellis God forbede.

Bileveth this as siker as your crede.
God thanke I, and in good tyme be it sayd,
That ther was nevere man yet yvele apayd
For gold ne silver that he to me lente,
Ne nevere falshede in myn herte I mente.

And sire, quod he, now of my pryvetee,
Syn ye so goodlich han been unto me,
And kithed to me so greet gentillesse,
Somwhat to quyte with youre kyndenesse
I wol yow shewe, and if yow list to leere,
I wol yow teche pleynly the manere
Yow I kan werken in philosophie.
Taketh good heede, ye shul wel seen at ye
That I wol doon a maistrie er I go.

Ye, quod the preest, ye, sire, and wol ye so?
Marie! therof I pray yow hertely.
At youre comandement, sire, trewely,
Quod the chanoun, and ellis God forbeede!

Loo, how this theef koude his service beede!
Ful sooth it is that swich profred servyse
Stynketh, as witnessen thise olde wyse,
And that, ful soone I wol it verifie
In this chanoun, roote of al trecherie,

*And on the appointed day I will pay you back.
If you find that I am lying,
On the next day you can have me hanged by the neck!"*

*This priest gave him a mark, very quickly,
And this canon gave him many thanks,
And left him, and went on his way,
And on the third day he brought his money,
Giving the priest back his gold,
And the priest was very happy about this.*

*"Certainly," he said, "it does me no harm
To lend a man a noble, or two or three,
Or whatever I happen to own,
When he is so true to his word
That he never fails to pay on the appointed day;
I can never say no to such a man."*

*"What!" said this canon, "would I be untrue?
No, that would be something completely new for me.
I will always keep my pledged word
Up to the date when I creep
Into my grave, and God forbid that it should be otherwise.
Believes this as you believe your creed.
I thank God, and it may be rightly said,
That no man yet ever suffered evil
From lending me gold or silver,
And I never intended any deception in my heart.
And Sir," he said, "now I shall tell you,
Since you have been so good to me,
And shown me such great courtesy,
Something to repay your kindness,
Some of my secrets, and if you want to learn,
I will teach you everything
I know about alchemy.
Look closely; you will see with your own eyes
That I will do something amazing before I leave."*

*"Yes," said the priest, "yes, sir, will you?
By St Mary, I beg you to do so."
"I'm at your command, Sir, truly,"
Said the canon, "God forbid it should be otherwise!"
Look at how this thief offered his services!
It's very true that the services offered
Stinks, as the old wise writers tell us,
And very soon I will prove it
With the deeds of this canon, the ritual treachery,*

That everemoore delit hath and gladnesse --	Who always takes delight and gladness
Swiche feendly thoghtes in his herte impresse --	In the devilish thoughts that are fixed in his heart—
How cristes peple he may to meschief brynge.	In ways in which he can bring the people of Christ into mischief.
God kepe us from his false dissymulynge!	God keep us from his deceptions!
Noght wiste this preest with whom that he delte,	This priest did not know whom he was dealing with,
Ne of his harm comynge he no thyng felte.	And of the harm that was coming to him he felt nothing.
O sely preest! o sely innocent!	Oh foolish priest! O foolish innocent!
With coveitise anon thou shalt be blent!	Soon you will be blinded by your greed!
O gracelees, ful blynd is thy conceite,	Graceless man, your mind is completely blind,
No thyng ne artow war of the deceite	In no way are you aware of the deceit
Which that this fox yshapen hath to thee!	Which this fox has lined up for you!
His wily wrenches thou ne mayst nat flee.	His cunning deceptions are inescapable.
Wherfore, to go to the conclusion,	So, to conclude,
That refereth to thy confusion,	This will bring your ruin,
Unhappy man, anon I wol me hye	Unhappy man, right now I will hurry
To tellen thyn unwit and thy folye,	To tell of your lack of common sense and stupidity,
And eek the falsnesse of that oother wrecche,	And also the falseness of that other wretch,
As ferforth as that my konnyng wol strecche.	As far as my skill allows me.
This chanon was my lord, ye wolden weene?	This canon was my lord, you imagine?
Sire hoost, in feith, and by the hevenes queene,	Sir host, I swear, by the Queen of Heaven,
It was another chanoun, and nat hee,	It was another canon, and not him,
That kan an hundred foold moore subtiltee.	Who is a hundred times more cunning.
He hath bitrayed folkes many tyme;	He has betrayed folks many times;
Of his falsnesse it dulleth me to ryme.	It distresses me to talk in rhyme of his falseness.
Evere whan that I speke of his falshede,	Every time I speak about his falsehood,
For shame of hym my chekes wexen rede.	I blush for the shame of him.
Algates they bigynnen for to glowe,	Or at least my cheeks begin to glow,
For reednesse have I noon, right wel I knowe,	For I have no redness, I well know,
In my visage; for fumes diverse	In my face; for different fumes
Of metals, whiche ye han herd me reherce,	Of metals, which you have heard me mention,
Consumed and wasted han my reednesse.	Have consumed and destroyed my complexion.
Now taak heede of this chanons cursednesse!	Now listen to what this cursed canon did!
Sire, quod he to the preest, lat youre man gon	"Sir," he said to the priest, "have your man go and fetch
For quyksilver, that we it hadde anon;	Some quicksilver, we need it at once;
And lat hym bryngen ounces two or three;	And let him bring two or three ounces;
And whan he comth, as faste shal ye see	And when he comes, you shall quickly see
A wonder thyng, which ye saugh nevere er this.	An amazing thing, which you never saw before."
Sire, quod the preest, it shal be doon, ywis.	"Sir," said the priest, "this shall be done, indeed."
He bad his servant fecchen hym this thyng,	He ordered his servant to fetch him this thing,
And he al redy was at his biddyng,	And he had everything ready as he asked,
And wente hym forth, and cam anon agayn	And he went out, and came straight back again
With this quyksilver, shortly for to sayn,	With this quicksilver, to say briefly,
And took thise ounces thre to the chanoun;	And he gave these three ounces to the canon;

And he hem leyde faire and wel adoun,	And he laid them down neatly and carefully,
And bad the servant coles for to brynge,	And ordered the servant to bring coals
That he anon myghte go to his werkynge.	So that he could get working at once.
The coles right anon weren yfet,	The coals were fetched at once,
And this chanoun took out a crosselet	And this canon took out a crucible
Of his bosom, and shewed it to the preest.	From his bosom, and showed it to the priest.
This instrument, quod he, which that thou seest,	"This instrument," he said, "which you see here,
Taak in thy hand, and put thyself therinne	Take it in your hand, and put in it
Of this quyksilver an ounce, and heer bigynne,	An ounce of this quicksilver, and start now,
In name of crist, to wexe a philosofre.	In the name of Christ, to become an alchemist.
Ther been ful fewe to whiche I wolde profre	There are very few to whom I would offer
To shewen hem thus muche of my science.	To show them so much of my art.
For ye shul seen heer, by experience,	For you shall see here, through experience,
That this quyksilver I wol mortifye	That this quicksilver will be hardened by me
Right in youre sighte anon, withouten lye,	Right before your eyes, in truth,
And make it as good silver and as fyn	And I shall turn it into silver as good and fine
As ther is any in youre purs or myn,	As any there is in your purse or mine,
Or ellesswhere, and make it malliable;	Or anywhere else, and make it workable;
And elles holdeth me fals and unable	Otherwise you can call me false and tell me
Amonges folk for evere to appeere.	That I cannot live amongst people.
I have poudre heer, that coste me deere,	I have a powder here, that was very expensive,
Shal make al good, for it is cause of al	Which will make everything good, for it is the root of all
My konnyng, which that I yow shewen shal.	My cunning, which I shall show to you.
Voyde youre man, and lat hym be theroute,	Send away your man, tell him to wait outside,
And shette the dore, whils we been aboute	And shut the door, while we are doing
Oure pryvetee, that no man us espie,	Our business, so that no man can spy on us,
Whils that we werke in this philosophie.	While we work at this science."
Al as he bad fulfilled was in dede.	Everything was organised as he ordered.
This ilke servant anonright out yede	The same servant went out at once,
And his maister shette the dore anon,	And his master quickly shut the door,
And to hire labour spedily the gon.	And very swiftly started with their labour.
This preest, at this cursed chanons biddyng,	This priest, at the request of this cursed canon,
Upon the fir anon sette this thyng,	Put this thing on the fire at once,
And blew the fir, and bisyed hym ful faste.	And blew on the fire, and worked very hard.
And this chanoun into the crosselet caste	And this canon threw into the crucible
A poudre, noot I wherof that it was	A powder, I don't know what it was
Ymaad, outher of chalk, outher of glas,	Made of, either chalk or glass,
Or somwhat elles, was nat worth a flye,	Or something else that was worthless,
To blynde with this preest; and bad hym hye	With which he could blind this priest; and he told him to hurry
The coles for to couchen al above	To heap the coals over
The crosselet. For in tokenyng I thee love,	The crucible. "As a sign of my love for you,"
Quod this chanoun, thyne owene handes two	Said this canon, "your two hands
Shul werche al thyng which that shal heer be do.	Will do everything which we do here."
Graunt mercy, quod the preest, and was ful glad,	"Thank you very much," said the priest, and he was very happy,
And couched coles as that the chanoun bad.	And he arranged the coals as the canon had ordered.
And while he bisy was, this feendly wrecche,	And while he was busy, this fiendish wretch,
This false chanoun -- the foule feend hym fecche! --	This false canon—maybe devil take him!—

Out of his bosom took a bechen cole,	Took a beech coal from his robe,
In which ful subtilly was maad an hole,	In which he had skilfully made a hole,
And therinne put was of silver lemaille	And put silver filings, an ounce
An ounce, and stopped was, withouten faille,	Of them, inside, and he had sealed
This hole with wex, to kepe the lemaille in.	The hole with wax, to keep them in.
And understondeth that this false gyn	You should understand that this false device
Was nat maad ther, but it was maad bifore;	Was not made there, he had already prepared it;
And othere thynges I shal tellen moore	Along with other things I shall tell you more of
Herafterward, whiche that he with hym broghte.	Later, which he brought with him.
Er he cam there, hym to bigile he thoghte,	Before he got there, he intended to trick him,
And so he dide, er that they wente at wynne;	And so he did, before they parted;
Til he had terved hym, koude he nat blynne.	Until he had skinned him, he would not stop.
It dulleth me whan that I of hym speke.	It distresses me to speak of him.
On his falshede fayn wolde I me wreke,	I would like to take revenge for his falsehood,
If I wiste how, but he is heere and there;	If I knew how, but he flits about from place to place;
He is so variaunt, be abit nowhere.	He is so changeable, he has no fixed abode.
But taketh heed now, sires, for goddes love!	But pay attention now, sirs, for the love of God!
He took his cole of which I spak above,	He took this coal which I have mentioned,
And in his hand he baar it pryvely.	And held it secretly in his hand.
And whiles the preest couched bisil	And while the priest busily arranged
The coles, as I tolde yow er this,	The coals, as I said before,
This chanoun seyde, freend, ye doon amys.	This canon said, "Friend, you are doing it wrong.
This is nat couched as it oghte be;	These are not arranged as they should be;
But soone I shal amenden it, quod he.	But I will soon make it right," he said.
Now lat me medle therwith but a while,	"Just let me work with it for a while,
For of yow have I pitee, by seint gile!	For I have pity on you, by St Giles!
Ye been right hoot; I se wel how ye swete.	You are very hot; I can see how you sweat.
Have heere a clooth, and wipe awey the wete.	Here, take a cloth and wipe away the wetness."
And whiles that the preest wiped his face,	And while the priest wiped his face,
This chanoun took his cole -- with sory grace! --	This canon took his coal—may he have no luck!—
And leyde it above upon the myddeward	And put it on top of the middle
Of the crosselet, and blew wel afterward,	Of the crucible, and then blew strongly
Til that the coles gonne faste brenne.	Until the coals began to burn hot.
Now yeve us drynke, quod the chanoun thenne;	"Now bring us some drink," the canon then said,
As swithe al shal be wel, I undertake.	"Soon all shall be well, I promise you.
Sitte we doun, and lat us myrie make.	Let's sit down, and make merry."
And whan that this chanounes bechen cole	And when this canon's beech coal
Was brent, al the lemaille out of the hole	Had burnt, all the filings fell out of the hole
Into the crosselet fil anon adoun;	Straight into the crucible;
And as it moste nedes, by resoun,	As they had to, by arrangement,
Syn it so even aboven it couched was.	Since it was balanced so exactly above.
But therof wiste the preest nothyng, alas!	But the priest knew nothing of this, alas!
He demed alle the coles yliche good;	He thought all the coals were as good as each other,
For of that sleighte he nothyng understood.	For he understood nothing about that trick.
And whan this alkamystre saugh his tyme,	And when this alchemist saw his chance,

Ris up, quod he, sire preest, and stondeth by me;	He said, "Rise up, sir priest, and stand by me;
And for I woot wel ingot have ye noon,	And because I know you don't have any moulds,
Gooth, walketh forth, and brynge us a chalk stoon;	Go outside, and bring me a chalk stone;
For I wol make it of the same shap	For I will make it into the shape
That is an ingot, if I may han hap.	Of a mould, if I can.
And bryngeth eek with yow a bolle or a panne	And also bring with you a bowl or pan
Ful of water, and ye shul se wel thanne	Full of water, and you will see well
How that oure bisynesse shal thryve and preeve.	How our business will thrive and succeed.
And yet, for ye shul han no mysbileeve	And yet, so that you will not suspect me
New wrong conceite of me in youre absence,	Or form a wrong opinion of me when you are away,
I ne wol nat been out of youre presence,	I will not leave you,
But go with yow, and come with yow ageyn.	I will go and come back with you."
The chambre dore, shortly for to seyn,	The door of the room, to say briefly,
They opened and shette, and wente hir weye.	They opened and shut, and went on their way.
And forth with hem they carieden the keye,	And they took the key with them,
And coome agayn withouten any delay.	And came back again as soon as possible.
What sholde I tarien al the longe day?	Why should I waste too much time?
He took the chalk, and shoop it in the wise	He took the chalk, and shaped it in the fashion
Of an ingot, as I shal yow devyse.	Of a mould, as I shall tell you.
I seye, he took out of his owene sleeve	I tell you, he took from his own sleeve
A teyne of silver -- yvele moot he cheeve! --	A small silver bar--may he have bad luck!--
Which that ne was nat but an ounce of weighte.	Which weighed not more than an ounce.
And taaketh heede now of his cursed sleighte!	And now see what a cursed trick he played!
He shoop his ingot, in lengthe and in breede	He shaped his mould the length and width
Of this teyne, withouten any drede,	Of this bar, it's certain,
So slyly that the preest it nat espide,	So slyly that the priest did not notice,
And in his sleve agayn he gan it hide,	And he hid it back in his sleeve,
And fro the fir he took up his mateere,	And from the fire he picked up his material,
And in th' yngot putte it with myrie cheere,	And with a merry face he poured it into the mould,
And in the water-vessel he it caste,	And then dipped it in the pan of water,
Whan that hym luste, and bad the preest as faste,	As he pleased, and he ordered the priest quickly,
Loke what ther is, put in thyn hand and grope.	"See what is there; put in your hand and feel.
Thow fynde shalt ther silver, as I hope.	I think that you will find silver there."
What, devel of helle! sholde it elles be?	What else, devil of hell, would it be?
Shaving of silver silver is, pardee!	Shavings of silver make silver, by God!
He putte his hand in and took up a teyne	He put his hand in and took out a small bar
Of silver fyn, and glad in every veyne	Of pure silver, and this priest was glad
Was this preest, whan he saugh that it was so.	With his whole heart, when he saw what had happened.
Goddes blessyng, and his moodres also,	"May the blessing of God, and his mother's also,
And alle halwes, have ye, sire chanoun,	And all of the saints, be upon you, Sir Canon,"
Seyde the preest, and I hir malisoun,	Said the priest, "and may I have their curse,
But, and ye vouche-sauf to techen me	If, if you agree to teach me
This noble craft and this subtilitee,	This noble craft and all its tricks,
I wol be youre in al that evere I may.	I am not yours in every way I can be."
Quod the chanoun, yet wol I make assay	The canon said, "But I will do this thing
The seconde tyme, that ye may taken heede	A second time, so that you can watch

And been expert of this, and in youre neede	And become an expert in this, and when you need
Another day assaye in myn absence	You can try out, when I am not here,
This disciplyne and this crafty science.	This discipline and this crafty science.
Lat take another ounce, quod he tho,	Let us take another ounce," he then said,
Of quyksilver, withouten wordes mo,	"Of quicksilver, without saying any more,
And do therwith as ye han doon er this	And do the same thing as you did before
With that oother, which that now silver is.	With the other, which is now silver."
This preest hym bisieth in al that he kan	The priest worked as hard as he could
To doon as this chanoun, this cursed man,	To do what this canon, this cursed man,
Comanded hym, and faste he blew the fir,	Ordered him, and blew hard on the fire,
For to come to th' effect of his desir.	So that he could get what he wanted.
And this chanon, right in the meene while,	And this canon, at exactly the same time,
Al redy was this preest eft to bigile,	Was prepared to trick the priest again,
And for a contenaunce in his hand he bar	And for show he carried in his hand
An holwe stikke -- taak kep and be war! --	A hollow stick–pay attention, beware!–
In the ende of which an ounce, and namoore,	In the end of which he had put an ounce, no more,
Of silver lemaille put was, as bifore	Of silver filings, as before
Was in his cole, and stopped with wex weel	He had in his coal, and it was well sealed with wax
For to kepe in his lemaille every deel.	To keep all the filings in.
And whil this preest was in his bisynesse,	And while the priest was busy with this,
This chanoun with his stikke gan hym dresse	This canon went to him with his stick
To hym anon, and his poudre caste in	At once, and threw his powder in
As he dide er -- the devel out of his skyn	As he had before–may the devil strip him
Hym terve, I pray to god, for his falshede!	Of his skin, I pray to God, for his falsehood!
For he was evere fals in thoght and dede --	For he was always false in thought and deed–
And with this stikke, above the crosselet,	And with this stick, above the crucible,
That was ordeyned with that false jet	That had been prepared falsely,
He stired the coles til relente gan	He stirred up the coals until it began to melt
The wex agayn the fir, as every man,	The wax next to the fire, as every man,
But it a fool be, woot wel it moot nede,	Unless he is a fool, knows has to happen,
And al that in the stikke was out yede,	And everything that was in the stick fell out
And in the crosselet hastily it fel.	And dropped straight into the crucible.
Now, good sires, what wol ye bet than wel?	Now, good sirs, what more do you want?
Whan that this preest thus was bigiled ageyn,	When this priest had been tricked this way again,
Supposynge noght but treuthe, sooth to seyn,	Imagining everything was true, I swear,
He was so glad that I kan nat expresse	He was so glad that I cannot express
In no manere his myrthe and his gladnesse;	In any way his happiness and jollity;
And to the chanoun he profred eftsoone	And he offered the canon once again
Body and good. Ye, quod the chanoun soone,	His body and his possessions. "Yes," the canon said quickly,
Though poure I be, crafty thou shalt me fynde.	"Although I am poor, you will find I am skilful.
I warne thee, yet is ther moore bihynde.	I warn you, there is more to come.
Is ther any coper herinne? seyde he.	Do you have any copper?" He said.
Ye, quod the preest, sire, I trowe wel ther be.	"Yes," said the priest, "Sir, I'm sure there is some."
Elles go bye us som, and that as swithe;	"If there is not go and buy some, and do it quickly;
Now, goode sire, go forth thy wey and hy the.	Now, good Sir, go on your way, and hurry."

He wente his wey, and with the coper cam,	He went on his way, and came back with the copper,
And this chanon it in his handes nam,	And this canon took it in his hands,
And of that coper weyed out but an ounce.	And weighed out just an ounce of copper.
Al to symple is my tonge to pronounce,	My tongue is too innocent to describe,
As ministre of my wit, the doublenesse	As a servant of my wit, the duplicity
Of this chanoun, roote of alle cursednesse!	Of this canon, such a cursed man!
He semed freendly to hem that knewe hym noght,	He seemed friendly to those who did not know him,
But he was feendly bothe in werk and thoght.	But he was devilish in his deeds and thoughts.
It weerieth me to telle of his falsnesse,	It makes me tired to tell of his falseness,
And nathelees yet wol I it expresse,	But nonetheless I will speak of it,
To th' entente that men may be war therby,	So that men can be warned by this,
And for noon oother cause, trewely.	Truly, I don't do it for any other reason.
He putte this ounce of coper in the crosselet,	He put this ounce of copper in the crucible,
And on the fir as swithe he hath it set,	And quickly put it on the fire,
And caste in poudre, and made the preest to blowe,	And threw in powder, and made the priest blow,
And in his werkyng for to stoupe lowe,	To bend down low as he worked,
As he dide er, -- and al nas but a jape;	As he did before—and this was just a trick;
Right as hym liste, the preest he made his ape!	Exactly as he wanted, he made a fool of the priest!
And afterward in the ingot he it caste,	And afterwards he cast it in the mould,
And in the panne putte it at the laste	And at the end put it in the pan
Of water, and in he putte his owene hand,	Of water, and put in his own hand,
And in his sleve (as ye biforen-hand	And in his sleeve (as I told you
Herde me telle) he hadde a silver teyne.	Before) he had a small bar of silver.
He slyly took it out, this cursed heyne,	He slyly took it out, this cursed rascal,
Unwityng this preest of his false craft,	With the priest not knowing of his trick,
And in the pannes botme he hath it laft;	And he left it in the bottom of the pan;
And in the water rombled to and fro,	And he splashed around in the water,
And wonder pryvely took up also	And very secretly he also picked up
The coper teyne, noght knowynge this preest,	The copper bar, without the priest knowing,
And hidde it, and hym hente by the breest,	And hid it, and grabbed him by his coat,
And to hym spak, and thus seyde in his game	And spoke to him, saying jokingly:
Stoupeth adoun, by god, ye be to balme!	"Bend down. By God, you are to blame!
Helpeth me now, as I dide yow whileer;	Help me now, as I helped you before;
Putte in youre hand, and looketh what is theer.	Put in your hand, and see what is there."
This preest took up this silver teyne anon,	The priest quickly picked up the silver bar,
And thanne seyde the chanoun, lat us gon	And said to the canon, "Let us go
With thise thre teynes, whiche that we han wroght,	With these three bars, which we have made,
To som goldsmyth, and wite if they been oght.	To some goldsmith and see if they are worth anything,
For, by my feith, I nolde, for myn hood,	For, I swear, I wouldn't swap my hood for them
But if that they were silver fyn and good,	Unless they are pure good silver,
And that as swithe preeved it shal bee.	And that can quickly be proved."
Unto the goldsmyth with thise teynes three	They went to the goldsmith with these
They wente, and putte thise teynes in assay	Three bars and had them tested
Fo fir and hamer; myghte no man seye nay,	By fire and hammer; no man could deny
But that they weren as hem oghte be.	That they were what they were supposed to be.

This sotted preest, who was gladder than he?	*This deluded priest, who was happier than him?*
Was nevere brid gladder agayn the day,	*No bird was ever more glad of daybreak,*
Ne nyghtyngale, in the sesoun of may,	*No nightingale, in the season of May,*
Was nevere noon that luste bet to synge;	*Was ever more eager to sing;*
Ne lady lustier in carolynge,	*No lady was ever lustier in singing carols*
Or for to speke of love and wommanhede,	*Or speaking of love and womanhood,*
Ne knyght in armes to doon an hardy dede,	*No knight in arms was ever so keen to do a manly deed,*
To stonden in grace of his lady deere,	*To gain the favour of his dear lady,*
Than hadde this preest this soory craft to leere.	*Than this priest was to learn this sorry craft.*
And to the chanoun thus he spak and seyde	*And he spoke to the canon and said:*
For love of god, that for us alle deyde,	*"For the love of God, who died for love of us,*
And as I may deserve it unto yow,	*If I deserve to have it from you,*
What shal this receite coste? telleth now!	*What will this recipe cost me? Tell me!"*
By oure lady, quod this chanon, it is deere,	*"By our Lady," said this canon, "it is expensive,*
I warne yow wel; for save I and a frere,	*I must warn you; except for me and a friar*
In engelond ther kan no man it make.	*There is no man in England who can make it."*
No fors, quod he, now, sire, for goddes sake,	*"It doesn't matter," he said, "now, sir, for God's sake,*
What shal I paye? telleth me, I preye.	*What shall I pay? Tell me, please."*
Ywis, quod he, it is ful deere, I seye.	*"Indeed," he said, "as I say, it is very expensive.*
Sire, at o word, if that thee list it have,	*Sir, in a nutshell, if you want it,*
Ye shul paye fourty pound, so God me save!	*You must pay me forty pounds, so help me God!*
And nere the freendshipe that ye dide er this	*And if it wasn't for the friendship you showed me previously*
To me, ye sholde paye moore, ywis.	*You would pay more, I swear."*
This preest the somme of fourty pound anon	*The priest immediately fetched the sum of*
Of nobles fette, and took hem everichon	*Forty pounds in nobles, and gave all of them*
To this chanoun, for this ilke receite.	*To this canon for this recipe.*
Al his werkyng nas but fraude and deceite.	*Everything had just been fraud and deceit.*
Sire preest, he seyde, I kepe han no loos	*"Sir priest," he said, "I don't want fame*
Of my craft, for I wolde it kept were cloos;	*For my skill, I want it kept secret;*
And, as ye love me, kepeth it secree.	*And, as you love me, don't tell anyone.*
For, and men knewen al my soutiltee,	*For, if men knew my unusual skill,*
By god, they wolden han so greet envye	*By God, they would be so envious*
To me, by cause of my philosophye,	*Of me because of my science*
I sholde be deed; ther were noon oother weye.	*I would be killed; that would be certain."*
God it forbeede, quod the preest, what sey ye?	*"God forbid," said the priest, "what are you saying?*
Yet hadde I levere spenden al the good	*I would rather spend all the wealth*
Which that I have, and elles wexe I wood,	*Which I have, I'd even rather go mad,*
Than that ye sholden falle in swich mescheef.	*Than let you have any distress."*
For youre good wyl, sire, have ye right good preef,	*"You have given me fine proof of your goodwill, sir,"*
Quod the chanoun, and farwel, grant mercy!	*Said the canon, "and farewell, many thanks!"*
He wente his wey, and never the preest hym sy	*He went on his way, and the priest never saw him*
After that day; and whan that this preest sholde	*After that day; and when this priest wanted,*

Maken assay, at swich tyme as he wolde,
Of this receit, farwel! it wolde nat be.
Lo, thus byjaped and bigiled was he!
Thus maketh he his introduccioun,
To brynge folk to hir destruccioun.

Considereth, sires, how that, in ech estaat,
Bitwixe men and gold ther is debaat
So ferforth that unnethes is ther noon.
This multiplying blent so many oon
That in good feith I trowe that it bee
The cause grettest of swich scarsetee.
Philosophres speken so mystily
In this craft that men kan nat come therby,
For any wit that men han now-a-dayes.
They mowe wel chiteren as doon thise jayes,
And in hir termes sette hir lust and peyne,

But to hir purpos shul they nevere atteyne.
A man may lightly lerne, if he have aught,

To multiplie, and brynge his good to naught!

Lo! swich a lucre is in this lusty game,
A mannes myrthe it wol turne unto grame,
And empten also grete and hevye purses,
And maken folk for to purchacen curses
Of hem that han hir good therto ylent.
O! fy, for shame! they that han been brent,

Allas! kan they nat flee the fires heete?

Ye that it use, I rede ye it leete,
Lest ye lese al; for bet than nevere is late.

Nevere to thryve were to long a date.
Though ye prolle ay, ye shul it nevere fynde.

Ye been as boold as is bayard the blynde,
That blondreth forth, and peril casteth noon.
He is as boold to renne agayn a stoon
As for to goon bisides in the weye.
So faren ye that multiplie, I seye.
If that youre eyen kan nat seen aright,
Looke that youre mynde lakke noght his sight.
For though ye looken never so brode and stare,
Ye shul nothyng wynne on that chaffare,
But wasten al that ye may rape and renne.
Withdraweth the fir, lest it to faste brenne;
Medleth namoore with that art, I mene,
For if ye doon, youre thrift is goon ful clene.
And right as swithe I wol yow tellen heere
What philosophres seyn in this mateere.
Lo, thus seith arnold of the newe toun,

At the time he chose, to make a trial
Of this recipe, no way! It wouldn't happen.
See how he was tricked and fooled!
That's how he introduces himself
So he can bring folk to their destruction.

Think, sirs, how, in every rank,
Men and their gold are so separated
That there is hardly any gold left.
This alchemy blinds so many
That I swear I believe it is
The greatest reason for this scarcity.
Philosophers speak so mystically
About this craft which men cannot achieve,
With any intelligence that men have nowadays.
They might well chatter like jays,
And use their technical terms for their desire and pain,
But they will never achieve their goal.
A man can easily learn, if he has anything to lose,
To perform alchemy, and reduce his wealth to nothing!

See! There is such profit in this jolly game,
It can turn a man's joy into sorrow,
And also empty fat purses,
And make people deserve the curses
Of those who lent them their wealth to use.
Oh, fie, for shame! Those who have been burned,
Alas, can they not run away from the heat of the fire?
Those who do this, I advise you to give it up,
In case you lose everything; it is better late than never.
To never prosper would be too long a time.
Although you search forever, you will never find it.
You are as foolish as Bayard the blind horse,
That blunders around and ignores all danger.
He is as likely to run into a stone
As to go around it in the road.
That's what you alchemists are like, I say.
If your eyes cannot see clearly,
At least make sure your mind is not blind.
For though you look so wide-eyed and staring,
You will gain nothing in the transaction,
You will waste everything that you can steal.
Give up the fire, in case it burns you;
I mean, give up that art,
For if you do, you will lose all your prosperity.
And I will tell you quickly here
What the alchemists say about this.
This is what Arnold of the New Town says,

As his rosarie maketh mencioun;
He seith right thus, withouten any lye
Ther may no man mercurie mortifie
But it be with his brother knowlechyng.
How be that he which that first seyde this thyng
Of philosophres fader was, hermes --

He seith how that the dragon, doutelees,
Ne dyeth nat, but if that he be slayn
With his brother; and that is for to sayn,
By the dragon, mercurie, and noon oother
He understood, and brymstoon by his brother,
That out of sol and luna were ydrawe.
And therfore, seyde he, -- taak heede to my sawe --
Lat no man bisye hym this art for to seche,
But if that he th' entencioun and speche
Of philosophres understonde kan;
And if he do, he is a lewed man.
For this science and this konnyng, quod he,
Is of the secree of secrees, pardee.

Also ther was a disciple of plato,
That on a tyme seyde his maister to,
As his book senior wol bere witnesse,
And this was his demande in soothfastnesse
Telle me the name of the privee stoon?
And plato answerde unto hym anoon,
Take the stoon that titanos men name.
Which is that? quod he. Magnasia is the same,

Seyde plato. Ye, sire, and is it thus?
This is ignotum per ignocius.
What is magnasia, good sire, I yow preye?
It is a water that is maad, I seye,
Of elementes foure, quod plato.
Telle me the roote, good sire, quod he tho,
Of that water, if it be youre wil.
Nay, nay, quod plato, certein, that I nyl.
The philosophres sworn were everychoon
That they sholden discovere it unto noon,
Ne in no book it write in no manere.
For unto crist it is so lief and deere
That he wol nat that it discovered bee,
But where it liketh to his deitee
Men for t' enspire, and eek for to deffende
Whom that hym liketh; lo, this is the ende.

Thanne conclude I thus, sith that God of hevene
Ne wil nat that the philosophres nevene
How that a man shal come unto this stoon,
I rede, as for the beste, lete it goon.
For whoso maketh God his adversarie,
As for to werken any thyng in contrarie
Of his wil, certes, never shal he thryve,

Which he mentions in his book Rosari;
He says straight out, truthfully:
"There is no man who can make mercury hard
Unless it is with his brother's knowledge";
Although the one who first said this thing
Was the father of philosophers, Hermes Trismegistus;
He says that the Dragon, doubtless,
Does not die unless it is killed
By his brother; so he means,
By the Dragon, Mercury, and nothing else,
He understood, and brimstone he meant as his brother,
That were drawn out of gold and silver.
"And therefore, he said–pay attention–
"let no man waste his time attempting this art,
Unless he can understand the meaning
And words of alchemists;
And if he does, he is an ignorant man.
For this science and this skill," he said,
"Concerns the greatest secrets, by God."

Also there was a disciple of Plato,
Who at one time said to his master,
As his book Senior tells us,
And this was the question he asked:
"Tell me the name of the philosopher's stone."
And Plato answered him at once,
"Take the stone that men call Titanos."
"Which one is that?" he asked. "Magnesia is the same,"
Said Plato. "Yes, sir, is that it?
You are explaining unknowns with unknowns.
What is magnesia, good sir, I beg you?
"It is a liquid that is made, I tell you,
Of the four elements," said Plato.
"Tell me the basis, good sir," he then said,
"Of that liquid, if you would."
"No, no," said Plato, "certainly, I will not.
The alchemists all swore
That they would reveal it to no-one,
Nor write it down in any book.
For it is so beloved of Christ and dear
That he does not want it to be discovered,
Except where it pleases his deity
To inspire men, and also to forbid it
To whomever he pleases; that is all."

So I conclude that, since God in heaven
Does not wish for the alchemist to tell
How anyone can get hold of this stone,
I advise, for the best, to leave it alone.
For anyone who makes an enemy of God,
By doing anything against
His will, certainly, he will never prosper,

Thogh that he multiplie terme of his lyve.	*Even if he practices alchemy all his life.*
And there a poynt; for ended is my tale.	*Put down a full stop, for this is the end of my tale.*
God sende every trewe man boote of his bale!	*May God send every true man relief from his troubles!*

Heere is ended the Chanouns Yemannes Tale — *The end of the Canon's Yeoman's tale*

The Manciple's Tale

Prologue

Here folweth the Prologe of the Maunciples Tale.   *The Manciple's Prologue*

Woot ye nat where ther stant a litel toun,	*Do you know a little town*
Which that ycleped is Bobbe-up-and-doun	*Which is called Bob-up-and-down,*
Under the Blee, in Caunterbury weye?	*Under Blee, in Canterbury Way?*
Ther gan oure Hooste for to jape and pleye,	*There our host began to joke and play,*
And seyde, Sires, what, Dun is in the Myre!	*And said, "What's this! Dun is in the mire!*
Is ther no man for preyere ne for hyre,	*Is there no man, for prayer or for hire,*
That wole awake oure felawe al bihynde?	*Who will wake up our friend behind us?*
A theef myghte hym ful lightly robbe and bynde.	*A thief could easily rob him and tie him up.*
See how he nappeth, see how for Cokkes bones,	*Look at him napping! See how, for cock's bones,*
That he wol falle fro his hors atones.	*He will soon fall from his horse!*
Is that a Cook of London, with meschaunce?	*Is that the cook of London, bad luck to him?*
Do hym com forth, he knoweth his penaunce,	*Make him come forward, he knows his punishment;*
For he shal telle a tale, by my fey,	*For I swear he shall tell a tale,*
Although it be nat worth a botel hey.	*Even if it's not worth the bundle of hay.*
Awake, thou Cook, quod he, God yeve thee sorwe,	*Wake up, you cook," he said, "may God bring you sorrow!*
What eyleth thee, to slepe by the morwe?	*What's wrong with you, sleeping in the morning?*
Hastow had fleen al nyght, or artow dronke?	*Have you been scratching all night, or are you drunk?*
Or hastow with som quene al nyght yswonke	*Or have you been screwing some prostitute all night,*
So that thow mayst nat holden up thyn heed?	*So that you can now can't hold your head up?"*
This Cook that was ful pale, and no thyng reed,	*This cook, who was very pale, not red,*
Seyde to oure Hoost, So God my soule blesse,	*Said to our host, "God bless my soul,*
As ther is falle on me swich hevynesse,	*Such a heavy feeling has fallen on me,*
Noot I nat why, that me were levere slepe	*I don't know why, that I would rather sleep*
Than the beste galon wyn in Chepe.	*Than have the best gallon of wine in Cheapside."*
Wel, quod the Maunciple, if it may doon ese	*"Well," said the manciple, "if it will bring relief*
To thee, Sire Cook, and to no wight displease	*To you, sir cook, and not displease anyone,*
Which that heere rideth in this compaignye,	*Who is riding in our company,*
And that oure Hoost wole of his curteisye,	*And if our host would kindly agree,*
I wol as now excuse thee of thy tale,	*I will excuse you from telling your tale for now.*
For, in good feith, thy visage is ful pale.	*For, certainly, your face is very pale,*
Thyne eyen daswen eek, as that me thynketh,	*Your eyes are also glazed over, it seems to me,*
And wel I woot, thy breeth ful soure stynketh.	*And I can smell that your breath stinks sour:*
That sheweth wel thou art nat wel disposed,	*This shows that you are not healthy.*
Of me, certeyn, thou shalt nat been yglosed.	*I certainly won't deceive you.*
See how he ganeth, lo, this dronken wight!	*See how he yawns, this drunken fellow,*
As though he wolde swolwe us anonright.	*As though he would swallow the lot of us.*
Hoold cloos thy mouth, man, by thy fader kyn,	*Keep your mouth closed, man, by your father's*

The devel of helle sette his foot therin.	A devil from hell has put his foot in there!
Thy cursed breeth infecte wole us alle,	Your cursed breath would infect us all.
Fy, stynkyng swyn! fy, foule moothe thou falle!	Fie, stinking swine! Fie, may bad fortune fall on you!
A, taketh heede, sires, of this lusty man!	Take heed, sirs, of this lusty man.
Now, sweete sire, wol ye justen atte fan?	Now, sweet sir, will you joust at a dummy?
Therto me thynketh ye been wel yshape,	It seems to me you are well set up for that,
I trowe that ye dronken han wyn-ape,	I believe that you have drunk until you act like an ape,
And that is, whan men pleyen with a straw.	And that is when men begin to fight with straws."
And with this speche the Cook wax wrooth and wraw,	At this speech the cook became extremely angry,
And on the Manciple he gan nodde faste,	And he began to shake his head vigourously at the manciple,
For lakke of speche, and doun the hors hym caste,	He couldn't speak, and the horse threw him off,
Where as he lay til that men up hym took;	Where he lay, until men lifted him up.
This was a fair chyvachee of a Cook!	That was excellent horsemanship by a cook!
Allas, he nadde holde hym by his ladel!	Alas, he should have stayed in his kitchen!
And er that he agayn were in his sadel	Before he was back in his saddle,
Ther was greet showvyng bothe to and fro,	There was great shoving to and fro
To lifte hym up, and muchel care and wo,	To lift him up, and much effort and trouble,
So unweeldy was this sory palled goost.	This pale ghost was so unwieldy.
And to the Manciple thanne spak oure hoost,	And our host spoke to the manciple:
By cause drynke hath dominacioun,	"Because drink is ruling over
Upon this man, by my savacioun,	This man, by my salvation,
I trowe he lewedly wolde telle his tale.	I think he would tell his tale badly.
For were it wyn, or oold or moysty ale,	For if it were wine or old or new ale
That he hath dronke, he speketh in his nose,	That he has drunk, he speaks through his nose,
And fneseth faste, and eek he hath the pose.	And sneezes, and he also has a cold.
He hath also to do moore than ynough	He has more than enough to do
To kepen hym and his capul out of slough,	Keeping himself and his horse out of the mud;
And if he falle from his capul eftsoone,	And if he falls from his horse again
Thanne shal we alle have ynogh to done	Then we shall have plenty of work
In liftyng up his hevy dronken cors.	Lifting up his heavy drunken body.
Telle on thy tale, of hym make I no fors;	You tell your tale, I won't pay any attention to him.
But yet, Manciple, in feith thou art to nyce,	But still, Manciple, you truly are too foolish,
Thus openly repreve hym of his vice.	To criticise him openly for his advice.
Another day he wole peraventure	On another day he would, perhaps,
Reclayme thee and brynge thee to lure.	Call you back and trap you,
I meene he speke wole of smale thynges,	I mean, he would speak of little things,
As for to pynchen at thy rekenynges,	Such as finding fault with your accounts,
That were nat honeste, if it cam to preef.	That wouldn't be honest, if put to the test."
No, quod the Manciple, that were a greet mescheef,	"No," said the manciple, "that would be terrible!
So myghte he lightly brynge me in the snare;	In that way he could easily trap me.
Yet hadde I levere payen for the mare,	Yet I would rather pay for the mare
Which that he rit on, than he sholde with me stryve	Which he is riding, than to fight with him.
I wol nat wratthen hym, al so moot I thryve;	I will not anger him, I swear!
That that I speke, I seyde it in my bourde.	What I said, I said it is a joke.

And wite ye what, I have heer in a gourde A draghte of wyn, ye, of a ripe grape, And right anon ye shul seen a good jape. This Cook shal drynke therof if that I may,	And do you know what? I have here in a gourd A draught of wine, yes, of a ripe grape, And at once you shall see a good joke. The cook will drink some of this, if I can make him.
Up peyne of deeth, he wol nat seye me nat. And certeynly, to tellen as it was, Of this vessel the Cook drank faste; allas, What neded hym? he drank ynough biforn!	On pain of death, he will not refuse me." And Certainly, to tell it as it was The cook drank deeply from this vessel, alas! Why did he do that? He had drunk enough before.
And whan he hadde pouped in this horn, To the Manciple he took the gourde agayn, And of that drynke the Cook was wonder fayn, And thanked hym in swich wise as he koude. Thanne gan oure Hoost to laughen wonder loude,	And when he had drained the horn, He gave the gourd back to the manciple; And the cook was delighted by the drink, And thanked him as best he could. Then our host began to laugh out wonderfully loud,
And seyde, I se wel it is necessarie Where that we goon, that drynke we with us carie. For that wol turne rancour and disese Tacord and love and many a wrong apese.	And said, "I see it is certainly necessary, Wherever we go, to carry good drink with us; For that will turn anger and strife To agreement and love, and make many wrong things right.
O thou Bacus, yblessed be thy name, That so kanst turnen ernest into game! Worship and thank be to thy deitee! Of that mateere ye gete namoore of me, Telle on thy tale, Manciple, I thee preye. Wel, sire, quod he, now herkneth what I seye.	O Bacchus, may your name be blessed, Who can turn serious things into fun! We worship and give thanks to your deity! Now I will say no more about that. Get on with your tale, manciple, I pray you." "Well, sir," he said, "now listen to what I say."

The Tale

Heere bigynneth the Maunciples Tale of the Crowe.	***The Manciple's Tale***
Whan Phebus dwelled heere in this world adoun, As olde bookes maken mencioun, He was the mooste lusty bachiler In al this world, and eek the beste archer. He slow Phitoun the serpent, as he lay Slepynge agayn the sonne upon a day; And many another noble worthy dede He with his bowe wroghte, as men may rede. Pleyen he koude on every mynstralcie, And syngen, that it was a melodie To heeren of his cleere voys the soun. Certes, the kyng of Thebes, Amphioun, That with his syngyng walled that citee, Koude nevere syngen half so wel as hee. Therto he was the semelieste man, That is or was sith that the world bigan.	When Phoebus lived down here on earth, As the old books tell us, He was the lustiest bachelor In the whole world, and also the best archer. He killed Phitoun, the serpent, as he laid Sleeping in the sun one day; And many other noble worthy deeds He did with his bow, as men may read. He could play on every instrument, And sing so that it was beautiful To hear the sound of his clear voice. Certainly the king of Thebes, Amphion, Who surrounded that city with his singing, Could never sing half as well as him. Also he was the best looking man That has ever been, since the beginning of the world.
What nedeth it hise fetures to discryve? For in this world was noon so fair on lyve.	What is the point in describing his features? In this whole world there was no one so handsome.

He was therwith fulfild of gentillesse,
Of honour, and of parfit worthynesse.
This Phebus that was flour of bachilrie,

As wel in fredom as in chivalrie,

Of Phitoun, so as telleth us the storie,
Was wont to beren in his hand a bowe.
Now hadde this Phebus in his hous a crowe,
Which in a cage he fostred many a day,

And taughte it speken as men teche a jay.
Whit was this crowe, as is a snow-whit swan,
And countrefete the speche of every man
He koude, whan he sholde telle a tale.
Therwith in al this world no nyghtngale

Ne koude, by an hondred thousand deel,

Syngen so wonder myrily and weel.
Now hadde this Phebus in his hous a wyf
Which that he lovede moore than his lyf;
And nyght and day dide evere his diligence
Hir for to plese and doon hire reverence.
Save oonly, if the sothe that I shal sayn,
Jalous he was, and wolde have kept hire fayn,

For hym were looth byjaped for to be-
And so is every wight in swich degree;
But al in ydel, for it availleth noght.

A good wyf that is clene of werk and thoght
Sholde nat been kept in noon awayt, certayn.

And trewely the labour is in vayn
To kepe a shrewe, for it wol nat bee.
This holde I for a verray nycetee,
To spille labour for to kepe wyves,
Thus writen olde clerkes in hir lyves.
But now to purpos, as I first bigan:
This worthy Phebus dooth al that he kan
To plesen hir, wenynge that swich plesaunce,

And for his manhede and his governaunce,

That no man sholde han put hym from hire grace.

But God it woot, ther may no man embrace
As to destreyne a thyng, which that nature
Hath natureelly set in a creature.
Taak any bryd, and put it in a cage,
And do al thyn entente and thy corage
To fostre it tendrely with mete and drynke,
Of alle deyntees that thou kanst bithynke;
And keepe it al so clenly as thou may,

He was also filled with nobility,
Of honour, and of perfect goodness.
This Phoebus, who was the flower of knighthood,
In generosity as well as in chivalry, victory
Over Phitoun, so the story tells us,
Used to carry a bow in his hand.
Now in his house this Phoebus had a crow
Which he had brought up for a long time in a cage,
And taught it to speak, as people teach jays.
This crow was as white as a snow white swan,
And imitated the speech of every man
When he was telling a tale.
Also there wasn't a nightingale in the whole world
Who, even if it was a hundred thousand times better,
Could sing as wonderfully jolly and well.
Now in his house Phoebus had a wife
Whom he loved more than his whole life,
And night and day he always toiled
To please her and show her respect,
Except, if I tell the truth,
He was jealous, and would gladly have kept her shut up.
He hated being tricked,
As does everyone in the same place;
But it's all in vain, it doesn't help.

A good wife, who is clean in thought and deed,
Doesn't have to be constantly watched, it's certain;
And truly it is a waste of time
Trying to control a shrew, it won't happen.
I think this is a very foolish thing,
To waste effort guarding wives:
That's what the ancient scholars wrote.
But now to the point, as I began:
This good Phoebus did all that he could
To please her, thinking of such pleasant things,
And with all his manly qualities and his fine behaviour,
No man should have been able to replace him in her affections.
But God knows, no man can contain
And control something which nature
Has naturally placed in a creature.
Take any bird, and put it in a cage,
And pay all your attention to it, and take pains
To tenderly raise it with food and drink,
With all the dainties that you can imagine,
And keep it as clean as you can,

Middle English	Modern English
Al though his cage of gold be nevere so gay,	And even if his golden cage is wonderfully beautiful,
Yet hath this bryd, by twenty thousand foold,	This bird would be twenty thousand times happier
Levere in a forest that is rude and coold	In a forest that is rough and cold,
Goon ete wormes, and swich wrecchednesse;	Eating worms and other such wretched food.
For evere this bryd wol doon his bisynesse	This bird will always be trying
To escape out of his cage, whan he may.	To escape from his cage, if he can.
His libertee this bryd desireth ay.	The bird always wants his freedom.
Lat take a cat, and fostre hym wel with milk,	Take a cat, and bring him up well with milk
And tendre flessh, and make his couche of silk,	And tender meat, and make him a silk bed,
And lat hym seen a mous go by the wal,	And let him see a mouse go past the wall,
Anon he weyveth milk and flessh and al,	At once he will reject the milk and meat and all,
And every deyntee that is in that hous,	And every delicacy in the house,
Swich appetit he hath to ete a mous.	He has such an appetite for eating the mouse.
Lo, heere hath lust his dominacioun,	See, his lust then rules over him,
And appetit fleemeth discrecioun.	And his appetite takes away his self-control.
A she wolf hath also a vileyns kynde,	A she wolf also has an evil nature.
The lewedeste wolf that she may fynde,	The most base wolf that she can find,
Or leest of reputacioun wol she take,	The one with the lowest reputation, she will take,
In tyme when hir lust to han a make.	When she is in heat.
Alle thise ensamples speke I by thise men,	All these examples I'm talking about are about men
That been untrewe, and no thyng by wommen,	Who are unfaithful, nothing about women.
For men han evere a likerous appetit	For men always have lecherous appetites
On lower thyng to parfourne hire delit,	For lower things to use for their delight
Than on hire wyves, be they nevere so faire,	Rather than their wives, however beautiful they are,
Ne nevere so trewe, ne so debonaire.	However faithful, however gracious.
Flessh is so newefangel, with meschaunce,	Flesh is so keen on new things, damnation to it,
That we ne konne in no thyng han plesaunce	That we cannot take pleasure in anything
That sowneth into vertu any while.	That remains virtuous for any length of time.
This Phebus, which that thoghte upon no gile,	This Phoebus, who did not imagine any trickery,
Deceyved was, for al his jolitee;	Was deceived, despite all his good qualities.
For under hym another hadde shee,	For under his nose she had another,
A man of litel reputacioun,	A man of low reputation,
Nat worth to Phebus in comparisoun.	Worth nothing compared to Phoebus.
The moore harm is, it happeth ofte so,	Curse it, this often happens,
Of which ther cometh muchel harm and wo.	And it brings much harm and sorrow.
And so bifel, whan Phebus was absent,	And so it happened, when Phoebus was absent,
His wyf anon hath for hir lemman sent;	Her wife immediately sent for her sweetheart.
Hir lemman? certes, this is a knavyssh speche,	Her sweetheart? This is certainly scandalous speech!
Foryeveth it me, and that I yow biseche.	Forgive me, I beg you.
The wise Plato seith, as ye may rede,	The wise Plato says, as you may read,
The word moot nede accorde with the dede.	The word must always match the deed.
If men shal telle proprely a thyng,	If a man is to tell a thing properly,
The word moot cosyn be to the werkyng.	The words and the deeds must match.

I am a boystous man, right thus seye I.
Ther nys no difference trewely
Bitwixe a wyf that is of heigh degree-
If of hire body dishoneste she bee-
And a povre wenche, oother than this,
If it so be they werke bothe amys,
But that the gentile in hire estaat above,
She shal be cleped his lady as in love,
And for that oother is a povre womman,
She shal be cleped his wenche, or his lemman;
And God it woot, myn owene deere brother,
Men leyn that oon as lowe as lith that oother.
Right so bitwixe a titlelees tiraunt

And an outlawe, or a theef erraunt,
The same I seye, ther is no difference.

To Alisaundre was toold this sentence,
That for the tiraunt is of gretter myght,
By force of meynee for to sleen dounright,
And brennen hous and hoom, and make al playn,

Lo, therfore is he cleped a capitayn!
And for the outlawe hath but smal meynee,
And may nat doon so greet an harm as he,
Ne brynge a contree to so greet meschcef,
Men clepen hym an outlawe or a theef.
But for I am a man noght textueel,
I wol noght telle of textes nevere a deel;
I wol go to my tale as I bigan.
Whan Phebus wyf had sente for hir lemman,

Anon they wroghten al hir lust volage.
The white crowe that heeng ay in the cage
Biheeld hire werk, and seyde nevere a word,

And whan that hoom was com Phebus the lord,
This crowe sang, Cokkow! Cokkow! Cokkow!
What bryd! quod Phebus, what song syngestow?

Ne were thow wont so myrily to synge
That to myn herte it was a rejoysynge
To heere thy voys? allas, what song is this?
By God, quod he, I synge nat amys.
Phebus, quod he, for al thy worthynesse,
For al thy beautee and thy gentillesse,
For al thy song and al thy mynstralcye,
For al thy waityng, blered is thyn eye
With oon of litel reputacioun
Noght worth to thee, as in comparisoun
The montance of a gnat, so moote I thryve,
For on thy bed thy wyf I saugh hym swyve.

What wol ye moore? the crowe anon hym tolde,

I am an unlearned man, I'm telling you:
There really is no difference
Between a wife of high position,
If she is dishonest with her body,
And a poor wretch, except this—
If both of them go astray—
Except the gentlewoman, higher in rank,
Will be called his lady, as in courtly love;
And because the other is a poor woman,
She will be called his wench or his sweetheart.
And, God knows, my own dear brother,
Men think that each is as bad as the other.
It's the same difference as between a usurping tyrant
And an outlaw or a filthy thief,
They are the same, I say: there is no difference.
Alexander was told this,
That, because the tyrant has more power,
With his forces to cause death,
And burn house and home, and raze everything,
See, then he is called a captain;
And because the outlaw only has a small force,
And can't do as much harm as him,
Or bring such damage to a country,
Men call him an outlaw or thief.
But because I am not an educated man,
I will not say anything of texts at all;
I will go on with my tale, as I began.
When the wife of Phoebus had sent for her sweetheart,
Straight away they satisfied their burning lust.
The white crow, that always hung in the cage,
Saw what they were doing, and never said a word.

And when Phoebus, the lord, came home,
This crow sang, "Cuckoo! Cuckoo! Cuckoo!"
"What, bird?" Said Phoebus. "What song are you singing?
Don't you usually sing so beautifully
That it made my heart rejoice
To hear your voice? Alas, what is this song?"
"By God," he said, "I am not singing wrongly.
Phoebus," he said, "for all your goodness,
For all your beauty and your nobility,
For all your songs and your music,
For all your wariness, you have been tricked
By one of low reputation,
Worth nothing, compared to you,
Just worth a gnat, I swear!
For I saw him screwing your wife on your bed."
What more do you want? The crow told him at

By sadde tokenes and by wordes bolde,	With clear evidence and bold words,
How that his wyf han doon hire lecherye,	How his wife had cheated on him,
Hym to greet shame and to greet vileynye,	To his great shame and dishonour,
And tolde hym ofte, he asugh it with hise eyen.	And he told him that he had often seen it with his eyes.
This Phebus gan aweyward for to wryen,	Then Phoebus began to turn away,
And thoughte his sorweful herte brast atwo,	And he thought his sorrowing heart would break in two.
His bowe he bente and sette ther inne a flo,	He drew back his bow, and notched an arrow,
And in his ire his wyf thanne hath he slayn.	And in his anger he then killed his wife.
This is theffect, ther is namoore to sayn,	That is all; there is no more to say:
For sorwe of which he brak his mynstralcie,	Sorrowing because of it he broke his musical instruments,
Bothe harpe, and lute, and gyterne, and sautrie,	His harp, his lute, his cither and psaltery;
And eek he brak hise arwes and his bowe,	And he also broke his arrows and his bow,
And after that thus spak he to the crowe.	And after that he said this to the crow:
Traitour, quod he, with tonge of scorpioun,	"Traitor," he said, "with your scorpion tongue,
Thou hast me broght to my confusioun,	You have brought about my downfall;
Allas, that I was wroght! why nere I deed?	Alas for the day I was born! Why did I not die?
O deere wyf, O gemme of lustiheed,	Oh dear wife! Oh gem of delight!
That were to me so sad and eek so trewe,	You were so good and true to me,
Now listow deed with face pale of hewe,	Now you're lying dead, with your pale face,
Ful giltelees, that dorste I swere, ywys.	Guiltless, I certainly swear to that!
O rakel hand, to doon so foule amys!	Oh you foolish hand, to have done such a foul crime!
O trouble wit, O ire recchelees!	You troubled mind, reckless anger,
That unavysed smyteth gilteles.	That without thinking struck the Innocent!
O wantrust, ful of fals suspecioun,	Oh mistrust, foul suspicion,
Where was thy wit and thy discrecioun?	Where was your intelligence and your sense?
O, every man, be war of rakelnesse,	Oh every man, beware of acting rashly!
Ne trowe no thyng withouten strong witnesse.	Don't believe anything without evidence.
Smyt nat to soone, er that ye witen why,	Don't strike too early, before you know why,
And beeth avysed wel and sobrely,	And be sensible and and sober
Er ye doon any execucioun	Before you do any act
Upon youre ire for suspecioun.	Because of the anger your suspicions have caused.
Allas, a thousand folk hath rakel ire	Alas, a thousand people have been undone
Fully fordoon, and broght hem in the mire!	By rash anger, it has brought them low.
Allas, for sorwe I wol myselven slee!	Alas! I will kill myself for sorrow!"
And to the crowe, O false theef, seyde he,	And to the crow, "Oh false thief!" he said,
I wol thee quite anon thy false tale;	"I will pay you back at once for your falsehood.
Thou songe whilom lyk a nyghtngale,	You once sang like a nightingale,
Now shaltow, false theef, thy song forgon,	Now, false thief, you will give up your song,
And eek thy white fetheres everichon.	And also all your white feathers,
Ne nevere in al thy lyf ne shaltou speke,	And you will never speak again in your life.
Thus shal men on a traytour been awreke.	So men will be revenged on a traitor;
Thou and thyn ofspryng evere shul be blake,	You and your offspring will always be black,
Ne nevere sweete noyse shul ye make,	And no more will you make any sweet noise,
But evere crie agayn tempest and rayn,	You will always cry out, anticipating the storm and rain,
In tokenynge that thurgh thee my wyf is slayn.	As a sign that it was you caused my wife's death."

And to the crowe he stirte, and that anon,
And pulled hise white fetheres everychon,
And made hym blak, and refte hym al his song,

And eek his speche, and out at dore hym slong,

Unto the devel-which I hym bitake!-
And for this caas been alle Crowes blake.
Lordynges, by this ensample I yow preye,
Beth war and taketh kepe what I seye:

Ne telleth nevere no man in youre lyf
How that another man hath dight his wyf;
He wol yow haten mortally, certeyn.
Daun Salomon, as wise clerkes seyn,
Techeth a man to kepen his tonge weel.
But as I seyde, I am noght textueel;
But nathelees, thus taughte me my dame;
My sone, thenk on the crowe, on Goddes name.

My sone, keepe wel thy tonge and keepe thy freend,

A wikked tonge is worse than a feend.
My sone, from a feend men may hem blesse.

My sone, God of his endelees goodnesse
Walled a tonge with teeth and lippes eke,
For man sholde hym avyse what he speeke.
My sone, ful ofte for to muche speche

Hath many a man been spilt, as clerkes teche.

But for litel speche, avysely,
Is no man shent, to speke generally.
My sone, thy tonge sholdestow restreyne
At alle tymes, but whan thou doost thy peyne
To speke of God in honour and in preyere;
The firste vertu sone, if thou wolt leere,
Is to restreyne and kepe wel thy tonge.
Thus lerne children, whan that they been yonge,

My sone, of muchel spekyng yvele avysed,
Ther lasse spekyng hadde ynough suffised,
Comth muchel harm-thus was me toold and taught.-

In muchel speche synne wanteth naught.
Wostow wherof a rakel tonge serveth?
Right as a swerd forkutteth and forkerveth
An arme atwo, my deere sone, right so
A tonge kutteth freendshipe al atwo.
A jangler is to God abhomynable;
Reed Salomon, so wys and honurable,
Reed David in hise psalmes, reed Senekke!
My sone, spek nat, but with thyn heed thou bekke;

And he rushed to the crow, straight away,
And pulled out every one of his white feathers,
And made him black, and took away all his song,

And also his speech, and threw him out the door

To the devil, which is where I send him;
And this is why all crows are black.
My Lords, I pray you to take warning
From this example, and take care what you say:

And never tell anyone in your whole life
How another man has screwed his wife;
He will make you his mortal enemy, certainly.
Don Solomon, the wise scholars say,
Told men to watch out for their tongues.
But, as I said, I am not educated.
But nonetheless, my mother taught me this:
"My son, think of the crow, in the name of God!

My son, hold your tongue well, and keep your friends.

A wicked tongue is worse than a devil;
My son, men can bless themselves and escape the devil.

My son, God in his endless goodness
Put a wall of teeth and lips around the tongue,
So that men could think about what they save.
My son, very often, through speaking too much,

Many men have been ruined, the scholars teach us,

But a little wise speech
Does no man harm, generally speaking.
My son, you should restrain your tongue
At all times, except when you are trying
To speak of God, in worship and prayer.
The primary virtue, son, if you will learn it,
Is to restrain and guard your tongue;
This is what children learn when they are young.

My son, from ill considered speaking,
Where less talk would have been enough,
There comes much harm; this was told and taught to me.

There is plenty of sin in too much talk.
Do you know what a rash tongue is like?
It is like a sword which cuts and carves
An arm in two, my dear son, in the same way
A tongue cuts friendship all in two.
God despises gossips.
Read Solomon, so wise and honourable;
Read the Psalms of David; read Seneca.
My son, do not speak, but nod your head.

Dissimule as thou were deef, it that thou heere
A jangler speke of perilous mateere.
The Flemyng seith, and lerne it if thee leste,
That litel janglyng causeth muchel reste.
My sone, if thou no wikked word hast seyd,

Thee thar nat drede for to be biwreyd;
But he that hath mysseyd, I dar wel sayn,
He may by no wey clepe his word agayn.;
Though hym repente, or be hym leef or looth,

He is his thral to whom that he hath sayd
A tale, of which he is now yvele apayd.

My sone, be war, and be noon auctour newe
Of tidynyges, wheither they been false or trewe,
Wherso thou com, amonges hye or lowe,
Kepe wel thy tonge, and thenk upon the Crowe.

Pretend you are deaf, if you hear
A gossip speaking of dangerous things.
The Flemish say, and you should learn it,
That the less gossip there is, the more peace.
My son, if you have never said anything wicked,
You don't have to dread being betrayed;
But someone who has spoken evil, I daresay,
He can never take his words back again.
Something that has been said remains said,
and out it goes,
Even if he repents, or doesn't want it known.
He is the slave of the person to whom he told
The story which he now wishes he hadn't.
My son, beware, and don't be the author
Of gossip, whether it is false or true.
Wherever you go, amongst high or low,
Hold your tongue well, and think of the crow."

The Parsons's Tale

Prologue

The Parson's Prologue

By that the Maunciple hadde his tale al ended,	By the time the Manciple had finished his tale,
The sonne fro the south lyne was descended	The sun had come down from the meridian;
So lowe, that he nas nat to my sighte	He was so low that as I looked
Degrees nyne and twenty as in highte.	He was not more than twenty-nine degrees high.
Ten of the clokke it was tho, as I gesse,	I imagine it was four o'clock then,
For ellevene foot, or litel moore or lesse,	For at that time my shadow was
My shadwe was at thilke tyme as there,	Eleven feet long, more or less,
Of swiche feet as my lengthe parted were	Of such feet that is if my height were divided
In sixe feet equal of proporcioun.	Into six sections of equal size.
Therwith the moones exaltacioun,	There the joy of the moon—
I meene Libra, alwey gan ascende,	I mean Libra–steadily rose
As we were entryng at a thropes ende.	As we were coming into a village;
For which our Hoost, as he was wont to gye,	And our host, as he was used to leading,
As in this caas, oure joly compaignye,	As on this occasion, our jolly company,
Seyde in this wise, Lordynges everichoon,	Said this: "My Lords, everyone,
Now lakketh us no tales mo than oon,	Now we are only lacking one tale.
Fulfilled is my sentence and my decree;	My plan and my orders have been fulfilled;
I trowe that we han herd of ech degree.	I think that we have heard from each social class;
Almoost fulfild is al myn ordinaunce,	My reign is almost done.
I pray to God, so yeve hym right good chaunce	I pray to God, may he have good luck,
That telleth this tale to us lustily!	Someone who tells such a pleasing tale.
Sire preest, quod he, artow a vicary,	Sir priest," he said, "are you a vicar?
Or arte a person? sey sooth by thy fey.	Or are you a parson? Tell the truth, in faith!
Be what thou be, ne breke thou nat oure pley;	Whoever you are, don't go against our rules;
For every man save thou hath toold his tale.	For every man, apart from you, has told his tale.
Unbokele and shewe us what is in thy male,	Untie your bag and show us what you have;
For trewely, me thynketh by thy cheere	For truly, it seems from your appearance
Thou sholdest knytte up wel a greet mateere.	That you could easily give us a great speech.
Telle us a fable anon, for Cokkes bones.	Tell us a story at once, for the bones of the cock!"
This Persoun him answerede, al atones,	The Parson answered, at once,
Thou getest fable noon ytoold for me,	"You will not get any story from me,
For Paul, that writeth unto Thymothee,	For Paul, writing to Timothy,
Repreveth hem that weyveth soothfastnesse,	Reproved those who abandon truthfulness
And tellen fables, and swich wrecchednesse.	And tell fictional tales and such wretched things.
Why sholde I sowen draf out of my fest	Why should I throw chaff from my fist,
Whan I may sowen whete, if that me lest?	When I can sow wheat, if I want to?
For which I seye, if that yow list to heere,	So I say, if you want to hear
Moralitee and vertuous mateere;	Of morality and virtue,
And thanne that ye wol yeve me audience,	Providing you will listen to me,

I wol ful fayn, at Cristes reverence,
Do yow plesaunce leefful, as I kan.
But trusteth wel I am a southren man,
I kan nat geeste Rum, Ram, Ruf by lettre,
Ne, God woot, rym holde I but litel bettre,
And therfore if yow list, I wol nat glose,
I wol yow telle a myrie tale in prose
To knytte up al this feeste, and make an ende,

And Jesu, for his grace, wit me sende
To shewe yow the wey, in this viage,
Of thilke parfit glorious pilgrymage
That highte Jerusalem celestial.
And if ye vouchesauf, anon I shal
Bigynne upon my tale, for which I preye,
Telle youre avys, I kan no bettre seye.
But nathelees, this meditacioun
I putte it ay under correccioun
Of clerkes, for I am nat textueel;
I take but sentence, trusteth weel.
Therfore I make a protestacioun
That I wol stonde to correccioun.
Upon this word we han assented soone;
For, as us semed, it was for to done
To enden in som vertuous sentence,
And for to yeve hym space and audience;
Adn bede oure Hoost he sholde to hym seye
That alle we to telle his tale hym preye.
Oure Hoost hadde the wordes for us alle:
Sire preest, quod he, now faire yow bifalle,

Sey what yow list, and we wol gladly heere.
And with that word he seyde in this manere,
Telleth, quod he, youre meditacioun;
But hasteth yow, the sonne wole adoun.
Beth fructuous, and that in litel space,
And to do wel God sende yow his grace.

*I will very gladly, for the worship of Christ,
Give you such lawful pleasure as I can.
But trust me, I am a southern man;
I cannot recite "ABC" letter by letter,
And, God knows, I'm no better at rhyming;
And so, if you wish—I won't pretend—
I will tell you a jolly tale in prose
To bring an end to all this festivity.*

*And Jesus, in his grace, send me wit
To show you the way, on this journey,
Of the perfect glorious pilgrimage
To the celestial Jerusalem.
And if you agree, I shall at once
Begin my tale, and I pray you
To tell me what you think; that's all I can say.
But nevertheless, this meditation,
I submit it to the correction
Scholars, for I am not book learned;
I only get the idea from them, trust me.
So I must declare
That I am willing to stand corrected."
We quickly agreed to what he said,
For it seemed that it was best to do so—
To finish with some virtuous subject,
And to give him our time and attention,
And we told our host to tell him
That we all prayed for him to tell us his tale.
Our host spoke for all of us;
"Sir priest," he said, "may you have good fortune!
Tell us your meditation," he said.
"But be quick, the sun is going down;
Be fruitful, in that little time,
And may God send you his grace to do well!
Say what you want, and we will gladly listen."
And with that said he spoke in this fashion.*

The Tale

First part

§1 Oure sweete lord God of hevene, that no man wole perisse, but wole that we comen alle to the knoweleche of hym, and to the blisful lif that is perdurable, amonesteth us by the prophete Jeremie, that seith in thys wyse: "stondeth upon the weyes, and seeth and axeth of olde pathes (that is to seyn, of olde sentences) which is the goode wey. And walketh in that wey, and ye shal fynde refresshynge for youre soules, etc." Manye been the weyes espirituels that leden fold to oure lord Jhesu Crist, and to the regne of glorie. Of whiche weyes, ther is a ful noble wey and ful

Our sweet Lord God in heaven, who wants no men to die but wants us to all gain knowledge of him and come to the blissful life eternal, admonishes us through the prophet Jeremiah, who says: "Stand on the road, and see and ask by looking at the old paths which is a good way, and walk that path, and you will find refreshment for your souls, etc." There are many spiritual ways which lead folk to our Lord Jesus Christ and to the reign of glory. Of these ways there is a very noble one, which cannot fail to guide a man or

475

covenable, which may nat fayle to man ne to wommon that thurgh synne hath mysgoon fro the righte wey of Jerusalem celestial; and this wey is cleped penitence, of which man sholde gladly herknen and enquere with his herte, to wyten what is penitence, and whennes it is cleped penitence, and in how manye maners been the accious or werkynges of penitence, and how manye speces ther been of penitence, and whiche thynges apertenen and bihoven to penitence, and whiche thynges destourben penitence.

woman who has gone astray to the celestial Jerusalem; and this way is called Penitence, which men should gladly listen to and ask with all his heart what is penitence, and why is it called penitence, and in what way does it work, and how many types of penitence are there, and which things are relevant to penitence, and which things prevent it.

§2 Seint Ambrose seith that penitence is the pleynynge of man for the gilt that he hath doon, and namoore to do any thyng for which hym oghte to pleyne. And som doctour seith. "penitence is the waymentynge of man that sorweth for his synne, and pyneth hymself for he hath mysdoon." Penitence, with certeyne circumstances, is verray repentance of a man that halt hymself in sorwe and oother peyne for his giltes. And for he shal be verray penitent, he shal first biwaylen the synnes that he hath doon, and stidefastly purposen in his herte to have shrift of mouthe, and to doon satisfaccioun, and nevere to doon thyng for which hym oghte moore to biwayle or to compleyne, and to continue in goode werkes, or elles his repentance may nat availle. For, as seith Seint Ysidre, "he is a japere and a gabbere, and no verray repentant, that eftsoone dooth thyng for which hym oghte repente." Wepynge, and nat for to stynte to do synne, may nat avayle. But nathelees, men shal hope that every tyme that man falleth, be it never so ofte, that he may arise thurgh penitence, if he have grace; but certeinly it is greet doute. For, as seith Seint Gregorie, "unnethe ariseth he out of his synne, that is charged with the charge of yvel usage." And therfore repentant folk, that stynte for to synne, and forlete synne er that synne forlete hem, hooly chirche holdeth hem siker of hir savacioun. And he that synneth and verraily repenteth hym in his laste, hooly chirche yet hopeth his savacioun, by the grete mercy of oure lord Jhesu Crist, for his repentaunce; but taak the siker wey.

St Ambrose says that penitence is when a man complains of the bad things which he has done, and when he has no longer any desire for things which he should complain of. And a certain theologian says, "Penitence is the moaning of a man who is sorry for his sins and who punishes himself for the wrong he has done." Penitence, with certain details, is the true repentance of a man who is sorry and in pain for what he has done. And because he must be truly penitent, he must first wail for the sins which he has committed, and have a true intention in his heart to confess in words, and to take his punishment, and never commit any more sins, and to carry out good works, for otherwise his repentance will do him no good. For as St Isidore (of Seville) says, "It is a trifler and a foolish talker, not a true repentant, who does something which he ought to repent over again." If you weep, but do not cease from sinning, that does no good. But nevertheless, men should hope that every time a man falls, however often he does, that he will rise up again through Penitence if he has grace; but certainly that is very doubtful. For, as St Gregory says, "The one who continues to commit sins hardly escapes his sin." And so repentant folk, who stop sinning and abandon sin before it leaves them, the holy Church says that they will definitely be saved. And someone who sins and truly repents in his last hours, the holy Church still hopes for his salvation, through the great mercy of our Lord Jesus Christ, because of his repentance; but it is best to go the certain way.

§3 And now, sith I have declared yow what thing is penitence, now shul ye understonde that ther been three accious of penitence. The firste is that if a man be baptized after that he hath synned, Seint Augustyn seith, "but he be penytent for his olde

Now that I have told you what penitence is, now you shall learn that there are three effects of penitence. Firstly, if a man is baptised after he has sinned. St Augustine says, "Unless he is penitent for his previous sinful life, he may not

synful lyf, he may nat bigynne the newe clene lif." For, certes, if he be baptized withouten penitence of his olde gilt, he receyveth the mark of baptesme, but nat the grace ne the remission of his synnes, til he have repentance verray. Another defaute is this, that men doon deedly synne after that they han receyved baptesme. The thridde defaute is that men fallen in venial synnes after hir baptesme, fro day to day. Therof seith Seint Augustyn that penitence of goode and humble folk is the penitence of every day.

§4 The speces of penitence been three. That oon of hem is solempne, another is commune, and the thridde is privee. Thilke penance that is solempne is in two maneres; as to be put out of hooly chirche in-lente, for slaughtre of children and swich maner thyng. Another is, whan a man hath synned openly, of which synne the fame is openly spoken in the contree, and thanne hooly chirche by juggement destreyneth hym for to do open penaunce. Commune penaunce is that preestes enjoynen men communly in certeyn caas, as for to goon peraventure naked in pilgrimages, or barefoot. Pryvee penaunce is thilke that men doon alday for privee synnes, of whiche we shryve us prively and receyve privee penaunce.

§5 Now shaltow understande what is bihovely and necessarie to verray perfit penitence. And this stant on three thynges: contricioun of herte, confessioun of mouth, and satisfaction. For which seith Seint John Crisostom "penitence destreyneth a man to accepte benygnely every peyne that hym is enjoyned, with contricioun of herte, and shrift of mouth, with satisfaccioun; and in werkynge of alle manere humylitee." And this is fruytful penitence agayn three thinges in which we wratthe oure lord Jhesu Crist: this is to seyn, by delit in thynkynge, by reccheleesnesse in spekynge, and by wikked synful werknyge. And agayns thise wikkede giltes is penitence, that may be likned unto a tree.

§6 The roote of this tree is contricioun, that hideth hym in the herte of hym that is verray repentaunt, right as the roote of a tree gydeth hym in the erthe. Of the roote of contricioun spryngeth a stalke that bereth braunches and leves of confessioun, and fruyt of satisfaccioun. For which Crist seith in his gospel: "dooth digne fruyt of penitence"; for by this fruyt may men knowe this tree, and nat by the roote that is hyd in the herte of man, ne by the

begin a new clean life." For certainly if he is baptised without repenting for his old sins, he receives the mark of baptism, but not the grace nor the forgiveness of his sins, until he truly repents. Another fault is this: if a man does a deadly sin after he has been baptised. The third problem is that men commit venial sins every day after they have been baptised. So St Augustine says that good and humble people must be penitent every day.

There are three types of penitence. One is solemn, one is common, and the third is private. There are two types of solemn penance; such as being refused entry to the holy Church in Lent for killing children; and suchlike things. Another is, when a man has openly sinned, so that everyone in the country knows of it, and then the holy Church orders that he must do his penance in public. Common penance is what priests order for men to do together in certain cases, such as going naked on pilgrimages, or barefoot. Private penance is what men do every day for their private sins, where we make our confession in private and do our penance the same way.

Now you must understand what is necessary for true, perfect penitence. This is made up of three things: contrition of the heart, confession by mouth, and satisfaction. St John Chrisostom says, "Penitence forces a man to accept calmly every pain that is given to him, with a contrite heart, confessing verbally, with satisfaction, and with every sort of humility." And this is effective penitence for the three things by which we anger our Lord Jesus Christ; that is to say, taking delight in thinking, being reckless in speech, and committing wicked sins. Penitence is set against this wicked guilt, and it can be compared to a tree.

The root of the tree is contrition, that is hidden in the hearts of the one who is truly repentant, just as the root of the tree is hidden in the earth. From the root of contrition there springs a stalk which holds the branches and leaves of confession, and the fruit of satisfaction. For Christ says in the gospel, "Do the worthy fruit of penitence"; for by this fruit men shall know this tree, not from the braunches, ne by the leves of confessioun. And therfore oure lord Jhesu Crist seith thus: "by the fruyt of hem shul ye knowen hem." Of this roote eek spryngeth a seed of grace, the which seed is mooder of sikernesse, and this seed is egre and hoot. The grace of this seed spryngeth of God thurgh remembrance of the day of doom and on the peynes of helle. Of this matere seith Salomon that in the drede of God man forleteth his synne. The heete of this seed is the love of God, and the desiryng of the joye perdurable. This heete draweth the herte of a man to God, and dooth hym haten his synne. For soothly ther is nothyng that savoureth so wel to a child as the milk of his norice, ne nothyng is to hym moore abhomnyable than thilke milk whan it is medled with oother mete. Right so the synful man that loveth his synne, hym semeth that it is to him moost sweete of any thyng; but fro that tyme that he loveth sadly oure lord Jhesu Crist, and desireth the lif perdurable, ther nys to him no thyng moore abhomynable. For soothly the lawe of God is the love of God; for which David the prophete seith: "I have loved thy lawe, and hated wikkednesse and hate"; he that loveth God kepeth his lawe and his Word. This tree saugh the prophete Daniel in spirit, upon the avysioun of the Kyng Nabugodonosor, whan he conseiled hym to do penitence. Penaunce is the tree of lyf to hem that is receyven, and he that holdeth hym in verray penitence is blessed, after the sentence of Solomon.

§7 In this penitence or contricioun man shal understonde foure thynges; that is to seyn, what is contricioun, and whiche been the causes that moeven a man to contricioun, and how he sholde be contrit, and what contricioun availleth to the soule. Thanne is it thus: that contricioun is the verray sorwe that a man receyveth in his herte for his synnes, with sad purpos to shryve hym, and to do penaunce, and neveremoore to do synne. And this sorwe shal been in this manere, as seith Seint Bernard: "it shal been hevy and grevous, and ful sharp and poynaunt in herte." First, for man hath agilt his lord and his creatour; and moore sharp and poynaunt, for he hath agilt hys fader celestial; and yet moore sharp and poynaunt, for he hath wrathed and agilt hym that boghte hym, that with his precious blood hath delivered us fro the bondes of synne, and fro the crueltee of the deve, and fro the peynes of helle.

§8 The causes that oghte moeve a man to contricioun been sixe. First a man shal remembre hym of his synnes; but looke he that thilke remembraunce ne be to hym no delit by no wey, but greet shame and sorwe for his gilt. For Job seith, "synful men doon werkes worthy of confusioun." And therfore seith Ezechie, "I wol remembre me alle the yeres of my lyf in bitternesse of myn herte." And God seith in the Apocalipse, "remembreth yow fro whennes that ye been falle"; for biforn that tyme that ye synned, ye were the children of God, and lymes of the regne of God; but for youre synne ye been woxen thral, and foul, and membres of the feend, hate of aungels, sclaundre of hooly chirche, and foode of the false serpent; prepetueel matere of the fir of helle: and yet moore foul and abhomynable, for ye trespassen so ofte tyme as dooth the hound that retourneth to eten his spewyng. And yet be ye fouler for youre longe continuyng in synne and youre synful usage, for which ye be roten in yore synne, as a beest in the dong. Swiche manere of thoghtes maken a man to have shame of his synne, and no delit, as God seith by the prophete Ezechiel: "ye shal remembre yow of youre weyes, and they shuln displese yow." Soothly synnes been the weyes that leden folk of helle.

There are six reasons for a man to be contrite. Firstly he should remind himself of his sins; but he must make sure that his remembering does not please him in any way, but that he has great shame and sorrow for his guilt. For Job says, "Sinful men do things for which they deserve to be dammed." And also Ezekiel says, "I will remember all the years of my life with bitterness in my heart." And God says in the Apocalypse, "Remember the place from which you have fallen"; for before you were sinners, you were children of God and his assistants; but because of your sin you have become slaves, and foul, and arms of the devil, hated by angels, a slander of the holy Church, food of the false serpent, fuel of the flames of hell; and yet you are more foul and horrible, for you sin as many times as the dog returning to eat his vomit. And yet you are even more foul because of your long persistence with sin and your sinful behaviour, you rot in your sin like a beast in his dung. Such thoughts should make a man be ashamed of his sin, not take delight in it, as God says through the prophet Ezekiel, "You shall remind yourself of what you have done, and the memory will upset you." Truly sin is the path that leads people to hell.

§9 The seconde cause that oghte make a man to have desdeyn of synne is this: that, as seith Seint Peter, "whoso that dooth synne is thral of synne"; and synne put a man in greet thraldom. And therfore seith the prophete Ezechiel: I wente sorweful in desdayn of myself. Certes, wel oghte a man have desdayn of synne, and withdrawe hym from that thraldom and vileynye. And lo, what seith Seneca in this matere? He seith thus: "though I wiste that neither God ne man ne sholde nevere knowe it, yet wolde I have desdeyn for to do synne." And the same Seneca also seith: "I am born to gretter thynges that to be thral to my body, or than for to maken of my body a thral." Ne a fouler thral may no man ne womman maken of his body that for to yeven his body to synne. Al were it the fouleste cherl or the fouleste womman that lyveth, and leest of value, yet is he thanne moore foul and moore in servitute. Evere fro the hyer degree that man falleth, the moore is he thral, and moore to God and to the world vile and abhomynable. O goode God, wel oghte man have desdeyn of synne, sith that thurgh synne, ther he was free, now is he maked bonde. And therfore seyth Seint Augustyn: if thou hast desdeyn of thy

The second reason for a man to reject sin is this: that, as St Peter says, "whoever sins is the slave of sin"; and sin deeply enslaves a man. That is why the prophet Ezekiel says: "I was sad in my hatred of myself." Certainly, a man should have great disdain for sin and keep away from that slavery and evil. And see what Seneca says in this matter. He says: Although I know that neither God nor man should ever know it, I want to hate the idea of sinning." And the same Seneca also says, "I am born for greater things than being a slave of my body, or to make my body into a slave." There is no more foul slavery a man or woman can do with their body than to give their body to sin. Even if they were the foulest peasant or the most horrible woman alive, the lowest, that would make them more foul and more of a slave. The further from the high degree that that man falls, the more he is a slave, and the more horrible to God and to the world. Oh good God, a man should certainly hate sin, since through sin he is a slave where once he was free. And that is why St Augustine says: "If you despise your servant, if he does wrong

servant, if he agilte or synne, have thou thanne desdayn that thou thyself sholdest do synne. Tak reward of thy value, that thou ne be foul to thyself. Allas! wel oghten they thanne have desdayn to been servauntz and thralles to synne, and soore been ashamed of hemself, that God of his endelees goodnesse hath set hem in heigh estaat, or yeven hem wit, strenghte of body, heele, beautee, prosperitee, and boghte hem fro the deeth with his herte-blood. That they so unkyndely, agayns his gentilesse, quiten hym so vileynsly to slaughtre of hir owene soules. O goode God, ye wommen that been of so greet beautee, remembreth yow of the proverbe of Salomon. He seith: "likneth a fair womman that is a fool of hire body lyk to a ryng of gold that were in the groyn of a soughe." For right as a soughe wrotheth in everich ordure, so wroteth she hire beautee in the stynkynge ordure of of synne.

§10 The thridde cause that oghte moeve a man to contricioun is drede of the day of doom and of the horrible peynes of helle. For, as Seint Jerome seith, "at every tyme that me remembreth of the day of doom I quake; for whan I ete or drynke, or what so that I do, evere semeth me that the trompe sowneth in myn ere: 'riseth up, ye that been dede, and cometh to the juggement.'" O goode God, muchel oghte a man to drede wich a juggement, ther as we shullen been alle, as Seint Poul seith, biforn the seete of oure lord Jhesu Crist; whereas he shal make a general congregacioun, whereas no man may been absent. For certes there availleth noon essoyne ne excusacioun. And nat oonly that oure defautes shullen be jugged, but eek that alle oure werkes shullen openly be knowe. And as seith Seint Bernard, "ther ne shal no pledynge availle, ne no sleighte; we shullen yeven rekenynge of everich ydel word." Ther shul we han a juge that may nat been deceyved ne corrput. And why? for, certes, alle oure thoghtes been discovered as to hym; ne for preyere ne for meede he shal nat been corrupt. And therfore seith Salomon, the wratthe of God ne wol nat spare no wight, for prevere ne for yifte; and therfore, at the day of doom, ther nys noon hope to escape. Wherfore, as seith Seint Anselm, "ful greet angwyssh shul the synful folk have at that tyme; Ther shal the stierne and wrothe juge sitte above, and under hym the horrible pit of helle open to destroyen hym that moot biknowen his synnes, whiche synnes openly been shewed biforn God and biforn every creature; and in the left syde mo develes that herte may bithynke, for the harye and drawe the synful soules to the peyne of helle; and withinne the hertes of folk shall be bitynge conscience, and withoute forth shal be the world al brennynge. Whider shall thanne the wrecched synful man flee to hiden hym? Certes, he may nat hyden hym; he moste come forth and shewen hym." For certes, as seith Seint Jerome, "the erthe shal casten hym out of hym, and the see also, and the eyr also, that shal be ful of thonder-clappes and lightnynges." Now soothly, whoso wel remembreth hym of thise thynges, I gesse that his synne shal nat turne hym into delit, but to greet sorwe, for drede of the peyne of helle. And therfore seith Job to God: "suffre, Lord, that I may a while biwaille and wepe. Er I go withoute returnyng to the derke lord, covered with the derknesse of deeth; to the lond of mysese and of derknesse, whereas is the shadwe of deeth; whereas ther is noon ordre or ordinaunce, but grisly drede that evere shal laste." Loo, heere may ye seen that Job preyde repit a while, to biwepe and waille his trespas; for soothly oo day of respit is bettre than al the tresor of this world. And forasmuche as a man may acquiten hymself biforn God by penitence in this world, and nat by tresor, therfore sholde he preye to God to yeve hym respit a while to biwepe and biwaillen his trespas. For certes, al the sorwe that a man myghte make fro the bigynnyng of the world nys but a litel thyng at regard of the sorwe of helle. The cause why that Job clepeth helle the "lond of derknesse"; understondeth that he clepeth it "lond" or erthe, for it is stable, and nevere shal faille; "derk", for he that is in helle hath defaute of light material. For certes, the derke light that shal come out of the fyr that evere shal brenne, shal furne hym al to peyne that is in helle; for it sheweth hym to the horrible develes that hym tormenten. Covered with the derknesse of deeth, that is to seyn, that he that is in helle shal have defaute of the sighte of God; for certes, the sighte of God is the lyf perdurable. The derknesse of deeth been the synnes that the wrecched man hath doon, whiche that destourben hym to see the face of God, right as dooth a derk clowde bitwixe us and the sonne. Lond of misese, by cause that ther been three maneres of defautes, agayn three thynges that folk of this world han in this present lyf, that is to seyn, honours, delices, and richesses. Agayns honour, have they in helle shame and confusioun. For wel ye woot that men clepen honour the reverence that man doth to man; but in helle is noon honour ne reverence. For certes, namoore reverence shal be doon there to a kyng than to a knave. For which God seith by the prophete Jeremye, thilke folk that me despisen shul been in despit. Honour is eek

can imagine, to harass and pull the sinful souls into the pain of hell; and in the hearts of those people their conscience will be biting them, and outside the whole world will be burning. Where will the wretched sinful man run to hide then? Certainly, he cannot hide; he come out and show himself." For certainly, as St Jerome says, "the Earth shall give him up, and also the sea, and the air, that will be full of thunder and lightning." Now truly, whoever thinks of these things, I guess that he will not then enjoy his sin, but being great sorrow for fear of the pain of hell. And therefore Job said to God, "Grant, Lord, that I'm a while and weep for a while, before I go without return to the dark land, coupled with the darkness of death, to the land of suffering and darkness, where there is the shadow of death, where there is no law, no order, just the grisly fear that will last for eternity." You see, here you can see that Job begged for a little time to weep and bemoan his sins, for truly one day of respite is better than the wealth of the entire world. And inasmuch as a man can get forgiveness from God for penitence in this world, not through giving wealth, so he should pray to God to give him respite for a while to weep and wail for his sins. For certainly, all the sorrow that a man could have from the beginning of the world is nothing compared to the sorrow of hell. That is why Job calls hell the "land of darkness.": You must understand he calls it "land" or earth, for it is solid and will never collapse; "dark," because someone who is in hell has no light. For certainly, the dark light that will come out of the fire that burns eternally shall give him great pain for it shows his position to the horrible devils which torture him. "Covered with the darkness of death"–that is to say, that the person who is in hell will not see God, for certainly seeing God is eternal life. "The darkness of death" of sins that the wretched man has done, which stop him from seeing the face of God, like a dark cloud between us and the sun. "Land of suffering," because there are three sorts of faults, encompassing the three things that people in this world want in this life; that is to say, honour, pleasure and riches. Instead of honour, in hell they will have shame and confusion. For you know well that what men call honour is the reverence that one man has for another, but in hell there is no honour nor reverence. For certainly, there will be no more cleped greet lordshipe; ther shal no wight serven other, but of harm and torment. Honour is eek cleped greet dignytee and heighnesse, but in helle shul they been al fortroden of develes. And God seith, "the horrible develes shulle goon and comen upon the hevedes of the dampned folk." And this is for as muche as the hyer that they were in this present lyf, the moore shulle they been abated and defouled in helle. Agayns the richesse of this world shul they han mysese of poverte, and this poverte shal been in foure thynges: in defaute of tresor, of which that David seith, "the riche folk, that embraceden and oneden al hire herte to tresor of this world, shul slepe in the slepynge of deeth; and nothyng ne shal they fynden in hir handes of al hir tresor." And moore-over the myseyse of helle shal been in defaute of mete and drinke. For God seith thus by Moyses: they shul been wasted with hunger, and the briddes of helle shul devouren hem with bitter deeth, and the galle of the dragon shal been hire drynke, and the venym of the dragon hire morsels. And forther over, hire myseyse shal been in defaute of clothyng; for they shulle be naked in body as of clothyng, save the fyr in which they bree and othere filthes; and naked shul they been of soule, as of alle manere vertues, which that is the clothyng of the soule. Where been thannne the gaye robes, and the softe shetes, and the smale shertes? Loo, what seith God of hem by the prophete Ysaye: that "under hem shul been strawed motthes, and hire covertures shulle been of womres of helle." And forther over, hir myseyse shal been in defaute of freendes. For he nys nat povre that hath goode freendes; but there is no frend, for neither God ne no creature shal been freend to hem. And everich of hem shal haten oother with deedly hat. The sones and the doghtren shullen rebellen agayns fader and mooder, and kynrede agauns kynrede, and chiden and despisen everich of hem oother bothe day nad nyght, as God seith by the prophete Michias. And the lovynge children, that whilom loveden so flesshly everich oother, wolden everich of hem eten oother if they myghte. For how sholden they love hem togidre in the peyne of helle, whan they hated everich of hem oother in the progenitee of this lyr? For truste wel, hir flesshly love was deedly hate, as seith the prophete David: "whoso that loveth wikkednesse, he hateth his soule." And whoso hateth his owene soule, certes, he may love noon oother wight in no manere. And therfore, in helle is no solas ne no freendshipe, but evere the moore flesshly kynredes that been in helle, the moore cursynges, the more chidynges, and the

reverence there than a king has for a lowly servant. Honour is also called great lordship; in hell no creature will serve any other, except to give them harm and torture. Honour is also called great dignity and high rank, but in hell they will all be stamped upon by devils. And God says, "The horrible Devils will walk to and fro on the heads of the damned." And the higher position they had in life on Earth, the more they will be debased and defiled in hell. For all the riches they had in this world they will have the misery of poverty and this poverty will be made of four things: in lack of treasure, of which David says, "The rich people, who embraced and assimilated in their hearts the treasure of this world, will sleep the sleep of death; and they will have none of their treasure in their hands." And moreover the misery of hell will be found in a lack of meat and drink. For God says through Moses: "They shall be wasted with hunger, and the birds of hell will eat them with bitter death, and the bile of the Dragon will be their drink, and the poison of the Dragon will be their food." And furthermore, they shall have misery in their lack of clothing, for they shall be naked, apart from the fire which they are burning in, and other filth; and their souls shall be naked, for they will have lost all virtue, which is the clothing of the soul. Where then are the gay robes, the soft sheets, and the delicate shirts? See what God says of them through the prophet Isaiah: that "they will have maggots underneath them, and their cover will be the worms of hell." Also, they will have misery in the lack of friends. For he who has good friends is not poor; but there is no friend, for neither God nor any other creature will be their friend, and they will all hate each other with deadly hate. "The sons and daughters will rebel against father and mother, and families against each other, and attack and despise every one of those others day and night," as God says through the prophet Micah. And the loving children, who once loved each other in the flesh, would eat each other if they could. For how will they have any love in the pain of hell, when they all hated each other in the prosperity of life? You should believe, their love of the flesh was deadly hatred, as the prophet David says: "Whoever loves wickedness, hates his own soul." And whoever hates his own soul, he can certainly not love any other creature. And so

moore deedly hate ther is among hem. And forther over, they shul have defaute of alle manere delices. For certes, delices been after the appetites of the fyve wittes, as sighte, herynge, smellynge, savorynge, and touchynge. But in helle hir sighte shal be ful of derknesse and of smoke, and therfore ful of teeres; and hir herynge ful of waymentynge and of gryntynge of teeth, as seith Jhesu Crist. Hir nose-thirles shullen be ful of stynkynge stynk; and as seith Ysaye the prophete, "hir savoryng shal be ful of bitter galle"; and touchynge of al hir body ycovered with "fir that nevere shal quenche, and with wormes that nevere shul dyen," as God seith by the mouth of Ysaye. And for as muche as they shul nat wene that they may dyen for peyne, and by hir deeth flee fro peyne, that may they understonden by the word of Job, that seith, "ther as is the shadwe of deeth." Certes, a shadwe hath the liknesse of the thyng of which it is shadwe, but shadwe is nat the same thyng of which it is shadwe. Right so fareth the peune of helle; it is lyk deeth for the horrible angwissh, and why? For it peyneth hem evere, as though they sholde dye anon; but certes, they shal nat dye. For, as seith Seint Gregorie, "to wrecche caytyves shal be deeth withoute deeth, and end withouten ende, and defaute withoute failynge. For hir deeth shal alwey lyven, and hir ende shal everemo bigynne, and hir defaute shal nat faille." And therfore seith Seint John the evaungelist: "they shullen folwe deeth, and they shul nat fynde hym; and they shul desiren to dye, and deeth shal flee fro hem." And eek Job seith that in helle is noon ordre of rule. And al be it so that God hath creat alle thynges in right ordre, and no thyng withouten ordre, but alle thynges been ordeyned and nombred; yet, nathelees, they that been dampned been nothyng in ordre, ne holden noon ordre. For the erthe ne shal bere hem no fruyt. For as the prophete David seith, "God shal destroie the fruyt of the erthe as fro hem; ne water ne shal yeve hem no moisture, ne the eyr no refresshyng, ne fyr no light." For, as seith Seint Basilie, "the brennynge of the fyr of this world shal God yeven in helle to hem that been dampned, but the light and the cleernesse shal be yeven in hevene to this children"; right as the goode man yeveth flessh to his children and bones to his houndes. And for they shullen have noon hope to escape, seith Seint Job atte laste that "ther shal horrour and grisly drede dwellen withouten ende." Horrour is alwey drede of harm that is to come, and this drede shal evere dwelle in the hertes of hem that been dampned. And therfore han they lorn al hire hope, for sevene causes. First, for God, that is hir juge, shal be withouten mercy to

there is no comfort or friendship in hell, the more of your family that is in hell, the more curses, the more attacks, and the more deadly hatred there is amongst them. And also, they will lack all sorts of pleasure, for pleasure comes from the appetites of the five wits, sight, hearing, smelling, tasting and touching. But in hell their sight will be full of darkness and smoke, and so full of tears; and their hearing will be full of wailing and the gnashing of teeth, as Jesus Christ said. Their nostrils will be full of foul stink; and, as Isaiah the prophet says, "their mouths shall be full of bitter bile"; and all over their body they will be covered with "a fire which will never go out and with worms which will never die," as God says through the mouth of Isaiah. Furthermore they will not be able to think that they will die of pain, and escape pain through death, because they will understand the words of Job, who said, "there is the shadow of death." Certainly a shadow has the likeness of the thing of which it is a shadow, but a shadow is not the same thing. That is the case with the pain of hell; it is like death in its horrible anguish, and why? For it gives them eternal pain, as if they were about to die; but certainly, they they shall not die. For, as St Gregory says, "These riches will find death without death, and without end, and starvation without end. For their death will always be living, and their end will always begin, and their starvation will not cease." That is why St John the Evangelist says, "They shall seek death, and they will not find him; they will want to die, and death will flee from them." And also Job says that in hell there is no hierarchy. And although it is the case that God has created all things in the right order, and nothing without order, all things are ordained and numbered; nonetheless, they who are damned have no order, cannot keep order, for the Earth will not bear them any fruit. For, as the prophet David says, "God will destroy the fruit of the Earth for them, and waters shall not give them any moisture, nor the air any refreshment, nor fire any light." For, as St Basil says, "the burning fire in this world God will give to the damned in hell, but light and clarity will be given to his children in heaven," just as a good man gives meat to his children and the bones to his dogs. And they will have no hope of escape, St Job says in the end that "horror and fear will live there eternally."

hem; and they may nat plese hym ne noon of his halwes; ne they ne may yeve no thyng for hir raunsoun; ne they have no voys to speke to hym; ne they may nat fle fro peyne; ne they have no goodnesse in hem, that they mowe shewe to delivere hem fro peyne. And therfore seith Salomon: "the wikked man dyeth, and whan he is deed, he shal have noon hope to escape fro peyne." Whoso thanne wolde wel understande thise peynes, and bithynke hym weel that he hath deserved thilke peynes for his synnes, certes, he sholde have moore talent to siken and to wepe, than for to syngen and to pleye. For, as that seith Salomon, "whoso that hadde the science to knowe the peynes that been establissed and ordeyned for synne, he wolde make sorwe." "Thilke science," as seith Seint Augustyn, "maketh a man to waymenten in his herte."

Horror is always the dread of harm that is coming, and this dread will always be in the hearts of the damned. And so they have lost all hope, for seven reasons. Firstly, because God, who is their judge, will not show them any mercy; and they cannot please him nor any of his saints; nor can they pay anything for him to forgive them; nor will they have a voice to speak to him; nor can they escape pain; nor will they have any goodness in them, that they can show to save them from pain. That is why Solomon says: "The wicked man dies, and when he is dead, he shall not be able to escape from pain." Anyone who would then understand his pain and think that he has deserved such pain for his sins, certainly, he should have more desire to sigh and weep than to sing and play. For, as Solomon says, "Whoever has the knowledge to know the pain that is coming for sin, he would lament." "This knowledge," as St Augustine says, "will make a man's sorrow in his heart."

§11 The fourthe point that oghte maken a man to have contricion is the sorweful remembraunce of the good that he hath left to doon heere in erthe, and eek the good that he hath lorn. Soothly, the goode werkes that he hath lost, outher they been the goode werkes that he wroghte er he fel into deedly synne, or elles the goode werkes that he wroghte while he lay in synne. Soothly, the goode werkes that he dide biforn that he fil in synne been al mortefied and astoned and dulled by the ofte synnyng. The othere goode werkes, that he wroghte whil he lay in deedly synne, thei been outrely dede, as to the lyf perdurable in hevene. Thanne thilke goode werkes that been mortefied by ofte synnyng, whiche goode werkes he dide whil he was in charitee, ne mowe nevere quyken agayn withouten verray penitence. And therof seith God by the mouth of Ezechiel, that "if the rightful man returne agayn from his rightwisnesse and werke wikkednesse, shal he lyve?" Nay, for alle the goode werkes that he hath wroght ne shul nevere been in remembraunce, for he shal dyen in this synne. And upon thilke chapitre seith Seint Gregorie thus: that "we shulle understonde this principally; that whan we doon deedly synne, it is for noght thanne to rehercen or drawen into memorie the goode werkes that we han wroght biforn. For certes, in the werkynge of the deedly synne, ther is no trust to no good werk that we can doon biforn; that is to seyn, as for to have therby the lyf perdurable in hevene. But nathelees, the goode werkes quyken a

The fourth point which should make a man be contrite is the sorrowful remembrance of the good that he has not done on earth, and also the good that he has lost. Truly, the good works that he has lost, they are either the good works that he did before he became a sinner or the good works he did while he was sinning. Truly, the good works that he did before he became a sinner are destroyed by his frequent sinning. The other good works, which he did while he lay in deadly sin, they are utterly dead, as far as regards gaining eternal life in heaven. Those good works that have been stained by frequent sinning, the good works he did while he was charitable, they can never be revived without true repentance. And so God says through the mouth of is Ezekiel that "if the righteous man comes back from his righteousness and does wicked things, will he live?" No, for all the good work he has done will not be remembered, for he will die as a sinner. St Gregory says this about this chapter: that "we must principally understand this; that when we do a deadly sin, it is then no good to try to call to mind the good works we have done before." For certainly, in committing deadly sin, the good work we have done before does no good; that is to say, it will not help us gain eternal life in heaven. But nonetheless, the good works will revive again, and come again, and help, and help

gayn, and comen agayn, and helpen, and availlen to have the lyf perdurable in hevene, whan we han contricioun. But soothly, the goode werkes that men doon whil they been in deedly synne, for as muche as they were doon in deedly synne, they may nevere quyke agayn. For certes thyng that nevere hadde lyf may nevere quykene; and nathelees, al be it that they ne availle noght to han the lyf perdurable, yet availlen they to abregge of the peyne of helle, or elles to geten temporal richesse, or elles that God wole the rather enlumyne and lightne the herte of the synful man to have repentaunce; and eek they availlen for to usen a man to doon goode werkes, that the feend have the lasse power of his soule. And thus the curteis lord Jhesu Crist ne wole that no good werk be lost; for in somwhat it shal availle. But, for as muche as the goode werkes that men doon whil they been in good lyf been al mortefied by synne folwynge, and eek sith that alle the goode werkes that men doon whil they been in deedly synne been outrely dede as for to have the lyf perdurable; wel may that man that no good werk ne dooth synge thilke newe frenshe song, "jay tout perdu mon temps et mon labour." For certes, synne birevith a man bothe goodnesse of nature and eek the goodnesse of grace. For soothly, the grace of the Hooly Goost fareth lyk fyr, that may nat been ydel; for fyr fayleth anoon as it forleteth his wirkynge, and right so grace fayleth anoon as it forleteth his werkynge. Then leseth the synful man the goodnesse of glorie, that oonly is bihight to goode men that labouren and werken. Wel may he be sory thanne, that oweth al his lif to God as longe as he hath lyved, and eek as longe as he shal lyve, that no goodnesse ne hath to paye with his dette to God to whom he oweth al his lyf. For trust wel, he shal yeven acountes, as seith Seint Bernard, of alle the goodes that han be yeven hym in this present lyf, and how he hath hem despended; in so muche that ther shal nat perisse an heer of his heed, ne a moment of an houre ne shal nat perisse of his tyme, that he ne shal yeve of it a rekenyng.

§12 The fifthe thyng that oghte moeve a man to contricioun is remembrance of the passioun that oure lord Jhesu Crist suffred for oure synnes. For, as seith Seint Bernard, whil that I lyve I shal have remembrance of the travailles that oure lord Crist suffred in prechyng; his werynesse in travaillyng, his temptaciouns whan he fasted, his longe wakynges whan he preyde, hise teeres whan that he

gain the life eternal in heaven, when we are contrite. But truly, the good works that men do while they are still committing deadly sins, as they were done during deadly sin, they will never be able to get credit for them. For certainly something which never had life can never be brought back to life; however, although they do not help anyone to get eternal life, they help to shorten the pain of hell, or else to get riches on earth, or otherwise God will light up the heart of the sinful man to guide him to repentance; and they also help to make a man accustomed to doing good works, so that the devil will have less power over his soul. And so the kind Lord Jesus Christ does not want any good work to go unrecognised, for it will help in some degree. But, inasmuch as the good works which men do when they are living a good life are all rendered powerless by the sin that follows, and also since all the good works that men do while they are committing deadly sins are utterly dead as far as the life eternal is concerned, a man who does no good works may well sing this new French song, which says I have wasted my time and my labour. For certainly, Sin takes away from a man both the goodness of nature and the goodness of grace. Truly, the grace of the Holy Ghost is like fire, it cannot be idle; for fire dies out as soon as it leaves its source, and in the same way Grace fails as soon as it leaves its source. Then the sinful man loses the goodness of glory, that only comes to good men who labour and work. He may well be sorry then, who owes his whole life to God as long as he has lived, and as long as he shall live, who has no goodness with which to pay his debts to the god to whom he owes all his life. For you can be certain, "He shall account for," as St Bernard says, "all the goods that he has been given in his present life, how he spent them, there will not be a hair on his head nor a moment of time that he will not have to account for."

The fifth thing that should make a man contrite is remembering the passion that our Lord Jesus Christ suffered for our sins. For, as Saint Bernard says, "while I am alive I shall remember the troubles that our Lord Christ had in preaching: how his work made him tired, how he was tempted when he fasted, his long vigils when he prayed, the tears he wept

weep for pitee of good peple; the wo and the shame and the filthe that men seyden to hym; of the foule spittyng that men spitte in his face, of the buffettes that men yaven hym, of the foule mowes, and of the repreves that men to hym seyden; of the nayles with whiche he was nayled to the croys, and of al the remenant of his passioun that he suffred for my synnes, and no thyng for his gilt. And ye shul understonde that in mannes synne is every manere of ordre or ordinaunce turned up-so-doun. For it is sooth that God, and resoun, and sensualitee, and the body of man been so ordeyned that everich of thise foure thynges sholde have lordshipe over that oother; as thus: God sholde have lordshipe over resoun, and resoun over sensualitee, and sensualitee over the body of man. But soothly, whan man synneth, al this ordre or ordinaunce is turned up-so-doun. And therfore, thanne, for as muche as the resoun of man ne wol nat be subget ne obeisant to God, that is his lord by right, therfore leseth it the lordshipe that it sholde have over sensualitee, and eek over the body of man. And why? For sensualitee rebelleth thanne agayns resoun, and by that way leseth resoun the lordshipe over sensualitee and over the body. For right as resoun is rebel to God, right so is bothe sensualitee rebel to resoun and the body also. And certes this disordinaunce and this rebellioun oure lord Jhesu Crist aboghte upon his precious body ful deere, and herkneth in which wise. For as muche thanne as resoun is rebel to God, therfore is man worthy to have sorwe and to be deed. This suffred oure lord Jhesu Crist for man, after that he hadde be bitraysed of his disciple, and distreyned and bounde, so that his blood brast out at every nayl of his handes, as seith Seint Augustyn. And forther over, for as muchel as resoun of man ne wol nat daunte sensualitee whan it may, therfore is man worthy to have shame; and this suffred oure lord Jhesu Crist for man, whan they spetten in his visage. And forther over, for as muchel thanne as the caytyf body of man is rebel bothe to resoun and to sensualitee, therfore is it worthy the deeth. And this suffred oure Lord Jhesu Crist for man upon the croys where as ther was no part of his body free withouten greet peyne and bitter passioun. And al this suffred Jhesu Crist, that nevere forfeted. And therfore resonably may be seyd Jhesu in this manere: "to muchel am I peyned for the thynges that I nevere deserved, and to muche defouled for shendshipe that man is worthy to have. And therfore may the synful man wel seye, as seith Seint Bernard, "acursed be the bitternesse of my synne, for which ther moste be suffred so muchel

as he pitied good people, the sorrow and shame and the filth of the things that men said to him, of the foul spitting in his face, of the blows that men gave him, of the foul looks and the insults that men said to him, of the nails with which he was nailed to the cross, and all the rest of his passion which he suffered for my sins, and not at all due to any guilt of his." And you must understand that in the sin of man every sort of order or regulation is reversed. For it is true that God, and reason, and sensuality, and men's bodies are so arranged that all of these four things should rule over each other, like this: God should rule over reason, and reason should rule over sensuality, and sensuality should rule over the body of man. But truly, when a man sins, this whole arrangement is turned upside down. And so, as the reason of man will not obey God, who is his Lord by right, so his reason loses its rule over sensuality, and also over the body of man. And why? Because sensuality then rebels against reason, and in that way reason loses its rule over sensuality and body. For just as reason rebels against God, sensuality rebels against reason and the body also. And certainly this disorder and this rebellion was paid for by our Lord Jesus Christ with his precious body, and you shall hear how. For when reason rebels against God, so a man deserves to be sorrowful and to die. Our Lord Jesus Christ suffered this for man, after he was betrayed by his disciple, and tied and bound so that blood burst out from every fingernail, as St Augustine says. Also, as the reason of man will not rule over sensuality when it can, so men deserve to be shamed; and our Lord Jesus Christ suffered this for mankind, when they spat in his face. And furthermore, as the wretched body of man rebels against both reason and sensuality, so it deserves to die. And our Lord Jesus Christ suffered this for mankind upon the cross, where there was no part of his body free from great pain and bitter suffering. And Jesus Christ suffered all this, the one who had never sinned. And therefore it is reasonable for Jesus to say, "I have been given too much pain for things I never deserved, and I have been too defiled by shame which rightfully belongs to mankind." And therefore a sinful man may well say, as St Bernard does, "May the bitterness of my sin be cursed, which has caused so much bitter suffering." For

bitternesse." For certes, after the diverse disordinaunces of oure wikkednesses was the passioun of Jhesu Crist ordeyned in diverse thynges, as thus. Certes, synful mannes soule is bitraysed of the devel by coveitise of temporeel prosperitee, and scorned by deceite whan he cheseth flesshly delices; and yet is it tormented by inpacience of adversitee, and bispet by servage and subjeccioun of synne; and atte laste it is slayn fynally. For this disordinaunce of synful man was Jhesu Crist first bitraysed, and after that was he bounde, that cam for to unbynden us of synne and peyne. Thanne was he byscorned, that oonly sholde han been honoured in alle thynges and of alle thynges. Thanne was his visage, that oghte be desired to be seyn of al mankynde, in which visage aungels desiren to looke, vileynsly bispet. Thanne was he scourged, that no thyng hadde agilt; and finally, thanne was he crucified and slayn. Thanne was acompliced the word of Ysaye, "he was wounded for oure mysdedes and defouled for oure felonies." Now sith that Jhesu Crist took upon hymself the peyne of alle oure wikkednesses, muchel oghte synful man wepen and biwayle, that for his synnes goddes sone of hevene sholde al this peyne endure.

§13 The sixte thyng that oghte moeve a man to contricioun is the hope of three thynges; that is to seyn, foryifnesse of synne, and the yifte to grace wel for to do, and the glorie of hevene, with which God shal gerdone man for his goode dedes. And for as muche as Jhesu Crist yeveth us thise yiftes of his largesse and of his sovereyn bountee, therfore is he cleped Jhesus Nazarenus Rex Judeorum. Jhesus is to seyn saveour or salvacioun, on whom men shul hope to have foryifnesse of synnes, which that is proprely salvacioun of synnes. And terfore seyde the aungel to Joseph, thou shalt clepen his name Jhesus, that shal saven his peple of hir synnes. And heerof seith Seint Peter: "ther is noon oother name under hevene that is yeve to any man, by which a man may be saved, but oonly Jhesus." Nazarenus is as muche for to seye as "florisshynge," in which a man shal hope that he that yeveth hym remissioun of synnes shal yeve hym eek grace wel for to do. For in the flour is hope of fruyt in tyme comynge, and in foryifnesse of synnes hope of grace wel for to do. "I was atte dore of thyn herte," seith Jhesus, "and cleped for to entre. He that openeth to me shal have foryifnesse of synne. I wol entre into hym by my grace, and soupe with hym," by the goode werkes that he

certainly, the passion of Jesus Christ was ordered in various ways according to the various rebellions of our wickedness. So soul soul of a sinful man is betrayed by the devil through coveting prosperity on earth, and mocked by deceit when he chooses pleasures of the flesh; and yet it is tormented by the impatience of adversity and spat upon by slavery an sin; and finally it is killed. For through this disorder of sinful man Jesus Christ was first betrayed, and after that he was bound, the one who came to unbind us from sin and pain. Then he was mocked, he who who should only have been honoured in everything by all creatures. Then his face, which all men should have wanted to see, the face on which angels wish to look, was villainously spat on. Then he was whipped, the one who had done no sin; and finally he was crucified and killed. Then the words of Isaiah were accomplished, "He was wounded for our misdeeds and insulted for our crimes." Now since Jesus Christ took upon himself the pain of all our wickedness, a sinful man ought to weep and moan very much, seeing the son of God enduring all this pain for his sins.

The sixth thing that ought to make a man contrite is the hope of three things; that is to say, forgiveness of sin, and the gift of grace to be good, and the glory of heaven, with which God shall reward man for good deeds. And as Jesus Christ gives us his gifts of his generosity and perfect goodness, so he is called Jesus of Nazareth, King of the Jews. Jesus means saviour or salvation, and it is through him that men hope to be forgiven their sins, which is the salvation of sin. And that is why the angel said to Joseph, "You shall call him Jesus, and he will save people from their sins." And St Peter says of this: "There is no other name under heaven that any man has, through which any man can be saved, only Jesus." Nazarenus can mean "flourishing," and it gives a man hope that the one who gives him forgiveness for his sins will also give him the grace to do well. For in the flower there is hope of fruit to come, and in forgiveness of sins there is the hope of grace to do well. "I was at the door of your heart," says Jesus, "and I called to let me in. The person who opens to me will be forgiven his sins. I will enter into him through my grace and eat with

shal doon, whiche werkes been the foode of God; "and he shal soupe with me" by the grete joye that I shal yeven hym. Thus shal man hope, for his werkes of penaunce, that God shal yeven hym his regne, as he bihooteth hym in the gospel.

§14 Now shal a man understonde in which manere shal been his contricioun. I seye that it shal been universal and total. This is to seyn, a man shal be verray repentaunt for alle his synnes that he hath doon in delit of his thoght; for delit is ful perilous. For ther been two manere of consentynges: that oon of hem is cleped consentynge of affeccioun, whan a man is moeved to do synne, and deliteth hym longe for to thynke on that synne; and his reson aperceyveth it wel that it is synne agayns the lawe of God, and yet his resoun refreyneth nat his foul delit or talent, though he se wel apertly that it is agayns the reverence of God. Although his resoun ne consente noght to doon that synne in dede, yet seyn somme doctours that swich delit that dwelleth longe, it is ful perilous, al be it nevere so lite. And also a man sholde sorwe namely for al that evere he hath desired agayn the lawe of God with perfit consentynge of his resoun; for therof is no doute, that it is deedly synne in consentynge. For certes, ther is no deedly synne, that it nas first in mannes thought, and after that in his delit, and so forth into consentynge and into dede. Wherfore I seye that many men ne repenten hem nevere of swiche thoghtes and delites, ne nevere shryven hem of it, but oonly of the dede of grete synnes outward. Wherfore I seye that swiche wikked delites and wikked thoghtes been subtile bigileres of hem that shullen be dampned.

Mooreover man oghte to sorwe for his wikkede wordes as wel as for his wikkede dedes. For certes, the repentaunce of a synguler synne, and nat repente of alle his other synnes, or elles repenten hym of alle his othere synnes, and nat of a synguler synne, may nat availle. For certes, God almyghty is al good; and therfore he foryeveth al, or elles right noght. And heerof seith Seint Augustyn: "I wot certeynly that God is enemy to everich synnere; and how thanne, he that observeth o synne, shal he have foryifnesse of the remenaunt of his othere synnes? Nay. And forther over, contricioun sholde be wonder sorweful and angwissous; and therfore yeveth hym God pleynly his mercy; and therfore, whan my soule was angwissous withinne me, I hadde remembrance of God that my preyere myghte come to hym. Forther over, contricioun moste be

him," by the good works which he shall do, which are the food of God, "and he shall sup with me" through the great joy which I will give him. This will give man hope, for in his works penance God will allow him to reign, as he promises in the gospel.

Now man shall understand how he should be contrite. I say that it must be universal and total. That is to say, a man must be truly repentant for all his sins which have pleased him, for delight is very dangerous. For there are two manners of consenting: one of them is called consenting of affection, when a man is inspired to sin, and takes delight for a long time in thinking of that sin; and in his reason he can see clearly that it is a sin against the law of God, and yet his reason does not stop his foul delight or desire, although he can clearly see that it is blasphemous against God. Although his reason does not agree to doing that sin, some theologians say that the delight he takes it, if it lasts a long time, is very dangerous, however little it is. And also a man should be especially sorrowful for everything which he has wanted against the law of God with his reason agreeing, for there is no doubt, that it is a deadly sin to consent. For certainly, there was no deadly sin that was not first in a man's thought, and after that in his delight, and so on to consent and to deed. So I say that many men never repent of such thoughts and enjoyment, nor never confess it, they only confess the outward deeds of great sins. So I say that such wicked delights and wicked thoughts are subtle deceivers of those who will be damned. Moreover, a man should be sorrowful over his wicked words as well as his wicked deeds. For certainly, the repentance of a single sin, without repenting all his other sins, or repenting all of his other sins and not of a single sin, will do no good. For certainly, God Almighty is all goodness, and so he forgives everything or nothing. And of this St Augustine says, "I know for certain that God is an enemy to every sinner." So what does this mean? Someone who confesses one sin, will he be forgiven for all his other sins? No. And furthermore, contrition should be wonderfully sorrowful and anxious; and that is how he gains little mercy of God; and therefore, when my soul was anxious inside me, I thought of God so that my prayers might go to him. Furthermore contrition must be

continueel, and that man have stedefast purpos to shriven hym, and for to amenden hym of his lyf. For soothly, whil contricioun lasteth, man may evere have hope of foryifnesse; and of this comth hate of synne, that destroyeth synne, bothe in himself, and eek in oother folk, at his power. For which seith David: "ye that loven God, hateth wikkednesse." For trusteth wel, to love God is for to love that he loveth, and hate that he hateth.

§15 The laste thyng that men shal understonde in contricioun is this: wherof avayleth contricioun. I seye that somtyme contricioun delivereth a man fro synne; of which that David seith, "I seye," quod David (that is to seyn, I purposed fermely) "to shryve me, and thow, lord, relessedest my synne." And right so as contricion availleth noght withouten sad purpos of shrifte, if man have oportunitee, right so litel worth is shrifte or satisfaccioun withouten contricioun. And mooreover contricion destroyeth the prisoun of helle, and maketh wayk and fieble alle the strengthes of the develes, and restoreth the yiftes of the hooly goost and of alle goode vertues; and it clenseth the soule of synne, and delivereth the soule fro the peyne of helle, and fro the compaignye of the devel, and fro the servage of synne, and restoreth it to alle goodes espirituels, and to the compaignye and communyoun of hooly chirche. And forther over, it maketh hym that whilom was sone of ire to be sone of grace; and alle thise thynges been preved by hooly writ. And therfore, he that wolde sette his entente to thise thynges, he were ful wys; for soothly he ne sholde nat thanne in al his lyf have corage to synne, but yeven his body and al his herte to the service of Jhesu Crist, and therof doon hym hommage. For soothly oure sweete lord Jhesu Crist hath spared us so debonairly in oure folies, that if he ne hadde pitee of mannes soule, a sory song we myghten alle synge.

Second part (beginning)

§16 The seconde partie of penitence is confessioun, that is signe of contricioun. Now shul ye understonde what is confessioun, and wheither it oghte nedes be doon or noon, whiche thynges been covenable to verray confessioun.

§17 First shaltow understonde that confessioun is verray shewynge of synnes to the preest. This is to seyn verray, for he moste confessen hym of alle the condiciouns that bilongen to his synne, as ferforth as he kan. Al moot be seyd, and no thyng excused ne hyd ne forwrapped, and noght avaunte thee of thy goode werkes. And forther over, it is necessarie to understonde whennes that synnes spryngen, and how they encreessen and whiche they been.

§18 Of the spryngynge of synnes seith Seint Paul in this wise: that "right as by a man synne entred first into this world, and thurgh that synne deeth, right so thilke deeth entred into alle men that synneden." And this man was Adam, by whom synne entred into this world, whan he brak the comaundementz of God. And therfore, he that first was so myghty that he sholde nat have dyed, bicam swich oon that he moste nedes dye, wheither he wolde or noon, and al his progenye in this world, that in thilke man synneden. Looke that in th' estaat of innocence, whan Adam and eve naked weren in paradys, and nothyng ne hadden shame of hir nakednesse, how that the serpent, that was moost wily of alle othere beestes that God hadde maked, seyde to the womman: "why comaunded God to yow ye sholde nat eten of every tree in paradys?" The womman answerde: "of the fruyt," quod she, "of the trees in paradys we feden us, but soothly, of the fruyt of the tree that is in the myddel of paradys, God forbad us for to ete, ne nat touchen it, lest per aventure we sholde dyen." The serpent seyde to the womman: nay, nay, ye shul nat dyen of deeth; for sothe, God woot that what day that ye eten therof, youre eyen shul opene, and ye shul been as goddes, knowynge good and harm." The womman thanne saugh that the tree was good to feedyng, and fair to the eyen, and delitable to the sighte. She took of the fruyt of the tree, and eet it, and yaf to hire housbonde, and he eet, and anoon the eyen of hem bothe openeden. And whan that they knewe that they were naked, they sowed of fige leves a maner of breches to hiden hire membres. There may ye seen that deedly synne hath, first, suggestion of the feend, as sheweth heere by the naddre; and afterward, the delit of the flessh, as sheweth heere by Eve; and after that, the consentynge of resoun, as sheweth heere by Adam. For trust wel, though so were that the feend tempted Eve, that is to seyn, the flessh, and the flessh hadde delit in the beautee of the fruyt defended, yet certes, til that resoun, that is to seyn, Adam, consented to the etynge of the fruyt, yet stood he in th' estaat of innocence. Of thilke Adam tooke we thilke wynne original; for of hym

true, for a man must confess everything about his sin, as much as he can. Everything must be said, nothing can be excused nor hid nor concealed, and you must not boast of your good works. Furthermore, you must understand where sins come from, how they increase, and what they are.

Of the creation of sin St Paul says this: "Just as man first came into the world through sin, and so did death, so death entered all men who committed sin." And this man was Adam, who first brought sin into the world, when he broke the commandments of God. And therefore, someone who was at first so great that he should not have died, became someone who must die, whether he wants or not, and all his children in this world, who sin through this man. You can see that in the state of innocence, when Adam and Eve were naked in paradise, and were in no way ashamed of it, how the serpent, who was the most cunning of all the animals that God had made, said to the woman, "Why has God ordered that you cannot eat the fruit of every tree in paradise?" The woman answered: "Of the fruit," she said, "of the trees in paradise we do feed, but certainly the fruit of the tree in the middle of paradise, God has forbidden us to eat it, and told us not to touch it, in case it should kill us." The serpent said to the woman, "No, no, you shall not die through death; truly, God knows that when you do eat from that tree, your eyes shall be opened and you will be like gods, knowing the difference between good and evil." The woman then saw that the fruit of the tree looked good to eat, beautiful and tasty to the sight. She took fruit from the tree, and ate it, and gave it to her husband, and he ate, and at once both of them had their eyes open. And when they knew that they were naked, they sewed a type of breeches out of fig leaves to hide their genitals. So there you can see that deadly sin was first caused at the suggestion of the devil, here in the person of a snake; and afterwards in the delight of the flesh, as shown here by Eve; and after that, through the agreement of reason, as shown by Adam. For certainly, although it was the devil who tempted Eve–that is to say, the flesh–and the flesh took delight in the beauty of the forbidden fruit, but certainly, until reason–that is to say we took the original sin from this

flesshly descended be we alle, and engendred of vile and corrupt mateere. and whan the soule is put in oure body, right anon is contract original synne; and that that was erst but oonly peyne of concupiscence, is afterward bothe peyne and synne. And therfore be we alle born sones of wratthe and of dampnacioun perdurable, if it nere baptesme that we receyven, which bynymeth us the culpe. But for sothe, the peyne dwelleth with us, as to temptacioun, which peyne highte concupiscence. And this concupiscence, whan it is wrongfully disposed or ordeyned in man, it maketh hym coveite, by coveitise of flessh, flesshly synne, by sighte of his eyen as to erthely thynges, and eek coveitise of hynesse by pride of herte.

§19 Now, as for to speken of the firste coveitise, that is concupiscence, after the lawe of oure membres, that weren lawefulliche ymaked and by rightful juggement of God; I seye, forasmuche as man is nat obeisaunt to God, that is his lord, therfore is the flessh to hym disobeisaunt thurgh concupiscence, whigh yet is cleped norrissynge, of synne and occasioun of synne. Therfore, al the while that a man hath in hym the peyne of concupiscence, it is impossible but he be tempted somtime and moeved in his flessh to synne. And this thyng may nat faille as longe as he lyveth; it may wel wexe fieble and faille by vertu of baptesme, and by the grace of God thurgh penitence; but fully ne shal it nevere quenche, that he ne shal som tyme be moeved in hymself, but if he were al refreyded by siknesse, or by malefice of sorcerie, or colde drynkes. For lo, what seith Seint Paul: "the flessh coveiteth agayn the spirit, and the spirit agayn the flessh; they been so contrarie and so stryven that a man may nat alway doon as he wolde." The same Seint Paul, after his grete penaunce in water and in lond, - in water by nyght and by day in greet peril and in greet peyne; in lond, in famyne and thurst, in coold and cloothelees, and ones stoned almoost to the deeth, - yet seyde he, "allas, I caytyf man! Who shal delivere me fro the prisoun of my caytyf body?" and Seint Jerome, whan he longe tyme hadde woned in desert, where as he hadde no compaignye but of wilde beestes, where as he ne hadde no mete but herbes, and water to his drynke, ne no bed but the naked erthe, for which his flessh was blak as an ethiopeen for heete, and ny destroyed for coold, yet seyde he that "the brennynge of lecherie boyled in al his body." Wherfore I woot wel sykerly that they been deceyved that seyn that they

—agreed to eat fruit, he was still in a state of innocence. For we are all descended from him him in the flesh, and made of vile corrupt matter. And when the soul is put in our body, at once original sin begins; and what was at first just the pain of desire afterwards becomes pain and sin. And so we are all sons of anger and eternal damnation, if we are not baptised, which removes the guilt from us. But truly, the pain stays with us, as a temptation, that pain is called concupiscence. And this concupiscence, when it affects a man in a bad way, it makes him covet, through coveting flesh, the sins of the flesh, through what he sees all earthly things, and it also makes him covet high position through pride.

Now, to speak of the first covetousness, that is concupiscence, according to the laws of our bodies which were lawfully made by the true judgement of God, I say that in as much as a man is not obedient to God, who is his Lord, so the flesh is disobedient to him due to concupisecence, which both nourishes and causes sin. So, the whole time that a man has within him the pain of concupiscence, he cannot avoid being sometimes tempted and inspired to sin through the flesh. And he cannot avoid this as long as he lives. It may well become feeble and frail through the power of baptism and the grace of God through penitence, but it will never be fully extinguished, at some time he will feel this, unless he is cooled by sickness, or by evil sorcery, or cold drinks. For see what St Paul says: "The flesh is covetous against the spirit, and the spirit against the flesh; they are so opposite and quarrel so that a man cannot always do as he wishes." The same St Paul, after his great penance on water and on land —on water by night and day in great danger and great pain; on land in starvation and thirst, in cold and naked, and once stoned almost to death—yet he said, "Alas, I am a wretched man excavation mark who will save me from the prison of my wretched body?" and St Jerome, when he had dwelt a long time in the desert, with no company but that of wild beasts, where he had neither food nor herbs, and only water to drink, and no bed but the bare earth, which made his flesh as black as an Ethiopian through the heat, and almost killed him with the cold, but he still said that "the burning of lechery boiled through his

ne be nat empted in hir body. Witnesse on Seint Jame the apostel, that seith that "every wight is tempted in his owene concupiscence"; that is to seyn, that everich of us hath matere and occasioun to be tempted of the norissynge of synne that is in his body. And therfore seith Seint John the evaungelist: "if that we seyn that we be withoute synne, we deceyve us selve, and trouthe is nat in us."

§20 Now hal ye understonde in what manere that synne wexeth or encreesseth in man. The firste thyng is thilke norissynge of synne of which I spak biforn, thilke flesshly concupiscence. And after that comth the subjeccioun of the devel, this is to seyn, the develes bely, with which he bloweth in man the fir of flesshly concupiscence. And after that, a man bithynketh hym wheither he wol doon, or no, thilke thing to which he is tempted. And thanne, if that a man withstonde and weyve the firste entisynge of his flessh and of the feend, thanne is it no synne; And if it so be that he do nat so, thanne feeleth he anoon a flambe of delit. And thanne is it good to be war, and kepen hym wel, or elles he wol falle anon into consentynge of synne; and thanne wol he do it, if he may have tyme and place. And of this matere seith Moyses by the devel in this manere: the feend seith, "I wole chace and pursue the man by wikked suggestioun, and I wole hente hym by moevynge or stirynge of synne. And I wol departe my prise or my praye by deliberacioun, and my lust shal been acomplised in delit. I wol drawe my swerd in consentynge" - for certes, right as a swerd departeth a thyng in two peces, right so consentynge departeth God fro man — "and thanne wol I sleen hym with myn hand in dede of synne; thus seith the feend. For certes, thanne is a man al deed in soule. And thus is synne acomplised by temptacioun, by delit, and by consentynge; and thanne is the synne cleped actueel.

§21 For sothe, synne is in two maneres; outher it is venial, or deedly synne. Soothly, whan man loveth any creature moore than Jhesu Crist oure creatour, thanne is it deedly synne. And venial synne is it, if man love Jhesu Crist lasse than hym oghte. For sothe, the dede of this venial synne is ful perilous; for it amenuseth the love that men sholde han to God moore and moore. And therfore, it a man charge hymself with manye swiche venial synnes, certes, but if so be that he somtyme descharge hym of hem by shrifte, they mowe ful lightly amenuse in hym al the love that he hath to Jhesu Crist; and in this wise skippeth venial into deedly synne. For certes, the moore that a man chargeth his soule with venial synnes, the moore is he enclyned to fallen into deedly synne. And therfore lat us nat be necligent to deschargen us of venial synnes. For the proverbe seith that "manye smale maken a greet." And herkne this ensample. A greet wawe of the see comth som tyme with so greet a violence that it drencheth the ship. And the same harm doon som tyme the smale dropes of water, that entren thurgh a litel crevace into the thurrok, and in the botme of the ship, if men be so necligent that they ne descharge hem nat by tyme. And therfore, although ther be a difference bitwixe thise two causes of drenchynge, algates the ship is dreynt. Right so fareth it somtyme of deedly synne, and of anoyouse veniale synnes, whan they multiplie in a man so greetly that the love of thilke worldly thynges that he loveth, thurgh whiche he synneth venyally, is as greet in his herte as the love of god, or moore. And therfore, the love of every thyng that is nat biset in God, ne doon principally for Goddes sake, although that a man love it lasse than God, yet is it venial synne; and deedly synne whan the love of any thyng weyeth in the herte of man as muchel as the love of God, or moore. "Deedly synne," as seith Seint Augustyn, "is whan a man turneth his herte fro God, which that is verray sovereyn bountee, that may nat chaunge, and yeveth his herte to thyng that may chaunge and flitte." And certes, that is every thyng save God of hevene. For sooth is that if a man yeve his love, the which that he oweth al to God with al his herte, unto a creature, certes, as muche of his love as he yeveth to thilke creature, so muche he bireveth fro God; and therfore dooth he synne. For he that is dettour to God ne yeldeth nat to God al his dette, that is to seyn, al the love of his herte.

love that he has in him for Jesus Christ; and in this way venial sin becomes deadly sin. For certainly, the more a man loads his soul with venial sins, the more he is likely to fall into deadly sin. And so we must not be negligent in offloading our venial sins. For the proverb says that "Many small things make one great one." And listen to this example. A great wave comes so violently that it sinks the ship. And the same thing will happen with little drops of water, which creep in through a little crack into the bilge and the bottom of the ship, if men are so negligent that they do not empty them in time. And so, although there is a difference between these two manners of sinking, either way the ship is sunk. That is how it sometimes goes with deadly sin, and harmful venial sins, when they increase so greatly in a man that the love of worldly things, through which he is sinning venially, is as great in his heart as the love of God, if not more. And so, the love of everything that is not part of God, nor done mainly for the sake of God, although a man loves it less than God, it is still venial sin; and deadly sin when the love of anything weighs as much in the heart of a man as the love of God, or even more. "Deadly sin," as St Augustine says, "is when a man turns his heart away from God, who is true perfect goodness, which cannot change, and gives his heart to something that can change and disappear." And certainly, that applies to everything except God in heaven. For it is true that if a man gives his love, which he owes all love to God with all of his heart, to a creature, certainly however much love he gives to that creature, that is the amount he takes away from God; and he is sending. For he who owes everything to God is not paying God everything; that is to say, all the love he has in his heart.

§22 Now sith man understondeth generally which is venial synne, thanne is it covenable to tellen specially of synnes whiche that many a man peraventure ne demeth hem nat synnes, and ne shryveth him nat of the same thynges, and yet natheless they been synnes; soothly, as thise clerkes writen, this is to seyn, that at every tyme that a man eteth or drynketh moore than suffiseth to the sustenaunce of his body, in certein he dooth synne. And eek whan he speketh moore than it nedeth, it is synne. Eke whan he herkneth nat benignely the compleint of the povre; eke whan he is in heele of

Now since man generally understands what venial sin is, then it is appropriate to mention specially sins which many men do not think are sins, and do not confess to, but they are still true sins, as the scholars say; that is to say, that every time a man eats or drinks more than he needs for his body, he is certainly sinning. And also when he speaks more than necessary, that is sin. And when he does not listen to the complaints of the poor with grace; also when he is healthy but does not fast when other folk do, without good cause; also when

body, and wol nat faste whan other folk faste, withouten cause resonable; eke whan he slepeth moore than nedeth, or whan he comth by thilke enchesoun to late to chirche, or to othere werkes of charite; eke whan he useth his wyf, withouten sovereyn desir of engendrure to the honour of God, or for the entente to yelde to his wyf the dette of his body; eke whan he wol nat visite the sike and the prisoner, if he may; eke if he love wyf or child, or oother worldly thyng, moore than resoun requireth; eke if he flatere or blandise moore than hym oghte for any necessitee; eke if he amenuse or withdrawe the almesse of the povre; eke if he apparailleth his mete moore deliciously than nede is, or ete it to hastily by likerousnesse; eke if he tale vanytees at chirche or at Goddes service, or that he be a talker of ydel wordes of folye or of vileynye, for he shal yelden acountes of it at the day of doom; eke whan he biheteth or assureth to do thynges that he may nat parfourne; eke whan that he by lightnesse or folie mysseyeth or scorneth his neighebor; eke whan he hath any wikked suspecioun of thyng ther he ne woot of it no soothfastnesse: thise thynges, and no withoute nombre, been synnes, as seith Seint Augustyn.

§23 Now shal men understonde that, al be it so that noon erthely man may eschue alle venial synnes, yet may be refreyne hym by the brennynge love that he hath to oure lord Jhesu Christ, and by preyeres and confessioun and othere goode werkes, so that it shal but litel greve. For, as seith Seint Augustyn, "if a man love God in swich manere that al that evere he dooth is in the love of god, and for the love of God, verraily, for he brenneth in the love of God, looke, how muche that a drope of water that falleth in a fourneys ful of fyr anoyeth or greveth, so muche anoyeth a venial synne unto a man that is parfit in the love of Jhesu Crist." Men may also refreyne venial synne by receyvynge worthily of the precious body of Jhesu Crist; by receyvynge eek of hooly water; by almesdede; by general confessioun of Confiteor at masse and at complyn; and by blessynge of bisshopes and of preestes, and by oothere goode werkes.

§24 Now is it bihovely thyng to telle whiche been the sevene deedly synnes, this is to seyn, chiefaynes of synnes. Alle they renne in o lees, but in diverse manneres. Now been they cleped chieftaynes, for as muche as they been chief and spryng of alle othere synnes. Of the roote of thise sevene synnes, thanne, is Pride the general roote

he sleeps more than he needs, and when for this reason he comes too late to church, or to other charitable works; also when he sleeps with his wife without wishing to procreate for the honour of God or with the intention of paying the debt of his body to his wife; also when he does not visit the sick and prisoners, when he can; also if he loves his wife or child, or any other worldly thing, more than is reasonable. Also if he flatters or begs more than he ought to for any necessity; also if he cuts down or completely stops paying alms to the poor; also if he prepares his food more deliciously than necessary, or eats it too quickly due to greed; also if he talks of trivialities at church or religious service, or if he talks idle words of folly or villainy, for he shall pay for it at Judgement Day; also when he promises to do things that he cannot do; also when through frivolity or stupidity he slanderers or scorns his neighbour; also when he retains wicked suspicions of things when he knows there is no basis for them: these things, and many others without number, are sins, as St Augustine says.

Now men must understand that, although it is impossible for any earthly man to avoid all venial sins, yet he can control himself through the burning love that he has for our Lord Jesus Christ, and through prayers and confession and other good work, so that it will do little harm. For, as St Augustine says, "If a man loves God in such a way that all he ever does is for the love of God, truly, because he burns with the love of God, see how much damage a drop of water does if it falls into a furnace, that is as much damage a venial sin does to a man who has perfect love for Jesus Christ." Men can also control venial sin by receiving in the right way be precious body of Jesus Christ; by receiving also holy water, through giving charity, by the general confession at mass and evening prayers, and through the blessings of bishops and priests, and through other good works.

Now it is suitable to describe the seven deadly sins, that is to say, the ruling sins. They all run together, but in different ways. Now they are called the chief sins, inasmuch as they are the greatest and the origin of all other sins. From the root of these seven sins, then, pride is the general root of all harm. For from this

of alle harmes. For of this roote spryngen certein braunches, as Ire, Envye, Accidie or Slewthe, Avarice or Coveitise (to commune understondynge), Glotonye, and Lecherye. And everich of thise chief synnes hath his braunches and his twigges, as shal be declared in hire chapitres folwynge.

De Superbia

§25 And thogh so be that no man kan outrely telle the nombre of the twigges and of the harmes that cometh of pride, yet wol I shewe a partie of hem, as ye shul understonde. Ther is inobedience, avauntynge, ypocrisie, despit, arrogance, inpudence, swellynge of herte, insolence, elacioun, inpacience, strif, contumacie, presumpcioun, irreverence, pertinacie, veyne glorie, and many another twig that I kan nat declare. Inobedient is he that disobeyeth for despit to the comandementz of God, and to his sovereyns, and to his goostly fader. Avauntour is he that bosteth of the harm or of the bountee that he hath doon. Ypocrite is he that hideth to shewe hym swich as he is, and sheweth hym swich as he noght is. Despitous is he that hath desdeyn of his neighebor, that is to seyn, of his evene-cristene, or hath despit to doon that hym oghte to do. Arrogant is he that thynketh that he hath thilke bountees in hym that he hath noght, or weneth that he sholde have hem by his desertes, or elles he demeth that he be that he nys nat. Inpudent is he that for his pride hath no shame of his synnes. Swellynge of herte is whan a man rejoyseth hym of harm that he hath doon. Insolent is he that despiseth in his juggement alle othere folk, as to regard of his value, and of his konnyng, and of his spekyng, and of his beryng. Elacioun is whan he ne may neither suffre to have maister ne felawe. Inpacient is he that wol nat been ytaught ne undernome of his vice, and by strif werreieth trouthe wityngly, and deffendeth his folye. Contumax is he that thurgh his indignacioun is agayns everich auctoritee or power of hem that been his sovereyns. Presumpcioun is whan a man undertaketh an emprise that hym oghte nat do, or elles that he may nat do; and this is called surquidrie. Irreverence is whan men do nat honoure there as hem oghte to doon, and waiten to be reverenced. Pertinacie is whan man deffendeth his folie, and truseth to muchel to his owene wit. Veyneglorie is for to have pompe and delit in his temporeel hynesse, and glorifie hym in this worldly estaat. Janglynge is whan a man speketh to muche biforn folk, and clappeth as a mille, and taketh no keep

root spring certain branches, such as anger, envy, sloth, avarice or covetousness (as commonly understood), gluttony and lechery. And each one of these chief sins has its branches and its twigs, as I shall show in the following chapters.

On Pride

Although it is the case that no man can completely count the number of twigs and the harm that comes from pride, but I will show you part of them, so you will understand. There is disobedience, boasting, hypocrisy, scorn, arrogance, impudence, swelling of the heart, insolence, elation, impatience, contumely, rebellion, presumption, irreverence, pertinacity, vainglory and many other twigs I cannot describe. Someone who disobeys the commandments of God out of spite, and those of his superiors and of his spiritual father, is disobedient. A boaster is someone who boasts of the harm or the good which he has done. A hypocrite is someone who hides his true nature and shows himself as he is not. Someone who is scornful is someone who disdains his neighbour–that is to say, his fellow Christian–or rejects what he ought to do. Someone who is arrogant thinks that he has good things which he does not have, or thinks that he deserves them, or otherwise he thinks that he is what he is not. Someone who is impudent has, because of his pride, no shame for his sins. The swelling of heart is when a man rejoices in the harm that he has done. Someone who is insolent despises all other folk, compared to himself, and his understanding, and his speech, and his bearing. Elation is when a man cannot tolerate having either a master nor an equal. Someone who is impatient will not be taught nor criticised for his vice, and through strife deliberately wages war on truth, and defends his foolishness. Someone who has contumely is someone who through his indignation rebels against all the authority and power of those who are superior to him. Presumption is when a man begins an enterprise which he should not undertake, or which he cannot undertake; that is what presumption is. Irreverence is when men do not honour the things which they ought to, and when they expect to be revered themselves. Pertinacity is when a man defends

what he seith.

§26 And yet is ther a privee spece of Pride, that waiteth first to be salewed er he wole salewe, al be be lasse worth than that oother is peraventure; and eek he waiteth or desireth to sitte, or elles to goon above hym in the wey, or kisse pax, or been encensed, or goon to offryng biforn his neighebor, and swiche semblable thynges, agayns his duetee, peraventure, but that he hath his herte and his entente in swich a proud desir to be magnified and honoured biforn the peple. Now been ther two maneres of pride: that oon of hem is withinne the herte of man, and that oother is withoute. Of whiche, soothly, thise forseyde thynges, and no that I have seyd, apertenen to pride that is in the herte of man; and that othere speces of Pride been withoute. But nathelees that oon of thise speces of pride is signe of that oother, right as the gaye leefsel atte taverne is signe of the wyn that is in the celer. And this is in manye thynges: as in speche and contenaunce, and in outrageous array of clothyng. For certes, if ther ne hadde be no synne in clothyng, Crist wolde nat so soone have noted and spoken of the clothyng of thilke riche man in the gospel. And as seith Seint Gregorie, that "precious clothyng is cowpable for the derthe of it, and for his softenesse, and for his strangenesse and degisynesse, and for the superfluitee, or for the inordinat scantnesse of it." Allas! may man nat seen, as in oure dayes, the synful costlewe array of clothynge, and namely in to muche superfluite, or elles in to desordinat scantnesse?

§27 As to the first synne, that is in superfluitee of clothynge, which that maketh it so deere, to harm of the peple; nat oonly the cost of embrowdynge, the degise endentynge or barrynge, owndynge, palynge, wyndynge or bendynge, and semblable wast of clooth in vanitee; but ther is also costlewe furrynge in hir gownes, so muche pownsonynge of chisels to maken holes, so muche daggynge of sheres; forthwith the superfluitee in lengthe of the forseide gowens, trailynge in the dong and in the mire, on horse and eek on foote, as wel of man as of womman, that al thilke trailyng is verraily as in effect wasted, consumed, thredbare, and roten with

his foolishness and trusts his own wits too much. Vainglory is taking pomp and delight in high rank on earth, and to rejoice in this worldly estate. Jangling is one man speaks too much to other folk, clattering like a mill, and does not care what he says.

And yet there is a secret form of pride which waits to be greeted before he will greet others, even though he is less worthy than the other; and also he expects or wishes to sit, or go ahead, or make the kiss of peace, or be blessed with incense, or go to the offertory before his neighbour, and other similar things, beyond what duty requires, because he has in his heart and his intentions such a proud desire to show off and be honoured before the people. Now there are two sorts of pride: one of them is in the heart of man, and the other is outside. Of which, truly, these previously mentioned things, and more than I have said, are attached to the pride that is in the heart of man; and there are outside that other species of pride. But nevertheless one of these types of pride is the sign of the other, just as a pretty bush at a tavern is a sign that they have wine in the cellar. And this is shown in many things: such as in speech and expression, and in outrageous clothes. For certainly, if there was no sin in clothes, Christ would not have been so quick to take note of and mention the clothing the rich man was wearing in the gospel. And, as Gregory says, "precious clothing is sinful due to the expense of it, and because of its softness, and its exotic style and elaborateness, and for the excess of it or the excess thinness of it." Alas, can't men see, in our current time, the sinful excessively expensive display of clothing, with far too much material, or otherwise with far too little?

As for the first sin, too much material, which makes it so expensive, which causes harm; not only for the cost of embroidery, the ostentatious ornamentation with bars, wavy stripes, vertical stripes, folding or decorative borders, and similar wastes of cloth on vanity, on their gowns, but there is also expensive fur trim, so much punching with chisels to make holes, so much cutting with shears; immediately the excess length of these gowns, trailing in the dung and the mud, whether riding or walking, for men as well as women, all this trailing cloth is truly wasted,

donge, rather than it is yeven to the povre, to greet damage of the forseyde povre folk. And that in sondry wise; this is to seyn that the moore that clooth is wasted, the moore moot it coste to the peple for the scarsnesse. And forther over, if so be that they wolde yeven swich pownsoned and dagged clothyng to the povre folk, it is nat convenient to were for hire estaat, ne suffisant to beete hire necessitee, to kepe hem fro the distemperance of the firmament. Upon that oother side, to speken of the horrible disordiant scantnesse of clothyng, as been thise kutted sloppes, or haynselyns, that thurgh hire shortnesse ne covere nat the shameful membres of man, to wikked entente. Allas! somme of hem shewen the boce or hir shap, and the horrible swollen membres, that semeth lik the maladie of hirnia, in the wrappynge of hir hoses; and eek the buttokes of hem faren as it were the hyndre part of a she-ape in the fulle of the moone. And mooreover, the wrecched swollen membres that they shewe thurgh disgisynge, in departynge of hire hoses in whit and reed, semeth that half hir shameful privee membres weren flayne. And if so be that they departen hire hoses in othere colours, as is whit and blak, or whit and blew, or blak and reed, and so forth, thanne semeth it, as by variaunce of colour, that half the partie of hire privee membres were corrupt by the fir of Seint Antony, or by cancre, or by oother swich meschaunce. Of the hyndre part of hir buttokes, it is ful horrible for to see. For certes, in that partie of hir body ther as they purgen hir stynkynge ordure, that foule partie shewe they to the peple prowdly in despit of honestitee, which honestitee that Jhesu Crist and his freendes observede to shewen in hir lyve. Now, as of the outrageous array of wommen, God woot that though the visages of somme of hem seme ful chaast and debonaire, yet notifie they in hire array of atyr likerousnesse and pride. I sey nat that honestitee in clothynge of man or womman is uncovenable, but certes the superfluitee or disordinat scantitee of clothynge is reprevable. Also the synne of aornement or of apparaille is in thynges that apertenen to ridynge, as in to manye delicat horses that been hoolden for delit, that been so faire, fatte, and costlewe; and also in many a vicious knave that is sustened by cause of hem, and in to curious harneys, as in sadeles, in crouperes, peytrels, and bridles coverd precious clothyng, and riche barres and plates of gold and of silver. For which God seith by Zakarie the prophete, "I wol confounde the rideres of swiche horses." This folk taken litel reward of the ridynge of Goddes sone of hevene, and of his

consumed, threadbare and rotten with dung, when it could have been given to the poor, and that causes great harm to the poor. This is seen in various ways; the more cloth that is wasted, the more it must cost for people due to to its scarcity. Furthermore, if they were to give such highly ornamental clothing to the poor, it is not the right sort of clothing for their position, nor enough for their needs, to keep them from the bad weather in the sky. With reference to the other thing, horribly scanty clothing, like these short coats, or short jackets, that through their shortness do not cover the shameful members of man, and that causes wickedness. Alas, some of them show the bulge of their shape, and their horribly swollen members, which makes them look like they have a hernia, in the wrapping of their leggings; and also you can see their buttocks as if they were the arse of a female ape under the full moon. And moreover, the wretched swollen members that they show in their clothes, when they have their stockings split between white and red, it seems that half of their shameful private members have been flayed. And if they divide their stockings into other colours, such as white and black, or white and blue, or black and red, and so forth, then it seems, through the different colours, that half of their private members have been corrupted by the fire of St Anthony, or by cancer, or by some other piece of bad luck. On the back of their arses, it is revolting to see. For certainly, on that part of the body where they get rid of their stinking excrement, those foul parts they show proudly to people, completely indecent, without the decency which Jesus Christ and his friends showed in their lives. Now, as for the outrageous dress of women, God knows that although some of them seem to have very pure and meek faces, through their clothing they show all their lechery and pride. I do not say that it is wrong for men and women to have decent clothes, but certainly too much or too little clothing is to be blamed. This is also seen in excessive adornment of horses, with too many delicate horses that are kept for delight, that are so fair, well fed and expensive; and also many vicious servants are maintained because of them; and they have too elaborate harnesses, saddles, croppers, collars and bridles covered with precious cloth, and rich bowls and plates of gold and silver. Through the prophet

harneys whan he rood upon the asse, and ne hadde noon oother harneys but the povre clother of his disciples; ne we ne rede nat that evere he rood on oother beest. I speke this for the synne of superfluitee, and nat for resonable honestitee, whan reson it requireth. And forther over, certes, pride is greetly notified in holdynge of greet meynee, whan they be of litel profit or of right no profit; and namely whan that meynee is felonous and damageous to the peple by hardynesse of heigh lordshipe or by wey of offices. For certes, swiche lordes sellen thanne hir lordshipe to the devel of helle, whanne they sustenen the wikkednesse of hir meynee. Or elles, whan this folk of lowe degree, as thilke that holden hostelries, sustenen the thefte of hire hostilers, and that is in many manere of deceites. Thilke manere of folk been the flyes that folwen the hony, or elles the houndes that folwen the careyne. Swich forseyde folk stranglen spiritually hir lordshipes; for which thus seith David the prophete: "wikked deeth moote come upon thilke lordshipes, and God yeve that they moote descenden into helle al doun; for in hire houses been iniquitees and shrewednesses, and nat God of hevene. And certes, but if they doon amendement, right as God yaf his benysoun to (Laban) by the service of Jacob, and to (Pharao) by the service of Joseph, right so God wol yeve his malisoun to swiche lordshipes as sustenen the wikkednesse of hir servauntz, but they come to amendement. Pride of the table appeereth eek ful ofte; for certes, riche men been cleped to festes, and povre folk been put awey and rebuked. Also in excesse of diverse metes and drynkes, and namely swich manere bake-metes and dissh-metes, brennynge of wilde fir and peynted and castelled with papir, and semblable wast, so that it is abusioun for to thynke. And eek in to greet preciousnesse of vessel and curiositee of mynstralcie, by whiche a man is stired the moore to delices of luxurie, if so be that he sette his herte the lasse upon oure lord Jhesu Crist, certeyn it is a synne; and certeinly the delices myghte been so grete in this caas that man myghte lightly falle by hem into deedly synne. The especes that sourden of Pride, soothly whan they sourden of malice ymagined, avised, and forncast, or elles of usage, been deedly synnes, it is no doute. And whan they sourden by freletee unavysed, and sodeynly withdrawen ayeyn, al been they grevouse synnes, I gesse that they ne been nat deedly.

Zechariah God says, "I will destroy the riders of horses like these." These folk take little notice of the way the son of Heaven rode, and of the harness he had when he rode on the ass, having no other harness but the poor clothes of his disciples; and we do not read that he ever rode any other animal. I am speaking of the sin of excess, not reasonable decent clothing, when it is reasonable to have it. And furthermore, certainly, pride is shown greatly in the great households, when there is little or no profit at all, particularly when a group of retainers steals and does harm to the people through the harshness of high Lordship or through what they have been told. For certainly, such lords are then selling their titles to the devil in hell, when they support the wickedness of their household. Or otherwise, when these lowly folk, such as innkeepers, they keep up many sorts of deceit. These sorts of people are flies that follow honey, or hounds that follow dead meat. These people I mention spiritually strangle their Lordships; and of them David the prophet says: "Wicked death must come to these lords, and God shall grant that they will all descend into hell, for their houses contain iniquities and wicked deeds and not almighty God." And certainly, unless they make things right, just as God gave his blessing to Laban due to the service of Jacob, and to Pharaoh due to the service of Joseph, so he will curse those lords who to support the wickedness of their servants, unless they make things right. Pride of the table also shows itself very often; for certainly, rich men are invited to feasts, and poor folk are pushed away and cursed. It is also shown in excess of different food and drink, such as meat pies and stews, burning with wild fir and painted and decorated with paper towers, and other wasteful things, so that is is ridiculous to think of. And also in excessive crockery and intricate performances of music, which makes a man feel more lecherous, if it means that he thinks less in his heart of our Lord Jesus Christ, then it is certainly a sin; and certainly the pleasures would be so great in this case that a man might easily be led into deadly sin by them. The types of pride which arise, truly when they arise from malice, plotted, considered and premeditated, or else by habit, are deadly sins, there is no doubt. And when they come from unplanned weakness, and are suddenly

§28 Now myghte men axe wherof that pride sourdeth and spryngeth, and I seye, somtyme it spryngeth of the goodes of nature, and somtyme of the goodes of fortune, and somtyme of the goodes of grace. Certes, the goodes of nature stonden outher in goodes of body or in goodes of soule. Certes, goodes of body been heele of body, strengthe, delivernesse, beautee, gentrice, franchise. Goodes of nature of the soule been good wit, sharp understondynge, subtil engyn, vertu natureel, good memorie. Goodes of fortune been richesse, hyghe degrees of lordshipes, preisynges of the peple. Goodes of grace been science, power to suffre spiritueel travaille, benignitee, vertuous contemplacioun, withstondynge of temptacioun, and semblable thynges. Of whiche forseyde goodes, certes it is a ful greet folye a man to priden hym in any of hem alle. Now as for to speken of goodes of nature, God woot that somtyme we han hem in nature as muche to oure damage as to oure profit. As for to speken of heele of body, certes it passeth ful lightly, and eek it is ful ofte enchesoun of the siknesse of oure soule. For, God woot, the flessh is a ful greet enemy to the soule; and therfore, the moore that the body is hool, the moore be we in peril to falle. Eke for to pride hym in his strengthe of body, it is an heigh folye. For certes, the flessh coveiteth agayn the spirit; and ay the moore strong that the flessh is, the sorier may the soule be. And over al this, strengthe of body and worldly hardynesse causeth ful ofte many a man to peril and meschaunce. Eek for to pride hym of his gentrie is ful greet folie; for ofte tyme the gentrie of the body binymeth the gentrie of the soule; and eek we ben alle of o fader and of o mooder, and alle we been of o nature, roten and corrupt, bothe riche and povre. For sothe, o manere gentrie is for to preise, that apparailleth mannes corage with vertues and moralitees, and maketh hym Cristes child. For truste wel that over what man that synne hath maistrie, he is a verray cherl to synne. Now been ther generale signes of gentillesse, as eschewynge of vice and ribaudye and servage of synne, in word, in werk, and contenaunce; and usynge vertu, curteisye, and clennesse, and to be liberal, that is to seyn, large by mesure; for thilke that passeth mesure is folie and synne. Another is to remembre hym of bountee, that he of oother folk hath receyved. Another is to be benigne to his goode subetis; wherfore seith Senek, "ther is no thing moore covenable to a man of heigh estaat than debonairetee and pitee. And therfore thise flyes

rejected, although they are grievous sins, I guess that they are not deadly.
Now men might ask where pride comes from, and I say that sometimes it comes from the goods of nature, and sometimes from Fortune, and sometimes from grace. Certainly, the goods of nature are seen in the goods of the body and the goods of the soul. Certainly, the goods of the body are health, strength, agility, beauty, nobility, freedom. The goods of nature nature of the soul are wit, understanding, ingenuity, power over the senses, good memory. The goods of fortune are riches, high rank, and praise of the people. The goods of grace are knowledge, power to suffer spiritual troubles, kindness, virtuous contemplation, resisting temptation and similar things. Of these goods I have mentioned, it is certainly very foolish of a man to pride himself on any of them. Now to speak of the goods of nature, God knows that sometimes they do us as much damage as they do good. To speak of the health of the body, certainly it is very little, and it is also often the cause of sickness in the soul. For, God knows, the flesh is a very great enemy of the soul, and so the healthier the body is, the more we are in danger of falling into pride. Also deprived oneself on the strength of the body, is great foolishness. For certainly, the flesh coverts against the spirit, and the stronger the flesh is, the worse the soul may be. And above all this, strength of body and worldly hardiness very often puts a man in danger and misfortune. Also to pride oneself on one's noble birth is very foolish indeed; for often the gentility of the body takes away the gentility of the soul; and also we are all born of one father and one mother, we are all of one nature, rotten and corrupt, the rich and the poor. For truly, one sort of nobility should be praised, that which gives a man determination, virtue and plurality, and makes him the child of Christ. For you can be sure that if sin rules over a man, then he is truly a slave of sin. Now there are general signs of nobility, such as avoiding vice and lewd behaviour and binding oneself to sin, in word and deed and manner, and using virtue, courtesy and cleanliness, and to be liberal —that is to say, reasonably generous, for anything excessive is foolishness and sin. Another thing is to remind oneself of good things that you have received from others. Another is to be gracious to one's good

that men clepen bees, whan they maken hir kyng, they chesen oon that hath no prikke wherwith he may stynge." Another is, a man to have a noble herte and a diligent, to attayne to heighe vertuouse thynges. Now certes, a man to pride hym in the goodes of grace is eek an outrageous folie; for thilke yifte of grace that sholde have turned hym to goodnesse and to medicine, turneth hym to venym and to confusioun, as seith Seint Gregorie. Certes also, whoso prideth hym in the goodes of fortune, he is a ful greet fool; for somtyme is a man a greet lord by the morwe, that is a caytyf and a wrecche er it be nyght; and somtyme the richesse of a man is cause of his deth; somtyme the delices of a man ben cause of the grevous maladye thurgh which he dyeth. Certes, the commendacioun of the peple is somtyme ful fals and ful brotel for to triste; this day they preyse, tomorwe they blame. God woot, desir to have commendacioun eek of the peple hath caused deeth to many a bisy man.

Remedium contra peccatum Superbie

§29 Now sith that so is that ye han understonde what is pride, and whiche been the speces of it, and whennes pride sourdeth and spryngeth, now shul ye understonde which is The remedie agayns the synne of pride; and that is hymylitee, or mekenesse. That is a vertu thurgh which a man hath verray knoweleche of hymself, and holdeth of hymself no pris ne deyntee, as in regard of his desertes, considerynge evere his freletee. Now been ther three maneres of hymylitee: as humylitee in herte; another hymylitee is in his mouth; the thridde in his werkes. The humilitee in herte is in foure maneres. That oon is whan a man holdeth hymself as noght worth biforn God of hevene. Another is whan he ne despiseth noon oother man. The thridde is whan he rekketh nat, though men holde hym noght worth. The ferthe is whan he nys nat sory of his humiliacioun. Also the humilitee of mouth is in foure thynges: in attempree speche, and in humblesse of speche, and whan he biknoweth with his owene mouth that he is swich as hym thynketh that he is in his herte. Another is whan he preiseth the bountee of another man, and nothyng therof amenuseth. Humilitee eek in werkes is in foure maneres. The firste is whan he putteth othere men biforn hym. The seconde is to chese the loweste place over al. The thridde is gladly to assente to good conseil. The ferthe is to stonde gladly to the award of his sovereyns, or of hym that is in hyer degree. Certein, this is a greet werk of hymylitee.

Envy

§30 After Pride wol I speken of the foule synne of Envye, which that is, as by the word of the Philosophre, "sorwe of oother mannes prosperitee"; and after the word of Seint Augustyn, it is sorwe of oother mennes wele, and joye of othere mennes harm. This foule synne is platly agayns the hooly goost. Al be it so that every synne is agayns the Hooly Goost, yet nathelees, for as muche as bountee aperteneth proprely to the Hooly Goost, and envye comth proprely of malice, therfore it is proprely agayn the bountee of the Hooly Goost. Now hath malice two speces; that is to seyn, hardnesse of herte in wikkednesse, or elles the flessh of man is so blynd that he considereth nat that he is in synne, or rekketh nat that he is in synne, which is the hardnesse of the devel. That oother spece of malice is whan a man werreyeth trouthe, whan he woot that it is trouthe; and eek whan he werreyeth the grace that God hath yeve to his neighebor; and al this is by Envye. Certes, thanne is Envye the worste synne that is. For soothly, alle othere synnes been somtyme oonly agayns o special vertu; but certes, envye is agayns alle vertues and agayns alle goodnesses. For it is sory of alle the bountees of his neighebor, and in this manere it is divers from alle othere synnes. For wel unnethe is ther any synne that it ne hath som delit in itself, save oonly envye, that evere hath in itself angwissh and sorwe. The speces of envye been thise. Ther is first, sorwe of oother mannes goodnesse and of his prosperitee; and prosperitee is kyndely matere of joye; thanne is envye a synne agayns kynde. The seconde spece of envye is joye of oother mannes harm; and that is proprely lyk to the devel, that evere rejoyseth hym of mannes harm. Of thise two speces comth bakbityng; and this synne of bakbityng or detraccion hath certeine speces, as thus. Som man preiseth his neighebor by a wikked entente; for he maketh alwey a wikked knotte atte laste ende. Alwey he maketh a but atte laste ende, that is digne of moore blame, than worth is al the preisynge. The seconde spece is that if a man be good, and dooth or seith a thing to good entente, the bakbitere wol turne al thilke goodnesse up-so-doun to his shrewed entente. The thridde is to amenuse the bountee of his neighebor. The fourthe spece of bakbityng is this, that if men speke goodnesse of a man, thanne wol the bakbitere seyn, parfey, swich a man is yet bet than he; in dispreisynge of hym that men preise. The fifte spece is this, for to consente gladly and herkne gladly to the harm that men speke of oother folk. This synne is ful greet, and ay encreesseth after the wikked entente of the bakbitere. After bakbityng cometh gruchchyng or murmuracioun; and somtyme it spryngeth of inpacience agayns god, and som-tyme agayns man. Agayn God it is, whan a man gruccheth agayn the peyne of helle, or agayns poverte, or los of catel, or agayn reyn or tempest; or elles gruccheth that shrewes han prosperitee, or elles for the goode men han adversitee. And alle thise thynges sholde man suffre paciently, for they comen by the rightful juggement and ordinaunce of God. Somtyme comth grucching of avarice; as Judas grucched agayns the Magdaleyne, whan she enoynted the heved of oure lord Jhesu Crist with hir precious oynement. This manere murmure is swich as whan man gruccheth of goodnesse that hymself dooth, or that oother folk doon of hir owene catel. Somtyme comth murmure of pride; as whan Simon the Pharisse gruchched agayn the Magdaleyne, whan she approched to Jhesu Crist, and weep at his feet for hire synnes. And somtyme grucchyng sourdeth of envye; whan men discovereth a mannes harm that was pryvee, or bereth hym on hond thyng that is fals. Murmure eek is ofte amonges servauntz that grucceh whan hir sovereyns bidden hem doon leveful thynges; and forasmuche as they dar nat openly withseye the comaundementz of hir sovereyns, yet wol they seyn harm, and grucche, and murmure prively for verray despit; whiche wordes men clepen the develes Pater noster, though so be that the devel ne hadde nevere Pater noster, but that lewed folk yeven it swich a name. Somtyme it comth of ire or prive hate, that norisseth rancour in herte, as afterward I shal declare. Thanne cometh eek bitternesse of herte, thurgh which bitternesse every good dede of his neighebor semeth to hym bitter and unsavory. Thanne cometh discord, that unbyndeth alle manere of freendshipe. Thanne comth scornynge of his neighebor, al do he never so weel. Thanne comth accusynge, as whan man seketh occasioun to anoyen his neighebor, which that is lyk the craft of the devel, that waiteth bothe nyght and day to accusen us alle. Thanne comth malignitee, thurgh which a man anoyeth his neighebor prively, if he may; and if he noght may, algate his wikked wil ne shal nat wante, as for to brennen his hous pryvely, or empoysone or sleen his beestes, and semblable thynges.

will turn it all upside down to suit his wicked intentions. The third type is to malign the goodness of his neighbour. The fourth type is that if men speak well of a man, then the backbiter will say, "Indeed, but so-and-so is better than him," putting down the one that men praise. The fifth type is this: to gladly agree and to gladly listen to the bad things that men say of others. This is a very great sin and always increases according to the wicked intentions of the backbiter. After backbiting comes grouching or grumbling; and sometimes that comes from impatience with God, and sometimes with man. It is against God when a man complains about the pain of hell, or about poverty, or losing possessions, or rain or storms; or otherwise complains that bad men are prosperous, or that good men suffer. All these are things which a man should suffer patiently, because they come from the true judgement and order of God. Sometimes the complaints come from greed; that was how Judas complained against the Magdalene when she anointed the head of our Lord Jesus Christ with her precious ointment. This is the sort of grumbling you get when a man complains of the goodness that he himself has done, or that other folk do with their own possessions. Sometimes there is the grumbling of pride, as when Simon the Pharisee complained about the Magdalene when she approached Jesus Christ and wept at his feet for their sins. And sometimes the complaints come from envy, when someone discovers something discreditable which was secret, or fools someone with something. There is also grumbling among servants who complain when their superiors tell them to do things which they should; and inasmuch as they do not openly defy the orders of their superiors, they will still say bad things, and complain, and grumble privately in their disobedience; these words are called the devil's prayer by men, although the devil has never had a prayer, but ignorant people call it that. Sometimes it comes from anger or secret hate that nourishes anger in the heart, as I shall later explain. Then there is also the bitterness of the heart, and through that bitterness every good deed of his neighbour seems to be bitter and unsavoury. Then there comes disagreements that tear apart all sorts of friendship. Then comes scorning of a neighbour, however well he is doing. Then comes accusing, when a man tries to aggravate his neighbour, which is the work of the devil, who waits both night and day to accuse all of us. Then comes malignity, where a man annoys his neighbour secretly, if he can, and if he cannot do so, he will still surely have plenty of wicked plans, such as secretly burning his house, or poisoning or killing his cattle, and such things.

The remedy for envy

Remedium contra peccatum Invidie

§31 Now wol I speke of remedie agayns this foule synne of envye. First is the love of God principal, and lovyng of his neighebor as hymself; for soothly, that oon ne may nat been withoute that oother. And truste wel that in the name of thy neighebor thou shalt understonde the name of thy brother; for certes alle we have o fader flesshly, and o mooder, that is to seyn, Adam and Eve; and eek o fader espiritueel, and that is God of hevene. Thy neighebor artow holden for to love, and wilne hym alle goodnesse; and therfore seith God, love thy neighebor as thyselve, that is to seyn, to salvacioun bothe of lyf and of soule. And mooreover thou shalt love hym in word, and in benigne amonestynge and chastisynge, and conforten hym in his anoyes, and preye for hym with al thyn herte. And in dede thou shalt love hym in swich wise that thou shalt doon to hym in charitee as thou woldest that it were doon to thyn owene persone. And therfore thou ne shalt doon hym no damage in wikked word, ne harm in his body, ne in his catel, ne in his soule, by entissyng of wikked ensample. Thou shalt nat desiren his wyf, ne none of his thynges. Understoond eek that in the name of neighebor is comprehended his enemy. Certes, man shal loven his enemy, by the comandement of God, and soothly thy freend shaltow love in God. I seye, thyn enemy shaltow love for Goddes sake, by his comandement. For if it were reson that man sholde haten his enemy, for so he God nolde nat receyven us to his love that been his enemys. Agayns three manere of wronges that his enemy dooth to hym, he shal doon three thynges, as thus. Agayns hate and rancour of herte, he shal love hym in herte. Agayns chidyng and wikkede wordes, he shal preye for his enemy. Agayns the wikked dede of his enemy, he shal doon hym bountee. For Crist seith: loveth youre enemys, and preyeth for hem that speke yow harm, and eek for hem that yow chacen and pursewen, and dooth bountee to hem that yow haten. Loo, thus comaundeth us oure lord Jhesu Crist to do to oure enemys. For soothly, nature

Now I will tell you of the remedy for this foul sin of envy. Firstly the love of God is the greatest and a man must love his neighbour as himself, for truly there cannot be one without the other. And you can be certain that in your neighbour you see your brother; for certainly we all have one earthly father and one mother–that is to say, Adam and Eve–and and also one spiritual father, and that is Almighty God. You are commanded to love your neighbour and wish for all goodness for him; and that is why God says, "Love your neighbour as yourself"–that is to say, for salvation of both life and soul. And moreover you will love him in words, and in gracious admonishing and chastisement, and comfort him in his troubles, and pray for him with all your heart. And in deeds you shall love him in such a way that you will treat him as as you would treat yourself. And so you will do him no damage with wicked words, nor harm to his body, nor to his possessions, nor his soul, by wicked examples. You shall not desire his wife nor any of his possessions. You must understand also that in the name of your neighbour you can see your enemy. Certainly, one must love your enemy, by the orders of God; and you shall also truly love your friend in God. I say, you shall love your enemy for the sake of God, through his commandment. Because if it was reasonable for a man to hate his enemy, truly God would not receive we who are enemies to his love. There are three wrongs that his enemy does to him, and he shall do three things in return, which are these: against hate and the angry heart, he will love him with his heart. Against criticism criticism and wicked words, he shall pray for for his enemy. Against the wicked deeds of his enemy, he shall do him good. For Christ says, "Love your enemies, and pray for those who speak against you, and also for those whom

dryveyh us to loven oure freends, and parfey, oure enemys han moore nede to love that oure freendes; and they that moore nede have, certes to hem shal men doon goodnesse; and certes, in thilke dede have we remembraunce of the love of Jhesu Crist that deyde for his enemys. And in as muche as thilke love is the moore grevous to perfourne, so muche is the moore gret the merite; and therfore the lovynge of oure enemy hath confounded the venym of the devel. For right as the devel is disconfited by humylitee, right so is he wounded to the deeth by love of oure enemy. Certes, thanne is love the medicine that casteth out the venym of envye fro mannes herte. The speces of this paas shullen be moore largely declared in hir chapitres folwynge.

you chase and persecute, and do good to those you hate." See, this is how our Lord Jesus Jesus Christ commands us to treat our enemies. For truly, nature makes us love our our friends, and indeed, our enemies have more need of love than our friends; and they who need more must have more, men should certainly be good to them; and certainly, in doing this we remember the love of Jesus Christ who died for his enemies. And inasmuch as this love is harder to do, so its merits are that much greater; and so loving our enemy confounds the poison of the devil. For just as the devil is upset by humility, so he is wounded to death by the love of our enemies. Certainly, then love is the medicine which drives the poison of envy from the hearts of men. The way in which this works will be more fully explained in the following chapters.

Wrath
§32 After Envye wol I discryven the synne Ire. For soothly, whoso hath envye upon his neighebor, anon he wole comunly fynde hym a matere of wratthe, in word or in dede, agayns hym to whom he hath envye. And as wel comth Ire of Pride, as of Envye; for soothly, he that is proud or envyous is lightly wrooth.

After envy I will describe the sin of anger. For truly, whoever is envious of his neighbour, he will soon find that he is angry, in word or deed, to him who he envies. And anger comes from pride as well as from envy, for truly he who is proud or envious is easily angered.

§33 This synne of ire, after the discryvyng of Seint Augustyn, is wikked wil to been avenged by word, or by dede. Ire, after the philosophre, is the fervent blood of man yquyked in his herte, thurgh which he wole harm to hym that he hateth. For certes, the herte of man, by eschawfynge and moevynge of his blood, wexeth so trouble that he is out of alle juggement of resoun. But ye shal understonde that Ire is in two maneres; that oon of hem is good, and that oother is wikked. The goode Ire is by jalousie of goodnesse, thurgh which a man is wrooth with wikkednesse and agayns wikkednesse; and therfore seith a wys man that Ire is bet than pley. This Ire is with debonairetee, and it is wrooth withouten bitternesse; nat wrooth agayns the man, but wrooth with the mysdede of the man, as seith the prophete David, "irascimini et nolite peccare." Now understondeth that wikked Ire is in two maneres; that is to seyn, sodeyn Ire or hastif Ire, withouten avisement and consentynge of resoun. The menyng and the sens of this is, that the resoun of a man ne consente nat to thilke sodeyn Ire; and thanne is it venial. Another Ire is ful wikked, that comth of felonie of herte avysed and cast biforn,

This sin of anger, according to the description of St Augustine, is a wicked desire to take revenge through words or deeds. Anger, according to Aristotle, is the hot blood of man brewing in his heart, through which he wishes to harm the one he hates. For certainly, the heart of man, through the heating and moving of his blood, becomes so troubled that he loses all reason. But you must understand that anger has two types; one of them is good, and the other is wicked. The good anger is the desire for good, through which a man becomes angry with wickedness and against wickedness; and so a wise man says that anger is better than leisure. This anger has grace, and it is without bitterness; it is not angry with the man, but with the misdeed of the man, as the prophet David said, "Be angry and do not not sin". Now you should understand that wicked anger has two types, that is to say, sudden anger or hasty anger, without thinking and without consulting reason. The meaning of this is that a man's reason does not agree with this sudden anger, and that is a venial sin.

with wikked wil to do vengeance, and therto his resoun consenteth; and soothly this is deedly synne. This Ire is so displesant to God that it troubleth his hous, and chaceth the hooly goost out of mannes soule, and wasteth and destroyeth the liknesse of God,- that is to seyn, the vertu that is in mannes soule, - and put in hym the liknesse of the devel, and bynymeth the man fro God, that is his rightful lord.

Another anger is very wicked, that comes with crime in the heart beforehand and preplanned, with a wicked will to take revenge, and so the reason of a man consents to it, and this is a deadly sin. This anger is so displeasing to God that it shakes his house and chases the Holy Ghost from the soul of a man, and lays waste to and destroys the likeness of God–that is to say, the virtue in the soul of man, and puts into him the likeness of the devil, and it takes away the man from God, who is his rightful lord.

§34 This Ire is a ful greet plesaunce to the devel; for it is the develes fourneys, that is eschawfed with the fir of helle. For certes, right so as fir is moore mighty to destroyen erthely thynges than any oother element, right so Ire is myghty to destroyen alle spiritueel thynges. Looke how that fir of smale gleedes, that been almost dede under asshen, wollen quike agayn when they been touched with brymstoon; right so Ire wol everemo quyken agayn, whan it is touched by the pride that is covered in mannes herte. For certes, fir ne may nat comen out of no thyng, but if it were first in the same thyng natureely, as fir is drawen out of flyntes with steel. And right so as pride is ofte tyme matere of Ire, right so is rancour norice and kepere of Ire. Ther is a maner tree, as seith seint Ysidre, that whan men maken fir of thilke tree, and covere the coles of with asshen, soothly the fir of it wol lasten a yeer or moore. And right so fareth it rancour; whan it is ones conceyved in the hertes of som men, certein, it wol lasten peraventure from oon estre day unto another estre day, and moore. But certes, thilke man is ful fer fro the mercy of God al thilke while.

This anger gives very much pleasure to the devil, for it is the devil's furnace, that is heated with the fire of hell. For certainly, just as fire is better at destroying earthly things than any other element, so anger is the best at destroying spiritual things. Look how a fire or small coals that are almost dead under the ashes will rekindle when they are touched with brimstone; just so anger will always rekindle again when it is touched by the fire that is hidden in the heart of a man. For certainly, fire cannot come from nothing, unless it was already naturally in the same thing, as fire is drawn out of flints with steel. And just as pride often causes anger, so so rancour also causes anger. There is a type of tree, so St Isidore says, and when men make a fire from this tree and cover its coals with ashes, truly the fire from it will last for a full or more. And this is the same with rancour; once it has been kindled in the hearts of some men, certainly it will last maybe from one day to another Easter day, and longer. But certainly, while this is going on the man will be very far from the mercy of God.

§35 In this forseyde develes fourneys ther forgen three shrewes: pride, that ay bloweth and encreesseth the fir by chidynge and wikked wordes; thanne stant envye, the holdeth the hoote iren upon the herte of man with a peire of longe toonges of long rancour; and thanne stant the synne of contumelie, or strif and cheeste, and batereth and forgeth by vileyns reprevynges. Certes, this cursed synne annoyeth bothe to the man hymself and eek to his neighebor. For soothly, almoost al the harm that any man dooth to his neighebor comth of wratthe. For certes, outrageous wratthe dooth al that evere the devel hym comaundeth; for he ne spareth neigher Crist ne his sweete mooder. And in his outrageous anger and Ire, allas! allas! ful many oon at that tyme feeleth in his herte ful

In the furnace of the devil which I have already mentioned there are three scoundrels working: pride, that always blows and increases the fire with its chiding and wicked words; then there is envy which places the hot iron in the heart of man with a pair of tongs made from rancour; then there is the sin of contentiousness, or quarrelling, which beats and forges with vulgar insults. Certainly, this horrible sin annoys both the man himself and his neighbour. For truly, almost all harm that a man does to his neighbour comes from anger. For certainly, outrageous anger does everything the devil tells it to, for he spares neither Christ nor his sweet mother. And in his outrageous anger–alas alas!–Many people

wikkedly, bothe of Crist and eek of alle his halwes. Is nat this a cursed vice? Yis, certes. Allas! it bynymeth from man his wit and his resoun, and al his debonaire lif espiritueel that sholde kepen his soule. Certes, it bynymeth eek goddes due lordshipe, and that is mannes soule, and the love of his neighebores. It stryveth eek alday agayn trouthe. It reveth hym the quiete of his herte, and subverteth his soule.

§36 Of Ire comen thise stynkynge engendrures: First, hate, that is oold wratthe; discord, thurgh which a man forsaketh his olde freend that he hath loved ful longe; and thanne cometh werre, and every manere of wrong that man dooth to his neighebor, in body or in catel. Of this cursed synne of Ire cometh eek manslaughtre. And understonde wel that homycide, that is manslaughtre, is in diverse wise. Som manere of homycide is spiritueel, and som is bodily. Spiritueel manslaughtre is in sixe thynges. First by hate, as seith Seint John: "he that hateth his brother is an homycide." Homycide is eek by babkbitynge, of whiche bakbiteres seith Salomon that "they han two swerdes with whiche they sleen hire neighebores. For soothly, as wikke is to bynyme his good name as his lyf. Homycide is eek in yevynge of wikked conseil by fraude; as for to yeven conseil to areysen wrongful custumes and taillages. Of whiche seith Salomon: "leon rorynge and bere hongry been like to the cruel lordshipes" in witholdynge or abreggynge of the shepe (or the hyre), or of the wages of sevauntz, or elles in usure, or in withdrawynge of the almesse of povre folk. For which the wise man seith, fedeth hym that almoost dyeth for honger; for soothly, but if thow feede hym, thou sleest hym; and alle thise been deedly synnes. Bodily manslaughtre is, whan thow sleest him with thy tonge in oother manere; as whan thou comandest to sleen a man, or elles yevest hym conseil to sleen a man. Manslaughtre in dede is in foure maneres. That oon is by lawe, right as a justice dampneth hym that is coupable to the deeth. But lat the justice be war that he do it rightfully, and that he do it nat for delit to spille blood, but for kepynge of rightwisnesse. Another homycide is that is doon for necessitee, as whan o man sleeth another is his defendaunt, and that he ne may noon ootherwise escape from his owene deeth. But certeinly if he may escape withouten slaughtre of his adversarie, and sleeth hym, he dooth synne and he shal bere penance as for deedly synne. Eek if a man, by caas or aventure, shete an arwe, or caste

feel wickedly disposed in their hearts to Christ and also his saints. Is this not a terrible vice? Yes, certainly. Alas! It takes intelligence and reason away from a man, and all his blessed spiritual life that should be guarding his soul. Certainly it takes away the recognition of the proper Lordship of God, which is a man's soul and the love of his neighbours. It also always fights against truth. It takes away from him the calm of his heart and overthrows his soul.

From anger there comes these stinking offspring: firstly, hate, that is ancient anger; discord, which makes a man abandon an old friend whom he has loved for a long time; then there is war and all these sorts of wrong that a man can do to his neighbour, to his body or his possessions. From this horrible sin of anger also comes manslaughter. You must understand that homicide, which is manslaughter, has various types. Some types of homicide are ordinary and some are spiritual. There are six types of spiritual manslaughter. Firstly there is hate, as St John says: "The man who hates his brother is a murderer." There is also a homicide by backbiting, Solomon says of such backbiters that "they have two swords with which they kill their neighbours." For truly, it is as wicked to take away the good name of a man as it is to take his life. It is also homicidal to give wicked advice through fraud, such as giving advice to impose wrongful rents and taxes. Solomon says of this, "The roaring lion lion and the hungry bear are similar to cruel lords" if they reduce or cut off payments or wages of servants, or otherwise lend money for interest, or do not give charity to poor people. Concerning this the wise man says, "Feed the one who is almost dying of hunger"; for truly, it lets you feed him, you will kill him; and these are all deadly sins. Bodily manslaughter is when you kill someone with your tongue in some way, such as when you give orders for someone to be killed, or otherwise give advice that a man should be killed. Manslaughter in deed comes in four types. One is through law, as when a judge sentences a guilty person to death. But the justice must make sure that he does it properly, and that he is doing it not for delight in spilling blood but in order to maintain the law. Another type of homicide is what is done out of necessity, as when one man kills another

a stoon, with which he sleeth a man, he is homycide. Eek if a womman by necligence overlyeth hire child in hir slepyng, it is homycide and deedly synne. Eek whan man destourbeth concepcioun of a child, and maketh a womman outher bareyne by drynkynge venenouse herbes thurgh which she may nat conceyve, or sleeth a child by drynkes wilfully, or elles putteth certeine material thynges in hire secree places to slee the child, or elles dooth unkyndely synne, by which man or womman shedeth hire nature in manere or in place ther as a child may nat be conceived, or elles if a woman have conceyved, and hurt hirself and sleeth the child, yet is it homycide. What seye we eek of wommen that mordren hir children for drede of worldly shame? Certes, an horrible homicide. Homycide is eek if a man approcheth to a womman by desir of lecherie, thurgh which the child is perissed, or elles smyteth a womman wityngly, thurgh which she leseth hir child. Alle thise been homycides and horrible deedly synnes. Yet comen ther of Ire manye mo synnes, as wel in word as in thoght and in dede; as he that arretteth upon God, or blameth God of thyng of which he is hymself gilty, or despiseth God and alle his halwes, as doon thise cursede hasardours in diverse contrees. This cursed synne doon they, whan they feelen in hir herte ful wikkedly of God and of his halwes. Also whan they treten unreverently the sacrement of the auter, thilke synne is so greet that unnethe may it been releessed, but that the mercy of God passeth alle his werkes; it is so greet, and he so benigne. Thanne comth of Ire attry angre.

in self defence when he could not otherwise escape death. But certainly, if he can escape killing his enemy, and he kills him, he is sinning and must do penance in the same way as for deadly sin. Also, if a man, by accident or chance, shoots an arrow, or throws a stone with which he kills a man, he is a homicide. Also, if a woman through her negligence smothers her child by rolling on it when she sleeps, that is homicide and a deadly sin. And a man prevents conception of a child, and makes a woman barren by making her drink poisonous herbs which means she cannot conceive, or deliberately kills a child by giving her drinks, or otherwise puts certain things in her secret places to kill the child, or otherwise does some unnatural sin, through which both men and women forget their true nature, in a way or in a place where a child cannot be conceived, or if a woman has conceived, and hurts herself and kills a child, that is homicide. And what do we say about women who murder their children because they dread shame in the world? Certainly, that is a horrible homicide. It is also homicide if a man approaches a woman, desiring lechery, and that kills the child, or otherwise deliberately hits a woman, which makes her lose their child. All these are homicides and horrible deadly sins. Yet there are many more sins which come from anger, in thought as well as in deed; such as the person who blames God, or blames God for something of which he himself is guilty, or despises God and all his saints, as cursed gamblers do in various countries. They do this cursed sin, when they feel very wicked in their hearts about God and his saints. Also when they treat the sacrament of the altar without reverence, this is such a great sin that it can hardly be forgiven, except through the mercy which God has in all his works; it is so great, and he is so gracious. Then poisonous anger comes from anger.

Whan a man is sharply amonested in his shrifte to forleten his synne, thanne wole he be angry, and answeren hokerly and angrily, and deffenden or excusen his synne by unstedefastnesse of his flessh; or elles he dide it for to holde compaignye with his felawes; or elles, he seith, the feend enticed hym; or elles he dide it for his youthe; or elles his compleccioun is so corageous that he may nat forbere; or elles it is his destinee, as he seith, unto a certein age; or eles, he seith, it

When a man is forcefully told in confession to abandon his sin, then he will be angry, and answer scornfully and angrily, and defend or excuse his sin by saying that his flesh is weak; or otherwise he did it in order to be the same as his friends; or otherwise, he says that the devil tempted him; or he did it because he was young; or else his temperament is so hot that he could not stop himself; or it was his fate, he says, at a certain age; or otherwise it comes

cometh hym of gentillesse of his auncestres; and semblable thynges. Alle thise manere of folk so wrappen hem in hir synnes that they ne wol nat delivere hemself. For soothly, no wight that excuseth hym wilfully of his synne may nat been delivered of his synne, til that he mekely biknoweth his synne. After this, thanne cometh sweryng, that is expres agayn the comandement of God; and this bifalleth ofte of anger and of Ire. God seith: "thow shalt nat take the name of thy lord God in veyn or in ydel." Also oure lord Jhesu Crist weith, by the word of Seint Mathew, "ne wol ye nat swere in alle manere; neither by hevene, for it is Goddes trone; ne by erthe, for it is the bench of his feet; ne by Jerusalem, for it is the citee of a greet kyng; ne by thyn heed, for thou mayst nat make an heer whit ne blak. But seyeth by youre word 'ye, ye,' and 'nay, nay'; and what that is moore, it is of yvel," - thus seith crist. For Cristes sake, ne swereth nat so synfully in dismembrynge of Crist by soule, herte, bones, and body. For certes, it semeth that ye thynke that the cursede jewes ne dismembred nat ynough the preciouse persone of Crist, but ye dismembre hym moore. And if so be that the lawe compelle yow to swere, thanne rule yow after the lawe of God in youre sweriyng, as seith Jeremye, quarto capitulo: "thou shalt kepe three condicions: thou shalt swere "in trouthe, in doom, and in rightwisnesse." This is to seyn, thou shalt swere sooth; for every lesynge is agayns Crist. For Crist is verray trouthe. And thynk wel this, that "every greet swerere nat compedded lawefully to swere, the wounde shal nat departe from his hous" whil he useth swich unleveful sweryng. Thou shalt sweren eek in doom, whan thou art constreyned by thy domesman to witnessen the trouthe. Eek thow shalt nat swere for envye, ne for favour, ne for meede, but for rightwisnesse, for declaracioun of it, to the worshipe of God and helpyng of thyne evene-cristene. And therefore every man that taketh goodes name in ydel, or falsly swereth with his mouth, or elles taketh on hym the name of Crist, to be called a cristen man, and lyveth agayns cristed lyvynge and his techynge, alle they taken Goddes name in ydel. Looke eek what Seint Peter seith, actuum, quarto, non est aliud nomen sub celo, etc., "ther nys noon oother name," seith Seint Peter, "under hevene yeven to men, in which they mowe be saved"; that is to seyn, but the name of Jhesu Crist. Take kep eek how precious is the name of Crist, as seith Seint Paul, ad philipenses, secundo, in nomine Jhesu, etc., "that in the name of Jhesu every knee of hevenely creatures, or erthely, or of helle sholde bowe," for it is so heigh and so

from his inheritance; and similar things. Always people wrap themselves up in their sins so that they cannot save themselves. For truly, no person who excuses himself often and obstinately can be saved until he humbly acknowledges that he has sinned. After this comes swearing, which is expressly against God's commandments; and this often happens due to wrath and anger. God says, "You shall not take the name of your Lord God in vain for idleness." Also our Lord Jesus Christ says, through St Matthew, "You will not swear in any fashion; neither by heaven, for it is the throne of God; nor by earth, for it is where he rests his feet; nor by Jerusalem, for it is the city of a great King; nor by your head, for you cannot change the colour of your hair. Let your yes be your yes and your no be your no, anything more is evil" –that is what Christ says. For the sake of Christ, do not sinfully swear in dismembering the soul of Christ, and his heart, his bones and his body. For certainly, it seems as though you think the cursed Jews did not tear the precious body of Christ enough, you have to tear him apart still further. And if it so happens that the law orders you to swear, then follow the laws of God as you swear, as Jeremiah says in his fourth chapter: you shall keep three conditions: you shall swear for truth, in a legal case, and for righteousness. That is to say, you shall swear what is truth, for every lie goes against Christ; for Christ is the truth. And think carefully about this: that "every great swearer, who is not legally forced to swear, the stain shall not leave his house" while he is unlawfully swearing. You can also swear in a legal case, when you are forced by the judge to bear witness to the truth. Also you must not swear for envy, nor for favour, nor reward, but for righteousness, to declare it, for the worship of God and to help your fellow Christians. And so every man who takes the name of God in vain, awfully swears, or otherwise uses the name of Christ, to be called a Christian man while he lives against the life and teaching of Christ, all of these people are taking the name of God in vain. Look what St Peter says in chapter four of Acts: "There is no other name given to men on earth through the name of Jesus Christ. Also observe how how precious the name of Jesus Christ is, as St Paul says, in the second chapter of the Epistle to the Philippians:

worshipful that the cursede feend in helle sholde tremblen to heeren it ynempned. Thanne semeth it that men that sweren so horribly by his blessed name, that they despise it moore booldely that dide the cursede jewes, or elles the devel, that trembleth when he heereth his name.

"in the name of Jesus every knee of heavenly creatures, or earthly ones, or of of hell should bow," for it is so high and worshipful that the cursed devil in hell will tremble when he hears it named. Then it seems if men swear so horribly by his blessed name that they are despising it more brazenly than the cursed Jews or the devil did, who tremble when they hear his name.

§37 Now certes, sith that sweryng, but if it be lawefully doon, is so heighly deffended, muche worse is forsweryng falsly, and yet nedelees.

Now certainly, since swearing, unless it is is legal, is so greatly forbidden, it is much worse to swear falsely, and it is needless.

§38 What seye we eek of hem that deliten hem in sweryng, and holden it a gentrie or a manly dede to swere grete others? And what of hem that of verray usage ne cesse nat to swere grete othes, al be the cause nat worth a straw? Certes, this is horrible synne. Swerynge sodeynly withoute avysement is eek a synne. But lat us go now to thilke horrible sweryng of adjuracioun and conjuracioun, as doon thise false enchauntours or nigromanciens in bacyns ful of water, or in a bright swerd, in a cercle, or in a fir, or in a shulderboon of a sheep. I kan nat seye but that they doon cursedly and dampnably agayns Crist and al the feith of hooly chirche. What seye we of hem that bileeven on divynailes, as by flight or by noyse of briddes, or of beestes, or by sort, by nigromancie, by dremes, by chirkynge of dores, or crakkynge of houses, by gnawynge of rattes, and swich manere wrecchednesse? Certes, al this thyng is deffended by God and by hooly chirche. For which they been acursed, til they come to amendement, that on swich filthe setten hire bileeve. Charmes for woundes or maladie of men or of beestes, if they taken any effect, it may be peraventure that God suffreth it, for folk sholden yeve the moore feith and reverence to his name. Now wol I speken of lesynges, which generally is fals signyficaunce of word, in entente to deceyven his evene-cristene. Som lesynge is of which ther comth noon avantage to no wight; and som lesynge turneth to the ese and profit of o man, and to disese and damage of another man. Another lesynge is for to saven his lyf of his catel. Another lesynge comth of delit for to lye, in which delit they wol forge a long tale, and peynten it with alle circumstaunces, where al the ground of the tale is fals. Som lesynge comth, for he wole sustene his word; and som lesynge comth of reccheleesnesse withouten avisement; and semblable thynges.

What do we say of those who take delight in swearing, and think it is a kind or a manly thing to swear great oaths? And what of them who off habitually continue to swear great oaths, even though the cause is worthless? Certainly, this is a horrible sin. Swearing suddenly without thinking is also a sin. But let us now go into this horrible swearing of exorcism and conjuring spirits, as those false enchanters or wizards do with basins full of water, or in a bright sword, in a circle, or in a fire, or in the shoulder bone of a sheep. I cannot say anything but that what they do is cursed and against Christ and the whole of the holy Church. What shall we say of those who believe in divination, seeing the future in the flight or noise of birds, or beasts, or of drawing lots, through wizardry, through dreams, through squeaking doors or creaking houses, by gnawing rats, and that sort of wretchedness? Certainly all these things are forbidden by God and his holy Church. Those who invest belief in such filth are cursed until illnesses of men or of beasts happen to work, it may perhaps be that God has allowed it, so that people should give more faith and worship to his name. Now I will speak of lies, which generally is giving false significance to words, with the intention of deceiving a fellow Christian. One sort of lie is one which brings no advantage to anybody; and some lies bring ease and profit to one man, and disease and damage to another. Another type of liar is one which attempts to save one's life or possessions. Another comes from delight in lying, in which delight he will make up a long story and decorate it with false details, when everything about the story is false. Some lies are told to back up what someone has said; and some come from recklessness

§39 Lat us now touche the vice of flaterynge, which ne comth nat gladly but for drede or for coveitise. Flaterye is generally wrongful preisynge. Flatereres been the develes norices, that norissen his children with milk losengerie. For sothe, Salomon seith that "flaterie is wors than detraccioun." For somtyme detraccion maketh an hauteyn man be the moore humble, for he dredeth detraccion; but certes flaterye, that maketh a man to enhauncen his herte and his contenance. Flatereres been the develes enchauntours; for they make a man to wene of hymself be lyk that he nys nat lyk. They been lyk to Judas that bitraysen a man to sellen hym to his enemy, that is to the devel. Flatereres been the develes chapelleyns, that syngen evere placebo. I rekene flaterie in the vices of Ire; for ofte tyme, if o man be wrooth with another, thanne wole he flatere som wight to sustene hym in his querele.

§40 Speke we now of swich cursynge as comth of irous herte. Malisoun generally may be seyd every maner power of harm. Swich cursynge bireveth man fro the regne of God, as seith Seint Paul. And ofte tyme swiche cursynge wrongfully retorneth agayn to hym that curseth, as a bryd that retorneth agayn to his owene nest. And over alle thyng men oghten eschewe to cursen hir children, and yeven to the devel hire engendrure, as ferforth as in hem is. Certes, it is greet peril and greet synne.

§41 Lat us thanne speken of chidynge and reproche, whiche been ful grete woundes in mannes herte, for they unsowen the semes of freendshipe in mannes herte. For certes, unnethes may a man pleynly been accorded with hym that hath hym openly revyled and repreved and disclaundred. This is a ful grisly synne, as Crist seith in the gospel. And taak kep now, that he that repreveth his neighebor, outher he repreveth hym by som harm of peyne that he hath on his body, as "mesel", "croked harlot", or by som synne that he dooth. Now if he repreve hym by harm of peyne, thanne turneth the repreve to Jhesu Crist, for peyne is sent by the rightwys sonde of God, and by his suffrance, be it meselrie, or maheym, or maladie. And if he repreve hym uncharitably of synne, as "thou holour," "thou dronkelewe harlot," and so forth, thanne aperteneth that to the rejoysynge of the devel, that evere hath joyde that men doon synne. And certes, chidynge may nat come but out of a vileyns herte.

without thinking, and suchlike things. Let us speak of the vice of flattery, which is not innate but comes from dread or covetousness. Flattery is generally praising the wrong things. Flatterers are the nurses of the devil, who nourishes children with the milk of deceit. For truly, Solomon says that, "Flattery is worse than criticism." For sometimes criticism makes a haughty man be more humble, for he dreads it, but certainly flattery, that will make a man's heart and his behaviour become proud. Flatterers are the enchanters of the devil; they make a man imagine he is something he is not. They are like Judas, betraying a man to sell him to his enemy; that is to the devil. Flatterers are the chaplains of the devil, who are forever singing "I shall please." I include flattery as one of the voices of anger, for often if a man is angry with another, then he will flatter some other person to gain his support in his dispute.

Now we shall speak of the cursing that comes from an angry heart. Cursing may generally be said to have every sort of power of harm. Such cursing takes a man away from the kingdom of God, as St Paul says. And often such cursing wrongfully comes back to the curser, like a bird returning to its nest. And above all men should avoid cursing their children, and giving their offspring to the devil, as much as they can. Certainly it is a great danger and a great sin.

Now let us speak of chiding and reproach, which are very wounding to the heart of man, for they tear the seams of friendship in the the heart of a man. Certainly, a man can hardly be fully reconciled with someone who has openly criticised and slandered him. This is a very horrid sin, as Christ says in the gospel. And observe now, that someone who criticises his neighbour, or criticises him due to some harm that has come to his body, such as calling him leper or crippled rascal, or because of some sin he does. If he criticises him for the pain he suffers, then the criticism is criticism of Jesus Christ, for pain is sent through the just order of God, and with his permission, whether it is leprosy, or bodily bodily injury, or illness. And if he criticises him uncharitably for sin, such as "you lecher, you drunken rascal" and so on, then he is celebrating the devil, who is always happy

For after the habundance of the herte speketh the mouth ful ofte. And ye shul understonde that looke, by the wey, whan any man shal chastise another, that he be war from chidynge or reprevynge. For trewely, but he be war, he may ful lightly quyken the fir of angre and of wratthe, which that he sholde quenche, and peraventure sleeth hym, which that he myghte chastise with benignitee. For as seith Salomon, "the amyable tonge is the tree of lyf," - that is to seyn, of lyf espiritueel; and soothly, a deslavee tonge sleeth spirites of hym that repreveth and eek of hym that is repreved. Loo, what seith Seint Augustyn: "ther is nothyng so lyk the develes child as he that ofte chideth." Seint Paul seith eek, "the servant of God bihoveth nat to chide." And how that chidynge be a vileyns thyng bitwixe alle manere folk, yet is it certes moost uncovenable bitwixe a man and his wyf; for there is nevere reste. And wherfore seith Salomon, "an hous that is uncovered and droppynge, and a chidynge wyf, been lyke." A man that is in a droppynge hous in manye places, though he eschewe the droppynge in a place, it droppeth on hym in another place. So fareth it by a chydynge wyf; but she chide hym in o place, she wol chide hym in another. And therfore, bettre is a morsel of breed with joye than an hous ful of delices with chidynge, seith Salomon. Seint Paul seith: "o ye wommen, be ye subgetes to youre housbondes as bihoveth in God, and ye men loveth youre wyves." Add colossenses, tertio.

when men sin. And certainly, criticism can only come from a vulgar hearts. For in proportion to the generosity of the heart the mouth speaks very often. And you shall understand, if you observe, when any man criticises another, that he must be careful of criticism or reproach. For truly, unless he is careful, he can very easily kindle the fire of anger and wrath, which he should quench, and perhaps he might kill the person whom he might chastise graciously. For as Solomon says, "The sweet tongue is the tree of life"–that is to say, of spiritual life–and truly, an unbridled tongue kills the spirits of the one who criticises and also the person who is criticised. See what St Augustine says: "There is nobody who is so like the child of the devil as somebody who often criticises." St Paul also says, "The servant of God should not criticise." And how that criticism is horrible between every sort of people, but it is certainly worse between a husband and his wife, for it will never rest. And so Solomon says, "A house that is without a roof and leaking and a nagging wife are the same thing." A man who has a house which leaks in many places, although he might avoid the drips in one place, it drips on him somewhere else. That is what it is like to have a criticising wife; if she doesn't nag him about one thing, she nags him about another. And so, "It is better to have a scrap of bread with joy than a house full of delicacies with criticism," says Solomon. St Paul says, "Oh you women, subject yourselves to your husbands as God orders, and you men must love your wives." This is in the Epistle to the Colossians, chapter three.

§42 Afterward speke we of scornynge, which is a wikked synne, and namely whan he scorneth a man for his goode werkes. For certes, swiche scorneres faren lyk the foule tode, that may nat endure to smelle the soote savour of the vyne whanne it florissheth. Thise scorneres been partyng felawes with the devel; for they han joye whan the devel wynneth, and sorwe whan he leseth. They been adversaries of Jhesu Crist, for they haten that he loveth, that is to seyn, salvacioun of soule.

Now let us speak of scorning, which is a wicked sin, and particularly when someone scorns a man for good works. For certainly, such scorn is awful like a foul toad, who cannot stand the sweet smelling savour of a flourishing vine. These scorners are equal partners with the devil; for they are happy when the devil wins and they are sad when he loses. They are enemies of Jesus Christ, for they hate the thing that he loves–that is, salvation of the soul.

§43 Speke we now of wikked conseil; for he that wikked conseil yeveth is a traytour. For he deceyveth hym that trusteth in hym, ut Achitofel

Now let us speak of wicked advice, for someone who gives wicked advice is a traitor, for he deceives the person who trusts him, as

ad Absolonem. But nathelees, yet is his wikked conseil first agayn hymself for, as seith the wise man, "every fals lyvynge hath this propertee in hymself, that he that wole anoye another man, he anoyeth first hymself." And men shul understonde that man shal nat taker his conseil of fals folk, ne of angry folk, or grevous folk, ne of folk that lovern specially to muchel hir owene profit, ne to muche worldly folk, namely in conseilynge of soules.

§44 Now comth the synne of hem that sowen and maken discord amounges folk, which is a synne that Crist hateth outrely. And no wonder is; for he deyde for to make concord. And moore shame do they to Crist, than dide they that hym crucifiede; for God loveth bettre that freendshipe be amonges folk, than he dide his owene body, the which that he yaf for unitee. Therfore been they likned to the devel, that evere is aboute to maken discord.

§45 Now comth the synne of double tonge; swiche as speken faire byforn folk, and wikkedly bihynde; or elles they maken semblant as though they speeke of good entencioun, or elles in game and pley, and yet they speke of wikked entente.

§46 Now comth biwreying of conseil, thurgh which a man is defamed; certes, unnethe may be restoore the damage. Now comth manace, that is an open folye; for he that ofte manaceth, he threteth moore than he may perfourne ful ofte tyme.

§47 Now cometh ydel wordes, that is withouten profit of hym that speketh tho wordes, and eek of hym that herkneth tho wordes. Or elles ydel wordes been tho that been nedelees, or withouten entente of natureel profit. And al be it that ydel wordes been somtyme venial synne, yet sholde men douten hem, for we shul yeve rekenynge of hem bifore God.

§48 Now comth janglynge, that may nat been withoute synne. And, as seith Salomon, "it is a sygne a apert folye." And therfore a philosophre seyde, whan men axed hym how that men sholde plese the peple, and he answerde "do manye goode werkes, and spek fewe jangles."

§49 After this comth the synne of japeres, that been the develes apes; for they maken folk to laughe at hire japerie as folk doon at the gawdes of an ape.

Achitofel did to Absolon. Nevertheless, in giving wicked advice he firstly harms himself. For, as the wise man says, "every false person alive has this property in himself, that if he will annoy another man, first of all he annoys himself." And men shall understand that a man should not take advice from false folk, nor from angry folk, nor hostile folk, nor folk that are too fond of their own profit, nor folk who are too worldly, giving advice to souls.

Now comes the sin of those who sow and cause discord amongst people, which is a sin that Christ utterly despises. And it is no wonder, for he died to have harmony. And they do more shame to Christ than the ones who had him crucified, for God loves amity amongst people more than he does his own body, which he gave to create it. So they are like the devil, who is always working to make discord.

Now comes the sin of the double tongue, which is when somebody speaks nicely to a person, and wickedly behind them, or otherwise they pretend they are speaking with good intent, or otherwise that there are joking, and yet they have wicked intentions.

Now comes the betraying of counsel, which makes a man horrible; certainly, he can hardly restore the damage he has done. Now comes menace, which is an open folly, for the person who menaces often, he often threatens more than he can do.

Now, idle words, which are of no profit to the person who speaks them, and also no use to to the one who listens to them. Or otherwise idle words are those that are needless and are not meant to be useful. And although idle words are sometimes a venial sin, men men must still fear them, for we will have to answer to God for them.

Now comes idle chattering, which can be a sin And, as Solomon says, "It is a sign of stupidity." And so a philosopher said, when men asked him how one should please others, he answered, "Do many good works, and speak a few idle words."

After this comes the sin of mockery, markers are the apes of the devil, for they persuade people to laugh at their mockery as they do

Swiche japes deffendeth Seint Paul. Looke how that vertuouse wordes and hooly conforten hem that travaillen in the service of Crist, right so conforten the vileyns wordes and knakkes of japeris hem that travaillen in the service of the devel. Thise been the synnes that comen of the tonge that comen of Ire and of othere synnes mo.

Sequitur remedium contra peccatum Ire
§50 The remedie agayns Ire is a vertu that men clepen mansuetude, that is debonairetee; and eek another vertu, that men callen pacience or suffrance.

§51 Debonairetee withdraweth and refreyneth the stirynges and the moevynges of mannes corage in his herte, in swich manere that they ne skippe nat out by angre ne by Ire. Suffrance suffreth swetely alle the anoyaunces and the wronges that men doon to man outward. Seint Jerome seith thus of debonairetee, that "it dooth noon harm to no wight ne seith; ne for noon harm that men doon or seyn, he ne eschawfeth nat agayns his resoun." This vertu somtyme comth of nature; for, as seith the philosophre, a man is a quyk thyng, by nature debonaire and tretable to goodnesse; but whan debonairetee is enformed of grace, thanne is it the moore worth.

§52 Pacience, that is another remedie agayns Ire, is a vertu that suffreth swetely every mannes goodnesse, and is nat wrooth for noon harm that is doon to hym. The philosophre seith that pacience is thilke vertu that suffreth debonairely alle the outrages of adversitee and every wikked word. This vertu maketh a man lyk to god, and maketh hym Goddes owene deere child, as seith grist. This vertu disconfiteth thyn enemy. And therfore seith the wise man, "if thow wolt venquysse thyn enemy, lerne to suffre." And thou shalt understonde that man suffreth foure manere of grevances in outward thynges, agayns the whiche foure he moot have foure manere of paciences.
§53 The firste grevance is of wikkede wordes. Thilke suffrede Jhesu Crist withouten grucchyng, ful paciently, whan the jewes despised and repreved hym ful ofte. Suffre thou therfore paciently; for the wise man seith, "if thou stryve with a fool, though the fool be wrooth or though he laughe, algate thou shalt have no reste." That oother grevance outward is to have damage of thy catel. Ther agayns suffred Crist ful paciently, whan he was despoyled of al that he hadde in this lyf, and that nas but his clothes. The thridde grevance is a

513

man to have harm in his body. That suffred crist ful paciently in al his passioun. The fourthe grevance is in outrageous labour in werkes. Wherfore I seye that folk that maken hir servantz to travaillen to grevously, or out of tyme, as on haly dayes, soothly they do greet synne. Heer-agayns suffred Crist ful paciently and taughte us pacience, whan he baar upon his blissed shulder the croys upon which he sholde uffren despitous deeth. Heere man men lerne to be pacient; for certes noght oonly Cristen men been pacient, for love of Jhesu Crist, and for gerdoun of the blisful lyf that is perdurable, but certes, the olde payens that nevere were Cristene, commendeden and useden the vertu of pacience.

§54 A philosophre upon a tyme, that wolde have beten his disciple for his grete trespas, for which he was greetly amoeved, broghte a yerde to scoure with the child; and whan this child saugh the yerde, he seyde to his maister, "what thenke ye do?" "I wol bete thee," quod the maister, "for thy correccioun." "For sothe," quod the child, "ye oghten first correcte youreself, that han lost al youre pacience for the gilt of a child." For sothe," quod the maister al wepynge, "thow seyst sooth. Have thow the yerde, my deere sone, and correcte me for myn impacience." Of pacience comth obedience, thurgh which a man is obedient to Crist and to alle hem to whiche he oghte to been obedient in Crist. And understond wel that obedience is perfit, whan that a man dooth gladly and hastily, with good herte entierly, al that he sholde do. Obedience generally is to perfourne the doctrine of God and of his sovereyns, to whiche hym oghte to ben obeisaunt in alle rightwisnesse.

Sloth
§55 After the synne of envye and of ire, now wol I speken of the synne of Accidie. For envye blyndeth the herte of a man, and ire troubleth a man, and Accidie maketh hym hevy, thoghtful, and wraw. Envye and ire maken bitternesse in herte, which bitternesse is mooder of Accidie, and bynymeth hym the love of alle goodnesse. Thanne is Accidie the angwissh of troubled herte; and Seint Augustyn seith, "it is anoy of goodnesse and joye of harm." Certes, this is a dampnable synne; for it dooth wrong to Jhesu Crist, in as muche as it bynymeth the service that men oghte doon to

Crist with alle diligence, as seith Salomon. But Accidie dooth no swich diligence. He dooth alle thyng with anoy, and with wrawnesse, slaknesse, and excusacioun, and with ydelnesse, and unlust; for which the book seith, "acursed be he that dooth the service of God necligently." Thanne is Accidie enemy to everich estaat of man; for certes, the estaat of man is in three maneres. Outher it is th'estaat of innocence, as was th'estaat of Adam biforn that he fil into synne, in which estaat he was holden to wirche as in heriynge and adowrynge of God. Another estaat is the estaat of synful men, in which estaat men been holden to laboure in preiynge to God for amendement of hire synnes, and that he wole graunte hem to arysen out of hir synnes. Another estaat is th'estaat of grace; in which estaat he is holden to werkes of penitence. And certes, to alle thise thynges is Accidie enemy and contrarie, for he loveth no bisynesse at al. Now certes, this foule synne, Accidie, is eek a ful greet enemy to the liflode of the body; for it ne hath no purveaunce agayn temporeel necessitee; for it forsleweth and forsluggeth and destroyeth alle goodes temporeles by reccheleesnesse.

§56 The fourthe thyng is that Accidie is lyk hem that been in the peyne of helle, by cause of hir slouthe and of hire hevynesse; for they that been dampned been so bounde that they ne may neither wel do ne wel thynke. Of Accidie comth first, that a man is anoyed and encombred for to doon any goodnesse, and maketh that God hath abhomynacion of swich Accidie, as seith Seint John.

§57 Now comth Slouthe, that wol nat suffre noon hardnesse ne no penaunce. For soothly, slouthe is so tendre and so delicaat, as seith Salomon, that he wol nat suffre noon hardnesse ne penaunce, and therfore he shendeth al that he dooth. Agayns this roten-herted synne of Accidie and slouthe sholde men exercise hemself to doon goode werkes, and manly and vertuously cacchen corage wel to doon, thynkynge that oure lord Jhesu Crist quiteth every good dede, be it never so lite. Usage of labour is a greet thyng, for it maketh, as seith Seint Bernard, the laborer to have stronge armes and harde synwes; and slouthe maketh hem feble and tendre. Thanne comth drede to bigynne to werke anye goode werkes. For certes, he that is enclyned to synne, hym thynketh it is so greet an emprise for to undertake to doon werkes of goodnesse, and casteth in his herte that the circumstances of goodnesse been so grevouse and so chargeaunt

service they ought to to Christ with their best efforts, as Solomon says. But sloth does no such work. He does everything with anger, distress, slowness, making excuses, idleness and disinclination; and the book says, "The one who does the service of God negligently is cursed." So sloth is the enemy to every state of man, for certainly there are three states of man. There is the state of innocence, which was the state of Adam before he sinned, and in that state he had to work as praise and adoration of God. Another state is the state of sinful men, and men in that state are obliged to work by praying to God to amend their sins, and to be forgiven from their sins. Another Another state is the state of grace, and in that state he has to work for penitence. And certainly, sloth is the enemy and antithesis of all these things, for he hates all work. Now certainly this foul sin is also a very great enemy against sustaining the body, for it does not make any preparation for the necessities of the world, it loses through delay and spoils through sluggishness and destroys all earthly goods through carelessness.

The fourth thing is that sloth makes men like those who are suffering in hell, because their sloth and their heaviness is like those who are damned, who are so burdened that they cannot either do or think well. Sloth is the first cause of a man being annoyed and prevented from doing good things, and that makes God hate sloth, as St John says.

Now we will talk of sloth that will not tolerate any hard treatment nor any penance. For truly, sloth is so tender and delicate, as Solomon says, that he cannot suffer any hardness or penance, and so he ruins everything he does. Men should occupy themselves with good works against this rotten hearted sin of sloth, and in a manly and virtuous way be determined to do well, remembering that our Lord Jesus Christ rewards every good deed, however small it is. Work is a great thing, for it makes, as Saint Bernard says, the labourer develop strong arms and hard muscles; sloth makes them feeble and tender. Then there is the dread of doing any good work. For certainly, someone who is inclined to sin, he thinks that doing good work is such a great effort, and he thinks in his heart that the circumstances of goodness

for to suffre, that he dar nat undertake to do werkes of goodnesse, as seith Seint Gregorie.

§58 Now comth wanhope, that is despeir of the mercy of God, that comth somtyme of to muche outrageous sorwe, and somtyme of to muche drede, ymaginynge that he hath doon so muche synne that it wol nat availlen hym, though he wolde repenten hym and forsake synne; thurgh which despeir or drede he abaundoneth al his herte to every maner synne, as seith Seint Augustin. Which dampnable synne, if that it continue unto his ende, it is cleped synnyng in the Hooly Goost. This horrible synne is so perilous that he that is despeired, ther nys no felonye ne no synne that he douteth for to do; as shewed wel by Judas. Certes, aboven alle synnes thanne is this synne moost displesant to crist, and moost adversarie. Soothly, he that despeireth hym is lyk the coward champious recreant, that seith, "creant" withoute nede, Allas! akkas! bedekes us he recreant and nedelees despeired. Certes, the mercy of God is evere redy to the penitent, and is aboven alle his werkes. Allas! kan a man nat bithynke hym on the gospel of Seint Luc, 15, where as Crist seith that "as wel shal ther be joye in hevene upon a synful man that dooth penitence, as upon nynty and nyne rightful men that neden no penitence." Looke forther, in the same gospel, the joye and the feeste of the goode man that hadde lost his sone, whan his sone with repentaunce was retourned to his fader. Kan they nat remembren hem eek that, as seith Seint Luc, 23, how that the theef that was hanged bisyde Jhesu Crist, seyde "lord, remembre of me, whan thow comest into thy regne? "For sothe," seyde Crist, "I seye to thee, to-day shaltow been with me in paradys." Certes, ther is noon so horrible synne of man that it ne may in his lyf be destroyed by penitence, thurgh vertu of the passion and of the deeth of Crist. Allas! what nedeth man thanne to been despeired, sith that his mercy so redy is and large? Axe and have. Thanne cometh sompnolence, that is, sloggy slombrynge, which maketh a man be hevy and dul in body and in soule; and this synne comth of slouthe. And certes, the tyme that, by wey of resoun, men sholde nat slepe, that is by the morwe, but if ther were cause resonable. For soothly, the morwe tyde is moost covenable a man to seye his preyeres, and for to thynken on God, and for to honoure God, and to yeven almesse to the povre that first cometh in the name of Crist. Lo, what seith

Salomon "whoso wolde by the morwe awaken and seke me, he shal fynde." Thanne cometh necligence, or reccheleesnesse, that rekketh of no thyng. And how that ignoraunce be mooder of alle harm, certes, necligence is the norice. Necligence ne dooth no fors, whan he shal doon a thyng, wheither he do it weel or baddely.

§59 Of the remedie of thise two synnes, as seith the wise man, that he that dredeth god, he spareth nat to doon that him oghte doon. And he that loveth god, he wol doon diligence to plese God by his werkes, and abaundone hymself, with al his myght, wel for to doon. Thanne comth ydelnesse, that is the yate of alle harmes. An ydel man is lyk to a place that hath no walles; the develes may entre on every syde, or sheten at hym at discovert, by temptacion on every syde. This ydelnesse is the thurrok of alle wikked and vileyns thoghtes, and of alle jangles, trufles, and of alle ordure. Certes, the hevene is yeven to hem that wol labourn, and nat to ydel folk. Eek David seith that "they ne been nat in the labour of men, ne they shul nat been whipped with men," that is to seyn, in purgatorie. Certes, thanne semeth it, they shul be tormented with the devel in helle, but if they doon penitence.

§60 Thanne comth the synne that men clepen tarditas, as whan a man is to laterede or tariynge, er he wole turne to God; and certes, that is a greet folie. He is lyk to hym that falleth in the dych, and wol nat arise. And this vice comth of a fals hope, that he thynketh that he shal lyve longe; but that hope faileth ful ofte.

§61 Thanne comth lachesse; that is he, that whan he biginneth any good werk, anon he shal forleten it and stynten; as doon they that han any wight to governe, and ne taken of hym namoore kep, anon as they fynden any contrarie or any anoy. Thise been the newe sheepherdes that leten hir sheep wityngly go renne to the wolf that is in the breres, or do no fors of hir owene governaunce. Of this comth poverte and destruccioun, bothe of spiritueel and temporeel thynges. Thanne comth a manere cooldnesse, that freseth al the herte of a man. Thanne comth devoccioun, thurgh which a man is so blent, as seith Seint Bernard, and hath swich languour in soule that he may neither rede ne singe in hooly chirche, ne heere ne thynke of no devoioun, ne travaille with his handes in no good werk, that it nys hym unsavory and al apalled. Thanne wexeth he slough and slombry, and soone wol be wrooth, and soone is enclyned to hate and to envye. Thanne comth the synne of worldly sorwe, swich as is cleped tristicia, that sleeth man, as seith Seint Paul. For certes, swich sorwe werketh to the deeth of the soule and of the body also; for therof comth that a man is anoyed of his owene lif. Wherfore swich sorwe shorteth ful ofte the lif of man, er that his tyme be come by wey of kynde.

Remedium contra peccatum Accidie
§62 Agayns this horrible synne of Accidie, an the branches of the same, ther is a vertu that is called fortitudo or strentthe, that is an affeccioun thurgh which a man despiseth anoyouse thinges. This vertu is so myghty and so vigerous that it dar withstonde myghtily and wisely kepen hymself fro perils that been wikked, and wrastle agayn the assautes of the devel. For it enhaunceth and enforceth the soule, right as Accidie abateth it and maketh it fieble. For this fortitudo may endure by long suffraunce the travailles that been covenable.

§63 This vertu hath manye speces; and the firste is cleped magnanimitee, that is to seyn, greet corage. For certes, ther bihoveth greet corage agains Accidie, lest that it ne swolwe the soule by the synne of sorwe, or destroye it by wanhope. This vertu maketh folk to undertake harde thynges and grevouse thynges, by hir owene wil, wisely and resonably. And for as muchel as the devel fighteth agayns a man moore by queyntise and by sleighte than by strengthe, therfore men shal withstonden hym by wit and by resoun and by discrecioun. Thanne arn ther the vertues of feith and hope in God and in his seintes, to acheve and acomplice the goode werkes in the whiche he purposeth fermely to continue. Thanne comth seuretee or sikernesse; and that is whan a man ne douteth no travaille in tyme comynge of the goode werkes that a man hath bigonne. Thanne comth magnificence, that is to seyn, whan a man dooth and perfourneth grete werkes of goodnesse; and that is the ende why that men sholde do goode werkes, for in the acomplissynge of grete goode werkes lith the grete gerdoun. Thanne is ther constaunce, that is, stablenesse of corage; and this sholde been in herte by stedefast feith, and in mouth, and in berynge, and in chiere, and in dede. Eke ther

can neither read nor sing in the holy Church nor hear nor think of any devotion, nor work with his hands in any good enterprise, everything to him is unsavoury and faded. Then he becomes slow and sleepy, and quick to anger, and will be quick to hate and to envy. Then there is the sin of worldly sorrow, which is called tristicia, as St Paul says. For certainly, this sorrow works for the death of the soul and the body also; for it causes a man to be annoyed with his own life. So sorrow very often shortens the life of a man, before his natural life is over.

The remedy for sloth
Against this horrible sinful sloth, and all types of it, there is a virtue called strength, through which a man can despise harmful things. This virtue is so great and so strong that it can withstand mightily and wisely keep away from wicked dangers, and wrestle with the assaults of the devil. For it enhances and strengthens the soul, just as sloth makes it weaker and lesser. For this strength can endure any suitable work.

This virtue has many types; the first is called magnanimity, which means, great bravery. For certainly, great bravery is needed to fight sloth, otherwise it will swallow the soul soul through the sin of sorrow, or destroy with despair. This virtue makes folk try to do hard and painful things, sensibly and intelligently, of their own volition. And inasmuch as the devil fights against men more with ingenuity and trickery than with strength, so men must withstand him through wit and reason and through discretion. Then there are the virtues of faith and hope in God and his saints to achieve and accomplish the good works which he faithfully plans to continue. Then comes security or self-confidence, which is when a man does not fear any suffering in doing good works in the future. Then there is magnificence, which is to say when a man does great good works; and that is why men should do good works, for the greater the work, the greater the reward. Then there is constancy, which means steadfast determination, and this should be represented in the heart by steadfast faith, and in speech, and bearing, and appearance and deed. There

been mo speciale remedies against Accidie in diverse werkes, and in consideracioun of the peynes of helle and of the joyes of hevene, and in the trust of the grace of the holy goost, that wole yeve hym myght to perfourne his goode entente.

are also other special ways of defeating sloth through different works, and in thinking of the pain of hell and the joy of heaven, and by placing trust in the grace of the Holy Ghost, they will give him the strength do his good works.

Avarice
§64 After accidie wol I speke of Avarice and of Coveitise, of which synne seith Seint Paul that "the roote of alle harmes is Coveitise." Ad thimotheum sexto. For soothly, whan the herte of a man is confounded in itself and troubled, and that the soule hath lost the confort of God, thane seketh he an ydel solas of worldly thynges. Avarice, after the descripcioun of Seint Augustyn, is a likerousnesse in herte to have erthely thynges. Som oother folk seyn that Avarice is for to purchacen manye erthely thynges, and no thyng yeve to hem that han nede. And understoond that Avarice ne stant nat oonly in lond ne catel, but somtyme in science and in glorie, and in every manere of outrageous thyng is Avarice and Coveitise. And the difference bitwixe Avarice and Coveitise is this: Coveitise is for to coveite swiche thynges as thou hast nat; and Avarice is for to withholde and kepe swiche thynges as thou hast, withoute rightful nede. Soothly, this Avarice is a synne that is ful dampnable; for al hooly writ curseth it, and speketh agayns that vice; for it dooth wrong to Jhesu Crist. For it bireveth hym the love that men to hym owen, and turneth it backward agayns alle resoun, and maketh that the avaricious man hath moore hope in his catel than in Jhesu Crist, and dooth moore observance in kepynge of his tresor than he dooth to the service of Jhesu Crist. And therfore seith Seint Paul ad ephesios, quinto, that an avaricious man is in the thraldom of ydolatrie.

After sloth I will speak of avarice and greed, of which sin St Paul says, "greed is the root of all evil." (In the sixth chapter of the Epistle to Timothy). For truly, when a man's heart is confused and troubled, and when his soul has lost the confidence of God, then he seeks idle solace in things of this world. Avarice, according to St Augustine, is an excessive desire in the heart to have the things of this earth. Some other folks say that greed is to purchase many earthly goods and not to give anything to those who are in need. You must understand that greed does not only refer to land and possessions, but sometimes to knowledge and glory, and every excessive thing involves avarice and greed. And the difference between avarice and greed is this: it is greedy to covet the things you do not have; to be avaricious is to hold onto the things which you have, of which you have no need. Truly, avarice is a very horrible sin, for all holy writings curse it and speak against it, for it wrongs Jesus Christ. For it takes the love that men owe him away, and takes away their reason, and makes the avaricious man think more of his possessions than he does of Jesus Christ, and he pays more attention to keeping his treasure than he does to serving Jesus Christ. And so St Paul says in the Epistle to the Ephesians, chapter five, that an avaricious man is an idolater.

§65 What difference is bitwixe an ydolastre and an avaricious man, but that an ydolastre, per aventure, ne hath but o mawmet or two, and the avaricious man hath manye? For certes, every floryn in his cofre is his mawmet. And certes, the synne of mawmettrie is the firste thyng that God deffended in the ten comaundementz as bereth witnesse in exodi capitulo vicesimo. Thou shalt have no false Goddes bifore me, ne thou shalt make to thee no grave thyng. Thus is an avaricious man, that loveth his tresor biforn God, an ydolastre, thurgh this cursed synne of Avarice. Of Coveitise comen thise harde lordshipes, thurgh whiche men been distreyned by taylages,

What difference is there between an idolater and an avaricious man, except that perhaps an idolater might have only a couple of idols, whereas an avaricious man has many? Certainly, every coin in his strongbox is his idol. And certainly idolatry is the first thing which God forbade in the ten Commandments, as we see in the twentieth chapter of Exodus: "You will have no false gods ahead of me, and you shall make no statues for yourself." So an avaricious man, who loves his treasure more than God, is an idolater, through his cursed sin of avarice. Greed causes these hard rulers, which makes men oppressed through taxes, custumes, and cariages, moore than hire duetee or resoun is. And eek taken they of hire boonde-men amercimentz, whiche myghten moore resonably ben cleped extorcions than amercimentz. Of whiche amercimentz and raunsonynge of boonde-men somme hordes stywards seyn that it is ryghtful, for as muche as a cherl hath no temporeel thyng that it ne is his lordes, as they seyn. But certes, thise lordshipes doon wrong that bireven hire bondefolk thynges that they nevere yave hem. Augustinus, De civitate, libro nono. Sooth is that the condicioun of thraldom and the firste cause of thraldom is for synne. Genesis nono. Thus may ye seen that the gilt disserveth thraldom, but nat nature. Wherfore thise lordes ne sholde nat muche glorifien hem in hir lordshipes, sith that by natureel condicion they been nat lordes over thralles, but that thraldom comth first by the desert of synne. And forther over, ther as the lawe seith that temporeel goodes of boonde-folk been the goodes of hir lordeshipes, ye, that is for to understonde, the goodes of the emperour, to deffenden hem in hir right, but nat for to robben hem ne reven hem. And therfore seith Seneca, "thy prudence sholde lyve benignely with thy thralles." Thilke that thou clepest thy thralles been Goddes peple; for humble folk been Cristes freendes; they been contubernyal with the lord.

rents and payments, more than their feudal duty, or any reasonableness, demands. And they also take payments from their bondsmen (in lieu of service) which could more reasonably be called extortion rather than than payment. These payments and forced payments of bondsmen some stewards say are legal, because they claim that no peasant has any earthly possessions, they all belong to his lord, they say. But certainly, these lords do wrong to take from their bondsmen things which they never gave them. In the ninth book of the City of God by St Augustine, he says "That is certainly slavery and the first cause of slavery is sin. You can see in the ninth chapter of Genesis that a man may deserve bondage through sin, but it is not natural." So these lords should not glorify themselves so much, since they are not naturally made to rule over their bondsmen, bondage only comes as punishment for sin. And furthermore, although the law says that all the earthly goods of bondsmen belong to their lords, what that means is that they are the goods of the Emperor, for him to defend, but he cannot rob them or take them from them. That is why Seneca says, "you should sensibly be kind to your bondsmen." Those whom you call your bondsmen are God's people, for humble folk are the friends of Christ; they are on familiar terms with the Lord.

§66 Thynk eek that of swich seed as cherles spryngen, of swich seed spryngen lordes. As wel may the cherl be saved as the lord. The same deeth that taketh the cherl, swich deeth taketh the lord. Wherfore I rede, do right so with the cherl, as thou woldest that thy lord dide with thee, if thou were in his plit. Every synful man is a cherl to synne. I rede thee, certes, that thou, lord, werke in swich wise with thy cherles that they rather love thee than drede. I woot wel ther is degree above degree, as reson is; and skile is that men do hir devoir ther as it is due; but certes, extorcions and despit of youre underlynges is dampnable.

Think also of the seed from which lowly people spring, lords come from the same seed. And a peasant can be saved just as well as a lord. The same death that comes for a peasant, this death comes for the lord. So I advise you, treat your subordinates just as you would wish your superiors to treat you, if you were in his place. Every sinful man is a peasant. I advise you, certainly, that you, lord, should rule in such a fashion that your serfs love you rather than fear you. I know that there is an order of things, as is reasonable, and it is reasonable that men should do their duty as they should, but certainly, extortion and contempt for your underlings is horrible.

§67 And forther over, understoond wel that thise conquerours or tirauntz maken ful ofte thralles of hem that been born of as roial blood as been they that hem conqueren. This name of thraldom was nevere erst kowth, til that Noe seyde that his sone Canaan sholde be thral to his bretheren for his

Furthermore, you must understand that these conquerors or tyrants very often make slaves of those who are just noble as themselves. Slavery was never known until Noah said that his son Ham should be in bondage to his brothers for his sins. What do we say then

synne. What seye we thanne of hem that pilen and doon extorcions to hooly chirche? Certes, the swerd that men yeven first to a knyght, whan he is newe dubbed, signifieth that he sholde deffenden hooly chirche, and nat robben it ne pilen it; and whoso dooth is traitour to Crist. And, as seith Seint Augustyn, they been the develes wolves that stranglen the sheep of Jhesu Crist; and doon worse than wolves. For soothly, whan the wolf hath ful his wombe, he stynteth to strangle sheep. But soothly, the pilours and destroyours of the Godes of hooly chirche no do nat so, for they ne stynte nevere to pile.

§68 Now as I have seyd, sith so is that synne was first cause of thraldom, thanne is it thus, that thilke tyme that al this world was in synne, thanne was al this world in thraldom and subjeccioun. But certes, sith the time of grace cam, God ordeyned that som folk sholde be moore heigh in estaat and in degree, and som folk moore lough, and that everich sholde be served in his estaat and in his degree. And therfore in somme contrees, ther they byen thralles, whan they han turned hem to the feith, they maken hire thralles free out of thraldom. And therfore, certes, the lord oweth to his man that the man oweth to his lord. The pope calleth hymself servant of the servantz of God; but for as muche as the estaat of hooly chirche ne myghte nat han be, ne the commune profit myghte nat han be kept, ne pees and rest in erthe, but if God hadde ordeyned that som men hadde hyer degree and som men lower, therfore was sovereyntee ordeyned, to kepe and mayntene and deffenden hire underlynges or hire subgetz in resoun, as ferforth as it lith in hire power, and nat to destroyen hem ne confounde. Wherfore I seye that thilke lordes that been lyk wolves, that devouren the possessiouns or the catel of povre folk wrongfully, withouten mercy or mesure, they shul receyven, by the same mesure that they han mesured to povre folk, the mercy of Jhesu Crist, but if it be amended. Now comth deciete bitwixe marchaunt and marchant. And thow shalt understonde that marchandise is in manye maneres; that oon is bodily, and that oother is goostly; that oon is honest and leveful, and that oother is deshonest and unleveful. Of thilke bodily marchandise that is leveful and honest is this that, there as God hath ordeyned that a regne or a contree is suffisaunt to hymself, thanne is it honest and leveful that of habundaunce of this contree, that men helpe another contree that is moore needy. And therfore ther moote been marchantz to bryngen fro that o contree to that oother hire

of those who rob and extort from the holy Church? Certainly, the sword that a knight is given when he is first created is to show that he should defend the holy Church, not rob or pillage it; whoever does that is a traitor to Christ. And, as St Augustine said, "They are the wolves of the devil if they destroy the sheep of Jesus Christ," and they are worse than wolves. For truly, when a wolf has had his fill, he stops killing sheep. But truly, the robbers and destroyers of the property of the holy Church do not, they never stop.

Now, as I have said, since sin was the first cause of bondage, this is how it is: have a time when all the world was sinning, then all the world was in bondage and subjection. But certainly, since the time of grace has come, God ordered that some folk should be higher in state and rank, and some folk lower, and that everyone should be treated according to his state and rank. And so in some countries, where slaves can be purchased, when they Christians, they free their slaves. And so, certainly, the lord owes his man what the man owes to his lord. The Pope calls himself the the servant of the servants of God; but because the holy Church might never have existed, and the common good could not have been kept, nor could there have been peace or rest on earth, unless God ordered that some men had higher rank and some lower, so a supreme power was ordained, to keep and maintain and defend their underlings and subjects in a reasonable fashion, as much as they were able, and not to destroy or harass them. So I say that these lords who are like wolves, who gobble up the possessions and belongings of poor folk wrongfully, without mercy or restraint, they will receive the same amount of mercy from Jesus Christ as they have given to the poor folk, unless they change their ways. Now we come to deceit between merchants. You must understand that merchandise has many types; there is bodily merchandise, and spiritual; one is honest and lawful, the other is dishonest and unlawful. Of the bodily merchandise that is lawful and honest there is this: that, where God has ordered for a kingdom or country to be well provided, then it is honest and lawful that from the abundance of this country, men should help another country that is more in

marchandises. That oother marchandise, that men haunten with fraude and trecherie and deceite, with lesynges and false othes, is cursed and dampnable. Espiritueel marchandise is proprely symonue, that is, ententif desir to byen thyng espiritueel, that is, thyng that aperteneth to the seintuarie of God and to cure of the soule. This desir, if so be that a man do his diligence to parfournen it, al be it that his desir ne take noon effect, yet is it to hym a deedly synne; and if he be ordred, he is irreguler. Certes symonye is cleped of Simon Magus, that wolde han boght for temporeel catel the yifte that God hadde yeven, by the Hooly Goost, to Seint Peter and to the apostles. And therfore understoond that bothe he that selleth and he that beyeth thynges espirituels been cleped symonyals, be it by catel, be it by procurynge, or by flesshly preyere of his freendes, flesshly freendes, or espiritueel freendes. Flesshly in two maneres; as by kynrede, or othere freendes. Soothly, if they praye for hym that is nat worthy and able, it is symonye, if he take the benefice; and if he be worthy and able, ther nys noon. That oother manere is whan men or wommen preyen for folk to avauncen hem, oonly for wikked flesshly affeccioun that they han unto the persone; and that is foul symonye. But certes, in service, for which men yeven thynges espirituels unto hir servauntz, it moot been understonde that the service moot been honest, and elles nat; and eek that it be withouten bargaynynge, and that the persone be able. For, as seith Seint Damasie, "alle the synnes of the world, at regard of this synne, arn as thyng of noght." For it is the gretteste synne that may be, after the synne of Lucifer and Antecrist. For by this synne God forleseth the chirche and the soule that he boghte with his precious blood, by hem that yeven chirches to hem that been nat digne. For they putten in theves that stelen the soules of Jhesu Crist and destroyen his patrymoyne. By swiche undigne preestes and curates han lewed men the lasse reverence of the sacramentz of hooly chirche; and swiche yeveres of chirches putten out the children of Crist, and putten into the chirche the develes owene sone. They sellen the soules that lambes sholde kepen to the wolf that strangleth hem. And therfore shul they nevere han part of the pasture of lambes, that is the blisse of hevene. Now comth hasardrie with his apurtenaunces, as tables and rafles, of which comth deceite, false othes, chidynges, and alle ravynes, blasphemynge and reneiynge of God, and hate of his neighebores, wast of goodes, mysspendynge of tyme, and

need. And so merchants must take their merchandise from one country to another. That other merchandise, that men trade in with fraud and treachery and deceit, with lies and false oaths, is cursed and damnable. Spiritual merchandise is simony, that is the eagerness to buy something spiritual; that is, something related to the sanctuary of God and to the care of the soul. This desire, if a man follows it through, although he will not get his desire, but it is a deadly sin; and if he is ordained, then he is going against the rules of his order. Simony is named after Simon Magus, who wanted to use earthly riches to buy the gift that God had given through the Holy Ghost to St Peter and the apostles. And so understand that the person who sells and the person who buys spiritual things are called simoniacs, whether through their wealth, through buying office for someone, or by purchasing worldly prayers from his friends, worldly or spiritual: worldly in two ways, by family relationship or friendship. Truly, praying for someone who is not worthy and suitable, that is simony, if he pays for it; and if he is worthy and suitable, it is not. The other type is when men or women pray for people to give them advancement, just due to the wicked fleshy affection they have for that person, and that is horrible simony. But certainly, in reward for service, when men give spiritual things to their servants, it must must be understood that the service must be honest; and also that there is no fraud in it, and that the person is suitable to receive it. For, as St Damasus says, "All the sins of the world are nothing, compared to this sin." For it is the greatest sin of all, after the sin of Lucifer and Antichrist. For through this sin God completely loses the church and soul that he purchased with his precious blood, due to people being given churches when they are not worthy. For they put thieves in place who steal the soul of Jesus Christ and destroy his legacy. Because of these unworthy priests and curates unlearned men have less respect for the sacraments of the holy Church, so people who give churches in this way drive out the children of Christ and put the son of the devil into the church. They sell the souls who should guard the lands to the wolf that will destroy them. And so they will never be be admitted to the pasture of the lambs, which is the bliss of heaven. Now we speak of

somtyme manslaughtre. Certes, hasardours ne mowe nat been withouten greet synne whiles they haunte that craft. Of Avarice comen eek lesynges, thefte, fals witnesse, and false othes. And ye shul understonde that thise been grete synnes, and expres agayn the comaundementz of God, as I have seyd. Fals witnesse is in word and eek in dede. In word, as for to bireve thy neighebores goode name by thy fals witnessyng, or bireven hym his catel or his heritage by thy fals witnessyng, whan thou for ire, or for meede, or for envye, berest fals witnesse, or accusest hym or excusest hym by thy fals witnesse, or elles excusest thyself falsly. Ware yow, questemongeres and notaries! Certes, for fals witnessyng was Susanna in ful gret sorwe and peyne, and many another mo. The synne of thefte is eek expres agayns Goddes heeste, and that in two maneres, corporeel or spiritueel. Corporeel, as for to take thy neighebores catel agayn his wyl, be it by force or by sleighte, be it by met or by mesure; by stelyng eek of false enditementz upon hym, and in borwynge of thy neighebores catel, in entente nevere to payen it agayn, and semblable thynges. Espiritueel thefte is sacrilege, that is to seyn, hurtynge of hooly thynges, or of thynges sacred to Crist, in two maneres - by reson of the hooly place, as chirches or chirche-hawes, for which every vileyns synne that men doon in swiche places may be cleped sacrilege, or every violence in the semblable places; also, they that withdrawen falsly the rightes that longen to hooly chirche. And pleynly and generally, sacrilege is to reven hooly thyng fro hooly place, or unhooly thyng out of hooly place, or hooly thing out of unhooly place.

Relevacio contra peccatum Avarice
§69 Now shul ye understonde that the releevynge of Avarice is misericorde, and pitee largely taken. And men myghten axe why that misericorde and pitee is releevynge of Avarice. Certes, the a vricious man sheweth no pitee ne misericorde to the nedeful man, for he deliteth hym in the kepynge of his tresor, and nat in the rescowynge ne releevynge of his evene-cristen. And therfore

speke I first of misericorde. Thanne is misericorde, as seith the philosophre, a vertu by which the corage of a man is stired by the mysese of hym that is mysesed. Upon which misericorde folweth pitee in parfournynge of charitable werkes of misericorde. And certes, thise thynges moeven a man to the misericorde of Jhesu Crist, that he yaf hymself for oure gilt, and suffred deeth for misericorde, and forgay us oure originale synnes, and therby relessed us fro the peynes of helle, and amenused the peynes of purgatorie by penitence, and yeveth grace wel to do, and atte laste the blisse of hevene. The speces of misericorde been, as for to lene and for to yeve, and to foryeven and relesse, and for to han pitee in herte and compassioun of the meschief of his evene-cristene, and eek to chastise, there as nede is. Another manere of remedie agayns Avarice is resonable largesse; but soothly, heere bihoveth the consideracioun of the grace of Jhesu Crist, and of his temporeel goodes, and eek of the goodes perdurables, that Crist yaf to us; and to han remembrance of the deeth that he shal receyve, he noot whanne, where, ne how; and eek that he shal forgon al that he hath, save oonly that he hath despended in goode werkes.

§70 But for as muche as som folk been unmesurable, men oghten eschue fool-largesse, that men clepen wast. Certes, he that is fool-large ne yeveth nat his catel, but he leseth is catel. Soothly, what thyng that he yeveth for veyne glorie, as to mynstrals and to folk, for to beren his renoun in the world, he hath synne therof, and noon almesse. Certes, he leseth foule his good, that ne seketh with the yifte of his good nothyng but synne. He is lyk to an hors that seketh rather to drynken drovy or trouble water than for to drynken water of the clere welle. And for as muchel as they yeven ther as they sholde nat yeven, to hem aperteneth thilke malisoun that Crist shal yeven at the day of doom to hem that shullen been dampned.

Gluttony
§71 After Avarice comth Glotonye, which is expres eek agayn the comandement of God. Glotonye is unmesurable appetit to ete or to drynke, or elles to doon ynogh to the unmesurable appetit and desordeynee coveitise to eten or to drynke. This synne corrumped al this world, as is wel shewed in the synne of Adam and of Eve. Looke eek what seith Seint Paul, of Glotonye "manye," seith Seint Paul, goon, of whiche I have

speak first of mercy. Mercy, as Aristotle says, is a virtue through which a man is moved by the distress of a person in distress. Pity follows mercy in the performance of charitable works of mercy. And certainly, in these things a man imitates the mercy of Jesus Christ, who gave himself for our sins, and suffered death so that we should have mercy, and forgave us our our original sins, and so released us from the pain of hell, and lessened the pain of Purgatory through penitence, and gives us the grace to do good, and ultimately the bliss of heaven. The types of mercy are generosity and giving, and forgiveness and releasing, and having pity in the heart and compassion for the suffering of a fellow Christian, and also to criticise, when there is need. Another remedy against avarice is reasonable generosity; truly, here we must consider the grace of Jesus Jesus Christ, and earthly goods, and also the eternal goods that he gave us; and we must remember the death we will receive, we do not know when or where or how; and so we will lose everything we have except what we have spent on good works.

But as some people are extravagant, men should avoid foolish generosity, which we call waste. Certainly, someone who is foolishly generous does not give his possessions, he loses them. Truly, anything that he gives for his own promotion, such as to minstrels and other people to keep his reputation in the world, that is a sin and he gets no credit for alms. Certainly, someone who only looks for sin with his wealth will lose his goods. He is like a horse that would rather drink dirty than drink from a clear well. And those who give in places where they should not, they shall be damned by Christ at the day day of judgement.

After avarice comes gluttony, which is also expressly against God's commandment. Gluttony is to have an immoderate appetite for food or drink, or to feed the immoderate appetite for food or drink. This sin corrupted the whole world, as was well demonstrated by the sins of Adam and Eve. See also what St Paul says about gluttony: "Many," says St Paul, "of whom I have often spoken to you,

ofte seyd to yow, and now I seye it wepynge, that been the enemys of the croys of Crist; of whiche the ende is deeth, and of whiche hire wombe is hire God, and hire glorie in confusioun of hem that so savouren erthely thynges. He that is usaunt to this synne of glotonye, he ne may no synne withstonde. He moot been in servage of alle vices, for it is the develes hoord ther he hideth hym and resteth. This synne hath manye speces. The firste is dronkenesse, that is the horrible sepulture of mannes resoun; and therfore, whan a man is dronken, he hath lost his resoun; and this is deedly synne. But soothly, whan that a man is nat wont to strong drynke, and peraventure ne knoweth nat the strengthe of the drynke, or hath feblesse in his heed, or hath travailed, thurgh which he drynketh the moore, al be he sodeynly caught with drynke, it is no deedly synne, but venyal. The seconde spece of glotonye is that the spirit of a man wexeth al trouble, for dronkenesse bireveth hym the discrecioun of his wit. The thridde spece of glotonye is whan a man devoureth his mete, and hath no rightful manere of etynge. The fourthe is whan, thurgh the grete habundaunce of his mete, the humours in his body been distempred. The fifthe is foryetelnesse by to muchel drynkynge; for which somtymee a man foryeteth er the morwe what he dide at even, or on the nyght biforn.

§72 In oother manere been distinct the speces of glotonye, after Seint Gregorie. The firste is for to ete biforn tyme to ete. The seconde is whan a man get hym to delicaat mete or drynke. The thridde is whan men taken to muche over mesure. The fourthe is curiositee, with greet entente to maken and apparaillen his mete. The fifthe is for to eten to gredily. Thise been the fyve fyngres of the develes hand, by whiche he draweth folk to synne.

Remedium contra peccatum Gule
§73 Agayns Glotonye is the remedie abstinence, as seith Galien; but that holde I nat meritorie, if he do it oonly for the heele of his body. Seint Augustyn wole that abstinence be doon for vertu and with pacience. "Abstinence," he seith, "is litel worth, but if a man have good wil therto, and but it be enforced by pacience and by charitee, and that men doon it for Godes sake, and in hope to have the blisse of hevene".

§74 The felawes of abstinence been attemperaunce, that holdeth the meene in alle

and I am weeping as I say it, our enemies of cross of Christ; they shall end in death, and there barely is there god, and they glory in the ruin of those who love earthly things." Someone who habitually commits this sin of gluttony, he cannot resist any sin. He must be a slave to all voices, for it is the hiding place of the devil, where he rests. This sin has many types. The 1st is drunkenness, that is the horrible grave of the reason of man; and so, a man is strong, he has lost his reason; and this is a deadly sin. But truly, when a man is not accustomed to strong drink, and perhaps does not know how strong the drink is, or has a weak head, or has been working, which has made him drink more, if he is suddenly caught by drink, that is not a deadly sin, but a venial one. The second type of gluttony is when a man becomes low spirited, for drunkenness takes away his intelligence. The third type of glass and me is when a man gobbles his food and does not eat in a reasonable manner. The fourth is when he gives himself poor health through eating too too much. The fifth is loss of memory because of too much drink, which sometimes makes a man forget before morning what he did in the evening, or on the previous night.

There is another way to define the types of gluttony, according to St Gregory. Firstly there is eating before it is a mealtime. Secondly there is being too picky over food or drink. Thirdly there is eating too much. Fourthly there is taking too much trouble over the preparation and elaboration of food. The fifth is to eat too greedily. These the five fingers of the hand of the devil, through which he draws men to sin.

The remedy for gluttony
The remedy for gluttony is abstinence, as Galen says; but I do not think that has merit, if it is only done for bodily health. St Augustine says that abstinence should be done for virtue, and patiently. "Abstinence," he says, "is worth nothing unless a man has goodwill, and unless it is backed up by patience and charity, and unless men do it for the sake of God, and in the hope of attaining the happiness of heaven."

The companions of abstinence are temperance, that holds the balance in all thynges; eek shame, that aschueth alle deshonestee; surfisance, that seketh no riche metes ne drynkes, ne dooth no fors of to outrageous appariailynge of mete; mesure also, that restreyneth by resoun the deslavee appetit of etynge; sobrenesse also, that restreyneth the outrage of drynke; sparynge also, that restreyneth the delacaat ese to sitte longe at his mete and softely, wherfore some folk stonden of hir owene wyl to eten at the lasse leyser.

Lust

§75 After Glotonye thanne comth Lecherie, for thise two synnes been so ny cosyns that ofte tyme they wol nat departe. God woot, this synne is ful displesaunt thyng to God; for he seyde hymself, "do no lecherie." And therfore he putte grete peynes agayns this synne in the olde lawe. If womman thral were taken in this synne, she sholde be beten with staves to the deeth; and if she were a gentil womman, she sholde be slayn with stones; and if she were a bisshoppes doghter, she sholde been brent, by Goddes comandement. Forther over, by the synne of lecherie God dreynte al the world at the diluge. And after that he brente fyve citees with thonder-leyt, and sak hem into helle.

§76 Now lat us speke thanne of thilke stynkynge synne of lecherie that men clepe avowtrie of wedded folk, that is to seyn, if that oon of hem be wedded, or elles bothe. Seint John seith that avowtiers shullen been in helle, in a stank brennynge of fyr and of brymston; in fyr, for hire lecherye; in brymston, for the stynk of hire ordure. Certes, the brekynge of this sacrement is an horrible thyng. It was maked of God hymself in paradys, and confermed by Jhesu Crist, as witnesseth Seint Mathew in the gospel: "a man shal lete fader and mooder, and taken hym to his wif, and they shullen be two in o flesh." This sacrement bitokneth the knyttynge togidre of Crist and of hooly chirche. And nat oonly that God forbad avowtrie in dede, but eek he comanded that thou sholdest nat coveite thy neighebores wyf. "In this heeste," seith Seint Augustyn, "is forboden alle manere coveitise to doon lecherie." Lo, what seith Seint Mathew in the gospel, that whose seeth a womman to coveitise of his lust, he hath doon lecherie with hire in his herte. Heere may ye seen that nat oonly the dede of this synne is forboden, but eek the desire to doon that synne. This cursed synne anoyeth grevousliche hem that it haunten. And first to hire soule, for he

---

things; also shame, that rejects all disgrace; satisfaction, that does not wish for rich food or drink, and does not want food excessively decorated; also moderation, that uses reason to rein in the unrestrained appetite; sobriety also, that stops excess of drink; frugality also, that stops excess of drink; frugality also, that stops a man from spending too long over his food in too much luxury, which is why some people will voluntarily stand to eat so it will take less time.

After gluttony comes lechery, things which are so close to each other that sometimes they can be separated. God knows that this is a sin whic is very displeasing to God, for he himself said, "Do no lechery." And so he created great great punishments for this sin in the ancient laws. If a bondswoman was caught committing this sin, she should be beaten to death with sticks; and if she were a gentlewoman, she should be killed with stones; and if she were a Bishop's daughter, she should be burned, by the commandment of God. Furthermore, it was the sin of lechery which caused God to drown the whole world in a flood. After that he burned five cities with lightning bolts, and sent them down to hell.

Now let us speak of that stinking sin of lechery which men call adultery by married folk; that is to say, if one of them is married, or both of them. St John says that adulterers shall go to hell, in a pool of burning fire and brimstone- fire for their lechery, brimstone because of the the stink of their filth. Certainly, breaking this commandment is a terrible thing. It was ordered by God himself in Paradise, and confirmed by Jesus Christ, as St Matthew tells us in the Gospel: "A man shall leave his father and mother and give himself to his wife, and they shall be of one flesh." This sacrament represents the joining together of Christ and the holy Church. And God did not only forbid adultery in deeds, but he also commanded that you must not covet the wife of your neighbour. "In this commandment," says St Augustine, "all desire to commit lechery is forbidden." See what St Matthew says in the Gospel, that "whenever a man desires a woman lustfully, he has committed lechery with her in his heart Here you can see that not only is committing this sin forbidden, but also the desire to do it. This horrid sin greatly pains those who

obligeth it to synne and to peyne of deeth that is perdurable. Unto the body anoyeth it grevously also, for it dreyeth hym, and wasteth him, and shent hym, and of his blood he maketh sacrifice to the feend of helle. It wasteth eek his catel and his substaunce. And certes, if it be a foul thyng a man to waste his catel on wommen, yet is it a fouler thyng whan that, for swich ordure, wommen dispenden upon men hir catel and substaunce. This synne, as seith the prophete, bireveth man and womman hir goode fame and al hire honour; and it is ful plesaunt to the devel, for therby wynneth he the mooste partie of this world. And right as a marchant deliteth hym moost in chaffare that he hath moost avantage of, right so deliteth the fend in this ordure.

commit it. Firstly it pains their soul, it commits to sin and to eternal death. It also annoys the body greviously, for it dries it out, and drains it, and ruins it, and makes his blood a sacrifice to the devil. It also wastes his cattle and possessions as well. And certainly, if it is a terrible thing for a man to throw away his possessions on women, it is still more horrid when, for filthy reasons, women spend their wealth on men. This sin, the prophet says, takes away from men and women their good reputation and all their honour, and it is very pleasing to the devil, for it helps him to win most of this world. And just as a merchant loves the business which brings him the best profit, so the devil loves this filth.

§77 This is that oother hand of the devel with fyve fyngres to cacche the peple to his vileynye. The firste fynger is the fool lookynge of the fool womman and of the fool man, that sleeth, right as the basilicok sleeth folk by the venym of his sighte; for the coveitise of eyen folweth the coveitise of the herte. The seconde fynger is the vileyns touchynge in wikkede manere. And therfore seith Salomon that whoso toucheth and handleth a womman, he fareth lyk hym that handleth the scorpioun that styngeth and sodeynly sleeth thurgh his envenymynge; as whoso toucheth warm pych, it shent his fyngres. The thridde is foule wordes, that fareth lyk fyr, that right anon brenneth the herte. The fourthe fynger is the kissynge; and trewely he were a greet fool that wolde kisse the mouth of a brennynge oven or of a fourneys. And moore fooles been they that kissen in vileynye, for that mouth is the mouth of helle; and namely thise olde dotardes holours, yet wol they kisse, though they may nat do, and smatre hem. Certes, they been lyk to houndes; for an hound, whan he comth by the roser or by othere (bushes), though he may nat pisse, yet wole he heve up his leg and make a contenaunce to pisse. And for that many man weneth that he may nat synne, for no likerousnesse that he dooth with his wyf, certes, that opinion is fals. God woot, a man may sleen hymself with his owene knyf, and make hymselve dronken of his owene tonne. Certes, be it wyf, be it child, or any worldly thyng that he loveth biforn God, it is his mawmet, and he is an ydolastre. Man sholde loven hys wyf by discrecioun, paciently and atemprely; and thanne is she as though it were his suster. The fifthe fynger of the develes hand is the stynkynge dede of leccherie.

That is the other hand of the devil with five fingers to catch people and turn them to his villainy. The first finger is the foolish looks of the foolish woman and foolish man; it kills, just as a basilisk kills folk with his poisonous sight, for the desire of the eyes follows the desire of the heart. The second finger is a vulgar touching in a wicked fashion. That is why Solomon says that "whoever touches and handles a woman, he will be treated like one who handles a stinging scorpion which suddenly kills with its poison"; like whoever touches warm tar, he will injure his fingers. The third is foul words, that are like fire and burn the heart at once. The fourth finger is kissing, and it would be a great fool who would kiss the mouth of a hot oven or a furnace. Those who kiss when doing this are even greater fools, for the mouth is the mouth of hell; and particularly that of these old lechers, who wish to kiss, even if they can't, and they foul themselves. Certainly, they are like dogs; for when a dog, when he passes a rose bush or any other sort, although he cannot piss, he will lift up his leg and act as if pissing. And because of that many men think that he cannot commit the sin of lechery with his wife, but he is wrong. God knows, a man can kill himself with his own knife, and he can drink from his own barrel. Certainly, whether it is a wife, a child, or any earthly thing that he loves before God, he makes it his idol, and he is therefore an idolater. A man should love his wife with discretion, patiently and moderately, and treat her as though she

Certes, the fyve fyngres of glotonie the feend put in the wombe of a man, and with his fyve fingres of lecherie he gripeth hym by the reynes, for to throwen hym into the fourneys of helle. Ther as they shul han the fyr and the wormes that evere shul lasten, and wepynge and wailynge sharp hunger and thurst, and grymnesse of develes, that shullen al totrede hem without repit and withouten ende.

Of leccherie, as I seyde, sourden diverse speces, as fornicacioun, that is bitwixe man and womman that been nat maried; and this is deedly synne, and agayns nature. Al that is enemy and destruccioun to nature is agayns nature. Parfay, the resoun of a man telleth eek hym wel that is is deedly synne, for as muche as God forbad leccherie. And Seint Paul yeveth hem the regne that nys dewe to no wight but to hem that doon deedly synne. Another synne of leccherie is to bireve a mayden of hir maydenhede, for he that so dooth, certes, he casteth a mayden out of the hyeste degree that is in this present lif, and bireveth hir thilke precious fruyt that the book clepeth the hundred fruyt. I ne kan seye it noon oother-wewyes in englissh, but in latyn it highte centesimus fructus. Certes, he that so dooth is cause of manye damages and vileynyes, mo than any man kan rekene; right as he somtyme is cause of alle damages that beestes don in the feeld, that breketh the hegge or the closure, thurgh which he destroyeth that may nat been restoored. For certes, namoore may maydenhede be restoored than a arm that is smyten fro the body may retourne agany to wexe. She may have mercy, this woot I wel, if she do penitence; but nevere shal it be that she nas corrupt. And al be it so that I have spoken somwhat of avowtrie, it is good to shewen mo perils that longen to avowtrie, for to eschue that foule synne. Avowtrie in latyn is for to seyn, approchynge of oother mannes bed, thurgh which tho that whilom weren a flessh abowndone hir bodyes to other persones. Of this synne, as seith the wise man, folwen manye harmes. First, brekynge of feith; and certes, in feith is the keye of cristendom. And whan that feith is broken and lorn, soothly cristendom stant veyn and withouten fruyt. This synne is eek a thefte; for thefte generally is for to reve a wight his thyng agayns his wille. Certes, this is the fouleste thefte that may be, whan a womman steleth hir body from hir housbonde, and yeveth it to hire holour to defoulen hire; and steleth hir soule fro Crist, and

were his sister. The fifth finger of the Devil's hand is the revolting deed of lechery. With the five fingers of gluttony the devil grabs the belly of a man, and with the five fingers of lechery he grabs him by the groin to throw him into the furnace of hell, where they will suffer fire and worms eternally, and weeping and wailing, sharp hunger and thirst, fierce devils, who will trample all of them without mercy for eternity.

As I said, there are various forms of lechery, such as fornication, between a man and a woman who are not married, and that is a deadly sin and unnatural. Everything that is an enemy of or destroys nature is against nature. Indeed, a man should be able to reason with himself that this is a deadly sin, because God forbade lechery. And St Paul puts them in the category where nobody goes except those who do deadly sin. Another sin of lechery is to take a girl's virginity, for the one who does so, certainly, he throws a maiden down from the highest rank in earthly life and takes from her that precious fruit which the book calls the hundredfold fruit. I can't say it any differently in English, but in Latin it is called Centesimus Fructus. Certainly the one who does so is the cause of much damage and villainy, more than any man can perceive; just as someone who breaks through a hedge or fence can sometimes be the cause of all the damage that beasts do in the field, and he destroys that which cannot be restored. For certainly, virginity cannot be restored any more than an arm cut off from the body can be made to grow again. She may receive mercy, certainly, if she is penitent; but she will never again be uncorrupted. And although I have spoken already something about adultery, it is good to show more dangers that go with adultery, so that you will shun that horrible sin. Adultery in Latin means going to the bed of another man, when those who once were were one flesh give their bodies to other people. As the wise man says, many harms come from this end. Firstly, breaking faith, and certainly faith is the cornerstone of Christianity. And when faith is broken and lost, truly Christianity is empty and fruitless. This sin is also a theft, for it is theft to deprive a person of his property without his permission. Certainly, this is the most horrible theft there can be, when a woman steals her

yeveth it to the devel. This is a fouler thefte than for to breke a chirche and stele the chalice; for thise avowtiers breken the temple of God spiritually and stelen the vessel of grace, that is the body and the soule, for which Crist shal destroyen hem, as seith Seint Paul. Soothly, of this thefte douted gretly Joseph, whan that his lordes wyf preyed hym of vileynye, whan he seyde, "lo, my lady, how my lord hath take to me under my warde al that he hath in this world, ne no thyng of his thynges is out of my power, but oonly ye, that been his wyf. And how sholde I thanne do this wikkednesse, and synne so horribly agayns God and agayns my lord? God it forbeede!" Allas! al to litel is swich trouthe now yfounde. The thridde harm is the filthe thurgh which they breken the comandement of God, and defoulen the auctour of matrimoyne, that is Crist. For certes, in so muche as the sacrement of mariage is so noble and so digne, so muche is it gretter synne for to breken it; for God made mariage in paradys, in the estaat of innocence, to multiplye mankynde to the service of God. And therfore is the brekynge therof the moore grevous; of which brekynge comen false heires ofte tyme, that wrongfully ocupien folkes heritages. And therfore wol Crist putte hem out of the regne of hevene, that is heritage to goode folk. Of this brekynge comth eek ofte tyme that folk unwar wedden or synnen with hire owene kynrede, and namely thilke harlotes that haunten bordels of thise fool wommen, that mowe be likned to a commune gong, where as men purgen hire ordure. What seve we eek of putours that lyven by the horrible synne of putrie, and constreyne wommen to yelden hem a certeyn rente of hire bodily puterie, ye, somtyme of his owene wyf or his child, as doon thise bawdes? Certes, thise been cursede synnes. Understoond eek that avowtrie is set gladly in the ten comandementz bitwixe thefte and manslaughtre; for it is the gretteste thefte that may be, for it is thefte of body and of soule. And it is lyk to homycide, for it herveth atwo and breketh atwo hem that first were maked o flessh. And therfore, by the olde lawe of God, they sholde by slayn. But nathelees, by the lawe of Jhesu Crist, that is lawe of pitee, whan he seyde to the womman that was founden in avowtrie, and sholde han been slayn with stones, after the wyl of the Jewes, as was hir lawe, "go," quod Jhesu Crist, "and have namoore wyl to synne, or, wille namoore to do synne. Soothly the vengeaunce of avowtrie is awarded to the peynes of helle, but if so be that it be destourbed by penitence. Yet been ther mo speces of this cursed synne; as whan that oon of hem is

body away from her husband and gives it to an adulterer to soil her, and she steals her soul from Christ and gives it to the devil. This is worse than breaking into a church and stealing the chalice, for these adulterers are breaking into the spiritual temple of God, and stealing the vessel of grace, the body and soul, and Christ shall destroy them for it, as St Paul says. Truly, Joseph was very afraid of this theft, when the wife of his Lord asked him to sin with her, when he said, "See, my lady, my lord has given me command over everything he has in this world, and all of his possessions are in my power, except for you, who are his wife. How could I then do this wicked thing, sinning so horribly against God and my lord? God forbid!" Alas, such faithfulness is now all too uncommon. The third harm is the filth through which they break God's commandment, and soil the originator of matrimony, who is Christ. Certainly, as the sacrament of marriage is so noble and worthy, it is that much greater sin to break it, for God made marriage in paradise, in the state of innocence, to make man multiply so that they could serve God. And so breaking that sacrament is all the worse; and from that breaking sometimes there will come false heirs, who wrongfully claim other people's inheritance. And so Christ will not allow them the kingdom of heaven, which is the inheritance of good people. Due to this breaking sometimes folk marry or sin with their own family, not knowing it, particularly those men who frequent brothels with these foolish women, which must be likened to a common lavatory, where men purge themselves of their filth. What should we say of pimps who live through the horrible sin of prostitution, and make women pay them a certain percentage of the money they get through prostitution, sometimes using his own wife or his child, as these bawds do? Certainly, these are horrible sins. You should understand also that adultery is usually placed in the ten commandments between theft and and manslaughter; for it is the worst theft imaginable, for it steals away body and soul. And it is similar to murder, for it carves in two and separates those who originally were of one flesh. And so, through the ancient law of God, they should be slain. However, by the Lord Jesus Christ, that is the law of pity, when he said to the woman who was caught

religious, or elles bothe; or of folk that been entred into ordre, as subdekne, or dekne, or preest, or hospitaliers. And evere the hyer that he is in ordre, the gretter is the synne. The thynges that gretly agreggen hire synne is the brekynge of hire avow of chastitee, whan they receyved the ordre. And forther over, sooth is that hooly ordre is chief of al the tresorie of good, and his especial signe and mark of chastitee, to shewe that they been joyned to chastitee, which that is the moost precious lyf that is. And thise ordred folk been specially titled to God, and of the special meignee of God, for which, whan they doon deedly synne, they been the special traytours of God and of his peple; for they lyven of the peple, to preye for the peple, and while they been suche traitours, here preyer avayleth nat to the peple.

committing adultery, and should have been killed with stones, as the Jews wanted to according to their law, "Go," said Jesus Christ, "and sin no more." Truly adultery is punished with the pains of hell, unless penitence intervenes. But there are more types of this horrible sin; such as when one of them is in a religious order, or both of them; or if they are in holy orders, such as being subdeacons, deacons, priests or Knights Hospitallers. And the higher somebody is in holy orders, the worse the sin is. The thing which makes their sin so much worse is that they break their vow of chastity, which they took when they joined their order. Furthermore, the holy orders are the greatest treasure which God possesses and their sign of chastity is to show that they are living a chaste life, which is the most precious life of all. And these folk who are ordained are especially dedicated to God, and they are part of the special household of God, and when they do deadly sins, they are especially traitorous to God and his people; because they live off the people, to pray for the people, and when they are traitors in this way, their prayer does no good for the people.

Preestes been aungels, as by the dignitee of hir mysterye; but for sothe, Seint Paul seith that Sathanas transformeth hym in an aungel of light. Soothly, the preest that haunteth deedly synne, he may be likned to the aungel of derknesse transformed in the aungel of light. He semeth aungel of light, but for sothe he is aungel of derknesse. Swiche preestes been the sones of helie, as sweweth in the book of kynges, that they weren the sones of Belial, that is the devel. Belial is to seyn, "withouten juge"; and so faren they; hem thynketh they been free, and han no juge, namoore than hath a free bole that taketh which cow that hym liketh in the town. So faren they by wommen. For right as a free bole is ynough for al a toun, right so is a wikked preest corrupcioun ynough for al a parisshe, or for al a contree. Thise preestes, as seith the book, ne konne nat the mysterie of preesthod to the peple, ne God ne knowe they nat. They ne helde hem nat apayd, as seith the book, of soden flessh that was to hem offred, but they tooke by force the flessh that is rawe. Certes, so thise shrewes ne holden hem nat apayd of roosted flessh and sode flessh, with which the peple feden hem in greet reverence, but they wole have raw flessh of folkes wyves and hir

Priests are angels, due to their profession; but truly, St Paul says that Satan can transform himself into an angel of light. Truly, the priest who practices deadly sins, he is like an angel of darkness changed into an angel of light. He looks like an angel of light, but truly he is an angel of darkness. These are priests who are like the sons of Belial, as shown in the Book of Kings—that is to say, the devil. Belial means "without yoke." And this is what they are like; it seems to them that they are free and unyoked, just as a bull who runs free and takes whichever cow he wants in the town. That's what they are like with women. For just one free bull is enough for a whole town, so a a wicked priest is enough to corrupt a whole parish, or a whole country. These priests, as the book says, do not know what a priest should do for the people, and they do not know God. They were not satisfied, as the book says, by the cooked meat that was offered to them, but by force they took the meat that was raw. Certainly, these rascals do not feel satisfied by roast meat or boiled meat, which the people feed then with great respect, but they wish for the raw flesh of people's wives and

doghtres. And certes, thise wommen that consenten to hire harlotrie doon greet wrong to Crist, and to hooly chirche, and alle halwes, and to alle soules; for they bireven alle thise hym that sholde worshipe Crist and hooly chirche, and preye for Cristene soules. And therfore han swiche preestes, and hire lemmanes eek that consenten to hir leccherie, the malisoun of al the court Cristien, til they come to amendement. The thridde spece of avowtrie is somtyme bitwixe a man and his wyf, and that is whan they take no reward in hire assemblynge but oonly to hire flesshly delit, as seith Seint Jerome, and ne rekken of nothyng but that they been assembled; by cause that they been maried, al is good ynough, as thynketh to hem. But in swich folk hath the devel power, as seyde the aungel Raphael to Thobie, for in hire assemblynge they putten Jhesu Crist out of hire herte, and yeven hemself to alle ordure. The fourthe spece is the assemblee of hem that been of hire kynrede, or of hem that been of oon affynytee, or elles with hem with whiche hir fadres or hir kynrede han deled in the synne of lecherie. This synne maketh hem lyk to houndes, that taken no kep to kynrede. And certes, parentele is in two maneres, outher goostly or flesshly; goostly, as for to deelen with his god-sibbes. For right so as he that engendreth a child is his flesshly fader, right so in his god-fader his fader espiritueel. For which a womman may in no lasse synne assemblen with hire godsib than with hire owene flesshly brother. The fifthe spece is thilke abhomynable synne, of which that no man unnethe oghte speke ne write; nathelees it is openly reherced in holy writ. This cursednesse doon men and wommen in diverse entente and in diverse manere; but though that hooly writ speke of horrible synne, certes hooly writ may nat been defouled, namoore than the sonne that shyneth on the mixne. Another synne aperteneth to leccherie, that comth in slepynge, and this synne cometh ofte to hem that been maydenes, and eek to hem that been corrupt; and this synne men clepen polucioun, that comth in foure maneres. Somtyme of langwissynge of body, for the humours been to ranke and to habundaunt in the body of man; somtyme of infermetee, for the fieblesse of the vertu retentif, as phisik maketh mencion; somtyme for surfeet of mete and drynke; and somtyme of vileyns thoghtes that been enclosed in mannes mynde whan he gooth to slepe, which may nat been withoute synne; for which men moste kepen hem wisely, or elles may men synnen ful grevously.

their daughters. And certainly, these women who agree to their lechery are severely wronging Christ, and the holy Church, and all the saints, and all souls; for they take away from Christ all those who should worship him and the holy church and pray for the souls of Christians. And so these priests, and the lovers that agree to their lechery, are the curse of the whole ecclesiastical court, until they change their ways. The third type of adultery is what happens sometimes between a man and his wife, and that is when they have intercourse thinking only of their fleshly pleasures, as St Jerome says, and all they are thinking about is that they have had intercourse; because they are married, they think that everything is good enough. But the devil has power over such folk, as the angel Raphael said to Tobias, for when they are committing intercourse they put Jesus Christ out of their heart and give themselves over to filth. The fourth type of intercourse of those who are related by blood, or related by marriage, all those who have been lecherous with their fathers or kinsmen. This sin makes them like dogs, who don't care about kinship. And certainly, there are two types of kinship, spiritual or fleshy; spiritual such as having dealings with the children of one's godparents. For just as someone who procreates a child is the father of his flesh, so his godfather is his spiritual father. So a woman having intercourse with her spiritual kinsman is just as sinful as if she was doing it with her actual brother. The fifth type of sin is that horrible sin which no man should hardly be able to speak of or write; but it is openly spoken of in holy writ. This cursed thing men and women do for different reasons and in different ways; but although the holy writ speaks of horrible sin, it cannot be befouled, any more than the sun can when it shines on a dunghill. Another sin of lechery comes through sleeping, and this sin often comes to those who are virgins, and also those who are corrupt; and men call this sin pollution, which comes in four types. Sometimes it can come from weakness of the body, when the humours are too abundant in the body of a man; sometimes from infirmity, when the man is too feeble to retain his fluid, as medical science as noted; sometimes through an excess of food and drink; and sometimes through vulgar thoughts that are held in a man's mind when he goes to

Remedium contra peccatum Luxurie
§78 Now comth the remedie agayns Leccherie, and that is generally chastitee and continence, that restreyneth alle the desordeynee moevynges that comen of flesshly talentes. And evere the gretter merite shal he han, that moost restreyneth the wikkede eschawfynges of the ardour of this synne. And this is in two maneres, that is to seyn, chastitee in mariage, and chastitee of widwehod. Now shaltow understonde that matrimoyne is leefful assemblynge of man and of womman that receyven by vertu of the sacrement the boond thurgh which they may nat be departed in al hir lyf, that is to seyn, whil that they lyven bothe. This, as seith the book, is a ful greet sacrement. God maked it, as I have seyd, in paradys, and wolde hymself be born in mariage. And for to halwen mariage he was at a weddynge, where as he turned water into wyn; which was the firste miracle that he wroghte in erthe biforn his disciples. Trewe effect of mariage clenseth fornicacioun and replenysseth hooly chirche of good lynage; for that is the ende of mariage; and it chaungeth deedly synne into venial synne bitwixe hem that been ywedded, and maketh the hertes al oon of hem that been ywedded, as wel as the bodies. This is verray mariage, that was establissed by God, er that synne bigan, whan natureel lawe was in his right poynt in paradys; and it was ordeyned that o man sholde have but o womman, and o womman but o man, as seith Seint Augustyn, by manye resouns. First, for mariage is figured bitwixe Crist and holy chirche. And that oother is for a man is heved of a womman; algate, by ordinaunce it sholde be so. For if a womman hadde mo men that oon, thanne sholde she have moo hevedes than oon, and that were an horrible thyng biforn God; and eek a womman ne myghte nat plese to many folk at oones. And also ther ne sholde nevere be pees ne reste amonges hem; for everich wolde axen his owene thyng. And forther over, no man ne sholde knowe his owene engendrure, ne who sholde have his heritage; and the womman sholde been the lasse biloved fro the tyme that she were conjoynt to many men.

§79 Now comth how that a man sholde bere hym

sleep, and so he cannot be innocent; men must guard themselves very carefully against this, or they will commit very grievous sin.

Now we come to the remedy against lechery, which in general terms is chastity and continence, which will restrain all the excessive inclinations which come from the desires of the flesh. And a man shall have even greater merit if he restrains the wicked inflammations of this sin. He can do this in two ways–that is to say, in the chastity of marriage, and the chastity of widowhood. They must understand that matrimony is the lawful joining of a man and woman who through the sacrament are bonded in such a way that they will not be separated throughout their lives–that is to say, while they are both alive. As the book says, this is a very great sacrament. God made it, as I have said, in paradise, and he himself was born from a marriage. And to make marriage holy he was at a wedding, where he turned water into wine, which was the first miracle he did on earth for his disciples. True marriage removes the need for fornication and repopulates the holy Church with good people, for that is the purpose of marriage; and it turns a deadly sin into a venial sin between those who are married, and completely unites the hearts of those who are married, as well as their bodies. This is true marriage, which was established by God, before sin came, when natural law was properly followed in Paradise; and it was decreed that one man should only have one woman, and one woman one man, as St Augustine says, for many reasons.
Firstly, because marriage symbolises the joining of Christ and the holy Church. The other is that man rules over women; or at least that is how it should be. For if a woman had more than one man, then she would have more than one head, and that would be a horrible thing to God; and also a woman could not please so many people at the same time. And also there would never be any peace between them, for each one would be asking for his own needs. And no man would know where he came from, nor who should have his inheritance; and the woman would be less loved if she was joined to many men.

Now we shall talk of how a man should behave

with his wif, and namely in two thynges, that is to seyn, in suffraunce and reverence, as shewed Crist whan he made first womman. For he ne made hire nat of the heved of Adam, for she sholde nat clayme to greet lordshipe. For ther as the womman hath the maistrie, she maketh to muche desray. Ther neden none ensamples of this; the experience of day by day oghte suffise. Also, certes, God ne made nat womman of the foot of Adam, for she ne sholde nat been holden to lowe; for she kan nat paciently suffre. But God made womman of the ryb of Adam, for womman sholde be felawe unto man. Man sholde bere hym to his wyf in feith, in trouthe, and in love, as seith Seint Paul, that a man sholde loven his wyf as Crist loved hooly chirche, that loved it so wel that he deyde for it. So sholde a man for his wyf, if it were nede.

§80 Now how that a womman sholde be subget to hire housbonde, that telleth Seint Peter. First, in obedience. And eek as seith the decree, a womman that is wyf, as longe as she is a wyf, she hath noon auctoritee to swere ne to bere witnesse withoute leve of hir housbonde, that is hire lord; algate, he sholde be so by resoun. She sholde eek serven hym in alle honestee, and been attempree of hire array. I woot wel that they sholde setten hire entente to plesen hir housbondes, but nat by hire queyntise of array. Seint Jerome seith that "wyves that been apparailled in silk and in precious purpre ne mowe nat clothen hem in Jhesu Crist." Loke what seith Seint John eek in thys matere? Seint Gregorie eek seith that "no wight seketh precious array but oonly for veyne glorie, to been honoured the moore biforn the peple. It is a greet folye, a womman to have a fair array outward and in hirself be foul inward. A wyf sholde eek be mesurable in lookynge and in berynge and in lawghynge, and discreet in alle hire wordes and hire dedes. And aboven alle worldy thyng she sholde loven hire houbonde with al hire herte, and to hym be trewe of hir body. So sholde an housbonde eek be to his wyf. For sith that al the body is the housbondes, so sholde hire herte been, or elles ther is bitwixe hem two, as in that, no parfit mariage. Thanne shal men understonde that for thre thynges a man and his wyf flesshly mowen assemble. The firste is in entente of engendrure of children to the service of God; for certes that is the cause final of matrimoyne. Another cause is to yelden everich of hem to oother the dette of hire bodies; for neither of hem hath power of his owene body. The thridde is for to eschewe

with his wife, and especially in two things; that is to say, with patience and reverence, as Christ showed when he first made women. For he did not make her from the head of Adam, so that she would not claim rule over him. For where woman is in charge, she makes too much chaos. We do not need to give examples of this, the experience of daily life should be enough. Also, certainly, God did not make woman from the foot of Adam, for she should not be thought of as too low, for she cannot suffer patiently. But God made woman from Adam's rib, for a woman should be a companion to man. A man should conduct himself towards his wife with faith, truth and love, as St Paul says, a man should love his as Christ loved the holy Church, and he loved it so well that he died for it. So a man should love his wife, if it is necessary.

Now we shall talk of how a woman should be the subject of her husband, as St Peter tells us. Firstly, in obedience. The law says, that a woman who is a wife, as long as she remains a wife, she has no authority to swear or to be a witness without permission of her husband, that is her lord; at any rate he ought to be. She should also serve him honestly, and be modest in her dress. I know that they ought to try to please their husbands, but not through elaborate dress. St Jerome says that, "wives who are dressed in silk and expensive purple cloth cannot dress themselves with Jesus Christ." Look what St John says about the matter. St Gregory also says that "nobody wants precious clothing except for vainglory, so that they can have greater honour before the people." It is very foolish for a woman to have nice clothing and to be disgusting inside. A wife should be moderate in her looks and her carriage and in her laughter, and discreet in all her words and deeds. She should love her husband with all her heart above all worldly things, and be faithful to him with her body. A husband should be the same to his wife. For since the whole body belongs to the husband, the same should apply to their hearts, or otherwise there will be between the two of them, in that respect, no perfect marriage. Then men must understand that there are three purposes for a man and his wife to be together in the flesh. The first is to create children for the service of God, since that is the final intent of matrimony. Another

leccherye and vileynye. The ferthe is for sothe deedly synne. As to the firste, it is mertorie; the seconde also, for, as seith the decree, that she hath merite of chastitee that yeldeth to hire housbonde the dette of hir body, ye, though it be agayn hir likynge and the lust of hire herte. The thridde manere is venyal synne; and, trewely, scarsly may ther any of thise be withoute venial synne, for the corrupcion and for the delit. The fourthe manere is for to understonde, as if they assemble oonly for amorous love and for noon of the foreseyde causes, but for to accomplice thilke brennynge delit, they rekke nevere how ofte. Soothly it is deedly synne; and yet, with sorwe, somme folk wol peynen hem moore to doon than to hire appetit suffiseth.

§81 The seconde manere of chastitee is for to been a clene wydewe, and eschue the embracynges of man, and desiren the embracynge of Jhesu Crist. Thise been tho that han been wyves and han forgoon hire housbondes, and eek wommen that han doon leccherie and been releeved by penitence. And certes, if that a wyf koude kepen hire al chaast by licence of hir housbonde, so that she yeve nevere noon occasion that he agilte, it were to hire a greet merite. Thise manere wommen that observen chastitee moste be clene in herte as wel as in body and in though, and mesurable in clothynge and in contenaunce; and been abstinent in etynge and drynkynge, in spekynge, and in dede. They been the vessel or the boyste of the blissed Magdelene, that fulfilleth hooly chirche of good odour. The thridde manere of chastitee is virginitee, and it bihoveth that she be hooly in herte and clene of body. Thanne is she spouse to Jhesu Crist, and she is the lyf of angeles. She is the preisynge of this world, and she is as thise martirs in egalitee; she hath in hire that tonge may nat telle ne herte thynke. Virginitee baar oure lord Jhesu Crist, and virgine was hymselve.

§82 Another remedie agayns leccherie is specially to withdrawen swiche thynges as yeve occasion to thilke vileynye, as ese, etynge, and drynkynge. For certes, whan the pot boyleth strongly, the beste remedie is to withdrawe the fyr. Slepynge longe in greet quiete is eek a greet norice to leccherie.

reason is to pay to each other the debt of their bodies, for neither of them has power over his own body. The third is to stop lechery and vulgarity. The fourth is to prevent truly deadly sin. As for the first, that is good, the second also, for, as the law says, someone who gives her body to her husband, even though it is against her will and her heart's desire, she can be called chaste. The third thing is venial sin, and surely none of these can exist without venial sin, because of the corruption and delight involved. The fourth type is present if they join only for amorous love and not for any of the reasons mentioned above, but to give themselves that burning delight, never counting how often. Truly it is a deadly sin; and yet, sadly, some people will try to do more than their appetite needs.

The second type of chastity is to be a clean widow, and reject the embraces of man, and wish to embrace Jesus Christ. These are the women who have been wives and lost their husbands, and also women who have been lecherous and have been forgiven through penitence. And certainly, if a wife can keep herself completely chaste through permission of her husband, so that she never gave him an opportunity to do wrong, that would be a great credit to her. These sorts of women who observe chastity must be clean of heart as well as body and thought, demure in clothing and behaviour, and moderate in eating and drinking, in speaking and in deeds. They are the vessel of the blessed Magdalene, that fills the holy Church with sweet scent. The third type of chastity is virginity, and that person should be wholly in her heart and queen of body. Then she is married to Jesus Christ, and she is an angel. She is the praise of the world, and she is the equal of the martyrs; she has things in her that the tongue cannot tell nor the heart think. Our Lord Jesus Christ came from virginity, and he was a virgin himself.

Another cure for lechery is to specifically take away things which give rise to that felony, such as leisure, eating and drinking. For certainly, when the plot is boiling over, the best thing to do is take away the fire. Sleeping too long and too peacefully is a great nurse of lechery.

§83 Another remedie agayns leccherie is that a man or a womman eschue the compaignye of hem by whiche he douteth to be tempted; for al be it so that the dede be withstonden, yet is ther greet temptacioun. Soothly, a whit wal, although it ne brenne noght fully by stikynge of a candele, yet is the wal blak of the leyt. Ful ofte tyme I rede that no man truste in his owene perfeccioun, but he be stronger than Sampson, and hoolier than David, and wiser than Salomon.

§84 Now after that I have declared yow, as I kan, the sevene deedly synnes, and somme of hire braunches and hire remedies, soothly, if I koude, I wolde telle yow the ten comandementz. But so heigh a doctrine I lete to divines. nathelees, I hope to God, they been touched in this tretice, everich of hem alle.

Second part (conclusion)

§85 Now for as muche as the seconde partie of penitence stant in confessioun of mouth, as I bigan in the firste chapitre, I seye, Seint Augustyn seith: synne is every word and every dede, and al that men coveiten, agayn the lawe of Jhesu Crist; and this is for to synne in herte, in mouth, and in dede, by thy fyve wittes, that been sighte, herynge, smellynge, tastynge or savourynge, and feelynge. Now is it good to understonde the circumstances that agreggen muchel every synne. Thou shalt considere what thow art that doost the synne, wheither thou be male or femele, yong or oold, gentil or thral, free or servant, hool or syk, wedded or sengle, ordred or unordred, wys or fool, clerk or seculeer; if she be of thy kynrede, bodily of goostly, or noon; if any of thy kynrede have

§86 Another circumstaunce is this: wheither it be doon in fornicacioun or in avowtrie or noon; incest or noon; mayden or noon; in manere of homicide or noon; horrible grete synnes or smale; and how longe thou hast continued in synne. The thridde circumstaunce is the place ther thou hast do synne; wheither in oother mennes hous or in thyn owene; in feeld or in chirche or in chirchehawe; in chirche dedicaat or noon. For if the chirche be halwed, and man or womman spille his kynde inwith that place, by wey or synne or by wikked temptacioun, the chirche is entredited til it be reconsiled by the bysshop. And the preest sholde be enterdited that

Another remedy for lechery is that a man or woman can reject the company of those whom he fears will tempt him, for although he may be able to withstand the deed, there is always great temptation. A white wall, although it will not be fully burned by placing a candle next to it, it will be blackened by the flame. I have often read that no man should trust his own perfection, unless he is stronger than Sampson, and holier than David, and wiser than Solomon.

Now, according to what I have told you, as far as I know, those are the seven deadly sins, and some of their variants and their cures. If I could I would tell you of the ten Commandments. But I leave such high doctrine to theologians. However, I hope to God, they have all appeared at different points in this treatise.

Now inasmuch as the second part of penitence is made up of confession by speaking, as I said in the first chapter, I tell you what St Augustine says, "Sin is every word and every deed, and everything that men covet, against the law of Jesus Christ; this is sinning in the heart, in speech, in deeds, through your five wits, sight, hearing, smelling, tasting, and feeling." It is useful to understand the circumstances that make every sin so much worse. You must think who you are who is sinning, whether you are man or woman, young or old, noble or serf, free or servant, healthy or sick, married or single, ordained or not, wise or foolish, scholar or secular; whether she is related to you, bodily or sinned with her, or not; and many other things.

Something else to consider is this: whether it is done through fornication or adultery, incest, whether she is a virgin, whether it is homicidal or not, whether it is a horrible great sin or small one, and how long you continued to sin. The third circumstance to consider is where you committed the sin, whether in someone else's house or your own, in a field or a church or a churchyard, in a consecrated place or not. For if the church has been sanctified, and a man or woman spill his semen in that place through sinful wicked temptation, the church is closed until it can be purified by the

dide swich a vileynye; to terme of al his lif he sholde namoore synge masse, and if he dide, he sholde doon deedly synne at every time that he so songe masse. The fourthe circumstaunce is by whiche mediatours, or by whiche messagers, as for enticement, or for consentement to bere compaignye with felaweshipe; for many a swecche, for to bere compaignye, wol go to the devel of helle. Wherfore they that eggen or consenten to the synne been parteners of the synne, and of the dampnacioun of the synnere.

§87 The fifthe circumstaunce is how manye tymes that he hath synne, if it be in his mynde, and how ofte that he hath falle. For he that ofte talleth in synne, he despiseth the mercy of God, and encreesseth hys synne, and is unkynde to Crist; and he wexeth the moore fieble to withstonde synne, and synneth the moore lightly, and the latter ariseth, and is the moore eschew for to shryven hym, and namely, to hym that is his confessour. For which that folk, whan they falle agayn in hir olde folies, outher they forleten hir olde confessours ol outrely, or eles they departen hir shrift in diverse places; but soothly, swich departed shrift deserveth no mercy of God of his synnes. The sixte sircumstaunce is why that a man synneth, as by which temptacioun; and if hymself procure thilke temptacioun, or by the excitynge of oother folk; or if he synne with a womman by force, or by hire owene assent; of if the womman, maugree hir heed, hath been afforced, or noon. This shal she telle: for coveitise, or for poverte, and if it was hire procurynge, or noon; and swich manere harneys. The seventhe circumstaunce is in what manere he hath doon his synne, or how that she hath suffred that folk han doon to hire. And the same shal the man telle pleynly with alle circumstaunces; and wheither he hath synned with comune bordel wommen, or noon; or doon his synne in hooly tymes, or noon; in fastyng tymes, or noon; or biforn his shrifte, or after his latter shrifte; and hath peraventure broken therfore his penance enjoyned; by whos help and whos conseil; by sorcerie or craft; al moste be toold. Alle thise thynges, after that they been grete or smale, engreggen the conscience of man. And eek the preest, that is thy juge, may the bettre been avysed of his juggement in yevynge of thy penaunce, and that is after thy contricioun. For understand wel that after tyme that a man hath defouled his baptesme by synne, if he wole come to salvacioun, ther is noon other wey but by penitence and shrifte and satisfaccioun; and namely by the two, if ther be a confessour to

bishop. And the priest should be banned who did such a crime; for the rest of his life he cannot sing the mass, and if he did he would be committing a deadly sin every time he did so. The fourth circumstance is who agreed to come with you as mediators to facilitate your sin or for companionship; for many wretches, to have company, will go to the devil. Anyone who incites or agrees to a sin is a partner in the sin, and of the damnation of the sinner.

The fifth circumstance is how many times a man has sinned, if he can remember, and how many times he has fallen. For someone who is often false through sin, he despises the mercy of God, and sins all the more, and rebels unnaturally against Christ; and his ability to fight off sin weakens, and he sins more easily, and he becomes reluctant to confess to the person who is his confessor. And so these people, when they fall back to their old sins, they either entirely forsake their old confessors or otherwise they split their confession amongst various people; but truly, a divided confession such as this will gain no mercy from God. The sixth circumstance is what temptation caused a man to sin, if he went after it himself, or if other people encouraged him; or if he sinned with a woman through force, or with her agreement, or if the woman, despite her watchfulness, has been forced, or not. She shall tell this, whether it was through greed, or poverty, whether she planned it or not; and all these sorts of things. The seventh circumstance is how he did his sin, or how she permitted what was done to her. In this the man must tell complete details; whether he has sinned with common prostitutes or not, or sinned at holy times or not, in fasting times or not, or before his confession, or after his most recent confession, and so he may perhaps have disobeyed the penance he was given, through his help and advice, what sorcery or cunning; he must tell everything. All these things, depending on their magnitude, weigh down the conscience of a man. And also the priest, who is your judge, will be better able to make his judgement as to your penance, which he will make according to your contrition. for you must understand that once a man has fouled his baptism through sin, if he wants salvation, there is no other way but penitence, confession and

which he may shriven hym, and the thridde, if he have lyf to parfournen it.

satisfaction, specifically by the first two, if there is a confessor to whom he may confess, and the third, if he has a life in which to perform it.

§88 Thanne shal man looke and considere that if he wole maken a trewe and a profitable confessioun, ther moste be foure condiciouns. First, it moot been in sorweful bitternesse of herte, as seyde the kyng Ezechias to God: "I wol remembre me alle the yeres of my lif in bitternesse of myn herte." This condicioun of bitternesse hath fyve signes. The firste is that confessioun moste be shamefast, nat for to coyere ne hyden his synne, for he hath agilt his God and defouled his soule. And herof seith Seint Augustyn: "the herte travailleth for shame of his synne; and for he hath greet shamefastnesse, he is digne to have greet mercy of God." Swich was the confessioun of the publican that wolde nat heven up his eyen to hevene, for he hadde offended God of hevene; for which shamefastnesse he hadde anon the mercy of god. And therof seith Seint Augustyn that swich shamefast folk been next foryevenesse and remissioun. Another signe is humylitee in confessioun; of which seith Seint Peter, "humbleth yow under the myght of God." The hond of God is myghty in confessioun, for therby God foryeveth thee thy synnes, for he allone hath the power. And this humylitee shal been in herte, and in signe outward; for right as he hath humylitee to God in his herte, right so sholde he humble his body outward to the preest, that sit in goddes place. For which in no manere, sith that Crist is sovereyn, and the preest meene and mediatour bitwixe Crist and the synnere, and the synnere is the laste by wey of resoun, thanne sholde nat the synnere sitte as heighe as his confessour, but knele biforn hym or at his feet, but if maladie destourbe it. For he shal nat taken kep who sit there, but in whos place that he sitteth. A man that hath trespased to a lord, and comth for to axe mercy and maken his accord, and set him doun anon by the lord, men wolde holden hym outrageous, and nat worthy so soone for to have remissioun ne mercy. The thridde signe is how that thy shrift sholde be ful of teeris, if man may, and if man may nat wepe with his bodily eyen, lat hym wepe in herte. Swich was the confession of Seint Peter, for after that he hadde forsake Jhesu Crist, he wente out and weep ful bitterly. The fourthe signe is that he ne lette nat for shame to shewen his confessioun. Swich was the confessioun of the Magdalene, that ne spared, for no shame of hem that weren atte feeste, for to go to oure lord Jhesu Crist and biknowe to hym hire

Then a man shall look and consider that if he wishes to make a true and profitable confession, there must be four conditions. Firstly, he must have sorrow and bitterness in his heart, as King Hezekiah said to God, "I will remember the bitterness in my heart all the years of my life." This condition of bitterness has five signs. The first is that confession must be made with shame, not trying to cover or hide his sin, for he has sinned against God and stained his soul. St Augustine says of this, "The heart suffers through shame at its sin"; someone who has a great sense of shame, he deserves great mercy from God. This was seen in the confession of the tax collector who would not raise his eyes to heaven, for he had offended Almighty God; and because of his sense of shame he was straightaway given the mercy of God. St Augustine says of this that people who are filled with shame are the closest to forgiveness and remission. Another sign is to be humble when you confess, and St Peter says, "Humble yourself before the might of God." The hand of God is mighty in confession, for that is how God forgives you your sins, he is the only one who has the power to do so. And this humility must be in your heart and in outward signs, for just as you are humbled to God in your heart, you should be humble with your body to the priest, who is God's representative. Since Christ is king, and the priest is the agent and the mediator between Christ and the sinner, and the sooner is obviously the lowest, the sinner should not sit as high as his confessor, but kneel down to him at his feet, unless illness prevents it. He will not care who sits there, he will only think of whose place he is sitting in. A man who has sinned against a lord, and comes to ask for mercy and to be reconciled, if he sat down at once next to the lord, men would think that he was presumptuous, and unworthy of forgiveness or mercy. The third sign is how many tears are shed during the confession, if a man can, and if he cannot weep with his physical eyes, let him weep in his heart. This was what St Peter confessed, for after he had forsaken Jesus Christ, he went out and bitterly wept. The

synne. The fifthe signe is that a man or a wommman be obeisant to receyven the penaunce that hym is enjoyned ofr his synnes, for certes, Jhesu Crist, for the giltes of o man, was obedient to the deeth.

§89 The seconde condicion of verray confession is that it be hastily doon. For certes, if a man hadde a deedly wounde, evere the lenger that he taried to warisshe hymself, the moore wolde it corrupte and haste hym to his deeth; and eek the wounde wolde be the wors for to heele. And right so fareth synne that longe tyme is in a man unshewed. Certes, a man oghte hastily shewen his synnes for manye causes; as for drede of deeth, that cometh ofte sodeynly, and no certeyn what tyme it shal be, ne in what place; and eek the drecchynge of o synne draweth in another; and eek the lenger that he tarieth, the ferther he is fro Crist. And if he abide to his laste day, scarsly may he shryven hym or remembre hym of his synnes or repenten hym, for the grevous maladie of his deeth. And for as muche as he ne hath nat in his lyf herkned Jhesu Crist whanne he hath spoken, he shal crie to Jhesu Crist at his laste day, and scarsly wol he herkne hym. And understond that this condicioun moste han foure thunges. Thi shrift moste be purveyed bifore and avysed; for wikked haste dooth no profit; and that a man konne shryve hym of his synnes, be it of pride, or of envye, and so forth with the speces and circumstances; and that he have comprehended in hys mynde the nombre and the greetnesse of his synnes, and how longe that he hath leyn in synne; and eek that he be contrit of his synnes, and in stidefast purpos, by the grace of God, nevere eft to falle in synne; and eek that he, drede and countrewaite hymself, that he fle the occasiouns of synne to whiche he is enclyned. Also thou shalt shryve thee of alle thy synnes to o man, and nat a parcel to o man and a parcel to another; that is to understonde, in entente to departe thy confessioun, as for shame of drede; for it nys but stranglynge of thy soule. For certes Jhesu Crist is entierly al good; in hym nys noon imperfeccioun; and therfore outher he foryeveth al parfitly or never a deel. I seye nat that if thow be assigned to the penitauncer for certein synne, that thow art bounde to shewen hym al the remenaunt fo thy synnes, of whiche thow hast be shryven of thy curaal, but if it like to thee of thyn humylitee; this is no departynge of shrifte. Ne I seye nat, ther as I speke of divisioun of confessioun, that if thou have licence for to shryve thee to a discreet and an honest preest, where thee liketh, and by licence of thy curaat, that thow ne mayst wel shryve thee to him al alle thy synnes. But lat no blotte be bihynde; lat no synne been untoold, fer as thow hast remembraunce. And whan thou shalt be shryven to thy curaat, telle hym eek alle the synnes that thow hast doon syn thou were last yshryven; this is no wikked entente of divisioun of shrifte.

priest who gives you penance for a certain sin, that you have to tell him all the rest of your sins, if you have confessed them to your curate, unless in your humility it pleases you to do so; this is not division of confession. And I do not say, when I speak of division of confession, that if you have permission to as confess yourself to a discrete and honest priest, curate, that you cannot make a good confession to him. But let no stain of sin remain; let no sin be unconfessed, as far as you can remember them. And when you confess to your curates, tell him all the sins that you have done since you last made confession; this does not come under the wickedness of division of confession.

§90 Also the verray shrifte axeth certeine condiciouns. First, that thow shryve thee by thy free wil, noght constreyned, ne for shame of folk, ne for maladie, ne swich thynges. For it is resound that he that trespaseth by his free wyl, that by his free wyl he confesse his trespas; and that noon oother man telle his synne but he hymself; ne he shal nat nayte ne denye his synne, ne wratthe hym agayn the preest for his amonestynge to lete synne. The seconde condicioun is that thy shrift be laweful, that is to seyn, that thow that shryvest thee, and eek the preest that hereth thy confessioun, been verraily in the feith of hooly chirche; and that a man ne be nat despeired of the mercy of Jhesu Crist, as caym or Judas. And eek a man moot accusen hymself of his owene trespas, and nat another; but he shal blame and wyten hymself and his owene malice of his synne, and noon oother. But nathelees, if that another man be occasioun or enticere of his synne, or the estaat of a persone be swich thurgh which his synne is agregged, or elles that he may nat pleynly shryven hym but he telle the persone with which he hath synned, thanne may he telle it, so that his entente ne be nat to bakbite the persone, but oonly to declaren his confessioun. Thou ne shalt nat eek make no lesynges in thy confessioun, for humylitee, peraventure, to seyn that thou hast doon synnes of whiche thow were nevere gilty. For Seint Augustyn seith, if thou, by cause of thyn hymylitee, makest lesynges on thyself, though thow ne were nat in synne biforn, yet artow thanne in synne thurgh thy lesynges. Thou most eek shewe thy synne by thyn owene propre mouth, but thow be woxe dowmb, and nat by no lettre; for thow that hast doon the synne, thou shalt have the shame therfore. Thow shalt nat eek peynte thy

Also there are certain conditions to true confession. Firstly, you must confess yourself of your own free will, not being constrained, nor out of public shame, nor due to illness, nor anything similar. For it is reasonable that he who trespasses through his free will, that he will confess through free will, and no other man should tell of his sins but himself; nor will he deny his shame, nor become angry with the priest for telling him to abandon sin. The second condition is that your confession should be lawful; which means, that you make your own confession and also the priest who hears it is truly in the faith of the holy Church, and that a man is not despairing of the mercy of Jesus Christ, as Cain or Judas were. And also a man must accuse himself of his own sins, not someone else; and he must be the one to blame and reproach himself for his evil sins, and nobody else. But nevertheless, if another man causes or entices him to sin, or if somebody else is in such a position that they aggravated his sin, or if he may not completely confess his sin until he names the person with whom he has sinned, then he may say the name, providing that he is not trying to get that person into trouble, but only to make his confession. You should also never lie in confession, for perhaps through humility you might say that you had committed sins which you had never done. For St Augustine says, "If you, because of your humility, lie against yourself, if you were not sinful before, you have then sinned through your lies." You must also tell your sins in your own voice, except if you have become dumb, and not through any writing; for you who have committed the sin,

confessioun by faire subtile wordes, to covere the moore thy synne; for thanne bigilestow thyself, and nat the preest. Thow most tellen it platly, be it nevere so foul ne so horrible. Thow shalt eek shryve thee to a preest that is discreet to conseille thee; and eek thou shalt nat shryve thee for veyne glorie, ne for ypocrisye, ne for no cause but oonly for the doute of Jhesu Crist and the heele of thy soule. Thow shalt nat eek renne to the preest sodeynly to tellen hym lightly thy synne, as whoso telleth a jape or a tale, but avysely and with greet devocioun. And generally, shryve thee ofte. If thou ofte falle, ofte thou arise by confessioun. And though thou shryve thee ofter than ones of synne of which thou hast be shryven, it is the moore merite. And, as seith Seint Augustyn, thow shalt have the moore lightly relessyng and grace of God, bothe of synne and of peyne. And certes, oones a yeere atte leeste wey it is lawful for to been housled; for certes, oones a yeere alle thynges renovellen.

§91 Now have I toold yow of verray confessioun, that is the seconde partie of penitence.

Third part

§92 The thridde partie of Penitence is Satisfaccioun, and that stant moost generally in almesse and in bodily peyne. Now been ther thre manere of almesse: contricion of herte, where a man offreth hymself to God; another is to han pitee of defaute of his neighebores; and the thridde is in yevynge of good conseil and comfort, goostly and bodily, where men han nede, and namely in sustenaunce of mannes foode. And tak kep that a man hath nede of thise thinges generally: he hath nede of foode, he hath nede of clothyng and herberwe, he hath nede of charitable conseil and visitynge in prisone and in maladie, and sepulture of his dede body. And if thow mayst nat visite the nedeful with thy persone, visite hym by thy message and by thy yiftes. Thise been general almesses or werkes of charitee of hem that han temporeel richesses or discrecioun in conseilynge. Of thise werkes shaltow heren at the day of doom.

§93 Thise almesses shaltow doon of thyne owene propre thynges, and hastily and prively, if thow mayst. But nathelees, if thow mayst ant doon it privively, thow shalt nat forbere to doon almesse though men seen it, so that it be nat doon for thank of the world, but oonly for thank of Jhesu Crist. For, as witnesseth Seint Mathew, capitulo quinto, "a citee may nat been hyd that is set on a montayne, ne men lighte nat a lanterne and put it under a busshel, but men sette it on a candle-stikke to yeve light to the men in the hous. Right so shal youre light lighten bifore men, that they may seen youre goode werkes, and glorifie youre fader that is in hevene.

§94 Now as to speken of bodily peyne, it stant in preyeres, in wakynges, in fastynges, in vertuouse techynges of orisouns. And ye shul understonde that orisouns or preyeres is for to seyn a pitous wyl of herte, that redresseth it in God and expresseth it by word outward, to remoeven harmes and to han thynges espiritueel and durable, and somtyme temporele thynges; of whiche orisouns, certes, in the orison of the pater noster hath jhesu crist enclosed moost thynges. Certes, it is privyleged of thre thynges in his dignytee, for which it is moore digne than any oother preyere; for that Jhesu Crist hymself maked it; and it is short, for it sholde be koud the moore lightly, and for to withholden it the moore esily in herte, and helpen hymself the ofter with the orisoun, and for a man sholde be the lasse wery to seyen it, and for a man may nat excusen hym to lerne it, it is so short and so esy; and for it comprehendeth in it self alle goode preyeres. The exposicioun of this hooly preyere, that is so excellent and digne, I bitake to thise maistres of theologie, save thus muchel wol I seyn; that whan thow prayest that God sholde for yeve thee thy giltes as thou foryevest hem that agilten to thee, be ful wel war that thow ne be nat out of charitee. This hooly orison amenuseth eek venyal synne, and therfore it aperteneth specially to penitence.

§95 This preyere moste be trewely seyd, and in verray feith, and that men preye to God ordinatly and discreetly and devoutly; and alwey a man shal putten his wyl to be subget to the wille of God. This orisoun moste eek been seyd with greet humblesse and ful pure; honestly, and nat to the anoyaunce of any man or wommman. It moste eek been continued with the werkes of charitee. It avayleth eek agayn the vices of the soule; for, as seith Seint Jerome, "by fastynge been saved the vices of the flessh, and by preyere the vices of the soule."

you should not withhold alms because men can see you, it should all be done for the gratitude of Jesus Christ, not for the gratitude of the world. For, as St Matthew says, in his fifth chapter, "A city that is on a mountain cannot hidden, nor can men light a lantern and put it under a bushel, they put it on a candlestick to give light to the men of the house. That is how your light will shine before men, so they can see your good works, and glorify your Father in heaven."

Now with reference to bodily pain, it consists of prayers, in keeping vigils, in fasting, and in good teaching of prayers. And you must understand that prayers mean a pious feeling in the heart, that directs itself to God and expresses itself through words, to take away harm and to gain spiritual and lasting things, and sometimes things of this earth; of all these prayers certainly the Our Father was the one in which Jesus Christ encapsulated most things. Certainly, it has three things in its favour, which make it worth more than any other prayer, because Jesus himself made it, and it is short, so that it can be learned easily, and kept more easily in the heart, so that it can be used more often, so that a man will not become tired of saying it, so that he cannot have any excuse for not learning it, it is so short and easy, and because it exemplifies all good prayers. The explanation of this holy prayer, that is so excellent and good, I will leave to the masters of theology, except that I will say that when you pray for God to forgive you your sins as you forgive those who sin against you, be very well aware that this does not excuse you from charity. This holy prayer also reduces venial sin, and so it is especially important with reference to penitence.

This prayer must be said truthfully and in good faith, so that men pray to God in an orderly fashion, discreetly and devoutly; and a man must always subject his will to the will of God. This prayer must be said with great humbleness and clearly, honestly and not to annoy any man or woman. It must also be sustained by works of charity. It also works against the vices of the soul, for, as St Jerome says, "Fasting stops the vices of the flesh, and prayer stops the vices of the soul."

§96 After this, thou shalt understonde that bodily peyne stant in wakynge; for Jhesu Crist seith, waketh and preyeth, that ye ne entre in wikked temptacioun. Ye shul understanden also that fastynge stant in thre thynges: in forberynge of bodily mete and drynke, and in forberynge of worldly jolitee, and in forberynge of deedly synne; this is to seyn, that a man shal kepen hym fro deedly synne with al his might.

After this, you must understand that bodily pain means keeping vigil, for Jesus Christ "Keep vigil and pray, so that you do not enter into wicked temptation." You must also understand that fasting consists of three things: in refraining from physical meat and drink, in refraining from earthly merriment, and refraining from deadly sin; this means, that a man will do everything he can to keep himself away from deadly sin.

§97 And thou shalt understanden eek that God ordeyned fastynge, and to fastynge appertenen foure thinges: largenesse to povre folk; gladnesse of herte espiritueel, nat to been angry ne anoyed, ne grucche for he fasteth; and also resonable houre for to ete; ete by mesure; that is for to seyn, a man shal nat ete in untyme, ne sitte the lenger at his table to ete for he fasteth.

And you should understand also that God ordered fasting, and for fasting to refer to four things: generosity to the poor, spiritual gladness of heart, not to be angry or annoyed, nor to be miserable because he is fasting, and also to eat at a reasonable time; to measure out your food carefully; that means, a man should not eat at the wrong time, and he should not spend longer eating just because he has fasted.

§98 Thanne shaltow understonde that bodily peyne stant in disciplyne or techynge, by word, or by writynge, or in ensample; also in werynge of heyres, or of stamyn, or of haubergeons on hire naked flessh, for Cristes sake, and swiche manere penances. But war thee wel that swiche manere penaunces on thy flessh ne make nat thyn herte bitter or angry or anoyed of thyself; for bettre is to caste awey thyn heytre, that for to caste awey the swetenesse of Jhesu Crist. And therfore seith Seint Paul, "clothe yow, as they that been chosen of God, in herte of misericorde, debonairetee, suffraunce, and swich manere of clothynge"; of whiche Jhesu Crist is moore apayed than of heyres, or haubergeouns, or hauberkes.

Then you must understand that bodily pain is made up of discipline of either teaching, words or writing or example; also in wearing hair shirts, or coarse cloth, or coats of mail on naked flesh, for the sake of Christ, and other such penances. But be very careful that this sort of penance of the flesh does not make you bitter or angry or annoyed, for it is better to throw away your hairshirt than to throw away the sweetness of Jesus Christ. And so St Paul says, "Clothe your heart with mercy, meekness, forbearance and such things, as do those who are chosen by God," and that pleases Jesus Christ more than hair shirts, or coats of mail, or plate armour.

§99 Thanne is discipline eek in knokkynge of thy brest, in scourgynge with yerdes, in knelynges, in tribulaciouns, in suffrynge paciently wronges that been doon to thee, and eek in pacient suffraunce of maladies, or lesynge of worldly catel, or of wyf, or of child, or othere freendes. Thanne shaltow understonde whiche thynges destourben penaunce; and this is in foure maneres, that is, drede, shame, hope, and wanhope, that is, desperacion. And for to speke first of drede; for which he weneth that he may suffre no penaunce; ther-agayns is remedie for to thynke that bodily penaunce is but short and litel at regard of the peyne of helle, that is so crueel and so long that it lasteth withouten ende.

Then there is discipline also in beating your breast, and whipping yourself with sticks, in kneeling, in suffering, in enduring patiently wrong is that have been done to you, and also patiently enduring illness, or losing earthly possessions, or your wife, or a child, or other friends. Now you must understand the things which disturb penance; and there are four types of things: fear, shame, hope and lack of hope, which is despair. To speak first of fear, for somebody who thinks that he cannot tolerate any penance; the remedy for that is to remember that bodily penance is just short and small compared to the pain of hell, that is so cruel and long as it lasts for eternity.

§100 Now again the shame that a man hath to shryven hym, and namely thise ypocrites that wolden been holden so parfite that they han no nede to shryven hem; agayns that shame sholde a man thynke that, by wey of resoun, that he that hath nat been shamed to doon foule thinges, certes hym oghte nat been ashamed to do faire thynges, and that is confessiouns. A man sholde eek thynke that God seeth and woot alle his thoghtes and alle his werkes; to hym may no thyng been hyd ne covered. Men sholden eek remembren hem of the shame that is to come at the day of doom to hem that been nat penitent and shryven in this present lyf. For alle the creatures in hevene, in erthe, and in helle shullen seen apertly al that they hyden in this world.

As for the shame when a man has to confess himself, and particularly these hypocrites who think they are so perfect there is no need to confess; a man should set against that shame the thought that, logically, he was not ashamed to do horrible things, so he certainly should not be ashamed to do good things, such as confession. A man should also think of how God sees and knows all his thoughts and all he does, nothing can be hidden from him. Men should also remind themselves of the shame that will come on Judgement Day to those who are not penitent and confessed here on earth. For all the creatures in heaven, on Earth and in hell will clearly see everything that they tried to hide in this world.

§101 Now for to speken of the hope of hem that been necligent and slowe to shryven hem, that stant in two maneres. That oon is that he hopeth for to lyve longe and for to purchacen muche richesse for his delit, and thanne he wol shryven hym; and as he seith, hym semeth thanne tymely ynough to come to shrifte. Another is of surquidrie that he hath in cristes mercy. Agayns the firste vice, he shal thynke that oure life is in no sikernesse, and eek that alle the richesses in this world ben in aventure, and passen as a shadwe on the wal; and, as seith Seint Gregorie, that it aperteneth to the grete righwisnesse of God that nevere shal the peyne stynte of hem that nevere wolde withdrawen hem fro synne, hir thankes, but ay continue in synne; for thilke perpetueel wil to do synne shul they han perpetueel peyne.

Now I shall speak of the hopes of they who are negligent and slow to confess; there are two types of these people. One type is the person hopes to live a long life and gain much wealth for his pleasure, and then confess himself; he says that the end of his life seems the right time to confess. The other type presumes that Christ will be merciful. The first type should consider that there is no security in our life, and that all the riches in the world are subject to fate and can disappear like a shadow on the wall; and, as St Gregory says, in the great great righteousness of God he will never spare from pain those who would never withdraw from sin, voluntarily, but carry on sinning; for those who perpetually sin will have perpetual pain.

§102 Wanhope is in two maneres; the firste wanhope is in the mercy of Crist; that oother is that they thynken that they ne myghte that longe persevere in goodnesse. The firste wanhope comth of that he demeth that he hath synned so greetly and so ofte, and so longe leyn in synne, that he shal nat be saved. Certes, agayns that cursed wanhope sholde he thynke that the passion of Jhesu Crist is moore strong for to bynde than synne is strong for to bynde. Agayns the seconde wanhope he shal thynke that as ofte as he falleth he may arise agayn by penitence. And though he never so longe have leyn in synne, the mercy of Crist is alwey redy to receiven hym to mercy. Agayns the wanhope that he demeth that he sholde nat longe persevere in goodnesse, he shal thynke that the feblesse of the devel may nothyng doon, but if men wol suffren hym; and

There are two sorts of despair: the first is in the mercy of Christ; the other is the thought that they cannot be good for long. The first form of despair comes from someone who thinks that he has sinned so greatly and so often, and been a sinner for such a long time, that he cannot be saved. Against that horrible despair he should remember that the passion of Jesus Christ has more strength to free him than sin has to tie him down. The second despair should always remember that however often he falls he can rise up again through penitence. And however long he may have been sinning, the mercy of Christ is always ready to receive him. The person who despairs in thinking that he will not be able to be good for long, he should remember that the devil is too weak to do anything, eek he shal han strengthe of the help of God, and of al hooly chirche, and of the proteccioun of aungels, if hym list. Thanne shal men understonde what is the fruyt of penaunce; and, after the word of Jhesu Crist, it is the endelees blisse of hevene, ther joye hath no contrarioustee of wo ne grevaunce; ther alle harmes been passed of this present lyf; ther as is the sikernesse fro the peyne of helle; ther as is the blisful compaignye that rejoysen hem everemo, everich of otheres joye; ther as the body of man, that whilom was foul and derk, is moore cleer than the sonne; ther as the body, that whilom was syk, freele, and fieble, and mortal, is inmortal, and so strong and so hool that ther may no thyng apeyren it; ther as ne is neither hunger, thurst, ne coold, but every soule replenyssed with the sighte of the parfit knowynge of God. This blisful regne may men purchace by poverte espiritueel, and the glorie by lowenesse, the plentee of joye by hunger and thurst, and the reste by travaille, and the lyf by deeth and mortificacion of synne.

unless men allow him; and also he will have the strength of God, and all the holy Church, and the protection of angels, if he wants them. Then men shall understand what they gain from penance; and, according to the word of Jesus Christ, it is the eternal bliss of heaven, where there is only joy and no sorrow or grief; where all the pain of earthly life is gone; there is safety there from the pain of hell; there is blissful company, rejoicing eternally, everyone celebrating the joy of all the others; there the body of man, that was formerly horrid and dark, is clearer than the sun; there that body, that before was sick, frail, feeble and mortal, is immortal, and so strong and healthy that nothing can injure it; there is no hunger, thirst or cold, every soul is reborn through perfect knowledge of God. This blissful kingdom can be gained by men through spiritual poverty, and the glory through humbleness, the excessive joy through hunger and thirst, and the rest through work, and the life through death and rejection of sin.

Chaucer's retraction

Now preye I to hem alle that herkne thai litel tretys or rede, that if ther be any thyng in it that liketh hem, that therof they thanken oure Lord Jesu Crist, of whom procedeth al wit and al goodnesse. And if ther be any thyng that displese hem, I preye hem also that they arrette it to the defaute of myn unkonnynge, and nat to my wyl, that wolde ful fayn have seyd bettre, if I hadde had konnynge. For oure Boke seith, `al that is writen, is writen for oure doctrine,' and that is myn entente. Wherfore, I biseke yow mekely for the mercy of God, that ye preye for me that Crist have mercy on me, and foryeve me my giltes; and namely, of my translaciouns and enditynges of worldly vanitees, the whiche I revoke in my retracciouns; As is the book of Troilus, the book also of Fame, the book of the .XXV. Ladies, the book of the Duchesse, the book of Seint Valentynes day of the Parlement of Briddes, the tales of Caunterbury (thilke that sownen into synne), the book of the Leoun, and many another book, if they were in my remembrance; and many a song and many a leccherous lay, that Crist for his grete mercy foryeve me the synne. But of the translaciouns of Boece de Consolacione, and othere bookes of Legendes of Seintes and omelies, and moralitee, and devocioun; that thanke I oure Lord Jesu Crist, and his blissful mooder, and alle the seintes of hevene; bisekynge hem that they from hennesforth unto my lyves ende sende me grace to biwayle my giltes, and to studie to the salvacioun of my soule; and graunte me grace of verray penitence, confessioun, and satisfaccioun to doon in this present lyf, thurgh the benigne grace of Hym, that is kyng of kynges, and preest over alle preestes, that boghte us with the precious blood of his herte, so that I may been oon of hem at the day of doome that shulle be saved. Qui cum patre, &cetera.

Now I beg all those who listen to this little treatise or read it, that if there is anything in it which pleases them, that they give thanks to our Lord Jesus Christ, from whom all wit and goodness comes. And if there's anything that displeases them, I beg that they blame it on my lack of wit, and not my desire, for I would have been much happier to have said something better if I had the ability. For the book says, "Everything that is written is written for our education," and that is my intention. So I beg you meekly, for God's mercy, that you pray to Christ that he will have mercy on me and forgive my sins; and particularly my translations and compositions of worldly vanity, such as the book of Troilus, the book of Fame, the book of the Fifteen Ladies, the book of the Duchess, the book of St Valentine's day, the Parliament of Fowls, the stories of Canterbury, those that may be sinful, the book of the Lion, and many other books, if I could remember them, and many songs and dirty lyrics, and may Christ in his great mercy forgive me my sin. But as for the translation of Boethius' Consolation of Philosophy, and other books of the stories of the saints, and homilies, and morality and devotion, I thank our Lord Jesus Christ for that, and his blissful mother, and all the saints in heaven, begging them that from now until the end of my life they will give me the grace to bemoan my sins and to study for the salvation of my soul, and that they give me the grace of true penitence, confession and satisfaction in this life, through the kind grace of him who is the king of kings and priest over all priests, who saved us with his precious heart's blood, so that when Judgement Day comes I shall be one of the saved. He who lives and rules with the father, etc.

Heere is ended the book of the tales of Caunterbury compiled by Geffrey Chaucer of whos soule Jesu Crist have mercy. Amen.

This is the end of the book of the Canterbury Tales, compiled by Geoffrey Chaucer, on whose soul may Jesus Christ have mercy. Amen.

Printed in Great Britain
by Amazon.co.uk, Ltd.,
Marston Gate.